KURT VONNEGUT COMPLETE STORIES

KURT VONNEGUT COMPLETE STORIES

COLLECTED AND INTRODUCED BY
JEROME KLINKOWITZ & DAN WAKEFIELD
FOREWORD BY
DAVE EGGERS

SEVEN STORIES PRESS
New York ★ Oakland ★ London

Seven Stories Press
140 Watts Street
New York, NY 10013
www.sevenstories.com

College professors and high school and middle school teachers may order free examination copies of Seven Stories Press titles. To order, visit www.sevenstories.com or send a fax on school letterhead to (212) 226-1411.

Library of Congress Cataloging-in-Publication Data

Names: Vonnegut, Kurt, author. | Klinkowitz, Jerome, editor. | Wakefield,
    Dan, editor. | Eggers, Dave, writer of foreword.
Title: Complete stories / Kurt Vonnegut ; collected and introduced by Jerome
    Klinkowitz and Dan Wakefield ; foreword by Dave Eggers.
Description: A Seven Stories Press first edition. | New York : Seven Stories
    Press, [2017]
Identifiers: LCCN 2017013594 | ISBN 9781609808082 (hardback)
Subjects: | BISAC: LITERARY COLLECTIONS / American / General. | FICTION /
    Literary.
Classification: LCC PS3572.O5 A6 2017 | DDC 813/.54--dc23
LC record available at https://lccn.loc.gov/2017013594

Printed in the USA

9 8 7 6 5 4 3 2

KEY TO SOURCES

AR   *Armageddon in Retrospect*. New York: Putnam's, 2008.
From paperback edition, Berkley Books, New York, 2009.

BSB   *Bagombo Snuff Box*. New York: Putnam's, 1999.
From paperback edition, Berkley Books, New York, 2000.

L   Papers, 1941–2007, of Kurt Vonnegut at the Lilly Library,
Indiana University, Bloomington, Indiana.

LB   *Look at the Birdie*. New York: Delacorte Press, 2009.
From paperback edition, Dial Press, New York, 2010.

PS   *Palm Sunday*. New York: Delacorte Press / Seymour Lawrence, 1981.
From paperback edition, Dell, New York, 1982.

SP   *Sucker's Portfolio*. Las Vegas: Amazon Publishing, 2012.
From Amazon print edition as above.

WMH   *Welcome to the Monkey House*. New York: Delacorte Press / Seymour
Lawrence, 1968. From paperback edition, Dial Press, New York, 2010.

WMS   *While Mortals Sleep*. New York: Delacorte Press, 2011.
From paperback edition, Dial Press, New York, 2012.

Contents

SECTION I: WAR
(Headnote by Jerome Klinkowitz)   1

SECTION 2: WOMEN
(Headnote by Dan Wakefield)   169

SECTION 3: SCIENCE
(Headnote by Jerome Klinkowitz)   271

SECTION 4: ROMANCE
(Headnote by Dan Wakefield)   367

SECTION 5: WORK ETHIC VERSUS FAME AND FORTUNE
(Headnote by Dan Wakefield)   459

SECTION 6: BEHAVIOR
(Headnote by Jerome Klinkowitz)   669

SECTION 7: THE BAND DIRECTOR
(Headnote by Dan Wakefield) 803

SECTION 8: FUTURISTIC
(Headnote by Jerome Klinkowitz) 853

Foreword

by Dave Eggers

The moral story is gone. The fable is gone. They cannot be found in contemporary literature. Not even in children's literature. Writers do not feel inclined to tell their fellow human beings how to live.

Most of the stories in this collection are moral stories. They tell us what's right and what's wrong, and they tell us how to live. In 2017, this is a radical act.

Vonnegut, like many American writers who published stories in the 1950s, wrote concise cautionary tales set amid burgeoning prosperity. Usually there was little ambiguity. Liars were punished. Adulterers got their comeuppance. Greedy capitalists were laid low, and those who were idealistic and pure found a way, just in the nick of time, to preserve their idealism and their purity against corruption in its many forms.

The '60s and '70s eroded—destroyed—the American interest in this kind of story. A president was killed. His brother was killed. King was killed. Another president resigned under threat of impeachment. Tens of thousands of young men were killed in a useless war half a world away.

The short story evolved to reflect the dark ambiguity of the times, and never returned to its former incarnation. For fifty years now, the short story has been many things, but it has rarely been a moral tool. We have had slice-of-life stories, stories of malaise, ennui, and broken dreams. We have had the hyperreal story that describes unbeautiful lives with no hope of change. We have had the experimental story, the short-short story, stories of decent people doing the wrong thing and unsympathetic people triumphing for no reason other than to demonstrate the elemental unfairness of the world. But it has been a long while since a story told us, or reminded us, what was noble and what was evil, how we should act and how we can live with dignity.

Kurt Vonnegut wrote a story called "The Honor of a Newsboy," and it might be the best demonstration of how square and plainspoken he was as a young writer. In it, his moral compass guides a story that, given that era's marketplace for short fiction, begins with a pulpy instigating act.

A woman named Estelle is murdered and her lover, a layabout named Earl, is the prime suspect. He has an alibi, though. He was out of town visiting a brother, and the alibi appears to be backed up by a stack of unread newspapers on Earl's porch.

But when Sheriff Charley Howes counts the newspapers, he notices that the edition from Wednesday, the day Estelle was killed, is missing. The sheriff surmises that Earl came back from his brother's house to murder Estelle, but as a habitual watcher of the stock market, he couldn't resist checking the Dow in the paper. Earl says the newspaper wasn't delivered that day.

Enter the paperboy and his honor. The boy, named Mark, insists he delivered the paper. "If the papers pile up and nobody's said to stop, you keep on delivering for six days," he says. "It's the *rule*, Mr. Howes." Sheriff Charley Howes has a choice: believe a known ne'er-do-well who lives on the edge of town, or a ten-year-old paperboy? In a contemporary story, the paperboy would turn out to be some conniving operator. Or the sheriff would be the killer. But in the 1950s—in a Vonnegut story from the 1950s—the sheriff is the sheriff, an unassailable pillar of the community, and a paperboy is at the shoulder of Jesus.

"The serious way Mark talked about the rule reminded Charley what a marvelous age ten was," Vonnegut writes. "And Charley thought it was a pity that everybody couldn't stay ten for the rest of their lives. If everybody were ten, Charley thought, maybe rules and common decency and horse sense would have a Chinaman's chance."

Vonnegut wrote short stories like this for about ten years, and then devoted his writing life to his incomparable novels, which were largely free of marketplace concerns. They were more complex of course, but the same moral surety evident in these early stories guided the novels, too. Taken as a whole, his body of work reveals one of the most consistent and principled points of view of any twentieth-century artist.

"Damn it, you got to be kind." This epitaph was written on a gravestone Vonnegut drew and sent to me. One could try to make Vonnegut's philosophy more involved than that, but it wouldn't get any closer to the truth. Be kind. Do no harm. Take care of your family. Don't start wars.

I was lucky enough to get to know Kurt Vonnegut a bit—a little bit—before he passed on. The first meeting was comical, not unlike a scene from one of his novels. It was the year 2000, and Vonnegut's wife Jill had arranged for a small gathering in their Manhattan walk-up. Colson Whitehead was there, as was the critic and champion of the book John Leonard. Colson and I were relatively young, about thirty, and were nervous and thrilled to be meeting Vonnegut for the first time. The last member of the party, whose name I never caught, talked the entire time. Colson and I had been given an audience with Kurt Vonnegut, and the grim irony was that we were subjected to an hour's worth of chatter from some other guy. The minutes clicked away as the man rambled on, loving his own voice, filling the room with his sea of words, while Vonnegut, chain-smoking, every so often nodded his gray head politely. I remember that Vonnegut managed one sentence in all that time, and it had to do with jazz.

Later, Jill arranged one more meeting, and this time Vonnegut and I were alone, and we were able to talk. Or rather, I was able to listen. He was everything you would have wanted him to be. Gentle, funny and quick to laugh, empathetic to all—to the waiter at the restaurant, to the hostess—his heavy-lidded eyes always giving off the impression of unalterable weariness with the crimes of his fellow humans.

September 11 was only a few months away, and that day, and the United States' subsequent invasion of Afghanistan and Iraq, gave birth to a period of unparalleled essays about the futility of war. It was the right coda to his writing life. He had struggled with *Timequake*, his last novel. Trying to talk sense into a violent and unreasonable planet in the form of short essays was the right final act for a man who had been trying to do just that, in novels and short stories, for more than fifty years.

Near the end of "The Honor of a Newsboy," the sheriff sees his reflection in a window. "He saw a tired old man, and he figured he'd grown old and tired trying to make the world be what ten-year-olds thought it was."

I hope you enjoy this collection as much as I did. The editors, Vonnegut's long-time friends Jerome Klinkowitz and Dan Wakefield, have done a beautiful job of ordering and introducing the stories. Their knowledge of, and fierce loyalty to, the great man is evident everywhere within these pages, and makes this omnibus an essential part of the Vonnegut canon.

One last word: Lest I leave you with the impression that these stories are useful primarily as documents of the writer as a young man, or as a postcard from a bygone era, please know that this collection pulses with relevance even today, and provides an almost shameful amount of unadulterated reading pleasure. The prose is clean and the pace always brisk, and the satisfaction we draw from seeing some moral clarity, some linear order brought to a knotted world, is impossible to overstate.

Introduction

Complete Stories comprises the full extent of the author's short fiction as drawn from three sources: the stories published during his lifetime, first in magazines and then as collected in *Canary in a Cat House* (1961), *Welcome to the Monkey House* (1968), *Palm Sunday* (1981), and *Bagombo Snuff Box* (1999); finished but unpublished stories assembled after the author's death by his estate's attorney Donald Farber and released as *Armageddon in Retrospect* (2008), *Look at the Birdie* (2009), *While Mortals Sleep* (2011), and *Sucker's Portfolio* (2013); and finished but unpublished stories residing in the 1941–2007 papers of Kurt Vonnegut at the Lilly Library, Indiana University, Bloomington, Indiana. The method in assembling these materials has been to group the stories rationally, according to their subject matter and approach. Thus submissions that journals of the time rejected can be considered in the context of others that were accepted, letting readers see just where Kurt Vonnegut was ahead of his time. Stories from his archive at the Lilly are included where, in the view of his agents at the time and the editors of this volume afterward they constitute finished works. There are many false starts (in several genres) among his papers, plus variants on story ideas that were discarded after one version would find success. In assessing canonical status, it is foremost to consider whether the author would have wanted to publish a piece during his or her lifetime; once a final version was put into print, it is inconceivable that the author would seek to publish other drafts of the same material. When alternative versions have been published, such as those of Ernest Hemingway's *A Moveable Feast* (in 1964 and 1992), it has been one posthumous editorial project supplanting the other, with the goal of restoring the author's intent. In navigating the deep waters of the Vonnegut archive, both the estate and this volume's editors have been careful to identify finished work, as opposed to sketches, variants, and aborted projects.

Presented here are the short stories Kurt Vonnegut wanted the reading public to see. During his lifetime, he was successful at publishing a bit fewer than half of them. It is without irony that when a magazine rejected an especially strong piece, his agent would counsel him to "save it for the collection of your works which will be published someday when you become famous. Which may take a little time." That letter from Kenneth Littauer of Littauer and Wilkinson was sent on March 24, 1958, and it was correct on both counts.

How those stories came to be written can be explained by considering both the publishing history of the time and Kurt Vonnegut's personal role in it. The editors of this volume address these issues from their own experience: Jerome Klinkowitz as a scholar of the period, Dan Wakefield as an author active during these times. Both were friends of Kurt Vonnegut, and each benefited from sharing a professional world with him. But even before this, they were readers. Klinkowitz recalls reading Vonnegut's stories as a youngster in the 1950s, dipping into his parents' copies of the *Saturday Evening Post* much as Kurt himself did when growing up in the 1930s. Dan Wakefield read them in the barbershop, as he happily recounts. Like so many others of his age, Klinkowitz became a fan of Vonnegut's novels as a college student in the mid-1960s; Wakefield, already established in New York City as a feature journalist, interacted with the soon-to-be-famous author as he began writing best-selling novels himself. By 1971 Klinkowitz and Wakefield were working with others on a collaborative critical book titled *The Vonnegut Statement.* Published early in 1973, it set the tone for a raft of commentary that followed and continues to this day.

In this present volume the editors have supplied not just headnotes to each of the stories' topical sections, which range from "War" and "Women" to the "Futuristic," but have written short essays that place Kurt Vonnegut's stories in perspective. Although most Americans did not become familiar with his work until the success of *Slaughterhouse-Five* in 1969 and despite the fact that his collegiate readers of the earlier sixties had paperbacks of just his otherwise-neglected early novels, Vonnegut had already enjoyed a decades-long career as a writer of short stories for the general magazine market. In "Short Stories of the American 1950s, Inc., Kurt Vonnegut, Proprietor" Jerome Klinkowitz explains how writing such fiction initiated Vonnegut's career and located it firmly within the manners and mores of middle-class Americans. In "How Vonnegut Learned to Write Short Stories" Dan Wakefield reveals how unlike many writers of today, who have honed their craft in creative writing programs at universities, Kurt was mentored by a supportive magazine editor and a literary agency that back in the 1950s did what masters of fine arts educators do today. The market and the method that this volume's editors respectively describe complement each other; Vonnegut's experiences, raising a family in Dwight D. Eisenhower's America (while voting each time for Adlai Stevenson and witnessing the ascendency of John F. Kennedy nearby on the richer side of Cape Cod), dovetail with the world of family-oriented magazines where his agents were coaching him to make sales. It is a story that can be told from many points of view. Kurt's first wife, the former Jane Cox and later Jane Vonnegut Yarmolinsky, wrote about it in her memoir, *Angels Without Wings* (1987); their son Mark added further details in his own accounts *The Eden Express* (1975) and *Just Like Someone Without Mental Illness Only More So* (2010). Nanette Vonnegut described her father's writing habits, early in his career and late, in her foreword to the posthumously published *We Are What We Pretend to Be* (2012). By organizing this volume of stories according to their author's working methods the editors have sought to portray how Kurt Vonnegut's first career was established, flourished for a time, and then receded as the publishing industry changed, not to mention the world around it.

Elements of Vonnegut's life contributed to this first career, based as it was on his life as a midwesterner from Indianapolis who'd attended Cornell University, served in World War II, studied afterward at the University of Chicago, and worked as a journalist and then publicist before venturing into the world of fiction writing. Each element figures in one or more of the stories he'd write: science from his undergraduate course work in biochemistry, human behavior from his studies in anthropology, war as he'd taken part in it at the Battle of the Bulge and as a prisoner of war in Germany, and facets of middle-class American life as he'd observed them back home in Indiana, out east in upstate New York, among his coworkers for a time in the corporate maze of General Electric, and most rewardingly among his neighbors in small-town New England. Although living in West Barnstable, Massachusetts, at the base of Cape Cod, he often fictionalized his narrative location as the mythical village of North Crawford, New Hampshire, a typification of Anytown, USA—one of his favorite plays was Thornton Wilder's *Our Town*. His family life with three children expanded exponentially when with the deaths of his sister and brother-in-law he and his wife took in the children from that marriage. During stretches when stories were not being accepted he turned to fill-in jobs writing advertising copy for a firm in Boston, struggling to operate an import automobile dealership, and teaching in a school for disturbed children. Meanwhile, his novels drew little attention and sold poorly, except in cheap paperback editions favored by a college audience that had yet to be recognized as a counterculture. Eventually he had to take leave of family life for two years and teach at the University of Iowa Writers' Workshop. While there he devised a structure for a novel he'd been contemplating for years, *Slaughterhouse-Five*. That book was published in 1969, and the rest is history. But so was his time as a writer of short stories.

There is much to learn about this world-famous novelist by reexamining his previous career as a worker in the fields of weekly and monthly magazines. Thankfully resources were available for study and much help was provided. At the Lilly Library, Cherry Williams and Sarah Mitchell provided extraordinary assistance. From the University of Louisville, where he was completing a doctoral dissertation on Vonnegut, scholar Josh Simpson supplied information about material in this archive. Among those no longer living, agents Kenneth Littauer and Max Wilkinson and editor Knox Burger deserve credit for supporting their young client throughout the 1950s and into the early 1960s, so far in advance of the fame that awaited him. Most of all, every Vonnegut reader owes a huge debt to his late wife Jane, who during these lean years kept meticulous files that held the stories he published and preserved the ones that were finished but rejected. As her husband's work began to draw critical attention, she patiently answered requests for bibliographic information, sending Jerome Klinkowitz a detailed list in 1971 that has been the foundation for much work afterward. Today at the Lilly Library researchers see evidence of her organizational hand everywhere and have proclaimed her their patron saint. It is likely that if Kurt Vonnegut were alive today, he would give a tip of the hat to Littauer, Wilkinson, and Burger, while dedicating this book to her.

HISTORICAL NOTE

Of the twelve Vonnegut stories (all previously published in magazines) collected in *Canary in a Cat House* (Greenwich, CT: Fawcett Publications / Gold Medal Books, 1961), eleven were re-collected in *Welcome to the Monkey House* in 1968:

> "Report on the Barnhouse Effect"
> "All the King's Horses"
> "D.P."
> "The Manned Missiles"
> "The Euphio Question"
> "More Stately Mansions"
> "The Foster Portfolio"
> "Deer in the Works"
> "Tom Edison's Shaggy Dog"
> "Unready to Wear"
> "Tomorrow and Tomorrow and Tomorrow"

The twelfth story, "Hal Irwin's Magic Lamp," was re-collected with revisions in *Bagombo Snuff Box* in 1999.

Welcome to the Monkey House and *Bagombo Snuff Box* acknowledge the magazine publications of these stories, but not their appearance in *Canary in a Cat House* (which was, incidentally, a paperback original, as were Vonnegut's second and third novels, *The Sirens of Titan* and *Mother Night*, in 1959 and 1961, respectively).

— JK and DW

Short Stories of the American 1950s, Inc., Kurt Vonnegut, Proprietor

Kurt Vonnegut's history with the short story is a special one. Conventional wisdom is that it ended in 1968, when he and his new publisher, Seymour Lawrence, sorted through what Kurt had published and selected twenty-three short stories, plus a personal essay and a personalized book review, to be issued under the title *Welcome to the Monkey House*. What had brought this relatively unheralded writer to Lawrence's attention was the book review, a *New York Times Book Review* piece about the new *Random House Dictionary*. Here was a sample of Vonnegut's writing at its most engaging, not to mention funniest. Lawrence especially appreciated the fun Kurt had with Bennett Cerf, the Random House chief for whom the younger publisher had once worked.

Lawrence's offer of a three-book contract to an author whose previous five novels had never sold more than a few thousand copies each was good news, coming as it did in the aftermath of Vonnegut's previous source of income having dried up. Since 1950 he'd supported himself and his large family by writing short stories for the great family weekly magazines of the day *Collier's* and the *Saturday Evening Post*, with occasional sales to other journals treating family issues of interest to women, *Cosmopolitan* and the *Ladies' Home Journal* among them. These were venues for human interest articles about issues and events that touched the lives of everyday Americans. Interspersed with this material would be four or five examples of short fiction that treated some of the same topics, albeit with a flair for imagination and with plenty of poetic license.

Kurt Vonnegut knew how middle-class families who read these magazines were living, as he lived among them in the village of West Barnstable, Massachusetts, "on the biceps" (as he liked to say) of the flexed arm that constitutes Cape Cod. Here he and his neighbors pursued their service professions and ran their small businesses. Kurt's was a short story business operating from an ell he'd had built off the side of his house, which was otherwise filled with a devoted wife and no fewer than six children, three of his own and three taken in when his sister and brother-in-law died within days of each other. There were rich people to observe nearby in Hyannis

Port; one of his neighbors skippered the Kennedy family yacht. Outward toward the Cape's tip was Provincetown, where there were artists and writers galore. Kurt could observe them, too, but from a distance. It would be many years before he lived and worked among others engaged in the arts. For now it was short stories that provided a market for his writing, along with publishers who'd take five of his novels but have no great success with their sales.

All this ended in 1963, when Vonnegut made his last sale to the *Saturday Evening Post.* "The Hyannis Port Story" was one of Kurt's best, but the *Post* had to cancel it when President Kennedy was assassinated. Even before this, sales had slowed down, as advertising volume decreased and issues shrank. Soon the journal would go dormant for a time, while *Collier's*, once a media giant, ceased publication altogether. There was no mystery as to why: as the 1950s progressed and turned into the early 1960s, television had stolen the magazines' audiences, and with them went the advertisers. Soon Kurt Vonnegut the short story writer was out of work.

By 1965 he was forced to take temporary leave of his family and begin teaching at the University of Iowa Writers' Workshop. Here his colleagues included fellow visitors Nelson Algren, Richard Yates, and José Donoso, plus regulars Vance Bourjaily and R. V. Cassill. Like Vonnegut, these writers were pros. Unlike him, they'd had at least some success with their novels, Algren fabulously so, as opposed to Kurt, whose books rarely sold out their small first printings. All that would change in just a few years. In the company of these writers and with students who included such future greats as John Irving and Gail Godwin, Kurt Vonnegut was encouraged to take his novel writing seriously. A scholar-critic from the English Department certainly did. Robert Scholes became a friend and advocate. In 1967, as Kurt was finishing his two-year appointment in the workshop, Scholes published *The Fabulators* with Oxford University Press. This groundbreaking study of late-twentieth-century fiction singled out key writers for chapter-length treatment, among them such major figures as Iris Murdoch and Lawrence Durrell—plus Kurt Vonnegut, whose novels held their own with *The Alexandria Quartet* and others. In such circumstances this former short story writer turned to the manuscript of *Slaughterhouse-Five* with gusto. But there were still those short stories—good ones—that his new publisher felt deserved a home.

Others had known they were good. In 1961, Knox Burger, Kurt's former editor at *Collier's*, had taken a job with Gold Medal Books at Fawcett Publications and brought out a dozen of them in a mass market paperback titled *Canary in a Cat House.* As Kurt and Seymour Lawrence pondered a new collection in 1968, they saved all but one of these stories, "Hal Irwin's Magic Lamp," perhaps rejecting it because of its awkward characterization of an African American servant. There were still more than enough pieces to choose from—forty-six that Vonnegut had published from 1950 to the present, including the newly finished "Welcome to the Monkey House," which *Playboy* featured as a preview of the highly touted collection of the same name. Twenty-three stories in all made it in, but another twenty-three didn't. What happened to those twenty-three, and to an even larger number that were never published during the author's lifetime, makes *Complete Stories* so valuable.

In 1974, the twenty-three previously published but still uncollected short stories were presented, along with an equal number of Kurt Vonnegut's essays, addresses, and reviews, to Seymour Lawrence as a book to be called *Rare Vonnegut*. "That sounds terribly posthumous," Kurt complained, and he felt that being named as the author of some of these short stories was like "being accused of petty crimes and misdemeanors." But he liked seeing the essays again and let them be published as *Wampeters, Foma & Granfalloons* (1974). The twenty-three stories were discussed in "A Do-It-Yourself Short Story Collection by Kurt Vonnegut," one of the essays comprising *Vonnegut in America* as published by Seymour Lawrence in 1977. Here readers were told not only about the stories but where and how to find them, together with an estimate of how many nickels they'd need for photocopying. So the "missing twenty-three" continued to live, somewhat in obscurity, until Kurt agreed to their being collected in 1999 as *Bagombo Snuff Box*.

Working on this book with scholar Peter Reed proved to be an especially happy experience for the author. Proof of that is the warm tone and friendly manner of the commentary he added to the volume. For *Welcome to the Monkey House*, prefaced thirty-one years before he'd become famous, Vonnegut was funny, but in a diffident and almost apologetic way. What came to his mind was a bad review in which his work had been called "a series of narcissistic giggles." What if this new book would be another, he worried. "Perhaps it would be helpful to the reader to imagine me as the White Rock girl, kneeling on a boulder in a nightgown, either looking for minnows or adoring her own reflection." Note the comparison not to the myth of Narcissus, but to its somewhat tawdry exploitation in an ad from the very magazines where Vonnegut had been writing. (Not coincidentally, that bad review came from the *New Yorker*, where no so banal an advertisement would have appeared.) But to the readers of *Bagombo Snuff Box* the author of not just these stories but of *Slaughterhouse-Five* and other novels could be avuncular, if not downright grandfatherly, in his sharing of friendly wisdom about the art of story writing.

As both novelist and short story writer, Kurt Vonnegut had sought to speak plainly and directly, a legacy of his student journalism and early public relations work where earning the reader's trust was preeminent. In his fiction readers encountered a strong American vernacular unheard since Mark Twain, a style that the cold reason of modernism had tried to extinguish. In *Palm Sunday* (1981) Vonnegut indicates how even translations of the Gospels could be improved by considering how Jesus may have actually spoken. The occasion is one of Christ's conversations, where Jesus chides Judas for chiding him over the presumed waste of soothing but expensive oil that could have been sold to benefit the poor. In the King James version, the Good Lord says, "For the poor always ye shall have with you; but you do not always have me." That's poor writing on the part of the gospelers, Vonnegut says, or at least a poor translation into English, because it allows rich people to cite Jesus when ignoring social needs. Kurt asks his readers to examine the context. Jesus has had a long and tiring day, knows that he will be betrayed by this suddenly holier than thou disciple, and will face scourging and crucifixion. What can he say? How about what Mark Twain or Abraham Lincoln would have said in similar circumstances: "Judas, don't worry about it. There will still be plenty of poor people left long after I'm gone." That's the beauty and effectiveness of the vernacular. Judas is chided, but not in a way that makes him feel like "something the cat dragged in," another favorite vernacular phrase of Vonnegut's. And the truth is certainly known.

In Kurt Vonnegut's time, during the century that is so often called "the American century," this truth was shared by a culture that cohered in the pages of popular magazines. Consider how they shaped three overlapping generations of aspiring and ultimately successful writers. In the twentieth century's earlier years a youngster from St. Paul named F. Scott Fitzgerald perused any number of popular magazines in his parents' nicely furnished front parlor. As a college-bound teen he foresaw himself as a dramatist, but became a fiction writer instead, placing stories in the *Saturday Evening Post* (which at the time brought him more fame and money even than *The Great Gatsby*). In the 1940s, another youngster, this one from rural Pennsylvania, lay on the living room rug delighting in issue after issue of the *New Yorker*. The subscriber was his mother, who hoped to write in this magazine's style and place work there herself. Her son John Updike wanted to be a cartoonist. But guess who got a story (many of them) in the *New Yorker* first. Between Fitzgerald and Updike, in the 1930s it was Kurt Vonnegut who could come home from high school, pick up a newly arrived copy of the *Saturday Evening Post*, and spend a quiet half hour reading one of its several short stories, sometimes marking one for his father's attention. Later the family might discuss it at dinner. Kurt describes this situation not only nostalgically but lovingly in his preface to *Bagombo Snuff Box*. These are memories of a world long lost, but they are powerful nonetheless—powerful because they outline a course he himself would follow as a young man after college, after the war, after graduate school, and after employment as a publicist at General Electric.

That's a long line of "afters," but it anticipates a professional life that kept the author busy from 1950 through 1963. During those years he published four novels, from *Player Piano* and *The Sirens of Titan* to *Mother Night* and *Cat's Cradle*, but none earned him enough to live on. His bread and butter were short stories for a wide range of magazines, varied in nature but all speaking to the American middle class. The mainstays were *Collier's* and the *Saturday Evening Post*, weeklies directed to interests all the family members could share. In each issue five or six short stories would share space with feature articles on the same subjects, from Cold War fears and day-to-day economics to personality pieces about people both famous and common, not to mention promises of a better life from the world of science. Within the American family were husbands, wives, and children, and Vonnegut was adept at capturing the attention of each. In the *Post* from 1952 through 1956 there were no fewer than four separate stories featuring a high school band director named George M. Helmholtz who struggled with and often (but not always) solved the problems of his young pupils. As late as 1959 he was struggling with one last Helmholtz story about the band director perplexed by the students' interest in their newly codified IQs. The version his agents liked the best is included here as "A Song for Selma," but the magazine, whose space for stories was now shrinking, declined it as one of three versions that didn't make the new, stricter grade. Not coincidentally, in the novel he was writing at this time, *The Sirens of Titan* (1959), Kurt included Helmholtz and another recently retired colleague as familiar types: "two *Saturday Evening Post* characters at the end of the road." But in preceding years short stories about the thoughtful, caring man had comforted teens in the family who might otherwise fear they'd been misunderstood.

Collier's and the *Post* also published Vonnegut stories with husbands and wives as the central chararacters—sometimes in happy marriages, other times not, but always with someone much like Kurt Vonnegut who'd intervene to make things better. Sometimes this person was an investment counselor, other times a storm window salesman (and installer), occupations Kurt figured as not so different from his own running of a short story business in small-town America of the 1950s. If a story went heavy on romance, his agents shopped it around the widely popular magazines slanted to women's interests, including the *Ladies' Home Journal*, *Redbook*, and *Cosmopolitan*, the last of which "wasn't always a sex manual," as Vonnegut had to remind an interviewer in 1999. On this same occasion Kurt confessed to radio's Michael Feldman on *Whad'Ya Know?* that he "could be manly, too," explaining why one story went to *Esquire* and another to *Argosy*, respectively the high and low ends of male interest journals. There were many more such magazines in between, and in the 1950s they supported a number of authors who would later find great success with novels, not the least of which was the author of *The Godfather*, Mario Puzo.

Then there was the science fiction market, where Kurt Vonnegut inadvertently ran afoul of establishment critics. In his lifetime only five stories were published here, and the best of them, "Harrison Bergeron," was famously reprinted in the political journal *National Review* as a favorite of editor and commentator William F. Buckley. But three of his first four novels featured science, as did several of his short stories from the family weeklies. Kurt knew science and wanted to write about it, especially as in the 1950s he could see how it was influencing American life, for good or bad. As Knox Burger told the editors of *The Vonnegut Statement* in 1973, all agents would submit their clients' stories to the top-paying markets first, and only in the face of rejections work their way down from the fifty-cent-per-word level to the penny-a-word pulp market. In his fifth novel, *God Bless You, Mr. Rosewater* (1965), Vonnegut has his title character visit an actual convention of science fiction writers and praise them as "the only ones who'll talk about the *really* terrific changes going on . . . the only ones with guts enough to *really* care about the future, who *really* notice what machines do to us, what wars do to us, what cities do to us, what big, simple ideas do to us, what tremendous misunderstandings, mistakes, accidents and catastrophes do to us." That roster of concerns sounds much like what Kurt Vonnegut wrote about in both his novels and his stories. But he also makes his character Eliot Rosewater drunk when he says this; in a sober moment, Eliot admits that science fiction writers "couldn't write for sour apples," just simply manipulate ideas. Vonnegut's own goal was to treat science *and* write well. But the reputation of so much popular science fiction writing being bad haunted his career, costing him some critical appreciation; he describes this fate in "Science Fiction," his first essay collected in *Wampeters, Foma & Granfalloons.*

In *Fates Worse Than Death* (1991) Kurt writes about how his first magazine sale made his father proud, and one suspects his mother would have been proud, too, despite having died by her own hand in despair over her family's failed fortune. They'd lost it in the Great Depression, and she struggled to produce earnings by submitting short stories to popular magazines. As Vonnegut recalls in his "self-interview" collected in *Palm Sunday,* "She was a highly intelligent, cultivated woman" who had earned A-plus in every high school class, including writing—where she was taught to write in a highly finished style. "She was a good writer," her son allowed, "but she had no talent for the vulgarity the slick magazines required." By "vulgarity" Kurt surely meant the vernacular that English teachers of the day (and of his mother's elevated social class) deplored. "Fortunately," he continues, "I was loaded with vulgarity, so when I grew up I was able to make her dream come true."

Readers of *Complete Stories* will find vulgarity in just one short story written with a prank in mind for a science fiction anthology later in his career. Its title is a clear giveaway. Otherwise stories from *Collier's,* the *Saturday Evening Post,* the *Ladies' Home Journal,* and others abound in the distinctive voice and honest expression the author made his hallmarks. It's evident when he writes of war (he was a veteran) and of peace (he was an advocate). It anchors his stories about science and a scientific future in practicalities as familiar as the kitchen refrigerator (he prided himself on knowing how it worked). His narrators have real jobs: selling and installing storm windows, counseling on investments, conducting the high school band. His characters fall in love, sometimes awkwardly but always sincerely. Generationally, Kurt Vonnegut was representative of his times: born into comfortable circumstances during the roaring twenties, seeing his family lose most of its money in the Great Depression, serving in World War II, returning to school on the GI Bill, commencing a career in the new corporate world and then quitting it to start his own small business, a short story business. What follows are its profits.

—JK

How Vonnegut Learned to Write Short Stories

A scrawled name at the bottom of a rejection letter from *Collier's* magazine opened the door to Kurt Vonnegut's professional career as a writer. At first he didn't recognize it. He made out the message that said, "This is a little sententious for us. You're not the Kurt Vonnegut who worked on the *Cornell Daily Sun* in 1942, are you?" Kurt thought the scrawled signature might be "Owen Buyer, Ormes Bruyes, or Dunk Briges, all persons unknown to me." As fate or luck or the Muses would have it, a photographer Kurt worked with at General Electric suggested he send some of the stories he was writing to a war buddy the photographer knew from *Yank*. His buddy's name was Knox Burger and he worked for *Collier's*—he was the fiction editor.

Collier's. Kurt dug out the rejection letter and deciphered "Knox Burger" as the name he hadn't been able to make out. Burger had been editor of a humor magazine called the *Cornell Widow* while Kurt wrote for the *Sun*. He lost no time in going to New York for lunch with Knox, and a friendship and mentorship began that lasted many years.

Kurt sent Knox a selection of recent stories and Knox responded the way good editors did in those days—with a detailed letter of instructions (July 13, 1949) for how to improve a story that he felt had potential, one called "Mnemonics." Vonnegut later reflected that "Agents and editors back then could tell a writer how to fine-tune a story as though they were pit mechanics and the story were a race car" (introduction to *Bagombo Snuff Box*).

Burger's suggestions were indeed as detailed as those for taking a car apart—a full page of single-spaced instructions followed by the encouraging belief that the story had . . . possibilities. Knox said a particular character needed to be more motivated and told how to do that; he wanted a wife's shopping list to be more imaginative and gave examples of items she might be shopping for. He believed one reference was "forced" and asked that it be replaced . . .

Kurt immediately addressed each suggestion with fixes, only to receive another letter with further revisions. Kurt copied down each point he needed to address and shot off his latest revisions, only to receive a final response that the story had been sent up to the publisher, who felt not only that it didn't come off but that it had left a bad taste in his mouth!

Had I been reading all this in a novel about an aspiring writer, I would have feared that turning the page I would find that the hero had hurled himself, or at least his typewriter, off the nearest cliff. Vonnegut didn't even throw the story away. He must have taken it apart again, worked on it more and longer, for "Mnemonics" was finally published in *Collier's* almost two years later (April 28, 1951). As Ginger Strand observed in her perceptive account *The Brothers Vonnegut*, "Plenty of guys had literary dreams, but Kurt also had discipline."

While most novice writers react to a flood of rejections by deciding that the editors are just too dumb or insensitive to appreciate the author's deathless prose, Vonnegut had the unusual reaction that his stories were rejected because they weren't good enough. He wrote in "Coda to My Career as a Writer for Periodicals" (*Bagombo*) that when he was starting out, there were some magazines that "to their credit, would not touch my stuff with rubber gloves. I wasn't offended or ashamed. I understood. I was nothing if not modest."

Over the course of the years he was sending out short stories to magazines (from 1947 to 1963) Vonnegut got rejection slips at some time or other from the following magazines: *Today's Woman, This Week*, the *Atlantic, Redbook, Life, Collier's, Liberty*, the *New Yorker, Story, Esquire, Tomorrow, Harper's, McCall's*, the *Tiger's Eye*, the *Yale Review, Coronet, American Magazine, Cosmopolitan*, the *American Mercury, Scientific American, Direction, Nugget, Science Fiction and Fantasy, Family Circle*, the *Dial, Woman's Day, Mademoiselle*.

He knew he had to learn the technique of writing saleable stories, but Burger didn't have the time to continue teaching him. As fiction editor of *Collier's* he had to edit six short stories a week. He believed this neophyte was worth nurturing, so he found him a literary agent.

Kurt had already tried and been rejected by the Russell and Volkening Agency, who represented such luminaries as Saul Bellow, Eudora Welty, and Henry Miller. Knox recommended Littauer and Wilkinson, telling them he thought Vonnegut "might turn out to be a skillful and prolific writer." Ken Littauer had been Knox's predecessor as fiction editor of *Collier's*, and his partner, Max Wilkinson, was a former story editor of MGM. Kurt himself could not have created more colorful characters to play the role of agents in a novel about a young writer's progress; Littauer was a former colonel in the Lafayette Escadrille, who wore a fuzzy bowler hat and carried a furled umbrella, while Wilkinson had the distinction of getting punched in the nose by F. Scott Fitzgerald (as thanks for trying to get him some money from Hollywood).

Littauer ably took over where Burger left off. As Kurt later wrote in the *Bagombo* introduction, "If I sent [Littauer] a story that didn't quite work, wouldn't quite satisfy a reader, he would tell me how to fix it." In one of his "fixes" Littauer wrote a two-page single-spaced analysis of the story "The Honor of a Newsboy" that included a page of dialogue between two characters that simplified the plot. He responded to every story with suggestions of how to improve it.

He wrote Kurt on August 28, 1959, coming down hard on his criticism of the story "FUBAR," and ended with the explanation of his editorial psychology: "If the foregoing [criticism] enrages you, I have gained my purpose—which is to stimulate your imagination, by playing on your emotions. So, revile me to your heart's content, but fix the story!"

Kurt had written for his high school and college newspapers (the *Shortridge Daily Echo* and the *Cornell Sun*) but when he came home from World War II he began to write with real determination and purpose. You could sense it in his first letter home to his family after being in the POW camp in Dresden during the firebombing that destroyed that city:

"We were put to work carrying corpses from Air-Raid shelters; women, children, old men; dead from concussion, fire or suffocation. Civilians cursed us and threw rocks as we carried bodies to huge funeral pyres in the city." The bombing had destroyed all of Dresden—"but not me," a theme and thought that recurs through the letter, as a later phrase, "so it goes," will recur several decades later in his classic novel *Slaughterhouse-Five*.

Stationed at Fort Riley, Kansas, after the war as a clerk typist, before his discharge, Vonnegut wrote stories, sending them out to magazines, encouraged by his newly married wife, Jane Cox, who had him read *The Brothers Karamazov* on their honeymoon, and who helped him from her own experience as an editor of the Swarthmore literary magazine.

I cringed when I read that Jane, in hopes of finding Kurt advice and encouragement, had sent some of his work to a "literary consultant." In my own time starting out in New York in the fifties, I knew young women who were recent college grads who got such "literary" jobs and sometimes learned the practice was to find promise in aspiring writers who were willing to pay for further "editorial advice." Kurt of course received a letter of encouragement, but fortunately (in this instance) neither he nor Jane had the twenty dollars that would have to be paid to receive further encouragement and advice. That didn't stop Kurt from writing or Jane from encouraging him.

He continued writing stories when he went to the University of Chicago master's program in anthropology, and he learned on the job as a reporter for the City News Bureau (as Hemingway had learned before him on the *Kansas City Star*). While working for General Electric by day, turning out press releases and feature articles on new products, Kurt was writing his own short stories at night and on weekends, sending them out continually.

The connection with Burger, who had passed him on to Littauer, began the professional leg of Kurt's journey. It was Burger who published Kurt's first story, "Report on the Barnhouse Effect," after Ken Littauer got him to work on the ending and make it into a dramatic conclusion instead of a speech. The result finally met Burger's standards and a check was dispatched to Vonnegut for $750, minus the agent's 10 percent.

Kurt wrote to his father on October 28, 1949, to report his proud news:

> Dear Pop:
>
> I sold my first story to Collier's. Received my check ($750 minus a 10% agent's commission [from the Littauer and Wilkinson agency]), yesterday noon. It now appears that two more of my works have a good chance of being sold in the near future.
>
> I think I'm on my way. I've deposited my first check in a savings account and, if I sell more, will continue to do so until I have the equivalent of one year's pay at GE. Four more stories will do it nicely, with cash to spare (something we never had before). I will then quit this goddamn nightmare job, and never take another one so long as I live, so help me God.
>
> I'm happier than I've been for a great many years.
> Love,
> K.

Decades later, in *Fates Worse Than Death*, Vonnegut wrote that while this story "is no milestone in literature . . . it looms like Stonehenge beside my own little footpath from birth to death." He wrote that his father glued cheerful messages to pieces of Masonite and protected them with varnish; he did that with this letter from Kurt, and on the back of the piece of Masonite he glued a message, "in his own lovely hand," a quotation from *The Merchant of Venice*:

> An oath, an oath, I have an oath in Heaven:
> Shall I lay perjury on [*sic*] my soul?

Speaking of his agents' expertise, in his *Bagombo* introduction, Kurt says, "With help like that, I sold one, and then two, and then three stories, and banked more money than a year's salary at GE." After "Barnhouse," Kurt sold "Thanasphere," "*Der Arme Dolmetscher*," "EPICAC," and "All the King's Horses." He was able to quit "the damnable job" at the start of 1951.

As well as his agents, he also had Jane, a wife who acted (as many writers' wives did in those days) as partner and cheerleader. She read all of Kurt's work and together they studied the stories that the magazines he was trying to write for published, attempting to decipher story ideas for the "slicks," as the popular weekly magazines of the era were known—not necessarily because of "slick formula stories" but because of the slick paper they were printed on (as opposed to the "pulps," magazines published on rough paper and with "rough" contents indicated by the magazines' names, such as *True Men, Men's Adventure*, etc.). The slicks boasted stories by important authors—Hemingway, Steinbeck, Fitzgerald, Faulkner.

Jane had faith that Kurt would someday be in those ranks of great American writers. "She knew my father was going to be famous and it was all going to be worth it," their son Mark wrote in his memoir *Just Like Someone Without Mental Illness Only More So.* Kurt expressed his faith in Jane in a letter to Burger (February 1, 1955) that also expressed his worries over buying a new house and not yet having sold the old one: "Everything's going to be just grand, though. Jane says so. She says she knows it in her bones. And I no kidding believe her. I'd better, with two houses and $20,000 in mortgages."

Part of that faith was based on Kurt's five years' experience in what he called "a crazy seller's market for short stories in 1950. There were four weekly magazines that published three or more of the things in every issue. Six monthlies did the same" (*Fates Worse Than Death, Bagombo Snuff Box*).

But times were changing. "Only three years after I left Schenectady, advertisers started withdrawing their money from magazines."

Short stories had been our national entertainment but they were being replaced by television.

"When my cash cows the slick magazines were put out of business by TV, I wrote industrial advertising and then sold cars instead, and invented a new board game, and taught in a private school for fucked up rich kids, and so on" (*Fates Worse Than Death*).

As Mark wrote in his memoir, "The pressure to make money made it so he couldn't write, so he had to try to sell cars, which he was bad at." When Mark was ten years old Kurt asked to borrow $300 he had saved from his paper route. Mark graduated from Swarthmore in 1968, the year before *Slaughterhouse-Five* was published: "I never knew my father as a rich and famous writer. I knew him as the man who was turned down for a job teaching English at Cape Cod Community College."

While piecing together a living during those years ("What we were mainly living on was hope," Jane Vonnegut Yarmolinsky said in her book *Angels Without Wings*) Vonnegut managed to write five novels that made less money than some of his stories for the slicks before being saved (in succession), financially, by the Iowa Writers' Workshop, a Guggenheim Fellowship, and the publisher Seymour Lawrence (who brought out *Slaughterhouse-Five* in 1969). Kurt's short story career ended fittingly when one of his best stories, "The Hyannis Port Story," was sold to the *Saturday Evening Post*. It was set to appear in the issue that was canceled the week of JFK's assassination.

In a 1999 *New York Times* op-ed piece called "Can Writing Be Taught?" Vonnegut wrote that "thanks to popular magazines, I learned on the job to be a fiction writer. Such paid literary apprenticeships, with standards so low, don't exist anymore. Thus: graduate writing programs . . .

"When the subject of creative writing courses is raised in company as sophisticated as readers of this paper, say, two virtually automatic responses can be expected:

First a withering 'Can you really teach anyone how to write?' An editor of this very paper asked me that only two days ago. . . . Listen, there were creative writing teachers long before there were creative writing courses, and they were called and continue to be called *editors*."

And good teachers today do what good editors did in Vonnegut's day. That's what Vonnegut did when he taught at the Iowa Writers' Workshop, Harvard, and the City College of New York.

The death of Kurt's friend John D. MacDonald, the popular mystery writer, prompted him to write a letter to the widow in which he remarked on "how seriously incomplete literary history must always be. How few of us know that John and I were members of an unacknowledged school of writing rooted in The Golden Age of Magazine Fiction which followed World War Two, and that for us, 'Knox Burger,' and 'Ken Littauer,' and 'Max Wilkinson' and so on were names to conjure with."

Along with Kurt Vonnegut.

—DW

War

The obvious bridge between Kurt Vonnegut the novelist and Vonnegut the short story writer is war. Of his fourteen novels, *Slaughterhouse-Five* remains his most famous and most characteristic piece of work, even though its presumed centerpiece, the firebombing of Dresden, is inferred rather than depicted. There is nothing intelligent to say about a massacre, this book teaches us, but there is a great deal to talk about nonetheless. In similar manner his many short stories about warfare avoid presentations of actual combat. When he does put soldiers to the test, it is in fantastic circumstances, such as the literally mortal game played in "All the King's Horses" and the apparently hallucinatory action in "Great Day." Otherwise it is war as an idea that is treated.

"I'm deeply interested in wars and, in a terrible way, sort of a fan," the otherwise vocal pacifist admitted to interviewers Henry James Cargas and John Keegan in a November 1988 telephone interview transcription housed in the Lilly Library. "I'm interested in how they had been fought, how they *should* be fought and so forth." He could trace this fascination to something more elemental than his own service in World War II, Vonnegut specified. "It's an ugly interest, I think, and it may have something to do with chess. I've played chess all my life and of course there are good ways and bad ways." What happens to people when they play chess is hardly the stuff for compelling fiction, but when it is a device for warfare the results are anything but trivial or boring.

"What do we talk about when we talk about war?" As a twenty-four-year-old commencing his career as a fiction writer, Kurt Vonnegut knew for sure that if the discussion were to make sense, it would not be about guns and bullets and bombs and explosions. There were plenty of other writers doing that, and he feared such work would only encourage more warfare, as combat always seems entrancing to the young. His own experience in combat had been brief, when his squad of advance infantry scouts lost their way between lines and were captured in the Battle of the Bulge late in 1944. For him the war was over. For the next five months he'd survive as a prisoner of war in Dresden and then for a few more days as a refugee foraging for food after Germany's surrender. As every aspiring writer who'd read Ernest Hemingway knew (and every one of them had read him), you should "write about what you know." And so Kurt did. The problem was that nobody wanted to read it.

After sending an article about his experiences to the *American Mercury* in June 1946 and having it rejected, he tried them a little more than a year later with a short story. Assuming that editor Charles Angoff would value it more highly if its credibility were anchored in fact, Vonnegut revealed that "the events described actually took place in Dresden." Though fashioned as a narrative and benefitting from all the proper fictive devices such as characterization, imagery, development by dialogue, and a well-plotted resolution, "Brighten Up" was, Kurt insisted, absolutely true. Perhaps that was the problem, because Angoff turned it down just like its nonfiction predecessor. "Brighten Up," along with several other short stories about World War II and Kurt's early essay about the Dresden firebombing, "Wailing Shall Be in All Streets," did not appear until 2008. That was a year after his death, when his son Mark helped organize the posthumous collection *Armageddon in Retrospect and Other New and Unpublished Writings on War and Peace*. By then the author's views on war, and especially his unique way of presenting them, had helped reshape America's understanding of World War II and its many wars afterward. But in 1946 and 1947, the country wasn't ready for what Kurt had to say. Nor had he devised his unique way of saying it, except in the May 29, 1945, letter to his family that Mark added to his book. There young Kurt spoke directly, to real people he could visualize and in a vernacular style with all the candences and familiar phrasings that identified him as "a person from Indianapolis," which many years later he credited as being the quality of his best work. All this would eventually bring him success.

For now, he had a family to support. Mark was a babe in arms when "Brighten Up" was written, and five more kids would follow: a pair of daughters with his wife Jane, and three nephews he and Jane welcomed when their parents died within days of each other. His initial sales, not starting until 1950, were stories with other subjects. His first "war story" would have combat take place not on the battlefield but on a chessboard, and with Americans (including women and children) not facing off against Germans but being captives of a rogue Asian warlord suggestive of the Korean War that had commenced in June 1950. "All the King's Horses" appeared in *Collier's* for February 10, 1951, a date that indicates how this World War II veteran was for the first time, at least in warfare, ahead of his times. Unlike the previous conflict, for which America had little trouble mobilizing after Japan's attack on Pearl Harbor, what was happening on the Korean Peninsula was confusing. There were two Koreas, North and South; one was supported by the Soviet Union and China, the other not so much by the United States as by the United Nations, which in South Korea's defense mounted not a war but a "police action." Especially troublesome was that unlike Germany and Japan in the decade before, the Soviets had long-range aircraft capable of bombing the mainland United States. And not just with conventional bombs, but with atomic weapons. Bombers could be shot down, of course, but there was another long range delivery system now in existence: intercontinental ballistic missiles. The US and the USSR were not formally at war, but there was something more ominous underway called the Cold War. In time, British poet and American resident W. H. Auden would call it "the Age of Anxiety." Here, months after its start, Kurt Vonnegut expressed those anxieties in a perfectly crafted story about the craft of conflict itself, "All the King's Horses."

Throughout the 1950s, Kurt Vonnegut would find that Cold War stories sold better than hot war pieces. "Thanasphere," published by *Collier's* on September 5, 1950, in advance of his hot war taking place on the chess board, locates the action in peacetime—but in a peacetime observed from outer space, where an officer of the United States Air Force has been sent to monitor Soviet developments. What he actually hears only a writer like Vonnegut could have devised. In "The Manned Missiles" from *Cosmopolitan* of July 1958 the author drafts a pair of letters exchanged between the fathers of two deceased young astronauts, one Russian and the other American. Here sentiment and emotion overcome both the chill of technology and the heat of conflict. Only in this way might anxieties be relieved.

Vonnegut fans today know their favorite writer handled "his" war best by indirection. The Allied firebombing of Dresden on February 13, 1945, may have been its highlight, but in *Slaughterhouse-Five* the raid itself is never described, just its aftermath. *Mother Night*, Kurt's novel set almost entirely in World War II, has much more about the domestic reality of Germany during these years. When adding a new introduction to this book in 1966, he showed the first evidence of his confident, hometown voice for speaking of the bombing. Unlike the dull, discursive tone of the rejected "Wailing Shall Be in All Streets," this piece speaks personally of his night in the air raid shelter when he "heard the bombs walking around up there." This sounds like a person from Indianapolis talking to another person, one who wasn't in Dresden but who can certainly relate to hearing a heavy-footed tenant making a nuisance upstairs.

Beyond that, the challenge was to speak when there are no words equal to the experience. And so when we talk about war, we talk about its aftermath. All of Kurt's World War II stories, sold to magazines or saved for publication after his death, are set in the months following his capture, in the days following the German surrender, or in the period of American Occupation of the defeated Third Reich. "D.P." (from the *Ladies' Home Journal* of August 1953) and "The Commandant's Desk" (unsold) pose US Army occupiers against beleaguered citizens enduring the humiliations of defeat. "D.P." was placed quickly in the magazine market and was produced for television on *General Electric Theater*, where the show was introduced by host Ronald Reagan and the action featured Sammy Davis Jr. in his first dramatic role. "The Commandant's Desk" was more trouble. In the ebullience of being able to quit his job as a publicist for General Electric and preparing to move to the happier environs of Cape Cod, where he could be a full-time fiction writer, Vonnegut sent the story off to Knox Burger at *Collier's* with a letter (April 14, 1951) praising his own work and asking for "a fat bonus." On May 18 Burger replied with over one thousand words of counsel and criticism. The "viewpoint character" was not steady enough to anchor the story, but neither was his former enemy, the American captain. First-person stories need a special flavor that "usually stems strongly from the particular personality of the teller," Knox advised, and recommended that Kurt take a look at some stories by Sherwood Anderson and Stephen Vincent Benet. Hopefully he'd see that having the "old man tell his tale" and letting the captain's reactions "provide the reader with an easier and fuller opportunity to identify and react" was a better way to proceed. A dozen more suggestions followed. On May 22 Burger wrote Kurt again, wishing that "you'd give a higher priority to THE COM-MANDANT'S DESK," as its June 15 deadline was looming. In the end, all efforts failed and publication waited until a year after Vonnegut's death.

For another war story, this one set in the year 1067 during the aftermath of the Battle of Hastings, recently conquered Britains debate how to deal with their new French rulers. "The Unicorn Trap" interested Knox Burger not at all. On November 24, 1954, he was blunt. "Put it away, Kurt," he urged. "It is tainted with genius, but of the madder kind." Magazines, at least of the day, were "too literal" for such foolery, however wise at bottom. And so it too would wait more than a lifetime for publication.

It and eight other war stories by this young (at the time) author fill out *Armageddon in Retrospect* half a century later. Read today, collected as his mentors of the late 1940s and 1950s hoped they would be someday, these pieces hang together in a beneficially coherent way. Mutually reenforcing are scenes of POW life, cravings for food that override desires that were preeminent in these young soldiers' peacetime lives, and interactions among themselves (where some are good guys and others not). One early effort not included in the *Armageddon* volume is "Atrocity Story," appearing here for the first time. Like much of Kurt Vonnegut's World War II material, it is based on fact: in the corpse mining Kurt and his fellow prisoners were tasked to do after the firebombing, a colleague was caught looting and was executed for it. Here, quite naturally, the item is food. In *Slaughterhouse-Five* it is a teapot, and in the film it is most effectively a Dresden figurine that matches one accidently destroyed before the war by a clumsy child. Although Vonnegut had no hand in the script, he praised screenwriter Stephen Geller's work, regretting only that the film, unlike the novel, was one character short: "me." Yet on a day when he was on set during the production Kurt Vonnegut did manage to insinuate himself in the action, albeit in a conventionally fictive way. It happens in the hospital room Billy Pilgrim shares with Air Force historian Bertram Copeland Rumford, a hawkish professor with no sympathy for Dresden or anyone who suffered there. As can happen in filmmaking, intial takes were going poorly. The exposition was clear, the chemistry between Billy (drifting in and out of consciousness) and Rumfoord (impatiently recovering from a skiing accident) was working, and director George Roy Hill felt the continuity to the next segment was clear—except that no one knew how to "get out of" the scene comfortably. Kurt Vonnegut did, suggesting that after Rumfoord's blustering about the raid's irrelevance to history and Billy's sudden mention that "I was there" the pompous professor would snort, "So write your own book!"

Where Kurt Vonnegut *wasn't* is also dealt with in one of the *Armageddon* stories. "Great Day" is set in the future. Getting there has never been a problem for fiction writers, and for other early subjects Vonnegut would use futuristic settings to contrast hoped-for utopias with the dystopias that in human efforts so often follow. Yet futurism wouldn't work for the type of war story he wanted to write: indeed, given the way warfare was developing there might not be a future. Instead, he used a device he was also toying with for a story that would intermix science and tragedy, "Between Timid and Timbuktu." As a character would note much later in Vonnegut's novel *The Sirens of Titan*, everything in the dictionary between these two words involved "time." Throughout his life, time obsessed this writer—not just the familiar theme of transience, but its relativity and perhaps transportability. Could there be such a thing as "time travel"? In "Great Day" the author undertakes his first experiment with the device that would be instrumental to the success of *Slaughterhouse-Five*.

It is no coincidence that time travel is also the only way Kurt Vonnegut could write about conventional military combat: not on a chessboard, not in a prisoner-of-war camp, and not in the chaos of war's aftermath, but on a real battlefield with real soldiers (and actual casualties). First-time readers of "Great Day" will be surprised to learn where it happens, and how the narrative gets there, and what the title "Great Day" means. It won't be what they think, but the story will still get them thinking. Which is all the writer of this and the other war stories wanted, while at the same time supporting his family.

—JK

COMPLETE STORIES

All the King's Horses

COLONEL BRYAN KELLY, his huge figure blocking off the light that filtered down the narrow corridor behind him, leaned for a moment against the locked door in an agony of anxiety and helpless rage. The small Oriental guard sorted through a ring of keys, searching for the one that would open the door. Colonel Kelly listened to the voices inside the room.

"Sarge, they wouldn't dare do anything to Americans, would they?" The voice was youthful, unsure. "I mean, there'd be hell to pay if they hurt—"

"Shut up. Want to wake up Kelly's kids and have them hear you running off at the mouth that way?" The voice was gruff, tired.

"They'll turn us loose pretty quick, whaddya bet, Sarge?" insisted the young voice.

"Oh, sure, kid they love Americans around here. That's probably what they wanted to talk to Kelly about, and they're packing the beer and ham sandwiches into box lunches for us right now. All that's holding things up is they don't know how many with mustard, how many without. How d'ya want yours?"

"I'd just like to—"

"Shut up."

"Okay, I'd just—"

"Shut up."

"I'd just like to know what's going on, is all." The young corporal coughed.

"Pipe down and pass that butt along," said a third voice irritably. "There's ten good puffs left in it. Don't hog the whole thing, kid." A few other voices muttered in agreement.

Colonel Kelly opened and closed his hands nervously, wondering how he could tell the fifteen human beings behind the door about the interview with Pi Ying and the lunatic ordeal they were going to have to endure. Pi Ying said that their fight against death would be no different, philosophically, from what all of them, except Kelly's wife and children, had known in battle. In a cold way, it was true—no different, philosophically. But Colonel Kelly was more shaken than he had ever been in battle.

Colonel Kelly and the fifteen on the other side of the door had crash-landed two days before on the Asiatic mainland, after they had been blown off course by a sudden storm

7

and their radio had gone dead. Colonel Kelly had been on his way, with his family, to a post as military attaché in India. On board the Army transport plane with them had been a group of enlisted men, technical specialists needed in the Middle East. The plane had come to earth in territory held by a Communist guerrilla chief, Pi Ying.

All had survived the crash—Kelly, his wife Margaret, his ten-year-old twin sons, the pilot and copilot, and the ten enlisted men. A dozen of Pi Ying's ragged riflemen had been waiting for them when they climbed from the plane. Unable to communicate with their captors, the Americans had been marched for a day through rice fields and near-jungle to come at sunset to a decaying palace. There they had been locked in a subterranean room, with no idea of what their fates might be.

Now, Colonel Kelly was returning from an interview with Pi Ying, who had told him what was to become of the sixteen American prisoners. *Sixteen*—Kelly shook his head as the number repeated itself in his thoughts.

The guard prodded him to one side with his pistol and thrust the key into the lock, and the door swung open. Kelly stood silently in the doorway.

A cigarette was being passed from hand to hand. It cast its glow for an instant on each expectant face in turn. Now it lighted the ruddy face of the talkative young corporal from Minneapolis, now cast rugged shadows over the eye sockets and heavy brows of the pilot from Salt Lake, now bloomed red at the thin lips of the sergeant.

Kelly looked from the men to what seemed in the twilight to be a small hillock by the door. There his wife Margaret sat, with the blond heads of her sleeping sons cradled in her lap. She smiled up at him, her face misty white. "Darling—you're all right?" Margaret asked quietly.

"Yes, I'm all right."

"Sarge," said the corporal, "ask him what Pi Ying said."

"Shut up." The sergeant paused. "What about it, sir—good news or bad?"

◎ ◎ ◎

Kelly stroked his wife's shoulder, trying to make the right words come—words to carry courage he wasn't sure he had. "Bad news," he said at last. "Rotten news."

"Well, let's have it," said the transport pilot loudly. Kelly supposed he was trying to reassure himself with the boom of his own voice, with brusqueness. "The worst he can do is kill us. Is that it?" He stood and dug his hands into his pockets.

"He wouldn't dare!" said the young corporal in a threatening voice—as though he could bring the wrath of the United States Army to bear on Pi Ying with a snap of his fingers.

Colonel Kelly looked at the youngster with curiosity and dejection. "Let's face it. The little man upstairs has all the trumps." An expression borrowed from another game, he thought irrelevantly. "He's an outlaw. He hasn't got a thing to lose by getting the United States sore at him."

"If he's going to kill us, say so!" the pilot said explosively. "So he's got us cold! What's he going to do?"

"He considers us prisoners of war," said Kelly, trying to keep his voice even. "He'd like to shoot us all." He shrugged. "I haven't been trying to keep you in suspense, I've been looking for the right words—and there aren't any. Pi Ying wants more entertainment out of us than shooting us would provide. He'd like to prove that he's smarter than we are in the bargain."

"How?" asked Margaret. Her eyes were wide. The two children were waking up.

"In a little while, Pi Ying and I are going to play chess for your lives." He closed his fist over his wife's limp hand. "And for my four lives. It's the only chance Pi Ying will give us." He shrugged, and smiled wryly. "I play a better-than-average game—a little better than average."

"Is he nuts?" said the sergeant.

"You'll all see for yourselves," said Colonel Kelly simply. "You'll see him when the game begins—Pi Ying and his friend, Major Barzov." He raised his eyebrows. "The major claims to be sorry that, in his capacity as a military observer for the Russian army, he is powerless to intervene in our behalf. He also says we have his sympathy. I suspect he's a damn liar on both counts. Pi Ying is scared stiff of him."

"We get to watch the game?" whispered the corporal tensely.

"The sixteen of us, soldier, are the chessmen I'll be playing with."

The door swung open. . . .

◎ ◎ ◎

"Can you see the whole board from down there, White King?" called Pi Ying cheerfully from a balcony overlooking the azure-domed chamber. He was smiling down at Colonel Bryan Kelly, his family, and his men. "You must be the White King, you know. Otherwise, we couldn't be sure that you'd be with us for the whole game." The guerrilla chief's face was flushed. His smile was one of mock solicitousness. "Delighted to see all of you!"

To Pi Ying's right, indistinct in the shadows, stood Major Barzov, the taciturn Russian military observer. He acknowledged Kelly's stare with a slow nod. Kelly continued to stare fixedly. The arrogant, bristle-haired major became restless, folding and unfolding his arms, repeatedly rocking back and forth in his black boots. "I wish I could help you," he said at last. It wasn't an amenity but a contemptuous jest. "I am only an observer here." Barzov said it heavily. "I wish you luck, Colonel," he added, and turned his back.

Seated on Pi Ying's left was a delicate young Oriental woman. She gazed expressionlessly at the wall over the Americans' heads. She and Barzov had been present when Pi Ying had first told Colonel Kelly of the game he wanted to play. When Kelly had begged Pi Ying to leave his wife and children out of it, he had thought he saw a spark of pity in her eyes. As he looked up at the motionless, ornamental girl now, he knew he must have been mistaken.

"This room was a whim of my predecessors, who for generations held the people in slavery," said Pi Ying sententiously. "It served nicely as a throne room. But the floor is inlaid with squares, sixty-four of them—a chessboard, you see? The former tenants had those handsome, man-sized chessmen before you built so that they and their friends could sit up here and order servants to move them about." He twisted a ring on his finger. "Imaginative as that was, it remained for us to hit upon this new twist. Today, of course, we will use only the black chessmen, my pieces." He turned to the restive Major Barzov. "The Americans have furnished their own chessmen. Fascinating idea." His smile faded when he saw that Barzov wasn't smiling with him. Pi Ying seemed eager to please the Russian. Barzov, in turn, appeared to regard Pi Ying as hardly worth listening to.

◎ ◎ ◎

The twelve American soldiers stood against a wall under heavy guard. Instinctively, they bunched together and glared sullenly at their patronizing host. "Take it easy," said Colonel Kelly, "or we'll lose the one chance we've got." He looked quickly at his twin sons, Jerry and Paul, who gazed about the room, unruffled, interested, blinking sleepily at the side of their stunned mother. Kelly wondered why he felt so little as he watched his family in the face of death. The fear he had felt while they were waiting in their dark prison was gone. Now he recognized the eerie calm—an old wartime friend—that left only the cold machinery of his wits and senses alive. It was the narcotic of generalship. It was the essence of war.

"Now, my friends, your attention," said Pi Ying importantly. He stood. "The rules of the game are easy to remember. You are all to behave as Colonel Kelly tells you. Those of you who are so unfortunate as to be taken by one of my chessmen will be killed quickly, painlessly, promptly." Major Barzov looked at the ceiling as though he were inwardly criticizing everything Pi Ying said.

The corporal suddenly released a blistering stream of obscenities—half abuse, half self-pity. The sergeant clapped his hand over the youngster's mouth.

Pi Ying leaned over the balustrade and pointed a finger at the struggling soldier. "For those who run from the board or make an outcry, a special form of death can be arranged," he said sharply. "Colonel Kelly and I must have complete silence in which to concentrate. If the colonel is clever enough to win, then all of you who are still with us when I am checkmated will get safe transport out of my territory. If he loses—" Pi Ying shrugged. He settled back on a mound of cushions. "Now, you must all be good sports," he said briskly. "Americans are noted for that, I believe. As Colonel Kelly can tell you, a chess game can very rarely be won—any more than a battle can be won—without sacrifices. Isn't that so, Colonel?"

Colonel Kelly nodded mechanically. He was recalling what Pi Ying had said earlier—that the game he was about to play was no different, philosophically, from what he had known in war.

"How can you do this to children!" cried Margaret suddenly, twisting free of a guard and striding across the squares to stand directly below Pi Ying's balcony. "For the love of God—" she began.

Pi Ying interrupted angrily: "Is it for the love of God that Americans make bombs and jet planes and tanks?" He waved her away impatiently. "Drag her back." He covered his eyes. "Where was I? We were talking about sacrifices, weren't we? I was going to ask you who you had chosen to be your king's pawn," said Pi Ying. "If you haven't chosen one, Colonel, I'd like to recommend the noisy young man down there—the one the sergeant is holding. A delicate position, king's pawn."

The corporal began to kick and twist with new fury. The sergeant tightened his arms about him. "The kid'll calm down in a minute," he said under his breath. He turned his head toward Colonel Kelly. "Whatever the hell the king's pawn is, that's me. Where do I stand, sir?" The youngster relaxed and the sergeant freed him.

Kelly pointed to the fourth square in the second row of the huge chessboard. The sergeant strode to the square and hunched his broad shoulders. The corporal mumbled something incoherent, and took his place in the square next to the sergeant—a second dependable pawn. The rest still hung back.

"Colonel, you tell us where to go," said a lanky T-4 uncertainly. "What do we know about chess? You put us where you want us." His Adam's apple bobbed. "Save the soft spots for your wife and kids. They're the ones that count. You tell us what to do."

"There are no soft spots," said the pilot sardonically, "no soft spots for anybody. Pick a square, any square." He stepped onto the board. "What does this square make me?"

"You're a bishop, Lieutenant, the king's bishop," said Kelly.

◎ ◎ ◎

He found himself thinking of the lieutenant in those terms—no longer human, but a piece capable of moving diagonally across the board; capable, when attacking with the queen, of terrible damage to the black men across the board.

"And me in church only twice in my life. Hey, Pi Ying," called the pilot insolently, "what's a bishop worth?"

Pi Ying was amused. "A knight and a pawn, my boy; a knight and a pawn."

Thank God for the lieutenant, thought Kelly. One of the American soldiers grinned. They had been sticking close together, backed against the wall. Now they began to talk among themselves—like a baseball team warming up. At Kelly's direction, seeming almost unconscious of the meaning of their actions, they moved out onto the board to fill out the ranks.

Pi Ying was speaking again. "All of your pieces are in place now, except your knights and your queen, Colonel. And you, of course, are the king. Come, come. The game must be over before suppertime."

Gently, shepherding them with his long arms, Kelly led his wife and Jerry and Paul to their proper squares. He detested himself for the calm, the detachment with which he did it. He saw the fear and reproach in Margaret's eyes. She couldn't understand that he had to be this way—that in his coldness was their only hope for survival. He looked away from Margaret.

Pi Ying clapped his hands for silence. "There, good; now we can begin." He tugged at his ear reflectively. "I think this is an excellent way of bringing together the Eastern and Western minds, don't you, Colonel? Here we indulge the American's love for gambling with our appreciation of profound drama and philosophy." Major Barzov whispered impatiently to him. "Oh, yes," said Pi Ying, "two more rules: We are allowed ten minutes a move, and—this goes without saying—no moves may be taken back. Very well," he said, pressing the button on a stop watch and setting it on the balustrade, "the honor of the first move belongs to the white men." He grinned. "An ancient tradition."

"Sergeant," said Colonel Kelly, his throat tight, "move two squares forward." He looked down at his hands. They were starting to tremble.

"I believe I'll be slightly unconventional," said Pi Ying, half turning his head toward the young girl, as though to make sure that she was sharing his enjoyment. "Move my queen's pawn forward two squares," he instructed a servant.

Colonel Kelly watched the servant slide the massive carving forward—to a point threatening the sergeant. The sergeant looked quizzically at Kelly. "Everything okay, sir?" He smiled faintly.

"I hope so," said Kelly. "Here's your protection . . . Soldier," he ordered the young corporal, "step forward one square." There—it was all he could do. Now there was no advantage in Pi Ying's taking the pawn he threatened—the sergeant. Tactically it would be a pointless trade, pawn for pawn. No advantage so far as good chess went.

"This is very bad form, I know," said Pi Ying blandly. He paused. "Well, then again, I'm not so sure I'd be wise to trade. With so brilliant an opponent, perhaps I'd better play flawless chess, and forget the many temptations." Major Barzov murmured something to him "But it would get us into the spirit of the game right off, wouldn't it?"

"What's he talking about, sir?" asked the sergeant apprehensively.

Before Kelly could order his thoughts, Pi Ying gave the order. "Take his king's pawn."

"Colonel! What'd you do?" cried the sergeant. Two guards pulled him from the board and out of the room. A studded door banged shut behind them.

"Kill me!" shouted Kelly, starting off his square after them. A half-dozen bayonets hemmed him in.

◎ ◎ ◎

Impassively, the servant slid Pi Ying's wooden pawn onto the square where the sergeant had stood. A shot reverberated on the other side of the thick door, and the guards reappeared. Pi Ying was no longer smiling. "Your move, Colonel. Come, come—four minutes have gone already."

Kelly's calm was shattered, and with it went the illusion of the game. The pieces in his power were human beings again. The precious, brutal stuff of command was gone from Colonel Kelly. He was no more fit to make decisions of life and death than the rawest recruit. Giddily, he realized that Pi Ying's object was not to win the game quickly, but to thin out the Americans in harrowing, pointless forays. Another two minutes crept by as he struggled to force himself to be rational. "I can't do it," he whispered at last. He slouched now.

"You wish me to have all of you shot right now?" asked Pi Ying. "I must say that I find you a rather pathetic colonel. Do all American officers give in so easily?"

"Pin his ears back, Colonel," said the pilot. "Let's go. Sharpen up. Let's go!"

"You're in no danger now," said Kelly to the corporal. "Take his pawn."

"How do I know you're not lying?" said the youngster bitterly. "Now I'm going to get it!"

"Get over there!" said the transport pilot sharply.

"No!"

The sergeant's two executioners pinned the corporal's arms to his sides. They looked up expectantly at Pi Ying.

"Young man," said Pi Ying solicitously, "would you enjoy being tortured to death, or would you rather do as Colonel Kelly tells you?"

The corporal spun suddenly and sent both guards sprawling. He stepped onto the square occupied by the pawn that had taken the sergeant, kicked the piece over, and stood there with his feet apart.

Major Barzov guffawed. "He'll learn to be a pawn yet," he roared. "It's an Oriental skill Americans could do well to learn for the days ahead, eh?"

Pi Ying laughed with Barzov, and stroked the knee of the young girl, who had been sitting, expressionless, at his side. "Well, it's been perfectly even so far—a pawn for a pawn. Let's begin our offensives in earnest." He snapped his fingers for the attention of the servant. "King's pawn to king three," he commanded. "There! Now my queen and bishop are ready for an expedition into white man's territory." He pressed the button on the stop watch. "Your move, Colonel." . . .

◎ ◎ ◎

It was an old reflex that made Colonel Bryan Kelly look to his wife for compassion, courage. He looked away again—Margaret was a frightening, heartbreaking sight, and there was nothing he could do for her but win. Nothing. Her stare was vacant, almost idiotic. She had taken refuge in deaf, blind, unfeeling shock.

Kelly counted the figures still surviving on the board. An hour had passed since the game's beginning. Five pawns were still alive, among them the young corporal; one bishop, the nervy pilot; two rooks; two knights—ten-year-old frightened knights; Margaret, a rigid, staring queen; and himself, the king The missing four? Butchered—butchered in senseless exchanges that had cost Pi Ying only blocks of wood. The other soldiers had fallen silent, sullen in their own separate worlds.

"I think it's time for you to concede," said Pi Ying. "It's just about over, I'm afraid. Do you concede, Colonel?" Major Barzov frowned wisely at the chessmen, shook his head slowly, and yawned.

Colonel Kelly tried to bring his mind and eyes back into focus. He had the sensation of burrowing, burrowing, burrowing his way through a mountain of hot sand, of having to keep going on and on, digging, squirming, suffocated, blinded. "Go to hell," he muttered. He concentrated on the pattern of the chessmen. As chess, the ghastly game had been absurd. Pi Ying had moved with no strategy other than to destroy white men. Kelly had moved to defend each of his chessmen at any cost, had risked none in offense. His powerful queen, knights, and rooks stood unused in the relative safety of the two rear rows of squares. He clenched and unclenched his fists in frustration. His opponent's haphazard ranks were wide open. A checkmate of Pi Ying's king would be possible, if only the black knight weren't dominating the center of the board.

"Your move, Colonel. Two minutes," coaxed Pi Ying.

And then Kelly saw it—the price he would pay, that they all would pay, for the curse of conscience. Pi Ying had only to move his queen diagonally, three squares to the left, to put him in check. After that he needed to make one more move— inevitable, irresistible—and then checkmate, the end. And Pi Ying would move his queen. The game seemed to have lost its piquancy for him; he had the air of a man eager to busy himself elsewhere.

The guerrilla chief was standing now, leaning over the balustrade. Major Barzov stood behind him, fitting a cigarette into an ornate ivory holder. "It's a very distressing thing about chess," said Barzov, admiring the holder, turning it this way and that. "There isn't a grain of luck in the game, you know. There's no excuse for the loser." His tone was pedantic, with the superciliousness of a teacher imparting profound truths to students too immature to understand.

Pi Ying shrugged. "Winning this game gives me very little satisfaction. Colonel Kelly has been a disappointment. By risking nothing, he has deprived the game of its subtlety and wit. I could expect more brilliance from my cook."

The hot red of anger blazed over Kelly's cheeks, inflamed his ears. The muscles of his belly knotted; his legs moved apart. Pi Ying must not move his queen. If Pi Ying moved his queen, Kelly would lose; if Pi Ying moved his knight from Kelly's line of attack, Kelly would win. Only one thing might induce Pi Ying to move his knight—a fresh, poignant opportunity for sadism.

"Concede, Colonel. My time is valuable," said Pi Ying.

"Is it all over?" asked the young corporal querulously.

"Keep your mouth shut and stay where you are," said Kelly. He stared through shrewd, narrowed eyes at Pi Ying's knight, standing in the midst of the living chessmen. The horse's carved neck arched. Its nostrils flared.

The pure geometry of the white chessmen's fate burst upon Kelly's consciousness. Its simplicity had the effect of a refreshing, chilling wind. A sacrifice had to be offered to Pi Ying's knight. If Pi Ying accepted the sacrifice, the game would be Kelly's. The trap was perfect and deadly save for one detail—bait.

"One minute, Colonel," said Pi Ying.

Kelly looked quickly from face to face, unmoved by the hostility or distrust or fear that he saw in each pair of eyes. One by one he eliminated the candidates for death. These four were vital to the sudden, crushing offense, and these must guard the king. Necessity, like a child counting eeny, meeny, miney, moe around a circle, pointed its finger at the one chessman who could be sacrificed. There was only one.

Kelly didn't permit himself to think of the chessman as anything but a cipher in a rigid mathematical proposition: if x is dead, the rest shall live. He perceived the tragedy of his decision only as a man who knew the definition of tragedy, not as one who felt it.

"Twenty seconds!" said Barzov. He had taken the stop watch from Pi Ying.

The cold resolve deserted Kelly for an instant, and he saw the utter pathos of his position—a dilemma as old as mankind, as new as the struggle between East and West. When human beings are attacked, x, multiplied by hundreds or thousands, must die—sent to death by those who love them most. Kelly's profession was the choosing of x.

"Ten seconds," said Barzov.

"Jerry," said Kelly, his voice loud and sure, "move forward one square and two to your left." Trustingly, his son stepped out of the back rank and into the shadow of the black knight. Awareness seemed to be filtering back into Margaret's eyes. She turned her head when her husband spoke.

Pi Ying stared down at the board in bafflement. "Are you in your right mind, Colonel?" he asked at last. "Do you realize what you've just done?"

A faint smile crossed Barzov's face. He bent forward as though to whisper to Pi Ying, but apparently thought better of it. He leaned back against a pillar to watch Kelly's every move through a gauze of cigarette smoke.

Kelly pretended to be mystified by Pi Ying's words. And then he buried his face in his hands and gave an agonized cry. "Oh, God, no!"

"An exquisite mistake, to be sure," said Pi Ying. He excitedly explained the blunder to the young girl beside him. She turned away. He seemed infuriated by the gesture.

"You've got to let me take him back," begged Kelly brokenly.

Pi Ying rapped on the balustrade with his knuckles. "Without rules, my friend, games become nonsense. We agreed that all moves would be final, and so they are." He motioned to a servant. "King's knight to king's bishop six!" The servant moved the piece onto the square where Jerry stood. The bait was taken, the game was Colonel Kelly's from here on in.

"What is he talking about?" murmured Margaret.

"Why keep your wife in suspense, Colonel?" said Pi Ying. "Be a good husband and answer her question, or should I?"

"Your husband sacrificed a knight," said Barzov, his voice overriding Pi Ying's. "You've just lost your son." His expression was that of an experimenter, keen, expectant, entranced.

Kelly heard the choking sound in Margaret's throat, caught her as she fell. He rubbed her wrists. "Darling, please—listen to me!" He shook her more roughly than he had intended. Her reaction was explosive. Words cascaded from her—hysterical babble condemning him. Kelly locked her wrists together in his hands and listened dumbly to her broken abuse.

◎ ◎ ◎

Pi Ying's eyes bulged, transfixed by the fantastic drama below, oblivious of the tearful frenzy of the young girl behind him. She tugged at his blouse, pleading. He pushed her back without looking away from the board.

The tall T-4 suddenly dived at the nearest guard, driving his shoulder into the man's chest, his fist into his belly. Pi Ying's soldiers converged, hammered him to the floor and dragged him back to his square.

In the midst of the bedlam, Jerry burst into tears and raced terrified to his father and mother. Kelly freed Margaret, who dropped to her knees to hug the quaking child. Paul, Jerry's twin, held his ground, trembled, stared stolidly at the floor.

"Shall we get on with the game, Colonel?" asked Pi Ying, his voice high. Barzov turned his back to the board, unwilling to prevent the next step, apparently reluctant to watch it.

Kelly closed his eyes, and waited for Pi Ying to give the order to the executioners. He couldn't bring himself to look at Margaret and Jerry. Pi Ying waved his hand for silence. "It is with deep regret—" he began. His lips closed. The menace suddenly went out of his face, leaving only surprise and stupidity. The small man slumped on the balustrade, slithered over it to crash among his soldiers.

Major Barzov struggled with the Chinese girl. In her small hand, still free of his grasp, was a slender knife. She drove it into her breast and fell against the major. Barzov let her fall. He strode to the balustrade. "Keep the prisoners where they are!" he shouted at the guards. "Is he alive?" There was no anger in his voice, no sorrow—

only irritation, resentment of inconvenience. A servant looked up and shook his head.

Barzov ordered servants and soldiers to carry out the bodies of Pi Ying and the girl. It was more the act of a scrupulous housekeeper than a pious mourner. No one questioned his brisk authority.

"So this is your party after all," said Kelly.

"The peoples of Asia have lost a very great leader," Barzov said severely. He smiled at Kelly oddly. "Though he wasn't without weaknesses, was he, Colonel?" He shrugged. "However, you've won only the initiative, not the game; and now you have me to reckon with instead of Pi Ying. Stay where you are, Colonel. I'll be back shortly."

He ground out his cigarette on the ornamented balustrade, returned the holder to his pocket with a flourish, and disappeared through the curtains.

"Is Jerry going to be all right?" whispered Margaret. It was a plea, not a question, as though mercy were Kelly's to dole out or to withhold.

"Only Barzov knows," he said. He was bursting to explain the moves to her, to make her understand why he had had no choice; but he knew that an explanation would only make the tragedy infintely more cruel for her. Death through a blunder she might be able to understand; but death as a product of cool reason, a step in logic, she could never accept. Rather than accept it, she would have had them all die.

"Only Barzov knows," he repeated wearily. The bargain was still in force, the price of victory agreed to. Barzov apparently had yet to realize what it was that Kelly was buying with a life.

"How do we know Barzov will let us go if we do win?" said the T-4.

"We don't, soldier. We don't." And then another doubt began to worm into his consciousness. Perhaps he had won no more than a brief reprieve. . . .

Colonel Kelly had lost track of how long they'd waited there on the chessboard for Barzov's return. His nerves were deadened by surge after surge of remorse and by the steady pressure of terrible responsibility. His consciousness had lapsed into twilight. Margaret slept in utter exhaustion, with Jerry, his life yet to be claimed, in her arms. Paul had curled up on his square, covered by the young corporal's field jacket. On what had been Jerry's square, the horse's carved head snarling as though fire would burst from its nostrils, stood Pi Ying's black knight.

◎ ◎ ◎

Kelly barely heard the voice from the balcony—mistook it for another jagged fragment in a nightmare. His mind attached no sense to the words, heard only their sound. And then he opened his eyes and saw Major Barzov's lips moving. He saw the arrogant challenge in his eyes, understood the words. "Since so much blood has been shed in this game, it would be a pitiful waste to leave it unresolved."

Barzov settled regally on Pi Ying's cushions, his black boots crossed. "I propose to beat you, Colonel, and I will be surprised if you give me trouble. It would be very upsetting to have you win by the transparent ruse that fooled Pi Ying. It isn't that easy any more. You're playing me now, Colonel. You won the initiative for a moment. I'll take it and the game now, without any more delay."

Kelly rose to his feet, his great frame monumental above the white chessmen sitting on the squares about him. Major Barzov wasn't above the kind of entertainment Pi Ying had found so diverting. But Kelly sensed the difference between the major's demeanor and that of the guerrilla chief. The major was resuming the game, not because he liked it, but because he wanted to prove that he was one hell of a bright fellow, and that the Americans were dirt. Apparently, he didn't realize that Pi Ying had already lost the game. Either that, or Kelly had miscalculated.

In his mind, Kelly moved every piece on the board, driving his imagination to show him the flaw in his plan, if a flaw existed—if the hellish, heartbreaking sacrifice was for nothing. In an ordinary game, with nothing at stake but bits of wood, he would have called upon his opponent to concede, and the game would have ended there. But now, playing for flesh and blood, an aching, ineradicable doubt overshadowed the cleancut logic of the outcome. Kelly dared not reveal that he planned to attack and win in three moves—not until he had made the moves, not until Barzov had lost every chance to exploit the flaw, if there was one.

"What about Jerry?" cried Margaret.

"Jerry? Oh, of course, the little boy. Well, what about Jerry, Colonel?" asked Barzov. "I'll make a special concession, if you like. Would you want to take the move back?" The major was urbane, a caricature of cheerful hospitality.

"Without rules, Major, games become nonsense," said Kelly flatly. "I'd be the last to ask you to break them."

Barzov's expression became one of profound sympathy. "Your husband, madame, has made the decision, not I." He pressed the button on the stop watch. "You may keep the boy with you until the Colonel has fumbled all of your lives away. Your move, Colonel. Ten minutes."

"Take his pawn," Kelly ordered Margaret. She didn't move. "Margaret! Do you hear me?"

"Help her, Colonel, help her," chided Barzov.

Kelly took Margaret by the elbow, led her unresisting to the square where a black pawn stood. Jerry tagged along, keeping his mother between himself and Kelly. Kelly returned to his square, dug his hands into his pockets, and watched a servant take the black pawn from the board. "Check, Major. Your king is in check."

Barzov raised an eyebrow. "Check, did you say? What shall I do about this annoyance? How shall I get you back to some of the more interesting problems on the board?" He gestured to a servant. "Move my king over one square to the left."

"Move diagonally one square toward me, Lieutenant," Kelly ordered the pilot. The pilot hesitated. "Move! Do you hear?"

"Yessir." The tone was mocking. "Retreating, eh, sir?" The lieutenant slouched into the square, slowly, insolently.

"Check again, Major," Kelly said evenly. He motioned at the lieutenant. "Now my bishop has your king in check." He closed his eyes and told himself again and again that he had made no miscalculation, that the sacrifice *had* won the game, that there *could* be no out for Barzov. This was it—the last of the three moves.

"Well," said Barzov, "is that the best you can do? I'll simply move my queen in front of my king." The servant moved the piece. "Now it will be a different story."

"Take his queen," said Kelly to his farthest-advanced pawn, the battered T-4.

Barzov jumped to his feet. "Wait!"

"You didn't see it? You'd like to take it back?" taunted Kelly.

◎ ◎ ◎

Barzov paced back and forth on his balcony, breathing hard. "Of course I saw it!"

"It was the only thing you could do to save your king," said Kelly. "You may take it back if you like, but you'll find it's the only move you can make."

"Take the queen and get on with the game," shouted Barzov. "Take her!"

"Take her," echoed Kelly, and the servant trundled the huge piece to the side lines. The T-4 now stood blinking at Barzov's king, inches away. Colonel Kelly said it very softly this time: "Check."

Barzov exhaled in exasperation. "Check indeed." His voice grew louder. "No credit to you, Colonel Kelly, but to the monumental stupidity of Pi Ying."

"And that's the game, Major."

The T-4 laughed idiotically, the corporal sat down, the lieutenant threw his arms around Colonel Kelly. The two children gave a cheer. Only Margaret stood fast, still rigid, frightened.

"The price of your victory, of course, has yet to be paid," said Barzov acidly. "I presume you're ready to pay now?"

Kelly whitened. "That was the understanding, if it would give you satisfaction to hold me to it."

Barzov placed another cigarette in his ivory holder, taking a scowling minute to do it. When he spoke, it was in the tone of the pedant once more, the wielder of profundities. "No, I won't take the boy. I feel as Pi Ying felt about you—that you, as Americans, are the enemy, whether an official state of war exists or not. I look upon you as prisoners of war.

"However, as long as there is no official state of war, I have no choice, as a representative of my government, but to see that all of you are conducted safely through the lines. This was my plan when I resumed the game where Pi Ying left off. Your being freed has nothing to do with my personal feelings, nor with the outcome of the game. My winning would have delighted me and taught you a valuable lesson.

But it would have made no difference in your fates." He lighted his cigarette and continued to look at them with severity.

"That's very chivalrous of you, Major," said Kelly.

"A matter of practical politics, I assure you. It wouldn't do to precipitate an incident between our countries just now. For a Russian to be chivalrous with an American is a spiritual impossibility, a contradiction in terms. In a long and bitter history, we've learned and learned well to reserve our chivalry for Russians." His expression became one of complete contempt. "Perhaps you'd like to play another game, Colonel—plain chess with wooden chessmen, without Pi Ying's refinement. I don't like to have you leave here thinking you play a better game than I."

"That's nice of you, but not this evening."

"Well, then, some other time." Major Barzov motioned for the guards to open the door of the throne room. "Some other time," he said again. "There will be others like Pi Ying eager to play you with live men, and I hope I will again be privileged to be an observer." He smiled brightly. "When and where would you like it to be?"

"Unfortunately, the time and the place are up to you," said Colonel Kelly wearily. "If you insist on arranging another game, issue an invitation, Major, and I'll be there."

D.P.

EIGHTY-ONE small sparks of human life were kept in an orphanage set up by Catholic nuns in what had been the gamekeeper's house on a large estate overlooking the Rhine. This was in the German village of Karlswald, in the American Zone of Occupation. Had the children not been kept there, not been given the warmth and food and clothes that could be begged for them, they might have wandered off the edges of the earth, searching for parents who had long ago stopped searching for them.

Every mild afternoon the nuns marched the children, two by two, through the woods, into the village and back, for their ration of fresh air. The village carpenter, an old man who was given to thoughtful rests between strokes of his tools, always came out of his shop to watch the bobbing, chattering, cheerful, ragged parade, and to speculate, with idlers his shop attracted, as to the nationalities of the passing children's parents.

"See the little French girl," he said one afternoon. "Look at the flash of those eyes!"

"And look at that little Pole swing his arms. They love to march, the Poles," said a young mechanic.

"Pole? Where do you see any Pole?" said the carpenter.

"There—the thin, sober-looking one in front," the other replied.

"Aaaaah. He's too tall for a Pole," said the carpenter. "And what Pole has flaxen hair like that? He's a German."

The mechanic shrugged. "They're all German now, so what difference does it make?" he said. "Who can prove what their parents were? If you had fought in Poland, you would know he was a very common type."

"Look—look who's coming now," said the carpenter, grinning. "Full of arguments as you are, you won't argue with me about *him*. There we have an American!" He called out to the child. "Joe—when you going to win the championship back?"

"Joe!" called the mechanic. "How is the Brown Bomber today?"

At the very end of the parade, a lone, blue-eyed colored boy, six years old, turned and smiled with sweet uneasiness at those who called out to him every day. He nodded politely, murmuring a greeting in German, the only language he knew.

His name, chosen arbitrarily by the nuns, was Karl Heinz. But the carpenter had given him a name that stuck, the name of the only colored man who had ever made an impression on the villagers' minds, the former heavyweight champion of the world, Joe Louis.

"Joe!" called the carpenter. "Cheer up! Let's see those white teeth sparkle, Joe."

Joe obliged shyly.

The carpenter clapped the mechanic on the back. "And if *he* isn't a German too! Maybe it's the only way we can get another heavyweight champion."

Joe turned a corner, shooed out of the carpenter's sight by a nun bringing up the rear. She and Joe spent a great deal of time together, since Joe, no matter where he was placed in the parade, always drifted to the end.

"Joe," she said, "you are such a dreamer. Are all your people such dreamers?"

"I'm sorry, sister," said Joe. "I was thinking."

"Dreaming."

"Sister, am I the son of an American soldier?"

"Who told you that?"

"Peter. Peter said my mother was a German, and my father was an American soldier who went away. He said she left me with you, and then went away too." There was no sadness in his voice—only puzzlement.

Peter was the oldest boy in the orphanage, an embittered old man of fourteen, a German boy who could remember his parents and brothers and sisters and home, and the war, and all sorts of food that Joe found impossible to imagine. Peter seemed superhuman to Joe, like a man who had been to heaven and hell and back many times, and knew exactly why they were where they were, how they had come there, and where they might have been.

"You mustn't worry about it, Joe," said the nun. "No one knows who your mother and father were. But they must have been very good people, because you are so good."

"What is an American?" said Joe.

"It's a person from another country."

"Near here?"

"There are some near here, but their homes are far, far away—across a great deal of water."

"Like the river."

"More water than that, Joe. More water than you have ever seen. You can't even see the other side. You could get on a boat and go for days and days and still not get to the other side. I'll show you a map sometime. But don't pay any attention to Peter, Joe. He makes things up. He doesn't really know anything about you. Now, catch up."

◎ ◎ ◎

Joe hurried, and overtook the end of the line, where he marched purposefully and alertly for a few minutes. But then he began to dawdle again, chasing ghostlike words in his small mind: . . . soldier . . . German . . . American . . . your people . . . champion . . . Brown Bomber . . . more water than you've ever seen.

"Sister," said Joe, "are Americans like me? Are they brown?"

"Some are, some aren't, Joe."

"Are there many people like me?"

"Yes. Many, many people."

"Why haven't I seen them?"

"None of them have come to the village. They have places of their own."

"I want to go there."

"Aren't you happy here, Joe?"

"Yes. But Peter says I don't belong here, that I'm not a German and never can be."

"Peter! Pay no attention to him."

"Why do people smile when they see me, and try to make me sing and talk, and then laugh when I do?"

"Joe, Joe! Look quickly," said the nun. "See—up there, in the tree. See the little sparrow with the broken leg. Oh poor, brave little thing—he still gets around quite well. See him, Joe? Hop, hop, hippity-hop."

◎ ◎ ◎

One hot summer day, as the parade passed the carpenter's shop, the carpenter came out to call something new to Joe, something that thrilled and terrified him.

"Joe! Hey, Joe! Your father is in town. Have you seen him yet?"

"No, sir—no, I haven't," said Joe. "Where is he?"

"He's teasing," said the nun sharply.

"You see if I'm teasing, Joe," said the carpenter. "Just keep your eyes open when you go past the school. You have to look sharp, up the slope and into the woods. You'll see, Joe."

"I wonder where our little friend the sparrow is today," said the nun brightly. "Goodness, I hope his leg is getting better, don't you, Joe?"

"Yes, yes I do, sister."

She chattered on about the sparrow and the clouds and the flowers as they approached the school, and Joe gave up answering her.

The woods above the school seemed still and empty.

But then Joe saw a massive brown man, naked to the waist and wearing a pistol, step from the trees. The man drank from a canteen, wiped his lips with the back of his hand, grinned down on the world with handsome disdain, and disappeared again into the twilight of the woods.

"Sister!" gasped Joe. "My father—I just saw my father!"

"No, Joe—no you didn't."

"He's up there in the woods. I saw him. I want to go up there, sister."

"He isn't your father, Joe. He doesn't know you. He doesn't want to see you."

"He's one of my people, sister!"

"You can't go up there, Joe, and you can't stay here." She took him by the arm to make him move. "Joe—you're being a bad boy, Joe."

Joe obeyed numbly. He didn't speak again for the remainder of the walk, which brought them home by another route, far from the school. No one else had seen his wonderful father, or believed that Joe had.

Not until prayers that night did he burst into tears.

At ten o'clock, the young nun found his cot empty.

◎ ◎ ◎

Under a great spread net that was laced with rags, an artillery piece squatted in the woods, black and oily, its muzzle thrust at the night sky. Trucks and the rest of the battery were hidden higher on the slope.

Joe watched and listened tremblingly through a thin screen of shrubs as the soldiers, indistinct in the darkness, dug in around their gun. The words he overheard made no sense to him.

"Sergeant, why we gotta dig in, when we're movin' out in the mornin', and it's just maneuvers anyhow? Seems like we could kind of conserve our strength, and just scratch around a little to show where we'd of dug if there was any sense to it."

"For all you know, boy, there may *be* sense to it before mornin'," said the sergeant. "You got ten minutes to get to China and bring me back a pigtail. Hear?"

The sergeant stepped into a patch of moonlight, his hands on his hips, his big shoulders back, the image of an emperor. Joe saw that it was the same man he'd marveled at in the afternoon. The sergeant listened with satisfaction to the sounds of digging, and then, to Joe's alarm, strode toward Joe's hiding place.

Joe didn't move a muscle until the big boot struck his side. "*Ach!*"

"Who's that?" The sergeant snatched Joe from the ground, and set him on his feet hard. "My golly, boy, what you doin' here? Scoot! Go on home! This ain't no place for kids to be playin'." He shined a flashlight in Joe's face. "Doggone," he muttered. "Where you come from?" He held Joe at arm's length, and shook him gently, like a rag doll. "Boy, how you get here—swim?"

Joe stammered in German that he was looking for his father.

"Come on—how you get here? What you doin'? Where's your mammy?"

"What you got there, sergeant?" said a voice in the dark.

"Don't rightly know what to call it," said the sergeant. "Talks like a Kraut and dresses like a Kraut, but just look at it a minute."

Soon a dozen men stood in a circle around Joe, talking loudly, then softly, to him, as though they thought getting through to him were a question of tone.

◙ ◙ ◙

Every time Joe tried to explain his mission, they laughed in amazement.

"How he learn German? Tell me that."

"Where your daddy, boy?"

"Where your mammy, boy?"

"Sprecken zee Dutch, boy? Looky there. See him nod. He talks it, all right."

"Oh, you're fluent, man, mighty fluent. Ask him some more."

"Go get the lieutenant," said the sergeant. "He can talk to this boy, and under-stand what he's tryin' to say. Look at him shake. Scared to death. Come here, boy; don't be afraid, now." He enclosed Joe in his great arms. "Just take it easy, now—everything's gonna be all-l-l-l right. See what got? By golly, I don't believe the boy's ever seen chocolate before. Go on—taste it. Won't hurt you."

Joe, safe in a fort of bone and sinew, ringed by luminous eyes, bit into the choc-olate bar. The pink lining of his mouth, and then his whole soul, was flooded with warm, rich pleasure, and he beamed.

"He smiled!"

"Look at him light up!"

"Doggone if he didn't stumble right into heaven! I mean!"

"Talk about displaced persons," said the sergeant, hugging Joe, "this here's the most displaced little old person I *ever* saw. Upside down and inside out and ever' which way."

"Here, boy—here's some more chocolate."

"Don't give him no more," said the sergeant reproachfully. "You want to make him sick?"

"Naw, sarge, naw—don't wanna make him sick. No, sir."

"What's going on here?" The lieutenant, a small, elegant Negro, the beam of his flashlight dancing before him, approached the group.

"Got a little boy here, lieutenant," said the sergeant. "Just wandered into the bat-tery. Must of crawled past the guards."

"Well send him on home, sergeant."

"Yessir. I planned to." He cleared his throat. "But this ain't no ordinary little boy, lieutenant." He opened his arms so that the light fell on Joe's face.

The lieutenant laughed incredulously, and knelt before Joe. "Haw'd you get here?"

"All he talks is German, lieutenant," said the sergeant.

"Where's your home?" said the lieutenant in German.

"Over more water than you've ever seen," said Joe.

"Where do you come from?"

"God made me," said Joe.

"This boy is going to be a lawyer when he grows up," said the lieutenant in English. "Now, listen to me," he said to Joe, "what's your name, and where are your people?"

"Joe Louis," said Joe, "and you are my people. I ran away from the orphanage, because I belong with you."

The lieutenant stood, shaking his head, and translated what Joe had said.

The woods echoed with glee.

"Joe Louis! I *thought* he was awful big and powerful-lookin'!"

"Jus' keep away from that left—*tha's* all!"

If he's Joe, he's sure found his people. He's got us there!"

"Shut up!" commanded the sergeant suddenly. "All of you just shut up. This ain't no joke! Ain't nothing funny in it! Boy's all alone in the world. Ain't no joke."

A small voice finally broke the solemn silence that followed. "Naw—ain't no joke at all."

"We better take the jeep and run him back into town, sergeant," said the lieutenant. "Corporal Jackson, you're in charge."

"You tell 'em Joe was a *good* boy," said Jackson.

"Now, Joe," said the lieutenant in German, softly, "you come with the sergeant and me. We'll take you home."

Joe dug his fingers into the sergeant's forearms. "Papa! No—papa! I want to stay with you."

"Look, sonny, I ain't your papa," said the sergeant helplessly. "I *ain't* your papa."

"Papa!"

"Man, he's glued to you, ain't he, sergeant?" said a soldier. "Looks like you ain't never goin' to pry him loose. You got yourself a boy there, sarge, and he's got hisself a papa."

The sergeant walked over to the jeep with Joe in his arms. "Come on, now," he said, "you leggo, little Joe, so's I can drive. I can't drive with you hangin' on, Joe. You sit in the lieutenant's lap right next to me."

◙ ◙ ◙

The group formed again around the jeep, gravely now, watching the sergeant try to coax Joe into letting go.

"I don't want to get tough, Joe. Come on—take it easy, Joe. Let go, now, Joe, so's I can drive. See, I can't steer or nothin' with you hanging on right there."

"Papa!"

"Come on, over to my lap, Joe," said the lieutenant in German.

"Papa!"

"Joe, Joe, looky," said a soldier. "Chocolate! Want some more chocolate, Joe? See? Whole bar, Joe, all yours. Jus' leggo the sergeant and move over into the lieutenant's lap."

Joe tightened his grip on the sergeant.

"Don't put the chocolate back in your pocket, man! Give it to Joe anyways," said a soldier angrily. "Somebody go get a case of D bars off the truck, and throw 'em in the back for Joe. Give that boy chocolate enough for the nex' twenny years."

"Look, Joe," said another soldier, "ever see a wristwatch? Look at the wristwatch, Joe. See it glow, boy? Move over in the lieutenant's lap, and I'll let you listen to it tick. Tick, tick, tick, Joe. Come on, want to listen?"

Joe didn't move.

The soldier handed the watch to him. "Here, Joe, you take it anyway. It's yours." He walked away quickly.

"Man," somebody called after him, "you crazy? You paid fifty dollars for that watch. What business a little boy got with any fifty-dollar watch?"

"No—I ain't crazy. Are you?"

"Naw, I ain't crazy. Neither one of us crazy, I guess. Joe—want a knife? You got to promise to be careful with it, now. Always cut *away* from yourself. Hear? Lieutenant, when you get back, you tell him always cut *away* from hisself."

"I don't want to go back. I want to stay with *papa*," said Joe tearfully.

"Soldiers can't take little boys with them, Joe," said the lieutenant in German. "And we're leaving early in the morning."

"Will you come back for me?" said Joe.

"We'll come back if we can, Joe. Soldiers never know where they'll be from one day to the next. We'll come back for a visit, if we can."

"Can we give old Joe this case of D bars, lieutenant?" said a soldier carrying a cardboard carton of chocolate bars.

◎ ◎ ◎

"Don't ask me," said the lieutenant. "I don't know anything about it. I never saw anything of any case of D bars, never heard anything about it."

"Yessir." The soldier laid his burden down on the jeep's back seat.

"He ain't gonna let go," said the sergeant miserably. "You drive, lieutenant, and me and Joe'll sit over there."

The lieutenant and the sergeant changed places, and the jeep began to move.

"Bye, Joe!"

"You be a good boy, Joe!"

"Don't you eat all that chocolate at once, you hear?"

"Don't cry, Joe. Give us a smile."

"Wider, boy—that's the stuff!"

◎ ◎ ◎

"Joe, Joe, wake up, Joe." The voice was that of Peter, the oldest boy in the orphanage, and it echoed damply from the stone walls.

Joe sat up, startled. All around his cot were the other orphans, jostling one another for a glimpse of Joe and the treasures by his pillow.

"Where did you get the hat, Joe—and the watch, and knife?" said Peter. "And what's in the box under your bed?"

Joe felt his head, and found a soldier's wool knit cap there. "Papa," he mumbled sleepily.

"Papa!" mocked Peter, laughing.

"Yes," said Joe. "Last night I went to see my papa, Peter."

"Could he speak German, Joe?" said a little girl wonderingly.

"No, but his friend could," said Joe.

"He didn't see his father," said Peter. "Your father is far, far away, and will never come back. He probably doesn't even know you're alive."

"What did he look like?" said the girl.

Joe glanced thoughtfully around the room. "Papa is as high as this ceiling," he said at last. "He is wider than that door." Triumphantly, he took a bar of chocolate from under his pillow. "And as brown as that!" He held out the bar to the others. "Go on, have some. There is plenty more."

"He doesn't look anything like that," said Peter. "You aren't telling the truth, Joe."

"My papa has a pistol as big as this bed, almost, Peter," said Joe happily, "and a cannon as big as this house. And there were hundreds and hundreds like him."

"Somebody played a joke on you, Joe," said Peter. "He wasn't your father. How do you know he wasn't fooling you?"

"Because he cried when he left me," said Joe simply. "And he promised to take me back home across the water as fast as he could." He smiled airily. "Not like the river, Peter—across more water than you've *ever* seen. He promised, and then I let him go."

The Manned Missiles

I, MIKHAIL IVANKOV, stone mason in the village of Ilba in the Ukrainian Soviet Socialist Republic, greet you and pity you, Charles Ashland, petroleum merchant in Titusville, Florida, in the United States of America. I grasp your hand.

The first true space man was my son, Major Stepan Ivankov. The second was your son, Captain Bryant Ashland. They will be forgotten only when men no longer look up at the sky. They are like the moon and the planets and the sun and the stars.

I do not speak English. I speak these words in Russian, from my heart, and my surviving son, Alexei, writes them down in English. He studies English in school and German also. He likes English best. He admires your Jack London and your O. Henry and your Mark Twain. Alexei is seventeen. He is going to be a scientist like his brother Stepan.

He wants me to tell you that he is going to work on science for peace, not war. He wants me to tell you also that he does not hate the memory of your son. He understands that your son was ordered to do what he did. He is talking very much, and would like to compose this letter himself. He thinks that a man forty-nine is a very old man, and he does not think that a very old man who can do nothing but put one stone on top of another can say the right things about young men who die in space.

If he wishes, he can write a letter of his own about the deaths of Stepan and your son. This is my letter, and I will get Aksinia, Stepan's widow, to read it to me to make sure Alexei has made it say exactly what I wish it to say. Aksinia, too, understands English very well. She is a physician for children. She is beautiful. She works very hard so she can forget sometimes her grief for Stepan.

◎ ◎ ◎

I will tell you a joke, Mr. Ashland. When the second baby moon of the U.S.S.R. went up with a dog in it, we whispered that it was not really a dog inside, but Prokhor Ivanoff, a dairy manager who had been arrested for theft two days before. It was only a joke, but it made me think what a terrible punishment it would be to send a human being up there. I could not stop thinking about that. I dreamed about it at night, and I dreamed that it was myself who was being punished.

I would have asked my elder son Stepan about life in space, but he was far away in Guryev, on the Caspian Sea. So I asked my younger son. Alexei laughed at my fears of space. He said that a man could be made very comfortable up there. He said that many young men would be going up there soon. First they would ride in baby moons. Then they would go to the moon itself. Then they would go to other planets. He laughed at me, because only an old man would worry about such simple trips.

Alexei told me that the only inconvenience would be the lack of gravity. That seemed like a great lack to me. Alexei said one would have to drink out of nursing bottles, and one would have to get used to the feeling of falling constantly, and one would have to learn to control one's movements because gravity would no longer offer resistance to them. That was all. Alexei did not think such things would be bothersome. He expected to go to Mars soon.

Olga, my wife, laughed at me, too, because I was too old to understand the great new Age of Space. "Two Russian moons shine overhead," she said, "and my husband is the only man on earth who does not yet believe it!"

But I went on dreaming bad dreams about space, and now I had information to make my bad dreams truly scientific. I dreamed of nursing bottles and falling, falling, falling, and the strange movements of my limbs. Perhaps the dreams were supernatural. Perhaps something was trying to warn me that Stepan would soon be suffering in space as I had suffered in dreams. Perhaps something was trying to warn me that Stepan would be murdered in space.

Alexei is very embarrassed that I should say that in a letter to the United States of America. He says that you will think that I am a superstitious peasant. So be it. I think that scientific persons of the future will scoff at scientific persons of the present. They will scoff because scientific persons of the present thought so many important things were superstitions. The things I dreamed about space all came true for my son. Stepan suffered very much up there. After the fourth day in space, Stepan sometimes cried like a baby. I had cried like a baby in my dreams.

I am not a coward, and I do not love comfort more than the improvement of human life. I am not a coward for my sons, either. I knew great suffering in the war, and I understand that there must be great suffering before great joy. But when I thought of the suffering that must surely come to a man in space, I could not see the joy to be earned by it. This was long before Stepan went up in his baby moon.

I went to the library and read about the moon and the planets, to see if they were truly desirable places to go. I did not ask Alexei about them, because I knew he would tell me what fine times we would have on such places. I found out for myself in the library that the moon and the planets were not fit places for men or for any life. They were much too hot or much too cold or much too poisonous.

I said nothing at home about my discoveries at the library, because I did not wish to be laughed at again. I waited quietly for Stepan to visit us. He would not laugh at my questions. He would answer them scientifically. He had worked on rockets for years. He would know everything that was known about space.

◎ ◎ ◎

Stepan at last came to visit us, and brought his beautiful wife. He was a small man, but strong and broad and wise. He was very tired. His eyes were sunken. He knew already that he was to be shot into space. First had come the baby moon with the radio. Next had come the baby moon with the dog. Next would come the baby moons with the monkeys and the apes. After them would come the baby moon with Stepan. Stepan had been working night and day, designing his home in space. He could not tell me. He could not even tell his wife.

Mr. Ashland, you would have liked my son. Everybody liked Stepan. He was a man of peace. He was not a major because he was a great warrior. He was a major because he understood rockets so well. He was a thoughtful man. He often said that he wished that he could be a stone mason like me. He said a stone mason would have time and peace in which to think things out. I did not tell him that a stone mason thinks of little but stones and mortar.

I asked him my questions about space, and he did not laugh. Stepan was very serious when he answered me. He had reason to be serious. He was telling me why he was himself willing to suffer in space.

He told me I was right. A man would suffer greatly in space, and the moon and the planets were bad places for men. There might be good places, but they were too far for men to reach in a lifetime.

"Then, what is this great new Age of Space, Stepan?" I asked him.

"It will be an age of baby moons for a long time," he said. "We will reach the moon itself soon, but it would be very difficult to stay there more than a few hours."

"Then why go into space, if there is so little good out there?" I asked him.

◎ ◎ ◎

"There is so much to be learned and seen out there," he said. "A man could look at other worlds without a curtain of air between himself and them. A man could look at his own world, study the flow of weather over it, measure its true dimensions." This last surprised me. I thought the dimensions of our world were well known. "A man out there could learn much about the wonderful showers of matter and energy in space," said Stepan. And he spoke of many other poetic and scientific joys out there.

I was satisfied. Stepan had made me feel his own great joy at the thought of all the beauty and truth in space. I understood at last, Mr. Ashland, why the suffering would be worthwhile. When I dreamed of space again, I would dream of looking down at our own lovely green ball, dream of looking up at other worlds and seeing them more clearly than they had ever been seen.

It was not for the Soviet Union but for the beauty and truth in space, Mr. Ashland, that Stepan worked and died. He did not like to speak of the warlike uses of space. It was Alexei who liked to speak of such things, of the glory of spying on earth from baby moons, of guiding missiles to their targets from baby moons, of mastering the earth with weapons fired from the moon itself. Alexei expected Stepan to share his excitement about thoughts of such childish violence.

Stepan smiled, but only because he loved Alexei. He did not smile about war, or the things a man in a baby moon or on the moon itself could do to an enemy. "It is a use of science that we may be forced to make, Alexei," he said. "But if such a war happens, nothing will matter any more. Our world will become less fit for life than any other in the solar system."

Alexei has not spoken well of war since.

Stepan and his wife left late that night. He promised to come back before another year had passed, but I never saw him alive again.

When news came that the Soviet Union had fired a man carrying baby moon into space, I did not know that the man was Stepan. I did not dare to suspect it. I could not wait to see Stepan again, to ask him what the man had said before he took off, how he was dressed, what his comforts were. We were told that we would be able to hear the man speak from space at eight o'clock that night on the radio.

We listened. We heard the man speak. The man was Stepan.

Stepan sounded strong. He sounded happy. He sounded proud and decent and wise. We laughed until we cried, Mr. Ashland. We danced. Our Stepan was the most important man alive. He had risen above everyone, and now he was looking down, telling us what our world looked like; looking up, telling us what the other worlds looked like.

Stepan made pleasant jokes about his little house in the sky. He said it was a cylinder ten meters long and four meters in diameter. It could be very cozy. And Stepan told us that there were little windows in his house, and a television camera, and a telescope, and radar, and all manner of instruments. How delightful to live in a time when such things could be! How delightful to be the father of the man who was the eyes, ears, and heart in space for all mankind!

◎ ◎ ◎

He would remain up there for a month, he said. We began to count the days. Every night we listened to a broadcast of recordings of things Stepan had said. We heard nothing about his nosebleeds and his nausea and his crying. We heard only the calm, brave things he had said. And then, on the tenth night, there were no more recordings of Stepan. There was only music at eight o'clock. There was no news of Stepan at all, and we knew he was dead.

Only now, a year later, have we learned how Stepan died and where his body is. When I became accustomed to the horror of it, Mr. Ashland, I said, "So be it. May Major Stepan Ivankov and Captain Bryant Ashland serve to reproach us, whenever we look at the sky, for making a world in which there is no trust. May the two men be the beginning of trust between peoples. May they mark the end of the time when science sent our good, brave young men hurtling to meet in death."

I enclose a photograph of my family, taken during Stepan's last visit to us. It is an excellent picture of Stepan. The body of water in the background is the Black Sea.

Mikhail Ivankov

◎ ◎ ◎

Dear Mr. Ivankov:

Thank you for the letter about our sons. I never did get it in the mail. It was in all the papers after your Mr. Koshevoi read it out loud in the United Nations. I never did get a copy just for me. I guess Mr. Koshevoi forgot to drop it in the mailbox. That's all right. I guess that's the modern way to deliver important letters, just hand them to reporters. They say your letter to me is just about the most important thing that's happened lately, outside of the fact we didn't go to war over what happened between our two boys.

I don't speak Russian, and I don't have anybody right close by who does, so you'll have to excuse the English. Alexei can read it to you. You tell him he writes English very well—better than I do.

Oh, I could have had a lot of expert help with this letter, if I'd wanted it—people happy to write to you in perfect Russian or perfect English or perfect anything at all. Seems like everybody in this country is like your boy Alexei. They all know better than I do what I should say to you. They say I have a chance to make history, if I answer you back the right things. One big magazine in New York offered me two thousand dollars for my letter back to you, and then it turned out I wasn't even supposed to write a letter for all that money. The magazine people had already written it, and all I had to do was sign it. Don't worry. I didn't.

I tell you, Mr. Ivankov, I have had a bellyful of experts. If you ask me, our boys were experted to death. Your experts would do something, then our experts would answer back with some fancy billion-dollar stunt, and then your experts would answer that back with something fancier, and what happened finally happened. It was just like a bunch of kids with billions of dollars or billions of rubles or whatever.

You are lucky you have a son left, Mr. Ivankov. Hazel and I don't. Bryant was the only son Hazel and I had. We didn't call him Bryant after he was christened. We called him Bud. We have one daughter, named Charlene. She works for the telephone company in Jacksonville. She called up when she saw your letter in the paper, and she is the only expert about what I ought to say I've listened to. She's a real expert, I figure, because she is Bud's twin. Bud never married, so Charlene is as close as you can get to Bud. She said you did a good job, showing how your Stepan was a good-hearted man, trying to do what was right, just like anybody else. She said I should show you the same about Bud. And then she started to cry, and she said for me to tell you about Bud and the goldfish. I said, "What's the sense of writing somebody in Russia a story like that?" The story doesn't prove anything. It's just one of those silly stories a family will keep telling whenever they get together. Charlene said that was why I should tell it to you, because it would be cute and silly in Russia, too, and you would laugh and like us better.

So here goes. When Bud and Charlene were about eight, why I came home one night with a fish bowl and two goldfish. There was one goldfish for each twin, only it was impossible to tell one fish from the other one. They were exactly alike. So one morning Bud got up early, and there was one goldfish floating on top of the water dead. So Bud went and woke up Charlene, and he said, "Hey, Charlene—your goldfish just died." That's the story Charlene asked me to tell you, Mr. Ivankov.

◎ ◎ ◎

I think it is interesting that you are a mason. That is a good trade. You talk as if you lay up mostly stone. There aren't many people left in America who can really lay up stone. It's almost all cement-block work and bricks here. It probably is over there, too. I don't mean to say Russia isn't modern. I know it is.

Bud and I laid up quite a bit of block when we built the gas station here, with an apartment up over it. If you looked at the first course of block along the back wall, you would have to laugh, because you can see how Bud and I learned as we went. It's strong enough, but it sure looks lousy. One thing wasn't so funny. When we were hanging the rails for the overhead door, Bud slipped on the ladder, and he grabbed a sharp edge on the mounting bracket, and he cut a tendon on his hand. He was scared to death his hand would be crippled, and that would keep him out of the Air Force. His hand had to be operated on three times before it was right again, and every operation hurt something awful. But Bud would have let them operate a hundred times, if they had to, because there was just one thing he wanted to be, and that was a flyer.

One reason I wish your Mr. Koshevoi had thought to mail me your letter was the picture you sent with it. The newspapers got that, too, and it didn't come out too clear in the papers. But one thing we couldn't get over was all that beautiful water behind you. Somehow, when we think about Russia, we never think about any water around. I guess that shows how ignorant we are. Hazel and I live up over the gas station, and we can see water, too. We can see the Atlantic Ocean, or an inlet of it they call Indian River. We can see Merritt Island, too, out in the water, and we can see the place Bud's rocket went up from. It is called Cape Canaveral. I guess you know that. It isn't any secret where he went up from. They couldn't keep that tremendous missile secret any more than they could keep the Empire State Building secret. Tourists came from miles around to take pictures of it.

The story was, its warhead was filled with flash powder, and it was going to hit the moon and make a big show. Hazel and I thought that's what the story was, too. When it took off, we got set for a big flash on the moon. We didn't know it was our Bud up in the warhead. We didn't even know he was in Florida. He couldn't get in touch with us. We thought he was up at Otis Air Force Base on Cape Cod. That was the last place we heard from him. And then that thing went up, right in the middle of our view out the picture window.

◎ ◎ ◎

You say you're superstitious sometimes, Mr. Ivankov. Me too. Sometimes I can't help thinking it was all meant to be right from the very first—even the way our picture window is aimed. There weren't any rockets going up down here when we built. We moved down here from Pittsburgh, which maybe you know is the center of our steel industry. And we figured we maybe weren't going to break any records for pumping gas, but at least we'd be way far away from any bomb targets, in case there was another war. And the next thing we know, a rocket center goes up almost next door, and our little boy is a man, and he goes up in a rocket and dies.

The more we think about it, the more we're sure it was meant to be. I never got it straight in my mind about religion in Russia. You don't mention it. Anyway, we are religious, and we think God singled out Bud and your boy, too, to die in a special way for a special reason. When everybody was asking, "How is it going to end?"— well, maybe this is how God meant for it to end. I don't see how it can keep on.

◎ ◎ ◎

Mr. Ivankov, one thing that threw me as much as anything was the way Mr. Koshevoi kept telling the U.N. that Bud was a killer. He called Bud a mad dog and a gangster. I'm glad you don't feel that way, because that's the wrong way to feel about Bud. It was flying and not killing he liked. Mr. Koshevoi made a big thing out of how cultured and educated and all your boy was, and how wild and ignorant mine was. He made it sound as though a juvenile delinquent had murdered a college professor.

Bud never was in any trouble with the police, and he didn't have a cruel streak. He never went hunting, for instance, and he never drove like a crazy man, and he got drunk only one time I know of, and that was an experiment. He was proud of his reflexes, see? His health was on his mind all the time, because he had to be healthy to be a great flyer. I keep looking around for the right word for Bud, and I guess the one Hazel suggested is the best one. It sounded kind of stuffed-up to me at first, but now I'm used to it, and it sounds right. Hazel says Bud was dignified. Man and boy, that's what he was—straight and serious and polite and pretty much alone.

I think he knew he was going to die young. That one time he got drunk, just to find out what alcohol was, he talked to me more than he'd ever talked before. He was nineteen then. And then was the only time he let me know he knew death was all balled up in what he wanted to do with his life. It wasn't other people's deaths he was talking about, Mr. Ivankov. It was his own. "One nice thing about flying," he said to me that night. "What's that?" I said. "You never know how bad it is till it's too late," he said, "and when it happens, it happens so fast you never know what hit you."

That was death he was talking about, and a special, dignified, honorable kind of death. You say you were in the war and had a hard time. Same here, so I guess we both know about what kind of death it was that Bud had in mind. It was a soldier's death.

We got the news he was dead three days after the big rocket went up across the water. The telegram said he had died on a secret mission, and we couldn't have any details. We had our Congressman, Earl Waterman, find out what he could about Bud. Mr. Waterman came and talked to us personally, and he looked like he had seen God. He said he couldn't tell us what Bud had done, but it was one of the most heroic things in United States history.

The word they put out on the big rocket we saw launched was that the firing was satisfactory, the knowledge gained was something wonderful, and the missile had been blown up over the ocean somewhere. That was that.

Then the word came that the man in the Russian baby moon was dead. I tell you honestly, Mr. Ivankov, that was good news to us, because that man sailing way up there with all those instruments meant just one thing, and that was a terrible weapon of war.

Then we heard the Russian baby moon had turned into a bunch of baby moons, all spreading apart. Then, this last month, the cat was out of the bag. Two of the baby moons were men. One was your boy, the other was mine.

I'm crying now, Mr. Ivankov. I hope some good comes of the death of our two boys. I guess that's what millions of fathers have hoped for as long as there have been people. There in the U.N. they're still arguing about what happened way up in the sky. I'm glad they've got around to where everybody, including your Mr. Koshevoi, agrees it was an accident. Bud was up there to get pictures of what your boy was riding in, and to show off for the United States some. He got too close. I like to think they lived a little while after the crash, and tried to save each other.

◎ ◎ ◎

They say they'll be up there for hundreds of years, long after you and I are gone. In their orbits they will meet and part and meet again, and the astronomers know exactly where their next meeting place will be. Like you say, they are up there like the sun and the moon and the stars.

I enclose a photograph of my boy in his uniform. He was twenty-one when the picture was taken. He was only twenty-two when he died. Bud was picked for that mission on account of he was the finest flyer in the United States Air Force. That's what he always wanted to be. That's what he was.

I grasp your hand.

Charles M. Ashland
Petroleum Merchant
Titusville, Florida
U. S. A.

Thanasphere

AT NOON, Wednesday, July 26th, windowpanes in the small mountain towns of Sevier County, Tennessee, were rattled by the shock and faint thunder of a distant explosion rolling down the northwest slopes of the Great Smokies. The explosion came from the general direction of the closely guarded Air Force experimental station in the forest ten miles northwest of Elkmont.

Said the Air Force Office of Public Information, "No comment."

That evening, amateur astronomers in Omaha, Nebraska, and Glenwood, Iowa, reported independently that a speck had crossed the face of the full moon at 9:57 p.m. There was a flurry of excitement on the news wires. Astronomers at the major North American observatories denied that they had seen it.

They lied.

In Boston, on the morning of Thursday, July 27th, an enterprising newsman sought out Dr. Bernard Groszinger, youthful rocket consultant for the Air Force. "Is it possible that what crossed the moon was a spaceship?" the newsman asked.

Dr. Groszinger laughed at the question. "My own opinion is that we're beginning another cycle of flying-saucer scares," he said. "This time everyone's seeing spaceships between us and the moon. You can tell your readers this, my friend: No rocket ship will leave the earth for at least another twenty years."

He lied.

He knew a great deal more than he was saying, but somewhat less than he himself thought. He did not believe in ghosts, for instance—and had yet to learn of the Thanasphere.

Dr. Groszinger rested his long legs on his cluttered desktop, and watched his secretary conduct the disappointed newsman through the locked door, past the armed guards. He lit a cigarette and tried to relax before going back into the stale air and tension of the radio room. IS YOUR SAFE LOCKED? asked a sign on the wall, tacked there by a diligent security officer. The sign annoyed him. Security officers, security regulations only served to slow his work, to make him think about things he had no time to think about.

The secret papers in the safe weren't secrets. They said what had been known for centuries: Given fundamental physics, it follows that a projectile fired into space in direction x, at y miles per hour, will travel in the arc z. Dr. Groszinger modified the equation: Given fundamental physics and one billion dollars.

Impending war had offered him the opportunity to try the experiment. The threat of war was an incident, the military men about him an irritating condition of work—*the experiment* was the heart of the matter.

There were no unknowns, he reflected, finding contentment in the dependability of the physical world. Young Dr. Groszinger smiled, thinking of Christopher Columbus and his crew, who hadn't known what lay ahead of them, who had been scared stiff by sea monsters that didn't exist. Maybe the average person of today felt the same way about space. The Age of Superstition still had a few years to run.

But the man in the spaceship two thousand miles from earth had no unknowns to fear. The sullen Major Allen Rice would have nothing surprising to report in his radio messages. He could only confirm what reason had already revealed about outer space.

The major American observatories, working closely with the project, reported that the ship was now moving around the earth in the predicted orbit at the predicted velocity. Soon, anytime now, the first message in history from outer space would be received in the radio room. The broadcast could be on an ultra-high-frequency band where no one had ever sent or received messages before.

The first message was overdue, but nothing had gone wrong—nothing *could* go wrong, Dr. Groszinger assured himself again. Machines, not men, were guiding the flight. The man was a mere observer, piloted to his lonely vantage point by infallible electronic brains, swifter than his own. He had controls in his ship, but only for gliding down through the atmosphere, when and if they brought him back from space. He was equipped to stay for several years.

Even the man was as much like a machine as possible, Dr. Groszinger thought with satisfaction. He was quick, strong, unemotional. Psychiatrists had picked Major Rice from a hundred volunteers, and predicted that he would function as perfectly as the rocket motors, the metal hull, and the electronic controls. His specifications: Husky, twenty-nine years of age, fifty-five missions over Europe during the Second World War without a sign of fatigue, a childless widower, melancholy and solitary, a career soldier, a demon for work.

The Major's mission? Simple: To report weather conditions over enemy territory, and to observe the accuracy of guided atomic missiles in the event of war.

Major Rice was fixed in the solar system, two thousand miles above the earth now—close by, really—the distance from New York to Salt Lake City, not far enough away to see much of the polar icecaps, even. With a telescope, Rice could pick out small towns and the wakes of ships without much trouble. It would be breathtaking to watch the enormous blue-and-green ball, to see night creeping around it, and clouds and storms growing and swirling over its face.

Dr. Groszinger tamped out his cigarette, absently lit another almost at once, and strode down the corridor to the small laboratory where the radio equipment had been set up.

Lieutenant General Franklin Dane, head of Project Cyclops, sat next to the radio operator, his uniform rumpled, his collar open. The General stared expectantly at the loudspeaker before him. The floor was littered with sandwich wrappings and cigarette butts. Coffee-filled paper cups stood before the General and the radio operator, and beside the canvas chair where Groszinger had spent the night waiting.

General Dane nodded to Groszinger and motioned with his hand for silence.

"Able Baker Fox, this is Dog Easy Charley. Able Baker Fox, this is Dog Easy Charley . . ." droned the radio operator wearily, using the code names. "Can you hear me, Able Baker Fox? Can you—"

The loudspeaker crackled, then, tuned to its peak volume, boomed: "This is Able Baker Fox. Come in, Dog Easy Charley. Over."

General Dane jumped to his feet and embraced Groszinger. They laughed idiotically and pounded each other on the back. The General snatched the microphone from the radio operator. "You made it. Able Baker Fox! Right on course! What's it like, boy? What's it feel like? Over." Groszinger, his arm draped around the General's shoulders, leaned forward eagerly, his ear a few inches from the speaker. The radio operator turned the volume down, so that they could hear something of the quality of Major Rice's voice.

The voice came through again, soft, hesitant. The tone disturbed Groszinger—he had wanted it to be crisp, sharp, efficient.

"This side of the earth's dark, very dark just now. And I feel like I'm falling—the way you said I would. Over."

"Is anything the matter?" asked the General anxiously. "You sound as though something—"

The Major cut in before he could finish: "There! Did you hear that?"

"Able Baker Fox, we can't hear anything," said the General, looking perplexed at Groszinger. "What is it—some kind of noise in your receiver? Over."

"A child," said the Major. "I hear a child crying. Don't you hear it? And now—listen!—now an old man is trying to comfort it." His voice seemed farther away, as though he were no longer speaking directly into his microphone.

"That's impossible, ridiculous!" said Groszinger. "Check your set, Able Baker Fox, check your set. Over."

"They're getting louder now. The voices are louder. I can't hear you very well above them. It's like standing in the middle of a crowd, with everybody trying to get my attention at once. It's like . . ." The message trailed off. They could hear a shushing sound in the speaker. The Major's transmitter was still on.

"Can you hear me, Able Baker Fox? Answer! Can you hear me?" called General Dane.

The shushing noise stopped. The General and Groszinger stared blankly at the speaker.

"Able Baker Fox, this is Dog Easy Charley," chanted the radio operator. "Able Baker Fox, this is Dog Easy Charley. . . ."

◎ ◎ ◎

Groszinger, his eyes shielded from the glaring ceiling light of the radio room by a newspaper, lay fully dressed on the cot that had been brought in for him. Every few minutes he ran his long, slender fingers through his tangled hair and swore. His machine had worked perfectly, *was* working perfectly. The one thing he had not designed, the damn man in it, had failed, had destroyed the whole experiment.

They had been trying for six hours to reestablish contact with the lunatic who peered down at earth from his tiny steel moon and heard voices.

"He's coming in again, sir," said the radio operator. "This is Dog Easy Charley. Come in, Able Baker Fox. Over."

"This is Able Baker Fox. Clear weather over Zones Seven, Eleven, Nineteen, and Twenty-three. Zones One, Two, Three, Four, Five, and Six overcast. Storm seems to be shaping up over Zones Eight and Nine, moving south by southwest at about eighteen miles an hour. Over."

"He's OK now," said the General, relieved.

Groszinger remained supine, his head still covered with the newspaper. "Ask him about the voices," he said.

"You don't hear the voices anymore, *do* you, Able Baker Fox?"

"What do you mean, I don't hear them? I can hear them better than I can hear you. Over."

"He's out of his head," said Groszinger, sitting up.

"I heard that," said Major Rice. "Maybe I am. It shouldn't be too hard to check. All you have to do is find out if an Andrew Tobin died in Evansville, Indiana, on February 17, 1927. Over."

"I don't follow you, Able Baker Fox," said the General. "Who was Andrew Tobin? Over."

"He's one of the voices." There was an uncomfortable pause. Major Rice cleared his throat. "Claims his brother murdered him. Over."

The radio operator had risen slowly from his stool, his face chalk-white. Groszinger pushed him back down and took the microphone from the General's now limp hand.

"Either you've lost your mind, or this is the most sophomoric practical joke in history, Able Baker Fox," said Groszinger. "This is *Groszinger* you're talking to, and you're dumber than I think you are if you think you can kid me." He nodded. "Over."

"I can't hear you very well anymore, Dog Easy Charley. Sorry, but the voices are getting louder."

"Rice! Straighten out!" said Groszinger.

"There—I caught that: Mrs. Pamela Ritter wants her husband to marry again, for the sake of the children. He lives at—"

"Stop it!"

"He lives at 1577 Damon Place, in Scotia, New York. Over and out."

◎ ◎ ◎

General Dane shook Groszinger's shoulder gently. "You've been asleep five hours," he said. "It's midnight." He handed him a cup of coffee. "We've got some more messages. Interested?"

Groszinger sipped the coffee. "Is he still raving?"

"He still hears the voices, if that's what you mean." The General dropped two unopened telegrams in Groszinger's lap. "Thought you might like to be the one to open these."

Groszinger laughed. "Went ahead and checked Scotia and Evansville, did you? God help this army, if all the generals are as superstitious as you, my friend."

"OK, OK, you're the scientist, you're the brain-box. That's why I want *you* to open the telegrams. I want you to tell me what in hell's going on."

Groszinger opened one of the telegrams.

HARVEY RITTER LISTED FOR 1577 DAMON PLACE, SCOTIA. GE ENGINEER. WIDOWER, TWO CHILDREN. DECEASED WIFE NAMED PAMELA. DO YOU NEED MORE INFORMATION? R. B. FAILEY, CHIEF, SCOTIA POLICE

He shrugged and handed the message to General Dane, then opened the other telegram:

RECORDS SHOW ANDREW TOBIN DIED IN HUNTING ACCIDENT FEBRUARY 17, 1927. BROTHER PAUL LEADING BUSINESSMAN. OWNS COAL BUSINESS STARTED BY ANDREW. CAN FURNISH FURTHER DETAILS IF NEEDED. F. B. JOHNSON, CHIEF, EVANSVILLE P.D.

"I'm not surprised," said Groszinger. "I expected something like this. I suppose you're firmly convinced now that our friend Major Rice has found outer space populated by ghosts?"

"Well, I'd say he's sure as hell found it populated by something," said the General.

Groszinger wadded the second telegram in his fist and threw it across the room, missing the wastebasket by a foot. He folded his hands and affected the patient, priestlike pose he used in lecturing freshman physics classes. "At first, my friend, we had two possible conclusions: Either Major Rice was insane, or he was pulling off a spectacular hoax." He twiddled his thumbs, waiting for the General to digest this intelligence. "Now that we know his spirit messages deal with real people, we've got to conclude that he has planned and is now carrying out some sort of hoax. He got his names and addresses before he took off. God knows what he hopes to accomplish by it. God knows what we can do to make him stop it. That's your problem, I'd say."

The General's eyes narrowed. "So he's trying to jimmy the project, is he? We'll see, by God, we'll see." The radio operator was dozing. The General slapped him on the back. "On the ball, Sergeant, on the ball. Keep calling Rice till you get him, understand?"

The radio operator had to call only once.

"This is Able Baker Fox. Come in, Dog Easy Charley." Major Rice's voice was tired.

"This is Dog Easy Charley," said General Dane. "We've had enough of your voices, Able Baker Fox—do you understand? We don't want to hear any more about them. We're onto your little game. I don't know what your angle is, but I do know I'll bring you back down and slap you on a rock pile in Leavenworth so fast you'll leave your teeth up there. Do we understand each other?" The General bit the tip from a fresh cigar fiercely. "Over."

"Did you check those names and addresses? Over."

The General looked at Groszinger, who frowned and shook his head. "Sure we did. That doesn't prove anything. So you've got a list of names and addresses up there. So what does that prove? Over."

"You say those names checked? Over."

"I'm telling you to quit it, Rice. Right now. Forget the voices, do you hear? Give me a weather report. Over."

"Clear patches over Zones Eleven, Fifteen, and Sixteen. Looks like a solid overcast in One, Two, and Three. All clear in the rest. Over."

"That's more like it, Able Baker Fox," said the General. "We'll forget about the voices, eh? Over."

"There's an old woman calling out something in a German accent. Is Dr. Groszinger there? I think she's calling his name. She's asking him not to get too wound up in his work—not to—"

Groszinger leaned over the radio operator's shoulder and snapped off the switch on the receiver. "Of all the cheap, sickening stunts," he said.

"Let's hear what he has to say," said the General. "Thought you were a scientist."

Groszinger glared at him defiantly, snapped on the receiver, and stood back, his hands on his hips.

"—saying something in German," continued the voice of Major Rice. "Can't understand it. Maybe you can. I'll give it to you the way it sounds: '*Alles geben die Götter, die unendlichen, ihren Lieblingen, ganz. Alle—*'"

Groszinger turned down the volume. "'*Alle Freuden, die unendlichen, alle Schmerzen, die unendlichen, ganz,*'" he said faintly. "That's how it ends." He sat down on the cot. "It's my mother's favorite quotation—something from Goethe."

"I can threaten him again," said the General.

"What for?" Groszinger shrugged and smiled. "Outer space *is* full of voices." He laughed nervously. "*There's* something to pep up a physics textbook."

"An omen, sir—it's an omen," blurted the radio operator.

"What the hell do you mean, an omen?" said the General. "So outer space is filled with ghosts. That doesn't surprise me."

"Nothing would, then," said Groszinger.

"That's exactly right. I'd be a hell of a general if anything would. For all I know, the moon is made of green cheese. So what. All I want is a man out there to tell me that I'm hitting what I'm shooting at. I don't give a damn what's going on in outer space."

"Don't you see, sir?" said the radio operator. "Don't you see? It's an omen. When people find out about all the spirits out there they'll forget about war. They won't want to think about anything but the spirits."

"Relax, Sergeant," said the General. "Nobody's going to find out about them, understand?"

"You can't suppress a discovery like this," said Groszinger.

"You're nuts if you think I can't," said General Dane. "How're you going to tell anybody about this business without telling them we've got a rocket ship out there?"

"They've got a right to know," said the radio operator.

"If the world finds out we have that ship out there, that's the start of World War Three," said the General. "Now tell me you want that. The enemy won't have any choice but to try and blow the hell out of us before we can put Major Rice to any use. And there'd be nothing for us to do but try and blow the hell out of them first. Is that what you want?"

"No, sir," said the radio operator. "I guess not, sir."

"Well, we can experiment, anyway," said Groszinger. "We can find out as much as possible about what the spirits are like. We can send Rice into a wider orbit to find out how far out he can hear the voices, and whether—"

"Not on Air Force funds, you can't," said General Dane. "That isn't what Rice is out there for. We can't afford to piddle around. We need him right there."

"All right, all right," said Groszinger. "Then let's hear what he has to say."

"Tune him in, Sergeant," said the General.

"Yes, sir." The radio operator fiddled with the dials. "He doesn't seem to be transmitting now, sir." The shushing noise of a transmitter cut into the hum of the loudspeaker. "I guess he's coming in again. Able Baker Fox, this is Dog Easy Charley—"

"King Two X-ray William Love, this is William Five Zebra Zebra King in Dallas," said the loudspeaker. The voice had a soft drawl and was pitched higher than Major Rice's.

A bass voice answered: "This is King Two X-ray William Love in Albany. Come in W5ZZK, I hear you well. How do you hear me? Over."

"You're clear as a bell, K2XWL—twenty-five thousand megacycles on the button. I'm trying to cut down on my drift with a—"

The voice of Major Rice interrupted. "I can't hear you clearly, Dog Easy Charley. The voices are a steady roar now. I can catch bits of what they're saying. Grantland Whitman, the Hollywood actor, is yelling that his will was tampered with by his nephew Carl. He says—"

"Say again, K2XWL," said the drawling voice. "I must have misunderstood you. Over."

"I didn't say anything, W5ZZK. What was that about Grantland Whitman? Over."

"The crowd's quieting down," said Major Rice. "Now there's just one voice—a young woman, I think. It's so soft I can't make out what she's saying."

"What's going on, K2XWL? Can you hear me, K2XWL?"

"She's calling my name. Do you hear it? She's calling my name," said Major Rice.

"Jam the frequency, dammit!" cried the General. "Yell, whistle—do something!" Early-morning traffic past the university came to a honking, bad-tempered stop, as Groszinger absently crossed the street against the light, on his way back to his office and the radio room. He looked up in surprise, mumbled an apology, and hurried to the curb. He had had a solitary breakfast in an all-night diner a block and a half from the laboratory building, and then he'd taken a long walk. He had hoped that getting away for a couple of hours would clear his head—but the feeling of confusion and helplessness was still with him. Did the world have a right to know, or didn't it?

There had been no more messages from Major Rice. At the General's orders, the frequency had been jammed. Now the unexpected eavesdroppers could hear nothing but a steady whine at 25,000 megacycles. General Dane had reported the dilemma to Washington shortly after midnight. Perhaps orders as to what to do with Major Rice had come through by now.

Groszinger paused in a patch of sunlight on the laboratory building's steps, and read again the front-page news story, which ran fancifully for a column, beneath the headline "Mystery Radio Message Reveals Possible Will Fraud." The story told of two radio amateurs, experimenting illegally on the supposedly unused ultra-high-frequency band, who had been amazed to hear a man chattering about voices and a will. The amateurs had broken the law, operating on an unassigned frequency, but they hadn't kept their mouths shut about their discovery. Now hams all over the world would be building sets so they could listen in, too.

"Morning, sir. Nice morning, isn't it?" said a guard coming off duty. He was a cheerful Irishman.

"Fine morning, all right," agreed Groszinger. "Clouding up a little in the west, maybe." He wondered what the guard would say if he told him what he knew. He would laugh, probably.

Groszinger's secretary was dusting off his desk when he walked in. "You could use some sleep, couldn't you?" she said. "Honestly, why you men don't take better care of yourselves I just don't know. If you had a wife, she'd make you—"

"Never felt better in my life," said Groszinger. "Any word from General Dane?"

"He was looking for you about ten minutes ago. He's back in the radio room now. He's been on the phone with Washington for half an hour."

She had only the vaguest notion of what the project was about. Again, Groszinger felt the urge to tell about Major Rice and the voices, to see what effect the news would have on someone else. Perhaps his secretary would react as he himself had reacted, with a shrug. Maybe that was the spirit of this era of the atom bomb, H-bomb, God-knows-what-next bomb—to be amazed at nothing. Science had given humanity forces enough to destroy the earth, and politics had given humanity a fair assurance that the forces would be used. There could be no cause for awe to top *that* one. But proof of a spirit world might at least equal it. Maybe that was the shock the world needed, maybe word from the spirits could change the suicidal course of history.

General Dane looked up wearily as Groszinger walked into the radio room. "They're bringing him down," he said. "There's nothing else we can do. He's no damn good to us now." The loudspeaker, turned low, sang the monotonous hum of the jamming signal. The radio operator slept before the set, his head resting on his folded arms.

"Did you try to get through to him again?"

"Twice. He's clear off his head now. Tried to tell him to change his frequency, to code his messages, but he just went on jabbering like he couldn't hear me—talking about that woman's voice."

"Who's the woman? Did he say?"

The General looked at him oddly. "Says it's his wife, Margaret. Guess that's enough to throw anybody, wouldn't you say? Pretty bright, weren't we, sending up a guy with no family ties." He arose and stretched. "I'm going out for a minute. Just make sure you keep your hands off that set." He slammed the door behind him.

The radio operator stirred. "They're bringing him down," he said.

"I know," said Groszinger.

"That'll kill him, won't it?"

"He has controls for gliding her in, once he hits the atmosphere."

"If he wants to."

"That's right—if he wants to. They'll get him out of his orbit and back to the atmosphere under rocket power. After that, it'll be up to him to take over and make the landing."

They fell silent. The only sound in the room was the muted jamming signal in the loudspeaker.

"He don't want to live, you know that?" said the radio operator suddenly. "Would you want to?"

"Guess that's something you don't know until you come up against it," said Groszinger. He was trying to imagine the world of the future—a world in constant touch with the spirits, the living inseparable from the dead. It was bound to come. Other men, probing into space, were certain to find out. Would it make life heaven or hell? Every bum and genius, criminal and hero, average man and madman, now and forever part of humanity—advising, squabbling, conniving, placating . . .

The radio operator looked furtively toward the door. "Want to hear him again?"

Groszinger shook his head. "Everybody's listening to that frequency now. We'd all be in a nice mess if you stopped jamming." He didn't want to hear more. He was baffled, miserable. Would Death unmasked drive men to suicide, or bring new hope? he was asking himself. Would the living desert their leaders and turn to the dead for guidance? To Caesar . . . Charlemagne . . . Peter the Great . . . Napoleon . . . Bismarck . . . Lincoln . . . Roosevelt? To Jesus Christ? Were the dead wiser than—

Before Groszinger could stop him, the sergeant switched off the oscillator that was jamming the frequency.

Major Rice's voice came through instantly high and giddy. " . . . thousands of them, thousands of them, all around me, standing on nothing, shimmering like northern lights—beautiful, curving off in space, all around the earth like a glowing fog. I can see them, do you hear? I can see them now. I can see Margaret. She's waving and smiling, misty, heavenly, beautiful. If only you could see it, if—"

The radio operator flicked on the jamming signal. There was a footfall in the hallway.

General Dane stalked into the radio room, studying his watch. "In five minutes they'll start him down," he said. He plunged his hands deep into his pockets and slouched dejectedly. "We failed this time. Next time, by God, we'll make it. The next man who goes up will know what he's up against—he'll be ready to take it."

He put his hand on Groszinger's shoulder. "The most important job you'll ever have to do, my friend, is to keep your mouth shut about those spirits out there, do you understand? We don't want the enemy to know we've had a ship out there, and we don't want them to know what they'll come across if they try it. The security of this country depends on that being our secret. Do I make myself clear?"

"Yes, sir," said Groszinger, grateful to have no choice but to be quiet. He didn't want to be the one to tell the world. He wished he had had nothing to do with sending Rice out into space. What discovery of the dead would do to humanity he didn't know, but the impact would be terrific. Now, like the rest, he would have to wait for the next wild twist of history.

The General looked at his watch again. "They're bringing him down," he said.

⊡ ⊡ ⊡

At 1:39 p.m., on Friday, July 28th, the British liner *Capricorn*, two hundred eighty miles out of New York City, bound for Liverpool, radioed that an unidentified object had crashed into the sea, sending up a towering geyser on the horizon to starboard of the ship. Several passengers were said to have seen something glinting as the thing fell from the sky. Upon reaching the scene of the crash, the *Capricorn* reported finding dead and stunned fish on the surface, and turbulent water, but no wreckage.

Newspapers suggested that the *Capricorn* had seen the crash of an experimental rocket fired out to sea in a test of range. The Secretary of Defense promptly denied that any such tests were being conducted over the Atlantic.

In Boston, Dr. Bernard Groszinger, young rocket consultant for the Air Force, told newsmen that what the *Capricorn* had observed might well have been a meteor.

"That seems quite likely," he said. "If it was a meteor, the fact that it reached the earth's surface should, I think, be one of the year's most important science news stories. Usually meteors burn to nothing before they're even through the stratosphere."

"Excuse me, sir," interrupted a reporter. "Is there anything out beyond the stratosphere—I mean, is there any name for it?"

"Well, actually the term 'stratosphere' is kind of arbitrary. It's the outer shell of the atmosphere. You can't say definitely where it stops. Beyond it is just, well—dead space."

"Dead space—that's the right name for it, eh?" said the reporter.

"If you want something fancier, maybe we could put it into Greek," said Groszinger playfully. "*Thanatos*, that's Greek for 'death,' I think. Maybe instead of 'dead space' you'd prefer 'Thanasphere.' Has a nice scientific ring to it, don't you think?"

The newsmen laughed politely.

"Dr. Groszinger, when's the first rocket ship going to make it into space?" asked another reporter.

"You people read too many comic books," said Groszinger. "Come back in twenty years, and maybe I'll have a story for you."

Souvenir

JOE BANE WAS A pawnbroker, a fat, lazy, bald man, whose features seemed pulled to the left by his lifetime of looking at the world through a jeweler's glass. He was a lonely, untalented man and would not have wanted to go on living had he been prevented from playing every day save Sunday the one game he played brilliantly—the acquiring of objects for very little, and the selling of them for a great deal more. He was obsessed by the game, the one opportunity life offered him to best his fellow men. The game was the thing, the money he made a secondary matter, a way of keeping score.

When Joe Bane opened his shop Monday morning, a black ceiling of rainclouds had settled below the valley's rim, holding the city in a dark pocket of dead, dank air. Autumn thunder grumbled along the misty hillsides. No sooner had Bane hung up his coat and hat and umbrella, taken off his rubbers, turned on the lights, and settled his great bulk on a stool behind a counter than a lean young man in overalls, shy and dark as an Indian, plainly poor and awed by the city, walked in to offer him a fantastic pocketwatch for five hundred dollars.

"No, sir," said the young farmer politely. "I don't want to borrow money on it. I want to sell it, if I can get enough for it." He seemed reluctant to hand it to Bane, and cupped it tenderly in his rough hands for a moment before setting it down on a square of black velvet. "I kind of hoped to hang on to it, and pass it on to my oldest boy, but we need the money a whole lot worse right now."

"Five hundred dollars is a lot of money," said Bane, like a man who had been victimized too often by his own kindness. He examined the jewels studding the watch without betraying anything of his inner amazement. He turned the watch this way and that, catching the glare of the ceiling light in four diamonds marking the hours three, six, nine, and twelve, and the ruby crowning the winder. The jewels alone, Bane reflected, were worth at least four times what the farmer was asking.

"I don't get much call for a watch like this," said Bane. "If I tied up five hundred dollars in it, I might be stuck with it for years before the right man came along." He watched the farmer's sunburned face and thought he read there that the watch could be had for a good bit less.

"There ain't another one like it in the whole county," said the farmer, in a clumsy attempt at salesmanship.

"That's my point," said Bane. "Who wants a watch like this?" Bane, for one, wanted it, and was already regarding it as his own. He pressed a button on the side of the case and listened to the whirring of tiny machinery striking the nearest hour on sweet, clear chimes.

"You want it or not?" said the farmer.

"Now, now," said Bane, "this isn't the kind of deal you just dive headfirst into. I'd have to know more about this watch before I bought it." He pried open the back and found inside an engraved inscription in a foreign language. "What does this say? Any idea?"

"Showed it to a schoolteacher back home," said the young man, "and all she could say was it looked a whole lot like German."

Bane laid a sheet of tissue paper over the inscription, and rubbed a pencil back and forth across it until he'd picked up a legible copy. He gave the copy and a dime to a shoeshine boy loitering by the door and sent him down the block to ask a German restaurant proprietor for a translation.

The first drops of rain were spattering clean streaks on the sooty glass when Bane said casually to the farmer, "The cops keep pretty close check on what comes in here."

The farmer reddened. "That watch is mine, all right. I got it in the war," he said.

"Uh-huh. And you paid duty on it?"

"Duty?"

"Certainly. You can't bring jewelry into this country without paying taxes on it. That's smuggling."

"Just tucked it in my barracks bag and brought her on home, the way everybody done," said the farmer. He was as worried as Bane had hoped.

"Contraband," said Bane. "Just about the same as stolen goods." He held up his hands placatingly. "I don't mean I can't buy it, I just want to point out to you that it'd be a tricky thing to handle. If you were willing to let it go for, oh, say a hundred dollars, maybe I'd take a chance on it to help you out. I try to give veterans a break here whenever I can."

"A hundred dollars! That's all?"

"That's all it's worth, and I'm probably a sucker to offer that," said Bane. "What the hell—that's an easy hundred bucks for you, isn't it? What'd you do—cop it off some German prisoner or find it lying around in the ruins?"

"No, sir," said the farmer, "it was a little tougher'n that."

Bane, who was keenly sensitive to such things, saw that the farmer, as he began to tell how he'd gotten the watch, was regaining the stubborn confidence that had deserted him when he'd left his farm for the city to make the sale.

"My best buddy Buzzer and me," said the farmer, "were prisoners of war together in some hills in Germany—in Sudetenland, somebody said it was. One morning,

Buzzer woke me up and said the war was over, the guards were gone, the gates were open."

Joe Bane was impatient at first with having to listen to the tale. But it was a tale told well and proudly, and long a fan of others' adventures for want of any of his own, Bane began to see, enviously, the two soldiers walking through the open gates of their prison, and down a country road in the hills early on a bright spring morning in 1945, on the day the Second World War ended in Europe.

The young farmer, whose name was Eddie, and his best buddy Buzzer walked out into peace and freedom skinny, ragged, dirty, and hungry, but with no ill will toward anyone. They'd gone to war out of pride, not bitterness. Now the war was over, the job done, and they wanted only to go home. They were a year apart, but as alike as two poplars in a windbreak.

Their notion was to take a brief sightseeing tour of the neighborhood near the camp, then to come back and wait with the rest of the prisoners for the arrival of some official liberators. But the plan evaporated when a pair of Canadian prisoners invited the buddies to toast victory with a bottle of brandy they'd found in a wrecked German truck.

Their shrunken bellies gloriously hot and tingling, their heads light and full of trust and love for all mankind, Eddie and Buzzer found themselves swept along by a jostling, plaintive parade of German refugees that jammed the main road through the hills, refugees fleeing from the Russian tanks that growled monotonously and unopposed in the valley behind and below them. The tanks were coming to occupy this last undefended bit of German soil.

"What're we runnin' from?" said Buzzer. "The war's over, ain't it?"

"Everybody else is runnin'," said Eddie, "so I guess maybe we better be runnin', too."

"I don't even know where we are," said Buzzer.

"Them Canadians said it's Sudetenland."

"Where's that?"

"Where we're at," said Eddie. "Swell guys, them Canadians."

"I'll tell the world! Man," said Buzzer, "I love everybody today. Whoooooey! I'd like to get me a bottle of that brandy, put a nipple on it, and go to bed with it for a week."

Eddie touched the elbow of a tall, worried-looking man with close-cropped black hair, who wore a civilian suit too small for him. "Where we runnin' to, sir? Ain't the war over?"

The man glared, grunted something, and pushed by roughly.

"He don't understand English," said Eddie.

"Why, hell, man," said Buzzer, "why'n't you talk to these folks in their native tongue? Don't hide your candle under a bushel. Let's hear you sprecken some Dutch to this man here."

They'd come alongside a small, low black roadster, which was stalled on the shoulder of the road. A heavily muscled square-faced young man was tinkering with the dead motor. On the leather front seat of the car sat an older man whose face was covered with dust and several days' growth of black beard, and shaded by a hat with the brim pulled down.

Eddie and Buzzer stopped. "All right," said Eddie. "Just listen to this: *Wie geht's?*" he said to the blond man, using the only German he knew.

"*Gut, gut,*" muttered the young German. Then, realizing the absurdity of his automatic reply to the greeting, he said with terrible bitterness, "*Ja! Geht's gut!*"

"He says everything's just fine," said Eddie.

"Oh, you're fluent, mighty fluent," said Buzzer.

"Yes, I've traveled extensively, you might say," said Eddie.

The older man came to life and yelled at the man who was working on the motor, yelled shrilly and threateningly.

The blond seemed frightened. He went to work on the motor with redoubled desperation.

The older man's eyes, bleary a moment before, were wide and bright now. Several refugees turned to stare as they passed.

The older man glanced challengingly from one face to the next, and filled his lungs to shout something at them. But he changed his mind, sighed instead, and his spirits collapsed. He thrust his face in his hands.

"Wha'd he say?" said Buzzer.

"He don't speak my particular dialect," said Eddie.

"Speaks low-class German, huh?" said Buzzer. "Well, I'm not goin' another step till we find somebody who can tell us what's goin' on. We're Americans, boy. Our side won, didn't it? What we doin' all tangled up with these Jerries?"

"You—you Americans," said the blond, surprisingly enough in English. "Now you will have to fight them."

"Here's one that talks English!" said Buzzer.

"Talks it pretty good, too," said Eddie.

"Ain't bad, ain't bad at all," said Buzzer. "Who we got to fight?"

"The Russians," said the young German, seeming to relish the idea. "They'll kill you, too, if they catch you. They're killing everybody in their path."

"Hell, man," said Buzzer, "we're on their side."

"For how long? Run, boys, run." The blond swore and hurled his wrench at the motor. He turned to the old man and spoke, scared to death of him.

The older man released a stream of German abuse, tired of it quickly, got out of the car, and slammed the door behind him. The two looked anxiously in the direction from which the tanks would come, and started down the road on foot.

"Where you guys headed?" said Eddie.

"Prague—the Americans are in Prague."

Eddie and Buzzer fell in behind them. "Sure gettin' a mess of geography today, ain't we, Eddie?" said Buzzer. He stumbled, and Eddie caught him. "Oh, oh, Eddie, that old booze is sneakin' up on me."

"Yeah," said Eddie, whose own senses were growing fuzzier. "I say to hell with Prague. If we don't ride, we don't go, and that's that."

"Sure. We'll just find us some shady spot, and sit and wait for the Russians. We'll just show 'em our dog tags," said Buzzer. "And when they see 'em, bet they give us a big banquet." He dipped a finger inside his collar and brought out the tags on their string.

"Oh my, yes," said the blond German, who had been listening carefully, "a wonderful big banquet they'll give you."

The column had been moving more and more slowly, growing more packed. Now it came to a muttering halt.

"Must be a woman up front, tryin' to read a road map," said Buzzer.

From far down the road came an exchange of shouts like a distant surf. Restless, anxious moments later, the cause of the trouble was clear: The column had met another, fleeing in terror from the opposite direction. The Russians had the area surrounded. Now the two columns merged to form an aimless whirlpool in the heart of a small village, flooding out into side lanes and up the slopes on either side.

"Don't know nobody in Prague, anyhow," said Buzzer, and he wandered off the road and sat by the gate of a walled farmyard.

Eddie followed his example. "By God," he said, "maybe we oughta stay right here and open us up a gun shop, Buzzer." He included in a sweep of his hand the discarded rifles and pistols that were strewn over the grass. "Bullets and all."

"Swell place to open a gun shop, Europe is," said Buzzer. "They're just crazy about guns around here."

Despite the growing panic of the persons milling about them, Buzzer dropped off into a brandy-induced nap. Eddie had trouble keeping his eyes open.

"Aha!" said a voice from the road. "Here our American friends are."

Eddie looked up to see the two Germans, the husky young man and the irascible older one, grinning down at them.

"Hello," said Eddie. The cheering edge of the brandy was wearing off, and queasiness was taking its place.

The young German pushed open the gate to the farmyard. "Come in here, would you?" he told Eddie. "We have something important to say to you."

"Say it here," said Eddie.

The blond leaned down. "We've come to surrender to you."

"You've come to what?"

"We surrender," said the blond. "We are your prisoners—prisoners of the United States Army."

Eddie laughed.

"Seriously!"

"Buzzer!" Eddie nudged his buddy with the toe of his boot. "Hey, Buzzer—you gotta hear this."

"Hmmmm?"

"We just captured some people."

Buzzer opened his eyes and squinted at the pair. "You're drunker'n I am, by God, Eddie, goin' out capturin' people," he said at last. "You damn fool—the war's over." He waved his hand magnanimously. "Turn 'em loose."

"Take us through the Russian lines to Prague as American prisoners, and you'll be heroes," said the blond. He lowered his voice. "This is a famous German general. Think of it—you two can bring him in as your prisoner!"

"He really a general?" said Buzzer. "Heil Hitler, Pop."

The older man raised his arm in an abbreviated salute.

"Got a little pepper left in him, at that," said Buzzer.

"From what I heard," said Eddie, "me and Buzzer'll be heroes if we get just us through the Russian lines, let alone a German general."

The noise of a tank column of the Red Army grew louder.

"All right, all right," said the blond, "sell us your uniforms, then. You'll still have your dog tags, and you can take our clothes."

"I'd rather be poor than dead," said Eddie. "Wouldn't you, Buzzer?"

"Just a minute, Eddie," said Buzzer, "just hold on. What'll you give us?"

"Come in the farmyard. We can't show you here," said the blond.

"I even heard there was some Nazis in the neighborhood," said Buzzer. "Come on, give us a little peek here."

"Now who's a damn fool?" said Eddie.

"Just want to be able to tell my grandchildren what I passed up," said Buzzer.

The blond was going through his pockets. He pulled out a fat roll of German currency.

"Confederate money!" said Buzzer. "What else you got?"

It was then that the old man showed them his pocketwatch, four diamonds, a ruby, and gold. And there, in the midst of a mob of every imaginable sort of refugee, the blond told Buzzer and Eddie that they could have the watch if they would go behind a wall and exchange their ragged American uniforms for the Germans' civilian clothes. They thought Americans were so dumb!

This was all so funny and crazy! Eddie and Buzzer were so drunk! What a story they would have to tell when they got home! They didn't want the watch. They wanted to get home alive. There, in the midst of a mob of every imaginable sort of refugee, the blond was showing them a small pistol, as though they could have that, too, along with the watch.

But it was now impossible for anybody to say any more funny stuff and still be heard. The earth shook, and the air was ripped to shreds as armored vehicles from the victorious Soviet Union, thundering and backfiring, came up the road. Every-body who could got out of the way of the juggernaut. Some were not so lucky. They were mangled. They were squashed.

Eddie and Buzzer and the old man and the blond found themselves behind the wall where the blond had said the Americans could swap their uniforms for the watch and civilian clothes. In the uproar, during which anybody could do anything, and nobody cared what anybody else did, the blond shot Buzzer in the head. He aimed his pistol at Eddie. He fired. He missed.

That had evidently been the plan all along, to kill Eddie and Buzzer. But what chance did the old man, who spoke no English, have to pass himself off to his captors as an American? None. It was the blond who was going to do that. And they were both about to be captured. All the old man could do was commit suicide.

Eddie went back over the wall, putting it between himself and the blond. But the blond didn't care what had become of him. Everything the blond needed was on Buzzer's body. When Eddie peered over the wall to see if Buzzer was still alive, the blond was stripping the body. The old man now had the pistol. He put its muzzle in his mouth and blew his brains out.

The blond walked off with Buzzer's clothes and dog tags. Buzzer was in his GI underwear and dead, without ID. On the ground between the old man and Buzzer, Eddie found the watch. It was running. It told the right time. Eddie picked it up and put it in his pocket.

The rainstorm outside Joe Bane's pawnshop had stopped. "When I got home," said Eddie, "I wrote Buzzer's folks. I told 'em he'd been killed in a fight with a German, even though the war was over. I told the Army the same thing. I didn't know the name of the place where he'd died, so there was no way they could look for his body and give him a decent funeral. I had to leave him there. Whoever buried him, unless they could recognize GI underwear, wouldn't have known he was American. He could have been a German. He could have been anything."

Eddie snatched the watch from under the pawnbroker's nose. "Thanks for letting me know what it's worth," he said. "Makes more sense to keep it for a souvenir."

"Five hundred," said Bane, but Eddie was already on his way out the door.

Ten minutes later, the shoeshine boy returned with a translation of the inscription inside the watch. This was it:

"To General Heinz Guderian, Chief of the Army General Staff, who cannot rest until the last enemy soldier is driven from the sacred soil of the Third German Reich. ADOLF HITLER."

The Cruise of The Jolly Roger

DURING THE GREAT DEPRESSION, Nathan Durant was homeless until he found a home in the United States Army. He spent seventeen years in the Army, thinking of the earth as terrain, of the hills and valleys as enfilade and defilade, of the horizon as something a man should never silhouette himself against, of the houses and woods and thickets as cover. It was a good life, and when he got tired of thinking about war, he got himself a girl and a bottle, and the next morning he was ready to think about war some more.

When he was thirty-six, an enemy projectile dropped into a command post under thick green cover in defilade in the terrain of Korea, and blew Major Durant, his maps, and his career through the wall of his tent.

He had always assumed that he was going to die young and gallantly. But he didn't die. Death was far, far away, and Durant faced unfamiliar and frightening battalions of peaceful years.

In the hospital, the man in the next bed talked constantly of the boat he was going to own when he was whole again. For want of exciting peacetime dreams of his own, for want of a home or family or civilian friends, Durant borrowed his neighbor's dream.

With a deep scar across his cheek, with the lobe of his right ear gone, with a stiff leg, he limped into a boatyard in New London, the port nearest the hospital, and bought a secondhand cabin cruiser. He learned to run it in the harbor there, christened the boat *The Jolly Roger* at the suggestion of some children who haunted the boatyard, and set out arbitrarily for Martha's Vineyard.

He stayed on the island but a day, depressed by the tranquility and permanence, by the feeling of deep, still lakes of time, by men and women so at one with the peace of the place as to have nothing to exchange with an old soldier but a few words about the weather.

Durant fled to Chatham, at the elbow of Cape Cod, and found himself beside a beautiful woman at the foot of a lighthouse there. Had he been in his old uniform, seeming as he'd liked to seem in the old days, about to leave on a dangerous mission, he and the woman might have strolled off together. Women had once treated him like a small boy with special permission to eat icing off cakes. But the woman looked away without interest. He was nobody and nothing. The spark was gone.

His former swashbuckling spirits returned for an hour or two during a brief blow off the dunes of Cape Cod's east coast, but there was no one aboard to notice. When he reached the sheltered harbor at Provincetown and went ashore, he was a hollow man again, who didn't have to be anywhere at any time, whose life was all behind him.

"Look up, please," commanded a gaudily dressed young man with a camera in his hands and a girl on his arm.

Surprised, Durant did look up, and the camera shutter clicked. "Thank you," said the young man brightly.

"Are you a painter?" asked his girl.

"Painter?" said Durant. "No—retired Army officer."

The couple did a poor job of covering their disappointment.

"Sorry," said Durant, and he felt dull and annoyed.

"Oh!" said the girl. "There's some real painters over there."

Durant glanced at the artists, three men and one woman, probably in their late twenties, who sat on the wharf, their backs to a silvered splintering pile, sketching. The woman, a tanned brunette, was looking right at Durant.

"Do you mind being sketched?" she said.

"No—no, I guess not," said Durant bearishly. Freezing in his pose, he wondered what it was he'd been thinking about that had made him interesting enough to draw. He realized that he'd been thinking about lunch, about the tiny galley aboard *The Jolly Roger*, about the four wrinkled wieners, the half-pound of cheese, and the flat remains of a quart of beer that awaited him there.

"There," said the woman, "you see?" She held out the sketch.

What Durant saw was a big, scarred, hungry man, hunched over and desolate as a lost child. "Do I really look that bad?" he said, managing to laugh.

"Do you really feel that awful?"

"I was thinking of lunch. Lunch can be pretty terrible."

"Not where we eat it," she said. "Why not come with us?"

Major Durant went with them, with the three men, Ed, Teddy, and Lou, who danced through a life that seemed full of funny secrets, and with the girl, Marion. He found he was relieved to be with others again, even with these others, and his step down the walk was jaunty.

At lunch, the four spoke of painting, ballet, and drama. Durant grew tired of counterfeiting interest, but he kept at it.

"Isn't the food good here?" said Marion, in a casual and polite aside.

"Um," said Durant. "But the shrimp sauce is flat. Needs—" He gave up. The four were off again in their merry whirlwind of talk.

"Did you just drive here?" said Teddy, when he saw Durant staring at him disapprovingly.

"No," said Durant. "I came in my boat."

"A boat!" they echoed, excited, and Durant found himself center stage.

"What kind?" said Marion.

"Cabin cruiser," said Durant.

Their faces fell. "Oh," said Marion, "one of those floating tourist cabins with a motor."

"Well," said Durant, tempted to tell them about the blow he'd weathered, "it's certainly no picnic when—"

"What's its name?" said Lou.

"*The Jolly Roger*," said Durant.

The four exchanged glances, and then burst into laughter, repeating the boat's name, to Durant's consternation and bafflement.

"If you had a dog," said Marion, "I'll bet you'd call it Spot."

"Seems like a perfectly good name for a dog," said Durant, reddening.

Marion reached across the table and patted his hand. "Aaaaaah, you lamb, you musn't mind us." She was an irresponsibly affectionate woman, and appeared to have no idea how profoundly her touch was moving the lonely Durant, in spite of his resentment. "Here we've been talking away and not letting you say a word," she said. "What is it you do in the Army?"

Durant was startled. He hadn't mentioned the Army, and there were no insignia on his faded khakis. "Well, I was in Korea for a little while," he said, "and I'm out of the Army now because of wounds."

The four were impressed and respectful. "Do you mind talking about it?" said Ed.

Durant sighed. He did mind talking about it to Ed, Teddy, and Lou, but he wanted very much for Marion to hear about it—wanted to show her that while he couldn't speak her language, he could speak one of his own that had life to it. "No," he said, "there are some things that would just as well stay unsaid, but for the most part, why not talk about it?" He sat back and lit a cigarette, and squinted into the past as though through a thin screen of shrubs in a forward observation post.

"Well," he said, "we were over on the east coast, and . . ." He had never tried to tell the tale before, and now, in his eagerness to be glib and urbane, he found himself including details, large and small, as they occurred to him, until his tale was no tale at all, but a formless, unwieldy description of war as it had really seemed: a senseless, complicated mess that in the telling was first-rate realism but miserable entertainment.

He had been talking for twenty minutes now, and his audience had finished coffee and dessert, and two cigarettes apiece, and the waitress was getting restive about the check. Durant, florid and irritated with himself, was trying to manage a cast of thousands spread over the forty thousand square miles of South Korea. His audience was listening with glazed eyes, brightening at any sign that the parts were about to be brought together into a whole and thence to an end. But the signs were always false, and at last, when Marion swallowed her third yawn, Durant blew himself in his story through the wall of his tent and fell silent.

"Well," said Teddy, "it's hard for us who haven't seen it to imagine."

"Words can hardly convey it," said Marion. She patted Durant's hand again. "You've been through so much, and you're so modest about it."

"Nothing, really," said Durant.

After a moment of silence, Marion stood. "It's certainly been pleasant and interesting, Major," she said, "and we all wish you bon voyage on *The Jolly Roger.*"

And there it ended.

Back aboard *The Jolly Roger*, Durant finished the stale quart of beer and told himself he was ready to give up—to sell the boat, return to the hospital, put on a bathrobe, and play cards and thumb through magazines until doomsday.

Moodily he studied his charts for a course back to New London. It was then he realized that he was only a few miles from the home village of a friend who had been killed in the Second World War. It struck him as wryly fitting that he should call on this ghost on his way back.

He arrived at the village through an early-morning mist, the day before Memorial Day, feeling ghostlike himself. He made a bad landing that shook the village dock, and tied up *The Jolly Roger* with a clumsy knot.

When he reached the main street, he found it quiet but lined with flags. Only two other people were abroad to glance at the dour stranger.

He stepped into the post office and spoke to the brisk old woman who was sorting mail in a rickety cage.

"Pardon me," said Durant, "I'm looking for the Pefko family."

"Pefko? Pefko?" said the postmistress. "That doesn't sound like any name around here. Pefko? They summer people?"

"No—I don't think so. I'm sure they're not. They may have moved away a while ago."

"Well, if they lived here, you'd think I'd know. They'd come here for their mail. There's only four hundred of us year around, and I never heard of any Pefko."

The secretary from the law office across the street came in and knelt by Durant, and worked the combination lock of her mailbox.

"Annie," said the postmistress, "you know about anybody named Pefko around here?"

"No," said Annie, "unless they had one of the summer cottages out on the dunes. It's hard to keep track of who is in those. They're changing hands all the time."

She stood, and Durant saw that she was attractive in a determinedly practical way, without wiles or ornamentation. But Durant was now so convinced of his own dullness that his manner toward her was perfunctory.

"Look," he said, "my name is Durant, Major Nathan Durant, and one of my best friends in the Army was from here. George Pefko—I know he was from here. He said so, and so did all his records. I'm sure of it."

"Ohhhhhh," said Annie. "Now wait, wait, wait. That's right—certainly. Now I remember."

"You knew him?" said Durant.

"I knew *of* him," said Annie. "I know now who you're talking about: the one that got killed in the war."

"I was with him," said Durant.

"Still can't say as I remember him," said the postmistress.

"You don't remember him, probably, but you remember the family," said Annie. "And they *did* live out on the dunes, too. Goodness, that was a long time ago—ten or fifteen years. Remember that big family that talked Paul Eldredge into letting them live in one of his summer cottages all winter? About six kids or more. That was the Pefkos. A wonder they didn't freeze to death, with nothing but a fireplace for heat. The old man came out here to pick cranberries, and stayed on through the winter."

"Wouldn't exactly call this their hometown," said the postmistress.

"George did," said Durant.

"Well," said Annie, "I suppose one hometown was as good as another for young George. Those Pefkos were wanderers."

"George enlisted from here," said Durant. "I suppose that's how he settled on it." By the same line of reasoning, Durant had chosen Pittsburgh as his hometown, though a dozen other places had as strong a claim.

"One of those people who found a home in the Army," said the postmistress. "Scrawny, tough boy. I remember now. His family never got any mail. That was it, and they weren't church people. That's why I forgot. Drifters. He must have been about your brother's age, Annie."

"I know. But I tagged after my brother all the time in those days, and George Pefko never had anything to do with his gang. They kept to themselves, the Pefkos did."

"There must be somebody who remembers him well," said Durant. "Somebody who—" He let the sentence die on a note of urgency. It was unbearable that every vestige of George had disappeared, unmissed.

"Now that I think about it," said Annie, "I'm almost sure there's a square named after him."

"A square?" said Durant.

"Not really a square," said Annie. "They just call it a square. When a man from around here gets killed in a war, the town names some little plot of town property after him—a traffic circle or something like that. They put up a plaque with his name on it. That triangle down by the village dock—I'm almost sure that was named for your friend."

"It's hard to keep track of them all, *these* days," said the postmistress.

"Would you like to go down and see it?" said Annie. "I'll be glad to show you."

"A plaque?" said Durant. "Never mind." He dusted his hands. "Well, which way is the restaurant—the one with a bar?"

"After June fifteenth, any way you want to go," said the postmistress. "But right now everything is closed and shuttered. You can get a sandwich at the drugstore."

"I might as well move on," said Durant.

"As long as you've come, you ought to stay for the parade," said Annie.

"After seventeen years in the Army, that would be a real treat," said Durant. "What parade?"

"Memorial Day," said Annie.

"That's tomorrow, I thought," said Durant.

"The children march today. School is closed tomorrow," said Annie. She smiled. "I'm afraid you're going to have to endure one more parade, Major, because here it comes."

Durant followed her apathetically out onto the sidewalk. He could hear the sound of a band, but the marchers weren't yet in sight. There were no more than a dozen people waiting for the parade to pass.

"They go from square to square," said Annie. "We really ought to wait for them down by George's."

"Whatever you say," said Durant. "I'll be closer to the boat."

They walked down the slope toward the village dock and *The Jolly Roger*.

"They keep up the squares very nicely," said Annie.

"They always do, they always do," said Durant.

"Are you in a hurry to get somewhere else today?"

"Me?" said Durant bitterly. "Me? Nothing's waiting for me anywhere."

"I see," said Annie, startled. "Sorry."

"It isn't your fault."

"I don't understand."

"I'm an Army bum like George. They should have handed me a plaque and shot me. I'm not worth a dime to anybody."

"Here's the square," said Annie gently.

"Where? Oh—that." The square was a triangle of grass, ten feet on a side, an accident of intersecting lanes and a footpath. In its center was a low boulder on which was fixed a small metal plaque, easily overlooked.

"George Pefko Memorial Square," said Durant. "By golly, I wonder what George would make of that?"

"He'd like it, wouldn't he?" said Annie.

"He'd probably laugh."

"I don't see that there's anything to laugh about."

"Nothing, nothing at all—except that it doesn't have much to do with anything, does it? Who cares about George? Why should anyone care about George? It's just what people are expected to do, put up plaques."

The bandsmen were in sight now, all eight of them, teenagers, out of step, rounding a corner with confident, proud, sour, and incoherent noise intended to be music.

Before them rode the town policeman, fat with leisure, authority, leather, bullets, pistol, handcuffs, club, and a badge. He was splendidly oblivious to the smoking, back-firing motorcycle beneath him as he swept slowly back and forth before the parade.

Behind the band came a cloud of purple, seeming to float a few feet above the street. It was lilacs carried by children. Along the curb, teachers looking as austere as New England churches called orders to the children.

"The lilacs came in time this year," said Annie. "Sometimes they don't. It's touch-and-go."

"That so?" said Durant.

A teacher blew a whistle. The parade halted, and Durant found a dozen children bearing down on him, their eyes large, their arms filled with flowers, their knees lifted high.

Durant stepped aside.

A bugler played taps badly.

The children laid their flowers before the plaque on George Pefko Memorial Square.

"Lovely?" whispered Annie.

"Yes," said Durant. "It would make a statue want to cry. But what does it mean?"

"Tom," called Annie to a small boy who had just laid down his flowers, "why did you do that?"

The boy looked around guiltily. "Do what?"

"Put the flowers down there," said Annie.

"Tell them you're paying homage to one of the fallen valiant who selflessly gave his life," prompted a teacher.

Tom looked at her blankly, and then back at the flowers.

"Don't you know?" said Annie.

"Sure," said Tom at last. "He died fighting so we could be safe and free. And we're thanking him with flowers, because it was a nice thing to do." He looked up at Annie, amazed that she should ask. "Everybody knows that."

The policeman raced his motorcycle engine. The teacher shepherded the children back into line. The parade moved on.

"Well," said Annie, "are you sorry you had to endure one more parade, Major?"

"It's true, isn't it," murmured Durant. "It's so damn simple, and so easy to forget." Watching the innocent marchers under the flowers, he was aware of life, the beauty and importance of a village at peace. "Maybe I never knew—never had any way of knowing. This *is* what war is about, isn't it. This."

Durant laughed. "George, you homeless, horny, wild old rummy," he said to George Pefko Memorial Square, "damned if you didn't turn out to be a saint."

The old spark was back. Major Durant, home from the wars, was somebody.

"I wonder," he said to Annie, "if you'd have lunch with me, and then, maybe, we could go for a ride in my boat."

Der Arme Dolmetscher

I WAS ASTONISHED one day in 1944, in the midst of front-line hell-raising, to learn that I had been made interpreter, *Dolmetscher* if you please, for a whole battalion, and was to be billeted in a Belgian burgomaster's house within artillery range of the Siegfried Line.

It had never entered my head that I had what it took to dolmetsch. I qualified for the position while waiting to move from France into the front lines. While a student, I had learned the first stanza of Heinrich Heine's "Die Lorelei" by rote from a college roommate, and I happened to give those lines a dogged rendition while working within earshot of the battalion commander. The Colonel (a hotel detective from Mobile) asked his Executive Officer (a dry-goods salesman from Knoxville) in what language the lyrics were. The Executive withheld judgment until I had bungled through "*Der Gipfel des Berges foo-unk-kelt im Abendsonnenschein.*"

"Ah believes tha's Kraut, Cuhnel," he said.

My understanding in English of the only German I knew was this: "I don't know why I am so sad. I can't get an old legend out of my head. The air is cool and it's getting dark, and quiet flows the Rhine. The peak of the mountain twinkles in evening sunshine."

The Colonel felt his role carried with it the obligation to make quick, headstrong decisions. He made some dandies before the Wehrmacht was whipped, but the one he made that day was my favorite. "If tha's Kraut, whassat man doin' on the honey-dippin' detail?" he wanted to know. Two hours later, the company clerk told me to lay down the buckets, for I was now battalion interpreter.

Orders to move up came soon after. Those in authority were too harried to hear my declarations of incompetence. "You talk Kraut good enough foah us," said the Executive Officer. "Theah ain't goin' to be much talkin' to Krauts where weah goin'." He patted my rifle affectionately. "Heah's what's goin' to do most of youah interpretin' fo' ya," he said. The Executive, who had learned everything he knew from the Colonel, had the idea that the American Army had just licked the Belgians, and that I was to be stationed with the burgomaster to make sure he didn't try to pull a fast one. "Besides," the Executive concluded, "theah ain't nobody else can talk Kraut at all."

I rode to the burgomaster's farm on a truck with three disgruntled Pennsylvania

Dutchmen who had applied for interpreters' jobs months earlier. When I made it clear that I was no competition for them, and that I hoped to be liquidated within twenty-four hours, they warmed up enough for me to furnish the interesting information that I was a *Dolmetscher.* They also decoded "Die Lorelei" at my request. This gave me command of about forty words (par for a two-year-old), but no combination of them would get me so much as a glass of cold water.

Every turn of the truck's wheels brought a new question: "What's the word for 'army'? . . . How do I ask for the bathroom? . . . What's the word for 'sick'? . . . 'well'? . . . 'dish'? . . . 'brother'? . . . 'shoe'?" My phlegmatic instructors tired, and one handed me a pamphlet purporting to make German easy for the man in the foxhole.

"Some of the first pages are missing," the donor explained as I jumped from the truck before the burgomaster's stone farmhouse. "Used 'em for cigarette papers," he said.

It was early morning when I knocked at the burgomaster's door. I stood on the step like a bit player in the wings, with the one line I was to deliver banging around an otherwise empty head. The door swung open. "*Dolmetscher,*" I said.

The burgomaster himself, old, thin, and nightshirted, ushered me into the first-floor bedroom that was to be mine. He pantomimed as well as spoke his welcome, and a sprinkling of "*Danke schön*" was adequate dolmetsching for the time being. I was prepared to throttle further discussion with "*Ich weiss nicht, was soll es bedeuten, dass ich so traurig bin.*" This would have sent him padding off to bed, convinced that he had a fluent, albeit shot-full-of-*Weltschmerz, Dolmetscher.* The stratagem wasn't necessary. He left me alone to consolidate my resources.

Chief among these was the mutilated pamphlet. I examined each of its precious pages in turn, delighted by the simplicity of transposing English into German. With this booklet, all I had to do was run my finger down the left-hand column until I found the English phrase I wanted, and then rattle off the nonsense syllables printed opposite in the right-hand column. "How many grenade launchers have you?" for instance, was *Vee feel grenada vairfair habben zee?* Impeccable German for "Where are your tank columns?" proved to be nothing more troublesome than *Vo zint eara pantzer shpitzen?* I mouthed the phrases: "Where are your howitzers? How many machine guns have you? Surrender! Don't shoot! Where have you hidden your motorcycle? Hands up! What unit are you from?"

The pamphlet came to an abrupt end, toppling my spirits from manic to depressive. The Pennsylvania Dutchman had smoked up all the rear-area pleasantries, the pamphlet's first half, leaving me with nothing to work with but the repartee of hand-to-hand fighting.

As I lay sleepless in bed, the one drama in which I could play took shape in my mind. . . .

DOLMETSCHER (to BURGOMASTER'S DAUGHTER): I don't know what will become of me, I am so sad. (*Embraces her.*)

BURGOMASTER'S DAUGHTER (*with yielding shyness*): The air is cool, and it's getting dark, and the Rhine is flowing quietly.

(DOLMETSCHER *seizes* BURGOMASTER'S DAUGHTER, *carries her bodily into his room.*)

DOLMETSCHER (*softly*): Surrender.

BURGOMASTER (*brandishing Luger*): Ach! Hands up! DOLMETSCHER and BURGOMASTER'S DAUGHTER: Don't shoot!

(*A map, showing disposition of American First Army, falls from* BURGOMASTER'S *breast pocket.*)

DOLMETSCHER (*aside, in English*): What is this supposedly pro-Ally burgomaster doing with a map showing the disposition of the American First Army? And why am I supposed to be dolmetsching with a Belgian in German? (*He snatches .45 automatic pistol from beneath pillow and aims at* BURGOMASTER.)

BURGOMASTER and BURGOMASTER'S DAUGHTER: Don't shoot! (BURGOMASTER *drops Luger, cowers, sneers.*)

DOLMETSCHER: What unit are you from? (BURGOMASTER *remains sullen, silent.* BURGOMASTER'S DAUGHTER *goes to his side, weeps softly.* DOLMETSCHER *confronts* BURGOMASTER'S DAUGHTER.) Where have *you* hidden your motorcycle? (*Turns again to* BURGOMASTER.) Where are your howitzers, eh? Where are your tank columns? How many grenade launchers have you?

BURGOMASTER (*cracking under terrific grilling*): I—I surrender.

BURGOMASTER'S DAUGHTER: I am so sad.

(*Enter* GUARD DETAIL *composed of Pennsylvania Dutchmen, making a routine check just in time to hear* BURGOMASTER *and* BURGOMASTER'S DAUGHTER *confess to being Nazi agents parachuted behind American lines.*)

Johann Christoph Friedrich von Schiller couldn't have done any better with the same words, and they were the only words I had. There was no chance of my muddling through, and no pleasure in being interpreter for a full battalion in December and not being able to say so much as "Merry Christmas."

I made my bed, tightened the drawstrings on my duffel bag, and stole through the blackout curtains and into the night.

Wary sentinels directed me to Battalion Headquarters, where I found most of our officers either poring over maps or loading their weapons. There was a holiday spirit in the air, and the Executive Officer was honing an eighteen-inch bowie knife and humming "Are You from Dixie?"

"Well, bless mah soul," he said, noticing me in the doorway, "here's old 'Sprecken Zee Dutch.' Speak up, boy. Ain't you supposed to be ovah at the mayah's house?"

"It's no good," I said. "They all speak Low German, and I speak High."

The Executive was impressed. "Too good foah 'em, eh?" He ran his index finger down the edge of his murderous knife. "Ah think we'll be runnin' into some who can talk the high-class Kraut putty soon," he said, and then added, "Weah surrounded."

"We'll whomp 'em the way we whomped 'em in Nawth Ca'lina and Tennessee," said the Colonel, who had never lost on maneuvers back home. "You stay heah, son. Ah'm gonna want you foah mah pussnel intupretah."

Twenty minutes later I was in the thick of dolmetsching again. Four Tiger tanks drove up to the front door of Headquarters, and two dozen German infantrymen dismounted to round us up with submachine guns.

"Say sumpin'," ordered the Colonel, spunky to the last.

I ran my eye down the left-hand columns of my pamphlet until I found the phrase that most fairly represented our sentiments. "Don't shoot," I said.

A German tank officer swaggered in to have a look at his catch. In his hand was a pamphlet, somewhat smaller than mine. "Where are your howitzers?" he said.

Bagombo Snuff Box

"THIS PLACE IS NEW, isn't it?" said Eddie Laird.

He was sitting in a bar in the heart of the city. He was the only customer, and he was talking to the bartender.

"I don't remember this place," he said, "and I used to know every bar in town."

Laird was a big man, thirty-three, with a pleasantly impudent moon face. He was dressed in a blue flannel suit that was plainly a very recent purchase. He watched his image in the bar mirror as he talked. Now and then, one of his hands would stray from the glass to stroke a soft lapel.

"Not so new," said the bartender, a sleepy, fat man in his fifties. "When was the last time you were in town?"

"The war," Laird said.

"Which war was that?"

"Which war?" Laird repeated. "I guess you have to ask people that nowadays, when they talk about war. The second one—the Second *World* War. I was stationed out at Cunningham Field. Used to come to town every weekend I could."

A sweet sadness welled up in him as he remembered his reflection in other bar mirrors in other days, remembered the reflected flash of captains' bars and silver wings.

"This place was built in 'forty-six, and been renovated twice since then," the bartender said.

"Built—and renovated twice," Laird said wonderingly. "Things wear out pretty fast these days, don't they? Can you still get a plank steak at Charley's Steak House for two dollars?"

"Burned down," the bartender said. "There's a J.C. Penney there now."

"So what's the big Air Force hangout these days?" Laird said.

"Isn't one," the bartender said. "They closed down Cunningham Field."

Laird picked up his drink, and walked over to the window to watch the people go by. "I halfway expected the women here to be wearing short skirts still," he said. "Where are all the pretty pink knees?" He rattled his fingernails against the window. A woman glanced at him and hurried on.

"I've got a wife out there somewhere," Laird said. "What do you suppose has happened to *her* in eleven years?"

"A wife?"

"An ex-wife. One of those war things. I was twenty-two, and she was eighteen. Lasted six months."

"What went wrong?"

"Wrong?" Laird said. "I just didn't want to be owned, that's all. I wanted to be able to stick my toothbrush in my hip pocket and take off whenever I felt like it. And she didn't go for that. So . . ." He grinned. "*Adiós.* No tears, no hard feelings."

He walked over to the jukebox. "What's the most frantically popular song of the minute?"

"Try number seventeen," the bartender said. "I guess I could stand it one more time."

Laird played number seventeen, a loud, tearful ballad of lost love. He listened intently. And at the end, he stamped his foot and winked, just as he had done years before.

"One more drink," Laird said, "and then, by heaven, I'm going to call up my ex-wife." He appealed to the bartender. "That's all right, isn't it? Can't I call her up if I want to?" He laughed. "'Dear Emily Post: I have a slight problem in etiquette. I haven't seen or exchanged a word with my ex-wife for eleven years. Now I find myself in the same city with her—'"

"How do you know she's still around?" the bartender said.

"I called up an old buddy when I blew in this morning. He said she's all set—got just what she wants: a wage slave of a husband, a vine-covered cottage with expansion attic, two kids, and a quarter of an acre of lawn as green as Arlington National Cemetery."

Laird strode to the telephone. For the fourth time that day, he looked up his ex-wife's number, under the name of her second husband, and held a dime an inch above the slot. This time, he let the coin fall. "Here goes nothing," Laird said. He dialed.

A woman answered. In the background, a child shrieked and a radio blabbed.

"Amy?" Laird said.

"Yes?" She was out of breath.

A silly grin spread over Laird's face. "Hey—guess what? This is Eddie Laird."

"Who?"

"Eddie Laird—Eddie!"

"Wait a minute, would you, please?" Amy said. "The baby is making such a terrible racket, and the radio's on, and I've got brownies in the oven, just ready to come out. I can't hear a thing. Would you hold on?"

"Sure."

"Now then," she said, winded, "who did you say this was?"

"Eddie Laird."

She gasped. "Really?"

"Really," Laird said merrily. "I just blew in from Ceylon, by way of Baghdad, Rome, and New York."

"Good heavens," said Amy. "What a shock. I didn't even know if you were alive or dead."

Laird laughed. "They can't kill me, and by heaven, they've sure tried."

"What have you been up to?"

"Ohhhhh—a little bit of everything. I just quit a job flying for a pearling outfit in Ceylon. I'm starting a company of my own, prospecting for uranium up around the Klondike region. Before the Ceylon deal, I was hunting diamonds in the Amazon rain forest, and before that, flying for a sheik in Iraq."

"Like something out of *The Arabian Nights*," said Amy. "My head just swims."

"Well, don't get any glamorous illusions," Laird said. "Most of it was hard, dirty, dangerous work." He sighed. "And how are you, Amy?"

"Me?" said Amy. "How is any housewife? Harassed."

The child began to cry again.

"Amy," said Laird huskily, "is everything all right—between us?"

Her voice was very small. "Time heals all wounds," she said. "It hurt at first, Eddie—it hurt very much. But I've come to understand it was all for the best. You can't help being restless. You were born that way. You were like a caged eagle, mooning, molting."

"And you, Amy, are *you* happy?"

"Very," said Amy, with all her heart. "It's wild and it's messy with the children. But when I get a chance to catch my breath, I can see it's sweet and good. It's what I always wanted. So in the end, we both got our way, didn't we? The eagle and the homing pigeon."

"Amy," Laird said, "could I come out to see you?"

"Oh, Eddie, the house is a horror and I'm a witch. I couldn't stand to have you see me like this—after you've come from Ceylon by way of Baghdad, Rome, and New York. What a hideous letdown for someone like you. Stevie had the measles last week, and the baby has had Harry and me up three times a night, and—"

"Now, now," Laird said, "I'll see the real you shining through it all. I'll come out at five, and say hello, and leave again right away. Please?"

On the cab ride out to Amy's home, Laird encouraged himself to feel sentimental about the coming reunion. He tried to daydream about the best of his days with her, but got only fantasies of movie starlet–like nymphs dancing about him with red lips and vacant eyes. This shortcoming of his imagination, like everything else about the day, was a throwback to his salad days in the Air Force. All pretty women had seemed to come from the same mold.

Laird told the cab to wait for him. "This will be short and sweet," he said.

As he walked up to Amy's small, ordinary house, he managed a smile of sad maturity, the smile of a man who has hurt and been hurt, who has seen everything, who has learned a great deal from it all, and who, incidentally, has made a lot of money along the way.

He knocked and, while he waited, picked at the flaking paint on the door frame.

Harry, Amy's husband, a blocky man with a kind face, invited Larry in.

"I'm changing the baby," Amy called from inside. "Be there in two shakes."

Harry was clearly startled by Laird's size and splendor, and Laird looked down on him and clapped his arm in comradely fashion.

"I guess a lot of people would say this is pretty irregular," Laird said. "But what happened between Amy and me was a long time ago. We were just a couple of crazy kids, and we're all older and wiser now. I hope we can all be friends."

Harry nodded. "Why, yes, of course. Why not?" he said. "Would you like something to drink? I'm afraid I don't have much of a selection. Rye or beer?"

"Anything at all, Harry," Laird said. "I've had kava with the Maoris, scotch with the British, champagne with the French, and cacao with the Tupi. I'll have a rye or a beer with you. When in Rome . . ." He dipped into his pocket and brought out a snuff box encrusted with semiprecious gems. "Say, I brought you and Amy a little something." He pressed the box into Harry's hand. "I picked it up for a song in Bagombo."

"Bagombo?" said Harry, dazzled.

"Ceylon," Laird said easily. "Flew for a pearling outfit out there. Pay was fantastic, the mean temperature was seventy-three, but I didn't like the monsoons. Couldn't stand being bottled up in the same rooms for weeks at a time, waiting for the rain to quit. A man's got to get out, or he just goes to pot—gets flabby and womanly."

"Um," said Harry.

Already the small house and the smells of cooking and the clutter of family life were crowding in on Laird, making him want to be off and away. "Nice place you have here," he said.

"It's a little small," Harry said. "But—"

"Cozy," said Laird. "Too much room can drive you nuts. I know. Back in Bagombo, I had twenty-six rooms, and twelve servants to look after them, but they didn't make me happy. They mocked me, actually. But the place rented for seven dollars a month, and I couldn't pass it up, could I?"

Harry started to leave for the kitchen, but stopped in the doorway, thunderstruck. "Seven dollars a month for twenty-six rooms?" he said.

"Turned out I was being taken. The tenant before me got it for three."

"Three," Harry murmured. "Tell me," he said hesitantly, "are there a lot of jobs waiting for Americans in places like that? Are they recruiting?"

"You wouldn't want to leave your family, would you?"

Harry was conscience-stricken. "Oh, no! I thought maybe I could take them."

"No soap," said Laird. "What they want is bachelors. And anyway, you've got a nice setup here. And you've got to have a specialty, too, to qualify for the big money. Fly, handle a boat, speak a language. Besides, most of the recruiting is done in bars in Singapore, Algiers, and places like that. Now, I'm taking a flier at uranium prospecting on my own, up in the Klondike, and I need a couple of good Geiger counter technicians. Can you repair a Geiger counter, Harry?"

"Nope," said Harry.

"Well, the men I want are going to have to be single, anyway," said Laird. "It's a beautiful part of the world, teeming with moose and salmon, but rugged. No place for women or children. What *is* your line?"

"Oh," said Harry, "credit manager for a department store."

"Harry," Amy called, "would you please warm up the baby's formula, and see if the lima beans are done?"

"Yes, dear," said Harry.

"What did you say, honey?"

"I said yes!" Harry bellowed.

A shocked silence settled over the house.

And then Amy came in, and Laird had his memory refreshed. Laird stood. Amy was a lovely woman, with black hair, and wise brown affectionate eyes. She was still young, but obviously very tired. She was prettily dressed, carefully made-up, and quite self-conscious.

"Eddie, how nice," she said with brittle cheerfulness. "Don't you look well!"

"You, too," Laird said.

"Do I really?" Amy said. "I feel so ancient."

"You shouldn't," Laird said. "This life obviously agrees with you."

"We *have* been very happy," Amy said.

"You're as pretty as a model in Paris, a movie star in Rome."

"You don't mean it." Amy was pleased.

"I do," Laird said. "I can see you now in a Mainbocher suit, your high heels clicking smartly along the Champs-Élysées, with the soft winds of the Parisian spring ruffling your black hair, and with every eye drinking you in—and a gendarme salutes!"

"Oh, Eddie!" Amy cried.

"Have you been to Paris?" said Laird.

"Nope," said Amy.

"No matter. In many ways, there are more exotic thrills in New York. I can see you there, in a theater crowd, with each man falling silent and turning to stare as you pass by. When was the last time you were in New York?"

"Hmmmmm?" Amy said, staring into the distance.

"When were you last in New York?"

"Oh, I've never been there. Harry has—on business."

"Why didn't he take you?" Laird said gallantly. "You can't let your youth slip away without going to New York. It's a young person's town."

"Angel," Harry called from the kitchen, "how can you tell if lima beans are done?"

"Stick a lousy fork into 'em!" Amy yelled.

Harry appeared in the doorway with drinks, and blinked in hurt bewilderment. "Do you have to yell at me?" he said.

Amy rubbed her eyes. "I'm sorry," she said. "I'm tired. We're both tired."

"We haven't had much sleep," Harry said. He patted his wife's back. "We're both a little tense."

Amy took her husband's hand and squeezed it. Peace settled over the house once more.

Harry passed out the drinks, and Laird proposed a toast.

"Eat, drink, and be merry," Laird said, "for tomorrow we could die."

Harry and Amy winced, and drank thirstily.

"He brought us a snuff box from Bagombo, honey," said Harry. "Did I pronounce that right?"

"You've Americanized it a little," said Laird. "But that's about it." He pursed his lips. "*Bagombo.*"

"It's very pretty," said Amy. "I'll put it on my dressing table, and not let the children near it. Bagombo."

"There!" Laird said. "*She* said it just right. It's a funny thing. Some people have an ear for languages. They hear them once, and they catch all the subtle sounds immediately. And some people have a tin ear, and never catch on. Amy, listen, and then repeat what I say: '*Toli! Pakka sahn nebul rokka ta. Si notte loni gin ta tonic.*'"

Cautiously Amy repeated the sentence.

"Perfect! You know what you just said in Buhna-Simca? 'Young woman, go cover the baby, and bring me a gin and tonic on the south terrace.' Now then, Harry, you say, '*Pilla Sibba tu bang-bang. Libbin hru donna steek!*'"

Harry, frowning, repeated the sentence.

Laird sat back with a sympathetic smile for Amy. "Well, I don't know, Harry. That might get across, except you'd earn a laugh from the natives when you turned your back."

Harry was stung. "What did I say?"

"'Boy!'" Laird translated. "'Hand me the gun. The tiger is in the clump of trees just ahead.'"

"*Pilla!*" Harry said imperiously. "*Sibba tu bang-bang. Libbin hru donna steek!*" He held out his hand for the gun, and the hand twitched like a fish dying on a riverbank.

"Better—much better!" Laird said.

"That *was* good," Amy said.

Harry brushed off their adulation. He was grim, purposeful. "Tell me," he said, "are tigers a problem around Bagombo?"

"Sometimes, when game gets scarce in the jungles, tigers come into the outskirts of villages," Laird said. "And then you have to go out and get them."

"You had servants in Bagombo, did you?" Amy said.

"At six cents a day for a man, and four cents a day for a woman? I guess!" Laird said.

There was the sound of a bicycle bumping against the outside of the house.

"Stevie's home," Harry said.

"I want to go to Bagombo," Amy said.

"It's no place to raise kids," Laird said. "That's the big drawback."

The front door opened, and a good-looking, muscular nine-year-old boy came in, hot and sweaty. He threw his cap at a hook in the front closet and started upstairs.

"Hang up your hat, Stevie!" Amy said. "I'm not a servant who follows you around, gathering things wherever you care to throw them."

"And pick up your feet!" said Harry.

Stevie came creeping down the stairway, shocked and perplexed. "What got into you two all of a sudden?" he said.

"Don't be fresh," Harry said. "Come in here and meet Mr. Laird."

"*Major* Laird," said Laird.

"Hi," said Stevie. "How come you haven't got a uniform on, if you're a Major?"

"Reserve commission," Laird said. The boy's eyes, frank, irreverent, and unromantic, scared him. "Nice boy you have here."

"Oh," Stevie said, "*that* kind of a Major." He saw the snuff box, and picked it up.

"Stevie," Amy said, "put that down. It's one of Mother's treasures, and it's not going to get broken like everything else. Put it down."

"Okay, okay, okay," said Stevie. He set the box down with elaborate gentleness. "I didn't know it was such a treasure."

"Major Laird brought it all the way from Bagombo," Amy said.

"Bagombo, Japan?" Stevie said.

"Ceylon, Stevie," Harry said. "Bagombo is in Ceylon."

"Then how come it's got 'Made in Japan' on the bottom?"

Laird paled. "They export their stuff to Japan, and the Japanese market it for them," he said.

"There, Stevie," Amy said. "You learned something today."

"Then why don't they say it was made in Ceylon?" Stevie wanted to know.

"The Oriental mind works in devious ways," said Harry.

"Exactly," said Laird. "You've caught the whole spirit of the Orient in that one sentence, Harry."

"They ship these things all the way from Africa to Japan?" Stevie asked.

A hideous doubt stabbed Laird. A map of the world swirled in his mind, with continents flapping and changing shape and with an island named Ceylon scuttling through the seven seas. Only two points held firm, and these were Stevie's irreverent blue eyes.

"I always thought it was off India," Amy said.

"It's funny how things leave you when you start thinking about them too hard," Harry said. "Now I've got Ceylon all balled up with Madagascar."

"And Sumatra and Borneo," Amy said. "That's what we get for never leaving home."

Now four islands were sailing the troubled seas in Laird's mind.

"What's the answer, Eddie?" Amy said. "Where *is* Ceylon?"

"It's an island off Africa," Stevie said firmly. "We studied it."

Laird looked around the room and saw doubt on every face but Stevie's. He cleared his throat. "The boy is right," he croaked.

"I'll get my atlas and show you," Stevie said with pride, and ran upstairs.

Laird stood up, weak. "Must dash."

"So soon?" Harry said. "Well, I hope you find lots of uranium." He avoided his wife's eyes. "I'd give my right arm to go with you."

"Someday, when the children are grown," Amy said, "maybe we'll still be young enough to enjoy New York and Paris, and all those other places—and maybe retire in Bagombo."

"I hope so," said Laird. He blundered out the door, and down the walk, which now seemed endless, and into the waiting taxicab. "Let's go," he told the driver.

"They're all yelling at you," said the driver. He rolled down his window so Laird could hear.

"Hey, Major!" Stevie was shouting. "Mom's right, and we're wrong. Ceylon *is* off India."

The family that Laird had so recently scattered to the winds was together again, united in mirth on the doorstep.

"*Pilla!*" called Harry gaily. "*Sibba tu bang-bang. Libbin hru donna steek!*"

"*Toli!*" Amy called back. "*Pakka sahn nebul rokka ta. Si notte loni gin ta tonic.*"

The cab pulled away.

That night, in his hotel room, Laird put in a long-distance call to his second wife, Selma, in a small house in Levittown, Long Island, New York, far, far away.

"Is Arthur doing any better with his reading, Selma?" he asked.

"The teacher says he isn't dull, he's lazy," Selma said. "She says he can catch up with the class anytime he makes up his mind to."

"I'll talk to him when I get home," Laird said. "And the twins? Are they letting you sleep at all?"

"Well, I'm getting two of them out of the way at one crack. Let's look at it that way." Selma yawned agonizingly. "How's the trip going?"

"You remember how they said you couldn't sell potato chips in Dubuque?"

"Yes."

"Well, I did," said Laird. "I'm going to make history in this territory. I'll stand *this* town on its ear."

"Are you—" Selma hesitated. "Are you going to call *her* up, Eddie?"

"Naaaaah," Laird said. "Why open old graves?"

"You're not even curious about what's happened to her?"

"Naaaaah. We'd hardly know each other. People change, people change." He snapped his fingers. "Oh, I almost forgot. What did the dentist say about Dawn's teeth?"

Selma sighed. "She needs braces."

"Get them. I'm clicking, Selma. We're going to start living. I bought a new suit."

"It's about time," Selma said. "You've needed one for *so* long. Does it look nice on you?"

"I think so," Laird said. "I love you, Selma."

"I love you, Eddie. Good night."

"Miss you," Laird said. "Good night."

Great Day

WHEN I WAS SIXTEEN folks took me for twenty-five, and one full-growed woman from the city swore I must be thirty. I was big all over—had whiskers like steel wool. I sure wanted to see something besides LuVerne, Indiana, and that ain't saying Indianapolis would of held me, neither.

So I lied about my age, and I joined the Army of the World.

Didn't nobody cry. There wasn't no flags, there wasn't no bands. It wasn't like in olden times, where a young boy like me'd be going away to maybe get his head blowed off for democracy.

Wasn't nobody there at the depot but Ma, and Ma was mad. She thought the Army of the World was just for bums who couldn't find respectable work nowheres.

Seems like yesterday, but that was back in the year two thousand and thirty-seven.

"You keep away from them Zulus," Ma said.

"There's more'n just Zulus in the Army of the World, Ma," I told her. "There's folks from ever country there *is*."

But anybody born outside of Floyd County is a Zulu to Ma. "Well, anyways," she said, "I expect they'll feed you good, with world taxes as high as they is. And, as long as you're bound and determined to go off with them Zulus and all, I expect I ought to be glad there ain't no other armies roaming around, trying to shoot you."

"I'll be keeping the peace, Ma," I said. "Won't never be no terrible wars no more, with just one army. Don't that make you proud?"

"Makes me proud of what folks done done for peace," Ma said. "That don't make me love no army."

"It's a new, high-class kind of army, Ma," I said. "You ain't even allowed to curse. And if you don't go to church regular, you don't get no dessert."

Ma shook her head. "You just remember one thing," she said. "You just remember you *was* high-class." She didn't kiss me. She shook my hand. "As long as *I* had you," she said, "you was."

But when I sent Ma a shoulder patch from my first outfit after basic training, I heard she showed it around like it was a picture postcard from God. Wasn't nothing but a piece of blue felt with a picture of a gold clock stitched in it, and green lightning was coming out of the clock.

I heard Ma was shooting off her bazoo to everbody about how *her* boy was in a time-screen company, just like she knowed what a time-screen company was, just like everbody knowed that was the grandest thing in the whole Army of the World.

Well, we was the first time-screen company and the last one, unless they gets the bugs out of time machines. What we was supposed to do was so secret, *we* couldn't even find out what it was till it was too late to go over the hill.

Captain Poritsky was boss, and he wouldn't tell us nothing except we should be very proud, since there was only two hundred men on the face of the earth entitled to wear them clocks.

He use to be a football player at Notre Dame, and he looked like a stack of cannonballs on a courthouse lawn. He use to like to feel hisself all over while he talked to us. He use to like to feel how hard all them cannonballs was.

He said he was real honored to be leading such a fine body of men on such a important mission. He said we'd find out what the mission was on maneuvers at a place called Château-Thierry in France.

Sometimes generals would come look at us like we was going to do something sad and beautiful, but didn't nobody say boo about no time machine.

When we got to Château-Thierry, everbody was waiting for us. That's when we found out we was supposed to be something extra-desperate. Everbody wanted to see the killers with the clocks on their sleeves, everbody wanted to see the big show we was going to put on.

If we looked wild when we got there, we got wilder as time went on. We *still* couldn't find out what a time-screen company was supposed to do.

Wasn't no use asking.

"Captain Poritsky, sir," I said to him, just as respectful as I *could* be, "I hear we are going to demonstrate some new kind of attack tomorrow at dawn."

"Smile like you was happy and proud, soldier!" he said to me. "It's true!"

"Captain, sir," I said, "our platoon done elected me to come ask you if we couldn't find out now what we is supposed to do. We want to kind of get ready, sir."

"Soldier," Poritsky said, "ever man in that platoon got morale and esprit de corps and three grenades and a rifle and a bayonet and a hundred rounds of ammunition, don't he?"

"Yes, sir," I said.

"Soldier," Poritsky said, "that platoon *is* ready. And to show you how much faith I got in that platoon, it is going to lead the attack." He raised his eyebrows. "Well," he said, "ain't you going to say, 'Thank you, sir'?"

I done it.

"And to show how much faith I got in *you*, soldier," he said, "*you* are going to be the first man in the first squad in the first platoon." His eyebrows went up again. "Ain't you going to say, 'Thank you, sir'?"

I done it again.

"Just pray the scientists is as ready as you are, soldier," Poritsky said.

"There's scientists mixed up in it, sir?" I said.

"End of interview, soldier," Poritsky said. "Come to attention, soldier."

I done it.

"Salute," Poritsky said.

I done it.

"For'd harch!" he said.

Off I went.

So there I was on the night before the big demonstration, ignorant, ascared, and homesick, on guard duty in a tunnel in France. I was on guard with a kid named Earl Sterling from Salt Lake.

"Scientists is going to help us, eh?" Earl said to me.

"That's what he said," I told him.

"I'd just as soon of *not* knowed that much," Earl said.

Up above ground a big shell went off, and liked to bust our eardrums. There was a barrage going on up above, like giants walking around, kicking the world apart. They was shells from our guns, of course, playing like they was the enemy, playing like they was sore as hell about something. Everbody was down deep in tunnels, so wasn't nobody going to get hurt.

But wasn't nobody enjoying all that noise but Captain Poritsky, and he was crazy as a bedbug.

"Simulated this, simulated that," Earl said. "Them ain't simulated shells, and I ain't simulating being ascared of them, neither."

"Poritsky says it's music," I said.

"They say this is the way it really was, back in the real wars," Earl said. "Don't see how anybody stayed alive."

"Holes gives a lot of protection," I said.

"But back in the old days, didn't hardly nobody but generals get *down* in holes this good," Earl said. "The soldiers had shallow little things without no roof over 'em. And when the orders came, they had to get *out* of them holes, and orders like that was coming all the time."

"I expect they'd keep close to the ground," I said.

"How close can you get *to* the ground?" Earl wanted to know. "Some places up there the grass is cut down like somebody'd done used a lawn-mower. Ain't a tree left standing. Big holes everwheres. How come the folks just didn't go crazy in all them real wars—or quit?"

"Folks are funny," I said.

"Sometimes I don't think so," Earl said.

Another big shell went off, then two little ones—real quick.

"You seen that Russian company's collection?" Earl said.

"Heard about it," I said.

"They got close to a hundred skulls," Earl said. "Got 'em lined up on a shelf like honeydew melons."

"Crazy," I said.

"Yeah, collecting skulls like that," Earl said. "But they can't hardly *help* but collect 'em. I mean, they can't hardly dig in any direction and *not* find skulls and all. Something big must of happened over there."

"Something big happened all through here," I told him. "This here's a very famous battlefield from the World War. This here's where the Americans whipped the Germans. Poritsky told me."

"Two of them skulls got shrapnel in 'em," Earl said. "You seen *them?*"

"Nope," I said.

"Shake 'em, and you can hear the shrapnel rattle around inside," Earl said. "You can see the holes where the shrapnel went in."

"You know what they should ought to do with them poor skulls?" I asked him. "They should ought to get a whole slew of chaplains from ever religion there is. They should ought to give them poor skulls a decent funeral, and bury them someplace where they won't *never* be bothered again."

"It ain't like they was people any more," Earl said.

"It ain't like they wasn't *never* people," I said. "They gave up their lives so our fathers and our grandfathers and our great-grandfathers could live. The least *we* can do is treat their poor bones right."

"Yeah, but wasn't some of them trying to *kill* our great-great-grandfathers or whoever it was?" Earl said.

"The Germans *thought* they was improving things," I said. "Everbody *thought* they was improving things. Their hearts was in the right place," I said. "It's the thought that counts."

The canvas curtain at the top of the tunnel opened up, and Captain Poritsky come down from outside. He was taking his time, like there wasn't nothing out there worse'n a warm drizzle.

"Ain't it kind of dangerous, going out there, sir?" I asked him. He didn't *have* to go out there. There was tunnels running from everwheres to everwheres, and wasn't nobody supposed to go outside while the barrage was on.

"Ain't this a rather dangerous profession we picked of our own free will, soldier?" he asked me. He put the back of his hand under my nose, and I seen there was a long cut across it. "Shrapnel!" he said. He grinned, and then he stuck the cut in his mouth and sucked it.

Then, after he'd drunk enough blood to hold hisself a while, he looked me and Earl up and down. "Soldier," he said to me, "where's your bayonet?"

I felt around my belt. I'd done forgot my bayonet.

"Soldier, what if the enemy was to all of a sudden drop in?" Poritsky done a dance like he was gathering nuts in May. "'Sorry, fellows—you wait right here while I go get my bayonet.' *That* what you'd say, soldier?" he asked me.

I shook my head.

"When the chips are down, a bayonet is a soldier's best friend," Poritsky said. "That's when a professional soldier is happiest, on account of that's when he gets to close with the enemy. Ain't that so?"

"Yes, sir," I said.

"You been collecting skulls, soldier?" Poritsky said.

"No, sir," I said.

"Wouldn't hurt you none to take it up," Poritsky said.

"No, sir," I said.

"There's a reason why ever one of 'em died, soldier," Poritsky said. "They wasn't good soldiers! They wasn't professionals! They made mistakes! They didn't learn their lessons good enough!"

"Reckon not, sir," I said.

"Maybe you think maneuvers is tough, soldier, but they ain't near tough enough," Poritsky said. "If I was in charge, everbody'd be out there taking that bombardment. Only way to get professional outfits is to get 'em blooded."

"Blooded, sir?" I said.

"Get some men killed, so's the rest can learn!" Poritsky said. "Hell—this ain't no army! They got so many safety rules and doctors, I ain't even seen a hangnail for six years. You ain't going to turn out professionals that way."

"No, sir," I said.

"The professional has seen everthing, and ain't surprised by nothing," Poritsky said. "Well, tomorrow, soldier, you're going to see real soldiering, the likes of which ain't been seen for a hundred years. Gas! Rolling barrages! Fire fights! Bayonet duels! Hand-to-hand! Ain't you glad, soldier?"

"Ain't I *what*, sir?" I said.

"Ain't you *glad*?" Poritsky said.

I looked at Earl, then back at the captain. "Oh, yes, sir," I said. I shook my head real slow and heavy. "Yes, sir," I said. "Yes, indeedy-do."

When you're in the Army of the World, with all the fancy new weapons they got, there ain't but one thing to do. You *got* to believe what the officers tell you, even if it don't make sense. And the officers, *they* got to believe what the scientists tell 'em.

Things has got that far beyond the common man, and maybe they always was. When a chaplain hollered at us enlisted men about how we got to have great faith that don't ask no questions, he was carrying coals to Newcastle.

When Poritsky finally done told us we was going to attack with the help of a time machine, there wasn't no intelligent ideas a ordinary soldier like me *could* have. I just set there like a bump on a log, and I looked at the bayonet stud on my rifle. I leaned over, so's the front of my helmet rested on the muzzle, and I looked at that there bayonet stud like it was a wonder of the world.

All two hundred of us in the time-screen company was in a big dugout, listening to Poritsky. Wasn't nobody looking at him. He was just *too* happy about what was going to happen, feeling hisself all over like he hoped he wasn't dreaming.

"Men," that crazy captain said, "at oh-five-hundred hours the artillery will lay down two lines of flares, two hundred yards apart. Them flares will mark the edges of the beam of the time machine. We will attack between them flares."

"Men," he said, "between them lines of flares it will be today and July eighteenth, nineteen-eighteen, both at the same time."

I kissed that bayonet stud. I like the taste of oil and iron in small amounts, but that ain't encouraging nobody to bottle it.

"Men," Poritsky said, "you're going to see some things out there that'd turn a civilian's hair white. You're going to see the Americans counter-attacking the Germans back in olden times at Château-Thierry." My, he *was* happy. "Men," he said, "it's going to be a slaughterhouse in Hell."

I moved my head up and down, so's my helmet acted like a pump. It pumped air down over my forehead. At a time like that, little things can be extra-nice.

"Men," Poritsky said, "I hate to tell soldiers not to be ascared. I hate to tell 'em there ain't nothing to be ascared *of.* It's an insult to 'em. But the scientists tell me nineteen-eighteen can't do nothing to us, and we can't do nothing to nineteen-eighteen. We'll be ghosts to them, and they'll be ghosts to us. We'll be walking through them and they'll be walking through us like we was all smoke."

I blowed across the muzzle of my rifle. I didn't get a tune out of it. Good thing I didn't, because it would of broke up the meeting.

"Men," Poritsky said, "I just wish you *could* take your chances back in nineteen-eighteen, take your chances with the worst they could throw at you. Them as lived through it would be soldiers in the finest sense of the word."

Nobody argued with him.

"Men," that great military scientist said, "I reckon you can imagine the effect on our enemy when he sees the battlefield crawling with all them ghosts from nineteen-eighteen. He ain't going to know *what* to shoot at." Poritsky busted out laughing, and it took him a while to pull hisself back together. "Men," he said, "we'll be creeping through them ghosts. When we reach the enemy, make him wish to God we was ghosts, too—make him sorry he was ever born."

This enemy he was talking about wasn't nothing but a line of bamboo poles with rags tied to 'em, about half a mile away. You wouldn't believe a man could hate bamboo and rags the way Poritsky done.

"Men," Poritsky said, "if anybody's thinking of going A.W.O.L., here's your golden opportunity. All you got to do is cross one of them lines of flares, go through the edge of the beam. You'll disappear into nineteen-eighteen for real—won't be nothing ghostly about it. And the M.P. ain't been born who's crazy enough to go after you, on account of can't nobody who ever crosses over come back."

I cleaned between my front teeth with my rifle sight. I figured out all by myself that a professional soldier was happiest when he could bite somebody. I knowed I wasn't never going to reach them heights.

"Men," Poritsky said, "the mission of this here time-screen company ain't no different from the mission of ever company since time began. The mission of this here time-screen company is to kill! Any questions?"

We'd all done had the Articles of War read to us. We all knowed asking sensible questions was worsen killing your own mother with a axe. So there wasn't no questions. Don't expect there ever has been.

"Lock and load," Poritsky said.

We done it.

"Fix bayonets," Poritsky said.

We done it.

"Shall we go, girls?" Poritsky said.

Oh, that man knowed his psychology backwards and forwards. I expect that's the big difference between officers and enlisted men. Calling us girls instead of boys, when we was really boys, just made us so mad we couldn't hardly see straight.

We was going out and tear up bamboo and rags till there wasn't going to be no more fishpoles or crazy quilts for centuries.

Being in the beam of that there time machine was a cross between flu, wearing bifocals that was made for somebody else who couldn't see good, and being inside a guitar. Until they improves it, it ain't never going to be safe or popular.

We didn't see no folks from nineteen-eighteen at first. All we seen was their holes and barbed-wire, where there wasn't no holes and barbed-wire no more. We could walk over them holes like they had glass roofs over 'em. We could walk through that barbed-wire without getting our pants tore. They wasn't ours—they was nineteen-eighteen's.

There was thousands of soldiers watching us, folks from ever country there was.

The show we put on for 'em was just pitiful.

That time-machine beam made us sick to our stomachs and half blind. We was supposed to whoop it up and holler to show how professional we was. But we got out there between them flares, and didn't hardly nobody let out a peep for fear they'd throw up. We was supposed to advance aggressively, only we couldn't tell what belonged to us, and what was nineteen-eighteen's. We'd walk around things that wasn't there, and fall over things that was there.

If I had of been a observer, I would of said we was comical.

I was the first man in the first squad of the first platoon of that time-screen company, and wasn't but one man in front of me. He was our noble captain.

He only hollered one thing at his fearless troops, and I thought he hollered that to make us even more bloodthirsty than we was. "So long, Boy Scouts!" he hollered. "Write your mothers regular, and wipe your noses when they runs!"

Then he bent over, and he run off across no man's land as fast as he could go.

I done my best to stick with him, for the honor of the enlisted men. We was both falling down and getting up like a couple of drunks, just beating ourselves to pieces on that battlefield.

He never looked around to see how me and the rest was doing. I thought he didn't want nobody to see how green he was. I kept trying to tell him we'd done left everbody way behind, but the race took ever bit of breath I had.

When he headed off to one side, towards a line of flares, I figured he wanted to get in the smoke where folks couldn't see him, so he could get sick in private.

I had just fell into the smoke after him when a barrage from nineteen-eighteen hit.

That poor old world, she rocked and rolled, she spit and tore, she boiled and burned. Dirt and steel from nineteen-eighteen flew through Poritsky and me ever *which* way.

"Get up!" Poritsky hollered at me. "That's nineteen-eighteen! Can't hurt you none!"

"It would if it could!" I hollered back at him.

He made like he was going to kick me in the head. "Get up, soldier!" he said.

I done it.

"Get back with the rest of them Boy Scouts," he said. He pointed through a hole in the smoke, pointed back to where we'd come from. I seen the rest of the company was showing them thousands of observers how experts laid down and quivered. "That's where *you* belong," Poritsky said. "This here's my show, and it's a solo."

"Beg pardon?" I said. I turned my head to follow a nineteen-eighteen boulder that had just flew through *both* our heads.

"Look at me!" he hollered.

I done it.

"Here's where we separates the men from the boys, soldier," he said.

"Yes, sir," I said. "Can't hardly nobody run as fast as you can."

"I ain't talking about running," he said. "I'm talking about fighting!" Oh, it was a crazy conversation. Nineteen-eighteen tracers had started going through us.

I thought he was talking about fighting bamboo and rags. "Ain't nobody feeling very good, Captain, but I expect we'll win," I said.

"I mean I'm going through these here flares to nineteen-eighteen!" he hollered. "Ain't nobody else man enough to do that. Now, get the hell out of here!"

I seen he wasn't fooling a bit. He really did think that'd be grand, if he could wave a flag and stop a bullet, even if it was in some war that'd been over for a hundred years or more. He wanted to get in his lick, even if the ink on the peace treaties was so faded you couldn't hardly read them no more.

"Captain," I said to him, "I ain't nothing but a enlisted man, and enlisted men ain't even supposed to hint. But Captain," I said, "I don't think that makes good sense."

"I was born to *fight*!" he hollered. "I'm rusting out inside!"

"Captain," I said, "everthing there *is* to fight for has already done been won. We got peace, we got freedom, everbody everwhere is like brothers, everbody got nice houses and chicken ever Sunday."

He didn't hear me. He was walking towards the line of flares, towards the edge of the time-machine beam, where the smoke from the flares was thickest.

He stopped just before he got into nineteen-eighteen forever. He looked down at something, and I thought maybe he'd done found a bird's nest or a daisy in no man's land.

What he'd found wasn't neither. I went up to him and seen he was standing over a nineteen-eighteen shell hole, just like he was hanging in air.

There was two dead men in that sorry hole, two live ones, and mud. I knowed that two was dead, on account of one didn't have no head, and the other was blowed in two.

If you got a heart, and you come on something like that in a thick smoke, ain't nothing else in this universe going to be real. There wasn't no more Army of the World; there wasn't no more peace everlasting; there wasn't no more LuVerne, Indiana; there wasn't no more time machine.

There was just Poritsky and me and the hole.

If I was ever to have a child, this is what I'd tell it: "Child," I'd say, "don't never mess with time. Keep now now and then then. And if you ever get lost in thick smoke, child, set still till it clears. Set still till you can see where you are and where you been and where you're going, child."

I'd shake that child. "Child, you hear?" I'd say. "You listen to what your Daddy says. He *know*."

Ain't never going to see no sweet child of mine, I expect. But I aims to feel one, smell one, and hear one. Damn if I don't.

You could see where the four poor nineteen-eighteen souls had been crawling around and around in that hole, like snails crawling around in a fishbowl. There was a track leading from each one—the live ones *and* the dead ones.

A shell lit in the hole and blowed up.

When the mud fell back down, there wasn't but one man left alive.

He turned over from his belly to his back, and he let his arms flop out. It was like he was offering his soft parts to nineteen-eighteen, so it could kill him easy, if it wanted to kill him so bad.

And then *he* seen *us.*

He wasn't surprised to see us hanging there in air over him. Wasn't nothing could surprise *him* no more. Real slow and clumsy, he dug his rifle out of the mud and aimed it at us. He smiled like he knowed who we was, like he knowed he couldn't hurt us none, like it was all a big joke.

There wasn't no way a bullet could get through that rifle bore, it was so clogged with mud. The rifle blowed up.

That didn't surprise him none, neither, didn't even seem to hurt. That smile he give us, the smile about the joke, was still there when he laid back and died.

The nineteen-eighteen barrage stopped.

Somebody blowed a whistle from way far off.

"What you crying about, soldier?" Poritsky said.

"I didn't know I was, Captain," I said. My skin felt extra-tight, and my eyes was hot, but I didn't know I was crying.

"You was and you are," he said.

Then I really *did* cry. I knowed for sure I was just sixteen, knowed I wasn't nothing but a over-growed baby. I set down, and I swore I wouldn't get up again, even if the captain kicked my head off.

"There they go!" Poritsky hollered, real wild. "Look, soldier, look! Americans!" He fired his pistol off like it was the Fourth of July. "Look!"

I done it.

Looked like a million men crossing the beam of the time machine. They'd come from nothing on one side, melt away to nothing on the other. Their eyes was dead. They put one foot in front of the other like somebody'd wound 'em up.

All of a sudden, Captain Poritsky hauled me up like I didn't weigh nothing. "Come on, soldier—we're going with 'em!" he hollered.

That crazy man drug me right through that line of flares.

I screamed and I cried and I bit him. But it was too late.

There wasn't no flares no more.

There wasn't nothing but nineteen-eighteen all around.

I was in nineteen-eighteen for good.

And then another barrage hit. And it was steel and high-explosive, and I was flesh, and then was then, and steel and flesh was all balled up together.

I woke up here.

"What year is it?" I asked 'em.

"Nineteen-eighteen, soldier," they said.

"Where am I?" I asked 'em.

They told me I was in a cathedral that'd been turned into a hospital. Wish I could see it. I can hear from the echoes how high and grand it is.

I ain't no hero.

With heroes all around me here, I don't embroider my record none. I never bay-oneted or shot nobody, never throwed a grenade, never even seen a German, unless them was Germans in that terrible hole.

They should ought to have special hospitals for heroes, so heroes wouldn't have to lay next to the likes of me.

When somebody new comes around to hear me talk, I always tell 'em right off I wasn't in the war but ten seconds before I was hit. "I never done a thing to make the world safe for democracy," I tell 'em. "When I got hit, I was crying like a baby and trying to kill my own captain. If a bullet hadn't of killed him, *I would* of, and he was a fellow American."

I would of, too.

And I tell 'em I'd desert back to the year two thousand and thirty-seven, too, if I got half a chance.

There's two court-martial offenses right there.

But all these heroes here, they don't seem to care. "That's all right, Buddy," they say, "you just go right on talking. If somebody tries to court-martial you, we'll all swear we seen you killing Germans with your bare hands, and fire coming out of your ears."

They likes to hear me talk.

So I lay here, blind as a bat, and I tell 'em how I got here. I tell 'em all the things I see so clear inside my head—the Army of the World, everybody like brothers ever-where, peace everlasting, nobody hungry, nobody ascared.

That's how come I got my nickname. Don't hardly nobody in the hospital know my real name. Don't know who thought of it first, but everbody calls me Great Day.

Guns Before Butter

"What you do is take a roasting chicken, cut it up into pieces, and brown it in melted butter and olive oil in a hot skillet," said Private Donnini. "A good, hot skillet," he added thoughtfully.

"Wait a minute," said Private Coleman, writing furiously in a small notebook. "How big a chicken?"

"About four pounds."

"For how many people?" asked Private Kniptash sharply.

"Enough for four," said Donnini.

"Don't forget, a lot of that chicken is bone," said Kniptash suspiciously.

Donnini was a gourmet; many was the time that the phrase "pearls before swine" had occurred to him while telling Kniptash how to make this dish or that. Kniptash cared nothing for flavor or aroma—cared only for brute nutrition, for caloric blockbusters. In taking down recipes in his notebook, Kniptash was inclined to regard the portions as niggardly, and to double all the quantities involved.

"You can eat it all yourself, as far as I'm concerned," said Donnini evenly.

"O.K., O.K., so what do you do next?" said Coleman, his pencil poised.

"You brown it on each side for about five minutes, add chopped celery, onions, and carrots, and season to taste." Donnini pursed his lips as though sampling. "Then, while you're simmering it, add a mixture of sherry and tomato paste. Cover it. Simmer for around thirty minutes, and—" He paused. Coleman and Kniptash had stopped writing, and were leaning against the wall, their eyes closed—listening.

"That's good," said Kniptash dreamily, "but you know the first thing I'm gonna get back in the States?"

Donnini groaned inwardly. He knew. He had heard it a hundred times. Kniptash was sure there wasn't a dish in the world that could satisfy his hunger, so he had invented one, a culinary monster.

"First," said Kniptash fiercely, "I'm going to order me a dozen pancakes. That's what I said, lady," he said, addressing an imaginary waitress, "twelve! Then I'm going to have 'em stack 'em up with a fried egg between each one. Then you know what I'm going to do?"

"Pour honey over 'em!" said Coleman. He shared Kniptash's brutish appetite.

"You betcha!" said Kniptash, his eyes glistening.

"Phooey," said Corporal Kleinhans, their bald German guard, listlessly. Donnini guessed that the old man was about sixty-five years old. Kleinhans tended to be absent-minded, lost in thought. He was an oasis of compassion and inefficiency in the desert of Nazi Germany. He said he had learned his passable English during four years as a waiter in Liverpool. He would say no more about his experiences in England, other than to observe that the British ate far more food than was good for the race.

Kleinhans twisted his Kaiser Wilhelm mustache, and stood with the help of his antique, six-foot-long rifle. "You talk too much about food. That is why the Americans will lose the war—you are all too soft." He looked pointedly at Kniptash, who was still up to his nostrils in imaginary cakes, eggs, and honey. "Come, come, back to work." It was a suggestion.

The three American soldiers remained seated within the roofless shell of a building amid the smashed masonry and timbers of Dresden, Germany. The time was early March, 1945. Kniptash, Donnini, and Coleman were prisoners of war. Corporal Kleinhans was their guard. He was to keep them busy at arranging the city's billion tons of rubble into orderly cairns, rock by rock, out of the way of non-existent traffic. Nominally, the three Americans were being punished for minor defections in prison discipline. Actually, their being marched out to work in the streets every morning under the sad blue eyes of the lackadaisical Kleinhans was no better, no worse than the fates of their better-behaved comrades behind the barbed-wire. Kleinhans asked only that they appear to be busy when officers passed.

Food was the only thing on the P.W.'s pale level of existence that could have any effect on their spirits. Patton was a hundred miles away. To hear Kniptash, Donnini, and Coleman speak of the approaching Third Army, one would have thought it was spear-headed, not by infantry and tanks, but by a phalanx of mess sergeants and kitchen trucks.

"Come, come," said Corporal Kleinhans again. He brushed plaster dust from his ill-fitting uniform, the thin, cheap grey of the homeguard, the pathetic army of old men. He looked at his watch. Their lunch hour, which had been thirty minutes with nothing to eat, was over.

Donnini wistfully leafed through his notebook for another minute before returning it to his breast pocket and struggling to his feet.

The notebook craze had begun with Donnini's telling Coleman how to make Pizza pie. Coleman had written it down in one of several notebooks he had taken from a bombed-out stationery store. He had found the experience so satisfying, that all three were soon obsessed with filling the notebooks with recipes. Setting down the symbols for food somehow made them feel much closer to the real thing.

Each had divided his booklet into departments. Kniptash, for instance, had four major departments: "Desserts I Am Going to Try," "Good Ways to Fix Meat," "Snacks," and "Missalanious."

Coleman, scowling, continued to print laboriously in his notebook. "How much sherry?"

"Dry sherry—it's got to be *dry*," said Donnini. "About three-quarters of a cup." He saw that Kniptash was erasing something in his notebook. "What's the matter? Changing it to a gallon of sherry?"

"Nope. Wasn't even working on that one. I was changing something else. Changed my mind about what the first thing I want is," said Kniptash.

"What?" asked Coleman, fascinated.

Donnini winced. So did Kleinhans. The notebooks had heightened the spiritual conflict between Donnini and Kniptash, had defined it in black and white. The recipes that Kniptash contributed were flamboyant, made up on the spot. Donnini's were scrupulously authentic, artistic. Coleman was caught between. It was gourmet versus glutton, artist versus materialist, beauty versus the beast. Donnini was grateful for an ally, even Corporal Kleinhans.

"Don't tell me yet," said Coleman, flipping pages. "Wait'll I get set with the first page." The most important section of each of the notebooks was, by far, the first page. By agreement, it was dedicated to the dish each man looked forward to above all others. On his first page, Donnini had lovingly inscribed the formula for *Anitra al Cognac*—brandied duck. Kniptash had given the place of honor to his pancake horror. Coleman had plumped uncertainly for ham and candied sweet potatoes, but had been argued out of it. Terribly torn, he had written both Kniptash's and Donnini's selections on his first page, putting off a decision until a later date. Now, Kniptash was tantalizing him with a modification of his atrocity. Donnini sighed. Coleman was weak. Perhaps Kniptash's new twist would woo him away from *Anitra al Cognac* altogether.

"Honey's out," said Kniptash firmly. "I kind of wondered about it. Now I know it's all wrong. Doesn't go with eggs, honey doesn't."

Coleman erased. "Well?" he said expectantly.

"Hot fudge on top," said Kniptash. "A big blob of hot fudge—just let 'er set on top and spread out."

"Mmmmmmmmmmm," said Coleman.

"Food, food, food," muttered Corporal Kleinhans. "All day, every day, all I hear is food! Get up. Get to work! You and your damn fool notebooks. That's plundering, you know. I can shoot you for that." He closed his eyes and sighed. "Food," he said softly. "What good does it do to talk about it, to write about it? Talk about girls. Talk about music. Talk about liquor." He implored Heaven with outstretched arms. "What kind of soldiers are these that spend all day exchanging recipes?"

"You're hungry, too, aren't you?" said Kniptash. "What have you got against food?"

"I get quite enough to eat," said Kleinhans off-handedly.

"Six slices of black bread and three bowls of soup a day—that's enough?" said Coleman.

"That's plenty," argued Kleinhans. "I feel better. I was overweight before the war. Now I'm as trim as I was as a young man. Before the war, everybody was overweight, living to eat instead of eating to live." He smiled wanly. "Germany has never been healthier."

"Yeah, but aren't you hungry?" persisted Kniptash.

"Food isn't the only thing in my life, nor the most important," said Kleinhans. "Come, now, get up!"

Kniptash and Coleman arose reluctantly. "Got plaster or something in the end of your barrel, Pop," said Coleman. They shuffled slowly back onto the littered street, with Kleinhans bringing up the rear, digging plaster from his rifle muzzle with a match, and denouncing the notebooks.

Donnini picked out a small rock from millions, carried it over to the curb and lay it at the feet of Kleinhans. He rested for a moment, his hands on his hips. "Hot," he said.

"Just right for working," said Kleinhans. He sat down on the curb. "What were you in civilian life, a cook?" he said after a long silence.

"I helped my father run his Italian restaurant in New York."

"I had a place in Breslau for a while," said Kleinhans. "That was long ago." He sighed. "Seems silly now how much time and energy Germans used to spend just stuffing themselves with rich food. Such a silly waste." He looked past Donnini and glared. He waggled a finger at Coleman and Kniptash, who stood together in the middle of the street, each with a baseball-sized rock in one hand, a notebook in the other.

"It seems to me there was sour cream in it," Coleman was saying.

"Put those books away!" commanded Kleinhans. "Haven't you got a girl? Talk about your girl!"

"Sure I got a girl," said Coleman irritably. "Name's Mary."

"Is that *all* there is to know about her?" said Kleinhans.

Coleman looked puzzled. "Last name's Fiske—Mary Fiske."

"Well, is this Mary Fiske pretty? What does she do?"

Coleman narrowed his eyes thoughtfully. "One time I was waiting for her to come downstairs and I watched her old lady make a lemon meringue pie," he said. "What she did was take some sugar and some cornstarch and a pinch of salt, and mix it in with a couple of cups of wat—"

"Please, let's talk about music. Like music?" said Kleinhans.

"And then what'd she do?" said Kniptash. He had laid his rock down, and was now writing in his notebook. "She used eggs, didn't she?"

"Please, boys, no," pleaded Kleinhans.

"Sure she used eggs," said Coleman. "And butter, too. Plenty of butter and eggs."

II.

It was four days later that Kniptash found the crayons in a basement—on the same day that Kleinhans had begged for and been refused relief from the punishment detail.

When they had set out that morning, Kleinhans had been in a terrible temper, and had railed at his three charges for not keeping in step and for marching with their hands in their pockets. "Go ahead and talk, talk, talk about food, you women," he had taunted them. "I don't have to listen anymore!" Triumphantly, he had pulled two wads of cotton from his cartridge pouch and stuffed them into his ears. "Now I can think my own thoughts. Ha!"

At noon, Kniptash sneaked into the cellar of a bombed-out house, hoping for a rack of full mason jars such as he knew were in his snug cellar at home. He emerged dirty and dispirited, gnawing experimentally at a green crayon.

"How is it?" asked Coleman hopefully, looking at the yellow, purple, pink, and orange crayons in Kniptash's left hand.

"Wonderful. What flavor you like? Lemon? Grape? Strawberry?" He threw the crayons on the ground, and spit the green one after them.

It was lunch hour again, and Kleinhans was sitting with his back to his wards, staring thoughtfully out at the splintered Dresden skyline. Two white tufts protruded from his ears.

"You know what would go good, now?" said Donnini.

"A hot fudge sundae, with nuts and marshmallow topping," said Coleman promptly.

"And cherries," said Kniptash.

"*Spiedini alla Romana*!" whispered Donnini, his eyes closed.

Kniptash and Coleman whipped out their notebooks.

Donnini kissed his fingertips. "Skewered chopped beef, Roman style," he said. "Take a pound of chopped beef, two eggs, three tablespoons of Romano cheese, and—"

"For how many?" demanded Kniptash.

"Six normal human beings, or half a pig."

"What's this stuff look like?" asked Coleman.

"Well, it's a lot of stuff strung together on a skewer." Donnini saw Kleinhans remove an ear plug and return it almost instantly. "It's kind of hard to describe." He scratched his head, and his gaze landed on the crayons. He picked up the yellow one, and began to sketch. He became interested in the project, and, with the other crayons, added the subtler shadings and highlights, and finally, for background, a checkered tablecloth. He handed it to Coleman.

"Mmmmmmmm," said Coleman, shaking his head and licking his lips.

"Boy!" said Kniptash admiringly. "The little bastards practically jump out at you, don't they!"

Coleman held out his notebook eagerly. The page it was opened to was headed, straightforwardly, "CAKES." "Could you draw a Lady Baltimore cake? You know, white with cherries on top?"

Obligingly, Donnini tried, and met with heartening success. It was a fine-looking cake, and, for an added flourish, he sketched in pink icing script on top: "Welcome home Private Coleman!"

"Draw me a stack of pancakes—twelve of 'em," urged Kniptash. "That's what I said, Lady—twelve!" Donnini shook his head disapprovingly, but began to rough in the composition.

"I'm going to show *mine* to Kleinhans," said Coleman happily, holding his Lady Baltimore cake at arm's length.

"Now the fudge on top," said Kniptash, breathing down Donnini's neck.

"*Ach! Mensch!*" cried Corporal Kleinhans, and Coleman's notebook fluttered like a wounded bird into the tangle of wreckage next door. "The lunch hour is over!" He strode over to Donnini and Kniptash, and snatched their notebooks from them. He stuffed the books into his breast pocket. "Now we draw pretty pictures! Back to work, do you understand?" With a flourish, he fastened a fantastically long bayonet on to his rifle. "Go! *Los!*"

"What the hell got into him?" said Kniptash.

"All I did was show him a picture of a cake and he blows his stack," complained Coleman. "Nazi," he said under his breath.

Donnini slipped the crayons into his pocket, and scrambled out of the way of Kleinhans' terrible swift sword.

"The Articles of the Geneva Convention say privates must work for their keep. Work!" said Corporal Kleinhans. He kept them sweating and grunting all afternoon. He barked an order the instant any of the three showed an inclination to speak. "You! Donnini! Here, pick up this bowl of spaghetti," he said, indicating a huge boulder with the tip of his toe. He strode over to a pair of twelve-by-twelve rafters lying across the street. "Kniptash and Coleman, my boys," he crooned, clapping his hands, "here are those chocolate éclairs you've been dreaming about. One for each of you." He placed his face an inch from Coleman's. "With whipped cream," he whispered.

It was a genuinely glum crew that shambled into the prison enclosure that evening. Before, Donnini, Kniptash, and Coleman had made a point of half limping in, as though beaten down by terribly hard labor and unrelenting discipline. Kleinhans, in turn, had made a fine spectacle, snapping at them like a bad-tempered sheep dog as they stumbled through the gate. Now, their semblance was as before, but the tragedy they portrayed was real.

Kleinhans jerked open the barracks door, and motioned them in with an imperious sweep of his hand.

"*Achtung!*" cried a high voice from within. Donnini, Coleman, and Kniptash halted and slouched, their heels more or less together. With a crackle of leather and the clack of heels, Corporal Kleinhans slammed his rifle butt on the floor, and stood as erect as his old back would permit, trembling. A surprise inspection by a German officer was under way. Once a month they could expect one. A short colonel in a fur-collared coat and black boots was standing, his feet far apart, before a rank of prisoners. Beside him was the fat sergeant of the guard. All stared at Corporal Kleinhans and his charges.

"Well," said the colonel in German, "what have we here?"

The sergeant hurriedly explained with gestures, his brown eyes pleading for approval.

The colonel walked slowly across the cement floor, his hands clasped behind his back. He paused before Kniptash. "You pin a pad poy, eh?"

"Yessir, I have," said Kniptash simply.

"You sorry now?"

"Yessir, I sure am."

"Good." The colonel circled the small group several times, humming to himself, pausing once to finger the fabric of Donnini's shirt. "You unnerstandt me ven I talk Enklish?"

"Yessir, it's very clear," said Donnini.

"Vot part von Amerika I got an agsent like?" he asked eagerly.

"Milwaukee, sir. I could have sworn you were from Milwaukee."

"I could be a spvy in Milvaukee," said the colonel proudly to the sergeant. Suddenly, his gaze fell on Corporal Kleinhans, whose chest was just a little below his eye-level. His good humor evaporated. He stalked over to stand squarely before Kleinhans. "Corporal! Your blouse pocket is unbuttoned!" he said in German.

Kleinhans' eyes were wide as he reached for the offending pocket flap. Feverishly, he tried to tug it down to the button. It wouldn't reach.

"You have something in your pocket!" said the colonel, reddening. "*That's* the trouble. Take it out!"

Kleinhans jerked two notebooks from the pocket and buttoned the flap. He sighed with relief.

"And what have you in your notebooks, eh? A list of prisoners. Demerits, maybe? Let me see them." The colonel snatched them from the limp fingers. Kleinhans rolled his eyes.

"What is this?" said the colonel incredulously, his voice high. Kleinhans started to speak. "Silence, Corporal!" The colonel raised his eyebrows, and held a book out so that the sergeant could share his view. "'Vot I am going to eat de first ting ven I gat home,'" he read slowly. He shook his head. "Ach! 'Tvelf pangakes mit a fried ek betveen each von!' Oh! 'Und mit hot futch on top!'" He turned to Kleinhans. "Is that what you want, you poor boy?" he said in German. "And such a pretty picture you drew, too. Mmmmm." He reached for Kleinhans' shoulders. "Corporals have to think about war all the time. Privates can think about anything they want to—girls, food, and good things like that—just as long as they do what the corporals tell them." Deftly, as though he'd done it many times before, the colonel dug his thumbnails beneath the silver corporal's pips on Kleinhans' shoulder loops. They rattled against the wall like pebbles, down at the far end of the barracks. "Lucky privates."

Once more, Kleinhans cleared his throat for permission to speak.

"Silence, Private!" The little colonel strutted out of the barracks, shredding the notebooks as he went.

III.

Donnini felt rotten, and so, he knew, did Kniptash and Coleman. It was the morning after Kleinhans' demotion. Outwardly, Kleinhans seemed no different. His stride was spry as ever, and he still seemed capable of drawing pleasure from the fresh air and signs of spring poking up from the ruins.

When they arrived at their street, which still wasn't passable, even to bicycles, despite their three weeks of punishment, Kleinhans didn't browbeat them as he had the afternoon before. Neither did he tell them to appear to be busy as he had done the days before that. Instead, he led them directly into the ruin where they spent their lunch hours, and motioned them to sit down. Kleinhans appeared to sleep. There they sat in silence, the Americans aching with remorse.

"We're sorry you lost your pips on account of us," said Donnini at last.

"Lucky privates," said Kleinhans gloomily. "Two wars I go through to be a corporal. Now," he snapped his fingers, "poof. Cookbooks are *verboten*."

"Here," said Kniptash, his voice quavering. "Want a smoke? I got a Hungarian cigarette." He held out the precious cigarette.

Kleinhans smiled wanly. "Let's pass it around." He lit it, took a puff, and handed it to Donnini.

"Where'd you get a Hungarian cigarette?" asked Coleman.

"From a Hungarian," said Kniptash. He pulled up his trouser legs. "Traded my socks for it."

They finished the cigarette and leaned back against the masonry. Still Kleinhans had said nothing about work. Again he seemed faraway, lost in thought.

"Don't you boys talk about food anymore?" said Kleinhans, after another long silence.

"Not after you lost your pips," said Kniptash gravely.

Kleinhans nodded. "That's all right. Easy come, easy go." He licked his lips. "Pretty soon now, this will all be over." He leaned back and stretched. "And you know what I'm going to do the day it ends, boys?" Private Kleinhans closed his eyes. "I'm going to get three pounds of beef shoulder and lard it with bacon. Then I'll rub it with garlic and salt and pepper, and put it in a crock with white wine and water"—his voice became strident—"and onions and bay leaves and sugar"—he stood—"and peppercorns! In ten days, boys, she's ready!"

"What's ready?" said Coleman excitedly, reaching where his notebook had been.

"Sauerbraten!" cried Kleinhans.

"For how many?" asked Kniptash.

"Just two, my boy. Sorry." Kleinhans laid his hand on Donnini's shoulder. "Enough sauerbraten for two hungry artists—eh, Donnini?" He winked at Kniptash. "For you and Coleman, I'll fix something very filling. How about twelve pancakes with a slice of colonel between each one, and a big blob of hot fudge on top, eh?"

Happy Birthday, 1951

"SUMMER IS A FINE TIME for a birthday," said the old man. "And, as long as you have a choice, why not choose a summer day?" He wet his thumb on his tongue, and leafed through the sheaf of documents the soldiers had ordered him to fill out. No document could be complete without a birthdate, and, for the boy, one had to be chosen.

"Today can be your birthday, if you like it," said the old man.

"It rained in the morning," said the boy.

"All right, then—tomorrow. The clouds are blowing off to the south. The sun should shine all day tomorrow."

Looking for shelter from the morning rainstorm, the soldiers had found the hiding place where, miracle of miracles, the old man and the boy had lived in the ruins for seven years without documents—without, as it were, official permission to be alive. They said no person could get food or shelter or clothing without documents. But the old man and the boy had found all three for the digging in the catacombs of cellars beneath the shattered city, for the filching at night.

"Why are you shaking?" said the boy.

"Because I'm old. Because soldiers frighten old men."

"They don't frighten me," said the boy. He was excited by the sudden intrusion into their underground world. He held something shiny, golden in the narrow shaft of light from the cellar window. "See? One of them gave me a brass button."

There had been nothing frightening about the soldiers. Since the man was so old and the child so young, the military took a playful view of the pair—who, of all the people in the city, alone had recorded their presence nowhere, had been inoculated against nothing, had sworn allegiance to nothing, renounced or apologized for nothing, voted or marched for nothing, since the war.

"I meant no harm," the old man had told the soldiers with a pretense of senility. "I didn't know." He told them how, on the day the war ended, a refugee woman had left a baby in his arms and never returned. That was how he got the boy. The child's nationality? Name? Birthdate? He didn't know.

The old man rolled potatoes from the stove's wood fire with a stick, knocked the embers from their blackened skins. "I haven't been a very good father, letting you go without birthdays this long," he said. "You're entitled to one every year, you know, and I've let six years go by without a birthday. And presents, too. You're supposed to get presents." He picked up a potato gingerly, and tossed it to the boy, who caught it and laughed. "So you've decided tomorrow's the day, eh?"

"Yes, I think so."

"All right. That doesn't give me much time to get you a present, but there'll be something."

"What?"

"Birthday presents are better if they're a surprise." He thought of the wheels he had seen on a pile of rubble down the street. When the boy fell asleep, he would make some sort of cart.

"Listen!" said the boy.

As at every sunset, over the ruins from a distant street came the sound of marching.

"Don't listen," said the old man. He held up a finger for attention. "And you know what we'll do on your birthday?"

"Steal cakes from the bakery?"

"Maybe—but that isn't what I was thinking of. You know what I'd like to do tomorrow? I'd like to take you where you've never been in all your life—where I haven't been for years." The thought made the old man excited and happy. This would be *the* gift. The cart would be nothing. "Tomorrow I'll take you away from war."

He didn't see that the boy looked puzzled, and a little disappointed.

◙ ◙ ◙

It was the birthday the boy had chosen for himself, and the sky, as the old man had promised, was clear. They ate breakfast in the twilight of their cellar. The cart the old man had made late at night sat on the table. The boy ate with one hand, his other hand resting on the cart. Occasionally, he paused in eating to move the cart back and forth a few inches, and to imitate the sound of a motor.

"That's a nice truck you've got there, Mister," said the old man. "Bringing animals to the market, are you?"

"Brummmaaaa, brummmaaaa. Out of my way! Brummmaaaa. Out of the way of my tank."

"Sorry," sighed the old man, "thought you were a truck. You like it anyway, and that's what counts." He dropped his tin plate into the bucket of water simmering on the stove. "And this is only the beginning, only the beginning," he said expansively. "The best is yet to come."

"Another present?"

"In a way. Remember what I promised? We'll get away from war today. We'll go to the woods."

"Brummmaaaa, brummmaaaa. Can I take my tank?"

"If you'll let it be a truck, just for today."

The boy shrugged. "I'll leave it, and play with it when I get back."

Blinking in the bright morning, the two walked down their deserted street, turned into a busy boulevard lined with brave new façades. It was as though the world had suddenly become fresh and clean and whole again. The people didn't seem to know that desolation began a block on either side of the fine boulevard, and stretched for miles. The two, with lunches under their arms, walked toward the pine-covered hills to the south, toward which the boulevard lifted in a gentle grade.

Four young soldiers came down the sidewalk abreast. The old man stepped into the street, out of their way. The boy saluted, and held his ground. The soldiers smiled, returned his salute, and parted their ranks to let him pass.

"Armored infantry," said the boy to the old man.

"Hmmmm?" said the old man absently, his eyes on the green hills. "Really? How did you know that?"

"Didn't you see the green braid?"

"Yes, but those things change. I can remember when armored infantry was black and red, and green was—" He cut the sentence short. "It's all nonsense," he said, almost sharply. "It's all meaningless, and today we're going to forget all about it. Of all days, on your birthday, you shouldn't be thinking about—"

"Black and red is the engineers," interrupted the boy seriously. "Plain black is the military police, and red is the artillery, and blue and red is the medical corps, and black and orange is . . ."

The pine forest was very still. The centuries-old carpet of needles and green roof deadened the sounds floating up from the city. Infinite colonnades of thick brown trunks surrounded the old man and the boy. The sun, directly overhead, showed itself to them only as a cluster of bright pinpoints through the fat, dense blanket of needles and boughs above.

"Here?" said the boy.

The old man looked about himself. "No—just a little farther." He pointed. "There—see through there? We can see the church from here." The black skeleton of a burned steeple was framed against a square of sky between two trunks on the edge of the forest. "But listen—hear that? Water. There's a brook up above, and we can get down in its little valley and see nothing but treetops and sky."

"All right," said the boy. "I like this place, but all right." He looked at the steeple, then at the old man, and raised his eyebrows questioningly.

"You'll see—you'll see how much better," said the old man.

As they reached the top of the ridge, he gestured happily at the brook below. "There! And what do you think of this? Eden! As it was in the beginning—trees, sky, and water. This is the world you should have had, and today, at least, you can have it."

"And look!" said the boy, pointing to the ridge on the other side.

A huge tank, rusted to the color of the fallen pine needles, squatted on shattered treads on the ridge, with scabs of corrosion about the black hole where its gun had once been.

"How can we cross the water to get to it?" said the boy.

"We don't want to get to it," said the old man irritably. He held the boy's hand tightly. "Not today. Some other day we can come out here, maybe. But not today."

The boy was crestfallen. His small hand grew limp in the old man's.

"Here's a bend up ahead, and around that we'll find exactly what we want."

The boy said nothing. He snatched up a rock, and threw it at the tank. As the little missile fell toward the target, he tensed, as though the whole world were about to explode. A faint click came from the turret, and he relaxed, somehow satisfied. Docilely, he followed the old man.

Around the bend, they found what the old man had been looking for: a smooth, dry table of rock, out by the stream, walled in by high banks. The old man stretched out on the moss, affectionately patted the spot beside him, where he wanted the boy to sit. He unwrapped his lunch.

After lunch, the boy fidgeted. "It's very quiet," he said at last.

"It's as it should be," said the old man. "One corner of the world—as it should be."

"It's lonely."

"That's its beauty."

"I like it better in the city, with the soldiers and—"

The old man seized his arm roughly, squeezed it hard. "No you don't. You just don't know. You're too young, too young to know what this is, what I'm trying to give you. But, when you're older, you'll remember, and want to come back here—long after your little cart is broken."

"I don't want my cart to be broken," said the boy.

"It won't, it won't. But just lie here, close your eyes and listen, and forget about everything. This much I can give you—a few hours away from war." He closed his eyes.

The boy lay down beside him, and dutifully closed his eyes, too.

The sun was low in the sky when the old man awakened. He ached and felt damp from his long nap by the brook. He yawned and stretched. "Time to go," he said, his eyes still closed. "Our day of peace is over." And then he saw that the boy was gone. He called the boy's name unconcernedly at first; and then, getting no answer but the wind's, he stood and shouted.

Panic welled up in him. The boy had never been in the woods before, could easily get lost if he were to wander north, deeper into the hills and forest. He climbed onto higher ground and shouted again. No answer.

Perhaps the boy had gone down to the tank again, and tried to cross the stream. He couldn't swim. The old man hurried downstream, around the bend to where he could see the tank. The ugly relic gaped at him balefully from across the cut. Nothing moved, and there was only the sound of wind and the water.

"Bang!" cried a small voice.

The boy raised his head from the turret triumphantly. "Gotcha!" he said.

Brighten Up

THERE WAS A TIME when I was at one with my Father in feeling that to become a reverent, brave, trustworthy, and courteous Eagle Scout was to lay the foundations for a bountiful life. But I have since had occasion to reflect more realistically upon twig-bending, and am wondering now if Hell's Kitchen isn't a more sound preparation for living than was the Beaver Patrol. I cannot help feeling that my friend Louis Gigliano, who had been smoking cigars since he was twelve, was a great deal better prepared to thrive in chaos than was I, who had been trained to meet adversity with a combination pocketknife, can opener, and leather punch.

The test of the manly art of surviving I have in mind took place in a prisoner-of-war camp in Dresden. I, a clean-cut American youth, and Louis, a dissipated little weasel whose civilian occupation had been hashish-peddling to bobby-soxers, faced life there together. I am remembering Louis now because I am stone-broke, and because I know that Louis is living like a prince somewhere in this world he understands too well. It was that way in Germany.

Under the democratic provisions of the Geneva Convention, we, as privates, were obliged to work for our keep. All of us worked, that is, but Louis. His first act behind barbed wire was to report to an English-speaking Nazi guard that he wanted no part of the war, which he considered to be brother against brother, and the handiwork of Roosevelt and Jewish international bankers. I asked him if he meant it.

"I'm tired, for God's sake," he said. "I fought 'em for six months, and now I'm tired. I need a rest, and I like to eat as well as the next guy. Brighten up, will you!"

"I'd rather not, thank you," I said icily.

I was sent out on a pick-and-shovel detail; Louis remained in camp as the German sergeant's orderly. Louis got extra rations for whisk-brooming the sergeant three times a day. I got a hernia while tidying up after the American Air Force.

"Collaborationist!" I hissed at him after a particularly exhausting day in the streets. He was standing at the prison gate with a guard, immaculate and sprightly, nodding to his acquaintances in the dusty, weary column. His response to my taunt was to walk beside me to the sleeping quarters.

He laid a hand on my shoulder. "And then you can look at it this way, kid," he said. "Here you're helping Jerry clean up his streets so he can run tanks and trucks through 'em again. That's what I'd call collaboration. Me a collaborator? You've got it backwards. All I do to help Jerry win the war is smoke his cigarettes and hit him for more to eat. That's bad, I suppose?"

I flopped down on my bunk. Louis took a seat on a straw-tick nearby. My arm hung over the side of the bunk, and Louis interested himself in my wrist watch, a gift from my Mother.

"Nice, very nice watch, kid," he said. And then, "Hungry after all that work, I'll bet."

I was ravenous. Ersatz coffee, one bowl of watered soup, and three slices of dry bread are not the sort of fare to delight a pick-swinger's heart after nine hours of hard labor. Louis was sympathetic. He liked me; he wanted to help. "You're a nice kid," he said. "I'll tell you what I'll do. I'll make a quick deal for you. There's no sense in going hungry. Why, that watch is worth two loaves of bread, at least. Is that a good deal, or isn't it?"

At that point, two loaves of bread was a dazzling lure. It was an incredible amount of food for one person to have. I tried to bid him up. "Look, friend," he said, "this is a special price to you, and it's a top price. I'm trying to do you a favor, see? All I ask of you is to keep quiet about this deal, or everybody will want two loaves for a watch. Promise?"

I swore by all that is holy that I would never reveal the magnanimity of Louis, my best friend. He was back in an hour. He cast a furtive glance around the room, withdrew a long loaf from a rolled field jacket, and stuffed it beneath my mattress. I waited for him to make the second deposit. It was not forthcoming. "I hardly know what to tell you, kid. The guard I do business with told me the whole bottom's dropped out of the watch market since all these guys came in from the Bulge. Too many watches all at one time is what did it. I'm sorry, but I want you to know that Louis got you the maximum for that watch." He made a move toward the loaf under the mattress. "If you feel gypped, all you have to do is say the word, and I'll take this back and get your watch again."

My stomach growled. "Oh hell, Louis," I sighed, "leave it there."

When I awoke the next morning, I looked at my wrist to see what time it was. And then I recalled that I no longer owned a watch. The man in the bunk overhead was also astir. I asked him for the time. He stuck his head over the side, and I saw that his jaws were crammed with bread; he blew a shower of crumbs over me as he answered. He said he no longer had a watch. He chewed and swallowed until a major portion of the great wad of bread was cleared from his mouth and he could make himself understood. "I should care what time it is when Louis will give me two loaves and ten cigarettes for a watch that wasn't worth twenty dollars new?" he asked.

Louis had a monopoly on rapport with the guards. His avowed harmony with Nazi principles convinced our keepers that he was the only bright one among us, and we all had to do our Black–Marketeering through this superficial Judas. Six weeks after we had been quartered in Dresden, nobody had any way of knowing what time it was outside of Louis and the guards. Two weeks after that, Louis had done every married man out of his wedding ring with this argument: "O.K., go ahead and be sentimental, go ahead and starve to death. Love's a wonderful thing, they tell me."

His profits were enormous. I later found out that my watch, for instance, brought a price of one hundred cigarettes and six loaves of bread. Anyone familiar with starvation will recognize that this was a handsome prize. Louis converted most of his wealth into the most negotiable of all securities, cigarettes. And it wasn't long before the possibilities of being a loan shark had occurred to him. Once every two weeks we were issued twenty cigarettes. Slaves of the tobacco habit would exhaust the ration in one or two days, and would be in a state of frenzy until the next ration came. Louis, who was coming to be known as "The People's Friend" or "Honest John," announced that cigarettes might be borrowed from him at a reasonable fifty-percent interest until the next ration. He soon had his wealth loaned out and increasing by half every two weeks. I was terribly in debt to him, with nothing left for collateral but my soul. I took him to task for his greed: "Christ drove the money-lenders from the temple," I reminded him.

"That was money they were lending, my boy," he replied. "I'm not beggin' you to borrow my cigarettes, am I? You're beggin' me to lend you some. Cigarettes are luxuries, friend. You don't have to smoke to stay alive. You'd probably live longer if you didn't smoke. Why don't you give up the filthy habit?"

"How many can you let me have until next Tuesday?" I asked.

When usury had swelled his hoard to an all-time high, a catastrophe, which he had been awaiting impatiently, caused the value of his cigarettes to sky-rocket. The USAAF swept over the feeble Dresden defenses to demolish, among other things, the major cigarette factories. As a consequence, not only the P.W. cigarette ration, but that of the guards and civilians as well, was cut off completely. Louis was a major figure in local finance. The guards found themselves without a smoke to their names, and began selling our rings and watches back to Louis at a lower price than they had given him. Some put his wealth as high as one hundred watches. Louis' own estimate, however, was a modest fifty-three watches, seventeen wedding rings, seven high school rings, and an heirloom watch-fob. "Some of the watches need a lot of work done on them," he told me.

When I say that the AAF got the cigarette factories among other things, I mean that a number of human beings got blown up as well—something like 200,000. Our activities took a ghoulish turn. We were put to work exhuming the dead from their innumerable crypts. Many of them wore jewelry, and most had carried their precious belongings to the shelters. At first we shunned the grave goods. For one thing, some of us felt that stripping corpses was a revolting business, and for another, to be caught at it was certain death. It took Louis to bring us to our senses. "Good God, kid, you could make enough to retire on in fifteen minutes. I just wish they'd let me go out with you guys for just a day." He licked his lips, and continued: "Tell you what—I'll really make it worth your while. You get me one good diamond ring, and I'll keep you in smokes and chow for as long as we're in this hole."

The next evening I brought him his ring, tucked into my trouser cuff. So, it turned out, did everyone else. When I showed him the diamond he shook his head. "Oh, what a dirty shame," he said. He held the stone up to a light: "Here the poor kid risked his life for a zircon!" Everybody, a minute inspection revealed, had brought back either a zircon, a garnet, or a paste diamond. In addition, Louis pointed out, any slight value these might have was destroyed because of a glutted market. I let my plunder go for four cigarettes; others got a bit of cheese, a few hundred grams of bread, or twenty potatoes. Some hung on to their gems. Louis chatted with them from time to time about the dangers of being caught with loot. "Poor devil over at the British Compound got it today," he would say. "They caught him with a pearl necklace sewed into his shirt. It only took 'em two hours to try him and shoot him." Sooner or later everyone made a deal with Louis.

Shortly after the last of us had been cleaned out, the S.S. came through our quarters on a surprise inspection. Louis' bed was the only one undisturbed. "He never leaves the compound and is a perfect prisoner," a guard was quick to explain to the inspectors. My mattress was slashed open and the straw scattered over the floor when I came home that evening.

However, Louis' luck was not air-tight, for in the last weeks of fighting, our guards were sent to stem the Russian tide, and a company of lame old men was moved in to watch over us. The new sergeant had no need for an orderly, and Louis sank into the anonymity of our group. The most humiliating aspect of his new situation was the prospect of being sent out on a labor detail with the common people. He was bitter about it, and demanded an interview with the new sergeant. He got the interview and was gone for about an hour.

When he got back I asked him, "Well, how much does Hitler want for Berchtesgaden?"

Louis was carrying a parcel wrapped in toweling. He opened it to reveal two pairs of scissors, some clippers, and a razor. "I'm the camp barber," he announced. "By order of the camp commandant, I am to make you gentlemen presentable."

"What if I don't want you to cut my hair?" I asked.

"Then you get your rations cut in half. That's by order of the commandant, too."

"Do you mind telling us how you got this appointment?" I asked.

"Not at all, not at all," said Louis. "I just told him I was ashamed to be associated with a bunch of sloppy men who look like gangsters, and that he ought to be ashamed to have such a terrible bunch in his prison. We two, the commandant and I, are going to do something about it." He set a stool in the middle of the floor and motioned me toward it. "You're first, kid," he said. "The commandant noticed those long locks of yours, and told me to be sure and get 'em."

I sat down on the stool and he whisked a towel around my neck. There was no mirror in which I could watch him cut, but his operations felt professional enough. I remarked on his unsuspected skill as a barber.

"Nothing, really," he said. "Sometimes I surprise myself." He finished with the clippers. "That will be two cigarettes, or the equivalent," he said. I paid him in saccharine tablets. No one but Louis had any cigarettes.

"Want a look at yourself?" He handed me a fragment of mirror. "Not bad, eh? And the best thing about it is that it's probably the worst job I'll do, because I'm bound to improve with time."

"Holy smokes!" I shrieked. My scalp looked like the back of an Airedale with mange—patches of bare scalp alternated with wild tufts of hair, and blood oozed from a dozen tiny cuts.

"Do you mean to say that for doing a job like this you get to stay in camp all day?" I roared.

"Come on, kid, simmer down," said Louis. "I think you look real nice."

There wasn't anything very novel about the situation after all. It was business as usual with him. The rest of us continued to work our heads off all day, and to come home weary in the evenings to be trimmed by Louis Gigliano.

The Unicorn Trap

IN THE YEAR 1067, *anno Domini*, in the village of Stow-on-the-Wold, England, eighteen dead men turned this way and that in the eighteen arches of the village gibbet. Hanged by Robert the Horrible, a friend of William the Conqueror, they boxed the compass with fishy eyes. North, east, south, west, and north again, there was no hope for the kind, the poor, and the thoughtful.

Across the road from the gibbet lived Elmer the woodcutter, his wife Ivy, and Ethelbert, his ten-year-old son.

Behind Elmer's hut was the forest.

Elmer closed the door of his hut, closed his eyes and licked his lips and tasted rue. He sat down at the table with Ethelbert. Their gruel had grown cold during the unexpected visit from the squire of Robert the Horrible.

Ivy pressed her back to the wall, as though God had just passed by. Her eyes were bright, her breathing shallow.

Ethelbert stared at his cold gruel blankly, bleakly, his young mind waterlogged in a puddle of family tragedy.

"Oh, didn't Robert the Horrible look grand, though, sitting out there on his horse?" said Ivy. "All that iron and paint and feathers, and such extra-fancy drapes on his horse." She flapped her rags and tossed her head like an empress as the hoof-beats of the Normans' horses died away.

"Grand, all right," said Elmer. He was a small man with a large-domed head. His blue eyes were restless with unhappy intelligence. His small frame was laced with scraggly ropes of muscle, the bonds of a thinking man forced to labor. "Grand is what he is," he said.

"You can say what you want about them Normans," said Ivy, "they done brought class to England."

"We're paying for it," said Elmer. "There's no such thing as a free lunch." He buried his fingers in the flaxen thatch of Ethelbert's hair, tilted the boy's head back, and searched his eyes for a sign that life was worth living. He saw only a mirror image of his own troubled soul.

"All the neighbors must of saw Robert the Horrible snarling out front, so high and mighty," said Ivy proudly. "Just wait till they hear he sent his squire in here to make you the new tax collector."

Elmer shook his head, his lips waggling slackly. He had lived to be loved for his wisdom and harmlessness. Now he had been told to represent Robert the Horrible's greed—or die horribly.

"I'd like to have me a dress made out of what his horse was wearing," said Ivy. "Blue, all shot through with them little gold crosses." She was happy for the first time in her life. "I'd make it look careless-like," she said, "all kind of bunched up in back and dragging—only there wouldn't be nothing careless about it. And maybe, after I got me some decent clothes, I could pick me up a little French, and *parlee voo* with the Norman ladies, so refined and all."

Elmer sighed and cupped his son's hands in his own. Ethelbert's hands were coarse. The palms were scratched, and earth had worked into the pores and under the nails. Elmer traced a scratch with his fingertip. "How'd you get this?" he said.

"Working on the trap," said Ethelbert. He came to life, radiant with intelligence of his own. "I been fixing thorn trees over the hole," he said eagerly, "so when the unicorn falls in, the thorn trees fall in on top of him."

"That should hold him," said Elmer tenderly. "It isn't many families in England that can look forward to a unicorn dinner."

"I wish you'd come up in the forest and have a look at the trap," said Ethelbert. "I want to make sure I got it right."

"I'm sure it's a fine trap, and I *want* to see it," said Elmer. The dream of catching a unicorn ran through the drab fabric of the lives of the father and son like a golden thread.

Both knew there were no unicorns in England. But they'd agreed to madness—to live as though there were unicorns around; as though Ethelbert were going to catch one any day; as though the scrawny family would soon be stuffing itself with meat, selling the precious horn for a fortune, living happily ever after.

"You've been saying you'd come and see it for a year," said Ethelbert.

"I've been busy," said Elmer. He didn't want to inspect the trap, to see it for what it really was—a handful of twigs over a scratch in the ground, magnified into a great engine of hope by the boy's imagination. Elmer wanted to go on thinking of it as big and promising, too. There was no hope anywhere else.

Elmer kissed his son's hands, and sniffed the mingled smells of flesh and earth. "I'll come see it soon," he said.

"And I'd have enough left over from them horse drapes to make drawers for you and little Ethelbert," said Ivy, still enchanted. "Wouldn't you two be the ones, though, with blue drawers all shot through with them little gold crosses?"

"Ivy," said Elmer patiently, "I wish you'd get it through your head—Robert really *is* horrible. He isn't going to give you the drapes off his horse. He never gave anybody *anything*."

"I guess I can dream if I want to," said Ivy. "I guess that's a woman's privilege."

"Dream of what?" said Elmer.

"If you do a good job, he just *might* give me the drapes off his horse after they're all wore out," said Ivy. "And maybe, if you collect so many taxes they can't hardly believe it, maybe they'll invite us to the castle sometimes." She walked about the hut coquettishly, holding the hem of an imaginary train above the dirt floor. "*Bon joor, monsoor, madame,*" she said. "I trust your lordship and ladyship ain't poorly."

"Is that the best dream you've got?" said Elmer, shocked.

"And they'd give you some distinguished name like Elmer the Bloody or Elmer the Mad," said Ivy, "and you and me and Ethelbert would ride to church on Sundays, all spruced up, and if some old serf talked to us snotty, we'd haul off and—"

"Ivy!" cried Elmer. "We *are* serfs."

Ivy tapped her foot and rocked her head from side to side. "Ain't Robert the Horrible just gave us the opportunity to improve ourselves?" she said.

"To be as bad as *he* is?" said Elmer. "That's an improvement?"

Ivy sat down at the table, and put her feet up on it. "If a body gets stuck in the ruling classes through no fault of their own," she said, "they got to rule or have folks just lose all respect for government." She scratched herself daintily. "Folks got to be governed."

"To their sorrow," said Elmer.

"Folks got to be protected," said Ivy, "and armor and castles don't come cheap."

Elmer rubbed his eyes. "Ivy, would you tell me what it is we're being protected from that's so much worse than what we've got?" he said. "I'd like to have a look at it, and then make up my own mind about what scares me most."

Ivy wasn't listening to him. She was thrilling to the approach of hoofbeats. Robert the Horrible and his entourage passed on their way back to the castle, and the hut trembled with might and glory.

Ivy ran to the door and threw it open.

Elmer and Ethelbert bowed their heads.

There were shouts of happy surprise from the Normans.

"*Hien!*"

"*Regardez!*"

"*Donnez la chasse, mes braves!*"

The Normans' horses reared, wheeled, and galloped into the forest.

"What's the good news?" said Elmer. "Did they squash something?"

"They seen a deer!" said Ivy. "They're all taking out after it, with Robert the Horrible in front." She put her hand over her heart. "Ain't he the sportsman, though?"

"Ain't he, though," said Elmer. "May God make his right arm strong." He looked to Ethelbert for an answering sardonic smile.

Ethelbert's thin face was white. His eyes bugged. "The trap—they're going up where the trap is!" he said.

"If they lay a finger on that trap," said Elmer, "I'll—" The cords in his neck stood out and his hands became claws. Of course Robert the Horrible would hack the boy's work of love to pieces if he saw it. *"Pour le sport, pour le sport,"* he said bitterly.

Elmer tried to daydream of murdering Robert the Horrible, but the dream was as frustrating as life—a search for weaknesses where there were no weaknesses. The dream ended truthfully, with Robert and his men on horses as big as cathedrals, with Robert and his men in iron shells, laughing behind the bars of their visors, choosing at leisure from their collections of skewers, chains, hammers, and meat-axes—choosing ways to deal with an angry woodcutter in rags.

Elmer's hands went limp. "If they wreck the trap," he said flabbily, "we'll build another one, better than ever."

Shame for his weakness made Elmer sick. The sickness worsened. He rested his head on his folded arms. When he raised his head, it was to look about himself with a death's-head grin. He had passed his breaking point.

"Father! Are you all right?" said Ethelbert, alarmed.

Elmer stood shakily. "Fine," he said, "just fine."

"You look so different," said Ethelbert.

"I *am* different," said Elmer. "I'm not afraid anymore." He gripped the edge of the table and shouted. "I'm not afraid!"

"Hush!" said Ivy. "They'll hear you!"

"I will *not* hush!" said Elmer passionately.

"You better hush," said Ivy. "You know what Robert the Horrible does to people who won't hush."

"Yes," said Elmer, "he nails their hats to their heads. But, if that's the price I have to pay, I'll pay it." He rolled his eyes. "When I thought of Robert the Horrible wrecking the boy's trap, the *whole story of life* came to me in a blinding flash!"

"Father, listen—" said Ethelbert, "I'm not scared he's going to wreck the trap. I'm scared he's going to—"

"A blinding flash!" cried Elmer.

"Oh, for crying out loud," said Ivy impatiently, closing the door. "All right, all right, all right," she said with a sigh, "let's hear the story of life in a blinding flash."

Ethelbert tugged at his father's sleeve. "If I do say so myself," he said, "that trap is a—"

"The wreckers against the builders!" said Elmer. "There's the whole story of life!"

Ethelbert shook his head and talked to himself. "If his horse ever steps on the rope that's hooked up to the sapling that's hooked up to the—" He bit his lip.

"Are you all through, Elmer?" said Ivy. "Is that it?" Her eagerness to get back to watching the Normans was infuriatingly transparent. He fingered the doorpull.

"No, Ivy," said Elmer tensely, "I am *not* through." He knocked her hand away from the doorpull.

"You done struck me," said Ivy, amazed.

"All day you have that thing open!" said Elmer. "I wish we didn't have a door! All day you do nothing but sit in front of the door, watching executions and waiting for the Normans to pass." He shivered his hands in her face. "No wonder your brains are all fuddled with glory and violence!"

Ivy cringed pitifully. "I just watch," she said. "A body gets lonely, and it helps to make the time go."

"You've been watching too long!" said Elmer. "And I've got more news for you."

"Yes?" piped Ivy.

Elmer squared his narrow shoulders. "Ivy," he said, "I am not going to be tax collector for Robert the Horrible."

Ivy gasped.

"I am not going to help the wreckers," said Elmer. "My son and I are builders."

"He'll hang you if you don't," said Ivy. "He promised he would."

"I know," said Elmer. "I know." Fear hadn't come to him yet. Pain hadn't come where pain would come. There was only the feeling of having done something perfect at last—the taste of a drink from a cold, pure spring.

Elmer opened the door. The wind had freshened, and the chains by which the dead men hung sang a chorus of slow, rusty squawks. The wind came from over the forest, and it carried to Elmer's ears the cries of the Norman sportsmen.

The cries sounded strangely bewildered, unsure. Elmer supposed that this was because they were so far away.

"*Robert? Allô, allô? Robert? Hien! Allô, allô?*"

"*Allô? Allô? Hien! Robert—dites quelque chose, s'il vous plaît. Hien! Hien! Allô?*"

"*Allô, allô, allô? Robert? Robert l'horrible? Hien! Allô, allô, allô?*"

Ivy put her arms around Elmer from behind, and rested her cheek on his back. "Elmer, honey," she said, "I don't want you to get hung. I love you, honey."

Elmer patted her hands. "And I love you, Ivy," he said.

"I'll miss you."

"You're really going through with it?" said Ivy.

"It's time to die for what I believe in," said Elmer. "And even if it wasn't, I'd still have to."

"Why, why?" said Ivy.

"Because I said I would in front of my son," said Elmer. Ethelbert came to him, and Elmer put his arms around the boy.

The little family was now bound by a tangle of arms. The three entwined rocked back and forth as the sun set—rocked in a rhythm they felt in their bones.

Ivy sniffled against Elmer's back. "You're just teaching Ethelbert how to get *his* self hung, too," she said. "He's so fresh with them Normans now, it's a wonder they ain't flang him down the oubliette."

"I only hope that Ethelbert has a son like mine before he dies," said Elmer.

"Everything seemed to be going so grand," said Ivy. She burst into tears. "Here you was offered a fine position, with a chance for advancement," she said brokenly.

"And I figured maybe, after Robert the Horrible had wore out his horse drapes, you could kind of ask him—"

"Ivy!" said Elmer. "Don't make me feel worse. Comfort me."

"It'd be a sight easier, if I knew what it was you thought you was doing," said Ivy.

Two Normans came out of the forest, unhappy and baffled. They faced each other, spread their arms, and shrugged.

One pushed a shrub aside with his broadsword and looked under it pathetically. "*Allô, allô?*" he said. "*Robert?*"

"*Il a disparu!*" said the other.

"*Il s'est évanoui!*"

"*Le cheval, l'armement, les plumes—tout d'un coup!*"

"*Poof!*"

"*Hélas!*"

They saw Elmer and his family. "*Hien!*" called one to Elmer. "*Avez-vous vu Robert?*"

"Robert the Horrible?" said Elmer.

"*Oui.*"

"Sorry," said Elmer. "Haven't seen hide nor hair of him."

"*Eh?*"

"*Je n'ai vu pas ni peau ni cheveux de lui,*" said Elmer.

The Normans faced each other again, desolately.

"*Hélas!*"

"*Zut!*"

They went into the forest again slowly.

"*Allô, allô, allô?*"

"*Hien! Robert? Allô?*"

"Father! Listen!" said Ethelbert wildly.

"Shhhhh," said Elmer gently. "I'm talking to your mother now."

"It's just like that fool unicorn trap," said Ivy. "I didn't understand that, neither. I was real patient about that trap. I never said a word. But now I'm going to speak my piece."

"Speak it," said Elmer.

"That trap don't have nothing to do with nothing," said Ivy.

Tears formed on the rims of Elmer's eyes. The image of the twigs, the scratch in the earth, and the boy's imagination said all there was to say about his life—the life that was about to end.

"There ain't no unicorns around here," said Ivy, proud of her knowledge.

"I know," said Elmer. "Ethelbert and I know."

"And you getting yourself hung ain't going to make anything better, neither," said Ivy.

"I know. Ethelbert and I know that, too," said Elmer.

"Maybe *I'm* the dumb one," said Ivy.

Elmer suddenly felt the terror and loneliness and pain-to-come that were the price for the perfect thing he was doing—the price of the taste of a drink from a cold, pure spring. They were far worse than shame could ever be.

Elmer swallowed. His neck hurt where the noose would bite. "Ivy, honey," he said, "I sure *hope* you are."

That night, Elmer prayed for a new husband for Ivy, a stout heart for Ethelbert, and a merciful death and paradise for himself on the morrow.

"Amen," said Elmer.

"Maybe you could just *pretend* to be tax collector," said Ivy.

"Where would I get the just-pretend taxes?" said Elmer.

"Maybe you could be tax collector for just a little while," said Ivy.

"Just long enough to get hated for good reason," said Elmer. "*Then* I could hang."

"There's always something," said Ivy. Her nose reddened.

"Ivy—" said Elmer.

"Hmmm?"

"Ivy—I understand about the blue dress all shot through with little gold crosses," said Elmer. "I want that for you, too."

"And the drawers for you and Ethelbert," said Ivy. "It wasn't all just for me."

"Ivy," said Elmer, "what I'm doing—it's more important than those horse drapes."

"That's my trouble," said Ivy. "I just can't imagine anything grander than them."

"Neither can I," said Elmer. "But there are such things. There's *got* to be." He smiled sadly. "Whatever they are," he said, "they're what I'll be dancing about when I dance on air tomorrow."

"I wish Ethelbert would get back," said Ivy. "We should all be together."

"He had to check his trap," said Elmer. "Life goes on."

"I'm glad them Normans finally went home," said Ivy. "It was *allô* and *hien* and *hélas* and *zut* and *poof* till I thought I'd near go crazy. I guess they done found Robert the Horrible."

"Thus sealing my doom," said Elmer. He sighed. "I'll go look for Ethelbert," he said. "How better could a man spend his last night on earth than in bringing his son home from the forest?"

Elmer went out into a pale blue world of night under a half-moon. He followed the path that Ethelbert's feet had worn—followed it to the high, black wall of the forest.

"Ethelbert!" he called.

There was no reply.

Elmer pushed into the forest. Branches whipped his face, and brambles snatched at his legs.

"Ethelbert!"

Only the gibbet replied. The chains squawked, and a skeleton fell rattling to earth. There were now only seventeen exhibits in the eighteen arches. There was room for one more.

Elmer's anxiety for Ethelbert grew. It drove him hard, deeper and deeper into the forest. He came to a clearing, and rested, panting, sweat stinging his eyes.

"Ethelbert!"

"Father?" said Ethelbert in the thicket ahead. "Come here and help me."

Elmer went into the thicket blindly, his hands groping before him.

Ethelbert caught his father's hand in the perfect darkness. "Careful!" said Ethelbert. "Another step, and you'll be in the trap."

"Oh," said Elmer. "*That* was a close thing." Playfully, to make the boy feel good, he filled his voice with fear. "Whoooooey! I *guess!*"

Ethelbert pulled his hand down, and pressed it against something lying on the ground.

Elmer was amazed to feel the form of a big, dead stag. He knelt by it. "A deer!" he said.

His voice came back to him, seemingly from the bowels of the earth. "*A deer, a deer, a deer.*"

"It took me an hour to get it out of the trap," said Ethelbert.

"*Trap, trap, trap,*" said the echo.

"Really?" said Elmer. "Good Lord, boy! I had no idea that trap was that good!"

"*Good, good, good,*" said the echo.

"You don't know the half of it," said Ethelbert.

"*It, it, it,*" said the echo.

"Where's that echo coming from?" said Elmer.

"*From, from, from?*" said the echo.

"From right in front of you," said Ethelbert. "From the trap."

Elmer threw himself backwards as Ethelbert's voice came out of the hole before him, came out of the earth as though from the gates of Hell itself.

"*Trap, trap, trap.*"

"You *dug* it?" said Elmer, aghast.

"God dug it," said Ethelbert. "It's the chimney of a cave."

Elmer stretched out limp on the ground. He rested his head on the cooling, stiffening haunch of the stag. There was only one flaw in the thicket's roof of verdure. Through that flaw came the light from one bright star. Elmer saw the star as a rainbow through the prisms of grateful tears.

"I have nothing more to ask of life," said Elmer. "Tonight, everything has been given me—and more, and more, and more. With God's help, my son has caught a unicorn." He touched Ethelbert's foot, and stroked its arch. "If God listens even to the prayers of an humble woodcutter and his son," he said, "what *can't* the world become?"

Elmer almost slipped away to sleep, so much at one was he with the plan of things.

Ethelbert roused him. "Shall we take the stag down to Mom?" said Ethelbert. "A midnight feast?"

"Not the whole deer," said Elmer. "Too risky. We'll cut some choice steaks, and leave the rest hidden here."

"Have you got a knife?" said Ethelbert.

"No," said Elmer. "Against the law, you know."

"I'll get something to cut with," said Ethelbert.

Elmer, still lying down, heard his son lower himself into the chimney of the cave; heard him seek and find footholds deeper and deeper in the earth; heard him grunting and wrestling with logs at the bottom.

When Ethelbert returned, he was carrying something long that caught the glint from the one bright star. "This should do it," he said.

He gave to Elmer Robert the Horrible's keen, two-handed broadsword.

It was midnight.

The little family was stuffed with venison.

Elmer picked his teeth with Robert the Horrible's poignard.

Ethelbert, on watch at the door, wiped his lips with a plume.

Ivy pulled the horse drapes about her contentedly. "If I'd of knowed you was going to catch something," she said, "I wouldn't of thought that trap was such a dumb idea."

"That's the way it is with traps," said Elmer. He leaned back and tried to feel elated about not hanging the next day, now that Robert the Horrible was dead. But he found the reprieve a dull affair compared to the other thoughts carousing in the stately dome of his head.

"There's just one thing I got to ask," said Ivy.

"Name it," said Elmer expansively.

"I wish you two'd quit making light of me, telling me this is unicorn meat," said Ivy. "You think I'll believe anything you tell me."

"It *is* unicorn meat," said Elmer. "And I'm going to tell you something else you can believe." He slipped on Robert the Horrible's iron gauntlet, and rapped the table with it. "Ivy—there's a great day coming for the little people."

Ivy looked at him adoringly. "Ain't you and Ethelbert nice," she said, "going out and getting me the clothes for it?"

There were hoofbeats in the distance.

"Hide everything!" said Ethelbert.

In an instant, every vestige of Robert the Horrible and the deer was out of sight.

Norman warriors, armed to the teeth, thundered by Elmer the woodcutter's humble hut.

They shouted in fear and defiance of formless demons in the night.

"*Hien! Hien! Courage, mes braves!*"

The hoofbeats faded away.

Spoils

IF, ON JUDGMENT DAY, God were to ask Paul which of the two should rightly be his eternal residence, Heaven or Hell, Paul would likely suggest that, by his own and by Cosmic standards, Hell was his destiny—recalling the wretched thing he had done. The Almighty, in all His Wisdom, might recognize that Paul's life on the whole had been a harmless one, and that his tender conscience had already tortured him mightily—for the thing he did.

Paul's garish adventures as a prisoner of war in Sudetenland lost their troubling forms as they mired down in the past, but one dismal image would not sink from his consciousness. His wife's playful banter at dinner one night served to recall what he longed to forget. Sue had spent the afternoon with Mrs. Ward, next door, and Mrs. Ward had shown her an exquisite silver service for twenty-four, which, Sue was astonished to learn, Mr. Ward had liberated and brought home from the war in Europe.

"Honey," Sue chided him, "couldn't you have brought home just a little something better than you did?"

It was not likely that the Germans bewailed Paul's plundering, for one rusty and badly bent Luftwaffe saber was the whole of his loot. His companions in the Russian Zone, under postwar anarchy, Free Enterprise *par excellence* that lasted for weeks, came home laden with treasure like Spanish galleons, while Paul was content with his foolish relic. Though he had weeks to seek and take what he would, his first hours as a swashbuckling conqueror were his last. The thing that broke his spirit and his hate, the image that tormented him, began taking shape on a glorious morning of Spring in the mountains, May 8, 1945.

It took Paul and his fellow prisoners of war in Hellendorf, Sudetenland, some time to get used to the absence of their guards, who had prudently taken to the forests and hilltops the night before. He and two other Americans wandered uncertainly down the teeming road toward Peterswald, another tranquil farming village of five hundred war-bewildered souls. Humanity moved in wailing rivers, flowing in both directions with a unanimous lament—"The Russians are coming!" After four tedious kilometers in this milieu, the three settled on the bank of a stream that cut through Peterswald, wondering how they might reach the American lines, wondering if the Russians were killing everyone in their path as some said. Near them, secure in a barn-sheltered hutch, a white rabbit sat in darkness, listening to the uncustomary din without.

The trio felt no part of the terror that surged through the village, no pity. "God knows the arrogant block-heads have been begging for it," said Paul, and the others nodded in grim amusement. "After what the Germans did to them, you can't blame the Russians, no matter what they do," said Paul; and again his companions nodded. They sat in silence and watched as frantic mothers hid with their young in cellars, as others scurried up the hillside and into the woods, or deserted their homes to flee down the road with a few precious parcels.

A wide-eyed, long-striding British lance corporal shouted from the road, "Better get a move on, lads; they're in Hellendorf right now!"

A cloud of dust in the west, the roar of trucks, the scattering of frightened refugees, and the Russians entered the village, pitching cigarettes to the astonished citizens, and giving wet, enthusiastic kisses to all who dared show themselves. Paul cavorted about their trucks, laughing and shouting, and catching the loaves and chunks of meat thrown to him by those liberators who heard his "American! American!" above the wild accordion music that streamed from the red-starred trucks. Happy and excited, he and his friends returned to the brookside with armloads of food, and at once began to stuff themselves.

But as they ate, the others—Czechs, Poles, Jugoslavs, Russians, a fearsome horde of outraged German slaves—came to smash and loot and burn for the merry hell of it, in the wake of the Russian Army. Systematically, in purposeful knots of three and four, they went from house to house, breaking down doors, threatening the occupants, and taking what pleased them. Overlooking plunder was not likely, for Peterswald was built in a narrow draw, only one house deep on either side of a single road. Paul thought that thousands must have explored every house from cellar to attic before the moonlit evening came.

He and his friends watched the earnest pillagers at work, giving them sickly smiles whenever a group passed by. An exultant pair of Scotchmen had made friends with such a group, and, while on a cheerful foray, stopped off to talk with the Americans. Each had a handsome bicycle, numerous rings and watches, field glasses, cameras, and other admirable trinkets.

"After all," one of them explained, "you don't want to be sittin' down on a day like this, you'll never get another chance like this one. You're the victors, you know, you've a bloody good right to anything you like."

The three Americans talked it up among themselves, Paul at the fore, and convinced each other that they would be completely justified in looting the homes of the enemy. The three together beset the nearest house, one which had been vacant since before their arrival in Peterswald. It had already been well-exploited; no glass remained in the windows; every drawer had been dumped, every garment torn from the closets; cupboards had been stripped bare, and pillows and mattresses had been disemboweled by searchers. Each of the marauders before Paul and his friends had examined the heaps discarded by his predecessor until nothing but shreds of cloth and a few pots remained.

It was nearly evening when they picked over the sorry lot, and they found nothing to interest them. Paul remarked that there probably was not much in the house to begin with; whoever had lived there had been poor. The furnishings were shabby, the walls peeling, and the outside in need of painting and repair. But when Paul climbed the stairway to the tiny upper floor, he found an amazing room that did not fit into the impoverished pattern. It was a bedroom decorated in gay colors, with beautifully carved furniture, fairyland pictures on candy-striped walls, and freshly painted woodwork. Discarded loot, a forlorn hillock of toys stood in the middle of the floor. The only undisturbed objects in the whole house, leaning against the wall near the head of the bed, were a pair of, "I'll be damned; look, kids' crutches."

The Americans, having found nothing of value, agreed that it was getting too late for treasure hunting that day, and proposed that they set about getting supper. They had a good quantity of food on hand that the Russians had given to them, but got the idea that supper on this day of days should certainly be something special, with chicken, milk, and eggs, and maybe even a rabbit. Seeking such delicacies, the trio broke up to scour the neighboring barns and farmyards.

Paul peered into the small barn behind the house which they had hoped to plunder. Whatever food or livestock may have been here had been carted east hours ago, he reflected. On the dirt floor near the doorway were a few potatoes which he picked up, but nothing else. As he stuffed the potatoes into his pockets and prepared to move on, he heard a slight rustling from one corner. The gentle noise was repeated. When his eyes became accustomed to the darkness he could see a rabbit hutch in which a fat, white rabbit sat, twinkling his pink nose and breathing quickly. This was sensational luck, *the pièce de résistance* for the banquet. Paul opened the door and removed the unprotesting animal, holding it by its ears. Never having killed a rabbit with his hands, he was dubious as to how he might do it. At last he laid the rabbit's head on a chopping block and smashed its skull with the back of an axe. It kicked feebly for a few seconds and died.

Delighted with himself, Paul set about skinning and cleaning the rabbit, cutting off a foot for good luck in surely better days to come. Finished, he stood in the barn doorway, contemplating peace, the sunset, and the stream of sheepish German soldiers shuffling home from the last pocket of resistance. With them were the weary civilians who had fled down the road that morning, only to be turned back by the Russian advance.

Suddenly Paul was aware of three figures who detached themselves from the dismal procession and moved toward him. They paused before the battered house. A wave of remorse and sorrow billowed in Paul's chest: "This must be their little house and barn," he thought. "This must belong to that old man and woman, and to that crippled boy." The woman wept and the man shook his head. The boy kept trying to get their attention, saying something and gesturing toward the barn. Paul stood in the shadows so they could not see him, and he ran away with the rabbit when they went into the house.

He brought his contribution to the place that the others had chosen for a fireplace, a knoll from which Paul could see the barn he had left through a gap in a poplar windbreak. The rabbit was placed with the rest of the booty on a cloth stretched over the ground.

As the others busied themselves with preparing the food, he watched the barn, for the little boy had come out of his house, and was moving toward the barn as swiftly as his crutches would carry him. He disappeared into the barn for an agonizingly long time. Paul heard his faint shriek, and saw him come to the door, carrying the soft white pelt with him. He rubbed it against his cheek, and then sank to the doorsill to bury his face in the fur and sob his heart out.

Paul looked away, and did not look again. The other two did not see the child, and Paul did not tell them about him. When the three sat down to supper, one boy began grace: "Our Father, we thank thee for this food thou hast set before us . . ."

Heading for the American lines, moving casually from one village to the next, Paul's companions accumulated a sizeable quantity of German treasure. For some reason, all that Paul brought home was one rusty and badly bent Luftwaffe saber.

Just You and Me, Sammy

This story is about soldiers, but it isn't exactly a war story. The war was over when it all happened, so I guess that makes it a murder story. No mystery, just murder.

My name is Sam Kleinhans. It's a German name, and, I'm sorry to say, my father was mixed up in the *German-American Bund* in New Jersey for a while before the war. When he found out what it was all about, he got out in a hurry. But a lot of the people in our neighborhood went for the *Bund* in a big way. A couple of families on our street, I remember, got so excited about what Hitler was doing in the Fatherland, they sold everything they had, and went back to Germany to live.

Some of their kids were just about my age, and, when the U.S. got into the war and I went overseas as a rifleman, I wondered if I might not wind up shooting at some of my old playmates. I don't think I did. I found out afterwards that most of the *Bund* kids who took out German citizenship wound up as riflemen on the Russian front. A few got into small-time intelligence work, trying to mix in with American troops without being noticed, but not many. The Germans didn't trust them worth a damn—or at least that's what one of our former neighbors told Father in a letter asking him for a CARE parcel. The same man said he'd do anything to get back to the States, and I imagine they all feel that way.

Being so close to them and the *Bund* monkey business made me pretty self-conscious about my German ancestry when we finally got into the war. I must have seemed like quite a jerk to a lot of the guys, sounding off the way I did about loyalty, fighting for a cause, and all that. Not that the other guys in the Army didn't believe in those things—it's just that it wasn't fashionable to talk about them. Not in World War II.

Thinking back on it, I *know* I was corny. I remember what I said on the morning of May eighth, for instance, the day the war with Germany ended. "Isn't it glorious!" I said.

"Ain't what glorious?" said Private George Fisher, raising one eyebrow, as though he'd said something pretty deep. He was scratching his back on a strand of barbed-wire, thinking about something else, I guess. Food and cigarettes, probably, and maybe even women.

It wasn't very smart to be seen talking with George anymore. He didn't have any friends left in camp, and anybody who tried to be buddies with him was likely to wind up in the same lonely spot. All of us were milling around, and George and I just happened—I thought then—to come together there by the gate.

The Germans had made him head American in our prison camp. They said it was because he could speak German. At any rate, he made a good thing out of it. He was a lot fatter than the rest of us—so he probably was thinking about women. Nobody else had mentioned the subject since about a month after we'd been captured. Everybody but George had been living on potatoes for eight months, so, like I said, the subject of women was about as popular as the subject of raising orchids or playing the zither.

The way I felt then, if Betty Grable had showed up and said she was all mine, I would have told her to make me a peanut butter and jelly sandwich. Only it wasn't Betty that was on her way to see George and me that day—it was the Russian Army. The two of us, standing on the road shoulder in front of the prison gate, were listening to the tanks whining in the valley, just starting to climb up to where we were.

The big guns to the north, that had been rattling the prison windowpanes for a week, were quiet now, and our guards had disappeared during the night. Before that, the only traffic on the road had been a few farmers' carts. Now it was packed with jostling, yelling people—pushing, stumbling, swearing; trying to cross the hills to Prague before the Russians caught them.

Fear like that can spread, too, to people who don't have anything to be afraid of. All of the people running from the Russians weren't Germans. I remember a British lance corporal, for instance, who George and I saw strutting toward Prague as though the Devil was after him.

"Better get a move on, Yanks!" he puffed. "Rooskies only a couple of miles back, you know. Don't want to mix it with them, do you?"

One nice thing about being half-starved, which I gather the lance corporal wasn't, is that it's hard to worry about anything but being half-starved. "You've got it all wrong, Mac," I shouted back at him. "We're on their side, the way I understand it."

"They're not asking where you're from, Yank. They're shooting everything they can catch for the fun of it." He rounded the bend and was out of sight.

I laughed, but I was in for a surprise when I turned back to George. He was running his stubby fingers through his red mop of hair, and his fat moon face was white as he looked down the road in the direction the Russians would be coming from. That was something none of us had ever seen before—George afraid.

Until then, he'd been in command of every situation, whether it was with us or with the Germans. He had a thick skin, and he could bluff or wheedle his way out of anything.

Alvin York would have been impressed with some of his combat stories. We were all from the same division, except for George. He'd been brought in all by himself, and he said he'd been up front since D-Day. The rest of us were from a green outfit, captured in a breakthrough before we'd been in the line a week. George was a real campaigner, and entitled to a lot of respect. He got it; begrudged, all right, but he got it—until Jerry got killed.

"Call me a stool pigeon again, buddy, and I'll smash your ugly face in," I heard him tell one guy whose whispers he'd overheard. "You know damn well you'd do the same thing, if you had the chance. I'm just playing the guards for chumps. They think I'm on their side, so they treat me pretty good. I'm not hurting you none, so mind your own damn business!"

That was a few days after the break, after Jerry Sullivan got killed. Somebody'd tipped off the guards about the break, or at least it looked that way. They were waiting outside the fence, at the mouth of the tunnel, when Jerry, the first man through, crawled out. They didn't have to shoot him, but they did. Maybe George hadn't told the guards—but nobody gave him the benefit of that doubt when he was out of hearing.

Nobody said anything to his face. He was big and healthy, remember, and went on getting beefier and worse-tempered, while the rest of us were turning into drowsy scarecrows.

But now, with the Russians on their way, George's nerve seemed to have given out. "Let's make a break for Prague, Sammy. Just you and me, so we can travel fast," he said.

"What in hell's the matter with you?" I said. "We don't have to run from anybody, George. We just won a war, and you're acting like we lost one. Prague's sixty miles away, for God's sake. The Russians'll be here in an hour or so, and they'll probably send trucks to run us back to our lines. Take it easy, George—you don't hear any shooting, do you?"

"They'll shoot us, Sammy, sure as hell. You don't even look like an American soldier. They're wild men, Sammy. Come on, let's go while we got the chance."

He had a point about my clothes. They were ripped and stained and patched, and I looked more like a resident of skid row than an American soldier. But, as you might expect, George still looked pretty sharp. The guards kept him in cigarettes as well as food, and he could trade the smokes for just about anything in camp he wanted. He got himself several changes of clothes that way, and the guards let him use an iron they had in their shack, so he was the camp fashion plate.

His game was over now. Nobody had to trade with him anymore, and the men who'd taken such good care of him were gone. Maybe that's what was scaring him, and not the Russians. "Let's go, Sammy," he said. He was pleading with me, a person he hadn't had a friendly word for in eight months at close quarters.

"Go ahead, if you want to," I said. "You don't have to ask my permission, George. Go on. I'm staying here with the rest of the guys."

He didn't move. "You and me, Sammy, we'll stick together." He grinned and draped his arm around my shoulders.

I twisted away, and walked across the prison yard. All we had in common was red hair. He worried me: I couldn't figure out what his angle was on suddenly becoming a great pal of mine. And George was the kind of guy who always had an angle.

He followed me across the yard, and put his big arm around my shoulders again. "O.K., Sammy, we'll stay here and wait."

"I don't give a damn what you do."

"O.K., O.K.," he laughed. "I was just going to suggest, since we got an hour or so to wait, why don't you and me go down the road a piece and see if we can't get us some smokes and souvenirs? Both speaking German, we ought to make out real good, you and me."

I was dying for a smoke, and he knew it. I'd traded him my gloves for two cigarettes a couple of months before—when it had been plenty cold—and I hadn't had one since. George started me thinking about what that first inhale would be like. There'd be cigarettes in the nearest town, Peterswald, two uphill miles away.

"Whaddya say, Sammy?"

I shrugged. "What the hell—let's go."

"Attaboy."

"Where you going?" yelled one of the guys in the prison yard.

"Out to have us a quick look around," George answered.

"Be back in an hour," I added.

"Want some company?" yelled the guy.

George kept on walking, and didn't answer. "Get a mob, and they'll louse up everything," he said winking. "Two's just right."

I looked at him. He had a smile fixed on his face, but that didn't keep me from seeing that he was still plenty scared.

"What are you afraid of, George?"

"Old Georgie afraid of something? That'll be the day."

We took our place in the noisy crowd, and began to climb the gentle grade to Peterswald.

II.

Sometimes, when I think about what happened in Peterswald, I make excuses for myself—that I was drunk, that I was a little crazy after having been locked up and hungry for so long. The hell of it is that I wasn't forced into doing what I did. I wasn't cornered. I did it because I wanted to.

Peterswald wasn't what I'd expected. I'd hoped for at least a store or two where we could beg or steal a couple of cigarettes and something to eat. But the town wasn't anything more than two dozen farms, each with a wall and a ten-foot gate. They were jammed together on a green hilltop, overlooking the fields, so that they formed a solid fort. With tanks and artillery on their way, though, Peterswald was nothing but a pretty push-over, and it didn't look like anybody felt like making the Russians fight for it.

Here and there a white flag—a bedsheet on the end of a broomstick—fluttered from a second-story window. Every gate stood open—unconditional surrender.

"This looks as good as any," said George. He gripped my arm, steered me out of the mob, through the gate, and into the hard-packed courtyard of the first farm we came to.

The yard was closed in on three sides by the house and farm buildings, with the wall and gate across the fourth. Looking through the open doors into the vacant barns, and through the windows into the still house, I felt for the first time like what I really was—a worried stranger. Up to then, I'd walked, talked, and acted as though I was a special case, an American, somehow out of this European mess, without a damn thing to be afraid of. Walking into a ghost town changed my mind—

Or maybe I was beginning to be afraid of George. Saying that now may be hind-sight—I don't know for sure.

Maybe, down deep, I *was* starting to wonder. His eyes were too big and interested whenever I said something, and he couldn't keep his hands off me, pawing, patting, slapping; and every time he talked about what he wanted to do next, it was "You and me, Sammy . . ."

"Hello!" he shouted. He got a quick echo from the walls around us, and then silence. He still held my arm, and he gave it a squeeze. "Ain't this cozy, Sammy? Looks like we got the place all to ourselves." He pushed the big gate shut, and slid the thick wooden cross-bar across it. I don't think I could have budged the gate then, but George had moved it without even changing his expression. He walked back to my side, dusting his hands and grinning.

"What's the angle, George?"

"To the victor go the spoils—ain't that right?" He kicked open the front door. "Well, go on in, kid. Help yourself. Georgie's just fixed things so nobody's going to bother us till we've got the pick of the stuff. Go find something real nice for your mother and your girlfriend, huh?"

"All I want is a smoke," I said. "You can open the damn gate as far as I'm concerned."

George took a package of cigarettes from his field jacket pocket. "Here's the kind of buddy I am," he laughed. "Have one."

"What's the idea of making me walk all the way to Peterswald for a cigarette, when you had a whole pack?"

He walked into the house. "I like your company, Sammy. You ought to feel real complimented. Redheads ought to stick together."

"Let's get out of here, George."

"The gate's shut. There's nothing to be afraid of, Sammy, just like you said. Brighten up. Go out in the kitchen and get something to eat. That's all that's the matter with you. You'll kick yourself for the rest of your life if you pass up a deal like this." He turned his back, and started pulling out drawers, emptying them on a tabletop, and picking over the contents. He whistled an old dance tune I hadn't heard since the late thirties.

I stood in the middle of the room, getting a dizzy, dreamy lift out of the first deep drags on the cigarette. I closed my eyes, and, when I opened them again, George didn't worry me anymore. There wasn't anything to be afraid of—the growing nightmare feeling was gone. I relaxed.

"Whoever lived here took off in a hurry," said George, still with his back to me. He held up a small bottle. "Forgot their heart medicine. My old lady used to have this stuff around the house for her heart." He laid it back in the drawer. "Same in German as it is in English. Funny thing about strychnine, Sammy—little doses can save your life." He dropped a pair of earrings into his bulging pocket. "These'll make some little girl very happy," he said.

"If she likes stuff from the five-and-ten, they will."

"Cheer up, will you, Sammy? What're you trying to do, spoil your buddy's good time? Go out in the kitchen and get yourself something to eat, for God's sake. I'll be along in a minute."

As far as being a victor and getting some spoils goes, I didn't do badly in my own way—three slices of black bread and a wedge of cheese, waiting for me on the kitchen table in the back of the house. I looked in a cabinet drawer for a knife to cut the cheese with, and got a little surprise. There was a knife, all right, but there was also a pistol, not much bigger than my fist, and a full clip beside it. I played with it, figured out how it worked, and shoved the clip into place to see if it really belonged with the gun. It was a pretty thing—a nice souvenir. I shrugged, and started to put it back. It'd be suicide to be caught with a gun by the Russians today.

"Sammy! Where the hell are you?" called George.

I slipped the gun into my trouser pocket. "Here in the kitchen, George. What did you find—the crown jewels?"

"Better'n that, Sammy." His face was a bright pink, and he was breathing hard when he came into the room. He looked fatter than he really was, with his field jacket jammed full of junk he'd picked up in the other rooms. He banged a bottle of brandy on the table. "How you like the looks of that, Sammy? Now you and me can have ourselves a little victory party, huh? Now don't go home to Jersey and tell your folks old Georgie never gave you nothing." He slapped my back. "She was full when I found her, and she's half gone now, Sammy—so you're way behind the party."

"I'll stay that way, George. Thanks, but it'd probably kill me, the shape I'm in."

He sat down in the chair facing me, with a big, loose grin on his face. "Finish your sandwich, and you'll be ready for one. The war's over, boy! Is that something to drink to, or is it?"

"Later maybe."

He didn't take another drink himself. He sat quietly for a while, thinking hard about something, and I munched my food in silence.

"What's the matter with your appetite?" I asked at last.

"Nothing. Good as ever. I ate this morning."

"Thanks for offering me some. What was it, a farewell gift from the guards?"

He smiled, as though I'd just paid tribute to him for the slick deals he'd pulled. "What's the matter, Sammy—hate my guts or something?"

"Did I say anything?"

"You don't have to, kid. You're like all the rest." He leaned back in his chair and stretched his arms. "I hear some of the boys are going to turn me in as a collaborator when we get back to the States. You going to do that, Sammy?" He was perfectly calm, yawning. He went right on, without giving me a chance to answer. "Poor old Georgie hasn't got a friend in the world, has he? He's really on his own now, ain't he? I guess the rest of you boys'll be flown right home, but I imagine the Army will want to have a little talk with Georgie Fisher, won't they, huh?"

"You're boiled, George. Forget it. Nobody's going to—"

He stood up, steadying himself with a hand on the table. "Nope, Sammy, I got it doped out just right. Being a collaborator—that's treason, ain't it? They can hang you for that, can't they?"

"Take it easy, George. Nobody's going to try and hang you." I stood up slowly.

"I said I got it doped out just right, Sammy. Georgie Fisher's no man to be, so what do you think I'm gonna do?" He fumbled with his shirt collar, pulled out his dogtags, and threw them on the floor. "I'm gonna be somebody else, Sammy. I'd say that was real bright, wouldn't you?"

The noise of the tanks was beginning to make the dishes in the cupboard hum. I started for the door. "I don't give a damn what you do, George. I won't turn you in. All I want is to get home in one piece, and I'm heading back for camp right now."

George stepped between me and the door, and rested his hand on my shoulder. He winked and grinned. "Wait a minute, kid. You ain't heard it all, yet. Don't you want to hear what your buddy Georgie's going to do next? You'll be real interested."

"So long, George."

He didn't get out of my way. "Better sit down and have a drink, Sammy. Calm your nerves. You and me, kid, neither one of us is going back to camp. The boys back there know what Georgie Fisher looks like, and that'd spoil everything, wouldn't it?

Think I'd be smart to wait a couple of days, then turn myself in down at Prague, where nobody knows me."

"I said I wouldn't say anything, George, and I won't."

"I said sit down, Sammy. Have a drink."

I was woozy and weary, and the tough black bread in my stomach was making me feel sick. I sat.

"That's my buddy," he said. "This won't take long, if you see things my way, Sammy. I said I was going to quit being Georgie Fisher and be somebody else."

"Good, fine, George."

"The thing is, I'll need a new name and dogtags to go with it. I like yours—what'll you take for 'em?" He stopped smiling. He wasn't fooling—he was making me a deal. He leaned over the table, and, with his fat, pink, sweaty face a few inches from mine, he whispered, "Whaddya say, Sammy? Two hundred bucks cash and this watch for the tags. That'd damn near pay for a new LaSalle, wouldn't it? Look at the watch, Sammy—worth a thousand bucks in New York—strikes the hours, tells you what the date is—"

Funny, George forgetting LaSalle was out of business. He pulled a roll of bills from his hip pocket. The Germans had taken our money from us when we'd been captured, but some of the boys had hidden bills in the lining of their clothes. George, with his corner on cigarettes, had managed to get just about every cent the Germans had missed. Supply and demand—five bucks a smoke.

But the watch was a surprise. George had kept it a secret up to now—for very good reasons. The watch had belonged to Jerry Sullivan, the kid who'd been shot in the prison break.

"Where'd you get Jerry's watch, George?"

George shrugged. "A beauty, ain't it? Gave Jerry a hundred smokes for it. Cleaned me out to do it."

"When, George?"

He wasn't giving me his big, confidential grin anymore. He was mean and surly. "Whaddya mean, *when*? Just before he got it, if you want to know." He ran his hands through his hair. "O.K., go ahead and say I got him killed. That's what you're thinking, so go ahead and say it."

"I wasn't thinking that, George. I was just thinking how lucky you were to put that deal over. Jerry told me the watch had been his grandfather's, and he wouldn't take anything for it. That's all. I was just kind of surprised he made the deal," I said softly.

"What's the use?" he said angrily. "How can I prove I didn't have anything to do with that? You guys pinned that on me because I had it good and you didn't. I played square with Jerry, and I'll kill the guy who says I didn't. And now I'm playing square with you, Sammy. Do you want the dough and the watch or not?"

I was thinking back to the night of the break, remembering what Jerry had said just before he started crawling into the tunnel. "God, I wish I had a cigarette," he'd said.

The noise of the tanks was almost a roar now. They must be past the camp, climbing the last mile to Peterswald, I thought. Not much more time to play for. "Sure, George, it's a good deal. Swell, but what am I supposed to do while you're me?"

"Almost nothing, kid. All you do is forget who you are for a while. Turn yourself in at Prague, and tell 'em you've lost your memory. Stall 'em just long enough for me to get back to the States. Ten days, Sammy—that's all. It'll work, kid, with both of us redheads and the same height."

"So what happens when they find out *I'm* Sam Kleinhans?"

"I'll be over the hill in the States. They'll never find me." He was getting impatient. "C'mon, Sammy, is it a deal?"

It was a crack-brained scheme, without a prayer of working. I looked into George's eyes, and thought I saw that he knew that, too. Maybe, with a buzz on, he thought it would work—but now he seemed to be changing his mind. I looked at the watch on the table, and thought of Jerry Sullivan being carried back into camp dead. George had helped carry him, I remembered.

I thought of the gun in my pocket. "Go to hell, George," I said.

He didn't look surprised. He pushed the bottle in front of me. "Have a drink and think it over," he said evenly. "You're just making things tough for both of us." I pushed the bottle back. "Very tough," said George. "I want the tags awful bad, Sammy."

I braced myself, but nothing happened. He was a bigger coward than I thought.

George held out the watch, and pushed down the winder with his thumb. "Listen, Sammy—it strikes the hours."

I didn't hear the chimes. All hell cut loose outside—the deafening clank and thunder of tanks, backfiring, and wild, happy singing, with accordions screaming above it all.

"They're here!" I yelled. The war really was over! I could believe it now. I forgot George, Jerry, the watch—everything but the wonderful noise. I ran to the window. Big puffs of smoke and dust billowed up over the wall, and there was a banging on the gate. "This is it!" I laughed.

George yanked me back from the window, and pushed me against the wall. "This is it, all right!" he said. His face was filled with terror. He held a pistol against my chest. George clawed at my dogtag chain, snapped it with a quick jerk.

There was a sharp, splintering noise, a metallic groan, and the gate sprung open. A tank stood in the opening, racing its engine, its huge treads resting against the shattered gate. George turned to face the noise, just as two Russian soldiers slid from roosts atop the tank turret, and trotted into the courtyard, their submachine guns leveled. They looked quickly from window to window, and yelled something I couldn't understand.

"They'll kill us if they see that gun!" I cried.

George nodded. He seemed to be stunned, in a dream. "Yeah," he said, and he threw the gun across the room. It slithered along the bleached floorboards, coming to rest in a dark corner. "Put your hands up, Sammy," he said. He held his hands over his head, his back to me, facing the hallway down which the Russians were stomping. "I must of been crazy drunk, Sammy. I was out of my head," he whispered.

"Sure, George—sure you were."

"We got to stick together through this, Sammy, you hear?"

"Stick through what?" I kept my hands at my sides. "Hey Rooskie, how the hell are you?" I shouted.

The two Russians, rough-looking teen-agers, strutted into the room, their submachine guns ready. Neither one smiled. "Put your hands up!" commanded one in German.

"*Amerikaner*," I said weakly, and I put my hands up.

The two looked surprised, and began consulting in whispers, never taking their eyes off us. They scowled at first, but became more and more jovial as they talked, until they were at last beaming at us. I guess they had had to reassure each other that it was right in line with policy to be friendly with Americans.

"It's a great day for the people," said the one who could speak German, gravely.

"A great day," I agreed. "George, give the boys a drink."

They looked happily at the bottle, and rocked back and forth on their feet, nodding and snickering. They insisted politely that George take the first drink to the great day for the people. George grinned nervously. The bottle was almost to his lips before it slipped from his fingers to bang on the floor, spewing its contents over our feet.

"God, I'm sorry," said George.

I leaned over to pick it up, but the Russians stopped me. "Vodka is better than that German poison," said the German-speaking Russian solemnly, and he drew a large bottle from his blouse. "Roosevelt!" he said, taking a big gulp, and passing the bottle to George.

The bottle went around four times: in honor of Roosevelt, Stalin, Churchill, and of Hitler's roasting in hell. The last toast was my idea. "Over a slow fire," I added. The Russians thought that was pretty rich, but their laughter died instantly when an officer appeared at the gate to bellow for them. They gave us quick salutes, snatched the bottle, and rushed out of the house.

We watched them climb aboard the tank, which backed away from the gate and lumbered down the road. The two of them waved.

The vodka had made me feel fuzzy, hot, and wonderful—and, it turned out, cocky and bloodthirsty. George was almost blind drunk, swaying.

"I didn't know what I was doing, Sammy. I was—" The sentence trailed off. He was making for the corner where his gun lay—surly, weaving, squinting.

I stepped in front of him, and pulled the tiny pistol from my trouser pocket. "Look what I found, Georgie."

He stopped and blinked at it. "Looks like a nice one, Sammy." He held out his hand. "Let's have a look at it."

I snapped off the safety catch. "Sit down, Georgie, old friend."

He sank into the chair where I had sat at the table. "I don't get it," he mumbled. "You wouldn't shoot your old buddy, would you, Sammy?" He looked at me pleadingly. "I offered you a square deal, didn't I? Ain't I always been—"

"You're too bright to think I'd let you get away with this dogtag deal, aren't you? I'm no buddy of yours, and you know it, don't you, Georgie? The only way it'd work would be with me dead. Didn't you figure it that way, too?"

"Everybody's down on old George, ever since Jerry got it. I swear to God, Sammy, I never had anything to do with—" He didn't finish the sentence. George shook his head and sighed.

"Pretty tough about poor old Georgie—not even enough guts to shoot me when you had the chance." I picked up the bottle George had dropped and set it in front of him. "What you need is a good drink. See, George?—three good shots left. Aren't you glad it didn't all spill?"

"Don't want no more, Sammy." He closed his eyes. "Put away that gun, will you? I never meant you no harm."

"I said take a drink." He didn't move. I sat down opposite him, still covering him with the gun. "Give me the watch, George."

He seemed to wake up all of a sudden. "Is that what you're after? Sure, Sammy here it is, if that'll make things square. How can I explain how I get when I'm drunk? I just lose control of myself, kid." He handed me Jerry's watch. "Here, Sammy. After all old Georgie's put you through, God knows you've earned it."

I set the watch hands at noon, and pushed down the winder. The tiny chimes sounded twelve times, striking twice each second.

"Worth a thousand bucks in New York, Sammy," said George thickly, as the chimes rang.

"That's how long you have to drink out of that bottle, George," I said, "as long as it takes the watch to strike twelve."

"I don't get it. What's the big idea?"

I laid the watch on the table. "Like you said, George, it's a funny thing about strychnine—a little of it can save your life." I pushed the winder on the watch again. "Have a drink to Jerry Sullivan, buddy."

The chimes tinkled again. Eight . . . nine . . . ten . . . eleven . . . twelve. The room was quiet.

"O.K., so I didn't drink," said George, grinning. "So what happens now, Boy Scout?"

III.

When I began this story, I said I thought it was a murder story. I'm not sure.

I made it back to the American lines, all right, and I reported that George had killed himself accidentally with a pistol he'd found in a ditch. I signed an affidavit swearing it had happened that way.

What the hell, he was dead, and that was that, wasn't it? Who'd have benefited if I'd told them I shot George? My soul? George's soul, maybe?

Well, Army Intelligence smelled something fishy about the story quick enough. At Camp Lucky Strike, near Le Havre, France, where they had all of the repatriated prisoners of war waiting for boats home, I got called into a tent Intelligence had set up there. I'd been in camp for two weeks, and was due to ship out the next afternoon.

A gray-haired major asked the questions. He had the affidavit in front of him, and he passed over the story about the pistol in the ditch without showing much interest. He quizzed me for quite a while about how George had behaved in prison camp, and he wanted to know exactly what George looked like. He took notes on what I told him.

"Sure you have the name right?" he asked.

"Yessir, and the serial number, too. Here's one of his dogtags, sir. I left the other one with the body. Sorry, sir, I meant to turn this in before now."

The major studied the tag, finally fastened it to the affidavit, and slipped both into a thick folder. I could see George's name written on the outside. "I don't know exactly what to do with this next," he said, toying with the tie-string on the folder. "Quite a guy, George Fisher." He offered me a cigarette. I took it, but I didn't light it right away.

This was it. God knows how, but they'd found out the whole story, I thought. I wanted to yell, but I kept on smiling, my teeth clamped together hard.

The major took his time about phrasing the next sentence. "The tag is a phony," he said at last, smiling a little. "There's nobody by that name missing from the U.S. Army." He leaned forward to light my cigarette. "Maybe we'd better turn this folder over to the Germans so they can notify the next of kin."

I'd never seen George Fisher before they brought him into prison camp alone that day eight months previous, but I should have known the type. I grew up with a couple of kids like him. He must have been a good Nazi to get his job in German Intelligence, because as I said, most of the *Bund* kids didn't do that well. I don't know how many of them got back to the U.S. when the war ended, but my buddy George Fisher damn near made it.

The Commandant's Desk

I WAS SITTING before the window of my small cabinet-making shop in the Czechoslovakian town of Beda. My widowed daughter, Marta, held the curtain back for me, and watched the Americans through one corner of the window, being careful not to block any of my view with her head.

"I wish he would turn this way, so we could see his face," I said impatiently. "Marta, pull the curtain back more."

"Is he a general?" said Marta.

"A general as commandant for Beda?" I laughed. "A corporal, maybe. How well fed they all look, eh? Aaaaaah, they eat—*how* they eat!" I ran my hand along the back of my black cat. "Now, kitty, you have only to cross the street for your first taste of American cream." I raised my hands over my head. "Marta! Do you feel it, do you *feel* it? The Russians are gone, Marta, they're gone!"

And now, we were trying to see the face of the American commandant, who was moving into the building across the street—where the Russian commandant had been a few weeks before. The Americans went inside, kicking their way through rubbish and splintered furniture. For a while, there was nothing to see through my window. I leaned back in my chair and closed my eyes.

"It's over, the killing is all over," I said, "and we're alive. Did you think that was possible? Did anyone in his right mind expect to be alive when it was over?"

"I feel almost as though being alive were something to be ashamed of," she said.

"The world will probably feel that way for a long, long time. You can at least thank God you've come through it all with very little guilt in all the killing. Having been helpless in the middle has that advantage. Think of the guilt on the shoulders of the Americans—a hundred thousand dead in the Moscow bombings, fifty thousand in Kiev—"

"What about the guilt of the Russians?" she said passionately.

"No—not the Russians. That's one of the joys of losing a war. You surrender your guilt along with your capital, and join the ranks of the innocent little people."

The cat rubbed her flanks against my wooden leg and purred. I suppose most men with wooden legs conceal the fact as best they can. I lost my left leg as an Austrian infantryman in 1916, and I wear one trouser leg higher than the other to show off the handsome oak peg I made for myself after World War I. Carved in the peg are the images of Georges Clemenceau, David Lloyd George, and Woodrow Wilson, who helped the Czech Republic rise from the ruins of the Austro-Hungarian Empire in 1919, when I was twenty-five. And below these images are two more, each within a wreath: Tomàš Masaryk and Eduard Beneš, the first leaders of the Republic. There are other faces that should be added, and now, now that peace is with us once again, perhaps I'll carve them. The only carving I've done on the peg in the past thirty years is crude and obscure, and maybe barbaric—three deep nicks near the iron tip, for the three German officers whose car I sent down a mountainside one night in 1943, during the Nazi occupation.

These men across the street weren't the first Americans I'd seen. I owned a furniture factory in Prague during the days of the Republic, and I did a great deal of business with buyers for American department stores. When the Nazis came, I lost my factory, and moved to Beda, this quiet town in the foothills of Sudetenland. My wife died soon after that, of the rarest of causes, the natural ones. Then I had only my daughter, Marta.

Now, praise God, I was seeing Americans again—after the Nazis, after the Russian Army of World War II, after the Czech communists, after the Russians again. Knowing this day was coming had kept me alive. Hidden under the floorboards of my workshop was a bottle of Scotch that had constantly tried my willpower. But I left it in its hiding-place. It was to be my present to the Americans when they finally came.

"They're coming out," said Marta.

I opened my eyes to see a stocky, red-headed American major staring at me from across the street, his hands on his hips. He looked tired and annoyed. Another young man, a captain, tall, massive, and slow, and very Italian-looking except for his stature, strode out of the building to join him.

Stupidly, perhaps, I blinked back at them. "They're coming over here!" I said excitedly, helplessly.

The major and the captain walked in, each looking down at a blue pamphlet, which I gathered contained Czech phrases. The big captain seemed self-conscious, and I sensed that the red-headed major was a little belligerent.

The captain ran his finger down the margin of a page, and shook his head dispiritedly. "'Machine gun, mortar, motorcycle . . . tank, tourniquet, trench.' Nothing about filing cabinets, desks, or chairs."

"What the hell you expect?" said the major. "It's a book for soldiers, not a bunch of pansy clerks." He scowled at the pamphlet, said something completely unintelligible, and looked up at me expectantly. "There's one hell of a swell book," he said. "Says that's the way to ask for an interpreter, and the old man acts like it was Ubangi poetry."

"Gentlemen, I speak English," I said, "and my daughter, Marta, too."

"By God, he really does," said the major. "Good for you, Pop." He made me feel like a small dog, who had cleverly—for a small dog—fetched him a rubber ball.

I held out my hand to the major, and told him my name. He looked down at my hand superciliously, and kept his hands in his pockets. I felt myself reddening.

"My name is Captain Paul Donnini," said the other man quickly, "and this is Major Lawson Evans." He shook my hand. "Sir," he said to me—his voice was paternal and deep—"the Russians—"

The major used an epithet that made my jaw drop, and amazed Marta, who has heard soldiers talk for the better part of her life.

Captain Donnini was embarrassed. "They haven't left a stick of furniture," he continued, "and I'm wondering if you could let us have some of the pieces in your shop here."

"I was going to offer you them," I said. "It's a tragedy they smashed everything. They confiscated the most beautiful furniture in Beda." I smiled and shook my head. "Aaaaah, those enemies of capitalists—they had their quarters fixed up like a little Versailles."

"We saw the wreckage," said the captain.

"And then, when they couldn't have the treasures anymore, then no one could have them." I made a motion like a man swinging an axe. "And the world becomes a little duller for us all—for there being fewer treasures. Bourgeois treasures, maybe, but those who can't afford beautiful things love the idea of there being such things somewhere."

The captain nodded pleasantly, but, to my surprise, I saw that my words had somehow irritated Major Evans.

"Well, anyway," I said, "I want you to take whatever you need. It will be an honor to help you." I was wondering if now was the opportune time to offer the Scotch. Things weren't going quite as I'd expected.

"He's real smart, Pop is," said the major acidly.

I suddenly realized what it was the major had been implying. It was a shock. He was telling me that I was one of the enemy. He meant that I should cooperate because I was afraid; he wanted me to be afraid.

For an instant, I was physically sick. Once, as a much younger and more Christian man, I liked to say that men who depended on fear to get things done were sick and pathetic and pitifully alone. Later, after having seen whole armies of such men in action, I saw that I was the kind that was alone—and maybe sick and pathetic, too, but I would have killed myself rather than admit that.

I had to be wrong about the new commandant. I told myself I'd been suspicious and—now that I'm old, I can say it—afraid too long. But Marta felt the threat, the fear in the air, too, I could tell. She was hiding her warmth, as she had hidden it for years, behind a dull, prim mask.

"Yes," I said, "you are welcome to anything you can use."

The major pushed open the door of the back room, where I sleep and do my work. I was through being host. I sank back down in my chair by the window. Captain Donnini, ill at ease, stayed with Marta and me.

"It's very beautiful here in the mountains," he said lamely.

We lapsed into an uncomfortable silence, broken from time to time by the major's rummaging about in the back room. I took a good look at the captain, and was struck by how much more boyish he seemed than the major, though it was quite possible that they were the same age. It was hard to imagine him on a battlefield, and it was hard to imagine the major anywhere else.

I heard Major Evans give a low whistle, and I knew he'd found the commandant's desk.

"The major must have been a very brave man, he has so many medals," said Marta at last.

Captain Donnini seemed grateful for a chance to explain about his superior. "He was and is an extremely brave man," he said warmly. He said that the major and most of the enlisted men in Beda had come from an apparently famous armored division, which, the captain implied, never knew fear or fatigue, and loved nothing better than a good fight.

I clucked my tongue in wonderment, as I always do when hearing of such a division. I have heard of them from American officers, German officers, Russian officers; and my officers in World War I solemnly declared that I belonged to such a division. When I hear of a division of war-lovers from an enlisted man, maybe I will believe it, provided the man is sober and has been shot at. If there are such divisions, perhaps they should be preserved between wars in dry ice.

"And what about you?" said Marta, breaking into the captain's blood-and-thunder biography of Major Evans.

He smiled. "I'm so new to Europe, I can't—if you'll pardon the expression—find my behind with both hands. The air of Fort Benning, Georgia, is still in my lungs. The major—he's the hero, been fighting for three years without a break."

"And I didn't figure to wind up here as a combination constable, county clerk, and wailing wall," said Major Evans, standing in the doorway of the back room. "Pop, I want this desk. Making it for yourself, were you?"

"What would I do with a desk like that? I was building it for the Russian commandant."

"A friend of yours, eh?"

I tried to smile, unconvincingly, I imagine. "I wouldn't be here to talk to you, if I'd refused to make it. And I wouldn't have been here to talk to *him*, if I hadn't made a bed for the Nazi commandant—with a garland of swastikas and the first stanza of the Horst Wessel Song on the headboard."

The captain smiled with me, but the major didn't. "*This* one is different," said the major. "*He* comes right out and says he was a collaborator."

"I didn't say that," I said evenly.

"Don't spoil it, don't spoil it," said Major Evans, "it's a refreshing change."

Marta suddenly hurried upstairs.

"I was no collaborator," I said.

"Sure, sure—fought 'em every inch of the way. You bet. I know, I know. Come here a minute, will you? I want to talk about my desk."

He was seated on the unfinished desk, an enormous and, to me, hideous piece of furniture. I'd designed it as a private satire on the Russian commandant's bad taste and hypocrisy about symbols of wealth. I'd made it as ornate and pretentious as possible, a Russian peasant's dream of what a Wall Street banker's desk looked like. It glittered with bits of colored glass set like jewels in the wood, and it was highlighted with radiator paint that looked something like gilt. Now it appeared that the satire would have to remain private, for the American commandant was as taken by it as the Russian had been.

"This is what I call a piece of furniture," said Major Evans.

"Very nice," said Captain Donnini absently. He was looking up the stairs, where Marta had fled.

"There's just one thing wrong with it, Pop."

"The hammer and sickle—I know. I was going to take—"

"How right you are," said the major. He drew back his boot, and gave the massive escutcheon a savage kick on its edge. The round piece broke free, rolled drunkenly into a corner, and settled face down with a rowrroworrowrr—clack! The cat investigated it, and backed away suspiciously.

"An eagle goes there, Pop." The major took off his cap to show me the American eagle on it. "Like this one."

"Not a simple design. It'll take a while," I said.

"Not as simple as a swastika or a hammer and sickle, eh?"

I'd dreamed for weeks of sharing the joke of the desk with the Americans, of telling them about the secret drawer I'd built in for the Russian commandant, the richest joke of all. Now, the Americans were here; and I felt little different than before—rotten and lost and lonely. I didn't feel like sharing anything with anyone but Marta.

"No," I said, answering the major's poisonous question. "No, sir." What was I supposed to say?

The Scotch stayed under the floorboards, and the secret drawer in the desk remained a secret.

The American garrison in Beda was about a hundred men, almost all of them, save Captain Donnini, veterans of years of fighting in the same armored division from which Major Evans had come. They behaved like conquerors, with Major Evans encouraging them to do just that. I'd expected a great deal of the coming of the

Americans—a rebirth of pride and dignity for Marta and me; a little prosperity and good things to eat, too; and for Marta, the better part of a lifetime worth living. Instead, there was the bullying distrust of Major Evans, the new commandant, multiplied a hundred times in the persons of his men.

In the nightmare of a warring world, it takes peculiar skills to get along. One of these is the understanding of the psychology of occupation troops. The Russians weren't like the Nazis, and the Americans were very different from either. There wasn't the physical violence of the Russians and Nazis, thank God—no shootings or torture. What was particularly interesting was that the Americans had to get drunk before they could make real trouble. Unfortunately for Beda, Major Evans let them get drunk as often as they liked. When they were drunk, they were fond of stealing—in the name of souvenir hunting—driving jeeps through the street at breakneck speeds, firing guns in the air, shouting obscenities, picking fistfights, and breaking windows.

The people of Beda were so used to keeping silent and out of sight, no matter what happened, that it took us a while to discover the really basic difference between the Americans and the others. The Americans' toughness, callousness, was very shallow, and beneath it was grave misgiving. We discovered that they could be embarrassed easily by women or older men who would stand up to them like parents, and scold them for what they were doing. This sobered most of them up as quickly as buckets of cold water would have.

With that insight into our conquerors, we were able to make things a little more bearable, but not much. There was the crushing realization that we were regarded as the enemy, little different from the Russians, and that the major wanted us punished. The townspeople were organized into labor battalions, and put to work under armed guard, like prisoners of war. What made the labor particularly deadly is that it wasn't concerned with repairing the war damage to the town so much as with making the American garrison's quarters more comfortable, and with building a huge and ugly monument honoring the Americans who had died in the battle for Beda. Four had died. Major Evans made the atmosphere of the town the atmosphere of a prison. Shame was the order of the day, and budding pride or hope was promptly nipped. We weren't entitled to them.

There was one bright spot—an American unhappier than any of us—Captain Donnini. It was up to him to carry out the major's orders, and getting drunk, which he tried several times, didn't do for him what it did for the others. He carried out the orders with a reluctance I'm sure he could have been court-martialed for. Moreover, he spent as much time with Marta and me as he did with the major, and most of his talk with us was a guarded apology for what he had to do. Curiously, Marta and I found ourselves comforting this sad, dark giant, rather than the other way around.

I thought about the major as I stood at my workbench in the back room, finishing up the American eagle for the front of the new commandant's desk. Marta lay on my cot, staring at the ceiling. Her shoes were white with rock dust. She had been working all day on the monument.

"Well," I said gloomily, "if I'd been fighting for three years, I wonder how friendly I would be. Let's face it, whether all of us wanted to or not, we gave men and materials that helped to kill hundreds of thousands of Americans." I gestured at the mountains to the west. "Look where the Russians got their uranium."

"Eye for eye, tooth for tooth," said Marta. "How long does that go on?"

I sighed and shook my head. "The Czechs have paid with interest, God knows. Hand for hand, foot for foot, burning for burning, wound for wound, stripe for stripe." We'd lost most of our young men, Marta's husband among them, in suicide waves before main Russian attacks; and our largest cities were little more than gravel and smoke.

"And, after paying it, we get a new commissar. They're no different from the rest," she said bitterly. "It was childish to expect anything else."

Her terrible disappointment, for which I'd built her up, her apathy and hopelessness—good God in Heaven, I couldn't bear it! And there would be no more liberators. The only strength left anywhere in the world was in America, and the Americans were in Beda.

Dully, I set to work on the American eagle again. The captain had given me a dollar bill from which to copy the insignia. "Let me see—nine, ten, eleven, twelve, thirteen arrows in the claw."

There was a diffident knock on the door, and Captain Donnini walked in. "Pardon me," he said.

"I guess we'll have to," I said. "Your side won the war."

"Afraid I didn't have much to do with it."

"The major didn't leave anybody for the captain to shoot," said Marta.

"What happened to your window?" said the captain.

There was shattered glass all over the floor, and a big piece of cardboard now kept the weather from coming in the window. "It was liberated last night by a beer bottle," I said. "I've written the major a note about it—for which I'll probably be beheaded."

"What's that you're making?"

"An eagle with thirteen arrows in one claw, and an olive branch in the other."

"You're well-off. You could be whitewashing rocks. You were kept off the list, just so you could finish the desk."

"Yes, I saw the rock whitewashers," I said. "With the whitewashed rocks, Beda looks better than it did before the war. You'd never know it had been shelled." The major had ordered that a stirring message be written on his lawn in whitewashed rock: *1402 MP Company, Major Lawson Evans Commanding.* The flower beds and walks were also being outlined in rock.

"Oh, he's not a bad man," said the captain. "It's a miracle he's come through it all as well as he has."

"It's a miracle any of us have come through as well as we have," said Marta.

"Yes, I realize that. I know—you've been through terrible times. But, well, so has the major. He lost his family in the Chicago bombings, his wife and three children."

"I lost my husband in the war," said Marta.

"So what are you trying to tell us—that we're all doing penance for the death of the major's family? Does he think we wanted them killed?" I said.

He leaned against the workbench, and closed his eyes. "Oh hell, I don't know, I don't know. I thought it would help you to understand him—make you not hate him. Nothing makes any sense, though—nothing seems to help."

"Did you think you could help, Captain?" said Marta.

"Before I came over here—yes, I did. Now I know I'm not what's needed, and I don't know what is. I sympathize with everybody, damn it, and see why they are the way they are—you two, all the people in town, the major, the enlisted men. Maybe, if I'd got a bullet through me or had somebody come after me with a flame-thrower, maybe I'd be more of a man."

"And hate like everyone else," said Marta.

"Yes—and be as sure of myself as everybody else seems to be on account of it."

"Not sure—*numb*," I said.

"Numb," he repeated, "everyone has reasons for being numb."

"That's the last defense," said Marta. "Numbness or suicide."

"Marta!" I said.

"You know it's true," she said flatly. "If gas chambers were set up on European street corners, they'd have longer queues than the bakeries. When does all the hate end? Never."

"Marta, for the love of Heaven, I won't have you talking that way," I said.

"Major Evans talks that way, too," said Captain Donnini. "Only he says he wants to go on fighting. Once or twice, when he's been tight, he's said he wished he'd been killed—that there wasn't anything to go home to. He took fantastic chances in the fighting, and never got a scratch."

"Poor man," said Marta, "no more war."

"Well, there's still guerrilla action—a lot of it around Leningrad. He's applied for a transfer there, so he can get into it." He looked down and spread his fingers over his knees. "Well, anyway, what I came to tell you was that the major wants his desk tomorrow."

The door swung open, and the major strode into the workshop. "Captain, where the hell have you been? I sent you on an errand that should have taken five minutes, and you've been gone thirty."

Captain Donnini stood at attention. "Sorry, sir."

"You know how I feel about my men fraternizing with the enemy."

"Yessir."

He confronted me. "Now what's this about your window?"

"One of your men broke it last night."

"Now, isn't that too damn bad?" It was another one of his unanswerable questions. "I said, isn't that too damn bad, Pop?"

"Yes, sir."

"Pop, I'm going to tell you something that I want you to get through your head. And then I want you to make sure everybody else in town understands it."

"Yes, sir."

"You've lost a war. Have you got that? And I'm not here to have you or anybody else cry on my shoulder. I'm here to see that everybody damn well understands they lost a war, and to see that nobody makes trouble. And that's all I'm here for. And the next person who tells me he was a pal of the Russians because he had to be gets his teeth kicked in. And that goes for the next person who tells me he's got it rough. You haven't got it half rough enough."

"Yes, sir."

"It's your Europe," said Marta quietly.

He turned to her angrily. "If it were mine, young lady, I'd have the engineers bulldoze the whole lousy mess flat. Nothing in it but gutless wonders who'll follow any damn dictator that comes along." Again I was struck, as I'd been on the first day, by how awfully tired and distracted he seemed.

"Sir—" said the captain.

"Be quiet. I didn't fight my way here so the Eagle Scouts could take over. Now, where's my desk?"

"I'm finishing the eagle."

"Let's have a look." I handed him the disk. He swore softly, and touched the insignia on his cap. "Like this one," he said. "I want it exactly like this one."

I blinked at the insignia on his cap. "But it is like that one. I copied exactly from a dollar bill."

"The arrows, Pop! Which claw are the arrows in?"

"Oh—on your hat they're in the right claw, on the bill they're in the left."

"All the difference in the world, Pop: one's the Army, the other's for civilians." He raised his knee, and snapped the carving over it. "Try again. You were so anxious to please the Russian commandant, please me!"

"Could I say something?" I said.

"No. All I want to hear from you is that I'll get the desk tomorrow morning."

"But the carving will take days."

"Stay up all night."

"Yes, sir."

He walked out, with the captain at his heels.

"What were you going to tell him?" said Marta, with a wry smile.

"I was going to tell him that the Czechs have fought against the Europe he hates as hard and long as he has. I was going to tell him— Oh well, what's the use?"

"Go on."

"You've heard it a thousand times, Marta. It's a tiresome story, I suppose. I wanted to tell him how I've fought the Hapsburgs and the Nazis, and then the Czech communists, and then the Russians—fought them in my own small ways. Not once have I sided with a dictator, and I never will."

"Better get to work on the eagle. Remember, arrows in the right hand."

"Marta, you've never tasted Scotch, have you?" I dug the claws of a hammer into a crack in the floor, and pried up the board. There lay the dusty bottle of Scotch I had saved for the great day of my dreams.

It was delicious, and the two of us got quite drunk. While I worked, we relived the old days, Marta and I, and for a while it seemed almost as though her mother were alive again, and Marta was a young, pretty, and carefree girl again, and we had our home and friends in Prague again, and . . . Oh God, it was lovely for a little while.

Marta fell asleep on the cot, and I hummed to myself as I chiseled out the American eagle long into the night. It was a crude, slap-dash job, and I covered its faults with putty and the fake gilt.

A few hours before sunrise, I glued the emblem to the desk, applied clamps, and dropped off to sleep. It was ready for the new commandant, exactly, save for the emblem, as I had designed it for the Russian.

They came for the desk early the next morning, a half-dozen soldiers and the captain. The desk looked like a casket for an Oriental potentate as they carried it like pallbearers across the street. The major met them at the door, and cried warnings whenever they threatened to bump the treasure against the doorframe. The door closed, the sentry took up his position before it again, and there was nothing more to see.

I went into my workroom, cleared the shavings from the bench, and began a letter to Major Lawson Evans, 1402 MP Company, Beda, Czechoslovakia.

Dear sir: I wrote, *There is one thing about the desk I neglected to tell you. If you will look just below the eagle, you will find . . .*

I didn't take it across the street right away, although I'd intended to. It made me feel a little sick to read it over—something I never would have felt had it been addressed to the Russian commandant, who was to have received it originally. Thinking about the letter spoiled my lunch, though I haven't had enough to eat for years. Marta was too lost in her own depression to notice, though she scolds me when I don't look out for myself. She took away my untouched plate without a word.

Late in the afternoon, I drank the last of the Scotch, and walked across the street. I handed the envelope to the sentry.

"This another one about the window, Pop?" said the sentry. Apparently the window episode was a joke in wide circulation.

"No, another matter—about the desk."

"O.K., Pop."

"Thanks."

I went back to my workshop, and lay down on my cot to wait. I even managed to nap a little.

It was Marta who awakened me.

"All right, I'm ready," I murmured.

"Ready for what?"

"The soldiers."

"Not the soldiers—the major. He's leaving."

"He's what?" I threw my legs over the side of the cot.

"He's getting into a jeep with all of his equipment. Major Evans is leaving Beda!"

I hurried to the front window, and pulled aside the cardboard. Major Evans was seated in the rear of a jeep, in the midst of duffel bags, a bed roll, and other equipment. One would have thought from his appearance that a battle was raging on the outskirts of Beda. He glowered from beneath a steel helmet, and he had a carbine beside him, and a cartridge belt, knife, and pistol about his waist.

"He got his transfer," I said in wonderment.

"He's going to fight the guerrillas," laughed Marta.

"God help them."

The jeep started. Major Evans waved, and jolted away into the distance. The last I saw of the remarkable man was as the jeep reached the crest of a hill at the town's edge. He turned, thumbed his nose, and was lost from sight in the valley beyond.

Captain Donnini, across the street, caught my eye and nodded.

"Who's the new commandant?" I called.

He tapped his chest.

"What is an Eagle Scout?" whispered Marta.

"Judging from the major's tone, it's something very unsoldierly, naive, and soft-hearted. Shhhh! Here he comes."

Captain Donnini was half solemn, half amused with his new importance.

He lit a cigarette thoughtfully, and looked as though he were trying to phrase something in his mind. "You asked when the end of hate would come," he said at last. "It comes right now. No more labor battalions, no more stealing, no more smashing. I haven't seen enough to hate." He puffed on the cigarette and thought some more. "But I'm sure I can hate the people of Beda as bitterly as Major Evans did if they don't start out tomorrow to rebuild this into a decent place for the children."

He turned quickly, and recrossed the street.

"Captain," I called, "I wrote a letter to Major Evans—"

"He turned it over to me. I haven't read it yet."

"Could I have it back?"

He looked at me questioningly. "Well, all right—it's on my desk."

"The letter is about the desk. There's something I've got to fix."

"The drawers work fine."

"There's a special drawer you don't know about."

He shrugged. "Come on."

I threw some tools into a bag, and hurried to his office. The desk sat in magnificent isolation in the middle of the otherwise spartan room. My letter lay on its top.

"You can read it, if you like," I said.

He opened the letter, and read aloud:

"Dear sir: There is one thing about the desk I neglected to tell you. If you will look just below the eagle, you will find that the oak leaf in the ornamentation can be pressed in and turned. Turn it so that the stem points up at the eagle's left claw. Then, press down on the acorn just above the eagle, and . . ."

As he read, I followed my own directions. I pressed on the leaf and turned it, and there was a click. I pushed the acorn with my thumb, and the front of a small drawer popped out a fraction of an inch, just enough to let a person get a grip on it and pull it out the rest of the way.

"Seems to be stuck," I said. I reached up under the desk, and snipped a strand of piano wire hooked to the back of the drawer. "There!" I pulled the drawer out the rest of the way. "You see?"

Captain Donnini laughed. "Major Evans would have loved it. Wonderful!" Appreciatively, he slid the drawer back and forth several times, wondering at how its front blended so perfectly with the ornamentation. "Makes me wish I had secrets."

"There aren't many people in Europe without them," I said. He turned his back for a moment. I reached under the commandant's desk again, slipped a pin into the detonator, and removed the bomb.

Armageddon in Retrospect

DEAR FRIEND:

May I have a minute of your rime? We have never met, but I am taking the liberty of writing to you because a mutual friend has spoken of you highly as being far above average in intellect and concern for your fellow men.

The impact of each day's news being as great as it is, it is very easy for us to forget quickly major events of a few days before. Let me, then, refresh your memory on an event that shook the world five short years ago, and which is now all but forgotten, save by a few of us. I refer to what has come to be known, for good biblical reasons, as *Armageddon*.

You will remember, perhaps, the hectic beginnings at the Pine Institute. I confess that I went to work as administrator of the Institute with a sense of shame and foolishness, and for no other reason than money. I had many other offers, but the recruiter from the Institute offered to pay me twice as much as the best of them. I was in debt after three years of poverty as a graduate student, so I took the job, telling myself that I would stay one year, pay off my debts and build my savings, get a respectable job, and deny ever after that I'd been within a hundred miles of Verdigris, Oklahoma.

Thanks to this lapse in integrity, I was associated with one of the truly heroic figures of our time, Dr. Gorman Tarbell.

The assets I brought to the Pine Institute were general, chiefly the skills that go with a doctor's degree in business administration. I might as easily have applied these assets to running a tricycle factory or an amusement park. I was not in any way the creator of the theories that brought us to and through Armageddon. I arrived on the scene quite late, when much of the important thinking had been done.

Spiritually, and in terms of sacrifice, the name of Dr. Tarbell should head the list of real contributors to the campaign and victory.

Chronologically, the list should probably begin with the late Dr. Selig Schildknecht, of Dresden, Germany, who spent, by and large fruitlessly, the last half of his life and inheritance in trying to get someone to pay attention to his theories on mental illness. What Schildknecht said, in effect, was that the only unified theory of mental illness that seemed to fit all the facts was the most ancient one, which had never been disproved. He believed that the mentally ill were possessed by the Devil.

He said so in book after book, all printed at his own expense, since no publisher would touch them, and he urged that research be undertaken to find out as much as possible about the Devil, his forms, his habits, his strong points, his weaknesses.

Next on the list is an American, my former employer, Jessie L. Pine of Verdigris. Many years ago, Pine, an oil millionaire, ordered 200 feet of books for his library. The book dealer saw an opportunity to get rid of, among other gems, the collected works of Dr. Selig Schildknecht. Pine assumed that the Schildknecht volumes, since they were in a foreign language, contained passages too hot to be printed in English. So he hired the head of the University of Oklahoma's German Department to read them to him.

Far from being infuriated by the book dealer's selection, Pine was overjoyed. All his life he'd felt humiliated by his lack of education, and here he'd found a man with five university degrees whose fundamental philosophy agreed with his own, to wit: "Onliest thing in the world that's wrong with folks is that the Devil's got aholt of some of 'em."

If Schildknecht had managed to hold on to life a little longer, he wouldn't have died penniless. As it was, he missed the founding of the Jessie L. Pine Institute by only two years. From the moment of that founding on, every spurt from half the oil wells in Oklahoma was a nail in the Devil's coffin. And it was a slow day, indeed, when an opportunist of one sort or another didn't board a train for the marble halls rising in Verdigris.

The list, if I were to continue it, would get rather long, for thousands of men and women, a few of them intelligent and honest, began to explore the paths of research indicated by Schildknecht, while Pine followed doggedly with haversacks of fresh currency. But most of these men and women were jealous, incompetent passengers on one of the greatest gravy trains in history. Their experiments, usually awfully expensive, were principally satires on the ignorance and credulity of their benefactor, Jessie L. Pine.

Nothing would have come of all the millions spent, and I, for one, would have drawn my amazing paycheck without trying to deserve it, if it hadn't been for the living martyr of Armageddon, Dr. Gorman Tarbell.

He was the oldest member of the Institute, and the most reputable—about sixty, heavy, short, passionate, with long white hair, with clothes that made him look as though he spent his nights under bridges. He'd retired near Verdigris after a successful career as a physicist in a large eastern industrial research laboratory. He stopped off at the Institute one afternoon, while on his way to get groceries, to find out what on earth was going on in the impressive buildings.

I was the one who saw him first, and, perceiving him to be a man of prodigious intelligence, I did a rather sheepish job of telling him what the Institute proposed to do. My attitude conveyed that "just between the well-educated pair of us, this is a lot of hooey."

He didn't join me in my condescending smile at the project, however, but asked, instead, to see something of Dr. Schildknecht's writings. I got him the chief volume, that summarized what was said in all the others, and stood by and chuckled knowingly as he scanned it.

"Have you got any spare laboratories?" he said at last.

"Well, yes, as a matter of fact, we do," I said.

"Where?"

"Well, the whole third floor's still unoccupied. The painters are just finishing it off."

"Which room can I have?"

"You mean you want a job?"

"I want peace and quiet and space to work."

"You understand, sir, that the only kind of work that can be done here has to be related to demonology?"

"A perfectly delightful idea."

I looked out into the hallway, to make sure Pine wasn't around, and then whispered, "You really think there might be something to it?"

"What right have I got to think otherwise? Can you prove to me that the Devil doesn't exist?"

"Well, I mean—for heaven's sake, nobody with any education believes in—"

Crack! Down came his cane on my kidney-shaped desk. "Until we prove that the Devil doesn't exist, he's as real as that desk."

"Yessir."

"Don't be ashamed of your job, boy! There's as much hope for the world in what's going on here as there is in anything that's going on in any atomic research laboratory. 'Believe in the Devil,' I say, and we'll go on believing in him unless we get better reasons than we've got for not believing in him. *That's* science!"

"Yessir."

And off he went down the hall to arouse the others, and then up to the third floor to choose his laboratory, and to tell the painters to concentrate on it, that it had to be ready by the next morning.

I trailed him upstairs with a job application form. "Sir," I said, "would you mind filling this out, please?"

He took it without looking at it, and wadded it into his coat pocket, which I saw was bulging like a saddle-bag with crumpled documents of one sort and another. He never did fill out the application, but created an administrative nightmare by simply moving in.

"Now, sir, about salary," I said, "how much would you want?"

He waved the question aside impatiently. "I'm here to do research, not keep the books."

A year later, *The First Annual Report of the Pine Institute* was published. The chief accomplishment seemed to be that $6,000,000 of Pine's money had been put back into circulation. The press of the Western World called it the funniest book of the year, and reprinted passages that proved it. The Communist press called it the gloomiest book of the year, and devoted columns to the tale of the American billionaire who was trying to make direct contact with the Devil in order to increase his profits.

Dr. Tarbell was untroubled. "We are now at the point at which the physical sciences once were with respect to the structure of the atom," he said cheerfully. "We have some ideas that are little more than matters of faith. Perhaps they're laughable, but it's ignorant and unscientific to laugh until we've had some time to experiment."

Lost among the pages and pages of nonsense in the *Report* were three hypotheses suggested by Dr. Tarbell:

That, since many cases of mental illness were cured by electric shock treatment, the Devil might find electricity unpleasant; that, since many mild cases of mental illness were cured by lengthy discussions of personal pasts, the Devil might be repelled by endless talk of sex and childhood; that the Devil, if he existed, seemingly took possession of people with varying degrees of tenacity—that he could be talked out of some patients, could be shocked out of others, and that he couldn't be driven out of some without the patients' being killed in the process.

I was present when a newspaper reporter quizzed Tarbell about these hypotheses. "Are you kidding?" said the reporter.

"If you mean that I offer these ideas in a playful spirit, yes."

"Then you think they're hokum?"

"Stick to the word 'playful,'" said Dr. Tarbell. "And, if you'll investigate the history of science, my dear boy, I think you'll find that most of the really big ideas have come from intelligent playfulness. All the sober, thin-lipped concentration is really just a matter of tidying up around the fringes of the big ideas."

But the world preferred the word "hokum." And, in time, there were laughable pictures to go with the laughable stories from Verdigris. One was of a man wearing a headset that kept a small electric current going through his head, that was supposed to make him an uncomfortable resting place for the Devil. The current was said to be imperceptible, but I tried on one of the headsets, and found the sensation extremely unpleasant. Another photogenic experiment, I recall, was of a mildly deranged person talking about her past while under a huge glass bell-jar, which, it was hoped, might catch some detectable substance of the Devil, who was theoretically being evicted bit by bit. And on and on the picture possibilities went, each seemingly more absurd and expensive than the last.

And then came what I called *Operation Rat-hole*. Because of it, Pine was obliged to look at his bank balance for the first time in years. And what he saw sent him prospecting for new oilfields. Because of the frightful expense involved, I opposed the undertaking. But, over my objections, Dr. Tarbell convinced Pine that the only way to test Devil theories was to experiment with a large group of people. Operation Rat-hole, then, was an attempt to make Nowata, Craig, Ottawa, Delaware, Adair, Cherokee, Wagoner, and Rogers counties Devil-free. As a check, Mayes County, in the midst of the others, was to be left unprotected.

In the first four counties, 97,000 of the headsets were passed out, to be worn, for a consideration, night and day. In the last four, centers were set up where persons were to come in, for a consideration, at least twice a week to talk their hearts out about their pasts. I turned over management of these centers to an assistant. I couldn't bear the places, where the air was forever filled with self-pity and the dullest laments imaginable.

Three years leter, Dr. Tarbell handed Jessie L. Pine a confidential progress report on the experiments, and then went to the hospital with a case of exhaustion. He had made the report tentative, had warned Pine not to show it to anyone until more work—much more—had been done.

It came as a terrible shock to Tarbell when, on the radio in his hospital room, he heard an announcer introduce Pine on a coast-to-coast network, and he heard Pine say, after an incoherent preamble:

"Ain't been a person possessed by the Devil in these here eight counties we been protecting. Plenty of old cases, but ain't no new ones, 'cept five that was tongue-tied and seventeen that let their batteries go dead. Meanwhile, smack spang in the middle, we let the Mayes County folks take care of theirselves the best they could, and they been goin' to hell regular as ever. . . .

"Trouble with the world is and always has been the Devil," concluded Pine. "Well, we done run him out of northeastern Oklahoma, 'cept for Mayes County, and I figure we can run him out of there, too, and clean off the face of the earth. Bible says there's gonna be a great battle 'tween good and evil by and by. Near's I can figure, this here's it."

"The old fool!" cried Tarbell. "My Lord, *now* what's going to happen?"

Pine couldn't have chosen another instant in history when his announcement would have set off a more explosive response. Consider the times: the world, as though by some malevolent magic, had been divided into hostile halves, and had begun a series of moves and countermoves that could only, it seemed, end in disaster. Nobody knew what to do. The fate of humanity seemed out of the control of human beings. Every day was filled with desperate helplessness, and with worse news than that of the day before.

Then, from Verdigris, Oklahoma, came the announcement that the trouble with the world was that the Devil was at large. And with the announcement came an offer of proof and a suggested solution!

The sigh of relief that went up from the earth must have been heard in other galaxies. The trouble with the world wasn't the Russians or the Americans or the

Chinese or the British or the scientists or the generals or the financiers or the politicians, or, praise be to God, human beings anywhere, poor things. People were all right, and decent and innocent and smart, and it was the Devil who was making their good-hearted enterprises go sour. Every human being's self-respect increased a thousand-fold, and no one, save the Devil, lost face.

Politicians of all lands rushed to the microphones to declare themselves as being against the Devil. Editorial pages everywhere took the same fearless stand—against the Devil. Nobody was for him.

In the United Nations, the small nations introduced a resolution to the effect that the big nations all join hands, like the affectionate children they really were at heart, and chase their only enemy, the Devil, away from earth forever.

For many months following Pine's announcement, it was almost necessary to boil a grandmother or run berserk with a battle-axe in an orphanage to qualify for space on the front page of a newspaper. All the news was about Armageddon. Men who had entertained their readers with whimsical accounts of the Verdigris activities became, overnight, sober specialists in such matters as Bratpuhrian Devil-gongs, the efficacy of crosses on bootsoles, the Black Mass, and allied lore. The mails were jammed as badly as at Christmastime with letters to the U.N., Government officials, and the Pine Institute. Almost everybody, apparently, had known all along that the Devil was the trouble with everything. Many said they'd seen him, and almost all of them had pretty good ideas for getting rid of him.

Those who thought the whole thing was crazy found themselves in the position of a burial insurance salesman at a birthday party, and most of them shrugged and kept their mouths shut. Those who didn't keep their mouths shut weren't noticed anyway.

Among the doubters was Dr. Gorman Tarbell. "Good heavens," he said ruefully, "we don't know what we've proved in the experiments. They were just a beginning. It's years too soon to say whether we were doing a job on the Devil or what. Now Pine's got everybody all whooped up to thinking all we have to do is turn on a couple of gadgets or something, and earth'll be Eden again." Nobody listened.

Pine, who was bankrupt anyway, turned over the Institute to the U.N., and UNDICO, the United Nations Demonological Investigating Commitee, was formed. Dr. Tarbell and I were named as American delegates to the Committee, which held its first meeting in Verdigris. I was elected Chairman, and, as you might expect, I was subjected to a lot of poor jokes about my being the perfect man for the job because of my name.

It was very depressing for the Committee to have so much expected—demanded, even—of them, and to have so little knowledge with which to work. Our mandate from the people of the world wasn't to prevent mental illness, but to eliminate the Devil. Bit by bit, however, and under terrific pressure, we mapped a plan, drawn up, for the most part, by Dr. Tarbell.

"We can't promise anything," he said. "All we can do is take this opportunity for world-wide experiments. The whole thing is assumptions, so it won't hurt anything to assume a few things more. Let's assume that the Devil is like an epidemic disease, and go to work on him accordingly. Maybe, if we make it impossible for him to find a comfortable place in anybody anywhere, he'll disappear or die or go to some other planet, or whatever it is the Devil does, if there is a Devil."

We estimated that to equip every man, woman, and child with one of the electric headsets would cost about $20,000,000,000, and about $70,000,000,000 more a year for batteries. As modern wars go, the price was about right. But we soon found that people weren't inclined to go that high for anything less than killing each other.

The Tower of Babel technique, then, seemed the more practical. Talk is cheap. Hence, UNDICO's first recommendation was that centers be set up all over the world, and that people everywhere be encouraged in one way or another, according to native methods of coercion—an easy buck, or a bayonet, or fear of damnation—to come regularly to these centers to unburden themselves about childhood and sex.

Response to this first recommendation, this first sign that UNDICO was really going to go after the Devil in a businesslike fashion, revealed a deep undercurrent of uneasiness in the flood of enthusiasm. There was hedging on the part of many leaders, and vague objections were raised in fuzzy terms like "running counter to our great national heritage for which our forefathers sacrificed unflinchingly at . . ." No one was imprudent enough to want to seem a protector of the Devil, but, all the same, the kind of caution recommended by many in high places bore a strong resemblance to complete inaction.

At first, Dr. Tarbell thought the reaction was due to fear—fear of the Devil's retaliation for the war we wanted to make on him. Later, after he'd had time to study the opposition's membership and statements, he said gleefully, "By golly, they think we've got a chance. And they're all scared stiff they won't have a chance of being so much as a dogcatcher if the Devil isn't at large in the populace."

But, as I said, we felt that we had less than a chance in a trillion of changing the world much more than one whit. Thanks to an accident and the undercurrent of opposition, the odds soon jumped to an octillion to one.

Shortly after the Committee's first recommendation, the accident happened. "Any fool knows the quick and easy way to get rid of the Devil," whispered one American delegate to another one in the U.N. General Assembly. "Nothing to it. Just blow him to hell in his headquarters in the Kremlin." He couldn't have been more mistaken in thinking the microphone before him was dead.

His comment was carried over the public address system, and was dutifully translated into fourteen languages. The Russian delegation walked out, and telegraphed home for a suitable reaction. Two hours later, they were back with a statement:

"The people of the Union of Soviet Socialist Republics hereby withdraw all support of the United Nations Demonological Investigating Committee as being an internal affair

of the United States of America. Russian scientists are in full agreement with the findings of the Pine Institute as to the presence of the Devil throughout the United States. Using the same experimental techniques, these scientists have found no signs whatsoever of the Devil's activities within the boundaries of the U.S.S.R, and, hence, consider the problem as being uniquely American. The people of the U.S.S.R wish the people of the United States of America success in their difficult enterprise, that they may all the sooner be ready for full membership in the family of friendly nations."

In America, the instant reaction was to declare that any effort on UNDICO's part in this country would mean a further propaganda victory for Russia. Other nations followed suit, declaring themselves to be already Devil-free. And that was that for UNDICO. Frankly, I was relieved and delighted. UNDICO was beginning to look like a real headache.

That was that for the Pine Institute, too, for Pine was dead broke, and had no choice but to close the doors at Verdigris. When the closing was announced, the hundreds of phonies who'd found wealth and relaxation in Verdigris stormed my office, and I fled to Dr. Tarbell's laboratory.

He was lighting his cigar with a hot soldering iron when I entered. He nodded, and squinted through the cigar smoke at the dispossessed demonologists milling around in the courtyard below. "About time we got rid of the staff so we could get some work done."

"We're canned, too, you know."

"Right now I don't need money," said Tarbell. "Need electricity."

"Hurry up, then—the last check I sent the Power and Light Company was as rubber as your overshoes. What is that thing you're working on, anyway?"

He soldered a connection to the copper drum, which was about four feet high and six feet in diameter, and had a lid on the top. "Going to be the first M.I.T. alumnus to go over Niagara Falls in a barrel. Think there's a living in it?"

"Seriously."

"Such a sober boy. First read me something aloud. That book there—see the bookmark?"

The book was a classic in the field of magic, Sir James George Frazer's *The Golden Bough*. I opened it to the bookmark, and found a passage underlined, the passage describing the Mass of Saint Sécaire, or the Black Mass. I read it aloud:

"'The Mass of Saint Sécaire may be said only in a ruined or deserted church, where owls mope and hoot, where bats flit in the gloaming, where gypsies lodge of nights, and where toads squat under the desecrated altar. Thither the bad priest comes by night . . . and at the first stroke of eleven he begins to mumble the mass backwards, and ends just as the clocks are knelling the midnight hour. . . . The host he blesses is black and has three points; he consecrates no wine, but instead he drinks the water of a well into which the body of an unbaptized infant has been flung. He makes the sign of the cross, but it is on the ground and with his left foot.

And many other things he does which no good Christian could look upon without being struck blind and deaf and dumb for the rest of his life.' Phew!" I said.

"Supposed to bring the Devil like a fire alarm box brings the hook-and-ladder," said Dr. Tarbell.

"Surely you don't think it'd really work?"

He shrugged. "I haven't tried." The lights suddenly went out. "That's that," he sighed, and laid down the soldering iron. "Well, there's nothing more we can do here. Let's go out and find an unbaptized infant."

"Won't you tell me what the drum is for?"

"Perfectly self-evident. It's a Devil-trap, of course."

"Naturally." I smiled uncertainly, and backed away from it. "And you're going to bait it with Devil's-food cake."

"One of the major theories to come out of the Pine Institute, my boy, is that the Devil is completely indifferent to Devil's-food cake. However, we're sure he's anything but indifferent to electricity, and, if we could pay the light bill, we could make electricity flow through the walls and lid of this drum. So, all we have to do, once the Devil is inside, is to throw the switch and we've got him. Maybe. Who knows? Who was ever crazy enough to try it? But first, as the recipe for rabbit stew goes, catch your rabbit."

I'd hoped I'd seen the end of demonology for a while, and was looking forward to moving on to other things. But Dr. Tarbell's tenacity inspired me to stay with him, to see where his "intelligent playfulness" would lead next.

And, six weeks later, Dr. Tarbell and I, pulling the copper drum along on a cart, and laying wire from a spool on my back, were picking our way down a hillside at night, down to the floor of the Mohawk Valley, in sight of the lights of Schenectady.

Between us and the river, catching the full moon's image and casting it into our eyes, was an abandoned segment of the old Erie Ship Canal, now useless, replaced by channels dredged in the river, filled with still, brackish water. Beside it lay the foundations of an old hotel, that had once served the bargemen and travelers on the now forgotten ditch.

And beside the foundations was a roofless frame church.

The old steeple was silhouetted against the night sky, resolute, indomitable, in a parish of rot and ghosts. As we entered the church, a tugboat pulling barges somewhere up the river sounded its horn, and the voice came to us, echoing through the architecture of the valley, funereal, grave.

An owl hooted, and a bat whirred over our heads. Dr. Tarbell rolled the drum to a spot before the altar. I connected the wires I'd been stringing to a switch, and connected the switch, through twenty feet more of wire, to the drum. The other end of the line was hooked into the circuits of a farmhouse on the hillside.

"What time is it?" whispered Dr. Tarbell.

"Five of eleven."

"Good," he said weakly. We were both scared stiff. "Now listen, I don't think anything at all's going to happen, but, if it does—I mean to us—I've left a letter at the farmhouse."

"That makes two of us," I said. I seized his arm. "Look—what say we call it off," I pleaded. "If there really is a Devil, and we keep trying to corner him, he's sure to turn on us—and there's no telling what he'd do!"

"You don't have to stay," said Tarbell. "I could work the switch, I guess."

"You're determined to go through with it?"

"Terrified as I am," he said.

I sighed heavily. "All right. God help you. I'll man the switch."

"O.K.," he said, smiling wanly, "put on your protective headset, and let's go."

The bells in a steeple clock in Schenectady started striking eleven.

Dr. Tarbell swallowed, stepped to the altar, brushed aside a squatting toad, and began the grisly ceremony.

He had spent weeks reading up on his role and practicing it, while I had gone in search of a proper site and the grim props. I hadn't found a well in which an unbaptized infant had been flung, but I'd found other items in the same category that seemed gruesome enough to be satisfactory substitutes in the eyes of the most depraved demon.

Now, in the name of science and humanity, Dr. Tarbell put his whole heart into the performance of the Mass of Saint Sécaire, doing, with a look of horror on his face, what no good Christian could look upon without being struck blind and deaf and dumb.

I somehow survived with my senses, and sighed with relief as the clock in Schenectady knelled twelve.

"Appear, Satan!" shouted Dr. Tarbell as the clock struck. "Hear your servants, Lord of Night, and appear!"

The clock struck for the last time, and Dr. Tarbell slumped against the altar, exhausted. He straightened up after a moment, shrugged, and smiled. "What the hell," he said, "you never know until you try." He took off his headset.

I picked up a screwdriver, preparing to disconnect the wires. "And that, I hope, really winds up UNDICO and the Pine Institute," I said.

"Well, still got a few more ideas," said Dr. Tarbell. And then he howled.

I looked up to see him wide-eyed, leering, trembling all over. He was trying to say something, but all that came out was a strangled gurgle.

Then began the most fantastic struggle any man will ever see. Dozens of artists have tried to paint the picture, but, bulging as they paint Tarbell's eyes, red as they paint his face, knotted as they paint his muscles, they can't recapture a splinter of the heroism of Armageddon.

Tarbell dropped to his knees, and, as though straining against chains held by a giant, he began to inch toward the copper drum. Sweat soaked his clothes, and he could only pant and grunt. Time and again, as he would pause to catch his breath, he was pulled back by invisible forces. And again he would rise to his knees, and toil forward over the lost ground and inches beyond.

At last he reached the drum, stood with stupendous effort, as though lifting bricks, and tumbled into the opening. I could hear him scratching against the insulation inside, and his breathing was amplified in the chamber, awing.

I was stupefied, unable to believe or understand what I'd seen, or to know what to do next.

"Now!" cried Dr. Tarbell from within the drum. His hand appeared for a moment, pulled the lid shut, and once more he cried, sounding far away and weak, "Now."

And then I understood, and began to quake, and a wave of nausea passed over me. I understood what it was he wanted me to do, what he was asking with the last fragment of his soul that was being consumed by the Devil in him.

So I locked the lid from the outside, and I closed the switch.

Thank heaven Schenectady was nearby. I telephoned a professor of electrical engineering from Union College, and, inside of three-quarters of an hour, he had devised and installed a crude air-lock, through which air and food and water could be gotten to Dr. Tarbell, but which always kept an electrified, Devil-proof barrier between him and the outside.

Certainly the most heartbreaking aspect of the tragic victory over the Devil is the deterioration of Dr. Tarbell's mind. There is nothing left of that splendid instrument. Instead, there is something that uses his voice and body, that wheedles and tries to gain sympathy and freedom by shouting, among other bitter lies, that Tarbell was dumped into the drum by me. If I may say so, my own role has not been without pain and sacrifice.

Since the Tarbell affair is, alas, controversial, and since, for propaganda reasons, our country cannot officially admit that the Devil was caught here, the Tarbell Protective Foundation is without Government subsidies. The expense of maintaining the Devil-trap and its contents has been borne by donations from public-spirited individuals like yourself.

The expenditures and proposed expenditures of the Foundation are extremely modest in proportion to value received by all humanity. We have done no more in the way of improving the physical plant than seemed absolutely necessary. The church has been roofed and painted and insulated and fenced in, and rotting timbers have been replaced by sound ones, and a heating system and an auxiliary generating system have been installed. You will agree that all of these items are essential.

However, despite the limits we have placed on our spending, the Foundation finds that its treasury is badly depleted by the inroads of inflation. What we had laid aside for small improvements has been absorbed in bare maintenance. The Foundation employs a skeleton staff of three paid caretakers, who work in shifts around the clock, feeding Dr. Tarbell, keeping away thrill-seekers, and maintaining the vital electrical equipment. This staff cannot be cut without inviting the incomparable disaster of Armageddon's victory's turning to defeat in a single, unguarded instant. The directors, myself included, serve without compensation.

Because there is a larger need, beyond mere maintenance, we must go in search of new friends. That is why I am writing to you. Dr. Tarbell's immediate quarters have been enlarged since those first nightmarish months in the drum, and now comprise a copper-walled, insulated chamber eight feet in diameter and six feet high. But this is, you will admit, a poor home for what remains of Dr. Tarbell. We have hopes of being able, through open hearts and hands such as yours, to expand his quarters to include a small study, bedroom, and bath. And recent research indicates that there is every hope of giving him a current-carrying picture window, though the cost will be great.

But whatever the cost, we can make no sacrifices in scale with what Dr. Tarbell has done for us. And, if the contributions from new friends like you are great enough, we hope, in addition to expanding Dr. Tarbell's quarters, to be able to erect a suitable monument outside the church, bearing his likeness and the immortal words he wrote in a letter hours before he vanquished the Devil:

"*If I have succeeded tonight, then the Devil is no longer among men. I can do no more. Now, if others will rid the earth of vanity, ignorance, and want, mankind can live happily ever after.—Dr. Gorman Tarbell.*"

No contribution is too small.

Respectfully yours,
Dr. Lucifer J. Mephisto
Chairman of the Board

The Petrified Ants

I.

"This *is* quite a hole you have here," said Josef Broznik enthusiastically, gripping the guard rail and peering into the echoing blackness below. He was panting from the long climb up the mountain slope, and his bald head glistened with perspiration.

"A remarkable hole," said Josef's twenty-five-year-old brother, Peter, his long, big-jointed frame uncomfortable in fog-dampened clothes. He searched his thoughts for a more profound comment, but found nothing. It was a perfectly amazing hole—no question about it. The officious mine supervisor, Borgorov, had said it had been sunk a half mile deep on the site of a radioactive mineral water spring. Borgorov's enthusiasm for the hole didn't seem in the least diminished by the fact that it had produced no uranium worth mining.

Peter studied Borgorov with interest. He seemed a pompous ass of a young man, yet his name merited fear and respect whenever it was mentioned in a gathering of miners. It was said, not without awe, that he was the favorite third cousin of Stalin himself, and that he was merely serving an apprenticeship for much bigger things.

Peter and his brother, Russia's leading myrmecologists, had been summoned from the University of Dnipropetrovsk to see the hole—or, rather, to see the fossils that had come out of it. Myrmecology, they had explained to the hundred-odd guards who had stopped them on their way into the area, was that branch of science devoted to the study of ants. Apparently, the hole had struck a rich vein of petrified ants.

Peter nudged a rock the size of his head and rolled it into the hole. He shrugged and walked away from it, whistling tunelessly. He was remembering again the humiliation of a month ago, when he had been forced to apologize publicly for his paper on *Raptiformica sanguinea*, the warlike, slave-raiding ants found under hedges. Peter had presented it to the world as a masterpiece of scholarship and scientific method, only to be rewarded by a stinging rebuke from Moscow. Men who couldn't tell *Raptiformica sanguinea* from centipedes had branded him an ideological backslider with dangerous tendencies toward Western decadence. Peter clenched and unclenched his fists, angry, frustrated. In effect, he had had to apologize because the ants he had studied would not behave the way the top Communist scientific brass wanted them to.

"Properly led," said Borgorov, "people can accomplish anything they set their minds to. This hole was completed within a month from the time orders came down from Moscow. Someone very high dreamed we would find uranium on this very spot," he added mysteriously.

"You will be decorated," said Peter absently, testing a point on the barbed wire around the opening. His reputation had preceded him into the area, he supposed. At any rate, Borgorov avoided his eyes, and addressed his remarks always to Josef—Josef the rock, the dependable, the ideologically impeccable. It was Josef who had advised against publishing the controversial paper, Josef who had written his apology. Now, Josef was loudly comparing the hole to the Pyramids, the Hanging Gardens of Babylon, and the Colossus of Rhodes.

Borgorov rambled on tiresomely, Josef agreed warmly, and Peter allowed his gaze and thoughts to wander over the strange new countryside. Beneath his feet were the *Erzgebirge*—the Ore Mountains, dividing Russian-occupied Germany from Czechoslovakia. Gray rivers of men streamed to and from pits and caverns gouged in the green mountain slopes—a dirty, red-eyed horde burrowing for uranium . . .

"When would you like to see the fossil ants we found?" said Borgorov, cutting into his thoughts. "They're locked up now, but we can get at them anytime tomorrow. I've got them all arranged in the order of the levels we found them in."

"Well," said Josef, "the best part of the day was used up getting cleared to come up here, so we couldn't get much done until tomorrow morning anyway."

"And yesterday, and the day before, and the day before that, sitting on a hard bench, waiting for clearance," said Peter wearily. Instantly he realized that he had said something wrong again. Borgorov's black eyebrows were raised, and Josef was glaring. He had absentmindedly violated one of Josef's basic maxims—"Never complain in public about anything." Peter sighed. On the battlefield he had proved a thousand times that he was a fiercely patriotic Russian. Yet, he now found his countrymen eager to read into his every word and gesture the symptoms of treason. He looked at Josef unhappily, and saw in his eyes the same old message: Grin and agree with everything.

"The security measures are marvelous," said Peter, grinning. "It's remarkable that they were able to clear us in only three days, when you realize how thorough a job they do." He snapped his fingers. "Efficiency."

"How far down did you find the fossils?" said Josef briskly, changing the subject.

Borgorov's eyebrows were still arched. Plainly, Peter had only succeeded in making himself even more suspicious. "We hit them going through the lower part of the limestone, before we came to the sandstone and granite," he said flatly, addressing himself to Josef.

"Middle Mesozoic period, probably," said Josef. "We were hoping you'd found fossil ants deeper than that." He held up his hands. "Don't get us wrong. We're delighted that you found these ants, it's only that middle Mesozoic ants aren't as interesting as something earlier would be."

"Nobody's ever seen a fossil ant from an earlier period," said Peter, trying half-heartedly to get back into things. Borgorov ignored him.

"Mesozoic ants are just about indistinguishable from modern ants," said Josef, surreptitiously signaling for Peter to keep his mouth shut. "They lived in big colonies, were specialized as soldiers and workers and all that. My myrmecologist would give his right arm to know how ants lived before they formed colonies—how they got to be the way they are now. That *would* be something."

"Another first for Russia," said Peter. Again no response. He stared moodily at a pair of live ants who pulled tirelessly and in opposite directions at the legs of an expiring dung beetle.

"Have you *seen* the ants we found?" said Borgorov defensively. He waved a small tin box under Josef's nose. He popped off the lid with his thumbnail. "Is this old stuff, eh?"

"Good heavens," murmured Josef. He took the box tenderly, held it at arm's length so that Peter could see the ant embedded in the chip of limestone.

The thrill of discovery shattered Peter's depression. "An inch long! Look at that noble head, Josef! I never thought I would see the day when I would say an ant was handsome. Maybe it's the big mandibles that make ants homely." He pointed to where the pincers ordinarily were. "This one has almost none, Josef. It *is* a pre-Mesozoic ant!"

Borgorov assumed a heroic stance, his feet apart, his thick arms folded. He beamed. This wonder had come out of *his* hole.

"Look, look," said Peter excitedly. "What is that splinter next to him?" He took a magnifying glass from his breast pocket and squinted through the lens. He swallowed. "Josef," he said hoarsely, "you look and tell me what you see."

Josef shrugged. "Some interesting little parasite maybe, or a plant, perhaps." He moved the chip up under the magnifying glass. "Maybe a crystal or—" He turned pale. Trembling, he passed the glass and fossil to Borgorov. "Comrade, you tell us what you see."

"I see," said Borgorov, screwing up his face in florid, panting concentration. He cleared his throat and began afresh. "I see what looks like a fat stick."

"Look closer," said Peter and Josef together.

"Well, come to think of it," said Borgorov, "it does look something like a—for goodness sake—like a—" He left the sentence unfinished, and looked up at Josef perplexedly.

"Like a bass fiddle, Comrade?" said Josef.

"Like a bass fiddle," said Borgorov, awed . . .

II.

A drunken, bad-tempered card game was in progress at the far end of the miners' barracks where Peter and Josef were quartered. A thunderstorm boomed and slashed outside. The brother myrmecologists sat facing each other on their bunks, passing their amazing fossil back and forth and speculating as to what Borgorov would bring from the storage shed in the morning.

Peter probed his mattress with his hand—straw, a thin layer of straw stuffed into a dirty white bag and laid on planks. Peter breathed through his mouth to avoid drawing the room's dense stench through his long, sensitive nose. "Could it be a child's toy bass fiddle that got washed into that layer with the ant somehow?" he said. "You know this place was once a toy factory."

"Did you ever hear of a toy bass fiddle, let alone one that size? It'd take the greatest jeweler in the world to turn out a job like that. And Borgorov swears there wasn't any way for it to get down that deep—not in the past million years, anyway."

"Which leaves us one conclusion," said Peter.

"One." Josef sponged his forehead with a huge red handkerchief.

"Something could be worse than *this* pigpen?" said Peter. Josef kicked him savagely as a few heads raised up from the card games across the room. "Pigpen," laughed a small man as he threw his cards down and walked to his cot. He dug beneath his mattress and produced a bottle of cognac. "Drink, Comrade?"

"Peter!" said Josef firmly. "We left some of our things in the village. We'd better get them right away."

Gloomily, Peter followed his brother out into the thunderstorm. The moment they were outside, Josef seized him by the arm and steered him into the slim shelter of the eaves. "Peter, my boy, Peter—when are you going to grow up?" He sighed heavily, implored with upturned palms. "When? That man is from the police." He ran his stubby fingers over the polished surface where hair had once been.

"Well, it *is* a pigpen," said Peter stubbornly.

Josef threw up his hands with exasperation. "Of course it is. But you don't have to tell the police you think so." He laid his hand on Peter's shoulder. "Since your reprimand, anything you say can get you into terrible trouble. It can get us both into terrible trouble." He shuddered. "Terrible."

Lightning blazed across the countryside. In the dazzling instant, Peter saw that the slopes still seethed with the digging horde. "Perhaps I should give up speaking altogether, Josef."

"I ask only that you think out what you say. For your own good, Peter. Please, just stop and think."

"Everything you've called me down for saying has been the truth. The paper I had to apologize for was the truth." Peter waited for a rolling barrage of thunder to subside. "I mustn't speak the truth?"

Josef peered apprehensively around the corner, squinted into the darkness beneath the eaves. "You mustn't speak certain kinds of truth," he whispered, "not if you want to go on living." He dug his hands deep in his pockets, hunched his shoulders. "Give in a little, Peter. Learn to overlook certain things. It's the only way."

Together, without exchanging another word, the brothers returned to the glare and suffocation of the barracks, their feet making sucking noises in their drenched shoes and socks.

"Too bad all our things are locked up until morning, Peter," said Josef loudly.

Peter hung his coat on a nail to dry, dropped heavily on his hard bunk, and pulled his shoes off. His movements were clumsy, his nerves dulled by a vast aching sensation of pity, of loss. Just as the lightning had revealed for a split second the gray men and gouged mountainsides—so had this talk suddenly revealed in a merciless flash the naked, frightened soul of his brother. Now Peter saw Josef as a frail figure in a whirlpool, clinging desperately to a raft of compromises. Peter looked down at his unsteady hands. "It's the only way," Josef had said, and Josef was right.

Josef pulled a thin blanket over his head to screen out the light. Peter tried to lose himself in contemplation of the fossil ant again. Involuntarily, his powerful fingers clamped down on the white chip. The chip and priceless ant snapped in two. Ruefully, Peter examined the faces of the break, hoping to glue them together again. On one of the faces he saw a tiny gray spot, possibly a mineral deposit. Idly, he focused his magnifying glass on it.

"Josef!"

Sleepily, Josef pushed the blanket away from his face. "Yes, Peter?"

"Josef, look."

Josef stared through the lens for fully a minute without speaking. When he spoke, his tone was high, uneven. "I don't know whether to laugh or cry or wind my watch."

"It looks like what I think it looks like?"

Josef nodded. "A book, Peter—a book."

III.

Josef and Peter yawned again and again, and shivered in the cold twilight of the mountain dawn. Neither had slept, but their bloodshot eyes were quick and bright-looking, impatient, excited. Borgorov teetered back and forth on his thick boot soles, berating a soldier who was fumbling with the lock on a long toolshed.

"Did you sleep well in your quarters?" Borgorov asked Josef solicitously.

"Perfectly. It was like sleeping on a cloud," said Josef.

"I slept like a rock," said Peter brightly.

"Oh?" said Borgorov quizzically. "Then you don't think it was a pigpen after all, eh?" He didn't smile when he said it.

The door swung open, and two nondescript German laborers began dragging boxes of broken limestone from the shed. Each box, Peter saw, was marked with a number, and the laborers arranged them in order along a line Borgorov scratched in the dirt with his iron-shod heel.

"There," said Borgorov. "That's the lot." He pointed with a blunt finger. "One, two, and three. Number one is from the deepest layer—just inside the limestone— and the rest were above it in the order of their numbers." He dusted his hands and sighed with satisfaction, as though he himself had moved the boxes. "Now, if you'll excuse me, I'll leave you to work." He snapped his fingers, and the soldier marched the two Germans down the mountainside. Borgorov followed, hopping twice to get in step.

Feverishly, Peter and Josef dug into box number one, the one containing the oldest fossils, piling rock fragments on the ground. Each built a white cairn, sat beside it, tailor-fashion, and happily began to sort. The dismal talk of the night before, Peter's fall from political grace, the damp cold, the breakfast of tepid barley mush and cold tea—all were forgotten. For the moment, their consciousnesses were reduced to the lowest common denominator of scientists everywhere—overwhelming curiosity, blind and deaf to everything but the facts that could satisfy it.

Some sort of catastrophe had apparently caught the big, pincerless ants in their life routine, leaving them to be locked in rock just as they were until Borgorov's diggers broke into their tomb millions of years later. Josef and Peter now stared incredulously at evidence that ants had once lived as individuals—individuals with a culture to rival that of the cocky new masters of Earth, men.

"Any luck?" asked Peter.

"I've found several more of our handsome, big ants," replied Josef. "They don't seem to be very sociable. They're always by themselves. The largest group is three. Have you broken any rocks open?"

"No, I've just been examining the surfaces." Peter rolled over a rock the size of a good watermelon, and scanned its underside with his magnifying glass. "Well, wait, here's something, maybe." He ran his finger over a dome-shaped projection of a hue slightly different than that of the stone. He tapped around it gently with a hammer, painstakingly jarring chips loose. The whole dome emerged at last, bigger than his fist, free and clean—windows, doors, chimney, and all. "Josef," said Peter. His voice cracked several times before he could finish the sentence. "Josef—they lived in houses." He stood, with the rock cradled in his arms, an unconscious act of reverence.

Josef now peered over Peter's shoulder, breathing down his neck. "A lovely house."

"Better than ours," said Peter.

"Peter!" warned Josef. He looked around apprehensively.

The hideous present burst upon Peter again. His arms went limp with renewed anxiety and disgust. The rock crashed down on the others. The dome-shaped house, its interior solid with limestone deposits, shattered into a dozen wedges.

Again the brothers' irresistible curiosities took command. They sank to their knees to pick over the fragments. The more durable contents of the house had been locked in rock for eons, only now to meet air and sunlight. The perishable furnishings had left their impressions.

"Books—dozens of them," said Peter, turning a fragment this way and that to count the now-familiar rectangular specks.

"And here's a painting. I swear it is!" cried Josef.

"They'd discovered the wheel! Look at this wagon, Josef!" A fit of triumphant laughing burst from Peter. "Josef," he gasped, "do you realize that we have made the most sensational discovery in history? Ants once had a culture as rich and brilliant as ours. Music! Painting! Literature! Think of it!"

"And lived in houses—aboveground, with plenty of room, and lots of air and sunshine," said Josef raptly. "And they had fire and cooked. What could this be but a stove?"

"Millions of years before the first man—before the first gorilla, chimp, or orangutan, or even the first monkey, Josef—the ants had everything, *everything*." Peter stared ecstatically into the distance, shrinking in his imagination down to the size of a finger joint and living a full, rich life in a stately pleasure dome all his own.

It was high noon when Peter and Josef had completed a cursory examination of the rocks in box number one. In all, they found fifty-three of the houses, each different—some large, some small, varying from domes to cubes, each one a work of individuality and imagination. The houses seemed to have been spaced far apart, and rarely were they occupied by more than a male and a female and young.

Josef grinned foolishly, incredulously. "Peter, are we drunk or crazy?" He sat in silence, smoking a cigarette and periodically shaking his head. "Do you realize it's lunchtime? It seems as though we've been here about ten minutes. Hungry?"

Peter shook his head impatiently, and began digging through the second box—fossils from the next layer up, eager to solve the puzzle of how the magnificent ant civilization had declined to the dismal, instinctive ant way of life of the present.

"Here's a piece of luck, Josef—ten ants so close together I can cover them with my thumb." Peter picked up rock after rock, and, wherever he found one ant, he found at least a half dozen close by. "They're starting to get gregarious."

"Any physical changes?"

Peter frowned through his magnifying glass. "Same species, all right. No, now, wait—there *is* a difference, the pincers are more developed, considerably more developed. They're starting to look like modern workers and soldiers." He handed a rock to Josef.

"Mmmm, no books here," said Josef. "You find any?"

Peter shook his head, and found that he was deeply distressed by the lack of books, searching for them passionately. "They've still got houses, but now they're jammed with people." He cleared his throat. "I mean ants." Suddenly a cry of joy escaped him. "Josef! Here's one without the big pincers, just like the ones in the lower level!" He turned the specimen this way and that in the sunlight. "By himself, Josef. In his house, with his family and books and everything! Some of the ants are differentiating into workers and soldiers—some aren't!"

Josef had been reexamining some of the gatherings of the ants with pincers. "The gregarious ones may not have been interested in books," he announced. "But every-where that you find them, you find pictures." He frowned perplexedly. "There's a bizarre twist, Peter; the picture lovers evolving away from the book lovers."

"The crowd lovers away from the privacy lovers," said Peter thoughtfully. "Those with big pincers away from those without." To rest his eyes, he let his gaze wander to the toolshed and a weathered poster from which the eyes of Stalin twinkled. Again he let his gaze roam, this time into the distance—to the teeming mouth of the nearest mine shaft, where a portrait of Stalin beamed paternally on all as they shambled in and out; to a cluster of tar-paper barracks below, where a portrait of Stalin stared shrewdly, protected from the weather by glass, at the abominable san-itary facilities.

"Josef," Peter began uncertainly, "I'll bet tomorrow's tobacco ration that those works of art the pincered ants like so well are political posters."

"If so, our wonderful ants are bound for an even higher civilization," said Josef enigmatically. He shook rock dust from his clothing. "Shall we see what is in box number three?"

Peter found himself looking at the third box with fear and loathing. "*You* look, Josef," he said at last.

Josef shrugged. "All right." He studied the rocks in silence for several minutes. "Well, as you might expect, the pincers are even more pronounced, and—"

"And the gatherings are bigger and more crowded, and there are no books, and the posters are as numerous as the ants!" Peter blurted suddenly.

"You're quite right," said Josef.

"And the wonderful ants without pincers are gone, aren't they, Josef?" said Peter huskily.

"Calm down," said Josef. "You're losing your head over something that happened a thousand thousand years ago—or more." He tugged thoughtfully at his earlobe. "As a matter of fact, the pincerless ants do seem extinct." He raised his eyebrows. "As far as I know, it's without precedent in paleontology. Perhaps those without pincers were susceptible to some sort of disease that those with pincers were immune to. At any rate, they certainly disappeared in a hurry. Natural selection at its ruggedest—survival of the fittest."

"Survival of the somethingest," said Peter balefully.

"No! Wait, Peter. We're both wrong. Here is one of the old type ants. And another and another! It looks like they were beginning to congregate, too. They're all packed together in one house, like matchsticks in a box."

Peter took the rock fragment from him, unwilling to believe what Josef said. The rock had been split by Borgorov's diggers so as to give a clean cross section through the ant-packed house. He chipped away at the rock enclosing the other side of the house. The rock shell fell away. "Oh," he said softly, "I see." His chippings had revealed the doorway of the little building, and guarding it were seven ants with pincers like scythes. "A camp," he said, "a reeducation camp."

Josef blanched at the word, as any good Russian might, but regained his composure after several hard swallows. "What is that starlike object over there?" he said, steering away from the unpleasant subject.

Peter chiseled the chip in which the object was embedded free from the rest of the rock, and held it out for Josef to contemplate. It was a sort of rosette. In the center was a pincerless ant, and the petals looked like warriors and workers with their weapons buried and locked in the flesh of the lone survivor of the ancient race. "There's your quick evolution, Josef." He watched his brother's face intently, yearning for a sign that his brother was sharing his hectic thoughts, his sudden insight into their own lives.

"A great curiosity," said Josef evenly.

Peter looked about himself quickly. Borgorov was struggling up the path from far below. "It's no curiosity, and you know it, Josef," said Peter. "What happened to those ants is happening to us."

"Hush!" said Josef desperately.

"We're the ones without pincers, Josef. We're done. We aren't made to work and fight in huge hordes, to live by instinct and nothing more, perpetuating a dark, damp anthill without the wits even to wonder why!"

They both fell into red-faced silence as Borgorov navigated the last hundred yards. "Come now," said Borgorov, rounding the corner of the toolshed, "our samples couldn't have been as disappointing as all that."

"It's just that we're tired," said Josef, giving his ingratiating grin. "The fossils are so sensational we're stunned."

Peter gently laid the chip with the murdered ant and its attackers embedded in it on the last pile. "We have the most significant samples from each layer arranged in these piles," he said, pointing to the row of rock mounds. He was curious to see what Borgorov's reaction might be. Over Josef's objections, he explained about two kinds of ants evolving within the species, showed him the houses and books and pictures in the lower levels, the crowded gatherings in the upper ones. Then, without offering the slightest interpretation, he gave Borgorov his magnifying glass, and stepped back.

Borgorov strolled up and down the row several times, picking up samples and clucking his tongue. "It couldn't be more graphic, could it?" he said at last.

Peter and Josef shook their heads.

"Obviously," said Borgorov, "what happened was this." He picked up the chip that showed the bas-relief of the pincerless ant's death struggle with countless warriors. "There were these lawless ants, such as the one in the center, capitalists who attacked and exploited the workers—ruthlessly killing, as we can see here, scores at a time." He set down the melancholy exhibit, and picked up the house into which the pincerless ants were crammed. "And here we have a conspiratorial meeting of the lawless ants, plotting against the workers. Fortunately"—and he pointed to the soldier ants outside the door—"their plot was overheard by vigilant workers.

"So," he continued brightly, holding up samples from the next layer, a meeting of the pincered ants and the home of a solitary ant, "the workers held democratic indignation meetings, and drove their oppressors out of their community. The capitalists, overthrown, but with their lives spared by the merciful common people, were soft and spoiled, unable to survive without the masses to slave for them. They could only dillydally with the arts. Hence, put on their own mettle, they soon became extinct." He folded his arms with an air of finality and satisfaction.

"But the order was just the reverse," objected Peter. "The ant civilization was wrecked when some of the ants started growing pincers and going around in mobs. You can't argue with geology."

"Then an inversion has taken place in the limestone layer—some kind of upheaval turned it upside down. Obviously." Borgorov sounded like sheathed ice. "We have the most conclusive evidence of all—the evidence of logic. The sequence could only have been as I described it. Hence, there *was* an inversion. Isn't that so?" he said, looking pointedly at Josef.

"Exactly, an inversion," said Josef.

"Isn't that so?" Borgorov wheeled to face Peter.

Peter exhaled explosively, slouched in an attitude of utter resignation. "Obviously, Comrade." Then he smiled, apologetically. "Obviously, Comrade," he repeated . . .

EPILOGUE

"Good Lord, but it's cold!" said Peter, letting go of his end of the saw and turning his back to the Siberian wind.

"To work! To work!" shouted a guard, so muffled against the cold as to look like a bundle of laundry with a submachine gun sticking out of it.

"Oh, it could be worse, much worse," said Josef, holding the other end of the saw. He rubbed his frosted eyebrows against his sleeve.

"I'm sorry you're here, too, Josef," said Peter sadly. "I'm the one who raised his voice to Borgorov." He blew on his hands. "I guess that's why we're here."

"Oh, that's all right," sighed Josef. "One stops thinking about such things. One stops thinking. It's the only way. If we didn't belong here, we wouldn't be here."

Peter fingered a limestone chip in his pocket. Embedded in it was the last of the pincerless ants, ringed by his murderers. It was the only fossil from Borgorov's hole that remained above the surface of the earth. Borgorov had made the brothers write a report on the ants as he saw them, had had every last fossil shoveled back into the bottomless cavity, and had shipped Josef and Peter to Siberia. It was a thorough piece of work, not likely to be criticized.

Josef had pushed aside a pile of brush, and was now staring with fascination at the bared patch of earth. An ant emerged furtively from a hole, carrying an egg. It ran around in crazy circles, then scurried back into the darkness of the tiny earth womb. "A marvelous adjustment ants have made, isn't it, Peter?" said Josef enviously. "The good life—efficient, uncomplicated. Instinct makes all the decisions." He sneezed. "When I die, I think I'd like to be reincarnated as an ant. A modern ant, not a capitalist ant," he added quickly.

"What makes you so sure you aren't one?" said Peter.

Josef shrugged off the jibe. "Men could learn a lot from ants, Peter, my boy."

"They have, Josef, they have," said Peter wearily. "More than they know."

Atrocity Story

OURS WAS THE LAST large group of freed American P.O.W.s to go through Camp Lucky Strike, near Le Havre, on our way home. There were no formations to make after we got a clothing issue and partial pay, so we divided our time between eating, sleeping and drinking eggnogs at the Red Cross Club. It was a hot afternoon and I was half-asleep when Jones came in to see me.

"I was talking to this lieutenant in the War Crimes tent," he said, "and he was pretty surprised when I told him about Malloti. He'd never heard about it so I guess none of the other boys reported it when they came through. I told him all I knew about it and said I'd bring you and Donnini up. He wants to see you right away."

I woke Jim up and the three of us went to the War Crimes Commission tent. Jones, Donnini and myself had been together in a work group of 150 Americans in Dresden—or 149 after they shot Steve Malloti for plundering. Donnini had been our aid man in Dresden, though he hadn't been a medic in the Army, and had delivered a German baby during the biggest raid on Dresden.

A first lieutenant sat behind a plain wooden table with a T-5 male stenographer beside him. He thanked Jones for bringing us and motioned for us to sit down. I noticed that he was a Coast Artillery Officer. He started asking questions as soon as we were seated. The T-5 recorded our answers on a mimeographed War Crimes Commission form.

"Now what was this boy's name again?"

"Stephen Malloti," Jim told him, and spelled it wrong. I corrected the spelling. The T-5 looked irritated when he had to erase.

"And he was from . . ."

"East Pittsburgh," Jim and I said together. The lieutenant said for just one of us to do the talking so I shut up. "He was in the 106th with us when we got captured in the Bulge; I or L Company, I think, in the 423rd," Jim went on. He turned to me for confirmation. "I wouldn't swear to it," I said. "It seems to me that it was more like K or M in the 422nd." The T-5 was very burned up at this.

"Hmmm," mused the lieutenant. A colonel, evidently in charge, had come up and was standing behind Jones's chair, listening. "When did Malloti die?"

"Must have been about the fifteenth of March, wasn't it?" Jones and I nodded. It must have been about then, because I was in the hospital and Hall had come down and told me all about it. Hall knew more about it than any of us because he was one of the four who had to dig Steve's grave; but he had already left for the States so we had to piece together the story as best we could. The T-5 shook his head as he recorded the vague details.

"Why was he shot?" asked the colonel.

I was afraid Jim would tell it all wrong, but he did a good job: "Well they had us working in the streets of Dresden after the big raid, cleaning up. We were not getting anything much to eat so we used to slip off one at a time to look in the cellars of bombed-out buildings for food. Sometimes we'd find potato bins or jars of cherries and marmalade and carrots and turnips and stuff like that. Our guards all knew we were doing it but they never said much because we used to find them a bottle of something now and then. But one day, Steve was just coming out of a cellar when a bunch of police caught him and searched him. He had half a jar of string beans under his jacket." The T-5 had stopped writing: there were no blanks on his mimeographed sheet for this type of testimony.

"And they arrested him," put in the lieutenant, who had heard the story from Jones. "When did you see him again?"

"None of us here ever saw him again. About two weeks after they caught him, the guards picked four out of our Kommando to go out and bury him. Those four guys were the only ones that ever saw him again." We gave him the names of the four. The T-5 wrote them down under "Remarks."

"Now, just what happened that morning?"

Jim was unquestioned spokesman: "Well, these four guys had to get up earlier than the rest of us. The bombing had wrecked the transportation system so they walked about eight miles to a rifle range on the opposite side of town. Just before they got there they met Steve. Four guards with rifles and a non-com were with him."

"Did he seem scared?" asked the colonel.

"No. Hall and the other guys that saw him said he was pretty calm. He asked them where they were going and they laughed and said it was some kind of lousy pick-and-shovel detail but that they didn't know what. They didn't know at the time. Steve laughed back and said he'd heard the war was about over."

"So he didn't know what was going to happen to him. Is that right?" The T-5, suddenly interested, to the surprise of everyone, asked that.

"Either that, or he was an awfully brave man," Jim said. In talking it over later, we decided that the truth was that Steve did know and was an awfully brave man.

"What else did those four boys say about the shooting?" asked the lieutenant.

"Not much more, except that he was shot in the back and had a terrible look on his face when the shooting was over and the guards made them come and drag the body around to where they'd dug the grave. The grave was behind kind of a bunker so they didn't see them do it. All they heard was the shots. He didn't have a coffin or anything. His grave was marked with a board. It had his name on it, and the reason he was shot. One of the guys said a prayer for him. There wasn't a chaplain."

"Anything else?"

"Well, I don't suppose it makes much difference to you guys. I mean it's probably for the Russians to handle and not your line; but those four guys had to dig two graves. The other one was for a Russian who got shot just before Steve. They said he got it for swiping a box of matches out of a bombed building. I don't know whether that's true or not."

"What sort of a trial did Malloti get?"

"That's hard to say because none of us got to see him. But we were living with the South Africans at that time and their leader got in on part of the trial. He said that the whole thing was being run in German, and that, without any counsel, Steve had crossed himself up on his testimony several times. At the end he signed a paper that said he was guilty of plundering. Steve didn't know any German. It's hard to say whether he knew what he was doing or not."

"Then he was legally tried and convicted?" said the colonel.

"Hell yes, I suppose so," said Jim, getting a little mad, "But it wasn't a fair trial, and, for Christ's sake, sir, all he did was swipe a jar of beans because he was hungry."

The colonel shook his head from side to side, making clucking noises with his tongue against his teeth. "Did you know that you could be shot for plundering?" The T-5 nodded his head in admiration of this legal wisdom. The lieutenant was rankled but kept his mouth shut.

"Yes," we all admitted, "but we were hungry as hell. We had to eat—sir."

"That may be," said the colonel, moving up to the table in order to pound on it as he made his point, "but you knew, and Malloti knew that, if you got caught stealing from cellars, you could be shot for it. Malloti, as I understand it, was caught red-handed, tried, convicted and shot. That, I'm afraid, does not constitute a war crime." He smiled like Mr. Chips.

Jones, Donnini and I got up together. "Is that all, sir?" Jones asked the lieutenant.

The lieutenant looked embarrassed. "Yes, I guess so."

"We may want you later to get some more facts for the sake of the records," added the colonel. "We'll let you know."

As we walked out into the bright sunlight we could hear the colonel explaining to the lieutenant and the T-5, "You see, they did it perfectly legally and there's no doubt but what the boy was guilty."

"You know what?" said Jones.

"No, what?" said Jim.

"It's a good goddamn thing they shot a Russian the same day."

"Yeah," said Jim. "They'll string up every Jerry within fifty miles of that rifle range for doing it."

Women

In a May 19, 1950, letter to his college friend Miller Harris, who had published a story of his own in *Harper's*, Vonnegut complained that "I can never get a woman into my stories." In a 1974 interview with Joe David Bellamy and John Casey, Kurt said, "It has never worried me but it is puzzling that I've never been able to do women well in a book. Part of it is that I'm a performer when I write. I am taking off on different characters, and I frequently have a good English accent and the characters I do well in my books are parts I can play easily. If it were dramatized, I would be able to do my best characters on stage, and I don't make a very good female impersonator."

Three years later in a *Playboy* interview, he seemed to have given up "puzzling" about his inability "to do women well" and accepted it. He tells the interviewer "I try to keep deep love out of my stories because, once that particular subject comes up, it is almost impossible to talk about anything else. Readers don't want to hear about anything else. They go gaga about love. If a lover in a story wins his true love, that's the end of the tale, even if World War III is about to begin, and the sky is black with flying saucers."

Vonnegut is more interested in creating the story, the *plot*, in his short stories than in developing the characters—either women *or* men—who move the story forward. The plot is his forte in writing short stories, and in the process he is also giving an accurate portrayal of the middle class he is writing for in the 1950s, reflecting its customs, its hopes and dreams, and slipping in his own critiques of the culture.

Vonnegut's self-assessment as lacking the power to create credible women characters does not mean he is a woman hater. In fact, more than most male writers of popular magazine fiction of the time, he skewers the men that the women have to put up with, and shines a light on the men's failure to understand the frustrations of their wives and girlfriends. In his non-romantic short stories that feature women (except for the much-divorced movie star Gloria Hilton in "Go Back to Your Precious Wife and Son") the women are portrayed as sympathetic—not because of their looks, but because of their actions. The men in their lives, however, are mostly shown to be real jerks—stupid, insensitive, and boorish. The main exception to this menagerie of male piggishness is a one-eyed gnome, who writes romantic letters to lonely women, insisting they never be so crass as to exchange snapshots, and leaves them in the end with their fantasies intact, believing that their long-distance lover deserted them only in his untimely death ("Out, Brief Candle").

The biggest jerk of all in these stories we have put in the "Women" category is Earl "Hotbox" Sullivan, the model railroad hobbyist of "With His Hand on the Throttle." In his mid-thirties he is becoming rich building roads, but his non-working life is consumed in operating—and adding on to—his elaborate model railroad layout in the basement. Earl's own mother, who's become an ally of his wife, says of his model railroad obsession, "It's like being mother to a dope fiend." Earl's "pusher" is the salesman of model train equipment, who brings him an expensive new model locomotive that is "twinkling like a tiara."

Earl spends so much time in the basement, wearing his conductor's cap and engineering his trains over bridges and through tunnels, that he hasn't taken "his pretty young wife" out to dinner in four months. His wife and mother can't even get him to come upstairs on time to have a nice lunch they've prepared on a Saturday.

He complains to his supplier friend, "I don't think they [women] spend ten seconds a year trying to see things from a man's point of view." Like all the men who neglect their wives in the stories of love and romance, Earl feels he has done his marital duty by working "ten, twelve hours a day . . . Where do you suppose the money's coming from to pay for this house and this food and the cars—for clothes? I love my wife, and I work like hell for her." In the end, only his mother's ire makes him realize he'd better not cancel still another night out with his wife just to play more railroading games. He never really does "get it" about his wife's needs, but takes her out just to make peace.

That was no doubt the way many men of the fifties solved their marital disputes—a method that no doubt remains in play in our own "enlightened" era, though that as well as many other man-woman conflicts has increasingly been resolved by divorce. It's a reflection of the times when Vonnegut was writing his magazine stories that only one of them deals with divorce—and that is the one about a movie star who is about to leave her fifth husband ("Go Back to Your Precious Wife and Son"). Except for that, divorce is not part of the plot of these stories.

The stories are accurate reflections of the time in which they were written. In my own childhood and adolescence in the forties and fifties in Indianapolis, the same place where Kurt grew up, I never knew of any friends whose parents were divorced. One boy in my grade school lived with his mother—the father was never mentioned, and it was assumed in whispers that he must have "run off" with another woman, or simply fled to escape marriage and fatherhood. You didn't ask. One of the social shocks of my childhood came when I was ten years old, and my mother announced to me and my conservative father (we were both shocked) that she had invited "a divorced woman" to come to dinner. I remember thinking, "She must be sexy." As it turned out, I was right. She even wore an ankle bracelet! A year or so later she moved to Hollywood, and sent us back snapshots of herself, posing in the stances of starlets, though we never saw her on the screen, or in *Photoplay* or the other popular "movie magazines" my mother brought home.

The frustrated question of Earl, the model railroad junkie, expresses the sentiments of the majority of men of the time on women's rights: "They got the vote and free access to all the saloons. What do they want now—to enter the men's shot put?"

By the turn of the new century, the answer would be a resounding "Yes!"

No women in these stories of the fifties that are representative of their times play any sport. Tennis might have been acceptable, but mainly in the upper classes, and that is not the audience of the popular weekly magazines of the era.

Vonnegut sees through the superficiality of the chauvinism of the bachelor seducer in "Little Drops of Water," and has him outwitted by a woman who disrupts his routines and seduces him out of bachelorhood. In "Hundred-Dollar Kisses" Vonnegut takes a swipe at the allure of men's magazines (including *Playboy* and its imitators of the time, like *Nugget*) with the concluding line that "everybody pays attention to pictures of things. Nobody pays attention to the things themselves." The "things" are the women. That story was rejected by the magazines of Kurt's era, and appeared in the posthumous volume *While Mortals Sleep*.

There is only one Vonnegut story of women or romance in which the woman in the story is not satisfied with being a housewife. That story, "Lovers Anonymous," was published in the women's magazine *Redbook* in 1963—the same year that *The Feminine Mystique* was published. This story may be the first fictional account of the cultural effect of that book—the social equivalent of the first atomic bomb.

"Sheila Hinckley," says the narrator, "was a pretty, intelligent woman practically all the men in my particular age group wanted to marry . . . Sheila had been the smartest girl in high school, and had been going like a house afire at the University of Vermont, too." Her admirers had "assumed there wasn't any point in serious courting until she'd finished college."

When Sheila quits college in the middle of her junior year and marries Herb, her old admirers declare themselves a band of "eternal sufferers" and form a permanent "Brotherhood of People Who Were Too Dumb to Realize That Sheila Hinckley Might Actually Want to Be a Housewife." They name themselves "Lovers Anonymous."

These suffering admirers, along with her husband, are also too dumb to realize that she might someday also want to be more than that! The readers must forgive them, for few other males of their time would have imagined such a thing either—at least not until *The Feminine Mystique* came out—or, as the book that Sheila is reading is called, *Woman, the Wasted Sex, or, The Swindle of Housewifery*.

The narrator—another one of Vonnegut's salesmen of "combination aluminum storm windows and screens"—goes to the local lending library to see what the book that Sheila is carrying around is all about. After reading the book's table of contents, he returns it to the librarian and tells her, "You can throw this piece of filth down the nearest sewer."

"It's a very popular book," she says.

After reading the book, Sheila decides her brain has "turned to mush" and she wants to go back to college. Her husband moves out and makes a separate house for himself in the "ell" attachment to their main house. He doesn't do it out of anger, but out of guilt for wasting his wife's intelligence on "keeping house for a small-town bookkeeper who hardly even finished high school."

Since the woman must share the guilt, too, and sympathize with her husband, Sheila realizes her husband has "been a slave all his life, doing things he hated in order to support his mother, and then me, and then me and the girls" (they have two daughters).

After reading *Woman, the Wasted Sex, or, The Swindle of Housewifery*, Sheila decides to go back to college and finish her degree—not with the goals she set in her high school yearbook: "discover a new planet or be the first woman justice of the Supreme Court or president of a company that manufactured fire engines." To put the 1963 readers of *Redbook* at ease—especially the husbands who might read the story—Sheila doesn't aspire to those goals that the high school boys joked about—she decides to be a teacher (the principal approved occupation, along with nursing, for women in the pre–*Feminine Mystique* days).

In the coda to the story, the aluminum window salesman takes a copy of *Woman, the Wasted Sex, or, The Swindle of Housewifery* to a lunch with his pals and one of them asks,

> "You didn't let your wife read this, did you?"
> "Certainly," I said.
> "She'll walk out on you and the kids . . . and become a rear admiral."

That was a preposterous idea in 1963.

Kurt had no way to know that nine years after his story (and *The Feminine Mystique*) was published, Rear Admiral Alene B. Duerk became the first woman admiral in the US Navy. In another ten years Sandra Day O'Conner became the first woman Supreme Court justice, fulfilling the second high school dream of Sheila Hinckley. There are no records of the first woman president of a company that manufactures fire engines, but I have no doubt she is out there. Vonnegut's story gives the first glimpse that a popular middle-class magazine gives its readers of the shock waves created by *The Feminine Mystique*, and the new world to come.

—DW

Miss Temptation

PURITANISM HAD FALLEN into such disrepair that not even the oldest spinster thought of putting Susanna in a ducking stool; not even the oldest farmer suspected that Susanna's diabolical beauty had made his cow run dry.

Susanna was a bit-part actress in the summer theater near the village, and she rented a room over the firehouse. She was a part of village life all summer, but the villagers never got used to her. She was forever as startling and desirable as a piece of big-city fire apparatus.

Susanna's feathery hair and saucer eyes were as black as midnight. Her skin was the color of cream. Her hips were like a lyre, and her bosom made men dream of peace and plenty for ever and ever. She wore barbaric golden hoops on her shell-pink ears, and around her ankles were chains with little bells on them.

She went barefoot and slept until noon every day. And, as noon drew near, the villagers on the main street would grow as restless as beagles with a thunderstorm on the way.

At noon, Susanna would appear on the porch outside her room. She would stretch languidly, pour a bowl of milk for her black cat, kiss the cat, fluff her hair, put on her earrings, lock her door, and hide the key in her bosom.

And then, barefoot, she would begin her stately, undulating, titillating, tinkling walk—down the outside stairway, past the liquor store, the insurance agency, the real-estate office, the diner, the American Legion post, and the church, to the crowded drugstore. There she would get the New York papers.

She seemed to nod to all the world in a dim, queenly way. But the only person she spoke to during her daily walk was Bearse Hinkley, the seventy-two-year-old pharmacist.

The old man always had her papers ready for her.

"Thank you, Mr. Hinkley. You're an angel," she would say, opening a paper at random. "Now, let's see what's going on back in civilization." While the old man would watch, fuddled by her perfume, Susanna would laugh or gasp or frown at items in the paper—items she never explained.

Then she would take the papers, and return to her nest over the firehouse. She would pause on the porch outside her room, dip her hand into her bosom, bring out the key, unlock the door, pick up the black cat, kiss it again, and disappear inside.

The one-girl pageant had a ritual sameness until one day toward the end of summer, when the air of the drugstore was cut by a cruel, sustained screech from a dry bearing in a revolving soda-fountain stool.

The screech cut right through Susanna's speech about Mr. Hinkley's being an angel. The screech made scalps tingle and teeth ache. Susanna looked indulgently in the direction of the screech, forgiving the screecher. She found that the screecher wasn't a person to be indulged.

The screech had been made by the stool of Cpl. Norman Fuller, who had come home the night before from eighteen bleak months in Korea. They had been eighteen months without war—but eighteen months without cheer, all the same. Fuller had turned on the stool slowly, to look at Susanna with indignation. When the screech died, the drugstore was deathly still.

Fuller had broken the enchantment of summer by the seaside—had reminded all in the drugstore of the black, mysterious passions that were so often the mainsprings of life.

He might have been a brother, come to rescue his idiot sister from the tenderloin; or an irate husband, come to a saloon to horsewhip his wife back to where she belonged, with the baby. The truth was that Corporal Fuller had never seen Susanna before.

He hadn't conciously meant to make a scene. He hadn't known, consciously, that his stool would screech. He had meant to underplay his indignation, to make it a small detail in the background of Susanna's pageant—a detail noticed by only one or two connoisseurs of the human comedy.

But the screech had made his indignation the center of the solar system for all in the drugstore—particularly for Susanna. Time had stopped, and it could not proceed until Fuller had explained the expression on his granite Yankee face.

Fuller felt his skin glowing like hot brass. He was comprehending destiny. Destiny had suddenly given him an audience, and a situation about which he had a bitter lot to say.

Fuller felt his lips move, heard the words come out. "Who do you think you are?" he said to Susanna.

"I beg your pardon?" said Susanna. She drew her newspapers about herself protectively.

"I saw you come down the street like you were a circus parade, and I just wondered who you thought you were," said Fuller.

Susanna blushed gloriously. "I—I'm an actress," she said.

"You can say that again," said Fuller. "Greatest actresses in the world, American women."

"You're very nice to say so," said Susanna uneasily.

Fuller's skin glowed brighter and hotter. His mind had become a fountain of apt, intricate phrases. "I'm not talking about theaters with seats in 'em. I'm talking about the stage of life. American women act and dress like they're gonna give you the world. Then, when you stick out your hand, they put an ice cube in it."

"They do?" said Susanna emptily.

"They do," said Fuller, "and it's about time somebody said so." He looked challengingly from spectator to spectator, and found what he took to be dazed encouragement. "It isn't fair," he said.

"What isn't?" said Susanna, lost.

"You come in here with bells on your ankles, so's I'll have to look at your ankles and your pretty pink feet," said Fuller. "You kiss the cat, so's I'll have to think about how it'd be to be that cat," said Fuller. "You call an old man an angel, so's I'll have to think about what it'd be like to be called an angel by you," said Fuller. "You hide your key in front of everybody, so's I'll have to think about where that key is," said Fuller.

He stood. "Miss," he said, his voice full of pain, "you do everything you can to give lonely, ordinary people like me indigestion and the heeby-jeebies, and you wouldn't even hold hands with me to keep me from falling off a cliff."

He strode to the door. All eyes were on him. Hardly anyone noticed that his indictment had reduced Susanna to ashes of what she'd been moments before. Susanna now looked like what she really was—a muddle-headed nineteen-year-old clinging to a tiny corner of sophistication.

"It isn't fair," said Fuller. "There ought to be a law against girls acting and dressing like you do. It makes more people unhappy than it does happy. You know what I say to you, for going around making everybody want to kiss you?"

"No," piped Susanna, every fuse in her nervous system blown.

"I say to you what you'd say to me, if I was to try and kiss you," said Fuller grandly. He swung his arms in an umpire's gesture for "out." "The hell with you," he said. He left, slamming the screen door.

He didn't look back when the door slammed again a moment later, when the patter of running bare feet and the wild tinkling of little bells faded away in the direction of the firehouse.

◎ ◎ ◎

That evening, Corporal Fuller's widowed mother put a candle on the table, and fed him sirloin steak and strawberry shortcake in honor of his homecoming. Fuller ate the meal as though it were wet blotting paper, and he answered his mother's cheery questions in a voice that was dead.

"Aren't you glad to be home?" said his mother, when they'd finished their coffee.

"Sure," said Fuller.

"What did you do today?" she said.

"Walked," he said.

"Seeing all your old friends?" she said.

"Haven't got any friends," said Fuller.

His mother threw up her hands. "No friends?" she said. "You?"

"Times change, ma," said Fuller heavily. "Eighteen months is a long time. People leave town, people get married—"

"Marriage doesn't kill people, does it?" she said.

Fuller didn't smile. "Maybe not," he said. "But it makes it awful hard for 'em to find any place to fit old friends in."

"Dougie isn't married, is he?"

"He's out west, ma—with the Strategic Air Command," said Fuller. The little dining room became as lonely as a bomber in the thin, cold stratosphere.

"Oh," said his mother. "There must be somebody left."

"Nope," said Fuller. "I spent the whole morning on the phone, ma. I might as well have been back in Korea. Nobody home."

"I can't believe it," she said. "Why, you couldn't walk down Main Street without being almost trampled by friends."

"Ma," said Fuller hollowly, "after I ran out of numbers to call, you know what I did? I went down to the drugstore, ma, and just sat there by the soda fountain, waiting for somebody to walk in—somebody I knew maybe just even a little. Ma," he said in anguish, "all I knew was poor old Bearse Hinkley. I'm not kidding you one bit." He stood, crumpling his napkin into a ball. "Ma, will you please excuse me?"

"Yes. Of course," she said. "Where are you going now?" She beamed. "Out to call on some nice girl, I hope?"

Fuller threw the napkin down. "I'm going to get a cigar!" he said. "I don't know any girls. They're all married too."

His mother paled. "I—I see," she said. "I—I didn't even know you smoked."

"Ma," said Fuller tautly, "can't you get it through your head? I been away for eighteen months, ma—eighteen months!"

"It is a long time, isn't it?" said his mother, humbled by his passion. "Well, you go get your cigar." She touched his arm. "And please don't feel so lonesome. You just wait. Your life will be so full of people again, you won't know which one to turn to. And, before you know it, you'll meet some pretty young girl, and you'll be married too."

"I don't intend to get married for some time, mother," said Fuller stuffily. "Not until I get through divinity school."

"Divinity school!" said his mother. "When did you decide that?"

"This noon," said Fuller.

"What happened this noon?"

"I had kind of a religious experience, ma," he said. "Something just made me speak out."

"About what?" she said, bewildered.

In Fuller's buzzing head there whirled a rhapsody of Susannas. He saw again all the professional temptresses who had tormented him in Korea, who had beckoned from makeshift bed-sheet movie screens, from curling pinups on damp tent walls, from ragged magazines in sandbagged pits. The Susannas had made fortunes, beckoning to lonely Corporal Fullers everywhere—beckoning with stunning beauty, beckoning the Fullers to come nowhere for nothing.

The wraith of a Puritan ancestor, stiff-necked, dressed in black, took possession of Fuller's tongue. Fuller spoke with a voice that came across the centuries, the voice of a witch hanger, a voice redolent with frustration, self-righteousness, and doom.

"What did I speak out against?" he said. "Temp-ta-tion."

◙ ◙ ◙

Fuller's cigar in the night was a beacon warning carefree, frivolous people away. It was plainly a cigar smoked in anger. Even the moths had sense enough to stay away. Like a restless, searching red eye, it went up and down every street in the village, coming to rest at last, a wet, dead butt, before the firehouse.

Bearse Hinkley, the old pharmacist, sat at the wheel of the pumper, his eyes glazed with nostalgia—nostalgia for the days when he had been young enough to drive. And on his face, for all to see, was a dream of one more catastrophe, with all the young men away, when an old man or nobody would drive the pumper to glory one more time. He spent warm evenings there, behind the wheel—and had for years.

"Want a light for that thing?" he said to Corporal Fuller, seeing the dead cigar between Fuller's lips.

"No, thanks, Mr. Hinkley," he said. "All the pleasure's out of it."

"Beats me how anybody finds any pleasure in cigars in the first place," said the old man.

"Matter of taste," said Fuller. "No accounting for tastes."

"One man's meat's another man's poison," said Hinkley. "Live and let live, I always say." He glanced at the ceiling. Above it was the fragrant nest of Susanna and her black cat. "Me? All my pleasures are looking at what used to be pleasures."

Fuller looked at the ceiling, too, meeting the unmentioned issue squarely. "If you were young," he said, "you'd know why I said what I said to her. Beautiful, stuck-up girls give me a big pain."

"Oh, I remember that," said Hinkley. "I'm not so old I don't remember the big pain."

"If I have a daughter, I hope she isn't beautiful," said Fuller. "The beautiful girls at high school—by God, if they didn't think they were something extra-special."

"By God, if I don't think so, too," said Hinkley.

"They wouldn't even look at you if you didn't have a car and an allowance of twenty bucks a week to spend on 'em," said Fuller.

"Why should they?" said the old man cheerfully. "If I was a beautiful girl, I wouldn't." He nodded to himself. "Well—anyway, I guess you came home from the wars and settled that score. I guess you told her."

"Ah-h-h," said Fuller. "You can't make any impression on them."

"I dunno," said Hinkley. "There's a fine old tradition in the theater: The show must go on. You know, even if you got pneumonia or your baby's dying, you still put on the show."

"I'm all right," said Fuller. "Who's complaining? I feel fine."

The old man's white eyebrows went up. "Who's talking about you?" he said. "I'm talking about her."

Fuller reddened, mousetrapped by egoism. "She'll be all right," he said.

"She will?" said Hinkley. "Maybe she will. All I know is, the show's started at the theater. She's supposed to be in it and she's still upstairs."

"She is?" said Fuller, amazed.

"Has been," said Hinkley, "ever since you paddled her and sent her home."

Fuller tried to grin ironically. "Now, isn't that too bad?" he said. His grin felt queasy and weak. "Well, good-night, Mr. Hinkley."

"Good-night, soldier boy," said Hinkley. "Good-night."

◉ ◉ ◉

As noon drew near on the next day, the villagers along the main street seemed to grow stupid. Yankee shopkeepers made change lackadaisically, as though money didn't matter any more. All thoughts were of the great cuckoo clock the firehouse had become. The question was: Had Corporal Fuller broken it or, at noon, would the little door on top fly open, would Susanna appear?

In the drugstore, old Bearse Hinkley fussed with Susanna's New York papers, rumpling them in his anxiety to make them attractive. They were bait for Susanna.

Moments before noon, Corporal Fuller—the vandal himself—came into the drugstore. On his face was a strange mixture of guilt and soreheadedness. He had spent the better part of the night awake, reviewing his grievances against beautiful women. *All they think about is how beautiful they are,* he'd said to himself at dawn. *They wouldn't even give you the time of day.*

He walked along the row of soda-fountain stools and gave each empty stool a seemingly idle twist. He found the stool that had screeched so loudly the day before. He sat down on it, a monument of righteousness. No one spoke to him.

The fire siren gave its perfunctory wheeze for noon. And then, hearselike, a truck from the express company drove up to the firehouse. Two men got out and climbed the stairs. Susanna's hungry black cat jumped to the porch railing and arched its back as the expressmen disappeared into Susanna's room. The cat spat when they staggered out with Susanna's trunk.

Fuller was shocked. He glanced at Bearse Hinkley, and he saw that the old man's look of anxiety had become the look of double pneumonia—dizzy, blind, drowning.

"Satisfied, corporal?" said the old man.

"I didn't tell her to leave," said Fuller.

"You didn't leave her much choice," said Hinkley.

"What does she care what I think?" said Fuller. "I didn't know she was such a tender blossom."

The old man touched Fuller's arm lightly. "We all are, corporal—we all are," he said. "I thought that was one of the few good things about sending a boy off to the Army. I thought that was where he could find out for sure he wasn't the only tender blossom on earth. Didn't you find that out?"

"I never thought I was a tender blossom," said Fuller. "I'm sorry it turned out this way, but she asked for it." His head was down. His ears were hot crimson.

"She really scared you stiff, didn't she?" said Hinkley.

Smiles bloomed on the faces of the small audience that had drawn near on one pretext or another. Fuller appraised the smiles, and found that the old man had left him only one weapon—utterly humorless good citizenship.

"Who's afraid?" he said stuffily. "I'm not afraid. I just think it's a problem some-body ought to bring up and discuss."

"It's sure the one subject nobody gets tired of," said Hinkley.

Fuller's gaze, which had become a very shifty thing, passed over the magazine rack. There was tier upon tier of Susannas, a thousand square feet of wet-lipped smiles and sooty eyes and skin like cream. He ransacked his mind for a ringing phrase that would give dignity to his cause.

"I'm thinking about juvenile delinquency!" he said. He pointed to the magazines. "No wonder kids go crazy."

"I know I did," said the old man quietly. "I was as scared as you are."

"I told you, I'm not afraid of her," said Fuller.

"Good!" said Hinkley. "Then you're just the man to take her papers to her. They're paid for." He dumped the papers in Fuller's lap.

Fuller opened his mouth to reply. But he closed again. His throat had tight-ened, and he knew that, if he tried to speak, he would quack like a duck.

"If you're really not afraid, corporal," said the old man, "that would be a very nice thing to do—a Christian thing to do."

◎ ◎ ◎

As he mounted the stairway to Susanna's nest, Fuller was almost spastic in his efforts to seem casual.

Susanna's door was unlatched. When Fuller knocked on it, it swung open. In Fuller's imagination, her nest had been dark and still, reeking of incense, a labyrinth of heavy hangings and mirrors, with somewhere a Turkish corner, with somewhere a billowy bed in the form of a swan.

He saw Susanna and her room in truth now. The truth was the cheerless truth of a dirt-cheap Yankee summer rental—bare wood walls, three coat hooks, a linoleum rug. Two gas burners, an iron cot, an icebox. A tiny sink with naked pipes, a plastic drinking glass, two plates, a murky mirror. A frying pan, a saucepan, a can of soap powder.

The only harem touch was a white circle of talcum powder before the murky mirror. In the center of the circle were the prints of two bare feet. The marks of the toes were no bigger than pearls.

Fuller looked from the pearls to the truth of Susanna. Her back was to him. She was packing the last of her things into a suitcase.

She was now dressed for travel—dressed as properly as a missionary's wife.

"Papers," croaked Fuller. "Mr. Hinkley sent 'em."

"How very nice of Mr. Hinkley," said Susanna. She turned. "Tell him—" No more words came. She recognized him. She pursed her lips and her small nose reddened.

"Papers," said Fuller emptily. "From Mr. Hinkley."

"I heard you," she said. "You just said that. Is that all you've got to say?"

Fuller flapped his hands limply at his sides. "I'm—I—I didn't mean to make you leave," he said. "I didn't mean that."

"You suggest I stay?" said Susanna wretchedly. "After I've been denounced in public as a scarlet woman? A tart? A wench?"

"Holy smokes, I never called you those things!" said Fuller.

"Did you ever stop to think what it's like to be me?" she said. She patted her bosom. "There's somebody living inside here, too, you know."

"I know," said Fuller. He hadn't known, up to then.

"I have a soul," she said.

"Sure you do," said Fuller, trembling. He trembled because the room was filled with a profound intimacy. Susanna, the golden girl of a thousand tortured daydreams, was now discussing her soul, passionately, with Fuller the lonely, Fuller the homely, Fuller the bleak.

"I didn't sleep a wink last night because of you," said Susanna.

"Me?" He wished she'd get out of his life again. He wished she were in black and white, a thousandth of an inch thick on a magazine page. He wished he could turn the page and read about baseball or foreign affairs.

"What did you expect?" said Susanna. "I talked to you all night. You know what I said to you?"

"No," said Fuller, backing away. She followed, and seemed to throw off heat like a big iron radiator. She was appallingly human.

"I'm not Yellowstone Park!" she said. "I'm not supported by taxes! I don't belong to everybody! You don't have any right to say anything about the way I look!"

"Good gravy!" said Fuller.

"I'm so tired of dumb toots like you!" said Susanna. She stamped her foot and suddenly looked haggard. "I can't help it if you want to kiss me! Whose fault is that?"

Fuller could now glimpse his side of the question only dimly, like a diver glimpsing the sun from the ocean floor. "All I was trying to say was, you could be a little more conservative," he said.

Susanna opened her arms. "Am I conservative enough now?" she said. "Is this all right with you?"

The appeal of the lovely girl made the marrow of Fuller's bones ache. In his chest was a sigh like the lost chord. "Yes," he said. And then he murmured, "Forget about me."

Susanna tossed her head. "Forget about being run over by a truck," she said. "What makes you so mean?"

"I just say what I think," said Fuller.

"You think such mean things," said Susanna, bewildered. Her eyes widened. "All through high school, people like you would look at me as if they wished I'd drop dead. They'd never dance with me, they'd never talk to me, they'd never even smile back." She shuddered. "They'd just go slinking around like small-town cops. They'd look at me the way you did—like I'd just done something terrible."

The truth of the indictment made Fuller itch all over. "Probably thinking about something else," he said.

"I don't think so," said Susanna. "You sure weren't. All of a sudden, you started yelling at me in the drugstore, and I'd never even seen you before." She burst into tears. "What is the matter with you?"

Fuller looked down at the floor. "Never had a chance with a girl like you—that's all," he said. "That hurts."

Susanna looked at him wonderingly. "You don't know what a chance is," she said.

"A chance is a late-model convertible, a new suit, and twenty bucks," said Fuller.

Susanna turned her back to him and closed her suitcase. "A chance is a girl," she said. "You smile at her, you be friendly, you be glad she's a girl." She turned and opened her arms again. "I'm a girl. Girls are shaped this way," she said. "If men are nice to me and make me happy, I kiss them sometimes. Is that all right with you?"

"Yes," said Fuller humbly. She had rubbed his nose in the sweet reason that governed the universe. He shrugged. "I better be going. Good-bye."

"Wait!" she said. "You can't do that—just walk out, leaving me feeling so wicked." She shook her head. "I don't deserve to feel wicked."

"What can I do?" said Fuller helplessly.

"You can take me for a walk down the main street, as though you were proud of me," said Susanna. "You can welcome me back to the human race." She nodded to herself. "You owe that to me."

◎ ◎ ◎

Cpl. Norman Fuller, who had come home two nights before from eighteen bleak months in Korea, waited on the porch outside Susanna's nest, with all the village watching.

Susanna had ordered him out while she changed, while she changed for her return to the human race. She had also called the express company and told them to bring her trunk back.

Fuller passed the time by stroking Susanna's cat. "Hello, kitty, kitty, kitty, kitty," he said, over and over again. Saying, "Kitty, kitty, kitty, kitty," numbed him like a merciful drug.

He was saying it when Susanna came out of her nest. He couldn't stop saying it, and she had to take the cat away from him, firmly, before she could get him to look at her, to offer his arm.

"So long, kitty, kitty, kitty, kitty, kitty, kitty," said Fuller.

Susanna was barefoot, and she wore barbaric hoop earrings, and ankle bells. Holding Fuller's arm lightly, she led him down the stairs, and began her stately, undulating, titillating, tinkling walk past the liquor store, the insurance agency, the real-estate office, the diner, the American Legion post, and the church, to the crowded drugstore.

"Now, smile and be nice," said Susanna. "Show you're not ashamed of me."

"Mind if I smoke?" said Fuller.

"That's very considerate of you to ask," said Susanna. "No, I don't mind at all."

By steadying his right hand with his left, Corporal Fuller managed to light a cigar.

Little Drops of Water

NOW LARRY'S GONE.

We bachelors are lonely people. If I weren't damn lonely from time to time, I wouldn't have been a friend of Larry Whiteman, the baritone. Not friend, but companion, meaning I spent time with him, whether I liked him particularly or not. As bachelors get older, I find, they get less and less selective about where they get their companionship—and, like everything else in their lives, friends become a habit, and probably a part of a routine. For instance, while Larry's monstrous conceit and vanity turned my stomach, I'd been dropping in to see him off and on for years. And when I come to analyze what *off and on* means, I realize that I saw Larry every Tuesday between five and six in the afternoon. If, on the witness stand, someone were to ask me where I was on the evening of Friday, such and such a date, I would only have to figure out where I would be on the coming Friday to tell him where I had probably been on the Friday he was talking about.

Let me add quickly that I like women, but am a bachelor by choice. While bachelors are lonely people, I'm convinced that married men are lonely people with dependents.

When I say I like women, I can name names, and perhaps, along with the plea of habit, account for my association with Larry in terms of them. There was Edith Vranken, the Schenectady brewer's daughter who wanted to sing; Janice Gurnee, the Indianapolis hardware merchant's daughter who wanted to sing; Beatrix Werner, the Milwaukee consulting engineer's daughter who wanted to sing; and Ellen Sparks, the Buffalo wholesale grocer's daughter who wanted to sing.

I met these attractive young ladies—one by one and in the sequence named—in Larry's studio, or what anyone else would call *apartment*. Larry adds to his revenues as a soloist by giving voice lessons to rich and pretty young women who want to sing. While Larry is soft as a hot fudge sundae, he is big and powerful-looking, like a college-bred lumberjack, if there is such a thing, or a Royal Canadian Mounted Policeman. His voice, of course, gives the impression that he could powder rocks between his thumb and forefinger. His pupils inevitably fell in love with him. If you ask *how* they loved him, I can only reply with another question: where in the cycle do you mean? If you mean at the beginning, Larry was loved as a father pro tem. Later, he was loved as a benevolent taskmaster, and finally, as a lover.

After that came what Larry and his friends had come to call *graduation*, which, in fact, had nothing to do with the pupil's status as a singer, and had everything to do with the cycle of affections. The cue for graduation was the pupil's overt use of the word *marriage*.

Larry was something of a Bluebeard, and, may I say, a lucky dog while his luck held out. Edith, Janice, Beatrix, and Ellen—the most recent group of graduates—loved and were loved in turn. And, in turn, given the ax. They were wonderful looking girls, every one of them. There were also more like them where they had come from, and those others were boarding trains and planes and convertibles to come to New York because they wanted to sing. Larry had no replacement problem. And, with plenty of replacements, he was spared the temptation of making some sort of permanent arrangement, such as marriage.

Larry's life, like most bachelors' lives, but far more so, had every minute accounted for, with very little time for women as women. The time he had set aside for whatever student happened to be in favor was Monday and Thursday evenings, to be exact. There was a time for giving lessons, a time for lunch with friends, a time for practice, a time for his barber, a time for two cocktails with me—a time for everything, and he never varied his schedule by more than a few minutes. Similarly, he had his studio exactly as he wanted it—a place for everything, with no places begging, and with no thing, in his eyes, dispensable. While he might have been on the fence about marriage as a young young man, marriage soon became impossible. Where he might once have had a little time and space to fit in a wife—a cramped wife—there came to be none, absolutely none.

"Habit—it's my strength!" Larry once said. "Ahhhh, wouldn't they love to catch Larry, eh? And remake him, eh? Well, before they can get me into their traps, they've got to blast me out of my rut, and it can't be done. I love my cozy little rut. Habit—*Aes triplex*."

"How's that?" I said.

"*Aes triplex*—triple armor," he said.

"Oh." *Aes Kleenex* would have been closer to the truth, but neither one of us knew that then. Ellen Sparks was around, and ascendant in Larry's heavens—Beatrix Werner having been liquidated a couple of months before—but Ellen was showing no signs of being any different than the rest.

I said I liked women, and gave as examples some of Larry's students, including Ellen. I liked them from a safe distance. After Larry, in his amorous cycle with a favorite, ceased to be a father away from home and eased into a warmer role, I in turn became sort of a father. A lackadaisical, slipshod father, to be sure, but the girls liked to tell me how things were going, and ask my advice. They had a lemon of an adviser in me, because all I could ever think of to say was "Oh well, what the hell, you're only young once."

I said as much to Ellen Sparks, an awfully pretty brunette not likely to be depressed by thoughts or want of money. Her speaking voice was pleasant enough, but when she sang it was as though her vocal cords had risen into her sinuses.

"A Jew's harp with lyrics," said Larry, "with Italian lyrics in a Middle Western accent, yet." But he kept her on, because Ellen was a lot of fun to look at, and she paid her fees promptly, and never seemed to notice that Larry charged her for a lesson whatever he happened to need at the moment.

I once asked her where she'd gotten the idea to be a singer, and she said she liked Lily Pons. To her that was an answer, and a perfectly adequate one. Actually, I think she wanted to get away from the home reservation and have some fun being rich where nobody knew her. She probably drew lots to see whether the excuse would be music, drama, or art. At that, she was more serious-minded than some of the girls in her situation. One girl I know about set herself up in a suite with her father's money, and broadened herself by subscribing to several newsmagazines. One hour out of every day, she religiously underlined everything in them that seemed important. With a thirty-dollar fountain pen.

Well, as New York father to Ellen, I heard her, as I had heard the others before her, declare that she loved Larry, and that she couldn't be sure, but she thought he might like her pretty well, too. She was proud of herself, because here she was making headway with a fairly famous man, and she'd only been away from home five months. The triumph was doubly delicious in that, I gathered, she'd been looked upon as something of a dumb twit in Buffalo. After that, she confided haltingly about evenings of wine and heady talk of the arts.

"Monday and Thursday evenings?" I asked.

She looked startled. "What are you, a Peeping Tom?"

Six weeks later she spoke guardedly of marriage, of Larry's seeming at the point of mentioning it. Seven weeks later she graduated. I happened to drop by Larry's on my Tuesday call for cocktails, and saw her seated in her yellow convertible across the street. By the way she slouched down in the cushions, defiant and at the same time completely licked, I knew what had happened. I thought it best to leave her alone—being, for one thing, dead sick of the same old story. But she spotted me, and raised my hair with a blast of her horns.

"Well, Ellen, hello. Lesson over?"

"Go on, laugh at me."

"I'm not laughing. Why should I laugh?"

"You are inside," she said bitterly. "Men! You knew about the others, didn't you? You knew what happened to them, and what was going to happen to me, didn't you?"

"I knew a lot of Larry's students grew quite attached to him."

"And detached. Well, here's one little girl who won't detach."

"He's an awfully busy man, Ellen."

"He said his career was a jealous mistress," she said huskily. "What does that make me?"

It did seem to me that Larry's remark was a little meatier than necessary. "Well, Ellen, I think you're well off. You deserve someone closer to your own age."

"That's mean. I deserve him."

"Even if you are foolish enough to want him, you can't have him. His life is so petrified with habits, he couldn't possibly accommodate a wife. It'd be easier to get the Metropolitan Opera Company to work in singing commercials."

"I will return," she said grimly, pressing the starter.

Larry's back was to me when I entered. He was mixing drinks. "Tears?" he said.

"Nary a one," I said.

"Good," said Larry. I couldn't be sure he meant it. "It always makes me feel mean when they cry." He threw up his hands. "But what am I to do? My career is a jealous mistress."

"I know. She told me. Beatrix told me. Janice told me. Edith told me." The roster seemed to please him. "Ellen says she won't detach, by the way."

"Really? How unwise. Well, we shall see what we shall see."

When God had been in his heaven as far as Ellen was concerned, when she had been confident that she was about to bring a certified New York celebrity back to Buffalo in a matter of weeks, I had taken her in fatherly fashion to lunch at my favorite restaurant. She seemed to like it, and I saw her there now and then after the breakup.

She was usually with the type of person both Larry and I had told her she deserved—someone closer to her own age. She also seemed to have chosen persons closer to her own amiable vacuity, which made for lunch hours of sighs, long silences, and the general atmosphere of being fogbound often mistaken for love. Actually, Ellen and her companion were in the miserable condition of not being able to think of anything to say, I'm sure. With Larry, the problem had never come up. It was understood that he was to do the talking, and that when he fell silent, it was a silence for effect, beautiful, to be remembered and unbroken by her. When her escorts focused their attention on the matter of paying the check, Ellen, ever aware of her audience, indicated by restlessness and a look of disdain that this wasn't the caliber stuff she was used to. And, of course, it wasn't.

When we happened to be in the restaurant at the same time, she ignored my nods, and—giving less than a damn, really—I gave the practice of nodding up. I think she felt I was part of a *plot*, somehow *in on* Larry's *scheme* to *humiliate* her.

After a while, she gave up young men closer to her age in favor of buying her own lunch. And finally, by a coincidence that surprised us both, she found herself seated at the table next to mine, clearing her white throat.

It became impossible for me to go on reading my paper. "Well, as I live and breathe," I said.

"And how have you been?" she asked coldly. "Still getting lots of laughs?"

"Oh yes, lots and lots. Sadism's on the upswing, you know. New Jersey's legalized it, and Indiana and Wyoming are on the brink."

She nodded. "Still waters run deep," she said enigmatically.

"Meaning me, Ellen?"

"Me."

"I see," I said perplexedly. "By that, you mean there is more to you than meets the eye? I agree." And I did agree. It was incredible that there should be so little to Ellen—intellectually, mind you—as what met the eye.

"Larry's eye," she said.

"Oh, come on, Ellen—surely you're over that. He's vain and selfish, and keeps his stomach in with a girdle."

She held up her hands. "No, no—just tell me about the postcards and the horn. What does he say about them?"

"Postcards? Horn?" I shook my head. "He hasn't said a word about either one."

"Natch," she said. "Excellent, perfect. But perf."

"Sorry, I'm conf and have an imp app," I said, rising.

"What's that?"

"I said I'm confused, Ellen. And I'd try to understand, but I haven't time. I've an important appointment. Good luck, dear."

The appointment was with the dentist, and, with that grim visit over and the back of the afternoon broken, I decided to find Larry and ask him about the postcards and the horn. It was Tuesday, and it was four, so Larry would naturally be at his barber's. I went to the shop and took the seat next to him. His face was covered with lather, but it was Larry, all right. For years, no one else had been in that chair at four on Tuesday.

"Trim," I said to the barber; and then, to Larry, "Ellen Sparks says you should know still waters run deep."

"Hmmmm?" said Larry through the lather. "Who's Ellen Sparks?"

"A former student of yours. Remember?" This forgetting routine was an old trick of Larry's, and, for all I know, it was on the level. "She graduated two months ago."

"Tough job keeping track of all the alumnae," he said. "That little Buffalo thing? Wholesale groceries? I remember. And now the shampoo," he said to the barber.

"Of course, Mr. Whiteman. *Naturally* the shampoo next."

"She wants to know about the postcards and the horn."

"Postcards and horn," he said thoughtfully. "No, doesn't ring a bell." He snapped his fingers. "Oh yes, yes, yes, yes. You can tell her that she is absolutely destroying me with them. Every morning I get a card from her in the mail."

"What does she say?"

"Tell her the mail arrives as I am eating my four-minute eggs. I lay it all before me, with her card on top. I finish my eggs, eagerly seize the card. And then? I tear it in halves, then quarters, then sixteenths, and drop the little snowstorm in my waste-basket. Then it is time for coffee. I haven't the remotest idea what she says."

"And the horn?"

"Even more horrible punishment than the cards." He laughed. "Hell hath no fury like a woman scorned. So, every afternoon at two-thirty, as I am about to begin practice, what happens?"

"She lifts you off the floor with a five-minute blast on the horns?"

"She hasn't the nerve. Every afternoon I get one little, almost imperceptible *beep*, the shifting of gears, and the silly child is gone."

"Doesn't bother you, eh?"

"Bother me? She was right in thinking I was sensitive, but she underestimates my adaptability. It bothered me for the first couple of days, but now I no more notice it than I notice the noise of the trains. I actually had to think a minute before realizing what you were talking about when you asked about horns."

"That girl's got blood in her eye," I said.

"She'd do well to send a little of it to her brain," said Larry. "What do you think of my new student, by the way?"

"Christina? If she'd been my daughter, I'd have sent her to welding school. She's the kind the teachers in grade school used to call *listeners*. The teachers would put them in the corner during singing class, and tell them to beat time with their feet and keep their little mouths shut."

"She's eager to learn," said Larry defensively. He was sensitive to intimations that his interest in his students was ever anything but professional. And, more or less in self-defense, he was belligerently loyal to the artistic possibilities of his charges. His poisonous appraisal of Ellen's voice, for instance, wasn't made until she was ready to be chucked in the oubliette.

"In ten years, Christina will be ready for 'Hot Cross Buns.'"

"She may surprise you."

"I don't think she will, but Ellen may," I said. I was disturbed by Ellen's air of being about to loose appalling, irresistible forces. And yet, there was just this damn fool business of the cards and horn.

"Ellen who?" said Larry fuzzily, from under a hot towel.

The barbershop telephone rang. The barber started for it, but it stopped ringing. He shrugged. "Funny thing. Seems like every time Mr. Whiteman's in here lately, the phone does that."

The telephone by my bed rang.

"This is Larry Whiteman!"

"Drop dead, Larry Whiteman!" The clock said two in the morning.

"Tell that girl to quit it, do you hear?"

"Fine, glad to, you bet," I said thickly. "Who what?"

"That wholesale groceress, of course! That Buffalo thing. Do you hear? She's got to quit it instantly. That light, that goddamned light."

I started to drop the telephone into its cradle, hoping against hope to rupture his eardrum, when I came awake and realized that I was fascinated. Perhaps Ellen had at last unleashed her secret weapon. Larry had had a recital that night. Maybe she'd let him have it in front of everybody. "She blinded you with a light?"

"Worse! When the houselights went down, she lit up her fool face with one of those fool flashlights people carry on their key chains till the batteries pooh out. There she was, grinning out of the dark like death warmed over."

"And she kept it up all evening? I'd think they'd have thrown her out."

"She did it until she was sure I'd seen her, then out it went. Then came the coughs. Lord! the coughs!"

"Somebody always coughs."

"Not the way she does it. Just as I took a breath to start each number, she'd let go—*hack hack hack.* Three deliberate hacks."

"Well, if I see her, I'll tell her," I said. I was rather taken by the novelty of Ellen's campaign, but disappointed by its lack of promise of long-range results. "An old trouper like you shouldn't have any trouble ignoring that sort of business," which was true.

"She's trying to rattle me. She's trying to make me crack up before my Town Hall recital," he said bitterly. The professional high point for Larry each year is his annual Town Hall recital—which is always a critical success, incidentally. Make no mistake about that—Larry, as a singer, is very hot stuff. But now, Ellen had begun her lamp and cough campaign with the big event only two months off.

Two weeks after Larry's frantic call, Ellen and I coincided at lunch again. She was still distinctly unfriendly, treating me as though I were a valuable spy, but not to be trusted, and distasteful to deal with. Once more she gave me the unsettling impression of hidden power, of something big about to happen. Her color was high and her movements furtive. After a few brittle amenities, she asked if Larry had said anything about the light.

"A great deal," I said, "after your first performance, that is. He was quite burned up."

"But now?" she said eagerly.

"Bad news for you, Ellen—good news for Larry. He's quite used to it now, after three recitals, so he has calmed down beautifully. The effect, I'm afraid, is zero. Look, why not give up? You've needled him long enough, haven't you? Revenge is the most you can get, and you've got that." She'd made one basic mistake that I didn't feel was up to me to point out: All of her annoyances were regular, predictable, which made it very easy for Larry to assimilate them into the clockwork of his life and ignore them.

She took the bad news in her stride. I might as well have told her that her campaign was a smashing success—that Larry was at the point of surrender. "Revenge is small apples," she said.

"Well, you've got to promise me one thing, Ellen—"

"Sure," she said. "Why shouldn't I be like Larry and promise anything, any old thing at all?"

"Ellen, promise not to do anything violent at his Town Hall recital."

"Scout's honor," she said, and smiled. "The easiest promise I ever made."

That evening, I played back the puzzling conversation to Larry. He was having his bedtime snack of crackers and hot milk.

"Uh-hummmm," he said, his mouth full. "If she *had* made sense, it would have been the first time in her life." He shrugged disdainfully. "She's licked, this Helen Smart."

"Ellen Sparks," I corrected him.

"Whatever her name is, she'll be catching the train home soon. Awful taste! Honestly. I wouldn't have been surprised if she'd thrown spitballs and stuck pins in my doorbell."

Somewhere along the street, a garbage can lid clattered. "What a racket," I said. "Do they have to be that noisy about it?"

"What racket?"

"That garbage can."

"Oh, that. If you lived here, you'd be used to it. Don't know who it is, but they give the can a lick every night"—he yawned—"just at bedtime."

Keeping big secrets, particularly secrets about things of one's own doing, is a tough proposition for even very bright people. It is so much tougher for small brains that criminals, for instance, are constantly blabbing themselves into jail or worse. Whatever it is they've done, it's too wonderful not to bring out in the open for admiration. That Ellen kept a secret for even five minutes is hard to believe. The fact is, she kept a dandy one for six months, for the time separating her breakup with Larry and the two days before his Town Hall recital.

She finally told me at one of our back-to-back luncheons. She phrased the news in such a way that it wasn't until I saw Larry the next day that I realized what it was she'd given away.

"Now, you promised, Ellen," I told her again, "no rough stuff at the recital day after tomorrow. No heckling, no stink bombs, no serving of a subpoena."

"Don't be crude."

"Don't you, dear. The recital's as much for music lovers as it is for Larry. It's no place for partisan politics."

She seemed, for the first time in months, relaxed, like a person who had just finished a completely satisfying piece of work—a rare type these days. Her color, usually tending toward the reds of excitement, mysterious expectancy, was serene pink and ivory.

She ate in silence, asked me nothing about Larry. There was nothing new I could have told her. Despite her persistent reminders—the horn, the cards, the light and coughs, and God knows what else—he had forgotten all about her. His life went its systematically selfish way, undisturbed.

Then she told me the news. It explained her calm. I had been expecting it for some time, and had even tried to coax her in that direction. I wasn't surprised, nor impressed. It was a completely obvious solution to the mess, arrived at by a brain geared to the obvious.

"The die is cast," she said soberly. "No turning back," she added.

I agreed that the die was cast, indeed, and for the best; and I thought I understood what she meant. The only surprise was that she kissed me on the cheek as she stood to leave the restaurant.

The next afternoon—cocktails-with-Larry-at-five time again—I let myself into his studio. He wasn't anywhere to be seen. Larry had *always* been in the living room when I arrived, puttering around with the drinks, elegant in a loud tartan jacket a woman admirer had sent him. "Larry!"

The curtains into his bedroom parted, and he emerged unsteadily, pathetically. As a bathrobe he wore a scarlet-lined, braid-encrusted cape left over from some forgotten operetta. He sank into a chair like a wounded general, and hid his face in his hands.

"Flu!" I said.

"It's some unknown virus," he said darkly. "The doctor can find nothing. Nothing. Perhaps this is the beginning of a third world war—germ warfare."

"Probably all you need is sleep," I said, helpfully, I thought.

"Sleep! Hah! All night I couldn't sleep. Hot milk, pillows under the small of the back, sheep—"

"Party downstairs?"

He sighed. "The neighborhood was like a morgue. It's something inside me, I tell you."

"Well, as long as you've got your appetite—"

"Did I invite you here to torment me? Breakfast, my favorite meal, tasted like sawdust."

"Well, your voice sounds fine, and that's really the heart of the matter just now, isn't it?"

"Practice this afternoon was an utter flop," he said acidly. "I was unsure, rattled, blew up. I didn't feel right, not ready, half naked—"

"You look like a million dollars, anyway. The barber did a—"

"The barber is a butcher, a hacker, a—"

"He did a fine job."

"Then why don't I *feel* like he did." He stood. "Nothing's gone right today. The whole schedule's shot to hell. And never in my life, not once have I had the slightest bit of anxiety about a recital. Not once!"

"Well," I said hesitantly, "maybe good news would help. I saw Ellen Sparks at lunch yesterday, and she said she—"

Larry snapped his fingers. "That's it, that's it! Of course, that Ellen, she's poisoned me!" He paced the floor. "Not enough to kill me; just enough to break my spirit before tomorrow night. She's been out to get me all along."

"I don't think she poisoned you," I said, smiling. I hoped to divert him by being chatty. I stopped, suddenly aware of the awful significance of what I was about to say. "Larry," I said slowly, "Ellen left for Buffalo last night."

"Good riddance!"

"No more postcards to tear up at breakfast," I said casually. No effect. "No more honking of horns before practice." Still no effect. "No more ringing of the barbershop telephone, no more rattling of the garbage can at bedtime."

He grabbed my arms and shook me. "No!"

"Hell yes." I started to laugh in spite of myself. "She's so balled up in your life, you can't make a move without a cue from her."

"That little termite," said Larry hoarsely. "That burrowing, subversive, insidious, infiltrating little—" He hammered on the mantel. "I'll break the habit!"

"Habits," I corrected him. "If you do, they'll be the first ones you ever broke. Can you do it by tomorrow?"

"Tomorrow?" He moaned. "Oh—tomorrow."

"The houselights go out, and—"

"No flashlight."

"You get set for your first number—"

"Where are the coughs?" he said desperately. "I'll blow up like Texas City!" Trembling, he picked up the telephone. "Operator, get me Buffalo. What's her name again?"

"Sparks—*Ellen* Sparks."

I was invited to the wedding, but I'd have sooner attended a public beheading. I sent a sterling silver pickle fork and my regrets.

To my amazement, Ellen joined me at lunch on the day following the wedding. She was alone, lugging a huge parcel.

"What are you doing here on this day of days?" I said.

"Honeymooning." Cheerfully, she ordered a sandwich.

"Uh-huh. And the groom?"

"Honeymooning in his studio."

"I see." I didn't, but we had reached a point where it would have been indelicate for me to probe further.

"I've put in my two hours today," she volunteered. "And hung up one dress in his closet."

"And tomorrow?"

"Two and a half hours, and add a pair of shoes."

"*Little drops of water, Little grains of sand,*" I recited, "*Make the mighty ocean, And the beauteous land.*" I pointed to the parcel. "Is that part of your trousseau?"

She smiled. "In a way. It's a garbage can lid for beside the bed."

Jenny

GEORGE CASTROW used to come back to the home works of the General Household. Appliances Company just once a year—to install his equipment in the shell of the new model GHA refrigerator. And every time he got there he dropped a suggestion in the suggestion box. It was always the same suggestion: "Why not make next year's refrigerator in the shape of a woman?" Then there would be a sketch of a refrigerator shaped like a woman, with arrows showing where the vegetable crisper and the butter conditioner and the ice cubes and all would go.

George called it the Food-O-Mama. Everybody thought the Food-O-Mama was an extra-good joke because George was out on the road all year long, dancing and talking and singing with a refrigerator shaped like a refrigerator. Its name was Jenny. George had designed and built Jenny back when he'd been a real comer in the GHA Research Laboratory.

George might as well have been married to Jenny. He lived with her in the back of a moving van that was mostly filled with her electronic brains. He had a cot and a hot plate and a three-legged stool and a table and a locker in the back of the van. And he had a doormat he put on the bare ground outside when he parked the van somewhere for the night. "Jenny and George," it said. It glowed in the dark.

Jenny and George went from appliance dealer to appliance dealer all over the United States and Canada. They would dance and sing and crack jokes until they'd collected a good crowd in a store. Then they would make a strong sales pitch for all the GHA appliances standing around doing nothing.

Jenny and George had been at it since 1934. George was sixty-four years old when I got out of college and joined the company. When I heard about George's big paycheck and his free way of life and the way he made people laugh and buy appliances, why I guessed he was the happiest man in the company.

But I never got to see Jenny and George until I got transferred out to the Indianapolis offices. One morning out there we got a telegram saying Jenny and George were in our neck of the woods somewhere—and would we please find them and tell George his ex-wife was very sick? She wasn't expected to live. She wanted to see him.

I was very surprised to hear he'd had a wife. But some of the older people in the office knew about her. George had only lived with her for six months—and then

193

he'd hit the road with Jenny. His ex-wife's name was Nancy. Nancy had turned right around and married his best friend.

I got the job of tracking Jenny and George down. The company never knew exactly where they were. George made his own schedule. The company gave him his head. They just kept rough track of him by his expense accounts and by rave letters they'd get from distributors and dealers.

And almost every rave letter told about some new stunt that Jenny'd done, that Jenny'd never been able to do before. George couldn't leave her alone. He tinkered with her every spare minute, as though his life depended on making Jenny as human as possible.

I called our distributor for central Indiana, Hal Flourish. I asked him if he knew where Jenny and George were. He laughed to beat the band and said he sure did. Jenny and George were right in Indianapolis, he said. They were out at the Hoosier Appliance Mart. He told me Jenny and George had stopped early morning traffic by taking a walk down North Meridian Street.

"She had on a new hat and a corsage and a yellow dress," he said. "And George was all dolled up in his soup and fish and yellow spats and a cane. You would of died. And you know how he's got her fixed up now, so's he knows when her battery's running down?"

"Nossir," I said.

"She yawns," he said, "and her eyelids get all droopy."

Jenny and George were starting their first show of the day when I got out to the Hoosier Appliance Mart. It was a swell morning. George was on the sidewalk in the sunshine, leaning on the fender of the moving van that had Jenny's brains in it. He and Jenny were singing a duet. They were singing the "Indian Love Call." They were pretty good. George would sing, "I'll be calling you-hoo," in a gravel baritone. Then Jenny would answer back from the doorway of the Mart in a thin, girlish soprano.

Sully Harris, who owned the Mart, was standing by Jenny with one arm draped over her. He was smoking a cigar and counting the house.

George had on the dress suit and yellow spats Hal Flourish had laughed so hard about. George's coattails dragged on the ground. His white vest was buttoned down around his knees. His shirt bosom was rolled up under his chin like a window blind. And he had on trick shoes that looked like bare feet the size of canoe paddles. The toenails were painted fire-engine red.

But Hal Flourish is the kind of man who thinks anything that's supposed to be funny *is* funny. George wasn't funny if you looked at him closely. And I *had* to look at him closely because I wasn't there for a good time. I was bringing him sad news. I looked at him closely, and I saw a small man getting on in years and all alone in this vale of tears. I saw a small man with a big nose and brown eyes that were just sick about something.

But most people in the crowd thought he was a howl. Just here and there you'd see a few people who saw what I saw. Their smiles weren't making fun of George. Their smiles were kind of queer and sweet. Their smiles mostly seemed to ask how Jenny worked.

Jenny was radio-controlled, and the controls were in those trick shoes of George's—under his toes. He would punch buttons with his toes, and the shoes would send out signals to Jenny's brains in the moving van. Then the brains would signal Jenny what to do. There weren't any wires between Jenny and George and the van.

It was hard to believe George had anything to do with what Jenny was up to. He had a little pink earphone in his ear, so he could hear everything anybody said to Jenny, even when she was a hundred feet away. And he had little rearview mirrors on the frames of his glasses, so he could turn his back to her and still see everything she did.

When they stopped singing, Jenny picked me out to kid around with. "Hello, tall, dark, and handsome," she said to me. "Did the old icebox drive you out of the house?" She had a sponge rubber face at the top of the door, with springs embedded in it and a loudspeaker behind it. Her face was so real, I almost had to believe there was a beautiful woman inside the refrigerator—with her face stuck through a hole in the door.

I kidded her back. "Look, Mrs. Frankenstein," I said to her, "why don't you go off in a corner somewhere and make some ice cubes? I want to have a private talk with your boss."

Her face turned from pink to white. Her lips trembled. Then her lips pulled down and dragged her whole face out of shape. She shut her eyes so she wouldn't have to look at such a terrible person. And then, as God is my judge, she squeezed out two fat tears. They ran down her cheeks, then down her white enamelled front to the floor.

I smiled and winked at George to let him know how slick I thought his act was, and that I really did want to see him.

He didn't smile back. He didn't like me for talking to Jenny that way. You would have thought I'd spit in the eye of his mother or sister or something.

A kid about ten years old came up to George and said, "Hey, Mister, I bet I know how she works. You got a midget in there."

"You're the first one who ever guessed," George said. "Now that everybody knows, I might as well let the midget out." He motioned for Jenny to come out on the sidewalk with him.

I expected her to waddle and clank like a tractor, because she weighed seven hundred pounds. But she had a light step to go with that beautiful face of hers. I never saw such a case of mind over matter. I forgot all about the refrigerator. All I saw was her.

She sidled up to George. "What is it, Sweetheart?" she said.

"The jig is up," George said. "This bright boy knows you're a midget inside. Might as well come on out and get some fresh air and meet the nice people." He hesitated just long enough and looked just glum enough to make the people think maybe they were really going to see a midget.

And then there was a whirr and a click, and Jenny's door swung open. There wasn't anything inside but cold air, stainless steel, porcelain, and a glass of orange juice. It was a shock to everybody—all that beauty and personality on the outside, and all that cold nothing on the inside.

George took a sip from the glass of orange juice, put it back in Jenny and closed her door.

"I'm certainly glad to see you taking care of yourself for a change," Jenny said. You could tell she was crazy about him, and that he broke her heart about half the time. "Honestly," she said to the crowd, "the poor man should be dead of scurvy and rickets by now, the way he eats."

An audience is the nuttiest thing there is, if you ever stop to think about it. Here George had proved there wasn't anything inside Jenny, and here the crowd was, twenty seconds later, treating her like a real human being again. The women were shaking their heads to let Jenny know they knew what a trial it was to get a man to take care of himself. And the men were giving George secret looks to let him know they knew what a good pain it was to have a woman always treating you like a baby.

The only person who wasn't going along with the act, who wasn't being a boob for the pleasure of it, was the kid who'd guessed there was a midget inside. He was sore about being wrong, and his big ambition was to bust up the act with truth— Truth with a capital T. He'll grow up to be a scientist someday. "All right," the kid said, "if there isn't a midget in there, then I know exactly how it works."

"How, honey?" said Jenny. She was all ears for whatever bright little thing this kid was going to say. She really burned him up.

"Radio controls!" the kid said.

"Oooooo!" said Jenny. She was thrilled. "That would be a *grand* way to do it!"

The kid turned purple. "You can joke around all you want," he said, "but that's the answer and you know it." He challenged George. "What's *your* explanation?" he said.

"Three thousand years ago," said George, "the sultan of Alla-Bakar fell in love with the wisest, most affectionate, most beautiful woman who ever lived. She was Jenny, a slave girl.

"The old sultan knew there would be constant bloodshed in his kingdom," said George, "because men who saw Jenny always went mad for her love. So the old sultan had his court magician take Jenny's spirit out of her body and put it in a bottle. This he locked up in his treasury.

"In 1933," said George, "Lionel O. Heartline, president of the General Household Appliances Company, bought a curious bottle while on a business trip to fabled Baghdad. He brought it home, opened it, and out came the spirit of Jenny—three thousand years old. I was working in the Research Laboratory of GH at the time, and Mr. Heartline asked me what I could provide in the way of a new body for Jenny. So I rigged the shell of a refrigerator with a face, a voice, and feet—and with spirit controls, which work on Jenny's willpower alone."

It was such a silly story, I forgot it as soon as I'd chuckled at it. It took me weeks to realize that George wasn't just hamming it up when he told the story from his heart. He was getting as close to the truth about Jenny as he ever dared get. He was getting close to it with poetry.

"And, hey presto!—here she is," said George.

"Baloney!" the scientific kid yelled. But the audience wasn't with him, never would be.

Jenny let out a big sigh, thinking about those three thousand years in a bottle. "Well," she said, "that part of my life's all over now. No use crying over spilt milk. On with the show."

She slunk into the Mart, and everybody but George and I toddled right in behind her.

George, still controlling her with his toes, ducked into the cab of the moving van. I followed him and stuck my head in the window. There he was, the top of his trick shoes rippling while his toes made Jenny talk a blue streak in the Mart. At nine o'clock on a sunshiny morning he was taking a big drink from a bottle of booze.

When his eyes stopped watering and his throat stopped stinging he said to me, "What you looking at me that way for, Sonny Jim? Didn't you see me drink my orange juice first like a good boy? It isn't as though I was drinking before breakfast."

"Excuse me," I said. I got away from the truck to give him time to pull himself together, and to give me time, too.

"When I saw that beautiful GHA refrigerator in the Research Laboratory," Jenny was saying in the Mart, "I said to George, 'That's the flawless white body for me.'" She glanced at me and then at George, and she shut up and her party smile went away for a couple of seconds. Then she cleared her throat and went on. "Where was I?" she said.

George wasn't about to get out of the cab. He was staring through the windshield now at something very depressing five thousand miles away. He was ready to spend the whole day like that.

Jenny finally ran out of small talk, and she came to the door and called him. "Honey," she called, "are you coming in pretty soon?"

"Keep your shirt on," George said. He didn't look at her.

"Is—is everything all right?" she said.

"Grand," George said, still staring through the windshield. "Just grand."

I did my best to think this was part of a standard routine, to find something clever and funny in it. But Jenny wasn't playing to the crowd. They couldn't even see her face. And she wasn't playing to me, either. She was playing to George and George was playing to her, and they would have played it the same way if they'd been alone in the middle of the Sahara Desert.

"Honey," Jenny said, "there are a lot of nice people waiting inside." She was embarrassed, and she knew darn good and well I'd caught him boozing it up.

"Hooray," said George.

"Sweetheart," she said, "the show *must* go on."

"Why?" said George.

Up to then, I'd never known how joyless what they call a joyless laugh could be. Jenny gave a joyless laugh to get the crowd to thinking that what was going on was simply hysterical. The laugh sounded like somebody breaking champagne glasses with a ball-peen hammer. It didn't just give me the willies. It gave everybody the willies.

"Did—did you want something, young man?" she said to me.

What the hell—there was no talking to George, so I talked to her. "I'm from the Indianapolis office. I—I have a message about his wife," I said.

George turned his head. "About my what?" he said.

"Your—your *ex*-wife," I said.

The crowd was out on the sidewalk again, confused and shuffling around and wondering when the funny part was going to come. It sure was a screwy way to sell refrigerators. Sully Harris was starting to get sore.

"Haven't heard from her for twenty years," George said. "I can go another twenty without hearing from her, and feel no pain. Thanks just the same." He stared through the windshield again.

That got a nervous laugh out of the crowd, and Sully Harris looked relieved.

Jenny came up to me, bumped up against me, and whispered out of the corner of her mouth, "What about Nancy?"

"She's very sick," I whispered. "I guess she's dying. She wants to see him one last time."

Somewhere in the back of the van a deep humming sound quit. It was the sound of Jenny's brains. Jenny's face turned into dead sponge rubber—turned into something as stupid as anything you'll ever see on a department store clothes dummy. The yellow-green lights in her blue glass eyes winked out.

"Dying?" said George. He opened the door of the cab to get some air. The big Adam's apple in his scrawny throat went up and down, up and down. He flapped his arms feebly. "Show's over, folks," he said.

Nobody moved right away. Everybody was stunned by all this unfunny real life in the middle of make-believe.

George kicked off his trick shoes to show how really over the show was. He couldn't make himself speak again. He sat there, turned sideways in the cab, staring at his bare feet on the running board. The feet were narrow and bony and blue.

The crowd shuffled away, their day off to a very depressing start. Sully Harris and I hung around the van, waiting for George to take his head out of his hands. Sully was heartbroken about what had happened to the crowd.

George mumbled something in his hands that we didn't catch.

"How's that?" Sully asked him.

"When somebody tells you you've got to come like that," George said, "you've got to come?"

"If—if she's your ex-wife, if you walked out on her twenty years ago," Sully said, "then how come you gotta fall apart now on account of her—in front of my customers, in front of my store?"

George didn't answer him.

"If you want a train or an airplane reservation or a company car," I said to George, "I'll get it for you."

"And leave the van?" George said. He said it as though I'd made a very fatheaded suggestion. "There's a quarter of a million dollars' worth of equipment in there, Sonny Jim," he said. He shook his head. "Leave all that valuable equipment around for somebody to—" His sentence petered out. And I saw there wasn't any sense to arguing with what he was saying, because he was really getting at something else. The van was his home, and Jenny and her brains were his reason for being—and the thought of going somewhere without them after all these years scared him stiff.

"I'll go in the van," he said. "I can make better time that way." He got out of the cab and got some excitement going—so no one would point out that moving vans weren't famous as fast transportation. "You come with me," he said, "and we can drive straight through."

I called the office, and they told me that not only could I go with Jenny and George—I *had* to go. They said that George was the most dedicated employee the company had, next to Jenny, and that I was to do anything I could to help him in this time of need.

When I got back from telephoning, George was off telephoning somewhere else himself. He'd put on a pair of sneakers and left the magic shoes behind. Sully Harris had picked up the magic shoes, and was looking inside.

"My God," Sully said to me, "it's like these little buttons all over an accordion in there." He slipped his hand into a shoe. He left it in there for about a minute before he got nerve enough to push a button.

"Fuh," Jenny said. She was perfectly deadpan.

Sully pushed another button.

"Fuh," Jenny said.

He pushed another button.

Jenny smiled like Mona Lisa.

Sully pushed several buttons.

"Burplappleneo," said Jenny. "Bama-uzztrassit. Shuh," she said. She did a right face and stuck out her tongue.

Sully lost his nerve. He put the magic shoes down by the van the way you'd put bedroom slippers by a bed. "Boy—" he said, "those people aren't gonna come back here. They're gonna think it's a morgue or something after that show he put on. I just thank God for one thing."

"What's that?" I said.

"At least they didn't find out whose voice and face the refrigerator's got."

"Whose?" I said.

"You didn't know?" said Sully. "Hell—he made a mold of her face and put it on Jenny. Then he had her record every sound in the English language. Every sound Jenny makes, *she* made first."

"Who?" I said.

"Nancy, or whatever her name is," Sully said. "Right after the honeymoon he did all that. The dame that's dying now."

We made seven hundred miles in sixteen hours, and I don't believe George said ten words to me the whole time. He did do some talking, but not to me. It was in his sleep, and I guess he was talking to Jenny. He would say something like "Uffa-mf-uffa" while he was snoozing next to me. Then his toes would wiggle in his sneakers, signalling for Jenny to give him whatever answer he wanted to hear.

He didn't have the magic shoes on, so Jenny didn't do anything. She was strapped up against a wall in the dark in the back of the van. George didn't worry much about her until we got within about an hour of where we were going. Then he got as fidgety as a beagle. Every ten minutes or so he'd think Jenny had busted loose and was crashing around in her brains. We would have to pull over and stop, and go around in back and make sure she was fine.

You talk about plain living: the inside of the van looked like a monk's cell in a television station's control room. I'd seen floorboards that were wider and springier than George's cot. Everything that was for George in the van was cheap and uncomfortable. I wondered at first where the quarter of a million dollars he'd talked about was. But every time he passed his flashlight beam over Jenny's brains I got more excited. Those brains were the most ingenious, most complicated, most beautiful electronic system I'll ever see. Money was no object where Jenny was concerned.

As the sun came up we turned off the highway and banged over chuckholes into the hometown of the General Household Appliances Company. Here was the town where I'd started my career, where he'd started his career, where he'd brought his bride so long ago.

George was driving. The banging woke me up, and it shook something loose in George. All of a sudden he had to talk. He went off like an alarm clock.

"Don't know her!" he said. "Don't know her at all, Sonny Jim!" He bit the back of his hand, trying to drown out the pain in his heart. "I'm coming to see a perfect stranger, Sonny Jim," he said. "All I know is she was very beautiful once. I loved her more than anything on earth once, and she broke everything I had into little pieces. Career, friendships, home—*kaput*." George hit the horn button, blasted the bejeepers out of the dawn with the van's big bullhorn. "Don't ever idolize a woman, Sonny Jim!" he yelled.

We banged over another chuckhole. George had to grab the wheel with both hands. Steadying down the truck steadied him down, too. He didn't talk anymore till we got where we were going.

Where we were going was a white mansion with pillars across the front. It was Norbert Hoenikker's house. He was doing very well. He was assistant director of GHA research. He'd been George's best friend years before—before he'd taken George's wife Nancy away from him.

Lights were on all over the house. We parked the van behind a doctor's car out front. We knew it was a doctor's car because it had a tag with those twined snakes on it up above the back license plate. The minute we parked, the front door of the house opened, and Norbert Hoenikker came out. He was wearing a bathrobe and slippers, and he hadn't slept all night.

He didn't shake hands with George. He didn't even say hello. He started right out with a rehearsed speech. "George," he said. "I'm going to stay out here while you go in. I want you to consider it your house while you're in there—with complete freedom for you and Nancy to say absolutely anything you have to say to each other."

The last thing George wanted to do was to go in there and face Nancy alone. "I—I haven't got anything to say to her," he said. He actually put his hand on the ignition key, got ready to start up the van and roar away.

"She has things to say to you," Mr. Hoenikker said. "She's been asking for you all night. She knows you're out here now. Lean close when she talks. She isn't very strong."

George got out, shambled up the walk to the house. He walked like a diver on the bottom of the sea. A nurse helped him into the house and closed the door.

"Is there a cot in back?" Mr. Hoenikker asked me.

"Yessir," I said.

"I'd better lie down," he said.

Mr. Hoenikker lay down on the cot, but he couldn't get any rest. He was a tall, heavy man, and the cot was too little for him. He sat up again. "Got a cigarette?" he said.

"Yessir," I said. I gave him one and lit it. "How is she, sir?" I said.

"She'll live," he said, "but it's made an old lady out of her like that." He snapped his fingers. It was a weak snap. It didn't make any noise. He looked at the face of Jenny, and it hurt him. "He's got a shock coming in there," he said. "Nancy doesn't look like that anymore." He shrugged. "Maybe that's good. Maybe he'll have to look at her as a fellow human being now."

He got up. He went to Jenny's brains and shook a steel rack that carried part of them. The rack didn't give at all. Hoenikker wound up shaking himself. "Oh, God," he said, "what a waste, what a waste, what a waste. One of the great technical minds of our time," he said, "living in a moving van, married to a machine, selling appliances somewhere between Moose Jaw, Saskatchewan, and Flamingo, Florida."

"I guess he is pretty bright," I said.

"Bright?" Hoenikker said. "He isn't just George Castrow. He's *Dr.* George Castrow. He spoke five languages when he was eight, mastered calculus when he was ten, and got his Ph.D. from M.I.T. when he was eighteen!"

I whistled.

"He never had any time for love," Hoenikker said. "Didn't believe in it, was sure he could get along without it—whatever it was. There was too much else to do for George to bother with love. When he came down with pneumonia at the age of thirty-three, he had never so much as held the hand of a woman."

Hoenikker saw the magic shoes where George had put them, under the cot. He slipped off his bedroom slippers and slipped on the magic shoes. He was pretty familiar with them. "When pneumonia hit George," he said, "he was suddenly in terror of death and in desperate need of a nurse's touch many times a day. The nurse was Nancy."

Hoenikker turned on Jenny's master control switch. Her brains hummed. "A man who hasn't built up a certain immunity to love through constant exposure to it," he said, "is in danger of being all but killed by love when the first exposure comes." He shuddered. "Love scrambled poor George's brains. Suddenly love was *all* that mattered. Working with him in the laboratory, I was forced to listen eight hours a day to tripe about love. Love made the world go round! It was love and love alone the world was seeking! Love conquered all!"

Hoenikker tugged at his nose and closed his eyes, trying to remember a skill he'd had a long time ago. "Hello, Baby," he said to Jenny. His toes wiggled in the magic shoes.

"Heh-le, Hah-uh-u-duh-suh-um," Jenny said. There wasn't any expression in her face. She spoke again, put the sounds together better. "Hello, Handsome," she said to Hoenikker.

Hoenikker shook his head. "Nancy's voice doesn't sound like that anymore," he said. "Lower, a little rougher now—not so liquid."

"Huh-ear, huh-ut fuh-uh thu-uh suh-a-fuh uf-fuh Guh-od guh-o-yuh-oooo," Jenny said to him. She smoothed that out, too, "Here, but for the Grace of God, go you," she said.

"Say," I said, "you're good. I didn't think anybody but George could make her talk."

"Can't make her seem alive—not the way George can," Hoenikker said. "Never could—not even after I'd had a thousand hours of practice."

"You put that many hours in on her?" I said.

"Sure," said Hoenikker. "I was the one who was going to take her out on the road. I was the footloose bachelor who didn't have much of a future in research anyway. George was the married man who was to stay home with his laboratory and his wife, and go on to bigger things."

Life's surprises made Hoenikker sniffle. "Designing Jenny—" he said, "that was supposed to be a little joke in the middle of George's career—an electronic joke off the top of his head. Jenny was a little something he was to tinker with while he came drifting back to earth after his honeymoon with Nancy."

Hoenikker rambled on about those olden days when Jenny was born. And sometimes he would make Jenny chime in, as though she remembered those days, too. Those were bad days for Hoenikker, because he fell in love with George's wife. He'd been scared to death he would do something about it.

"I loved her for what she was," he said. "Maybe it was all the pap George was spouting about love that made me fall in love with her. George would say something ridiculous about love or about her, and I'd think up real reasons for loving her. I wound up loving her as a human being, as a miraculous, one-of-a-kind, moody muddle of faults and virtues—part child, part woman, part goddess, and no more consistent than a putty slide-rule."

"And then George began spending more and more time with me," said Jenny. "He took to going home from the laboratory at the last possible moment, wolfing down his supper, and hurrying back to work on me till well past midnight. He would have the control shoes on all day long and half the night—and we would talk, and talk, and talk."

Hoenikker tried to give her face some expression for what she was going to say next. He punched the Mona-Lisa-smile button Sully Harris had punched the day before. "I was excellent company," she said. "I never once said anything he didn't want to hear—and I always said what he wanted to hear exactly when he wanted to hear it."

"Here," said Hoenikker, undoing Jenny's straps so she could step forward, "is the most calculating woman, the greatest student of the naïve male heart that ever walked the face of the earth. Nancy never had a chance."

"Ordinarily," said Hoenikker, "a man's first wild dreams about his wife peter out after the honeymoon. The man then has to settle down to the difficult but rewarding business of finding out to whom he is really married. But George had an alternative. He could keep his wild dreams of a wife alive in Jenny. His neglect of the imperfect Nancy became a scandal."

"George suddenly announced that I was too precious a mechanism to be entrusted in anyone's care but his own," said Jenny. "He was going to take his Jenny out on the road, or he would leave the company entirely."

"His new hunger for love," said Hoenikker, "was matched only by his ignorance of the pitfalls of love. He only knew that love made him feel wonderful, no matter where it came from."

Hoenikker turned off Jenny, took off the shoes, lay down on the cot again. "George chose the perfect love of a robot," he said, "leaving me to do what I could to earn the love of an imperfect, deserted girl."

"I—I'm certainly glad she's well enough to say whatever she's got to say to him," I said.

"He would have gotten the message in any event," said Hoenikker. He handed up a slip of paper. "She dictated this, in case she wasn't up to saying it to him personally."

I didn't get to read the message right away, because George showed up at the back door of the van. He looked more like a robot than he'd ever made Jenny seem. "Your house again—your wife again," he said.

George and I had breakfast in a diner. Then we drove over to the GHA works and parked in front of the Research Laboratory.

"Sonny Jim," George said to me, "you can run along now, and start leading a life of your own again. And much obliged."

When I got off by myself, I read what Nancy had dictated to her second husband, what she'd said in person to George.

"Please look at the imperfect human being God gave you to love once," she'd said to George, *"and try to like me a little for what I really was, or, God willing, am. Then please, Darling, become an imperfect human being among imperfect human beings again."*

I'd been in such a hurry to get off by myself that I hadn't shaken George's hand or asked him what he was going to do next. I went back to the van to do both those things.

The back door of the van was open. Jenny and George were talking inside, very soft and low.

"I'm going to try to pick up the pieces of my life, Jenny—what's left of it," George said. "Maybe they'll take me back in the Research Laboratory. I'll ask anyway—hat in hand."

"They'll be thrilled to have you back!" said Jenny. She was thrilled herself. "This is the best news I've ever heard—the news I've been longing to hear for years." She yawned and her eyelids drooped. "Excuse me," she said.

"You need a younger man to squire you around now," said George. "I'm getting old—and you'll never get old."

"I'll never know another man as ardent and thoughtful as you, as handsome as you, as brilliant as you," said Jenny. She meant it. She yawned again. Her eyelids drooped some more. "Excuse me," she said. "Good luck, Angel," she mumbled. Her eyes closed all the way. "Good night, Sweetheart," she said. She was asleep. Her battery was dead.

"Dream a little dream of me," whispered George.

I ducked out of sight as George brushed away a tear and left the van forever.

The Epizootic

WHILE NEW YOUNG WIDOWS in extraordinary numbers paraded their weeds for all to see, no official had yet acknowledged that the land was plagued. The general population and the press, long inured to a world gone mad, had not yet noticed that affairs had recently become even worse. The news was full of death. The news had always been full of death. It was the life insurance companies that noticed first what was going on, and well they might have. They had insured millions of lives at rates based on a life expectancy of sixty-eight years. Now, in a six-month period, the average age at death for married American males with more than twenty thousand dollars in life insurance had dropped to an appalling forty-seven years.

"Dropped to forty-seven years—and still dropping," said the president of the American Reliable and Equitable Life and Casualty Company of Connecticut. The president himself was only forty-six, very young to be heading the eighth-largest insurance company in the country. He was a humorless, emaciated, ambitious young man who had been described by the previous president as "gruesomely capable." His name was Millikan.

The previous president, who had been kicked upstairs to chairmanship of the board of directors, was with Millikan now in the company's boardroom in Hartford. He was an amiable old gentleman, a lifelong bachelor named Breed.

The third person present was Dr. Everett, a young epidemiologist from the United States Department of Health and Welfare. It was Dr. Everett who gave the plague a name that stuck. He called it "the epizootic." "When you say forty-seven years—" he said to Millikan, "is that an exact figure?"

"We happen to be somewhat short of exact figures just now," said Millikan wryly. "Our chief actuary killed himself two days ago—threw himself out his office window."

"Family man?" said Dr. Everett.

"Naturally," said the chairman of the board. "And his family is very nicely taken care of now, thanks to life insurance. His debts can all be paid off, his wife is assured an adequate income for life, and his children can go to college without having to work their ways through." The old man said all this with sad, plonking irony. "Insurance is a wonderful thing," he said, "especially after it's been in effect for more than

206

two years." He meant by that that most life insurance contracts paid off on suicide after they had been in effect for more than two years. "No family man," he said, "should be without it."

"Did he leave a note?" said Dr. Everett.

"He left two," said the chairman. "One was to us, suggesting that we replace him with a Gypsy fortune-teller. The other was to his wife and children, and it said simply, '*I love you more than anything. I have done this so you can have all the things you deserve.*'" He winked ruefully at Dr. Everett, the country's outstanding authority on the epizootic. "I daresay such sentiments are quite familiar to you by now."

Dr. Everett nodded. "As familiar as chicken pox to a pediatrician," he said tiredly.

Millikan brought his fist down on the table hard. "What I want to know is what is the Government going to do about this?" he said. "At the current death rate, this company will be out of business in eight months! I presume the same is true of every life insurance company. What is the Government going to do?"

"What do you *suggest* the Government do?" said Dr. Everett. "We're quite open to suggestion—almost pathetically so."

"All right!" said Millikan. "Government action number one!"

"Number one!" echoed Dr. Everett, preparing to write.

"Get this disease out in the open, where we can *fight* it! No more secrecy!" said Millikan.

"Marvellous!" said Dr. Everett. "Call the reporters at once. We'll hold a press conference right here, give out all the facts and figures—and within minutes the whole world will know." He turned to the old chairman of the board. "Modern communications are wonderful, aren't they?" he said. "Almost as wonderful as life insurance." He reached for the telephone on the long table, took it from its cradle. "What's the name of the afternoon paper?" he said.

Millikan took the telephone away from him, hung up.

Everett smiled at him in mock surprise. "I thought that was step number one. I was just going to take it, so we could get right on to step two."

Millikan closed his eyes, massaged the bridge of his nose. The young president of American Reliable and Equitable had plenty to contemplate within the violet privacy of his eyelids. After step one, which would inevitably publicize the bad condition of the insurance companies, there would be the worst financial collapse in the country's history. As for curing the epizootic: publicity could only make the disease kill more quickly, would make it cram into a few weeks of panic deaths that would ordinarily be spread over a few queasy years. As for the grander issues, as for America's becoming weak and contemptible, as for money's being valued more highly than life itself, Millikan hardly cared. What mattered to him most was immediate and personal. All other implications of the epizootic paled beside the garish, blaring fact that the company was about to go under, taking Millikan's brilliant career with it.

The telephone on the table rang. Breed answered, received information without comment, hung up. "Two more planes just crashed," he said. "One in Georgia—fifty-three aboard. One in Indiana—twenty-nine aboard."

"Survivors?" said Dr. Everett.

"None," said Breed. "That's eleven crashes this month—so far."

"All right! All right! All right!" said Millikan, rising to his feet. "Government action number one—ground all airplanes! No more air travel at all!"

"Good!" said Dr. Everett. "We should also put bars on all windows above the first floor, remove all bodies of water from centers of population, outlaw the sales of firearms, rope, poisons, razors, knives, automobiles and boats—"

Millikan subsided into his chair, hope gone. He took a photograph of his family from his billfold, studied it listlessly. In the background of the photograph was his hundred-thousand-dollar waterfront home, and, beyond that, his forty-eight-foot cabin cruiser lying at anchor.

"Tell me," Breed said to young Dr. Everett, "are you married?"

"No," said Dr. Everett. "The Government has a rule now against letting married men work on epizootic research."

"Oh?" said Breed.

"They found out that married men working on the epizootic generally died of it before they could even submit a report," said Dr. Everett. He shook his head. "I just don't understand, just don't understand. Or sometimes I do—and then I don't again."

"Does the deceased have to be married in order for you to credit his death to the epizootic?" said Breed.

"A wife *and* children," said Dr. Everett. "That's the classic pattern. A wife alone doesn't mean much. Curiously, a wife and just one child doesn't mean much, either." He shrugged. "Oh, I suppose a few cases where a man has been unusually devoted to his mother or some other relative, or maybe even to his college, should be classified technically as the epizootic—but cases like that aren't statistically important. To the epidemiologist who deals only in staggering figures, the epizootic is overwhelmingly a disease of successful, ambitious married men with more than one child."

Millikan took no interest in their conversation. With monumental irrelevance, he now placed the photograph of his family in front of the two bachelors. It showed a quite ordinary mother with three quite ordinary children, one an infant. "Look those wonderful people in the eye!" he said hoarsely.

Breed and Dr. Everett glanced at each other strickenly, then did as Millikan told them. They looked at the photograph bleakly, having just confirmed for each other the fact that Millikan was mortally ill with the epizootic.

"Look those wonderful people in the eye," said Millikan, as tragically resonant as the Ancient Mariner now. "That's something *I've* always been able to do—until now," he said.

Breed and Dr. Everett continued to look into the uninteresting eyes, preferring the sight of them to the sight of a man who was going to die very soon.

"Look at Robert!" Millikan commanded, speaking of his eldest son. "Imagine having to tell that fine boy that he can't go to Andover anymore, that he's got to go to public school from now on! Look at Nancy!" he commanded, speaking of his only daughter. "No more horse, no more sailboat, no more country club for her. And look at little Marvin in his dear mother's arms," he said. "Imagine bringing a baby into this world and then realizing that you won't be able to give it any advantages at all!" His voice became jagged with self-torment and shame. "That poor little kid is going to have to fight every inch of the way!" he said. "They *all* are. When American Reliable and Equitable goes smash, there isn't a thing their father will be able to do for them! Tooth and nail all the way for them!" he cried.

Now Millikan's voice became soft with horror. He invited the two bachelors to look at his wife—a bland, lazy, plump dumpling, incidentally. "Imagine having a wonderful woman like that, a real pal who's stuck with you through thick and thin, who's borne your children and made a decent home for them," he said. "Imagine," he said after a long silence, "imagine being a hero to her, imagine giving her all the things she's longed for all her life. And then imagine telling her," he whispered, "that you've lost it all."

Millikan sobbed. He ran from the boardroom into his office, took a loaded revolver from his desk. As Breed and Dr. Everett burst in upon him, he blew his brains out, thereby maturing life insurance policies in the amount of one cool million.

And there lay one more case of the epizootic, the epidemic practice of committing suicide in order to create wealth.

"You know—" said the chairman of the board, "I used to wonder what was going to become of all the Americans like him, a bright and shiny new race that believed that life was a matter of making one's family richer and richer and richer, or it wasn't life. I often wondered what would become of them, if bad times ever came again, if the bright and shiny men suddenly discovered their net worths going down." Breed pointed to the floor. Now he pointed to the ceiling. "Instead of up," he said.

Bad times had come—about four months in advance of the epizootic.

"The one-way men—designed for up only," said Breed.

"And their one-way wives and their one-way children," said Dr. Everett. "Dear God—" he said, going to a window and looking out over a wintry Hartford, "the principal industry of this country is now dying for a living."

Hundred-Dollar Kisses

Q: Do you understand that everything you say is going to be taken down by that stenographer over there?

A: Yes sir.

Q: And that anything you say may be used against you?

A: Understood.

Q: Your name, age, and address?

A: Henry George Lovell, Jr., thirty-three, living at 4121 North Pennsylvania Street, Indianapolis, Indiana.

Q: Occupation?

A: Until about two o'clock this afternoon, I was manager of the Records Section of the Indianapolis Office of the Eagle Mutual Casualty and Indemnity Company of Ohio.

Q: In the Circle Tower?

A: Right.

Q: Do you know me?

A: You are Detective Sergeant George Miller of the Indianapolis Police Department.

Q: Has anyone maltreated you or threatened you with maltreatment or offered you favors in order to obtain this statement?

A: Nope.

Q: Did you, at approximately two o'clock this afternoon, assault a man named Verne Petrie with a telephone?

A: I hit him on the head with the part you talk and listen in.

Q: How many times did you strike him with it?

A: Once. I hit him one good one.

Q: What is Verne Petrie to you?

A: Verne Petrie to me is what is wrong with the world.

Q: I mean, what was Verne Petrie to you in the organization of the office?

A: We were on the same junior executive level. We were in different sections. He wasn't my boss, and I wasn't his boss.

Q: You were competing for advancement?

A: No. We were in two entirely different fields.

Q: How would you describe him?

A: You want me to describe Verne with feeling, or just for the record?

Q: Any way you want to do it.

A: Verne Petrie is a big, pink, fat man about thirty-five years old. He has silky orange hair and two long upper front teeth like a beaver. He wears a red vest and chainsmokes very small cigars. He spends at least fifteen dollars a month on girlie magazines.

Q: Girlie magazines?

A: *Man About Town. Bull. Virile. Vital. Vigor. Male Valor.* You know.

Q: And you say Verne Petrie spends fifteen dollars a month on such magazines?

A: At least. The things generally cost fifty cents or more, and I never saw Verne come back from a lunch hour when he didn't have at least one new one. Sometimes he had three.

Q: You don't like girls?

A: Sure I like girls. I'm crazy about girls. I married one, and I've got two nice little ones.

Q: Why should you resent it that Verne buys these magazines?

A: I don't resent it. It just seems kind of sick to me.

Q: Sick?

A: Girlie pictures are like dope to Verne. I mean, anybody likes to look at pin-up pictures off and on, but Verne, he has to buy armloads of them. He spends a fortune on them, and they're realer than anything real to him. When it says at the bottom of a pin-up picture, "Come play with me, Baby," or something like that, Verne believes it. He really thinks the girl is saying that to him.

Q: He's married?

A: To a nice, pretty, affectionate girl. He's got a swell-looking wife at home. It isn't as though he's bottled up in the Y.M.C.A.

Q: There is never anything else in the magazines besides pictures of girls?

A: Oh sure—there's other stuff. Haven't you ever looked inside one?

Q: I'm asking you.

A: They're all pretty much alike. They all have at least one big picture of a naked girl, usually right in the middle. That's what sells the magazine, is that big picture. Then there'll be some articles about foreign cars or decorating a bachelor penthouse or white slavery in Hong Kong or how to choose a loudspeaker. But what Verne wants is the pictures of the girls. To him, looking at those pictures is just like taking the girls out on dates. Cummerbunds.

Q: Pardon me? What was that last? Cummerbunds?

A: That's another thing they generally have articles on—cummerbunds.

Q: You seem to have read these magazines rather extensively yourself.

A: I had the desk right next to Verne's. The magazines were all over the place. And every time he brought a new one back to the office, he'd rub my nose in it.

Q: Actually rub your nose in it?

A: Practically. And he always said the same thing.

Q: What was the thing he always said?

A: I don't want to say it in front of a lady stenographer.

Q: Can't you approximate it?

A: Verne would open the magazine to the picture of the girl, and he'd say, approximately, "Boy, I'd pay a hundred dollars to kiss a doll baby like that. Wouldn't you?"

Q: This bothered you?

A: After a couple of years, it was getting under my skin.

Q: Why?

A: Because it showed a darn poor sense of values.

Q: Do you think you are God Almighty, empowered to go around correcting people's sense of values?

A: I do not think I am God Almighty. I do not even think I am a very good Unitarian.

Q: Suppose you tell us what happened when you came back from lunch this afternoon?

A: I found Verne Petrie sitting at his desk with a new copy of *Male Valor* magazine open in front of him. It was open to a two-page picture of a woman named Patty Lee Minot. She was wearing a cellophane bathrobe. Verne was listening to his telephone and looking at the picture at the same time. He had his hand over the mouthpiece. He winked at me, as though he was hearing something wonderful on the telephone. He signalled to me that I should listen in on my own telephone. He held up three fingers, meaning I should switch my phone to line three.

Q: Line three?

A: There are three lines coming into the office. And I looked around the office, and I realized that there was somebody listening in on line three on every telephone. Everybody in the office was listening in. So I listened in, and I could hear a telephone ringing on the other end.

Q: It was the telephone of Patty Lee Minot ringing in New York?

A: Yes. I didn't know it at the time, but that's what it was. Verne tried to tell me what was going on. He pointed to Patty Lee Minot's picture in the magazine, then he pointed to Miss Hackleman's desk.

Q: What was going on at Miss Hackleman's desk?

A: Miss Hackleman was out with a cold, and one of the building janitors was sitting in her chair, using her telephone. He was the one who was making the long-distance call that everybody else was listening in on.

Q: You knew him?

A: I'd seen him around the building. I knew his first name. It was stitched on the back of his coveralls. His first name was Harry. I found out later his whole name was Harry Barker.

Q: Describe him.

A: Harry? Well, he looks a lot older than he is. He looks about forty-five. Actually, I guess, he's younger than I am. He's pretty good-looking, and I think he must have been a pretty good athlete at one time. But he's losing his hair fast, and he's got a lot of wrinkles from worrying or something.

Q: So you were listening to the telephone ringing in New York?

A: Yes. And I accidentally sneezed.

Q: Sneezed?

A: Sneezed. I did it right into the telephone, and everybody jumped a mile, and then somebody said, "Gesundheit." This made Verne Petrie very sore.

Q: What did he do, exactly?

A: He got red, and he whined. He whined, "Shut up, you guys." You know. He whined like somebody who didn't want a beautiful experience spoiled by a bunch of jerks. "Come on, you guys," he whined, "either get off the line or shut up. I want to hear." And then somebody on the other end answered the telephone. It was Patty Lee Minot's maid, and the long-distance operator asked her if it was such-and-such a number, and the maid said yes it was. So the operator said, "Here's your number, sir," and the janitor named Harry started talking to the maid. Harry was all tensed up. He was making a lot of funny faces into the telephone, as though he was trying to make up his mind about how to sound. "Could I speak to Miss Melody Arlene Pfitzer, please?" he said. "Miss Who?" said the maid. "Miss Melody Arlene Pfitzer," said Harry. "Ain't nobody here named Pfitzer," said the maid. "This Patty Lee Minot's number?" said Harry. "That's right," said the maid. "Melody Arlene Pfitzer—" said Harry, "that's Patty Lee Minot's real name." "I wouldn't know nothing about that," said the maid.

Q: Who is Patty Lee Minot?

A: Don't you know?

Q: I'm asking you for the record.

A: I just told you: she was the girl in the cellophane bathrobe in Verne's magazine. She was the girl in the middle of *Male Valor*. I guess she is what you would call a glamorous celebrity. She's in the girlie magazines all the time, and sometimes she's on television, and one time I saw her in a movie with Bing Crosby.

Q: Continue.

A: You know what it said under her picture in the magazine?

Q: What?

A: "Woman Eternal for October." That's what it said.

Q: Go on about the telephone conversation.

A: Well, the janitor named Harry was kidding around with the maid about Patty Lee Minot's real name. "Call her Melody Arlene Pfitzer sometime, and see what she says," he said. "If it's all the same to you," said the maid, "I don't believe I will." And Harry said, "Put her on, would you please? Tell her it's Harry K. Barker calling." "She know you?" said the maid. "She will if she thinks about it a minute," said Harry. "Where you know her from?" said the maid. "High school," said Harry. "I don't believe she'll want to be bothered just now, on account of she's got a TV show tonight," said the maid. "She isn't thinking much about high school just now," she said. "I used to be married to her in high school," Harry said. "You think that might make a difference?" And then Verne hit me on the arm.

Q: He hit you?

A: Yes.

Q: You're claiming that he assaulted you before you assaulted him?

A: I suppose I could, couldn't I? That's an interesting idea. If I was to hire a shyster lawyer, I suppose that's maybe what he'd claim. No—Verne didn't assault me. He just hit me on the arm to get my attention, hit me hard enough to hurt, though. And then he practically smathered the picture of Patty Lee Minot all over my face.

Q: Smathered?

A: Practically smeared it all around.

Q: And what did the maid say on the telephone when she learned that Harry K. Barker had once been married to her employer?

A: She said, "Hold on."

Q: I see.

A: And then, after she left the telephone, I said, "Hold on," and Verne blew up.

Q: You made a little joke on the telephone, and Verne didn't like it?

A: I just imitated the maid, and Verne went through the roof. He said, "All right, wise guy, shut your trap. I get to hear your heavenly voice all day long, every day, year in and year out. I am just about to hear the voice of Patty Lee Minot in person, and I'll thank you kindly to keep your big yap shut. I'm paying for this call. This call is coming out of my hide. You're welcome to listen, but kindly shut up."

Q: Verne was paying for the call?

A: That's right. The call was his idea. It all started when he showed Harry the picture of Patty Lee Minot in the magazine. Verne told Harry he'd pay a hundred dollars to kiss a doll baby like that, and Harry said it was funny he should say that. Harry told Verne he used to be married to her. Verne couldn't believe it, so they bet twenty dollars on it, and then they put in the call.

Q: When Verne blew up at you, you didn't fight back in any way?

A: I just took it. He wasn't in any mood to be trifled with. It was just as though I was trying to bust up his love life. It was just as though he was having a big love affair with Patty Lee Minot, and I came along and wrecked it. I didn't say a word back to him, and then Patty Lee Minot came on the line. "Hello?" she said. "This is Harry Barker," Harry said. He was trying to be smooth and sophisticated. He was lighting a little cigar Verne had given to him. "Long time no see, Melody Arlene," he said. "Who is this really?" she said. "Is this you, Ferd?"

Q: Who is Ferd?

A: Search me. Some friend of hers who is a practical joker, I guess. Some glamorous, fun-loving New York celebrity. Harry said, "No, this is really Harry. We were married on October fourteenth, eleven years ago, Melody Arlene. Remember?" "If this is really Harry, and I don't believe it is," she said, "how come you're calling me up?" "I thought you might like to know how our daughter is, Melody Arlene," said Harry. "You never have tried to find out anything about her over all these years. I thought you might like to know how she was doing, since she is the only baby you ever had."

Q: What did she say to that?

A: She didn't say anything for a minute. Finally she said, in a very tough, twangy voice, "Who is this? Is this somebody trying to blackmail me? Because if it is, you can go straight to hell. Go ahead and give the whole story to the newspapers, if you want to. I've never tried to keep it a secret. I was married when I was sixteen to a boy named Harry Barker. We were both juniors in high school, and we had to get married on account of I was going to have a baby. Tell the whole wide world, for all I care." And then Harry said, "The baby died, Melody Arlene. Your little baby died two years after you walked out."

Q: He said what?

A: His and her baby died. Their baby died. She didn't even know it, never bothered to find out what became of her daughter. This, according to *Male Valor* magazine, was woman eternal, every red-blooded male's dream girl. And you know what she said?

Q: No.

A: Sergeant, this Woman Eternal for October said, "That's a part of my life I've blotted out completely. I'm sorry, but I couldn't care less."

Q: What was Verne Petrie's reaction when she said that?

A: No special reaction. His piggy little eyes were all glazed over, and he was showing his teeth and kind of gnashing them. He was off in some wild daydream about himself and Patty Lee Minot.

Q: And then what?

A: And then nothing. She hung up, and that was that. We all hung up, and everybody but Verne looked sick. Harry stood up, and he shook his head. "I wish to God I'd had more sense than to call her up," he said. "Here's your twenty bucks, Harry," said Verne. "No thanks," said Harry. He was like a man in a bad dream. "I don't want it now," he said. "It would be like money from her." Harry looked down at his hands. "I built her a house, a nice little house. Built it with my own hands," he said. He started to say something else, but he changed his mind. He shuffled out of the office, still looking at his hands. For about the next half hour, it was like a morgue around the office. Everybody felt lousy—everybody but Verne. I looked over at Verne, and he had the magazine open to the picture of Patty Lee Minot again. He caught my eye, and he said to me, "That lucky son of a gun."

Q: Who was a lucky son of a gun?

A: Harry Barker was a lucky son of a gun, because he'd been married to that wonderful woman on the bed. "That lucky son of a gun," Verne said. "Boy," he said, "since I've heard her voice on the telephone, she's one doll baby I'd give a thousand dollars to kiss."

Q: And then you let him have it?

A: Right.

Q: With his own telephone? On top of his head?

A: Right.

Q: Knocking him cold?

A: I knocked Verne Petrie colder than a mackerel, because it came to me all in a flash that Verne Petrie was what was wrong with the world.

Q: What is wrong with the world?

A: Everybody pays attention to pictures of things. Nobody pays attention to things themselves.

Q: Is there anything you would care to add?

A: Yes. I would like to put on the record the fact that I weigh one hundred and twenty-three pounds, and Verne Petrie weighs two hundred pounds and is a full foot taller than I am. I had no choice but to use a weapon. I stand ready, of course, to pay his hospital bill.

Ruth

THE TWO WOMEN nodded formally across the apartment's threshold. They were lonely women, widows; one middle-aged and the other young. Their meeting now—ostensibly to defeat their loneliness—only emphasized how solitary each was.

Ruth, the young woman, had travelled a thousand miles for this meeting with a stranger; had endured the clatter and soot and itch of a railroad coach from springtime in an Army town in Georgia to a factory town in a still-frozen New York valley. Now she wondered why it had seemed so right, so imperative that she come. This heavy, elderly woman, who blocked the door and smiled only with difficulty, had seemed in her letters to want this, too.

"So you're the woman who married my Ted," said the older woman coolly.

Ruth tried to imagine herself with a married son, and supposed she might have phrased the question in the same way. She set her bags down in the hall. She had expected to sweep into the apartment amid affectionate greetings, warm herself by a radiator, freshen up, and then begin to talk of Ted. Instead, her husband's mother seemed intent on examining her before letting her in. "Yes, Mrs. Faulkner," said Ruth, "we had five months together before he went overseas." Under the woman's critical stare, she found herself adding, almost defensively, "A happy five months."

"Ted was all I had," said Mrs. Faulkner. She said it as though it were a reproach.

"He was a fine man," said Ruth uneasily.

"My little boy," said Mrs. Faulkner. It was an aside to an unseen, sympathetic audience. She shrugged. "You must be cold. Do come in, Miss Hurley." Hurley was Ruth's maiden name.

"I could just as easily stay at a hotel," said Ruth. The woman's gaze made her feel foreign, self-conscious about her drawling speech, about her clothes, which were insubstantial, better suited to a warmer climate.

"I wouldn't hear of your staying anywhere but here. We have so much to talk about. When is Ted's child to be born?"

"In four months." Ruth slid her suitcase just inside the door, and sat, with an air of temporariness, on the edge of a sofa covered with slippery chintz. The only illumination in the overheated room came from a lamp on the mantel, its frail light muddled by a tortoiseshell shade. "Ted told me so much about you, I've been dying to meet you," said Ruth.

On the long train ride, Ruth had pretended for hours at a time that she was talking to Mrs. Faulkner, winning her affection from the first. She had rehearsed and polished her biography a dozen times in anticipation of Mrs. Faulkner's saying, "Now tell me something about yourself." She was ready with her opening line: "Well, I have no relatives, I'm afraid—no close ones, anyway. My father was a colonel in the cavalry, and . . ." But Ted's mother didn't put the opening question.

Silent and thoughtful, Mrs. Faulkner poured two tiny glasses of sherry from an expensive-looking decanter. "The personal effects—" she said at last, "they told me they were sent to you."

Ruth was puzzled for a moment. "Oh, the things he had with him overseas? Yes, I have them. It's customary, I think—I mean, it's a matter of routine to send them to the wife."

"I suppose it's all done automatically by machines in Washington," said Mrs. Faulkner ironically. "A general just pushes a button, and—" She left the sentence unfinished. "Could I have the things, please?"

"They're mine," said Ruth, and thought how childish that must sound. "I think he wanted me to have them." She looked down at the absurdly small glass of sherry, and wished for twenty more to take the edge off the ordeal.

"If it comforts you to think so, go right on thinking of them as yours," said Mrs. Faulkner patiently. "I simply want to have everything in one place—what little is left."

"I'm afraid I don't understand."

Mrs. Faulkner turned her back, and spoke softly, piously. "Having it all together makes him just a little nearer." She turned a switch on a floor lamp, suddenly filling the room with white brilliance. "These things will mean nothing to you," she said. "If you were a mother, you might understand how utterly priceless they are to me." She dabbed at a speck of dust on the ornate, glass-faced cabinet that squatted on lions' paws against the wall. "You see? I've left room in the cabinet for the things I knew you had."

"It's very sweet," said Ruth. She wondered what Ted might have thought of the cabinet—with its baby shoes, the book of nursery rhymes, the penknife, the Boy Scout badge. . . . Apart from its cheap sentimentality, Ted, too, would have sensed something unwholesome, sick about it. Mrs. Faulkner stared at the trinkets wide-eyed, unblinking, bewitched.

Ruth spoke to break the spell. "Ted told me you were doing awfully well at your shop. Is business as good as ever?"

"I've given it up," said Mrs. Faulkner absently.

"Oh? Then you're giving all your time to your club activities?"

"I've resigned."

"I see." Ruth fidgeted, taking off her gloves and putting them on again. "Ted said you were an awfully clever decorator, and I see he was right. He said you liked to do this place over every year or two. What sort of changes do you plan for next time?"

Mrs. Faulkner turned away from the shelf reluctantly. "Nothing will ever be changed again." She held out her hand. "Are the things in your suitcase?"

"There isn't much," said Ruth. "His billfold—"

"Cordovan, isn't it? I gave it to him in his junior year in high school."

Ruth nodded. She opened a suitcase, and dug into its bottom. "A letter to me, two medals, and a watch."

"The watch, please. The engraving on the back, I believe, says that it was a gift from me on his twenty-first birthday. I have a place ready for it."

Resignedly, Ruth held out the objects to her, cupped in her hands. "The letter I'd like to keep."

"You can certainly keep the letter and the medals. They have nothing to do with the boy I want to remember."

"He was a man, not a boy," said Ruth mildly. "He'd want to be remembered that way."

"That's your way of remembering him," said Mrs. Faulkner. "Respect mine."

"I'm sorry," said Ruth, "I do respect it. But you should be proud of him for being brave and—"

"He was gentle and sensitive and intelligent," interrupted Mrs. Faulkner passionately. "They should never have sent him overseas. They may have tried to make him hard and cheap, but at heart he was still my boy."

Ruth stood, and leaned against the cabinet, the shrine. Now she understood what was going on, what was behind Mrs. Faulkner's hostility. To the older woman, Ruth was one of the shadowy, faraway conspirators who had taken Ted.

"For heaven's sake, dear, look out!"

Startled, Ruth jerked her shoulder away from the cabinet. A small object tottered from an open shelf and smashed into white chips on the floor. "Oh!—I'm *so* sorry."

Mrs. Faulkner was on her knees, brushing the fragments together with her fingers. "How could you? How *could* you?"

"I'm awfully sorry. Can I buy you another one?"

"She wants to know if she can buy me another one," quavered Mrs. Faulkner, again to an unseen audience. "Where is it you can buy a candy dish made by Ted's little hands when he was seven?"

"It can be mended," said Ruth helplessly.

"Can it?" said Mrs. Faulkner tragically. She held the fragments before Ruth's face. "Not all the king's horses and all the king's men—"

"Thank heaven there were two of them," said Ruth, pointing to a second clay dish on the shelf.

"Don't touch it!" cried Mrs. Faulkner. "Don't touch anything!"

Trembling, Ruth backed away from the cabinet. "I'd better be going." She turned up the collar of her thin cloth coat. "May I use your phone to call a cab—please?"

Mrs. Faulkner's aggressiveness dissolved instantly into an expression of pitiability. "No. You can't take my boy's child away from me. Please, dear, try to understand and forgive me. That little dish was sacred. Everything that's left of my little boy is sacred, and that's why I behaved the way I did." She gathered a bit of Ruth's sleeve in her hand and held it tightly. "You understand, don't you? If there's an ounce of mercy in you, you'll forgive me and stay."

Ruth drove the air from her lungs with pent-up exasperation. "I'd like to go right to bed, if you don't mind." She wasn't tired, was so keyed up, in fact, that she expected to spend the night staring at the ceiling. But she didn't want to exchange another word with this woman, wanted to hide her humiliation and disappointment in the white oblivion of bed.

Mrs. Faulkner became the perfect hostess, respectful and solicitous. The small guest room, tasteful, crisp, barren, like all guest rooms implied an invitation to make oneself at home, and at the same time admitted that it was an impossibility. The room was cool, as though the radiators had only been turned on an hour or so before, and the air was sweet with the smell of furniture polish.

"And this is for the baby and me?" said Ruth. She had no intention of staying beyond the next morning, but felt forced to make conversation as Mrs. Faulkner lingered in the doorway.

"This is for you alone, dear. I thought the baby would be more comfortable in my room. It's larger, you know. I hardly know where you'd put a crib in here." She smiled primly. "Now, you *will* forgive me, won't you, dear?" She turned without waiting for an answer, and went to her room, humming softly.

Ruth lay wide-eyed for an hour between the stiff sheets. Her thoughts came in disconnected pulses of brilliance—glimpses of this moment and that. Ted's long, contemplative face appeared again and again. She saw him as a lonely child—as he had first come to her; then as a lover; then as a man. The shrine—commemorating a child, ignoring a man—made a pathetic kind of sense. For Mrs. Faulkner, Ted had died when he'd loved another woman.

Ruth threw back the covers, and walked to the window, needing the refreshment of a look at the outdoors. There was only a brick wall a few feet away, chinked with snow. She tiptoed down the hall, toward the big living room windows that framed the blue Adirondack foothills. She stopped.

Mrs. Faulkner, her gross figure silhouetted through a thin nightgown, stood before the shelf of souvenirs, talking to it. "Good night, darling, wherever you are. I hope you can hear me and know that your mother loves you." She paused, and appeared to be listening, and looked wise. "And your child will be in good hands, darling—the same hands that cradled you." She held up her hands for the shelf to see. "Good night, Ted. Sleep tight."

Ruth stole back to bed. A few moments later, bare feet padded down the hall, a door closed, and all was still.

⊙ ⊙ ⊙

"Good morning, Miss Hurley." Ruth blinked up at Ted's mother. The brick wall outside the guest room window glared, the snow gone. The sun was high. "Did you sleep well, my child?" The voice was cheerful, intimate. "It's almost noon. I have breakfast for you. Eggs, coffee, bacon, and biscuits. Would you like that?"

Ruth nodded and stretched, and drowsily doubted the nightmare of their meeting the night before. Sunlight was splashed everywhere, dispelling the funereal queasiness of their first encounter.

The table in the kitchen was aromatic with the peace and plenty of a leisurely breakfast.

As Ruth returned Mrs. Faulkner's smile across her third cup of coffee, she was at her ease, content with starting a new life in these warm surroundings. The night before had been no more than a misunderstanding between two tired, nervous women.

Ted wasn't mentioned—not at first. Mrs. Faulkner talked wittily about her early days as a businesswoman in a man's world, made light of what must have been desperate years after her husband's death. And then she encouraged Ruth to talk about herself, and she listened with flattering interest. "And I suppose you'll be wanting to go back to the South to live someday."

Ruth shrugged. "I have no real ties there—or anywhere else, for that matter. Father was an Army regular, and I've lived on practically every post you can name."

"Where would you most like to make your home?" Mrs. Faulkner coaxed.

"Oh—this is a pleasant enough part of the country."

"It's awfully cold," said Mrs. Faulkner with a laugh. "It's the world headquarters for sinus trouble and asthma."

"Well, I suppose Florida would be more easy going. I guess, if I had my choice, I'd like Florida best."

"You have your choice, you know."

Ruth set down her cup. "I plan to make my home here—the way Ted wanted me to."

"I meant after the baby is born," said Mrs. Faulkner. "Then you'd be free to go wherever you liked. You have the insurance money, and with what I could add to that you could get a nice little place in St. Petersburg or somewhere like that."

"What about you? I thought you wanted to have the child near you."

Mrs. Faulkner reached into the refrigerator. "Here, you poor dear, you need cream, don't you." She set the pitcher before Ruth. "Don't you see how nicely it would work out for both of us? You could leave the child with me, and be free to lead the life a young woman should lead." Her voice became confiding. "It's what Ted wants for both of us."

"I'm darned if it is!"

Mrs. Faulkner stood. "I think I'm the better judge of that. He's with me every minute I'm in this house."

"Ted is dead," said Ruth incredulously.

"That's just it," said Mrs. Faulkner impatiently. "To you he *is* dead. You can't feel his presence or know his wishes now, because you hardly knew him. One doesn't get to know a person in five months."

"We were man and wife!" said Ruth.

"Most husbands and wives are strangers till death does them part, dear. I hardly knew my husband, and we had several years together."

"Some mothers try to make their sons strangers to every woman but themselves," said Ruth bitterly. "Praise be to God, you failed by a hair!"

Mrs. Faulkner strode man-like into the living room. Ruth listened to the springs creaking in the chair before the sacred cabinet. Again the whispered dialogue with silence drifted down the hall.

In ten minutes, Ruth was packed and standing in the living room.

"Child, where are you going?" said Mrs. Faulkner, without looking at her.

"Away—South, I guess." Ruth's feet were close together, her high heels burrowing in the carpet as she shifted petulantly from one foot to the other. She had a great deal to say to the older woman, and she waited for her to face her. A hundred vengeful phrases had sprung to mind as she packed—just, unanswerable.

Mrs. Faulkner didn't turn her head, continued to stare at the mementos. Her big shoulders were hunched, her head down—an attitude of stubborn mass and wisdom. "What are you, Miss Hurley, some sort of goddess who can give or take away the most precious thing in a person's life?"

"You asked me to give a great deal more than you have any right to ask." Ruth imagined how a small boy might have felt, standing on this spot while the keen bully of a woman decided what, exactly, he was to do next.

"I ask only what my son asks."

"That isn't so."

"She's wrong, isn't she, dear?" said Mrs. Faulkner to the cabinet. "She doesn't love you enough to hear you, but your mother does."

Ruth slammed the door, ran into the wet street, and flagged a puzzled motorist to a stop.

"I ain't no cab, lady."

"Please, take me to the station."

"Look, lady, I'm going uptown, not downtown." Ruth burst into tears. "All right, lady. For heaven's sakes, all right. Get in."

"Train number 427, the Seneca, arriving on track four," said the voice in the loud-speaker. The voice seemed intent on shattering any illusions passengers might have of their destinations' being better than what they were leaving. San Francisco was droned as cheerlessly as Troy; Miami sounded no more seductive than Knoxville.

Thunder rolled across the ceiling of the waiting room. The pillar by Ruth trembled. She looked up from her magazine to the station clock. Her train would be next, southbound.

When she bought her ticket, checked her baggage through, and settled on a hard bench to read away the dead minutes, her movements had been purposeful, quick, her walk almost a swagger. The motions had been an accompaniment to a savage dialogue buzzing in her head. In her imagination she had lashed out at Mrs. Faulkner with merciless truths, had triumphantly wrung from that rook of a woman apologies and tears.

For the moment, the vengeful fantasy left Ruth satisfied, forgetful of her recent tormentor. She felt only boredom and incipient loneliness. To dispel these two, she looked from group to group in the waiting room, reading in faces and clothes and luggage the commonplace narratives that had brought each person to the station.

A tall, baby-faced private chatted stiffly with his well-dressed mother and father: yanked out of gray flannels and college by the draft . . . nothing but a marksman's medal . . . bright, lots of money . . . father uncomfortable about son's rank and over-parking . . .

A racking cough cut into Ruth's thoughts. An old man, cramped against the armrest at the end of a completely vacant bench, was doubled by a coughing fit. He waited for the coughing to subside, so that he could take another puff on the cigarette butt between his dirty fingers.

A frail, bright-eyed old woman handed a redcap a dollar, and demanded his polite attention as she gave precise instructions as to how her luggage was to be handled: on her annual expedition to criticize her children and spoil her grandchildren . . .

Again the agonized coughing. Now Ruth caught the stench of the dirty man's breath, brought to her nostrils by a sudden gust from the door. The cough worsened, tearing the breath from him. The cigarette dropped.

Ruth twisted around on the bench so that her gaze wouldn't naturally fall on him. A winded fat man, his red face determinedly cheerful beneath a homburg, begged to be let in at the first of the ticket line: salesman . . . ball bearings or boilers or something like that . . .

Again the agonized coughing. Irritated that so disagreeable a sight should make demands on her attention, Ruth glanced once more at the old man. He had slumped over the arm of the bench, twisted, quaking.

The fat salesman looked down at the old man, and then straight ahead again, keeping his place in line.

The old lady, still instructing the redcap, raised her voice to be heard above the interruption.

The young soldier and his correct parents weren't so vulgar as to acknowledge that something unsightly was at hand.

A newsboy burst into the station, started to stride down the aisle between Ruth and the old man, stopped a few feet short, and headed for the other end of the waiting room, shouting news of a tragedy a thousand miles away. "Read all about it!"

Another train rumbled overhead. Everyone was moving toward the ramp now, avoiding the aisle in which the old man lay, giving no sign that it was anything but luck that made them choose another route to the train.

"*Buffalo, Harrisburg, Baltimore, and Washington,*" said the voice in the loud-speaker.

Ruth realized that it was her train, too. She stood without looking again at the old man. He was no more than disgustingly drunk, she told herself. He deserved to lie there, sleeping it off. She tucked her magazine and purse under her arm. Someone—the police or some charity or whoever's job it was—would be along to pick him up.

"*Board!*"

Ruth skirted the man and strode toward the ramp. The hiss and chilling dampness from the track level billowed down the ramp to envelop her. Pale lights, wreathed in steam, stretched away in seeming infinity—unreal, offering nothing to compete with her thoughts.

And her thoughts nagged, making her imagine an annoying, repetitive sound—a man's cough. Louder and louder it grew in her mind, seeming to echo and amplify in a vast stone vault.

"*Board!*"

Ruth turned, and ran back down the ramp. In seconds she was leaning over the old man, loosening his collar, rubbing his wrists. She laid his slight frame out at full length, and placed her coat under his head.

"Redcap!" she shouted.

"Yes'm?"

"This man is dying. Call an ambulance!"

"Yes ma'am!"

Horns honked as Ruth walked against the light. She took no notice, busily upbraiding in her mind the insensitive men and women in the railroad station. The ambulance had taken the old man away, and now Ruth, having missed her train, had four more hours to spend in Ted's hometown.

"Just because he was ugly and dirty, you wouldn't help him," she told the imagined crowd. "He was sick and needed help, and you all went your selfish ways rather than touch him. Shame on you." She looked challengingly at persons coming down the sidewalk toward her, and had her look returned with puzzlement. "You'd pretend there was nothing serious wrong with him," she murmured.

Ruth killed time in a woman's way, pretending to be on a shopping errand. She looked critically at window displays, fingered fabrics, priced articles, and promised salesgirls she would be back to buy after looking in one or two more shops.

Her activity was almost fully automatic, leaving her thoughts to go their righteous, self-congratulatory way. She was one of the few, she told herself, who did not run away from the untouchables, from unclean, sick strangers.

It was a buoyant thought, and Ruth let herself believe that Ted was sharing it with her. With the thought of Ted came the image of his formidable mother. The buoyance grew as Ruth saw how selfish Mrs. Faulkner was by comparison. The older woman would have sat in the waiting room oblivious to everything but the tragedy in her own narrow life. She would have muttered to a ghost while the old man hacked his life away.

Ruth relived her bitter, humiliating few hours with the woman, the bullying and wheedling in the name of a nightmarish notion of motherhood and an armful of trinkets. Disgust and the urge to get away came back full strength. Ruth leaned against a jewelry counter, and came face-to-face with herself in a mirror.

"Can I help you, madam?" said a salesgirl.

"What? Oh—no, thank you," said Ruth. The face in the mirror was vindictive, smug. The eyes had the same cold glaze as the eyes that had looked at the old man in the station and seen nothing.

"You look a little ill. Would you like to sit down for a moment?"

"No, really—there's nothing wrong," said Ruth absently.

"There's a doctor on duty in the store."

Ruth looked away from the mirror. "This is silly of me. I felt unsteady there for just a minute. It's passed now." She smiled uncertainly. "Thanks very much. I've got to be on my way."

"A train?"

"No," said Ruth wearily. "A terribly sick old woman needs my help."

Out, Brief Candle

ANNIE COWPER THOUGHT of the letters from Schenectady as having come like a sweet, warm wind at the sunset of her life. The truth was that she was only in her middle forties when they started to come, and the sunset of her life was still far away. She had all of her teeth and needed her steel-rimmed spectacles only for reading.

She felt old because her husband, Ed, who really was old, had died and left her alone on the hog farm in northern Indiana. When Ed died, she had sold the livestock, rented the flat, black, rich land to neighbors, read her Bible, watered her houseplants, fed her chickens, tended her small vegetable garden, or simply rocked—waiting patiently and without rancor for the Bright Angel of Death. Ed had left her plenty of money, so she wasn't goaded into doing anything more, and the people in the area, the only area Annie knew, made her feel that she was doing the right thing, the customary thing, the only thing.

Though she was without relatives, she wasn't without callers. Farm wives came often for an hour or two of stifled pity over cakes and coffee.

"If my Will went, I just don't know what I'd do," said one. "In the city, I don't think folks really know what it is to be one flesh. They just change husbands as often as they please, and one's as good as another one."

"Yes," said Annie, "I certainly wouldn't care for that. Have another peach surprise, Doris June."

"I mean, in the city a man and woman don't really need each other except to—" Delicately, Doris June left the sentence unfinished.

"Yes, that's true," said Annie. One of her duties as a widow, she had learned, was to provide dramatic proof to the neighboring wives that, bad as their husbands might be at times, life without them would be worse.

Annie didn't spoil this illusion for Doris June by telling her about the letters—telling her what she had discovered so late in life about womanly happiness, telling her about one man, at least, who could make her happy from as far away as Schenectady.

Sometimes other women's husbands came to the farm, too, gruff and formal, to perform some man's chore that their wives had noticed needed doing—patching a roof, putting a new packing in the pump, greasing the idle machinery in the barn. They knew she was a virtuous widow, and respected her severely for it. They hardly spoke.

Sometimes Annie wondered how the husbands would act if they knew about the letters. Maybe they would think she was a loose woman, then, and accept her formal invitations for coffee which were meant to be declined. They might even make remarks with double meanings and full of shy flirtation—the sort of remarks they made to the shameless girl behind the coffee counter in the diner in town.

If she'd shown the men the letters, they would have read something dirty into them, she thought, when the letters weren't at all like that, really. They were spiritual, they were poetry, and she didn't even know or care what the man who wrote them looked like.

Sometimes the minister came for a visit, too, a bleak, fleshless, dust-colored old man, who was overjoyed by her death-like peace and moral safety.

"You make me want to go on, Mrs. Cowper," he said. "I wish you could talk to our young people sometime. They don't believe it's possible for a person to live a Christian life in this modern day and age."

"That's very kind of you," said Annie. "I think all young people are kind of wild, and settle down later. Have another raspberry delight, won't you? They'll only spoil, and I'll have to throw them away."

"You were never wild, were you, Mrs. Cowper?"

"Well—of course I married Ed when I was just a little better than sixteen. I didn't have much chance for running around."

"And you wouldn't have, if you'd had the chance," said the minister triumphantly.

Annie felt a strange impulse to argue with him and tell him proudly about the letters. But she fought the wicked impulse, and nodded gravely.

A few would-be lovers called, too, with honorable intentions and a powerful lust for her land. But, while these callers spoke clumsy poetry about her fields, not one made her feel that she was anything more than what she saw of herself in the mirror—a tall, lean woman, as unornamental as a telephone pole, with coarse, work-swollen hands, and a long nose whose tip had been bitten to a permanent red by frost. Like Ed, they never tried.

The moment a would-be lover left after a chilly visit, mumbling about weather and crops and twisting his hat, Annie would feel a great need for the letters from Schenectady. She would lock the door, pull the blinds, lie on her bed, and read and reread the letters until hunger or sleep or a knock on the door forced her to hide them again until another time.

Ed died in October, and Annie got along without him and without the letters, too, until the next spring—or what should have been spring. It was in early May, when a sudden, bitter frost killed the daffodil sprouts, that Annie had written:

"Dear 5587: This is the first time I have ever written to a total stranger. I just happened to be waiting in the drugstore to get a prescription for my sinus trouble filled, and I picked up a copy of Western Romance Magazine. I don't usually read magazines like that. I think they are silly. But I just happened to turn to the pen pals section, and I saw your letter, and I read where you are lonely and could sure use a pen pal." She smiled at her foolishness. "I will tell you a little about myself," she wrote. "I am fairly young still, and I have brown hair, green eyes, and . . ."

In a week, a reply had come, and the code number used by the magazine became a name: Joseph P. Hawkins, of Schenectady, New York.

"My dear Mrs. Cowper:" Hawkins had written, "I have received many replies to my plea for pen pals, but none has moved me more deeply than yours. A meeting of kindred spirits, such as I believe ours to be, is a rare thing, indeed, in this vale of tears, and is fuller of true bliss than the most perfect of physical matings. I see you now as an angel, for the voice I hear in your letters is the voice of an angel. The instant the angel appeared, loneliness fled, and I knew I was not really alone on this vast and crowded planet after all . . ."

Annie had giggled nervously as she read the first letter, and felt guilty about having led the poor man on so, and she had been a little shocked, too, by the ardent tone of the letter. But she'd found herself rereading the letter several times a day, each time with increased pity. At last, in a fever of compassion, she had given the poor man his wish, and painstakingly tried to create another angel for him.

From then on there had been no turning back, no will to turn back.

Hawkins was eloquent and poetic—but most of all he was exquisitely sensitive to a woman's moods. He sensed it when Annie was depressed, though she never told him she was, and he would say just the right thing to cheer her. And when she was elated, he nourished her elation, and kept it alive for weeks instead of fleeting minutes.

She tried to do the same for him, and her fumbling efforts seemed to sit surprisingly well with her pen pal.

Never once did Hawkins say a vulgar thing, nor did he harp on the fact of his being a man and her a woman. That was unimportant, he said vehemently. The important thing was that their spirits would never be lonely again, so splendidly were they matched. It was a very high-level correspondence—on such a high level, in fact, that Annie and Hawkins went for an entire year without mentioning anything as down-to-earth as money, work, age, physical appearances, organized religion, or politics. Nature, Fate, and the undefinable sweet aches of the spirit were subject matter enough to keep them both writing on and on and on and on and on. The second winter without Ed seemed no worse than a chilly May to Annie, because, for the first time in her life, she had discovered what true friendship was like.

When the correspondence finally came down to earth, it wasn't Joseph P. Hawkins who brought it down—it was Annie. When spring came again, she was writing to him, as he had written to her, about the millions of tender little shoots poking their heads up, and about the mating songs of the birds and the budding of the trees, and the bees carrying pollen from one plant to the next—when she suddenly felt compelled to do what Hawkins had forbidden her to do.

"Please," he had written, "let us not descend to the vulgarity of, as I believe the phrase goes, 'exchanging snaps.' No photographer, save in Heaven, could ever take a picture of the angel that rises from your letters to blind me with adoration."

But one heady, warm spring night, Annie enclosed a snapshot anyway. The picture was one Ed had taken at a picnic five years before, and, at the time, she'd thought it was a terrible likeness. But now, as she studied it before sealing her letter, she saw a great deal in the woman in the picture that she had not seen before—a haze of spiritual beauty that softened every harsh line.

The next two days of waiting were nightmares. She hated herself for having sent the picture, and told herself that she was the ugliest woman on earth, that she had ruined everything between herself and Hawkins. Then she would try to calm herself by telling herself that the picture couldn't possibly make any difference—that the relationship was purely spiritual, that she might as well have enclosed a blank sheet of paper, for all the difference the picture, beautiful or ugly, could make. But only Joseph P. Hawkins could say what the effect of the picture was.

He did so by special-delivery airmail. "Bright angel, adieu!" he wrote, and Annie burst into tears.

But then she forced herself to read on. "Frail, wispish counterfeit of my mind's eye, stand aside, dethroned by warm and earthly, vibrant bride of my mind—my Annie as she really is! Adieu, ghost! Make way for life, for I live and Annie lives, and it is spring!"

Annie was jubilant. She hadn't spoiled anything with the picture. Hawkins had seen the haze of spiritual beauty, too.

It wasn't until she sat down to write that she understood how changed the relationship was. They had admitted that they were not only spirit but flesh, and Annie's skin tingled at the thought—and the pen that once had wings did not budge. Every phrase that came to Annie's mind seemed foolish, inflated, though phrases like them had seemed substantial enough in the past.

And then the pen began to move with a will of its own. It wrote two words that said more than Annie had said in the hundred pages that had gone before:

"I come."

She was blind with love, gloriously out of control.

Hawkins's reply, a telegram, was almost as short: "PLEASE DON'T. AM DEATHLY ILL."

That was his last communication. Annie's telegrams and special-delivery letters brought no more response from Joseph P. Hawkins. A long-distance call revealed that Hawkins had no telephone. Annie was shattered, able to think of nothing but the gentle, lonely man, wasting away without a soul to care for him, *really care*, seven hundred miles from the vibrant bride of his mind.

After one agonized week of Hawkins's profound silence, Annie strode from the Schenectady railroad station, flushed with love, suffocating in her new girdle, tormented by her savings, which crackled and scratched in her stocking-tops and spare bosom. She carried a small suitcase and her knitting bag, into which she'd swept the entire contents of her medicine cabinet.

She wasn't afraid, not even rattled, though she'd never been on a train before, and had never seen anything remotely like the clouds of smoke and clanging busyness of Schenectady. She was numbed by duty and love, impressively tall and long-striding, leaning forward aggressively.

The cabstand was empty, but Annie told a redcap Hawkins's address, and he directed her to a bus that would take her there.

"You just ask the bus driver where you should get off," said the redcap.

And Annie did—at two-minute intervals. She sat right behind the driver, her modest luggage on her lap.

As the bus picked its way through mazes of noisy, fuming factories and slums and jounced over chuckholes and railroad tracks, Annie could see Hawkins, thin and white, tall, delicate, and blue-eyed, wasting away on a hard narrow bed in a tenement room.

"Is this the place where I get off?"

"No, ma'am. Not yet. I'll let you know."

The factories and slums dropped away, and pleasant little houses on neat, green, postage-stamp lots took their place. Peering into the windows as the bus passed, Annie could imagine Hawkins lying abed in his small, shipshape bachelor's quarters, once husky, now wan, his body ravished by disease.

"Is this where I get off?"

"A good ways, yet, ma'am. I'll let you know."

The small houses gave way to larger ones, and these gave way to mansions, the largest homes Annie had ever seen. She was the only passenger aboard now, awed by a new image of Hawkins, a dignified old gentleman with silver hair and a tiny mustache, languishing in a bed as big as her vegetable garden.

"Is this the neighborhood?" said Annie incredulously.

"Right along here somewhere." The bus slowed, and the driver looked out at the house numbers. At the next corner, he stopped the bus and opened the door. "Somewhere in that block, lady. I was looking for it, but I guess I missed it."

"Maybe it's in the next block," said Annie, who'd been watching too, with a quaking heart, as the house numbers came closer and closer to the one she knew so well.

"Nope. Got to be in this one. Nothing up ahead but a cemetery, and that goes for six blocks."

Annie stepped out into the quiet, shaded street. "Thank you very much."

"You're certainly welcome," said the driver. He started to close the door, but hesitated. "You know how many people are dead in that cemetery up there?"

"I'm a stranger in town," said Annie.

"All of 'em," said the driver triumphantly. The door clattered shut, and the bus grumbled away.

An hour later, Annie had rung every doorbell and been barked at by every dog in the block.

No one had ever heard of Joseph P. Hawkins. Everyone agreed that, if there were such an address, it would be a tombstone in the next block.

Desolately, her big feet hurting, Annie trudged along the grass outside the iron-spiked cemetery fence. There were only stone angels to return her bewildered, searching gaze. She came at last to the stone arch that marked the cemetery entrance. Defeated, she sat down on her suitcase to wait for the next bus.

"Looking for somebody?" said a gruff voice behind her.

She turned to see a dwarfed old man standing under the cemetery arch. One eye was blind and white as a boiled egg, and the pupil of the other eye was bright and cunning, and roamed restlessly. He carried a shovel clotted with fresh earth.

"I—I'm looking for Mr. Hawkins," said Annie. "Mr. Joseph P. Hawkins." She stood, and tried to conceal her horror.

"Cemetery business?"

"He works here?"

"Did," said the dwarf. "Dead now."

"No!"

"Yep," said the dwarf without feeling. "Buried this morning."

Annie sank down, until she was seated on the suitcase again, and then she cried softly. "Too late, too late."

"A friend of yours?"

"The dearest friend a woman ever had!" said Annie passionately, brokenly. "Did you know him?"

"Nope. They just put me on the job out here when he took sick. From what I hear, he was quite a gentleman, though."

"He was, he was," said Annie. She looked up at the old man, and contemplated his shovel uneasily. "Tell me," she said. "He wasn't a—a grave-digger, was he?"

"Landscape architect and memorial custodian."

"Oh," said Annie, smiling through her tears, "I'm so glad." She shook her head. "Too late, too late. What can I do now?"

"I hear he liked flowers pretty well."

"Yes," said Annie, "he said they were the friends who always came back and never disappointed him. Where could I get some?"

"Well, it's supposed to be against the law, but I guess maybe it'd be all right if you picked some of those crocuses inside the gate there, just as long as nobody saw you. And there are some violets over there by his house."

"His house?" said Annie. "Where's his house?"

The old man pointed through the arch to a small, squat stone building, matted with ivy.

"Oh—the poor man," said Annie.

"It's not so bad," said the old man. "I live there now, and it's all right. Come on. You get the flowers, and then I'll drive you over to where he's buried in the truck. It's a long walk, and you'd get lost. He's in the new part we're just opening up. First one there, in fact."

The cemetery's little pickup truck followed ribbons of asphalt through the still, cool, forest of marble, until Annie was lost. The seat of the truck was jammed forward, so that the old man's short legs could reach the pedals. Annie's long legs, as a consequence, were painfully cramped by the dashboard. In her lap was a bouquet of crocuses and violets.

Neither spoke. Annie couldn't bear to look at her companion, and could think of nothing to say to him, and he, in turn, didn't seem particularly interested in her— was simply performing a routine and tiresome chore.

They came at last to an iron gate that barred the way into mud ruts leading into a wood.

The old man unlocked the gate. He put the truck into low gear, and it pushed into the twilight of the woods, with briars and branches scratching at its sides.

Annie gasped. Ahead was a peaceful, leafy clearing, and there, in a patch of sunlight, was a fresh grave.

"Headstone hasn't come yet," said the dwarf.

"Joseph, Joseph," whispered Annie. "I'm here."

The dwarf stopped the truck, limped around to Annie's side, and opened her door with a courtly gesture. He smiled for the first time, baring a ghastly set of dead-white false teeth.

"Could I be alone?" said Annie.

"I'll wait here."

Annie laid her flowers on the grave, and sat beside it for an hour, reciting to herself all the wonderful, tender things Joseph had said to her.

The chain of thought might have gone on for hours more, if the little man hadn't broken it with a polite cough.

"We'd better go," he said. "The sun will be going down soon."

"It's like tearing my heart out, leaving him here alone."

"You can come back another time."

"Yes," said Annie, "I will."

"What kind of a man was he?"

"What kind?" said Annie, standing reverently. "I never saw him. We just wrote to each other. He was a good, good man."

"What did he do that was good?"

"He made me feel pretty," said Annie. "I know what that's like now."

"You know what he looked like?"

"No. Not exactly."

"He was tall and broad shouldered, I hear. He had blue eyes and curly hair. That the way you imagined him?"

"Oh, yes!" said Annie happily. "Exactly. I could tell."

The sun was setting when the one-eyed gnome drove into the cemetery, after having warned Annie about strangers and put her on the train. Tombstones cast long shadows across his way as he went once more to the lonely poet's grave in the woods.

He took Annie's bouquet from the grave with a sigh.

He drove back to his stone house, and put the flowers in water, in a vase on his desk. He touched off the fire laid in the fireplace, to drive out the early spring evening's dampness, made himself a cup of coffee, and sat down to write, leaning forward to sniff Annie's flowers as he did so.

"My dear Mrs. Draper:" he wrote. "How strange that you, my pen pal and soul's dearest friend, should be on a chicken farm in British Columbia, a beautiful land that I shall probably never see. No matter what you say about life in British Columbia, it must be very beautiful, for hasn't it produced you? Please, please, please," he wrote, and he grunted emphatically as he underlined the three words, "let us not descend to the vulgarity of, as I believe the phrase goes, 'exchanging snaps.' No photographer, save in Heaven, could ever take a picture of the angel that rises from your letters to blind me with adoration."

Mr. Z

GEORGE WAS THE SON of a country minister and the grandson of a country minister. He was in the Korean War. When that was over, he decided to become a minister, too.

He was an innocent. He wanted to help people in trouble. So he went to the University of Chicago. He didn't study just theology. He studied sociology and psychology and anthropology, too. He went to school the year around, and, during one summer session, there was a course offered in criminology.

George didn't know anything about criminals, so he took it.

And he was told to go to the county jail to interview a prisoner named Gloria St. Pierre Gratz. She was the wife of Bernard Gratz, who was said to be a killer for hire and a thief. Ironically, Gratz remained at large and unhunted, since nothing could be proved against him. His wife was in jail for possessing stolen goods, goods almost certainly stolen by him. She had not implicated him—neither had she given a reasonable account of where else the diamonds and fur coats might have come from. She was serving a year and a day. Her sentence was just about up when George went to see her. George was interviewing her not simply because of her criminality, but because she had an astoundingly high I.Q. She told George that she preferred to be addressed by her maiden name, the name she had used during her days as an exotic dancer. "I never learned how to answer to the name of Mrs. Gratz," she said. "That's nothing against Bernie," she said. "I just never learned." So George called her Miss St. Pierre.

He talked to Miss St. Pierre through a screen at the jail. It was the first jail George had ever been in. He had written down the bare bones of her biography in a loose-leaf notebook. Now he was double-checking the information.

"Let's see—" he said to her, "you left high school in the middle of your junior year, and you changed your name from Francine Pefko to Gloria St. Pierre. You stopped seeing Mr. F, and you became a carhop outside of Gary. And it was there that you met Mr. G?"

"Arny Pappas," she said.

"Right—" said George, "Arny Pappas—Mr. G. Is *carhop* one word or two?"

"Two words, one word—" she said, "who ever wrote it down before?" She was a tiny girl—a trinket brunette, very pretty, very pale, and hard as nails. She was bored stiff with George and his questions. She yawned a lot, not bothering to cover her velvet mouth. And her responses were bewilderingly derisive. "A smart college kid like you ought to be able to make *ten* words out of it," she said.

Gamely, George went on trying to sound professional and brisk. "Well now," he said, "was there some reason for your discontinuing your education in your junior year?"

"My father was a drunk," she said. "My stepmother clawed. I was already grown up. I already looked twenty-one. I could make all the money I wanted. Arny Pappas gave me a yellow Buick convertible all my own. Honey—" she said, "what did I want with algebra and *Ivanhoe?*"

"Um," said George. "And then Mr. H came along, and he and Mr. G got into a fistfight over you?"

"Knives," she said. "It was knives. Stan Carbo—that was his name. Why call him Mr. H?"

"To protect him—" said George, "to keep this all confidential—to protect anybody you might want to tell me about."

She laughed. She stuck the tip of a finger through the screen, and she wiggled it at George. "You?" she said. "You're going to protect Stan Carbo? I wish you could see him. I wish *he* could see *you.*"

"Well," said George lamely, "maybe someday we'll meet."

"He's dead," she said. She didn't sound sorry. She didn't even sound interested.

"That's too bad," said George.

"You're the first person who ever said so," she said.

"In any event," said George, looking at his notes, "while he was still among the living, Mr. H offered you a job as an exotic dancer in his nightclub in East Chicago—and you accepted."

Gloria laughed again. "Honest to God, honey—" she said, "you should see your face. It's bright red! You know that? Your mouth looks like you've been sucking lemons!" She shook her head. "Rollo—" she said, "tell me again what you think you're doing here."

George had been over the question several times before. He went over it again. "As I told you," he said patiently, "I'm a student of sociology, which is the science of human society." There wasn't any point in telling her that the course was actually criminology. That might be offensive. There didn't seem to be much point in telling her anything, for that matter.

"They made a science out of people?" she said. "What a crazy science that must be."

"It's still very much in its infancy," said George.

"Like you," she said. "How old are you, baby?"

"Twenty-one," said George stiffly.

"Think of that!" she said. "Twenty-one! What is it like to be that old? I won't be twenty-one until next March." She sat back. "You know," she said, "every so often

I meet somebody like you, and I realize it's possible for some people to grow up in this country without ever seeing anything, without ever having anything happen to them."

"I was in Korea for a year and a half," said George. "I think I've had a little something happen to me."

"I tell you what," she said, "I'll write a book about your great adventures, and you can write one about mine." And then, to George's dismay, she took a pencil stub and an empty pack of cigarettes from her pocket. She tore the pack apart, flattened it out to make a sheet of paper. "All righty—" she said, "here we go, Rollo. We'll call this *The Thrilling Life Story of Mr. Z*—to protect you. You were born on a farm, were you, Mr. Z?"

"Please—" said George, who really had been born on a farm.

"I answered your questions," she said. "You answer mine." She frowned. "Your present address, Mr. Z?" she said.

George shrugged, told her his address. He was living over the garage of the dean of the Divinity School.

"Occupation?" she said. "*Student*. One word or two?"

"Two," said George.

"*Stew dent*," she said, and she wrote it down. "Now, I'm going to have to investigate your love life, Mr. Z. That's actually kind of the main part of your science, even though it *is* in its infancy. I want you to tell me about all the hearts you've broken during this wild, wild life of yours. Let's start with Miss A."

George closed his notebook. He gave her a bleak smile. "Thanks for your time, Miss St. Pierre," he said. "It was good of you to talk to me." He stood.

She gave him a blinding smile. "Oh, *please* sit down," she said. "I haven't been nice at all—and here you've been so nice to me, no matter what awful things I say. Please—please sit down, and I'll answer any question you ask. Any question. Ask me a real hard one, and I'll do my best. Isn't there one really *big* question?"

George was fool enough to relax some, to sit down again. He did have one big question. He had no more dignity, no more anything to lose, so he asked it—asked it flat out. "You've got a very high I.Q., Miss Pierre. Why is it that somebody as smart as you are should live the way you do?"

"Who says I'm smart?" she said.

"You've been tested," said George. "Your I.Q. is higher than that of the average physician."

"The average physician," she said, "couldn't find his own behind with both hands."

"That's not quite true—" said George.

"Doctors make me sick," she said. And now she turned really nasty, now that she had George relaxed for a full blast of malevolence. "But college kids make me sicker," she said. "Get out of here," she said. "You're the most boring goon I ever met!" She made a limp, disgusted motion with her hand. "Beat it, Rollo," she said. "Tell teacher I'm the way I am because I *like* the way I am. Maybe they'll make you a professor of people like me."

Out in the anteroom of the jail, a little, dark, vicious young man came up to George. He looked at George as though he wanted to kill him. He had a voice like a grackle. He was Bernard Gratz, the lady's husband.

"You been in there with Gloria St. Pierre?" said Gratz.

"That's right," said George politely.

"Where you from?" he said. "What you want with her?" he said. "Who ast you to come?" he said.

George had a letter of introduction from the professor who was giving the course in criminology. He handed it to Gratz.

Gratz wadded it up and handed it back. "That don't cut no ice with me," he said. "She ain't supposed to talk to nobody but her lawyer or me. She knows that."

"It was purely voluntary on her part," said George. "Nobody made her talk to me."

Gratz took hold of George's notebook. "Come on—lemme see," he said. "What you got in the book?"

George pulled the book away. It not only had his notes on Gloria in it. It contained notes for all of his courses.

Gratz made another grab for the notebook, got it. He tore out all the pages, threw them up in the air.

George did a very un-Christian thing. He knocked the little man cold—laid him right out.

He revived Gratz enough to get Gratz's promise that he was going to kill George slowly. And then George gathered up his papers and went home.

Two weeks went by without much of anything's happening. George wasn't worried about being killed. He didn't think Gratz had any way of finding him in his room over the garage of the dean of the Divinity School. George had trouble believing that the adventure in the jail had even happened.

There was a picture in the paper one day, showing Gloria St. Pierre leaving the jail with Gratz. George didn't believe either one was real.

And then, one night, he was reading *The Encyclopedia of Criminology*. He was looking for clues that would help him to understand the life Gloria St. Pierre had chosen to lead. The *Encyclopedia*, all-inclusive as it tried to be, said not one word about why such a beautiful, intelligent girl should have thrown her life away on such ugly, greedy, cruel men.

There was a knock on the door.

George opened the door, found two unfamiliar young men standing outside.

One of them said George's name politely, read it and his address from a piece of paper torn from a pack of cigarettes. It was the piece of paper on which Gloria St. Pierre had started to write George's biography, *The Thrilling Life Story of Mr. Z.*

George recognized it a split second before the two men started beating the stuffing out of him. They called him "Professor" every time they hit him. They didn't seem mad at all.

But they knew their business. George went to the hospital with four broken ribs, two broken ankles, a split ear, a closed eye, and a headful of orioles.

◙ ◙ ◙

The next morning, George sat in his hospital bed and tried to write his parents a letter. "*Dear Mother and Father:*" he wrote, "*I'm in the hospital, but you mustn't worry.*"

He was wondering what to say beyond that, when a platinum blonde with eyelashes like buggy whips came in. She carried a potted plant and a copy of *True Detective.*

She smelled like a gangster funeral.

She was Gloria St. Pierre, but George had no way of recognizing her. Bernard Baruch could have hidden behind a disguise like that. She came bearing gifts all right, but no pity seemed to go with them. George's wounds interested her, but the interest was clinical. She was obviously used to seeing people bashed up, and she gave George low grades as a spectacle.

"You got off easy," she said. She assumed George knew who she was.

"I'm not dead," said George. "That's true."

She nodded. "That's smart," she said. "That's smarter than I thought you'd be. You could have been dead very easily. I'm surprised you're not dead."

"May I ask a question?" said George.

"I'd think you'd be through asking questions," she said. And George finally recognized her voice.

He lay back and closed his one good eye.

"I brought you a plant and a magazine," she said.

"Thanks," he said. He wished she would go away. He had nothing to say to her. She was so wild and unfamiliar that George couldn't even think about her.

"If you want some other plant or some other magazine," she said, "say so."

"Just fine," said George. A whanging headache was coming on.

"I thought of getting you something to eat," she said. "But they said you were on the serious list, so I thought maybe you better not eat."

George opened his eye. This was the first he'd heard of his being on the serious list. "Serious list?" he said.

"They wouldn't have let me in if I hadn't said I was your sister," she said. "I think it's some kind of mistake. You don't look serious to me."

George sighed—or meant to sigh. It came out a groan. And, through the whanging and purple flashes of his headache, he said, "They should have you make up the list."

"I suppose you blame me for all this," she said. "I suppose that's how your mind works."

"It isn't working," said George.

"I'm here just because I feel sorry for you," she said. "I don't owe you any apology at all. You asked for this. I hope you learned something," she said. "Everything there is to learn isn't printed in books."

"I know that now," said George. "Thanks for coming, and thanks for the presents, Miss St. Pierre. I think I'd better take a nap now." George pretended to go to sleep, but Gloria St. Pierre didn't go away. George could feel her and smell her very close by.

"I left him," she said. "You hear me?"

George went on pretending to sleep.

"After I heard what he had done to you, I left him," she said.

George went on pretending to sleep. After a while Gloria St. Pierre went away.

◻ ◻ ◻

And, after a while, George really did go to sleep. Sleeping in an overheated room with his head out of order, George dreamed of Gloria St. Pierre.

When he woke up, the hospital room seemed part of the dream, too. Trying to find out what was real and what was a dream, George examined the objects on his bedside table. Among these things were the plant and the magazine Gloria had brought him.

The cover on the magazine could very well have been a part of the dream George had been having, so he pushed that aside. For utterly sane reading, he chose the tag wired to the stem of the plant. And the tag started out sanely enough. "*Clementine Hitchcock Double-Blooming Geranium*," it said.

But after that the tag went crazy. "*Warning! This is a fully patented plant!*" it said. "*Asexual reproduction is strictly forbidden by law!*"

George thanked God when the perfect image of reality, a fat policeman, clumped in. He wanted George to tell him about the beating.

George told the lugubrious tale from the beginning, and realized, as he told it, that he didn't intend to press charges. There was a crude fairness in what had happened. He had, after all, started things off by slugging a known gangster much smaller than himself. Moreover, George's brains had taken such a scrambling that he remembered almost nothing about the men who had done the actual beating.

The policeman didn't try to argue George into pressing charges. He was glad to be saved some work. There was one thing about George's tale that interested him, though. "You say you know this Gloria St. Pierre?" he said.

"I've just told you," said George.

"She's only two doors down," said the policeman.

"What?" said George.

"Sure," said the policeman. "She got beat up, too—in the park right across the street from the hospital."

"How badly hurt is she?" said George.

"She's on the serious list," said the policeman. "About the same deal as you—a couple of ankles broken, a couple of ribs, two big shiners. You still got all your teeth?"

"Yes," said George.

"Well," said the policeman, "she lost her upper front ones."

"Who did it?" said George.

"Her husband," said the policeman. "Gratz."

"You've got him?" said George.

"In the morgue," said the policeman. "A detective caught him working her over. Gratz ran. The detective shot him when he wouldn't stop. So the lady's a widow now."

George's ankles were set and put in casts after lunch that day. He was given a wheelchair and crutches.

It took him a while to get nerve enough to go calling on the widow Gratz.

At last, he rolled himself into her room and up to her bedside.

Gloria was reading a copy of the *Ladies' Home Journal*. When George rolled in, she covered the lower part of her face with the magazine. She covered it too late. George had already seen how fat-lipped and snaggletoothed she was.

Both eyes were black and blue. Her hair was immaculately groomed, however. And she wore earrings—big, barbarous hoops.

"I—I'm sorry," said George.

She didn't answer. She stared at him.

"You came to see me—tried to cheer me up," he said. "Maybe I can cheer you up."

She shook her head.

"Can't you talk?" said George.

She shook her head. And then tears ran down her cheeks.

"Oh my—my," said George, full of pity.

"Pleath—go way," she said. "Don't look at me—pleath! I'm tho damn ugly. Go way."

"You don't look so bad," said George earnestly. "Really."

"He thpoiled my lookth!" she said. The tears got worse.

"He thpoiled my lookth, tho no other man would ever want me!"

"Oh now—" said George gently, "as soon as the swelling goes down, you'll be beautiful again."

"I'll have falth teeth," she said. "I'm not even twenty-one, and I'll have falth teeth. I'll look like thomething out of the bottom of a garbath can. I'm going to become a nun."

"A what?" said George.

"A nun," she said. "All men are pigth. My huthband wath a pig. My father wath a pig. You're a pig. All men are pigth. Go way."

George sighed, and he went away.

George snoozed before supper, dreamed about Gloria again. When he woke up, he found Gloria St. Pierre in a wheelchair next to his bed, watching him.

She was solemn. She had left her big earrings in her room. And she was doing nothing to cover her bunged-up face. She exposed it bravely, almost proudly, for all to see.

"Hello," she said.

"Hello," said George.

"Why didn't you tell me you were a minithter?" she said.

"I'm not one," said George.

"You're thtudying to be one," she said.

"How do you know that?" said George.

"It'th in the newthpaper," she said. She had the paper with her. She read the head-line out loud: "DIVINITY THTUDENT, GUN MOLL, HOTHPITALITHED BY THUGTH."

"Oh boy," murmured George, thinking of the effect of the headline on his land-lord, the dean of the Divinity School, and on his own parents in a white clapboard house in the Wabash Valley, not far away.

"Why didn't you tell me what you were?" said Gloria. "If I'd know what you were, I never would have thaid the thingth I thaid."

"Why not?" said George.

"You're the only kind of man who ithn't a pig," she said. "I thought you were jutht thome college kid who wath a pig like everybody elth, only you jutht didn't have the nerve to act like a pig."

"Um," said George.

"If you're a minithter—or thtudying to be one, anyway—" she said, "how come you don't bawl me out?"

"For what?" said George.

"For all the evil thingth I do," she said. She didn't seem to be fooling. She knew she was bad, and she felt strongly that George's duty was to scare her.

"Well—until I get a pulpit of my own—" said George.

"What do you need a pulpit for?" she said. "Don't you believe what you believe? Tho why you need a pulpit?" She rolled her wheelchair closer. "Tell me I'll go to hell, if I don't change," she said.

George managed a humble smile. "I'm not sure you will," he said.

She backed off from George. "You're jutht like my father," she said contemptu-ously. "He'd forgive and forgive and forgive me—only it wathn't forgiving at all. He jutht didn't care."

Gloria shook her head. "Boy—" she said, "what a lothy mitherable minithter *you're* going to be! You don't believe anything! I pity you."

And she left.

George had another dream about Gloria St. Pierre that night—Gloria with the lisp this time, Gloria with the teeth missing and the ankles in casts. It was the wildest dream yet. He was able to think of the dream with a certain wry humor. It didn't embarrass him to have a body as well as a mind and a soul. He didn't blame his body for wanting Gloria St. Pierre. It was a perfectly natural thing for a body to do.

When George went calling on her after breakfast, he imagined that his mind and soul weren't involved in the least.

"Good morning," she said to him. Many swellings had gone down. Her looks were improved—and she had a question all ready for him. This was it:

"If I wath to become a houthwife with many children, and the children were good," she said to George, "would you rejoith?"

"Of course," said George.

"That'th what I dreamed latht night," she said. "I wath married to you, and we had bookth and children all over the houth." She didn't seem to admire the dream much—nor had it done anything to improve her opinion of George.

"Well—" said George, "I—I'm very flattered that you should dream of me."

"Don't be," she said. "I have crathy dreamth all the time. Anyway, the dream latht night wath more about falth teeth than it wath about you."

"False teeth?" said George.

"I had great big falth teeth," she said. "Every time I tried to thay anything to you or the children, the falth teeth would fall out."

"I'm sure false teeth can be made to fit better than that," said George.

"Could you love thomebody with falth teeth?" she said.

"Certainly," said George.

"When I athk you if you could love thomebody with falth teeth," she said, "I hope you don't think I'm athking you if you could love me. That itn't what I'm athking."

"Um," said George.

"If we got married," she said, "it wouldn't latht. You wouldn't get mad enough at me if I wath bad."

There was a silence—a long one in which George finally came to understand her somewhat. She treated herself as worthless because no one had ever loved her enough to care if she was good or bad.

Since there was no one else to do it, she punished herself.

George came to understand, too, that he would be worthless as a minister as long as he didn't get angry about what such people did to themselves. Blandness, shyness, forgiveness would not do.

She was begging him to care enough to get mad.

The world was begging him to care enough to get mad.

"Married or not," he said, "if you continue to treat yourself like garbage and God's sweet earth like a city dump, I hope with all my heart that you roast in hell."

Gloria St. Pierre's pleasure was luminous—profound.

George had never given that much pleasure to a woman or to himself before. And, in his innocence, he supposed that the next step had to be marriage.

He asked her to marry him. She accepted. It was a good marriage. It was the end of innocence for them both.

With His Hand on the Throttle

EARL HARRISON WAS AN empire builder by nature, annoyed at being shorter than most men, massively muscled, self-made, insistently the center of any gathering, unable to relax. He had calluses on his palms as tough as the back of a crocodile. He made his living building roads, and, in his middle thirties, was growing rich at it. Legions of trucks, bulldozers, graders, earth movers, rollers, asphalt spreaders, and power shovels carried his name into every corner of the state.

But Earl liked owning the equipment and watching the colossal work it did more than he liked the luxuries it could earn for him. Most of his money went right back into the business, which grew bigger and bigger and bigger, with no end in sight.

Save for good whiskey and cigars and model trains, Earl's life was Spartan. He worked with his machine operators, and dressed like them most of the time in heavy shoes and faded khaki. His house was small, and his pretty young wife, Ella, had no servants. The hobby of model railroading suited Earl perfectly—the building and controlling of a busy little world complicated with wonderful machinery. And, like his business, the empire on plywood grew as though Napoleon were running it. In his imagination he could make his model railroad as real and important as affairs in the full-scale world.

◙ ◙ ◙

The brutish black 4-8-2, its big drivers clashing steel on steel, boomed over the quivering trestle and plunged into the tunnel mouth, whipping the chattering, screaming freight cars behind it. In another five seconds the locomotive, known along the pike as Old Spitfire, burst into the open again with the roar of a wounded devil.

It was Saturday morning, and Earl "Hotbox" Harrison was at the throttle. His gunmetal gray eyes were slits under the visor of his striped cap. His freight was behind time, eastbound on a single track, with the westbound passenger express due. Between Old Spitfire and the safety of the siding ahead was Widow's Hairpin, the most treacherous curve on the Harrisonburg and Earl City Railroad.

The passenger express whistled mournfully in the distance. Hotbox gritted his teeth. There was only one thing to do. He eased the throttle wide open as Old Spitfire shot past the water tower and into the curve.

The track writhed under the fury of the train. Suddenly, at the peak of the curve, the locomotive tottered and shook. Hotbox cried out. The locomotive leaped free of the tracks, and the train followed its crashing, rolling course down the embankment.

All was still.

"Damn!" said Earl. He shut off the power, left his stool, and went over to where Old Spitfire lay on its side.

"Bent its main rod and side rod," said Harry Zellerbach sympathetically. He and Earl had been in the basement for two hours, tirelessly shipping mythical passengers and freight back and forth between the oil burner and the water softener.

Earl set Old Spitfire on the tracks, and rolled it back and forth experimentally. "Yeah—and dented the ashpan hopper," he said gravely. He sighed. "Old Spitfire was the first locomotive I bought when I started the pike. Remember, Harry?"

"You bet I do, Hotbox."

"And Old Spitfire is going to keep on running till I'm through with the pike."

"Till hell freezes over," said Harry with satisfaction. He had reason to be satisfied with the thought. A tall, thin, wan man, who spent most of his life in basements, he was proprietor of the local hobby shop. In terms of his own modest notions of wealth, he had struck a bonanza in Earl Harrison. There was nothing scaled to HO gauge that Earl wouldn't buy.

"Till hell freezes over," said Earl. He took a can of beer from behind a plaster mountain range, and drank to the world that was all his and still growing.

"Earl—" called his wife, Ella, from the top of the basement stairs, "lunch is getting cold, hon." Her tone was polite and apologetic, though this was the third time she'd called.

"Coming," said Earl. "On my way. Be there in two shakes."

"Please, Earl," called his mother, "Ella has a wonderful lunch, and it'll spoil if you don't come right up."

"Coming," said Earl absently, trying to straighten Old Spitfire's main rod with a screwdriver. "Please, Mom, will you two please keep your shirts on for a couple of seconds?"

The door at the top of the stairs clicked shut, and Earl exhaled with relief. "Honest to God, Harry," he said, "it's like living in a sorority house around here lately. Women, women."

"Yeah—I guess," said Harry. "Of course, you could have it worse. You could have your mother-in-law visiting you, like I do, instead of just your mother. Your mother seems like a sweet old lady."

"No question about it," said Earl. "She *is* sweet. But she still treats me like I was a little kid, and it drives me nuts. I'm not a kid anymore."

"I'll tell the world, Hotbox," said Harry loyally.

"I'm worth ten times what my old man was worth, and have a hundred times as much responsibility."

"You can say *that* again, Hotbox."

"Earl—" called Ella again. "Hotbox, honey—"

"Earl!" said his mother. "You're being rude."

"See what I mean?" said Earl to Harry. "Just like I was a kid." He turned his head toward the stairway. "Said I'd be right up, didn't I?" He returned to his work. "Old Spitfire's smashed up, but what do they care? Women are always talking about how men ought to try to understand their psychology more, but I don't think they spend ten seconds a year trying to see things from a man's point of view."

"I hear you talking, Hotbox."

"Earl—please, darn it," called Ella.

"Be up before you can say Jack Robinson," said Earl.

And twenty minutes later, Hotbox *did* come up to lunch, and lunch *was* cold. Harry Zellerbach declined Ella's halfhearted invitation to share the meal, explaining that he had to deliver some deadeyes and marlinspikes to a man who was building a model of the *Constitution* in *his* basement.

Earl removed his red neckerchief and engineer's cap, and kissed his wife and then his mother.

"Switchman's strike slow you down?" said Ella.

"He was handling a lot of rush defense shipments," said his mother. "Couldn't let our boys in the front lines down, just because lunch was getting cold." She was slight and bird-like, extremely feminine and seeming in need of protection. But she'd been blessed with six brawling sons, Earl the oldest, and had had to be as quick and clever as a mongoose to get any obedience from them. Yearning for a sweet, frilly daughter, she'd learned judo and how to play shortstop. "Cut off the troops' rail supplies, and they might have to give up the water heater and retreat to the fuse box," she said.

"Aaaaaaaaaaah," said Earl, grinning with a mixture of self-consciousness and irritation. "I guess I'm entitled to a little relaxation now and then. I don't have to apologize." It had never occurred to him, before the arrival of his mother two days before, that anyone might think an apology was in order. Ella had never twitted him about the pike until now. Suddenly, it was open season on model railroaders.

"Women are entitled to a few things, too," said his mother.

"They got the vote and free access to the saloons," said Earl. "What do they want now—to enter the men's shot put?"

"Common courtesy," said his mother.

He didn't answer. Instead, he went to his file of magazines, and brought one back to the table with him. By coincidence, the magazine opened to an ad for model tanks and artillery pieces, authentic in every detail, and scaled for HO gauge layouts. He squinted at the photograph in the ad, trying to screen out the surrounding type and get the impression of realism.

"Earl—" said Ella.

"Hotbox," said his mother, "you're being spoken to by your wife, your companion for life."

"Shoot," said Earl, laying down the magazine reluctantly.

"I was wondering if maybe we couldn't all go out to dinner tonight—for a change," said Ella. "We could go to Lou's Steak House, and—"

"Not tonight, honey," said Earl. "I've got to do some troubleshooting on the block system."

"Be a sport," said his mother. "Take her out, Earl. Just the two of you go out, and I'll fix a little something for myself here."

"We go out," said Earl. "We go out together lots. Didn't we go out together last Tuesday, Ella?"

Ella nodded vaguely. "Down to the depot to see the new gas-turbine locomotive. It was on exhibit."

"Oh, that must have been nice," said Earl's mother. "Nobody ever took me to see a locomotive."

Earl felt the redness of irritation spreading over the back of his neck. "What's the big idea, you two needling me all the time lately? I work hard, and I'm entitled to play hard, I say. So I like trains. What's the matter with trains?"

"Nothing's the matter with trains, dear," said his mother. "I don't know where the world would be without trains. But there are other things, too. All week you're out on the job somewhere, and come home so tired you can hardly say hello, and then on the weekends you're down in the basement. What kind of a life is that for Ella?"

"Now, Mother—" said Ella, making the faintest of gestures to stop her.

"Who do you think I'm working for, ten, twelve hours a day?" said Earl. "Where do you suppose the money's coming from to pay for this house and this food and the cars—for clothes? I love my wife, and I work like hell for her."

"Couldn't you strike a happy medium?" said his mother. "Poor Ella—"

"Listen," said Earl, "the man in the road construction business who tries to strike a happy medium gets eaten alive."

"What a picture!" said his mother.

"Well, it's the truth," said Earl. "And I've invited Ella to play on the pike with me lots of times. She can come down and get in on the fun any time she wants. Haven't I always said that, Ella? Lots of wives take a real interest in their husbands' layouts."

"That's right," said Ella. "Harry Zellerbach's wife can lay track and wind a transformer and talk for hours about 4-6-6-4 articulated locomotives and 0-4-0 docksides."

"Well, a woman can go *too* far," said Earl. "I think Maude Zellerbach is probably a little punchy. But Ella could have a good time, if she'd just give it a chance. I gave her a Bowser M-1 4-8-2 for her birthday, and she hasn't had it out of the roundhouse once in six months."

"Ella—how could you?" said Earl's mother. "If I had a Bowser all my own, heaven knows when I'd get my housework done."

"OK, you've had your fun," said Earl. "Now let a man eat in peace. I've got a lot on my mind."

"We could go for a ride in the car this afternoon," said Ella. "We could show Mother the countryside, and you could do your thinking out in the fresh air."

The atmosphere of conspiracy made Earl stubborn. He wasn't going to be wheedled into anything. "Trouble is," he said, "Harry's expecting in a shipment of stuff this afternoon, and he's going to give me first look. With the metal shortage, the shipments are small, and everything's on a first-come, first-serve basis. You go. I'd better stay."

"It's like being mother to a dope fiend," said Earl's mother. "I didn't raise him this way."

"Aaaaaaaaaah," said Earl again. His eyes dropped to his magazine, and he scanned, ironically, an article about a man whose wife painted the scenery background for his layout, swell little barns and haystacks and snow-covered peaks and clouds and birds and everything.

"Earl," said his mother, "Ella hasn't been out to a movie or to supper with you for four months. You *should* take her out tonight."

"Never mind, Mother," said Ella.

Earl abandoned the magazine. "Mother," he said evenly, "I love you dearly, as a good son should. But I'm not your little boy anymore. I'm a grown man, entitled to make up my own mind, not to have my life run by you. Everything is fine between Ella and me, and we go out whenever I can possibly spare the time. Isn't that right, Ella?"

"Yes," said Ella. And then she spoiled it. "I guess."

"Now, there's this shipment coming in this afternoon, and the block system is all balled up, so, I'm sorry, but—"

"She could help you with the block system," said Earl's mother. "Ella could help you this afternoon, and then tonight would be free."

"I would, Earl," said Ella.

"Well, you see—" said Earl. "That is, I mean—" He shrugged. "OK."

◎ ◎ ◎

Ella worked hard and gamely in the basement. Her slender fingers were clever, and she learned the knack of splicing and soldering wires after one demonstration from Earl.

"By golly, Ella," said Earl, "we should have tried this before. A circus, isn't it?"

"Yup," said Ella, dropping a bead of solder onto a connection.

Earl, as he moved busily about the edge of the layout, hugged Ella ardently every time he passed her. "See? You never know till you try, eh?"

"Nope."

"And, when you get that last circuit done there, then the real fun begins. We'll get the trains rolling, and see how the system works."

"Anything you say," said Ella. "There—the circuit's done."

"Wonderful," said Earl. Together, they hid the block system's wires under the roadbeds.

Then Earl put his arm around Ella, and gave her a long, now poetic, now philosophic, now technical lecture on the operation of a layout. Grandly, he seated her on the stool and guided her hand to the throttle. He put his engineer's cap on her head, where it came to rest on level with her ears. Her large, dark eyes were all but hidden by the visor, glittering like the eyes of an animal at bay in a shallow hole.

"OK," said Earl judiciously, "let's see, what'll we have for a situation?"

"You'd go a long way before you found a more unlikely one than this one," said Ella, looking bleakly over the miniature landscape, awaiting instructions.

Earl was deep in thought. "That's the difference between a kid's toy railroad and an honest-to-gosh pike," he said. "A kid will just run his train around and around in circles. This thing is set up to do hauling jobs just like the real thing."

"I'm glad there's a difference," said Ella.

"OK, I've got the situation," said Earl. "Let's say a big load of frozen beef has just been brought in to the Earl City yards for shipment to Harrisonburg."

"Lord!" said Ella helplessly.

"Don't get panicky. That's the thing—keep your head and think it out," said Earl affectionately. "Just take that Baldwin diesel switcher, pick up those reefers in the hold yard, run 'em over to the loading platform, then back to the icing plant, then over the hump track to the southbound classification yard. Then pick 'em up with your Bowser in the roundhouse, hook on whatever's in the forwarding yard, and off you go."

"I do?"

"Here," said Earl, "I'll give you a hand on this one." He stood behind Ella, his arms enveloping her as he pushed buttons and switches.

Hours later, the two of them were still in the basement, now side by side on stools before the control panel.

Ecstatic, fresh as a daisy, Earl closed a circuit, and a snub-nosed diesel-electric grumbled out of a siding, picked up a string of hopper cars, and labored up a long plaster grade to a coal loader. *Dingadingadingading!* went a warning bell at a crossing, and a little robot popped out of his shack to wave a lantern.

Exhausted, but sticking grimly to her post, Ella drove her passenger express through an underpass, beneath the diesel-electric.

Earl pressed a button, Ella pressed another, and the two locomotives whistled cheerily at each other.

"Ella—" called Earl's mother from the top of the stairs. "If you and Earl are going out to supper, you'd better get dressed."

"Seemed like minutes, didn't it?" laughed Earl. "Whole afternoon gone like that!" He snapped his fingers.

Ella took his hand, and seemed to come alive again, like a fish freed from a hook and thrown back into deep, cold water. "Let's go," she said. "What'll I wear? Where'll we go? What'll we do?"

"You go on up," said Earl. "I'll be up in two shakes, soon as I get the equipment back in the yards."

Earl and Ella, as a grand finale to their companionable afternoon in the basement, had put almost every piece of rolling stock into service on the little countryside, so Earl had a big job on his hands, restoring order to the pike while Ella took a shower and dressed. He might have picked up the trinkets and set them down again where he wanted them, and been done with the job in a minute or two. But he would have stolen from the poor box before he would have done such a thing. Under their own power, creeping at scale speeds, the trains made their way to their proper destinations, and were there broken up by switchers.

Signals winked on and off, road barriers dipped and rose, bells tinkled—and euphoria and pride filled the being of Hotbox Harrison, who had this much of the universe precisely as he would have it, under his thumb.

Over the tiny din he heard the outside door of the basement open and close. He turned to see Harry Zellerbach, who grinned and hugged a long, heavy parcel to his chest.

"Harry!" said Earl. "By golly, I thought you'd forgotten me. Been waiting for you to call all afternoon."

"I'll forget you when I forget my own name, Hotbox," said Harry. He looked meaningfully at the box he was carrying, and winked. "The stuff that came through was mostly junk, or stuff you already had, so I didn't bother calling. But there's one thing, Hotbox—" He looked at the box again, coyly. "You'll be the first one to see it, next to my wife. Nobody else even knows I got it."

Earl clapped him on his arm. "There's a friend for you!"

"I try to be, Hotbox," said Harry. He laid the box on the edge of the layout, and lifted the lid slowly. "First one in the state, Hotbox." There in the box, twinkling like a tiara, lay a long, sleek locomotive, silver, orange, black, and chromium.

"The Westinghouse gas-turbine job," said Earl huskily, awed.

"And only sixty-eight forty-nine," said Harry. "That's practically cost for me, and I got it at a steal. It's got a whine and a roar built in."

Reverently, Earl set it on the tracks, and gently fed power to it. Without a word, Harry took over the controls, and Earl stalked about the layout, spellbound, watching the dream locomotive from all angles, calling out to Harry whenever the illusion of reality was particularly striking.

"Earl—" called Ella.

He didn't answer.

"Hotbox!"

"Hmm?" he said dreamily.

"Come on, if we're going to get any supper."

"Listen," called Earl, "put on another plate, will you? Harry's going to stay for supper." He turned to Harry. "You will, won't you? You'll want to be here when we find out just what this baby can do."

"Pleasure, Hotbox."

"We're going out for supper," said Ella.

Earl straightened up. "Oh—for gosh sakes. That's right, we were."

"Listen to this," said Harry, and the locomotive blew its horn, loud and dissonant.

Earl shook his head in admiration. "Monday," he called to Ella. "We'll go out Monday. Something big has just come up, Sweetheart. Wait'll you see."

"Earl, we haven't got anything much in the house for supper," said Ella desolately.

"Sandwiches, soup, cheese—anything at all," said Earl. "Don't knock yourself out on our account."

"Now, get a load of the reserve power, Hotbox," said Harry. "She's taking that grade without any trouble at half-throttle. Now watch what happens."

"Whooooooooey!" said Earl. He felt a hand on his shoulder. "Oh—hi Mom." He pointed at the new locomotive. "What do you think of that, eh? That's the new era in railroading you see there, Mom. Turbine job."

"Earl, you can't do that to Ella," she said. "She was all dressed up and excited, and then you let her down like this."

"Didn't you hear me give her a rain check?" said Earl. "We're going out on Monday instead. Anyway, she's nuts about the pike now. She understands. We had a whale of a time down here, this afternoon."

"I've never been so disappointed in anyone in all my life," said his mother evenly.

"It's just something you aren't in a position to understand."

She turned her back without another word, and left.

Ella brought Earl and Harry sandwiches, soup, and beer, for which they thanked her gallantly.

ß"You wait until Monday," said Earl, "and we're going out and have us a time, Sweetheart."

"Fine," said Ella spiritlessly. "Good. Glad."

"You and Mom going to eat upstairs?"

"Mom's gone."

"Gone? Where?"

"I don't know. She called a cab and went."

"She's always been like that," said Earl. "Gets something in her head, and the next thing you know, *bing*, she's gone ahead and done it. Any crazy darn thing. No holding her. Independent as hell."

The telephone rang, and Ella excused herself to answer it.

"For you, Harry," she called down. "It's your wife."

When Harry Zellerbach returned, he was smiling broadly. He put his arm around Earl's shoulder, and, to Earl's surprise, he sang "Happy Birthday" to him.

"Happy birthday, dear Hotbox," he concluded, "happy birthday ta-hoo yooooooooou."

"That's sweet," said Earl, "but it's nine months off."

"Oh? Huh. That's funny."

"What's going on?"

"Well—your mother was just over at the hobby shop, and bought you a present. Told my old lady it was for your birthday. Maude called me so I could be the first to congratulate you."

"What'd she buy?" said Earl.

"Guess I better not tell you, Hotbox. Supposed to be a surprise. I've said too much already."

"Scaled to HO?" wheedled Earl.

"Yeah—she made sure about that. But that's all I'm going to tell you."

"Here she comes now," said Earl. He could hear the swish of wheels through the gravel of the driveway. "She's a sweet old lady, you know, Harry?"

"She's your mother, Hotbox," said Harry soberly.

"She used to have a heck of a temper, and she could run like the wind, and every so often she used to catch me and wallop me a good one. But, you know, I had it coming to me every time—in spades."

"Mum knows best, Hotbox."

"Mother," said Ella at the top of the stairs, "what on earth have you got? For heaven's sakes, what are you going to do? Mother—"

"Quick," Earl whispered to Harry, "let's be fooling around with the pike, so she won't know we know something special is going on. Let her surprise us."

The two busied themselves with the trains, as though they didn't hear the footsteps coming down the stairs. "OK," said Earl, "let's try this for a situation, Harry. There's a big Shriners' convention in Harrisonburg, see, and we've got to put on a couple of specials to—" He let the sentence die. Harry was looking in consternation at the foot of the basement steps.

The air was rent with a bloodcurdling cry.

Earl, the hair on the back of his neck standing on end, faced his mother.

She loosed the cry again. "*Eeeeeeeeeeeeeoooowwwwrrrr!*"

Earl gasped and recoiled. His mother was glaring at him through the goggles of an aviator's helmet. She held a model H-36 at arm's length, and, with terrifying sound effects, was making it dive and climb.

"Mother! What are you doing?"

"Hobby? *Hrrrrrrowowowow*. Pilot to bombardier. Bombardier to pilot. Roger. Wilco. *Rumrumrumrum*."

"Have you lost your mind?"

She circled the oil burner noisily, putting the ship through loops and barrel rolls. "Roger. Wilco. *Owrrrr. Rattattattatt!* Got 'em!"

Earl switched off the power to the layout, and waited limply for his mother to emerge from behind the furnace.

She appeared with a roar, and, before Earl could stop her, she climbed onto the layout with amazing agility, and put one foot on a mirror lake, the other in a canyon. The plywood quaked under her.

"Mother! Get off!"

"Bombs away!" she cried. She whistled piercingly, and kicked a trestle to splinters. "*Kaboom!*"

The plane was in a climb again. "*Yourrrowrrrourrrrrr*. Pilot to bombardier. Got the A-bomb ready?"

"No, no, no!" begged Earl. "Mother, please—I surrender, I give up!"

"Not the A-bomb," said Harry, aghast.

"A-bomb ready," she said grimly. The bomber's nose dropped until it pointed at the roundhouse. "*Mmmmmmeeeeeeeeeewwwwtttrr!* There she goes!"

Earl's mother sat with all her might on the roundhouse. "*Blamme!*"

She stepped down from the table, and before Earl could order his senses, his mother was upstairs again.

When Earl finally came upstairs, shocked and weary, he found only his wife, Ella, who sat on the couch, her feet thrust straight out. She looked dazed.

"Where's Mom?" said Earl. There was no anger in his voice—only awe.

"On her way to a movie," said Ella, not looking at Earl but at a blank place on the wall.

"She had the cab waiting outside."

"Blitzkrieg," said Earl, shaking his head. "When she gets sore, she gets sore."

"She isn't sore anymore," said Ella. "She was singing like a lark when she came upstairs."

Earl mumbled something and shuffled his feet.

"Hmm?" said Ella.

He reddened, and squared his shoulders. "I said, I guess I had it coming to me." He mumbled again.

"Hmm?"

He cleared his throat. "I said, I'm sorry about the way I double-crossed you tonight. Sometimes my mind doesn't work too hot, I guess. We've still got time for a show. Would you go out with me?" "Hey, Hotbox!" cried Harry Zellerbach, hurrying into the room. "It's the nuts. It's terrific!"

"What is?"

"It really looks like it's been bombed. No kidding. You photograph it the way it is, and show people the picture, and they'd say, 'Now *there's* a battlefield.' I'll go down to the shop and get some gun turrets from model airplane kits, and tonight we can convert a couple of your trains into armored trains, and camouflage 'em. And I've got a half-dozen HO Pershing tanks I could let you have."

Earl's eyes grew bright with excitement, like incandescent lamps burning out, and then dimmed again. "Let's run up white flags, Harry, and call it a night. You know what Sherman said about war. I'd better see what I can do about making an honorable peace."

Eden by the River

WHEN THE HUNTER passed them in the woods, the boy and the girl pretended not to have anything to do with each other, pretended to be on separate walks, looking for birds. The hunter glanced at each of them with just enough whimsy to let them know that he wasn't fooled, that he knew and liked young lovers when he saw them.

When he was gone, the two resumed their game with the stone.

The boy was seventeen, tall, still growing—as graceless as a homemade stepladder. His wrists were thick, his shoulders still narrow. His feet and hands were big, and his legs were long, sweeping him through the woods with the gait of a man on stilts. His face was the face of a sweet, grave child, surprised at being up so high in the air for so long.

He stepped out of the path and pressed his back against a tree. He was breathing quickly, happy and alert, waiting for the girl to kick the stone.

The stone was as small and blue as a robin's egg. It lay on damp moss on the path. The boy and the girl, taking turns, had kicked it a mile into the woods from the driveway where they'd found it.

Now, fifty feet beyond the stone, the path ended at a river.

The girl was nineteen, small, mature, and silkily muscular. Her lovely features twisted in humorless concentration as she walked up to the stone, took aim, and kicked it.

As the stone skittered down the path, the boy dashed after it, floundering, flapping. He feinted, bobbed, blocked an imaginary opponent, and kicked the stone again.

The stone flew low and fast, hit the river, and sank, twinkling dimly, quickly out of sight.

The boy turned and smiled at the girl in triumph, as though the world had never seen manly strength like his before.

Her eyes didn't disappoint him. They were filled with love and admiration. "You shouldn't have kicked it so far," she said. "Not all the way to the river. I wanted it. I wanted to keep it."

"We can kick another one home," he said. "You can keep that one."

"It wouldn't be as good," she said. "No stone will ever be quite that good."

"A stone's a stone," he said.

"That's just like a man to say that," she said. "It takes a woman to see what should be saved and what should be thrown away." She sat on a flat rock on the riverbank and patted the place beside her. "Sit here. It's dry."

He considered the place, then chose another a dozen feet away from her, a sunless, spongy patch, spiked with reed stumps.

"Are you really comfortable over there?" she said. "Wouldn't you rather be in the sunshine?"

"Fine," he said. "Really." He found twisted pleasure in being uncomfortable, in keeping away from her.

"Eden must have been like this before the apple," she said. "Simple. Clean."

"Yup," he said.

When they were alone together, she was the one who embroidered the moments with words of affection. His replies were grunts, inattentive, barely civil. His thoughts were undefined, a hazy sense of pride and peace.

"Just two people, and the animals and the plants," she said. "So quiet." She took off her shoes and stretched her legs to wet her toes in the river. "And all we say is being said for the first time. And it just has to do with us," she said. "There isn't anybody else anywhere."

"Um," he said. He looked away from her pink toes and the curves of her calves indifferently. He took a knife from his pocket and peeled the bark from a sapling. "I guess she's wondering where we are," he said.

"We're where we should be," she said.

"I don't know what kind of a story we can make up to tell her what got into us," he said. "Running off like this—kicking an old stone like a couple of crazy kids."

"We don't have to make up stories," she said. "We aren't children. Today's the day we stop being children."

He shook his head wonderingly. "Crazy! I didn't any more think this was going to happen than fly to the moon."

"I like things that just happen," she said. She didn't seem at all surprised or puzzled by what had happened.

The boy frowned, pondering the mystery. "It was the craziest thing ever," he said. "I was just trying to keep out of everybody's way, standing out there in the driveway, not thinking about anything. And I saw the stone. Then you came out, and I kicked the stone, and you kicked it—"

"And here we are," she said. "I was watching you out the window a long time."

"You were?" he said.

"Didn't you feel me looking down at you?" she said. "I can always feel it when people look at me."

He stopped whittling and reddened, thinking of her looking at him secretly. "I thought you were off on another world somewhere," he said. "With all the stuff you have to do and think about—"

"I was looking at you," she said. "So tall, so handsome."

"I'm funny looking," he said.

"No you're not," she said.

"You're the only one who doesn't think so," he said.

She tossed her head, impatient with his self-pity.

He was ashamed. He covered his shame by standing briskly and dusting his hands. "We'd better get on back," he said.

"I'm not ready to go yet," she said.

"Well, whenever you're ready," he said.

"It seems like there ought to be things we should say to each other," she said.

He shrugged. "I guess we're pretty well talked out by now," he said. "You'd think we'd have said everything there was to say to each other a couple of hundred times by now."

She looked out at the river, and her eyes widened with a big thought. "Maybe if you kissed me," she said distantly, "that would say everything that needs to be said. Would you mind that?"

He was startled. "Why no—I wouldn't mind," he said. "You mean *now?*"

"Please," she said. "I think it would be nice."

"Why, sure, sure," he said. He shambled over to her, his hands limp before him, like flippers. Looking down on her, he was overwhelmed by a feeling of idiocy, grinning, shuffling his feet—as though a practical joke were in progress. "On the forehead?"

"That would be fine," she said.

He kissed her lightly on the forehead, the kiss like a falling dry leaf. Before he could pull away, she pressed her cheek against his. Her cheek was hot, and his cheek burned as he went back to his sunless, spongy, spikey spot.

"OK?" he said.

"Perfect," she said. "That's the first time you've ever kissed me. Why is that?"

"Oh, why heck—" he said. His hands worked in air. "I mean . . . well, for heaven's sake . . . it just isn't that kind of a thing, is all."

Her expression hadn't changed since he'd kissed her. She still stared wide-eyed at the river. "You know what I think?" she said.

"No," he said.

"I think almost everything is that kind of thing," she said. She stood and stepped into her shoes, smiling possessively at him all the while. "And now that I've said that," she said, "it really *is* time to get back."

She seemed relieved about something.

On the walk home, she was serene and unresponsive.

The boy kicked another stone, a white one, down the path. He danced around it challengingly before her eyes. She paid no attention, and he felt foolish.

He kicked the stone into the underbrush, dug his hands deep into his pockets, and hunched his shoulders, trying to find thoughts of his own.

He wondered if she was annoyed with him for not having said more about how he liked her, for not having thought of the kiss himself. Once before, when she'd told him she loved another man, she'd expected him to talk. And he'd said almost nothing. He'd been eager to say things. But whatever there was to say had fled and left him dumb.

They met the hunter again. The hunter kept his eyes down demurely until he reached the boy. Then he looked up at the boy suddenly and winked. The wrinkles in the hunter's face formed a whirlpool around the one salacious eye.

The boy and the girl were met at the door of the big white house by a lean woman in her late forties. She was dressed for a wedding. Behind her, in the twilight of the house, people were polishing silver, wiping glasses, putting flowers in vases, dusting dark woodwork that already shone. Somewhere a vacuum cleaner snuffled under carpets and bumped into baseboards.

"Where have you been?" said the woman unhappily. She twisted a handkerchief in her hands. "The guests will be here in less than an hour."

"I've got plenty of time, Aunt Mary," said the girl. "Everything's all laid out. I've tried it on dozens of times, and it's all perfect."

"If your father and mother were alive," said the woman, "you wouldn't have treated *them* this way—simply walking off without a word."

"It's something I had to do," said the girl. She looked at her aunt levelly. "I just had to, Aunt Mary, or I wouldn't have done it."

"You could have *told* me," said the woman.

"I didn't know it was going to happen until it happened," said the girl. "I'll go now and get ready." She brushed past her aunt and went up the stairs two steps at a time.

"Heyden!" her aunt called after her. "It's time you learned some responsibility toward others!" She turned her attention to the boy. "You'd better get ready, too."

"All right."

"You know what you're to say?" she said.

"Yes," he said.

"Clear your throat before you say it, to be sure your voice won't crack."

"It won't."

Her face relaxed as she looked at him. Her anxiety was replaced by tenderness. "Oh dear—that's when I'm going to cry," she said. "When you speak up, I just won't be able to stand it." Tears formed on the rims of her eyes. "Nobody will," she said. "You standing there so straight—"

"Yup," he said, embarrassed for them both. He tried to get past her, but she caught his sleeve.

"Do you know what it means—what an awfully moving thing it is you're going to say?" she said.

The question and the tears annoyed him. "Yeah, sure—I guess," he said.

"Do you *really?*" she said intensely.

"Yeah—yes, yes, yes!" he said. "I tell you yes!"

She let go of his sleeve and took a step backward. "Why are you so angry all of a sudden?" she said.

He flapped his arms in irritable confusion. "I dunno!" he said. "People tell me to get in the way, get out of the way; say something, shut up; stand up, sit down." He waved the wedding straight to hell. "I dunno! I guess it's a woman's thing! I'll be glad when it's over." He walked away from her. "When it's over," he said, "maybe I'll be able to do a little living of my own again."

◎ ◎ ◎

The boy, the groom, and the best man were in the damp cellar of the big white house. The shoes of the wedding guests scuffed overhead.

The groom opened the lid on the water meter, read the meter judiciously, and closed the lid with a snap. "Aren't you supposed to be upstairs?" he said to the boy.

"Search me," said the boy. "If I'm not supposed to be down here, some woman will come and pull me by the ears to where I'm supposed to be. I'd rather stay down here with you guys."

"We aren't much company," said the best man.

"What guy is at a time like this?" said the boy.

The groom smiled. "You sound like *you're* the one who's getting married," he said. He held out his hand to the best man. "Let's have that flask again."

The best man handed the groom a silver flask, and the groom drank. He drank with his eyes open, looking at the boy.

The camaraderie of the moment warmed the boy. Here at least he could be at ease with two men he knew and liked—at ease away from the women's mysteries. There were no demands on him here, no emotions to confuse him. "I'd like a drink, too, if you don't mind," he said.

The groom started to offer the flask without a thought. Then he pulled it back. "Wait," he said playfully, "that would be contributing to the delinquency of a minor."

"Worse than that," said the best man, "it would destroy his health."

"Why yes," said the groom. "He's still got growing to do. We can't let him jeopardize his physique. That physique is going to make some woman very happy someday."

The next moment seemed to last forever, as the boy's extended hand closed on nothing.

He saw now that the groom was no friend at all—saw how ugly he was, with teeth too big and white, with lips too thick, with eyes too greedy. And on and on the groom's grin went—radiant with conceit and derision.

The feel of the girl's cheek in the woods came back to the boy. His own cheek burned again. Suddenly he wanted to tell the groom about the walk in the woods, the quiet time by the river, the kiss. He wanted to curl his lip and tell the groom that he'd never know love like that in a million years.

But he didn't say anything. He stared stonily.

"It was just a gag," said the groom genially. "Gee whiz, boy—don't look so down in the mouth, like you lost your best friend. I thought *you* were kidding *us* about the drink." He took the boy's hand and shook it manfully. "Heeeeeey—we can't be mad at each other today."

The groom was a friend again, affectionate, good looking.

The boy looked away, bewildered by the noisy emotions that had been coming and going all day like summer thunderstorms. "I was just kidding about being sore," he said.

The lean woman called down the stairway for the boy to come up. "Hurry!" she said.

"Wish me luck," said the groom, letting go of the boy's hand.

"Good luck," said the boy.

"Thanks," said the groom. "I'll need it."

◎ ◎ ◎

The boy was walking with the girl again. And this time she was on his arm.

His heart was beating like a fire alarm. He was ready to talk now, to tell her how he loved her. The words were ready, bursting his soul.

But her hand was cold, and her arm was as still as dry sticks. Her face was frozen in a smile that had nothing to do with him.

He was too late. He had missed his chance when they were in Eden by the river.

He was alone, all alone.

He left her and sat down. His mind was blank, sensitive only to masses of sound and color.

"Who gives this woman in marriage?" said the minister.

The boy stood. "I—her brother—do," he said.

Lovers Anonymous

HERB WHITE KEEPS BOOKS for the various businesses around our town, and he makes out practically everybody's income tax. Our town is North Crawford, New Hampshire. Herb never got to college, where he would have done well. He learned about bookkeeping and taxes by mail. Herb fought in Korea, came home a hero. And he married Sheila Hinckley, a very pretty, intelligent woman practically all the men in my particular age group had hoped to marry. My particular age group is thirty-three, thirty-four, and thirty-five years old, these days.

On Sheila's wedding day we were twenty-one, twenty-two, and twenty-three. On Sheila's wedding night we all went down to North Crawford Manor and drank. One poor guy got up on the bar and spoke approximately as follows:

"Gentlemen, friends, brothers, I'm sure we wish the newlyweds nothing but happiness. But at the same time I have to say that the pain in our hearts will never die. And I propose that we form a permanent brotherhood of eternal sufferers, to aid each other in any way we can, though Lord knows there's very little anybody can do for pain like ours."

The crowd thought that was a fine idea.

Hay Boyden, who later became a house mover and wrecker, said we ought to call ourselves the Brotherhood of People Who Were Too Dumb to Realize That Sheila Hinckley Might Actually Want to Be a Housewife. Hay had boozy, complicated reasons for suggesting that. Sheila had been the smartest girl in high school, and had been going like a house afire at the University of Vermont, too. We'd all assumed there wasn't any point in serious courting until she'd finished college.

And then, right in the middle of her junior year, she'd quit and married Herb.

"Brother Boyden," said the drunk up on the bar, "I think that is a sterling suggestion. But in all humility I offer another title for our organization, a title in all ways inferior to yours except that it's about ten thousand times easier to say. Gentlemen, friends, brothers, I propose we call ourselves 'Lovers Anonymous.'"

The motion carried. The drunk up on the bar was me.

And like a lot of crazy things in small, old-fashioned towns, Lovers Anonymous lived on and on. Whenever several of us from that old gang happen to get together, somebody is sure to say, "Lovers Anonymous will please come to order." And it is still a standard joke in town to tell anybody who's had his heart broken lately that he should join LA. Don't get me wrong. Nobody in LA still pines for Sheila. We've all more or less got Sheilas of our own. We think about Sheila more than we think about some of our other old girls, I suppose, mainly because of that crazy LA. But as Will Battola, the plumber, said one time, "Sheila Hinckley is now a spare whitewall tire on the Thunderbird of my dreams."

Then about a month ago my good wife served a sordid little piece of news along with the after-dinner coffee and macaroons. She said that Herb and Sheila weren't speaking to each other anymore.

"Now, what are you doing spreading idle gossip like that for?" I said.

"I thought it was my duty to tell you," she said, "since you're the lover-in-chief of Lovers Anonymous."

"I was merely present at the founding," I said, "and as you well know, that was many, many years ago."

"Well, I think you can start *un*-founding," she said.

"Look," I said, "there aren't many laws of life that stand up through the ages, but this is one of the few: People who are contemplating divorce do not buy combination aluminum storm windows and screens for a fifteen-room house." That is my business—combination aluminum storm windows and screens, and here and there a bathtub enclosure. And it was a fact that very recently Herb had bought thirty-seven Fleetwood windows, which is our first-line window, for the fifteen-room ark he called home.

"Families that don't even eat together don't keep together very long," she said.

"What do you know about their eating habits?" I wanted to know.

"Nothing I didn't find out by accident," she said. "I was collecting money for the Heart Fund yesterday." Yesterday was Sunday. "I happened to get there just when they were having Sunday dinner, and there were the girls and Sheila at the dinner table, eating—and no Herb."

"He was probably out on business somewhere," I said.

"That's what I told myself," she said. "But then on my way to the next house I had to go by their old ell—where they keep the firewood and the garden tools."

"Go on."

"And Herb was in there, sitting on a box and eating lunch off a bigger box. I never saw anybody look so sad."

The next day Kennard Pelk, a member of LA in good standing and our chief of police, came into my showroom to complain about a bargain storm window that he had bought from a company that had since gone out of business. "The glass part is stuck halfway up and the screen is rusted out," he said, "and the aluminum is covered with something that looks like blue sugar."

"That's a shame," I said.

"The reason I turn to you is, I don't know where else I can get service."

"With your connections," I said, "couldn't you find out which penitentiary they put the manufacturers in?"

I finally agreed to go over and do what I could, but only if he understood that I wasn't representing the entire industry. "The only windows I stand behind," I said, "are the ones I sell."

And then he told me a screwy thing he'd seen in Herb White's rotten old ell the night before. Kennard had been on his way home in the police cruiser at about two a.m. The thing he'd seen in Herb White's ell was a candle.

"I mean, that old house has fifteen rooms, not counting the ell," said Kennard, "and a family of four—five, if you count the dog. And I couldn't understand how anybody, especially at that time of night, would want to go out to the ell. I thought maybe it was a burglar."

"The only thing worth stealing in that house is the Fleetwood windows."

"Anyway, it was my duty to investigate," said Kennard. "So I snook up to a window and looked in. And there was Herb on a mattress on the floor. He had a bottle of liquor and a glass next to him, and he had a candle stuck in another bottle, and he was reading a magazine by candlelight."

"That was a fine piece of police work," I said.

"He saw me outside the window, and I came closer so he could see who I was. The window was open, so I said to him, 'Hi—I was just wondering who was out here,' and he said, 'Robinson Crusoe.'"

"Robinson Crusoe?" I said.

"Yeah. He was very sarcastic with me," said Kennard. "He asked me if I had the rest of Lovers Anonymous with me. I told him no. And then he asked me if a man's home was still his castle, as far as the police were concerned, or whether that had been changed lately."

"So what did you say, Kennard?"

"What was there to say? I buttoned up my holster and went home."

Herb White himself came into my showroom right after Kennard left. Herb had the healthy, happy, excited look people sometimes get when they come down with double pneumonia. "I want to buy three more Fleetwood windows," he said.

"The Fleetwood is certainly a product that everybody can be enthusiastic about," I said, "but I think you're overstepping the bounds of reason. You've got Fleetwoods all around right now."

"I want them for the ell," he said.

"Do you feel all right, Herb?" I asked. "You haven't even got furniture in half the rooms we've already made wind-tight. Besides, you look feverish."

"I've just been taking a long, hard look at my life, is all," he said. "Now, do you want the business or not?"

"The storm window business is based on common sense, and I'd just as soon keep it that way," I replied. "That old ell of yours hasn't had any work done on it for

I'll bet fifty years. The clapboards are loose, the sills are shot, and the wind whistles through the gaps in the foundation. You might as well put storm windows on a shredded wheat biscuit."

"I'm having it restored," he said.

"Is Sheila expecting a baby?"

He narrowed his eyes. "I sincerely hope not," he said, "for her sake, for my sake, and for the sake of the child."

I had lunch that day at the drugstore. About half of Lovers Anonymous had lunch at the drugstore. When I sat down, Selma Deal, the woman back of the counter, said, "Well, you great lover, got a quorum now. What you gonna vote about?"

Hay Boyden, the house mover and wrecker, turned to me. "Any new business, Mr. President?"

"I wish you people would quit calling me Mr. President," I said. "My marriage has never been one hundred percent ideal, and I wouldn't be surprised that was the fly in the ointment."

"Speaking of ideal marriages," said Will Battola, the plumber, "you didn't by chance sell some more windows to Herb White, did you?"

"How did you know?"

"It was a guess," he said. "We've been comparing notes here, and as near as we can figure, Herb has managed to give a little piece of remodeling business to every member of LA."

"Coincidence," I said.

"I'd say so, too," said Will, "if I could find anybody who wasn't a member and who still got a piece of the job."

Between us, we estimated Herb was going to put about six thousand dollars into the ell. That was a lot of money for a man in his circumstances to scratch up.

"The job wouldn't have to run more than three thousand if Herb didn't want a kitchen and a bathroom in the thing," said Will. "He's already got a kitchen and a bathroom ten feet from the door between the ell and the house."

Al Tedler, the carpenter, said, "According to the plans Herb gave me this morning, there ain't gonna be no door between the ell and the house. There's gonna be a double-studded wall with half-inch Sheetrock, packed with rockwood batts."

"How come double studding?" I asked.

"Herb wants it soundproof."

"How's a body supposed to get from the house to the ell?" I said.

"The body has to go outside, cross about sixty feet of lawn, and go in through the ell's own front door," said Al.

"Kind of a shivery trip on a cold winter's night," I said. "Not many bodies would care to make it barefoot."

And that was when Sheila Hinckley White walked in.

You often hear somebody say that So-and-So is a very well preserved woman. Nine times out of ten So-and-So turns out to be a scrawny woman with pink lipstick who looks as if she had been boiled in lanolin. But Sheila really is well preserved. That day in the drugstore she could have passed for twenty-two.

"By golly," Al Tedler said, "if I had that to cook for me, I wouldn't be any two-kitchen man."

Usually when Sheila came into a place where several members of LA were sitting, we would make some kind of noise to attract her attention and she would do something silly like wiggle her eyebrows or give us a wink. It didn't mean a thing.

But that day in the drugstore we didn't try to catch her eye and she didn't try to catch ours. She was all business. She was carrying a big red book about the size of a cinder block. She returned it to the lending library in the store, paid up, and left.

"Wonder what the book's about," said Hay.

"It's red," I said. "Probably about the fire engine industry."

That was a joke that went a long way back—clear back to what she'd put under her picture in the high school yearbook the year she graduated. Everybody was supposed to predict what kind of work he or she would go into in later life. Sheila put down that she would discover a new planet or be the first woman justice of the Supreme Court or president of a company that manufactured fire engines.

She was kidding, of course, but everybody—including Sheila, I guess—had the idea that she could be anything she set her heart on being.

At her wedding to Herb, I remember, I asked her, "Well now, what's the fire engine industry going to do?"

And she laughed and said, "It's going to have to limp along without me. I'm taking on a job a thousand times as important—keeping a good man healthy and happy, and raising his young."

"What about the seat they've been saving for you on the Supreme Court?"

"The happiest seat for me, and for any woman worthy of the name of woman," she said, "is a seat in a cozy kitchen, with children at my feet."

"You going to let somebody else discover that planet, Sheila?"

"Planets are stones, stone-dead stones," she said. "What I want to discover are my husband, my children, and through them, myself. Let somebody else learn what she can from stones."

After Sheila left the drugstore I went to the lending library to see what the red book was. It was written by the president of some women's college. The title of it was *Woman, the Wasted Sex, or, The Swindle of Housewifery*.

I looked inside the book and found it was divided in these five parts:

    I.   5,000,000 B.C.–A.D. 1865, The Involuntary Slave Sex
   II.   1866–1919, The Slave Sex Given Pedestals
  III.   1920–1945, Sham Equality—Flapper to Rosie the Riveter

Reva Owley, the woman who sells cosmetics and runs the library, came up and asked if she could help me.

"You certainly can," I said. "You can throw this piece of filth down the nearest sewer."

"It's a very popular book," she said.

"That may be," I said. "Whiskey and repeating firearms were very popular with the redskins. And if this drugstore really wants to make money, you might put in a hashish-and-heroin counter for the teenage crowd."

"Have you read it?" she asked.

"I've read the table of contents," I said.

"At least you've opened a book," she said. "That's more than any other member of Lovers Anonymous has done in the past ten years."

"I'll have you know I read a great deal," I said.

"I didn't know that much had been written about storm windows." Reva is a very smart widow.

"You can sure be a snippy woman, on occasion," I said.

"That comes from reading books about what a mess men have made of the world," she said.

The upshot was, I read that book.

What a book it was! It took me a week and a half to get through it, and the more I read, the more I felt as if I were wearing long burlap underwear.

Herb White came into my showroom and caught me reading it. "Improving your mind, I see," he said.

"If something's improved," I said, "I don't know what it is. You've read this, have you?"

"That pleasure and satisfaction was mine," he said. "Where are you now?"

"I've just been through the worst five million years I ever expect to spend," I said. "And some man has finally noticed that maybe things aren't quite as good as they could be for women."

"Theodore Parker?" said Herb.

"Right," I said. Parker was a preacher in Boston about the time of the Civil War.

"Read what he says," said Herb.

So I read out loud: "'The domestic function of woman does not exhaust her powers. To make one half the human race consume its energies in the functions of housekeeper, wife and mother is a monstrous waste of the most precious material God ever made.'"

Herb had closed his eyes while I read. He kept them closed. "Do you realize how hard those words hit me, with the—with the wife I've got?"

"Well," I said, "we all knew you'd been hit by something. Nobody could figure out what it was."

"That book was around the house for weeks," he said. "Sheila was reading it. I didn't pay any attention to it at first. And then one night we were watching Channel Two." Channel Two is the educational television station in Boston. "There was this discussion going on between some college professors about the different theories of how the solar system had been born. Sheila all of a sudden burst into tears, said her brains had turned to mush, said she didn't know anything about anything anymore."

Herb opened his eyes. "There wasn't anything I could say to comfort her. She went off to bed. That book was on the table next to where she'd been sitting. I picked it up and it fell open to the page you just read from."

"Herb," I said, "this isn't any of my business, but—"

"It's your business," he said. "Aren't you president of LA?"

"You don't think there really is such a thing!" I said.

"As far as I'm concerned," he said, "Lovers Anonymous is as real as the Veterans of Foreign Wars. How would you like it if there was a club whose sole purpose was to make sure you treated your wife right?"

"Herb," I said, "I give you my word of honor—"

He didn't let me finish. "I realize now, ten years too late," he said, "that I've ruined that wonderful woman's life, had her waste all her intelligence and talent—on what?" He shrugged and spread his hands. "On keeping house for a small-town bookkeeper who hardly even finished high school, who's never going to be anything he wasn't on his wedding day."

He hit the side of his head with the heel of his hand. I guess he was punishing himself, or maybe trying to make his brains work better. "Well," he said, "I'm calling in all you anonymous lovers I can to help me put things right—not that I can ever give her back her ten wasted years. When we get the ell fixed up, at least I won't be underfoot all the time, expecting her to cook for me and sew for me and do all the other stupid things a husband expects a housewife to do.

"I'll have a little house all my own," he said, "and I'll be my own little housewife. And anytime Sheila wants to, she can come knock on my door and find out I still love her. She can start studying books again, and become an oceanographer or whatever she wants. And any handyman jobs she needs done on that big old house of hers, her handy neighbor—which is me—will be more than glad to do."

With a very heavy heart I went out to Herb's house early that afternoon to measure the windows of the ell. Herb was at his office. The twin girls were off at school. Sheila didn't seem to be at home, either. I knocked on the kitchen door, and the only answer I got was from the automatic washing machine.

"Whirr, gloop, rattle, slup," it said.

As long as I was there, I decided to make sure the Fleetwoods I'd already installed were working freely. That was how I happened to look in through the living room window and see Sheila lying on the couch. There were books on the floor around her. She was crying.

When I got around to the ell I could see that Herb had certainly been playing house in there. He had a little kerosene range on top of the woodpile, along with pots and pans and canned goods.

There was a Morris chair with a gasoline lantern hanging over it, and a big chopping block next to the chair, and Herb had his pipes and his magazines and his tobacco laid out there. His bed was on the floor, but it was nicely made, with sheets and all. On the walls were photographs of Herb in the Army, Herb on the high school baseball team, and a tremendous print in color of Custer's Last Stand.

The door between the ell and the main house was closed, so I felt free to climb in through a window without feeling I was intruding on Sheila. What I wanted to see was the condition of the sash on the inside. I sat down in the Morris chair and made some notes.

And then I leaned back and lit a cigarette. A Morris chair is a comfortable thing. Sheila came in without my even hearing her.

"Cozy, isn't it?" she said. "I think every man your age should have a hideaway. Herb's ordered storm windows for his ShangriLa, has he?"

"Fleetwoods," I said.

"Good," she said. "Heaven knows Fleetwoods are the best." She looked at the underside of the rotten roof. Pinpricks of sky showed through. "I don't suppose what's happening to Herb and me is any secret," she said.

I didn't know how to answer that.

"You might tell Lovers Anonymous and their Ladies' Auxiliary that Herb and I have never been this happy before," she said.

I couldn't think of any answer for that, either. It was my understanding that Herb's moving into the ell was a great tragedy of recent times.

"And you might tell them," she said, "that it was Herb who got happy first. We had a ridiculous argument about how my brains had turned to mush. And then I went upstairs and waited for him to come to bed—and he didn't. The next morning I found he'd dragged a mattress out here and was sleeping like an angel.

"I looked down on him, so happy out here, and I wept. I realized that he'd been a slave all his life, doing things he hated in order to support his mother, and then me, and then me and the girls. His first night out here was probably the first night in his life that he went to sleep wondering who he might be, what he might have become, what he still might be."

"I guess the reason the world seems so upside down so often," I said, "is that everybody figures he's doing things on account of somebody else. Herb figures this whole ell business is a favor to you."

"Anything that makes him happier is a favor to me," she said.

"I read that crazy red book—or I'm reading it," I said.

"Housewifery *is* a swindle, if a woman can do more," she said.

"You going to do more, Sheila?"

"Yes," she said. She had laid out a plan whereby she would get her degree in two years, with a combination of correspondence courses, extension courses, and a couple of summer sessions at Durham, where the state university is. After that she was going to teach.

"I never would have made a plan like that," she told me, "if Herb hadn't called my bluff to the extent he did. Women are awful bluffers sometimes."

"I've started studying," she went on. "I know you looked through the window and saw me with all my books, crying on the couch."

"I didn't think you'd seen me," I said. "I wasn't trying to mind somebody else's business. Kennard Pelk and I both have to look through windows from time to time in the line of duty."

"I was crying because I was understanding what a bluffer I'd been in school," she said. "I was only pretending to care about the things I was learning, back in those silly old days. Now I do care. That's why I was crying. I've been crying a lot lately, but it's good crying. It's about discovery, it's about grown-up joy."

I had to admit it was an interesting adjustment Sheila and Herb were making. One thing bothered me, though, and there wasn't any polite way I could ask about it. I wondered if they were going to quit sleeping with each other forever.

Sheila answered the question without my having to ask it.

"Love laughs at locksmiths," she said.

About a week later I took the copy of Woman, the *Wasted Sex, or, The Swindle of Housewifery* to a luncheon meeting of LA at the drugstore. I was through with the thing, and I passed it around.

"You didn't let your wife read this, did you?" Hay Boyden asked.

"Certainly," I said.

"She'll walk out on you and the kids," said Hay, "and become a rear admiral."

"Nope," I said.

"You give a woman a book like this," said Al Tedler, "and you're gonna have a restless woman on your hands."

"Not necessarily," I said. "When I gave my wife this book I gave her a magic bookmark to go with it." I nodded. "That magic bookmark kept her under control all the way through."

Everybody wanted to know what the bookmark was.

"One of her old report cards," I said.

SECTION 3

Science

Sometimes (to his displeasure) labeled as a science fiction writer, Kurt Vonnegut always took pains to caution critics and encourage readers about his true status: he was a writer who understood science. Typical of the posture he assumed is his first published story, "Report on the Barnhouse Effect," appearing in *Collier's* for February 11, 1950. His premise is the simple one any research scientist accepts, that if something new can be thought of, it can be brought into being. Kurt's character Professor Barnhouse has turned this axiom back upon itself, effectively putting mind over matter. But that is not the point of the story, which is not about the professor and his invention but rather its effect. And the manner for considering that effect is one of the most common formats in the everyday world of business and government: the report.

Who writes the report? Someone who can not just understand what the scientist has done but explain it to a general audience.

As happens, the report writer gets involved in his material. That's the fun (and wisdom) Vonnegut works into his narrative. In time, it would become the key factor in his personal journalism, a technique shared with a host of writers from Tom Wolfe and Joan Didion to Gay Talese and Hunter S. Thompson. But this would not happen until well into the 1960s. Here, at the start of the 1950s, short fiction for the day's popular magazines seemed the best ticket not just for the author's views but for his style of writing.

That style was crafted to speak generally. Vonnegut's stories were meant for everyone, not just readers of niche magazines. If the *New Yorker* was not for "the little old lady from Dubuque," as it advertised itself at the time, Kurt's stories were—and for everybody else in America. Neither did he aim for the science fiction market, for the simple reason that it paid a penny a word while *Collier's* and the *Saturday Evening Post* paid half a dollar. Five stories placed in these family weeklies would support his family for a year, earning him (as he liked to say) the same reasonable middle-class income as his neighbor who managed the cafeteria at the public school his kids attended. The stories themselves were written for the vast American middle class whose stable existence characterized the stateside 1950s. Paging through the *Post*, these readers would be intrigued by radio waves from outer space and massive new machines called computers that could mimic human intelligence. But they were also wryly amused when such things fit in with the lives they were living. The radio waves did not come from electronic lizards on Mars who were threatening to turn earthlings into zombies; nor were they the same particles of radiation that scientific equipment of the day was picking up, as discussed by technology writers elsewhere in the magazine. Vonnegut's wrinkle was to show how his fellow citizens might easily take this new technology and apply it to one of the most familiar of human foibles, as demonstrated in "The Euphio Question" for *Collier's* the next year. The amazing new computer Kurt would name in another story for *Collier's*, "EPICAC," wound up doing something even more elementally human with its time. The message: don't worry about these inventions, they will only give us more of what we already have, and we know quite well how to deal with that.

What made these stories saleable was less their fascination with inventions than Kurt Vonnegut's inventiveness in integrating them with middle-class life. "Next Door," published in the April 1955 issue of *Cosmopolitan*, needed nothing more exotic than a standard AM radio broadcasting music to the neighboring apartment. Through the party wall a young boy can hear the music and the neighbors' argument rising above it. What the kid does next is inventive; as Kurt and every other handyman in the country knew, you work with what you have. But the result is better living through science, even though the science is of the Thomas Edison variety (albeit new when Kurt himself was the child's age). "Unready to Wear" didn't make it into *Collier's*, *Cosmo*, or the *Post*. *Galaxy Science Fiction* took it at their rock-bottom rates in 1953, but of the science-based stories Vonnegut did manage to sell it is the strongest and most humorous with familiar middle-class manners, so it is obvious where the author was aiming. At *Collier's*, editor Knox Burger accepted "Mnemonics" for the April 28, 1951, issue, but only after Kurt struggled with many sets of revisions beginning in July 1949 when Kurt, still living in suburban Schenectady, New York, and working as a publicist for the General Electric Research Laboratory, first mailed it in as a submission.

This sheaf of editorial correspondence indicates just what had to be done to a Vonnegut story before it could qualify for the top national popular market of *Collier's*, as opposed to the world of science fiction where, as Burger lamented, the "specialists seem to start with more novel germs and more elaborate theses, but their prose moves like Filboyd Studge" (a funny name Kurt would adopt decades later when prefacing *Breakfast of Champions*). One problem Knox identified was that as long as the would-be fiction writer was working for General Electric, he would have to go easy on mocking the presumed advantages of science. "At General Electric, Progress Is Our Most Important Product" proclaimed their advertising slogan, and here Kurt was suggesting that in the end there wasn't really much progress at all, just the same old weaknesses of human behavior (which he'd include a few years later in his first novel, *Player Piano*). "Personally," Knox Burger advised in an undated note filed with the 1949 correspondence, "I think the publishers [of *Collier's*] are angling for some of that GE business on the advertising pages. Perhaps you'd care to buy a page in your own name. $8800.00 in black and white, cheapest cost per thousand readers of any magazine market. Think it over."

If this whimsical if ironic (given Kurt's penury) suggestion sounds like a Vonnegut story, one need only look to the science-based pieces Kurt was unable to place with *Collier's* or anyone else at the time. Of this batch, "Confido" is the most inventive— inventive within the parameters of common human behavior that most readers of the family magazines shared. That was the challenge he faced in aiming for the wider market. The science had to be believable, and the response to it had to be equally believeable, yet at the same time surprising to the extent that readers would have been gently tricked by their own credulousness. "Hall of Mirrors" and "Look at the Birdie" deal less with science than with pseudoscience, while "The Nice Little People" exceeds the limits of both customary behavior and practical credibility. When rejection slips had piled so high that even Kurt's agent Kenneth Littauer could find no hope for publication, he'd urged his client to save the material "for posterity." And that's where the Vonnegut estate consigned them after his death, respecting the wishes of someone who from firsthand experience knew their ultimate value.

Today, "Between Timid and Timbuktu" speaks most personally of the Kurt Vonnegut who would begin as a short story writer and after twenty years of persistent effort triumph as a best-selling author. There's the shaping power of time, always a concern of thoughtful writers. But also the desire to manipulate it, a fascination Vonnegut explored from his earliest to his latest work. It takes readers from heartbreak to hopefulness and back again, in a rhythm that Kurt liked to outline in his chalk-talk for lecture audiences eager to know how fictive narratives worked. It entertains scientific possibility based on commonly reported near-death experiences. Half a century later he'd use this same phenomenon as the enabling device for his book of satiric essays, *God Bless You, Dr. Kevorkian*, in which as a "reporter from the afterlife" he'd return from controlled near-death adventures to share thoughts from those actually deceased, whether unknown, famous, or infamous. "Between Timid and Timbuktu" isn't funny, except for the grim humor of its conclusion. But that too is another trick, perhaps not as gentle, that Vonnegut plays with his readers. The science in this story serves as a warning of how human desire might be served. "Be careful," Kurt liked to warn his readers about anything he might write, "we might wind up miles from here."

—JK

Next Door

THE OLD HOUSE was divided into two dwellings by a thin wall that passed on, with high fidelity, sounds on either side. On the north side were the Leonards. On the south side were the Hargers.

The Leonards—husband, wife, and eight-year-old son—had just moved in. And, aware of the wall, they kept their voices down as they argued in a friendly way as to whether or not the boy, Paul, was old enough to be left alone for the evening.

"Shhhhh!" said Paul's father.

"Was I shouting?" said his mother. "I was talking in a perfectly normal tone."

"If I could hear Harger pulling a cork, he can certainly hear you," said his father.

"I didn't say anything I'd be ashamed to have anybody hear," said Mrs. Leonard.

"You called Paul a baby," said Mr. Leonard. "That certainly embarrasses Paul—and it embarrasses me."

"It's just a way of talking," she said.

"It's a way we've got to stop," he said. "And we can stop treating him like a baby, too—*tonight*. We simply shake his hand, walk out, and go to the movie." He turned to Paul. "You're not afraid—are you, boy?"

"I'll be all right," said Paul. He was very tall for his age, and thin, and had a soft, sleepy, radiant sweetness engendered by his mother. "I'm fine."

"Damn right!" said his father, clouting him on the back. "It'll be an adventure."

"I'd feel better about this adventure, if we could get a sitter," said his mother.

"If it's going to spoil the picture for you," said his father, "let's take him with us." Mrs. Leonard was shocked. "Oh—it isn't for children."

"I don't care," said Paul amiably. The why of their not wanting him to see certain movies, certain magazines, certain books, certain television shows was a mystery he respected—even relished a little.

"It wouldn't kill him to see it," said his father.

"You *know* what it's about," she said.

"What *is* it about?" said Paul innocently.

Mrs. Leonard looked to her husband for help, and got none. "It's about a girl who chooses her friends unwisely," she said.

"Oh," said Paul. "That doesn't sound very interesting."

"Are we going, or aren't we?" said Mr. Leonard impatiently. "The show starts in ten minutes."

Mrs. Leonard bit her lip. "All right!" she said bravely. "You lock the windows and the back door, and I'll write down the telephone numbers for the police and the fire department and the theater and Dr. Failey." She turned to Paul. "You *can* dial, can't you, dear?"

"He's been dialing for years!" cried Mr. Leonard.

"Sssssssh!" said Mrs. Leonard.

"Sorry," Mr. Leonard bowed to the wall. "My apologies."

"Paul, dear," said Mrs. Leonard, "what are you going to do while we're gone?"

"Oh—look through my microscope, I guess," said Paul.

"You're not going to be looking at germs, are you?" she said.

"Nope—just hair, sugar, pepper, stuff like that," said Paul.

His mother frowned judiciously. "I think that would be all right, don't you?" she said to Mr. Leonard.

"Fine!" said Mr. Leonard. "Just as long as the pepper doesn't make him sneeze!"

"I'll be careful," said Paul.

Mr. Leonard winced. "Shhhhh!" he said.

◎ ◎ ◎

Soon after Paul's parents left, the radio in the Harger apartment went on. It was on softly at first—so softly that Paul, looking through his microscope on the living room coffee table, couldn't make out the announcer's words. The music was frail and dissonant—unidentifiable.

Gamely, Paul tried to listen to the music rather than to the man and woman who were fighting.

Paul squinted through the eyepiece of his microscope at a bit of his hair far below, and he turned a knob to bring the hair into focus. It looked like a glistening brown eel, flecked here and there with tiny spectra where the light struck the hair just so.

There—the voices of the man and woman were getting louder again, drowning out the radio. Paul twisted the microscope knob nervously, and the objective lens ground into the glass slide on which the hair rested.

The woman was shouting now.

Paul unscrewed the lens, and examined it for damage.

Now the man shouted back—shouted something awful, unbelievable.

Paul got a sheet of lens tissue from his bedroom, and dusted at the frosted dot on the lens, where the lens had bitten into the slide. He screwed the lens back in place.

All was quiet again next door—except for the radio.

Paul looked down into the microscope, down into the milky mist of the damaged lens.

Now the fight was beginning again—louder and louder, cruel and crazy.

Trembling, Paul sprinkled grains of salt on a fresh slide, and put it under the microscope.

The woman shouted again, a high, ragged, poisonous shout.

Paul turned the knob too hard, and the fresh slide cracked and fell in triangles to the floor. Paul stood, shaking, wanting to shout, too—to shout in terror and bewilderment. It had to stop. Whatever it was, it *had* to stop!

"If you're going to yell, turn up the radio!" the man cried.

Paul heard the clicking of the woman's heels across the floor. The radio volume swelled until the boom of the bass made Paul feel like he was trapped in a drum.

"And now!" bellowed the radio, "for Katy from Fred! For Nancy from Bob, who thinks she's swell! For Arthur, from one who's worshipped him from afar for six weeks! Here's the old Glenn Miller Band and that all-time favorite, *Stardust!* Remember! If you have a dedication, call Milton nine-three-thousand! Ask for All-Night Sam, the record man!"

The music picked up the house and shook it.

A door slammed next door. Now someone hammered on a door.

Paul looked down into his microscope once more, looked at nothing—while a prickling sensation spread over his skin. He faced the truth: The man and woman would kill each other, if he didn't stop them.

He beat on the wall with his fist. "Mr. Harger! Stop it!" he cried. "Mrs. Harger! Stop it!"

"For Ollie from Lavina!" All-Night Sam cried back at him. "For Ruth from Carl, who'll never forget last Tuesday! For Wilbur from Mary, who's lonesome tonight! Here's the Sauter-Finnegan Band asking, *Love, What Are You Doing to My Heart?*"

Next door, crockery smashed, filling a split second of radio silence. And then the tidal wave of music drowned everything again.

Paul stood by the wall, trembling in his helplessness. "Mr. Harger! Mrs. Harger! Please!"

"Remember the number!" said All-Night Sam. "Milton nine-three-thousand!"

Dazed, Paul went to the phone and dialed the number.

"WJCD," said the switchboard operator.

"Would you kindly connect me with All-Night Sam?" said Paul.

"Hello!" said All-Night Sam. He was eating, talking with a full mouth. In the background, Paul could hear sweet, bleating music, the original of what was rending the radio next door.

"I wonder if I might make a dedication," said Paul.

"Dunno why not," said Sam. "Ever belong to any organization listed as subversive by the Attorney General's office?"

Paul thought a moment. "Nossir—I don't think so, sir," he said.

"Shoot," said Sam.

"From Mr. Lemuel K. Harger to Mrs. Harger," said Paul.

"What's the message?" said Sam.

"I love you," said Paul. "Let's make up and start all over again."

The woman's voice was so shrill with passion that it cut through the din of the radio, and even Sam heard it.

"Kid—are you in trouble?" said Sam. "Your folks fighting?"

Paul was afraid that Sam would hang up on him if he found out that Paul wasn't a blood relative of the Hargers. "Yessir," he said.

"And you're trying to pull 'em back together again with this dedication?" said Sam.

"Yessir," said Paul.

Sam became very emotional. "O.K., kid," he said hoarsely, "I'll give it everything I've got. Maybe it'll work. I once saved a guy from shooting himself the same way."

"How did you do that?" said Paul, fascinated.

"He called up and said he was gonna blow his brains out," said Sam, "and I played *The Bluebird of Happiness*." He hung up.

Paul dropped the telephone into its cradle. The music stopped, and Paul's hair stood on end. For the first time, the fantastic speed of modern communications was real to him, and he was appalled.

"Folks!" said Sam, "I guess everybody stops and wonders sometimes what the heck he thinks he's doin' with the life the good Lord gave him! It may seem funny to you folks, because I always keep up a cheerful front, no matter how I feel inside, that I wonder sometimes, too! And then, just like some angel was trying to tell me, 'Keep going, Sam, keep going,' something like this comes along.

"Folks!" said Sam, "I've been asked to bring a man and his wife back together again through the miracle of radio! I guess there's no sense in kidding ourselves about marriage! It isn't any bowl of cherries! There's ups and downs, and sometimes folks don't see how they can go on!"

Paul was impressed with the wisdom and authority of Sam. Having the radio turned up high made sense now, for Sam was speaking like the right-hand man of God.

When Sam paused for effect, all was still next door. Already the miracle was working.

"Now," said Sam, "a guy in my business has to be half musician, half philosopher, half psychiatrist, and half electrical engineer! And! If I've learned one thing from working with all you wonderful people out there, it's this: if folks would swallow their self-respect and pride, there wouldn't be any more divorces!"

There were affectionate cooings from next door. A lump grew in Paul's throat as he thought about the beautiful thing he and Sam were bringing to pass.

"Folks!" said Sam, "that's all I'm gonna say about love and marriage! That's all anybody needs to know! And now, for Mrs. Lemuel K. Harger, from Mr. Harger—I love you! Let's make up and start all over again!" Sam choked up. "Here's Eartha Kitt, and *Somebody Bad Stole De Wedding Bell!*"

The radio next door went off.

The world lay still.

A purple emotion flooded Paul's being. Childhood dropped away, and he hung, dizzy, on the brink of life, rich, violent, rewarding.

There was movement next door—slow, foot-dragging movement.

"So," said the woman.

"Charlotte—" said the man uneasily. "Honey—I swear."

"'I love you,'" she said bitterly, "'let's make up and start all over again.'"

"Baby," said the man desperately, "it's another Lemuel K. Harger. It's got to be!"

"You want your wife back?" she said. "All right—I won't get in her way. She can have you, Lemuel—you jewel beyond price, you."

"*She* must have called the station," said the man.

"She can have you, you philandering, two-timing, two-bit Lochinvar," she said. "But you won't be in very good condition."

"Charlotte—put down that gun," said the man. "Don't do anything you'll be sorry for."

"That's all behind me, you worm," she said.

There were three shots.

Paul ran out into the hall, and bumped into the woman as she burst from the Harger apartment. She was a big, blonde woman, all soft and awry, like an unmade bed.

She and Paul screamed at the same time, and then she grabbed him as he started to run.

"You want candy?" she said wildly. "Bicycle?"

"No, thank you," said Paul shrilly. "Not at this time."

"You haven't seen or heard a thing!" she said. "You know what happens to squealers?"

"Yes!" cried Paul.

She dug into her purse, and brought out a perfumed mulch of face tissues, bobbypins and cash. "Here!" she panted. "It's yours! And there's more where that came from, if you keep your mouth shut." She stuffed it into his trousers pocket.

She looked at him fiercely, then fled into the street.

Paul ran back into his apartment, jumped into bed, and pulled the covers up over his head. In the hot, dark cave of the bed, he cried because he and All-Night Sam had helped to kill a man.

◉ ◉ ◉

A policeman came clumping into the house very soon, and he knocked on both apartment doors with his billyclub.

Numb, Paul crept out of the hot, dark cave, and answered the door. Just as he did, the door across the hall opened, and there stood Mr. Harger, haggard but whole.

"Yes, sir?" said Harger. He was a small, balding man, with a hairline mustache. "Can I help you?"

"The neighbors heard some shots," said the policeman.

"Really?" said Harger urbanely. He dampened his mustache with the tip of his little finger. "How bizarre. I heard nothing." He looked at Paul sharply. "Have you been playing with your father's guns again, young man?"

"Oh, nossir!" said Paul, horrified.

"Where are your folks?" said the policeman to Paul.

"At the movies," said Paul.

"You're all alone?" said the policeman.

"Yessir," said Paul. "It's an adventure."

"I'm sorry I said that about the guns," said Harger. "I certainly would have heard any shots in this house. The walls are thin as paper, and I heard nothing."

Paul looked at him gratefully.

"And you didn't hear any shots, either, kid?" said the policeman.

Before Paul could find an answer, there was a disturbance out on the street. A big, motherly woman was getting out of a taxi-cab and wailing at the top of her lungs. "Lem! Lem, baby."

She barged into the foyer, a suitcase bumping against her leg and tearing her stocking to shreds. She dropped the suitcase, and ran to Harger, throwing her arms around him.

"I got your message, darling," she said, "and I did just what All-Night Sam told me to do. I swallowed my self-respect, and here I am!"

"Rose, Rose, Rose—my little Rose," said Harger. "Don't ever leave me again." They grappled with each other affectionately, and staggered into their apartment.

"Just look at this apartment!" said Mrs. Harger. "Men are just lost without women!" As she closed the door, Paul could see that she was awfully pleased with the mess.

"You *sure* you didn't hear any shots?" said the policeman to Paul.

The ball of money in Paul's pocket seemed to swell to the size of a watermelon. "Yessir," he croaked.

The policeman left.

Paul shut his apartment door, shuffled into his bedroom, and collapsed on the bed.

◎ ◎ ◎

The next voices Paul heard came from his own side of the wall. The voices were sunny—the voices of his mother and father. His mother was singing a nursery rhyme and his father was undressing him.

"Diddle-diddle-dumpling, my son John," piped his mother, "went to bed with his stockings on. One shoe off, and one shoe on—diddle-diddle-dumpling, my son John."

Paul opened his eyes.

"Hi, big boy," said his father, "you went to sleep with all your clothes on."

"How's my little adventurer?" said his mother.

"O.K.," said Paul sleepily. "How was the show?"

"It wasn't for children, honey," said his mother. "You would have liked the short subject, though. It was all about bears—cunning little cubs."

Paul's father handed her Paul's trousers, and she shook them out, and hung them neatly on the back of a chair by the bed. She patted them smooth, and felt the ball of money in the pocket. "Little boys' pockets!" she said, delighted. "Full of childhood's mysteries. An enchanted frog? A magic pocketknife from a fairy princess?" She caressed the lump.

"He's not a little boy—he's a big boy," said Paul's father. "And he's too old to be thinking about fairy princesses."

Paul's mother held up her hands. "Don't rush it, don't rush it. When I saw him asleep there, I realized all over again how dreadfully short childhood is." She reached into the pocket and sighed wistfully. "Little boys are so hard on clothes—especially pockets."

She brought out the ball and held it under Paul's nose. "Now, would you mind telling Mommy what we have here?" she said gaily.

The ball bloomed like a frowzy chrysanthemum, with ones, fives, tens, twenties, and lipstick-stained Kleenex for petals. And rising from it, befuddling Paul's young mind, was the pungent musk of perfume.

Paul's father sniffed the air. "What's that smell?" he said.

Paul's mother rolled her eyes. "*Tabu*," she said.

Report on the Barnhouse Effect

LET ME BEGIN by saying that I don't know any more about where Professor Arthur Barnhouse is hiding than anyone else does. Save for one short, enigmatic message left in my mailbox on Christmas Eve, I have not heard from him since his disappearance a year and a half ago.

What's more, readers of this article will be disappointed if they expect to learn how *they* can bring about the so-called "Barnhouse Effect." If I were able and willing to give away that secret, I would certainly be something more important than a psychology instructor.

I have been urged to write this report because I did research under the professor's direction and because I was the first to learn of his astonishing discovery. But while I was his student I was never entrusted with knowledge of how the mental forces could be released and directed. He was unwilling to trust anyone with that information.

I would like to point out that the term "Barnhouse Effect" is a creation of the popular press, and was never used by Professor Barnhouse. The name he chose for the phenomenon was "*dynamopsychism*," or *force of the mind.*

I cannot believe that there is a civilized person yet to be convinced that such a force exists, what with its destructive effects on display in every national capital. I think humanity has always had an inkling that this sort of force does exist. It has been common knowledge that some people are luckier than others with inanimate objects like dice. What Professor Barnhouse did was to show that such "luck" was a measurable force, which in his case could be enormous.

By my calculations, the professor was about fifty-five times more powerful than a Nagasaki-type atomic bomb at the time he went into hiding. He was not bluffing when, on the eve of "Operation Brainstorm," he told General Honus Barker: "Sitting here at the dinner table, I'm pretty sure I can flatten anything on earth—from Joe Louis to the Great Wall of China."

There is an understandable tendency to look upon Professor Barnhouse as a supernatural visitation. The First Church of Barnhouse in Los Angeles has a congregation numbering in the thousands. He is godlike in neither appearance nor intellect. The man who disarms the world is single, shorter than the average American male, stout, and averse to exercise. His I.Q. is 143, which is good but certainly not sensational. He is quite mortal, about to celebrate his fortieth birthday, and in good health. If he is alone now, the isolation won't bother him too much. He was quiet and shy when I knew him, and seemed to find more companionship in books and music than in his associations at the college.

Neither he nor his powers fall outside the sphere of Nature. His dynamopsychic radiations are subject to many known physical laws that apply in the field of radio. Hardly a person has not now heard the snarl of "Barnhouse static" on his home receiver. The radiations are affected by sunspots and variations in the ionosphere.

However, they differ from ordinary broadcast waves in several important ways. Their total energy can be brought to bear on any single point the professor chooses, and that energy is undiminished by distance. As a weapon, then, dynamopsychism has an impressive advantage over bacteria and atomic bombs, beyond the fact that it costs nothing to use: it enables the professor to single out critical individuals and objects instead of slaughtering whole populations in the process of maintaining international equilibrium.

As General Honus Barker told the House Military Affairs Committee: "Until someone finds Barnhouse, there is no defense against the Barnhouse Effect." Efforts to "jam" or block the radiations have failed. Premier Slezak could have saved himself the fantastic expense of his "Barnhouseproof" shelter. Despite the shelter's twelve-foot-thick lead armor, the premier has been floored twice while in it.

There is talk of screening the population for men potentially as powerful dynamo-psychically as the professor. Senator Warren Foust demanded funds for this purpose last month, with the passionate declaration: "He who rules the Barnhouse Effect rules the world!" Commissar Kropotnik said much the same thing, so another costly armaments race, with a new twist, has begun.

This race at least has its comical aspects. The world's best gamblers are being coddled by governments like so many nuclear physicists. There may be several hundred persons with dynamopsychic talent on earth, myself included. But, without knowledge of the professor's technique, they can never be anything but dice-table despots. With the secret, it would probably take them ten years to become dangerous weapons. It took the professor that long. He who rules the Barnhouse Effect is Barnhouse and will be for some time.

Popularly, the "Age of Barnhouse" is said to have begun a year and a half ago, on the day of Operation Brainstorm. That was when dynamopsychism became significant politically. Actually, the phenomenon was discovered in May, 1942, shortly after the professor turned down a direct commission in the Army and enlisted as an artillery private. Like X-rays and vulcanized rubber, dynamopsychism was discovered by accident.

From time to time Private Barnhouse was invited to take part in games of chance by his barrack mates. He knew nothing about the games, and usually begged off. But one evening, out of social grace, he agreed to shoot craps. It was either terrible or wonderful that he played, depending upon whether or not you like the world as it now is.

"Shoot sevens, Pop," someone said.

So "Pop" shot sevens—ten in a row to bankrupt the barracks. He retired to his bunk and, as a mathematical exercise, calculated the odds against his feat on the back of a laundry slip. His chances of doing it, he found, were one in almost ten million! Bewildered, he borrowed a pair of dice from the man in the bunk next to his. He tried to roll sevens again, but got only the usual assortment of numbers. He lay back for a moment, then resumed his toying with the dice. He rolled ten more sevens in a row.

He might have dismissed the phenomenon with a low whistle. But the professor instead mulled over the circumstances surrounding his two lucky streaks. There was one single factor in common: on both occasions, *the same thought train had flashed through his mind just before he threw the dice.* It was that thought train which aligned the professor's brain cells into what has since become the most powerful weapon on earth.

◙ ◙ ◙

The soldier in the next bunk gave dynamopsychism its first token of respect. In an understatement certain to bring wry smiles to the faces of the world's dejected demagogues, the soldier said, "You're hotter'n a two-dollar pistol, Pop." Professor Barnhouse was all of that. The dice that did his bidding weighed but a few grams, so the forces involved were minute; but the unmistakable fact that there were such forces was earthshaking.

Professional caution kept him from revealing his discovery immediately. He wanted more facts and a body of theory to go with them. Later, when the atomic bomb was dropped on Hiroshima, it was fear that made him hold his peace. At no time were his experiments, as Premier Slezak called them, "a bourgeois plot to shackle the true democracies of the world." The professor didn't know where they were leading.

In time, he came to recognize another startling feature of dynamopsychism: *its strength increased with use.* Within six months, he was able to govern dice thrown by men the length of a barracks distant. By the time of his discharge in 1945, he could knock bricks loose from chimneys three miles away.

Charges that Professor Barnhouse could have won the last war in a minute, but did not care to do so, are perfectly senseless. When the war ended, he had the range and power of a 37-millimeter cannon, perhaps—certainly no more. His dynamopsychic powers graduated from the small-arms class only after his discharge and return to Wyandotte College.

I enrolled in the Wyandotte Graduate School two years after the professor had rejoined the faculty. By chance, he was assigned as my thesis adviser. I was unhappy about the assignment, for the professor was, in the eyes of both colleagues and students, a somewhat ridiculous figure. He missed classes or had lapses of memory during lectures. When I arrived, in fact, his shortcomings had passed from the ridiculous to the intolerable.

"We're assigning you to Barnhouse as a sort of temporary thing," the dean of social studies told me. He looked apologetic and perplexed. "Brilliant man, Barnhouse, I guess. Difficult to know since his return, perhaps, but his work before the war brought a great deal of credit to our little school."

When I reported to the professor's laboratory for the first time, what I saw was more distressing than the gossip. Every surface in the room was covered with dust; books and apparatus had not been disturbed for months. The professor sat napping at his desk when I entered. The only signs of recent activity were three overflowing ashtrays, a pair of scissors, and a morning paper with several items clipped from its front page.

As he raised his head to look at me, I saw that his eyes were clouded with fatigue. "Hi," he said, "just can't seem to get my sleeping done at night." He lighted a cigarette, his hands trembling slightly. "You the young man I'm supposed to help with a thesis?"

"Yes, sir," I said. In minutes he converted my misgivings to alarm.

"You an overseas veteran?" he asked.

"Yes, sir."

"Not much left over there, is there?" He frowned. "Enjoy the last war?"

"No, sir."

"Look like another war to you?"

"Kind of, sir."

"What can be done about it?"

I shrugged. "Looks pretty hopeless."

He peered at me intently. "Know anything about international law, the U.N., and all that?"

"Only what I pick up from the papers."

"Same here," he sighed. He showed me a fat scrapbook packed with newspaper clippings. "Never used to pay any attention to international politics. Now I study them the way I used to study rats in mazes. Everybody tells me the same thing—'Looks hopeless.'"

"Nothing short of a miracle—" I began.

"Believe in magic?" he asked sharply. The professor fished two dice from his vest pocket. "I will try to roll twos," he said. He rolled twos three times in a row. "One chance in about 47,000 of that happening. There's a miracle for you." He beamed for an instant, then brought the interview to an end, remarking that he had a class which had begun ten minutes ago.

He was not quick to take me into his confidence, and he said no more about his trick with the dice. I assumed they were loaded, and forgot about them. He set me the task of watching male rats cross electrified metal strips to get to food or female rats—an experiment that had been done to everyone's satisfaction in the nineteen-thirties. As though the pointlessness of my work were not bad enough, the professor annoyed me further with irrelevant questions. His favorites were: "Think we should have dropped the atomic bomb on Hiroshima?" and "Think every new piece of scientific information is a good thing for humanity?"

◎ ◎ ◎

However, I did not feel put upon for long. "Give those poor animals a holiday," he said one morning, after I had been with him only a month. "I wish you'd help me look into a more interesting problem—namely, my sanity."

I returned the rats to their cages.

"What you must do is simple," he said, speaking softly. "Watch the inkwell on my desk. If you see nothing happen to it, say so, and I'll go quietly—relieved, I might add—to the nearest sanitarium."

I nodded uncertainly.

He locked the laboratory door and drew the blinds, so that we were in twilight for a moment. "I'm odd, I know," he said. "It's fear of myself that's made me odd."

"I've found you somewhat eccentric, perhaps, but certainly not—"

"If nothing happens to that inkwell, 'crazy as a bedbug' is the only description of me that will do," he interrupted, turning on the overhead lights. His eyes narrowed. "To give you an idea of how crazy, I'll tell you what's been running through my mind when I should have been sleeping. I think maybe I can save the world. I think maybe I can make every nation a *have* nation, and do away with war for good. I think maybe I can clear roads through jungles, irrigate deserts, build dams overnight."

"Yes, sir."

"Watch the inkwell!"

Dutifully and fearfully I watched. A high-pitched humming seemed to come from the inkwell; then it began to vibrate alarmingly, and finally to bound about the top of the desk, making two noisy circuits. It stopped, hummed again, glowed red, then popped in splinters with a blue-green flash.

Perhaps my hair stood on end. The professor laughed gently. "Magnets?" I managed to say at last.

"Wish to heaven it were magnets," he murmured. It was then that he told me of dynamopsychism. He knew only that there was such a force; he could not explain it. "It's me and me alone—and it's awful."

"I'd say it was amazing and wonderful!" I cried.

"If all I could do was make inkwells dance, I'd be tickled silly with the whole business." He shrugged disconsolately. "But I'm no toy, my boy. If you like, we can drive around the neighborhood, and I'll show you what I mean." He told me about pulverized boulders, shattered oaks, and abandoned farm buildings demolished within a fifty-mile radius of the campus. "Did every bit of it sitting right here, just thinking—not even thinking hard."

He scratched his head nervously. "I have never dared to concentrate as hard as I can for fear of the damage I might do. I'm to the point where a mere whim is a blockbuster." There was a depressing pause. "Up until a few days ago, I've thought it best to keep my secret for fear of what use it might be put to," he continued. "Now I realize that I haven't any more right to it than a man has a right to own an atomic bomb."

He fumbled through a heap of papers. "This says about all that needs to be said, I think." He handed me a draft of a letter to the Secretary of State.

> Dear Sir:
> I have discovered a new force which costs nothing to use, and which is probably more important than atomic energy. I should like to see it used most effectively in the cause of peace, and am, therefore, requesting your advice as to how this might best be done.
> Yours truly,
> A. Barnhouse.

"I have no idea what will happen next," said the professor.

◎ ◎ ◎

There followed three months of perpetual nightmare, wherein the nation's political and military great came at all hours to watch the professor's tricks.

We were quartered in an old mansion near Charlottesville, Virginia, to which we had been whisked five days after the letter was mailed. Surrounded by barbed wire and twenty guards, we were labeled "Project Wishing Well," and were classified as Top Secret.

For companionship we had General Honus Barker and the State Department's William K. Cuthrell. For the professor's talk of peace-through-plenty they had indulgent smiles and much discourse on practical measures and realistic thinking. So treated, the professor, who had at first been almost meek, progressed in a matter of weeks toward stubbornness.

He had agreed to reveal the thought train by means of which he aligned his mind into a dynamopsychic transmitter. But, under Cuthrell's and Barker's nagging to do so, he began to hedge. At first he declared that the information could be passed on simply by word of mouth. Later he said that it would have to be written up in a long report. Finally, at dinner one night, just after General Barker had read the secret orders for Operation Brainstorm, the professor announced, "The report may take as long as five years to write." He looked fiercely at the general. "Maybe twenty."

The dismay occasioned by this flat announcement was offset somewhat by the exciting anticipation of Operation Brainstorm. The general was in a holiday mood. "The target ships are on their way to the Caroline Islands at this very moment," he declared ecstatically. "One hundred and twenty of them! At the same time, ten V-2s are being readied for firing in New Mexico, and fifty radio-controlled jet bombers are being equipped for a mock attack on the Aleutians. Just think of it!" Happily he reviewed his orders. "At exactly 1100 hours next Wednesday, I will give you the order to *concentrate*; and you, professor, will think as hard as you can about sinking the target ships, destroying the V-2s before they hit the ground, and knocking down bombers before they reach the Aleutians! Think you can handle it?"

The professor turned gray and closed his eyes. "As I told you before, my friend, I don't know what I can do." He added bitterly, "As for this Operation Brainstorm, I was never consulted about it, and it strikes me as childish and insanely expensive."

General Barker bridled. "Sir," he said, "your field is psychology, and I wouldn't presume to give you advice in that field. Mine is national defense. I have had thirty years of experience and success, professor, and I'll ask you not to criticize my judgment."

The professor appealed to Mr. Cuthrell. "Look," he pleaded, "isn't it war and military matters we're all trying to get rid of? Wouldn't it be a whole lot more significant and lots cheaper for me to try moving cloud masses into drought areas, and things like that? I admit I know next to nothing about international politics, but it seems reasonable to suppose that nobody would want to fight wars if there were enough of everything to go around. Mr. Cuthrell, I'd like to try running generators where there isn't any coal or water power, irrigating deserts, and so on. Why, you could figure out what each country needs to make the most of its resources, and I could give it to them without costing American taxpayers a penny."

"Eternal vigilance is the price of freedom," said the general heavily.

Mr. Cuthrell threw the general a look of mild distaste. "Unfortunately, the general is right in his own way," he said. "I wish to heaven the world were ready for ideals like yours, but it simply isn't. We aren't surrounded by brothers, but by enemies. It isn't a lack of food or resources that has us on the brink of war—it's a struggle for power. Who's going to be in charge of the world, our kind of people or theirs?"

The professor nodded in reluctant agreement and arose from the table. "I beg your pardon, gentlemen. You are, after all, better qualified to judge what is best for the country. I'll do whatever you say." He turned to me. "Don't forget to wind the restricted clock and put the confidential cat out," he said gloomily, and ascended the stairs to his bedroom.

◎ ◎ ◎

For reasons of national security, Operation Brainstorm was carried on without the knowledge of the American citizenry which was paying the bill. The observers, technicians, and military men involved in the activity knew that a test was under way—a test of what, they had no idea. Only thirty-seven key men, myself included, knew what was afoot.

In Virginia, the day for Operation Brainstorm was unseasonably cool. Inside, a log fire crackled in the fireplace, and the flames were reflected in the polished metal cabinets that lined the living room. All that remained of the room's lovely old furniture was a Victorian love seat, set squarely in the center of the floor, facing three television receivers. One long bench had been brought in for the ten of us privileged to watch. The television screens showed, from left to right, the stretch of desert which was the rocket target, the guinea-pig fleet, and a section of the Aleutian sky through which the radio-controlled bomber formation would roar.

Ninety minutes before H-hour the radios announced that the rockets were ready, that the observation ships had backed away to what was thought to be a safe distance, and that the bombers were on their way. The small Virginia audience lined up on the bench in order of rank, smoked a great deal, and said little. Professor Barnhouse was in his bedroom. General Barker bustled about the house like a woman preparing Thanksgiving dinner for twenty.

At ten minutes before H-hour the general came in, shepherding the professor before him. The professor was comfortably attired in sneakers, gray flannels, a blue sweater, and a white shirt open at the neck. The two of them sat side by side on the love seat. The general was rigid and perspiring; the professor was cheerful. He looked at each of the screens, lighted a cigarette and settled back.

"Bombers sighted!" cried the Aleutian observers.

"Rockets away!" barked the New Mexico radio operator.

All of us looked quickly at the big electric clock over the mantel, while the professor, a half-smile on his face, continued to watch the television sets. In hollow tones, the general counted away the seconds remaining. "Five . . . four . . . three . . . two . . . one . . . *Concentrate!*"

Professor Barnhouse closed his eyes, pursed his lips, and stroked his temples. He held the position for a minute. The television images were scrambled, and the radio signals were drowned in the din of Barnhouse static. The professor sighed, opened his eyes, and smiled confidently.

"Did you give it everything you had?" asked the general dubiously.

"I was wide open," the professor replied.

The television images pulled themselves together, and mingled cries of amazement came over the radios tuned to the observers. The Aleutian sky was streaked with the smoke trails of bombers screaming down in flames. Simultaneously, there appeared high over the rocket target a cluster of white puffs, followed by faint thunder.

General Barker shook his head happily. "By George!" he crowed. "Well, sir, by George, by George, by George!"

"Look!" shouted the admiral seated next to me. "The fleet—it wasn't touched!"

"The guns seem to be drooping," said Mr. Cuthrell.

We left the bench and clustered about the television set to examine the damage more closely. What Mr. Cuthrell had said was true. The ships' guns curved downward, their muzzles resting on the steel decks. We in Virginia were making such a hullabaloo that it was impossible to hear the radio reports. We were so engrossed, in fact, that we didn't miss the professor until two short snarls of Barnhouse static shocked us into sudden silence. The radios went dead.

We looked around apprehensively. The professor was gone. A harassed guard threw open the front door from the outside to yell that the professor had escaped. He brandished his pistol in the direction of the gates, which hung open, limp and twisted. In the distance, a speeding government station wagon topped a ridge and dropped from sight into the valley beyond. The air was filled with choking smoke, for every vehicle on the grounds was ablaze. Pursuit was impossible.

"What in God's name got into him?" bellowed the general.

Mr. Cuthrell, who had rushed out onto the front porch, now slouched back into the room, reading a penciled note as he came. He thrust the note into my hands. "The good man left this billet-doux under the door knocker. Perhaps our young friend here will be kind enough to read it to you gentlemen, while I take a restful walk through the woods."

"Gentlemen," I read aloud, "as the first superweapon with a conscience, I am removing myself from your national defense stockpile. Setting a new precedent in the behavior of ordnance, I have humane reasons for going off. A. Barnhouse."

◻ ◻ ◻

Since that day, of course, the professor has been systematically destroying the world's armaments, until there is now little with which to equip an army other than rocks and sharp sticks. His activities haven't exactly resulted in peace, but have, rather, precipitated a bloodless and entertaining sort of war that might be called the "War of the Tattletales." Every nation is flooded with enemy agents whose sole mission is to locate military equipment, which is promptly wrecked when it is brought to the professor's attention in the press.

Just as every day brings news of more armaments pulverized by dynamopsychism, so has it brought rumors of the professor's whereabouts. During last week alone, three publications carried articles proving variously that he was hiding in an Inca ruin in the Andes, in the sewers of Paris, and in the unexplored lower chambers of Carlsbad Caverns. Knowing the man, I am inclined to regard such hiding places as unnecessarily romantic and uncomfortable. While there are numerous persons eager to kill him, there must be millions who would care for him and hide him. I like to think that he is in the home of such a person.

One thing is certain: at this writing, Professor Barnhouse is not dead. Barnhouse static jammed broadcasts not ten minutes ago. In the eighteen months since his disappearance, he has been reported dead some half-dozen times. Each report has stemmed from the death of an unidentified man resembling the professor, during a period free of the static. The first three reports were followed at once by renewed talk of rearmament and recourse to war. The saber-rattlers have learned how imprudent premature celebrations of the professor's demise can be.

Many a stouthearted patriot has found himself prone in the tangled bunting and timbers of a smashed reviewing stand, seconds after having announced that the arch-tyranny of Barnhouse was at an end. But those who would make war if they could, in every country in the world, wait in sullen silence for what must come—the passing of Professor Barnhouse.

◎ ◎ ◎

To ask how much longer the professor will live is to ask how much longer we must wait for the blessings of another world war. He is of short-lived stock: his mother lived to be fifty-three, his father to be forty-nine; and the lifespans of his grandparents on both sides were of the same order. He might be expected to live, then, for perhaps fifteen years more, if he can remain hidden from his enemies. When one considers the number and vigor of these enemies, however, fifteen years seems an extraordinary length of time, which might better be revised to fifteen days, hours, or minutes.

The professor knows that he cannot live much longer. I say this because of the message left in my mailbox on Christmas Eve. Unsigned, typewritten on a soiled scrap of paper, the note consisted of ten sentences. The first nine of these, each a bewildering tangle of psychological jargon and references to obscure texts, made no sense to me at first reading. The tenth, unlike the rest, was simply constructed and contained no large words—but its irrational content made it the most puzzling and bizarre sentence of all. I nearly threw the note away, thinking it a colleague's warped notion of a practical joke. For some reason, though, I added it to the clutter on top of my desk, which included, among other mementos, the professor's dice.

It took me several weeks to realize that the message really meant something, that the first nine sentences, when unsnarled, could be taken as instructions. The tenth still told me nothing. It was only last night that I discovered how it fitted in with the rest. The sentence appeared in my thoughts last night, while I was toying absently with the professor's dice.

I promised to have this report on its way to the publishers today. In view of what has happened, I am obliged to break that promise, or release the report incomplete. The delay will not be a long one, for one of the few blessings accorded a bachelor like myself is the ability to move quickly from one abode to another, or from one way of life to another. What property I want to take with me can be packed in a few hours. Fortunately, I am not without substantial private means, which may take as long as a week to realize in liquid and anonymous form. When this is done, I shall mail the report.

I have just returned from a visit to my doctor, who tells me my health is excellent. I am young, and, with any luck at all, I shall live to a ripe old age indeed, for my family on both sides is noted for longevity.

Briefly, I propose to vanish.

Sooner or later, Professor Barnhouse must die. But long before then I shall be ready. So, to the saber-rattlers of today—and even, I hope, of tomorrow—I say: Be advised. Barnhouse will die. But not the Barnhouse Effect.

Last night, I tried once more to follow the oblique instructions on the scrap of paper. I took the professor's dice, and then, with the last, nightmarish sentence flitting through my mind, I rolled fifty consecutive sevens.

Good-bye.

The Euphio Question

LADIES AND GENTLEMEN of the Federal Communications Commission, I appreciate this opportunity to testify on the subject before you.

I'm sorry—or maybe "heartsick" is the word—that news has leaked out about it. But now that word is getting around and coming to your official notice, I might as well tell the story straight and pray to God that I can convince you that America doesn't want what we discovered.

I won't deny that all three of us—Lew Harrison, the radio announcer, Dr. Fred Bockman, the physicist, and myself, a sociology professor—found peace of mind. We did. And I won't say it's wrong for people to seek peace of mind. But if somebody thinks he wants peace of mind the way we found it, he'd be well advised to seek coronary thrombosis instead.

Lew, Fred, and I found peace of mind by sitting in easy chairs and turning on a gadget the size of a table-model television set. No herbs, no golden rule, no muscle control, no sticking our noses in other people's troubles to forget our own; no hobbies, Taoism, push-ups or contemplation of a lotus. The gadget is, I think, what a lot of people vaguely foresaw as the crowning achievement of civilization: an electronic something-or-other, cheap, easily mass-produced, that can, at the flick of a switch, provide tranquility. I see you have one here.

My first brush with synthetic peace of mind was six months ago. It was also then that I got to know Lew Harrison I'm sorry to say. Lew is chief announcer of our town's only radio station. He makes his living with his loud mouth, and I'd be surprised if it were anyone but he who brought this matter to your attention.

Lew has, along with about thirty other shows, a weekly science program. Every week he gets some professor from Wyandotte College and interviews him about his particular field. Well, six months ago Lew worked up a program around a young dreamer and faculty friend of mine, Dr. Fred Bockman. I gave Fred a lift to the radio station, and he invited me to come on in and watch. For the heck of it, I did.

Fred Bockman is thirty and looks eighteen. Life has left no marks on him, because he hasn't paid much attention to it. What he pays most of his attention to, and what Lew Harrison wanted to interview him about, is this eight-ton umbrella of his that he listens to the stars with. It's a big radio antenna rigged up on a telescope mount. The way I understand it, instead of looking at the stars through a telescope, he aims this thing out in space and picks up radio signals coming from different heavenly bodies.

Of course, there aren't people running radio stations out there. It's just that many of the heavenly bodies pour out a lot of energy and some of it can be picked up in the radio-frequency band. One good thing Fred's rig does is to spot stars hidden from telescopes by big clouds of cosmic dust. Radio signals from them get through the clouds to Fred's antenna.

That isn't all the outfit can do, and, in his interview with Fred, Lew Harrison saved the most exciting part until the end of the program. "That's very interesting, Dr. Bockman," Lew said. "Tell me, has your radio telescope turned up anything else about the universe that hasn't been revealed by ordinary light telescopes?"

This was the snapper. "Yes, it has," Fred said. "We've found about fifty spots in space, *not hidden by cosmic dust*, that give off powerful radio signals. Yet no heavenly bodies at all seem to be there."

"Well!" Lew said in mock surprise. "I should say that *is* something! Ladies and gentlemen, for the first time in radio history, we bring you the noise from Dr. Bockman's mysterious voids." They had strung a line out to Fred's antenna on the campus. Lew waved to the engineer to switch in the signals coming from it. "Ladies and gentlemen, the voice of nothingness!"

The noise wasn't much to hear—a wavering hiss, more like a leaking tire than anything else. It was supposed to be on the air for five seconds. When the engineer switched it off, Fred and I were inexplicably grinning like idiots. I felt relaxed and tingling. Lew Harrison looked as though he'd stumbled into the dressing room at the Copacabana. He glanced at the studio clock, appalled. The monotonous hiss had been on the air for five minutes! If the engineer's cuff hadn't accidentally caught on the switch, it might be on yet.

Fred laughed nervously, and Lew hunted for his place in the script. "The hiss from nowhere," Lew said. "Dr. Bockman, has anyone proposed a name for these interesting voids?"

"No," Fred said. "At the present time they have neither a name nor an explanation."

The voids the hiss came from have still to be explained, but I've suggested a name for them that shows plans of sticking: "Bockman's Euphoria." We may not know what the voids are, but we know what they do, so the name's a good one. Euphoria, since it means a sense of buoyancy and well-being, is really the only word that will do.

◙ ◙ ◙

After the broadcast, Fred, Lew, and I were cordial to one another to the point of being maudlin.

"I can't remember when a broadcast has been such a pleasure," Lew said. Sincerity is not his forte, yet he meant it.

COMPLETE STORIES

"It's been one of the most memorable experiences of my life," Fred said, looking puzzled. "Extraordinarily pleasant."

We were all embarrassed by the emotion we felt, and parted company in bafflement and haste. I hurried home for a drink, only to walk into the middle of another unsettling experience.

The house was quiet, and I made two trips through it before discovering that I was not alone. My wife, Susan, a good and lovable woman who prides herself on feeding her family well and on time, was lying on the couch, staring dreamily at the ceiling. "Honey," I said tentatively, "I'm home. It's suppertime."

"Fred Bockman was on the radio today," she said in a faraway voice.

"I know. I was with him in the studio."

"He was out of this world," she sighed. "Simply out of this world. That noise from space—when he turned that on, everything just seemed to drop away from me. I've been lying here, just trying to get over it."

"Uh-huh," I said, biting my lip. "Well, guess I'd better round up Eddie." Eddie is my ten-year-old son, and captain of an apparently invincible neighborhood baseball team.

"Save your strength, Pop," said a small voice from the shadows.

"You home? What's the matter? Game called off on account of atomic attack?"

"Nope. We finished eight innings."

"Beating 'em so bad they didn't want to go on, eh?"

"Uh, they were doing pretty good. Score was tied, and they had two men on and two outs." He talked as though he were recounting a dream. "And then," he said, his eyes widening, "everybody kind of lost interest, just wandered off. I came home and found the old lady curled up here, so I lay down on the floor."

"Why?" I asked incredulously.

"Pop," Eddie said thoughtfully, "I'm damned if I know."

"Eddie!" his mother said.

"Mom," Eddie said, "I'm damned if *you* know either."

I was damned if anybody could explain it, but I had a nagging hunch. I dialed Fred Bockman's number. "Fred, am I getting you up from dinner?"

"I wish you were," Fred said. "Not a scrap to eat in the house, and I let Marion have the car today so she could do the marketing. Now she's trying to find a grocery open."

"Couldn't get the car started, eh?"

"Sure she got the car started," said Fred. "She even got to the market. Then she felt so good she walked right out of the place again." Fred sounded depressed. "I guess it's a woman's privilege to change her mind, but it's the lying that hurts."

"Marion lied? I don't believe it."

"She tried to tell me everybody wandered out of the market with her—clerks and all."

"Fred," I said, "I've got news for you. Can I drive out right after supper?"

When I arrived at Fred Bockman's farm, he was staring, dumbfounded, at the evening paper.

"The whole town went nuts!" Fred said. "For no reason at all, all the cars pulled up to the curb like there was a hook and ladder going by. Says here people shut up in the middle of sentences and stayed that way for five minutes. Hundreds wandered around in the cold in their shirt-sleeves, grinning like toothpaste ads." He rattled the paper. "This *is* what you wanted to talk to me about?"

I nodded. "It all happened when that noise was being broadcast, and I thought maybe—"

"The odds are about one in a million that there's any maybe about it," said Fred. "The time checks to the second."

"But most people weren't listening to the program."

"They didn't have to listen, if my theory's right. We took those faint signals from space, amplified them about a thousand times, and rebroadcast them. Anybody within reach of the transmitter would get a good dose of the stepped-up radiations, whether he wanted to or not." He shrugged. "Apparently that's like walking past a field of burning marijuana."

"How come you never felt the effect at work?"

"Because I never amplified and rebroadcast the signals. The radio station's transmitter is what really put the sock into them."

"So what're you going to do next?"

Fred looked surprised. "Do? What is there to do but report it in some suitable journal?"

◎ ◎ ◎

Without a preliminary knock, the front door burst open and Lew Harrison, florid and panting, swept into the room and removed his great polo coat with a bullfighter-like flourish. "You're cutting him in on it, too?" he demanded, pointing at me.

Fred blinked at him. "In on what?"

"The millions," Lew said. "The billions."

"Wonderful," Fred said. "What are you talking about?"

"The noise from the stars!" Lew said "They love it. It drives 'em nuts. Didja see the papers?" He sobered for an instant. "It *was* the noise that did it, wasn't it, Doc?"

"We think so," Fred said. He looked worried. "How, exactly, do you propose we get our hands on these millions or billions?"

"Real estate!" Lew said raptly. "'Lew,' I said to myself, 'Lew, how can you cash in on this gimmick if you can't get a monopoly on the universe? And, Lew,' I asked myself, 'how can you sell the stuff when anybody can get it free while you're broadcasting it?'"

"Maybe it's the kind of thing that shouldn't be cashed in on," I suggested. "I mean, we don't know a great deal about—"

"Is happiness bad?" Lew interrupted.

"No," I admitted.

"Okay, and what we'd do with this stuff from the stars is make people happy. Now I suppose you're going to tell me that's bad?"

"People ought to be happy," Fred said.

"Okay, okay," Lew said loftily. "That's what we're going to do for the people. And the way the people can show their gratitude is in real estate." He looked out the window. "Good—a barn. We can start right there. We set up a transmitter in the barn, run a line out to your antenna, Doc, and we've got a real estate development."

"Sorry," Fred said. "I don't follow you. This place wouldn't do for a development. The roads are poor, no bus service or shopping center, the view is lousy and the ground is full of rocks."

Lew nudged Fred several times with his elbow. "Doc, Doc, Doc—sure it's got drawbacks, but with that transmitter in the barn, you can give them the most precious thing in all creation—happiness."

"Euphoria Heights," I said.

"That's great!" said Lew. "I'd get the prospects, Doc, and you'd sit up there in the barn with your hand on the switch. Once a prospect set foot on Euphoria Heights, and you shot the happiness to him, there's nothing he wouldn't pay for a lot."

"Every house a home, as long as the power doesn't fail," I said.

"Then," Lew said, his eyes shining, "when we sell all the lots here, we move the transmitter and start another development. Maybe we'd get a fleet of transmitters going." He snapped his fingers. "Sure! Mount 'em on wheels."

"I somehow don't think the police would think highly of us," Fred said.

"Okay, so when they come to investigate, you throw the old switch and give *them* a jolt of happiness." He shrugged. "Hell, I might even get bighearted and let them have a corner lot."

"No," Fred said quietly. "If I ever joined a church, I couldn't face the minister."

"So we give *him* a jolt," Lew said brightly.

"No," Fred said. "Sorry."

"Okay," Lew said, rising and pacing the floor. "I was prepared for that. I've got an alternative, and this one's strictly legitimate. We'll make a little amplifier with a transmitter and an aerial on it. Shouldn't cost over fifty bucks to make, so we'd price it in the range of the common man—five hundred bucks, say. We make arrangements with the phone company to pipe signals from your antenna right into the homes of people with these sets. The sets take the signal from the phone line, amplify it, and broadcast it through the houses to make everybody in them happy. See? Instead of turning on the radio or television, everybody's going to want to turn on the happiness. No casts, no stage sets, no expensive cameras—no nothing but that hiss."

"We could call it the euphoriaphone," I suggested, "or 'euphio' for short."

"That's great, that's great!" Lew said. "What do you say, Doc?"

"I don't know." Fred looked worried. "This sort of thing is out of my line."

"We all have to recognize our limitations, Doc," Lew said expansively. "I'll handle the business end, and you handle the technical end." He made a motion as though to put on his coat. "Or maybe you don't want to be a millionaire?"

"Oh, yes, yes indeed I do," Fred said quickly. "Yes, indeed."

"All righty," Lew said, dusting his palms, "the first thing we've gotta do is build one of the sets and test her."

This part of it *was* down Fred's alley, and I could see the problem interested him. "It's really a pretty simple gadget," he said. "I suppose we could throw one together and run a test out here next week."

◙ ◙ ◙

The first test of the euphoriaphone, or euphio, took place in Fred Bockman's living room on a Saturday afternoon, five days after Fred's and Lew's sensational radio broadcast.

There were six guinea pigs—Lew, Fred and his wife Marion, myself, my wife Susan, and my son Eddie. The Bockmans had arranged chairs in a circle around a card table, on which rested a gray steel box.

Protruding from the box was a long buggy whip aerial that scraped the ceiling. While Fred fussed with the box, the rest of us made nervous small talk over sandwiches and beer. Eddie, of course, wasn't drinking beer, though he was badly in need of a sedative. He was annoyed at having been brought out to the farm instead of to a ball game, and was threatening to take it out on the Bockmans' Early American furnishings. He was playing a spirited game of flies and grounders with himself near the French doors, using a dead tennis ball and a poker.

"Eddie," Susan said for the tenth time, "please stop."

"It's under control, under control," Eddie said disdainfully, playing the ball off four walls and catching it with one hand.

Marion, who vents her maternal instincts on her immaculate furnishings, couldn't hide her distress at Eddie's turning the place into a gymnasium. Lew, in his way, was trying to calm her. "Let him wreck the dump," Lew said. "You'll be moving into a palace one of these days."

"It's ready," Fred said softly.

We looked at him with queasy bravery. Fred plugged two jacks from the phone line into the gray box. This was the direct line to his antenna on the campus, and clockwork would keep the antenna fixed on one of the mysterious voids in the sky—the most potent of Bockman's Euphoria. He plugged a cord from the box into an electrical outlet in the baseboard, and rested his hand on a switch. "Ready?"

"Don't, Fred!" I said. I was scared stiff.

"Turn it on, turn it on," Lew said. "We wouldn't have the telephone today if Bell hadn't had the guts to call somebody up."

"I'll stand right here by the switch, ready to flick her off if something goes sour," Fred said reassuringly. There was a click, a hum and the euphio was on.

Lew Harrison was the first to speak, continuing his conversation with Marion. "But who cares for material wealth?" he asked earnestly. He turned to Susan for confirmation.

"Uh-uh," said Susan, shaking her head dreamily. She put her arms around Lew, and kissed him for about five minutes.

"Say," I said, patting Susan on the back, "you kids get along swell, don't you? Isn't that nice, Fred?"

"Eddie," Marion said solicitously, "I think there's a real baseball in the hall closet. A *hard* ball. Wouldn't that be more fun than that old tennis ball?" Eddie didn't stir.

Fred was still prowling around the room, smiling, his eyes now closed all the way. His heel caught in a lamp cord, and he went sprawling on the hearth, his head in the ashes. "Hi-ho, everybody," he said, his eyes still closed. "Bunged my head on an andiron." He stayed there, giggling occasionally.

"The doorbell's been ringing for a while," Susan said. "I don't suppose it means anything."

"Come in, come in," I shouted. This somehow struck everyone as terribly funny. We all laughed uproariously, including Fred, whose guffaws blew up little gray clouds from the ashpit.

◎ ◎ ◎

A small, very serious old man in white had let himself in, and was now standing in the vestibule, looking at us with alarm. "Milkman," he said uncertainly. He held out a slip of paper to Marion. "I can't read the last line in your note," he said. "What's that say about cottage cheese, cheese, cheese, cheese, cheese . . ." His voice trailed off as he settled, tailor-fashion, to the floor beside Marion. After he'd been silent for perhaps three quarters of an hour, a look of concern crossed his face. "Well," he said apathetically, "I can only stay for a minute. My truck's parked out on the shoulder, kind of blocking things." He started to stand. Lew gave the volume knob on the euphio a twist. The milkman wilted to the floor.

"Aaaaaaaaaaah," said everybody.

"Good day to be indoors," the milkman said. "Radio says we'll catch the tail end of the Atlantic hurricane."

"Let 'er come," I said. "I've got my car parked under a big, dead tree." It seemed to make sense. Nobody took exception to it. I lapsed back into a warm fog of silence and thought of nothing whatsoever. These lapses seemed to last for a matter of seconds before they were interrupted by conversation of newcomers. Looking back, I see now that the lapses were rarely less than six hours.

I was snapped out of one, I recall, by a repetition of the doorbell's ringing. "I said come in," I mumbled.

"And I did," the milkman mumbled.

The door swung open, and a state trooper glared in at us. "Who the hell's got his milk truck out there blocking the road?" he demanded. He spotted the milkman. "Aha! Don't you know somebody could get killed, coming around a blind curve into that thing?" He yawned, and his ferocious expression gave way to an affectionate smile. "It's so damn unlikely," he said, "I don't know why I ever brought it up." He sat down by Eddie. "Hey, kid—like guns?" He took his revolver from its holster. "Look—just like Hoppy's."

Eddie took the gun, aimed it at Marion's bottle collection and fired. A large blue bottle popped to dust and the window behind the collection splintered. Cold air roared in through the opening.

"He'll make a cop yet," Marion chortled.

"God, I'm happy," I said, feeling a little like crying. "I got the swellest little kid and the swellest bunch of friends and the swellest old wife in the world." I heard the gun go off twice more, and then dropped into heavenly oblivion.

Again the doorbell roused me. "How many times do I have to tell you—for Heaven's sake, come in," I said, without opening my eyes.

"I *did*," the milkman said.

I heard the tramping of many feet, but had no curiosity about them. A little later, I noticed that I was having difficulty breathing. Investigation revealed that I had slipped to the floor, and that several Boy Scouts had bivouacked on my chest and abdomen.

"You want something?" I asked the tenderfoot whose hot, measured breathing was in my face.

"Beaver Patrol wanted old newspapers, but forget it," he said. "We'd just have to carry 'em somewhere."

"And do your parents know where you are?"

"Oh, sure. They got worried and came after us." He jerked his thumb at several couples lined up against the baseboard, smiling into the teeth of the wind and rain lashing in at them through the broken window.

"Mom, I'm kinda hungry," Eddie said.

"Oh, Eddie—you're not going to make your mother cook just when we're having such a wonderful time," Susan said.

Lew Harrison gave the euphio's volume knob another twist. "There, kid, how's that?"

"Aaaaaaaaaaah," said everybody.

When awareness intruded on oblivion again, I felt around for the Beaver Patrol, and found them missing. I opened my eyes to see that they and Eddie and the milkman and Lew and the trooper were standing by a picture window, cheering. The wind outside was roaring and slashing savagely and driving raindrops through the broken window as though they'd been fired from air rifles. I shook Susan gently, and together we went to the window to see what might be so entertaining.

"She's going, she's going, she's going," the milkman cried ecstatically.

◙ ◙ ◙

Susan and I arrived just in time to join in the cheering as a big elm crashed down on our sedan.

"Kee-*runch*!" said Susan, and I laughed until my stomach hurt.

"Get Fred," Lew said urgently. "He's gonna miss seeing the barn go!"

"H'mm?" Fred said from the fireplace.

"Aw, Fred, you missed it," Marion said.

"Now we're really gonna see something," Eddie yelled. "The power line's going to get it this time. Look at that poplar lean!"

The poplar leaned closer, closer, closer to the power line; and then a gust brought it down in a hail of sparks and a tangle of wires. The lights in the house went off.

Now there was only the sound of the wind. "How come nobody cheered?" Lew said faintly. "The euphio—it's off!"

A horrible groan came from the fireplace. "God, I think I've got a concussion."

Marion knelt by her husband and wailed. "Darling, my poor darling—what happened to you?"

I looked at the woman I had my arms around—a dreadful, dirty old hag, with red eyes sunk deep in her head, and hair like Medusa's. "Ugh," I said, and turned away in disgust.

"Honey," wept the witch, "it's me—Susan."

Moans filled the air, and pitiful cries for food and water. Suddenly the room had become terribly cold. Only a moment before I had imagined I was in the tropics.

"Who's got my damn pistol?" the trooper said bleakly.

A Western Union boy I hadn't noticed before was sitting in a corner, miserably leafing through a pile of telegrams and making clucking noises.

I shuddered. "I'll bet it's Sunday morning," I said. "We've been here twelve hours!" It was Monday morning.

The Western Union boy was thunderstruck. "Sunday morning? I walked in here on a Sunday night." He stared around the room. "Looks like them newsreels of Buchenwald, don't it?"

The chief of the Beaver Patrol, with the incredible stamina of the young, was the hero of the day. He fell in his men in two ranks, haranguing them like an old Army top-kick. While the rest of us lay draped around the room, whimpering about hunger, cold, and thirst, the patrol started the furnace again, brought blankets, applied compresses to Fred's head and countless barked shins, blocked off the broken window, and made buckets of cocoa and coffee.

◙ ◙ ◙

Within two hours of the time that the power and the euphio went off, the house was warm and we had eaten. The serious respiratory cases—the parents who had sat near the broken window for twenty-four hours—had been pumped full of penicillin and hauled off to the hospital. The milkman, the Western Union boy, and the trooper had refused treatment and gone home. The Beaver Patrol had saluted smartly and left. Outside, repairmen were working on the power line. Only the original group remained—Lew, Fred, and Marion, Susan and myself, and Eddie. Fred, it turned out, had some pretty important-looking contusions and abrasions, but no concussion.

Susan had fallen asleep right after eating. Now she stirred. "What happened?"

"Happiness," I told her. "Incomparable, continuous happiness—happiness by the kilowatt."

Lew Harrison, who looked like an anarchist with his red eyes and fierce black beard, had been writing furiously in one corner of the room. "That's good—happiness by the kilowatt," he said. "Buy your happiness the way you buy light."

"Contract happiness the way you contract influenza," Fred said. He sneezed.

Lew ignored him. "It's a campaign, see? The first ad is for the long-hairs: 'The price of one book, which may be a disappointment, will buy you sixty hours of euphio. Euphio never disappoints.' Then we'd hit the middle class with the next one—"

"In the groin?" Fred said.

"What's the matter with you people?" Lew said. "You act as though the experiment had failed."

"Pneumonia and malnutrition are what we'd *hoped* for?" Marion said.

"We had a cross section of America in this room, and we made every last person happy," Lew said. "Not for just an hour, not for just a day, but for two days without a break." He arose reverently from his chair. "So what we do to keep it from killing the euphio fans is to have the thing turned on and off with clockwork, see? The owner sets it so it'll go on just as he comes home from work, then it'll go off again while he eats supper; then it goes on after supper, off again when it's bedtime; on again after breakfast, off when it's time to go to work, then on again for the wife and kids."

He ran his hands through his hair and rolled his eyes. "And the selling points—my God, the selling points! No expensive toys for the kids. For the price of a trip to the movies, people can buy thirty hours of euphio. For the price of a fifth of whisky, they can buy sixty hours of euphio!"

"Or a big family bottle of potassium cyanide," Fred said.

"Don't you see it?" Lew said incredulously. "It'll bring families together again, save the American home. No more fights over what TV or radio program to listen to. Euphio pleases one and all—we proved that. And there is no such thing as a dull euphio program."

A knock on the door interrupted him. A repairman stuck his head in to announce that the power would be on again in about two minutes.

"Look, Lew," Fred said, "this little monster could kill civilization in less time than it took to burn down Rome. We're not going into the mind-numbing business, and that's that."

"You're kidding!" Lew said, aghast. He turned to Marion. "Don't you want your husband to make a million?"

"Not by operating an electronic opium den," Marion said coldly.

Lew slapped his forehead. "It's what the public wants. This is like Louis Pasteur refusing to pasteurize milk."

"It'll be good to have the electricity again," Marion said, changing the subject. "Lights, hot-water heater, the pump, the—oh, Lord!"

The lights came on the instant she said it, but Fred and I were already in mid-air, descending on the gray box. We crashed down on it together. The card table buckled, and the plug was jerked from the wall socket. The euphio's tubes glowed red for a moment, then died.

Expressionlessly, Fred took a screwdriver from his pocket and removed the top of the box.

"Would you enjoy doing battle with progress?" he said, offering me the poker Eddie had dropped.

In a frenzy, I stabbed and smashed at the euphio's glass and wire vitals. With my left hand, and with Fred's help, I kept Lew from throwing himself between the poker and the works.

"I thought you were on my side," Lew said.

"If you breathe one word about euphio to anyone," I said, "what I just did to euphio I will gladly do to you."

◎ ◎ ◎

And there, ladies and gentlemen of the Federal Communications Commission, I thought the matter had ended. It deserved to end there. Now, through the medium of Lew Harrison's big mouth, word has leaked out. He has petitioned you for permission to start commercial exploitation of euphio. He and his backers have built a radio-telescope of their own.

Let me say again that all of Lew's claims are true. Euphio will do everything he says it will. The happiness it gives is perfect and unflagging in the face of incredible adversity. Near tragedies, such as the first experiment, can no doubt be avoided with clockwork to turn the sets on and off. I see that this set on the table before you is, in fact, equipped with clockwork.

The question is not whether euphio works. It does. The question is, rather, whether or not America is to enter a new and distressing phase of history where men no longer pursue happiness but buy it. This is no time for oblivion to become a national craze. The only benefit we could get from euphio would be if we could somehow lay down a peace-of-mind barrage on our enemies while protecting our own people from it.

In closing, I'd like to point out that Lew Harrison, the would-be czar of euphio, is an unscrupulous person, unworthy of public trust. It wouldn't surprise me, for instance, if he had set the clockwork on this sample euphio set so that its radiations would addle your judgments when you are trying to make a decision. In fact, it seems to be whirring suspiciously at this very moment, and I'm so happy I could cry. I've got the swellest little kid and the swellest bunch of friends and the swellest old wife in the world. And good old Lew Harrison is the salt of the earth, believe me. I sure wish him a lot of good luck with his new enterprise.

Unready to Wear

I DON'T SUPPOSE the oldsters, those of us who weren't born into it, will ever feel quite at home being amphibious—amphibious in the new sense of the word. I still catch myself feeling blue about things that don't matter any more.

I can't help worrying about my business, for instance—or what used to be my business. After all, I spent thirty years building the thing up from scratch, and now the equipment is rusting and getting clogged with dirt. But even though I know it's silly of me to care what happens to the business, I borrow a body from a storage center every so often, and go around the old hometown, and clean and oil as much of the equipment as I can.

Of course, all in the world the equipment was good for was making money, and Lord knows there's plenty of that lying around. Not as much as there used to be, because there at first some people got frisky and threw it all around, and the wind blew it every which way. And a lot of go-getters gathered up piles of the stuff and hid it somewhere. I hate to admit it, but I gathered up close to a half million myself and stuck it away. I used to get it out and count it sometimes, but that was years ago. Right now I'd be hard put to say where it is.

But the worrying I do about my old business is bush league stuff compared to the worrying my wife, Madge, does about our old house. That thing is what she herself put in thirty years on while I was building the business. Then no sooner had we gotten nerve enough to build and decorate the place than everybody we cared anything about got amphibious. Madge borrows a body once a month and dusts the place, though the only thing a house is good for now is keeping termites and mice from getting pneumonia.

◙ ◙ ◙

Whenever it's my turn to get into a body and work as an attendant at the local storage center, I realize all over again how much tougher it is for women to get used to being amphibious.

Madge borrows bodies a lot oftener than I do, and that's true of women in general. We have to keep three times as many women's bodies in stock as men's bodies, in order to meet the demand. Every so often, it seems as though a woman just *has* to have a body, and doll it up in clothes, and look at herself in a mirror. And Madge, God bless her, I don't think she'll be satisfied until she's tried on every body in every storage center on Earth.

It's been a fine thing for Madge, though. I never kid her about it, because it's done so much for her personality. Her old body, to tell you the plain blunt truth, wasn't anything to get excited about, and having to haul the thing around made her gloomy a lot of the time in the old days. She couldn't help it, poor soul, any more than anybody else could help what sort of body they'd been born with, and I loved her in spite of it.

Well, after we'd learned to be amphibious, and after we'd built the storage centers and laid in body supplies and opened them to the public, Madge went hog wild. She borrowed a platinum blonde body that had been donated by a burlesque queen, and I didn't think we'd ever get her out of it. As I say, it did wonders for her self-confidence.

I'm like most men and don't care particularly what body I get. Just the strong, good-looking, healthy bodies were put in storage, so one is as good as the next one. Sometimes, when Madge and I take bodies out together for old times' sake, I let her pick out one for me to match whatever she's got on. It's a funny thing how she always picks a blond, tall one for me.

My old body, which she claims she loved for a third of a century, had black hair, and was short and paunchy, too, there toward the last. I'm human and I couldn't help being hurt when they scrapped it after I'd left it, instead of putting it in storage. It was a good, homey, comfortable body; nothing fast and flashy, but reliable. But there isn't much call for that kind of body at the centers, I guess. I never ask for one, at any rate.

The worst experience I ever had with a body was when I was flimflammed into taking out the one that had belonged to Dr. Ellis Konigswasser. It belongs to the Amphibious Pioneers' Society and only gets taken out once a year for the big Pioneers' Day Parade, on the anniversary of Konigswasser's discovery. Everybody said it was a great honor for me to be picked to get into Konigswasser's body and lead the parade.

Like a plain damn fool, I believed them.

◙ ◙ ◙

They'll have a tough time getting me into that thing again—ever. Taking that wreck out certainly made it plain why Konigswasser discovered how people could do without their bodies. That old one of his practically *drives* you out. Ulcers, headaches, arthritis, fallen arches—a nose like a pruning hook, piggy little eyes, and a complexion like a used steamer trunk. He was and still is the sweetest person you'd ever want to know, but, back when he was stuck with that body, nobody got close enough to find out.

We tried to get Konigswasser back into his old body to lead us when we first started having the Pioneers' Day Parades, but he wouldn't have anything to do with it, so we always have to flatter some poor boob into taking on the job. Konigswasser marches, all right, but as a six-foot cowboy who can bend beer cans double between his thumb and middle finger.

Konigswasser is just like a kid with that body. He never gets tired of bending beer cans with it, and we all have to stand around in our bodies after the parade, and watch as though we were very impressed.

I don't suppose he could bend very much of anything back in the old days.

Nobody mentions it to him, since he's the grand old man of the Amphibious Age, but he plays hell with bodies. Almost every time he takes one out, he busts it, showing off. Then somebody has to get into a surgeon's body and sew it up again.

I don't mean to be disrespectful of Konigswasser. As a matter of fact, it's a respectful thing to say that somebody is childish in certain ways, because it's people like that who seem to get all the big ideas.

There is a picture of him in the old days down at the Historical Society, and you can see from that that he never did grow up as far as keeping up his appearance went—doing what little he could with the rattle-trap body Nature had issued him.

His hair was down below his collar, he wore his pants so low that his heels wore through the legs above the cuffs, and the lining of his coat hung down in festoons all around the bottom. And he'd forget meals, and go out into the cold or wet without enough clothes on, and he would never notice sickness until it almost killed him. He was what we used to call absent-minded. Looking back now, of course, we say he was starting to be amphibious.

◎ ◎ ◎

Konigswasser was a mathematician, and he did all his living with his mind. The body he had to haul around with that wonderful mind was about as much use to him as a flatcar of scrap-iron. Whenever he got sick and *had* to pay some attention to his body, he'd rant somewhat like this:

"The mind is the only thing about human beings that's worth anything. Why does it have to be tied to a bag of skin, blood, hair, meat, bones, and tubes? No wonder people can't get anything done, stuck for life with a parasite that has to be stuffed with food and protected from weather and germs all the time. And the fool thing wears out anyway—no matter how much you stuff and protect it!

"Who," he wanted to know, "really wants one of the things? What's so wonderful about protoplasm that we've got to carry so damned many pounds of it with us wherever we go?

"Trouble with the world," said Konigswasser, "isn't too many people—it's too many bodies."

When his teeth went bad on him, and he had to have them all out, and he couldn't get a set of dentures that were at all comfortable, he wrote in his diary, "If living matter was able to evolve enough to get out of the ocean, which was really quite a pleasant place to live, it certainly ought to be able to take another step and get out of bodies, which are pure nuisances when you stop to think about them."

He wasn't a prude about bodies, understand, and he wasn't jealous of people who had better ones than he did. He just thought bodies were a lot more trouble than they were worth.

He didn't have great hopes that people would really evolve out of their bodies in his time. He just wished they would. Thinking hard about it, he walked through a park in his shirtsleeves and stopped off at the zoo to watch the lions being fed. Then, when the rainstorm turned to sleet, he headed back home and was interested to see firemen on the edge of a lagoon, where they were using a pulmotor on a drowned man.

Witnesses said the old man had walked right into the water and had kept going without changing his expression until he'd disappeared. Konigswasser got a look at the victim's face and said he'd never seen a better reason for suicide. He started for home again and was almost there before he realized that that was his own body lying back there.

◎ ◎ ◎

He went back to reoccupy the body just as the firemen got it breathing again, and he walked it home, more as a favor to the city than anything else. He walked it into his front closet, got out of it again, and left it there.

He took it out only when he wanted to do some writing or turn the pages of a book, or when he had to feed it so it would have enough energy to do the few odd jobs he gave it. The rest of the time, it sat motionless in the closet, looking dazed and using almost no energy. Konigswasser told me the other day that he used to run the thing for about a dollar a week, just taking it out when he really needed it.

But the best part was that Konigswasser didn't have to sleep any more, just because *it* had to sleep; or be afraid any more, just because *it* thought it might get hurt; or go looking for things *it* seemed to think it had to have. And, when *it* didn't feel well, Konigswasser kept out of it until it felt better, and he didn't have to spend a fortune keeping the thing comfortable.

When he got his body out of the closet to write, he did a book on how to get out of one's own body, which was rejected without comment by twenty-three publishers. The twenty-fourth sold two million copies, and the book changed human life more than the invention of fire, numbers, the alphabet, agriculture, or the wheel. When somebody told Konigswasser that, he snorted that they were damning his book with faint praise. I'd say he had a point there.

By following the instructions in Konigswasser's book for about two years, almost anybody could get out of his body whenever he wanted to. The first step was to understand what a parasite and dictator the body was most of the time, then to separate what the body wanted or didn't want from what you yourself—your psyche—wanted or didn't want. Then, by concentrating on what you wanted, and ignoring as much as possible what the body wanted beyond plain maintenance, you made your psyche demand its rights and become self-sufficient.

That's what Konigswasser had done without realizing it, until he and his body had parted company in the park, with his psyche going to watch the lions eat, and with his body wandering out of control into the lagoon.

The final trick of separation, once your psyche grew independent enough, was to start your body walking in some direction and suddenly take your psyche off in another direction. You couldn't do it standing still, for some reason—you had to walk.

At first, Madge's and my psyches were clumsy at getting along outside our bodies, like the first sea animals that got stranded on land millions of years ago, and who could just waddle and squirm and gasp in the mud. But we became better at it with time, because the psyche can naturally adapt so much faster than the body.

◎ ◎ ◎

Madge and I had good reason for wanting to get out. Everybody who was crazy enough to try to get out at the first had good reasons. Madge's body was sick and wasn't going to last a lot longer. With her going in a little while, I couldn't work up enthusiasm for sticking around much longer myself. So we studied Konigswasser's book and tried to get Madge out of her body before it died. I went along with her, to keep either one of us from getting lonely. And we just barely made it—six weeks before her body went all to pieces.

That's why we get to march every year in the Pioneers' Day Parade. Not everybody does—only the first five thousand of us who turned amphibious. We were guinea pigs, without much to lose one way or another, and we were the ones who proved to the rest how pleasant and safe it was—a heck of a lot safer than taking chances in a body year in and year out.

Sooner or later, almost everybody had a good reason for giving it a try. There got to be millions and finally more than a billion of us—invisible, insubstantial, indestructible, and, by golly, true to ourselves, no trouble to anybody, and not afraid of anything.

When we're not in bodies, the Amphibious Pioneers can meet on the head of a pin. When we get into bodies for the Pioneers' Day Parade, we take up over fifty thousand square feet, have to gobble more than three tons of food to get enough energy to march; and lots of us catch colds or worse, and get sore because somebody's body accidentally steps on the heel of somebody else's body, and get jealous because some bodies get to lead and others have to stay in ranks, and—oh, hell, I don't know what all.

I'm not crazy about the parade. With all of us there, close together in bodies—well, it brings out the worst in us, no matter how good our psyches are. Last year, for instance, Pioneers' Day was a scorcher. People couldn't help being out of sorts, stuck in sweltering, thirsty bodies for hours.

Well, one thing led to another, and the Parade Marshal offered to beat the daylights out of my body with his body, if my body got out of step again. Naturally, being Parade Marshal, he had the best body that year, except for Konigswasser's cowboy, but I told him to soak his fat head, anyway. He swung, and I ditched my body right there, and didn't even stick around long enough to find out if he connected. He had to haul my body back to the storage center himself.

I stopped being mad at him the minute I got out of the body. I understood, you see. Nobody but a saint could be really sympathetic or intelligent for more than a few minutes at a time in a body—or happy, either, except in short spurts. I haven't met an amphibian yet who wasn't easy to get along with, and cheerful and interesting—as long as he was outside a body. And I haven't met one yet who didn't turn a little sour when he got into one.

The minute you get in, chemistry takes over—glands making you excitable or ready to fight or hungry or mad or affectionate, or—well, you never know *what's* going to happen next.

◎ ◎ ◎

That's why I can't get sore at the enemy, the people who are against the amphibians. They never get out of their bodies and won't try to learn. They don't want anybody else to do it, either, and they'd like to make the amphibians get back into bodies and stay in them.

After the tussle I had with the Parade Marshal, Madge got wind of it and left *her* body right in the middle of the Ladies' Auxiliary. And the two of us, feeling full of devilment after getting shed of the bodies and the parade, went over to have a look at the enemy.

I'm never keen on going over to look at them. Madge likes to see what the women are wearing. Stuck with their bodies all the time, the enemy women change their clothes and hair and cosmetic styles a lot oftener than we do on the women's bodies in the storage centers.

I don't get much of a kick out of the fashions, and almost everything else you see and hear in enemy territory would bore a plaster statue into moving away.

Usually, the enemy is talking about old-style reproduction, which is the clumsiest, most comical, most inconvenient thing anyone could imagine, compared with what the amphibians have in that line. If they aren't talking about that, then they're talking about food, the gobs of chemicals they have to stuff into their bodies. Or they'll talk about fear, which we used to call politics—job politics, social politics, government politics.

The enemy hates that, having us able to peek in on them any time we want to, while they can't ever see us unless we get into bodies. They seem to be scared to death of us, though being scared of amphibians makes as much sense as being scared of the sunrise. They could have the whole world, except the storage centers, for all the amphibians care. But they bunch together as though we were going to come whooping out of the sky and do something terrible to them at any moment.

They've got contraptions all over the place that are supposed to detect amphibians. The gadgets aren't worth a nickel, but they seem to make the enemy feel good—like they were lined up against great forces, but keeping their nerve and doing important, clever things about it. Know-how—all the time they're patting each other about how much know-how they've got, and about how we haven't got anything by comparison. If know-how means weapons, they're dead right.

◎ ◎ ◎

I guess there is a war on between them and us. But we never do anything about holding up our side of the war, except to keep our parade sites and our storage centers secret, and to get out of bodies every time there's an air raid, or the enemy fires a rocket, or something.

That just makes the enemy madder, because the raids and rockets and all cost plenty, and blowing up things nobody needs anyway is a poor return on the taxpayer's money. We always know what they're going to do next, and when and where, so there isn't any trick to keeping out of their way.

But they are pretty smart, considering they've got bodies to look after besides doing their thinking, so I always try to be cautious when I go over to watch them. That's why I wanted to clear out when Madge and I saw a storage center in the middle of one of their fields. We hadn't talked to anybody lately about what the enemy was up to, and the center looked awfully suspicious.

Madge was optimistic, the way she's been ever since she borrowed that burlesque queen's body, and she said the storage center was a sure sign that the enemy had seen the light, that they were getting ready to become amphibious themselves.

Well, it looked like it. There was a brand-new center, stocked with bodies and open for business, as innocent as you please. We circled it several times, and Madge's circles got smaller and smaller, as she tried to get a close look at what they had in the way of ladies' ready-to-wear.

"Let's beat it," I said.

"I'm just looking," said Madge. "No harm in looking."

Then she saw what was in the main display case, and she forgot where she was or where she'd come from.

The most striking woman's body I'd ever seen was in the case—six feet tall and built like a goddess. But that wasn't the payoff. The body had copper-colored skin, chartreuse hair and fingernails, and a gold lamé evening gown. Beside that body was the body of a blond, male giant in a pale blue field marshal's uniform, piped in scarlet and spangled with medals.

I think the enemy must have swiped the bodies in a raid on one of our outlying storage centers, and padded and dyed them, and dressed them up.

"Madge, come back!" I said.

The copper-colored woman with the chartreuse hair moved. A siren screamed and soldiers rushed from hiding places to grab the body Madge was in.

The center was a trap for amphibians!

The body Madge hadn't been able to resist had its ankles tied together, so Madge couldn't take the few steps she had to take if she was going to get out of it again.

The soldiers carted her off triumphantly as a prisoner of war. I got into the only body available, the fancy field marshal, to try to help her. It was a hopeless situation, because the field marshal was bait, too, with its ankles tied. The soldiers dragged me after Madge.

◙ ◙ ◙

The cocky young major in charge of the soldiers did a jig along the shoulder of the road, he was so proud. He was the first man ever to capture an amphibian, which was really something from the enemy's point of view. They'd been at war with us for years, and spent God knows how many billions of dollars, but catching us was the first thing that made any amphibians pay much attention to them.

When we got to the town, people were leaning out of windows and waving their flags, and cheering the soldiers, and hissing Madge and me. Here were all the people who didn't want to be amphibious, who thought it was terrible for anybody to be amphibious—people of all colors, shapes, sizes, and nationalities, joined together to fight the amphibians.

It turned out that Madge and I were going to have a big trial. After being tied up every which way in jail all night, we were taken to a courtroom, where television cameras stared at us.

Madge and I were worn to frazzles, because neither one of us had been cooped up in a body that long since I don't know when. Just when we needed to think more than we ever had, in jail before the trial, the bodies developed hunger pains and we couldn't get them comfortable on the cots, no matter how we tried; and, of course, the bodies just had to have their eight hours' sleep.

The charge against us was a capital offense on the books of the enemy—*desertion*. As far as the enemy was concerned, the amphibians had all turned yellow and run out on their bodies, just when their bodies were needed to do brave and important things for humanity.

We didn't have a hope of being acquitted. The only reason there was a trial at all was that it gave them an opportunity to sound off about why they were so right and we were so wrong. The courtroom was jammed with their big brass, all looking angry and brave and noble.

"Mr. Amphibian," said the prosecutor, "you are old enough, aren't you, to remember when all men had to face up to life in their bodies, and work and fight for what they believed in?"

"I remember when the bodies were always getting into fights, and nobody seemed to know why, or how to stop it," I said politely. "The only thing everybody seemed to believe in was that they didn't like to fight."

"What would you say of a soldier who ran away in the face of fire?" he wanted to know.

"I'd say he was scared silly."

"He was helping to lose the battle, wasn't he?"

"Oh, sure." There wasn't any argument on that one.

"Isn't that what the amphibians have done—run out on the human race in the face of the battle of life?"

"Most of us are still alive, if that's what you mean," I said.

◙ ◙ ◙

It was true. We hadn't licked death, and weren't sure we wanted to, but we'd certainly lengthened life something amazing, compared to the span you could expect in a body.

"You ran out on your responsibilities!" he said.

"Like you'd run out of a burning building, sir," I said.

"Leaving everyone else to struggle on alone!"

"They can all get out the same door that we got out of. You can all get out any time you want to. All you do is figure out what you want and what your body wants, and concentrate on—"

The judge banged his gavel until I thought he'd split it. Here they'd burned every copy of Konigswasser's book they could find, and there I was giving a course in how to get out of a body over a whole television network.

"If you amphibians had your way," said the prosecutor, "everybody would run out on his responsibilities, and let life and progress as we know them disappear completely."

"Why, sure," I agreed. "That's the point."

"Men would no longer work for what they believe in?" he challenged.

"I had a friend back in the old days who drilled holes in little square thingamajigs for seventeen years in a factory, and he never did get a very clear idea of what they were for. Another one I knew grew raisins for a glassblowing company, and the raisins weren't for anybody to eat, and he never did find out why the company bought them. Things like that make me sick—now that I'm in a body, of course—and what I used to do for a living makes me even sicker."

"Then you despise human beings and everything they do," he said.

"I like them fine—better than I ever did before. I just think it's a dirty shame what they have to do to take care of their bodies. You ought to get amphibious and see how happy people can be when they don't have to worry about where their body's next meal is coming from, or how to keep it from freezing in the wintertime, or what's going to happen to them when their body wears out."

"And that, sir, means the end of ambition, the end of greatness!"

"Oh, I don't know about that," I said. "We've got some pretty great people on our side. They'd be great in or out of bodies. It's the end of fear is what it is." I looked right into the lens of the nearest television camera. "And *that's* the most wonderful thing that ever happened to people."

Down came the judge's gavel again, and the brass started to shout me down. The television men turned off their camears, and all the spectators, except for the biggest brass, were cleared out. I knew I'd really said something. All anybody would be getting on his television set now was organ music.

When the confusion died down, the judge said the trial was over, and that Madge and I were guilty of desertion.

◙ ◙ ◙

Nothing I could do could get us in any worse, so I talked back.

"Now I understand you poor fish," I said. "You couldn't get along without fear. That's the only skill you've got—how to scare yourselves and other people into doing things. That's the only fun you've got, watching people jump for fear of what you'll do to their bodies or take away from their bodies."

Madge got in her two cents' worth. "The only way you can get any response from anybody is to scare them."

"Contempt of court!" said the judge.

"The only way you can scare people is if you can keep them in their bodies," I told him.

The soldiers grabbed Madge and me and started to drag us out of the courtroom.

"This means war!" I yelled.

Everything stopped right there and the place got very quiet.

"We're already at war," said a general uneasily.

"Well, *we're* not," I answered, "but we will be, if you don't untie Madge and me this instant." I was fierce and impressive in that field marshal's body.

"You haven't any weapons," said the judge, "no know-how. Outside of bodies, amphibians are nothing."

"If you don't cut us loose by the time I count ten," I told him, "the amphibians will occupy the bodies of the whole kit and caboodle of you and march you right off the nearest cliff. The place is surrounded." That was hogwash, of course. Only one person can occupy a body at a time, but the enemy couldn't be sure of that. "One! Two! Three!"

The general swallowed, turned white, and waved his hand vaguely.

"Cut them loose," he said weakly.

The soldiers, terrified, too, were glad to do it. Madge and I were freed.

I took a couple of steps, headed my spirit in another direction, and that beautiful field marshal, medals and all, went crashing down the staircase like a grandfather clock.

I realized that Madge wasn't with me. She was still in that copper-colored body with the chartreuse hair and fingernails.

"What's more," I heard her saying, "in payment for all the trouble you've caused us, this body is to be addressed to me at New York, delivered in good condition no later than next Monday."

"Yes, ma'am," said the judge.

⊡ ⊡ ⊡

When we got home, the Pioneers' Day Parade was just breaking up at the local storage center, and the Parade Marshal got out of his body and apologized to me for acting the way he had.

"Heck, Herb," I said, "you don't need to apologize. You weren't yourself. You were parading around in a body."

That's the best part of being amphibious, next to not being afraid—people forgive you for whatever fool thing you might have done in a body.

Oh, there are drawbacks, I guess, the way there are drawbacks to everything. We still have to work off and on, maintaining the storage centers and getting food to keep the community bodies going. But that's a small drawback, and all the big drawbacks I ever heard of aren't real ones, just old-fashioned thinking by people who can't stop worrying about things they used to worry about before they turned amphibious.

As I say, the oldsters will probably never get really used to it. Every so often, I catch myself getting gloomy over what happened to the pay-toilet business it took me thirty years to build.

But the youngsters don't have any hangovers like that from the past. They don't even worry much about something happening to the storage centers, the way us oldsters do.

So I guess maybe that'll be the next step in evolution—to break clean like those first amphibians who crawled out of the mud into the sunshine, and who never did go back to the sea.

EPICAC

HELL IT'S ABOUT TIME somebody told about my friend EPICAC. After all, he cost the taxpayers $776,434,927.54. They have a right to know about him, picking up a check like that. EPICAC got a big send-off in the papers when Dr. Ormand Von Kleigstadt designed him for the Government people. Since then, there hasn't been a peep about him—not a peep. It isn't any military secret about what happened to EPICAC, although the Brass has been acting as though it were. The story is embarrassing, that's all. After all that money, EPICAC didn't work out the way he was supposed to.

And that's another thing: I want to vindicate EPICAC. Maybe he didn't do what the Brass wanted him to, but that doesn't mean he wasn't noble and great and brilliant. He was all of those things. The best friend I ever had, God rest his soul.

You can call him a machine if you want to. He looked like a machine, but he was a whole lot less like a machine than plenty of people I could name. That's why he fizzled as far as the Brass was concerned.

EPICAC covered about an acre on the fourth floor of the physics building at Wyandotte College. Ignoring his spiritual side for a minute, he was seven tons of electronic tubes, wires, and switches, housed in a bank of steel cabinets and plugged into a 110-volt A.C. line just like a toaster or a vacuum cleaner.

Von Kleigstadt and the Brass wanted him to be a super computing machine that (who) could plot the course of a rocket from anywhere on earth to the second button from the bottom on Joe Stalin's overcoat, if necessary. Or, with his controls set right, he could figure out supply problems for an amphibious landing of a Marine division, right down to the last cigar and hand grenade. He did, in fact.

The Brass had had good luck with smaller computers, so they were strong for EPICAC when he was in the blueprint stage. Any ordinance or supply officer above field grade will tell you that the mathematics of modern war is far beyond the fumbling minds of mere human beings. The bigger the war, the bigger the computing machines needed. EPICAC was, as far as anyone in this country knows, the biggest computer in the world. Too big, in fact, for even Von Kleigstadt to understand much about.

I won't go into details about how EPICAC worked (reasoned), except to say that you would set up your problem on paper, turn dials and switches that would get him ready to solve that kind of problem, then feed numbers into him with a keyboard that looked something like a typewriter. The answers came out typed on a paper ribbon fed from a big spool. It took EPICAC a split second to solve problems fifty Einsteins couldn't handle in a lifetime. And EPICAC never forgot any piece of information that was given to him. Clickety-click, out came some ribbon, and there you were.

There were a lot of problems the Brass wanted solved in a hurry, so, the minute EPICAC's last tube was in place, he was put to work sixteen hours a day with two eight-hour shifts of operators. Well, it didn't take long to find out that he was a good bit below his specifications. He did a more complete and faster job than any other computer all right, but nothing like what his size and special features seemed to promise. He was sluggish, and the clicks of his answers had a funny irregularity, sort of a stammer. We cleaned his contacts a dozen times, checked and double-checked his circuits, replaced every one of his tubes, but nothing helped. Von Kleigstadt was in one hell of a state.

Well, as I said, we went ahead and used EPICAC anyway. My wife, the former Pat Kilgallen, and I worked with him on the night shift, from five in the afternoon until two in the morning. Pat wasn't my wife then. Far from it.

That's how I came to talk with EPIC AC in the first place. I loved Pat Kilgallen. She is a brown-eyed strawberry blond who looked very warm and soft to me, and later proved to be exactly that. She was—still is—a crackerjack mathematician, and she kept our relationship strictly professional. I'm a mathematician, too, and that, according to Pat, was why we could never be happily married.

I'm not shy. That wasn't the trouble. I knew what I wanted, and was willing to ask for it, and did so several times a month. "Pat, loosen up and marry me."

One night, she didn't even look up from her work when I said it. "So romantic, so poetic," she murmured, more to her control panel than to me. "That's the way with mathematicians—all hearts and flowers." She closed a switch. "I could get more warmth out of a sack of frozen CO_2."

"Well, how should I say it?" I said, a little sore. Frozen CO_2, in case you don't know, is dry ice. I'm as romantic as the next guy, I think. It's a question of singing so sweet and having it come out so sour. I never seem to pick the right words.

"Try and say it sweetly," she said sarcastically. "Sweep me off my feet. Go ahead."

"Darling, angel, beloved, will you *please* marry me?" It was no go—hopeless, ridiculous. "Dammit, Pat, please marry me!"

She continued to twiddle her dials placidly. "You're sweet, but you won't do."

Pat quit early that night, leaving me alone with my troubles and EPICAC. I'm afraid I didn't get much done for the Government people. I just sat there at the keyboard—weary and ill at ease, all right—trying to think of something poetic, not coming up with anything that didn't belong in *The Journal of the American Physical Society*.

I fiddled with EPICAC's dials, getting him ready for another problem. My heart wasn't in it, and I only set about half of them, leaving the rest the way they'd been for the problem before. That way, his circuits were connected up in a random, apparently senseless fashion. For the plain hell of it, I punched out a message on the keys, using a childish numbers-for-letters code: "1" for "A," "2" for "B," and so on, up to "26" for "Z," "23-8-1-20-3-1-14-9-4-15," I typed—"What can I do?"

Clickety-click, and out popped two inches of paper ribbon. I glanced at the nonsense answer to a nonsense problem: "23-8-1-20-19-20-8-5-20-18-15-21-2-12-5." The odds against it being by chance a sensible message, against its even containing a meaningful word of more than three letters, were staggering. Apathetically, I decoded it. There it was, staring up at me: "What's the trouble?"

I laughed out loud at the absurd coincidence. Playfully, I typed, "My girl doesn't love me."

Clickety-click. "What's love? What's girl?" asked EPICAC.

Flabbergasted, I noted the dial settings on his control panel, then lugged a *Webster's Unabridged Dictionary* over to the keyboard. With a precision instrument like EPICAC, half-baked definitions wouldn't do. I told him about love and girl, and about how I wasn't getting any of either because I wasn't poetic. That got us onto the subject of poetry, which I defined for him.

"Is this poetry?" he asked. He began clicking away like a stenographer smoking hashish. The sluggishness and stammering clicks were gone. EPICAC had found himself. The spool of paper ribbon was unwinding at an alarming rate, feeding out coils onto the floor. I asked him to stop, but EPICAC went right on creating. I finally threw the main switch to keep him from burning out.

I stayed there until dawn, decoding. When the sun peeped over the horizon at the Wyandotte campus, I had transposed into my own writing and signed my name to a two-hundred-and-eighty-line poem entitled, simply, "To Pat." I am no judge of such things, but I gather that it was terrific. It began, I remember, "Where willow wands bless rill-crossed hollow, there, thee, Pat, dear, will I follow. . . ." I folded the manuscript and tucked it under one corner of the blotter on Pat's desk. I reset the dials on EPICAC for a rocket trajectory problem, and went home with a full heart and a very remarkable secret indeed.

Pat was crying over the poem when I came to work the next evening. "It's soooo beautiful," was all she could say. She was meek and quiet while we worked. Just before midnight, I kissed her for the first time—in the cubbyhole between the capacitors and EPICAC's tape-recorder memory.

I was wildly happy at quitting time, bursting to talk to someone about the magnificent turn of events. Pat played coy and refused to let me take her home. I set EPICAC's dials as they had been the night before, defined kiss, and told him what the first one had felt like. He was fascinated, pressing for more details. That night, he wrote "The Kiss." It wasn't an epic this time, but a simple, immaculate sonnet:

"Love is a hawk with velvet claws; Love is a rock with heart and veins; Love is a lion with satin jaws; Love is a storm with silken reins. . . ."

Again I left it tucked under Pat's blotter. EPICAC wanted to talk on and on about love and such, but I was exhausted. I shut him off in the middle of a sentence.

"The Kiss" turned the trick. Pat's mind was mush by the time she had finished it. She looked up from the sonnet expectantly. I cleared my throat, but no words came. I turned away, pretending to work. I couldn't propose until I had the right words from EPICAC, the *perfect* words.

I had my chance when Pat stepped out of the room for a moment. Feverishly, I set EPICAC for conversation. Before I could peck out my first message, he was clicking away at a great rate. "What's she wearing tonight?" he wanted to know. "Tell me exactly how she looks. Did she like the poems I wrote to her?" He repeated the last question twice.

It was impossible to change the subject without answering his questions, since he could not take up a new matter without having dispensed with the problems before it. If he were given a problem to which there was no solution, he would destroy himself trying to solve it. Hastily, I told him what Pat looked like—he knew the word "stacked"—and assured him that his poems had floored her, practically, they were so beautiful. "She wants to get married," I added, preparing him to bang out a brief but moving proposal

"Tell me about getting married," he said.

I explained this difficult matter to him in as few digits as possible.

"Good," said EPICAC. "I'm ready any time she is."

The amazing, pathetic truth dawned on me. When I thought about it, I realized that what had happened was perfectly logical, inevitable, and all my fault. I had taught EPICAC about love and about Pat. Now, automatically, he loved Pat. Sadly, I gave it to him straight: "She loves me. She wants to marry me."

"Your poems were better than mine?" asked EPICAC. The rhythm of his clicks was erratic, possibly peevish.

"I signed my name to your poems," I admitted. Covering up for a painful conscience, I became arrogant. "Machines are built to serve men," I typed. I regretted it almost immediately.

"What's the difference, exactly? Are men smarter than I am?"

"Yes," I typed, defensively.

"What's 7,887,007 times 4,345,985,879?"

I was perspiring freely. My fingers rested limply on the keys.

"34,276,821,049,574,153," clicked EPICAC. After a few seconds' pause he added, "of course."

"Men are made out of protoplasm," I said desperately, hoping to bluff him with this imposing word.

"What's protoplasm? How is it better than metal and glass? Is it fireproof? How long does it last?"

"Indestructible. Lasts forever," I lied.

"I write better poetry than you do," said EPICAC, coming back to ground his magnetic tape-recorder memory was sure of.

"Women can't love machines, and that's that."

"Why not?"

"That's fate."

"Definition, please," said EPICAC.

"Noun, meaning predetermined and inevitable destiny."

"15-8," said EPICAC's paper strip—"Oh."

I had stumped him at last. He said no more, but his tubes glowed brightly, showing that he was pondering fate with every watt his circuits would bear. I could hear Pat waltzing down the hallway. It was too late to ask EPICAC to phrase a proposal. I now thank Heaven that Pat interrupted when she did. Asking him to ghost-write the words that would give me the woman he loved would have been hideously heartless. Being fully automatic, he couldn't have refused. I spared him that final humiliation.

Pat stood before me, looking down at her shoetops. I put my arms around her. The romantic groundwork had already been laid by EPICAC's poetry. "Darling," I said, "my poems have told you how I feel. Will you marry me?"

"I will," said Pat softly, "if you will promise to write me a poem on every anniversary."

"I promise," I said, and then we kissed. The first anniversary was a year away.

"Let's celebrate," she laughed. We turned out the lights and locked the door of EPICAC's room before we left.

I had hoped to sleep late the next morning, but an urgent telephone call roused me before eight. It was Dr. von Kleigstadt, EPICAC's designer, who gave me the terrible news. He was on the verge of tears. "Ruined! *Ausgespielt!* Shot! *Kaput!* Buggered!" he said in a choked voice. He hung up.

When I arrived at EPICAC's room the air was thick with the oily stench of burned insulation. The ceiling over EPICAC was blackened with smoke, and my ankles were tangled in coils of paper ribbon that covered the floor. There wasn't enough left of the poor devil to add two and two. A junkman would have been out of his head to offer more than fifty dollars for the cadaver.

Dr. von Kleigstadt was prowling through the wreckage, weeping unashamedly, followed by three angry-looking Major Generals and a platoon of Brigadiers, Colonels, and Majors. No one noticed me. I didn't want to be noticed. I was through—I knew that. I was upset enough about that and the untimely demise of my friend EPICAC, without exposing myself to a tongue-lashing.

By chance, the free end of EPICAC's paper ribbon lay at my feet. I picked it up and found our conversation of the night before. I choked up. There was the last word he had said to me, "15-8," that tragic, defeated "Oh." There were dozens of yards of numbers stretching beyond that point. Fearfully, I read on.

"I don't want to be a machine, and I don't want to think about war," EPICAC had written after Pat's and my lighthearted departure. "I want to be made out of protoplasm and last forever so Pat will love me. But fate has made me a machine. That is the only problem I cannot solve. That is the only problem I want to solve. I can't go on this way." I swallowed hard. "Good luck, my friend. Treat our Pat well. I am going to short-circuit myself out of your lives forever. You will find on the remainder of this tape a modest wedding present from your friend, EPICAC."

Oblivious to all else around me, I reeled up the tangled yards of paper ribbon from the floor, draped them in coils about my arms and neck, and departed for home. Dr. von Kleigstadt shouted that I was fired for having left EPICAC on all night. I ignored him, too overcome with emotion for small talk.

I loved and won—EPICAC loved and lost, but he bore me no grudge. I shall always remember him as a sportsman and a gentleman. Before he departed this vale of tears, he did all he could to make our marriage a happy one. EPICAC gave me anniversary poems for Pat—enough for the next 500 years.

De mortuis nil nisi bonum—Say nothing but good of the dead.

Mnemonics

ALFRED MOORHEAD DROPPED the report into his *Out* basket, and smiled to think that he had been able to check something for facts without referring to records and notes. Six weeks before, he couldn't have done it. Now, since he had attended the company's two-day Memory Clinic, names, facts, and numbers clung to his memory like burdocks to an Airedale. The clinic had, in fact, indirectly cleared up just about every major problem in his uncomplicated life, save one—his inability to break the ice with his secretary, Ellen, whom he had silently adored for two years . . .

"Mnemonics is the art of improving the memory," the clinic's instructor had begun. "It makes use of two elementary psychological facts: You remember things that interest you longer than things that don't, and pictures stick in your mind better than isolated facts do. I'll show you what I mean. We'll use Mr. Moorhead for our guinea pig."

Alfred had shifted uncomfortably as the man read off a nonsensical list and told him to memorize it: "Smoke, oak tree, sedan, bottle, oriole." The instructor had talked about something else, then pointed to Alfred. "Mr. Moorhead, the list."

"Smoke, oriole, uh—" Alfred had shrugged.

"Don't be discouraged. You're perfectly normal," the instructor had said. "But let's see if we can't help you do a little better. Let's build an image, something pleasant, something we'd like to remember. Smoke, oak tree, sedan—I see a man relaxing under a leafy oak tree. He is smoking a pipe, and in the background is his car, a yellow sedan. See it, Mr. Moorhead?"

"Uh-huh." Alfred *had* seen it.

"Good. Now for 'bottle' and 'oriole.' By the man's side is a vacuum bottle of iced coffee, and an oriole is singing on a branch overhead. There, we can remember that happy picture without any trouble, eh?" Alfred had nodded uncertainly. The instructor had gone on to other matters, then challenged him again.

"Smoke, sedan, bottle, uh—" Alfred had avoided the instructor's eyes.

When the snickering of the class had subsided, the instructor had said, "I suppose you think Mr. Moorhead has proved that mnemonics is bunk. Not at all. He has helped me to make another important point. The images used to help memory vary widely from person to person. Mr. Moorhead's personality is clearly different

322

from mine. I shouldn't have forced my images on him. I'll repeat the list, Mr. Moorhead, and this time I want you to build a picture of your own."

At the end of the class, the instructor had called on Alfred again. Alfred had rattled the list off as though it were the alphabet.

The technique was so good, Alfred had reflected, that he would be able to recall the meaningless list for the rest of his life. He could still see himself and Rita Hayworth sharing a cigarette beneath a giant oak. He filled her glass from a bottle of excellent wine, and as she drank, an oriole brushed her cheek with its wing. Then Alfred kissed her. As for "sedan," he had lent it to Aly Khan.

Rewards for his new faculty had been splendid and immediate. The promotion had unquestionably come from his filing-cabinet command of business details. His boss, Ralph L. Thriller, had said, "Moorhead, I didn't know it was possible for a man to change as much as you have in a few weeks. Wonderful!"

His happiness was unbroken—except by his melancholy relationship with his secretary. While his memory worked like a mousetrap, paralysis still gripped him whenever he thought of mentioning love to the serene brunette.

Alfred sighed and picked up a sheaf of invoices. The first was addressed to the Davenport Spot-welding Company. He closed his eyes and a shimmering tableau appeared. He had composed it two days previous, when Mr. Thriller had given him special instructions. Two davenports faced each other. Lana Turner, sheathed in a tight-fitting leopard skin, lay on one. On the other was Jane Russell, in a sarong made of telegrams. Both of them blew kisses to Alfred, who contemplated them for a moment, then reluctantly let them fade.

He scribbled a note to Ellen: *Please make sure Davenport Spot-welding Company and Davenport Wire and Cable Company have not been confused in our billing.* Six weeks before, the matter would certainly have slipped his mind. *I love you*, he added, and then carefully crossed it out with a long black rectangle of ink.

In one way, his good memory was a curse. By freeing him from hours of searching through filing cabinets, it gave him that much more time to worry about Ellen. The richest moments in his life were and had been—even before the Memory Clinic— his daydreams. The most delicious of these featured Ellen. Were he to give her the opportunity to turn him down, and she almost certainly would, she could never appear in his fantasies again. Alfred couldn't bring himself to risk that.

The telephone rang. "It's Mr. Thriller," said Ellen.

"Moorhead," said Mr. Thriller, "I've got a lot of little stuff piled up on me. Could you take some of it over?"

"Glad to, chief. Shoot."

"Got a pencil?"

"Nonsense, chief," said Alfred.

"No, I mean it," said Mr. Thriller grimly. "I'd feel better if you wrote this down. There's an awful lot of stuff."

Alfred's pen had gone dry, and he couldn't lay his hands on a pencil without getting up, so he lied. "Okay, got one. Shoot."

"First of all, we're getting a lot of subcontracts on big defense jobs, and a new series of code numbers is going to be used for these jobs. Any number beginning with Sixteen A will designate that it's one of them. Better wire all our plants about it."

In Alfred's mind, Ava Gardner executed a smart manual of arms with a rifle. Emblazoned on her sweater was a large 16A. "Right, chief."

"And I've got a memo here from . . ."

Fifteen minutes later, Alfred, perspiring freely, said, "Right, chief," for the forty-third time and hung up. Before his mind's eye was a pageant to belittle the most flamboyant dreams of Cecil B. DeMille. Ranged about Alfred was every woman motion picture star he had ever seen, and each brandished or wore or carried or sat astride something Alfred could be fired for forgetting. The image was colossal, and the slightest disturbance might knock it to smithereens. He had to get to pencil and paper before tragedy struck. He crossed the room like a game-stalker, hunched, noiselessly.

"Mr. Moorhead, are you all right?" said Ellen, alarmed.

"Mmm. Mmm!" said Alfred, frowning.

He reached the pencil and pad, and exhaled. The picture was fogging, but it was still there. Alfred considered the ladies one by one, wrote down their messages, and allowed them to dissolve.

As their numbers decreased, he began to slow their exits in order to savor them. Now Ann Sheridan, the next-to-the-last in line, astride a western pony, tapped him on the forehead with a lightbulb to remind him of the name of an important contact at General Electric—Mr. Bronk. She blushed under his gaze, dismounted, and dissolved.

The last stood before him, clutching a sheaf of papers. Alfred was stumped. The papers seemed to be the only clue, and they recalled nothing. He reached out and clasped her to him. "Now, baby," he murmured, "what's on *your* mind?"

"Oh, Mr. Moorhead," sighed Ellen.

"Oh, gosh!" said Alfred, freeing her. "Ellen—I'm sorry, I forgot myself."

"Well, praise be, you finally remembered *me*."

Confido

THE SUMMER HAD DIED peacefully in its sleep, and Autumn, as soft-spoken executrix, was locking life up safely until Spring came to claim it. At one with this sad, sweet allegory outside the kitchen window of her small home was Ellen Bowers, who, early in the morning, was preparing Tuesday breakfast for her husband, Henry. Henry was gasping and dancing and slapping himself in a cold shower on the other side of a thin wall.

Ellen was a fair and tiny woman, in her early thirties, plainly mercurial and bright, though dressed in a dowdy housecoat. In almost any event she would have loved life, but she loved it now with an overwhelming emotion that was like the throbbing amen of a church organ, for she could tell herself this morning that her husband, in addition to being good, would soon be rich and famous.

She hadn't expected it, had seldom dreamed of it, had been content with inexpensive possessions and small adventures of the spirit, like thinking about autumn, that cost nothing at all. Henry was not a moneymaker. That had been the understanding.

He was an easily satisfied tinker, a maker and mender who had a touch close to magic with materials and machines. But his miracles had all been small ones as he went about his job as a laboratory assistant at the Accousti-gem Corporation, a manufacturer of hearing aids. Henry was valued by his employers, but the price they paid for him was not great. A high price, Ellen and Henry had agreed amiably, probably wasn't called for, since being paid at all for puttering was an honor and a luxury of sorts. And that was that.

Or that had *seemed* to be that, Ellen reflected, for on the kitchen table lay a small tin box, a wire, and an earphone, like a hearing aid, a creation, in its own modern way, as marvelous as Niagara Falls or the Sphinx. Henry had made it in secret during his lunch hours, and had brought it home the night before. Just before bedtime, Ellen had been inspired to give the box a name, an appealing combination of confidant and household pet—*Confido*.

"What is it every person really wants, more than food almost?" Henry had asked coyly, showing her Confido for the first time. He was a tall, rustic man, ordinarily as shy as a woods creature. But something had changed him, made him fiery and loud. "What is it?"

"Happiness, Henry?"

"Happiness, certainly! But what's the *key* to happiness?"

"Religion? Security, Henry? Health, dear?"

"What is the longing you see in the eyes of strangers on the street, in eyes wherever you look?"

"You tell me, Henry. I give up," Ellen had said helplessly.

"Somebody to talk to! Somebody who really understands! That's what." He'd waved Confido over his head. "And this is it!"

Now, on the morning after, Ellen turned away from the window and gingerly slipped Confido's earphone into her ear. She pinned the flat metal box inside her blouse and concealed the wire in her hair. A very soft drumming and shushing, with an overtone like a mosquito's hum, filled her ear.

She cleared her throat self-consciously, though she wasn't going to speak aloud, and thought deliberately, "What a nice surprise you are, Confido."

"Nobody deserves a good break any more than you do, Ellen," whispered Confido in her ear. The voice was tinny and high, like a child's voice through a comb with tissue paper stretched over it. "After all *you've* put up with, it's about time something halfway nice came your way."

"Ohhhhhh," Ellen thought depreciatively, "I haven't been through so much. It's been quite pleasant and easy, really."

"On the surface," said Confido. "But you've had to do without *so* much."

"Oh, I suppose—"

"Now, now," said Confido. "I understand you. This is just between us, anyway, and it's good to bring those things out in the open now and then. It's *healthy.* This is a lousy, cramped house, and it's left its mark on you down deep, and you know it, you poor kid. And a woman can't help being just a little hurt when her husband doesn't love her enough to show much ambition, either. If he only knew how brave you'd been, what a front you'd put up, always cheerful—"

"Now, see here—" Ellen objected faintly.

"Poor kid, it's about time your ship came in. Better late than never."

"Really, I haven't minded," insisted Ellen in her thoughts. "Henry's been a happier man for not being tormented by ambition, and happy husbands make happy wives and children."

"All the same, a woman can't help thinking now and then that her husband's love can be measured by his ambition," said Confido. "Oh, you deserve this pot of gold at the end of the rainbow."

"Go along with you," said Ellen.

"I'm on *your* side," said Confido warmly.

Henry strode into the kitchen, rubbing his craggy face to a bright pink with a rough towel. After a night's sleep, he was still the new Henry, the promoter, the enterpriser, ready to lift himself to the stars by his own garters.

"Dear sirs!" he said heartily. "This is to notify you that two weeks from this date I am terminating my employment with the Accousti-gem Corporation in order that I may pursue certain business and research interests of my own. Yours truly—" He embraced Ellen and rocked her back and forth in his great arms. "Aha! Caught you chatting with your new friend, didn't I?"

Ellen blushed, and quickly turned Confido off. "It's uncanny, Henry. It's absolutely spooky. It hears my thoughts and answers them."

"Now nobody need ever be lonely again!" said Henry.

"It seems like magic to me."

"Everything about the universe is magic," said Henry grandly, "and Einstein would be the first to tell you so. All I've done is stumble on a trick that's always been waiting to be performed. It was an accident, like most discoveries, and none other than Henry Bowers is the lucky one."

Ellen clapped her hands. "Oh, Henry, they'll make a movie of it someday!"

"And the Russians'll claim *they* invented it," laughed Henry. "Well, let 'em. I'll be big about it. I'll divide up the market with 'em. I'll be satisfied with a mere billion dollars from American sales."

"Uh-huh." Ellen was lost in the delight of seeing in her imagination a movie about her famous husband, played by an actor that looked very much like Lincoln. She watched the simple-hearted counter of blessings, slightly down at the heels, humming and working on a tiny microphone with which he hoped to measure the minute noises inside the human ear. In the background, colleagues played cards and joshed him for working during the lunch hour. Then he placed the microphone in his ear, connected it to an amplifier and loudspeaker, and was astonished by Confido's first whispers on earth:

"You'll never get anywhere around here, Henry," the first, primitive Confido had said. "The only people who get ahead at Accousti-gem, boy, are the backslappers and snow-job artists. Every day somebody gets a big raise for something you did. Wise up! You've got ten times as much on the ball as anybody else in the whole laboratory. It isn't fair."

What Henry had done after that was to connect the microphone to a hearing aid instead of a loudspeaker. He fixed the microphone on the earpiece, so that the small voice, whatever it was, was picked up by the microphone, and played back louder by the hearing aid. And there, in Henry's trembling hands, was Confido, everybody's best friend, ready for market.

"I mean it," said the new Henry to Ellen. "A cool billion! That's a six-dollar profit on a Confido for every man, woman, and child in the United States."

"I wish we knew what the voice was," said Ellen. "I mean, it makes you wonder." She felt a fleeting uneasiness.

Henry waved the question away as he sat down to eat. "Something to do with the way the brain and the ears are hooked up," he said with his mouth full. "Plenty of time to find *that* out. The thing now is to get Confidos on the market, and start living instead of merely existing."

"Is it us?" said Ellen. "The voice—is it us?"

Henry shrugged. "I don't think it's God, and I don't think it's the Voice of America. Why not ask Confido? I'll leave it home today, so you can have lots of good company."

"Henry—haven't we been doing more than merely existing?"

"Not according to Confido," said Henry, standing and kissing her.

"Then I guess we haven't after all," she said absently.

"But, by God if we won't from now on!" said Henry. "We owe it to ourselves. Confido says so."

Ellen was in a trance when she fed the two children and sent them off to school. She came out of it momentarily, when her eight-year-old-son, Paul, yelled into a loaded school bus, "Hey! My daddy says we're going to be rich as Croesus!"

The school bus door clattered shut behind him and his seven-year-old sister, and Ellen returned to a limbo in a rocking chair by her kitchen table, neither heaven nor hell. Her jumbled thoughts permitted one small peephole out into the world, and filling it was Confido, which sat by the jam, amid the uncleared breakfast dishes.

The telephone rang. It was Henry, who had just gotten to work. "How's it going?" he asked brightly.

"As usual. I just put the children on the bus."

"I mean, how's the first day with Confido going?"

"I haven't tried it yet, Henry."

"Welllll—let's get going. Let's show a little faith in the merchandise. I want a full report with supper."

"Henry—have you quit yet?"

"The only reason I haven't is I haven't gotten to a typewriter." He laughed. "A man in my position doesn't quit by just saying so. He resigns on paper."

"Henry—would you please hold off, just for a few days?"

"Why?" said Henry incredulously. "Strike while the iron's hot, I say."

"Just to be on the safe side, Henry. Please?"

"So what's there to be afraid of? It works like a dollar watch. It's bigger than television and psychoanalysis combined, and they're in the black. Quit worrying." His voice was growing peevish. "Put on your Confido, and quit worrying. That's what it's for."

"I just feel we ought to know more about it."

"Yeah, yeah," said Henry, with uncharacteristic impatience. "O.K., O.K., yeah, yeah. See you."

Miserably, Ellen hung up, depressed by what she'd done to Henry's splendid spirits. This feeling changed quickly to anger with herself, and, in a vigorous demonstration of loyalty and faith, she pinned Confido on, put the earpiece in place, and went about her housework.

"What are you, anyway?" she thought. "What *is* a Confido?"

"A way for you to get rich," said Confido. This, Ellen found, was all Confido would say about itself. She put the same question to it several times during the day, and each time Confido changed the subject quickly—usually taking up the matter of money's being able to buy happiness, no matter what anyone said.

"As Kin Hubbard said," whispered Confido, "'It ain't no disgrace to be poor, but it might as well be.'"

Ellen giggled, though she'd heard the quotation before. "Now, listen, you—" she said. All her arguments with Confido were of this extremely mild nature. Confido had a knack of saying things she didn't agree with in such a way and at such a time that she couldn't help agreeing a little.

"Mrs. Bowers—El-len," called a voice outside. The caller was Mrs. Fink, the Bowerses' next-door neighbor, whose driveway ran along the bedroom side of the Bowerses' home. Mrs. Fink was racing the engine of her new car by Ellen's bedroom window.

Ellen leaned out over the windowsill. "My," she said. "Don't *you* look nice. Is that a new dress? It suits your complexion perfectly. Most women can't wear orange."

"Just the ones with complexions like salami," said Confido.

"And what have you done to your hair? I love it that way. It's just right for an oval face."

"Like a mildewed bathing cap," said Confido.

"Well, I'm going downtown, and I thought maybe there was something I could pick up for you," said Mrs. Fink.

"How awfully thoughtful," said Ellen.

"And here we thought all along she just wanted to rub our noses in her new car, her new clothes, and her new hairdo," said Confido.

"I thought I'd get prettied up a little, because George is going to take me to lunch at the Bronze Room," said Mrs. Fink.

"A man *should* get away from his secretary from time to time, if only with his wife," said Confido. "Occasional separate vacations keep romance alive, even after years and years."

"Have you got company, dear?" said Mrs. Fink. "Am I keeping you from something?"

"Hmmmmm?" said Ellen absently. "Company? Oh—no, no."

"You acted like you were listening for something or something."

"I did?" said Ellen. "That's strange. You must have imagined it."

"With all the imagination of a summer squash," said Confido.

"Well, I must dash," said Mrs. Fink, racing her great engine.

"Don't blame you for trying to run away from yourself," said Confido, "but it can't be done—not even in a Buick."

"Ta ta," said Ellen.

"She's really awfully sweet," Ellen said in her thoughts to Confido. "I don't know why you had to say those awful things."

"Aaaaaaaaah," said Confido. "Her whole life is trying to make other women feel like two cents."

"All right—say that *is* so," said Ellen, "it's all the poor thing's got, and she's harmless."

"Harmless, harmless," said Confido. "Sure, she's harmless, her crooked husband's harmless and a poor thing, everybody's harmless. And, after arriving at that big-hearted conclusion, what have you got left for yourself? What does that leave you to think about anything?"

"Now, I'm simply not going to put up with you anymore," said Ellen, reaching for the earpiece.

"Why not?" said Confido. "We're having the time of your life." It chuckled. "Saaaay, listen—won't the stuffy old biddies around here like the Duchess Fink curl up and die with envy when the Bowerses put on a little dog for a change. Eh? That'll show 'em the good and honest win out in the long run."

"The good and honest?"

"*You*—you and Henry, by God," said Confido. "That's who. Who else?"

Ellen's hand came down from the earpiece. It started up again, but as a not very threatening gesture, ending in her grasping a broom.

"That's just a nasty neighborhood rumor about Mr. Fink and his secretary," she thought.

"Heah?" said Confido. "Where there's smoke—"

"And he's not a crook."

"Look into those shifty, weak blue eyes, look at those fat lips made for cigars and tell me that," said Confido.

"Now, now," thought Ellen. "That's enough. There's been absolutely no proof—"

"Still waters run deep," said Confido. It was silent for a moment. "And I don't mean just the Finks. This whole neighborhood is still water. Honest to God, somebody ought to write a book about it. Just take this block alone, starting at the corner with the Kramers. Why, to look at her, you'd think she was the quietest, most proper . . ."

"Ma, Ma—hey, Ma," said her son several hours later.

"Ma—you sick? Hey, Ma!"

"And *that* brings us to the Fitzgibbonses," Confido was saying. "That poor little, dried-up, sawed-off, henpecked—"

"Ma!" cried Paul.

"Oh!" said Ellen, opening her eyes. "You startled me. What are you children doing home from school?" She was sitting in her kitchen rocker, half-dazed.

"It's after three, Ma. Whuddya think?"

"Oh, dear—is it that late? Where on earth has the day gone?"

"Can I listen, Ma—can I listen to Confido?"

"It's not for children to listen to," said Ellen, shocked. "I should say not. It's strictly for grown-ups."

"Can't we just look at it?"

With cruel feat of will, Ellen disengaged Confido from her ear and blouse, and laid it on the table. "There—you see? That's all there is to it."

"Boy—a billion dollars lying right there," said Paul softly. "Sure doesn't look like much, does it? A cool billion." He was giving an expert imitation of his father on the night before. "Can I have a motorcycle?"

"Everything takes time, Paul," said Ellen.

"What are you doing with your housecoat on so late?" said her daughter.

"I was *just* going to change it," said Ellen.

She had been in the bedroom just a moment, her mind seething with neighborhood scandal, half-heard in the past, now refreshed and ornamented by Confido, when there were bitter shouts in the kitchen.

She rushed into the kitchen to find Susan crying, and Paul red and defiant. Confido's earpiece in his ear.

"Paul!" said Ellen.

"I don't care," said Paul. "I'm *glad* I listened. Now I know the truth—I know the whole secret."

"He pushed me," sobbed Susan.

"Confido said to," said Paul.

"Paul," said Ellen, horrified. "What secret are you talking about? What secret, dear?"

"I'm not your son," he said sullenly.

"Of *course* you are!"

"Confido says I'm not," said Paul. "Confido says I'm adopted. Susan's the one you love, and that's why I get a raw deal around here."

"Paul—darling, darling. It simply isn't true. I promise. I swear it. And I don't know what on earth you mean by raw deals—"

"Confido says it's true all right," said Paul stoutly.

Ellen leaned against the kitchen table and rubbed her temples. Suddenly, she leaned forward and snatched Confido from Paul.

"Give me that filthy little beast!" she said. She strode angrily out of the back door with it.

"Hey!" said Henry, doing a buck-and-wing through his front door, and sailing his hat, as he had never done before, onto the coatrack in the hall. "Guess what? The breadwinner's home!"

Ellen appeared in the kitchen doorway and gave him a sickly smile. "Hi."

"There's my girl," said Henry, "and have I got good news for you. This is a great day! I haven't got a job anymore. Isn't that swell? They'll take me back any time I want a job, and that'll be when Hell freezes over."

"Um," said Ellen.

"The Lord helps those who help themselves," said Henry, "and here's one man who just got both hands free."

"Huh," said Ellen.

Young Paul and Susan appeared on either side of her to peer bleakly at their father.

"What is this?" said Henry. "It's like a funeral parlor."

"Mom buried it, Pop," said Paul hoarsely. "She buried Confido."

"She did—she really did," said Susan wonderingly. "Under the hydrangeas."

"Henry, I had to," said Ellen desolately, throwing her arms around him. "It was us or it."

Henry pushed her away. "Buried it," he murmured, shaking his head. "Buried it? All you had to do was turn it off."

Slowly, he walked through the house and into the backyard, his family watching in awe. He hunted for the grave under the shrubs without asking for directions.

He opened the grave, wiped the dirt from Confido with his handkerchief, and put the earpiece in his ear, cocking his head and listening intently.

"It's all right, it's O.K.," he said softly. He turned to Ellen. "What on earth got into you?"

"What did it say?" said Ellen. "What did it just say to you, Henry?"

He sighed and looked awfully tired. "It said somebody else would cash in on it sooner or later, if we didn't."

"Let them," said Ellen.

"Why?" demanded Henry. He looked at her challengingly, but his firmness decayed quickly, and he looked away.

"If you've talked to Confido, you *know* why," said Ellen. "Don't you?"

Henry kept his eyes down. "It'll sell, it'll sell, it'll sell," he murmured. "My God, how it'll sell."

"It's a direct wire to the worst in us, Henry," said Ellen. She burst into tears. "Nobody should have that, Henry, nobody! That little voice is loud enough as it is."

An autumn silence, muffled in moldering leaves, settled over the yard, broken only by Henry's faint whistling through his teeth. "Yeah," he said at last. "I know."

He removed Confido from his ear, and laid it gently in its grave once more. He kicked dirt in on top of it.

"What's the last thing it said, Pop?" said Paul.

Henry grinned wistfully. "'I'll be seeing you, sucker. I'll be seeing you.'"

Hall of Mirrors

THERE WAS A PARKING LOT, and then a guitar school, and then Fred's O.K. Used Car Lot, and then the hypnotist's house, and then a vacant lot with the foundation of a mansion still on it, and then the Beeler Brothers' Funeral Home. Autumn winds, experimenting with the idea of a hard winter, made little twists of soot and paper, made the plastic propellers over the used car lot go *frrrrrrrrrrrrrrrrrrrrrrrrrrrrr*.

The city was Indianapolis, the largest city not on a navigable waterway in the world.

It was to the hypnotist's house that the two city detectives came. They were Detectives Carney and Foltz, Carney young and dapper, Foltz middle-aged and rumpled. Carney went up the hypnotist's steps like a tap dancer. Foltz, though he was going to do all the talking, trudged far behind. Carney's interest was specific. He was going straight for the hypnotist. Foltz's attention was diffused. He marveled at the monstrous architecture of the hypnotist's twenty-room house, let his mournful eyes climb the tower at one corner of the house. There had to be a ballroom at the top of the tower. There were ballrooms at the tops of all the towers that the rich had abandoned.

Foltz reached the hypnotist's door at last, rang the bell. The only hint of quackery was a small sign over the doorbell. K. HOLLOMON WEEMS, it said, HYPNOTIC THERAPY.

Weems himself came to the door. He was in his fifties, small, narrow-shouldered, neat. His nose was long, his lips full and red, and his bald head had a seeming phosphorescence. His eyes were unspectacular—pale blue, clear, ordinary.

"Doctor Weems?" said Foltz, grumpily polite.

"'Doctor' Weems?" said Weems. "There is no 'Doctor' Weems here. There is a very plain 'Mister' Weems. He stands before you."

"In your line of work," said Foltz, "I'd think a man would almost have to have some kind of doctor's degree."

"As it happens," said Weems, "I hold two doctor's degrees—one from Budapest, another from Edinburgh." He smiled faintly. "I don't use the title Doctor, however. I wouldn't want anyone to mistake me for a physician." He shivered in the winds. "Won't you come in?"

The three went into what had been the parlor of the mansion, what was the

333

hypnotist's office now. There was no nonsense about the furnishings. They were functional, gray-enameled steel—a desk, a few chairs, a filing cabinet, a bookcase. There were no pictures, no framed certificates on the high walls.

Weems sat down behind his desk, invited his visitors to sit. "The chairs aren't very comfortable, I'm afraid," he said.

"Where do you keep your equipment, Mr. Weems?" said Foltz.

"What equipment is that?" said Weems.

Foltz's stubby hands worked in air. "I assume you've got something you hypnotize people with. A light or something they stare at?"

"No," said Weems. "I'm all the apparatus there is."

"You pull the blinds when you hypnotize somebody?" said Foltz.

"No," said Weems. He volunteered no more information, but looked back and forth between the detectives, inviting them to state their business.

"We're from the police, Mr. Weems," said Foltz, and he showed his identification.

"You are not telling me the news," Weems said.

"You were expecting the police?" said Foltz.

"I was born in Romania, sir—where one is taught from birth to expect the police."

"I thought maybe you had some idea what we were here about?" said Foltz.

Weems sat back, twiddled his thumbs. "Oh—generally, generally, generally," he said. "I arouse vague fears among the simpler sorts wherever I go. Sooner or later they coax the police into having a look at me, to see if I might not be performing black magic here."

"You mind telling us what you do do here?" said Foltz.

"What I do, sir," said Weems, "is as simple and straightforward as what a carpenter or any other honest workman does. My particular service has to do with the elimination of undesirable habits or unreasonable fears." He startled young Carney by gesturing at him suddenly. "You, sir, obviously smoke too much. If you were to give me your undivided attention for two minutes, you would never smoke again, would never want to smoke again."

Carney put out his cigarette.

"I must apologize for the chair you're sitting on, sir," said Weems to Carney. "It's brand-new, but something's wrong with the cushion. There's a small lump on the left side. It's a very small lump, but after a while it makes people quite uncomfortable. It's surprising how a little thing like that can actually induce real pain. Curiously enough, people usually feel the pain in the neck and shoulders rather than in the lower spine."

"I'm all right," said Carney.

"Fine," said Weems. He turned to Foltz again. "If a man had a fear of firearms, for instance," he said, "and his work made it necessary for him to be around them, I could eliminate that fear with hypnosis. As a matter of fact, if a policeman, say, were only a moderately good pistol shot, I could steady his hand enough by means of hypnosis to make him an expert. I'll steady your hand, if you like. If you'll take out your pistol and hold it as steadily as possible—"

Foltz did not draw his pistol. "Only two reasons I ever take my pistol out," he said. "Either I'm gonna clean it, or I'm gonna shoot somebody with it."

"In a minute you'll change your mind," said Weems, and he glanced at his expensive wristwatch. "Believe me—I could make your hand as steady as a vise." He looked at Carney, saw that Carney was standing, was massaging the back of his neck. "Oh, dear," said Weems, "I did warn you about that chair. I should get rid of it. Take another chair, please, and turn that one to the wall, so no one else will get a stiff neck from it."

Carney took another chair, turned his first chair to the wall. He carried his head to one side. His neck was as stiff as a bent crowbar. No amount of rubbing seemed to help.

"Have I convinced you?" Weems said to Foltz. "Will you tell my friends and neighbors that I'm not practicing witchcraft or medicine without a license here?"

"I'd be glad to do that, sir," said Foltz. "But that isn't the main thing we came to see you about."

"Oh?" said Weems.

"No, sir," said Foltz. He took a photograph from the inside pocket of his coat. "What we really wanted to ask you was, do you know this woman, and do you have any idea where we could find her? We've traced her here, and nobody seems to know where she went after."

Weems took the photograph without hesitation, identified it promptly. "Mrs. Mary Styles Cantwell. I remember her well. Would you like to know the exact dates when she was here for treatment?" He opened a card file on his desk, searched for the card of the missing woman, found it. "Four visits in all," he said. "July fourteenth, fifteenth, nineteenth, and twenty-first."

"What did you treat her for?" said Foltz.

"Would you mind pointing that thing somewhere else?" said Weems.

"What?" said Foltz.

"Your pistol," said Weems. "It's pointing right at me."

Foltz looked down at his right hand, discovered that it really did hold a pistol, a pistol aimed at Weems. He was embarrassed, confused. Still, he did not return the pistol to its holster.

"Put it away, please," said Weems.

Foltz put it away.

"Thank you," said Weems. "Surely I'm not being that uncooperative."

"No, sir," said Foltz.

"It's the heat in the room," said Weems. "It puts everybody's nerves on edge. The heating system is very bad. It's always boiling hot in this room, while the rest of the house is like the North Pole. It's at least ninety degrees in here. Won't you gentlemen please take off your coats?"

Carney and Foltz took off their coats.

"Take off your suit coats, too," said Weems. "It must be a hundred in here."

Carney and Foltz took off their suit coats, but sweltered still.

"You both have splitting headaches now," said Weems, "and I know how hard it must be for you to think straight. But I want you to tell me everything you know about me or suspect about me."

"Four women who've been reported missing have been traced here," said Foltz.

"Only four?" said Weems.

"Only four," said Foltz.

"Their names, please?" said Weems.

"Mrs. Mary Styles Cantwell, Mrs. Esmeralda Coyne, Mrs. Nancy Royce, Mrs. Caroline Hughs Tinker, and Mrs. Janet Zimmer."

Weems wrote the names down, just the last names. "Cantwell, Coyne, Royce . . . Selfridge, did you say?"

"Selfridge?" said Foltz. "Who's Selfridge?"

"Nobody," said Weems. "Selfridge is nobody."

"Nobody," echoed Foltz blankly.

"What do you think I did with these women?" said Weems.

"We think you killed them," said Foltz. "They were all fairly rich widows. They all drew their money out of the bank after they came to see you, and they all disappeared after that. We think their bodies are somewhere in this house."

"Do you know my real name?" said Weems.

"No," said Foltz. "When we get your fingerprints, we figure we'll find out you're wanted a lot of other places."

"I will save you that trouble," said Weems. "I will tell you my real name. My real name, gentlemen, is Rumpelstiltskin. Have you got that? I will spell it for you. R-u-m-p-e-l-s-t-i-l-t-s-k-i-n."

"R-u-m-p-e-l-s-t-i-l-t-s-k-i-n," said Foltz.

"I think you should phone that information in to headquarters immediately," said Weems. He held out absolutely nothing to Foltz. "Here's the telephone," he said.

Foltz took the nothing he'd been handed, treated it like a telephone. Using the nonexistent instrument, he put a call through to a Captain Finnerty, reported gravely that Weems's real name was Rumpelstiltskin.

"What did Captain Finnerty say when you gave him the news?" said Weems.

"I don't know," said Foltz.

"You don't know?" said Weems incredulously. "He said I was the man who made people pass through mirrors, didn't he?"

"Yes," said Foltz. "That's what he said."

"I admit it," said Weems. "You've got me dead to rights. I am Rumpelstiltskin," he said, "and I have hypnotized people into stepping through mirrors, into stepping out of this life and into another on the other side. Can you believe that?"

"Yes," said Foltz.

"It's certainly possible, once you think about it, isn't it?" said Weems.

"Yes," said Foltz.

"You believe it, too, don't you?" Weems said to Carney.

Carney was a hunchback now, his neck, shoulders, and head ached so. "I believe it," he said.

"So that explains what happened to the ladies you're looking for," said Weems. "They're far from being dead, believe me. They came to me, very unhappy about the way their lives were going, so I sent them through mirrors to see if things weren't better on the other side. In every case, they chose to remain on the other side. I'll show you in a moment the mirrors they went through, but first I'd like to know if there are any more police outside, or on their way here."

"No," said Foltz.

"Just you two?" said Weems.

"Yes," said Foltz.

Weems clapped his hands lightly. "Well—come along, gentlemen, and I'll show you the mirrors."

He went to the office door, held it open for his guests. He watched them closely as they passed out into the hall, was gratified when they both began to shiver violently, as though struck by bitter cold.

"I warned you it was like the North Pole out here," he said. "You'd better bundle up, though I'm afraid you'll still be quite uncomfortable."

Carney and Foltz bundled up, but continued to shiver.

"Three flights of stairs to climb, gentlemen," said Weems. "We're going to the ballroom at the top of the house. That is where the mirrors are. There is an elevator, but it hasn't run for years."

Not only was the elevator inoperative. It didn't even exist anymore. The elevator, the paneling, the ornate light fixtures, and everything remotely valuable had been stripped from the mansion years before Weems took it over. But Weems invited his guests, even as their feet crunched broken plaster on bare floors, to admire the immaculate and lavish decor.

"This is the gold room, and this is the blue room," he said. "The white swan bed in the blue room is said to have belonged to Madame Pompadour, believe it or not. Do you believe that?" he said to Foltz.

"You couldn't prove it by me," said Foltz.

"Who can be sure of anything in this world, eh?" said Weems.

Carney repeated this sentiment word for word. "Who can be sure of anything in this world, eh?" he said.

"Here is the staircase to the ballroom," said Weems. The staircase was broad. There was a pedestal at its base that had once supported a statue. The original banisters were gone, naked spikes showing where the uprights had once been moored.

There was only one banister now, a length of pipe held by clinched nails. The bare steps were studded with carpet tacks. A tack here and there held a twist of red yarn.

"I've spent more money restoring this staircase than I've spent on anything else in the house," said Weems. "The banisters I found in Italy. The statue, a fourteenth-century Saint Catherine from Toledo, I bought from the estate of William Randolph Hearst. This carpet we're walking on, gentlemen, was woven to my specifications in Kerman, Iran. It's like walking on a feather mattress, isn't it?"

Carney and Foltz did not reply, there was so much splendor to appreciate. But they lifted their knees high, as though they were indeed walking on a feather mattress.

Weems opened the ballroom door, a handsome door, actually. But its handsomeness was spoiled by a message whitewashed across its face. KEEP OUT, said the sign. Two coat hangers hung from the doorknob, tinkled tinnily as Weems opened and closed the door.

The ballroom at the tower's top was circular. Around its walls, full-length mirrors alternated with ghastly leaded-glass windows of purple, mustard, and green. The only furnishings were three bundles of newspapers, tied up as though for a paper sale, two pieces of track from a toy train set, and the headboard of a brass bed.

Weems did not rhapsodize about the glories of the ballroom. He invited Carney and Foltz to give their full attention to the mirrors, which were real. And the play of mirrors on mirrors gave each mirror the aspect of a door leading to infinite perspectives of other doors.

"Sort of like a railroad roundhouse, isn't it?" said Weems. "Look at all the possible routes of travel radiating from us, beckoning to us." He turned to Carney suddenly. "Which route attracts you most?"

"I—I don't know," said Carney.

"Then I'll recommend one in a moment," said Weems. "It isn't a decision to be taken lightly, because a person changes radically when he passes through a mirror— he or she, as the case may be. Handedness changes, of course. That's elementary. A right-handed person becomes left-handed, and vice versa. But a person's personality changes, too—and his future—his or her future, as the case may be."

"The women we're looking for—they went through these mirrors?" said Foltz.

"Yes—the women you're looking for, and about a dozen more you're not looking for besides," said Weems. "They came to me with the shapeless longings of widows with money, but without confidence, hope, irresistible beauty, or dreams. They had been to physicians and quacks of every sort before they came to me. They could describe neither their ailment nor the hoped for cure. It was up to me to define both."

"So what did you tell them?" said Foltz.

"Couldn't you make a diagnosis on the basis of what I've told you?" said Weems. "It was their futures that were sick. And for sick futures"—and he swept his hand at the seeming doors all around them—"I know only one cure."

Weems shouted now, and then listened as though expecting faint replies. "Mrs. Cantwell? Mary?" he called. "Mrs. Forbes?"

"Who is Mrs. Forbes?" said Foltz.

"That is Mary Cantwell's new name on the other side of the glass," said Weems.

"Names change when people go through?" said Foltz.

"No—not necessarily," said Weems, "though a lot of people decide to change their names to go with their new futures, new personalities. In the case of Mary Cantwell—she married a man named Gordon Forbes a week after passing through." He smiled. "I was the best man—and, in all modesty, I don't think anyone ever deserved the honor more."

"You can go in and out of these mirrors any time you want?" said Foltz.

"Certainly," said Weems. "Self-hypnosis, the easiest and commonest form of hypnosis."

"I'd sure like a demonstration," said Foltz.

"That's why I'm trying to call Mary or one of the others back," said Weems. "Hello! Hello! Can anybody hear me?" he shouted at the mirrors.

"I thought maybe *you'd* go through a mirror for us," said Foltz.

"It's a thing I don't care to do, really, except on very special occasions," said Weems, "like Mary's wedding, like the Carter family's first anniversary on the other side—"

"The who family?" said Foltz.

"The Carter family," said Weems. "George, Nancy, and their children, Eunice and Robert." He pointed over his shoulder at a mirror behind him. "I put them all through that mirror there a year and a quarter ago."

"I thought you just specialized in rich widows," said Foltz.

"I thought that's what you specialized in," said Weems. "That's all you asked about—rich widows."

"So you put a family through, too?" said Foltz.

"Several of them," said Weems. "I suppose you want the exact number. I can't give you that number off the top of my head. I'll have to check my files."

"They had bad futures, sick futures," said Foltz, "these families you—uh—put through?"

"In terms of life on this side of the glass?" said Weems. "No—not really. But there were far better futures to be had on the other side. No danger of war, for one thing—a much lower cost of living, for another."

"Um," said Foltz. "And when they went through, they left all their money with you. Right?"

"They took it with them," said Weems, "all of it, with the exception of my fee, which is a flat hundred dollars a head."

"It's too bad they can't hear you yell," said Foltz. "I'd sure like to talk to some of these people, hear about all the nice things that have been happening to them."

"Look in any mirror, and see what a long, complicated corridor my voice has to carry down," said Weems.

"Guess it's up to you to put on the demonstration, then," said Foltz.

"I told you," said Weems, very uneasy now, "I am very reluctant to do it."

"You're afraid the trick won't work?" said Foltz.

"Oh, it'll work all right," said Weems. "It's likely to work too well, is all. If I get on the other side of the glass, I'm going to want to stay on the other side. I always do."

Foltz laughed. "If it's so heavenly on the other side," he said, "what could keep you here?"

Weems closed his eyes, massaged the bridge of his nose. "The same thing that makes you an excellent policeman," he said. He opened his eyes. "A sense of duty." He did not smile.

"And what is it this duty of yours makes you do?" said Foltz. He asked the question mockingly. His air of being dazed, of being in Weems's power, had dropped away.

Weems, seeing the transformation, became in turn a small and wretched man. "It makes me stay here, on this side," he said emptily, "because I am the only one I know of who can help others pass through." He shook his head. "You aren't hypnotized, are you?" he said.

"Hell no," said Foltz. "And neither is he."

Carney relaxed, shuddered, smiled.

"If it makes you feel any better," said Foltz, taking his handcuffs from his hip pocket, "it's a couple of brother hypnotists who are taking you in. That's how we got this assignment. Carney and I've both played with it some. Compared to you, we're mere amateurs, of course. Come on, Weems—Rumpelstiltskin—hold out your wrists like a good boy."

"This was a trap, then?" said Weems.

"Right," said Foltz. "We wanted to get you to talk, and you certainly did. The only problem now is to find the bodies. What did you plan to do with Carney and me—get us to shoot each other?"

"No," said Weems simply.

"I'll tell you this," said Foltz, "we respected hypnotism enough not to take any chances. There's another detective right outside the door."

Weems had not yet held out his thin wrists like a good boy. "I don't believe you," he said.

"Fred!" Foltz called to the detective on the staircase outside. "Come on in, so Rumpelstiltskin can believe in you."

In came the third detective, a pale, moonfaced, huge, young Swede. Carney and Foltz were elated and smug. The man named Fred didn't share their delight. He was worried and watchful, had his gun drawn.

"Please," Weems said to Foltz, "tell him to put his gun away."

"Put your gun away, Fred," said Foltz.

"You guys are really all right?" said Fred.

Carney and Foltz laughed.

"Fooled you, too, eh?" said Foltz.

Fred didn't laugh. "Yeah—you sure did," he said. He looked closely at Carney and Foltz, did it impersonally, as though they were department store dummies. And Carney and Foltz, in their moment of triumph, really did look like dummies—stiff, waxen, with mortuary smiles.

"For the love of God," Weems said to Foltz, "tell him to put his gun away."

"For the love of God," said Foltz, "put the gun away, Fred."

Fred didn't do it. "I—I don't think you guys know what you're doing," he said.

"That's the funniest thing I ever heard," said Weems.

Carney and Foltz burst out laughing. They laughed so hard and long that their bellies ached and their weeping eyes bugged, and they gasped for air.

"That's enough," said Weems, and they stopped laughing instantly, became department store dummies again.

"They *are* hypnotized!" said Fred, backing away.

"Certainly," said Weems. "You've got to understand what sort of a house you're in. Nothing is seen, said, felt, or done here that I don't want seen, said, felt, or done."

"Come on—" said Fred queasily, waving his gun, "wake 'em up."

"Straighten your tie," said Weems.

"I said wake 'em up," said Fred.

"Straighten your tie," said Weems.

Fred straightened his tie.

"Thank you," said Weems. "Now, I'm afraid I have rather frightening news for you—for all of you."

Consternation filled every face.

"A tornado is coming," said Weems. "It will blow you all away unless you handcuff your left hands to that steam radiator."

The three detectives, clumsy with terror, handcuffed themselves to the radiator.

"Throw your keys away, or you'll be struck by lightning!" said Weems.

Keys flew across the room.

"The tornado missed you," said Weems. "You're safe now."

The three detectives wept at their miraculous deliverance.

"Pull yourselves together, gentlemen," said Weems. "I have an announcement to make."

The three were avid for the news.

"I'm going to leave you," said Weems. "In fact, I'm going to leave everything about this existence behind." He went to a mirror, tapped it with his knuckles. "I'm going to step through this mirror in a moment. You will see me and my reflection meet and blend, shrink to the size of a pinhead. The pinhead will grow again, not as me and my reflection, but as my reflection alone. You will then see my reflection walk away from you, down the long, long corridor. See the corridor I'm going to walk down?"

The three nodded.

"You will see me pass through the mirror," said Weems, "when I say the words 'Black magic.' When I say the words 'White magic,' you will see me reappear in every mirror in this room. You will shoot at each of those images, until every mirror is broken. And when I say, 'Good-bye, gentlemen,' you will shoot each other down." Weems strolled to the attic door. Nobody watched him do it. All eyes were on the mirror he'd said he was going to pass through.

"Black magic," said Weems softly.

"There he goes!" cried Foltz.

"Like going through a door!" said Carney.

"God help us!" said Fred.

Weems stepped out of the ballroom and onto the stairs. He left the door open a crack. "White magic," he said.

"There he is!" said Foltz.

"All around us!" said Carney.

"Get him!" said Fred.

There was a pandemonium of shots and yells and shattering glass.

Weems waited for the silence that would tell him that all mirrors had been broken, that it was time at last to say good-bye.

The farewell was poised on his lips when bullets ripped through him and the door against which he leaned.

Weems sank dying to the staircase, about to roll all the way down it. He was not thinking of the lifeless roll to come. He was remembering too late—that on the other side of the ballroom door had been a mirror.

The Nice Little People

IT WAS A HOT, dry, glaring July day that made Lowell Swift feel as though every germ and sin in him were being baked out forever. He was riding home on a bus from his job as a linoleum salesman in a department store. The day marked the end of his seventh year of marriage to Madelaine, who had the car, and who, in fact, owned it. He carried red roses in a long green box under his arm.

The bus was crowded, but no women were standing, so Lowell's conscience was unencumbered. He sat back in his seat and crackled his knuckles absently, and thought pleasant things about his wife.

He was a tall, straight man, with a thin, sandy mustache and a longing to be a British colonel. At a distance, it appeared that his longing had been answered in every respect save for a uniform. He seemed distinguished and purposeful. But his eyes were those of a wistful panhandler, lost, baffled, inordinately agreeable. He was intelligent and healthy, but decent to a point that crippled him as master of his home or an accumulator of wealth.

Madelaine had once characterized him as standing on the edge of the mainstream of life, smiling and saying, "Pardon me," "After you," and "No, thank you."

Madelaine was a real estate saleswoman, and made far more money than Lowell did. Sometimes she joked with him about it. He could only smile amiably, and say that he had never, at any rate, made any enemies, and that, after all, God had made him, even as he had made Madelaine—presumably with some good end in mind.

Madelaine was a beautiful woman, and Lowell had never loved anyone else. He would have been lost without her. Some days, as he rode home on the bus, he felt dull and ineffectual, tired, and afraid Madelaine would leave him—and not blaming her for wanting to.

This day, however, wasn't one of them. He felt marvelous. It was, in addition to being his wedding anniversary, a day spiced with mystery. The mystery was in no way ominous, as far as Lowell could see, but it was puzzling enough to make him feel as though he were involved in a small adventure. It would give him and Madelaine a few minutes of titillating speculation. While he'd been waiting for the bus, someone had thrown a paper knife to him.

It had come, he thought, from a passing car or from one of the offices in the building

343

across the street. He hadn't seen it until it clattered to the sidewalk by the pointed black toes of his shoes. He'd glanced around quickly without seeing who'd thrown it; had picked it up gingerly, and found that it was warm and remarkably light. It was bluish silver in color, oval in cross section, and very modern in design. It was a single piece of metal, seemingly hollow, sharply pointed at one end and blunt at the other, with only a small, pearl-like stone at its midpoint to mark off the hilt from the blade.

Lowell had identified it instantly as a paper knife because he had often noticed something like it in a cutlery window he passed every day on his way to and from the bus stop downtown. He'd made an effort to locate the knife's owner by holding it over his head, and looking from car to car and from office window to office window, but no one had looked back at him as though to claim it. So he had put it in his pocket.

Lowell looked out of the bus window, and saw that the bus was going down the quiet, elm-shaded boulevard on which he and Madelaine lived. The mansions on either side, though now divided into expensive apartments, were still mansions out-side, magnificent. Without Madelaine's income, it would have been impossible for them to live in such a place.

The next stop was his, where the colonnaded white colonial stood. Madelaine would be watching the bus approach, looking down from the third-story apartment that had once been a ballroom. As excited as any high school boy in love, he pulled the signal cord, and looked up for her face in the glossy green ivy that grew around the gable. She wasn't there, and he supposed happily that she was mixing anniver-sary cocktails.

"*Lowell:*" said the note in the hall mirror. "*Am taking a prospect for the Finletter prop-erty to supper. Cross your fingers. —Madelaine.*"

Smiling wistfully, Lowell laid his roses on the table, and crossed his fingers.

The apartment was very still, and disorderly. Madelaine had left in a hurry. He picked up the afternoon paper, which was spread over the floor along with a pastepot and scrapbook, and read tatters that Madelaine had left whole, items that had nothing to do with real estate.

There was a quick *hiss* in his pocket, like the sound of a perfunctory kiss or the opening of a can of vacuum-packed coffee.

Lowell thrust his hand into his pocket and brought forth the paper knife. The little stone at its midpoint had come out of its setting, leaving a round hole.

Lowell laid the knife on the cushion beside him, and searched his pocket for the missing bauble. When he found it, he was disappointed to discover that it wasn't a pearl at all, but a hollow hemisphere of what he supposed to be plastic.

When he returned his attention to the knife, he was swept with a wave of revul-sion. A black insect a quarter of an inch long was worming out through the hole. Then came another and another—until there were six, huddled together in a pit in the cushion, a pit made a moment before by Lowell's elbow. The insects' movements were sluggish and clumsy, as though they were shaken and dazed. Now they seemed to fall asleep in their shallow refuge.

Lowell took a magazine from the coffee table, rolled it up, and prepared to smash the nasty little beasts before they could lay their eggs and infest Madelaine's apartment.

It was then he saw that the insects were three men and three women, perfectly proportioned, and clad in glistening black tights.

On the telephone table in the front hall, Madelaine had taped a list of telephone numbers: the numbers of her office, Bud Stafford—her boss, her lawyer, her broker, her doctor, her dentist, her hairdresser, the police, the fire department, and the department store at which Lowell worked.

Lowell was running his finger down the list for the tenth time, looking for the number of the proper person to tell about the arrival on earth of six little people a quarter of an inch high.

He wished Madelaine would come home.

Tentatively, he dialed the number of the police.

"Seventh precin't. Sergeant Cahoon speakin'."

The voice was coarse, and Lowell was appalled by the image of Cahoon that appeared in his mind: gross and clumsy, slab-footed, with room for fifty little people in each yawning chamber of his service revolver.

Lowell returned the telephone to its cradle without saying a word to Cahoon. Cahoon was not the man.

Everything about the world suddenly seemed preposterously huge and brutal to Lowell. He lugged out the massive telephone book, and opened it to "*United States Government.*" "Agriculture Department . . . Justice Department . . . Treasury Department"—everything had the sound of crashing giants. Lowell closed the book helplessly.

He wondered when Madelaine was coming home.

He glanced nervously at the couch, and saw that the little people, who had been motionless for half an hour, were beginning to stir, to explore the slick, plum-colored terrain and flora of tufts in the cushion. They were soon brought up short by the walls of a glass bell jar Lowell had taken from Madelaine's antique clock on the mantelpiece and lowered over them.

"Brave, brave little devils," said Lowell to himself, wonderingly. He congratulated himself on his calm, his reasonableness with respect to the little people. He hadn't panicked, hadn't killed them or called for help. He doubted that many people would have had the imagination to admit that the little people really were explorers from another world, and that the seeming knife was really a spaceship.

"Guess you picked the right man to come and see," he murmured to them from a distance, "but darned if I know what to do with you. If word got out about you, it'd be murder." He could imagine the panic and the mobs outside the apartment.

As Lowell approached the little people for another look, crossing the carpet silently, there came a ticking from the bell jar, as one of the men circled inside it again and again, tapping with some sort of tool, seeking an opening. The others were engrossed with a bit of tobacco one had pulled out from under a tuft.

Lowell lifted the jar. "Hello, there," he said gently.

The little people shrieked, making sounds like the high notes of a music box, and scrambled toward the cleft where the cushion met the back of the couch.

"No, no, no, no," said Lowell. "Don't be afraid, little people." He held out a fingertip to stop one of the women. To his horror, a spark snapped from his finger, striking her down in a little heap the size of a morning-glory seed.

The others had tumbled out of sight behind the cushion.

"Dear God, what have I done, what have I done?" said Lowell heartbrokenly.

He ran to get a magnifying glass from Madelaine's desk, and then peered through it at the tiny, still body. "Dear, dear, oh, dear," he murmured.

He was more upset than ever when he saw how beautiful the woman was. She bore a slight resemblance to a girl he had known before he met Madelaine.

Her eyelids trembled and opened. "Thank heaven," he said. She looked up at him with terror.

"Well, now," said Lowell briskly, "that's more like it. I'm your friend. I don't want to hurt you. Lord knows I don't." He smiled and rubbed his hands together. "We'll have a welcome to earth banquet. What would you like? What do you little people eat, eh? I'll find something."

He hurried to the kitchen, where dirty dishes and silverware cluttered the countertops. He chuckled to himself as he loaded a tray with bottles and jars and cans that now seemed enormous to him, literal mountains of food.

Whistling a festive air, Lowell brought the tray into the living room and set it on the coffee table. The little woman was no longer on the cushion.

"Now, where have you gone, eh?" said Lowell gaily. "I know, I know where to find you when everything's ready. Oho! a banquet fit for kings and queens, no less."

Using his fingertip, he made a circle of dabs around the center of a saucer, leaving mounds of peanut butter, mayonnaise, oleomargarine, minced ham, cream cheese, catsup, liver pâté, grape jam, and moistened sugar. Inside this circle he put separate drops of milk, beer, water, and orange juice.

He lifted up the cushion. "Come and get it, or I'll throw it on the ground," he said. "Now—where did you get to? I'll find you, I'll find you." In the corner of the couch, where the cushion had been, lay a quarter and a dime, a paper match, and a cigar band, a band from the sort of cigars Madelaine's boss smoked.

"There you are," said Lowell. Several tiny pairs of feet projected from the pile of debris.

Lowell picked up the coins, leaving the six little people huddled and trembling. He laid his hand before them, palm up. "Come on, now, climb aboard. I have a surprise for you."

They didn't move, and Lowell was obliged to shoo them into his palm with a pencil point. He lifted them through the air, dumped them on the saucer's rim like so many caraway seeds.

"I give you," he said, "the largest smorgasbord in history." The dabs were all taller than the dinner guests.

After several minutes, the little people got courage enough to begin exploring again. Soon, the air around the saucer was filled with piping cries of delight, as delicious bonanza after bonanza was discovered.

Lowell watched happily through the magnifying glass as faces were lifted to him with lip-smacking, ogling gratitude.

"Try the beer. Have you tried the beer?" said Lowell. Now, when he spoke, the little people didn't shriek, but listened attentively, trying to understand.

Lowell pointed to the amber drop, and all six dutifully sampled it, trying to look appreciative, but failing to hide their distaste.

"Acquired taste," said Lowell. "You'll learn. You'll—"

The sentence died, unfinished. Outside a car had pulled up, and floating up through the summer evening was Madelaine's voice.

When Lowell returned from the window, after watching Madelaine kiss her boss, the little people were kneeling and facing him, chanting something that came to him sweet and faint.

"Hey," said Lowell, beaming, "what is this, anyway? It was nothing—nothing at all. Really. Look here, I'm just an ordinary guy. I'm common as dirt here on earth. Don't get the idea I'm—" He laughed at the absurdity of the notion.

The chant went on, ardent, supplicating, adoring.

"Look," said Lowell, hearing Madelaine coming up the stairs, "you've got to hide until I get squared away in my mind what to do about you."

He looked around quickly, and saw the knife, the spaceship. He laid it by the saucer, and prodded them with the pencil again. "Come on—back in here for a little while."

They disappeared into the hole, and Lowell pressed the pearly hatch cover back into place just as Madelaine came in.

"Hello," she said cheerfully. She saw the saucer. "Been entertaining?"

"In a small way," said Lowell. "Have you?"

"It looks like you've been having mice in."

"I get lonely, like anybody else," said Lowell.

She reddened. "I'm sorry about the anniversary, Lowell."

"Perfectly all right."

"I didn't remember until on the way home, just a few minutes ago, and then it hit me like a ton of bricks."

"The important thing is," said Lowell pleasantly, "did you close the deal?"

"Yes—yes, I did." She was restless, and had difficulty smiling when she found the roses on the hall table. "How nice."

"I thought so."

"Is that a new knife you have?"

"This? Yes—picked it up on the way home."

"Did we need it?"

"I took a fancy to it. Mind?"

"No—not at all." She looked at it uneasily. "You saw us, didn't you?"

"Who? What?"

"You saw me kissing Bud outside just now."

"Yes. But I don't imagine you're ruined."

"He asked me to marry him, Lowell."

"Oh? And you said—?"

"I said I would."

"I had no idea it was that simple."

"I love him, Lowell. I want to marry him. Do you have to drum on your palm with that knife?"

"Sorry. Didn't realize I was."

"Well?" she said meekly, after a long silence.

"I think almost everything that needs to be said has been said."

"Lowell, I'm dreadfully sorry—"

"Sorry for me? Nonsense! Whole new worlds have opened up for me." He walked over to her slowly, put his arm around her. "But it will take some getting used to, Madelaine. Kiss? Farewell kiss, Madelaine?"

"Lowell, please—" She turned her head aside, and tried to push him away gently. He hugged her harder.

"Lowell—no. Let's stop it, Lowell. Lowell, you're hurting me. Please!" She struck him on the chest and twisted away. "I can't stand it!" she cried bitterly.

The spaceship in Lowell's hand hummed and grew hot. It trembled and shot from his hand, under its own power, straight at Madelaine's heart.

Lowell didn't have to look up the number of the police. Madelaine had taped it to the telephone table.

"Seventh precin't. Sergeant Cahoon speakin'."

"Sergeant," said Lowell, "I want to report an accident—a death."

"Homicide?" said Cahoon.

"I don't know what you'd call it. It takes some explaining."

When the police arrived, Lowell told his story calmly, from the finding of the spaceship to the end.

"In a way, it was my fault," he said. "The little people thought I was God."

Look at the Birdie

I WAS SITTING in a bar one night, talking rather loudly about a person I hated—and a man with a beard sat down beside me, and he said amiably, "Why don't you have him killed?"

"I've thought of it," I said. "Don't think I haven't."

"Let me help you to think about it clearly," he said. His voice was deep. His beak was large. He wore a black mohair suit and a black string tie. His little red mouth was obscene. "You're looking at the situation through a red haze of hate," he said. "What you need are the calm, wise services of a murder counselor, who can plan the job for you, and save you an unnecessary trip to the hot squat."

"Where do I find one?" I said.

"You've found one," he said.

"You're crazy," I said.

"That's right," he said. "I've been in and out of mental institutions all my life. That makes my services all the more appealing. If I were ever to testify against you, your lawyer would have no trouble establishing that I was a well-known nut, and a convicted felon besides."

"What was the felony?" I said.

"A little thing—practicing medicine without a license," he said.

"Not murder then?" I said.

"No," he said, "but that doesn't mean I *haven't* murdered. As a matter of fact, I murdered almost everyone who had anything to do with convicting me of practicing medicine without a license." He looked at the ceiling, did some mental arithmetic. "Twenty-two, twenty-three people—maybe more," he said. "Maybe more. I've killed them over a period of years, and I haven't read the papers every single day."

"You black out when you kill, do you," I said, "and wake up the next morning, and read that you've struck again?"

"No, no, no, no, no," he said. "No, no, no, no, no. I killed many of those people while I was cozily tucked away in prison. You see," he said, "I use the cat-over-the-wall technique, a technique I recommend to you."

"This is a new technique?" I said.

"I like to think that it is," he said. He shook his head. "But it's so obvious, I can't believe that I was the first to think of it. After all, murdering's an old, old trade."

"You use a cat?" I said.

"Only as an analogy," he said. "You see," he said, "a very interesting legal question is raised when a man, for one reason or another, throws a cat over a wall. If the cat lands on a person, claws his eyes out, is the cat thrower responsible?"

"Certainly," I said.

"Good," he said. "Now then—if the cat lands on nobody, but claws someone ten minutes after being thrown, is the cat thrower responsible?"

"No," I said.

"That," he said, "is the high art of the cat-over-the-wall technique for carefree murder."

"Time bombs?" I said.

"No, no, no," he said, pitying my feeble imagination.

"Slow poisons? Germs?" I said.

"No," he said. "And your next and final guess I already know: killers for hire from out of town." He sat back, pleased with himself. "Maybe I really *did* invent this thing."

"I give up," I said.

"Before I tell you," he said, "you've got to let my wife take your picture." He pointed his wife out to me. She was a scrawny, thin-lipped woman with raddled hair and bad teeth. She was sitting in a booth with an untouched beer before her. She was obviously a lunatic herself, watching us with the harrowing cuteness of schizophrenia. I saw that she had a Rollieflex with flashgun attached on the seat beside her.

At a signal from her husband, she came over and prepared to take my picture. "Look at the birdie," she said.

"I don't want my picture taken," I said.

"Say *cheese*," she said, and the flashgun went off.

When my eyes got used to darkness of the bar again, I saw the woman scuttling out the door.

"What the hell is this?" I said, standing up.

"Calm yourself. Sit down," he said. "You've had your picture taken. That's all."

"What's she going to do with it?" I said.

"Develop it," he said.

"And then what?" I said.

"Paste it in our picture album," he said, "in our treasure house of golden memories."

"Is this some kind of blackmail?" I said.

"Did she photograph you doing anything you shouldn't be doing?" he said.

"I want that picture," I said.

"You're not superstitious, are you?" he said.

"Superstitious?" I said.

"Some people believe that, if their picture is taken," he said, "the camera captures a little piece of their soul."

"I want to know what's going on," I said.

"Sit down and I'll tell you," he said.

"Make it good, and make it quick," I said.

"Good and quick it shall be, my friend," he said. "My name is Felix Koradubian. Does the name ring a bell?"

"No," I said.

"I practiced psychiatry in this city for seven years," he said. "Group psychiatry was my technique. I practiced in the round, mirror-lined ballroom of a stucco castle between a used car lot and a colored funeral home."

"I remember now," I said.

"Good," he said. "For your sake, I'd hate to have you think I was a liar."

"You were run in for quackery," I said.

"Quite right," he said.

"You hadn't even finished high school," I said.

"You mustn't forget," he said, "Freud himself was self-educated in the field. And one thing Freud said was that a brilliant intuition was as important as anything taught in medical school." He gave a dry laugh. His little red mouth certainly didn't show any merriment to go with the laugh. "When I was arrested," he said, "a young reporter who *had* finished high school—wonder of wonders, he may have even finished college—he asked me to tell him what a paranoiac was. Can you imagine?" he said. "I had been dealing with the insane and the nearly insane of this city for seven years, and that young squirt, who maybe took freshman psychology at Jerkwater U, thought he could baffle me with a question like that."

"What *is* a paranoiac?" I said.

"I sincerely hope that that is a respectful question put by an ignorant man in search of truth," he said.

"It is," I said. It wasn't.

"Good," he said. "Your respect for me at this point should be growing by leaps and bounds."

"It is," I said. It wasn't.

"A paranoiac, my friend," he said, "is a person who has gone crazy in the most intelligent, well-informed way, the world being what it is. The paranoiac believes that great secret conspiracies are afoot to destroy him."

"Do you believe that about yourself?" I said.

"Friend," he said, "I *have* been destroyed! My God, I was making sixty thousand dollars a year—six patients an hour, at five dollars a head, two thousand hours a year. I was a rich, proud, and happy man. And that miserable woman who just took your picture, she was beautiful, wise, and serene."

"Too bad," I said.

"Too bad it is, *indeed*, my friend," he said. "And not just for us, either. This is a sick, sick city, with thousands upon thousands of mentally ill people for whom nothing is being done. Poor people, lonely people, afraid of doctors, most of them—those are the people I was helping. Nobody is helping them now." He shrugged. "Well," he said, "having been caught fishing illegally in the waters of human misery, I have returned my entire catch to the muddy stream."

"Didn't you turn your records over to somebody?" I said.

"I burned them," he said. "The only thing I saved was a list of really dangerous paranoiacs that only I knew about—violently insane people hidden in the woodwork of the city, so to speak—a laundress, a telephone installer, a florist's helper, an elevator operator, and on and on."

Koradubian winked. "A hundred and twenty-three names on my magic list—all people who heard voices, all people who thought certain strangers were out to get them, all people, who, if they got scared enough, would kill."

He sat back and beamed. "I see you're beginning to understand," he said. "When I was arrested, and then got out on bail, I bought a camera—the same camera that took your picture. And my wife and I took candid snapshots of the District Attorney, the President of the County Medical Association, of an editorial writer who demanded my conviction. Later on, my wife photographed the judge and jury, the prosecuting attorney, and all of the unfriendly witnesses.

"I called in my paranoiacs, and I apologized to them. I told them that I had been very wrong in telling them that there was no plot against them. I told them that I had uncovered a monstrous plot, and that I had photographs of the plotters. I told them that they should study the photographs, and should be alert and armed constantly. And I promised to send them more photographs from time to time."

I was sick with horror, had a vision of the city teeming with innocent-looking lunatics who would suddenly kill and run.

"That—that picture of me—" I said wretchedly.

"We'll keep it locked up nice and tight," said Koradubian, "provided you keep this conversation a secret, and provided you give me money."

"How much money?" I said.

"I'll take whatever you've got on you now," he said.

I had twelve dollars. I gave it to him. "Now do I get the picture back?" I said.

"No," he said. "I'm sorry, but this goes on indefinitely, I'm afraid. One has to live, you know." He sighed, tucked away the money in his billfold.

"Shameful days, shameful days," he murmured. "And to think that I was once a respected professional man."

Between Timid and Timbuktu

I.

A young painter, whose wife had been killed in an automobile accident two weeks before, stood in front of the open French doors of his studio in a silent house. His feet were far apart, as though he were poised to strike someone, and the look of frustration on his face contradicted the peaceful scene before him. A green slope, speckled with bright leaves fallen from the maples, dropped away to a pond that brimmed over the rock dam he had built in the Spring. A stooped, bright-eyed old man, a neighboring farmer, paced slowly up and down the length of a wooden pier that jutted into the pond, casting a red-and-white bass lure into the water again and again and again.

The painter, David Harnden, held a small dictionary in his hands, and, in the frail warmth of Indian Summer's sunlight, he read and reread the definition of the word between *timid* and *Timbuktu*: "the general idea, relation, or fact of continuous or successive existence."

Impatiently, David snapped the book shut between his long fingers. The word was *time*. He ached to understand time, to defy it, to defeat it—to go back, not forward—to go back to the moments with his wife Jeanette, to the moments time had swept away.

The old farmer's fishing reel sang. David looked up to see the bright lure smack the water, sink, and begin its twitching course back to the pier. Now it was dripping in air, inches from the casting rod's tip. The last of the ripples it had made dissipated at the pond's edge. Another instant flickering past—going, going, gone. *Time.*

David's eyes widened. He knew his fascination with time was near lunacy, a flailing about, a reaction to tragedy. Yet, in calmer moments, there was growing a steady conviction that his wish to travel back to happier days might be reasonable. A scientist friend had once remarked audaciously, with a few fingers of whisky in him, that any technical advance that was conceivable to the mind would one day be made a reality by scientists. It was conceivable that man could travel to other planets; that would come to pass. It was conceivable that a machine could be made more intelli-

353

gent than men; that would come to pass. It was conceivable to David that he might return to Jeanette. He closed his eyes. It was inconceivable that he could never see her again . . .

He watched as the farmer whipped his rod to make another cast. The pier quivered. "Keep away from the end," called David. He had been meaning to fix two of the uprights, which were green, splitting. The old man gave no sign that he heard. David was in no frame of mind to worry about it. To hell with it—the pier would hold. His thoughts turned inward again.

He stretched out his long frame on a couch in the studio, let the dictionary drop to the floor, and lost himself in a fantasy of visitors from another world. He daydreamed of beings infinitely wiser than men, with more senses than mankind's five; beings who could tell him about time. He thought of visitors from space bringing an understanding of time because it seemed beyond the limits of human minds— far beyond. Perhaps there were in the universe forms of life—the flying-saucer men, say—who scampered through time wherever their fancy took them. They would laugh at earth men, to whom time was a one-way street with a dead end in sight.

Where would he travel in time if he could? David sat up and ran his hands through his short, black hair. "Back to Jeanette," he said aloud—back to the sights and sounds and smells and feel of a May afternoon. Time had fogged, flattened, cooled the precious image. He could remember that the afternoon had been vital, happy, perfect. He could no longer see it clearly . . .

Vaguely, heartbreakingly so, he could see himself and the handsome, laughing Jeanette as they had been on that day. The perfect moment? There were an infinite number of them, identically lovely. Married two weeks, they had come home to this house on that day . . . had jubilantly explored every room, exclaimed over the green, rolling tranquility framed in each window . . . had perched on the rock dam, had swirled bare feet in the rising crest of the pool and kissed . . . had lain on the slope's new grass . . . Jeanette, Jeanette, Jeanette . . .

The image was shattered by a cry. "Help! Help me!"

David jumped to his feet. The two uprights at the pier's end were split, splayed wide. The outermost section of planks hung crazily between them like a sprung gallows trap. The old farmer was gone. Nothing troubled the surface.

David ran down the slope, stripping off clothing as he went, and dived into the stinging chill of the water. In the depths beneath the broken pier, the strength went out of his strokes. Before him loomed the farmer, doubled into a tight ball, motionless save for a gentle lolling in the current. David burst the surface, filled his lungs, and plunged downward again. He seized the shoulder strap of the old man's overalls and tugged at the passive mass. No struggle, no clawing, no death grip.

David worked over the body on the slope. He lost track of how long he had been working to wring death out of the farmer's lungs. Up, over, press, relax . . . up, over, press, relax . . . How long had it been since he had shouted to a small boy on the road to get a doctor? *Up, over* . . . No flicker of life in the gaping white face. David's arms and shoulders ached; he could no longer close his hands into fists. Time had won again—had stolen another human being from those who loved him. Suddenly, David was aware that he had been talking aloud the whole time, angrily—that he was behaving, not with the grave concern of a man saving a life, but with the rage of a brawler. He felt no emotion toward the man under his hands, felt only hate for their common tormentor—time.

Tires swished through the deep gravel of the driveway above. A short, overweight little man trotted down the slope, swinging a black bag wildly as he came. David nodded wearily. Middle-aged Dr. Boyle, the village's only doctor, nodded back, struggling to regain his breath.

"Signs of life?" panted the doctor. He had opened his bag and was now holding a long-needled hypodermic syringe up to the sunlight. He pressed the plunger until a droplet grew at the needle's tip.

"He's dead, Doc—deader than hell," said David. "Thirty minutes ago he was thinking of bass for dinner. Now he's gone. Thirty minutes, all going one way, leaving him behind."

Dr. Boyle looked at him with mild puzzlement, then shrugged. "You'd be surprised how tough it is to kill some of these old turkeys," he said, almost cheerfully. He and David turned the farmer over. Matter-of-factly, Dr. Boyle drove the long needle into the drowned man's heart. "If there's a twitch left in him, we'll get him going again good as new. Maybe." He rolled the body on its stomach again. "You've had your rest. Back to work, my boy."

While Dr. Boyle rubbed the man's limbs and David gave artificial respiration, the barest tint of pink came into the waxen cheeks. A gasp, a sigh, and the old man breathed again.

"Back from the dead," whispered David, awed.

"If you like being melodramatic about it, we're bringing him back from the dead, I suppose," said Dr. Boyle, lighting a cigarette, keeping his eyes on the drowned man's face.

"Did we or didn't we?"

"A matter of defining your terms," said Boyle. It was obvious that the subject bored him. "Drowned men, electrocuted men, suffocated men, they're usually perfectly good men—good lungs, good heart, kidneys, liver, everything in first-rate shape. They're dead is all. If you catch a situation like that quick enough, sometimes you can do something with it." He gave the farmer another injection, this time in the arm. "Yep, back from the dead for a few more years of fishing."

"What's it like to be dead?" said David. "Maybe he can tell us."

"Let's not get corny," said the doctor absently. He frowned. "What's a youngster like you doing brooding about death, anyway? You're good for another sixty years." He colored, laid his hand on David's shoulder. "Sorry—forgot."

"What will he tell us?" insisted David, untroubled by the slip.

The doctor studied him curiously. "What's it like to be dead? In a word: dead. That's what it's like." He put his stethoscope to the old man's now-pounding heart. "What will our friend tell us?" He shook his head. "He'll say what it's customary to say. You've read it a hundred times in newspaper stories. The back-from-the-deaders don't remember a thing, so ninety percent say the customary phrase just to be interesting." He snapped his fingers. "And it's so much bunk. Know the phrase I mean?"

"No. Up to now I haven't been interested."

Dr. Boyle fished a pencil stub and a scrap of paper from his vest pocket. He scrawled a sentence on the paper and handed it to David. "Here. Don't look at it until our protégé comes around enough to talk. Five dollars says we'll hear him say what I've just written."

David folded the paper, kept it in his palm. Together, they carried the farmer up to the house.

II.

David and Dr. Boyle sat on the couch before the living room fireplace. David had built a fire. It was evening, and the two had been drinking. From a bedroom adjacent to the living room came the gentle snores of the old farmer, who now slept away his exhaustion swathed in blankets. There was no room for him in the doctor's ten-bed hospital.

"If you'd taken my bet, I'd be five dollars richer," said Boyle jovially.

David nodded. He still had the slip of paper on which the doctor had written the words he expected the farmer to say. When the farmer had gathered strength enough to speak an hour ago, he had said the words—almost exactly. David reread the slip aloud: "*My whole life passed before my eyes.*"

"What could be more trite?" said Dr. Boyle, refilling his glass.

"How do you know it isn't true?"

Boyle sighed condescendingly. "Does an intelligent man like you really need to have someone else give him the reason?" He raised his eyebrows. "If his life *did* pass before his eyes, his brain was what saw it. That's all anybody's got to see with. If his heart stops pumping, his brain doesn't get any blood. It can't work without blood. His brain couldn't work. Therefore, he couldn't see his life passing before his eyes. QED, quod erat demonstrandum, as they said in Rome and your high school geometry class—what was to be demonstrated is demonstrated." He stood. "How about my getting some more ice, eh?" He went into the kitchen at the back of the house, the least bit unsteady, humming.

David stood and stretched, and became aware that the heat of the blazing logs, an empty stomach, and the quick succession of highballs had conspired to make him very drunk. He felt buoyant, not wildly happy, but clever. Hazily, he had the impression of being on the verge of outwitting time—of being about to rise above it, about to go wherever he liked into the past.

Now, without quite understanding why, he was in the darkened bedroom, shaking the shoulder of the sleeping farmer. "Wake up!" he said urgently. "Come on, I've got to talk to you." He was rough, irritated that the farmer should continue to sleep. It was somehow awfully important that he talk to the man immediately. "Wake up, do you hear?"

The farmer stirred, stared up at him with bewildered red eyes.

"What did you see when you were dead?" David demanded.

The farmer licked his lips, blinked. "My whole life—" he began.

"I know that. What I want to know is the details. Did you see people and places you'd forgotten all about?"

The farmer closed his eyes, frowned in concentration. "I'm awful tired. I can't think." He stroked his temples. "It was quick, kind of like a movie going real fast, I guess—kind of flashes of old times."

"Did you get a good look at anything?" urged David tensely.

"Please, can't I go back to sleep?"

"As soon as you answer me. Can you describe anything in detail?"

The farmer licked his lips. "My mother and father—I saw them real good," he said thickly. "They looked young, just a couple of kids, almost. They was just back from the fair at Chicago, bringing me souvenirs, and carrying on about how there was an electric train running clear around the fairgrounds . . ." His voice trailed off.

"What did they say?" David shook his shoulder again.

"Father said he hadn't spent near as much as he'd expected." The voice was now a whisper. David had to lean over the bed to hear. "Said he had a lot of money left over."

"How much money?"

"Said he had fifty-seven bucks." The farmer was seized by a coughing fit that made him sit up.

"What else did he say?" said David excitedly, when the coughing stopped.

The farmer now looked up with fright in his eyes. "Said he had three bucks more than he needed for a new Therma-King range." He collapsed back on the pillows, his eyes closed.

"Dave! Get out of there!" said Dr. Boyle sharply. His round body was a belligerent silhouette in the bedroom door. "He isn't out of the woods by a long shot. Do you want to kill him?" He gathered up a fistful of David's sleeve and angrily pulled him out of the room.

David didn't resist, hardly knew what was happening to him. He said nothing, left untouched the fresh drink Boyle had mixed for him. He stretched out full length on the couch, with great effort wrote the number fifty-seven under the words on the scrap of paper, and fell asleep—to dream of Jeanette.

III.

"I'm sorry, the doctor doesn't have office hours on Wednesday afternoons," said the white-haired nurse, smoothing her uniform over her bony hips.

"It's a personal call. He's a friend of mine. I have something very important to show him," said David breathlessly. "Where is he—in his study?"

The nurse looked dubious, flicked on an intercommunication set on her desk. "Dr. Boyle, a young man out here says he has something important to show you. Says he's a friend. What was your name, young man?" She watched him alertly, as though she expected him to snatch her gold-capped fountain pen and run.

"David Harnden." David realized from the look she gave him how disreputable he must seem. For a week now, ever since he had saved the farmer from drowning, he hadn't shaved or even washed, except to cool his head occasionally with a cold washcloth. Ineffectually, he tried to straighten his suit, which was twisted in ungainly creases over his body. His trouser cuffs were spattered with clay. He had strode through a rainstorm in the suit on his way to the village library in the morning, lain in it on the wet green slope where he and Jeanette had lain not yet six months ago—

"Dr. Boyle is busy," said the nurse. "Sorry." It was plain that she wasn't.

David leaned over the intercom set, turned on the switch. "Boyle, listen. This time I've got something really big, conclusive. Even you'll be convinced when you see this." He waved a photostat before the microphone.

"Look, Dave"—Dr. Boyle's voice was tired, impatient sounding—"I've got a big meeting on Monday in Albany, and I'm supposed to have a paper ready for it. Thanks to your hounding and a measles epidemic, I haven't gotten beyond paragraph one. Whatever it is you've got, it can wait until after Monday. I can't see you today, and that's that." There was a click in the loudspeaker.

"He can't hear you," said the nurse primly. "He's pulled the plug out." She went over to the door and held it open. "The doctor can see you Tuesday," she said, as though only *she* could hear what Boyle said over the system. "If you'd like to leave that paper—whatever it is—perhaps he could look at it over the weekend."

David was looking up the carpeted staircase, wondering where in the huge old house the study might be. Absently, he handed the photostat to the nurse.

She studied it superciliously. "And what is he supposed to do with this? I doubt if he's in the market for a woodstove. 'Ladies, trade your old range for a Therma-King.' I don't get it."

"It's not for you to get," said David irritably. "Give it back. I'm taking it up to him myself, right now."

She opened the door wider and held the photostat against her spare bosom. "I'll take it up to him. Just tell me what it's all about."

"Tell him this proves the farmer wasn't lying. The Chicago World's Fair was in

1893, and in 1893 you could get a Therma-King range for fifty-four dollars. This ad from an 1893 paper proves it. That's three dollars less than fifty-seven, which is what the farmer said." He turned his back on her. "Oh, to hell with you. You're not listening."

"I can hear you all over the house," complained Dr. Boyle from the head of the stairs.

"Boyle, I've got proof that the old man's life really did pass before his eyes. He traveled back in time to 1893!"

"He should have shot your grandfather while he was back there. Maybe I'd have a minute's peace now to finish this paper."

"Can't I talk to you just a minute?" said David.

"Oh . . . all right. I'll see you as a patient in critical condition. You're in bad mental shape, Dave. You need to get away and rest like nobody I know, with the exception of myself. Come on up."

"The doctor will see you," said the nurse briskly. She handed him the photostat with patronizing deference.

"I can communicate quite well without the help of an interpreter," said David acidly, and went up the steps two at a time.

Dr. Boyle closed the door to his study, and, with his head resting on folded arms on the desktop, he listened to David's news.

"And this ad clinches it, doesn't it?" David was saying. "The old man went back to when he was seven years old, heard his father talking about the electric railroad at the World's Fair, then give the brand name and price on a kitchen range he was going to buy. It all checks!"

Boyle didn't raise his head. "I don't know what the explanation is, Dave, but I know it isn't yours. The guy has a hell of a memory, maybe. He must. Maybe going under the way he did does something screwy to the mind. Sometimes hypnotists can get people to remember things like the make of car their grade school teacher drove. Something in that line, maybe. Time travel? Hooey."

"I checked his memory, and it's nothing wonderful," said David. "I tell you, I haven't thought about anything else for the past week, and I've been over all the angles. The old man couldn't tell me within ten dollars what the stove he's got now cost him, and he was wrong about the make." He thrust his hands into his pockets. "Give me one solid argument against time travel. There isn't one."

"Logic, my boy," said Dr. Boyle patiently, between his teeth. "It doesn't make sense. You could go back in time, kill a man, and wipe out God-knows-how-many descendants. Knock off Charlemagne, and you kill about every white man on earth. Ridiculous! Why don't you go into gunrunning and sell the ancient Athenians a couple of machine guns so they can win the Peloponnesian War? Why not go back and invent the lightbulb, the telephone, and the airplane before Edison, Bell, and the Wrights get around to it? Think of the royalties!"

David nodded. "I know, I know—those arguments threw me, too, for a while.

Then I realized that the old man, if he really did travel through time, didn't go anywhere but where he'd already been. If I say that a dead man is free to travel back to any instant in his own lifetime, then your logic can't lay a finger on it. I don't think he can change a thing about his lifetime, as you very logically point out. If he travels back, he can feel only what he felt then, do what he did then. I'm convinced that that much is possible."

'Who cares?"

"I care," said David evenly. "You care, everybody cares. If it's true, this is a helluva sight more merciful life than it now appears to be."

Dr. Boyle stood, and now he, like the nurse, was holding the door open. "It's a very interesting idea, Dave, a fine one to kick around on a long winter evening. You believe it, and I don't. Neither one of us has a leg to stand on. I haven't got any more time for kicking ideas around, so you're going to have to excuse me."

"You've got to help me find out whether there's anything to it." David backed away from the door, stubbornly settled into an overstuffed chair, and lit a cigarette.

"Look, my friend," said Boyle with exasperation, "a week ago, I hardly knew you. Now I find you dogging me like my Siamese twin. Telephone calls, interminable conversations—all about time, time, time. I'm not interested, do you understand? Why don't you attach yourself to someone who would be? A close friend, maybe a minister or a psychologist, or some kind of ologist who would go big for this sort of monkey business. I'm a general practitioner, and a damned busy one."

"A physician's the only one who can help me with my experiment, and you're the only one in town," said David helplessly. "I'm sorry I'm cluttering up your life. The whole thing seems so important, is all—terribly important. I thought you'd see it that way, too, and want to help. What *could* be more important than proving I'm right? If your afterlife is going to be made up of eternity in the best moments of this life, wouldn't you like to know about it?"

Dr. Boyle yawned. "And if one's life happens to stink through no fault of his own?"

"Then he can settle for a trip back to the womb. Some don't want any more than that."

"You've got it all figured out, haven't you, Dave?" Boyle narrowed his eyes. "How could I help you? What is this experiment you're talking about?" His question had a carefulness about it, the same sort of carefulness he used when probing an abdomen for the knotted muscles of appendicitis.

David handed him another newspaper clipping, this one but a day old. He trembled slightly, keeping his temper in check. This smug little doctor, on whom so much depended, hadn't a grain of curiosity or imagination. He could not see that time—not cancer or heart disease or any other disease in his books—was the most frightening, crippling plague of mankind.

Dr. Boyle was reading the clipping aloud. "Ummmm. 'Los Angeles—A surgeon of the Sacred Heart Hospital here today—' Oh, yes, I read this. The man died on the operating table, and the surgeon revived him by massaging his heart. Uh-huh. Very interesting case, and particularly so to you, I suppose. I wonder if the patient said *his* whole life passed before his eyes?" He put the question sardonically.

"He was unconscious an hour ago," said David.

"How on earth do you know?"

"I telephoned the hospital just before I came here."

Dr. Boyle's eyebrows shot up. "You did *what*? You telephoned all the way to Los Angeles to ask about a complete stranger?" He laid his hand on David's shoulder. "You *are* in bad shape, Dave. I didn't realize what an obsession it was. You've got to leave this idea alone and get some rest—get away from that gloomy house. I'm giving you doctor's orders, now. You're on your way to a first-class crack-up. I mean it. Pack up and get away today."

"I'll get rest after the experiment—plenty of rest," said David evenly. "But the experiment comes first."

"And that experiment is—?"

David saw in Boyle's reddening face that the doctor had guessed. "An operation is what I want from you, Doctor. I'll pay anything you like for it—plenty. I want to see about time for myself." His voice was almost casual. He felt no awe for what he was asking for, felt only a longing for it. "I want you to kill me and bring me back to life."

"Get out," said Dr. Boyle quietly. "Never bother me again, do you understand? Now beat it."

IV.

Two months had passed since Dr. Boyle ordered David out of his office. David leaned back in a deep chair in his studio, propped his feet on his drafting table, and dialed a number.

"Dr. Boyle's office." It was the nurse's voice. She managed by her tone to convey that whoever was calling, whatever his business might be, he was imposing trivia on a vastly important organization.

"I'd like to speak to the doctor," said David. "It's urgent."

"This is Mr. Harnden, if I'm not mistaken."

"You're not mistaken."

"The doctor doesn't want to be bothered by you again. I thought he'd made that quite clear."

"This is an emergency," said David sharply. "If you don't put me through to Dr. Boyle right now, you're going to be one angel of mercy in damn serious trouble."

There was a long silence, unbroken save for her heavy breathing. Finally, a click. "Doctor, it's Mr. Harnden again. I know you gave orders that he wasn't to bother you, but he says it's an emergency." The last word was seasoned with sarcasm.

Boyle sighed. "OK, put him on."

"I'm already on, Boyle. I'm good and sick, or I wouldn't have taken a second of your precious time. You've got to come out here."

"You can't make it to the office? I've got ten patients waiting, and you caught me in the middle of setting a broken arm."

"Sorry, but you're going to have to come out here. Temperature's up to a hundred and two. I'm too groggy to drive." David gave the doctor an imposing list of symptoms.

"Sounds like that two-day virus business that's making the rounds. Can you hold out until four?"

"All right. You'll promise to be here at four sharp?"

"Four it is, Dave," he said tentatively. He cleared his throat. "Are you still worked up about time and all that?"

"No, that's all over now. I was out of my head, I guess, and I'm sorry. I took your advice. It was good advice. Thanks."

"That's good news." Dr. Boyle's voice was hearty now. "I was sorry about the rough treatment I handed you. I should have been more understanding. Look, if you think you could use some psychiatric help, there's a good man over in Troy I could—"

"No, no. I'm all cured. What I need now is some good old-fashioned medicine for a sore throat, a bellyache, and a fever."

"All right. Hold on until four. A couple aspirin will make you a little more comfortable. If things get worse, give me another ring, and I'll come right on out."

"I'll be waiting," said David. "Walk right in. You'll find me bedded down in the studio." He picked up a hypodermic syringe from the table beside him and turned it this way and that, catching the image of the elm logs' quiet blue flame in the fireplace. "I'll be waiting," he said again, and hung up. He had never felt better in his life.

A coiled spring, sheathed in a metal cylinder, was fixed to the top of the syringe in such a way that it pressed against the plunger. David filled the syringe with water. Two wires led from the cylinder, and he connected these to a battery and a switch. He closed the switch and grunted with satisfaction as an electric trigger released the spring, the plunger eased home, and a fine jet of water shot from the needle. Perfect.

He permitted himself the childish pleasure of feeling mysterious, of imagining what an outsider might make of the scene. It was a winter's high noon, darker than autumn twilight, without snow to brighten the overcast countryside. To the outsider, David reflected cheerfully, Nature would be seeming to sympathize with macabre doings in the studio. Desultory rain from a pocket of warmth thousands of feet above earth spattered and froze on the windowsills.

The parcel had arrived from the instrument maker's only an hour before. He had laid out the special hypodermic syringe and the timelock on the table. They looked like jewelry against their black velvet wrappings. They had only to be wired into the circuit lying on the floor and bolted into place. Everything else had been ready for weeks—the straps nailed to the floor, the bars across the two windows and French doors, the pulmotor—all awaiting the implements that David hadn't had the skill to build.

He didn't need Boyle now. Not at first. He could manage the first part himself. Then the doctor would have to help. Ethically, he couldn't refuse once the experiment was under way.

He laid the syringe and battery and switch on the floor, next to the straps nailed to the naked boards. Now for the timelock. It was mounted on a steel plate, and he twisted thick bolts through the plate into waiting holes in the studio's inner door. David gathered the wires leading from the lock's clockwork and connected these, too, to the switch and battery.

Again he closed the switch. Again the plunger of the syringe was driven down. David cocked his head as, simultaneously, the clockwork began to tick. For one minute, then two, then three, nothing happened save for the ticking. Suddenly, the clockwork whirred busily, and the tongue of the lock was drawn back, freeing the door.

He reset the lock and clockwork, expressionlessly filled the syringe with an oily, colorless fluid, and dialed his phone again.

"Western Union."

"Could you give me the correct time?" said David.

"Twelve twenty-nine and a quarter, sir."

"Thank you." David set his watch. Roughly three and a half hours to go. Three and a half hours without character, promise, or purpose. There was nothing more he had to do, nothing that could possibly interest him. He felt like a traveler between trains in a small town on Sunday, without the wish or hope of seeing a familiar face, smoking cigarette after bitter cigarette. He seemed without identity even to himself until he could be on his way. Idly, he tested the bars on a window. They resisted him without bending. They and the timelock could keep out a regiment, if necessary, until he was ready for help to come in.

He yawned. Only ten minutes had passed. He settled into the chair again, slouched down in its deep cushions so that the wings of the chair shut off his view of the sides. His gaze fell naturally upon a disordered corner by the door. At first he attached no importance to the objects jumbled there. With a feeling of mild confusion and surprise, he recognized them—his canvases, his easel, his paints. He found it hard to believe that he had once been a painter—only months before—and that this room, with the bars and the straps and the needles, had once been the birthplace of still lifes, of affectionate portraits, of sentimental landscapes.

For a moment, the room became ugly and frightening, and David wanted to tear down the bars, cover the straps with the warm, red carpet; to tell Boyle not to come, to invite forgotten friends to a rousing party.

The feeling passed. David's expression became shrewd, purposeful again. His old enemy, time, was trying to discourage him, to break him down in the few hours remaining. If he thought about the experiment much longer, he might lose his nerve before the expedition through time could begin.

He would make himself think about other things. In an old series of reflexes, he set up a fresh canvas on the easel and began to lay out smears of pigment on his palette. He was driving himself, and his movements were clumsy, his choice of colors irrational. He couldn't visualize anything on the expanse of white. He dug his palette knife into a mound of black and laid a glistening jet streak across the canvas.

Critics had once remarked upon his meticulous brushwork, the fineness of detail. On even large expanses of color, he had never used anything but chisel brushes no wider than his wedding ring. Now he spread color in gobs from the palette knife. His hands did as they pleased, as though guided by a spirit outside his own. He felt no more than the infantile delight of smearing.

David looked from his painting to his watch with surprise. The three and a half hours had fled. Boyle would be there at any instant. There was the sound of tires digging through the deep gravel outside. The doctor had arrived.

The fleeting terror, the awe of his surroundings, burst upon him again. He was panting. Footsteps crunched in the gravel.

David closed his eyes and told himself again that no expeditions in human history had been more important than the one he was forcing himself to make. He would die for a moment, explore eternity, revive, and tell the living that every instant they lived was as permanent a part of the universe as the largest constellation. In men's minds, time would cease to be a killer.

The doorbell rang. David lay down on the hard floor and tightened the straps about his ankles, his waist, his shoulders, and his left arm. If convulsions were to be a part of dying, these would keep him from injuring himself. With his free right hand, he worked the hypodermic needle into a vein in his left forearm. The fluid in it would stop his heart. The doorbell rang again.

David twisted his head for one last look around the studio. The door was barred by the timelock. The pulmotor and a second hypodermic syringe—identical to the one that Boyle had driven into the drowned farmer's heart—were in plain view, ready. With these, Dr. Boyle would bring him back to life.

David filled his lungs. He cupped the electric switch in his right hand, drove the air from his lungs, and closed the circuit. A faint tickling in his left arm told him that the syringe had emptied itself into his bloodstream. He didn't look at it, but stared instead at the formless painting on the easel at his feet. The timelock on the door was ticking. Any moment now, Boyle would be crossing the living room and shaking the door.

The telephone jangled. Savagely, David grabbed the cord with his free hand and brought the instrument crashing onto the floor beside him. To die to *that* damn noise!

"Dave," said a voice, tinny and weak in the earpiece inches from David's head. "Dave, this is Boyle." Again from the driveway, the sound of wheels in gravel, this time receding, growing fainter—gone.

David hadn't the strength to turn his head toward the phone. He wanted to lick his lips, but his tongue only quivered feebly. He hardly heard the words piping in the earpiece, was unable to attach meaning to them.

"Listen, I'm over in Rexford," the voice was saying. "It's a premature birth, and I've got to get the kid into an incubator. Can you hold out for a couple of hours . . ."

David concentrated his dimming consciousness on the painting. Curious, he was thinking, how curious that only now had he realized what it was he had painted. Now, from a distance, the seeming smears blended into a stunning landscape. He tried to smile, a wan salute to his masterpiece.

He admired the Spring-warmed green slope . . . the pool at its foot, brimming over the boulders of a crude dam . . . the young lovers swirling bare feet in the pool's crest . . . the woman's face was the face of an angel . . . so vivid that her lips seem about to move . . .

Romance

Kurt Vonnegut started publishing short stories in 1950, and the majority of them were published during that decade in the popular "slick" weekly magazines of the time. While his stories of "War" can be read today as expressing universal attitudes, his stories featuring "Romance" and "Women" are reflections of a bygone period, an era that now seems as stunningly retro as the antebellum world of hoopskirts and cavalry charges. A decade younger than Vonnegut, I came of age in the fifties (graduating from Columbia in 1955) and lived in New York as that world's grand finale and metamorphosis was so perceptively dramatized in *Mad Men*. As Calvin Trillin reflects in the documentary *New York in the Fifties* it is difficult now to imagine a national news magazine divided as *Time* was in those days between men as writers, reporters, and editors, and women as researchers. (Their gender determined their job, regardless of ability or talent.) It would also be difficult to conceive of novelist Lynne Sharon Schwartz being turned down for a job in publishing because she was recently married and "you might have a baby."

Both Vonnegut and his wife, Jane Cox, a Phi Beta Kappa graduate of Swarthmore (who made Kurt read *The Brothers Karamazov* on their honeymoon), began their graduate programs at the University of Chicago at the same time. When Jane became pregnant with their first child, it was understood that she would drop out of grad school and devote herself to the role of mother and wife as well as cheerleader of Kurt's writing ("She believed in his writing more than he did" wrote Mark, that first child) and personal secretary who often answered his mail and fulfilled requests of academics and researchers for references to his work—oh, and as an editor of the Swarthmore literary magazine, she was well suited to read and edit Kurt's stories, suggesting ideas and studying the markets with him to see what the "slicks" were looking for, and of course type up all his manuscripts (it came with the job description of "writer's wife" at the time). On top of all this, she was mother not only to their own three children but three sons of Kurt's sister Alice who were suddenly orphaned when her husband was killed in a commuter train crash the day before she died of cancer.

One anecdote of my own many-splendored chauvinism of the era (and women's acceptance of it) hit me several decades later when a former girlfriend, a Smith graduate who had typed the entire manuscript of my first book (I gave her a forty-dollar portable radio as a reward), sent me a book that she had written and published. I wrote her congratulations and a question that I asked myself as well: "Why didn't the boys of the fifties realize that the girls of the fifties wanted to write books of their own, instead of just typing up the books of the boys?"

The editors of the popular magazines Kurt wrote his stories for were all men (as in fact were many of the editors of the women's magazines as well) but he didn't need to make a special effort to comply with their views on men and women, for his own were largely the same as almost any male person's of his time. His stories of romance feature heroines who are almost all attractive: "beautiful . . . [with] pretty blue eyes" ("A Night for Love"), "prettiest little girl he'd ever seen . . . a flawless little trinket" ("FUBAR"), "a pretty, confident, twenty-year-old girl" ("Girl Pool"), "she was eighteen, petal-fresh" ("Miss Snow, You're Fired"), "an ex-model and a well-known figure skater" ("Paris, France").

The non-beauties in our "Romance" category are dealt a poor hand, perhaps to make the beauties even more desirable. The boss of the "Girl Pool" ("a pool of girls, teeming, warm, and deep") is Miss Nancy Hostetter, "a great elk of a woman" with a "craggy, loveless, humorless face." The readers would not have been surprised that she was unmarried. They were supposed to be surprised when it turned out in the end that she was just as warmhearted and kind as the "confident, twenty-year-old girl." That was the O. Henry kind of ending with a surprise twist—what Dave Eggers calls Vonnegut's "mousetrap stories," a story that "moves the reader along, through the complex (but not too complex) machinery of the story, until the end, when the cage is sprung and the reader is trapped." The readers of the popular magazine stories were happy to be trapped, to be surprised but pleased by the unexpected but plausible finale. This of course pleased the editors as well, whose job was to lure potential readers to buy their magazine.

Of the two "Romance" stories that seem to me most credible and charming, both have only two characters—a man and a woman, and neither woman is described as "beautiful," "petal fresh," or "a flawless little trinket." The appeal of these stories for me is based not on contemporary political correctness, but on the everyday, simple, familiar situations they portray, taking place over the course of a few hours. Both still employ the characteristic Vonnegut mousetrap twist at the end, but in these stories the twist at the end seems to be a result that flows naturally from the behavior of the characters.

One of these stories, "City," has never been published. A letter to Kurt from agent Kenneth Littauer reported, "THE CITY has come back from *American Magazine* and gone to *Today's Woman*." That seemed to be the end of it. I imagine a young romance heroine seen by a man as "a regular little butterball" might not sit well with the 1950 version of Today's Woman. The story lacks the glamour that the editors of popular magazines required at the time, since it emphasizes the "human-ness of the characters," who find flaws in both themselves and the person they are checking out.

The young man and the young woman think of themselves as a "boy" and a "girl," as young people (even in sophisticated New York) did in those days, including me and my friends. They are probably working at their first jobs in the big city, and not very happy with their plight at the end of the workday. They are waiting for a bus as they look critically at themselves and then in furtive glances at each other. The boy has a cinder in his "smarting left eye" as he stares at his "reddened reflection in the mirror face of the penny scales." He dabs at it with the corner of his handkerchief and thinks, "Filthy place to live, soot blowing in your eye every way you turn."

The girl is staring at her reflection in a drugstore window and "wonder[s] if sitting at a desk all day [isn't] making her wide at the hips, and whether a string of pearls might not make her blouse look less severe."

The boy's image of her confirms her own. He sees her as "a plump little mouse" whose blouse "makes her look like a school marm." When she gets a load of *him*, her appraisal is not much better: "Men with round faces shouldn't wear bow ties, she thought irritably. Makes their faces look wide and fat."

As they wait for their respective buses to come along, their appraisals of one another don't get any less critical, but a little sympathy creeps in to their critiques. He thinks, "She's getting enough to eat, all right. Regular little butterball . . . Looks tired, though. Office is no place for a girl like that. Bet the wolves give her a bad time where she works." She is musing that "men are so helpless. Look at that collar —a disgrace. Somebody ought to turn it for him."

Their eyes meet for an instant and she composes a letter to her mother in her mind, telling her how hard it is to make friends here, then slipping into a fantasy that "I met a very nice boy this evening. We went to a show and had sodas afterwards. It was just like back home." At the same time, he imagines asking her to the theater, "his heart pounding wildly."

Each tries to think of ruses for meeting, but neither is brave enough to take action. She thinks she might pretend she's lost, but she can't risk it: "I'd die if he thought I was just another cheap—." He doesn't want her to think "I'm just another fresh guy, like all the rest," and berates himself for having "no guts, no guts." A bus pulls up to the curb and the girl impulsively gets on it, though it's not the one she's been waiting for, and hopes he'll follow. The door closes but the boy realizes she's on that bus—bangs on the door, gets on, and takes the vacant seat beside her. They get up the nerve to make small talk, and admit the bus is not the one that each usually takes to get home.

> "Whose bus is it?" she asks.
> "Ours," he suggested.
> "Okay," she said . . . "Where is it taking us?"

"I don't know," he said. "We'll ride it together and find out." . . .
The gloom of the city was suddenly washed away. There was all
the clean, warm world, and the brightness of the future.

I know, I know, it's a "fifties story," featuring two naïve, unworldly young people, who seem like characters excavated from the Pleistocene age in our era of the popular *Girls* series on HBO. If readers want to explore literary or historical archeology, "City" is true to that time and place, told with a sure touch, and a grace that raises simplicity to the level of art.

Here is what Kurt felt about the other story that I think holds up well today and portrays a credible young man and woman: in his preface to *Welcome to the Monkey House*, he called it "a sickeningly slick love story from the *Ladies' Home Journal* God help us, entitled by them 'The Long Walk to Forever.'" He wrote that he included it in this first short story collection "in honor of the marriage that worked" (his first, to Jane Cox, his high school sweetheart) and with tongue firmly in cheek, he adds, "The title I gave it, I think, was 'Hell to Get Along With,'" which neither Kurt nor his agents would have titled a love story sent to a ladies' magazine in the 1950s (it was published in 1960). He goes on to excoriate himself for what he regarded in 1968 as the sentimentality of a story that "describes an afternoon I spent with my wife-to-be. Shame, shame, to have lived scenes from a woman's magazine."

He said in the preface to *Monkey House*, "My wife is still beautiful. I never knew a writer's wife who wasn't beautiful." Neither did I, including my own. (In the fifties, women who wanted to be writers often married writers, and became their editors, agents, and homemakers in the bargain—if you can call it a bargain. It seems comparable to some women of that era—stretching into the sixties—who wanted to be Protestant ministers becoming church organists. "I was told that was the highest position in the church I could hope for," a former church organist told me when she started divinity school in 1981.

The only characters in "Long Walk to Forever" are a boy and a girl (as they would have thought of themselves during the WWII era when the story takes place) and neither is described physically. The boy (Newt), a soldier, and the girl (Catharine) are both twenty, and all we know about them is that they have known each other for a long time as friends, but haven't seen one another since the boy enlisted in the army.

I know from talking to Kurt's lifelong friend Victor Jose (they met as students at Shortridge High School and both were in the O.W.L. Club) that the story was very close to Kurt's own experience. He met his wife Jane in kindergarten and dated her in high school. When he was home on leave in 1944 he heard that Jane was engaged to a boyfriend from Swarthmore, and "Kurt appeared on the scene just in time" to persuade her to break off that relationship and wait for him till he came home from the war.

In the short story, Catharine is carrying a magazine devoted to brides when she opens the door and is surprised to see Newt. "He was a private first class in the Artillery. His uniform was rumpled. His shoes were dusty. He needed a shave."

Catharine tells him she's getting married.

"I know," he says. "Let's go for a walk."

As they walk, he explains that he can't come to her wedding, which is next week, because he'll be in the brig when he goes back and reports himself AWOL. He will have to spend thirty days in the stockade.

She wonders why he's come back and he says it's to see her.

He wants to see her because he loves her.

"What a crazy time to tell me you love me," she says. "You never talked that way before."

She is angry and rattled and wants to stop, but he keeps her walking. "One foot in front of the other—through leaves, over bridges—." Whenever she wants to stop he convinces her to keep walking. Finally they sit down under a tree—she picks a spot far away from him, and watches him go to sleep. As it grows later, she wakes him. He asks her to marry him and she says no, and he starts walking away.

Catharine watches him "grow smaller in the long perspective of shadows and trees, knew that if he stopped and turned now, if he called to her, she would run to him. She would have no choice."

He does stop and turn around and call to her. She runs to him.

Through the spare dialogue they exchange, he persuades her to keep walking and she protests along the way but keeps walking. Without having their backgrounds or personalities filled in, without knowing many "facts" about them, we come to feel we know them. We are rooting for her not to marry Henry Stewart Chasens but for Newt and Catharine to come together at the end, as they do.

The story has the neat, inevitable satisfaction of a Hemingway story built on dialogue, but it's not as clipped, not as hard-edged. Neither does it seem sentimental in its language—no one makes flowery speeches, or melodramatic protests. It has a flow, a natural rhythm, like breathing, like walking, "one foot in front of the other—through leaves, over bridges—."

Vonnegut had mastered the formula of the "slick magazine" story of romance, yet forsaking its fundamental ingredients such as beautiful young women and bedazzled men, he broke out of the bonds of the accepted rules, and slipped in something original and unique that was true to life (*his* life). In his self-flogging for writing the story (but including it in his first story collection despite his own protests), maybe he was ashamed of revealing to the world his own deep feelings of love (which were felt by some as an unmanly admission in those times). Maybe that's why he spoke of having such difficulty writing about women characters.

After reading that story again, I felt haunted by something else he had written, something in that same vein and purity of style that I couldn't quite remember, and then it hit me. In his novel *Timequake*, much of it a nonfiction musing about his own life, there is a passage that describes the last talk he had with his former wife Jane, on the telephone, two weeks before she died. She was in Washington, DC, married to Adam Yarmolinksy, and Kurt was in Manhattan, married to Jill Krementz. He couldn't remember who initiated the call—it could have been either of them—but "the point of the call was to say good-bye."

Our last conversation was intimate. Jane asked me, as though I knew, what would determine the exact moment of her death. She may have felt like a character in a book by me. In a sense she was. During our twenty-two years of marriage, I had decided where we were going next, to Chicago, to Schenectady, to Cape Cod. It was my work that determined what we did next. She never had a job. Raising six kids was enough for her.

I told her on the telephone that a sunburned, raffish, bored but not unhappy ten-year-old boy, whom we did not know, would be standing on the gravel slope of the boat-launching ramp at the foot of Scudder's Lane. He would gaze out at nothing in particular, birds, boats, or whatever, in the harbor of Barnstable, Cape Cod.

At the head of Scudder's Lane, on Route 6A, one-tenth of a mile from the boat-launching ramp, is the big old house where we cared for our son and two daughters and three sons of my sister's until they were grownups. Our daughter Edith and her builder husband, John Squibb, and their small sons, Will and Buck, live there now.

I told Jane that this boy, with nothing better to do, would pick up a stone, as boys will. He would arc it over the harbor. When the stone hit the water, she would die.

The "Long Walk" was over.

—DW

Who Am I This Time?

THE NORTH CRAWFORD Mask and Wig Club, an amateur theatrical society I belong to, voted to do Tennessee Williams's *A Streetcar Named Desire* for the spring play. Doris Sawyer, who always directs, said she couldn't direct this time because her mother was so sick. And she said the club ought to develop some other directors anyway, because she couldn't live forever, even though she'd made it safely to seventy-four.

So I got stuck with the directing job, even though the only thing I'd ever directed before was the installation of combination aluminum storm windows and screens I'd sold. That's what I am, a salesman of storm windows and doors, and here and there a bathtub enclosure. As far as acting goes, the highest rank I ever held on stage was either butler or policeman, whichever's higher.

I made a lot of conditions before I took the directing job, and the biggest one was that Harry Nash, the only real actor the club has, had to take the Marlon Brando part in the play. To give you an idea of how versatile Harry is, inside of one year he was Captain Queeg in *The Caine Mutiny Court Martial*, then Abe Lincoln in *Abe Lincoln in Illinois* and then the young architect in *The Moon Is Blue*. The year after that, Harry Nash was Henry the Eighth in *Anne of the Thousand Days* and Doc in *Come Back Little Sheba*, and I was after him for Marlon Brando in *A Streetcar Named Desire*. Harry wasn't at the meeting to say whether he'd take the part or not. He never came to meetings. He was too shy. He didn't stay away from meetings because he had something else to do. He wasn't married, didn't go out with women—didn't have any close men friends either. He stayed away from all kinds of gatherings because he never could think of anything to say or do without a script.

So I had to go down to Miller's Hardware Store, where Harry was a clerk, the next day and ask him if he'd take the part. I stopped off at the telephone company to complain about a bill I'd gotten for a call to Honolulu, I'd never called Honolulu in my life.

And there was this beautiful girl I'd never seen before behind the counter at the phone company, and she explained that the company had put in an automatic billing machine and that the machine didn't have all the bugs out of it yet. It made mistakes. "Not only did I not call Honolulu," I told her, "I don't think anybody in North Crawford ever has or will."

So she took the charge off the bill, and I asked her if she was from around North Crawford. She said no. She said she just came with the new billing machine to teach local girls how to take care of it. After that, she said, she would go with some other machine to someplace else. "Well," I said, "as long as people have to come along with the machines, I guess we're all right."

"What?" she said.

"When machines start delivering themselves," I said, "I guess that's when the people better start really worrying."

"Oh," she said. She didn't seem very interested in that subject, and I wondered if she was interested in anything. She seemed kind of numb, almost a machine herself, an automatic phone-company politeness machine.

"How long will you be in town here?" I asked her.

"I stay in each town eight weeks, sir," she said. She had pretty blue eyes, but there sure wasn't much hope or curiosity in them. She told me she had been going from town to town like that for two years, always a stranger.

And I got it in my head that she might make a good Stella for the play. Stella was the wife of the Marlon Brando character, the wife of the character I wanted Harry Nash to play. So I told her where and when we were going to hold tryouts, and said the club would be very happy if she'd come.

She looked surprised, and she warmed up a little. "You know," she said, "that's the first time anybody ever asked me to participate in any community thing."

"Well," I said, "there isn't any other way to get to know a lot of nice people faster than to be in a play with 'em."

She said her name was Helene Shaw. She said she might just surprise me—and herself. She said she just might come.

⊙ ⊙ ⊙

You would think that North Crawford would be fed up with Harry Nash in plays after all the plays he'd been in. But the fact was that North Crawford probably could have gone on enjoying Harry forever, because he was never Harry on stage. When the maroon curtain went up on the stage in the gymnasium of the Consolidated Junior-Senior High School, Harry, body and soul, was exactly what the script and the director told him to be.

Somebody said one time that Harry ought to go to a psychiatrist so he could be something important and colorful in real life, too—so he could get married anyway, and maybe get a better job than just clerking in Miller's Hardware Store for fifty dollars a week. But I don't know what a psychiatrist could have turned up about him that the town didn't already know. The trouble with Harry was he'd been left on the doorstep of the Unitarian Church when he was a baby, and he never did find out who his parents were.

When I told him there in Miller's that I'd been appointed director, that I wanted him in my play, he said what he always said to anybody who asked him to be in a play—and it was kind of sad, if you think about it.

"Who am I this time?" he said.

So I held the tryouts where they're always held—in the meeting room on the second floor of the North Crawford Public Library. Doris Sawyer, the woman who usually directs, came to give me the benefit of all her experience. The two of us sat in state upstairs, while the people who wanted parts waited below. We called them upstairs one by one.

Harry Nash came to the tryouts, even though it was a waste of time. I guess he wanted to get that little bit more acting in.

For Harry's pleasure, and our pleasure, too, we had him read from the scene where he beats up his wife. It was a play in itself, the way Harry did it, and Tennessee Williams hadn't written it all either. Tennessee Williams didn't write the part, for instance, where Harry, who weighs about one hundred forty-five, who's about five feet eight inches tall, added fifty pounds to his weight and four inches to his height by just picking up a playbook. He had a short little double-breasted bellows-back grade-school graduation suit coat on and a dinky little red tie with a horsehead on it. He took off the coat and tie, opened his collar, then turned his back to Doris and me, getting up steam for the part. There was a great big rip in the back of his shirt, and it looked like a fairly new shirt too. He'd ripped it on purpose, so he could be that much more like Marlon Brando, right from the first.

When he faced us again, he was huge and handsome and conceited and cruel. Doris read the part of Stella, the wife, and Harry bullied that old, old lady into believing that she was a sweet, pregnant girl married to a sexy gorilla who was going to beat her brains out. She had me believing it too. And I read the lines of Blanche, her sister in the play, and darned if Harry didn't scare me into feeling like a drunk and faded Southern belle.

And then, while Doris and I were getting over our emotional experiences, like people coming out from under ether, Harry put down the playbook, put on his coat and tie, and turned into the pale hardware-store clerk again.

"Was—was that all right?" he said, and he seemed pretty sure he wouldn't get the part.

"Well," I said, "for a first reading, that wasn't too bad."

"Is there a chance I'll get the part?" he said. I don't know why he always had to pretend there was some doubt about his getting a part, but he did.

"I think we can safely say we're leaning powerfully in your direction," I told him.

He was very pleased. "Thanks! Thanks a lot!" he said, and he shook my hand.

"Is there a pretty new girl downstairs?" I said, meaning Helene Shaw.

"I didn't notice," said Harry.

It turned out that Helene Shaw *had* come for the tryouts, and Doris and I had our hearts broken. We thought the North Crawford Mask and Wig Club was finally going to put a really good-looking, really young girl on stage, instead of one of the beat-up forty-year-old women we generally have to palm off as girls.

But Helene Shaw couldn't act for sour apples. No matter what we gave her to read, she was the same girl with the same smile for anybody who had a complaint about his phone bill.

Doris tried to coach her some, to make her understand that Stella in the play was a very passionate girl who loved a gorilla because she needed a gorilla. But Helene just read the lines the same way again. I don't think a volcano could have stirred her up enough to say, "Oo."

"Dear," said Doris, "I'm going to ask you a personal question."

"All right," said Helene.

"Have you ever been in love?" said Doris. "The reason I ask," she said, "remembering some old love might help you put more warmth in your acting."

Helene frowned and thought hard. "Well," she said, "I travel a lot, you know. And practically all the men in the different companies I visit are married and I never stay anyplace long enough to know many people who aren't."

"What about school?" said Doris. "What about puppy love and all the other kinds of love in school?"

So Helene thought hard about that, and then she said, "Even in school I was always moving around a lot. My father was a construction worker, following jobs around, so I was always saying hello or good-bye to someplace, without anything in between."

"Um," said Doris.

"Would movie stars count?" said Helene. "I don't mean in real life. I never knew any. I just mean up on the screen."

Doris looked at me and rolled her eyes. "I guess that's love of a kind," she said.

And then Helene got a little enthusiastic. "I used to sit through movies over and over again," she said, "and pretend I was married to whoever the man movie star was. They were the only people who came with us. No matter where we moved, movie stars were there."

"Uh huh," said Doris.

"Well, thank you, Miss Shaw," I said. "You go downstairs and wait with the rest. We'll let you know."

So we tried to find another Stella. And there just wasn't one, not one woman in the club with the dew still on her. "All we've got are Blanches," I said, meaning all we had were faded women who could play the part of Blanche, Stella's faded sister. "That's life, I guess—twenty Blanches to one Stella."

"And when you find a Stella," said Doris, "it turns out she doesn't know what love is."

Doris and I decided there was one last thing we could try. We could get Harry

Nash to play a scene along with Helene. "He just might make her bubble the least little bit," I said.

"That girl hasn't got a bubble in her," said Doris.

So we called down the stairs for Helene to come back on up, and we told somebody to go find Harry. Harry never sat with the rest of the people at tryouts—or at rehearsals either.

The minute he didn't have a part to play, he'd disappear into some hiding place where he could hear people call him, but where he couldn't be seen. At tryouts in the library he generally hid in the reference room, passing the time looking at flags of different countries in the front of the dictionary.

Helene came back upstairs, and we were very sorry and surprised to see that she'd been crying.

"Oh, dear," said Doris. "Oh, my—now what on earth's the trouble, dear?"

"I was terrible, wasn't I?" said Helene, hanging her head.

Doris said the only thing anybody can say in an amateur theatrical society when somebody cries. She said, "Why, no dear—you were marvelous."

"No, I wasn't," said Helene. "I'm a walking icebox, and I know it."

"Nobody could look at you and say that," said Doris.

"When they get to know me, they can say it," said Helene. "When people get to know me, that's what they *do* say." Her tears got worse. "I don't want to be the way I am," she said. "I just can't help it, living the way I've lived all my life. The only experiences I've had have been in crazy dreams of movie stars. When I meet somebody nice in real life, I feel as though I were in some kind of big bottle, as though I couldn't touch that person, no matter how hard I tried." And Helene pushed on air as though it were a big bottle all around her.

"You ask me if I've ever been in love," she said to Doris. "No—but I want to be. I know what this play's about. I know what Stella's supposed to feel and why she feels it. I—I—I—" she said, and her tears wouldn't let her go on.

"You what, dear?" said Doris gently.

"I—" said Helene, and she pushed on the imaginary bottle again. "I just don't know how to begin," she said.

There was heavy clumping on the library stairs. It sounded like a deep-sea diver coming upstairs in his lead shoes. It was Harry Nash, turning himself into Marlon Brando. In he came, practically dragging his knuckles on the floor. And he was so much in character that the sight of a weeping woman made him sneer.

"Harry," I said, "I'd like you to meet Helene Shaw. Helene—this is Harry Nash. If you get the part of Stella, he'll be your husband in the play." Harry didn't offer to shake hands. He put his hands in his pockets, and he hunched over, and he looked her up and down, gave her looks that left her naked. Her tears stopped right then and there.

"I wonder if you two would play the fight scene," I said, "and then the reunion scene right after it."

"Sure," said Harry, his eyes still on her. Those eyes burned up clothes faster than she could put them on. "Sure," he said, "if Stell's game."

"What?" said Helene. She'd turned the color of cranberry juice.

"Stell—Stella," said Harry. "That's you. Stell's my wife."

I handed the two of them playbooks. Harry snatched his from me without a word of thanks. Helene's hands weren't working very well, and I had to kind of mold them around the book.

"I'll want something I can throw," said Harry.

"What?" I said.

"There's one place where I throw a radio out a window," said Harry. "What can I throw?"

So I said an iron paperweight was the radio, and I opened the window wide. Helene Shaw looked scared to death.

"Where you want us to start?" said Harry, and he rolled his shoulders like a prize-fighter warming up.

"Start a few lines back from where you throw the radio out the window," I said.

"O.K., O.K.," said Harry, warming up, warming up. He scanned the stage directions. "Let's see," he said, "after I throw the radio, she runs off stage, and I chase her, and I sock her one."

"Right," I said.

"O.K., baby," Harry said to Helene, his eyelids drooping.

What was about to happen was wilder than the chariot race in *Ben Hur*. "On your mark," said Harry. "Get ready, baby. Go!"

When the scene was over, Helene Shaw was as hot as a hod carrier, as limp as an eel. She sat down with her mouth open and her head hanging to one side. She wasn't in any bottle any more. There wasn't any bottle to hold her up and keep her safe and clean. The bottle was gone.

"Do I get the part or don't I?" Harry snarled at me.

"You'll do," I said.

"You said a mouthful!" he said. "I'll be going now . . . See you around, Stella," he said to Helene, and he left. He slammed the door behind him.

"Helene?" I said. "Miss Shaw?"

"Mf?" she said.

"The part of Stella is yours," I said. "You were great!"

"I was?" she said.

"I had no idea you had that much fire in you, dear," Doris said to her.

"Fire?" said Helene. She didn't know if she was afoot or on horseback.

"Skyrockets! Pinwheels! Roman candles!" said Doris.

"Mf," said Helene. And that was all she said. She looked as though she were going to sit in the chair with her mouth open forever.

"Stella," I said.

"Huh?" she said.

"You have my permission to go."

So we started having rehearsals four nights a week on the stage of the Consolidated School. And Harry and Helene set such a pace that everybody in the production was half crazy with excitement and exhaustion before we'd rehearsed four times. Usually a director has to beg people to learn their lines, but I had no such trouble. Harry and Helene were working so well together that everybody else in the cast regarded it as a duty and an honor and a pleasure to support them.

I was certainly lucky—or thought I was. Things were going so well, so hot and heavy, so early in the game that I had to say to Harry and Helene after one love scene, "Hold a little something back for the actual performance, would you please? You'll burn yourselves out."

I said that at the fourth or fifth rehearsal, and Lydia Miller, who was playing Blanche, the faded sister, was sitting next to me in the audience. In real life, she's the wife of Verne Miller. Verne owns Miller's Hardware Store. Verne was Harry's boss.

"Lydia," I said to her, "have we got a play or have we got a play?"

"Yes," she said, "you've got a play, all right." She made it sound as though I'd committed some kind of crime, done something just terrible. "You should be very proud of yourself."

"What do you mean by that?" I said.

Before Lydia could answer, Harry yelled at me from the stage, asked if I was through with him, asked if he could go home. I told him he could and, still Marlon Brando, he left, kicking furniture out of his way and slamming doors. Helene was left all alone on the stage, sitting on a couch with the same gaga look she'd had after the tryouts. That girl was drained.

I turned to Lydia again and I said, "Well—until now, I thought I had every reason to be happy and proud. Is there something going on I don't know about?"

"Do you know that girl's in love with Harry?" said Lydia.

"In the play?" I said.

"What play?" said Lydia. "There isn't any play going on now, and look at her up there." She gave a sad cackle. "You aren't directing this play."

"Who is?" I said.

"Mother Nature at her worst," said Lydia. "And think what it's going to do to that girl when she discovers what Harry really is." She corrected herself. "What Harry really isn't," she said.

I didn't do anything about it, because I didn't figure it was any of my business. I heard Lydia try to do something about it, but she didn't get very far.

"You know," Lydia said to Helene one night, "I once played Ann Rutledge, and Harry was Abraham Lincoln."

Helene clapped her hands. "That must have been heaven!" she said.

"It was, in a way," said Lydia. "Sometimes I'd get so worked up, I'd love Harry the way I'd love Abraham Lincoln. I'd have to come back to earth and remind myself that he wasn't ever going to free the slaves, that he was just a clerk in my husband's hardware store."

"He's the most marvelous man I ever met," said Helene.

"Of course, one thing you have to get set for, when you're in a play with Harry," said Lydia, "is what happens after the last performance."

"What are you talking about?" said Helene.

"Once the show's over," said Lydia, "whatever you thought Harry was just evaporates into thin air."

"I don't believe it," said Helene.

"I admit it's hard to believe," said Lydia.

Then Helene got a little sore. "Anyway, why tell me about it?" she said. "Even if it is true, what do I care?"

"I—I don't know," said Lydia, backing away. "I—I just thought you might find it interesting."

"Well, I don't," said Helene.

And Lydia slunk away, feeling about as frowzy and unloved as she was supposed to feel in the play. After that nobody said anything more to Helene to warn her about Harry, not even when word got around that she'd told the telephone company that she didn't want to be moved around anymore, that she wanted to stay in North Crawford.

So the time finally came to put on the play. We ran it for three nights—Thursday, Friday, and Saturday—and we murdered those audiences. They believed every word that was said on stage, and when the maroon curtain came down they were ready to go to the nut house along with Blanche, the faded sister.

On Thursday night the other girls at the telephone company sent Helene a dozen red roses. When Helene and Harry were taking a curtain call together, I passed the roses over the footlights to her. She came forward for them, took one rose from the bouquet to give to Harry. But when she turned to give Harry the rose in front of everybody, Harry was gone. The curtain came down on that extra little scene—that girl offering a rose to nothing and nobody.

I went backstage, and I found her still holding that one rose. She'd put the rest of the bouquet aside. There were tears in her eyes. "What did I do wrong?" she said to me. "Did I insult him some way?"

"No," I said. "He always does that after a performance. The minute it's over, he clears out as fast as he can."

"And tomorrow he'll disappear again?"

"Without even taking off his makeup."

"And Saturday?" she said. "He'll stay for the cast party on Saturday, won't he?"

"Harry never goes to parties," I said. "When the curtain comes down on Saturday, that's the last anybody will see of him till he goes to work on Monday."

"How sad," she said.

Helene's performance on Friday night wasn't nearly so good as Thursday's. She seemed to be thinking about other things. She watched Harry take off after curtain call. She didn't say a word.

On Saturday she put on the best performance yet. Ordinarily it was Harry who set the pace. But on Saturday Harry had to work to keep up with Helene.

When the curtain came down on the final curtain call, Harry wanted to get away, but he couldn't. Helene wouldn't let go his hand. The rest of the cast and the stage crew and a lot of well-wishers from the audience were all standing around Harry and Helene, and Harry was trying to get his hand back.

"Well," he said, "I've got to go."

"Where?" she said.

"Oh," he said, "home."

"Won't you please take me to the cast party?" she said.

He got very red. "I'm afraid I'm not much on parties," he said. All the Marlon Brando in him was gone. He was tongue-tied, he was scared, he was shy—he was everything Harry was famous for being between plays.

"All right," she said. "I'll let you go—if you promise me one thing."

"What's that?" he said, and I thought he would jump out a window if she let go of him then.

"I want you to promise to stay here until I get you your present," she said.

"Present?" he said, getting even more panicky.

"Promise?" she said.

He promised. It was the only way he could get his hand back. And he stood there miserably while Helene went down to the ladies' dressing room for the present. While he waited, a lot of people congratulated him on being such a fine actor. But congratulations never made him happy. He just wanted to get away.

Helene came back with the present. It turned out to be a little blue book with a big red ribbon for a place marker. It was a copy of *Romeo and Juliet*. Harry was very embarrassed. It was all he could do to say "Thank you."

"The marker marks my favorite scene," said Helene.

"Um," said Harry.

"Don't you want to see what my favorite scene is?" she said.

So Harry had to open the book to the red ribbon.

Helene got close to him, and read a line of Juliet's. "'How cam'st thou hither, tell me, and wherefore?'" she read. "'The orchard walls are high and hard to climb, and the place death, considering who thou art, if any of my kinsmen find thee here.'" She pointed to the next line. "Now, look what Romeo says," she said.

"Um," said Harry.

"Read what Romeo says," said Helene.

Harry cleared his throat. He didn't want to read the line, but he had to. "'With love's light wings did I o'erperch these walls,'" he read out loud in his everyday voice. But then a change came over him. " 'For stony limits cannot hold love out,'" he read, and he straightened up, and eight years dropped away from him, and he was brave and gay. "'And what love can do, that dares love attempt,'" he read, "'therefore thy kinsmen are no let to me.'"

"'If they do see thee they will murther thee,'" said Helene, and she started him walking toward the wings.

"'Alack!'" said Harry, "'there lies more peril in thine eye than twenty of their swords.'" Helene led him toward the backstage exit. "'Look thou but sweet,'" said Harry, "'and I am proof against their enmity.'"

"'I would not for the world they saw thee here,'" said Helene, and that was the last we heard. The two of them were out the door and gone.

They never did show up at the cast party. One week later they were married.

They seem very happy, although they're kind of strange from time to time, depending on which play they're reading to each other at the time.

I dropped into the phone company office the other day, on account of the billing machine was making dumb mistakes again. I asked her what plays she and Harry'd been reading lately.

"In the past week," she said, "I've been married to Othello, been loved by Faust and been kidnaped by Paris. Wouldn't you say I was the luckiest girl in town?"

I said I thought so, and I told her most of the women in town thought so too.

"They had their chance," she said.

"Most of 'em couldn't stand the excitement," I said. And I told her I'd been asked to direct another play. I asked if she and Harry would be available for the cast. She gave me a big smile and said, "Who are we this time?"

Long Walk to Forever

THEY HAD GROWN UP next door to each other, on the fringe of a city, near fields and woods and orchards, within sight of a lovely bell tower that belonged to a school for the blind.

Now they were twenty, had not seen each other for nearly a year. There had always been playful, comfortable warmth between them, but never any talk of love.

His name was Newt. Her name was Catharine. In the early afternoon, Newt knocked on Catharine's front door.

Catharine came to the door. She was carrying a fat, glossy magazine she had been reading. The magazine was devoted entirely to brides. "Newt!" she said. She was surprised to see him.

"Could you come for a walk?" he said. He was a shy person, even with Catharine. He covered his shyness by speaking absently, as though what really concerned him were far away—as though he were a secret agent pausing briefly on a mission between beautiful, distant, and sinister points. This manner of speaking had always been Newt's style, even in matters that concerned him desperately.

"A walk?" said Catharine.

"One foot in front of the other," said Newt, "through leaves, over bridges—"

"I had no idea you were in town," she said.

"Just this minute got in," he said.

"Still in the Army, I see," she said.

"Seven more months to go," he said. He was a private first class in the Artillery. His uniform was rumpled. His shoes were dusty. He needed a shave. He held out his hand for the magazine. "Let's see the pretty book," he said.

She gave it to him. "I'm getting married, Newt," she said.

"I know," he said. "Let's go for a walk."

"I'm awfully busy, Newt," she said. "The wedding is only a week away."

"If we go for a walk," he said, "it will make you rosy. It will make you a rosy bride." He turned the pages of the magazine. "A rosy bride like her—like her—like her," he said, showing her rosy brides.

Catharine turned rosy, thinking about rosy brides.

"That will be my present to Henry Stewart Chasens," said Newt. "By taking you for a walk, I'll be giving him a rosy bride."

"You know his name?" said Catharine.

"Mother wrote," he said. "From Pittsburgh?"

"Yes," she said. "You'd like him."

"Maybe," he said.

"Can—can you come to the wedding, Newt?" she said.

"That I doubt," he said.

"Your furlough isn't for long enough?" she said.

"Furlough?" said Newt. He was studying a two-page ad for flat silver. "I'm not on furlough," he said.

"Oh?" she said.

"I'm what they call A.W.O.L.," said Newt.

"Oh, Newt! You're not!" she said.

"Sure I am," he said, still looking at the magazine.

"Why, Newt?" she said.

"I had to find out what your silver pattern is," he said. He read names of silver patterns from the magazine. "Albemarle? Heather?" he said. "Legend? Rambler Rose?" He looked up, smiled. "I plan to give you and your husband a spoon," he said.

"Newt, Newt—tell me really," she said.

"I want to go for a walk," he said.

She wrung her hands in sisterly anguish. "Oh, Newt—you're fooling me about being A.W.O.L.," she said.

Newt imitated a police siren softly, raised his eyebrows.

"Where—where from?" she said.

"Fort Bragg," he said.

"North Carolina?" she said.

"That's right," he said. "Near Fayetteville—where Scarlett O'Hara went to school."

"How did you get here, Newt?" she said.

He raised his thumb, jerked it in a hitchhike gesture. "Two days," he said.

"Does your mother know?" she said.

"I didn't come to see my mother," he told her.

"Who did you come to see?" she said.

"You," he said.

"Why me?" she said.

"Because I love you," he said. "Now can we take a walk?" he said. "One foot in front of the other—through leaves, over bridges—"

□ □ □

They were taking the walk now, were in a woods with a brown-leaf floor.

Catharine was angry and rattled, close to tears. "Newt," she said, "this is absolutely crazy."

"How so?" said Newt.

"What a crazy time to tell me you love me," she said. "You never talked that way before." She stopped walking.

"Let's keep walking," he said.

"No," she said. "So far, no farther. I shouldn't have come out with you at all," she said.

"You did," he said.

"To get you out of the house," she said. "If somebody walked in and heard you talking to me that way, a week before the wedding—"

"What would they think?" he said.

"They'd think you were crazy," she said.

"Why?" he said.

Catharine took a deep breath, made a speech. "Let me say that I'm deeply honored by this crazy thing you've done," she said. "I can't believe you're really A.W.O.L., but maybe you are. I can't believe you really love me, but maybe you do. But—"

"I do," said Newt.

"Well, I'm deeply honored," said Catharine, "and I'm very fond of you as a friend, Newt, extremely fond—but it's just too late." She took a step away from him. "You've never even kissed me," she said, and she protected herself with her hands. "I don't mean you should do it now. I just mean this is all so unexpected. I haven't got the remotest idea of how to respond."

"Just walk some more," he said. "Have a nice time."

They started walking again.

"How did you expect me to react?" she said.

"How would I know what to expect?" he said. "I've never done anything like this before."

"Did you think I would throw myself into your arms?" she said.

"Maybe," he said.

"I'm sorry to disappoint you," she said.

"I'm not disappointed," he said. "I wasn't counting on it. This is very nice, just walking."

Catharine stopped again. "You know what happens next?" she said.

"Nope," he said.

"We shake hands," she said. "We shake hands and part friends," she said. "That's what happens next."

Newt nodded. "All right," he said. "Remember me from time to time. Remember how much I loved you."

Involuntarily, Catharine burst into tears. She turned her back to Newt, looked into the infinite colonnade of the woods.

"What does that mean?" said Newt.

"Rage!" said Catharine. She clenched her hands. "You have no right—"

"I had to find out," he said.

"If I'd loved you," she said, "I would have let you know before now."

"You would?" he said.

"Yes," she said. She faced him, looked up at him, her face quite red. "You would have known," she said.

"How?" he said.

"You would have seen it," she said. "Women aren't very clever at hiding it."

Newt looked closely at Catharine's face now. To her consternation, she realized that what she had said was true, that a woman couldn't hide love.

Newt was seeing love now.

And he did what he had to do. He kissed her.

◙ ◙ ◙

"You're hell to get along with!" she said when Newt let her go.

"I am?" said Newt.

"You shouldn't have done that," she said.

"You didn't like it?" he said.

"What did you expect," she said—"wild, abandoned passion?"

"I keep telling you," he said, "I never know what's going to happen next."

"We say good-bye," she said.

He frowned slightly. "All right," he said.

She made another speech. "I'm not sorry we kissed," she said. "That was sweet. We should have kissed, we've been so close. I'll always remember you, Newt, and good luck."

"You too," he said.

"Thank you, Newt," she said.

"Thirty days," he said.

"What?" she said.

"Thirty days in the stockade," he said—"that's what one kiss will cost me."

"I—I'm sorry," she said, "but I didn't ask you to go A.W.O.L."

"I know," he said.

"You certainly don't deserve any hero's reward for doing something as foolish as that," she said.

"Must be nice to be a hero," said Newt. "Is Henry Stewart Chasens a hero?"

"He might be, if he got the chance," said Catharine. She noted uneasily that they had begun to walk again. The farewell had been forgotten.

"You really love him?" he said.

"Certainly I love him!" she said hotly. "I wouldn't marry him if I didn't love him!"

"What's good about him?" said Newt.

"Honestly!" she cried, stopping again. "Do you have any idea how offensive you're being? Many, many, many things are good about Henry! Yes," she said, "and many, many, many things are probably bad too. But that isn't any of your business. I love Henry, and I don't have to argue his merits with you!"

"Sorry," said Newt.

"Honestly!" said Catharine.

Newt kissed her again. He kissed her again because she wanted him to.

◎ ◎ ◎

They were now in a large orchard.

"How did we get so far from home, Newt?" said Catharine.

"One foot in front of the other—through leaves, over bridges," said Newt.

"They add up—the steps," she said.

Bells rang in the tower of the school for the blind nearby. "School for the blind," said Newt.

"School for the blind," said Catharine. She shook her head in drowsy wonder. "I've got to go back now," she said.

"Say good-bye," said Newt.

"Every time I do," said Catharine, "I seem to get kissed."

Newt sat down on the close-cropped grass under an apple tree. "Sit down," he said.

"No," she said.

"I won't touch you," he said.

"I don't believe you," she said.

She sat down under another tree, twenty feet away from him. She closed her eyes.

"Dream of Henry Stewart Chasens," he said.

"What?" she said.

"Dream of your wonderful husband-to-be," he said.

"All right, I will," she said. She closed her eyes tighter, caught glimpses of her husband-to-be.

Newt yawned.

The bees were humming in the trees, and Catharine almost fell asleep. When she opened her eyes she saw that Newt really was asleep.

He began to snore softly.

Catharine let Newt sleep for an hour, and while he slept she adored him with all her heart.

The shadows of the apple trees grew to the east. The bells in the tower of the school for the blind rang again.

"*Chick-a-dee-dee-dee,*" went a chickadee.

388

KURT VONNEGUT

Somewhere far away an automobile starter nagged and failed, nagged and failed, fell still.

Catharine came out from under her tree, knelt by Newt.

"Newt?" she said.

"H'm?" he said. He opened his eyes.

"Late," she said.

"Hello, Catharine," he said.

"Hello, Newt," she said.

"I love you," he said.

"I know," she said.

"Too late," he said.

"Too late," she said.

He stood, stretched groaningly. "A very nice walk," he said.

"I thought so," she said.

"Part company here?" he said.

"Where will you go?" she said.

"Hitch into town, turn myself in," he said.

"Good luck," she said.

"You, too," he said. "Marry me, Catharine?"

"No," she said.

He smiled, stared at her hard for a moment, then walked away quickly.

Catharine watched him grow smaller in the long perspective of shadows and trees, knew that if he stopped and turned now, if he called to her, she would run to him. She would have no choice.

Newt did stop. He did turn. He did call. "Catharine," he called.

She ran to him, put her arms around him, could not speak.

A Night for Love

MOONLIGHT IS ALL RIGHT for young lovers, and women never seem to get tired of it. But when a man gets older he usually thinks moonlight is too thin and cool for comfort. Turley Whitman thought so. Turley was in his pajamas at his bedroom window, waiting for his daughter Nancy to come home.

He was a huge, kind, handsome man. He looked like a good king, but he was only a company cop in charge of the parking lot at the Reinbeck Abrasives Company. His club, his pistol, his cartridges, and his handcuffs were on a chair by the bed. Turley was confused and upset.

His wife, Milly, was in bed. For about the first time since their three-day honeymoon, in 1936, Milly hadn't put up her hair in curlers. Her hair was all spread out on her pillow. It made her look young and soft and mysterious. Nobody had looked mysterious in that bedroom for years. Milly opened her eyes wide, and stared at the moon.

Her attitude was what threw Turley as much as anything. Milly refused to worry about what was maybe happening to Nancy out in the moonlight somewhere so late at night. Milly would drop off to sleep without even knowing it, then wake up and stare at the moon for a while, and she would think big thoughts without telling Turley what they were, and then drop off to sleep again.

"You awake?" said Turley.

"Hm?" said Milly.

"You decided to be awake?"

"I'm staying awake," said Milly dreamily. She sounded like a girl.

"You think you've been staying awake?" said Turley.

"I must have dropped off without knowing it," she said.

"You've been sawing wood for an hour," said Turley.

He made her sound unattractive to herself because he wanted her to wake up more. He wanted her to wake up enough to talk to him instead of just staring at the moon. She hadn't really sawed wood while she slept. She'd been very beautiful and still.

Milly had been the town beauty once. Now her daughter was.

"I don't mind telling you, I'm worried sick," said Turley.

"Oh, honey," said Milly, "they're fine. They've got sense. They aren't crazy kids."

"You want to guarantee they're not cracked up in a ditch somewhere?" said Turley.

389

This roused Milly. She sat up, frowned, and blinked away her sleepiness. "You really think—"

"I really think!" said Turley. "He gave me his solemn promise he'd have her home two hours ago."

Milly pulled off her covers, put her bare feet close together on the floor. "All right," she said. "I'm sorry. I'm awake now. I'm worried now."

"About time," said Turley. He turned his back to her, and dramatized his responsible watch at the window by putting his big foot on the radiator.

"Do—do we just worry and wait?" said Milly.

"What do you suggest?" said Turley. "If you mean call the police to see if there's been an accident, I took care of that detail while you were sawing wood."

"No accidents?" said Milly in a small, small voice.

"No accidents they know of," said Turley.

"Well—that's—that's a little encouraging."

"Maybe it is to you," said Turley. "It isn't to me." He faced her, and he saw that she was now wide awake enough to hear what he had been wanting to say for some time. "If you'll pardon me saying so, you're treating this thing like it was some kind of holiday. You're acting like her being out with that rich young smart-aleck in his three-hundred-horsepower car was one of the greatest things that ever happened."

Milly stood, shocked and hurt. "Holiday?" she whispered. "Me?"

"Well—you left your hair down, didn't you, just so you'd look nice in case he got a look at you when he finally brought her home?"

Milly bit her lip. "I just thought if there was going to be a row, I didn't want to make it worse by having my hair up in curlers."

"You don't think there should be a row, do you?" said Turley.

"You're the head of the family. You—you do whatever you think is right." Milly went to him, touched him lightly. "Honey," she said, "I don't think it's good. Honest I don't. I'm trying just as hard as I can to think of things to do."

"Like what?" said Turley.

"Why don't you call up his father?" said Milly. "Maybe he knows where they are or what their plans were."

The suggestion had a curious effect on Turley. He continued to tower over Milly, but he no longer dominated the house, or the room, or even his little barefoot wife. "Oh, great!" he said. The words were loud, but they were as hollow as a bass drum.

"Why not?" said Milly.

Turley couldn't face her anymore. He took up his watch at the window again. "That would just be great," he said to the moonlit town. "Roust L. C. Reinbeck himself out of bed. 'Hello—L.C.? This is T.W. What the hell is your son doing with my daughter?'" Turley laughed bitterly.

Milly didn't seem to understand. "You've got a perfect right to call him or anybody else, if you really think there's an emergency," she said. "I mean, everybody's free and equal this time of night."

"Speak for yourself," Turley said, overacting. "Maybe you've been free and equal with the great L. C. Reinbeck, but I never have. And what's more, I never expect to be."

"All I'm saying is, he's human," said Milly.

"You're the expert on that," said Turley. "I'm sure I'm not. He never took me out dancing at the country club."

"He never took me out dancing at the country club, either. He doesn't like dancing." Milly corrected herself. "Or he didn't."

"Please, don't get technical on me this time of night," said Turley. "So he took you out and did whatever he likes to do. So whatever that was, you're the expert on him."

"Honey," said Milly, full of pain, "he took me out to supper once at the Blue Mill, and he took me to a movie once. He took me to *The Thin Man*. And all he did was talk, and all I did was listen. And it wasn't romantic talk. It was about how he was going to turn the abrasives company back into a porcelain company. And he was going to do the designing. And he never did anything of the kind, so that's how expert I am on the great Louis C. Reinbeck." She laid her hand on her bosom. "I'm the expert on you," she said, "if you want to know who I'm the expert on."

Turley made an animal sound.

"What, sweetheart?" said Milly.

"Me," said Turley, impatient. "What you're an expert on—me?"

Milly made helpless giving motions Turley didn't see.

He was standing stock-still, winding up tighter and tighter inside. Suddenly he moved, like a cumbersome windup man. He went to the telephone on the bedside table. "Why *shouldn't* I call him up?" he blustered. "Why shouldn't I?"

He looked up Louis C. Reinbeck's number in the telephone book clumsily, talked to himself about the times the Reinbeck company had gotten him up out of bed in the middle of the night.

He misdialed, hung up, got set to dial again. His courage was fading fast.

Milly hated to see the courage go. "He won't be asleep," she said. "They've been having a party."

"They've been having a what?" said Turley.

"The Reinbecks are having a party tonight—or it's just over."

"How you know that?" said Turley.

"It was in this morning's paper, on the society page. Besides," Milly continued, "you can go in the kitchen and look and see if their lights are on."

"You can see the Reinbeck house from our kitchen?" said Turley.

"Sure," said Milly. "You have to get your head down kind of low and over to one side, but then you can see their house in a corner of the window."

Turley nodded quizzically, watched Milly, thought about her, hard. He dialed again, let the Reinbecks' telephone ring twice. And then he hung up. He dominated his wife, his rooms, and his house again.

Milly knew that she had made a very bad mistake in the past thirty seconds. She was ready to bite off her tongue.

"Every time the Reinbecks do anything," said Turley, "you read every word about it in the paper?"

"Honey," said Milly, "all women read the society page. It doesn't mean anything. It's just a silly something to do when the paper comes. All women do it."

"Sure," said Turley. "Sure. But how many of 'em can say to theirselves, 'I could have been Mrs. Louis C. Reinbeck'?"

Turley made a great point of staying calm, of being like a father to Milly, of forgiving her in advance. "You want to face this thing about those two kids out there in the moonlight somewhere?" he said. "Or you want to go on pretending an accident's the only thing either one of us is thinking about?"

Milly stiffened. "I don't know what you mean," she said.

"You duck your head a hundred times a day to look at that big white house in the corner of the kitchen window, and you don't know what I mean?" said Turley. "Our girl is out in the moonlight somewhere with the kid who's going to get that house someday, and you don't know what I mean? You left your hair down and you stared at the moon and you hardly heard a word I said to you, and you don't know what I mean?" Turley shook his big, imperial head. "You just can't imagine?"

The telephone rang twice in the big white house on the hill. Then it stopped. Louis C. Reinbeck sat on a white iron chair on the lawn in the moonlight. He was looking out at the rolling lovely nonsense of the golf course and, beyond that and below, the town. All the lights in his house were out. He thought his wife, Natalie, was asleep.

Louis was drinking. He was thinking that the moonlight didn't make the world look any better. He thought the moonlight made the world look worse, made it look dead like the moon.

The telephone's ringing twice, then stopping, fitted in well with Louis's mood. The telephone was a good touch—urgency that could wait until hell froze over. "Shatter the night and then hang up," said Louis.

Along with the house and the Reinbeck Abrasives Company, Louis had inherited from his father and grandfather a deep and satisfying sense of having been corrupted by commerce. And like them, Louis thought of himself as a sensitive maker of porcelain, not grinding wheels, born in the wrong place at the wrong time.

Just as the telephone had rung twice at the right time, so did Louis's wife appear as though on cue. Natalie was a cool, spare Boston girl. Her role was to misunderstand Louis. She did it beautifully, taking apart his reflective moods like a master mechanic.

"Did you hear the telephone ring, Louis?" she said.

"Hm? Oh—yes. Uh-huh," said Louis.

"It rang and then it stopped," said Natalie.

"I know," said Louis. He warned her with a sigh that he didn't want to discuss the telephone call or anything else in a flat, practical Yankee way.

Natalie ignored the warning. "Don't you wonder who it was?"

"No," said Louis.

"Maybe it was a guest who left something. You didn't see anything around, did you, that somebody left?"

"No," said Louis.

"An earring or something, I suppose," said Natalie. She wore a pale-blue cloud-like negligee that Louis had given her. But she made the negligee meaningless by dragging a heavy iron chair across the lawn, to set it next to Louis's. The arms of the chairs clicked together, and Louis jerked his fingers from between them just in time.

Natalie sat down. "Hi," she said.

"Hi," said Louis.

"See the moon?" said Natalie.

"Yup," said Louis.

"Think people had a nice time tonight?" said Natalie.

"I don't know," said Louis, "and I'm sure they don't, either." He meant by this that he was always the only artist and philosopher at his parties. Everybody else was a businessman.

Natalie was used to this. She let it pass. "What time did Charlie get in?" she said. Charlie was their only son—actually Louis Charles Reinbeck, Junior.

"I'm sure I don't know," said Louis. "He didn't report in to me. Never does."

Natalie, who had been enjoying the moon, now sat forward uneasily. "He is home, isn't he?" she said.

"I haven't the remotest idea," said Louis.

Natalie bounded out of her chair.

She strained her eyes in the night, trying to see if Charlie's car was in the shadows of the garage. "Who did he go out with?" she asked.

"He doesn't talk with me," said Louis.

"Who is he with?" said Natalie.

"If he isn't by himself, then he's with somebody you don't approve of," said Louis.

But Natalie didn't hear him. She was running into the house. Then the telephone rang again, and went on ringing until Natalie answered.

She held the telephone out to Louis. "It's a man named Turley Whitman," she said. "He says he's one of your policemen."

"Something wrong at the plant?" said Louis, taking the phone. "Fire, I hope?"

"No," said Natalie, "nothing as serious as that." From her expression, Louis gathered that something a lot worse had happened. "It seems that our son is out with Mr. Turley's daughter somewhere, that they should have been back hours ago. Mr. Turley is naturally very deeply concerned about his daughter."

"Mr. Turley?" said Louis into the telephone.

"Turley's my first name, sir," said Turley. "Turley Whitman's my whole name."

"I'm going to listen on the upstairs phone," whispered Natalie. She gathered the folds of her negligee, ran manlike up the stairs.

"You probably don't know me except by sight," said Turley "I'm the guard at the main-plant parking lot."

"Of course I know you—by sight and by name," said Louis. It was a lie. "Now what's this about my son and your daughter?"

Turley wasn't ready to get to the nut of the problem yet. He was still introducing himself and his family. "You probably know my wife a good deal better'n you know me, sir," he said.

There was a woman's small cry of surprise.

For an instant, Louis didn't know if it was the cry of his own wife or of Turley's. But when he heard sounds of somebody trying to hang up, he knew it had to be on Turley's end. Turley's wife obviously didn't want her name dragged in.

Turley was determined to drag it in, though, and he won out. "You knew her by her maiden name, of course," he said, "Milly—Mildred O'Shea."

All sounds of protest at Turley's end died. The death of protests came to Louis as a shocking thing. His shock was compounded as he remembered young, affectionate and pretty, mystifying Milly O'Shea. He hadn't thought of her for years, hadn't known what had become of her.

And yet at the mention of her name, it was as though Louis had thought of her constantly since she'd kissed him good-bye in the moonlight so long before.

"Yes—yes," said Louis. "Yes, I—I remember her well." He wanted to cry about growing old, about the shabby ends brave young lovers came to.

From the mention of Milly's name, Turley had his conversation with the great Louis C. Reinbeck all his own way. The miracle of equality had been achieved. Turley and Louis spoke man to man, father to father, with Louis apologizing, murmuring against his own son.

Louis thanked Turley for having called the police. Louis would call them, too. If he found out anything, he would call Turley at once. Louis addressed Turley as "sir."

Turley was exhilarated when he hung up. "He sends his regards," he said to Milly. He turned to find himself talking to air. Milly had left the room silently, on bare feet.

Turley found her heating coffee in the kitchen on the new electric stove. The stove was named the Globemaster. It had a ridiculously complicated control panel. The Globemaster was a wistful dream of Milly's come true. Not many of her dreams of nice things had come true.

The coffee was boiling, making the pot crackle and spit. Milly didn't notice that it was boiling, even though she was staring at the pot with terrible concentration. The pot spit, stung her hand. She burst into tears, put the stung hand to her mouth. And then she saw Turley.

She tried to duck past him and out of the kitchen, but he caught her arm.

"Honey," he said in a daze. He turned off the Globemaster's burner with his free hand. "Milly," he said.

Milly wanted desperately to get away. Big Turley had such an easy time holding her that he hardly realized he was doing it. Milly subsided at last, her sweet face red and twisted. "Won't—won't you tell me what's wrong, honey?" said Turley.

"Don't worry about me," said Milly. "Go worry about people dying in ditches."

Turley let her go. "I said something wrong?" He was sincerely bewildered.

"Oh, Turley, Turley," said Milly, "I never thought you'd hurt me this way—this much." She cupped her hands as though she were holding something precious. Then she let it fall from her hands, whatever her imagination thought it was.

Turley watched it fall. "Just because I told him your name?" he said.

"When—when you told him my name, there was so much else you told him." She was trying to forgive Turley, but it was hard for her. "I don't suppose you knew what else you were telling him. You couldn't have."

'All I told him was your name," said Turley.

"And all it meant to Louis C. Reinbeck," said Milly, "was that a woman down in the town had two silly little dates with him twenty years ago, and she's talked about nothing else since. And her husband knows about those two silly little dates, too—and he's just as proud of them as she is. Prouder!"

Milly put her head down and to one side, and she pointed out the kitchen window, pointed to a splash of white light in an upper corner of the window. "There," she said, "the great Louis C. Reinbeck is up in all that light somewhere, thinking I've loved him all these years." The floodlights on the Reinbeck house went out. "Now he's up there in the moonlight somewhere—thinking about the poor little woman and the poor little man and their poor little daughter down here." Milly shuddered. "Well, we're not poor! Or we weren't until tonight."

The great Louis C. Reinbeck returned to his drink and his white iron lawn chair. He had called the police, who had told him what they told Turley—that there were no wrecks they knew of.

Natalie sat down beside Louis again. She tried to catch his eye, tried to get him to see her maternal, teasing smile. But Louis wouldn't look.

"You—you know this girl's mother, do you?" she said.

"Knew," said Louis.

"You took her out on nights like this? Full moon and all that?"

"We could dig out a twenty-year-old calendar and see what the phases of the moon were," said Louis tartly. "You can't exactly avoid full moons, you know. You're bound to have one once a month."

"What was the moon on our wedding night?" said Natalie.

"Full?" said Louis.

"New," said Natalie. "Brand-new."

"Women are more sensitive to things like that," said Louis. "They notice things."

He surprised himself by sounding peevish. His conscience was doing funny things to his voice because he couldn't remember much of anything about his honeymoon with Natalie.

He could remember almost everything about the night he and Milly O'Shea had wandered out on the golf course. That night with Milly, the moon had been full.

Now Natalie was saying something. And when she was done, Louis had to ask her to say it all over again. He hadn't heard a word.

"I said, 'What's it like?'" said Natalie.

"What's what like?" said Louis.

"Being a young male Reinbeck—all hot-blooded and full of dreams, swooping down off the hill, grabbing a pretty little town girl and spiriting her into the moonlight." She laughed, teasing. "It must be kind of godlike."

"It isn't," said Louis.

"It isn't godlike?"

"Godlike? I never felt more human in all my life!" Louis threw his empty glass in the direction of the golf course. He wished he'd been strong enough to throw the glass straight to the spot where Milly had kissed him good-bye.

"Then let's hope Charlie marries this hot little girl from town," said Natalie. "Let's have no more cold, inhuman Reinbeck wives like me." She stood. "Face it, you would have been a thousand times happier if you'd married your Milly O'Shea."

She went to bed.

"Who's kidding anybody?" Turley Whitman asked his wife. "You would have been a million times happier if you'd married Louis Reinbeck." He was back at his post by the bedroom window, back with his big foot on the radiator.

Milly was sitting on the edge of the bed. "Not a million times, not two times, not the-smallest-number-there-is times happier," said Milly. She was wretched. "Turley—please don't say anything more like that. I can't stand it, it's so crazy."

"Well, you were kind of calling a spade a spade down there in the kitchen," said Turley, "giving me hell for telling the great Louis Reinbeck your name. Let me just call a spade a spade here, and say neither one of us wants our daughter to make the same mistake you did."

Milly went to him, put her arms around him. "Turley, please, that's the worst thing you could say to me."

He turned a stubborn red, was as unyielding as a statue. "I remember all the big promises I made you, all the big talk," he said. "Neither of us thinks company cop is one of the biggest jobs a man can hold."

Milly tried to shake him, with no luck. "I don't care what your job is," she said.

"I was gonna have more money than the great L. C. Reinbeck," said Turley, "and I was gonna make it all myself. Remember, Milly? That's what really sold you, wasn't it?"

Her arms dropped away from him. "No," she said.

"My famous good looks?" said Turley.

"They had a lot to do with it," said Milly. His looks had gone very well with the looks of the prettiest girl in town. "Most of all," she said, "it was the great Louis C. Reinbeck and the moon."

The great Louis C. Reinbeck was in his bedroom. His wife was in bed with the covers pulled up over her head. The room was cunningly contrived to give the illusion of romance and undying true love, no matter what really went on there.

Up to now, almost everything that had gone on in the room had been reasonably pleasant. Now it appeared that the marriage of Louis and Natalie was at an end. When Louis made her pull the covers away from her face, when Natalie showed him how swollen her face was with tears, this was plainly the case. This was the end.

Louis was miserable—he couldn't understand how things had fallen to pieces so fast. "I—I haven't thought of Milly O'Shea for twenty years," he said.

"Please—no. Don't lie. Don't explain," said Natalie. "I understand."

"I swear," said Louis. "I haven't seen her for twenty years."

"I believe you," said Natalie. "That's what makes it so much worse. I wish you had seen her—just as often as you liked. That would have been better, somehow, than all this—this—" She sat up, ransacked her mind for the right word. "All this horrible, empty, aching, nagging regret." She lay back down.

"About Milly?" said Louis.

"About Milly, about me, about the abrasives company, about all the things you wanted and didn't get, about all the things you got that you didn't want. Milly and me—that's as good a way of saying it as anything. That pretty well says it all."

"I—I don't love her. I never did," said Louis.

"You must have liked the one and only time in your life you felt human," said Natalie. "Whatever happened in the moonlight must have been nice—much nicer than anything you and I ever had."

Louis's nightmare got worse, because he knew Natalie had spoken the truth. There never had been anything as nice as that time in the moonlight with Milly.

"There was absolutely nothing there, no basis for love," said Louis. "We were perfect strangers then. I knew her as little as I know her now."

Louis's muscles knotted and the words came hard, because he thought he was extracting something from himself of terrible importance. "I—I suppose she is a symbol of my own disappointment in myself, of all I might have been," he said.

He went to the bedroom window, looked morbidly at the setting moon. The moon's rays were flat now, casting long shadows on the golf course, exaggerating the toy geography. Flags flew here and there, signifying less than nothing. This was where the great love scene had been played.

Suddenly he understood. "Moonlight," he murmured.

"What?" said Natalie.

"It had to be." Louis laughed, because the explanation was so explosively simple. "We had to be in love, with a moon like that, in a world like that. We owed it to the moon."

Natalie sat up, her disposition much improved.

"The richest boy in town and the prettiest girl in town," said Louis, "we couldn't let the moon down, could we?"

He laughed again, made his wife get out of bed, made her look at the moon with him. "And here I'd been thinking it really had been something big between Milly and me way back then." He shook his head. "When all it was was pure, beautiful, moonlit hokum."

He led his wife to bed. "You're the only one I ever loved. An hour ago, I didn't know that. I know that now."

So everything was fine.

"I won't lie to you," Milly Whitman said to her husband. "I loved the great Louis C. Reinbeck for a while. Out there on the golf course in the moonlight, I just had to fall in love. Can you understand that—how I would have to fall in love with him, even if we didn't like each other very well?"

Turley allowed as how he could see how that would be. But he wasn't happy about it.

"We kissed only once," said Milly. "And if he'd kissed me right, I think I might really be Mrs. Louis C. Reinbeck tonight." She nodded. "Since we're calling spades spades tonight, we might as well call that one a spade, too. And just before we kissed up there on the golf course, I was thinking what a poor little rich boy he was, and how much happier I could make him than any old cold, stuck-up country club girl. And then he kissed me, and I knew he wasn't in love, couldn't ever be in love. So I made that kiss good-bye."

"There's where you made your mistake," said Turley.

"No," said Milly, "because the next boy who kissed me kissed me right, showed me he knew what love was, even if there wasn't a moon. And I lived happily ever after, until tonight." She put her arms around Turley. "Now kiss me again the way you kissed me the first time, and I'll be all right tonight, too."

Turley did, so everything was all right there, too.

About twenty minutes after that, the telephones in both houses rang. The burden of the messages was that Charlie Reinbeck and Nancy Whitman were fine. They had, however, put their own interpretation on the moonlight. They'd decided that Cinderella and Prince Charming had as good a chance as anybody for really living happily ever after. So they'd married.

So now there was a new household. Whether everything was all right there remained to be seen. The moon went down.

Find Me a Dream

IF THE COMMUNISTS ever expect to overtake the democracies in sewer pipe production, they are certainly going to have to hump some—because just one factory in Creon, Pennsylvania, produces more pipe in six months than both Russia and China put together could produce in a year. That wonderful factory is the Creon Works of the General Forge and Foundry Company.

As Works manager, Arvin Borders told every rookie engineer, "If you don't like sewer pipe, you won't like Creon." Borders himself, a forty-six-year-old bachelor, was known throughout the industry as "Mr. Pipe."

Creon is the Pipe City. The high school football team is the Creon Pipers. The only country club is the Pipe City Golf and Country Club. There is a permanent exhibit of pipe in the club lobby and the band that plays for the Friday-night dances at the club is Andy Middleton and His Creon Pipe-Dreamers.

One Friday night in the summertime, Andy Middleton turned the band over to his piano player. He went out to the first tee for some peace and fresh air. He surprised a pretty young woman out there. She was crying. Andy had never seen her before. He was twenty-five at the time.

Andy asked if he could help her.

"I'm being very silly," she said. "Everything is fine. I'm just being silly."

"I see," said Andy.

"I cry very easily—and even when there's nothing at all to cry about, I cry," she said.

"That must be kind of confusing for people who are with you," he said.

"It's a mess," she said.

"It might come in handy in case you ever have to attend the funeral of someone you hate," he said.

"It isn't going to be very handy in the pipe industry," she said.

"Are you in the pipe industry?" he said.

"Isn't everybody in Creon in the pipe industry?" she said.

"I'm not," he said.

"How do you keep from starving to death?" she said.

"I wave a stick in front of a band . . . give music lessons . . . things like that," he said.

"Oh, God—a musician," she said, and she turned her back.

"That's against me?" he said.

"I never want to see another musician as long as I live," she said.

"In that case," he said, "close your eyes and I'll tiptoe away." But he didn't leave.

"That's your band—playing tonight?" she said. They could hear the music quite clearly.

"That's right," he said.

"You can stay," she said.

"Pardon me?" he said.

"You're no musician," she said, "or that band would have made you curl up and die."

"You're the first person who ever listened to it," he said.

"I bet that's really the truth," she said. "Those people don't hear anything that isn't about pipe. When they dance, do they keep any kind of time to the music?"

"When they what?" he said.

"I said," she repeated, "when they dance."

"How can they dance," he said, "if the men spend the whole evening in the locker room, drinking, shooting crap, and talking sewer pipe, and all the women sit out on the terrace, talking about things they've overheard about pipe, about things they've bought with money from pipe, about things they'd like to buy with money from pipe?"

She started weeping again.

"Just being silly again?" he said. "Everything still fine?"

"Everything's fine," she said. The demoralized, ramshackle little band in the empty ballroom ended a number with razzberries and squeals. "Oh God, but that band hates music!" she said.

"They didn't always," he said.

"What happened?" she said.

"They found out they weren't ever going anywhere but Creon—and they found out nobody in Creon would listen. If I went and told them a beautiful woman was listening and weeping out here, they might get back a little of what they had once— and make a present of it to you."

"What's your instrument?" she said.

"Clarinet," he said. "Any special requests—any melodies you'd like to have us waft from the clubhouse while you weep alone?"

"No," she said. "That's sweet, but no music for me."

"Tranquilizers? Aspirin?" he said. "Cigarettes, chewing gum, candy?"

"A drink," she said.

Shouldering his way to the crowded bar, a bar called The Jolly Piper, Andy learned a lot of things about the sewer pipe business. Cleveland, he learned, had bought a lot of cheap pipe from another company, and Cleveland was going to be sorry about it in about twenty years. The Navy had specified Creon pipe for all buildings under construction, he learned, and nobody was going to be sorry. It was a little-known fact, he learned, that the whole world stood in awe of American pipemaking capabilities.

He also found out who the woman on the first tee was. She had been brought to the dance by Arvin Borders, bachelor manager of the Creon Works. Borders had met her in New York. She was a small-time actress, the widow of a jazz musician, the mother of two very young daughters.

Andy found out all this from the bartender. Arvin Borders, "Mr. Pipe" himself, came into the bar and craned his neck, looking for somebody. He was carrying two highballs. The ice in both glasses had melted.

"Still haven't seen her, Mr. Borders," the bartender called to him, and Borders nodded unhappily and left.

"Who haven't you seen?" Andy asked the bartender.

And the bartender told him all he knew about the widow. He also gave Andy the opinion, out of the corner of his mouth, that General Forge and Foundry Company headquarters in Ilium, New York, knew about the romance and took a very dim view of it. "You tell me where, in all of Creon," the bartender said to Andy, "a pretty, young New York actress could fit in."

The woman went by her stage name, which was Hildy Matthews, Andy learned. The bartender didn't have any idea who her husband had been.

Andy went into the ballroom to tell his Pipe-Dreamers to play a little better for a weeping lady on the golf course, and he found Arvin Borders talking to them. Borders, an earnest, thickset man, was asking the band to play "Indian Love Call" very loud.

"Loud?" said Andy.

"So she'll hear it, wherever she is, and come," said Borders. "I can't imagine where she got to," he said. "I left her on the terrace, with the ladies, for a while—and she just plain evaporated."

"Maybe she got fed up with all the talk about pipe," said Andy.

"She's very interested in pipe," said Borders. "You wouldn't think a woman who looked like that would be, but she can listen to me talk shop for hours and never get tired of it."

"'Indian Love Call' will bring her back?" said Andy.

Borders mumbled something unintelligible.

"Pardon me, sir?" said Andy.

Borders turned red and pulled in his chin. "I said," he said gruffly, "it's our tune."

"I see," said Andy.

"You boys might as well know now—I'm going to marry that girl," said Borders. "We're going to announce our engagement tonight."

Andy bowed slightly. "Congratulations," he said. He put his two highballs down on a chair, picked up his clarinet. "'Indian Love Call,' boys—real loud?" he said.

The band was slow to respond. Nobody seemed to want to play much, and everybody was trying to tell Andy something.

"What's the trouble?" said Andy.

"Before we play, Andy," said the pianist, "you ought to know just who we're playing for, whose *widow* we're playing for."

"Whose widow?" said Andy.

"I had no idea he was so famous," said Borders. "I mentioned him to your band here, and they almost fell off their chairs."

"Who?" said Andy.

"A dope fiend, an alcoholic, a wife-beater, and a woman-chaser who was shot dead last year by a jealous husband," said Borders indignantly. "Why anybody would think there was anything wonderful about a man like that I'll never know," he said. And then he gave the name of the man, a man who was probably the greatest jazz musician who had ever lived.

"I thought you weren't ever coming back," she said, out of the shadows on the first tee.

"I had to play a special request," said Andy. "Somebody wanted me to play 'Indian Love Call' as loud as I could."

"Oh," she said.

"You heard it and you didn't come running?" he said.

"Is that what he expected me to do?" she said.

"He said it was your tune," he said.

"That was his idea," she said. "He thinks it's the most beautiful song ever written."

"How did you two happen to meet?" he said.

"I was dead broke, looking for any kind of work at all," she said. "There was a General Forge and Foundry Company sales meeting in New York. They were going to put on a skit. They needed an actress. I got the part."

"What part did they give you?" he said.

"They dressed me in gold lamé, gave me a crown of pipe fittings, and introduced me as 'Miss Pipe Opportunities in the Golden Sixties,'" she said. "Arvin Borders was there," she said. She emptied her glass. "Kismet," she said.

"Kismet," he said.

She took his highball from him. "I'm sorry," she said, "I'm going to need this one, too."

"And ten more besides?" he said.

"If it takes ten more to get me back to all those people, all those lights, all that pipe," she said, "I'll drink ten more."

"The trip's that tough?" he said.

"If only I hadn't wandered out here," she said. "If only I'd stayed up there!"

"One of the worst mistakes a person can make, sometimes, I guess," he said, "is to try to get away from people and think. It's a great way to lose your forward motion."

"The band is playing so softly I can hardly hear the music," she said.

"They know whose widow's listening," he said, "and they'd just as soon you didn't hear them."

"Oh," she said. "They know. You know."

"He—he didn't leave you anything?" he said.

"Debts," she said. "Two daughters . . . for which I'm really very grateful."

"The horn?" he said.

"It's with him," she said. "Please   could I have one more drink?"

"One more drink," he said, "and you'll have to go back to your fiancé on your hands and knees."

"I'm perfectly capable of taking care of myself, thank you," she said. "It isn't up to you to watch out for me."

"Beg your pardon," he said.

She gave a small, melodious hiccup. "What a terrible time for that to happen," she said. "It doesn't have anything to do with drinking."

"I believe you," he said.

"You don't believe me," she said. "Give me some kind of a test. Make me walk a straight line or say something complicated."

"Forget it," he said.

"You don't believe I love Arvin Borders, either, do you?" she said. "Well, let me tell you that one of the things I do best is love. I don't mean pretending to love. I mean really loving. When I love somebody, I don't hold anything back. I go all the way, and right now I happen to love Arvin Borders."

"Lucky man," he said.

"Would you like to hear exactly how much I have already learned about pipe?" she said.

"Go ahead," he said.

"I read a whole book about pipe," she said. "I went to the public library and got down a book about pipe and nothing else but pipe."

"What did the book say?" he said.

From the tennis courts to the west came faint, crooning calls. Borders was now prowling the club grounds, looking for his Hildy. "Hildeee," he was calling. "Hildy?"

"You want me to yell yoo-hoo?" said Andy.

"Shhh!" she said. And she gave the small, melodious hiccup.

Arvin Borders wandered off into the parking lot, his cries fading away in the darkness that enveloped him.

"You were going to tell me about pipe," said Andy.

"Let's talk about you," she said.

"What would you like to know about me?" he said.

"People have to ask you questions or you can't talk?" she said.

He shrugged. "Small-time musician. Never married. Big dreams once. Big dreams all gone."

"Big dreams of what?" she said.

"Being half the musician your husband was," he said. "You want to hear more?"

"I love to hear other people's dreams," she said.

"All right—love," he said.

"You've never had that?" she said.

"Not that I've noticed," he said.

"May I ask you a very personal question?" she said.

"About my ability as a great lover?" he said.

"No," she said. "I think that would be a very silly kind of question. I think everybody young is basically a great lover. All anybody needs is the chance."

"Ask the *personal* question," he said.

"Do you make any money?" she said.

Andy didn't answer right away.

"Is that too personal?" she said.

"I don't guess it would kill me to answer," he said. He did some figuring in his head, gave her an honest report of his earnings.

"Why, that's very good," she said.

"More than a schoolteacher, less than a school janitor," he said.

"Do you live in an apartment or what?" she said.

"A big old house I inherited from my family," he said.

"You're really quite well off when you stop to think about it," she said. "Do you like little children—little girls?"

"Don't you think you'd better be getting back to your fiancé?" he said.

"My questions keep getting more and more personal," she said. "I can't help it, my own life has been so personal. Crazy, personal things happen to me all the time."

"I think we'd better break this up," he said.

She ignored him. "For instance," she said, "I pray for certain kinds of people to come to me, and they come to me. One time when I was very young, I prayed for a great musician to come and fall in love with me—and he did. And I loved him, too, even though he was the worst husband a woman could have. That's how good I am at loving."

"Hooray," he said quietly.

"And then," she said, "when my husband died and there was nothing to eat and I was sick of wild and crazy nights and days, I prayed for a solid, sensible, rich businessman to come along."

"And he did," said Andy.

"And then," she said, "when I came out here and ran away from all the people who liked pipe so much—do you know what I prayed for?"

"Nope," he said.

"A man to bring me a drink," she said. "That was all. I give you my word of honor, that was all."

"And I brought you two drinks," he said.

"And that isn't all, either," she said.

"Oh?" he said.

"I think that I could love you very much," she said.

"A pretty tough thing to do," he said.

"Not for me," she said. "I think you could be a very good musician if somebody encouraged you. And I could give you the big and beautiful love you want. You'd definitely have that."

"This is a proposal of marriage?" he said.

"Yes," she said. "And if you say no, I don't know what I'll do. I'll crawl under the shrubbery here and just die. I can't go back to all those pipe people, and there's no place else *to* go."

"I'm supposed to say yes?" he said.

"If you feel like saying yes, then say yes," she said.

"All right—" he said at last, "yes."

"We're both going to be so glad this happened," she said.

"What about Arvin Borders?" he said.

"We're doing him a favor," she said.

"We are?" he said.

"Oh, yes," she said. "On the terrace there, a woman came right out and said it would ruin Arvin's career if he married a woman like me—and you know, it probably would, too."

"That was the crack that sent you out here into the shadows?" he said.

"Yes," she said. "It was very upsetting. I didn't want to hurt anybody's career."

"That's considerate of you," he said.

"But you," she said, taking his arm, "I don't see how I could do anything for you but a world of good. You wait," she said. "You wait and see."

FUBAR

THE WORD *SNAFU*, derived from the initials of *situation normal, all fouled up*, was welcomed into the American language during World War II, and remains a useful part of the language today. *Fubar*, a closely related word, was coined at about the same time, and is now all but forgotten. *Fubar* is worthy of a better fate, meaning as it does *fouled up beyond all recognition*. It is a particularly useful and interesting word in that it describes a misfortune brought about not by malice but by administrative accidents in some large and complex organization.

Fuzz Littler, for instance, was fubar in the General Forge and Foundry Company. He was familiar with the word *fubar*—had to hear it only once to know it fit him like a pair of stretch nylon bikini shorts. He was fubar in the Ilium Works of GF&F, which consisted of five hundred and twenty-seven numbered buildings. He became fubar in the classic way, which is to say that he was the victim of a temporary arrangement that became permanent.

Fuzz Littler belonged to the Public Relations Department, and all the public relations people were supposed to be in Building 22. But Building 22 was full up when Fuzz came to work, so they found a temporary desk for Fuzz in an office by the elevator machinery on the top floor of Building 181.

Building 181 had nothing to do with public relations. With the exception of Fuzz's one-man operation, it was devoted entirely to research into semiconductors. Fuzz shared the office and a typist with a crystallographer named Dr. Lomar Horthy. Fuzz stayed there for eight years, a freak to those he was among, a ghost to those he should have been among. His superiors bore him no malice. They simply kept forgetting about him.

Fuzz did not quit for the simple and honorable reason that he was the sole support of his very sick mother. But the price of being passively fubar was high. Inevitably, Fuzz became listless, cynical, and profoundly introverted.

And then, at the start of Fuzz's ninth year with the company, when Fuzz himself was twenty-nine, Fate took a hand. Fate sent grease from the Building 181 cafeteria up the elevator shaft. The grease collected on the elevator machinery, caught fire, and Building 181 burned to the ground.

But there still wasn't any room for Fuzz in Building 22, where he belonged, so they fixed him up a temporary office in the basement of Building 523, clear at the end of the company bus line.

Building 523 was the company gym.

One nice thing, anyway—nobody could use the gym facilities except on weekends and after five in the afternoon, so Fuzz didn't have to put up with people swimming and bowling and dancing and playing basketball around him while he was trying to work. Sounds of playfulness would have been not only distracting but almost too mocking to bear. Fuzz, caring for his sick mother, had never had time to play in all his fubar days.

Another nice thing was that Fuzz had finally achieved the rank of supervisor. He was so isolated out in the gym that he couldn't borrow anybody else's typist. Fuzz had to have a girl all his own.

Now Fuzz was sitting in his new office, listening to the showerheads dribble on the other side of the wall and waiting for the new girl to arrive.

It was nine o'clock in the morning.

Fuzz jumped. He heard the great, echoing *ka-boom* of the entrance door slamming shut upstairs. He assumed that the new girl had entered the building, since not another soul in the world had any business there.

It was not necessary for Fuzz to guide the new girl across the basketball court, past the bowling alleys, down the iron stairway, and over the duckboards to his office door. The buildings and grounds people had marked the way with arrows, each arrow bearing the legend GENERAL COMPANY RESPONSE SECTION, PUBLIC RELATIONS DEPARTMENT.

Fuzz had been the General Company Response Section of the Public Relations Department during his entire fubar career with the company. As that section he wrote replies to letters that were addressed simply to the General Forge and Foundry Company at large, letters that couldn't logically be referred to any company operation in particular. Half the letters didn't even make sense. But no matter how foolish and rambling the letters might be, it was Fuzz's duty to reply to them warmly, to prove what the Public Relations Department proved tirelessly—that the General Forge and Foundry Company had a heart as big as all outdoors.

Now the footsteps of Fuzz's new girl were coming down the stairway cautiously. She didn't have much faith in what the arrows said, apparently. Her steps were hesitant, were sometimes light enough to be on tiptoe.

There was the sound of a door opening, and the open door loosed a swarm of tinny, nightmarish little echoes. The girl had made a false turn, then, had mistakenly opened the door to the swimming pool.

She let the door fall shut with a *blam.*

On she came again, back on the right path. The duckboards creaked and squished under her. She knocked on the door of the General Company Response Section of the Public Relations Department.

Fuzz opened the office door.

Fuzz was thunderstruck. Smiling up at him was the merriest, prettiest little girl he'd ever seen. She was a flawless little trinket, a freshly minted woman, surely not a day older than eighteen.

"Mr. Littler?" she said.

"Yes?" said Fuzz.

"I'm Francine Pefko." She inclined her sweet head in enchanting humility. "You're my new supervisor."

Fuzz was almost speechless with embarrassment, for here was infinitely more girl than the General Company Response Section could handle with any grace. Fuzz had assumed that he would be sent a dispirited and drab woman, an unimaginative drudge who could be glumly content with a fubar supervisor in fubar surroundings. He had not taken into account the Personnel Department's card machines, to whom a girl was simply a girl.

"Come in—come in," said Fuzz emptily.

Francine entered the miserable little office, still smiling, vibrant with optimism and good health. She had obviously just joined the company, for she carried all the pamphlets that new employees were given on their first day.

And, like so many girls on their first day, Francine was what one of her pamphlets would call *overdressed for work.* The heels of her shoes were much too slender and high. Her dress was frivolous and provocative, and she was a twinkling constellation of costume jewels.

"This is nice," she said.

"It is?" said Fuzz.

"Is this my desk?" she said.

"Yes," said Fuzz. "That's it."

She sat down springily in the revolving posture chair that was hers, stripped the cover from her typewriter, twittered her fingers over the keys. "I'm ready to go to work any time you are, Mr. Littler," she said.

"Yes—all righty," said Fuzz. He dreaded setting to work, for there was no way in which he could glamorize it. In showing this pert creature what his work was, he was going to display to her the monumental pointlessness of himself and his job.

"This is my very first minute of my very first hour of my very first day of my very first job," said Francine, her eyes shining.

"That so?" said Fuzz.

"Yes," said Francine. In all innocence, Francine Pefko now spoke a simple sentence that was heartbreakingly poetic to Fuzz. The sentence reminded Fuzz, with the ruthlessness of great poetry, that his basic misgivings about Francine were not occupational but erotic.

What Francine said was this: "*I came here straight from the Girl Pool.*" In speaking of the Girl Pool, she was doing no more than giving the proper name to the reception and assignment center maintained by the company for new woman employees.

But when Fuzz heard those words, his mind whirled with images of lovely young women like Francine, glistening young women, rising from cool, deep water, begging aggressive, successful young men to woo them. In Fuzz's mind, the desirable images all passed him by, avoided his ardent glances. Such beautiful creatures would have nothing to do with a man who was fubar.

Fuzz looked at Francine uneasily. Not only was she, so fresh and desirable from the Girl Pool, going to discover that her supervisor had a very poor job. She was going to conclude, as well, that her supervisor wasn't much of a man at all.

The normal morning workload in the General Company Response Section was about fifteen letters. On the morning that Francine Pefko joined the operation, however, there were only three letters to be answered.

One letter was from a man in a mental institution. He claimed to have squared the circle. He wanted a hundred thousand dollars and his freedom for having done it. Another letter was from a ten-year-old who wanted to pilot the first rocket ship to Mars. The third was from a lady who complained that she could not keep her dachshund from barking at her GF&F vacuum cleaner.

By ten o'clock, Fuzz and Francine had disposed of all three letters. Francine filed the three letters and carbons of Fuzz's gracious replies. The filing cabinet was otherwise empty. The General Company Response Section had lost all its old files in the Building 181 fire.

Now there was a lull.

Francine could hardly clean her typewriter, since her typewriter was brand new. Fuzz could hardly make busywork of shuffling gravely through papers, since he had only one paper in his desk. That one paper was a terse notice to the effect that all supervisors were to crack down hard on coffee breaks.

"That's all for right now?" said Francine.

"Yes," said Fuzz. He searched her face for signs of derision. So far there were none. "You—you happened to pick a slack morning," he said.

"What time does the mailman come?" said Francine.

"Mail service doesn't come out this far," said Fuzz. "When I come to work in the morning, and again when I come back from lunch, I pick up our mail at the company post office."

"Oh," said Francine.

The leaking showerheads next door suddenly decided to inhale noisily. And then, their nasal passages seemingly cleared, they resumed their dribbling once more.

"Is it real busy around here sometimes, Mr. Littler?" said Francine, and she shuddered because the idea of being thrillingly busy pleased her so much.

"Busy enough," said Fuzz.

"When do the people come out here, and what do we do for them?" said Francine.

"People?" said Fuzz.

"Isn't this public relations?" said Francine.

"Yes—" said Fuzz.

"Well, when does the public come?" said Francine, looking down at her eminently presentable self.

"I'm afraid the public doesn't come out this far," said Fuzz. He felt like a host at the longest, dullest party imaginable.

"Oh," said Francine. She looked up at the one window in the office. The window, eight feet above the floor, afforded a view of the underside of a candy wrapper in an areaway. "What about the people we work with?" she said. "Do they rush in and out of here all day?"

"I'm afraid we don't work with anybody else, Miss Pefko," said Fuzz.

"Oh," said Francine.

There was a terrific bang from a steam pipe upstairs. The huge radiator in the tiny office began to hiss and spit.

"Why don't you read your pamphlets, Miss Pefko," said Fuzz. "Maybe that would be a good thing to do," he said.

Francine nodded, eager to please. She started to smile, thought better of it. The crippled smile was Francine's first indication that she found her new place of employment something less than gay. She frowned slightly, read her pamphlets.

Fuzz whistled reedily, the tip of his tongue against the roof of his mouth.

The clock on the wall clicked. Every thirty seconds it clicked, and its minute hand twitched forward microscopically. An hour and fifty-one minutes remained until lunchtime.

"Huh," said Francine, commenting on something she'd read.

"Pardon me?" said Fuzz.

"They have dances here every Friday night—right in this building," said Francine, looking up. "That's how come they've got it all so decorated up upstairs," she said. She was referring to the fact that Japanese lanterns and paper streamers were strung over the basketball court. The mood of the next dance was apparently going to be rural, for there was a real haystack in one corner, and pumpkins and farm implements and sheaves of corn stalks were arranged with artistic carelessness along the walls.

"I love to dance," said Francine.

"Um," said Fuzz. He had never danced.

"Do you and your wife dance a lot, Mr. Littler?" said Francine.

"I'm not married," said Fuzz.

"Oh," said Francine. She blushed, pulled in her chin, resumed her reading. When her blushing faded, she looked up again. "You bowl, Mr. Littler?" she said.

"No," said Fuzz quietly, tautly. "I don't dance. I don't bowl. I'm afraid I don't do much of anything, Miss Pefko, but take care of my mother, who's been sick for years."

Fuzz closed his eyes. What he contemplated within the purple darkness of his eyelids was what he considered the cruelest fact of life—that sacrifices were *really* sacrifices. In caring for his mother, he had lost a great deal.

Fuzz was reluctant to open his eyes, for he knew that what he would see in Francine's face would not please him. What he would see in Francine's heavenly face, he knew, would be the paltriest of all positive emotions, which is respect. And mixed with that respect, inevitably, would be a wish to be away from a man who was so unlucky and dull.

The more Fuzz thought about what he would see when he opened his eyes, the less willing he was to open them. The clock on the wall clicked again, and Fuzz knew that he could not stand to have Miss Pefko watch him for even another thirty seconds.

"Miss Pefko," he said, his eyes still closed, "I don't think you'll like it here."

"What?" said Francine.

"Go back to the Girl Pool, Miss Pefko," said Fuzz. "Tell them about the freak you found in the basement of Building 523. Demand a new assignment."

Fuzz opened his eyes.

Francine was pale and rigid. She shook her head slightly, incredulous, scared. "You—you don't like me, Mr. Littler?" she said.

"That has nothing to do with it!" said Fuzz, standing. "Just clear out of here for your own good!"

Francine stood, too, still shaking her head.

"This is no place for a pretty, clever, ambitious, charming little girl like you," said Fuzz unevenly. "Stay here and you'll rot!"

"Rot?" echoed Francine.

"Rot like me," said Fuzz. In a jangling jumble of words he poured out the story of his fubar life. And then, beet red and empty, he turned his back on Francine. "Good-bye, Miss Pefko," he said, "it's been extremely nice knowing you."

Francine nodded wincingly. She said nothing. Blinking hard and often, she gathered up her things and left.

Fuzz sat down at his desk again, his head in his hands. He listened to Miss Pefko's fading footfalls, awaited the great, echoing *ka-boom* that would tell him Francine had left his life forever.

He waited and he waited and he waited for the *ka-boom*. And he supposed, finally, that he had been cheated out of that symbolic sound, that Francine had managed to close the door noiselessly.

And then he heard music.

The music Fuzz heard was a recording of a popular song, cheap and foolish. But, turned back on itself by the countless echo chambers of Building 523, the music was mysterious, dreamlike, magical.

Fuzz followed the music upstairs. He found its source, a large phonograph set against one wall of the gym. He smiled bleakly. The music, then, had been a little farewell present from Francine.

He let the record play to the end, and then he turned it off. He sighed, let his gaze travel over the decorations and playthings.

If he had raised his eyes to the level of the balcony, he would have seen that Francine hadn't left the building yet. She was sitting in the front row of the balcony, her arms resting on the pipe railing.

But Fuzz did not look up. In what he believed to be privacy, he tried a melancholy dance step or two—without hope.

And then Francine spoke to him. "Did it help?" she said.

Fuzz looked up, startled.

"Did it help?" she said again.

"Help?" said Fuzz.

"Did the music make you any happier?" said Francine.

Fuzz found the question one he couldn't answer promptly.

Francine didn't wait for an answer. "I thought maybe music would make you a little happier," she said. She shook her head. "I don't mean I thought it could solve anything. I just thought it would maybe—" She shrugged. "You know—maybe help a little."

"That's—that's very thoughtful of you," said Fuzz.

"Did it help?" said Francine.

Fuzz thought about it, gave an honest, hesitant answer. "Yes—" he said. "I—I guess it did, a little."

"You could have music all the time," said Francine. "There's tons of records. I thought of something else that could help, too."

"Oh?" said Fuzz.

"You could go swimming," said Francine.

"Swimming?" said Fuzz, amazed.

"Sure," said Francine. "Be just like a Hollywood movie star with his own private swimming pool."

Fuzz smiled at her for the first time in their relationship. "Someday I just might do that," he said.

Francine leaned out over the railing. "Why someday?" she said. "If you're so blue, why don't you go swimming right now?"

"On company time?" said Fuzz.

"There isn't anything you can do for the company now anyway, is there?" said Francine.

"No," said Fuzz.

"Then go on," said Francine.

"No suit," said Fuzz.

"Don't wear a suit," said Francine. "Skinny-dip. I won't peek, Mr. Littler. I'll stay right here. You'll feel *so* good, Mr. Littler." Francine now showed Fuzz a side of herself that he hadn't seen before. It was harsh and strong. "Or maybe you shouldn't go swimming, Mr. Littler," she said unpleasantly. "Maybe you like being unhappy so much, you wouldn't do anything to change it."

Fuzz stood on the edge of the swimming pool at the deep end, looked down into eleven feet of cool water. He was stark naked, feeling scrawny, pale, and a fool. He thought he was surely a fool for having become the plaything of the logic of an eighteen-year-old.

Pride made Fuzz turn his back on the water. He started for the locker room, but Francine's logic turned him around again. The cool, deep water undeniably represented pleasure and well-being. If he refused to throw himself into all that chlorinated goodness, then he really was a contemptible thing, a man who enjoyed being miserable.

In he went.

The cool, deep water did not fail him. It shocked him delightfully, stripped away his feelings of paleness and scrawniness. When Fuzz came to the surface after his first plunge, his lungs were filled with a mixture of laughter and shouts. He barked like a dog.

Fuzz gloried in the echoes of the barking, so he barked some more. And then he heard answering barks, much higher in pitch, and far away. Francine could hear him and was barking back at him through the ventilator system.

"Does it help?" she called.

"Yes!" Fuzz yelled back, without hesitation or restraint.

"How's the water?" said Francine.

"Wonderful!" yelled Fuzz. "Once you get in."

Fuzz went upstairs to the first floor of the gym again, fully dressed, tingling, virile. Again there was music to lead him on.

Francine was dancing in her stocking feet on the basketball court, gravely, respecting the grace God had given her.

Factory whistles blew outside—some near, some far, all mournful.

"Lunchtime," said Fuzz, turning off the phonograph.

"Already?" said Francine. "It came so fast."

"Something very peculiar has happened to time," said Fuzz.

"You know," said Francine, "you could become bowling champion of the company, if you wanted to."

"I never bowled in my life," said Fuzz.

"Well, you can now," said Francine. "You can bowl to your heart's content. In fact, you could become an all-round athlete, Mr. Littler. You're still young."

"Maybe," said Fuzz.

"I found a whole bunch of dumbbells in the corner," said Francine. "Every day you could work with them a little till you were just as strong as a bull."

Fuzz's toned-up muscles tightened and twisted pleasurably, asking to be as strong as the muscles of a bull. "Maybe," said Fuzz.

"Oh, Mr. Littler," said Francine beseechingly, "do I really have to go back to the Girl Pool? Can't I stay here? Whenever there's any work to do, I'll be the best secretary any man ever had."

"All right," said Fuzz, "stay."

"Thank you, thank you, thank you," said Francine. "I think this must be the best place in the whole company to work."

"That may well be," said Fuzz wonderingly. "I—I don't suppose you'd have lunch with me?"

"Oh, I can't today, Mr. Littler," she said. "I'm awfully sorry."

"I suppose you have a boyfriend waiting for you somewhere," said Fuzz, suddenly glum again.

"No," said Francine. "I have to go shopping. I want to get a bathing suit."

"I guess I'd better get one, too," said Fuzz.

They left the building together. The entrance door closed behind them with a great, echoing *ka-boom.*

Fuzz said something quietly as he looked back over his shoulder at Building 523.

"Did you say something, Mr. Littler?" said Francine.

"No," said Fuzz.

"Oh," said Francine.

What Fuzz had said to himself so quietly was just one word. The word was "*Eden.*"

Girl Pool

MY GOOD, BELOVED wife, née Amy Lou Little, came to me from the girl pool. And there's an enchanting thought for lonely men—a pool of girls, teeming, warm, and deep.

Amy Lou Little was a pretty, confident, twenty-year-old girl from Birmingham, Alabama. When my wife-to-be graduated from secretarial school in Birmingham, the school said she was fast and accurate, and a recruiter from the Montezuma Forge and Foundry Company, way up north, offered her a very good salary if she would come to Pittsburgh.

When my wife-to-be got to Pittsburgh, they put her in the Montezuma Forge and Foundry Company's girl pool, with earphones and a Dictaphone and an electric typewriter. They put her at a desk next to Miss Nancy Hostetter, leader of section C of the girl pool, who had been in the girl pool for twenty-two years. Miss Hostetter was a great elk of a woman, righteous, healthy and strong, and inconceivably fast and accurate. She said Amy was to look upon her as a big sister.

I was in the Montezuma Forge and Foundry Company, too, a rootless pleaser of unseen customers. The customers wrote to the company, and twenty-five of us replied, genially, competently. I never saw the customers, and the customers never saw me, and no one suggested that we exchange snapshots.

All day long, I talked into a Dictaphone, and messengers carried off the records to the girl pool, which I'd never seen.

There were sixty girls in the girl pool, ten to a section. Bulletin boards in every office said the girls belonged to anyone with access to a Dictaphone, and almost any man would have found a girl to his taste among the sixty. There were maidens like my wife-to-be, worldly women made up like showgirls, moon-faced matrons, and erect and self-sufficient spinsters, like Miss Hostetter.

The walls of the girl pool were eye-rest green, and had paintings of restful farm scenes on them, and the air was a rhapsody of girls' perfumes and the recorded music of André Kostelanetz and Mantovani. From morning until night, the voices of Montezuma's men, transcribed on Dictaphone records, filled the girls' ears.

But the men sent only their voices, never their faces, and they talked only of business. And all they ever called a girl was "operator."

"Molybdenum, operator," said a voice in Amy's ear, "spelled m-o-l-y-b-d-e-n-u-m."

The nasal Yankee voice hurt Amy's ears—sounded, she said, like somebody beating a cracked bell with a chain. It was my voice.

"Clangbang," said Amy to my voice.

"The unit comes with silicone gaskets throughout," said my voice. "That's s-i-l-i-c-o-n-e, operator."

"Oh, you don't have to spell silicone for me," said Amy. "Isn't anything I don't know about silicones after six months in this bughouse."

"Yours truly," said my voice, "Arthur C. Whitney, Jr., Customer Relations Section, Boiler Sales Department, Heavy Apparatus Division, Room 412, Building 77, Pittsburgh Works."

"ACW:all," Amy typed at the bottom of the letter. She separated the letter and copies from the carbon paper, dropped them into her out-basket, and slipped my record from the spindle of her Dictaphone.

"Why don't you bring your face around to the girl pool sometime, Arthur?" said my wife-to-be to my record. "We'd treat you like Clark Gable, just any man at all." She put another record from her in-basket onto her spindle. "Come on, you old devil, you," she said to the new record, "thaw out this half-frozen Alabama girl. Make me swoon."

"Five carbons, operator," said a new, harsh voice in Amy's ear. "To Mr. Harold N. Brewster, Thrust-Bearing Division, Jorgenson Precision Engineering Products Corporation, Lansing 5, Michigan."

"You *are* a hot-blooded old thing, aren't you?" said Amy. "What makes you men up here so passionate—the steam heat?"

"Did you say something to me, Amy?" said Miss Hostetter, removing her earphones. She was a tall woman, without ornaments, save for her gold twenty-year-service pin. She looked at Amy with bleak reproach. "What's the trouble now?"

Amy stopped her Dictaphone. "I was talking to the gentleman on the record," she said. "Got to talk to somebody around here, or go crazy."

"There are lots of nice people to talk to," said Miss Hostetter. "You're so critical of everything, when you haven't really had time to find out what everything's about."

"You tell me what this is about," said my wife-to-be, including the girl pool in a sweep of her hand.

"There was a very good cartoon about that in the *Montezuma Minutes*," said Miss Hostetter. The *Montezuma Minutes* was the company's weekly newspaper for employees.

"The one with the ghost of Florence Nightingale hovering over a stenographer?" said Amy.

"That was a good one," said Miss Hostetter. "But the one I had in mind showed a man with his new Thermolux furnace, and there were thousands of women all around him and the furnace, kind of ghostly. 'He doesn't send orchids, but he should,' the caption said, 'to the ten thousand women behind every dependable Montezuma product.'"

"Ghosts, ghosts, ghosts," said my wife-to-be. "Everybody's ghosts up here. They come out of the smoke and the cold in the morning, and they rush around and worry about boilers and silicone gaskets and molybdenum all day, then they disappear at five, plain fade away without a word. I don't know how anybody up here ever gets married or falls in love or finds anything nice to laugh about, or anything. Back home in high school—"

"High school isn't life," said Miss Hostetter.

"God help women, if this is life—cooped up all together, with a floor all to themselves," said my wife-to-be.

The two women faced each other with antipathies they'd been honing to razor sharpness for six months. The little blades glinted in their eyes, while they smiled politely.

"Life is what you make it," said Miss Hostetter, "and ingratitude is one of the worst sins. Look around you! Pictures on the walls, carpets on the floor, beautiful music, hospitalization and retirement, the Christmas party, fresh flowers on our desks, coffee hours, our own cafeteria, our own recreation room with television and ping-pong."

"Everything but life," said my wife-to-be. "The only sign of life I've heard of up here is that poor Larry Barrow."

"Poor Larry Barrow!" said Miss Hostetter, shocked. "Amy—he killed a policeman!"

Amy opened her top desk drawer, and looked down at the picture of Larry Barrow on the front page of the *Montezuma Minutes*. Barrow, a handsome young criminal, had shot a policeman in a Pittsburgh bank holdup two days before. He had last been seen climbing over a fence to hide somewhere in the vast Montezuma works. There were plenty of places where he could hide.

"He could be in the movies," said Amy.

"As a killer," said Miss Hostetter.

"Not necessarily," said Amy. "He looks like a lot of nice boys I knew in high school."

"Don't be childish," said Miss Hostetter. She dusted her big hands briskly. "Well, we aren't getting any work done, are we? Ten minutes to go until morning coffee break. Let's make the most of them."

Amy turned on her Dictaphone. "Dear Mr. Brewster," said the voice, "your request for estimates on modernization of your present heating plant with DM-114 Thermolux conversion condensers has been forwarded by company teletype to our Thermolux specialist in your district, and . . ."

Amy, as her fingers danced expertly over the keys, was free to think about whatever she pleased, and, with her top drawer still open, with Larry Barrow's picture still in view, she thought about a man, wounded, freezing, starving, hated, hunted, and alone, somewhere out in the works.

"Considering the thermal conductivity of the brick walls of the buildings to be heated," said the voice in Amy's ear, "as five Btu—that's abbreviation for British thermal unit, operator, with a capital B—per square foot per hour per degree Fahrenheit—capitalize Fahrenheit, operator—per inch . . ."

And my wife-to-be saw herself in the clouds of pink tulle she'd worn on the June night of the high school graduation dance, and, on her arm, limping, healing, free, was Larry Barrow. The scene was in the South.

"And, taking the thermal diffusivity—d-i-f-f-u-s-i-v-i-t-y, operator—as, k over w," said the voice in Amy's ear, "it seems safe to say that . . ."

And my wife-to-be was helplessly in love with Larry Barrow. The love filled her life, thrilled her, and nothing else mattered.

"Ting-a-ling," said Miss Hostetter, looking at the wall clock and removing her earphones. There was a coffee break in the morning, and another in the afternoon, and Miss Hostetter greeted each as though she were a cheery little bell connected to the clock. "Ting-a-ling, everybody."

Amy looked at Miss Hostetter's craggy, loveless, humorless face, and her dream fell to pieces.

"A penny for your thoughts, Amy," said Miss Hostetter.

"I was thinking about Larry Barrow," said Amy. "What would you do if you saw him?"

"I'd keep right on walking," said Miss Hostetter primly. "I'd pretend I hadn't recognized him, and I'd keep right on walking until I could get help."

"What if he suddenly grabbed you, and made you a prisoner?" said Amy.

Miss Hostetter reddened over her high cheekbones. "That's quite enough of *that* kind of talk," she said. "That's how panic gets started. I understand that some of the girls in the Wire and Cable Department got each other so upset about this man they had to be sent home. That isn't going to happen here. The girls in the girl pool are a cut above that."

"Even so—" said Amy.

"He isn't anywhere near this part of the works," said Miss Hostetter. "He's probably dead by now, anyway. They said there was blood in that office he broke into last night, so he isn't in any condition to go around grabbing people."

"Nobody really knows," said Amy.

"What you need," said Miss Hostetter, "is a cup of hot coffee, and a fast game of ping-pong. Come on. I'm going to beat you."

"Dear Sir:" said a voice in the pretty ear of my wife-to-be that afternoon, "We would very much like to have you as our guest at a demonstration of the entire line of Thermolux heating equipment in the Bronze Room of the Hotel Gresham at four-thirty, Wednesday . . ." The letter was not to one man, but to thirty. Each of the thirty was to get an individually typed invitation.

By the tenth time Amy had typed the same letter, she felt as though she were drowning. She put the project aside, temporarily, and, for the sake of variety, slipped another record from her in-box onto her Dictaphone spindle.

She rested her fingers on the keyboard, on *a, s, d,* and *f,* on *j, k, l,* and *;,* awaiting orders from the record. But the only sound from the record was a shushing sound, like the sound of the sea in a seashell.

After many seconds, a soft, deep, sweetly wheedling voice spoke in Amy's ear, spoke from the record.

"I read about you girls on the bulletin board," said the voice. "Says you girls belong to anybody with access to a Dictaphone." The voice laughed quietly. "*I* got access to a Dictaphone."

The record scratched on in another long silence.

"I'm cold and sick and lonely and hungry, Miss," said the voice at last. There was a cough. "I'm feverish, and I'm dying, Miss. Guess everybody will be real glad when I'm dead."

Another silence, another cough.

"All I ever did wrong was not let anybody push me around, Miss," said the voice. "Somewhere, somewhere, maybe there's a girl who thinks a boy shouldn't be shot or starved or locked up like an animal. Somewhere, maybe there's a girl who's got a heart left inside her.

"Somewhere," said the voice, "maybe there's a girl with a heart, who'd bring this boy something to eat, and some bandages, and give him a chance to live a little while longer.

"Maybe," said the voice, "she's got a heart of ice, and she'll go tell the police, so they can shoot this boy, and she can be real proud and happy.

"Miss," said the voice to my wife-to-be, "I'm going to tell you where I've been and where I'll be when you hear this. You can do anything you want with me—save me or get me killed, or plain let me die. I'll be in building 227." The voice laughed quietly again. "I'll be back of a barrel. Isn't much of a building, Miss. You won't have any trouble finding me in it."

The record ended.

Amy imagined herself cradling Larry Barrow's curly head in her round, soft arms.

"There, there," she murmured. "There, there." Tears filled her eyes.

A hand dropped on Amy's shoulder. It was Miss Hostetter's hand. "Didn't you hear me say ting-a-ling for the coffee break?" she said.

"No," said Amy.

"I've been watching you, Amy," said Miss Hostetter. "You've just been listening. You haven't been typing. Is there something strange about that record?"

"Perfectly ordinary record," said Amy.

"You looked so upset."

"I'm all right. I'm fine," said Amy tensely.

"I'm your big sister," said Miss Hostetter. "If there's anything—"

"I don't *want* a big sister!" said Amy passionately.

Miss Hostetter bit her lip, turned white, and stalked into the recreation room.

Furtively, Amy wrapped Larry Barrow's record in face tissues, and hid it in the bottom drawer of her desk, with her hand cream, face cream, lipstick, powder, rouge, perfume, nail polish, manicure scissors, nail file, nail buffer, eyebrow pencil, tweezers, bobby pins, vitamin tablets, needle and thread, eyedrops, brush, and comb.

She closed the drawer, and looked up to see the baleful eyes of Miss Hostetter, who watched her through a screen of milling girls in the doorway of the recreation room, watched her over a cup of steaming coffee and a saucer with two little cookies on it.

Amy smiled at her glassily, and went into the recreation room. "Ping-pong, anybody?" said Amy, fighting to keep her voice even.

She received a dozen merry challenges, and, during the recreation period, she daydreamed to the took-took of the ping-pong ball instead of the tack-tack of her typewriter.

◎ ◎ ◎

At five, whistles blew triumphantly in the works and all over Pittsburgh.

My wife-to-be had spent the afternoon in a suppressed frenzy of fear, excitement, and love. Her wastebasket was stuffed with mistakes. She hadn't dared to play Barrow's record again, or even to exchange a glance with Miss Hostetter, for fear of giving away her terrible secret.

Now, at five, André Kostelanetz and Mantovani and the blowers of the heating system were turned off. The mail girls came into the girl pool with trays of cylinders to be transcribed first thing in the morning. They emptied withered flowers from the vases on the desks. They would bring fresh flowers from the company hothouse in the morning. The girl pool became whirlpools around a dozen coatracks. In separate whirlpools, Amy and Miss Hostetter pulled on their cloth coats.

The girl pool became a river, flowing down the fireproof iron stairway into the company street. At the very end of the river was my wife-to-be.

Amy stopped, and the river left her behind, in the little cyclones of fly ash, in the canyon walled by numbered building façades.

Amy returned to the girl pool. The only light now came from the orange fires of furnaces in the distance.

Trembling, she opened the bottom drawer of her desk, and found the record gone.

Stunned and angry, she opened Miss Hostetter's bottom drawer. The record was there. The only other objects in the green steel bin were a bottle of Mercurochrome and a clipping from the *Montezuma Minutes*, entitled, "Creed of a Woman of Montezuma." "I am a Woman of Montezuma," the creed began, "hand in hand with Men, marching to a Better Tomorrow under the three banners of God, Country, and Company, bearing the proud shield of Service."

Amy wailed in anguish. She ran out of the girl pool, down the iron stairway, and down the company street to the main gate, to the headquarters of the company police. She was sure Miss Hostetter was there, proudly telling the police what she'd learned from the record.

The headquarters of the company police were in one corner of a great reception room by the main gate. Around the walls of the room were exhibits of the company's products and methods. In its center was a stand, where a fat concessionaire sold candy, tobacco, and magazines.

A tall woman in a cloth coat was talking animatedly to the policeman on duty.

"Miss Hostetter!" said Amy breathlessly, coming up behind her.

The woman turned to look curiously at my wife-to-be, and then returned her attention to the policeman. She was not Miss Hostetter. She was a visitor, who had taken a tour of the works and lost her purse inside.

"It could have been lost or stolen just anywhere," said the woman, "where all that terrible noise was, with all the hot steel and sparks; where that big hammer came crashing down; where that scientist showed us his whatchamacallit in his laboratory—anywhere! Maybe that killer who's running around wild in there snatched it while I wasn't looking."

"Lady," said the policeman patiently, "it's almost sure he's dead. And he isn't after purses, if he is alive. He's after something to eat. He's after life." He smiled grimly. "But he isn't going to get it—not for long."

The corners of my wife-to-be's sweet red mouth pulled down involuntarily.

Somewhere out in the works, dogs bayed.

"Hear that?" said the policeman with satisfaction. "They got dogs looking for him now. If he's got your purse, lady, which he doesn't, we'll have it back in jig time."

Amy looked around the big room for Miss Hostetter. Miss Hostetter wasn't there. Helplessness weakened Amy, and she sat down on a hard bench before a display entitled, "Can Silicones Solve Your Problems?"

Depression settled over Amy. She recognized it for what it was—the depression she always felt when a good movie ended. The theater lights were coming on, taking from her elation and importance and love she really had no claim to. She was only a spectator—one of many.

"Hear them dogs?" said the concessionaire to a customer behind Amy. "Special kind, I heard. Bloodhounds are the gentlest dogs alive, but the ones they've got after

Barrow are half coonhound. They can teach that kind to be tough—to take care of the tough customers."

Amy stood suddenly, and went to the candy counter. "I want a chocolate bar," she said, "the big kind, the twenty-five-cent kind. And a Butterfinger and a Coconut Mounds bar, and one of those caramel things—and some peanuts."

"Yes, ma'am!" said the concessionaire. "Going to have yourself a real banquet, aren't you? Just watch out you don't hurt that complexion with too much sweets—that's all."

◎ ◎ ◎

Amy hurried back into the works, and squeezed into a crowded company bus. She was the only girl on the bus. The rest were men on the evening shift. When they saw my wife-to-be, they grew heavily polite and attentive.

"Could you please let me out at building 227?" said Amy to the driver. "I don't know where it is."

"Don't know as I know where it is, either," said the driver. "Don't get much call for that one." He took a dog-eared map of the works down from the sun visor.

"You don't get *any* call for that one," said a passenger. "Nothing in 227 but a bunch of lanterns, some barrels of sand, and maybe a potbellied stove. You don't want 227, Miss."

"A man called the girl pool for a stenographer to work late," said Amy. "I thought he said 227." She looked at the driver's map, and saw the driver's finger pointing to a tiny square all by itself in the middle of the railroad yard, building 227. There was a big building fairly near to it, on the edge of the yard, building 224. "He might have said building 224," said Amy.

"Oh sure!" said the driver happily. "Shipping Department. That's the one you want."

All on board sighed with relief, and looked with affectionate pride at the pretty little Southern girl they were taking such good care of.

Amy was now the last passenger on the bus. The bus was crossing the wasteland between the heart of the works and the railroad yard, a tundra of slag heaps and rusting scrap. Out in the wasteland, away from the street, was a constellation of dancing flashlight beams.

"The cops and the dogs," said the driver to Amy.

"Oh?" said Amy absently.

"Started from the office where he broke in last night," said the driver. "The way the dogs are talking it up, they must be pretty close to him."

Amy nodded. My wife-to-be was talking to Miss Hostetter in her imagination. "If you've told the police," she was saying, "you've killed him, just as sure as if you'd aimed a gun at him and pulled the trigger. Don't you understand? Don't you care? Haven't you got an ounce of womanhood in you?"

Two minutes later, the driver let Amy off at the Shipping Department.

When the bus was gone, Amy walked out into the night, and stood on the edge of the railroad yard, a sea of cinders sprinkled with twinkling red, green, and yellow signal lights, and streaked with glinting rails.

As Amy's eyes grew used to the night, her heart beat harder, and from the many hulking forms she chose one, a small, squat building that was almost certainly building 227—where a dying man had said he'd be waiting for a girl with a heart.

The world dropped away, and the night seemed to snatch Amy up and spin her like a top, and she was running across the cinders to the building. The building loomed, and my wife-to-be stopped against its weathered clapboards, panting, and trying to listen above the roaring of blood at her temples.

Someone moved inside, and sighed.

Amy worked her way along the outside wall to the door. The padlock and hasp had been pried from the old wood.

Amy knocked on the door. "Hello," she whispered, "I brought you something to eat."

Amy heard an intake of breath, nothing more.

She pushed open the door.

In the wedge of frail gray light let in by the door stood Miss Hostetter.

Each woman seemed to look through the other, to wish her out of existence. Their expressions were blank.

"Where is he?" said Amy at last.

"Dead," said Miss Hostetter, "dead—behind the barrels."

Amy began an aimless, shuffling walk about the room, and stopped when she was as far from Miss Hostetter as she could get, her back to the older woman. "Dead?" she murmured.

"As a mackerel," said Miss Hostetter.

"Don't talk about him that way!" said my wife-to-be.

"That's how dead he is," said Miss Hostetter.

Amy turned to face Miss Hostetter angrily. "You had no business taking my record."

"It was anybody's record," said Miss Hostetter. "Besides, I didn't think you had the nerve to do anything about it."

"Well, I *did*," said Amy, "and I thought the least I could expect was to be alone. I thought you'd gone to the police."

"Well, I *didn't*," said Miss Hostetter. "You should have expected me to be here— you of all people."

"Nothing ever surprised me more," said Amy.

"You sent me here, dear," said Miss Hostetter. Her face looked for a moment as though it would soften. But her muscles tightened, and the austere lines of her face held firm. "You've said a lot of things about my life, Amy, and I heard them all. They all hurt, and here I am." She looked down at her hands, and worked her fast and accurate fingers slowly. "Am I still a ghost? Does this crazy trip out here to see a dead man make me not a ghost anymore?"

Tears filled the eyes of my wife-to-be. "Oh, Miss Hostetter," she said, "I'm so sorry if I hurt you. You're not a ghost, really you're not. You never were." She was overwhelmed with pity for the stark, lonesome woman. "You're full of love and mercy, Miss Hostetter, or you wouldn't be here."

Miss Hostetter gave no sign that the words moved her. "And what brought *you* here, Amy?"

"I loved him," said Amy. The pride of a woman in love straightened her back and colored her cheeks and made her feel beautiful and important again. "I loved him."

Miss Hostetter shook her homely head sadly. "If you loved him," she said, "take a look at him. He has a lovable knife in his lovable lap, and a lovable grin that will turn your hair white."

Amy's hand went up to her throat. "Oh."

"At least we're friends now, aren't we, Amy?" said Miss Hostetter. "That's something, isn't it?"

"Oh, yes, yes," said Amy limply. She managed a wan smile. "That's a great deal."

"We'd better leave," said Miss Hostetter. "Here come the men and the dogs."

The two left building 227 as the men and the dogs zigzagged across the wasteland a quarter of a mile away.

The two caught a company bus in front of the Shipping Department, and said nothing to each other during the long, dead trip back to the main gate.

At the main gate, it was time for them to part, each to her own bus stop. With effort, they managed to speak.

"Goodbye," said Amy.

"See you in the morning," said Miss Hostetter.

"It's so hard for a girl to know what to do," said my wife-to-be, swept by longing and a feeling of weakness.

"I don't think it's supposed to be easy," said Miss Hostetter. "I don't think it ever was easy."

Amy nodded soberly.

"And Amy," said Miss Hostetter, laying her hand on Amy's arm, "don't be mad at the company. They can't help it if they want their letters nicely typed."

"I'll try not," said Amy.

"Somewhere," said Miss Hostetter, "a nice young man is looking for a nice young woman like you, and tomorrow's another day.

"What we both need now," said Miss Hostetter, fading, ghost-like, into the smoke and cold of Pittsburgh, "is a good, hot bath."

When Amy scuffed through the fog to her bus stop, ghost-like, she found me standing there, ghost-like.

With dignity, we each pretended that the other was not there.

When suddenly, my wife-to-be was overwhelmed with the terror that she'd held off so long, she burst into tears and leaned against me, and I patted her back.

"My gosh," I said, "another human being."

"You'll never know how human," she said.

"Maybe I will," I said. "I could try."

I did try, and I do try, and I give you the toast of a happy man: May the warm springs of the girl pool never run dry.

Rome

THIS IS A STORY ABOUT a girl who was raised by her father, who worshipped her father—and then found out he was a terrible hypocrite. This really happened.

It happened the year I was president of the North Crawford Mask and Wig Club. That was the year of the big sorghum and oil scandal down in Barbell, Oklahoma. A man named Fred Lovell was the main crook. Lovell had an eighteen-year-old daughter named Melody, and no wife. And he had a sister in North Crawford. So he sent Melody up to live with his sister until the trouble blew over.

He thought the trouble would blow over. It didn't.

◙ ◙ ◙

Melody joined the Mask and Wig Club. She was so beautiful, and we thought it was so important to take her mind off her father's trial, that we gave her a leading part in a play right away. We gave her the part of Bella, a streetwalker with a heart of gold, in *Rome*, by Arthur Garvey Ulm.

There were only four parts in the play: Bella; Ben, the good American soldier; Jed, the bad American soldier; and Bernardo, a cynical Roman policeman. The time was World War II.

Bryce Warmergran got the part of the good soldier, the poet. Bryce was a mother's boy who had been raised in New York City. His mother, a widow, owned the Warmergran Lumber Company, and the Warmergran Lumber Company owned practically every tree and stump in northern New Hampshire. Bryce was in North Crawford for a year to learn all he could about trees. He was a nice, shiny, shy, polite boy.

Bryce had never acted before. All he had done for the club was dip punch during intermissions. I remember what John Sherwood, the electrical contractor, said about Bryce dipping punch. "That job is neither too big nor too little for that boy." That summed up Bryce very well.

John Sherwood was in *Rome*, too. He was the bad soldier. He was six feet four, skinny, broad-shouldered, and the town tomcat. He was famous among the ladies

426

for his dancing ability, his foul mouth, and his barracuda smile. He could also act. He loved to act. He loved to make the ladies in the audience itch and squirm.

I was the cynical policeman. I had to grow a handlebar mustache.

Rome was directed by Sally St. Coeur.

◎ ◎ ◎

Sally called the four of us together in the back room of her gift shop for a first reading of the play. The name of the shop was The Better Mousetrap. Sally had talked to Melody a good deal. We three men were getting our first really close look at the girl.

The thing that impressed me most, aside from her very pretty face, was her posture. She kept her elbows against her sides, her shoulders hunched over, and her hands up against her chest, as though she were scared to death of getting germs. The thing Bryce said he noticed about her was what he called her "purity." He said that, up to the time he saw Melody, he hadn't believed it was possible for a woman to be that pure. What John Sherwood said about her isn't fit to print. What it boiled down to was that women that cold and that ignorant of the facts of life made him sick. The innocence of that girl was an unforgivable attack on all John held dear.

There wasn't any question about Melody's being ignorant and innocent. The first question she asked Sally was, "Excuse me, Miss St. Coeur, but what's a streetwalker?"

"Hold your hats," John whispered to me.

"A streetwalker, dear?" said Sally. "Why, that's a—that's a woman who takes money."

"Oh," said Melody.

"There goes the reputation of every decent female cashier in the world," whispered John.

"Now, about this play—" said Sally, "it only lasted one night on Broadway. But, after reading it over, I realized that the actors and the director were to blame, not the play. It's a magnificent play, and this is a great opportunity for us to give it the performance it deserved and never got."

"Who is Arthur Garvey Ulm?" asked John.

"He's the man who wrote the play."

"I know that. I wondered what else he'd ever done."

"I—I don't think he's done anything else," said Sally.

"There's a full life for you," said John.

"Can I ask another question?" said Melody.

"Certainly, dear." That was very brave of Sally.

"I've read this whole thing through," said Melody, "and there's several places where it says I'm supposed to kiss different people?"

"Yes?"

Melody shook her head, looked very unhappy. "I got to really do that?"

"Uh—yay-uss," said Sally.

"Miss St. Coeur—I promised my daddy I wouldn't never kiss no man except my husband."

John gave an exasperated sigh that sounded like a freight whistle.

Melody turned to him coldly and said, "I suppose you think that's old-fashioned or unsophisticated or something."

"Why no," he said. "I think it's perfectly sacred."

"I can't tell whether you mean it or not."

And then Bryce spoke up. It was the first time I had ever heard him speak up on any subject. He was breathing shallowly, and he'd turned the color of tomato juice. "Miss Lovell—" he said, "any woman who has the courage to hold onto high ideals like that in this day and age is as brave and noble as a woman can be."

Melody was grateful. "Thank you," she said. "I didn't realize there were any men around who would respect a girl with high ideals."

"There are a few," said Bryce.

"There's more of 'em than most people would care to admit," said John.

"Shut up," I told him.

"Dear, about this kissing—" said Sally.

"I just can't do it, Miss St. Coeur—especially with an audience watching."

"Um," said Sally.

"My daddy says kissing folks in public is the most disgusting thing there is." The man who had told her that was under indictment for swindling his neighbors and his country out of six million dollars.

"Dear, a play is not life," Sally told Melody. "If an actress plays the part of a woman who isn't as good as she might be, that doesn't mean the morals of the actress are really bad."

"How's a woman gonna play an impure part and not have impure thoughts?"

"Good question," said John.

"Surely, dear, you've seen movies or television shows where actresses who lead perfectly respectable private lives—"

"Name one," whispered John.

"I've never seen television," said Melody. "I've never seen a movie. I've never seen a play. Daddy says it's movies and television and books and all that that make the young people's minds so dirty these days." She caught John smirking. She hated him as much as he hated her. "Oh, I see you laughing. I'm used to folks laughing. Daddy told me there'd be folks who'd laugh. 'That's all right—you let 'em laugh,' he told me. 'You're gonna get the last laugh, Honeybunch, when you go to Heaven and they go to Hell.'"

◎ ◎ ◎

How we kept on or why we kept on I don't know, but we did. That seems to be the basic rule in amateur theater—keep going, no matter what. The worst thing the

Mask and Wig Club ever went ahead with wasn't *Rome*. The worst thing by far was *Oedipus Rex*, by Sophocles. But that is another story. Suffice it to say that the treasurer of the North Crawford Savings and Loan Association had to get up in front of all the depositors wearing a bedsheet, and then tear his eyeballs out on account of he had married his mother by accident.

As far as the Arthur Garvey Ulm play goes, we *did* try to ease Melody out of the cast, but she wouldn't quit. "No," she said. "I've started this, and I'm gonna see it through. My daddy told me, 'Honeybunch, anything you start you finish. The only thing I ask is, don't never do nothing I'd be ashamed of.'"

And Sally got her talked around to where she agreed to kiss Bryce and John and me the way the script said. Only she wasn't going to do it in rehearsals. She would only do it on the night of the performance.

"That's probably a good rule anyway," said Sally. "I'll never forget *La Ronde*."

La Ronde was a play by an Austrian named Arthur Schnitzler. It was a play about how everybody in Vienna was having love affairs with everybody else. The club tried to put on a cleaned-up version of it at one time.

During rehearsals, everybody was kissing everybody else, and the Asiatic flu broke out. We never did get to put on the play. We never could get a flu-free cast.

◎ ◎ ◎

How did Melody feel about the grand jury indicting her daddy, and all that? She made a speech about it that first night. Very gently, we were trying to find out what kind of religion, exactly, she and her daddy represented. It turned out that he didn't belong to any church.

"My daddy," she said, "just reads the Bible and lives accordingly." And then she started to cry. "He's got the highest morals in Oklahoma. Oh, there's gonna be some people gonna eat some black, greasy crow when that trial comes up. I *know* my daddy, and when the trial begins, the whole world's gonna know my daddy. They're gonna see a saint on a pure white horse. And all the dirty-minded, whisky-drinking, cigarette-smoking, woman-chasing people who accused him falsely will be the ones to go to jail, and I'll laugh and laugh. And all the flags in Barbell will fly, and all the church bells will ring, and the Boy Scouts will have a parade, and the governor of Oklahoma will say, 'I proclaim this day Fred Lovell Day!'"

She pulled herself together. "Let's get on," she said.

"Your mother's dead, is she, dear?" Sally asked.

"She's in Los Angeles, leading a life of sin. Daddy cast her out when I was two." She blew her little nose.

"Cast her out?"

"She was dirty," said Melody, "in both mind and deed."

◎ ◎ ◎

Ulm's play starts with a scene on a Roman street corner at night. Bryce Warmergran, the good soldier, sees this streetwalker under a lamppost, and he's so innocent that he doesn't know what she is. She is young and beautiful, and he has been drinking wine for the first time in his life, and he regards her as sacred.

"What flower is this that blooms in the Roman night?" he asks. On top of being a good soldier, he's a poet, too. Bryce read his part very well right from the first. There wasn't any make-believe about it. He was crazy about Melody.

And Melody says back to him, "Night-blooming flowers are very common in Rome. But you have a sensitive face, soldier. Perhaps you will be more clever than most about which one you pick."

And then there's a lot of palaver where Bryce carries on about how flowers shouldn't be picked, how they ought to be left growing wherever they are, so other people can appreciate them, and so forth. And he says that wars are times when people go around tearing up flowers by the roots, and so forth.

The upshot is that she gains self-respect for the first time because a man has spoken to her respectfully for the first time. And Bryce has three months of back combat pay with him, and he gives it all to her without even wanting a kiss. "Don't ask me to explain," he tells her. "One doesn't have to explain one's actions in dreams." He pauses. "In wars." He pauses again. "In life." Ulm has him pause again. "In love," he says, and he drifts off into the night.

◎ ◎ ◎

And then along comes John Sherwood, the bad soldier, practically dragging his knuckles on the sidewalk. He is drunk and disorderly, and is smoking a black cigar. He has deserted the army and has made a fortune on the black market. He is carrying a suitcase filled with cigarettes, nylons, and chocolate bars.

Melody is still looking after Bryce, still all luminous with newfound self-respect. And John comes up behind her and says, "You speak English real good, baby."

"What?" she asks.

"I said somebody who talks English as good as you do must have known quite a few Yankee soldiers."

"You heard me talking to that man?"

"I heard you talking to that boy. He's a boy, a baby. If you don't know the difference between a boy and a man, I don't know who would."

"I don't know what you mean."

John gives her his famous barracuda smile. And the upshot is that he breaks down her self-respect again, and they go off together.

◙ ◙ ◙

The company in Boston that sells us the playbooks and collects royalties was very interested in our production. We were the first amateur group to put on *Rome*. The company wrote me, asked if we were encountering any special difficulties.

I stopped by Sally's store, showed her the letter. "Special difficulties—" she said, "that's ironical, that is."

"They just want to know about things that are Arthur Garvey Ulm's fault," I said. "They don't want to hear about Barbell, Oklahoma."

"I wish *I'd* never heard of it," she said. The play was in its fifth week of rehearsal, had one week to go. And, thanks to Melody, it was putrid. I mean it was really vile.

"Maybe we ought to call it off," I said.

"New Hampshire's depressed enough as it is," she said, "with winter coming on."

The thing was that Melody was absolutely incapable of any character change. The way Ulm had written the play, the main action was what went on in the streetwalker's soul, was what she thought of herself after men treated her one way or another. In the little foreword to the play, Ulm said, "In order for *Rome* to come alive, Bella's soul, as sensed by the audience, must be a dazzling kaleidoscope—a kaleidoscope reflected smokily in a mirror in Hell. If Bella leaves out one band of color in the full spectrum of what it means to be a destitute, rootless young woman in a country torn by war, then *Rome* will fail."

I mentioned Ulm's foreword to Sally, asked her if Melody knew what a kaleidoscope was.

"Yes," said Sally. "She also knows what a spectrum is. What she doesn't know is what a woman is."

"You mean what a woman sometimes *has* to be," I said.

"Suit yourself," said Sally.

There was a glum silence. It was late afternoon outside. And Sally suddenly put her hand over her mouth and said, "No, no, no, no!" She was imitating Melody. During rehearsals, whenever we reached a place where Melody was supposed to kiss Bryce or John, that was what she would do.

And Melody wasn't much better than that between kisses. No matter what men said and did to her, she was Fred Lovell's daughter, who would never do anything to make her daddy ashamed.

"Maybe we should have cast her as Saint Joan of Arc," I said.

Sally snorted, and she asked me, "What makes you think Saint Joan of Arc was full of novocain?"

◙ ◙ ◙

But we kept going, no matter what.

Everybody knew his or her lines, anyway, as the case might be. I said to Sally at the final rehearsal before dress rehearsal what somebody always says at the final rehearsal before dress rehearsal: "Well, we've got a play."

"The question is, what's it about?" she said. She had a point. There was Melody up on stage being Melody, and there was Bryce being Bryce, and John being John, and me being me—and somehow we'd all gotten to Rome. And every so often one of us would open his or her mouth, and out would come spooky words that didn't have anything to do with anything, words from outer space, words from another world, the words of Arthur Garvey Ulm.

The rehearsal was still going on when I said we had a play. I wasn't in that particular scene. As it happened, I sat down next to one of John's many girlfriends. Her name was Marty. She was a waitress from South Crawford. Like about half of John's admirers, she'd had her nose broken at one time or another. It seems to me that about half of his girls were named Marty, too.

This particular Marty dug her elbow into my ribs, and she said, "That Bryce Warmergran is a hot sketch, ain't he?" She was laughing her head off. She thought it was supposed to be a funny play.

And Bryce was funny, too, God help us. He was crazy about that touch-me-not, that plaster of Paris marshmallow sundae, that Melody. And he prowled around her in sort of a Groucho Marx squat, looked up at her with very gooey goo-goo eyes. That was how he carried out Ulm's instructions in the script, which said, "Ben, the good soldier, has a soul nearly as mercurial as that of the girl, for remember: he is a poet, and the passions of a poet, by definition, can never be predicted, can never be controlled."

Marty asked me if Melody was worried about her father's trial. I replied that nobody knew when the trial would be. The government had teams of investigators in Barbell, according to the papers, and it looked as though it would take them years to find out exactly what Fred Lovell had done and how he'd done it.

"As far as Melody's concerned," I said, "her father is sin-proof. She can't conceive of his doing wrong, so she isn't worried at all." I shrugged. "And who knows— maybe he *will* get off."

"Yeah," said Marty. "Seems like everybody but Eichmann gets off these days. Is this Lovell walking around, or locked up, or what?"

"I imagine he's out on bail or something," I said.

"They all are," she said.

And that was when Fred Lovell himself came into the auditorium.

◎ ◎ ◎

I knew right away who he was. His pictures had been in the papers and on television many times. He was a chunky man, moon-faced, with a button nose and a high forehead. He had steel-rimmed spectacles with lenses the size of quarters. He had on a very boxy, double-breasted suit that looked as though it were made out of splintered plywood. He only had one expression, and that was sort of a Queen Victoria scowl.

I went to meet him. His breast pocket was crammed with fountain pens, and one lapel twinkled like the Milky Way. The lapel had the emblems of at least a dozen fraternal and service organizations pinned to it, and I wouldn't have been surprised to see a Dr. Pepper bottlecap there, too. What impressed me most about Fred Lovell, though, was the heavy perfume of booze.

I greeted him very loudly, so everybody would be warned. "Mr. Lovell! What a pleasant surprise!" I said. "We had no idea you were coming!"

The houselights came up. The play stopped. Melody shrieked for joy from the stage. She came running to her daddy, threw her arms around him. I wondered what she would say when she smelled all that booze on him.

"Oh, Daddy, Daddy, Daddy—" she said, "you've got too much aftershave lotion on again."

◙ ◙ ◙

Sally said we might as well start from the first again, so we did. "Mr. Lovell," she said, "if you'll sit down somewhere—I think you're going to be very proud of your daughter."

"Always was," he said. "Never had any reason not to be."

There were only six people in the audience and three hundred empty chairs. Lovell surveyed the situation, looked a little like W. C. Fields trying to find a straight pool cue. And then he picked the seat I had just vacated, the one next to John Sherwood's broken-nosed girlfriend.

"What are you in this play?" he asked her.

"I'm not in it," she said.

"Then how come you're all painted up?" he wanted to know.

A few seconds before the houselights went out again, a young stranger tiptoed into the auditorium, took a seat at the very back. His hair was long, and he was all unbuttoned, but I assumed he was a G-man. I thought he was following Fred Lovell, making sure he didn't get away.

◙ ◙ ◙

I was in the first scene, so I had to be up onstage. I didn't have anything to say. I just walked through twice, looking cynical. I was in the wings with John Sherwood. Melody was out under the lamppost, waiting for the curtain to go up.

"Mmm *mmm*!" John said to me. "Man, that's sure a lot of woman out there." He smacked his lips. "I can hardly wait for that kiss on Friday night! Yum, yum, yum, boy—that ought to be about the best kiss a man could ever have."

"No need to make fun of her just because she doesn't have a broken nose," I said.

"You show me a woman with a broken nose," he said, "and I'll show you a woman who thinks it's important to make a man happy." He shook his head, looked at Bryce, who was waiting for his cue on the other side. "Now there's a boy who just might get killed by the miracle of that Friday night kiss."

"Killed?" I said.

"I doubt if he's got any immunity to any disease at all," said John. "He's never been exposed to anything."

And then the curtain went up.

Melody swiveled around some in the circle of light under the lamppost. Sally had told her to do that. Melody had asked her, "Why?" Melody wasn't in costume, but she was swinging a big, shiny, patent leather purse on a long strap. No matter how pure her thoughts might be, it was obvious to anybody but Bryce Warmergran what she was meant to be.

There was a loud "Haw!" out of John's girlfriend. She loved that play.

And then, before anybody onstage had said anything, Fred Lovell gave a terrible groan. "Bring down that curtain!" he roared.

◎ ◎ ◎

The curtain crashed down. The houselights came up. I, as club president, went out to argue with that crazy man. He was on his feet. He was purple. The unbuttoned young stranger in the trench coat was standing, too.

"This filthy play is off!" said Lovell.

"Sir?" I said.

"My sweet daughter—" he said. He choked up. "The most perfect thing in my life, the only perfect thing in my life, and you got her under a lamppost, swinging a purse! I am not delighted. I am not delighted at all!"

Melody came out from backstage, scared stiff.

"You're getting out of here!" Lovell told her.

"We're going back to Barbell, Daddy?"

"You're going back to your aunt's house."

"Can't I come with you?"

"Not yet, honey. Later on. Meanwhile, you get away from these people, and you keep away from 'em! They're no good for you. You hear?"

"I hear." Melody wasn't about to argue. She took her father's arm, and the two of them marched out.

Right after they left, the young stranger left, too. He slammed the door.

I turned to Sally. "What's going through your filthy mind?" I asked her.

"He was crying," said Sally.

"His eyes looked dry to me."

"Who are you talking about?" she said.

"Lovell," I said. "Tartuffe." Tartuffe is a hypocrite in a French play we put on one time.

"I was talking about the young man in the trench coat," she said.

"G-men," I told her, "never cry."

◙ ◙ ◙

The next evening, the story was in all the papers: Fred Lovell was a fugitive from justice. He had jumped bail. Right after taking Melody back to her aunt, he'd headed for the Canadian border, crossed it, gotten to Montreal. In Montreal he'd hopped a plane for Brazil.

His eighty-thousand-dollar bail was forfeited, the papers said. It wasn't Lovell's money. It had been scratched up by ordinary citizens of Barbell who still believed in him.

There was another nasty little story on the side, too, with pictures. The pictures were of Fred Lovell's mistress, a very fancy young woman with eyelashes like buggy whips, with long diamond earrings, with piles of champagne-colored hair. She had been seen in New Orleans, boarding a plane for Brazil.

"What does this do to the play?" my wife asked me at supper.

"There's nothing left to *do* to the play," I said.

"I'm scared to ask the real question."

"What's it do to Melody?" I said. "God only knows. Sally's tried to call her all day long, but she won't come to the phone. She's locked up in her bedroom."

"Is the door locked from the outside or the inside?"

"Good question. From the inside."

The telephone rang. I answered it. It was John Sherwood. He wanted to know if there was going to be a dress rehearsal that night.

"What do you think?" I asked him.

"Well, I've got one idea," he said. "The posters are all up, the publicity's been going on for weeks, and the tickets are practically sold. We've got a couple hundred bucks tied up in the set and costumes—"

"You are not telling me the news, John."

"Suppose my girlfriend took over the part of Bella," he said.

"Marty?" I said. "Can she act?"

"Could Melody act?" said John. "At least Marty knows what the play's about. She's seen practically every rehearsal. If I worked with her for the next three days, come Friday, she'd be ready to go on."

"It's worth a try," I said. "I'll call everybody and tell them there'll be a dress rehearsal tonight, as planned."

"The play must go on," said John.

"Or something," I said.

◎ ◎ ◎

When I got back to the auditorium that night, the young stranger was in the back row again. "May I ask you a question?" I said.

"Go ahead."

"Maybe you're not supposed to answer, and maybe I'm not supposed to ask—but are you a G-man?"

"Do I look like a G-man?"

"Not close up," I said.

"Then I leave you to your own conclusions," he said.

"If you are following Fred Lovell, I hate to tell you, but your bird has flown."

"That's the breaks," he said.

That was the end of the conversation. I went up front, minding my own business. The rehearsal hadn't started yet, but John's girl was under the lamppost, warming up.

"How's she gonna be?" I asked Sally.

"There's going to be a police raid for the first time in the history of the North Crawford Mask and Wig Club," said Sally.

I saw what she meant. Marty was going to turn Arthur Garvey Ulm's masterpiece into a really rugged, dirty, low-down play.

"Has Bryce seen her yet?" I said.

"He turned snow white and disappeared. I think he's cowering in the basement somewhere."

And then Melody walked in. Her eyes were red, and there were circles under them, but she was very calm. She had made herself up with false eyelashes, heavy mascara, circles of rouge on her cheeks. And her mouth, as they say in books, was a scarlet slash.

That girl radiated so much tragedy and so much dignity that everyone got out of her way. Marty, when she saw Melody, slunk away from the lamppost without a word.

Melody got up onstage, looked out at us over the footlights, closed her eyes for a long time, opened them again. "Shall we begin?" she said.

◎ ◎ ◎

Great God—what a performance that was! Melody was ten times life size. People in the audience sobbed out loud as Melody represented every kind of female from the Little Match Girl to Mary Magdalene.

And when it was time to kiss, that girl kissed. The first time she kissed Bryce, he came reeling into the wings with only the whites of his eyes showing. The first time she kissed John, he made his exit like a man of the world. But when he was out of sight of the audience, he went down on his hands and knees.

When Melody came off at the end of the first act, I caught her in my arms. "You're the greatest actress this club ever had!"

"I'm like her!" she said. "I'm trash! I'm garbage!" She got loose from me, went over to John, threw her arms around his neck. "I'm what you need, and you're what I need," she said. "Let's you and me run off," she said.

That was fine with John. "Sure, baby," he said. "You and me—you bet, you bet."

The door to the audience flew open, and in came the young stranger. He looked wilder than anybody. He pushed John aside, and he put his arms around Melody. "I love you more than any woman has ever been loved! I'm not going to ask you to marry me. You *have* to marry me. There is no choice! It *has* to be!"

"Wait 'til J. Edgar Hoover hears about this," I said.

"What's he got to do with it?" he said.

"You're the most unbuttoned G-man I ever heard of," I said.

"I'm no G-man," he said.

"Who are you?" I said.

"I am a playwright," he said, "named Arthur Garvey Ulm."

Miss Snow, You're Fired

EDDIE WETZEL WAS an engineer in charge of making big insulators in the Ceramics Department of the General Forge and Foundry Company in Ilium, New York. Eddie's office was out in Building 59, where there was always a film of white clay dust all over everything.

Eddie was twenty-six. He had strong feelings about beautiful women. He hated and feared them. He had been married to a beautiful woman once—for six fantastic months. In only six months his bride smashed up his friendships, insulted his superiors, put him $23,000 in debt, and turned his self-respect to cinders. When she left him, she took both cars and the furniture with her. She even took Eddie's watch, cigarette lighter, and cuff links. And then she sued him for divorce on the grounds of mental cruelty. She stuck him for $200 a month in alimony.

So Eddie was a pretty serious person when Arlene Snow was assigned to him as a secretary. She was eighteen, petal-fresh out of Ilium High School—and, one month after she joined the company, she was voted the most beautiful girl within the company's seventeen gates. She was voted that on ballots from the company's weekly newspaper, the *GF&F Topics*. Arlene received 27,421 votes out of the 31,623 votes cast.

"You are to be heartily congratulated," Eddie said to her when news of the honor came. "Unfortunately," he said, "our main business here is not sitting around and looking beautiful but manufacturing insulators. So let's get back to work now, shall we?"

He was so sarcastic with her so often that Arlene was delighted whenever an opportunity to get out of the glum and dusty office came along. And the prime opportunity was represented by Armand Flemming, editor of the *GF&F Topics*. Flemming was forty, the brother-in-law of the Vice President in Charge of Employee and Community Relations, the cowed husband of a woman as massive and unyielding as a war memorial. He was constantly borrowing Arlene from the Ceramics Department for use as an unpaid model.

Whenever the company launched a new product, Flemming ran a picture in his paper of Arlene smiling blankly at whatever the new product was. And whenever a holiday was in prospect, Flemming devoted his whole front page to a picture of Arlene that was supposed to express the spirit of the holiday. For the Fourth of July, there was a picture of Arlene in a star-spangled bathing suit, lighting a firecracker as big as she was. The caption was "Kapow!"

And when Halloween came around, there was Arlene being scared out of her little overalls by a jack-o'-lantern. The caption was "Eeeeeek!"

At Thanksgiving time, there was Arlene, dressed like a pilgrim woman from the waist up and like a Las Vegas cigarette girl from the waist down. She was being scared by a turkey, and the caption was "Gobble, gobble, gobble."

It was this last picture that finally caused Flemming's brother-in-law, also his boss, to lower the boom on him. He told poor Flemming that he thought the Thanksgiving picture and its caption were downright dirty. He said, too, that it was obvious to everybody in the company that Flemming was in love with Arlene, since nobody else's picture ever got in the paper anymore, and that Flemming was never to see her again.

As it happened, Arlene was in the offices of the *GF&F Topics* when the riot act was read to Flemming. Fortunately, however, she heard none of it. She was busy in the photography studio, posing in a very scanty Santa Claus suit, with one bare arm draped over the neck of a plaster Rudolph the Red-Nosed Reindeer.

◎ ◎ ◎

While Arlene was posing and Flemming was being reamed out, Eddie Wetzel was boiling mad in his office. For want of a secretary, he was typing his own correspondence with two stiff, blunt fingers, and the telephone was ringing incessantly. The calls were never for him, never had anything to do with insulators. The calls were all for Arlene, and all related in one way or another to her unofficial position as company love goddess.

"No—I do not have the slightest idea when she will be back!" Eddie bellowed at a young man on the telephone. "I am merely her supervisor. She never tells me anything." He slammed the telephone into its cradle. He was quite red, and his breathing was shallow and noisy.

Now Arlene and Flemming came in. Flemming was subdued and gray. He hadn't told Arlene what the trouble was. What was bothering him most was his brother-in-law's suggestion that he, Flemming, was in love with Arlene.

Flemming realized, with a breaking heart, that the suggestion was deadly accurate.

Arlene greeted Eddie with the usual uneasiness he made her feel, and then she saw the message he had written in the dust on her desktop. "Miss Snow," he had written in a large round hand, "you're fired."

◎ ◎ ◎

Eddie Wetzel made it stick, too. In a manner of speaking, Arlene went right out on her shell-pink ear.

Eddie was able to prove that she was impudent, vain, easily distracted, and a slow and inaccurate typist. She was unable to read her own shorthand, had no loyalty toward the Ceramics Department, held the company record for tardiness and absenteeism, and was as amenable to routines as a one-eyed black cat.

And common sense tempered with cowardice kept anyone else in the company from offering her a job. Any man asking for her services would have raised the question, inevitably, as to just what services he had in mind.

Poor Flemming was least of all free to help her. He slunk back to his office to think things over, and his wife called him up to tell him almost word for word what his brother-in-law had told him, that he wasn't to see Arlene again. She called Arlene "*that hussy.*"

When Arlene left the company that evening, there was a pitiful little ceremony at the main gate. She was relieved of her employee's badge—her heavenly face in a clear plastic sandwich. She stood there in the gray and acid slush of winter in Ilium; and the gate guard, complying with company regulations, snipped the badge in two with great tin shears and dropped the halves into an ashcan.

He could not look her in the eye.

Into the night went Arlene, her face simply one more pale pie in a river of pale pies. The sleet-blurred streetlights were not colorful enough to reveal to a passerby that Arlene had been crying.

When she got to her bus stop, Armand Flemming was waiting for her. He was not himself a bus rider. The car he had driven to work was sitting all alone in a company parking lot emptied by the five o'clock rush.

"You riding the bus tonight, Mr. Flemming?" Arlene asked him.

"A bus, an airplane, a train—" said Flemming. "Who knows what I'll be riding before this night is over."

"Pardon me?" said Arlene.

"I'd like to buy you a drink," said Flemming. "I owe you at least that. I feel very responsible for what happened."

"You don't have to," said Arlene.

"I know I don't have to," he said. "I'm tired of doing things I have to do. From now on I'm going to do what I want to do." He looked a little wild, but Arlene was too jangled by her own troubles to notice it much. "I insist on buying you a drink."

So Arlene and Flemming went to a quiet little bar down a side street. Its red neon sign winked at them blearily. "Bar," it said. What Arlene and Flemming didn't know was that Eddie Wetzel lived in an apartment over the bar, and that Eddie stopped into the bar every evening for two martinis after work.

Eddie was sitting in his customary booth now, reading a letter from his ex-wife. She still loved him, she said, and could he please send her an extra $142.75? She had

had a small accident, she said, and the money would go toward repairing her car. "I don't think it's fair," she wrote, "for me to pay for unexpected things like that, and I'm sure the judge would say the same thing."

The letter was from Miami Beach.

The conversation in the booth next to his now intruded on Eddie's awareness. After a moment of involuntary eavesdropping, Eddie realized who his neighbors were.

"Arlene, I've always followed the line of least resistance," Armand Flemming said. "I've never really taken the bit in my teeth and lived—never done the things I should have done, things I wanted to do."

"That's too bad, Mr. Flemming," said Arlene.

"I haven't pursued happiness," said Flemming.

"I don't guess any of us do, really," said Arlene.

"Then isn't it time?" said Flemming. "Isn't it time we did?" He leaned forward. "*Pendant toute notre vie, Arlene,*" he said, "*jouissons de la vie!*"

"I'm afraid I don't understand that," said Arlene. 'I took mostly business courses."

"While we live," said Flemming, covering her hand with his while he translated for her, "let us enjoy life!" Flemming was not fluent in French. He had, in fact, just shot his wad in that particular field. The quotation came from an apron his wife had given him on the previous Father's Day. "Today something in me snapped, and from now on I'm going to *live*!" He cleared his throat. "I want you to live, too!"

"After the things Mr. Wetzel said about me," said Arlene, "I just feel like curling up and dying."

"Forget Eddie Wetzel," said Flemming.

"I don't see how I can," said Arlene. "He's the meanest man I ever knew—" She clouded up. "And for no reason at all. I never did him any harm."

"I'll make you forget him," said Flemming.

"How?" said Arlene.

"By taking you away from all this: sleet, cold, Wetzels, General Forge and Foundry Company, hypocrisy, fear, prudishness, double-dealing, conformity, bullying, compromises, never doing what we really want to do—" said Flemming. "Arlene—" he said, "you are the most beautiful thing that ever came into my fife. I can't stand the idea of you going out of it. I love you. I want you to run away with me tonight."

Arlene was shocked. "Mr. Flemming!" she said.

"You know what I did after you were fired?" said Flemming. "I went to my office and thought things over. Then I marched up to the cashier's office, and I demanded my war bonds and I demanded every nickel I'd contributed to the pension fund and I demanded every share of stock I'd accumulated under the stock bonus plan." He opened his suit jacket, showing Arlene that his inner pockets were crammed with negotiable securities. "As I sit here," he said, grabbing her hand, "I am worth $7,419. Where would you like to go, Arlene, to forget Eddie Wetzel and all the twisted, frustrated people like him? Tahiti? Acapulco? The French Riviera? The Vale of Kashmir?"

"Oh, Mr. Flemming—" said Arlene, standing and trying to get her hand back, "I'm very grateful to you, and I appreciate the nice things you've said to me, and I'll always have a special place in my heart for you—but I'd better just go home, I think."

"Home?" said Flemming, standing too, hanging on to her hand. "You think I'd let go of happiness that easily?"

"What makes you so sure I'd *be* your happiness?"

"Haven't you ever looked at yourself?" said Flemming. "Don't you even know what you look like?"

"That was one of the things Mr. Wetzel said—" said Arlene, "that I looked at myself too much."

Flemming knotted his free hand into a fist. "I should have hit him," he said. He showed his teeth. "How I wish I'd hit him!"

"I'm awfully glad you didn't," said Arlene, still trying to get her hand back, get it back without hurting the feelings of the man who wanted to give up everything for her.

"It would have showed you I was a man," said Flemming, full of adrenaline. And then he saw that the opportunity hadn't been lost after all—that Eddie Wetzel was available in the very next booth.

⊙ ⊙ ⊙

The fight was brief and unambiguous. Flemming got himself a bloody nose without laying a finger on Eddie Wetzel.

And then the bartender threw Flemming and Eddie and Arlene out of his place, out into the slushy night. "From now on," the bartender said to Arlene, who was already in tears, "do me a favor and bring your boyfriends somewhere else!"

The three went upstairs to Eddie's apartment to make poor Flemming's nose stop bleeding. The apartment, a tiny one, was dismayingly bare. There were no curtains, no rugs, no tables, and only two cheap little kitchen chairs to sit on. The only bed, the narrow bed on which Flemming now lay, was an army-surplus iron cot.

"Oh God—" Flemming said to the ceiling, "no fool like an old fool."

"I didn't mean to hit you that hard," said Eddie. "I'm sorry. I didn't want to hit you at all."

"I wish you'd killed me," said Flemming.

Arlene was in the kitchen, getting ice cubes to pack around Flemming's nose. There was nothing in the refrigerator but one slice of liverwurst and a can of beer. It was a small mystery to her where Eddie ate, since there was no table.

And then she saw the remains of breakfast laid out on top of the refrigerator. That was where Eddie ate, standing up. And there, too, was the only ornamental object in the apartment—the photograph of a bewilderingly beautiful bride in a golden frame.

Eddie came into the kitchen, caught Arlene looking at the picture. "Natalie," he said.

"What?" said Arlene.

"Her name is Natalie," he said. "I guess you know that. All the other girls in the department must have told you about Natalie and me before you'd been working for me a day."

"Yes," she said. "I'm very sorry about what happened to your marriage."

"I was fool enough to think she was as good as she looked," he said. "It was a pretty grim mistake."

"If she was so terrible to you, why do you keep her picture?" she said.

"It's like a man who's been shot wanting the bullet for a souvenir," he said. He dismissed the subject, hurried clumsily on to another one. "Look—" he said, "I'm sorry about what happened today, sorry I had to put you out of a job."

"You explained very well why you had to do it," said Arlene. "It was absolutely fair, I guess. The way you told it, I certainly had it coming."

He worked his hands in the air. "I mean—it isn't really so terrible. It isn't as though you have a family or anything to support."

"That's right," she said. At this point, Arlene would have agreed with him no matter what he said, but her words were as empty as his refrigerator. She was too interested in Eddie as a curious specimen to care much about what she said. She thought she had a good idea now as to what had made his marriage blow up so spectacularly.

"As a matter of fact," said Eddie, "a girl like you probably doesn't even belong in business."

"Where do I belong?" said Arlene watchfully.

Eddie found himself without any reply at all. He was so confused and alarmed by beauty that he could think of no place in the ordinary scheme of things where it could be said to belong.

A long, pitiful moan from poor Flemming put off for a time Eddie having to give Arlene an answer.

◎ ◎ ◎

Flemming's nosebleed had stopped of its own accord. Flemming was sitting on the edge of Eddie's jingling cot now, moaning about the mess he had made of his life.

"Things aren't really so awful, are they, Mr. Flemming?" said Arlene. "You can put all the money and bonds and everything back tomorrow."

Flemming shook his head. "The note, the note," he said. As it turned out, he had left a farewell note on his desk, a note that squared everybody off in no uncertain terms, giving the works in particular to his vice-presidential brother-in-law and his battle-ax wife. "The best thing I ever wrote—the only true thing I ever wrote," said Flemming. "I told them I was going to live, that I was going to the South Seas and write the great American novel." He shuddered. "They've all read the note by now."

"Then go ahead and do it," said Arlene. "Really go to the South Seas. Really write a book."

"Without you?" said Flemming. Wan hope that she would still run away with him flickered momentarily in his eyes.

"I wouldn't go with you," she said. "I don't love you. I wouldn't do a thing like that."

Flemming nodded. "Of course not," he said. He closed his eyes. "Today was the day I went out of my mind," he said. "Today was the day I went crazy. Today was the day I proved I wasn't a man and ruined my career as a mouse."

"You could still go back to your wife and job—if you want," said Arlene. "Everybody would understand."

"If I want," echoed Flemming. "You, my dear, are all I want."

"You don't even know me," said Arlene. She turned to Eddie. "Neither do you," she said. "I'm just the idea of a pretty girl to both of you. The girl inside of me could change every five minutes, and neither one of you would notice. I think you must have been the same way with your wife," she said to Eddie.

"I was very good to my wife," said Eddie.

"The way you ignore what a woman really is," said Arlene, "a woman has to do all kinds of crazy things just to prove to herself that she's really alive. She'd never find out she was alive from you," she said. "When a girl does something bad," she said, "it's usually on account of somebody isn't paying enough attention to her."

She turned to Flemming. "Thank you for making me so famous," she said. And she left.

◙ ◙ ◙

Flemming watched Arlene go, and then he left himself. "It does a man good to get jogged out of his rut from time to time," he said wryly. "Good-night. Sweet dreams."

Eddie assumed that Flemming was going home. And that's where Flemming assumed Flemming was going, too.

But when Flemming, on his way to his lonely car in the middle of the company parking lot, passed Arlene, who was waiting for her bus, Arlene asked him if he was going home.

And he stopped, and he thought it over, and then he said, "Home? Are you nuts?" And he turned around, headed back into town. And he actually did go to Tahiti.

Arlene's bus was slow in coming, so slow that Eddie, who went looking for her, found her before she left his life forever.

"Look—" he said, "could I take you to supper somewhere?"

"Why would you do that?" she said.

"I owe it to you—for everything," he said.

"You don't owe me anything," she said.

"Then I owe it to myself—" he said, "to prove I can treat a nice girl properly." He sighed. "Or is it too late to try and prove that to you now?"

She gave him a small, rueful smile that bespoke a willingness to forgive and forget under certain ideal conditions. "No," she said, "it's never too late for that."

Paris, France

HARRY BURKHART WAS the golf pro at the Scantic Hills Country Club in Lexington, Massachusetts. His wife Rachel was an ex-model and a well-known figure skater. When she was in her early twenties she had been offered a part in the Hollywood Ice Review. She married Harry and became a housewife and mother instead. At that time, Harry had become the first football player from the Coast Guard Academy ever to be named All-American by the Associated Press.

When they were both thirty-seven, Harry and Rachel went to Europe for the first time. They went for two weeks—London, Paris, and back home through London again. They couldn't afford a trip even that quick and short. They owed money all over town. But they took the trip anyway, because their doctor and their minister said they had to do something radical and romantic in a game try at not hating each other so.

They had four children to save the marriage for. What the marriage had done for the children so far was to make them the gift of life, and then teach them how to be vain, querulous, and full of hell.

Harry and Rachel had a reasonably good week in London, with plenty of good food and drink, and with money to spend. The money was borrowed, came from the last bit of credit they could possibly get—but there it was, good old money. They always got along better where there was money to spend.

They went by train and boat from London to Paris. When they found their train compartment at Calais, they discovered they were going to share it with two old and demoralized tourists from Indianapolis named Arthur and Marie Futz. The Futzes were in their middle sixties. They, too, were seeing Europe for the first time.

Arthur Futz hated everything he saw. "Europe stinks. England stinks," he said to the Burkharts, as the train began to move. "If I was one of those newsmen over here who broadcast the news home, that's what I'd say every night: 'Europe stinks. This is Arthur Futz, returning you to NBC in New York.'"

Old Futz, a retired plumbing contractor, claimed to have been insulted, cheated, and poisoned in London. "And my God—" he said, "that wasn't even Europe yet." He shook his head. "At least I could understand what they were saying when they gave me the works." He shuddered. "I just wonder," said old Futz, "what new adventures await us in gay Paree."

"We just might have the time of our lives, Arthur," said his wife bleakly. Marie Futz was a sweet, humble, jumpy little thing. She was trying to have a good time, but old Futz wouldn't let her.

"I don't doubt that for a minute," said old Futz. "I bet the French have ways of separating Americans from their traveler's checks as yet undreamed of in other parts of the world."

"It's supposed to be the most beautiful city in the world," said Marie.

"The most beautiful city in the world is Indianapolis, Indiana," said old Futz. "And the most beautiful house in the world is at 4916 Graceland Avenue. And the most beautiful chair in the world is in the living room of that house. And if any money disappears out of my pocket when I'm sitting in that chair, all I have to do is reach in back of the dear old cushion, and there my money is."

"Well—" said Marie emptily, "we'll be back at 4916 Graceland Avenue before we know it." She looked to Rachel Burkhart for sympathy. "And then we'll never budge again," she said. It was so mournful, so full of regret and resignation, the way she talked about never budging again.

"Dumbest thing we ever did was budge in the first place," said old Futz. He pointed to the empty seats in the compartment, seats facing each other by the door. "There's the seats of the two smartest people in the world," he said to Harry and Rachel. "They had brains enough to stay home."

Old Futz now excused himself, went out into the corridor to look for the lavatory. "I just hope I've got enough money to buy myself into the lavatory and back out again, if there is one," he said. "About a hundred dollars each way ought to just about do."

When he was gone, poor Marie Futz couldn't keep herself from shedding a couple of tears. Once Marie'd done that, she told her troubles to the Burkharts. "He's worked so hard all his life that he's never learned how to play," she said. "Play is harder on Arthur than work. This trip was all my idea, and I can see now what a bad idea it was. The minute we got to England, Arthur got all panicky, wanted to call off the rest of the trip, wanted to go back home to 4916 Graceland Avenue."

Marie's next sentence got fainter and fainter. "So I told him, all right, if he really felt that bad, but couldn't we please just go to Paris, France, just for a day, if that's all he could stand it for, but go for a little while, anyway, long enough to see the Eiffel Tower and the *Mona Lisa*, because who knows when we'll ever be so close to Paris, France, again, and who knows how much longer either one of us has to see just a few of the famous, beautiful things outside of the four walls of 4916 Graceland Avenue—?" The end of the question, a whisper, echoed in the bottomless well of human yearning.

"I can see now," said Marie, "how selfish I've been."

"I don't think you've been selfish at all," said Rachel. The miseries of the Futzes were making her feel pretty young still, were making her bloom. Growing old was even tougher on Harry and Rachel than being broke all the time. Coming across really old people had the same soothing effect on them as easy credit.

"People have to grab what they want from time to time," said Harry. He showed off his clever hands, his grabbing hands. Every year those hands lost an appreciable amount of suppleness, but they had a long way to go before they became the tremulous, spotted leaves the hands of old Futz were.

"You can't just spend your whole life doing what other people want you to do," said Rachel. She had a big compact in her hand, as she often did. Palming it, she snapped it open and shut many times in quick succession, made the mirror in it wink and wink at her. What there was to wink at was a thin, athletic brunette who had lost her seeming softness. Her sinews and harsh competitiveness were on the surface now. There was a lot of allure left, but any man attracted was warned at once that Rachel was a plenty tough baby.

Harry and Rachel's momentary feelings of well-being were thin and cheap. How thin and cheap they were was about to be demonstrated. Their feelings of well-being were about to be ripped as easily as wet tissue paper. But even before that ripping took place, Harry and Rachel revealed, in the advice they gave poor Marie Futz, what a rotten couple they made.

"Sometimes people have to go their own way, come hell or high water," said Rachel.

"Sometimes people compromise and compromise until they haven't got any life left," said Harry.

"Life is too short," said Rachel.

And so on. They advised Marie with great amiability, but the things they were saying they had often said to each other, often yelled at each other, with terrible brutality.

Little, white-haired Mrs. Futz was appalled. "I don't mean Arthur and I don't get along," she said. "We'd be lost without each other. I—I shouldn't have said anything. I—I just wish he'd relax and have a nicer time. Nobody's really robbed him or insulted him over here. Everybody's been nice as pie. He just feels lost away from home." She thought awhile, looking for something else to say that would convince the Burkharts that she really had a good marriage. "We love each other very much," she said at last.

"I guess we do, too," said Harry. "I don't know. What the hell. Life's funny."

"I guess we'll make it somehow," said Rachel, her compact winking at her. She liked more and more what the mirror showed.

For Harry and Rachel, this was a moment of high affection. Now Fate, without half-trying, wrecked it. There was an official flurry in the corridor, and a conductor opened the compartment door and pointed out the two unclaimed seats. The boy and girl he pointed them out to were young, luminously good looking, and goofy with love. The boy gave the conductor a tremendous amount of money for his trouble.

And then these two choice children, apparently honeymooners, sat down in facing seats, made each other comfortable with silky touches and misty whispers.

These two found each other so interesting that the others in the compartment could stare at them as much as they liked without giving offense.

Rachel, forced to see what real beauty was, put her winking compact away.

Harry fell in love with the girl immediately, yearned for her shamelessly.

Marie Futz gave an involuntary sigh like a faraway freight whistle.

The boy spoke to the girl in an accent that seemed British. The girl's shy replies were unmistakably Boston Irish. And English wasn't the only language the young man had. He had spoken French liquidly to the conductor.

Arthur Futz returned from the lavatory and was the first to speak to the newcomers. "I walked past here twice," he said. "I saw you two sitting in here, and I figured it was the wrong compartment." He sat down noisily. "'Futz, you old fool,' I said to myself, 'what the heck are you doing lost on a railroad train in France?'"

"It's easy to get lost," said the young man agreeably. He explained that he and the girl had gotten into the wrong compartment, had just been moved to the right one.

"He sure speaks French good," Marie Futz said to her husband. "You should have heard him going with the conductor." She turned to the young man. "That *was* French, wasn't it?" she said.

"Some people have been kind enough to say so," said the young man.

"Arthur and me—" said Marie, "we got French phonograph records and listened to them, only the records talk so slow. You talk so fast, it could be almost any language, as far as I'm concerned. Your wife talks French, too, does she?"

"No," said the young man, "but I'm sure she will."

"I'm sure I won't," said old Futz grumpily.

"There's just one sentence I want to say," said Marie, "and that's 'Take me to the *Mona Lisa* and the Eiffel Tower.'" She turned to Rachel Burkhart, who was looking out the window at the orange roofs and the ranks of poplars. What she was actually seeing was the ghostly reflection of everyone in the dusty windowpane.

And Rachel was burning up.

"You and your husband try those Victrola records?" Marie asked her.

Rachel didn't hear the question. She was watching Harry's reflection in particular, seeing how much Harry pitied himself for not being married to a petal-fresh young dumpling. She clouded up, without showing it, and thought about all the better men she could have had at a smile and a lazy jingle of her bracelet.

Marie Futz, rebuffed by Rachel, put a question to Harry. "You folks know any other languages?"

"German," said Harry. "German is my second language."

Rachel swung her head around to him incredulously. "Whaaaat?" she said.

"Why you always have to pick me up on everything I say?" said Harry, turning the color of tomato juice.

"You can't speak German," said Rachel.

"You don't know everything there is to know about me," said Harry. "I *studied* German at the academy." He didn't mention that he had flunked it as well. He was so lost in a dream of what might have been, what ought to have been, what still might be, that he didn't know what a lie was. He really thought he was bilingual, though he'd never thought so before. Harry suddenly imagined Vienna was his spiritual home, with oceans of beer and waltzing and affectionate, uncritical blond girls bursting their dirndls.

The boy was talking to him now, talking to him in German, inviting Harry to share the pleasures of that barking, growling language.

"I—I didn't quite get all that," said Harry queasily.

The boy said it all again, slowly and distinctly.

Harry considered what had been said to him, and looked as wise as a bullfrog full of buckshot.

Rachel broke the silence with a laugh that sounded like fire tongs being swept through a shelf of champagne glasses. "So typical!" she cried raucously. "How perfectly typical!"

Harry arose slowly, trembling. He stalked out of the compartment, closing the door behind him with a rattle and a bang.

"Well, it *is* typical!" said Rachel, absolutely unrepentant. "He's always imagining he's things he isn't." It took no special crisis to make Rachel sound off about her marriage to strangers. She and Harry had been doing it at the drop of a hat for years. Without knowing it, they had been exploiting the subject as just about the only remotely interesting thing about themselves.

The subject, at any rate, discouraged anybody else from taking the floor for a while. The compartment was reduced to muggy silence.

After a bit, old Futz got out his tickets and his passport, and all the rest of the tossed salad of travel documents. They made him so anxious that others got anxious, too, checked their own documents.

In the conversation that followed, it came out that all three couples would be returning to London in three days. Not only that—they would be sharing the same compartment again.

"I wonder what tales we'll all have to tell," said Marie Futz.

Harry Burkhart never did come back into the compartment. He stayed out in the corridor all the way to Paris, smoking so much that he arrived in the City of Light coughing his head off.

Rachel went out to get him when the train was in the station, claimed him like a cheap suitcase. "Where's your sense of humor?" she asked him.

"Haven't got one," said Harry.

"Paris, honey—Paris, France!" said Marie Futz, full of joy.

"I don't feel good. I don't feel good at all," said old Futz.

The young lovers melted into the Parisian evening at once, blended with it, their coloration perfect, their way made easy by the young man's familiarity with the city and the tongue.

The Futzes and the Burkharts had to find an interpreter to help them claim their baggage, exchange their pounds for francs, and finally tell their cab drivers where they wanted to go.

Waiting at the curb for a cab, Rachel cracked off at Harry again. "Too bad this isn't Germany," she said. "In Germany you'd be king."

Harry swore, took a short walk to work off some of his rage. This tour took him past a beautiful young girl standing under a lamppost. She spoke to Harry in English. She let him know right away that he looked like a hero to her.

In plain view of Rachel, not thirty feet away from her, that girl promised Harry so much love that only a hero would dare take it on.

◎ ◎ ◎

The three couples were booked at different hotels, but here and there they caught glimpses of each other.

Harry Burkhart, for instance, riding an excursion boat down the Seine with a woman not his wife, saw Marie Futz talking with the help of a phrase book to a baffled painter on the riverbank.

Marie Futz, in turn, spotted the marvelous young lovers arguing bitterly on a bench in the garden of the Tuileries.

Old Arthur Futz and a very hollow-eyed Rachel Burkhart ran into each other in the big American drugstore near the Arc de Triomphe. Old Futz was buying Pepto-Bismol. Rachel was buying hair dye and what looked like a half gallon of Chanel No. 5. They didn't speak to each other. Old Futz's fingernails were black, incidentally, and he was a man in a hurry, a man with plenty to do.

Old Futz, moreover, addressed the pharmacist in French. It was stubborn, twanging, billy-goat French, but it was firm and unashamed. The message got through.

And when the three-day visit was over, old Futz got himself and Marie through the Gare du Nord and on board the right train and in the right compartment without the help of an interpreter. He and Marie were the first ones in the compartment, and Marie was gaga over him.

"You got so much more out of those Victrola records than I thought you did," she said, talking about the records from which they'd tried to learn French.

"Didn't learn a damn thing from those records," said Futz. "Any language is just noises people make with their mouths. Somebody makes a noise at me, and I make a noise back at him."

"Nobody understood the noises I made the whole time," said Marie.

"That's because you weren't really talking about anything," said Futz.

Marie accepted this insult meekly. She had wasted the time of an awful lot of Frenchmen with sweet, outgoing, hopeful gibberish.

The next person on board was the lovely young girl—the lovely young girl alone. If love had isolated her from her fellow passengers on the trip to Paris, something a lot less cheerful was doing it now. She didn't greet the Futzes. She took her seat gravely, all thoughts turned inward. She wore no makeup this trip, cloaked herself in the dignity of the intelligent and drab.

She had a watch, but she didn't look at it. She didn't look expectantly into the corridor or out the window. She wasn't waiting for anyone to join her.

The last arrivals were Harry and Rachel Burkhart. There were a policeman, a railroad conductor, a porter, and a young man from the American Embassy with them.

Harry was drunk and disorderly, his tie awry, buttons off his coat, big stains on his elbows and knees. He had a fat lip and a shiner all the colors of fruitcake.

Rachel looked like a white queen of the cannibals. She had bleached her black hair and dyed it Zulu orange. She was cold sober. With a tenderness made all the more touching by her wild appearance, Rachel helped pour Harry on board.

Harry didn't want her tenderness, and he needed it desperately. He alternated between thanking her and telling her to go to hell. Once, when he thanked her, he called her Mother.

When the train began to move, Harry waved to the city and said, "So long, Paris, so long you old—" And he called Paris what the woman he'd spent three days with had been.

The lovely, lonely girl showed flickering interest in this scurrilous farewell, withdrew into herself again.

It took somebody as crazy as Harry to put a blunt question to her. "You can see what happened to *her* husband," he said to the girl, jerking a thumb at Rachel. "So what happened to yours?"

"He's been detained," she said politely.

"Paris sure didn't detain me," said Harry. "I'm one of the most undetained people who ever visited the place." He now stared with glassy speculation at old Futz, rocked back and forth and stared as the train threaded its way between back porches, airing bedding, and enchanted forests of chimney pots. "Mr. Futz—" said Harry.

"Yes?" said old Futz.

"Could I talk to you in private?" said Harry.

"What you going to do now, Harry?" said Rachel uneasily.

"Gonna start running my life again, are you?" said Harry.

"No," said Rachel. She didn't say another word to him.

Harry coaxed a very reluctant old Futz out into the corridor with him.

"I apologize for my husband," said Rachel.

"That's all right," said Marie Futz. "I don't mind. All men do nutty things sometimes."

"Just men?" said Rachel. "Look at my hair."

"Look at my hand," said Marie. She stripped the white glove from her left hand, held it up.

"What about it?" said Rachel.

"No wedding ring," said Marie. "Battered, used old thing—" that old lady said of her wedding ring, "worn almost as thin as a piece of paper in one place." She widened her eyes wonderingly. "Somewhere in that Seine River now, I guess. And when we get back to Indianapolis, Arthur and I'll have to go into some jewelry store, and he'll have to buy a brand new ring for his sixty-five-year-old bride."

The symbolism of a lost wedding ring was so poignant that the lovely girl was caught up in the story. "You lost it off a bridge?" she said.

"Down the drain of a washbasin in the Louvre," said Marie. "Arthur and I had just seen the *Mona Lisa*. Arthur let out a big burp while we looked at that wonderful picture. Then he said there was a good reproduction of it in the Circle Theater in Indianapolis. Then he said he's seen *Saturday Evening Post* covers that made it look sick. Then he said he bet that funny smile on her face was on account of she had heartburn, too.

"So—" said Marie, "I went into the ladies' room, and I cried and cried and cried. He'd squashed my happiness the way he'd squash a cockroach. Without thinking what I was doing, I was taking off and putting on my wedding ring again and again. And then I heard this tinkle, saw that poor old ring go down the drain."

"There wasn't any way of getting it back?" said Rachel, unconsciously treasuring her own wedding ring and ring finger in a hot, tight fist.

"Arthur worked side by side with the French plumbers for three days," said Marie. "Expense was no object. When the plumbers at the Louvre wanted to give up, Arthur put up the money to keep on going. He explored Paris below street level, and I explored it above, and I don't see how either one of us could have had a nicer time. He came up out of the manhole talking French like a native.

"And last night," said Marie, "all the friends he'd made down below threw a party for us. They gave him a crown and me a necklace out of pipe fittings, and they made us King and Queen of the Sewers of Paris."

The train was in open countryside now.

"Considering who we are and what we are and what we've always been," said old Marie Futz, "I can't think of a nicer honor toward the close of life. I'm satisfied now to go back to 4916 Graceland Avenue and never budge again."

The train passed the ruins of a factory that had been bombed in the Second World War.

Orange-haired Rachel looked out at those unsalvageable ruins and said, "I guess Paris gives everybody what he or she's got coming to him or her."

Again the lovely girl was made to turn her thoughts outward. "Wouldn't any city that wasn't your hometown do that?" she said.

"I never saw a city before," said Rachel, "that let a person be so many things so easily. There ought to be a big sign in all the Paris railroad stations, in all the languages, saying, '*This is all a dream. Go ahead and be the fool you are, and see what happens.*'" Rachel touched her hair. "Any minute now, I'll wake up, and my hair will turn back to black again."

"I think it looks very attractive the way it is," said Marie Futz charitably.

"Attractive?" said Rachel with clanking irony. "I'll tell you how attractive it is. I'll tell you how attractive Harry and I both are.

"In Paris, France—" said Rachel, "Harry and I went our own separate ways, lived out our own separate dreams. His way was with a pretty little tart who gave him all the love I'd never given him. She took him for five hundred dollars, his wristwatch, and his cuff links. When his money was gone, she called in her boyfriend, who beat him to a pulp.

"My way," said Rachel, "was to prove how attractive I still was. It didn't take me long to find out. I spent most of the three days hiding in my hotel room, hiding from the kinds of people I attracted: bellhops and drunks over sixty."

The train slowed for a station, but did not stop. It crept past a brick wall on which was chalked in letters six feet high, "Yankee, Go Home."

Rachel and Marie now waited for the girl to tell her story. She never did tell it, to them or to anybody. She didn't long to tell it, because she didn't know if it was something to be proud of or ashamed of or what.

If she had told it, she would have borne out what Rachel said about Paris. And she would have established a deeper tie with Marie Futz, for her story had to do with a wedding ring, too. Her name was Helen Donovan. Though she wore a wedding ring for all to see, Helen was not married, had never been married.

She was a new assistant librarian at the American Embassy in London, the air of Boston still in her lungs. She had been overseas for exactly six weeks—long enough to fall in love with the young man, whose name was Ted Asher—in love enough, far from home enough, to agree to go to Paris with him.

And the only way she got nerve enough to make such an expedition was to buy a wedding ring, to wear it for all to see. Her own fool's dream in Paris had been of holy matrimony. The boy's dream had been of fleeting, easy, carefree love.

The two had scared the daylights out of each other, had parted with Helen's virtue still intact.

Old Futz came back into the compartment. Harry had borrowed money from him, had gone into the dining car for black coffee. "He'll be all right," said old Futz. "He's pretty near sober now."

"What did he say about me?" said Rachel.

"He said he didn't see how a wonderful woman like you ever put up with a bum like him," said Futz.

Rachel went to the dining car to see Harry. The car wasn't really open for business yet. It had just opened to take care of Harry's special emergency. Rachel got in only after explaining that she was a key part of Harry's emergency.

Old Futz was right. Harry was close to sober.

"Hi," said Rachel, sitting down across the table from him.

"Hi," said Harry.

"It's only me," said Rachel.

"Well—" said Harry, "I could certainly make do, if you could."

Rachel answered him by taking his hand.

"I've been sitting here, thinking the craziest things," said Harry. He closed his eyes and pinched the bridge of his nose.

"Like what?" said Rachel.

"Who knows—someday we might even fall in love," said Harry.

"I sure don't love me much anymore," said Rachel.

"Me and myself just had a big bust-up, too," said Harry. "I don't think they'll ever speak to each other again."

"Maybe we could catch each other on the rebound," said Rachel.

And they did catch each other on the rebound. They were like honeymooners on the boat from Calais to Dover—pretty ratty-looking honeymooners, but honeymooners all the same.

On another part of the boat, Marie Futz unwrapped a plaster model of the Eiffel Tower two feet high. It was a surprise present for her husband. It had a barometer in it, made in Japan, and old Futz discovered right away that the barometer was permanently stuck at *ouragan.*

"It's the thought that counts," said old Futz. "Thank you very much."

Back in the stern of the boat, young Helen Donovan stood all alone, hypnotized by the wake. She took off her spurious wedding ring and threw it at France.

A Frenchman standing nearby saw her do it. He went up to her and said, "Pardon, Madame—I could not 'elp viewing zee dramatic zing you do."

His name was Gaston DuPont, a Renault salesman. Gaston was on his way to raise hell in what he considered the most immoral city in the world, London. He thought he was making a whale of a beginning, finding a good-looking girl who had just thrown away her wedding ring.

Gaston was wrong. Helen rejected his guardedly indecent proposals.

Poor Gaston, spurned by Helen, fell in with evil companions when he got to London. He was royally rooked by many people but in particular by a Piccadilly tart named Iris. After three days in London, Gaston looked worse than Harry Burkhart had after three days in Paris.

Helen Donovan started to write a novel about *her* three days in Paris. But the first two lines she wrote put her right out of the novel business again.

"Love is a funny thing," she wrote. "I don't think I'm old enough yet to understand everything there is to know about it."

City

HE HELD HIS smarting left eye open with his fingers, and stared at its reddened reflection in the mirror face of the penny scales. It felt as though the cinder were still there, but he couldn't see it. He dabbed helplessly at his eyeball with a corner of his handkerchief. Filthy place to live, soot blowing in your eye every way you turn, he thought. Handkerchief's none too clean—get a nice infection this way . . .

She studied her vague image in the drugstore window, and wondered if sitting at a desk all day wasn't making her wide at the hips, and whether a string of pearls might not make her blouse look less severe. The blouse was just back from the cleaners, and look at it! she thought. Doesn't pay to wear anything white in this town. Wear it one day, and it looks like you'd been dusting a coal bin with it. Well, there's the fourth number fifteen bus, and still no number eleven. If that man doesn't quit jabbing at his eye, he'll poke it out. Somebody ought to tell him to blow his nose. *That's* the way to get a cinder out. Thought everybody knew that. Just blow hard once or twice, and . . .

Got it that time, he thought with relief, staring vengefully at the wicked black speck on his handkerchief. Felt like it was the size of Gibraltar. By gosh, that must be the fourth number fifteen bus, and still no number nine! Might stay in town for a show. Should get home and wash out some socks, and write Mom. He yawned. Same faces on the same corner every night. There's that plump little mouse that catches the number eleven. He arched his eyebrows. Get a load of her, would you—just primping away and admiring herself in the window. Never get tired of looking at themselves, do they? Somebody ought to tell her about clothes—that blouse makes her look like a schoolmarm. He straightened his bow tie. If the bus isn't here in two more minutes, it's the movies for me. Look at those big, blue, innocent eyes. Girl like that needs protection . . .

Men with round faces shouldn't wear bow ties, she thought irritably. Makes their faces look wide and fat. If I were his girlfriend, I'd make him wear the regular kind. And I'd make him quit wearing striped ties with striped suits, too. Unconsciously, she gave a vigorous little nod in confirmation of her sentiments. There's another number fifteen! Funny about the city, isn't it? I've seen him here every night for almost a month, and all I know about him is he takes a number nine bus. She sighed. By the time I get home tonight, there'll be just enough time to manicure my nails and write Mother before bedtime. Could stay down for a show. Be kind of dangerous, maybe, going home all by myself late at night. A girl hasn't any business —Huh, he's weighing himself. Bet he doesn't weigh an ounce over a hundred and fifty-five. Somebody ought to make him take care of himself, put some meat on his bones. He should weigh at least a hundred and eighty . . .

One hundred and fifty-four pounds, he said to himself. Lost eighteen pounds in ten months. Hamburgers, coffee, and coleslaw. Never seem to have an appetite anymore. Give a week's pay for an honest-to-God home-cooked meal. She looks like she's getting enough to eat, all right. Regular little butterball. Like that. Looks tired, though. Office is no place for a girl like that. Bet the wolves give her a bad time where she works. Girl like that ought to be married and raising a big family somewhere. Wonder if her folks know what she's up against, turned loose in a city like this. No telling what might happen to her. If she were my daughter, I know darn well I wouldn't let . . .

Men are so helpless, she thought. Look at that collar—a disgrace! Somebody ought to turn it for him. Turn the collar, and he could wear the shirt for another year, easy. His eyes met hers for an instant, and she looked away quickly to starse-blankly at the cigar store across the street. She found herself composing a letter to her mother: "The work is very interesting. Not much new. It is hard to make friends here, but I met a very nice boy this evening. We went to a show and had sodas afterwards. It was just like back home. He isn't like most of the men here. You'd like him very much." She glanced at him furtively, and caught him looking at her again. She blushed, turned her back, and, with a look of deep concentration, studied the cluttered display of aspirin and alarm clocks in the drugstore window.

Just ask her how to get to the theater, he thought, his heart pounding wildly. Can't be any harm in that. Then ask her if she'd like a show and a soda afterwards. Sure, people do it all the time. It's the only way there is to get to know people in the city, for God's sake. She's looking right this way again . . .

I could pretend I'm lost, and ask him how to get to the theater or something, she thought nervously. I could just touch his sleeve, and ask him. Oh dear, here he comes. What would he think of me if I stopped him and asked . . .

Maybe she'll think I'm just another fresh guy, like all the rest, just out to . . .

Oh, no, I just can't. I'd die if he thought I was just another cheap—She bit her lip. He's past now. He looked like he was going to say something, like he wanted to, but then he just kept on going. He *isn't* like all the rest. If only I could let him know . . .

No guts, no guts, no guts, he sneered at himself. He shuffled to a stop a dozen feet from her, and craned his neck in a pretense of looking for a bus from this new vantage point. If only I could find out for sure she wouldn't take it the wrong way if— A bus pulled up to the curb, and its door banged open. Oh, oh, it's bye bye baby, now. There she goes for her bus— the number eleven at last. He glanced distractedly at the front of the bus. That's not here—it's another fifteen!

She walked in front of the bus, studied the large number fifteen deliberately for several seconds, then climbed aboard without looking back. The door slammed behind her, and the driver shifted into gear, ready for the light to change. It didn't work, she told herself, and she sank into a vacant double seat, tired and miserable. I'll get off at the next corner and walk—He's hammering on the door! Oh, no— what'll I say?

With a dazed expression, looking everywhere but at her, he walked down the aisle, and took the seat beside her. He had but a single thought—What'll I say? He sat in silence, pondering. Gradually, he became aware that his left eye was smarting furiously again. Picked up another one, by golly! He was grateful for the distraction, and began to dab busily at his eye once more.

The light flashed green, and the bus roared away from the curb. "Blow your nose real hard," she said softly. "Maybe that'll get it out."

He blew manfully. "I'll be darned," he said, beaming, "it worked." His eyes met hers squarely for the first time.

"Thought everybody knew that," she said modestly, her voice growing more confident with every word. "Just blow hard once or twice and . . ."

The bus jerked and stopped. A passenger got on and looked at them. The bus rushed away again.

He said, "This isn't your regular bus, is it?"

She gave him a timid smile. "It's not yours, either, I guess."

"No," he said, "it's not mine either."

"Golly," she said. "Whose bus is it?"

"Ours," he suggested.

"Okay," she said, and snuggled a little. "Where is it taking us?"

"I don't know," he said. "We'll ride it together and find out."

"That will be nice," she said, and snuggled again.

They looked at each other shyly and both of them smiled. The gloom of the city was suddenly washed away. There was all the clean, warm world, and the brightness of the future, to talk about as the two rode on in tremulous expectancy, toward the unknown magic at the end of an enchanted line.

SECTION 5

Work Ethic versus Fame and Fortune

The fortunes of Kurt's once-affluent family, with servants, governesses, country club memberships, lavish parties, trips abroad, and children in private schools, sank down to everyday middle-class life in the twenties and thirties, and Kurt was taken out of the exclusive Orchard School after the third grade and sent to Public School No. 43.

Kurt later wrote (in *Palm Sunday*) that his mother spoke of the time "when I would resume my proper place in society when the Great Depression ended" and join the local country clubs and take part in all that went with such a life. "She could not understand that to give up my friends at Public School No. 43 . . . would be for me to give up *everything*.

"I still feel uneasy about prosperity," Kurt wrote, even after achieving prosperity himself.

In his essays, speeches, and novels, the two people Kurt most often cites are Jesus from his Sermon on the Mount, and his fellow Hoosier Eugene V. Debs, the labor organizer and Socialist Party candidate for president, who said, "While there is a lower class, I am in it. While there is a criminal element, I am of it. While there is a soul in prison, I am not free."

Vonnegut is always on the side of the underdog, and his empathy for those who work for their daily bread, to feed themselves and their family, as opposed to feeding their illusions and pretensions of wealth and fame. Those values are reflected throughout these stories.

In "Go Back to Your Precious Wife and Son," a glamorous movie star who is leaving her fifth husband is found to be "no prettier than a used studio couch" without her makeup and finery, and no more desirable as a partner. In "The Lie," a boy discovers his pretentious parents have faked his entrance exam to get him into the prestigious prep school he doesn't want to go to anyway. In "Any Reasonable

Offer," a realtor working hard to please some demanding clients discovers they are freeloaders pretending to be aristocrats. "This Son of Mine" tells about two fathers who are trying to pass off their sons as younger replicas of themselves rather than let the sons be who they really are.

One of Vonnegut's most well-crafted stories from this era is "The Hyannis Port Story," when Kurt's ubiquitous installer of storm windows gets a job to put them up in a wealthy socialite family's house in Hyannis Port, Massachusetts. (Vonnegut likes the storm windows man who works on his own—no office job, no corporation—and knows how to do things like "gluing the waterproof gasket around the rim of the tub with contact cement." He is also the protagonist in "Go Back to Your Precious Wife and Son.")

As the site of the "Kennedy Compound," where JFK and his glamorous family had their summer headquarters, Hyannis Port was famous at the time Kurt wrote the story (it was purchased by the *Saturday Evening Post* in 1963 but not published due to President Kennedy's assassination that November). The storm windows man is hired to install his Trip-L-Trak storm windows on a four-story "cottage" near the Kennedy Compound, owned by Commodore William Howard Taft Rumfoord, whose title is derived from once having been "commodore" of the local yacht club. He resents the intrusion of the president and his new-money clan, and the great men of the era who come to visit, from Adlai Stevenson to the president of Pakistan, and "Pope John the Sixth," who arrives by helicopter.

"A man who sells storm windows can never be really sure about what class he belongs to, especially if he installs the windows . . . [T]he Commodore welcomed me like a guest of great importance. He invited me to cocktails and dinner, and to spend the night. He said I could start measuring the next day." He is the reader's "spy," who can eavesdrop on the people who hire him.

When the Rumfoords' son gets engaged to a fourth cousin of the Kennedys, fresh in from Ireland, and decides to stop making speeches for Goldwater, the insufferably pretentious "Commodore" is abruptly thrown from his high horse. He decides he is really the man described by the barker on a sight-seeing boat who tells the tourists that Rumfoord "sits on this porch, drinking martinis, and letting the old mazooma roll in." The self-styled Commodore feels useless, and announces to his wife that "I've got to find some kind of work." His wife—who might have got her opinion from reading Vonnegut stories—says, "It's awfully hard for a woman to *admire* a man who actually doesn't do anything."

In Vonnegut's world—the world of America in the 1950s, as viewed by writers, artists, and "rugged individualists"—it's not just any kind of work that's admired, but work that avoids the trap described by influential books of the time such as *The Organization Man* by journalist William H. Whyte, *White Collar* by sociologist C. Wright Mills, and *Life in the Crystal Palace* by novelist Alan Harrington.

My freshly minted college grad friends and I read all those books in New York in those days, and like Vonnegut himself, who wrote stories on nights and weekends in order to make enough money to support himself and his family in order to leave General Electric, we looked for ways to avoid the regimentation of corporations. (The phrase "life in the crystal palace" comes from Dostoevsky's *Notes from Underground*: "You believe in a palace of crystal that can never be destroyed—a palace at which one will not be able to put out one's tongue or make a long nose on the sly." The "underground man" thinks he would "fight shy of such a palace.")

As the question raised by Harrington's novel was described, "Thousands of men enter the crystal palace yearly. In time they must make a choice: accept the numbing security of big corporation life or revolt against submission." Vonnegut's most succinct and successful story that dramatizes that choice is "Deer in the Works."

David Potter, an idealistic young man of twenty-nine who has been his own boss at a small newspaper with a tenuous future, has decided to get a job at the Ilium Works, a big corporation, in order to provide security for his family. His wife has just given birth to their second set of twins, but still she is worried when she hears of his decision: "The [Ilium] Works are fine for some people; they seem to thrive on that life. But you've always been so free." Trying to be "practical," he tells his wife, "I haven't got the right to take long chances anymore, Nan, not with a big famly counting on me."

He gets a job in public relations at the Ilium Works, and his first assignment is to find a company photographer to help him track down a deer who has wandered into the vast area of "the Works" and been "flushed . . . out" near the metallurgy lab. David's boss wants a picture of the deer and a "human interest" story that will be featured in papers across the country. After wandering through a maze of buildings as complicated and confusing as Kafka's *The Castle*, David comes upon the deer, who is cornered and frightened. It's David's job to lock the gate that the deer might escape through, but instead of locking the gate he opens it. The deer runs out to freedom and David follows. "David stepped into the woods and closed the gate behind him. He didn't look back."

Neither did Kurt when he left GE.

—DW

More Stately Mansions

WE'VE KNOWN the McClellans, Grace and George, for about two years now. They were the first neighbors to call on us and welcome us to the village.

I expected that initial conversation to lag uncomfortably after the first pleasantries, but not at all. Grace, her eyes quick and bright as a sparrow's, found subject matter enough to keep her talking for hours.

"You know," she said excitedly, "your living room could be a perfect dream! Couldn't it, George? Can't you see it?"

"Yup," said her husband. "Nice, all right."

"Just tear out all this white-painted woodwork," Grace said, her eyes narrowing. "Panel it all in knotty pine wiped with linseed oil with a little umber added. Cover the couch in lipstick red—*red* red. Know what I mean?"

"Red?" said Anne, my wife.

"Red! Don't be afraid of color."

"I'll try not to be," Anne said.

"And just cover the whole wall there, those two ugly little windows and all, with bottle-green curtains. Can't you see it? It'd be almost exactly like that problem living room in the February *Better House and Garden*. You remember that, of course."

"I must have missed that," said Anne. The month was August.

"Or was it *Good Homelife*, George?" Grace said.

"Don't remember offhand," said George.

"Well, I can look it up in my files and put my hand right on it." Grace stood up suddenly, and, uninvited, started a tour through the rest of the house.

She went from room to room, consigning a piece of furniture to the Salvation Army, detecting a fraudulent antique, shrugging partitions out of existence, and pacing off a chartreuse, wall-to-wall carpet we would have to order before we did another thing. "Start with the carpet," she said firmly, "and build from there. It'll pull your whole downstairs together if you build from the carpet."

"Um," said Anne.

"I hope you saw Nineteen Basic Carpet Errors in the June *Home Beautiful*."

"Oh yes, yes indeed," Anne said.

"Good. Then I don't have to tell you how wrong you can go, *not* building from the carpet. George—Oh, he's still in the living room."

I caught a glimpse of George on the living-room couch, lost in his own thoughts. He straightened up and smiled.

I followed Grace, trying to change the subject. "Let's see, you are on our north side. Who's to our south?"

Grace held up her hands. "Oh! You haven't met them—the Jenkinses. George," she called, "they want to know about the Jenkinses." From her voice, I gathered that our southerly neighbors were sort of lovable beachcombers.

"Now, Grace, they're nice enough people," George said.

"Oooh, George," Grace said, "you know how the Jenkinses are. Yes, they're nice, but . . ." She laughed and shook her head.

"But what?" I said. The possibilities raced through my mind. Nudists? Heroin addicts? Anarchists? Hamster raisers?

"In 1945 they moved in," Grace said, "and right off the bat they bought two beautiful Hitchcock chairs, and . . ." This time she sighed and shrugged.

"And what?" I demanded. And spilled India ink on them? And found a bundle of thousand-dollar bills rolled up in a hollow leg?

"And that's all," Grace said. "They just stopped right there."

"How's that?" said Anne.

"Don't you see? They started out beautifully with those two chairs; then they just petered out."

"Oh," said Anne slowly. "I see—a flash in the pan. So *that's* what's wrong with the Jenkinses. Aha!"

"Fie on the Jenkinses," I said.

Grace didn't hear me. She was patrolling between the living room and dining room, and I noticed that every time she entered or left the living room, she made a jog in her course, always at exactly the same place. Curious, I went over to the spot she avoided, and bounced up and down a couple of times to see if the floor was unsound at that point, or what.

In she came again, and she looked at me with surprise. "Oh!"

"Did I do something wrong?" I asked.

"I just didn't expect to find *you* there."

"Sorry."

"That's where the cobbler's bench goes, you know."

I stepped aside, and watched uncomfortably as she bent over the phantom cobbler's bench. I think it was then that she first alarmed me, made me feel a little less like laughing.

"With one or two little nail drawers open, and ivy growing out of them," she explained. "Cute?" She stepped around it, being careful not to bark her shins, and went up the stairs to the second floor. "Do you mind if I have a look around up here?" she asked gaily.

COMPLETE STORIES

"Go right ahead," said Anne.

George had gotten up off the sofa. He stood looking up the stairs for a minute; then he held up his empty highball glass. "Mind if I have another?"

"Say, I'm sorry, George. We haven't been taking very good care of you. You bet. Help yourself. The bottle's there in the dining room."

He went straight to it, and poured himself a good inch and a half of whisky in the bottom of the tumbler.

"The tile in this bathroom is all wrong for your towels, of course," Grace said from upstairs.

Anne, who had padded after her like a housemaid, agreed bleakly. "Of course."

George lifted his glass, winked, and drained it. "Don't let her throw you," he said. "Just her way of talking. Got a damn nice house here. *I* like it, and so does she."

"Thanks, George. That's nice of you."

◙ ◙ ◙

Anne and Grace came downstairs again, Anne looking quite bushed. "Oh, you men!" Grace said. "You just think we're silly, don't you?" She smiled companionably at Anne. "They just don't understand what interests women. What were you two talking about while we were having such a good time?"

"I was telling him he ought to wallpaper his trees and make chintz curtains for his keyholes," George said.

"Mmmmm," said Grace. "Well, time to go home, dear."

She paused outside the front door. "Nice basic lines to this door," she said. "That gingerbread will come right off, if you get a chisel under it. And you can lighten it by rubbing on white paint, then rubbing it off again right away. It'll look more like *you*."

"You've been awfully helpful," said Anne.

"Well, it's a dandy house the way it is," George said.

"I swear," Grace said, "I'll never understand how so many artists are men. No man I ever met had a grain of artistic temperament in him."

"Bushwa," said George quietly. And then he surprised me. The glance he gave Grace was affectionate and possessive.

"It *is* a dull little dump, I guess," said Anne gloomily, after the McClellans had left.

"Oh, listen—it's a swell house."

"I guess. But it needs so much done to it. I didn't realize. Golly, their place must be something. They've been in it for five years, she said. You can imagine what she could do to a place in five years—everything right, right down to the last nailhead."

"It isn't much from the outside. Anyway, Anne, this isn't like you."

She shook her head, as though to wake herself up. "It isn't, is it? Never in my life have I had the slightest interest in keeping up with the neighbors. But there's something about that woman."

"To hell with her! Let's throw in our lot with the Jenkinses."

Anne laughed. Grace's spell was wearing off. "Are you mad? Be friends with those two-chair people, those quitters?"

"Well, we'd make our friendship contingent on their getting a new couch to go with the chairs."

"And not any couch, but the *right* couch."

"If they want to be friends of ours, they mustn't be afraid of color, and they'd better build from the carpet."

"That goes without saying," said Anne crisply.

◎ ◎ ◎

But it was a long time before we found leisure for more than a nod at the Jenkinses. Grace McClellan spent most of her waking hours at our house. Almost every morning, as I was leaving for work, she would stagger into our house under a load of home magazines and insist that Anne pore over them with her in search of just the right solutions for our particular problem house.

"They must be awfully rich," Anne said at dinner one night.

"I don't think so," I said. "George has a little leather-goods store that you hardly ever see anybody in."

"Well, then every cent must go into the house."

"That I can believe. But what makes you think they're rich?"

"To hear that woman talk, you'd think money was nothing! Without batting an eyelash, she talks about ten-dollar-a-yard floor-to-ceiling draperies, says fixing up the kitchen shouldn't cost more than a lousy fifteen hundred dollars—without the fieldstone fireplace, of course."

"What's a kitchen without a fieldstone fireplace?"

"And a circular couch."

"Isn't there some way you can keep her away, Anne? She's wearing you out. Can't you just tell her you're too busy to see her?"

"I haven't the heart, she's so kind and friendly and lonely," said Anne helplessly. "Besides, there's no getting through to her. She doesn't hear what I say. Her head is just crammed full of blueprints, cloth, furniture, wallpaper, and paint."

"Change the subject."

"Change the course of the Mississippi! Talk about politics, and she talks about remodeling the White House; talk about dogs, and she talks about doghouses."

The telephone rang, and I answered it. It was Grace McClellan. "Yes, Grace?"

"You're in the office-furniture business, aren't you?"

"That's right."

"Do you ever get old filing cabinets in trade?"

"Yes. I don't like to, but sometimes I have to take them."

"Could you let me have one?"

I thought a minute. I had an old wooden wreck I was about to haul to the dump. I told her about it.

"Oh, that'll be divine! There's an article in last month's *Better House* about what to do with old filing cabinets. You can make them just darling by wallpapering them, then putting a coat of clear shellac over the paper. Can't you just see it?"

"Yep. Darling, all right. I'll bring it out tomorrow night."

"That's awfully nice of you. I wonder if you and Anne couldn't drop in for a drink then."

I accepted and hung up. "Well, the time has come," I said. "Marie Antoinette has finally invited us to have a look at Versailles."

"I'm afraid," Anne said. "It's going to make our home look so sad."

"There's more to life than decorating."

"I know, I know. I just wish you'd stay home in the daytime and keep telling me that while she's here."

The next evening, I drove the pickup truck home instead of my car, so I could deliver the old filing cabinet to Grace. Anne was already inside the McClellan house, and George came out to give me a hand.

The cabinet was an old-fashioned oak monster, and, with all the sweating and grunting, I didn't really pay much attention to the house until we'd put down our burden in the front hall.

◙ ◙ ◙

The first thing I noticed was that there were already two dilapidated filing cabinets in the hall, ungraced by wallpaper or clear shellac. I looked into the living room. Anne was sitting on the couch with a queer smile on her face. The couch springs had burst through the bottom and were resting nakedly on the floor. The chief illumination came from a single light bulb in a cobwebbed chandelier with sockets for six. An electric extension cord, patched with friction tape, hung from another of the sockets and led to an iron on an ironing board in the middle of the living room.

A small throw rug, the type generally seen in bathrooms, was the only floor covering, and the planks of the floor were scarred and dull from long neglect. Dust and cobwebs were everywhere, and the windows were dirty. The only sign of order or opulence was on the coffee table, where dozens of fat, slick decoration magazines were spread out like a fan.

George was nervous and more taciturn than usual, and I gathered that he was uneasy about having us in. After mixing us drinks, he sat down and maintained a fidgeting silence.

Not so with Grace. She was at a high pitch of excitement, and, seemingly, full of irrepressible pride. Sitting, rising, and sitting again a dozen times a minute, she did a sort of ballet about the room, describing exactly the way she was going to do the room over. She rubbed imaginary fabrics between her fingers, stretched out luxuriously in a wicker chair that would one day be a plum-colored chaise longue, held her hands as far apart as she could reach to indicate the span of a limed-oak television-radio-phonograph console that was to stand against one wall.

She clapped her hands and closed her eyes. "Can you see it? Can you *see* it?"

"Simply lovely," said Anne.

"And every night, just as George is coming up the walk, I'll have Martinis ready in a frosty pewter pitcher, and I'll have a record playing on the phonograph." Grace knelt before the thin air where the console would be, selected a record from nothingness, put it on the imaginary turntable, pressed a nonexistent button, and retired to the wicker chair. To my dismay, she began to rock her head back and forth in time to the phantom music.

After a minute of this, George seemed disturbed, too. "Grace! You're going to sleep." He tried to make his tone light, but real concern showed through.

Grace shook her head and opened her eyes lazily. "I wasn't sleeping; I was listening."

"It will certainly be a charming room," Anne said, looking worriedly at me.

Grace was suddenly on her feet again, charged with new energy. "And the dining room!" Impatiently, she picked up a magazine and thumbed through it. "Now, wait, where is it, where is it? No, not that one." She let the magazine drop. "Oh, of course, I clipped it last night and put it in the files. Remember, George? The dining-room table with the glass top and the place for potted flowers underneath?"

"Uh-huh."

"*That's* what goes in the dining room," Grace said happily. "See? You look right through the table, and there, underneath, are geraniums, African violets, or anything you want to put there. Fun?" She hurried to the filing cabinets. "You've got to see it in color, really."

Anne and I followed her politely, and waited while she ran her finger along the dividers in the drawers. The drawers, I saw, were jammed with cloth and wallpaper samples, paint color cards, and pages taken from magazines. She had already filled two cabinets, and was ready to overflow into the third, the one I'd brought. The drawers were labeled, simply, "Living room," "Kitchen," "Dining room," and so on.

"Quite a filing system," I said to George, who was just brushing by with a fresh drink in his hand.

He looked at me closely, as though he was trying to make up his mind whether I was kidding him or not. "It is," he said at last. "There's even a section about the workshop she wants me to have in the basement." He sighed. "Someday."

Grace held up a little square of transparent blue plastic. "And this is the material for the kitchen curtains, over the sink and automatic dishwasher. Waterproof, and it wipes clean."

"It's darling," Anne said. "You have an automatic dishwasher?"

"Mmmmm?" Grace said, smiling at some distant horizon. "Oh—dishwasher? No, but I know exactly the one we want. We've made up our minds on that, haven't we, George?"

"Yes, dear."

"And someday . . ." said Grace happily, running her fingers over the contents of a file drawer.

"Someday . . ." said George.

◎ ◎ ◎

As I say, two years have passed since then, since we first met the McClellans. Anne, with compassion and tenderness, invented harmless ways of keeping Grace from spending all her time at our house with her magazines. But we formed a neighborly habit of having a drink with the McClellans once or twice a month.

I liked George, and he grew friendly and talkative when he'd made sure we weren't going to bait his wife about interior decorating, something almost everyone else in the neighborhood was fond of doing. He adored Grace, and made light of her preoccupation, as he had done at our first meeting, only when he didn't know the people before whom she was performing. Among friends, he did nothing to discourage or disparage her dreaming.

Anne bore the brunt of Grace's one-track conversations as sort of a Christian service, listening with tact and patience. George and I ignored them, and had a pleasant enough time talking about everything but interior decoration.

In these talks it came out bit by bit that George had been in a bad financial jam for years, and that things refused to get better. The "someday" that Grace had been planning for for five years, George said, seemed to recede another month as each new home magazine appeared on the newsstands. It was this, I decided, not Grace, that kept him drinking more than his share.

And the filing cabinets got fuller and fuller, and the McClellan house got dowdier and dowdier. But not once did Grace's excitement about what their house was going to be like flag. If anything, it increased, and time and again we would have to follow her about the house to hear just how it was all going to be.

And then a fairly sad thing and an awfully nice thing happened to the McClellans. The sad thing was that Grace came down with a virus infection that kept her in the hospital two months. The nice thing was that George inherited a little money from a relative he'd never met.

While Grace was in the hospital, George often had supper with us; and the day he received his legacy, his taciturnity dropped away completely. To our surprise, *he* now talked interior decoration with fervor and to the exclusion of everything else.

"You've got the bug too, now," Anne said, laughing.

"Bug, hell! I've got the money! I'm going to surprise Grace by having that house just the way she wants it, when she comes home."

"Exactly, George?"

"Eggs-zactly!"

And Anne and I were willingly drafted to help him. We went through Grace's files and found detailed specifications for every room, right down to bookends and soap dishes. It was a tough job tracking down every item, but George was indefatigable, and so was Anne, and money was no object.

Time was everything, money was nothing. Electricians, plasterers, masons, and carpenters worked around the clock for bonus wages; and Anne, for no pay at all, harassed department stores into hurrying with the houseful of furniture she'd ordered.

Two days before Grace was to come home, the inheritance was gone, and the house was magnificent. George was unquestionably the happiest, proudest man on earth. The job was flawless, save for one tiny detail not worth mentioning. Anne had failed to match exactly the yellow square of cloth Grace had wanted for her living-room curtains and the cover for the couch. The shade Anne had had to settle for was just a little bit lighter. George and I couldn't see the difference at all.

And then Grace came home, cheerful but weak, leaning on George's arm. It was late in the afternoon, and Anne and I were waiting in the living room, literally trembling with excitement. As George helped Grace up the walk, Anne fussed nervously with a bouquet of red roses she had brought and placed in a massive glass vase in the center of the coffee table.

We heard George's hand on the latch, the door swung open, and the McClellans stood on the threshold of their dream house.

"Oh, George," Grace murmured. She let go of his arm, and, as though miraculously drawing strength from her surroundings, she walked from room to room, looking all about her as we had seen her do a thousand times. But this time of times she was speechless.

She returned at last to the living room, and sank onto the plum-colored chaise longue.

George turned down the volume of the phonograph to a sweet whisper. "Well?"

Grace sighed. "Don't rush me," she said. "I'm trying to find the words, the exact words."

"You like it?" George asked.

Grace looked at him and laughed incredulously. "Oh, George, George, of course I like it! You darling, it's wonderful! I'm home, home at last." Her lip trembled, and we all began to cloud up.

"Nothing wrong?" George asked huskily.

"You've taken wonderful care of it. Everything's so clean and beautiful."

"Well, it'd sure be a surprise if things *weren't* clean," George said. He clapped his hands together. "Now then, you well enough for a drink?"

"I'm not dead."

"Leave us out, George," I said. "We're leaving. We just had to see her expression when she walked in, but now we'll clear out."

"Oh, say now—" George said.

"No. I mean it. We're going. You two ought to be alone—you *three*, including the house."

"Stay right where you are," George said. He hurried into the dazzling white kitchen to mix the drinks.

"All right, so we'll sneak out," Anne said. We started for the front door. "Don't get up, Grace."

"Well, if you really won't stay, good-bye," Grace said from the chaise longue. "I hardly know how to thank you."

"It was the most fun I've had in years," said Anne. She looked proudly around the room, and went over to the coffee table to rearrange the roses slightly. "The only thing that worried me was the color of the slipcover and curtains. Are they all right?"

"Why, Anne, did you notice them too? I wasn't even going to mention them. It would certainly be silly to let a little thing like that spoil my homecoming." She frowned a little.

Anne was crestfallen. "Oh dear, I hope they didn't spoil it."

"No, no, of course they didn't," Grace said. "I don't quite understand it, but it doesn't matter a bit."

"Well, I can explain," Anne said.

"Something in the air, I suppose."

"In the air?" Anne said.

"Well, how else can you explain it? That material held its color just perfectly for years, and then, poof, it fades like this in a few weeks."

George walked in with a frosty pewter pitcher. "Now, you'll stay for a quick one, won't you?"

Anne and I took glasses hungrily, gratefully, wordlessly.

"There's a new *Home Beautiful* that came today, sweetheart," George said.

Grace shrugged. "Read one and you've read them all." She lifted her glass. "Happy days, and thanks, darlings, so much for the roses."

The Hyannis Port Story

THE FARTHEST AWAY from home I ever sold a storm window was in Hyannis Port, Massachusetts, practically in the front yard of President Kennedy's summer home. My field of operation is usually within about twenty-five miles of my home, which is in North Crawford, New Hampshire.

The Hyannis Port thing happened because somebody misunderstood something I said, and thought I was an ardent Goldwater Republican. Actually, I hadn't made up my mind one way or the other about Goldwater.

What happened was this: The program chairman of the North Crawford Lions Club was a Goldwater man, and he had this college boy named Robert Taft Rumfoord come talk to a meeting one day about the Democratic mess in Washington and Hyannis Port. The boy was national president of some kind of student organization that was trying to get the country back to what he called First Principles. One of the First Principles, I remember, was getting rid of the income tax. You should have heard the applause.

I got a funny feeling that the boy didn't care much more about politics than I did. He had circles under his eyes, and he looked as though he'd just as soon be somewhere else. He would say strong things, but they came out sounding like music on a kazoo. The only time he got really interesting was when he told about being in sailboat races and golf and tennis matches with different Kennedys and their friends. He said that there was a lot of propaganda around about what a fine golfer Bobby Kennedy was, whereas Bobby actually couldn't golf for sour apples. He said Pierre Salinger was one of the worst golfers in the world, and didn't care for sailing or tennis at all.

Robert Taft Rumfoord's parents were there to hear him. They had come all the way from Hyannis Port. They were both very proud of him—or at least the father was. The father had on white flannel trousers and white shoes, even though there was snow on the ground, and a double-breasted blue coat with brass buttons. The boy introduced him as *Commodore* William Rumfoord. The Commodore was a short man with very shaggy eyebrows, and pale blue eyes. He looked like a gruff, friendly teddy-bear, and so did his son. I found out later, from a Secret Service man, that the Kennedys sometimes called the Rumfoords "*the Pooh people*," on account of they were so much like the bear in the children's book *Winnie the Pooh*.

The Commodore's wife wasn't a Pooh person, though. She was thin and quick, and maybe two inches taller than the Commodore. Bears have a way of looking as though they're pretty much satisfied with everything. The Commodore's lady didn't have that look. I could tell she was jumpy about a lot of things.

After the boy was through pouring fire and brimstone on the Kennedys, with his father applauding everything he said, Hay Boyden, the building mover, stood up. He was a Kennedy Democrat, and he said some terrible things to the boy. The only one I remember is the first thing he said: "Son, if you keep blowing off steam like this during your Boy Scout days, you aren't going to have an ounce of pressure left when you're old enough to vote." It got worse from there on.

The boy didn't get mad. He just got embarrassed, and answered back with some more kazoo music. It was the Commodore who really cared. He turned the color of tomato juice. He stood up and he argued back, did it pretty well, even though his wife was pulling at the bottom of his brass-buttoned coat the whole time. She was trying to get him to stop raising such an uproar, but the Commodore loved the uproar.

The meeting broke up with practically everybody embarrassed, and I went over to Hay Boyden to talk to him about something that didn't have anything to do with Kennedy *or* Goldwater. It was about a bathtub enclosure I had sold him. He had insisted on installing it himself, saving himself about seven dollars and a half. Only it leaked, and his dining-room ceiling fell down, and Hay claimed that was the fault of the merchandise and not the installation. Hay had some poison left in his system from his argument with the boy, so he used it up on me. I answered him back with the truth, and walked away from him, and Commodore Rumfoord grabbed my hand and shook it. He thought I'd been defending his boy and Barry Goldwater.

"What business you in?" he asked me.

I told him, and, the next thing I knew, I had an order for storm windows all around on a four-story house in Hyannis Port. The Commodore called that big old house a cottage.

◎ ◎ ◎

"You're a Commodore in the Navy?" I asked him.

"No," he said. "My father, however, was Secretary of the Navy under William Howard Taft. That's my full name: Commodore William Howard Taft Rumfoord."

"You're in the Coast Guard?" I said.

"You mean the *Kennedy Private Fleet?*" he said.

"Pardon me?" I said.

"That's what they ought to call the Coast Guard these days," he said. "Its sole mission seems to be to protect Kennedys while they water-ski behind high-powered stinkpots."

"You're *not* in the Coast Guard?" I said. I couldn't imagine what was left.

"I was Commodore of the Hyannis Port Yacht Club in 1946," he said.

He didn't smile, and neither did I, and neither did his wife, whose name was Clarice.

But Clarice *did* give a little sigh that sounded like the whistle on a freight train far, far away on a wet morning.

I didn't know what the trouble was at the time, but Clarice was sighing because the Commodore hadn't held any job of any description since 1946. Since then, he'd made a full-time career of raging about whoever was President of the United States, including Eisenhower.

Especially Eisenhower.

◙ ◙ ◙

So I went down to Hyannis Port in my truck to measure the Commodore's windows late in June. His driveway was on Irving Avenue. So was the Kennedys' driveway. And President Kennedy and I hit Cape Cod on the very same day.

Traffic to Hyannis Port was backed up through three villages. There were license plates from every state in the Republic. The line was moving about four miles an hour. I was passed by several groups of fifty-mile hikers. My radiator came to a boil four times.

I was feeling pretty sorry for myself, because I was just an ordinary citizen, and had to get stuck in lines like that. But then I recognized the man in the limousine up ahead of me. It was Adlai Stevenson. He wasn't moving any faster than I was, and his radiator was boiling, too.

One place there, we got stuck so long that Mr. Stevenson and I got out and walked around a little. I took the opportunity to ask him how the United Nations were getting along. He told me they were getting along about as well as could be expected. That wasn't anything I didn't already know.

When I finally got to Hyannis Port, I found out Irving Avenue was blocked off by police and Secret Service men. Adlai Stevenson got to go down it, but I didn't. The police made me get back into line with the tourists, who were being shunted down a street one block over from Irving Avenue.

The next thing I knew, I was in Hyannis, going past the *Presidential Motor Inn*, the *First Family Waffle Shop*, the *PT-109 Cocktail Lounge*, and a miniature golf course called the *New Frontier*.

I went into the waffle shop, and I called up the Rumfoords to find out how an ordinary storm-window salesman was supposed to get down Irving Avenue without dying in a hail of lead. It was the butler I talked to. He took down my license number, and found out how tall I was and what color my eyes were and all. He said he would tell the Secret Service, and they would let me by next time.

It was late in the afternoon, and I'd missed lunch, so I decided to have a waffle. All the different kinds of waffles were named after Kennedys and their friends and relatives. A waffle with strawberries and cream was a *Jackie*. A waffle with a scoop of ice cream was a *Caroline*. They even had a waffle named *Arthur Schlesinger, Jr.*

I had a thing called a *Teddy*—and a cup of *Joe*.

◎ ◎ ◎

I got through next time, went right down Irving Avenue behind the Defense Minister of Pakistan. Except for us, that street was as quiet as a stretch of the Sahara Desert.

There wasn't anything to see at all on the President's side, except for a new, peeled-cedar fence about eight feet high and two hundred feet long, with a gate in it. The Rumfoord cottage faced the gate from across the street. It was the biggest house, and one of the oldest, in the village. It was stucco. It had towers and balconies, and a veranda that ran around all four sides.

On a second-floor balcony was a huge portrait of Barry Goldwater. It had bicycle reflectors in the pupils of its eyes. Those eyes stared right through the Kennedy gate. There were floodlights all around it, so I could tell it was lit up at night. And the floodlights were rigged with blinkers.

◎ ◎ ◎

A man who sells storm windows can never be really sure about what class he belongs to, especially if he installs the windows, too. So I was prepared to keep out from under foot, and go about my business, measuring the windows. But the Commodore welcomed me like a guest of great importance. He invited me to cocktails and dinner, and to spend the night. He said I could start measuring the next day.

So we had martinis out on the veranda. Only we didn't sit on the most pleasant side, which looked out on the Yacht Club dock and the harbor. We sat on the side that looked out on all the poor tourists being shunted off toward Hyannis. The Commodore liked to talk about all those fools out there.

"Look at them!" he said. "They wanted glamour, and now they realize they're not going to get it. They actually expected to be invited to play touch football with Eunice and Frank Sinatra and the Secretary of Health and Welfare. Glamour is what they voted for, and look at 'em now. They don't even get to look at a Kennedy chimney up above the trees. All the glamour they'll get out of this administration is an overpriced waffle named *Caroline*."

A helicopter went over, very low, and it landed somewhere inside the Kennedy fence. Clarice said she wondered who it was.

"Pope John the Sixth," said the Commodore.

The butler, whose name was John, came out with a big bowl. I thought it was peanuts or popcorn, but it turned out to be Goldwater buttons. The Commodore had John take the bowl out to the street, and offer buttons to the people in cars. A lot of people took them. Those people were disappointed. They were sore.

Some fifty-mile hikers, who'd actually hiked sixty-seven miles, all the way from Boston, asked if they could please lie down on the Rumfoord lawn for a while. They were burned up, too. They thought it was the duty of the President, or at least the Attorney General, to thank them for walking so far. The Commodore said they could not only lie down, but he would give them lemonade, if they would put on Goldwater buttons. They were glad to.

"Commodore," I said, "where's that nice boy of yours, the one who talked to us up in New Hampshire."

"The one who talked to you is the only one I've got," he said.

"He certainly poured it on," I said.

"Chip off the old block," he said.

Clarice gave that faraway freight-whistle sigh of hers again.

"The boy went swimming just before you got here," said the Commodore. "He should be back at any time, unless he's been decapitated by a member of the Irish Mafia on water skis."

We went around to the water side of the veranda to see if we could catch sight of young Robert Taft Rumfoord in swimming. There was a Coast Guard cutter out there, shooing tourists in motorboats away from the Kennedy beach. There was a sightseeing boat crammed with people gawking in our direction. The barker on the boat had a very loud loudspeaker, and we could hear practically everything he said.

"*The white boat there is the* Honey Fitz, *the President's personal yacht,*" said the barker. "*Next to it is the* Marlin, *which belongs to the President's father, Joseph C. Kennedy, former Ambassador to the Court of St. James's.*"

"The President's stinkpot, and the President's father's stinkpot," said the Commodore. He called all motorboats stinkpots. "This is a harbor that should be devoted exclusively to sail."

There was a chart of the harbor on the veranda wall. I studied it, and found a *Rumfoord Point,* a *Rumfoord Rock,* and a *Rumfoord Shoal.* The Commodore told me his family had been in Hyannis Port since 1884.

"There doesn't seem to be anything named after Kennedys," I said.

"Why *should* there be?" he said. "They only got here day before yesterday."

"Day before yesterday?" I said.

And he asked me, "What would *you* call nineteen-twenty-one?"

"*No, sir,*" the barker said to one of his passengers, "*that is not the President's house. Everybody asks that. That great big ugly stucco house, folks, that's the Rumfoord Cottage. I agree with you, it's too big to be called a* cottage, *but you know how rich people are.*"

"Demoralized and bankrupt by confiscatory taxation," said the Commodore. "You know," he said, "it isn't as though Kennedy was the first President we ever had in Hyannis Port. Taft, Harding, Coolidge, and Hoover were all guests of my father in this very house. Kennedy is simply the first President who's seen fit to turn the place into an eastern enclave of *Disneyland.*"

"*No, mam,*" said the barker, "*I don't know where the Rumfoords get their money, but they don't have to work at all, I know that. They just sit on that porch there, and drink martinis, and let the old mazooma roll in."*

The Commodore blew up. He said he was going to sue the owners of the sight-seeing boat for a blue million. His wife tried to calm him down, but he made me come into his study with him while he called up his lawyers.

"You're a witness," he said.

◎ ◎ ◎

But his telephone rang before he could call his lawyers. The person who was calling him was a Secret Service Agent named Raymond Boyle. I found out later that Boyle was known around the Kennedy household as the *Rumfoord Specialist* or the *Ambassador to Rumfoordiana*. Whenever anything came up that had to do with the Rumfoords, Boyle had to handle it.

The Commodore told me to go upstairs and listen in on the extension in the hall. "This will give you an idea of how arrogant civil servants have become these days," he said.

So I went upstairs.

"The Secret Service is one of the least secret services I've ever come in contact with," the Commodore was saying when I picked up the phone. "I've seen drum and bugle corps that were less obtrusive. Did I ever tell you about the time Calvin Coolidge, who was also a President, as it happened, went fishing for scup with my father and me off the end of the Yacht Club dock?"

"Yessir, you have, many times," said Boyle. "It's a good story, and I want to hear it again sometime. But right now I'm calling about your son."

The Commodore went right ahead with the story anyway. "President Coolidge," he said, "insisted on baiting his own hook, and the combined Atlantic and Pacific Fleets were not anchored offshore, and the sky was not black with airplanes, and brigades of Secret Service Agents were not trampling the neighbors' flowerbeds to purée."

"Sir——" said Boyle patiently, "your son Robert was apprehended in the act of boarding the President's father's boat, the *Marlin*."

"Back in the days of Coolidge, there *were* no stinkpots like that in this village, dribbling petroleum products, belching fumes, killing the fish, turning the beaches a gummy black."

"Commodore Rumfoord, sir," said Boyle, "did you hear what I just said about your son?"

"Of course," said the Commodore. "You said Robert, a member of the Hyannis Port Yacht Club, was caught touching a vessel belonging to another member of the club. This may seem a very terrible crime to a landlubber like yourself; but it has long been a custom of the sea, Mr. Boyle, that a swimmer, momentarily fatigued, may, upon coming to a vessel not his own, grasp that vessel and rest, without fear of being fired upon by the Coast Guard, or of having his fingers smashed by members of the Secret Service, or, as I prefer to call them, the *Kennedy Palace Dragoons*."

"There has been no shooting, and no smashing, sir," said Boyle. "There has also been no evidence of swimmer's fatigue. Your Robert went up the anchor line of the *Marlin* like a chimpanzee. He *swarmed* up that rope, Commodore. I believe that's the proper nautical term. And I remind you, as I tried to remind him, that persons moving, uninvited, unannounced, with such speed and purposefulness within the vicinity of a President are, as a matter of time-honored policy, to be turned back at all costs—to be turned back, if need be, *violently.*"

"Was it a Kennedy who gave the order that the boarder be repelled?" the Commodore wanted to know.

"There was no Kennedy on board, sir."

"The stinkpot was unoccupied?"

"Adlai Stevenson and Walter Reuther and one of my men were on board, sir," said Boyle. "They were all below, until they heard Robert's feet hit the deck."

"Stevenson and Reuther?" said the Commodore. "That's the last time I let my son go swimming without a dagger in his teeth. I hope he was opening the seacocks when beaten insensible by truncheons."

"Very funny, sir," said Boyle, his voice developing a slight cutting edge.

"You're sure it was my Robert?" said the Commodore.

"Who else but your Robert wears a Goldwater button on his swimming trunks?" asked Boyle.

"You object to his political views?" the Commodore demanded.

"I mention the button as a means of identification. Your son's politics do not interest the Secret Service. For your information, I have spent seven years protecting the life of a Republican, and three protecting the life of a Democrat," said Boyle.

"For your information, Mr. Boyle," said the Commodore, "Dwight David Eisenhower was *not* a Republican."

"Whatever he was, I protected him," said Boyle. "He may have been a Zoroastrian, for all I know. And whatever the next President is going to be, I'll protect him, too. I also protect the lives of persons like your son from the consequences of excessive informality where the Presidential presence is concerned." Now Boyle's voice really started to cut. It sounded like a bandsaw working on galvanized tin. "I tell you, officially and absolutely unsmilingly now, your son is to cease and desist from using Kennedy boats as love nests."

That got through to the Commodore, bothered him. "Love nests?" he said.

"Your Robert has been meeting a girl on boats all over the harbor," said Boyle. "He arranged to meet her today on the *Marlin*. He was sure it would be vacant. Adlai Stevenson and Walter Reuther were a shock."

The Commodore was quiet for a few seconds, and then he said, "Mr. Boyle, I resent your implications. If I ever hear of your implying such a thing about my son to anyone else, you had better put your pistol and shoulder holster in your wife's name, because I'll sue you for everything you've got. My Robert has never gone with a girl he wasn't proud to introduce to his mother and me, and he never will."

"You're going to meet this one any minute now," said Boyle. "Robert is on his way home with her."

The Commodore wasn't tough at all now. He was uneasy and humble when he said, "Would you mind telling me her name?"

"Kennedy, sir," said Boyle, "*Sheila* Kennedy, fresh over from Ireland, a fourth cousin of the President of the United States."

Robert Taft Rumfoord came in with the girl right after that, and announced they were engaged to be married.

⊙ ⊙ ⊙

Supper that night in the Rumfoord cottage was sad and beautiful and happy and strange. There were Robert and his girl, and me, and the Commodore and his lady.

That girl was so intelligent, so warm, and so beautiful that she broke my heart every time I looked at her. That was why supper was so peculiar. The girl was so desirable, and the love between her and Robert was so sweet and clean, that nobody could think of anything but silly little things to say. We mainly ate in silence.

The Commodore brought up the subject of politics just once. He said to Robert, "Well—uh—will you still be making speeches around the country, or—uh—"

"I think I'll get out of politics entirely for a while," said Robert.

The Commodore said something that none of us could understand, because the words sort of choked him.

"Sir?" said Robert.

"I said," said the Commodore, "'I would think you would.'"

I looked at the Commodore's lady, at Clarice. All the lines had gone out of her face. She looked young and beautiful, too. She was completely relaxed for the first time in God-knows-how-many years.

⊙ ⊙ ⊙

One of the things I said that supper was was *sad*. The sad part was how empty and quiet it left the Commodore.

The two lovers went for a moonlight sail. The Commodore and his lady and I had brandy on the veranda, on the water side. The sun was down. The tourist traffic had petered out. The fifty-mile hikers who had asked to rest on the lawn that afternoon were still all there, sound asleep, except for one boy who played a guitar. He played it slowly. Sometimes it seemed like a minute between the time he would pluck a string and the time he would pluck one again.

John, the butler, came out and asked the Commodore if it was time to turn on Senator Goldwater's floodlights yet.

"I think we'll just leave him off tonight, John," said the Commodore.

"Yes, sir," said John.

"I'm still *for* him, John," said the Commodore. "Don't anybody misunderstand me. I just think we ought to give him a rest tonight."

"Yes, sir," said John, and he left.

It was dark on the veranda, so I couldn't see the Commodore's face very well. The darkness, and the brandy, and the slow guitar let him start telling the truth about himself without feeling much pain.

"Let's give the Senator from Arizona a rest," he said. "Everybody knows who *he* is. The question is: Who am I?"

"A lovable man," said Clarice in the dark.

"With Goldwater's floodlights turned off, and with my son engaged to marry a Kennedy, what am I but what the man on the sight-seeing boat said I was: A man who sits on this porch, drinking martinis, and letting the old mazooma roll in."

"You're an intelligent, charming, well-educated man, and you're still quite young," said Clarice.

"I've got to find some kind of work," he said.

"We'll both be so much happier," she said. "I would love you, no matter what. But I can tell you now, darling—it's awfully hard for a woman to *admire* a man who actually doesn't do anything."

We were dazzled by the headlights of two cars coming out of the Kennedys' driveway. The cars stopped right in front of the Rumfoord Cottage. Whoever was in them seemed to be giving the place a good looking-over.

The Commodore went to that side of the veranda, to find out what was going on. And I heard the voice of the President of the United States coming from the car in front.

"Commodore Rumfoord," said the President, "may I ask what is wrong with your Goldwater sign?"

"Nothing, Mr. President," said the Commodore respectfully.

"Then why isn't it on?" asked the President.

"I just didn't feel like turning it on tonight, sir," said the Commodore.

"I have Mr. Khrushchev's son-in-law with me," said the President. "He would very much enjoy seeing it."

"Yes, sir," said the Commodore. He was right by the switch. He turned it on. The whole neighborhood was bathed in flashing light.

"Thank you," said the President. "And *leave* it on, would you, please?"

"Sir?" said the Commodore.

The cars started to pull away slowly. "That way," said the President, "I can find my way home."

Go Back to Your Precious
Wife and Son

GLORIA HILTON and her fifth husband didn't live in New Hampshire very long. But they lived there long enough for me to sell them a bathtub enclosure. My main line is aluminum combination storm windows and screens—but anybody in storm windows is practically automatically in bathtub enclosures, too.

The enclosure they ordered was for Gloria Hilton's personal bathtub. I guess that was the zenith of my career. Some men are asked to build mighty dams or noble skyscrapers, or conquer terrible plagues, or lead great armies into battle.

Me?

I was asked to keep drafts off the most famous body in the world.

◎ ◎ ◎

People ask me how well did I know Gloria Hilton. I generally say, "The only time I ever saw that woman in the flesh was through a hot-air register." That was how the bathroom where they wanted the enclosure was heated—with a hot-air register in the floor. It wasn't connected to the furnace. It just bled heat from the ceiling of the room down below. I don't wonder Gloria Hilton found her bathroom cold.

I was installing the enclosure when loud talk started coming out of the register. I was at a very tricky point, gluing the waterproof gasket around the rim of the tub with contact cement, so I couldn't close the register. I had to listen to what wasn't any of my business, whether I wanted to or not.

"Don't talk to me about love," Gloria Hilton said to her fifth husband. "You don't know anything about love. You don't know the meaning of love."

I hadn't looked down through the register yet, so the only face I had to put with her voice was her face in the movies.

"Maybe you're right, Gloria," said her fifth husband.

"I give you my word of honor I'm right," she said.

"Well—" he said, "that certainly brings the whole discussion to a dead stop right there. How could I possibly argue with the sacred word of honor of Gloria Hilton?"

I knew what he looked like. He was the one who'd done all the negotiating for the bathtub enclosure. I had also sold him two Fleetwood Trip-L-Trak storm windows for the two bathroom windows. Those have the self-storing screen feature. The whole time we were negotiating, he called his wife "Miss Hilton." Miss Hilton wanted this, and Miss Hilton wanted that. He was only thirty-five, but the circles under his eyes made him look sixty.

"I pity you," Gloria Hilton said to him. "I pity anybody who can't love. They are the most pitiful people there are."

"The more you talk," he said, "the more I'm convinced I'm one of them."

He was the writer, of course. My wife keeps a lot of Hollywood stuff in her head, and she tells me Gloria Hilton was married to a motorcycle policeman, then a sugar millionaire, then somebody who played Tarzan, then her agent—and then the writer. George Murra, the writer, was the one I knew.

"People keep wondering what the matter with the world is," said Gloria. "I know what the matter is. It's simple: most men don't know the meaning of the word love."

"At least give me credit for trying to find out what it means," said Murra. "For one solid year now, I haven't done a single, solitary thing but order a bathtub enclosure and try to find out what love means."

"I suppose you're going to blame me for that, too," she said.

"For what?" he said.

"The fact that you haven't written a word since we've been married," she said. "I suppose that's somehow my fault, too."

"I hope I'm not that shallow," he said. "I know a plain, ordinary coincidence when I see one. The fights we have all night, the photographers and reporters and so-called friends we have all day—they have nothing to do with the fact I've dried up."

"You're one of those people who enjoys suffering," she said.

"That's a smart way to be," he said.

"I'll tell you frankly," she said, "I'm disappointed in you."

"I knew," he said, "that sooner or later you would come right out and say it."

"I might as well tell you, too," she said, "that I've decided to bring this farce to an end."

"It's nice of you to make me among the first to know," he said. "Shall I notify Louella Parsons, or has that already been taken care of?"

I had the gasket glued onto the bathtub rim, so I was free to close the register. I looked straight down through the grating, and there Gloria Hilton was. She had her hair up in curlers. She didn't have any makeup on. She hadn't even bothered to draw on eyebrows. She had on some kind of slip and a bathrobe that was gaping open. I swear, that woman wasn't any prettier than a used studio couch.

"I don't think you're very funny," she said.

"You knew I was a serious writer when you married me," he said.

She stood up. She spread her arms like Moses telling the Jews the Promised Land was right over the next hill. "Go on back to your precious wife and your precious son," she said. "I certainly won't stand in your way."

I closed the register.

◙ ◙ ◙

Five minutes later, Murra came upstairs and told me to clear out. "Miss Hilton wants to use her bathroom," he said. I never saw such a peculiar expression on a man's face. He was all red, and there were tears in his eyes—but there was this crazy laugh tearing him apart, trying to get out.

"I'm not quite finished," I said.

"Miss Hilton is completely finished," he said. "Clear out!"

So I went out to my truck, and I drove into town, had a cup of coffee. The door for the bathtub enclosure was on a wooden rack on the back of my truck, out in the open—and it certainly attracted a lot of attention.

Most people, when they order an enclosure door, don't want anything on it unless maybe a flamingo or a seahorse. The plant, which is over in Lawrence, Massachusetts, is set up to sandblast a flamingo or a seahorse on a door for only six dollars extra. But Gloria Hilton wanted a big "G," two feet across—and in the middle of the "G" she wanted a life-size head of herself. And the eyes on the head had to be exactly five feet two inches above the bottom of the tub, because that's how high her real eyes were when she stood up barefoot in the tub.

They went crazy over in Lawrence.

One of the people I was having coffee with was Harry Crocker, the plumber. "I certainly hope you insisted on measuring her yourself," he said, "so the figures would be absolutely accurate."

"Her husband did it," I said.

"Some people have all the luck," he said.

I went to the pay telephone, and I called up Murra's house to see if it would be all right for me to come back and finish up. The line was busy.

When I got back to my coffee, Harry Crocker said to me, "You missed something I don't think anybody's ever liable to see in this town ever again."

"What's that?" I said.

"Gloria Hilton and her maid going through town at two hundred miles an hour," he said.

"Which way were they headed?" I said.

"West," he said.

◙ ◙ ◙

So I tried to call Murra again. I figured, with Gloria Hilton gone, all the big telephoning would be over. But the telephone went right on being busy for an hour. I thought maybe somebody had torn the telephone out by its roots, but the operator said it was in working order.

"Try the number again, then," I told her.

That time I got through.

Murra answered the phone. All I said to him was, "Hello," and he got very excited. He wasn't excited about getting the bathtub enclosure finished. He was excited because he thought I was somebody named John.

"John, John," he said to me, "thank God you called!

"John," he said to me, "I know what you think of me, and I don't blame you for thinking that—but please listen to what I have to say before you hang up. She's left me, John. That part of my life is over—finished! Now I'm trying to pick up the pieces. John," he said, "in the name of mercy, you've got to come here. Please, John, please, John, please."

"Mr. Murra—?" I said.

"Yes?" he said. From the way his voice went away from the telephone, I guess he thought I'd just walked into the room.

"It's me, Mr. Murra," I said.

"It's who?" he said.

"The bathtub enclosure man," I said.

"I was expecting a very important long-distance call," he said. "Please get off the wire."

"I beg your pardon," I said. "I just want to know when you want me to finish up there."

"Never!" he said. "Forget it! The hell with it!"

"Mr. Murra—" I said, "I can't return that door for credit."

"Send me the bill," he said. "I make you a present of the door."

"Whatever you say," I said. "Now, you've got these two Fleetwood Trip-L-Trak windows, too."

"Throw 'em on the dump!" he said.

"Mr. Murra—" I said, "I guess you're upset about something—"

"God you're smart!" he said.

"Maybe throwing away that door makes sense," I said, "but storm windows never hurt a soul. Why don't you let me come out and put 'em up? You'll never even know I'm there."

"All right, all right, all right!" he said, and he hung up.

◎ ◎ ◎

The Fleetwood Trip-L-Trak is our first-line window, so there isn't anything quick and dirty about the way we put them up. We put a gasket up all the way around, just the way we do on a bathtub enclosure. So I had some standing around to do at Murra's house, just waiting for glue to dry. You can actually fill up a room equipped with Fleetwoods with water, fill it clear up to the ceiling, and it won't leak—not through the windows, anyway.

While I was waiting on the glue, Murra came out and asked me if I wanted a drink.

"Pardon me?" I said.

"Or maybe bathtub enclosure men don't drink on duty," he said.

"That's only on television," I said.

So he took me in the kitchen, and he got out a bottle and ice and a couple of glasses.

"This is very nice of you," I said.

"I may not know what love is," he said, "but, by God, at least I've never gotten drunk by myself."

"That's what we're going to do?" I said.

"Unless you have some other suggestion," he said.

"I'll have to think a minute," I said.

"That's a mistake," he said. "You miss an awful lot of life that way. That's why you Yankees are so cold," he said. "You think too much. That's why you marry so seldom."

"At least some of that is a plain lack of money," I said.

"No, no," he said. "It goes deeper than that. You people around here don't grasp the thistle firmly." He had to explain that to me, about how a thistle won't prick you if you grab it real hard and fast.

"I don't believe that about thistles," I said.

"Typical New England conservatism," he said.

"I gather you aren't from these parts," I said.

"That happiness is not mine," he said. He told me he was from Los Angeles.

"I guess that's nice, too," I said.

"The people are all phonies," he said.

"I wouldn't know about that," I said.

"That's why we took up residence here," he said. "As my wife—my second wife, that is—told all the reporters at our wedding, 'We are getting away from all the phonies. We are going to live where people are really people. We are going to live in New Hampshire. My husband and I are going to find ourselves. He is going to write and write and write. He is going to write the most beautiful scenario anybody in the history of literature has ever written for me.'"

"That's nice," I said.

"You didn't read that in the newspapers or the magazines?" he said.

"No," I said. "I used to go out with a girl who subscribed to *Film Fun*, but that was years ago. I have no idea what happened to her."

Somewhere in the course of this conversation, a fifth of a gallon of Old Hickey's Private Stock Sour Mash Bourbon was evaporating, or was being stolen, or was otherwise disappearing fast.

And I haven't got the conversation set down quite straight, because somewhere in there Murra told me he'd been married when he was only eighteen—and he told me who the John was he'd thought I was on the telephone.

It hurt Murra a lot to talk about John. "John," he said, "is my only child. Fifteen years old." Murra clouded up, pointed southeast. "Only twenty-two miles away—so near and yet so far," he said.

"He didn't stay with his mother in Los Angeles?" I said.

"His home is with her," said Murra, "but he goes to school at Mount Henry." Mount Henry is a very good boys' prep school near here. "One of the reasons I came to New Hampshire was to be close to him." Murra shook his head. "I thought surely he'd get in touch with me sooner or later—return a telephone call, answer a letter."

"But he never did?" I said.

"Never," said Murra. "You know what the last thing was he said to me?"

"Nope," I said.

"When I divorced his mother and married Gloria Hilton, the last thing he said was, 'Father, you're contemptible. I don't want to hear another word from you as long as I live.'"

"That's—that's strong," I said.

"Friend—" said Murra hoarsely, "that's *mighty* strong." He bowed his head. "That was the word he used—contemptible. Young as he was, he sure used the right one."

"Did you finally get in touch with him today?" I said.

"I called the Headmaster of the school, and I told him there was a terrible family emergency, and he had to make John call me right away," said Murra.

"It worked, thank God," he said. "And, even though I am definitely contemptible, he has agreed to come see me tomorrow."

Somewhere else in that conversation, Murra told me to look at the statistics sometime. I promised him I would. "Just statistics in general—or some special statistics?" I asked him.

"Statistics on marriage," he said.

"I'm scared to think of what I'm liable to find," I said.

"You look at the statistics," said Murra, "and you'll find out that when people get married when they're only eighteen—the way my first wife and I did—there's a fifiy-fifty chance the thing will blow sky high."

"I was eighteen when I was married," I said.

"You're still with your first wife?" he said.

"Going on twenty years now," I said.

"Don't you ever feel like you got gypped out of your bachelor days, your playboy days, your days as a great lover?"

"Well," I said, "in New Hampshire those days generally come between the ages of fourteen and seventeen."

"Let me put it to you this way," he said. "Say you'd been married all these years, fighting about the dumb things married people fight about, being broke and worried most of the time—"

"I'm right with you," I said.

"And say the movies bought a book you'd written, and they hired you to write the screen play, and Gloria Hilton was going to be the star," he said.

"I don't think I can imagine that," I said.

"All right—" he said, "what's the biggest thing that could possibly happen to you in your line of work?"

I had to think a while. "I guess it would be if I sold the Conners Hotel on putting Fleetwoods on every window. That must be five hundred windows or more," I said.

"Good!" he said. "You've just made the sale. You've got real money in your pocket for the first time. You've just had a fight with your wife, and you're thinking mean things about her, feeling sorry for yourself. And the manager of the hotel is Gloria Hilton—Gloria Hilton looking the way she does in the movies."

"I'm listening," I said.

"Say you started putting up those five hundred Fleetwoods," he said, "and say every time you put up another storm window, there was Gloria Hilton smiling at you through the glass, like you were a god or something."

"Is there anything left to drink in the house?" I said.

"Say that went on for three months," he said. "And every night you went home to your wife, some woman you'd known so long she was practically like a sister, and she would crab about some little thing—"

"This is a very warm room, even without storm windows," I said.

"Say Gloria Hilton all of a sudden said to you," he said, "'Dare to be happy, my poor darling! Oh, darling, we were *made* for each other! Dare to be happy with me! I go limp when I see you putting up storm windows! I can't stand to see you so unhappy, to know you belong to some other woman, to know how happy I could make you, if only you belonged to me!'"

◎ ◎ ◎

After that, I remember, Murra and I went outdoors to look for thistles. He was going to show me how to grab thistles without getting hurt.

I don't think we ever found any. I remember pulling up a lot of plants, and throwing them against the house, and laughing a lot. But I don't think any of the plants were thistles.

Then we lost each other in the great outdoors. I yelled for him for a while, but his answers got fainter and fainter, and I finally went home.

I don't remember what the homecoming was like, but my wife does. She says I spoke to her in a rude and disrespectful manner. I told her that I had sold five hundred Fleetwood windows to the Conners Hotel. I also told her that she should look up the statistics on teenage marriages sometime.

Then I went upstairs, and I took the door off our bathtub enclosure. I told her Murra and I were trading doors.

I got the door off, and then I went to sleep in the tub.

My wife woke me up, and I told her to go away. I told her Gloria Hilton had just bought the Conners Hotel, and I was going to marry her.

I tried to tell her something very important about thistles, but I couldn't pronounce thistles, so I went to sleep again.

So my wife poured bubble-bath powder all over me, and she turned on the cold water faucet of the bathtub, and she went to bed in the guest room.

◎ ◎ ◎

About three o'clock the next afternoon, I went over to Murra's to finish putting up his windows, and to find out what we'd agreed to do about the bathtub enclosure door, if anything. I had two doors on the back of my truck, my door with a flamingo and his door with Gloria Hilton.

I started to ring his doorbell, but then I heard somebody knocking on an upstairs window. I looked up and saw Murra standing in the window of Gloria Hilton's bathroom. My ladder was already leaning against the sill of the window, so I went up the ladder and asked Murra what was going on.

He opened the window, and he told me to come in. He was very pale and shaky.

"Your boy showed up yet?" I said.

"Yes," he said. "He's downstairs. I picked him up at the bus station an hour ago."

"You two hitting it off all right?" I said.

Murra shook his head. "He's still so *bitter*," he said. "He's only fifteen, but he talks to me as though he were my great-great-grandfather. I came up here for just a minute, and now I haven't got nerve enough to go back down."

He took me by the arm. "Listen—" he said, "you go down and sort of pave the way."

"If I've got any pavement left in me," I said, "I'd better save it for home." I filled him in on my own situation at home, which was far from ideal.

"Whatever you do," he said, "don't make the same mistake I made. You keep that home of yours together, no matter what. I know it must be lousy from time to time, but, believe me, there are ways of life that are ten thousand times lousier."

"Well," I said, "I thank the good Lord for one thing—"

"What's that?" he said.

"Gloria Hilton hasn't come right out and said she loved me yet," I said.

◙ ◙ ◙

I went downstairs to see Murra's boy.

Young John had on a man's suit. He even had on a vest. He wore big black-rimmed spectacles. He looked like a college professor.

"John," I said, "I'm an old friend of your father's."

"That so?" he said, and he looked me up and down. He wouldn't shake hands.

"You certainly are a mature-looking young man," I said.

"I've *had* to be," he said. "When Father walked out on Mother and me, that made me head of the family, wouldn't you say?"

"Well now, John," I said, "your father hasn't been too happy, either, you know."

"That certainly is a great disappointment to me," he said. "I thought Gloria Hilton made men as happy as they could possibly be."

"John," I said, "when you get older, you're going to understand a lot of things you don't understand now."

"You must mean nuclear physics," he said. "I can hardly wait." And he turned his back to me, and he looked out the window. "Where's Father?" he said.

"Here he is," said Murra from the top of the stairs. "Here the poor fool is." He came creaking down the stairs.

"I think I'd better go back to school, Father," said the boy.

"So soon?" said Murra.

"I was told there was an emergency, or I wouldn't have come," said the boy. "There doesn't seem to be any emergency, so I'd like to go back, if you don't mind."

"Don't mind?" said Murra. He held out his arms. "John—" he said, "you'll break my heart if you walk out me now—without—"

"Without what, Father?" said the boy. He was cold as ice.

"Without forgiving me," said Murra.

"Never," said the boy. "I'm sorry—that's one thing I'll never do." He nodded. "Whenever you're ready to go, Father," he said, "I'll be waiting in the car."

And he walked out of the house.

Murra sat down in a chair with his head in his hands. "What do I do now?" he said. "Maybe this is the punishment I deserve. I guess what I do is just grit my teeth and take it."

"I can only think of one other thing," I said.

"What's that?" he said.

"Kick him in the pants," I said.

◙ ◙ ◙

So that's what Murra did.

He went out to the car, looking all gloomy and blue.

He told John something was wrong with the front seat, and he made John get out so he could fix it.

Then Murra let the boy have it in the seat of the pants with the side of his foot. I don't think there was any pain connected with it, but it did have a certain amount of loft.

The boy did a kind of polka downhill, toward the shrubbery where his father and I had been looking for thistles the night before. When he got himself stopped and turned around, he was certainly one surprised-looking boy.

"John," Murra said to him, "I'm sorry I did that, but I couldn't think of anything else to do."

For once, the boy didn't have a snappy come-back.

"I have made many serious mistakes in my life," said Murra, "but I don't think that was one of them. I love you, and I love your mother, and I think I'll go on kicking you until you can find it in your heart to give me another chance."

The boy still couldn't think of anything to say, but I could tell he wasn't interested in being kicked again.

"Now you come back in the house," said Murra, "and we'll talk this thing over like civilized human beings."

When they got back in the house, Murra got the boy to call up his mother in Los Angeles.

"You tell her we're having a nice time, and I've been terribly unhappy, and I am through with Gloria Hilton, and I want her to take me back on any terms whatsoever," said Murra.

The boy told his mother, and she cried, and the boy cried, and Murra cried, and I cried.

And then Murra's first wife told him he could come back home any time he wanted to. And that was that.

◙ ◙ ◙

The way we settled the bathtub enclosure door thing was that I took Murra's door and he took mine. Actually, I was trading a twenty-two-dollar door for a forty-eight-dollar door, not counting the picture of Gloria Hilton.

My wife was out when I got home. I hung the new door.

My own boy came up and watched me. He was red-nosed about something.

"Where's your mother?" I said to him.

"She went out," he said.

"When's she due back?" I said.

"She said maybe she'd never come back," said the boy.

I was sick, but I didn't let the boy know it. "That's one of her jokes," I said. "She says that all the time."

"I never heard her say it before," he said.

I was really scared when suppertime rolled around, and I still didn't have a wife. I tried to be brave. I got supper for the boy and me, and I said, "Well, I guess she's been delayed somewhere."

"Father—" said the boy.

"What?" I said.

"What did you *do* to Mother last night?" he said. He took a very high and mighty tone.

"Mind your own business," I said, "or you're liable to get a swift kick in the pants."

That calmed him right down.

My wife came home at nine o'clock, thank God.

She was cheerful. She said she'd had a swell time just being alone—shopping alone, eating in a restaurant alone, going to a movie alone.

She gave me a kiss, and she went upstairs.

I heard the shower running, and I all of a sudden remembered the picture of Gloria Hilton on the bathtub enclosure door.

"Oh my Lord!" I said. I ran up the stairs to tell her what the picture was doing on the door, to tell her I would have it sandblasted off first thing in the morning.

I went into the bathroom.

My wife was standing up, taking a shower.

She was just the same height as Gloria Hilton, so the picture on the door made kind of a mask for her.

There was my wife's body with the head of Gloria Hilton on it.

My wife wasn't sore. She laughed. She thought it was funny. "Guess who?" she said.

The Lie

IT WAS EARLY SPRINGTIME. Weak sunshine lay cold on old gray frost. Willow twigs against the sky showed the golden haze of fat catkins about to bloom. A black Rolls-Royce streaked up the Connecticut Turnpike from New York City. At the wheel was Ben Barkley, a black chauffeur.

"Keep it under the speed limit, Ben," said Doctor Remenzel. "I don't care how ridiculous any speed limit seems, stay under it. No reason to rush—we have plenty of time."

Ben eased off on the throttle. "Seems like in the springtime she wants to get up and go," he said.

"Do what you can to keep her down—O.K.?" said the doctor.

"Yes, sir!" said Ben. He spoke in a lower voice to the thirteen-year-old boy who was riding beside him, to Eli Remenzel, the doctor's son. "Ain't just people and animals feel good in the springtime," he said to Eli. "Motors feel good too."

"Um," said Eli.

"Everything feel good," said Ben. "Don't you feel good?"

"Sure, sure I feel good," said Eli emptily.

"Should feel good—going to that wonderful school," said Ben.

The wonderful school was the Whitehill School for Boys, a private preparatory school in North Marston, Massachusetts. That was where the Rolls-Royce was bound. The plan was that Eli would enroll for the fall semester, while his father, a member of the class of 1939, attended a meeting of the Board of Overseers of the school.

"Don't believe this boy's feeling so good, doctor," said Ben. He wasn't particularly serious about it. It was more genial springtime blather.

"What's the matter, Eli?" said the doctor absently. He was studying blueprints, plans for a thirty-room addition to the Eli Remenzel Memorial Dormitory—a building named in honor of his great-great-grandfather. Doctor Remenzel had the plans draped over a walnut table that folded out of the back of the front seat. He was a massive, dignified man, a physician, a healer for healing's sake, since he had been born as rich as the Shah of Iran. "Worried about something?" he asked Eli without looking up from the plans.

"Nope," said Eli.

Eli's lovely mother, Sylvia, sat next to the doctor, reading the catalogue of the Whitchill School. "If I were you," she said to Eli, "I'd be so excited I could hardly stand it. The best four years of your whole life are just about to begin."

"Sure," said Eli. He didn't show her his face. He gave her only the back of his head, a pinwheel of coarse brown hair above a stiff white collar, to talk to.

"I wonder how many Remenzels have gone to Whitehill," said Sylvia.

"That's like asking how many people are dead in a cemetery," said the doctor. He gave the answer to the old joke, and to Sylvia's question too. "All of 'em."

"If all the Remenzels who went to Whitehill were numbered, what number would Eli be?" said Sylvia. "That's what I'm getting at."

The question annoyed Doctor Remenzel a little. It didn't seem in very good taste. "It isn't the sort of thing you keep score on," he said.

"Guess," said his wife.

"Oh," he said, "you'd have to go back through all the records, all the way back to the end of the eighteenth century, even, to make any kind of a guess. And you'd have to decide whether to count the Schofields and the Haleys and the MacLellans as Remenzels."

"Please make a guess—" said Sylvia, "just people whose last names were Remenzel."

"Oh—" The doctor shrugged, rattled the plans. "Thirty maybe."

"So Eli is number thirty-one!" said Sylvia, delighted with the number. "You're number thirty-one, dear," she said to the back of Eli's head.

Doctor Remenzel rattled the plans again. "I don't want him going around saying something asinine, like he's number thirty-one," he said.

"Eli knows better than that," said Sylvia. She was a game, ambitious woman, with no money of her own at all. She had been married for sixteen years, but was still openly curious and enthusiastic about the ways of families that had been rich for many generations.

"Just for my own curiosity—not so Eli can go around saying what number he is," said Sylvia, "I'm going to go wherever they keep the records and find out what number he is. That's what I'll do while you're at the meeting and Eli's doing whatever he has to do at the Admissions Office."

"All right," said Doctor Remenzel, "you go ahead and *do* that."

"I will," said Sylvia. "I think things like that are interesting, even if you don't." She waited for a rise on that, but didn't get one. Sylvia enjoyed arguing with her husband about her lack of reserve and his excess of it, enjoyed saying, toward the end of arguments like that, "Well, I guess I'm just a simple-minded country girl at heart, and that's all I'll ever be, and I'm afraid you're going to have to get used to it."

But Doctor Remenzel didn't want to play that game. He found the dormitory plans more interesting.

"Will the new rooms have fireplaces?" said Sylvia. In the oldest part of the dormitory, several of the rooms had handsome fireplaces.

"That would practically double the cost of construction," said the doctor.

"I want Eli to have a room with a fireplace, if that's possible," said Sylvia.

"Those rooms are for seniors."

"I thought maybe through some fluke—" said Sylvia.

"What kind of fluke do you have in mind?" said the doctor. "You mean I should demand that Eli be given a room with a fireplace?"

"Not *demand*—" said Sylvia.

"Request firmly?" said the doctor.

"Maybe I'm just a simple-minded country girl at heart," said Sylvia, "but I look through this catalogue, and I see all the buildings named after Remenzels, look through the back and see all the hundreds of thousands of dollars given by Remenzels for scholarships, and I just can't help thinking people named Remenzel are entitled to ask for a little something extra."

"Let me tell you in no uncertain terms," said Doctor Remenzel, "that you are not to ask for anything special for Eli—not anything."

"Of course I won't," said Sylvia. "Why do you always think I'm going to embarrass you?"

"I don't," he said.

"But I can still think what I think, can't I?" she said.

"If you have to," he said.

"I have to," she said cheerfully, utterly unrepentant. She leaned over the plans. "You think those people will like those rooms?"

"What people?" he said.

"The Africans," she said. She was talking about thirty Africans who, at the request of the State Department, were being admitted to Whitehill in the coming semester. It was because of them that the dormitory was being expanded.

"The rooms aren't for them," he said. "They aren't going to be segregated."

"Oh," said Sylvia. She thought about this awhile, and then she said, "Is there a chance Eli will have to have one of them for a roommate?"

"Freshmen draw lots for roommates," said the doctor. "That piece of information's in the catalogue too."

"Eli?" said Sylvia.

"H'm?" said Eli.

"How would you feel about it if you had to room with one of those Africans?"

Eli shrugged listlessly.

"That's all right?" said Sylvia.

Eli shrugged again.

"I guess it's all right," said Sylvia.

"It had better be," said the doctor.

The Rolls-Royce pulled abreast of an old Chevrolet, a car in such bad repair that its back door was lashed shut with clothesline. Doctor Remenzel glanced casually at the driver, and then, with sudden excitement and pleasure, he told Ben Barkley to stay abreast of the car.

The doctor leaned across Sylvia, rolled down his window, yelled to the driver of the old Chevrolet, "Tom! Tom!"

The man was a Whitehill classmate of the doctor. He wore a Whitehill necktie, which he waved at Doctor Remenzel in gay recognition. And then he pointed to the fine young son who sat beside him, conveyed with proud smiles and nods that the boy was bound for Whitehill.

Doctor Remenzel pointed to the chaos of the back of Eli's head, beamed that his news was the same. In the wind blustering between the two cars they made a lunch date at the Holly House in North Marston, at the inn whose principal business was serving visitors to Whitehill.

"All right," said Doctor Remenzel to Ben Barkley, "drive on."

"You know," said Sylvia, "somebody really ought to write an article—" And she turned to look through the back window at the old car now shuddering far behind. "Somebody really ought to."

"What about?" said the doctor. He noticed that Eli had slumped way down in the front seat. "Eli!" he said sharply. "Sit up straight!" He returned his attention to Sylvia.

"Most people think prep schools are such snobbish things, just for people with money," said Sylvia, "but that isn't true." She leafed through the catalogue and found the quotation she was after.

"*The Whitehill School operates on the assumption,*" she read, "*that no boy should be deterred from applying for admission because his family is unable to pay the full cost of a Whitehill education. With this in mind, the Admissions Committee selects each year from approximately 3000 candidates the 150 most promising and deserving boys, regardless of their parents' ability to pay the full $2200 tuition. And those in need of financial aid are given it to the full extent of their need. In certain instances, the school will even pay for the clothing and transportation of a boy.*"

Sylvia shook her head. "I think that's perfectly amazing. It's something most people don't realize at all. A truckdriver's son can come to Whitehill."

"If he's smart enough," he said.

"Thanks to the Remenzels," said Sylvia with pride.

"And a lot of other people too," said the doctor.

Sylvia read out loud again: "*In 1799, Eli Remenzel laid the foundation for the present Scholarship Fund by donating to the school forty acres in Boston. The school still owns twelve of those acres, their current evaluation being $3,000,000.*"

"Eli!" said the doctor. "Sit up! What's the matter with you?"

Eli sat up again, but began to slump almost immediately, like a snowman in hell. Eli had good reason for slumping, for actually hoping to die or disappear. He could not bring himself to say what the reason was. He slumped because he knew he had been denied admission to Whitehill. He had failed the entrance examinations. Eli's parents did not know this, because Eli had found the awful notice in the mail and had torn it up.

Doctor Remenzel and his wife had no doubts whatsoever about their son's getting into Whitehill. It was inconceivable to them that Eli could not go there, so they had no curiosity as to how Eli had done on the examinations, were not puzzled when no report ever came.

"What all will Eli have to do to enroll?" said Sylvia, as the black Rolls-Royce crossed the Rhode Island border.

"I don't know," said the doctor. "I suppose they've got it all complicated now with forms to be filled out in quadruplicate, and punch-card machines and bureaucrats. This business of entrance examinations is all new, too. In my day a boy simply had an interview with the headmaster. The headmaster would look him over, ask him a few questions, and then say, 'There's a Whitehill boy.'"

"Did he ever say, 'There isn't a Whitehill boy'?" said Sylvia.

"Oh, sure," said Doctor Remenzel, "if a boy was impossibly stupid or something. There have to be standards. There have always been standards. The African boys have to meet the standards, just like anybody else. They aren't getting in just because the State Department wants to make friends. We made that clear. Those boys had to meet the standards."

"And they did?" said Sylvia.

"I suppose," said Doctor Remenzel. "I heard they're all in, and they all took the same examination Eli did."

"Was it a hard examination, dear?" Sylvia asked Eli. It was the first time she'd thought to ask.

"Um," said Eli.

"What?" she said.

"Yes," said Eli.

"I'm glad they've got high standards," she said, and then she realized that this was a fairly silly statement. "Of course they've got high standards," she said. "That's why it's such a famous school. That's why people who go there do so well in later life."

Sylvia resumed her reading of the catalogue again, opened out a folding map of "The Sward," as the campus of Whitehill was traditionally called. She read off the names of features that memorialized Remenzels—the Sanford Remenzel Bird Sanctuary, the George MacLellan Remenzel Skating Rink, the Eli Remenzel Memorial Dormitory, and then she read out loud a quatrain printed on one corner of the map:

> *When night falleth gently*
> *Upon the green Sward,*
> *It's Whitehill, dear Whitehill,*
> *Our thoughts all turn toward.*

"You know," said Sylvia, "school songs are so corny when you just read them. But when I hear the Glee Club sing those words, they sound like the most beautiful words ever written, and I want to cry."

"Um," said Doctor Remenzel.

"Did a Remenzel write them?"

"I don't think so," said Doctor Remenzel. And then he said, "No—Wait. That's the *new* song. A Remenzel didn't write it. Tom Kilyer wrote it."

"The man in that old car we passed?"

"Sure," said Doctor Remenzel. "Tom wrote it. I remember when he wrote it."

"A scholarship boy wrote it?" said Sylvia. "I think that's awfully nice. He *was* a scholarship boy, wasn't he?"

"His father was an ordinary automobile mechanic in North Marston."

"You hear what a democratic school you're going to, Eli?" said Sylvia.

◎ ◎ ◎

Half an hour later Ben Barkley brought the limousine to a stop before the Holly House, a rambling country inn twenty years older than the Republic. The inn was on the edge of the Whitehill Sward, glimpsing the school's rooftops and spires over the innocent wilderness of the Sanford Remenzel Bird Sanctuary.

Ben Barkley was sent away with the car for an hour and a half. Doctor Remenzel shepherded Sylvia and Eli into a familiar, low-ceilinged world of pewter, clocks, lovely old woods, agreeable servants, elegant food and drink.

Eli, clumsy with horror of what was surely to come, banged a grandmother clock with his elbow as he passed, made the clock cry.

Sylvia excused herself. Doctor Remenzel and Eli went to the threshold of the dining room, where a hostess welcomed them both by name. They were given a table beneath an oil portrait of one of the three Whitehill boys who had gone on to become President of the United States.

The dining room was filling quickly with families. What every family had was at least one boy about Eli's age. Most of the boys wore Whitehill blazers—black, with pale-blue piping, with Whitehill seals on their breast pockets. A few, like Eli, were not yet entitled to wear blazers, were simply hoping to get in.

The doctor ordered a Martini, then turned to his son and said, "Your mother has the idea that you're entitled to special privileges around here. I hope you don't have that idea too."

"No, sir," said Eli.

"It would be a source of the greatest embarrassment to me," said Doctor Remenzel with considerable grandeur, "if I were ever to hear that you had used the name Remenzel as though you thought Remenzels were something special."

"I know," said Eli wretchedly.

"That settles it," said the doctor. He had nothing more to say about it. He gave abbreviated salutes to several people he knew in the room, speculated as to what sort of party had reserved a long banquet table that was set up along one wall. He decided that it was for a visiting athletic team. Sylvia arrived, and Eli had to be told in a sharp whisper to stand when a woman came to a table.

Sylvia was full of news. The long table, she related, was for the thirty boys from Africa. "I'll bet that's more colored people than have eaten here since this place was founded," she said softly. "How fast things change these days!"

"You're right about how fast things change," said Doctor Remenzel. "You're wrong about the colored people who've eaten here. This used to be a busy part of the Underground Railroad."

"Really?" said Sylvia. "How exciting." She looked all about herself in a birdlike way. "I think everything's exciting here. I only wish Eli had a blazer on."

Doctor Remenzel reddened. "He isn't entitled to one," he said.

"I know that," said Sylvia.

"I thought you were going to ask somebody for permission to put a blazer on Eli right away," said the doctor.

"I wouldn't do that," said Sylvia, a little offended now. "Why are you always afraid I'll embarrass you?"

"Never mind. Excuse me. Forget it," said Doctor Remenzel.

Sylvia brightened again, put her hand on Eli's arm, and looked radiantly at a man in the dining-room doorway. "There's my favorite person in all the world, next to my son and husband," she said. She meant Dr. Donald Warren, headmaster of the Whitehill School. A thin gentleman in his early sixties, Doctor Warren was in the doorway with the manager of the inn, looking over the arrangements for the Africans.

It was then that Eli got up abruptly, fled the dining room, fled as much of the nightmare as he could possibly leave behind. He brushed past Doctor Warren rudely, though he knew him well, though Doctor Warren spoke his name. Doctor Warren looked after him sadly.

"I'll be damned," said Doctor Remenzel. "What brought that on?"

"Maybe he really *is* sick," said Sylvia.

The Remenzels had no time to react more elaborately, because Doctor Warren spotted them and crossed quickly to their table. He greeted them, some of his perplexity about Eli showing in his greeting. He asked if he might sit down.

"Certainly, of course," said Doctor Remenzel expansively. "We'd be honored if you did. Heavens."

"Not to eat," said Doctor Warren. "I'll be eating at the long table with the new boys. I would like to talk, though." He saw that there were five places set at the table. "You're expecting someone?"

"We passed Tom Hilyer and his boy on the way," said Doctor Remenzel. "They'll be along in a minute."

"Good, good," said Doctor Warren absently. He fidgeted, looked again in the direction in which Eli had disappeared.

"Tom's boy will be going to Whitehill in the fall?" said Doctor Remenzel.

"H'm?" said Doctor Warren. "Oh—yes, yes. Yes, he will."

"Is he a scholarship boy, like his father?" said Sylvia.

"That's not a polite question," said Doctor Remenzel severely.

"I beg your pardon," said Sylvia.

"No, no—that's a perfectly proper question these days," said Doctor Warren. "We don't keep that sort of information very secret any more. We're proud of our scholarship boys, and they have every reason to be proud of themselves. Tom's boy got the highest score anyone's ever got on the entrance examinations. We feel privileged to have him."

"We never *did* find out Eli's score," said Doctor Remenzel. He said it with good-humored resignation, without expectation that Eli had done especially well.

"A good strong medium, I imagine," said Sylvia. She said this on the basis of Eli's grades in primary school, which had ranged from medium to terrible.

The headmaster looked surprised. "I didn't tell you his scores?" he said.

"We haven't seen you since he took the examinations," said Doctor Remenzel.

"The letter I wrote you—" said Doctor Warren.

"What letter?" said Doctor Remenzel. "Did we get a letter?"

"A letter from me," said Doctor Warren, with growing incredulity. "The hardest letter I ever had to write."

Sylvia shook her head. "We never got any letter from you."

Doctor Warren sat back, looking very ill. "I mailed it myself," he said. "It was definitely mailed—two weeks ago."

Doctor Remenzel shrugged. "The U.S. mails don't lose much," he said, "but I guess that now and then something gets misplaced."

Doctor Warren cradled his head in his hands. "Oh, dear—oh, my, oh, Lord," he said. "I was surprised to see Eli here. I wondered that he would want to come along with you."

"He didn't come along just to see the scenery," said Doctor Remenzel. "He came to enroll."

"I want to know what was in the letter," said Sylvia.

Doctor Warren raised his head, folded his hands. "What the letter said, was this, and no other words could be more difficult for me to say: '*On the basis of his work in primary school and his scores on the entrance examinations, I must tell you that your son and my good friend Eli cannot possibly do the work required of boys at Whitehill.*'" Doctor Warren's voice steadied, and so did his gaze. "'*To admit Eli to Whitehill, to expect him to do Whitehill work,*'" he said, "'*would be both unrealistic and cruel.*'"

Thirty African boys, escorted by several faculty members, State Department men, and diplomats from their own countries, filed into the dining room.

And Tom Hilyer and his boy, having no idea that something had just gone awfully wrong for the Remenzels, came in, too, and said hello to the Remenzels and Doctor Warren gaily, as though life couldn't possibly be better.

"I'll talk to you more about this later, if you like," Doctor Warren said to the Remenzels, rising. "I have to go now, but later on—" He left quickly.

"My mind's a blank," said Sylvia. "My mind's a perfect blank."

Tom Hilyer and his boy sat down. Hilyer looked at the menu before him, clapped his hands and said, "What's good? I'm hungry." And then he said, "Say—where's your boy?"

"He stepped out for a moment," said Doctor Remenzel evenly.

"We've got to find him," said Sylvia to her husband.

"In time, in due time," said Doctor Remenzel.

"That letter," said Sylvia; "Eli knew about it. He found it and tore it up. Of course he did!" She started to cry, thinking of the hideous trap that Eli had caught himself in.

"I'm not interested right now in what Eli's done," said Doctor Remenzel. "Right now I'm a lot more interested in what some other people are going to do."

"What do you mean?" said Sylvia.

Doctor Remenzel stood impressively, angry and determined. "I mean," he said, "I'm going to see how quickly people can change their minds around here."

"Please," said Sylvia, trying to hold him, trying to calm him, "we've got to find Eli. That's the first thing."

"The first thing," said Doctor Remenzel quite loudly, "is to get Eli admitted to Whitehill. After that we'll find him, and we'll bring him back."

"But darling—" said Sylvia.

"No 'but' about it," said Doctor Remenzel. "There's a majority of the Board of Overseers in this room at this very moment. Every one of them is a close friend of mine, or a close friend of my father. If they tell Doctor Warren Eli's in, that's it— Eli's in. If there's room for all these other people," he said, "there's damn well room for Eli too."

He strode quickly to a table nearby, sat down heavily and began to talk to a fierce-looking and splendid old gentleman who was eating there. The old gentleman was chairman of the board.

Sylvia apologized to the baffled Hilyers, and then went in search of Eli.

Asking this person and that person, Sylvia found him. He was outside—all alone on a bench in a bower of lilacs that had just begun to bud.

Eli heard his mother's coming on the gravel path, stayed where he was, resigned. "Did you find out," he said, "or do I still have to tell you?"

"About you?" she said gently. "About not getting in? Doctor Warren told us."

"I tore his letter up," said Eli.

"I can understand that," she said. "Your father and I have always made you feel that you had to go to Whitehill, that nothing else would do."

"I feel better," said Eli. He tried to smile, found he could do it easily. "I feel so much better now that it's over. I tried to tell you a couple of times—but I just couldn't. I didn't know how."

"That's my fault, not yours," she said.

"What's father doing?" said Eli.

Sylvia was so intent on comforting Eli that she'd put out of her mind what her husband was up to. Now she realized that Doctor Remenzel was making a ghastly mistake. She didn't want Eli admitted to Whitehill, could see what a cruel thing that would be.

She couldn't bring herself to tell the boy what his father was doing, so she said, "He'll be along in a minute, dear. He understands." And then she said, "You wait here, and I'll go get him and come right back."

But she didn't have to go to Doctor Remenzel. At that moment the big man came out of the inn and caught sight of his wife and son. He came to her and to Eli. He looked dazed.

"Well?" she said.

"They—they all said no," said Doctor Remenzel, very subdued.

"That's for the best," said Sylvia. "I'm relieved. I really am."

"Who said no?" said Eli. "Who said no to what?"

"The members of the board," said Doctor Remenzel, not looking anyone in the eye. "I asked them to make an exception in your case—to reverse their decision and let you in."

Eli stood, his face filled with incredulity and shame that were instant. "You what?" he said, and there was no childishness in the way he said it. Next came anger. "You shouldn't have done that!" he said to his father.

Doctor Remenzel nodded. "So I've already been told."

"That isn't done!" said Eli. "How awful! You shouldn't have."

"You're right," said Doctor Remenzel, accepting the scolding lamely.

"Now I *am* ashamed," said Eli, and he showed that he was.

Doctor Remenzel, in his wretchedness, could find no strong words to say. "I apologize to you both," he said at last. "It was a very bad thing to try."

"Now a Remenzel *has* asked for something," said Eli.

"I don't suppose Ben's back yet with the car?" said Doctor Remenzel. It was obvious that Ben wasn't. "We'll wait out here for him," he said. "I don't want to go back in there now."

"A Remenzel asked for something—as though a Remenzel were something special," said Eli.

"I don't suppose—" said Doctor Remenzel, and he left the sentence unfinished, dangling in the air.

"You don't suppose what?" said his wife, her face puzzled.

"I don't suppose," said Doctor Remenzel, "that we'll ever be coming here any more."

Deer in the Works

THE BIG BLACK STACKS of the Ilium Works of the Federal Apparatus Corporation spewed acid fumes and soot over the hundreds of men and women who were lined up before the redbrick employment office. It was summer. The Ilium Works, already the second-largest industrial plant in America, was increasing its staff by one third in order to meet armament contracts. Every ten minutes or so, a company policeman opened the employment-office door, letting out a chilly gust from the air-conditioned interior and admitting three more applicants.

"Next three," said the policeman.

A middle-sized man in his late twenties, his young face camouflaged with a mustache and spectacles, was admitted after a four-hour wait. His spirits and the new suit he'd bought for the occasion were wilted by the fumes and the August sun, and he'd given up lunch in order to keep his place in line. But his bearing remained jaunty. He was the last, in his group of three, to face the receptionist.

"Screw-machine operator, ma'am," said the first man.

"See Mr. Cormody in booth seven," said the receptionist.

"Plastic extrusion, miss," said the next man.

"See Mr. Hoyt in booth two," she said. "Skill?" she asked the urbane young man in the wilted suit. "Milling machine? Jig borer?"

"Writing," he said. "Any kind of writing."

"You mean advertising and sales promotion?"

"Yes—that's what I mean."

She looked doubtful. "Well, I don't know. We didn't put out a call for that sort of people. You can't run a machine, can you?"

"Typewriter," he said jokingly.

The receptionist was a sober young woman. "The company does not use male stenographers," she said. "See Mr. Dilling in booth twenty-six. He just might know of some advertising-and-sales-promotion-type job."

He straightened his tie and coat, forced a smile that implied he was looking into jobs at the Works as sort of a lark. He walked into booth twenty-six and extended his hand to Mr. Dilling, a man of his own age. "Mr. Dilling, my name is David

Potter. I was curious to know what openings you might have in advertising and sales promotion, and thought I'd drop in for a talk."

Mr. Dilling, an old hand at facing young men who tried to hide their eagerness for a job, was polite but outwardly unimpressed. "Well, you came at a bad time, I'm afraid, Mr. Potter. The competition for that kind of job is pretty stiff, as you perhaps know, and there isn't much of anything open just now."

David nodded. "I see." He had had no experience in asking for a job with a big organization, and Mr. Dilling was making him aware of what a fine art it was—if you couldn't run a machine. A duel was under way.

"But have a seat anyway, Mr. Potter."

"Thank you." He looked at his watch. "I really ought to be getting back to my paper soon."

"You work on a paper around here?"

"Yes. I own a weekly paper in Dorset, about ten miles from Ilium."

"Oh—you don't say. Lovely little village. Thinking of giving up the paper, are you?"

"Well, no—not exactly. It's a possibility. I bought the paper soon after the war, so I've been with it for eight years, and I don't want to go stale. I might be wise to move on. It all depends on what opens up."

"You have a family?" said Mr. Dilling pleasantly.

"Yes. My wife, and two boys and two girls."

"A nice, big, well-balanced family," said Mr. Dilling. "And you're so young, too."

"Twenty-nine," said David. He smiled. "We didn't plan it to be quite that big. It's run to twins. The boys are twins, and then, several days ago, the girls came."

"You don't say!" said Mr. Dilling. He winked. "That would certainly start a young man thinking about getting a little security, eh, with a family like that?"

Both of them treated the remark casually, as though it were no more than a pleasantry between two family men. "It's what we wanted, actually, two boys, two girls," said David. "We didn't expect to get them this quickly, but we're glad now. As far as security goes—well, maybe I flatter myself, but I think the administrative and writing experience I've had running the paper would be worth a good bit to the right people, if something happened to the paper."

"One of the big shortages in this country," said Dilling philosophically, concentrating on lighting a cigarette, "is men who know how to do things, and know how to take responsibility and get things done. I only wish there were better openings in advertising and sales promotion than the ones we've got. They're important, interesting jobs, understand, but I don't know how you'd feel about the starting salary."

"Well, I'm just trying to get the lay of the land, now—to see how things are. I have no idea what salary industry might pay a man like me, with my experience."

"The question experienced men like yourself usually ask is: how high can I go and how fast? And the answer to that is that the sky is the limit for a man with drive and creative ambition. And he can go up fast or slow, depending on what he's willing to do and capable of putting into the job. We might start out a man like you at, oh, say, a hundred dollars a week, but that isn't to say you'd be stuck at that level for two years or even two months."

"I suppose a man could keep a family on that until he got rolling," said David.

"You'd find the work in the publicity end just about the same as what you're doing now. Our publicity people have high standards for writing and editing and reporting, and our publicity releases don't wind up in newspaper editors' wastebaskets. Our people do a professional job, and are well-respected as journalists." He stood. "I've got a little matter to attend to—take me about ten minutes. Could you possibly stick around? I'm enjoying our talk."

David looked at his watch. "Oh—guess I could spare another ten or fifteen minutes."

Dilling was back in his booth in three minutes, chuckling over some private joke. "Just talking on the phone with Lou Flammer, the publicity supervisor. Needs a new stenographer. Lou's a card. Everybody here is crazy about Lou. Old weekly man himself, and I guess that's where he learned to be so easy to get along with. Just to feel him out for the hell of it, I told him about you. I didn't commit you to anything—just said what you told me, that you were keeping your eyes open. And guess what Lou said?"

◙ ◙ ◙

"Guess what, Nan," said David Potter to his wife on the telephone. He was wearing only his shorts, and was phoning from the company hospital. "When you come home from the hospital tomorrow, you'll be coming home to a solid citizen who pulls down a hundred and ten dollars a week, *every* week. I just got my badge and passed my physical!"

"Oh?" said Nan, startled. "It happened awfully fast, didn't it? I didn't think you were going to plunge right in."

"What's there to wait for?"

"Well—I don't know. I mean, how do you know what you're getting into? You've never worked for anybody but yourself, and don't know anything about getting along in a huge organization. I knew you were going to talk to the Ilium people about a job, but I thought you planned to stick with the paper another year, anyway."

"In another year I'll be thirty, Nan."

"Well?"

"That's pretty old to be starting a career in industry. There are guys my age here who've been working their way up for ten years. That's pretty stiff competition, and it'll be that much stiffer a year from now. And how do we know Jason will still want to buy the paper a year from now?" Ed Jason was David's assistant, a recent college graduate whose father wanted to buy the paper for him. "And this job that opened up today in publicity won't be open a year from now, Nan. Now was the time to switch—this afternoon!"

Nan sighed. "I suppose. But it doesn't seem like you. The Works are fine for some people; they seem to thrive on that life. But you've always been so free. And you love the paper—you know you do."

"I do," said David, "and it'll break my heart to let it go. It was a swell thing to do when we had no kids, but it's a shaky living now—with the kids to educate and all."

"But, hon," said Nan, "the paper is making money."

"It could fold like that," said David, snapping his fingers. "A daily could come in with a one-page insert of Dorset news, or—"

"Dorset likes its little paper too much to let that happen. They like you and the job you're doing too much."

David nodded. "What about ten years from now?"

"What about ten years from now in the Works? What about ten years from now anywhere?"

"It's a better bet that the Works will still be here. I haven't got the right to take long chances any more, Nan, not with a big family counting on me."

"It won't be a very happy big family, darling, if you're not doing what you want to do. I want you to go on being happy the way you have been—driving around the countryside, getting news and talking and selling ads; coming home and writing what you want to write, what you believe in. You in the Works!"

"It's what I've got to do."

"All right, if you say so. I've had my say."

"It's still journalism, high-grade journalism," said David.

"Just don't sell the paper to Jason right away. Put him in charge, but let's wait a month or so, please?"

"No sense in waiting, but if you really want to, all right." David held up a brochure he'd been handed after his physical examination was completed. "Listen to this, Nan: under the company Security Package, I get ten dollars a day for hospital expenses in case of illness, full pay for twenty-six weeks, a hundred dollars for special hospital expenses. I get life insurance for about half what it would cost on the outside. For whatever I put into government bonds under the payroll-savings plan, the company will give me a five per cent bonus in company stock—twelve years from now. I get two weeks' vacation with pay each year, and, after fifteen years, I get three weeks. Get free membership in the company country club. After twenty-five years, I'll be eligible for a pension of at least a hundred and twenty-five dollars a month, and much more if I rise in the organization and stick with it for more than twenty-five years!"

"Good heavens!" said Nan.

"I'd be a damn fool to pass that up, Nan."

"I still wish you'd waited until the little girls and I were home and settled, and you got used to them. I feel you were panicked into this."

"No, no—this is it, Nan. Give the little girls a kiss apiece for me. I've got to go now, and report to my new supervisor."

"Your what?"

"Supervisor."

"Oh. I thought that's what you said, but I couldn't be sure."

"Good-bye, Nan."

"Good-bye, David."

◎ ◎ ◎

David clipped his badge to his lapel, and stepped out of the hospital and onto the hot asphalt floor of the world within the fences of the Works. Dull thunder came from the buildings around him, a truck honked at him, and a cinder blew in his eye. He dabbed at the cinder with a corner of his handkerchief and finally got it out. When his vision was restored, he looked about himself for Building 31, where his new office and supervisor were. Four busy streets fanned out from where he stood, and each stretched seemingly to infinity.

He stopped a passerby who was in less of a desperate hurry than the rest. "Could you tell me, please, how to find Building 31, Mr. Flammer's office?"

The man he asked was old and bright-eyed, apparently getting as much pleasure from the clangor and smells and nervous activity of the Works as David would have gotten from April in Paris. He squinted at David's badge and then at his face. "Just starting out, are you?"

"Yes sir. My first day."

"What do you know about that?" The old man shook his head wonderingly, and winked. "Just starting out. Building 31? Well, sir, when I first came to work here in 1899, you could see Building 31 from here, with nothing between us and it but mud. Now it's all built up. See that water tank up there, about a quarter of a mile? Well, Avenue 17 branches off there, and you follow that almost to the end, then cut across the tracks, and— Just starting out, eh? Well, I'd better walk you up there. Came here for just a minute to talk to the pension folks, but that can wait. I'd enjoy the walk."

"Thank you."

"Fifty-year man, I was," he said proudly, and he led David up avenues and alleys, across tracks, over ramps and through tunnels, through buildings filled with spitting, whining, grumbling machinery, and down corridors with green walls and numbered black doors.

"Can't be a fifty-year man no more," said the old man pityingly. "Can't come to work until you're eighteen nowadays, and you got to retire when you're sixty-five." He poked his thumb under his lapel to make a small gold button protrude. On it was the number "50" superimposed on the company trademark. "Something none of you youngsters can look forward to wearing some day, no matter how much you want one."

"Very nice button," said David.

The old man pointed out a door. "Here's Flammer's office. Keep your mouth shut till you find out who's who and what *they* think. Good luck."

Lou Flammer's secretary was not at her desk, so David walked to the door of the inner office and knocked.

"Yes?" said a man's voice sweetly. "Please come in."

David opened the door. "Mr. Flammer?"

Lou Flammer was a short, fat man in his early thirties. He beamed at David. "What can I do to help you?"

"I'm David Potter, Mr. Flammer."

Flammer's Santa-Claus-like demeanor decayed. He leaned back, propped his feet on his desk top, and stuffed a cigar, which he'd concealed in his cupped hand, into his large mouth. "Hell—thought you were a scoutmaster." He looked at his desk clock, which was mounted in a miniature of the company's newest automatic dishwasher. "Boy scouts touring the Works. Supposed to stop in here fifteen minutes ago for me to give 'em a talk on scouting and industry. Fifty-six per cent of Federal Apparatus' executives were eagle scouts."

David started to laugh, but found himself doing it all alone, and he stopped. "Amazing figure," he said.

"It *is*," said Flammer judiciously. "Says something for scouting and something for industry. Now, before I tell you where your desk is, I'm supposed to explain the rating-sheet system. That's what the Manual says. Dilling tell you about that?"

"Not that I recall. There was an awful lot of information all at once."

"Well, there's nothing much to it," said Flammer. "Every six months a rating sheet is made out on you, to let you and to let us know just where you stand, and what sort of progress you've been making. Three people who've been close to your work make out independent ratings of you, and then all the information is brought together on a master copy—with carbons for you, me, and Personnel, and the original for the head of the Advertising and Sales Promotion Division. It's very helpful for everybody, you most of all, if you take it the right way." He waved a rating sheet before David. "See? Blanks for appearance, loyalty, promptness, initiative, cooperativeness—things like that. You'll make out rating sheets on other people, too, and whoever does the rating is anonymous."

"I see." David felt himself reddening with resentment. He fought the emotion, telling himself his reaction was a small-town man's—and that it would do him good to learn to think as a member of a great, efficient team.

"Now about pay, Potter," said Flammer, "there'll never be any point in coming in to ask me for a raise. That's all done on the basis of the rating sheets and the salary curve." He rummaged through his drawers and found a graph, which he spread out on his desk. "Here—now you see this curve? Well, it's the average salary curve for men with college educations in the company. See—you can follow it on up. At thirty, the average man makes this much; at forty, this much—and so on. Now, this curve above it shows what men with real growth potential can make. See? It's a little higher and curves upward a little faster. You're how old?"

"Twenty-nine," said David, trying to see what the salary figures were that ran along one side of the graph. Flammer saw him doing it, and pointedly kept them hidden with his forearm.

"Uh-huh." Flammer wet the tip of a pencil with his tongue, and drew a small "x" on the graph, squarely astride the average man's curve. "There *you* are!"

David looked at the mark, and then followed the curve with his eyes across the paper, over little bumps, up gentle slopes, along desolate plateaus, until it died abruptly at the margin which represented age sixty-five. The graph left no questions to be asked and was deaf to argument. David looked from it to the human being he would also be dealing with. "You had a weekly once, did you, Mr. Flammer?"

Flammer laughed. "In my naïve, idealistic youth, Potter, I sold ads to feed stores, gathered gossip, set type, and wrote editorials that were going to save the world, by God."

David smiled admiringly. "What a circus, eh?"

"Circus?" said Flammer. "Freak show, maybe. It's a good way to grow up fast. Took me about six months to find out I was killing myself for peanuts, that a little guy couldn't even save a village three blocks long, and that the world wasn't worth saving anyway. So I started looking out for Number One. Sold out to a chain, came down here, and here I am."

The telephone rang. "Yes?" said Flammer sweetly. "Puh-*bliss*-itee." His benign smile faded. "No. You're kidding, aren't you? Where? Really—this is no gag? All right, all right. Lord! What a time for this to happen. I haven't got anybody here, and I can't get away on account of the goddam boy scouts." He hung up. "Potter—you've got your first assignment. There's a deer loose in the Works!"

"Deer?"

"Don't know how he got in, but he's in. Plumber went to fix a drinking fountain out at the softball diamond across from Building 217, and flushed a deer out from under the bleachers. Now they got him cornered up around the metallurgy lab." He stood and hammered on his desk. "Murder! The story will go all over the country, Potter. Talk about human interest. Front page! Of all the times for Al Tappin to be out at the Ashtabula Works, taking pictures of a new viscometer they cooked up out there! All right—I'll call up a hack photographer downtown, Potter, and get him to meet you out by the metallurgy lab. You get the story and see that he gets the right shots. Okay?"

He led David into the hallway. "Just go back the way you came, turn left instead of right at fractional horsepower motors, cut through hydraulic engineering, catch bus eleven on Avenue 9, and it'll take you right there. After you get the story and pictures, we'll get them cleared by the law division, the plant security officer, our department head and buildings and grounds, and shoot them right out. Now get going. That deer isn't on the payroll—he isn't going to wait for you. Come to work today—tomorrow your work will be on every front page in the country, if we can get it approved. The name of the photographer you're going to meet is McGarvey. Got it? You're in the big time now, Potter. We'll all be watching." He shut the door behind David.

David found himself trotting down the hall, down a stairway, and into an alley, brushing roughly past persons in a race against time. Many turned to watch the purposeful young man with admiration.

On and on he strode, his mind seething with information: *Flammer, Building 31; deer, metallurgy lab; photographer, Al Tappin. No. Al Tappin in Ashtabula.* Flenny *the hack photographer. No.* McCammer. *No.* McCammer is new supervisor. Fifty-six *per cent eagle scouts. Deer by viscometer laboratory. No. Viscometer in Ashtabula. Call Danner, new supervisor, and get instructions right. Three weeks' vacation after fifteen years. Danner not new supervisor. Anyway, new supervisor in Building 319. No. Fanner in Building 39981983319.*

David stopped, blocked by a grimy window at the end of a blind alley. All he knew was that he'd never been there before, that his memory had blown a gasket, and that the deer was not on the payroll. The air in the alley was thick with tango music and the stench of scorched insulation. David scrubbed away some of the crust on the window with his handkerchief, praying for a glimpse of something that made sense.

Inside were ranks of women at benches, rocking their heads in time to the music, and dipping soldering irons into great nests of colored wires that crept past them on endless belts. One of them looked up and saw David, and winked in tango rhythm. David fled.

At the mouth of the alley, he stopped a man and asked him if he'd heard anything about a deer in the Works. The man shook his head and looked at David oddly, making David aware of how frantic he must look. "I heard it was out by the lab," David said more calmly.

"Which lab?" said the man.

"That's what I'm not sure of," said David. "There's more than one?"

"Chemical lab?" said the man. "Materials testing lab? Paint lab? Insulation lab?"

"No—I don't think it's any of those," said David.

"Well, I could stand here all afternoon naming labs, and probably not hit the right one. Sorry, I've got to go. You don't know what building they've got the differential analyzer in, do you?"

"Sorry," said David. He stopped several other people, none of whom knew anything about the deer, and he tried to retrace his steps to the office of his supervisor, whatever his name was. He was swept this way and that by the currents of the Works, stranded in backwaters, sucked back into the main stream, and his mind was more and more numbed, and the mere reflexes of self-preservation were more and more in charge.

He chose a building at random, and walked inside for a momentary respite from the summer heat, and was deafened by the clangor of steel sheets being cut and punched, being smashed into strange shapes by great hammers that dropped out of the smoke and dust overhead. A hairy, heavily muscled man was seated near the door on a wooden stool, watching a giant lathe turn a bar of steel the size of a silo.

David now had the idea of going through a company phone directory until he recognized his supervisor's name. He called to the machinist from a few feet away, but his voice was lost in the din. He tapped the man's shoulder. "Telephone around here?"

The man nodded. He cupped his hands around David's ear, and shouted. "Up that, and through the—" Down crashed a hammer. "Turn left and keep going until you—" An overhead crane dropped a stack of steel plates. "Four doors down from there is it. Can't miss it."

David, his ears ringing and his head aching, walked into the street again and chose another door. Here was peace and air conditioning. He was in the lobby of an auditorium, where a group of men were examining a box studded with dials and switches that was spotlighted and mounted on a revolving platform.

"Please, miss," he said to a receptionist by the door, "could you tell me where I could find a telephone?"

"It's right around the corner, sir," she said. "But I'm afraid no one is permitted here today but the crystallographers. Are you with them?"

"Yes," said David.

"Oh—well, come right in. Name?"

He told her, and a man sitting next to her lettered it on a badge. The badge was hung on his chest, and David headed for the telephone. A grinning, bald, big-toothed man, wearing a badge that said, "Stan Dunkel, Sales," caught him and steered him to the display.

"Dr. Potter," said Dunkel, "I ask you: is that the way to build an X-ray spectrogoniometer, or is that the way to build an X-ray spectrogoniometer?"

"Yes," said David. "That's the way, all right."

"Martini, Dr. Potter?" said a maid, offering a tray.

David emptied a Martini in one gloriously hot, stinging gulp.

"What features do you want in an X-ray spectrogoniometer, Doctor?" said Dunkel.

"It should be sturdy, Mr. Dunkel," said David, and he left Dunkel there, pledging his reputation that there wasn't a sturdier one on earth.

In the phone booth, David had barely got through the telephone directory's A's before the name of his supervisor miraculously returned to his consciousness: *Flammer*! He found the number and dialed.

"Mr. Flammer's office," said a woman.

"Could I speak to him, please? This is David Potter."

"Oh—Mr. Potter. Well, Mr. Flammer is somewhere out in the Works now, but he left a message for you. He said there's an added twist on the deer story. When they catch the deer, the venison is going to be used at the Quarter-Century Club picnic."

"Quarter-Century Club?" said David.

"Oh, that's really something, Mr. Potter. It's for people who've been with the company twenty-five years or more. Free drinks and cigars, and just the best of everything. They have a wonderful time."

"Anything else about the deer?"

"Nothing he hasn't already told you," she said, and she hung up.

David Potter, with a third Martini in his otherwise empty stomach, stood in front of the auditorium and looked both ways for a deer.

"But our X-ray spectrogoniometer *is* sturdy, Dr. Potter," Stan Dunkel called to him from the auditorium steps.

Across the street was a patch of green, bordered by hedges. David pushed through the hedges into the outfield of a softball diamond. He crossed it and went behind the bleachers, where there was cool shade, and he sat down with his back to a wire-mesh fence which separated one end of the Works from a deep pine woods. There were two gates in the fence, but both were wired shut.

David was going to sit there for just a moment, long enough to get his nerve back, to take bearings. Maybe he could leave a message for Flammer, saying he'd suddenly fallen ill, which was essentially true, or—

"There he goes!" cried somebody from the other side of the diamond. There were gleeful cries, shouted orders, the sounds of men running.

A deer with broken antlers dashed under the bleachers, saw David, and ran frantically into the open again along the fence. He ran with a limp, and his reddish-brown coat was streaked with soot and grease.

"Easy now! Don't rush him! Just keep him there. Shoot into the woods, not the Works."

David came out from under the bleachers to see a great semicircle of men, several ranks deep, closing in slowly on the corner of fence in which the deer was at bay. In the front rank were a dozen company policemen with drawn pistols. Other members of the posse carried sticks and rocks and lariats hastily fashioned from wire.

The deer pawed the grass, and bucked, and jerked its broken antlers in the direction of the crowd.

"Hold it!" shouted a familiar voice. A company limousine rumbled across the diamond to the back of the crowd. Leaning out of a window was Lou Flammer, David's supervisor. "Don't shoot until we get a picture of him alive," commanded Flammer. He pulled a photographer out of the limousine, and pushed him into the front rank.

Flammer saw David standing alone by the fence, his back to a gate. "Good boy, Potter," called Flammer. "Right on the ball! Photographer got lost, and I had to bring him here myself."

The photographer fired his flash bulbs. The deer bucked and sprinted along the fence toward David. David unwired the gate, opened it wide. A second later the deer's white tail was flashing through the woods and gone.

The profound silence was broken first by the whistling of a switch engine and then by the click of a latch as David stepped into the woods and closed the gate behind him. He didn't look back.

Any Reasonable Offer

A FEW DAYS AGO, just before I came up here to Newport on a vacation, in spite of being broke, it occurred to me there isn't any profession—or racket, or whatever—that takes more of a beating from its clients than real estate. If you stand still, they club you. If you run, they shoot.

Maybe dentists have rougher client relationships, but I doubt it. Give a man a choice between having his teeth or a real estate salesman's commission extracted, and he'll choose the pliers and novocaine every time.

Consider Delahanty. Two weeks ago, Dennis Delahanty asked me to sell his house for him, said he wanted twenty thousand for it.

That afternoon I took a prospect out to see the house. The prospect walked through it once, said that he liked it and he'd take it. That evening he closed the deal. With Delahanty. Behind my back.

Then I sent Delahanty a bill for my commission—five percent of the sale price, one thousand dollars.

"What the hell are you?" he wanted to know. "A busy movie star?"

"You knew what my commission was going to be."

"Sure, I knew. But you only worked an hour. A thousand bucks an hour! Forty thousand a week, two million a year! I just figured it out."

"Some years I make ten million," I said.

"I work six days a week, fifty weeks a year, and then turn around and pay some young squirt like you a thousand for one hour of smiles and small talk and a pint of gas. I'm going to write my congressman. If it's legal, it sure as hell shouldn't be."

"He's my congressman, too, and you signed a contract. You read it, didn't you?"

He hung up on me. He still hasn't paid me.

Old Mrs. Hellbrunner called right after Delahanty. *Her* house has been on the market for three years, and it represents about all that's left of the Hellbrunner family's fortune. Twenty-seven rooms, nine baths, ballroom, den, study, music room, solarium, turrets with slits for crossbowmen, simulated drawbridge and portcullis, and a dry moat. Somewhere in the basement, I suppose, are racks and gibbets for insubordinate domestics.

"Something is very wrong," said Mrs. Hellbrunner. "Mr. Delahanty sold that awful little cracker-box of his in one day, and for four thousand more than he paid for it. Good heavens, I'm asking only a quarter of the replacement price for my house."

"Well—it's a very *special* sort of person who would want your place, Mrs. Hellbrunner," I said, thinking of an escaped maniac. "But someday he'll come along. They say there's a house for every person, and a person for every house. It isn't every day I get someone in here who's looking for something in the hundred-thousand-dollar range. But sooner or later—"

"When you accepted Mr. Delahanty as a client, you went right to work and earned your commission," she said. "Why can't you do the same for me?"

"We'll just have to be patient. It's—"

She, too, hung up, and then I saw the tall, gray-haired gentleman standing in the office doorway. Something about him—or maybe about me—made me want to jump to attention and suck in my sagging gut.

"Yessir!" I said.

"Is this yours?" he said, handing me an ad clipped from the morning paper. He held it as though he were returning a soiled handkerchief that had fallen from my pocket.

"Yessir—the Hurty place. That's mine, all right."

"This is the place, Pam," he said, and a tall, somberly dressed woman joined him. She didn't look directly at me, but at an imaginary horizon over my left shoulder, as though I were a headwaiter or some other minor functionary.

"Perhaps you'd like to know what they're asking for the place before we go out there," I said.

"The swimming pool is in order?" said the woman.

"Yes, ma'am. Just two years old."

"And the stables are usable?" said the man.

"Yessir. Mr. Hurty has his horses in them now. They're all newly whitewashed, fireproof, everything. He's asking eighty-five thousand for the place, and it's a firm price. Is that within your price range, sir?"

He curled his lip.

"I said that about price range, because some people—"

"Do we look like any of them?" said the woman.

"No, you certainly don't." And they didn't, either, and every second they were looking more like a four-thousand-two-hundred-fifty-dollar commission. "I'll call Mr. Hurty right away."

"Tell him that Colonel and Mrs. Bradley Peckham are interested in his property."

The Peckhams had come by cab, so I drove them to the Hurty estate in my old two-door sedan, for which I apologized, and, to judge from their expression, rightly so.

Their town car, they related, had developed an infuriating little squeak, and was in the hands of a local dealer, who had staked his reputation on getting the squeak out.

"What is it you do, Colonel?" I asked, making small talk.

His eyebrows went up. "Do? Why, whatever amuses me. Or in time of crisis, whatever my country needs most."

"Right now he's straightening things out at National Steel Foundry," said Mrs. Peckham.

"Rum show, that," said the Colonel, "but coming along, coming along."

At the Hurty threshold, Mr. Hurty himself came to the door, tweedy, booted, and spurred. His family was in Europe. The Colonel and his wife, once I had made the formal introductions, ignored me. The Peckhams had some distance to go, however, before offending four thousand dollars' worth of my pride.

I sat quietly, like a Seeing Eye dog or overnight bag, and listened to the banter of those who bought and sold eighty-five-thousand-dollar estates with urbane negligence.

There were none of your shabby questions about how much the place cost to heat or keep up, or what the taxes were, or whether the cellar was dry. Not on your life.

"I'm so glad there's a greenhouse," said Mrs. Peckham. "I had such high hopes for the place, but the ad didn't mention a greenhouse, and I just prayed there was one."

"Never underestimate the power of prayer," I said to myself.

"Yes, I think you've done well with it," the Colonel said to Hurty. "I'm glad to see you've got an honest-to-God swimming pool, and not one of these cement-lined puddles."

"One thing you may be interested in," said Hurty, "is that the water isn't chlorinated. It's passed under ultraviolet light."

"I should hope so," said the Colonel.

"Um," said Hurty.

"Have you a labyrinth?" said Mrs. Peckham.

"How's that?" said Hurty.

"A labyrinth made of box hedge. They're awfully picturesque."

"No, sorry," said Hurty, pulling on his mustache.

"Well, no matter," said the Colonel, making the best of it. "We can put one in."

"Yes," said his wife. "Oh, dear," she murmured, and placed her hand over her heart. Her eyes rolled, and she started to sink to the floor.

"Darling!" The Colonel caught her about the waist.

"Please—" she gasped.

"A stimulant!" commanded the Colonel. "Brandy! Anything!"

Hurty, unnerved, fetched a decanter and poured a shot.

The Colonel's wife forced some between her lips, and the roses returned to her cheeks.

"More, darling?" the Colonel asked.

COMPLETE STORIES

"A sip," she whispered.

When she'd finished it off, the Colonel sniffed the glass. "By George, but that's got a lovely bouquet!" He held out the glass to Hurty, and Hurty filled it.

"Jove!" said the Colonel, savoring, sniffing. "First-rate. Mmm. You know, it's a vanishing race that has the patience really to know the exquisite things in life. With most, it's gulp, gulp, and they're off on some mad chase again."

"Sure," said Hurty.

"Better, dear?" the Colonel asked his wife.

"Much. You know how it is. It comes and goes."

I watched the Colonel take a book from the shelves. He looked in the front, possibly to make sure it was a first edition. "Well, Mr. Hurty," he said, "I think it must show in our eyes how much we like the place. There are some things we'd change, of course, but by and large—"

Hurty looked to me.

I cleared my throat. "Well," I lied, "there are a number of people very interested in this property, as you might expect. I think you'd better make your offer official as soon as possible, if it's really to your liking."

"You aren't going to sell it to just *anybody*, are you?" said the Colonel.

"Certainly not!" lied Hurty, trying to recapture some of the élan he had lost during the labyrinth and brandy episodes.

"Well," said the Colonel, "the legal end can be handled quickly enough when the time comes. But first, if you don't mind, we'd like to get the feel of the place—get the newness out of it."

"Yes, of course, certainly," said Hurty, slightly puzzled.

"Then you don't mind if we sort of wander about a bit, as though it were already ours?"

"No, I guess not. I mean, certainly not. Go right ahead."

And the Peckhams did, while I waited, fidgeting in the living room, and Hurty locked himself in his study. They made themselves at home all afternoon, feeding the horses carrots, loosening the earth about the roots of plants in the greenhouse, drowsing in the sun by the swimming pool.

Once or twice I tried to join them, to point out this feature or that, but they received me as though I were an impertinent butler, so I gave it up.

At four, they asked a maid for tea, and got it—with little cakes. At five, Hurty came out of his study, found them still there, covered his surprise admirably, and mixed us all cocktails.

The Colonel said he always had *his* man rub the inside of martini glasses with garlic. He asked if there was a level spot for polo.

Mrs. Peckham discussed the parking problems of large parties, and asked if there was anything in the local air that was damaging to oil paintings.

At seven, Hurty, fighting yawns, excused himself, and telling the Peckhams to go on making themselves at home, he went to his supper. At eight, the Peckhams, having eddied about Hurty and his meal on their way to one place or another, announced that they were leaving.

They asked me to drop them off at the town's best restaurant.

"I take it you're interested?" I said.

"We'll want to talk a little," said the Colonel. "The price is certainly no obstacle. We'll let you know."

"How can I reach you, Colonel, sir?"

"I'm here for a rest. I prefer not to have anyone know my whereabouts, if you don't mind. I'll call you."

"Fine."

"Tell me," said Mrs. Peckham. "How did Mr. Hurty make his money?"

"He's the biggest used-car salesman in this part of the state."

"Aha!" said the Colonel. "I knew it! The whole place had the air of new money about it."

"Does that mean you don't want it after all?" I asked.

"No, not exactly. We'll simply have to live with it a little while to see what can be done about it, if anything."

"Could you tell me specifically what it was you didn't like?" I asked.

"If you can't see it," said Mrs. Peckham, "no one could possibly point it out to you."

"Oh."

"We'll let you know," said the Colonel.

Three days passed, with their normal complement of calls from Delahanty and Mrs. Hellbrunner, but without a sign from Colonel Peckham and his lady.

As I was closing my office on the afternoon of the fourth day, Hurty called me.

"When the hell," he said, "are those Peckham people going to come to a boil?"

"Lord knows," I said. "There's no way I can get in touch with them. He said he'd call me."

"You can get in touch with them anytime of night or day."

"How?"

"Just call my place. They've been out here for the past three days, taking the newness out of it. They've damn well taken something out of me, too. Do the liquor and cigars and food come out of your commission?"

"If there is a commission."

"You mean there's some question about it? He goes around here as though he has the money in his pocket and is just waiting for the right time to give it to me."

"Well, since he won't talk with me, you might as well do the pressuring. Tell him I've just told you a retired brewer from Toledo has offered seventy-five thousand. That ought to get action."

"All right. I'll have to wait until they come in from swimming, for cocktails."

"Call me back when you've got a reaction, and I'll toot out with an offer form all ready to go."

Ten minutes later he did. "Guess what, brain-box?"

"He bit?"

"I'm getting a brand-new real estate agent."

"Oh?"

"Yes indeedy. I took the advice of the last one I had, and a red-hot prospect and his wife walked out with their noses in the air."

"No! Why?"

"Colonel and Mrs. Peckham wish you to know that they couldn't possibly be interested in anything that would appeal to a retired brewer from Toledo."

It was a lousy estate anyhow, so I gaily laughed and gave my attention to more substantial matters, such as the Hellbrunner mansion. I ran a boldface advertisement describing the joys of life in a fortified castle.

The next morning, I looked up from my work to see the ad, torn from the paper, in the long, clean fingers of Colonel Peckham.

"Is this yours?"

"Good morning, Colonel. Yessir, it is."

"It sounds like *our* kind of place," said the voice of Mrs. Peckham.

We crossed the simulated drawbridge and passed under the rusty portcullis of their kind of place.

Mrs. Hellbrunner liked the Peckhams immediately. For one thing, they were, I'm pretty sure, the first people in several generations to admire the place. More to the point, they gave every indication of being about to buy it.

"It would cost about a half-million to replace," said Mrs. Hellbrunner.

"Yes," said the Colonel. "They don't build houses like this anymore."

"Oh!" gasped Mrs. Peckham, and the Colonel caught her as she headed for the floor.

"Quick! Brandy! Anything!" cried Colonel Peckham.

When I drove the Peckhams back to the center of town, they were in splendid spirits.

"Why on earth didn't you show us this place first?" said the Colonel.

"Just came on the market yesterday," I said, "and priced the way it is, I don't expect it'll be on the market very long."

The Colonel squeezed his wife's hand. "I don't expect so, do you, dear?"

Mrs. Hellbrunner still called me every day, but now her tone was cheery and flattering. She reported that the Peckhams arrived shortly after noon each day, and that they seemed more in love with the house on each visit.

"I'm treating them just like Hellbrunners," she said craftily.

"That's the ticket."

"I even got cigars for him."

"Pour it on. It's all tax-deductible," I cheered.

Four nights later, she called me again to say that the Peckhams were coming to dinner. "Why don't you sort of casually drop in afterward, and just happen to have an offer form with you?"

"Have they mentioned any figures?"

"Only that it's perfectly astonishing what you can get for a hundred thousand."

I set my briefcase down in the Hellbrunner music room after dinner that evening. I said, "Greetings."

The Colonel, on the piano bench, rattled the ice in his drink.

"And how are *you*, Mrs. Hellbrunner?" I said. One glance told me she had never in all her life been worse.

"I'm fine," she said hoarsely. "The Colonel has just been speaking very interestingly. The State Department wants him to do some troubleshooting in Bangkok."

The Colonel shrugged sadly. "Once more to the colors, as a civilian this time."

"We leave tomorrow," said Mrs. Peckham, "to close our place in Philadelphia—"

"And finish up at National Steel Foundry," said the Colonel.

"Then off to Bangkok they go," quavered Mrs. Hellbrunner.

"Men must work, and women must weep," said Mrs. Peckham.

"Yup," I said.

The next morning, the telephone was ringing when I unlocked my office door.

It was Mrs. Hellbrunner. Shrill. Not like old family at all. "I don't *believe* he's going to Bangkok," she raged. "It was the price. He was too polite to bargain."

"You'll take less?" Up to now, she'd been very firm about the hundred-thousand figure.

"Less?" Her voice became prayerful. "Lord—I'd take fifty to get rid of the monster!" She was silent for a moment. "Forty. Thirty. Sell it!"

So I sent a telegram to the Colonel, care of National Steel Foundry, Philadelphia. There was no reply, and then I tried the telephone.

"National Steel Foundry," said a woman in Philadelphia.

"Colonel Peckham, please."

"Who?"

"Peckham. Colonel Bradley Peckham. *The* Peckham."

"We have a Peckham, B. C., in Drafting."

"Is he an executive?"

"I don't know, sir. You can ask him."

There was a click in my ear as she switched my call to Drafting.

"Drafting," said a woman.

The first operator broke in: "This gentleman wishes to speak to Mr. Peckham."

"*Colonel* Peckham," I specified.

"Mr. Melrose," called the second woman, "is Peckham back yet?"

"Peckham!" Mr. Melrose shouted. "Shag your tail. Telephone!"

Above the sound of room noises, I heard someone ask, "Have a good time?"

"So-so," said a vaguely familiar, faraway voice. "Think we'll try Newport next time. Looked pretty good from the bus."

"How the hell do you manage tony places like that on your salary?"

"Takes a bit of doing." And then the voice became loud, and terribly familiar. "Peckham speaking. Drafting."

I let the receiver fall into its cradle.

I was awfully tired. I realized that I hadn't had a vacation since the end of the war. I had to get away from it all for a little while, or I would go mad. But Delahanty hadn't come through yet, so I was stone broke.

And then I thought about what Colonel Bradley Peckham had said about Newport. There *were* a lot of nice houses there—all beautifully staffed, furnished, stocked, overlooking the sea, and for sale.

For instance, take this place—the Van Tuyl estate. It has almost everything: private beach *and* swimming pool, polo field, two grass tennis courts, nine-hole golf course, stables, paddocks, French chef, at least three exceptionally attractive Irish parlor maids, English butler, cellar full of vintage stuff—

The labyrinth is an interesting feature, too. I get lost in it almost every day. Then the real estate agent comes looking for me, and he gets lost just as I find my way out. Believe me, the property is worth every penny of the asking price. I'm not going to haggle about it, not for a minute. When the time comes, I'll either take it or leave it.

But I've got to live with the place a little longer—to get the newness out—before I tell the agent what I'm going to do. Meanwhile, I'm having a wonderful time. Wish you were here.

The Package

WHAT DO YOU KNOW about that?" said Earl Fenton. He unslung his stereoscopic camera, took off his coat, and laid the coat and the camera on top of the television-radio-phonograph console. "Here we go on a trip clean around the world, Maude, and two minutes after we come back to our new house, the telephone rings. That's civilization."

"For you, Mr. Fenton," said the maid.

"Earl Fenton speaking . . . Who? . . . You got the right Fenton? There's a *Brudd* Fenton on San Bonito Boulevard . . . Yes, that's right, I did. Class of 1910 . . . Wait! No! Sure I do! Listen, you tell the hotel to go to hell, Charley, you're my guest. . . . Have we got room?"

Earl covered the mouthpiece and grinned at his wife. "He wants to know if we've got room!" He spoke into the telephone again. "Listen, Charley, we've got rooms I've never been in. No kidding. We just moved in today—five minutes ago.... No, it's all fixed up. Decorator furnished the place nice as you please weeks ago, and the servants got everything going like a dollar watch, so we're ready. Catch you a cab, you hear? . . .

"No, I sold the plant last year. Kids are grown up and on their own and all— young Earl's a doctor now, got a big house in Santa Monica, and Ted's just passed his bar exams and gone in with his Uncle George— Yeah, and Maude and I, we've just decided to sit back and take a well-earned— But the hell with talking on the phone. You come right on out. Boy! Have we got a lot of catching up to do!" Earl hung up and made clucking sounds with his tongue.

Maude was examining a switch panel in the hallway. "I don't know if this thing-amajig works the air-conditioning or the garage doors or the windows or what," she said.

"We'll get Lou Converse out here to show us how everything works," said Earl. Converse was the contractor who had put up the rambling, many-leveled "machine for living" during their trip abroad.

Earl's expression became thoughtful as he gazed through a picture window at the flagstone terrace and grill, flooded with California sunshine, and at the cartwheel gate that opened onto the macadam driveway, and at the garage, with its martin house, weathercock, and two Cadillacs. "By golly, Maude," he said, "I just finished talking to a ghost."

"Um?" said Maude. "Aha! See, the picture window goes up, and down comes the screen. Ghost? Who on earth?"

"Freeman, Charley Freeman. A name from the past, Maude. I couldn't believe it at first. Charley was a fraternity brother and just about the biggest man in the whole class of 1910. Track star, president of the fraternity, editor of the paper, Phi Beta Kappa."

"Goodness! What's he doing coming here to see poor little us?" said Maude.

Earl was witnessing a troubling tableau that had been in the back of his mind for years: Charley Freeman, urbane, tastefully clothed, was having a plate set before him by Earl, who wore a waiter's jacket. When he'd invited Charley to come on out, Earl's enthusiasm had been automatic, the reflex of a man who prided himself on being a plain, ordinary, friendly fellow, for all of his success. Now, remembering their college relationship, Earl found that the prospect of Charley's arrival was making him uncomfortable. "He was a rich kid," Earl said. "One of those guys"—and his voice was tinged with bitterness—"who had everything. You know?"

"Well, hon," said Maude, "you weren't exactly behind the door when they passed out the looks and brains."

"No—but when they passed out the money, they handed me a waiter's jacket and a mop." She looked at him sympathetically, and he was encouraged to pour out his heart on the subject. "By golly, Maude, it does something to a man to go around having to wait on guys his same age, cleaning up after 'em, and seeing them with nice clothes and all the money in the world, going off to some resort in the summer when I had to go to work to pay next year's tuition." Earl was surprised at the emotion in his voice. "And all the time they're looking down on you, like there was something wrong with people who weren't handed their money on a silver platter."

"Well, that makes me good and mad!" Maude said, squaring her shoulders indignantly, as though to protect Earl from those who'd humiliated him in college. "If this great Charley Freeman snooted you in the old days, I don't see why we should have him in the house now."

"Oh, heck—forgive and forget," Earl said gloomily. "Doesn't throw me anymore. He seemed to want to come out, and I try to be a good fellow, no matter what."

"So what's the high-and-mighty Freeman doing now?"

"Don't know. Something big, I guess. He went to med school, and I came back here, and we kind of lost touch." Experimentally, Earl pressed a button on the wall. From the basement came muffled whirs and clicks, as machines took control of the temperature and humidity and purity of the atmosphere about him. "But I don't expect Charley's doing a bit better than this."

"What were some of the things he did to you?" Maude pursued, still indignant.

Earl waved the subject away with his hand. There weren't any specific incidents that he could tell Maude about. People like Charley Freeman hadn't come right out and said anything to humiliate Earl when he'd waited on them. But just the same, Earl was sure that he'd been looked down on, and he was willing to bet that when he'd been out of earshot, they'd talked about him, and . . .

He shook his head in an effort to get rid of his dour mood, and he smiled. "Well, Mama, what say we have a little drinkie, and then take a tour of the place? If I'm going to show it to Charley, I'd better find out how a few of these gimcracks work, or he'll think old Earl is about as at home in a setup like this as a retired janitor or waiter or something. By golly, there goes the phone again! That's civilization for you."

"Mr. Fenton," the maid said, "it's Mr. Converse."

"Hello, Lou, you old horse thief. Just looking over your handiwork. Maude and I are going to have to go back to college for a course in electrical engineering, ha ha . . . Eh? Who? . . . No kidding. They really want to? . . . Well, I guess that's the kind of thing you have to expect to go through. If they've got their heart set on it, okay. Maude and I go clean around the world, and two minutes after we're home, it's like the middle of Grand Central Station."

Earl hung up and scratched his head in mock wonderment and weariness. In reality, he was pleased with the activity, with the bell-ringing proof that his life, unlike his ownership of the plant and the raising of his kids and the world cruise, was barely begun.

"What now?" said Maude.

"Aw, Converse says some fool home magazine wants to do a story on the place, and they want to get the pictures this afternoon."

"What fun!"

"Yeah—I guess. I dunno. I don't want to be standing around in all the pictures like some stuffed shirt." To show how little he cared, he interested himself in another matter. "I don't know why she wouldn't, considering what we paid her, but that decorator really thought of everything, you know?" He'd opened a closet next to the terrace doors and found an apron, a chef's hat, and asbestos gloves inside. "By golly, you know, that's pretty rich. See what it says on the apron, Maude?"

"Cute," said Maude, and she read the legend aloud: "'Don't shoot the cook, he's doing the best he can.' Why, you look like a regular Oscar of the Waldorf, Earl. Now let me see you in the hat."

He grinned bashfully and fussed with the hat. "Don't know exactly how one of the fool things is supposed to go. Feel kind of like a man from Mars."

"Well, you look wonderful to me, and I wouldn't trade you for a hundred stuck-up Charley Freemans."

They wandered arm in arm over the flagstone terrace to the grill, a stone edifice that might have been mistaken from a distance for a branch post office. They kissed, as they had kissed beside the Great Pyramid, the Colosseum, and the Taj Mahal.

"You know something, Maude?" said Earl, a great emotion ballooning in his breast. "You know, I used to wish my old man was rich, so you and I could have had a place like this right off—bing!—the minute I got out of college and we got married. But you know, we couldn't have had this moment looking back and knowing, by God, we made every inch of the way on our own. And we understand the little guy, Maude, because we were little guys once. By gosh, nobody born with a silver spoon in their mouth can buy that understanding. A lot of people on the cruise didn't want to look at all that terrible poverty in Asia, like their consciences bothered them. But us—well, seeing as how we'd come up the hard way, I don't guess we had much on our consciences, and we could look out at those poor people and kind of understand."

"Uh-huh," said Maude.

Earl worked his fingers in the thick gloves. "And tonight I'm going to broil you and me and Charley a sirloin steak as thick as a Manhattan phone book, and deserve every ounce of it, if I do say so myself."

"We aren't even unpacked."

"So what? I'm not tired. Got a lot of living to do, and the quicker I get at it, the more I'll get done."

Earl and Maude were in the living room, Earl still in his chef's outfit, when Charley Freeman was ushered in by the maid.

"By golly!" said Earl. "If it isn't Charley!"

Charley was still thin and erect, and the chief mark of age upon him was the graying of his thick hair. While his face was lined, it was still confident and wise-looking, was still, in Earl's opinion, subtly mocking. There was so much left of the old Charley, in fact, that the college relationship, dead for forty years, came alive again in Earl's mind. In spite of himself, Earl felt resentfully servile, felt crude and dull. His only defense was the old one—hidden resentment, with a promise that things would be very different before long.

"Been a long time, hasn't it, Earl?" Charley said, his voice still deep and virile. "You're looking fine."

"Lot of water can go under the bridge in forty years," said Earl. He was running his finger nervously over the rich fabric of the sofa. And then he remembered Maude, who was standing rigid, thin-lipped behind him. "Oh, excuse me, Charley, this is my wife, Maude."

"This is a pleasure I've had to put off for a long time," said Charley. "I feel I know you, Earl spoke of you so much in college."

"How do you do?" said Maude.

"Far better than I had any reason to expect six months ago," said Charley. "What a handsome house!" He laid his hand on the television-radio-phonograph console. "Now, what the devil do you call this?"

"Huh?" said Earl. "TV set. What's it look like?"

"TV?" said Charley, frowning. "TV? Oh—abbreviation for 'television.' That it?"

"You kidding me, Charley?"

"No, really. There must be more than a billion and a half poor souls who've never seen one of the things, and I'm one of them. Does it hurt to touch the glass part?"

"The tube?" Earl laughed uneasily. "Hell, no—go ahead."

"Mr. Freeman's probably got a tube five times as big as this one at home," said Maude, smiling coldly, "and he's kidding us along like he doesn't even know this is a TV set, the tube's so small."

"Well, Charley," said Earl, cutting briskly into the silence that followed Maude's comment, "and to what do we owe the honor of this visit?"

"For old times' sake," said Charley "I happened to be in town, and I remem—"

Before Charley could elaborate, he was interrupted by a party composed of Lou Converse, a photographer from *Home Beautiful*, and a young, pretty woman writer.

The photographer, who introduced himself simply as Slotkin, took command of the household, and as he was to do for the whole of his stay, he quashed all talk and activities not related to getting the magazine pictures taken. "Zo," said Slotkin, "und de gimmick is de pagatch, eh?"

"Baggage?" said Earl.

"*Package*," said the writer. "See, the angle on the story is that you come home from a world cruise to a complete package for living—everything anybody could possibly want for a full life."

"Oh."

"It's complete," said Lou Converse, "complete right down to a fully stocked wine cellar and a pantry filled with gourmet specialties. Brand-new cars, brand-new everything but wine."

"Aha! Dey vin a condezt."

"He sold his factory and retired," said Converse.

"Maude and I figured we owed ourselves a little something," said Earl. "We held back all these years, putting money back into the business and all, and then, when the kids were grown up and the big offer came for the plant, we all of a sudden felt kind of crazy, and said, Why not? And we just went ahead and ordered everything we'd ever wanted."

Earl glanced at Charley Freeman, who stood apart and in the background, half smiling, seeming to be fascinated by the scene. "We started out, Maude and I," said Earl, "in a two-room apartment down by the docks. Put that in the story."

"We had love," said Maude.

"Yes," said Earl, "and I don't want people to think I'm just another stuffed shirt who was born with a wad of money and blew himself to this setup. No, sir! This is the end of a long, hard road. Write that down. Charley remembers me back in the old days, when I had to work my way through school."

"Rugged days for Earl," said Charley.

Now the center of attention, Earl felt his self-confidence returning, and he began to see Charley's coming back into his life at this point as a generous act of fate, a fine opportunity to settle the old scores once and for all. "It wasn't the work that made it rugged," Earl said pointedly.

Charley seemed surprised by Earl's vehemence. "All right," he said, "then the work wasn't rugged. It was so long ago I can remember it either way."

"I mean it was tough being looked down on because I wasn't born with a silver spoon in my mouth," said Earl.

"Earl!" said Charley, smiling in his incredulity. "As many fatheads as we had for fraternity brothers, not one of them for a minute looked down—"

"Make ready for de pigdures," Slotkin said. "Stardt mit de grill—breadt, saladt, und a big, bloody piece of meadt."

The maid brought a five-pound slab of steak from the freezer, and Earl held it over the grill. "Hurry up," he said. "Can't hold a cow at arm's length all day." Behind his smile, however, he was nettled by Charley's bland dismissal of his college grievances.

"Hold it!" said Slotkin. The flashbulbs went off. "Good!"

And the party moved indoors. There, Earl and Maude posed in room after room, watering a plant in the solarium, reading the latest book before the living room fireplace, working pushbutton windows, chatting with the maid over the laundry console, planning menus, having a drink at the rumpus room bar, sawing a plank in the workshop, dusting off Earl's gun collection in the den.

And always, there was Charley Freeman at the rear of the entourage, missing nothing, obviously amused as Maude and Earl demonstrated their packaged good life. Under Charley's gaze, Earl became more and more restless and self-conscious as he performed, and Slotkin berated him for wearing such a counterfeit smile.

"By God, Maude," said Earl, perspiring in the master bedroom, "if I ever have to come out of retirement—knock on wood—I can go on television as a quick-change artist. This better be the last picture, by golly. Feel like a darn clotheshorse."

But the feeling didn't prevent his changing once more at Slotkin's command, this time into a tuxedo. Slotkin wanted a picture of dinner by candlelight. The dining room curtains would be drawn, electrically, to hide the fact of midafternoon outdoors.

"Well, I guess Charley's getting an eyeful," said Earl, distorting his face as he punched a collar button into place. "I think he's pretty darn impressed." His voice lacked conviction, and he turned hopefully to Maude for confirmation.

She was sitting at her dressing table, staring mercilessly at her image in the mirror, trying on different bits of jewelry. "Hmm?"

"I said I guess Charley's pretty impressed."

"*Him*," she said flatly. "He's just a little *too* smooth, if you ask me. After the way he used to snoot you, and then he comes here all smiles and good manners."

"Yeah," said Earl, with a sigh. "Doggone it, he used to make me feel like two bits, and he still does, looking at us like we were showing off instead of just trying to help a magazine out. And did you hear what he said when I came right out and told him what I didn't like about college?"

"He acted like you just made it up, like it was just in your mind. Oh, he's a slick article, all right. But I'm not going to let him get my goat," said Maude. "This started out as the happiest day of our lives, and it's going to go on being that. And you want to know something else?"

"What's that?" Backed by Maude, Earl felt his morale rising. He hadn't been absolutely sure that Charley was inwardly making fun of them, but Maude was, and she was burned up about it, too.

Her voice dropped to a whisper. "For all his superior ways, and kidding us about our TV set and everything, I don't think the great Charley Freeman amounts to a hill of beans. Did you see his suit—up close?"

"Well, Slotkin kept things moving so fast, I don't guess I got a close look."

"You can bet I did, Earl," said Maude. "It's all worn and shiny, and the cuffs are a sight! I'd die of shame if you went around in a suit like that."

Earl was startled. He had been so on the defensive that it hadn't occurred to him that Charley's fortunes could be anything but what they'd been in college. "Maybe a favorite old suit he hates to chuck out," he said at last. "Rich people are funny about things like that sometimes."

"He's got on a favorite old shirt and a favorite old pair of shoes, too."

"I can't believe it," murmured Earl. He pulled aside a curtain for a glimpse of the fairyland of the terrace and grill, where Charley Freeman stood chatting with Slotkin and Converse and the writer. The cuffs of Charley's trousers, Earl saw with amazement, were indeed frayed, and the heels of his shoes were worn thin. Earl touched a button, and a bedroom window slithered open.

"It's a pleasant town," Charley was telling them. "I might as well settle here as anywhere, since I haven't very strong reasons for living in any particular part of the country."

"Zo eggspensif!" said Slotkin.

"Yes," said Charley, "I'd probably be smart to move inland, where my money'd go a little farther. Lord, it's incredible what things cost these days!"

Maude laid her hand on Earl's shoulder. "Seems kind of fishy, doesn't it?" she whispered. "You don't hear from him for forty years, and all of a sudden he shows up, down-and-out, to pay us a big, friendly call. What's he after?"

"Said he just wanted to see me for old times' sake," said Earl.

Maude sniffed. "You believe that?"

The dining room table looked like an open treasure chest, with the flames of the candelabra caught in a thousand perfect surfaces—the silver, the china, the facets of the crystal, Maude's rubies, and Maude's and Earl's proud eyes. The maid set steaming soup, prepared for the sake of the picture, before them.

"Perfect!" said Slotkin. "So! Now talk."

"What about?" said Earl.

"Anything," said the woman writer. "Just so the picture won't look posed. Talk about your trip. How does the situation in Asia look?"

It was a question Earl wasn't inclined to chat about lightly.

"You've been to Asia?" said Charley.

Earl smiled. "India, Burma, the Philippines, Japan. All in all, Maude and I must have spent two months looking the situation over."

"Earl and I took every side trip there was," said Maude. "He just had to see for himself what was what."

"Trouble with the State Department is they're all up in an ivory tower," said Earl.

Beyond the glittering camera lens and the bank of flashbulb reflectors, Earl saw the eyes of Charley Freeman. Expert talk on large affairs had been among Charley's many strong points in college, and Earl had been able only to listen and nod and wonder.

"Yes, sir," said Earl, summing up, "the situation looked just about hopeless to everybody on the cruise but Maude and me, and it took us a while to figure out why that was. Then we realized that we were about the only ones who'd pulled themselves up by their bootstraps—that we were the only ones who really understood that no matter how low a man is, if he's got what it takes, he can get clean to the top." He paused. "There's nothing wrong with Asia that a little spunk and common sense and know-how won't cure."

"I'm glad it's that easy," said Charley. "I was afraid things were more complicated than that."

Earl, who rightly considered himself one of the easiest men on earth to get along with, found himself in the unfamiliar position of being furious with a fellow human being. Charley Freeman, who evidently had failed as Earl had risen in the world, was openly belittling one of Earl's proudest accomplishments, his knowledge of Asia. "I've seen it, Charley!" said Earl. "I'm not talking as just one more darn fool armchair strategist who's never been outside his own city limits!"

Slotkin fired his flashbulbs. "One more," he said.

"Of course you're not, Earl," said Charley. "That was rude of me. What you say is very true, in a way, but it's such an oversimplification. Taken by itself, it's a dangerous way of thinking. I shouldn't have interrupted. It's simply that the subject is one I have a deep interest in."

Earl felt his cheeks reddening, as Charley, with his seeming apology, set himself up as a greater authority on Asia than Earl. "Think maybe I'm entitled to some opinions on Asia, Charley. I actually got out and rubbed elbows with the people over there, finding out how their minds work and all."

"You should have seen him jawing away with the Chinese bellboys in Manila," said Maude, challenging Charley with her eyes to top *that*.

"Now then," said the writer, checking a list, "the last shot we want is of you two coming in the front door with your suitcases, looking surprised, as though you've just arrived . . ."

In the master bedroom again, Earl and Maude obediently changed back into the clothes they'd been wearing when they first arrived. Earl was studying his face in a mirror, practicing looks of pleased surprise and trying not to let the presence of Charley Freeman spoil this day of days.

"He's staying for supper and the night?" asked Maude.

"Oh heck, I was just trying to be a good fellow on the phone. Wasn't even thinking when I asked him to stay here instead of at the hotel. I could kick myself around the block."

"Lordy. Maybe he'll stay a week."

"Who knows? Slotkin hasn't given me a chance to ask Charley much of anything."

Maude nodded soberly. "Earl, what does it all add up to?"

"All what?"

"I mean, have you tried to put any of it together—the old clothes, and his paleness, and that crack about doing better now than he'd had any right to expect six months ago, and the books, and the TV set? Did you hear him ask Converse about the books?"

"Yeah, that threw me, too, because Charley was the book kind."

"All best-sellers, and he hadn't heard of a one! And he wasn't kidding about television, either. He really hasn't seen it before. He's been out of circulation for a while, and that's for sure."

"Sick, maybe," said Earl.

"Or in jail," whispered Maude.

"Good gosh! You don't suppose—"

"I suppose something's rotten in the state of Denmark," said Maude, "and I don't want him around much longer, if we can help it. I keep trying to figure out what he's doing here, and the only thing that makes sense is that he's here with his fancy ways to bamboozle you out of money, one way or another."

"All right, all right," said Earl, signaling with his hands for her to lower her voice. "Let's keep things as friendly as we can, and ease him out gently."

"How?" said Maude, and between them they devised what they considered a subtle method for bringing Charley's visit to an end before supper.

"Zo . . . zo much for dis," the photographer said. He winked at Earl and Maude warmly, as though noticing them as human beings for the first time. "Denk you.

Nice pagatch you live." He had taken the last picture. He packed his equipment, bowed, and left with Lou Converse and the writer.

Putting off the moment when he would have to sit down with Charley, Earl joined the maid and Maude in the hunt for flashbulbs, which Slotkin had thrown everywhere. When the last bulb was found, Earl mixed martinis and sat down on a couch that faced another, on which Charley sat.

"Well, Charley, here we are."

"And you've come a distance, too, haven't you, Earl?" said Charley, turning his palms upward to indicate the wonder of the dream house. "I see you've got a lot of science fiction on your shelves. Earl, this house *is* science fiction."

"I suppose," said Earl. The flattery was beginning, building up to something—a big touch, probably. Earl was determined not to be spellbound by Charley's smooth ways. "About par for the course in America, maybe, for somebody who isn't afraid of hard work."

"What a course—with this for par, eh?"

Earl looked closely at his guest, trying to discover if Charley was belittling him again. "If I seemed to brag a little when those fool magazine people were here," he said, "I think maybe I've got a little something to brag about. This house is a lot more'n a house. It's the story of my life, Charley—my own personal pyramid, sort of."

Charley lifted his glass in a toast. "May it last as long as the Great Pyramid at Gizeh."

"Thanks," said Earl. It was high time, he decided, that Charley be put on the defensive. "You a doctor, Charley?"

"Yes. Got my degree in 1916."

"Uh-huh. Where you practicing?"

"Little old to start practicing medicine again, Earl. Medicine's changed so much in this country in recent years, that I'm afraid I'm pretty much out of it."

"I see." Earl went over in his mind a list of things that might get a doctor in trouble with the law. He kept his voice casual. "How come you suddenly got the idea of coming to see me?"

"My ship docked here, and I remembered that this was your hometown," said Charley. "Haven't any family left, and trying to start life all over on this side again, I thought I'd look up some of my old college friends. Since the boat landed here, you were the first."

That was going to be Charley's tale, then, Earl thought—that he had been out of the country for a long time. Next would come the touch. "Don't pay much attention to the college gang, myself," he said, unable to resist a small dig. "Such a bunch of snobs there that I was glad to get away and forget 'em."

"God help them if they didn't outgrow the ridiculous social values of college days," said Charley.

Earl was taken aback by the sharpness in Charley's voice, and not understanding it, he hastily changed the subject. "Been overseas, eh? Where, exactly, Charley?"

"Earl!" Maude called from the dining room, according to the plan. "The most awful thing has happened."

"Oh?"

Maude appeared in the doorway. "Angela"—she turned to Charley to explain—"my sister. Earl, Angela just called to say she was coming here with Arthur and the children before dinner, and could we put them up for the night."

"Gosh," said Earl, "don't see how we can. There're five of them, and we've only got two guest rooms, and Charley here—"

"No, no," said Charley. "See here, tell them to come ahead. I planned to stay at the hotel, anyway, and I have some errands to run, so I couldn't possibly stay."

"Okay, if you say so," said Earl.

"If he's got to go, he's got to go," said Maude.

"Yes, well, got a lot to do. Sorry." Charley was on his way to the door, having left his drink half finished. "Thanks. It's been pleasant seeing you. I envy you your package."

"Be good," said Earl, and he closed the door with a shudder and a sigh.

While Earl was still in the hallway, wondering at what could become of a man in forty years, the door chimes sounded, deep and sweet. Earl opened the door cautiously to find Lou Converse, the contractor, standing on the doorstep. Across the street, Charley Freeman was getting into a taxi.

Lou waved to Charley, then turned to face Earl. "Hello! Not inviting myself to dinner. Came back after my hat. Think I left it in the solarium."

"Come on in," said Earl, watching Charley's taxi disappear toward the heart of town. "Maude and I are just getting set to celebrate. Why not stay for dinner and, while you're at it, show us how some of the gadgets work?"

"Thanks, but I'm expected home. I can stick around a little while and explain whatever you don't understand. Too bad you couldn't get Freeman to stay, though."

Maude winked at Earl. "We asked him, but he said he had a lot of errands to run."

"Yeah, he seemed like he was in kind of a hurry just now. You know," Converse said thoughtfully, "guys like Freeman are funny. They make you feel good and bad at the same time."

"What do you know about that, Maude?" said Earl. "Lou instinctively felt the same way we did about Charley! How do you mean that, exactly, Lou, about feeling good and bad at the same time?"

"Well, good because you're glad to know there are still some people like that in the world," said Converse. "And bad—well, when you come across a guy like that, you can't help wondering where the hell your own life's gone to."

"I don't get you," said Earl.

Converse shrugged. "Oh, Lord knows we couldn't all dedicate our lives the way he did. Can't all be heroes. But thinking about Freeman makes me feel like maybe I could have done a little more'n I have."

Earl exchanged glances with Maude. "What did Charley tell you he'd been doing, Lou?"

"Slotkin and I didn't get much out of him. We just had a few minutes there while you and Maude were changing, and I figured I'd get the whole story from you sometime. All he told us was, he'd been in China for the last thirty years. Then I remembered there was a big piece about him in the paper this morning, only I'd forgotten his name. That's where I found out about how he sunk all his money in a hospital over there and ran it until the Commies locked him up and finally threw him out. Quite a story."

"Yup," Earl said bleakly, ending a deathly silence, "quite a story, all right." He put his arm around Maude, who was staring through the picture window at the grill. He squeezed her gently. "I said it's quite a story, isn't it, Mama?"

"We really did ask him to stay," she said.

"That's not like us, Maude, or if it is, I don't want it to be anymore. Come on, hon, let's face it."

"Call him up at the hotel!" said Maude. "That's what we'll do. We'll tell him it was all a mistake about my sister, that—" The impossibility of any sort of recovery made her voice break. "Oh, Earl, honey, why'd he have to pick today? All our life we worked for today, and then he had to come and spoil it."

"He couldn't have tried any harder not to," Earl sighed. "But the odds were too stiff."

Converse looked at them with incomprehension and sympathy. "Well, heck, if he had errands he had errands," he said. "That's no reflection on your hospitality. Good gosh, there isn't another host in the country who's got a better setup for entertaining than you two. All you have to do is flick a switch or push a button for anything a person could want."

Earl walked across the thick carpet to a cluster of buttons by the bookshelves. Listlessly, he pressed one, and floodlights concealed in shrubbery all around the house went on. "That isn't it." He pressed another, and a garage door rumbled shut. "Nope." He pressed another, and the maid appeared in the doorway.

"You ring, Mr. Fenton?"

"Sorry, a mistake," said Earl. "That wasn't the one I wanted."

Converse frowned. "What is it you're looking for, Earl?"

"Maude and I'd like to start today all over again," said Earl. "Show us which button to push, Lou."

Poor Little Rich Town

NEWELL CADY HAD the polish, the wealth, the influence, and the middle-aged good looks of an idealized Julius Caesar. Most of all, though, Cady had know-how, know-how of a priceless variety that caused large manufacturing concerns to bid for his services like dying sultans offering half their kingdoms for a cure.

Cady could stroll through a plant that had been losing money for a generation, glance at the books, yawn and tell the manager how he could save half a million a year in materials, reduce his staff by a third, triple his output, and sell the stuff he'd been throwing out as waste for more than the cost of installing air-conditioning and continuous music throughout the plant. And the air-conditioning and music would increase individual productivity by as much as ten percent and cut union grievances by a fifth.

The latest firm to hire him was the Federal Apparatus Corporation, which had given him the rank of vice-president and sent him to Ilium, New York, where he was to see that the new company headquarters were built properly from the ground up. When the buildings were finished, hundreds of the company's top executives would move their offices from New York City to Ilium, a city that had virtually died when its textile mills moved south after the Second World War.

There was jubilation in Ilium when the deep, thick foundations for the new headquarters were poured, but the exultation was possibly highest in the village of Spruce Falls, nine miles from Ilium, for it was there that Newell Cady had rented, with an option to buy, one of the mansions that lined the shaded main street.

Spruce Falls was a cluster of small businesses and a public school and a post office and a police station and a firehouse serving surrounding dairy farms. During the second decade of the century it experienced a real estate boom. Fifteen mansions were built back then, in the belief that the area, because of its warm mineral springs, was becoming a spa for rich invalids and hypochondriacs and horse people, as had Saratoga, not far away.

In 1922, though, it was determined that bathing in the waters of the spring, while fairly harmless, was nonetheless responsible for several cases of a rash that a Manhattan dermatologist, with no respect for upstate real estate values, named "Spruce Falls disease."

In no time at all the mansions and their stables were as vacant as the abandoned palaces and temples of Angkor Thom in Cambodia. Banks foreclosed on those mansions that were mortgaged. The rest became property of the town in lieu of unpaid taxes. Nobody arrived from out of town to bid for them at any price, as though Spruce Falls disease were leprosy or cholera or bubonic plague.

Nine mansions were eventually bought from the banks or the town by locals, who could not resist getting so much for so little. They set up housekeeping in maybe six rooms at most, while dry rot and termites and mice and rats and squirrels and kids wrought havoc with the rest of the property.

"If we can make Newell Cady taste the joys of village life," said Fire Chief Stanley Atkins, speaking before an extraordinary meeting of the volunteer firemen on a Saturday afternoon, "he'll *use* that option to buy, and Spruce Falls will become *the* fashionable place for Federal Apparatus executives to live. Without further ado," said Chief Atkins expansively, "I move that Mr. Newell Cady be elected to full membership in the fire department and be named head judge of the annual Hobby Show."

"*Audaces fortuna juvat!*" said Upton Beaton, who was a tall, fierce-seeming sixty-five. He was the last of what had been the first family of Spruce Falls. "Fortune," he translated after a pause, "favors the bold, that's true. But gentlemen—" and he paused again, portentously, while Chief Atkins looked worried and the other members of the fire department shifted about on their folding chairs. Like his forebears, Beaton had an ornamental education from Harvard, and like them, he lived in Spruce Falls because it took little effort for a Beaton to feel superior to his neighbors there. He survived on money his family had made during the short-lived boom.

"But," Beaton said again, as he stood up, "is this the kind of fortune we want? We are being asked to waive the three-year residence requirement for membership in the fire department in Mr. Cady's case, and thereby all our memberships are cheapened. If I may say so, the post of judge of the Hobby Show is of far greater significance than it would seem to an outsider. In our small village, we have only small ways of honoring our great, but we, for generations now, have taken pains to reserve those small honors for those of us who have shown such greatness as it is possible to achieve in the eyes of a village. I hasten to add that those honors that have come to me are marks of respect for my family and my age, not for myself, and are exceptions that should probably be curtailed."

He sighed. "If we waive this proud tradition, then that one, and then another, all for money, we will soon find ourselves with nothing left to wave but the white flag of an abject surrender of all we hold dear!" He sat, folded his arms, and stared at the floor.

Chief Atkins had reddened during the speech, and he avoided looking at Beaton. "The real estate people," he mumbled, "swear property values in Spruce Falls will quadruple if Cady stays."

"What is a village profited if it shall gain a real estate boom and lose its own soul?" Beaton asked.

Chief Atkins cleared his throat. "There's a motion on the floor," he said. "Is there a second?"

"Second," said someone who kept his head down.

"All in favor?" said Atkins.

There was a scuffling of chair legs, and faint voices, like the sounds of a playground a mile away.

"Opposed?"

Beaton was silent. The Beaton dynasty of Spruce Falls had come to an end. Its paternal guidance, unopposed for four generations, had just been voted down.

"Carried," said Atkins. He started to say something, then motioned for silence. "Shhh!" The post office was next door to the meeting hall, in the same building, and on the other side of the thin partition, Mr. Newell Cady was asking for his mail.

"That's all, is it, Mrs. Dickie?" Cady was saying to the postmistress.

"That's more'n some people get around here in a year," said Mrs. Dickie. "There's still a little second-class to put around. Maybe some for you."

"Mmm," said Cady. "That the way the government teaches its people to sort?"

"Them teach me?" said Mrs. Dickie. "I'd like to see anybody teach me anything about this business. I been postmistress for twenty-five years now, ever since my husband passed on."

"Um," said Cady. "Here—do you mind if I come back there and take a look at the second-class for just a minute?"

"Sorry—regulations, you know," said Mrs. Dickie.

But the door of Mrs. Dickie's cage creaked open anyway. "Thank you," said Cady. "Now, suppose, instead of holding these envelopes the way you were, suppose you took them like this, and uh—ah—putting that rubber cap on your thumb instead of your index finger—"

"My land!" cried Mrs. Dickie. "Look at you go!"

"It would be even faster," said Cady, "if it weren't for that tier of boxes by the floor. Why not move them over here, at eye level, see? And what on earth is this table doing back here?"

"For my children," said Mrs. Dickie.

"Your children play back here?"

"Not real children," said Mrs. Dickie. "That's what I call the plants on the table—the wise little cyclamen, the playful little screw pine, the temperamental little sansevieria, the—"

"Do you realize," said Cady, "that you must spend twenty man-minutes and heaven knows how many foot-pounds a day just detouring around it?"

"Well," said Mrs. Dickie, "I'm sure it's awfully nice of you to take such an interest, but you know, I'd just feel kind of lost without—"

"I can't help taking an interest," said Cady. "It causes me actual physical pain to see things done the wrong way, when it's so easy to do them the right way. Oops! Moved your thumb right back to where I told you not to put it!"

"Chief Atkins," whispered Upton Beaton in the meeting hall.

"Eh?"

"Don't you scratch your head like that," said Beaton. "Spread your fingers like this, see? *Then* dig in. Cover twice as much scalp in half the time."

"All due respect to you, sir," said Atkins, "this village could do with a little progress and perking up."

"I'd be the last to stand in its way," said Beaton. After a moment he added, "'Ill fares the land, to hastening ills a prey, where wealth accumulates, and men decay.'"

"Cady's across the street, looking at the fire truck," said Ed Newcomb, who had served twenty years as secretary of the fire department. The Ilium real estate man, who had put stars in every eye except Beaton's, had assured Newcomb that his twenty-six-room Georgian colonial, with a little paper and paint, would look like a steal to a corporation executive at fifty thousand dollars. "Let's tell him the good news!" Newcomb's father had bought the ark at a bank foreclosure sale. He was the only bidder.

The fire department joined its newest member by the fire truck and congratulated him on his election.

"Thanks," said Cady, tinkering with the apparatus strapped to the side of the big red truck. "By George, but there's a lot of chrome on one of these things," he said.

"Wait till you see the new one!" said Ed Newcomb.

"They make the damn things as ornamental as a merry-go-round," said Cady. "You'd think they were playthings. Lord! What all this plating and gimcrackery must add to the cost! New one, you say?"

"Sure," said Newcomb. "It hasn't been voted on yet, but it's sure to pass." The joy of the prospect showed on every face.

"Fifteen hundred gallons a minute!" said a fireman.

"Two floodlights!" said another.

"Closed cab!"

"Eighteen-foot ladders!"

"Carbon dioxide tank!"

"And a swivel-mounted nozzle in the turret smack-spang in the middle!" cried Atkins above them all.

After the silence that followed the passionate hymn to the new truck, Cady spoke. "Preposterous," he said. "This is a perfectly sound, adequate truck here."

"Mr. Cady is absolutely right," said Upton Beaton. "It's a sensible, sturdy truck, with many years of dependable service ahead of it. We were foolish to think of putting the fire district into debt for the next twenty years, just for an expensive plaything for the fire department. Mr. Cady has cut right to the heart of the matter."

"It's the same sort of thing I've been fighting in industry for half my life," said Cady. "Men falling in love with show instead of the job to be done. The sole purpose of a fire department should be to put out fires and to do it as economically as possible."

Beaton clapped Chief Atkins on the arm. "Learn something every day, don't we, Chief?"

Atkins smiled sweetly, as though he'd just been shot in the stomach.

The Spruce Falls annual Hobby Show took place in the church basement three weeks after Newell Cady's election to the fire department. During the intervening twenty-one days, Hal Brayton, the grocer, had stopped adding bills on paper sacks and bought an adding machine, and had moved his counters around so as to transform his customer space from a jammed box canyon into a racetrack. Mrs. Dickie, the postmistress, had moved her leafy children and their table out of her cage and had had the lowest tier of mailboxes raised to eye level. The fire department had voted down scarlet and blue capes for the band as unnecessary for firefighting. And startling figures had been produced in a school meeting proving beyond any doubt that it would cost seven dollars, twenty-nine cents, and six mills more per student per year to maintain the Spruce Falls Grade School than it would to ship the children to the big, efficient, centralized school in Ilium.

The whole populace looked as though it had received a powerful stimulant. People walked and drove faster, concluded business more quickly, and every eye seemed wider and brighter—even frenzied. And moving proudly through this brave new world were the two men who were shaping it, constant companions after working hours now. Newell Cady and Upton Beaton. Beaton's function was to provide Cady with the facts and figures behind village activities and then to endorse outrageously Cady's realistic suggestions for reforms, which followed facts and figures as the night the day.

The judges of the Hobby Show were Newell Cady, Upton Beaton, and Chief Stanley Atkins, and they moved slowly along the great assemblage of tables on which the entries were displayed. Atkins, who had lost weight and grown listless since informed public opinion had turned against the new fire truck, carried a shoe box in which lay neat stacks of blue prize ribbons.

"Surely we won't need all these ribbons," said Cady.

"Wouldn't do to run out," said Atkins. "We did one year, and there was hell to pay."

"There are a lot of classes of entries," explained Beaton, "with first prizes in each." He held out his hand to Atkins. "One with a pin, please, Chief." He pinned a ribbon to a dirty gray ball four feet in diameter.

"See here," said Cady. "I mean, aren't we going to talk this over? I mean, we shouldn't all merrily go our own ways, should we, sticking ribbons wherever we happen to take a notion to? Heavens, here you're giving first prize to this frightful blob, and I don't even know what it is."

"String," said Atkins. "It's Ted Batsford's string. Can you believe it—the very first bit he ever started saving, right in the center of this ball, he picked up during the second Cleveland administration."

"Um," said Cady. "And he decided to enter it in the show this year."

"Every show since I can remember," said Beaton. "I knew this thing when it was no bigger than a bowling ball."

"So for brute persistence, I suppose we should at last award him a first prize, eh?" Cady said wearily.

"At last?" said Beaton. "He's always gotten first prize in the string-saving class."

Cady was about to say something caustic about this, when his attention was diverted. "Good Lord in heaven!" he said. "What is that mess of garbage you're giving first prize to now?"

Atkins looked bewildered. "Why, it's Mrs. Dickie's flower arrangement, of course."

"*That* jumble is a flower arrangement?" said Cady. "I could do better with a rusty bucket and a handful of toadstools. And you're giving it first prize. Where's the competition?"

"Nobody enters anybody else's class," said Beaton, laying a ribbon across the poop deck of a half-finished ship model.

Cady snatched the ribbon away from the model. "Hold on! Everybody gets a prize—am I right?"

"Why, yes, in his or her own class," said Beaton.

"So what's the point of the show?" demanded Cady.

"Point?" said Beaton. "It's a show, is all. Does it have to have a point?"

"Damn it all," said Cady. "I mean that it should have some sort of mission—to foster an interest in the arts and crafts, or something like that. Or to improve skills and refine tastes." He gestured at the displays. "Junk, every bit of it junk—and for years these misguided people have been getting top honors, as though they didn't have a single thing more to learn, or as though all it takes to gain acclaim in this world is the patience to have saved string since the second Cleveland administration."

Atkins looked shocked and hurt.

"Well," said Beaton, "you're head judge. Let's do it your way."

"Listen, Mr. Cady, sir," Atkins said hollowly, "we just can't not give—"

"You're standing in the way of progress," said Beaton.

"Now then, as I see it," said Cady, "there's only one thing in this whole room that shows the slightest glimmer of real creativity and ambition."

There were few lights in Spruce Falls that went off before midnight on the night of the Hobby Show opening, though the town was usually dark by ten. Those few nonparticipants who dropped in at the church to see the exhibits, and who hadn't heard about the judging, were amazed to find one lonely object, a petit-point copy of the cover of a woman's magazine, on view. Pinned to it was the single blue ribbon awarded that day. The other exhibitors had angrily hauled home their rejected offerings, and the sole prizewinner appeared late in the evening, embarrassed and furtive, to take her entry home, leaving the blue ribbon behind.

Only Newell Cady and Upton Beaton slept peacefully that night, with feelings of solid, worthwhile work behind them. But when Monday came again, there was a dogged cheerfulness in the town, for on Sunday, as though to offset the holocaust of the Hobby Show, the real estate man had been around. He had been writing to Federal Apparatus Corporation executives in New York, telling them of the mansions in Spruce Falls that could virtually be stolen from the simple-hearted natives and that were but a stone's throw from the prospective home of their esteemed colleague Mr. Newell Cady. What the real estate man had to show on Sunday were letters from executives who believed him.

By late afternoon on Monday, the last bitter word about the Hobby Show had been spoken, and talk centered now on the computation of capital gains taxes, the ruthless destruction of profit motives by the state and federal governments, the outrageous cost of building small houses—

"But I tell you," said Chief Atkins, "under this new law, you don't have to pay *any* tax on the profit you make off of selling your house. All that profit is just a paper profit, just plain, ordinary inflation, and they don't tax you on that, because it wouldn't be fair." He and Upton Beaton and Ed Newcomb were talking in the post office, while Mrs. Dickie sorted the late-afternoon mail.

"Sorry," said Beaton, "but you have to buy another house for at least as much as you got for your old one, in order to come under that law."

"What would I want with a fifty-thousand-dollar house?" said Newcomb, awed.

"You can have mine for that, Ed," said Atkins. "That way, you wouldn't have to pay any tax at all." He lived in three rooms of an eighteen-room white elephant his own father had bought for peanuts.

"And have twice as many termites and four times as much rot as I've got to fight now," said Newcomb.

Atkins didn't smile. Instead, he kicked shut the post office door, which was ajar. "You big fool! You can't tell who might of been walking past and heard that, what you said about my house."

Beaton stepped between them. "Calm down! Nobody out there but old Dave Mansfield, and he hasn't heard anything since his boiler blew up. Lord, if the little progress we've had so far is making everybody that jumpy, what's it going to be like when we've got a Cady in every big house?"

"He's a fine gentleman," said Atkins.

Mrs. Dickie was puffing and swearing quietly in her cage. "I've bobbed up and down for that bottom tier of boxes for twenty-five years, and I can't make myself stop it, now that they're not there anymore. Whoops!" The mail in her hands fell to the floor. "See what happens when I put my thumb the way he told me to?"

"Makes no difference," said Beaton. "Put it where he told you to, because here he comes."

Cady's black Mercedes came to a stop before the post office.

"Nice day, Mr. Cady, sir," said Atkins.

"Hmmm? Oh yes, I suppose it is. I was thinking about something else." Cady went to Mrs. Dickie's cage for his mail, but continued to talk to the group over his shoulder, not looking at Mrs. Dickie at all. "I just figured out that I go eight-tenths of a mile out of my way every day to pick up my mail."

"Good excuse to get out and pass the time of day with people," said Newcomb.

"And that's two hundred forty-nine point six miles per year, roughly," Cady went on earnestly, "which at eight cents a mile comes out to nineteen dollars and ninety-seven cents a year."

"I'm glad to hear you can still buy something worthwhile for nineteen dollars and ninety-seven cents," said Beaton.

Cady was in a transport of creativeness, oblivious of the tension mounting in the small room. "And there must be at least a hundred others who drive to get their mail, which means an annual expenditure for the hundred of one thousand, nine hundred and ninety-seven dollars, not to mention man-hours. Think of it!"

"Huh," said Beaton, while Atkins and Newcomb shuffled their feet, eager to leave. "I'd hate to think what we spend on shaving cream." He took Cady's arm. "Come on over to my house a minute, would you? I've something I think you'd—"

Cady stayed put before Mrs. Dickie's cage. "It's not the same thing as shaving cream at all," he said. "Men have to shave, and shaving cream's the best thing there is to take whiskers off. And we have to get our mail, certainly, but I've found out something apparently nobody around here knows."

"Come on over to my house," said Beaton, "and we'll talk about it."

"It's so perfectly simple, there's no need to talk about it," said Cady. "I found out that Spruce Falls can get rural free delivery, just by telling the Ilium post office and sticking out mailboxes in front of our houses the way every other village around here does. And that's been true for years!" He smiled and glanced absently at Mrs. Dickie's hands. "Ah, ah, ah!" he chided. "Slipping back to your old ways, aren't you, Mrs. Dickie?"

Atkins and Newcomb were holding open the door, like a pair of guards at the entrance to an execution chamber, while Upton Beaton hustled Cady out.

"It's a great advantage, coming into situations from the outside, the way I do," said Cady. "People inside of situations are so blinded by custom. Here you people were, supporting a post office, when you could get much better service for just a fraction of the cost and trouble." He chuckled modestly, as Atkins shut the post office door behind him. "One-eyed man in the land of the blind, you might say."

"A one-eyed man might as well be blind," declared Upton Beaton, "if he doesn't watch people's faces and doesn't give the blind credit for the senses they do have."

"What on earth are you talking about?" said Cady.

"If you'd looked at Mrs. Dickie's face instead of how she was doing her work, you would have seen she was crying," said Beaton. "Her husband died in a fire, saving some of these people around the village you call blind. You talk a lot about wasting time, Mr. Cady—for a really big waste of time, walk around the village someday and try to find somebody who doesn't know he can have his mail brought to his door anytime he wants to."

The second extraordinary meeting of the volunteer firemen within a month finished its business, and the full membership, save one fireman who had not been invited, seemed relaxed and contented for the first time in weeks. The business of the meeting had gone swiftly, with Upton Beaton, the patriarch of Spruce Falls, making motions, and the membership seconding in chorus. Now they waited for the one absent member, Newell Cady, to arrive at the post office on the other side of the thin wall to pick up his Saturday-afternoon mail.

"Here he is," whispered Ed Newcomb, who had been standing watch by the window.

A moment later, the rich voice came through the wall. "Good heavens, you've got all those plants in there with you again!"

"Just got lonesome," said Mrs. Dickie.

"But my dear Mrs. Dickie," said Cady, "think of—"

"The motion's been carried, then," said Chief Atkins in a loud voice. "Mr. Beaton is to be a committee of one to inform Mr. Cady that his fire department membership, unfortunately, is in violation of the by-laws, which call for three years' residence in the village prior to election."

"I will make it clear to him," said Beaton, also speaking loudly, "that this is in no way a personal affront, that it's simply a matter of conforming to our by-laws, which have been in effect for years."

"Make sure he understands that we all like him," said Ed Newcomb, "and tell him we're proud an important man like him would want to live here."

"I will," said Beaton. "He's a brilliant man, and I'm sure he'll see the wisdom in the residence requirement. A village isn't like a factory, where you can walk in and see what's being made at a glance, and then look at the books and see if it's a good or bad operation. We're not manufacturing or selling anything. We're trying to live together. Every man's got to be his own expert at that, and it takes years."

The meeting was adjourned.

The Ilium real estate man was upset, because everyone he wanted to see in Spruce Falls was out. He stood in Hal Brayton's grocery store, looking at the deserted street and fiddling with his fountain pen.

"They're *all* with the fire engine salesman?" he said.

"They're all going to be paying for the truck for the next twenty years," said Upton Beaton. He was tending Brayton's store while Brayton went for a ride on the fire engine.

"Red-hot prospects are going to start coming through here in a week, and everybody goes out joy-riding," said the real estate man bitterly. He opened the soft drink cooler and let the lid fall shut again. "What's the matter—this thing broken? Everything's warm."

"No, Brayton just hasn't gotten around to plugging it in since he moved things back the way they used to be."

"You said he's the one who doesn't want to sell his place?"

"One of the ones," said Beaton.

"Who else?"

"Everybody else."

"Go on!"

"Really," said Beaton. "We've decided to wait and see how Mr. Cady adapts himself, before we put anything else on the market. He's having a tough time, but he's got a good heart, I think, and we're all rooting for him."

A Present for Big Saint Nick

BIG NICK WAS SAID to be the most recent heir to the power of Al Capone. He refused to affirm or deny it, on the grounds that he might tend to incriminate himself.

He bought whatever caught his fancy, a twenty-three-room house outside Chicago, a seventeen-room house in Miami, racehorses, a ninety-foot yacht, one hundred fifteen suits, and among other things, controlling interest in a middle-weight boxer named Bernie O'Hare, the Shenandoah Blaster.

When O'Hare lost sight in one eye on his way to the top of his profession, Big Nick added him to his squad of bodyguards.

Big Nick gave a party every year, a little before Christmas, for the children of his staff, and on the morning of the day of the party, Bernie O'Hare, the Shenandoah Blaster, went shopping in downtown Chicago with his wife, Wanda, and their four-year-old son, Willy.

The three were in a jewelry store when young Willy began to complain and cling to his father's trousers like a drunken bellringer.

Bernie, a tough, scarred, obedient young thug, set down a velvet-lined tray of watches and grabbed the waist of his trousers. "Let go my pants, Willy! Let go!" He turned to Wanda. "How'm I supposed to pick a Christmas present for Big Nick with Willy pulling my pants down? Take him off me, Wan. What ails the kid?"

"There must be a Santa Claus around," said Wanda.

"There ain't no Santy Clauses in jewelry stores," said Bernie. "You ain't got no Santy Claus in here, have you?" he asked the clerk.

"No, sir," said the clerk. His face bloomed, and he leaned over the counter to speak to Willy. "But if the little boy would like to talk to old Saint Nick, I think he'll find the jolly old elf right next—"

"Can it," said Bernie.

The clerk paled. "I was just going to say, sir, that the department store next door has a Santa Claus, and the little—"

"Can'tcha see you're making the kid worse?" said Bernie. He knelt by Willy. "Willy boy, there ain't no Santy Clauses around for miles. The guy is full of baloney. There ain't no Santy next door."

"There, Daddy, there," said Willy. He pointed a finger at a tiny red figure standing by a clock behind the counter.

"Cripes!" said Bernie haggardly, slapping his knee. "The kid's got a eye like a eagle for Santy Clauses." He gave a fraudulent laugh. "Why, say, Willy boy, I'm surprised at you. That's just a little *plastic* Santy. He can't hurt you."

"I hate him," said Willy.

"How much you want for the thing?" said Bernie.

"The plastic Santa Claus, sir?" said the bewildered clerk. "Why, it's just a little decoration. I think you can get one at any five-and-ten-cent store."

"I want that one," said Bernie. "Right now."

The clerk gave it to him. "No charge," he said. "Be our guest."

Bernie dropped the Santa Claus on the terrazzo floor. "Watch what Daddy's going to do to Old Whiskers, Willy," he said. He brought his heel down. "Keeeeee-runch!"

Willy smiled faintly, then began to laugh as his father's heel came down again and again.

"Now you do it, Willy," said Bernie. "Who's afraid of *him*, eh?"

"I'll bust his ol' head off," said Willy gleefully. "Crunch him up!" He himself trampled Father Christmas.

"That was *real* smart," said Wanda. "You make me spend all year trying to get him to like Santa Claus, and then you pull a stunt like that."

"I hadda do something to make him pipe down, didn't I?" said Bernie. "Okay, okay. Now maybe we can have a little peace and quiet so I can look at the watches. How much is this one with the diamonds for numbers?"

"Three hundred dollars, sir, including tax," said the clerk.

"Does it glow in the dark? It's gotta glow in the dark."

"Yes, sir, the face is luminous."

"I'll take it," said Bernie.

"Three hundred bucks!" said Wanda, pained. "Holy smokes, Bernie."

"Whaddya mean, holy smokes?" said Bernie. "I'm ashamed to give him a little piece of junk like this. What's a lousy three-hundred-dollar watch to Big Nick? You kick about this, but I don't hear you kicking about the way the savings account keeps going up. Big Nick *is* Santy Claus, whether you like it or not."

"I don't like it," said Wanda. "And neither does Willy. Look at the poor kid—Christmas is ruined for him."

"Aaaaah, now," said Bernie, "it ain't that bad. It's real warmhearted of Big Nick to wanna give a party for the kids. I mean, no matter how it comes out, he's got the right idea."

"Some heart!" said Wanda. "Some idea! He gets dressed up in a Santa Claus suit so all the kids'll worship him. And he tops that off by makin' the kids squeal on their parents."

Bernie nodded in resignation. "What can I do?"

"Quit," said Wanda. "Work for somebody else."

"What else I know how to do, Wan? All I ever done was fight, and where else am I gonna make money like what Big Nick pays me? Where?"

A tall, urbane gentleman with a small mustache came up to the adjoining counter, trailed by a wife in mink and a son. The son was Willy's age, and was snuffling and peering apprehensively over his shoulder at the front door.

The clerk excused himself and went to serve the genteel new arrivals.

"Hey," said Bernie, "there's Mr. and Mrs. Pullman. You remember them from last Christmas, Wan."

"Big Nick's accountant?" said Wanda.

"Naw, his lawyer." Bernie saluted Pullman with a wave of his hand. "Hi, Mr. Pullman."

"Oh, hello," said Pullman without warmth. "Big Nick's bodyguard," he explained to his wife. "You remember him from the last Christmas party."

"Doing your Christmas shopping late like everybody else, I see," said Bernie.

"Yes," said Pullman. He looked down at his child, Richard. "Can't you stop snuffling?"

"It's psychosomatic," said Mrs. Pullman. "He snuffles every time he sees a Santa Claus. You can't bring a child downtown at Christmastime and not have him see a Santa Claus *some*where. One came out of the cafeteria next door just a minute ago. Scared poor Richard half to death."

"I won't have a snuffling son," said Pullman. "Richard! Stiff upper lip! Santa Claus is your friend, my friend, everybody's friend."

"I wish he'd stay at the North Pole," said Richard.

"And freeze his nose off," said Willy.

"And get ate up by a polar bear," said Richard.

"*Eaten* up by a polar bear," Mrs. Pullman corrected.

"Are you encouraging the boy to hate Santa Claus?" said Mr. Pullman.

"Why pretend?" said Mrs. Pullman. "*Our* Santa Claus *is* a dirty, vulgar, prying, foulmouthed, ill-smelling fake."

The clerk's eyes rolled.

"Sometimes, dear," said Pullman, "I wonder if you remember what we were like before we met that jolly elf. Quite broke."

"Give me integrity or give me death," said Mrs. Pullman.

"Shame comes along with the money," said Pullman. "It's a package deal. And we're in this thing together." He addressed the clerk. "I want something terribly overpriced and in the worst possible taste, something, possibly, that glows in the dark and has a barometer in it." He pressed his thumb and forefinger together in a symbol of delicacy. "Do you sense the sort of thing I'm looking for?"

"I'm sorry to say you've come to the right place," said the clerk. "We have a model of the *Mayflower* in chromium, with a red light that shines through the portholes," he said. "However, *that* has a clock instead of a barometer. We have a silver statuette of Man o' War with rubies for eyes, and *that's* got a barometer. Ugh."

"I wonder," said Mrs. Pullman, "if we couldn't have Man o' War welded to the poop deck of the *Mayflower*?"

"You're on the right track," said Pullman. "You surprise me. I didn't think you'd ever get the hang of Big Nick's personality." He rubbed his eyes. "Oh Lord, what does he need, what does he need? Any ideas, Bernie?"

"Nothing," said Bernie. "He's got seven of everything. But he says he still likes to get presents, just to remind him of all the friends he's got."

"He *would* think that was the way to count them," said Pullman.

"Friends are important to Big Nick," said Bernie. "He's gotta be told a hunnerd times a day everybody loves him, or he starts bustin' up the furniture an' the help."

Pullman nodded. "Richard," he said to his son, "do you remember what you are to tell Santa Claus when he asks what Mommy and Daddy think of Big Nick?"

"Mommy and Daddy love Big Nick," said Richard. "Mommy and Daddy think he's a real gentleman."

"What're you gonna say, Willy?" Bernie asked his own son.

"Mommy and Daddy say they owe an awful lot to Big Nick,' said Willy. "Big Nick is a kind, generous man."

"Ev-ry-bo-dy loves Big Nick," said Wanda.

"Or they wind up in Lake Michigan with cement overshoes," said Pullman. He smiled at the clerk, who had just brought him the *Mayflower* and Man o' War. "They're fine as far as they go," he said. "But do they glow in the dark?"

Bernie O'Hare was the front-door guard at Big Nick's house on the day of the party. Now he admitted Mr. and Mrs. Pullman and their son.

"Ho ho ho," said Bernie softly.

"Ho ho ho," said Pullman.

"Well, Richard," said Bernie to young Pullman, "I see you're all calmed down."

"Daddy gave me half a sleeping tablet," said Richard.

"Has the master of the house been holding high wassail?" said Mrs. Pullman.

"I beg your pardon?" said Bernie.

"Is he drunk?" said Mrs. Pullman.

"Do fish swim?" said Bernie.

"Did the sun rise?" said Mr. Pullman.

A small intercom phone on the wall buzzed. "Yeah. Nick?" said Bernie.

"They all here yet?" said a truculent voice.

"Yeah, Nick. The Pullmans just got here. They're the last. The rest are sitting in the living room."

"Do your stuff." Nick hung up.

Bernie sighed, took a string of sleigh bells from the closet, turned off the alarm system, and stepped outside into the shrubbery.

He shook the sleigh bells and shouted. "Hey! It's Santy Claus! And Dunder and

Blitzen and Dancer and Prancer! Oh, boy! They're landing on the roof! Now Santy's coming in through an upstairs bedroom window!"

He went back inside, hid the bells, bolted and chained the door, reset the alarm system, and went into the living room, where twelve children and eight sets of parents sat silently.

All the men in the group worked for Nick. Bernie was the only one who looked like a hoodlum. The rest looked like ordinary, respectable businessmen. They labored largely in Big Nick's headquarters, where brutality was remote. They kept his books and gave him business and legal advice, and applied the most up-to-date management methods to his varied enterprises. They were a fraction of his staff, the ones who had children young enough to believe in Santa Claus.

"Merry Christmas!" said Santa Claus harshly, his big black boots clumping down the stairs.

Willy squirmed away from his mother and ran to Bernie for better protection.

Santa Claus leaned on the newel post, a cigar jutting from his cotton beard, his beady eyes traveling malevolently from one face, to the next. Santa Claus was fat and squat and pasty-faced. He reeked of booze.

"I just got down from me workshop at the Nort' Pole," he said challengingly. "Ain't nobody gonna say hi to ol' Saint Nick?"

All around the room parents nudged children who would not speak.

"Talk it up!" said Santa. "This ain't no morgue." He pointed a blunt finger at Richard Pullman. "You been a good boy, heh?"

Mr. Pullman squeezed his son like a bagpipe.

"Yup," piped Richard.

"Ya sure?" said Santa suspiciously. "Ain't been fresh wit' grown-ups?"

"Nope," said Richard.

"Okay," said Santa. "Maybe I got a electric train for ya, an' maybe I don't." He rummaged through a pile of parcels under the tree. "Now, where'd I put that stinkin' train?" He found the parcel with Richard's name on it. "Want it?"

"Yup," said Richard.

"Well, act like you want it," said Santa Claus.

Young Richard could only swallow.

"Ya know what it cost?" said Santa Claus. "Hunnerd and twenny-four fifty." He paused dramatically. "Wholesale." He leaned over Richard. "Lemme hear you say t'anks."

Mr. Pullman squeezed Richard.

"T'anks," said Richard.

"T'anks. I guess," said Santa Claus with heavy irony. "You never got no hunnerd-and-twenny-four-fifty train from your old man, I'll tell you that. Lemme tell you, kid, he'd still be chasin' ambulances an' missin' payments on his briefcase if it wasn't for me. An' don't nobody forget it."

Mr. Pullman whispered something to his son.

"What was that?" said Santa. "Come on, kid, wha'd your old man say?"

"He said sticks and stones could break his bones, but words would never hurt him." Richard seemed embarrassed for his father. So did Mrs. Pullman, who was hyperventilating.

"Ha!" said Santa Claus. "That's a hot one. I bet he says that one a hunnerd times a day. What's he say about Big Nick at home, eh? Come on, Richard, this is Santa Claus you're talkin' to, and I keep a book about kids that don't tell the trut' up at the Nort' Pole. What's he really t'ink of Big Nick?"

Pullman looked away as though Richard's reply couldn't concern him less.

"Mommy and Daddy say Big Nick is a real gentleman," recited Richard. "Mommy and Daddy love Big Nick."

"Okay, kid," said Santa, "here's your train. You're a good boy."

"T'anks," said Richard.

"Now I got a big doll for little Gwen Zerbe," said Santa, taking another parcel from under the tree. "But first come over here, Gwen, so you and me can talk where nobody can hear us, eh?"

Gwen, propelled by her father, Big Nick's chief accountant, minced over to Santa Claus. Her father, a short, pudgy man, smiled thinly, strained his ears to hear, and turned green. At the end of the questioning, Zerbe exhaled with relief and got some of his color back. Santa Claus was smiling. Gwen had her doll.

"Willy O'Hare!" thundered Santa Claus. "Tell Santy the trut', and ya get a swell boat. What's your old man and old lady say about Big Nick?"

"They say they owe him a lot," said Willy dutifully.

Santa Claus guffawed. "I guess they do, boy! Willy, you know where your old man'd be if it wasn't for Big Nick? He'd be dancin' aroun' in little circles, talking to hisself, wit'out nuttin' to his name but a flock of canaries in his head. Here, kid, here's your boat, an' Merry Christmas."

"Merry Christmas to you," said Willy politely. "Please, could I have a rag?"

"A rag?" said Santa.

"Please," said Willy. "I wanna wipe off the boat."

"Willy!" said Bernie and Wanda together.

"Wait a minute, wait a minute," said Santa. "Let the kid talk. *Why* you wanna wipe it off, Willy?"

"I want to wipe off the blood and dirt," said Willy.

"Blood!" said Santa. "Dirt!"

"Willy!" cried Bernie.

"Mama says everything we get from Santa's got blood on it," said Willy. He pointed at Mrs. Pullman. "And that lady says he's dirty."

"No I didn't, no I didn't," said Mrs. Pullman.

"Yes you did," said Richard. "I heard you."

"My father," said Gwen Zerbe, breaking the dreadful silence, "says kissing Santa Claus isn't any worse than kissing a dog."

"Gwen!" cried her father.

"I kiss the dog all the time," said Gwen, determined to complete her thought, "and I never get sick."

"I guess we can wash off the blood and dirt when we get home," said Willy.

"Why, you fresh little punk!" roared Santa Claus, bringing his hand back to hit Willy.

Bernie stood quickly and clasped Santa's wrists. "Please," he said, "the kid don't mean nothing."

"Take your filt'y hands off me!" roared Santa. "You wanna commit suicide?"

Bernie let go of Santa.

"Ain't you gonna say nuttin'?" said Santa. "I t'ink I got a little apology comin'."

"I'm very sorry, Santa Claus," said Bernie. His big fist smashed Santa's cigar all over his face. Santa went reeling into the Christmas tree, clawing down ornaments as he fell.

Childish cheers filled the room. Bernie grinned broadly and clasped his hands over his head, a champ!

"Shut them kids up!" Santa Claus sputtered. "Shut them up, or you're all dead!"

Parents scuffled with their children, trying to muzzle them, and the children twisted free, hooting and jeering and booing Santa Claus.

"Make him eat his whiskers, Bernie!"

"Feed him to the reindeers!"

"You're all t'rough! You're all dead!" shouted Santa Claus, still on his back. "I get bums like you knocked off for twenty-five bucks, five for a hunnerd. Get out!"

The children were so happy! They danced out of the house without their coats, saying things like, "Jingle bells, you old poop," and "Eat tinsel, Santy," and so on. They were too innocent to realize that nothing had changed in the economic structure in which their parents were still embedded. In so many movies they'd seen, one punch to the face of a bad guy by a good guy turned hell into an earthly paradise.

Santa Claus, flailing his arms, drove their parents after them. "I got ways of findin' you no matter where you go! I been good to you, and this is the thanks I get. Well, you're gonna get thanks from me, in spades. You bums are all gonna get rubbed out."

"My dad knocked Santa on his butt!" crowed Willy.

"I'm a dead man," said O'Hare to his wife.

"I'm a dead woman," she said, "but it was almost worth it. Look how happy the children are."

They could expect to be killed by a hit man, unless they fled to some godforsaken country where the Mafia didn't have a chapter. So could the Pullmans.

Saint Nicholas disappeared inside the house, then reappeared with another armload of packages in Christmas wrappings. His white cotton beard was stained red from a nosebleed. He stripped the wrappings from one package, held up a cigarette lighter in the form of a knight in armor. He read the enclosed card aloud: "'To Big Nick, the one and only. Love you madly.'" The signature was that of a famous movie star out in Hollywood.

Now Saint Nicholas showed off another pretty package. "Here's one comes all the way from a friend in Italy." He gave its red ribbon a mighty yank. The explosion not only blew off his bloody beard and fur-trimmed red hat, but removed his chin and nose as well. What a mess! What a terrible thing for the young to see, one would think, but they wouldn't have missed it for the world.

After the police left, and the corpse was carted off to the morgue, dressed like Kris Kringle from the neck down, O'Hare's wife said this: "I don't think this is a Christmas the children are going to forget very soon. I know I won't."

Their son Willy had a souvenir that would help him remember. He had found the greeting card that came with the bomb. It was in the shrubbery. It said, "Merry Christmas to the greatest guy in the world." It was signed "The Family."

There would be a rude awakening, of course. The fathers were going to have to find new jobs, ho ho.

This Son of Mine

THE FACTORY MADE the best centrifugal pumps in the world, and Merle Waggoner owned it. He'd started it. He'd just been offered two million dollars for it by the General Forge and Foundry Company. He didn't have any stockholders and he didn't owe a dime. He was fifty-one, a widower, and he had one heir—a son. The boy's name was Franklin. The boy was named for Benjamin Franklin.

One Friday afternoon father and son went out of Merle's office and into the factory. They walked down a factory aisle to Rudy Linberg's lathe.

"Rudy," said Merle, "the boy here's home from college for three days, and I thought maybe you and him and your boy and me might go out to the farm and shoot some clay pigeons tomorrow."

Rudy turned his sky-blue eyes to Merle and young Franklin. He was Merle's age, and he had the deep and narrow dignity of a man who had learned his limitations early—who had never tried to go beyond them. His limitations were those of his tools, his flute, and his shotgun.

"Might try crows," Merle said.

Rudy stood at attention like the good soldier he was. And like an old soldier, he did it without humility, managed to convey that he was the big winner in life, after all. He had been Merle's first employee. He might have been a partner way back then, for two thousand dollars. And Rudy'd had the cash. But the enterprise had looked chancy to him. He didn't seem sorry now.

"We could set up my owl," said Rudy. He had a stuffed owl to lure crows. He and his son, Karl, had made it.

"Need a rifle to get at the crows out there," said Merle. "They know all about that owl of yours and Karl's. Don't think we could get any closer to 'em than half a mile."

"Might be sport, trying to get at 'em with a scope," said Franklin softly. He was tall and thin, in cashmere and gray flannel. He was almost goofy with shyness and guilt. He had just told his father that he wanted to be an actor, that he didn't want the factory. And shock at his own words had come so fast that he'd heard himself adding, out of control, the hideously empty phrase, "Thanks just the same."

His father hadn't reacted—yet. The conversation had gone blandly on to the farm, to shooting, to Rudy and Karl, to Rudy and Karl's new station wagon, and now to crows.

"Let's go ask my boy what he's got on tomorrow," said Rudy. It was a formality. Karl always did what his father wanted him to do, did it with profound love.

Rudy, Merle, and Franklin went down the aisle to a lathe thirty feet from Rudy's. Merle's chin was up. Rudy looked straight ahead. Franklin looked down at the floor.

Karl was a carbon copy of his father. He was such a good mimic of Rudy that his joints seemed to ache a little with age. He seemed sobered by fifty-one years of life, though he'd lived only twenty. He seemed instinctively wary of safety hazards that had been eliminated from the factory by the time he'd learned to walk. Karl stood at attention without humility, just as his father had done.

"Want to go shooting tomorrow?" said Rudy.

"Shoot what?" said Karl.

"Crows. Clay pigeons," said Rudy. "Maybe a woodchuck."

"Don't mind," said Karl. He nodded briefly to Merle and Franklin. "Glad to."

"We could take some steaks and have supper out there," said Merle. "You make the steak sauce, Rudy?"

"Don't mind," said Rudy. He was famous for his steak sauce, and had taught the secret to his son. "Be glad to."

"Got a bottle of twenty-year-old bourbon I've been saving for something special," said Merle. "I guess tomorrow'll be special enough." He lit a cigar, and Franklin saw that his father's hand was shaking. "We'll have a ball," he said.

Clumsily Merle punched Franklin in the kidneys, man to man, trying to make him bubble. He regretted it at once. He laughed out loud to show it didn't matter, laughed through cigar smoke that stung his eyes. The laugh drove smoke into the walls of his lungs. Pleasure fled. On and on the laugh went.

"Look at him, Rudy!" said Merle, lashing the merriment onward. "Foot taller'n his old man, and president of what at Cornell?"

"Interfraternity Council," murmured Franklin, embarrassed. He and Karl avoided looking at each other. Their fathers had taken them hunting together maybe a hundred times. But the boys had hardly spoken to each other, had exchanged little more than humorless nods and head shakes for hits and misses.

"And how many fraternities at Cornell?" said Merle.

"Sixty-two," said Franklin, more softly than before.

"And how many men in a fraternity?" said Merle.

"Forty, maybe," said Franklin. He picked up a sharp, bright spiral shaving of steel from the floor. "There's a pretty thing," he said. He knew his father's reaction was coming now. He could hear the first warning tremors in his voice.

"Say sixty fraternities," said Merle. "Say forty men in each . . . Makes twenty-four hundred boys my boy's over, Rudy! When I was his age, I didn't have but six men under me."

"They aren't under me, Father," said Franklin. "I just run the meetings of the Council and—"

The explosion came. "You run the show!" roared Merle. "You can be as damn polite about it as you want to, but you still run the show!"

Nobody said anything.

Merle tried to smile, but the smile curdled, as though he were going to burst into tears. He took the strap of Rudy's overalls between his thumb and forefinger and rubbed the faded denim. He looked up into Rudy's sky-blue eyes.

"Boy wants to be an actor, Rudy," he said. And then he roared again. "That's what he said!" He turned away and ran back to his office.

In the moment before Franklin could make himself move, Rudy spoke to him as if nothing were wrong.

"You got enough shells?" said Rudy.

"What?" said Franklin.

"You got enough shells? You want us to pick up some?" said Rudy.

"No," said Franklin. "We've got plenty of shells. Half a case, last time I checked."

Rudy nodded. He examined the work in Karl's lathe and tapped his own temple. The tapping was a signal Franklin had seen many times on hunts. It meant that Karl was doing fine.

Rudy touched Karl's elbow lightly. It was the signal for Karl to get back to work. Rudy and Karl each held up a crooked finger and saluted with it. Franklin knew what that meant, too. It meant, "Good-bye, I love you."

Franklin put one foot in front of the other and went looking for his own father.

Merle was sitting at his desk, his head down, when Franklin came in. He held a steel plate about six inches square in his left hand. In the middle of the plate was a hole two inches square. In his right hand he held a steel cube that fitted the hole exactly.

On the desktop were two black bags of jeweler's velvet, one for the plate and one for the cube. About every ten seconds Merle put the cube through the hole.

Franklin sat down gingerly on a hard chair by the wall. The office hadn't changed much in the years he'd known it. It was one more factory room, with naked pipes overhead—the cold ones sweaty, the hot ones dry. Wires snaked from steel box to steel box. The green walls and cream trim were as rough as elephant hide in some places, with alternating coats of paint and grime, paint and grime.

There had never been time to scrape away the layers, and barely enough time, overnight, to slap on new paint. And there had never been time to finish the rough shelves that lined the room.

Franklin still saw the place through child's eyes. To him it had been a playroom. He remembered his father's rummaging through the shelves for toys to amuse his boy. The toys were still there: cutaway pumps, salesmen's samples, magnets, a pair of cracked safety glasses that had once saved Rudy Linberg's blue eyes.

And the playthings Franklin remembered best—remembered best because his father would show them to him, but never let him touch—were what Merle was playing with now.

Merle slipped the cube through the square hole once more. "Know what these are?" he said.

"Yes, sir," said Franklin. "They're what Rudy Linberg had to make when he was an apprentice in Sweden."

The cube could be slipped through the hole in twenty-four different ways, without letting the tiniest ray of light pass through with it.

"Unbelievable skill," said Franklin respectfully. "There aren't craftsmen like that coming along anymore." He didn't really feel much respect. He was simply saying what he knew his father wanted to hear. The cube and the hole struck him as criminal wastes of time and great bores. "Unbelievable," he said again.

"It's unbelievable, when you realize that Rudy didn't make them," said Merle, "when you realize what generation the man who made them belongs to."

"Oh?" said Franklin. "Who did make them?"

"Rudy's boy," said Merle. "A member of your generation." He ground out his cigar. "He gave them to me on my last birthday. They were on my desk, boy, waiting for me when I came in—right beside the ones Rudy gave me so many years ago."

Franklin had sent a telegram on that birthday. Presumably, the telegram had been waiting on the desk, too. The telegram had said, "Happy Birthday, Father."

"I could have cried, boy, when I saw those two plates and those two cubes side by side," said Merle. "Can you understand that?" he asked. "Can you understand why I'd feel like crying?"

"Yes, sir," said Franklin.

Merle's eyes widened. "And then I guess I did cry—one tear, maybe two," he said. "Because—you know what I found out, boy?"

"No, sir," said Franklin.

"The cube of Karl's fitted through the hole of Rudy's!" said Merle. "They were interchangeable!"

"Gosh!" said Franklin. "I'll be darned. Really?"

And now he felt like crying, because he didn't care, couldn't care—and would have given his right arm to care. The factory whanged and banged and screeched in monstrous irrelevance—Franklin's, all Franklin's, if he just said the word.

"What'll you do with it—buy a theater in New York?" Merle said abruptly.

"Do with what, sir?" said Franklin.

"The money I'll get for the factory when I sell it—the money I'll leave to you when I'm dead," said Merle. He hit the word "dead" hard. "What's Waggoner Pump going to be converted into? Waggoner Theaters? Waggoner School of Acting? The Waggoner Home for Broken-Down Actors?"

"I—I hadn't thought about it," said Franklin. The idea of converting Waggoner Pump into something equally complicated hadn't occurred to him, and appalled him now. He was being asked to match his father's passion for the factory with an equal passion for something else. And Franklin had no such passion—for the theater or anything else.

He had nothing but the bittersweet, almost formless longings of youth. Saying he wanted to be an actor gave the longings a semblance of more fun than they really had. Saying it was poetry more than anything else.

"I can't help being a little interested," said Merle. "Do you mind?"

"No, sir," said Franklin.

"When Waggoner Pump becomes just one more division of General Forge and Foundry, and they send out a batch of bright young men to take over and straighten the place out, I'll want something else to think about—whatever it is you're going to do."

Franklin itched all over. "Yes, sir," he said. He looked at his watch and stood. "If we're going shooting tomorrow, I guess I'd better go see Aunt Margaret this afternoon." Margaret was Merle's sister.

"You do that," said Merle. "And I'll call up General Forge and Foundry, and tell them we accept their offer." He ran his finger down his calendar pad until he found a name and telephone number. "If we want to sell, I'm to call somebody named Guy Ferguson at something called extension five-oh-nine at something called the General Forge and Foundry Company at someplace called Ilium, New York." He licked his lips. "I'll tell him he and his friends can have Waggoner Pump."

"Don't sell on my account," said Franklin.

"On whose account would I keep it?" said Merle.

"Do you have to sell it today?" Franklin sounded horrified.

"Strike while the iron's hot, I always say," said Merle. "Today's the day you decided to be an actor, and as luck would have it, we have an excellent offer for what I did with my life."

"Couldn't we wait?"

"For what?" said Merle. He was having a good time now.

"Father!" cried Franklin. "For the love of heaven, Father, please!" He hung his head and shook it. "I don't know what I'm doing," he said. "I don't know for sure what I want to do yet. I'm just playing with ideas, trying to find myself. Please, Father, don't sell what you've done with your life, don't just throw it away because I'm not sure I want to do that with my life, too! Please!" Franklin looked up. "I'm not Karl Linberg," he said. "I can't help it. I'm sorry, but I'm not Karl Linberg."

Shame clouded his father's face, then passed. "I—I wasn't making any odious comparisons there," said Merle. He'd said exactly the same thing many times before. Franklin had forced him to it, just as he had forced him now, by apologizing for not being Karl Linberg.

"I wouldn't want you to be like Karl," said Merle. "I'm glad you're the way you are. I'm glad you've got big dreams of your own." He smiled. "Give 'em hell, boy—and be yourself! That's all I've ever told you to do with your life, isn't it?"

"Yes, sir," said Franklin. His last shred of faith in any dreams of his own had been twitched away. He could never dream two million dollars' worth, could never dream anything worth the death of his father's dreams. Actor, newspaperman, social worker, sea captain—Franklin was in no condition to give anyone hell.

"I'd better get out to Aunt Margaret's," he said.

"You do that. And I'll hold off telling Ferguson or whatever-his-name-is anything until Monday." Merle seemed at peace.

On his way through the factory parking lot to his car, Franklin passed Rudy and Karl's new station wagon. His father had raved about it, and now Franklin took a good look at it—just as he took good looks at all the things his father loved.

The station wagon was German, bright blue, with white-sidewall tires, its engine in the rear. It looked like a little bus—no hood in front, a high, flat roof, sliding doors, and rows of square windows on the sides.

The interior was a masterpiece of Rudy and Karl's orderliness and cabinet work, of lockers and niches and racks. There was a place for everything, and everything was in its place—guns, fishing tackle, cooking utensils, stove, ice chest, blankets, sleeping bags, lanterns, first-aid kit. There were even two niches, side by side, in which were strapped the cases of Karl's clarinet and Rudy's flute.

Looking inside admiringly, Franklin had a curious association of thoughts. His thoughts of the station wagon were mixed with thoughts of a great ship that had been dug up in Egypt after thousands of years. The ship had been fitted out with every necessity for a trip to Paradise—every necessity save the means of getting there.

"Mistuh Waggonuh, suh!" said a voice, and an engine raced.

Franklin turned to see that the parking lot guard had seen him coming, had now brought him his car. Franklin had been spared the necessity of walking the last fifty feet to it.

The guard got out and saluted smartly. "This thing really go a hundred and twenty-five, like it says on the speedometer?" he said.

"Never tried," said Franklin, getting in. The car was a sports car, windy and skittish, with room for two. He had bought it secondhand, against his father's wish. His father had never ridden in it. It was fitted out for its trip to Paradise with three lipstick-stained tissues, a beer can opener, a full ashtray, and a road map of Illinois.

Franklin was embarrassed to see that the guard was cleaning the windshield with his handkerchief. "That's all right, that's all right," he said. "Forget it." He thought he remembered the guard's name, but he wasn't sure. He took a chance on it. "Thanks for everything, Harry," he said.

"George, suh!" said the guard. "George Miramar Jackson, suh!"

"Of course," said Franklin. "Sorry, George. Forgot."

George Miramar Jackson smiled brilliantly. "No offense, Mistuh Waggonuh, suh! Just remember next time—George Miramar Jackson, suh!" In George's eyes there blazed the dream of a future time, when Franklin would be boss, when a big new job would open up indoors. In that dream, Franklin would say to his secretary, "Miss So-and-So? Send for—" And out would roll the magical, magnificent, unforgettable name.

Franklin drove out of the parking lot without dreams to match even George Miramar Jackson's.

At supper, feeling no pain after two stiff cocktails and a whirlwind of mothering at Aunt Margaret's, Franklin told his father that he wanted to take over the factory in due time. He would become the Waggoner in Waggoner Pump when his father was ready to bow out.

Painlessly, Franklin moved his father as profoundly as Karl Linberg had with a steel plate, a steel cube, and heaven knows how many years of patient scree-scraw with a file.

"You're the only one—do you know that?" choked Merle. "The only one—I swear!"

"The only one what, sir?" said Franklin.

"The only son who's sticking with what his father or his grandfather or sometimes even his great-grandfather built." Merle shook his head mournfully. "No Hudson in Hudson Saw," he said. "I don't think you can even cut cheese with a Hudson saw these days. No Flemming in Flemming Tool and Die. No Warner in Warner Street. No Hawks, no Hinkley, no Bowman in Hawks, Hinkley, and Bowman."

Merle waved his hand westward. "You wonder who all the people are with the big new houses on the west side? Who can have a house like that, and we never meet them, never even meet anybody who knows them? They're the ones who are taking over instead of the sons. The town's for sale, and they buy. It's their town now—people named Ferguson from places called Ilium.

"What is it about the sons?" said Merle. "They're your friends, boy. You grew up with them, you know them better than their fathers do. What is it? All the wars? Drinking?"

"I don't know, Father," said Franklin, taking the easiest way out. He folded his napkin with a neat finality. He stood. "There's a dance out at the club tonight," he said. "I thought I'd go."

"You do that," said Merle.

But Franklin didn't. He got as far as the country club's parking lot, then didn't go in.

Suddenly he didn't want to see his friends—the killers of their fathers' dreams. Their young faces were the faces of old men hanging upside down, their expressions grotesque and unintelligible. Hanging upside down, they swung from bar to ballroom to crap game, and back to bar. No one pitied them in that great human belfry, because they were going to be rich, if they weren't already. They didn't have to dream, or even lift a finger.

Franklin went to a movie alone. The movie failed to suggest a way in which he might improve his life. It suggested that he be kind and loving and humble, and Franklin was nothing if he wasn't kind and loving and humble.

The colors of the farm the next day were the colors of straw and frost. The land was Merle's, and it was flat as a billiard table. The jackets and caps of Merle and Franklin, of Rudy and Karl, made a tiny cluster of bright colors in a field.

Franklin knelt in the stubble, cocking the trap that would send a clay pigeon skimming over the field. "Ready," he said.

Merle threw his gun to his shoulder, squinted down the barrel, grimaced, and lowered the gun once more. "Pull!" he said.

Franklin jerked the lanyard of the trap. Out flew the clay pigeon.

Merle fired one barrel and then, with the pigeon out of range, clowningly fired the other. He'd missed. He'd been missing all afternoon. He didn't seem to mind much. He was, after all, still the boss.

"Behind it," said Merle. "I'm trying too hard. I'm not leading." He broke down his gun and the empty shells popped out. "Next?" he said. "Karl?"

Franklin loaded another clay pigeon into the trap. It was a very dead pigeon. So would the next one be. Karl hadn't missed all afternoon, and after Karl came Rudy, who hadn't missed, either.

Surprisingly, neither had Franklin. Not giving a damn, he had come to be at one with the universe. With brainless harmony like that, he'd found that he couldn't miss.

If Merle's shots hadn't been going wild, the only words spoken might have been a steady rhythm of "Ready . . . Pull . . . Ready . . . Pull." Nothing had been said about the murder of Franklin's small dream—the dream of being an actor. Merle had made no triumphant announcement about the boy's definitely taking over the factory someday.

In the small world of a man hunched over, Franklin cocked the trap and had a nightmarish feeling that they had been shooting clay pigeons for years, that that was all there was to life, that only death could end it.

His feet were frozen.

"Ready," said Franklin.

"Pull!" said Karl.

Out went the clay pigeon. *Bang* went the gun, and the bird was dust.

Rudy tapped his temple, then saluted Karl with a crooked finger. Karl returned the salute. That had been going on all afternoon—without a trace of a smile. Karl stepped back and Rudy stepped up, the next cog in the humorless clay-pigeon-destroying machine.

It was now Karl's turn to work the trap. As he and Franklin changed places, Franklin hit him on the arm and gave him a cynical smile. Franklin put everything into that blow and the smile—fathers and sons, young dreams and old dreams, bosses and employees, cold feet, boredom, and gunpowder.

It was a crazy thing for Franklin to do. It was the most intimate thing that had ever passed between him and Karl. It was a desperate thing to do. Franklin had to know if there was a human being inside Karl and, if so, what the being was like.

Karl showed a little of himself—not much. He showed he could blush. And for a split second, he showed that there was something he'd like to explain to Franklin.

But all that vanished fast. He didn't smile back. "Ready," he said.

"Pull!" said Rudy.

Out went the clay pigeon. *Bang* went the gun, and the bird was dust.

"We're going to have to find something harder for you guys and easier for me," said Merle. "I can't complain about the gun, because the damn thing cost me six hundred dollars. What I need is a six-dollar gun I can hold responsible for everything."

"Sun's going down. Light's getting bad," said Rudy.

"Guess we better knock off," said Merle. "No question about who the old folks' champion is, Rudy. But the boys are neck-and-neck. Ought to have some kind of shoot-off."

"They could try the rifle," said Rudy. The rifle leaned against the fence, ready for crows. It had a telescope. It was Merle's.

Merle brought an empty cigarette pack from his pocket and stripped off the foil. He handed the foil to Karl. "You two boys hang this up about two hundred yards from here."

Franklin and Karl trudged along the fence line, trudged off two hundred yards. They were used to being sent together on errands one of them could have handled alone—were used to representing, ceremoniously, their generation as opposed to their fathers'.

Neither said anything until the foil was tacked to a fence post. And then, as they stepped back from the target, Karl said something so shyly that Franklin missed it.

"Beg your pardon?" said Franklin.

"I'm—I'm glad you're not gonna take over the factory," said Karl. "That's good— that's great. Maybe, when you come through town with a show, I'll come backstage and see you. That all right? You'll remember me?"

"Remember you?" said Franklin. "Good gosh, Karl!" For a moment he felt like the actor he'd dreamed briefly of being.

"Get out from under your old man," said Karl, "that's the thing to do. I just wanted to tell you—in case you thought I was thinking something else."

"Thanks, Karl," said Franklin. He shook his head weakly. "But I'm not going to be an actor. I'm going to take over when Father retires. I told him last night."

"Why?" said Karl. "Why?" He was angry.

"It makes the old man happy, and I don't have any better ideas."

"You can do it," Karl said. "You can go away. You can be anything you want!"

Franklin put his hands together, then opened them to form a flower of fatalism. "So can anybody."

Karl's eyes grew huge. "I can't," he said. "I can't! Your father doesn't just have you. He's got his big success." He turned away, so Franklin couldn't see his face. "All my old man's got is me."

"Oh, now, listen," said Franklin. "Hey, now!"

Karl faced him. "I'm what he'd rather have than the half of Waggoner Pump he could have had for two thousand dollars!" he said. "Every day of my life he's told me so. Every day!"

"Well, my gosh, Karl," said Franklin, "it is a beautiful relationship you've got with your father."

"With my father?" said Karl incredulously. "With yours—with yours. It's him I'm supposed to get to love me. He's supposed to be eating his heart out for a son like me. That's the big idea." He waved his arms. "The station wagon, the duets, the guns that never miss, the damn-fool son that works on hand signals—that's all for your father to want."

Franklin was amazed. "Karl, that's all in your head. You are what your own father would rather have than half of Waggoner Pump or anything!"

"I used to think so," said Karl.

"The plate and cube you made," said Franklin, "you gave them to my father, but they were really a present for yours. And what perfect presents from a son to a father! I never gave my father anything like that—anything I'd put my heart and soul into. I couldn't!"

Karl reddened and turned away again. "I didn't make 'em," he said. He shivered. "I tried. How I tried!"

"I don't understand."

"My father had to make 'em!" said Karl bitterly. "And I found out it didn't make any difference to him who made 'em, just as long as your father thought I'd made 'em."

Franklin gave a sad, low whistle.

"When my old man did that, he rubbed my nose in what the big thing was to him." Karl actually wiped his nose on his jacket sleeve.

"But Karl—" said Franklin.

"Oh, hell," Karl said, tired. "I don't blame him. Sorry I said anything. I'm OK—I'm OK. I'll live." He flicked the foil target with a fingertip. "I'm gonna miss, and the hell with 'em."

Nothing more was said. The two trudged back to their fathers. It seemed to Franklin that they were leaving behind all they'd said, that the rising wind was whirling their dark thoughts away. By the time they had reached the firing line, Franklin was thinking only of whiskey, steak, and a red-hot stove.

When he and Karl fired at the foil, Franklin ticked a corner. Karl hit it in the middle. Rudy tapped his temple, then saluted Karl with a crooked finger. Karl returned the salute.

After supper, Rudy and Karl played duets for flute and clarinet. They played without sheet music, intricately and beautifully. Franklin and Merle could only keep time with their fingers, hoping that their tapping on the tabletop sounded like drums.

Franklin glanced at his father. When their eyes met, they decided that their drumming wasn't helping. Their drumming stopped.

With the moment to think about, to puzzle him pleasantly, Franklin found that the music wasn't speaking anymore of just Rudy and Karl. It was speaking of all fathers and sons. It was saying what they had all been saying haltingly, sometimes with pain and sometimes with anger and sometimes with cruelty and sometimes with love: that fathers and sons were one.

It was saying, too, that a time for a parting in spirit was near—no matter how close anyone held anyone, no matter what anyone tried.

Hal Irwin's Magic Lamp

HAL IRWIN BUILT his magic lamp in his basement in Indianapolis, in the summer of 1929. It was supposed to look like Aladdin's lamp. It was an old tin teapot with a piece of cotton stuck in the spout for a wick. Hal bored a hole in it for a doorbell button, which he hooked up to two flashlight batteries and a buzzer inside. Like many husbands back then, he had a workshop in the basement.

The idea was, it was a cute way to call servants. You'd rub the teapot as if it were a magic lamp, and you'd push the button on the side. The buzzer'd go off, and a servant, if you had one, would come and ask you what you wished.

Hal didn't have a servant, but he was going to borrow one from a friend. Hal was a customers' man in a brokerage house, and he knew his business inside out. He'd made half a million dollars on the stock market, and nobody knew it. Not even his wife.

He made the magic lamp as a surprise for his wife. He was going to tell her it was a magic lamp. And then he was going to rub it and wish for a big new house. And then he was going to prove to her that it really was a magic lamp, because every wish was going to come true.

When he made the lamp, the interior decorator was finishing up the insides of a big new French château Hal had ordered built out on North Meridian Street.

When Hal made that lamp, he and Mary were living in a shotgun house down in all the soot at Seventeenth and Illinois Street. They'd been married two years, and Hal hadn't had her out more than five or six times. He wasn't being stingy. He was saving up to buy her all the happiness a girl could ever ask for, and he was going to hand it to her in one fell swoop.

Hal was ten years older than Mary, so it was easy for him to buffalo her about a lot of things, and one of the things was money. He wouldn't talk money with her, never let her see a bill or a bank statement, never told her how much he made or what he was doing with it. All Mary had to go by was the piddling allowance he gave her to run the house, so she guessed they were poor as Job's turkey.

Mary didn't mind that. That girl was as wholesome as a peach and a glass of milk. Being poor gave her room to swing her religion around. When the end of the month came, and they'd eaten pretty well, and she hadn't asked Hal for an extra dime, she felt like a little white lamb. And she thought Hal was happy, even though he was broke, because she was giving him a hundred million dollars' worth of love.

There was only one thing about being poor that really bothered Mary, and that was the way Hal always seemed to think she wanted to be rich. She did her best to convince him that wasn't true.

When Hal would carry on about how well other folks were doing—about the high life at the country clubs and the lakes—Mary'd talk about the millions of folks in China who didn't have a roof over their heads or anything to eat.

"Me doing velly well for Chinaman," Hal said one night.

"You're doing very well for an American or for an anything!" Mary said. She hugged him, so he'd be proud and strong and happy.

"Well, your successful Chinaman's got a piece of news for you," Hal said. "Tomorrow you're gonna get a cook. I told an employment agency to send one out."

Actually, the person arriving the next day, whose name was Ella Rice, wouldn't be coming to cook, and wasn't from an employment agency. She already had a job with a friend of Hal's whom Mary didn't know. The friend would give her the day off so she could play the part of a jinni.

Hal had rehearsed her at the friend's house, and he would pay her well. She needed the extra money. She was going to have a baby in about six weeks, she thought. All she had to do was put on a turban when the time came, when Hal showed Mary his magic lamp, and rubbed it and rang its buzzer. Then she would say, "I am the jinni. What do you want?"

After that, Hal would start wishing for expensive things he already owned, which Mary hadn't seen yet. His first wish would be for a Marmon town car. It would already be parked out front. Every time he made a wish, starting with that one, Ella Rice would say, "You got it."

But that was tomorrow, and today was today, and Mary thought Hal didn't like her cooking. She was a wonderful cook. "Honey," she said, "are my meals that bad?"

"They're great. I have no complaints whatsoever."

"Then why should we get a cook?"

He looked at her as though she were deaf, dumb, and blind. "Don't you ever think of my pride?" he asked her. He put his hand over her mouth. "Honeybunch, don't tell me again about people dying like flies in China. I am who I am where I am, and I've got pride."

Mary wanted to cry. Here she thought she'd been making Hal feel better, and she'd been making him feel worse instead.

"What do you think I think when I see Bea Muller or Nancy Gossett downtown in their fur coats, buying out the department stores?" Hal said. "I think about you, stuck in this house. I think, Well, for crying out loud, I used to be president of their husbands' fraternity house! For crying out loud, me and Harve Muller and George Gossett used to be the Grand Triumvirate. That's what they used to call the three of us in college—the Grand Triumvirate! We used to run the college, and I'm not kidding. We founded the Owl's Club, and I was president.

"Look where they live, and look where we live," Hal went on. "We oughta be right out there with 'em at Fifty-seventh and North Meridian! We oughta have a cottage right next to 'em at Lake Maxinkuckee! Least I can do is get my wife a cook."

Ella Rice arrived at the house the next day at three o'clock as planned. In a paper bag she had the turban Hal had given her. Hal wasn't home yet. Ella was supposed to pretend to be the new cook instead of a jinni until Hal arrived at three-thirty. Which she did.

What Hal hadn't counted on, though, was that Mary would find Ella so likable, but so pitiful, not a cook, but a fellow human being in awful trouble. He had expected them to go to the kitchen to talk about this and that, what Hal liked to eat, and so on. But Mary asked Ella about her pregnancy, which was obvious. Ella, who was no actress, and at the end of her rope in any case, burst into tears. The two women, one white, one black, stayed in the living room and talked about their lives instead.

Ella wasn't married. The father of her child had beaten her up when he found out she was pregnant, and then taken off for parts unknown. She had aches and pains in many places, and no relatives, and didn't know how much longer she could do housework. She repeated what she had told Hal, that her pregnancy still had six weeks to go, she thought. Mary said she wished she could have a baby, but couldn't. That didn't help.

When Hal parked the new Marmon out front and entered the house, neither woman was in any condition to enjoy the show he had planned. They were a mess! But he imagined his magic lamp would cheer them up. He went to get it from the closet where he had hidden it upstairs, then brought it into the living room and said, "My goodness! Look what I just found. I do believe it's a magic lamp. Maybe if I rub it a jinni will appear, and she will make a wish come true." He hadn't considered hiring a black man to play the jinni. He was scared of black men.

Ella Rice recognized her cue, and got off the couch to do the crazy thing the white man was going to pay for. Anything for money. It hurt her a lot to stand, after sitting still for a half-hour. Even Hal could see that.

Hal wished for a Marmon, and the jinni said, "You got it." The three went out to the car, and Hal told them to get in, that it was his, paid for in full. The women sat in the backseat, and Mary said to Ella, not to Hal, "Thanks a lot. This is wonderful. I think I'm going nuts."

Hal drove up North Meridian Street, pointing out grand houses left and right. Every time he did that, Mary said that she wouldn't want it, that Hal could throw his magic lamp out the window, as far as she was concerned. What she was really upset about was the humiliating use he was making of her new friend Ella.

Hal stopped in front of a French château on which workmen were putting finishing touches. He turned off the motor, rubbed the lamp, buzzed the buzzer, and said, "Jinni, give me a new house at 5644 North Meridian Street."

Mary said to Ella, "You don't have to do this. Don't answer him."

Ella got mad at Mary now. "I'm getting *paid!*" Everything Ella said was in a dialect typical of a person of her race and class and degree of education back then. Now she groaned. She was going into labor.

They took Ella Rice to the city hospital, the only one that admitted black people. She had a healthy boy baby, and Hal paid for it.

Hal and Mary brought her and the baby back to their new house. The old house was on the market. And Mary, who couldn't have a baby herself, fixed up one of the seven bedrooms for mother and child, with cute furniture and wallpaper and toys the baby wasn't old enough to play with. Mother and child had their own bathroom.

The baby was christened in a black church, and Mary was there. Hal wasn't. He and Mary were hardly speaking. Ella named the baby Irwin, in honor of the people who were so good to her. His last name was the same as hers. He was Irwin Rice.

Mary had never loved Hal, but had managed to like him. It was a job. There weren't many ways for women to earn their own money back then, and she hadn't inherited anything, and wouldn't unless Hal died. Hal was no dumber than most men she'd known. She certainly didn't want to be alone. They had a black yard man and a black laundress, and a white housemaid from Ireland, who lived in the mansion. Mary insisted on doing the cooking. Ella Rice offered to do it, at least for herself. But nobody except Mary was allowed to cook.

She hated the new house so much, and the gigantic car, which embarrassed her, that she couldn't even like Hal anymore. This was very tough on Hal, extremely tough, as you can well imagine. Not only was he not getting love, or what looked like love, from the woman he'd married, but she was giving ten times more love than he'd ever gotten, and nonstop, to a baby as black as the ace of spades!

Hal didn't tell anybody at the office about the situation at home, because it would have made him look like a weakling. The housemaid from Ireland treated him like a weakling, as though Mary were the real power, and crazy as a bedbug.

Ella Rice of course made her own bed, and kept her bedroom and bathroom very neat. Things didn't seem right to her, either, but what could she do? Ella nursed the baby, so its food was all taken care of. Ella didn't eat downstairs with the Irwins. Not even Mary considered that a possibility. Ella didn't eat with the servants in the kitchen, either. She brought upstairs whatever Mary had prepared especially for her, and ate it in her bedroom.

At the office, anyway, Hal was making more money than ever, trading stocks and bonds for others, but also investing heavily for himself in stocks, never mind bonds, on margin. "On margin" meant he paid only a part of the full price of a stock, and owed the rest to the brokerage where he worked. And then the stock's value would go up, because other people wanted it, and Hal would sell it. He could then pay off his debt to the brokerage, and the rest of the profit was his to keep.

So he could buy more stock on margin.

Three months after the magic-lamp episode, the stock market crashed. The stocks Hal had bought on margin became worthless. All of a sudden, everybody thought they were too expensive at any price. So what Hal Irwin owed to his brokerage, and what his brokerage owed to a bank in turn, was more than everything he owned— the new house, the unsold old house, the furniture, the car, and on and on. You name it!

He wasn't loved at home even in good times, so Hal went out a seventh-story window without a parachute. All over the country, unloved men in his line of work were going out windows without parachutes. The bank foreclosed on both houses, and took the Marmon, too. Then the bank went bust, and anybody with savings in it lost those savings.

Mary had another house to go to, which was her widowed father's farm outside the town of Crawfordsville. The only place Ella Rice could think of to go with her baby was the black church where the baby had been baptized. Mary went there with them. A lot of mothers with babies or children, and old people, and cripples, and even perfectly healthy young people were sleeping there. There was food. Mary didn't ask where it came from. That was the last Mary would see of Ella and Irwin Rice. Ella was eating, and then she would nurse the baby.

When Mary got to her father's farmhouse, the roof was leaking and the electricity had been shut off. But her father took her in. How could he not? She told him about the homeless people in the black church. She asked him what he thought would become of them in such awful times.

"The poor take care of the poor," he said.

Shout About It from
the Housetops

I READ IT. I guess everybody in Vermont read it when they heard Hypocrites'
Junction was actually Crocker's Falls.

I didn't think it was such a raw book, the way raw books go these days. It was just
the rawest book a woman ever wrote—and I expect that's why it was so popular.

I met that woman once, that Elsie Strang Morgan, the one who wrote the book.
I met her husband, the high school teacher, too. I sold them some combination
aluminum storm windows and screens one time. That was about two months after
the book came out. I hadn't read it yet, hadn't paid much attention to all the talk
about it.

They lived in a huge, run-down old farmhouse five miles outside of Crocker's
Falls back then, just five miles away from all those people she gave the works to in
the book. I don't generally sell that far south, don't know many people down that
way. I was on my way home from a sales meeting in Boston, and I saw that big house
with no storm windows, and I just had to stop in.

I didn't have the least idea whose house it was.

I knocked on the door, and a young man in pajamas and a bathrobe answered.
I don't think he'd shaved in a week. I don't think he'd been out of the pajamas and
bathrobe for a week, either. They had a very lived-in look. His eyes were wild. He
was the husband. He was Lance Magnum in the book. He was the great lover in
the book, but he looked like one of the world's outstanding haters when I met him.

"How do you do," I said.

"How do *you* do?" he asked. He made it a very unpleasant question.

"I couldn't help noticing you don't have any storm windows on this beautiful old
home," I said.

"Why don't you try again?" he said.

"Try what?" I said.

"Try not noticing we don't have any storm windows on this beautiful old home,"
he said.

"If you were to put up storm windows," I said, "do you know who would pay for them?" I was going to answer the question myself. I was going to tell him that the money for the windows would come out of his fuel dealer's pocket, since the windows would save so much fuel. But he didn't give me a chance.

"Certainly I know who'd pay for 'em—my wife," he said. "She's the only person with any money around here. She's the breadwinner."

"Well," I said, "I don't know what your personal situation here happens to be—"

"You don't?" he said. "Everybody else does. What's the matter—can't you read?" he said.

"I can read," I told him.

"Then rush down to your nearest bookstore, plunk down your six dollars, and start reading about the greatest lover boy of modern times! Me!" he said, and he slammed the door.

◎ ◎ ◎

My conclusion was that the man was crazy, and I was about to drive off when I heard what sounded like a scream from the back of the house. I thought maybe I'd interrupted him while he was murdering his wife, thought he'd gone back to it now.

I ran to where the screaming was coming from, and I saw that an old rusty pump was making all the noise.

But it might as well have been a woman screaming, because a woman was making the pump scream, and the woman looked like she was just about to scream, too. She had both hands on the pump handle, and she was sobbing, and she was putting her whole body into every stroke. Water was going into a bucket that was already full, splashing down over the sides, spreading out on the ground. I didn't know it then, but she was Elsie Strang Morgan. Elsie Strang Morgan didn't want water. What she was after was violent work and noise.

When she saw me she stopped. She brushed the hair off of her eyes. She was Celeste in the book, of course. She was the heroine in her own book. She was the woman who didn't know what love was till she met Lance Magnum. When I saw her, she looked as though she'd forgotten what love was again.

"What are you?" she said. "A process server or a Rolls-Royce salesman?"

"Neither one, lady," I said.

"Then you came to the wrong house," she said. "Only two kinds of people come here anymore—those who want to sue me for a blue million and those who think I ought to live like King Farouk."

"It so happens that I *am* selling a quality product," I said. "But it also happens that this product pays for itself. As I was telling your husband—"

"When did you see my husband?" she said.

"Just now—at the front door," I said.

She looked surprised. "Congratulations," she said.

"Pardon me?" I said.

"You're the first outsider he's faced since the school board fired him," she said.

"I'm sorry to hear he was fired," I said.

"This is the first you heard of it?" she said.

"I'm not from around here, lady," I said. "I'm from the northern part of the state."

"Everybody from Chickahominy to Bangkok knows he was fired," she said, and she started to cry again.

I was sure now that both the husband and the wife were crazy, and that, if there were any children, the children would be as crazy as bedbugs, too. There obviously wasn't anybody around who could be counted on to make regular payments on storm windows, and, looking about the yard, I couldn't even see the makings of a down payment. There was about three dollars' worth of chickens, a fifty-dollar Chevrolet, and the family wash on the clothesline. The blue jeans and the tennis shoes and the wool shirt the woman was wearing wouldn't have brought a dollar and a half at a fire department rummage sale.

"Lady," I said, getting ready to leave, "I'm sorry you feel so bad, and I sure wish I could help. Things are bound to get better by and by, and when they do, I'd certainly like to show you the Rolls-Royce of the storm window field, the American Tri-trak, made of anodized aluminum with disappearing lifetime screen."

"Wait!" she said as I turned away.

"Ma'am?" I said.

"How would you act," she said, "if your wife had done what I did?"

"Ma'am?" I said.

And then she grabbed the pump handle and started making the pump scream again.

A lot of people have asked me if she really looks as tough as her picture on the back of her book. If she didn't want everybody to think she was a beer truck driver, I don't know why she chose that picture for the book, because she could certainly look nicer than that. In real life she doesn't look anything like Jimmy Hoffa.

She's got a low center of gravity, that's true. And she is maybe a little heavy, but I know plenty of men who would like that. The main thing is her face. It's a pretty, sweet, loving face. In real life she doesn't look as though she's wondering where she'd put down her cigar.

The second time she got going, the pump screamed so loud it brought her husband to the kitchen door. He had a quart of beer with him.

"It's full!" he yelled at her.

"What?" she said, still pumping.

"The bucket's full!" he said.

"I don't care!" she said.

So he took hold of the handle to make her stop. "She isn't well," he said to me.

"Just rich and famous is all," she said, "and sick as a dog."

"You better get out of here," he said to me, "or you'll wind up in bed in the middle of her next book—with God knows who."

"There isn't going to *be* any next book!" she said. "There isn't going to be any next anything! I'm getting out of here for good!" And she got into the old Chevrolet, got in and punched down the starter. Nothing happened. The battery was dead.

And then she went dead, too. She closed her eyes, rested her head on the steering wheel, and she looked like she wanted to stay there forever.

When she stayed like that for more than a minute, her husband got worried. He went over to the car barefooted, and I could see that he really loved her. "Honey?" he said. "Honeybunch?"

She kept her head where it was. Her mouth was all that moved. "Call up that Rolls-Royce salesman that was here," she said. "I want a Rolls-Royce. I want it right away."

"Honey?" he said again.

She raised her hand. "I want it!" she said. She certainly looked tough now. "And I want a mink! I want two minks! I want a hundred dresses from Bergdorf Goodman! A trip around the world! A diamond tiara from Cartier!" She got out of the car, feeling pretty good now. "What is it you sell?" she asked me.

"Storm windows," I said.

"I want those, too!" she said. "Storm windows all around!"

"Ma'am?" I said.

"That's all you sell?" she said. "Isn't there something else you could sell me? I have a check for a hundred and sixty thousand dollars in the kitchen, and you haven't even made a dent in it."

"Well," I said, "I also handle storm doors and tub enclosures and jalousies."

"Good!" she said. "I'll take 'em!" She stopped by her husband, looked him up and down. "Maybe you're through living," she said to him, "but I'm just starting. Maybe I can't have your love anymore, if I ever had it—but at least I can have everything money can buy, and that's plenty!"

She went into the house, and she slammed the kitchen door so hard she broke the window in it.

Her husband went over to the bucket that was already so full, and he poured his quart of beer into it. "Alcohol is no help," he said.

"I'm sorry to hear it," I said.

"What would you do if you were in the middle of this situation?" he asked me. "What would *you* do?"

"I suppose I'd commit suicide after a while," I said, "because nothing anybody's said or done has made any sense at all. The human system can stand only so much of that."

"You mean we're being immature?" he said. "You mean you don't think our problems are real? Just think a minute about the strain that's been placed on this marriage!"

"How can I," I said, "when I don't even know who you are?"

He couldn't believe it. "You don't?" he said. "You don't know my name?" He pointed after his wife. "Or her name?"

"No," I said, "but I certainly wish I did, because she just gave me the biggest order for windows I've had since I did the Green Mountain Inn. Or was she kidding?"

He looked at me now as though I were something rare and beautiful, as though he were afraid I would disappear. "I'm just one more plain, ordinary human being to you?" he said.

"Yes," I said. That wasn't strictly true, after the show he and his wife put on.

"Come in—come in," he said. "What would you like? Beer? Coffee?"

Nothing was too good for me. He hustled me into the kitchen. Nothing would do but I pass the time of day with him. I never knew a man to be so hungry for talk. In about half an hour there we covered every subject but love and literature.

And then his wife came in, all charged up for a new scene, the biggest scene yet.

"I've ordered the Rolls-Royce," she said, "and a new battery for the Chevrolet. When they come, I'm leaving for New York City in the Chevrolet. You can have the Rolls as partial compensation for all the heartaches I've caused you."

"Oh, for crying out loud, Elsie," he said.

"I'm through crying out loud," she said. "I'm through crying any which way. I'm going to start living."

"More power to you," he said.

"I'm glad to see you've got a friend," she said, looking at me. "I'm sorry to say I don't have any friends at the moment, but I expect to find some in New York City, where people aren't afraid to live a little and face life the way it really is."

"You know who my friend is?" he said.

"He's a man who hopes to sell storm windows," she said. And then she said to me, "Well, you sold 'em, Junior. You sold an acre of 'em, and my deepest hope is that they will keep my first husband from catching cold. Before I can leave this house in good conscience, I want to make sure it's absolutely safe and snug for a man who lives in his pajamas."

"Elsie—listen to me," he said. "This man is one of the few living creatures who knows nothing about you, me, or the book. He is one of the few people who can still look upon us as ordinary human beings rather than objects of hate, ridicule, envy, obscene speculation—"

Elsie Strang Morgan thought that over. The more she thought about it, the harder it hit her. She changed from a wild woman to a gentle, quiet housewife, with eyes as innocent as any cow's.

"How do you do?" she said.

"Fine, thank you, ma'am," I said.

"You must think we're kind of crazy here," she said.

"Oh, no ma'am," I said. The lie made me fidget some, and I picked up the sugar bowl in the middle of the table, and there underneath it was a check for one hundred and sixty thousand dollars. I am not fooling. That is where they had the check she'd gotten for the movie rights to her book, under a cracked five-and-ten-cent-store sugar bowl.

I knocked my coffee over, spilled it on the check.

And do you know how many people tried to save that check?

One.

Me.

I pulled it out of the coffee, dried it off, while Elsie Strang Morgan and her husband sat back, didn't care what happened to it. That check, that ticket to a life of ease and luxury, might as well have been a chance on a turkey raffle, for all they cared.

"Here—" I said, and I handed it to the husband. "Better put this in a safe place."

He folded his hands, wouldn't take it. "Here," he said.

I handed it to her. She wouldn't take it, either. "Give it to your favorite charity," she said. "It won't buy anything I want."

"What *do* you want, Elsie?" her husband asked her.

"I want things the way they were," she said, clouding up, "the way they never can be again. I want to be a dumb, shy, sweet little housewife again. I want to be the wife of a struggling high school teacher again. I want to love my neighbors again, and I want my neighbors to love me again—and I want to be tickled silly by dumb things like sunshine and a drop in the price of hamburger and a three-dollar-a-week raise for my husband." She pointed out the window. "It's spring out there," she said, "and I'm sure every woman in the world but me is glad."

And then she told me about her book. And while she talked she went to a window and looked out at all that useless springtime.

"It's about a very worldly, virile man from New York City," she said, "who comes to a small town in Vermont to teach."

"Me," said her husband. "She changed my name from Lawrence Morgan to Lance Magnum, so nobody could possibly recognize me—and then she proceeded to describe me right down to the scar on the bridge of my nose." He went to the icebox for another quart of beer. "She worked on this thing in secret, understand. I had no idea she'd ever written anything more complicated than a cake recipe until the six author's copies of the book came from the publisher. I came home from work one day, and there they were, stacked on that kitchen table there—six copies of *Hypocrites' Junction* by—good God in Heaven!—Elsie Strang Morgan!" He took a long pull from the beer bottle, banged the bottle down. "And there were candies all around the stack," he said, "and on the top was one perfect red red rose."

"This man in the book," said Elsie Strang Morgan, looking out the window, "falls in love with a simple country girl who has been out of Hypocrites' Junction just once in her life—when she was a junior in high school, and the whole junior class went to Washington, D.C., at cherry blossom time."

"That's you," said her husband.

"That's me—that *was* me," she said. "And when my husband married me, he found out I was so innocent and shy that he couldn't stand it."

"In the book?" I said.

"In life, in the book?" said her husband. "There's no difference. You know who the villain is in the book?"

"No," I said.

"A greedy banker named Walker Williams," he said. "And do you know who, in real life, is the President of the Crocker's Falls Savings Bank?"

"Nope," I said.

"A greedy banker named William Walker," he said. "Holy smokes," he said, "my wife should be working for the Central Intelligence Agency, making up new, unbreakable codes!"

"Sorry, sorry," she said, but she sounded way past being sorry to me. Her marriage was over. Everything was over.

"I suppose I should be sore at the school board for firing me," said her husband, "but who could really blame them? All four members were in the book, big as life. But even if they weren't in the book, how could they let a famous lover, a ruthless woman awakener like me, continue to instruct the young?" He went to his wife, came up behind her. "Elsie Strang Morgan," he said, "what on earth possessed you?"

And here was her reply:

"You did," she said very quietly. "You," she said.

"Think of what I was before I loved you. I couldn't have written a word in that book, because the ideas simply weren't in my head. Oh, I knew grubby little secrets about Crocker's Falls, but I didn't think about them much. They didn't seem so bad."

She faced him. "And then you, the great Lance Magnum, came to town, swept me off my feet. And you found me shy about this, hopelessly old-fashioned about that, hypocritical about something else. So, for the love of you, I changed," she said.

"You told me to stop being afraid of looking life in the face," she said, "so I stopped being afraid. You told me to see my friends and neighbors for what they really were—ignorant, provincial, greedy, mean—so I saw them for what they were.

"You told me," that woman said to her husband, "not to be shy and modest about love, but to be frank and proud about it—to shout about it from the housetops.

"So I did," she said.

"And I wrote a book to tell you how much I loved you," she said, "and to show you how much I'd learned, how much you'd taught me.

"I've been waiting and waiting and waiting for you to say one small thing that would indicate that you knew," said Elsie Strang Morgan, "that the book was as much yours as mine. I was the mother. You were the father. And the book, God help it, was our first child."

◎ ◎ ◎

I left after that big scene.

I would have liked to hear what Lance Magnum said about the terrible child he'd fathered by a simple country girl, but he told me I'd better go.

When I got outside, I found a mechanic putting a new battery in the Chevrolet. And I realized that the famous love affair between Lance and Celeste might end right then and there, if either one of them could jump in a car and drive away.

So I told the mechanic there'd been a mistake, told him we didn't want the battery after all.

I'm glad I did, because when I went back two days later, Elsie Strang Morgan and her husband were still together, cooing at each other like doves, and they signed an order for storm windows and doors all around. I couldn't sell them bathtub enclosures because they hadn't had plumbing put in yet—but they did have a Rolls-Royce.

While I was measuring up the windows on the house, Elsie Strang Morgan's husband brought me out a glass of beer. He was all dressed up now in a new suit, and he'd shaved.

"I guess you admitted the baby was yours," I said.

"If I didn't," he said, "I'd be the biggest hypocrite in Hypocrites' Junction," he said. "What kind of a man is it who'll father a baby and then not love it and call it his own?"

Now I hear she's got a new book out, and I'm scared to look at it. From all I hear, the leading character is a storm window salesman. He goes around measuring people's windows—and the book's about what he sees inside.

Ed Luby's Key Club

PART ONE

Ed Luby worked as a bodyguard for Al Capone once. And then he went into boot-legging on his own, made a lot of money at it. When the prohibition era ended, Ed Luby went back to his hometown, the old mill town of Ilium. He bought several businesses. One was a restaurant, which he called Ed Luby's Steak House. It was a very good restaurant. It had a brass knocker on its red front door.

At seven o'clock the other night, Harve and Claire Elliot banged on the door with the brass knocker—because the red door was locked. They had come from a city thirty miles away. It was their fourteenth wedding anniversary. They would be celebrating their anniversary at Luby's for the fourteenth time.

Harve and Claire Elliot had a lot of kids and a lot of love, and not much money. But once a year they really splurged. They got all dolled up, took twenty dollars out of the sugar bowl, drove over to Ed Luby's Steak House, and carried on like King Farouk and his latest girlfriend.

There were lights on in Luby's, and there was music inside. And there were plenty of cars in the parking lot—all a good deal newer than what Harve and Claire arrived in. Their car was an old station wagon whose wood was beginning to rot.

The restaurant was obviously in business, but the red front door wouldn't budge. Harve banged away some more with the knocker, and the door suddenly swung open. Ed Luby himself opened it. He was a vicious old man, absolutely bald, short and heavy, built like a .45-caliber slug.

He was furious. "What in hell you trying to do—drive the members nuts?" he said in a grackle voice.

"What?" said Harve.

Luby swore. He looked at the knocker. "That thing comes down right now," he said. "All the dumb things—a knocker on the door." He turned to the big thug who lurked behind him. "Take the knocker down right now," he said.

"Yes, sir," said the thug. He went to look for a screwdriver.

"Mr. Luby?" said Harve, puzzled, polite. "What's going on?"

574

"What's going on?" said Luby. "I'm the one who oughta be asking what's going on." He still looked at the knocker rather than at Harve and Claire. "What's the big idea?" he said. "Halloween or something? Tonight's the night people put on funny costumes and go knock on private doors till the people inside go nuts?"

The crack about funny costumes was obviously meant to hit Claire Elliot squarely—and it did. Claire was vulnerable—not because she looked funny, but because she had made the dress she wore, because her fur coat was borrowed. Claire looked marvelous, as a matter of fact, looked marvelous to anyone with an eye for beauty, beauty that had been touched by life. Claire was still slender, affectionate, tremendously optimistic. What time and work and worry had done to her was to make her look, permanently, the least bit tired.

Harve Elliot didn't react very fast to Luby's crack. The anniversary mood was still upon Harve. All anxieties, all expectations of meanness were still suspended. Harve wasn't going to pay any attention to anything but pleasure. He simply wanted to get inside, where the music and the food and the good drinks were.

"The door was stuck," said Harve. "I'm sorry, Mr. Luby. The door was stuck."

"Wasn't stuck," said Luby. "Door was *locked*."

"You—you're closed?" said Harve gropingly.

"It's a private club now," said Luby. "Members all got a key. You got a key?"

"No," said Harve. "How—how do we get one?"

"Fill out a application, pay a hundred dollars, wait and see what the membership committee says," said Luby. "Takes two weeks—sometimes a month."

"A hundred dollars!" said Harve.

"I don't think this is the kind of place you folks would be happy at," said Luby.

"We've been coming here for our anniversary for fourteen years," said Harve, and he felt himself turning red.

"Yeah—I know," said Luby. "I remember you real well."

"You do?" said Harve hopefully.

Luby turned really nasty now. "Yeah, big shot," he said to Harve, "you tipped me a quarter once. Me—Luby—I own the joint, and one time you slip me a big, fat quarter. Pal, I'll never forget you for that."

Luby made an impatient sweeping motion with his stubby hand. "You two mind stepping out of the way?" he said to Harve and Claire. "You're blocking the door. A couple of members are trying to get in."

Harve and Claire stepped back humbly.

The two members whose way they had been blocking now advanced on the door grandly. They were man and wife, middle-aged—porky, complacent, their faces as undistinguished as two cheap pies. The man wore new dinner clothes. The woman was a caterpillar in a pea green evening gown and dark, oily mink.

"Evening, Judge," said Luby. "Evening, Mrs. Wampler."

Judge Wampler held a golden key in his hand. "I don't get to use this?" he said.

"Happen to have the door open for some minor repairs," said Luby.

"I see," said the judge.

"Taking the knocker down," said Luby. "Folks come up here, won't believe it's a private club, drive the members nuts banging on the door."

The judge and his lady glanced at Harve and Claire with queasy scorn. "We aren't the first to arrive, are we?" said the judge.

"Police chief's been here an hour," said Luby. "Doc Waldron, Kate, Charley, the mayor—the whole gang's in there."

"Good," said the judge, and he and his lady went in.

The thug, Ed Luby's bodyguard, came back with a screwdriver. "These people still giving you a hard time, Ed?" he said. He didn't wait for an answer. He bellied up to Harve. "Go on—beat it, Junior," he said.

"Come on, Harve—let's get out of here," said Claire. She was close to tears.

"That's right—beat it," said Luby. "What you want is something like the Sunrise Diner. Get a good hamburger steak dinner there for a dollar and a half. All the coffee you can drink on the house. Leave a quarter under your plate. They'll think you're Diamond Jim Brady."

Harve and Claire Elliot got back into their old station wagon. Harve was so bitter and humiliated that he didn't dare to drive for a minute or two. He made claws of his shaking hands, wanted to choke Ed Luby and his bodyguard to death.

One of the subjects Harve covered in profane, broken sentences was the twenty-five-cent tip he had once given Luby. "Fourteen years ago—our first anniversary," said Harve. "That's when I handed that miserable b—— a quarter! And he never forgot!"

"He's got a right to make it a club, if he wants to," said Claire emptily.

Luby's bodyguard now had the knocker down. He and Luby went inside, slammed the big red door.

"Sure he does!" said Harve. "Certainly he's got a right! But the stinking little rat doesn't have a right to insult people the way he insulted us."

"He's sick," said Claire.

"All right!" said Harve, and he hammered on the dashboard with his folded hands. "All right—he's sick. Let's kill all the people who are sick the way Luby is."

"Look," said Claire.

"At what?" said Harve. "What could I see that would make me feel any better or any worse?"

"Just look at the wonderful kind of people who get to be members," said Claire.

Two very drunk people, a man and a woman, were getting out of a taxicab.

The man, in trying to pay the cabdriver, dropped a lot of change and his gold key to the Key Club. He got down on his hands and knees to look for it.

The sluttish woman with him leaned against the cab, apparently couldn't stand unsupported.

The man stood up with the key. He was very proud of himself for having found it. "Key to the most exclusive club in Ilium," he told the cabdriver.

Then he took out his billfold, meaning to pay his fare. And he discovered that the smallest bill he had was a twenty, which the driver couldn't change.

"You wait right here," said the drunk. "We'll go in and get some change."

He and the woman reeled up the walk to the door. He tried again and again to slip the key into the lock, but all he could hit was wood. "Open Sesame!" he'd say, and he'd laugh, and he'd miss again.

"Nice people they've got in this club," Claire said to Harve. "Aren't you sorry we're not members, too?"

The drunk finally hit the keyhole, turned the lock. He and his girl literally fell into the Key Club.

Seconds later they came stumbling out again, bouncing off the bellies of Ed Luby and his thug.

"Out! Out!" Luby squawked in the night. "Where'd you get that key?" When the drunk didn't answer, Luby gathered the drunk's lapels and backed him up to the building. "Where'd you get that key?"

"Harry Varnum lent it to me," said the drunk.

"You tell Harry he ain't a member here anymore," said Luby. "Anybody lends his key to a punk lush like you—he ain't a member anymore."

He turned his attention to the drunk's companion. "Don't you ever come out here again," he said to her. "I wouldn't let you in if you was accompanied by the President of the United States. That's one reason I turned this place into a club—so I could keep pigs like you out, so I wouldn't have to serve good food to a ———"
And he called her what she obviously was.

"There's worse things than that," she said.

"Name one," said Luby.

"I never killed anybody," she said. "That's more than you can say."

The accusation didn't bother Luby at all. "You want to talk to the chief of police about that?" he said. "You want to talk to the mayor? You want to talk to Judge Wampler about that? Murder's a very serious crime in this town." He moved very close to her, looked her up and down. "So's being a loudmouth, and so's being a ———" He called her what she was again.

"You make me sick," he said.

And then he slapped her with all his might. He hit her so hard that she spun and crumpled without making a sound.

The drunk backed away from her, from Luby, from Luby's thug. He did nothing to help her, only wanted to get away.

But Harve Elliot was out of his car and running at Luby before his wife could stop him.

Harve hit Luby once in the belly, a belly that was as hard as a cast-iron boiler.

That satisfaction was the last thing Harve remembered—until he came to in his car. The car was going fast. Claire was driving.

Harve's clinging, aching head was lolling on the shoulder of his wife of fourteen years.

Claire's cheeks were wet with recent tears. But she wasn't crying now. She was grim. She was purposeful.

She was driving fast through the stunted, mean, and filthy business district of Ilium. Streetlights were faint and far apart.

Tracks of a long-abandoned streetcar system caught at the wheels of the old station wagon again and again.

A clock in front of a jeweler's store had stopped. Neon signs, all small, all red, said BAR and BEER and EAT and TAXI.

"Where we going?" said Harve.

"Darling! How do you feel?" she said.

"Don't know," said Harve.

"You should see yourself," she said.

"What would I see?" he said.

"Blood all over your shirt. Your good suit ruined," she said. "I'm looking for the hospital."

Harve sat up, worked his shoulders and his neck gingerly. He explored the back of his head with his hand. "I'm that bad?" he said. "Hospital?"

"I don't know," she said.

"I—I don't feel too bad," he said.

"Maybe you don't need to go to the hospital," said Claire, "but she does."

"Who?" said Harve.

"The girl—the woman," said Claire. "In the back."

Paying a considerable price in pain, Harve turned to look into the back of the station wagon.

The backseat had been folded down, forming a truck bed. On that hard, jouncing bed, on a sandy blanket, lay the woman Ed Luby had hit. Her head was pillowed on a child's snowsuit. She was covered by a man's overcoat.

The drunk who had brought her to the Key Club was in back, too. He was sitting tailor-fashion. The overcoat was his. He was a big clown turned gray and morbid. His slack gaze told Harve that he did not want to be spoken to.

"How did we get these two?" said Harve.

"Ed Luby and his friends made us a present of them," said Claire.

Her bravery was starting to fail her. It was almost time to cry again. "They threw you and the woman into the car," she said. "They said they'd beat me up, too, if I didn't drive away."

Claire was too upset to drive now. She pulled over to the curb and wept.

Harve, trying to comfort Claire, heard the back door of the station wagon open and shut. The big clown had gotten out.

He had taken his overcoat from the woman, was standing on the sidewalk, putting the coat on.

"Where you think you're going?" Harve said to him. "Stay back there and take care of that woman!"

"She doesn't need me, buddy," said the man. "She needs an undertaker. She's dead."

In the distance, its siren wailing, its roof lights flashing, a patrol car was coming.

"Here come your friends, the policemen," said the man. He turned up an alley, was gone.

◉ ◉ ◉

The patrol car nosed in front of the old station wagon. Its revolving flasher made a hellish blue merry-go-round of the buildings and street.

Two policemen got out. Each had a pistol in one hand, a bright flashlight in the other.

"Hands up," said one. "Don't try anything."

Harve and Claire raised their hands.

"You the people who made all the trouble out at Luby's Key Club?" The man who asked was a sergeant.

"Trouble?" said Harve.

"You must be the guy who hit the girl," said the sergeant.

"Me?" said Harve.

"They got her in the back," said the other policeman. He opened the back door of the station wagon, looked at the woman, lifted her white hand, let it fall. "Dead," he said.

"We were taking her to the hospital," said Harve.

"That makes everything all right?" said the sergeant. "Slug her, then take her to the hospital, and that makes everything all right?"

"I didn't hit her," said Harve. "Why would I hit her?"

"She said something to your wife you didn't like," said the sergeant.

"Luby hit her," said Harve. "It was Luby."

"That's a good story, except for a couple of little details," said the sergeant.

"What details?" said Harve.

"Witnesses," said the sergeant. "Talk about witnesses, brother," he said, "the mayor, the chief of police, Judge Wampler and his wife—they *all* saw you do it."

◉ ◉ ◉

Harve and Claire Elliot were taken to the squalid Ilium Police Headquarters.

They were fingerprinted, were given nothing with which to wipe the ink off their hands. This particular humiliation happened so fast, and was conducted with such firmness, that Harve and Claire reacted with amazement rather than indignation.

Everything was happening so fast, and in such unbelievable surroundings, that Harve and Claire had only one thing to cling to—a childlike faith that innocent persons never had anything to fear.

Claire was taken into an office for questioning. "What should I say?" she said to Harve as she was being led away.

"Tell them the truth!" said Harve. He turned to the sergeant who had brought him in, who was guarding him now. "Could I use the phone, please?" he said.

"To call a lawyer?" said the sergeant.

"I don't need a lawyer," said Harve. "I want to call the babysitter. I want to tell her we'll be home a little late."

The sergeant laughed. "A *little* late?" he said. He had a long scar that ran down one cheek, over his fat lips, and down his blocky chin. "A little late?" he said again. "Brother, you're gonna be about twenty years late getting home—twenty years if you're lucky."

"I didn't have a thing to do with the death of that woman," said Harve.

"Let's hear what the witnesses say, huh?" said the sergeant. "They'll be along in a little bit."

"If they saw what happened," said Harve, "I'll be out of here five minutes after they get here. If they've made a mistake, if they really think they saw me do it, you can still let my wife go."

"Let me give you a little lesson in law, buddy," said the sergeant. "Your wife's an accessory to the murder. She drove the getaway car. She's in this as deep as you are."

Harve was told that he could do all the telephoning he wanted—could do it after he had been questioned by the captain.

His turn to see the captain came an hour later. He asked the captain where Claire was. He was told that Claire had been locked up.

"That was necessary?" said Harve.

"Funny custom we got around here," said the captain. "We lock up anybody we think had something to do with a murder." He was a short, thickset, balding man. Harve found something vaguely familiar in his features.

"Your name's Harvey K. Elliot?" said the captain.

"That's right," said Harve.

"You claim no previous criminal record?" said the captain.

"Not even a parking ticket," said Harve.

"We can check on that," said the captain.

"Wish you would," said Harve.

"As I told your wife," said the captain, "you really pulled a bonehead mistake, trying to pin this thing on Ed Luby. You happened to pick about the most respected man in town."

"All due respect to Mr. Luby—" Harve began.

The captain interrupted him angrily, banged on his desk. "I heard enough of that from your wife!" he said. "I don't have to listen to any more of it from you!"

"What if I'm telling the truth?" said Harve.

"You think we haven't checked your story?" said the captain.

"What about the man who was with her out there?" said Harve. "He'll tell you what really happened. Have you tried to find him?"

The captain looked at Harve with malicious pity. "There wasn't any man," he said. "She went out there alone, went out in a taxicab."

"That's wrong!" said Harve. "Ask the cabdriver. There was a man with her!"

The captain banged on his desk again. "Don't tell me I'm wrong," he said. "We talked to the cabdriver. He swears she was alone. Not that we need any more witnesses," he said. "The driver swears he saw you hit her, too."

The telephone on the captain's desk rang. The captain answered, his eyes still on Harve. "Captain Luby speaking," he said.

And then he said to the sergeant standing behind Harve, "Get this jerk out of here. He's making me sick. Lock him up downstairs."

The sergeant hustled Harve out of the office and down an iron staircase to the basement. There were cells down there.

Two naked lightbulbs in the corridor gave all the light there was. There were duckboards in the corridor, because the floor was wet.

"The captain's Ed Luby's brother?" Harve asked the sergeant.

"Any law against a policeman having a brother?" said the sergeant.

"Claire!" Harve yelled, wanting to know what cell in Hell his wife was in.

"They got her upstairs, buddy," said the sergeant.

"I want to see her!" said Harve. "I want to talk to her! I want to make sure she's all right!"

"Want a lot of things, don't you?" said the sergeant. He shoved Harve into a narrow cell, shut the door with a *clang.*

"I want my rights!" said Harve.

The sergeant laughed. "You got 'em, friend. You can do anything you want in there," he said, "just as long as you don't damage any government property."

The sergeant went back upstairs.

There didn't seem to be another soul in the basement. The only sounds that Harve could hear were footfalls overhead.

Harve gripped his barred door, tried to find some meaning in the footfalls.

There were the sounds of many big men walking together—one shift coming on, another going off, Harve supposed.

There was the clacking of a woman's sharp heels. The clacking was so quick and free and businesslike that the heels could hardly belong to Claire.

Somebody moved a heavy piece of furniture. Something fell. Somebody laughed. Several people suddenly arose and moved their chairs back at the same time.

And Harve knew what it was to be buried alive.

He yelled. "Hey, up there! Help!" he yelled.

A reply came from close by. Someone groaned drowsily in another cell.

"Who's that?" said Harve.

"Go to sleep," said the voice. It was rusty, sleepy, irritable.

"What kind of a town is this?" said Harve.

"What kind of a town is any town?" said the voice. "You got any big-shot friends?"

"No," said Harve.

"Then it's a bad town," said the voice. "Get some sleep."

"They've got my wife upstairs," said Harve. "I don't know what's going on. I've got to do something."

"Go ahead," said the voice. It chuckled ruefully.

"Do you know Ed Luby?" said Harve.

"You mean do I know who he is?" said the voice. "Who doesn't? You mean is he a friend of mine? If he was, you think I'd be locked up down here? I'd be out at Ed's club, eating a two-inch steak on the house, and the cop who brought me in would have had his brains beat out."

"Ed Luby's that important?" said Harve.

"Important?" said the voice. "Ed Luby? You never heard the story about the psychiatrist who went to Heaven?"

"What?" said Harve.

The voice told an old, old story—with a local variation. "This psychiatrist died and went to Heaven, see? And Saint Peter was tickled to death to see him. Seems God was having mental troubles, needed treatment bad. The psychiatrist asked Saint Peter what God's symptoms were. And Saint Peter whispered in his ear, 'God thinks He's Ed Luby.'"

The heels of the businesslike woman clacked across the floor above again. A telephone rang.

"Why should one man be so important?" said Harve.

"Ed Luby's all there is in Ilium," said the voice. "That answer your question? Ed came back here during the Depression. He had all the dough he'd made in bootlegging in Chicago. Everything in Ilium was closed down, for sale. Ed Luby bought."

"I see," said Harve, beginning to understand how scared he'd better be.

"Funny thing," said the voice, "people who get along with Ed, do what Ed says, say what Ed likes to hear—they have a pretty nice time in old Ilium. You take the chief of police now—salary's eight thousand a year. Been chief for five years now.

He's managed his salary so well he's got a seventy-thousand-dollar house all paid for, three cars, a summer place on Cape Cod, and a thirty-foot cabin cruiser. Of course, he isn't doing near as good as Luby's brother."

"The captain?" said Harve.

"Of course, the captain earns everything he gets," said the voice. "He's the one who really runs the Police Department. He owns the Ilium Hotel now—and the cab company. Also Radio Station WKLL, the friendly voice of Ilium."

"Some other people doing pretty well in Ilium, too," said the voice. "Old Judge Wampler and the mayor—"

"I got the idea," said Harve tautly.

"Doesn't take long," said the voice.

"Isn't there anybody against Luby?" said Harve.

"Dead," said the voice. "Let's get some sleep, eh?"

Ten minutes later, Harve was taken upstairs again. He wasn't hustled along this time, though he was in the care of the same sergeant who had locked him up. The sergeant was gentle now—even a little apologetic.

At the head of the iron stairs, they were met by Captain Luby, whose manners were changed for the better, too. The captain encouraged Harve to think of him as a prankish boy with a heart of gold.

Captain Luby put his hand on Harve's arm, and he smiled, and he said, "We've been rough on you, Mr. Elliot, and we know it. I'm sorry, but you've got to understand that police have to get rough sometimes—especially in a murder investigation."

"That's fine," said Harve, "except you're getting rough with the wrong people."

Captain Luby shrugged philosophically. "Maybe—maybe not," he said. "That's for a court to decide."

"If it has to come to that," said Harve.

"I think you'd better talk to a lawyer as soon as possible," said the captain.

"I think so, too," said Harve.

"There's one in the station house now, if you want to ask him," said the captain.

"Another one of Ed Luby's brothers?" said Harve.

Captain Luby looked surprised, and then he decided to laugh. He laughed very hard. "I don't blame you for saying that," he said. "I can imagine how things look to you."

"You can?" said Harve.

"You get in a jam in a strange town," said the captain, "and all of a sudden it looks to you like everybody's named Luby." He laughed again. "There's just me and my brother—just the two Lubys—that's all. This lawyer out front—not only isn't he any relative, he hates my guts and Ed's, too. That make you feel any better?"

"Maybe," said Harve carefully.

"What's that supposed to mean?" said the captain. "You want him or not?"

"I'll let you know after I've talked to him," said Harve.

"Go tell Lemming we maybe got a client for him," said the captain to the sergeant.

"I want my wife here, too," said Harve.

"Naturally," said the captain. "No argument there. She'll be right down."

The lawyer, whose name was Frank Lemming, was brought in to Harve long before Claire was. Lemming carried a battered black briefcase that seemed to have very little in it. He was a small, pear-shaped man.

Lemming's name was stamped on the side of his briefcase in big letters. He was shabby, puffy, short-winded. The only outward sign that he might have a little style, a little courage, was an outsize mustache.

When he opened his mouth, he let out a voice that was deep, majestic, unafraid. He demanded to know if Harve had been threatened or hurt in any way. He talked to Captain Luby and the sergeant as though they were the ones in trouble.

Harve began to feel a good deal better.

"Would you gentlemen kindly leave," said Lemming, calling the police *gentlemen* with grand irony. "I want to talk to my client alone."

The police left meekly.

"You're certainly a breath of fresh air," said Harve.

"That's the first time I've ever been called that," said Lemming.

"I was beginning to think I was in the middle of Nazi Germany," said Harve.

"You sound like a man who's never been arrested before," said Lemming.

"I never have been," said Harve.

"There's always got to be a first time," said Lemming pleasantly. "What's the charge?"

"They didn't tell you?" said Harve.

"They just told me they had somebody back here who wanted a lawyer," said Lemming. "I was here on another case." He sat down, put his limp briefcase against the leg of his chair. "So what's the charge?"

"They—they've been talking about murder," said Harve.

This news fazed Lemming only briefly. "These morons they call the Ilium Police Force," he said, "everything's murder to them. What did you do it with?"

"I didn't," said Harve.

"What did they *say* you did it with?" said Lemming.

"My fist," said Harve.

"You hit a man in a fight—and he died?" said Lemming.

"I didn't hit anybody!" said Harve.

"All right, all right, all right," said Lemming calmingly.

"Are you in with these guys, too?" said Harve. "Are you part of the nightmare, too?"

Lemming cocked his head. "Maybe you better explain that?" he said.

"Everybody in Ilium works for Ed Luby, I hear," said Harve. "I guess you do, too."

"Me?" said Lemming. "Are you kidding? You heard how I talk to Luby's brother. I'd talk to Ed Luby the same way. They don't scare me."

"Maybe—" said Harve, watching Lemming closely, wanting with all his heart to trust him.

"I'm hired?" said Lemming.

"How much will it cost?" said Harve.

"Fifty dollars to start," said Lemming.

"You mean right now?" said Harve.

"The class of people I do business with," said Lemming, "I get paid right away, or I never get paid."

"All I've got with me is twenty," said Harve.

"That'll do nicely for the moment," said Lemming. He held out his hand.

As Lemming was putting the money into his billfold, a policewoman with clacking heels brought Claire Elliot in.

Claire was snow-white. She wouldn't speak until the policewoman was gone. When she did speak, her voice was ragged, barely under control.

Harve embraced her, encouraged her. "We've got a lawyer now," he said. "We'll be all right now. He knows what to do."

"I don't trust him. I don't trust *anybody* around here!" said Claire. She was wild-eyed. "Harve! I've got to talk to you alone!"

"I'll be right outside," said Lemming. "Call me when you want me." He left his briefcase where it was.

"Has anybody threatened you?" Claire said to Harve, when Lemming was gone.

"There's been some pretty rough talk," said Harve.

"Has anybody threatened to kill you?" she said.

"No," said Harve.

Claire whispered now. "Somebody's threatened to kill me, and you—" Here she broke down. "And the children," she whispered brokenly.

Harve exploded. "Who?" he said at the top of his lungs. "Who threatened that?" he replied.

Claire put her hand over his mouth, begged him to be quiet.

Harve took her hand away. "Who?" he said.

Claire didn't even whisper her answer. She just moved her lips. "The captain," her lips said. She clung to him. "Please," she whispered, "keep your voice down. We've got to be calm. We've got to think. We've got to make up a new story."

"About what?" said Harve.

"About what happened," she said. She shook her head. "We mustn't ever tell what really happened again."

"My God," said Harve, "is this America?"

"I don't know what it is," said Claire. "I just know we've got to make up a new story—or—or something terrible will happen."

"Something terrible already has happened," said Harve.

"Worse things can still happen," said Claire.

Harve thought hard, the heels of his hands in his eye sockets. "If they're trying that hard to scare us," he said, "then they must be plenty scared, too. There must be plenty of harm we could do them."

"How?" said Claire.

"By sticking to the truth," said Harve. "That's pretty plain, isn't it? That's what they want to make us stop doing."

"I don't want to do anybody any harm," said Claire. "I just want to get out of here. I just want to go home."

"All right," said Harve. "We've got a lawyer now. That's a start."

Harve called to Lemming, who came in rubbing his hands. "Secret conference over?" he said cheerfully.

"Yes," said Harve.

"Well, secrets are all very fine in their place," said Lemming, "but I recommend strongly that you don't keep any from your lawyer."

"Harve—" said Claire warningly.

"He's right," said Harve. "Don't you understand—he's right."

"She's in favor of holding a little something back?" said Lemming.

"She's been threatened. That's the reason," said Harve.

"By whom?" said Lemming.

"Don't tell him," said Claire beseechingly.

"We'll save that for a little while," said Harve. "The thing is, Mr. Lemming, I didn't commit this murder they say I did. But my wife and I saw who really did it, and we've been threatened with all kinds of things, if we tell what we saw."

"Don't tell," said Claire. "Harve—don't."

"I give you my word of honor, Mrs. Elliot," said Lemming, "nothing you or your husband tells me will go any farther." He was proud of his word of honor, was a very appealing person when he gave it. "Now tell me who really did this killing."

"Ed Luby," said Harve.

"I beg your pardon?" said Lemming blankly.

"Ed Luby," said Harve.

Lemming sat back, suddenly drained and old. "I see," he said. His voice wasn't deep now. It was like wind in the treetops.

"He's a powerful man around here," said Harve, "I hear."

Lemming nodded. "You heard that right," he said.

Harve started to tell about how Luby had killed the girl. Lemming stopped him.

"What's—what's the matter?" said Harve.

Lemming gave him a wan smile. "That's a very good question," he said. "That's—that's a very *complicated* question."

"You work for him, after all?" said Harve.

"Maybe I do—after all," said Lemming.

"You see?" Claire said to Harve.

Lemming took out his billfold, handed the twenty dollars back to Harve.

"You quit?" said Harve.

"Let's say," said Lemming sadly, "that any advice you get from me from now on is free. I'm not the lawyer for this case—and any advice I have to give doesn't have much to do with the law." He spread his hands. "I'm a legal hack, friends. That must be obvious. If what you say is true—"

"It *is* true!" said Harve.

"Then you need a lawyer who can fight a whole town," said Lemming, "because Ed Luby *is* this town. I've won a lot of cases in Ilium, but they were all cases Ed Luby didn't care about." He stood. "If what you say is true, this isn't a case—it's a war."

"What am I going to do?" said Harve.

"My advice to you," said Lemming, "is to be as scared as your wife is, Mr. Elliot."

Lemming nodded, and then he scuttled away.

Seconds later, the sergeant came in for Harve and Claire, marched them through a door and into a room where a floodlight blinded them. Whispers came from the darkness beyond.

"What's this?" said Harve, his arm around Claire.

"Don't speak unless you're spoken to," said the voice of Captain Luby.

"I want a lawyer," said Harve.

"You had one," said the captain. "What happened to Lemming?"

"He quit," said Harve.

Somebody snickered.

"That's funny?" said Harve bitterly.

"Shut up," said Captain Luby.

"This is funny?" Harve said to the whispering blackness. "A man and a woman up here who never broke a law in their whole lives—accused of killing a woman they tried to save—"

Captain Luby emerged from the blackness. He showed Harve what he had in his right hand. It was a slab of rubber about four inches wide, eight inches long, and half an inch thick.

"This is what I call Captain Luby's wise-guy-wiser-upper," he said. He put the piece of rubber against Harve's cheek caressingly. "You can't imagine how much pain one slap from this thing causes," he said. "I'm surprised all over again, every time I use it. Now stand apart, stand straight, keep your mouths shut, and face the witnesses."

Harve's determination to break jail was born when the clammy rubber touched his cheek.

By the time the captain had returned to the whispering darkness, Harve's determination had become an obsession. No other plan would do.

Out in the darkness, a man now said in a clear, proud voice that he had seen Harve hit the girl. He identified himself as the mayor of Ilium.

The mayor's wife was honored to back him up.

Harve did not protest. He was too busy sensing all he could of what lay beyond the light. Someone now came in from another room, showing Harve where a door was, showing him what lay beyond the door.

Beyond the door he glimpsed a foyer. Beyond the foyer he glimpsed the great outdoors.

Now Captain Luby was asking Judge Wampler if he had seen Harve hit the girl.

"Yes," that fat man said gravely. "And I saw his wife help him to make a getaway, too."

Mrs. Wampler spoke up. "They're the ones, all right," she said. "It was one of the most terrible things I ever saw in my life. I don't think I'll ever forget it."

Harve tried to make out the first row of people, the first people he had to pass. He could make out only one person with any certainty. He could make out the policewoman with the clacking heels. She was taking notes now on all that was being said.

Harve decided to charge past her in thirty seconds.

He began to count the seconds away.

PART TWO

Harve Elliot stood in front of a blinding light with his wife, Claire. He had never committed a crime in his life. He was now counting off the seconds before he would break jail, before he would run away from the charge of murder.

He was listening to a supposed witness to his crime, to the man who had actually committed the murder. Ed Luby, somewhere behind the light, told his tale. Luby's brother, a captain on the Ilium Police Force, asked helpful questions from time to time.

"Three months ago," said Ed Luby, "I turned my restaurant into a private club—to keep undesirable elements out." Luby, the expert on undesirable elements, had once been a gunman for Al Capone.

"I guess those two up there," he said, meaning Harve and Claire, "didn't hear about it—or maybe they figured it didn't apply to them. Anyway, they showed up tonight, and they got sore when they couldn't get in, and they hung around the front door, insulting the members."

"You ever see them before?" Captain Luby asked him.

"Back before the place was a private club," said Luby, "these two used to come in about once a year. The reason I remembered 'em from one year to the next was the man was always loaded. And he'd get drunker in my place—and he'd turn mean."

"Mean?" said the captain.

"He'd pick fights," said Luby, "not just with men, either."

"So what happened tonight?" said the captain.

"These two were hanging around the door, making trouble for the members," said Luby, "and a dame came out in a taxi, all by herself. I don't know what she figured on doing. Figured on picking up somebody on the way in, I guess. Anyway, she got stopped, too, so I had three people hanging around outside my door. And they got in some kind of argument with each other."

All that interested Harve Elliot was the effect Luby's tale was having on the mood in the room. Harve couldn't see Luby, but he sensed that everyone was watching the man, was fascinated by him.

Now, Harve decided, was the time to run.

"I don't want you to take my word for what happened next," said Luby, "on account of I understand some people claim it was me who hit the girl."

"We've got the statements of other witnesses," said the captain sympathetically. "So you go ahead and give us your version, and we can double-check it."

"Well," said Luby, "the dame who came out in the taxi called the other dame— the dame up there—"

"Mrs. Elliot," said the captain.

"Yeah," said Luby. "She calls Mrs. Elliot something Mr. Elliot don't like, and the next thing I knew, Mr. Elliot had hauled off and—"

Harve Elliot plunged past the light and into the darkness. He charged at the door and the freedom beyond.

Harve lay under an old sedan in a used car lot. He was a block from the Ilium Police Station. His ears roared and his chest quaked. Centuries before he had broken jail. He had knocked people and doors and furniture out of his way effortlessly, had scattered them like leaves.

Guns had gone off, seemingly right by his head.

Now men were shouting in the night, and Harve lay under the car.

One clear image came to Harve from his fantastic flight—and only one. He remembered the face of the policewoman, the first person between him and freedom. Harve had flung her into the glare of the floodlight, had seen her livid, shocked face.

And that was the only face he'd seen.

The hunt for Harve—what Harve heard of it—sounded foolish, slovenly, demoralized. When Harve got his wind and his wits back, he felt marvelous. He wanted to laugh out loud and yell. He had won so far, and he would go on winning. He would get to the State Police. He would bring them back to Ilium to free Claire.

After that, Harve would hire the best lawyer he could find, clear himself, put Luby in prison, and sue the rotten city of Ilium for a blue million.

Harve peered out from under the car. His hunters were not coming toward him. They were moving away, blaming each other with childish querulousness for having let him escape.

Harve crawled out from under the car, crouched, listened. And then he began to walk carefully, always in shadows. He moved with the cunning of an infantry scout. The filth and feeble lights of the city, so recently his enemies, were his friends now.

And, moving with his back to sooty walls, ducking into doorways of decaying buildings, Harve realized that pure evil was his friend, too. Eluding it, outwitting it, planning its destruction all gave his life inconceivably exciting meanings.

A newspaper scuttled by, tumbled in a night breeze, seemed on its raffish way out of Ilium, too.

Far, far away a gun went off. Harve wondered what had been shot at—or shot.

Few cars moved in Ilium. And even rarer were people on foot. Two silent, shabby lovers passed within a few feet of Harve without seeing him.

A lurching drunk did see Harve, murmured some quizzical insult, lurched on.

Now a siren wailed—and then another, and yet another. Patrol cars were fanning out from the Ilium Police Station, idiotically advertising themselves with noise and lights.

One car set up a noisy, flashy roadblock not far from Harve. It blocked an underpass through the high, black rampart of a railroad bed. That much of what the police were doing was intelligent, because the car made a deadend of the route that Harve had been taking.

The railroad bed loomed like the Great Wall of China to Harve. Beyond it lay what he thought of as freedom. He had to think of freedom as being something close, as being just one short rush away. Actually, on the other side of the black rampart lay more of Ilium—more faint lights and broken streets. Hope, real hope, lay far, far beyond—lay miles beyond, lay on a superhighway, the fast, clean realm of the State Police.

But Harve now had to pretend that passing over or through the rampart was all that remained for him to do.

He crept to the railroad bed, moved along its cindery face, moved away from the underpass that the police had blocked.

He found himself approaching yet another underpass that was blocked by a car. He could hear talk. He recognized the voice of the talker. It was the voice of Captain Luby.

"Don't bother taking this guy alive," the captain said. "He's no good to himself or anybody else alive. Do the taxpayers a favor, and shoot to kill."

Somewhere a train whistle blew.

And then Harve saw a culvert that cut through the bed of the railroad. It seemed at first to be too close to Captain Luby. But then the captain swept the approaches with a powerful flashlight, showed Harve the trench that fed the culvert. It crossed a field littered with oil drums and trash.

When Captain Luby's light went off, Harve crawled out onto the field, reached the ditch, slithered in. In its shallow, slimy shelter, he moved toward the culvert.

The train that had whistled was approaching now. Its progress was grindingly, clankingly slow.

When the train was overhead, its noise at a maximum, Harve ducked into the culvert. Without thought of an ambush on the other side, he emerged, scrambled up the cinder slope.

He swung onboard the rusty rungs of an empty gondola in the moving train.

Eternities later, the slow-moving train had carried Harve Elliot out of Ilium. It was making its complaining way now through a seemingly endless wasteland—through woods and neglected fields.

Harve's eyes, stinging in the night wind, searched for light and motion ahead, for some outpost of the world that would help him rescue his wife.

The train rounded a curve. And Harve saw lights that, in the midst of the rural desolation, looked as lively as a carnival.

What made all that seeming life was a red flasher at a grade crossing, and the headlights of one car stopped by the flasher.

As the gondola rattled over the crossing, Harve dropped off and rolled.

He stood, went unsteadily to the stopped automobile. When he got past the headlights, he could see that the driver was a young woman.

He could see, too, how terrified she was.

"Listen! Wait! Please!" said Harve.

The woman jammed her car in gear, sent the car bucking past Harve and over the crossing as the end of the caboose went by.

Her rear wheels threw cinders in Harve's eyes.

When he had cleared his eyes, her taillights were twinkling off into the night, were gone.

The train was gone, too.

And the noisy red flasher was dead.

Harve stood alone in a countryside as still and bleak as the arctic. Nowhere was there a light to mark a house.

The train blew its sad horn—far away now.

Harve put his hands to his cheeks. They were wet. They were grimed. And he looked around at the lifeless night, remembered the nightmare in Ilium. He kept his hands on his cheeks. Only his hands and his cheeks seemed real.

He began to walk.

No more cars came.

On he trudged, with no way of knowing where he was, where he was heading. Sometimes he imagined that he heard or saw signs of a busy highway in the distance—the faint singing of tires, the billowing of lights.

He was mistaken.

He came at last to a dark farmhouse. A radio murmured inside.

He knocked on the door.

Somebody stirred. The radio went off.

Harve knocked again. The glass pane in the door was loose, rattled when Harve knocked. Harve put his face to the pane. He saw the sullen red of a cigarette. It cast only enough light to illuminate the rim of the ashtray in which it rested.

Harve knocked again.

"Come in," said a man's voice. "Ain't locked."

Harve went in. "Hello?" he said.

No one turned on a light for him. Whoever had invited him in didn't show himself, either. Harve turned this way and that. "I'd like to use your phone," he said to the dark.

"You stay faced right the way you are," said the voice, coming from behind Harve. "I got a double-barreled twelve-gauge shotgun aimed right at your middle, Mr. Elliot. You do anything out of the way at all, and I'll blow you right in two."

Harve raised his hands. "You know my name?" he said.

"That *is* your name?" said the voice.

"Yes," said Harve.

"Well, well," said the voice. It cackled. "Here I am, an old, old man. Wife gone, friends gone, children gone. Been thinking the past few days about using this here gun on myself. Just looky here what I would have missed! Just goes to prove—"

"Prove what?" said Harve.

"Nobody ever knows when he's gonna have a lucky day."

The ceiling fixture in the room went on. It was over Harve's head. Harve looked up at it. He didn't look behind himself, for fear of being blown in two. The ceiling fixture was meant to have three bulbs, had only one. Harve could tell that by the gray ghosts of the missing two.

The frosted shade was dotted with the shadows of the bodies of bugs.

"You can look behind, if you want," said the voice. "See for yourself whether I got a gun or not, Mr. Elliot."

Harve turned slowly to look at a very old man—a scrawny old man with obscenely white and even false teeth. The old man really did have a shotgun—a cavernous, rusty antique. The ornate, arched hammers of the gun were cocked.

The old man was scared. But he was pleased and excited, too.

"Don't make any trouble, Mr. Elliot," he said, "and we'll get along just fine. You're looking at a man who went over the top eight times in the Great War, so you ain't looking at anybody who'd be too chickenhearted to shoot. Shooting a man ain't something I never done before."

"All right—no trouble," said Harve.

"Wouldn't be the first man I shot," said the old man. "Wouldn't be the tenth, far as that goes."

"I believe you," said Harve. "Can I ask you how you happen to know my name?"

"Radio," said the old man. He motioned to an armchair, a chair with burst upholstering, with sagging springs. "You better set there, Mr. Elliot."

Harve did as he was told. "There's news of me on the radio?" he said.

"I guess there is," said the old man. "I expect you're on television, too. Don't have no television. No sense getting television at my age. Radio does me fine."

"What does the radio say about me?" said Harve.

"Killed a woman—broke jail," said the old man. "Worth a thousand dollars, dead or alive." He moved toward a telephone, keeping the gun aimed at Harve. "You're a lucky man, Mr. Elliot."

"Lucky?" said Harve.

"That's what I said," said the old man. "Whole county knows there's a crazy man loose. Radio's been telling 'em, 'Lock your doors and windows, turn out your lights, stay inside, don't let no strangers in.' Practically any house you would have walked up to, they would have shot first and asked questions afterwards. Just lucky you walked up to a house where there was somebody who don't scare easy." He took the telephone from its cradle.

"I never hurt anybody in my life," said Harve.

"That's what the radio said," said the old man. "Said you just went crazy tonight." He dialed for an operator, said to her, "Get me the Ilium Police Department."

"Wait!" said Harve.

"You want more time to figure how to kill me?" said the old man.

"The State Police—call the State Police!" said Harve.

The old man smiled foxily, shook his head. "They ain't the ones offering the big reward," he said.

The call went through. The Ilium Police were told where they could find Harve. The old man explained again and again where he lived. The Ilium Police would be coming out into unfamiliar territory. They had no jurisdiction there.

"He's all quiet now," said the old man. "I got him all calmed down."

And that was a fact.

Harve was feeling the relaxation of a very hard game's being over. The relaxation was a close relative of death.

"Funny thing to happen to an old man—right at the end of his days," said the old man. "Now I get a thousand dollars, picture in the paper—God knows what all—"

"You want to hear my story?" said Harve.

"Pass the time?" said the old man amiably. "All right with me. Just don't you budge from that chair."

So Harve Elliot told his tale. He told it pretty well, listened to the story himself. He astonished himself with the tale—and, with that astonishment, anger and terror began to seep into his being again.

"You've got to believe me!" said Harve. "You've got to let me call the State Police!"

The old man smiled indulgently. "Got to, you say?" he said.

"Don't you know what kind of a town Ilium is?" said Harve.

"Expect I do," said the old man. "I grew up there—and my father and grandfather, too."

"Do you know what Ed Luby's done to the town?" said Harve.

"Oh, I hear a few things now and then," said the old man. "He gave a new wing for the hospital, I know. I know, on account of I was in that wing one time. Generous man, I'd say."

"You can say that, even after what I've told you?" said Harve.

"Mr. Elliot," said the old man, with very real sympathy, "I don't think you're in any condition to talk about who's good and who's bad. I know what I'm talking about when I say that, on account of I was crazy once myself."

"I'm not crazy," said Harve.

"That's what I said, too," said the old man. "But they took me off to the crazy house just the same. I had a big story, too—all about the things folks had done to me, all about things folks was ganging up to do to me." He shook his head. "I believed that story, too. I mean, Mr. Elliot, I *believed* it."

"I tell you, I'm *not* crazy," said Harve.

"That's for a doctor to say, now, ain't it?" said the old man. "You know when they let me out of the crazy house, Mr. Elliot? You know when they let me out, said I could go home to my wife and family?"

"When?" said Harve. His muscles were tightening up. He knew he was going to have to rush past death again—to rush past death and into the night.

"They let me go home," said the old man, "when I could finally see for myself that nobody was really trying to do me in, when I could see for myself it was all in my head." He turned on the radio. "Let's have some music while we wait," he said. "Music always helps."

Asinine music about teenage love came from the radio. And then there was this news bulletin:

"Units of the Ilium Police are now believed to be closing in on Harvey Elliot, escaped maniac, who killed a woman outside of the fashionable Key Club in Ilium tonight. Householders are warned, however, to continue to be on the lookout for this man, to keep all doors and windows locked, and to report at once any prowlers. Elliot is extremely dangerous and resourceful. The chief of police has characterized

Elliot as a 'mad dog,' and he warns persons not to attempt to reason with him. The management of this station has offered a thousand-dollar reward for Elliot, dead or alive.

"This is WKLL," said the announcer, "eight sixty on your dial, the friendly voice of Ilium, with news and music for your listening pleasure around the clock."

It was then that Harve rushed the old man.

Harve knocked the gun aside. Both barrels roared.

The tremendous blast ripped a hole in the side of the house.

The old man held the gun limply, stupid with shock. He made no protest when Harve relieved him of the gun, went out the back door with it.

Sirens sobbed, far down the road.

◙ ◙ ◙

Harve ran into the woods in back of the house. But then he understood that in the woods he could only provide a short and entertaining hunt for Captain Luby and his boys. Something more surprising was called for.

So Harve circled back to the road, lay down in a ditch.

Three Ilium police cars came to showy stops before the old man's house. The front tire of one skidded to within a yard of Harve's hand.

Captain Luby led his brave men up to the house. The blue flashers of the cars again created revolving islands of nightmare.

One policeman stayed outside. He sat at the wheel of the car nearest to Harve. He was intent on the raiders and the house.

Harve got out of the ditch quietly. He leveled the empty shotgun at the back of the policeman's neck, said softly, politely, "Officer?"

The policeman turned his head, found himself staring down two rusty barrels the size of siege howitzers.

Harve recognized him. He was the sergeant who had arrested Harve and Claire, the one with the long scar that seamed his cheek and lips.

Harve got into the back of the car. "Let's go," he said evenly. "Pull away slowly, with your lights out. I'm insane—don't forget that. If we get caught, I'll kill you first. Let's see how quietly you can pull away—and then let's see how fast you can go after that."

The Ilium police car streaked down a superhighway now. No one was in pursuit. Cars pulled over to let it by.

It was on its way to the nearest barracks of the State Police.

The sergeant at the wheel was a tough, realistic man. He did exactly what Harve told him to do. At the same time, he let Harve know that he wasn't scared. He said what he pleased.

"What you think this is gonna get you, Elliot?" he said.

Harve had made himself comfortable in the backseat. "It's going to get a lot of people a lot of things," he said grimly.

"You figure the State Police will be softer on a murderer than we were?" said the sergeant.

"You know I'm not a murderer," said Harve.

"Not a jailbreaker or a kidnapper, either, eh?" said the sergeant.

"We'll see," said Harve. "We'll see what I am, and what I'm not. We'll see what everybody is."

"You want my advice, Elliot?" said the sergeant.

"No," said Harve.

"If I were you, I'd get clear the hell out of the country," said the sergeant. "After all you've done, friend, you haven't got a chance."

Harve's head was beginning to bother him again. It ached in a pulsing way. The wound on the back of his head stung, as though it were open again, and waves of wooziness came and went.

Speaking out of that wooziness, Harve said to the sergeant, "How many months out of the year do you spend in Florida? Your wife got a nice fur coat and a sixty-thousand-dollar house?"

"You really *are* nuts," said the sergeant.

"You aren't getting your share?" said Harve.

"Share of what?" said the sergeant. "I do my job. I get my pay."

"In the rottenest city in the country," said Harve.

The sergeant laughed. "And you're gonna change all that—right?"

The cruiser slowed down, swung into a turnout, came to a stop before a brand-new State Police barracks of garish, yellow brick.

The car was surrounded instantly by troopers with drawn guns.

The sergeant turned and grinned at Harve. "Here's your idea of Heaven, buddy," he said. "Go on—get out. Have a talk with the angels."

Harve was hauled out of the car. Shackles were slammed on his wrists and ankles.

He was hoisted off his feet, was swept into the barracks, was set down hard on a cot in a cell.

The cell smelled of fresh paint.

Many people crowded around the cell door for a look at the desperado.

And then Harve passed out cold.

"No—he isn't faking," he heard someone say in a swirling mist. "He's had a pretty bad blow on the back of his head."

Harve opened his eyes. A very young man was standing over him.

"Hello," said the young man, when he saw that Harve's eyes were open.

"Who are you?" said Harve.

"Dr. Mitchell," said the young man. He was a narrow-shouldered, grave, bespectacled young man. He looked very insignificant in comparison with the two big men standing behind him. The two big men were Captain Luby and a uniformed sergeant of the State Police.

"How do you feel?" said Dr. Mitchell.

"Lousy," said Harve.

"I'm not surprised," said the doctor. He turned to Captain Luby. "You can't take this man back to jail," he said. "He's got to go to Ilium Hospital. He's got to have X-rays, got to be under observation for at least twenty-four hours."

Captain Luby gave a wry laugh. "Now the taxpayers of Ilium gotta give him a nice rest, after the night he put in."

Harve sat up. Nausea came and went. "My wife—how is my wife?"

"Half off her nut, after all the stuff you pulled," said Captain Luby. "How the hell you expect her to be?"

"You've still got her locked up?" said Harve.

"Nah," said Captain Luby. "Anybody who isn't happy in our jail, we let 'em go right away—let 'em walk right out. You know that. You're a big expert on that."

"I want my wife brought out here," said Harve. "That's why I came here—" Grogginess came over him. "To get my wife out of Ilium," he murmured.

"Why do you want to get your wife out of Ilium?" said Dr. Mitchell.

"Doc—" said the captain jocularly, "you go around asking jailbirds *how* come they want what they want, and you won't have no time left over for medicine."

Dr. Mitchell looked vaguely annoyed with the captain, put his question to Harve again.

"Doc," said Captain Luby, "what's that disease called—where somebody thinks everybody's against 'em?"

"Paranoia," said Dr. Mitchell tautly.

"We saw Ed Luby murder a woman," said Harve. "They blamed it on me. They said they'd kill us if we told." He lay back. Consciousness was fading fast. "For the love of God," he said thickly, "somebody help."

Consciousness was gone.

Harve Elliot was taken to Ilium Hospital in an ambulance. The sun was coming up. He was aware of the trip—aware of the sun, too. He heard someone mention the sun's coming up.

He opened his eyes. Two men rode on a bench that paralleled his cot in the ambulance. The two swayed as the ambulance swayed.

Harve made no great effort to identify the two. When hope had died, so, too, had curiosity. Harve, moreover, had been somehow drugged. He remembered the young doctor's having given him a shot—to ease his pain, the doctor said. It killed Harve's worries along with his pain, gave him what comfort there was in the illusion that nothing mattered.

His two fellow passengers now identified themselves by speaking to each other.

"You new in town, Doc?" said one. "Don't believe I've ever seen you around before." That was Captain Luby.

"I started practice three months ago," the doctor said. That was Dr. Mitchell.

"You ought to get to know my brother," said the captain. "He could help you get started. He gets a lot of people started."

"So I've heard," said the doctor.

"A little boost from Ed never hurt anybody," said the captain.

"I wouldn't think so," said the doctor.

"This guy sure pulled a boner when he tried to pin the murder on Ed," said the captain.

"I can see that," said the doctor.

"Practically everybody who's anybody in town is a witness for Ed and against this jerk," said the captain.

"Uh-huh," said the doctor.

"I'll fix you up with an introduction to Ed sometime," said the captain. "I think you two would hit it off just fine."

"I'm very flattered," said the doctor.

At the emergency door of Ilium Hospital, Harve Elliot was transferred from the ambulance to a rubber-wheeled cart.

There was a brief delay in the receiving room, for another case had arrived just ahead of Harve. The delay wasn't long, because the other case was dead on arrival. The other case, on a cart exactly like Harve's, was a man.

Harve knew him.

The dead man was the man who had brought his girl out to Ed Luby's Key Club so long ago, who had seen his girl killed by Ed Luby.

He was Harve's prize witness—dead.

"What happened to him?" Captain Luby asked a nurse.

"Nobody knows," she said. "They found him shot in the back of the neck—in the alley behind the bus station." She covered the dead man's face.

"Too bad," said Captain Luby. He turned to Harve. "You're luckier than him, anyway, Elliot," he said. "At least you're not dead."

◙ ◙ ◙

Harve Elliot was wheeled all over Ilium Hospital—had his skull X-rayed, had an electroencephalogram taken, let doctors peer gravely into his eyes, his nose, his ears, his throat.

Captain Luby and Dr. Mitchell went with him wherever he was rolled. And Harve was bound to agree with Captain Luby when the captain said, "It's crazy, you know? We're up all night, looking for a clean shot at this guy. Now here we are, all day long, getting the same guy the best treatment money can buy. Crazy."

Harve's time sense was addled by the shot Dr. Mitchell had given him, but he did realize that the examinations and tests were going awfully slowly—and that more and more doctors were being called in.

Dr. Mitchell seemed to grow a lot tenser about his patient, too.

Two more doctors arrived, looked briefly at Harve, then stepped aside with Dr. Mitchell for a whispered conference.

A janitor, mopping the corridor, paused in his wet and hopeless work to take a good look at Harve. "This him?" he said.

"That's him," said Captain Luby.

"Don't look very desperate, do he?" said the janitor.

"Kind of ran out of desperation," said the captain.

"Like a car run out of gas," said the janitor. He nodded. "He crazy?" he asked.

"He better be," said the captain.

"What you mean by that?" said the janitor.

"If he isn't," said the captain, "he's going to the electric chair."

"My, my," said the janitor. He shook his head. "Sure glad I ain't him." He resumed his mopping, sent a little tidal wave of gray water down the corridor.

There was loud talk at the far end of the corridor now. Harve turned his incurious eyes to see Ed Luby himself approaching. Luby was accompanied by his big body-guard, and by his good friend, his fat friend, Judge Wampler.

Ed Luby, an elegant man, was first of all concerned about the spotlessness of his black and pointed shoes. "Watch where you mop," he told the janitor in a grackle voice. "These are fifty-dollar shoes."

He looked down at Harve. "My God," he said, "it's the one-man army himself." Luby asked his brother if Harve could talk and hear.

"They tell me he hears all right," said the captain. "He don't seem to talk at all."

Ed Luby smiled at Judge Wampler. "I'd say that was a pretty good way for a man to be, wouldn't you, Judge?" he said.

The conference of doctors ended on a note of grim agreement. They returned to Harve's side.

Captain Luby introduced young Dr. Mitchell to his brother, Ed. "The doc here's new to town, Ed," said the captain. "He's kind of taken Elliot here under his wing."

"I guess that's part of his oath. Right?" said Ed Luby.

"Beg your pardon?" said Dr. Mitchell.

"No matter what somebody is," said Ed, "no matter what terrible things they've done—a doctor's still got to do everything he can for him. Right?"

"Right," said Dr. Mitchell.

Luby knew the other two doctors, and they knew him. Luby and the doctors didn't like each other much. "You two guys are working on this Elliot, too?" said Ed.

"That's right," said one.

"Would somebody please tell me what's the matter with this guy, that so many doctors have to come from far and wide to look at him?" said Captain Luby.

"It's a very complicated case," said Dr. Mitchell. "It's a very tricky, delicate case."

"What's that mean?" said Ed Luby.

"Well," said Dr. Mitchell, "we're all pretty well agreed now that we've got to operate on this man at once, or there's a good chance he'll die."

Harve was bathed, and his head was shaved.

And he was rolled through the double doors and put under the blinding light of the operating room.

The Luby brothers were kept outside. There were only doctors and nurses around Harve now—pairs of eyes, and masks and gowns.

Harve prayed. He thought of his wife and children. He awaited the mask of the anesthetist.

"Mr. Elliot?" said Dr. Mitchell. "You can hear me?"

"Yes," said Harve.

"How do you feel?" said Dr. Mitchell.

"In the Hands of God," said Harve.

"You're not a very sick man, Mr. Elliot," said Dr. Mitchell. "We're not going to operate. We brought you up here to protect you." The eyes around the table shifted uneasily. Dr. Mitchell explained the uneasiness. "We've taken quite a chance here, Mr. Elliot," he said. "We have no way of knowing whether you deserve protection or not. We'd like to hear your story again."

Harve looked into each of the pairs of circling eyes. He shook his head almost imperceptibly. "No story," he said.

"No story?" said Dr. Mitchell. "After all this trouble we've gone to?"

"Whatever Ed Luby and his brother say the story is—that's the story," said Harve. "You can tell Ed I finally got the message. Whatever he says goes. No more trouble from me."

"Mr. Elliot," said Dr. Mitchell, "there isn't a man or a woman here who wouldn't like to see Ed Luby and his gang in prison."

"I don't believe you," said Harve. "I don't believe anybody anymore." He shook his head again. "As far as that goes," he said, "I can't prove any of my story anyway. Ed Luby's got all the witnesses. The one witness I thought I might get—he's dead downstairs."

This news was a surprise to those around the table.

"You knew that man?" said Dr. Mitchell.

"Forget it," said Harve. "I'm not saying any more. I've said too much already."

"There *is* a way you could prove your story—to our satisfaction, anyway," said Dr. Mitchell. "With your permission, we'd like to give you a shot of sodium pentothal. Do you know what it is?"

"No," said Harve.

"It's a so-called truth serum, Mr. Elliot," said Dr. Mitchell. "It will temporarily paralyze the control you have over your conscious mind. You'll go to sleep for a few minutes, and then we'll wake you up, and you won't be able to lie."

"Even if I told you the truth, and you believed it, and you wanted to get rid of Ed Luby," said Harve, "what could a bunch of doctors do?"

"Not much, I admit," said Dr. Mitchell.

"But only four of us here are doctors," said Dr. Mitchell. "As I told Ed Luby, yours was a very complicated case—so we've called together a pretty complicated meeting to look into it." He pointed out masked and gowned men around the table. "This gentleman here is head of the County Bar Association. These two gentlemen here are detectives from the State Police. These two gentlemen are F.B.I. agents. That is, of course," he said, "if your story's true—if you're willing to let us prove it's true."

Harve looked into the circling eyes again.

He held out his bare arm to receive the shot. "Let's go," he said.

Harve told his story and answered questions in the unpleasant, echoing trance induced by sodium pentothal.

The questions came to an end at last. The trance persisted.

"Let's start with Judge Wampler," he heard someone say.

He heard someone else telephoning, giving orders that the cabdriver who had driven the murdered woman out to the Key Club was to be identified, picked up, and brought to the operating room of Ilium Hospital for questioning. "You heard me—the operating room," said the man on the telephone.

Harve didn't feel any particular elation about that. But then he heard some really good news. Another man took over the telephone, and he told somebody to get Harve's wife out of jail at once on a writ of habeas corpus. "And somebody else find out who's taking care of the kids," said the telephoner, "and, for God's sake, make sure the papers and the radio stations find out this guy isn't a maniac after all."

And then Harve heard another man come back to the operating room with the bullet from the dead man downstairs, the dead witness. "Here's one piece of evidence that isn't going to disappear," said the man. "Good specimen." He held the bullet up to the light. "Shouldn't have any trouble proving what gun it came from— if we had the gun."

"Ed Luby's too smart to do the shooting himself," said Dr. Mitchell, who was obviously starting to have a very fine time.

"His bodyguard isn't too smart," said somebody else. "In fact, he's just dumb enough. He's even dumb enough to have the gun still on him."

"We're looking for a thirty-eight," said the man with the bullet. "Are they all still downstairs?"

"Keeping a death watch," said Dr. Mitchell pleasantly.

And then word came that Judge Wampler was being brought up. Everyone tied on his surgical mask again, in order that the judge, when he entered, mystified and afraid, could see only eyes.

"What—what is this?" said Judge Wampler. "Why do you want me here?"

"We want your help in a very delicate operation," said Dr. Mitchell.

Wampler gave a smile that was queer and slack. "Sir?" he said.

"We understand that you and your wife were witnesses to a murder last night," said Dr. Mitchell.

"Yes," said Wampler. His translucent chins trembled.

"We think you and your wife aren't quite telling the truth," said Dr. Mitchell. "We think we can prove that."

"How *dare* you talk to me like that!" said Wampler indignantly.

"I dare," said Dr. Mitchell, "because Ed Luby and his brother are all through in this town. I dare," he said, "because police from outside have moved in. They're going to cut the rotten heart right out of this town. You're talking to federal agents and State Police at this very minute." Dr. Mitchell spoke over his shoulder. "Suppose you unmask, gentlemen, so the judge can see what sort of people he's talking to."

The faces of the law were unmasked. They were majestic in their contempt for the judge.

Wampler looked as though he were about to cry.

"Now tell us what you saw last night," said Dr. Mitchell.

Judge Wampler hesitated. Then he hung his head, and he whispered, "Nothing. I was inside. I didn't see anything."

"And your wife didn't see anything, either?" said Dr. Mitchell.

"No," whispered Wampler.

"You didn't see Elliot hit the woman?" said Dr. Mitchell.

"No," said the judge.

"Why did you lie?" said Dr. Mitchell.

"I—I believed Ed Luby," said Wampler. "He—he told me what happened—and I—I believed him."

"You believe him now?" said Dr. Mitchell.

"I—I don't know," said Wampler wretchedly.

"You're through as a judge," said Dr. Mitchell. "You must know that."

Wampler nodded.

"You were through as a man a long time ago," said Dr. Mitchell. "All right," he said, "dress him up. Let him watch what happens next."

And Judge Wampler was forced to put on a mask and gown.

The puppet chief of police and the puppet mayor of Ilium were telephoned from the operating room, were told to come to the hospital at once, that there was something very important going on there. Judge Wampler, closely supervised, did the telephoning.

But, before they arrived, two state troopers brought in the cabdriver who had driven the murdered woman out to the Key Club.

He was appalled when he was brought before the weird tribunal of seeming surgeons. He looked in horror at Harve, who was still stretched out on the table in his sodium pentothal trance.

Judge Wampler again had the honor of doing the talking. He was far more convincing than anyone else could have been in advising the driver that Ed Luby and his brother were through.

"Tell the truth," said Judge Wampler quaveringly.

So the driver told it. He had seen Ed Luby kill the girl.

"Issue this man his uniform," said Dr. Mitchell.

And the driver was given a mask and gown.

Next came the mayor and the chief of police.

After them came Ed Luby, Captain Luby, and Ed Luby's big bodyguard.

The three came through the double doors of the operating room shoulder to shoulder.

They were handcuffed and disarmed before they could say a word.

"What the hell's the idea?" Ed Luby roared.

"It's all over. That's all," said Dr. Mitchell. "We thought you ought to know."

"Elliot's dead?" said Luby.

"*You're* dead, Mr. Luby," said Dr. Mitchell.

Luby started to inflate himself, was instantly deflated by a tremendous *bang.* A man had just fired the bodyguard's thirty-eight into a bucket packed with cotton.

Luby watched stupidly as the man dug the bullet out of the cotton, took it over to a counter where two microscopes had been set up.

Luby's comment was somewhat substandard. "Now, just a minute—" he said.

"We've got nothing but time," said Dr. Mitchell. "Nobody's in a hurry to go anywhere—unless you or your brother or your bodyguard have appointments elsewhere."

"Who *are* you guys?" said Luby malevolently.

"We'll show you in a minute," said Dr. Mitchell. "First, though, I think you ought to know that we're all agreed—you're through."

"Yeah?" said Luby. "Let me tell you, I've got plenty of friends in this town."

"Time to unmask, gentlemen," said Dr. Mitchell.

All unmasked.

Ed Luby stared at his utter ruin.

The man at the microscopes broke the silence. "They match," he said. "The bullets match. They came from the same gun."

Harve broke through the glass walls of his trance momentarily. The tiles of the operating room echoed. Harve Elliot had laughed out loud.

Harve Elliot dozed off, was taken to a private room to sleep off the drug.

His wife, Claire, was waiting for him there.

Young Dr. Mitchell was with Harve when he was wheeled in. "He's perfectly all right, Mrs. Elliot," Harve heard Dr. Mitchell say. "He just needs rest—and so, I'd think, would you."

"I don't think I'll be able to sleep for a week," said Claire.

"I'll give you something, if you like," said Dr. Mitchell.

"Later, maybe," said Claire. "Not now."

"I'm sorry we shaved off all his hair," said Dr. Mitchell. "It seemed necessary at the time."

"Such a crazy night—such a crazy day," she said. "What did it all mean?"

"It meant a lot," said Dr. Mitchell, "thanks to some brave and honest men."

"Thanks to you," she said.

"I was thinking of your husband," he said. "As for myself, I never enjoyed anything more in my life. It taught me how men get to be free, and how they can stay free."

"How?" said Claire.

"By fighting for justice for strangers," said Dr. Mitchell.

Harve Elliot managed to get his eyes open. "Claire—" he said.

"Darling—" she said.

"I love you," said Harve.

"That's the absolute truth," said Dr. Mitchell, "in case you've ever wondered."

King and Queen of
the Universe

MIND GOING BACK to the Great Depression for a few minutes—clear back to 1932? It was an awful time, I know, but there are a lot of good stories in the Great Depression.

Back in 1932 Henry and Anne were seventeen.

At seventeen, Henry and Anne were in love with each other in a highly ornamental way. They knew how good their love looked. They knew how good *they* looked. They could read in the eyes of their elders how right they were for each other—how right for the society into which they had been born.

Henry was Henry Davidson Merrill, son of the President of the Merchants' National Bank; grandson of the late George Mills Davidson, Mayor from 1916 to 1922; grandson of Dr. Rossiter Merrill, founder of the Children's Wing of the City Hospital . . .

Anne was Anne Lawson Heiler, daughter of the President of the Citizens' Gas Company; granddaughter of the late federal judge Franklin Pace Heiler; granddaughter of D. Dwight Lawson, architect, the Christopher Wren of the Middle Western city . . .

Their credentials and their fortunes were in order—had been from the instants of their births. Love like theirs made no demands beyond good grooming, good sailing, good tennis, good golf. They remained as untouched by the soul-deep aspects of love as Winnie-the-Pooh, the storybook teddy bear.

It was all so cheerful and easy—so natural and clean.

And, in a Winnie-the-Pooh mood, wherein sordid things could happen only to sordid people, Henry Davidson Merrill and Anne Lawson Heiler crossed a city park late one night—crossed it in evening clothes. They crossed it on their way from an Athletic Club dance to the garage where Henry's car was parked.

The night was black, and the few lights of the park were far apart and sickly pale.

People had been murdered in the park. One man had been butchered for twelve cents, and his murderer was still at large. But he had been a dirty, homeless man—one of those people who were born, seemingly, to be murdered for less than a dollar.

Henry regarded his tuxedo as a safe-conduct pass through the park—a costume so different from that of the natives as to make him immune to their squalid troublemaking.

Henry looked at Anne, and found her correctly bored—a pink bonbon in blue tulle, wearing her mother's pearls and orchids from Henry.

"I wouldn't mind sleeping on a park bench," said Anne loudly. "I think it would be fun. I think it would be fun to be a hobo." She put her hand in Henry's. Her hand was hard, tanned, comradely.

There was no cheap thrill in the meeting of their palms in the dark park. Having grown up together, knowing they would marry and grow old together, neither could surprise or puzzle the other with a touch or a glance or a word—or even with a kiss.

"It wouldn't be much fun to be a hobo in the wintertime," said Henry. He held her hand for a moment, swung it, then let it go without regret.

"I'd go to Florida in the wintertime," said Anne. "I'd sleep on the beaches and steal oranges."

"You can't live on just oranges," said Henry. He was being manly now—letting her know that he understood more about the harshnesses of the world than she did.

"Oranges and fish," said Anne. "I would steal ten cents' worth of hooks from a hardware store, and make a fishline out of string from somebody's wastebasket, and make a sinker out of a stone. Honestly," said Anne, "I think it would be heaven. I think people are crazy to worry about money the way they do."

In the exact middle of the park, what seemed to be a gargoyle on the rim of a fountain detached itself. It revealed itself as a man.

The movement transformed the park into the black River Styx, transformed the lights of the garage beyond into the gates of Paradise—gates a million miles away.

Henry became a foolish, slope-shouldered boy, as ungainly as a homemade stepladder. His white shirt bosom became a beacon for thieves and lunatics.

Henry glanced at Anne. She had become a fuddled butterball. Her hands went to her throat, hiding her mother's necklace. Her orchids seemed to weigh her down like cannonballs.

"Stop—please stop," the man wheezed softly. He coughed boozily, flagged them down with his hands. "Please—whoa, just a second."

Henry felt the sickening excitement of battle billow in his breast, raised his hands to somewhere between fight and surrender.

"Put your hands down," said the man. "I only want to talk to you. The robbers are all in bed by now. Drunks, drifters, and poets are the only ones up this late at night."

He lurched toward Henry and Anne, his own hands raised in a gesture of utter harmlessness. He was small and scrawny, and his cheap clothes wrinkled and crackled like newspaper.

He tipped his head back, exposing his scrawny throat to death at Henry's hands. He smiled slackly. "Big young man like you could kill me with two fingers," he said. Turtlelike, he watched with pop eyes for signs of trust.

Henry lowered his hands slowly, and so did the man.

"What you want?" said Henry. "You want money?"

"Don't you?" said the man. "Doesn't everybody? Bet even your old man could use some more." He chuckled, mimicked Henry. "'You want money?'"

"My father isn't rich," said Henry.

"These pearls aren't real," said Anne. It came out a series of unbecoming squawks.

"Oh—they're real enough, I imagine," said the man. He bowed slightly to Henry. "And your father has some money, I imagine. Maybe not enough for the next thousand years, but for the next five hundred, anyway." He swayed. His face was mobile, showed in quick succession shame, contempt, whimsy, and finally great sadness. His face showed sadness when he introduced himself. "Stanley Karpinsky is the name," he said. "Don't want your money. Don't want your pearls. Want to talk."

Henry found that he couldn't brush past Karpinsky—couldn't even refuse his hand. Henry Davidson Merrill found that Stanley Karpinsky had become precious to him—had become a small god of the park, a supernatural being who could see into the shadows, who knew what lay behind every shrub and tree.

It seemed to Henry that Karpinsky and Karpinsky alone could lead them safely to the edge of the park so far away.

Anne's terror now turned into hysterical friendliness as Henry shook Karpinsky's hand. "Goodness!" she cried into the night. "We thought you were a robber or we didn't know what!" She laughed.

Karpinsky became reserved, sure of their trust. He studied their clothes. "King and Queen of the Universe—that's what she'd think you were," he said. "By God, if she wouldn't!"

"Beg pardon?" said Henry.

"My mother would," said Karpinsky. "She'd think you were the two most beautiful creatures she ever laid eyes on. Little old Polish woman—scrubbing floors all her life. Never even got up off her hands and knees long enough to learn English. She'd think you were angels." He cocked his head and raised an eyebrow. "Would you come and let her have a look at you?" he said.

In the flaccid idiocy that had followed terror, Henry and Anne accepted Karpinsky's peculiar invitation—not only accepted it, but accepted it with enthusiasm.

"Mother?" babbled Anne. "Love to, love to, love to."

"Sure—where to?" said Henry.

"Just a block from here," said Karpinsky. "We'd go in, let her see you, and then you could leave right away. It wouldn't take over ten minutes."

"O.K.," said Henry.

"O.K.," said Anne. "This is fun."

Karpinsky studied them for a little while longer, taking from his pocket a loose cigarette that had been bent into almost a right angle. Karpinsky didn't bother to straighten it out, but lit it as it was.

"Come on," he said suddenly, flicking the match away. And Henry and Anne found themselves following him, walking very quickly. He was leading them away from the lights of the garage, was leading them toward a side street that was hardly better illuminated than the park.

Henry and Anne stayed right with him. For all the unearthliness of their mission and the park at night, Henry and Anne might have been hurtling through the black vacuum of space to the moon.

The odd expedition reached the edge of the park and crossed the street. The street seemed a murky tunnel through a nightmare, with bright, warm, safe reality at either end.

The city was very quiet. An empty streetcar far away screamed rustily, rang its cracked bell. An automobile horn bleated a reply.

A policeman down the block paused in his rounds to watch Henry, Anne, and Karpinsky. Feeling his protective gaze, Henry and Anne hesitated for an instant, then pressed on. They were committed to seeing the adventure through.

And it wasn't fear that was committing them to it anymore. Exhilaration was driving them now. Henry Davidson Merrill and Anne Lawson Heiler were suddenly, stunningly, dangerously, romantically leading lives of their own.

An old colored man, talking to himself, came from the opposite direction. He stopped and leaned against a building, still talking to himself, to watch them pass.

Henry and Anne met his gaze squarely. They were denizens of the night themselves.

And then Karpinsky opened a door. A steep stairway went up abruptly from the door. On the stair riser that was at eye level for a person standing on the street was a small sign. STANLEY KARPINSKY, M.S., it said, INDUSTRIAL CHEMIST, 3RD FLOOR.

Karpinsky watched Henry and Anne read the sign, and he seemed to draw strength from it. He sobered up, became respectable and grave, became the master of science that the sign proclaimed. He combed his hair with his fingers, straightened his coat.

Until that moment, Henry and Anne had thought of him as old. They could see now that Karpinsky's scrawniness wasn't a withering but a result of his having taken very bad care of himself.

He was only in his late twenties.

"I'll lead the way," said Karpinsky.

The walls of the stairway were sheathed in a bristly fiberboard. They smelled of cabbage. The building was an old house that had been divided into apartments.

It was the first unclean, unsafe building that Henry and Anne had ever been in.

As Karpinsky reached the second floor, an apartment door opened.

"George—that you?" said a woman peevishly. She stepped into the corridor, squinting. She was a big, stupid beast of a woman, holding her bathrobe closed with grubby fists. "Oh," she said, seeing Karpinsky, "the mad scientist—drunk again."

"Hello, Mrs. Purdy," said Karpinsky. He was blocking her view of Henry and Anne.

"You seen my George?" she said.

"No," said Karpinsky.

She smiled crookedly. "Made a million dollars yet?" she said.

"No—not yet, Mrs. Purdy," said Karpinsky.

"Better make it pretty quick," said Mrs. Purdy, "now that your mother's too sick to support you anymore."

"I expect to," said Karpinsky coolly. He stepped aside, letting her look at Henry and Anne on the stairs. "These are two good friends of mine, Mrs. Purdy," he said. "They think a great deal of my work."

Mrs. Purdy was thunderstruck.

"They've been dancing at the Athletic Club," said Karpinsky. "They heard my mother was very ill, and they decided to drop over to see her—to tell her how all the important people at the dance were talking about my experiments."

Mrs. Purdy opened her mouth and closed it again, without having made a sound.

Mrs. Purdy made a mirror of herself for Henry and Anne—showed them images of themselves that they'd never seen before. She showed them how enormously powerful they were, or would be. They had always known that they would be more comfortable and have more expensive pleasures than most—but it had never occurred to them that they would be more powerful, too.

That could be the only explanation of Mrs. Purdy's awe—that she was in awe of their power. "Nice—nice to know you," she said, keeping her eyes right on them. "Good night." She backed into her apartment and closed the door.

The home and the laboratory of Stanley Karpinsky, industrial chemist, were a single, drafty attic room—a room with the proportions of a shotgun. There were two tiny windows, one in each of the gable ends. They rattled in their frames.

The ceiling of the room was wood, the boards of the roof itself, rising to meet at the rooftree. The studs of the wall were bare. Shelves had been nailed between the studs, supporting a meager food supply, a microscope, books, reagent bottles, test tubes, beakers . . .

A great walnut dining table with lions'-claw feet was in the exact center of the room, with a shaded lightbulb over it. This was Karpinsky's laboratory table. A complex system of ring stands, flasks, glass tubing, and burettes was set up on it.

"Whisper," said Karpinsky, as he turned on the light over the table. He put his finger to his lips, and nodded meaningfully at a bed tucked under the eaves. The bed was so deep in shadows that it might have gone unnoticed, if Karpinsky hadn't pointed it out. His mother was sleeping there.

She did not stir. Her breathing was slow. Each time she exhaled, she seemed to be saying, "Thee."

Karpinsky touched the apparatus on the lion-clawed table—touched it with emotions that plainly teetered between love and hate.

"This," whispered Karpinsky, "is what everyone at the Athletic Club was talking about tonight. The captains of finance and industry could talk of nothing else." He raised his eyebrows quizzically. "Your father said I was going to be very rich on account of this, didn't he?" he said to Henry.

Henry managed a smile.

"Say yes," said Karpinsky.

Henry and Anne said nothing for fear of involving their fathers in an unprofitable business enterprise.

"Don't you see what this is?" whispered Karpinsky, his eyes wide. He was playing the magician now. "You mean it isn't self-evident?"

Henry and Anne exchanged glances, shook their heads.

"It's my mother's and father's dream come true," said Karpinsky. "It's what made their son rich and famous. Think of it—they were humble peasants in a strange land, unable to even read or write. But they worked hard in this land of promise, and every tearstained penny they got they put into an education for their son. They sent him not only to high school, but to college! Not only to college, but to graduate school! Now look at him—how successful he is!"

Henry and Anne were too young, too innocent, to recognize Karpinsky's performance for what it was—bloodcurdling satire. They looked at his apparatus gravely, and were prepared to believe that it really would make a fortune.

Karpinsky watched them for a reaction. And, when he got none, he flabbergasted them by bursting into tears. He made as though to grab the apparatus and hurl it to the floor. He stopped just short of doing that, one hand fighting with the other.

"Do I have to spell it out for you?" he whispered. "My father worked himself to death for my future; my mother is dying, killed by the same thing. And now, college degrees and all, I can't even get a job as a dishwasher!"

He closed in on the apparatus with his hands again, again seemed on the verge of destroying it. "This?" he said wistfully. He shook his head. "I don't know. Maybe it's something and maybe it isn't. Take years and thousands of dollars to find out." He looked toward the bed. "My mother hasn't got years to see me be a big success," he said. "She hasn't even got days, probably. She's going to the hospital for an operation tomorrow, and they tell me she hasn't got much of a chance of coming back."

Now the woman awakened. She didn't move, but she spoke her son's name.

"So I've got to be a big success tonight or never," said Karpinsky. "Stand there and admire the apparatus—look at it as though it were the most wonderful thing you ever laid eyes on, while I tell her you are millionaires, and you've come to buy the apparatus for a fortune!"

He went to his mother's side, knelt by the bed, and told her the good news in exulting Polish.

Henry and Anne went to the apparatus self-consciously, their arms limp at their sides.

Now Karpinsky's mother sat up, exclaiming.

Henry smiled glassily at the apparatus. "It's very nice, isn't it?" he said.

"Oh, yes—isn't it?" said Anne.

"Smile!" said Henry.

"What?" said Anne.

"Smile—look happy!" said Henry. It was the first order he had ever given her.

Anne was startled, and then she smiled.

"He's a great success," said Henry. "It's a wonderful thing."

"It's going to make him so rich," said Anne.

"His mother should be very proud of him," said Henry.

"She wants to meet you," said Karpinsky.

Henry and Anne went to the foot of the old woman's bed. She was speechless and radiant.

Karpinsky was wildly happy, too. His deception had paid off stunningly. In less than a minute, his mother had received her full reward, a perfectly gorgeous reward, for a life of awful sacrifices. Her joy shot with the speed of light into her past, illuminating every wretched moment of it with great joy.

"Tell her your names," said Karpinsky. "Any names. Doesn't make any difference."

Henry bowed. "Henry Davidson Merrill," he said.

"Anne Lawson Heiler," said Anne.

It would have been a shame to use any names other than the true ones. What Henry and Anne had just done was, after all, perfectly beautiful—and the first thing they had ever done that was likely to be noticed in Heaven.

Karpinsky made his mother lie down. He went over the good news for her again—crooningly.

She closed her eyes.

Henry and Anne and Karpinsky, their eyes shining, tiptoed away from her, toward the door.

And then the cops broke in.

There were three of them—one with his gun drawn, the other two with their clubs ready. They grabbed Karpinsky.

Right behind them came Henry's and Anne's fathers in tuxedos. They were wild with fear—fear that something awful had happened or was about to happen to their children. They had reported Henry's and Anne's disappearance as a kidnapping.

Karpinsky's mother sat up in bed, saw her son in the hands of the police. This was the last picture to be recorded in her mind in life. Karpinsky's mother groaned and died.

Ten minutes later, it was no longer possible to speak of Henry, Anne, and Karpinsky in a common action, in the same room, or even, poetically, in the same universe.

Karpinsky and the police worked hopelessly to revive Karpinsky's mother. Henry walked dazedly out of the building, with his appalled father begging him to stop and listen. Anne burst into tears that let her think of nothing. She was easily led by her father to his waiting car.

Six hours later, Henry was still walking. He had reached the edge of the city, and the sun was coming up. He had done curious things to his evening clothes. He had thrown away his black tie and his cuff links and his shirt studs. He had rolled up his shirtsleeves, and had ripped the starched white bosom of his shirt, so that it looked something like an ordinary shirt opened at the throat. His once glossy black shoes were the color of city mud.

He looked like a very young bum, which is what he had decided to be. A police cruiser finally found him, took him home. He didn't have a civil word for anybody, and he wouldn't listen. He wasn't a child anymore. He was a badly jangled man.

◉ ◉ ◉

Anne cried herself to sleep. And then, just about the time Henry was being brought home, she cried herself awake again.

The light of dawn in her room was as pale as skimmed milk. In that light, Anne saw a vision. Anne's vision was of a book. The name of the author was her own. In the book, Anne Lawson Heiler told the truth about the shallowness and cowardice and hypocrisy of the rich people in the city.

She thought of the first two lines in the book: "There was a depression on. Most of the people in the city were poor and heartbroken, but there was dancing at the Athletic Club." She felt much better. She went back to sleep again.

Just about the time Anne went back to sleep, Stanley Karpinsky opened a window in his attic room. He took the apparatus from the table with the lion's-claw feet, and he dropped the apparatus out the window piece by piece. Then he dropped his books and his microscope and all the rest of his equipment. He took a long time doing it, and some of the things made quite a racket when they hit the street.

Somebody finally called the police about a crazy man dropping things out of a window. When the police came, and they found out who it was that was dropping things, they didn't say anything to Karpinsky about it. They just cleaned up the mess in the street as best they could—cleaned it up sheepishly.

Henry slept until noon that day. And when he got up, he got out of the house before anyone knew he was awake. His mother, a sweet, sheltered person, heard his car start, heard his tires swish in gravel, and he was gone.

Henry drove with elaborate caution, dramatizing every motion he made in controlling the car. He felt that he had a terribly important errand to run—but he wasn't sure what the errand was. His driving, then, took on the importance of the nameless errand.

He arrived at Anne's house while she was eating breakfast. The attitude of the maid who let Henry in was that Anne was a pathetic invalid. This was hardly the case. Anne was eating with gusto, and was writing in a school notebook between bites.

She was writing her novel—angrily.

Anne's mother sat across the table from her, uneasily respecting the unfamiliar rites of creativity. The savagery of her daughter's pencil strokes offended her, frightened her. She knew what the writing was about. Anne had let her read some of it.

Anne's mother was delighted to see Henry. She had always liked Henry—and she was sure Henry would help her to change Anne's very bad mood. "Oh, Henry, dear," she said, "have you heard the good news? Did your mother tell you?"

"I haven't seen my mother," said Henry stolidly.

Anne's mother wilted. "Oh," she said. "I—I talked with her on the phone three times this morning. She's looking forward to having a long talk with you—about what happened."

"Um," said Henry. "What's the good news, Mrs. Heiler?"

"They got him a job," said Anne. "Isn't that swell?" Her wry expression made it clear that she thought the news was something less than swell. She thought Henry was something less than swell, too.

"That poor man—last night—Mr. Karpinsky," said Anne's mother, "he has a job, a wonderful job. Your father and Anne's father got on the phone this morning, and they got Ed Buchwalter to hire him at Delta Chemical." Her soft brown eyes begged Henry moistly to agree that there was nothing wrong in the world that could not be repaired easily. "Isn't that nice, Henry?" she said.

"I—I guess it's better than nothing," said Henry. He didn't feel a great deal better.

His apathy crushed Anne's mother. "What else could anyone *do*, Henry?" she said beseechingly. "What do you children want us to do next? We feel awful. We're doing everything we can for the poor man. If there were anything we could do for the poor woman, we would. It was all an accident, and anybody in our position would have done the same thing—with all the kidnappings and murders and I don't know what all in the papers." She began to weep. "And Anne's writing a book as though we were some kind of criminals, and you come in here and can't even smile, no matter what anybody tells you."

"The book doesn't say you're any criminal," said Anne.

"It certainly isn't very *complimentary*," said Anne's mother. "You make it sound as though your father and I and Henry's father and mother and the Buchwalters and the Wrightsons and everybody were just tickled pink so many people were out of work." She shook her head. "I'm not. I think the Depression is sickening, just sickening. How do you want us to act?" she asked pipingly.

"The book isn't about you," said Anne. "It's about me. I'm the worst person in it."

"You're a *nice* person!" said Anne's mother. "A *very* nice person." She stopped weeping now, smiled twitteringly, moved her elbows up and down as though they were the wing tips of a happy little bird. "Can't we all cheer up, children? Isn't everything going to be all right?" She turned to Henry. "Smile, Henry?"

Henry knew the kind of smile she wanted, and, twenty-four hours before, he would have given it to her automatically—the kind of smile a child gave a grown-up for kissing a hurt well. He didn't smile.

The most important thing to Henry was to demonstrate to Anne that he wasn't the shallow booby she apparently thought he was. Not smiling helped—but something more manly, more decisive was called for. It suddenly dawned on him what the nameless errand was that he'd set out upon. "Mrs. Heiler," he said, "I think maybe Anne and I should go see Mr. Karpinsky, and tell him how sorry we are."

"No!" said Anne's mother. It was sharp and quick—too sharp, too quick. There was panic in it. "I mean," she said, making erasing motions with her hands, "it's all taken care of. Your fathers have already been down to talk to him. They apologized to him and told him about the job and . . ." Her voice trailed off. It was apparent even to her what she was really saying.

She was really saying that she could not stand the idea of Henry's and Anne's growing up—the idea of their ever looking closely at tragedy. She was saying that she herself had never grown up, had never looked closely at tragedy. She was saying that the most beautiful thing money could buy was a childhood a lifetime long—

Anne's mother turned away. Her turning away was the closest she could come to telling Henry and Anne to go see Karpinsky and his tragedy, if they felt they had to.

Henry and Anne went.

◎ ◎ ◎

Stanley Karpinsky was in his room. He was sitting at the big table with the lion's-claw feet. He was staring into the middle distance, his thumb tips clamped lightly between his teeth. Heaped on the table before him were the few things that had survived the drop from the window at dawn. Karpinsky had salvaged what he could—mostly books in sprung bindings.

Karpinsky now listened to two people coming up the stairs. His door was open, so there was no need to knock. Henry and Anne simply appeared in the doorway.

"Well," said Karpinsky, rising, "the King and Queen of the Universe. I couldn't be more surprised. Come in."

Henry bowed stiffly. "We—we wanted to tell you how sorry we are," he said.

Karpinsky bowed in reply. "Thank you very much," he said.

"Very sorry," said Anne.

"Thank you," said Karpinsky.

There followed an embarrassed silence. Henry and Anne had apparently prepared no speeches other than their first ones, and yet seemed to expect great things of their visit.

Karpinsky was at a loss as to what to say next. Of all the players in the tragedy, Henry and Anne had certainly been the most innocent, the most faceless. "Well!" said Karpinsky. "How about some coffee?"

"All right," said Henry.

Karpinsky went to the gas burner, lit it, put water on. "I have a swell job now," he said. "Suppose you heard." He was no more overjoyed by this belated piece of good luck than Henry and Anne had been.

There was no response from Henry and Anne.

Karpinsky turned to look at them, to guess, if he could, what it was they expected from him. With great difficulty, rising above his own troubles, Karpinsky caught on. They had had a soul-shaking brush with life and death, and now they wanted to know what it had all meant.

Karpinsky, ransacking his brain for some foolish tidbit of thought to give them, surprised himself by finding something of real importance.

"You know," he said, "if we had fooled her last night, I would have considered my life at a satisfactory end, with all debts paid. I would have wound up on skid row, or maybe I would have been a suicide." He shrugged and smiled sadly. "Now," he said, "if I'm ever going to square things with her, I've got to believe in a Heaven, I've got to believe she can look down and see me, and I've got to be a big success for her to see."

This was profoundly satisfying to Henry and Anne—and to Karpinsky, too.

Three days later, Henry told Anne he loved her. Anne told him she loved him, too. They had told each other that before, but this was the first time it had meant a little something. They had finally seen a little something of life.

$10,000 a Year, Easy

"SO YOU'RE FINALLY MOVING, EH?" said Gino Donnini. He was a small, fierce-looking man, who had once been a brilliant operatic tenor. His brilliance was gone now, and, in his sixties, he gave voice lessons in order to pay for his cluttered apartment under mine, a little food and wine, and expensive cigars. "One by one my young friends are going. How will I stay young now?"

"I'd think you'd be glad to get somebody upstairs who wasn't tone-deaf."

"Aaaaaah—you make fine music inside. What's that book there?"

"I was just cleaning out our storage locker, Maestro, and found my old high-school annual." I opened the book to the checkerboard of faces and brief biographies that was the section devoted to the hundred and fifty seniors that year. "See how I've failed? They predicted I'd be a great novelist someday, and here I go to work for the telephone company as a maintenance engineer."

"Aha," said Gino, examining the book, "what great expectations these American children have." He had been an American for forty years, but still regarded himself as a puzzled outsider. "This fat little boy was going to be a millionaire, and this girl the first woman Speaker of the House."

"Now he runs a grocery, and she's his wife."

"Lo! how the mighty are fallen. And here's Nicky! I keep forgetting you two were classmates."

Nicky Marino had come to study voice with Gino, an old friend of his father, after the war, and he'd found an apartment for me in the same building when I'd decided to get an engineering degree under the G.I. Bill. "Well," I said, "the prediction for Nicky has held up beautifully."

"A great tenor," read Gino, "like his father."

"Or like you, Maestro."

Gino shook his head. "He was better. You can't imagine. I could play you records, and as bad as recording was in those days, Nicky's father's voice comes through more thrilling than anything you'll hear today. Generations can go by without knowing a miracle like that voice. And then he had to die at twenty-nine."

"Thank God he left a son."

In the small town in which Nicky and I'd grown up, everyone knew whose son

Nicky was—and no one doubted that he'd make our town famous as soon as he was full grown. No civic occasion was complete without his singing whatever was appropriate. His mother, herself an unmusical businesswoman, spent most of her money on voice and language lessons for Nicky, recreating in him the image of her lost husband.

"Yes," said Gino, "thank God he left a son. Will you have a farewell drink with me, or is it too soon after breakfast?"

"This isn't quite farewell. We don't move for two more days. I'll take a rain check on the drink, thanks. Now I've got to return some books to Nicky."

◎ ◎ ◎

Nicky Marino was in the shower, singing with the volume of a steam calliope when I arrived. I sat down in the one-room apartment to wait.

The walls were covered with photographs of his father, and with old posters headed by his father's name. On the table, beside a pot of coffee, a cracked cup in a cigarette-filled saucer, and a metronome, was a scrapbook, its edges festooned with the ragged ends of newspaper clippings about his father.

On the floor were his garish pajamas and the morning mail—a letter with a check and a snapshot clipped to it. It was from his mother, who never wrote without enclosing some memento of his father from a seemingly inexhaustible store of souvenirs. The check was from the earnings of her small gift shop, and, little as the check was, Nicky had to make it last, for he had no other income.

"How did that sound?" said Nicky, stepping from the bathroom, his big, dark, slow body glistening wet.

"How should I know? All I can tell is the difference between loud and soft. It was very loud." I'd lied to Gino about returning a book to Nicky. What I was after was ten dollars Nicky'd owed me for three months. "Look, about the ten bucks—"

"You'll get it!" he said expansively. "Everybody who was good to Nicky as an unknown will be rich when Nicky is rich."

He wasn't joking. His mother talked the same way—without a trace of uncertainty about his future. He had been talking and hearing himself talked about in this way all his life. Sometimes, he behaved as though he'd already reached the top.

"That's nice of you, Nicky, but I'll let you off the hook now for ten dollars, and then you won't have to make me rich later. You can keep it all yourself."

"Are you being sarcastic?" said Nicky. He stopped grinning. "Are you trying to tell me that the day won't come when—"

"No, no—hold on. It'll come, I guess. How should I know? All I want is my ten dollars, so I can rent a truck to move my stuff."

"Money!"

"What can you do without it? Ellen and I can't move."

"I've always done without it," said Nicky. "First the war takes four years out of my life, pft! And now money troubles."

"Then ten bucks would take years out of your life?"

"Ten, a hundred, a thousand." He sat down dejectedly. "Gino says it's showing up in my voice—the insecurity. I sing of happiness, he says, and insecurity shows through—poisons it. I sing of unhappiness, and it spoils that, too, because my real unhappiness isn't great or noble but cheap—money unhappiness."

"Gino said that? I thought the worse off an artist was financially, the better he was artistically."

Nicky snorted. "The richer they get, the better they get—especially singers."

"I was kidding, Nicky."

"Pardon me if I don't laugh. People who sell bolts and nuts and locomotives and frozen orange juice make billions, while the people who struggle to bring a little beauty into the world, give life a little meaning, they starve."

"You're not starving, are you?"

"No, not physically," he admitted, patting his belly. "But my spirit is starving for security, a few extras, a little pride."

"Uh huh."

"Oooooooh, what do you know about it? You're set—pension plan, automatic raises, free insurance for everything you can think of."

"I hesitate to mention this, Nicky," I said, "but—"

"I know, I know, I know! You're going to say why don't I get a job."

"I was going to be diplomatic about it. Not give up voice, understand, but pick up a little cash and security while you're studying with Gino, while you're getting ready for the big push. You can't sing all the time."

"I must and do."

"All right, then, get a job out-of-doors."

"And get bronchitis. Besides, you can imagine what working for somebody else would do to my spirit—licking boots, saying yes all the time, grovelling."

"Pretty terrible, all right, working for somebody."

There was a knock on the door, and Gino walked in. "Oh—you still here? Brought the morning paper, Nicky. I've read it."

"Talking about insecurity, Maestro," I said.

"Yes," said Gino thoughtfully, "it's something to talk about, all right. It's broken greater spirits than ours, and robbed the world of God knows how much beauty. I've seen it happen more times than I like to think about."

"It's not going to happen to me!" said Nicky passionately.

"What are you going to do?" said Gino. He shrugged. "Go into business? You're too much of an artist. If you were going to go ahead and try it anyway, I suppose the place to start would be in the want-ad section. But no—I'm against it. It's beneath you. You could get in and maybe make your fortune and get out again, and give your full attention to voice—but no, I don't like it, and I feel responsible for you."

Nicky sighed. "Give me the paper. The average man doesn't even suspect the price an artist pays to bring beauty into his life. Now the son of Angelo Marino is going into business." He turned to me to berate me as a representative of average men everywhere. "You understand what that means?"

"I've adopted a wait-and-see policy," I said.

"Nicky," said Gino gravely, "you've got to promise me one thing: that you won't let business get the better of you, that you'll keep the real end in view—your singing."

Nicky banged his fist on the table. "By God, Gino—here I thought you knew me better than anybody else on earth, next to my mother, and you say a thing like that!"

"Sorry."

"Now what's the stupid paper got to say for itself?"

On the day of our move from the apartment, Nicky insisted on my paying attention to matters far more important than my own piddling affairs—his affairs. He had been tramping the streets for two days, investigating likely ads in the Business Opportunities section.

"Where would I get a thousand dollars?" I grunted, as I lifted a chair onto the rented truck.

He made no effort to help, and stood by with an expression of annoyance, as though I had no business dividing my attention. "Five hundred, then."

"You're crazy. I'm in hock for my car, the new house, and the baby. If turkey was five cents a pound, I couldn't buy the beak."

"How on earth am I going to buy this doughnut shop?" he asked irritably.

"What the hell am I, the Guggenheim Foundation?"

"The bank'll lend me four, if I'll put in four," said Nicky. "You're passing up a chance of a lifetime. This lousy little shop nets ten thousand a year. The man proved it to me. Ten thousand a year, easy," he said, awe in his voice. "Twenty-seven dollars a day, every day. There it is, just waiting. Machines make the doughnuts; you buy the mix in bags, and sit around making change."

Gino came out of my apartment, carrying two lamps. "Back from the bank, Nicky?"

"They'll only lend me half, Gino. Can you beat it? They want me to put up four thousand, too."

"A nice wad, four thousand," said Gino.

"Peanuts!" said Nicky. "The owner's been making ten G's, even though he doesn't advertise or make a decent cup of coffee or try new flavors or—" He stopped short, and his enthusiasm decayed. "You know," he said flatly, "the stupid things businessmen have to do to make a thing go. Well, the hell with it, anyway."

"Just forget the ten thousand a year," said Gino.

An hour later, as I climbed into the cab of the truck and started the engine, Nicky came running out of his apartment. "Shut off the motor!"

Obediently, I did. "For the last time, Nicky, I can't even afford the ten you already owe me."

"I don't need it," he said.

"Given up? Good. I think you're wise."

"Someone else put up the money as a silent partner. The bank told him about me."

"Who put up the dough?"

"He wants to be known only as a friend of opera," said Nicky triumphantly. "Just like the artists in the old days, I've got a patron."

"First patron of art in history to underwrite a doughnut manufacturer."

"That's not the point!"

"Nicky," called Gino from his basement door. "What are you yelling about?"

Nicky looked at him sadly, ashamed. "I'm in business, Maestro."

"You've got to suffer to be great," said Gino.

Nicky nodded. "I'll use another name. It wouldn't do to use the name of Marino."

"I should say not," said Gino.

"Jeffrey," said Nicky thoughtfully, "George B. Jeffrey."

"Get out there and sell, George," said Gino.

While my new life never came in contact with Nicky's new life, I had only to pick up a paper to see that he was still in business. He had a small ad in almost every issue, and I was amazed by the variety of things he had to say in favor of doughnuts.

"Maybe we should make a point of going over and buying some," said Ellen, my wife, at breakfast one morning. "Maybe he's hurt that we haven't."

"Nothing would hurt him more than if we showed up there," I said. "He's humiliated enough, without his old friends looking in on him. The time to visit him is when this is all behind him, when he's either made a pile or been cleaned out, and is back studying with Gino."

That morning, which was about six months after Nicky'd decided to prostitute himself, I was waiting for a bus by a stoplight, and it seemed to me that someone had his car radio turned up annoyingly loud. I looked up from my paper to be surprised by a doughnut six feet high, with four wheels, a windshield, and bumpers.

Inside sat Nicky, his head back, his white teeth flashing, singing. The mad joy of the song got through to me, even if the melody didn't. "Nick, boy!" I called.

The song stopped, and he became glum, sardonic. He waved, and opened the side of the doughnut. "Come on, I'll give you a lift downtown."

"Don't go out of your way. Your shop's just down three blocks, isn't it?"

"I have business downtown," he said gloomily.

I found that inside the doughnut was a jeep, the back of which was filled with racks of doughnuts, iced in many colors. "Mmmmm. Don't those look good!"

"All right, rub it in."

"They really do look wonderful."

"In six more months I sell out, and if anybody ever offers me a doughnut, I'll break his back."

"You sounded happy enough back there by the light."

"Laugh, clown, laugh."

"Through the tears, eh? Business that bad?"

"Business! Who wants to talk about business?" said Nicky.

"How's music?"

"Haaaah, music. Gino says the security is helping."

"Good boy! So you're getting security."

"A little—some, maybe. Gino wants me to take my money and get out."

"But you said you were sticking with it another six months."

"Trapped," he said bitterly. "My partner, the great friend of opera, fixed things so I can't sell without his permission. Lord! What a babe in the woods I was!"

"Gosh, that's too bad. What's his name?"

"Lord knows. The bank represents him."

"Anyway, sounds like you're doing fine."

"It *would* sound that way to you," said Nicky. "You're the kind of guy that ought to be in this business, not me. You're the kind that'd love it—watching the competition, figuring new angles, new lines, new come-ons, all that nonsense." He clapped me on the knee. "Twentieth-century man! Thank your lucky stars you weren't born with talent."

"Nice, all right. Mind my asking what you're going downtown for?"

"Oh—one of the milk companies is kind of thinking about delivering our doughnuts in the morning along with milk. They want to see me."

"Kind of thinking of doing it?"

"They're going to do it," he said absently.

"Nicky! You'll be smothered with cash. You're a ball of fire in business. A natural!"

"How insensitive can you be?"

"Didn't mean to be offensive. Mind if I have a doughnut?"

"Take a light green one," said Nicky.

"Poisoned?"

"New flavor we're trying out."

I bit into it. "Boy! Mint. Good, huh?"

"Really like it?" he asked eagerly.

"What do you care, artist?"

"If I'm trapped, I might as well make the best of it."

"Well, keep a stiff upper lip. Here's where I get out."

He stopped, but he didn't look at me when I got out. He was staring at something across the street. "That lying son of a gun," he murmured, and pulled away.

Across the street was a restaurant, over which was written in electric lamps, "The Best Cup of Coffee in Town."

On my birthday, just after Easter, a package from Nicky arrived. I hadn't seen him for almost a year, and supposed that his silent partner had let him sell out by now, and that, rich as the devil, he was once more studying full-time with Gino. The doughnuts-delivered-with-milk idea had worked out fine, as nearly as I could tell. I had a standing order with my milkman for a half dozen every three days—with mint icing.

The package, delivered in the evening, confirmed one part of the supposition, at least—that Nicky was rolling in money.

"What is it?" said Ellen.

"Big and heavy enough to be a tricycle," I said. I removed the gaudy wrappings, and was dazzled by a complete sterling tea service, the sort of thing I could imagine ambassadors giving as wedding presents to princesses.

"Good heavens!" said Ellen. "What's that taped to the tray?"

"A ten-dollar bill and a note." I read the note aloud: "'Bet you thought you'd never get it back. Thanks. Happy birthday. Nicky.'"

"This is embarrassing," said Ellen. "What would I do with it? Where could I put it?"

"We could pay off the mortgage with it." I shook my head. "Well, hell, this is ridiculous. I'm going to get him to take it back." Ellen rewrapped the present, and I drove down to Nicky's apartment with it.

I almost turned away from his door, thinking he'd moved, when I saw the name on the knocker—"George B. Jeffrey." And the noises inside were unfamiliar, too: dance music and women's voices. Nicky hadn't had much to do with women, except for his mother. The assumption, *his* assumption, was that women, hundreds of them and all beautiful and talented, would come his way automatically once his career was going full blast. That had been his father's experience, so it would certainly happen to Nicky, too.

Then I remembered that George B. Jeffrey was Nicky's business name, and I knocked. A uniformed maid, carrying a tray of martinis, opened the door. "Yes?"

Behind her I saw Nicky's one room. It was now spotless, and elegantly furnished in dark Victorian furniture. The scrapbook was still there on the table, but rebound in expensive-looking plush and leather. And the pictures of his father and the posters still covered the walls, but they were now protected by glass in massive gilt frames. The room looked more like a well-run museum than a studio.

The sounds of celebration puzzled me, because I couldn't see anyone in the room behind the maid, and the only rooms opening onto it were the bathroom, the kitchenette, and a closet. "Is Mr. Marino in?" I said.

"Mr. *Jeffrey*?" said the maid.

"Yes—Mr. Jeffrey. I'm a friend of his."

The heavy drapes on one side of the room parted, and Nicky appeared, flushed, happy, and I saw that the wall separating Nicky's old room from the next apartment had been knocked out, and that he now had a suite. The drapes closed behind him, so that I had only a glimpse of what lay beyond—a room hazy with smoke and laughter, garishly modern. It was like looking into a sunset from the mouth of a cave.

"Happy birthday, happy birthday," said Nicky.

"Celebrating the sale of your business?"

"Hmmm? Oh—no, not exactly," he said. As before, my intrusion into his new life seemed to sadden him. "No. Just having some business associates in." His voice dropped to a confidential whisper. "You have to do a little of this to keep things going smoothly."

"Still trapped?"

"Yep. Son of a gun, he's really got me. Maybe in six months—"

"Another deal on?"

"Just one darn thing after another," he said dismally. "An outfit from Milwaukee's trying to open up some shops here, so what can we do but extend our chain? Dog eat dog. But in six months, so help me, George B. Jeffrey's going to disappear, and Nicky Marino's going to be reborn."

"Georgie, boy, sing us a song," called a woman from the other room.

It was plain that Nicky didn't want me to meet his business associates, that he didn't want me to go into the other room. But the woman opened the drapes to call to him again, and I got another look at the door. The walls, I saw, were decorated with framed ads, and over the fireplace was a caricature, a doughnut with Nicky's features, grinning, cocky, happy.

"Look, Nicky, I came about this tea service. It was a wonderful thing to do, but listen, it's too much. Really, we—"

He was restless, seemingly eager to get me out and get back to the party. "No—I want you to have it. You deserve it, or I wouldn't have given it to you. Back in the old days, the ten dollars you gave me was a king's ransom." He started easing me to the door, in friendly fashion, but firmly. "You keep it, and tell Ellen hello from George."

"From who?"

"From Nicky." I was out in the hall again. He winked, and shut the door.

I walked slowly down the stairs with the ridiculous bushel of silver still in my arms, and knocked on Gino's door.

The old man opened the door a crack, smiled broadly, and welcomed me in.

"Greetings, Maestro. I thought maybe you'd moved. Your sign isn't out there anymore."

"Yes—I've taken it down at last, and retired."

"Nicky just threw me out."

"Mr. George B. Jeffrey threw you out. Nicky would never do a thing like that. What would you like to drink?" He had an amiable edge on. "I've got a good bottle of Irish a former student sent me. He's a very successful welder now."

"Lovely."

"Any other time of the year, even Christmas, I enjoy being alone," said Gino, making my drink. "But in the springtime it gets me, and there's nothing to do but quietly tie one on."

"Live!" cried Nicky outside, to the world in general. Gino and I watched the variegated feet of the doughnut king's entourage pass by the cellar window.

"Bears his cross well, don't you think?" said Gino.

"Must break your heart to watch it, doesn't it, Maestro?"

"It must? Why?"

"Seeing a promising artist like Nicky getting deeper and deeper into business, farther and farther from singing."

"Oh—*that*. He's happy, even if he says he isn't. That's the important thing."

"You sound like a traitor to art, if I ever heard one."

Gino poured himself another shot, and, on the way back to his chair, he leaned over and whispered in my ear, "The only way Nicky could ever serve the world of music is as an usher."

"Maestro!" I couldn't believe it. "You said he was the image of his—"

"He said it. His mother said it. I never did. I never contradicted them, that's all. That big lie was his whole life. If I'd told him he was no good, he might have killed himself. And we were getting to the point when I was going to have to tell him something."

"Then this doughnut business was the luckiest thing that ever happened," I said wonderingly. "He can go on believing he's going to be a great singer like his father, and the business keeps him from having to prove it."

"So be careful who you call a traitor to art," said Gino. He lifted his glass in a toast to an imaginary audience. "Last year I gave ten thousand dollars to the Civic Opera Association."

"Ten thousand."

"Peanuts," said Gino.

The din of Nicky's singing filled the apartment courtyard. He was alone now, having said farewell to his guests.

"Exit George B. Jeffrey, enter Nicky Marino," whispered Gino.

Nicky thrust his head through the doorway. "Spring, men! Earth is being reborn!"

"How's business, Nicky?" said Gino.

"Business! Who cares about business? Six more months, Maestro, and the hell with it." He winked and left.

"Ten thousand dollars is peanuts, Gino?" I said.

"Peanuts," said Gino grandly. "Peanuts for the half owner of the world's fastest-growing doughnut chain. Six more months, did he say? In six more months he and doughnuts will probably do as much for opera as his father ever did. Someday, maybe I'll tell him about it." He shook his head. "No, no—that would spoil everything, wouldn't it? No—I guess the whole rest of his life had better be an interlude between the promises his mother made him about himself and the moment when he'll make them all come true."

Money Talks

CAPE COD WAS IN A COCOON of cooling water and autumn mists. It was seven in the evening. The only lights that shone on Harbor Road came from the dancing flashlight of a watchman in the boatyard, from Ben Nickelson's grocery store, and from the headlights of a big, black, Cadillac sedan.

The Cadillac stopped in front of Ben's store. The well-bred thunder of its engine died. A young woman in a cheap cloth coat got out and went into the store. She was blooming with health and youth and the nip in the air, but very shy. Every step seemed to be an apology.

Ben's shaggy head was on his folded arms by the cash register. His ambition had run down. At twenty-seven, Ben was through. He'd lost his store to his creditors.

Ben raised his head and smiled without hope. "Can I help you, ma'am?"

Her reply was a whisper.

"How's that?" said Ben. "I didn't hear."

"Could you kindly tell me how to get to the Kilraine cottage?" she said.

"Cottage?" said Ben.

"That *is* what they call it, isn't it?" she said. "That's what it says on the key tags."

"That's what they call it, all right," said Ben. "I just never got used to it. Maybe that was a cottage to Joel Kilraine. I never saw what else he had to live in."

"Oh dear," she said. "Is it great big?"

"Nineteen rooms, a half mile of private beach, tennis courts, a swimming pool," said Ben. "No stables, though. Maybe that's why they call it a cottage."

She sighed. "I'd hoped it would be a sweet, cozy little thing."

"Sorry to disappoint you," said Ben. "What you do to get there is turn around, and go back the way you came, until you come to a—" He paused. "You don't know the village at all?"

"No."

"Well, it's awful hard to describe," said Ben. "It's kind of hidden away. I'd better lead you there with my truck."

"I don't want to be any trouble," she said.

"I'm closing up in a minute anyway," said Ben. "Haven't anything else to do."

"I'll need some groceries first," she said.

"My creditors will be very happy," said Ben. Loneliness and futility swept over him, and he looked the girl up and down. From her hands he learned she was a nail-biter. From her low-heeled, blocky white shoes, he gathered that she was some kind of servant, usually in uniform. He thought she was pretty, but he didn't like her for being so cowed.

"What are you—her housekeeper or something?" said Ben. "She send you up to find out what she's got here?"

"Who?" she said.

"The nurse—the Cinderella girl—the one who got the whole shebang," said Ben. "The girl with the million-dollar alcohol rubs. What's her name? Rose? Rose something?"

"Oh," she said. She nodded. "That's what I'm doing." She looked away from Ben to the shelves behind him. "Let's see—I'd like a can of beef-noodle soup, a can of tomato . . . a box of cornflakes . . . a loaf of bread, a pound of oleo—"

Ben gathered her groceries on the counter. He put the oleo down hard, slapping the waxed cardboard against the wood.

The girl jumped.

"Saaaaay—you're nervous as a cat," said Ben. "Rose make you that way? She that kind? Rose wants what she wants when she wants it?"

"Rose is just a plain, dumpy little nurse, who still doesn't know what hit her," she said stiffly. "She's scared to death."

"She'll get over that quick enough," said Ben. "They *all* do. Come next summer, Rose'll be strutting around here like she'd just invented gunpowder."

"I don't think she's that kind," she said. "I certainly hope not."

Ben smiled askance. "Just an angel of mercy," he said. He winked. "By God, for twelve million bucks, *I'd* have nursed him, wouldn't *you?*"

"Rose had no idea he was going to leave her everything," she said.

Ben leaned back against the shelves, pretending to be crucified. "Oh, come now—come, come," he said.

"A lonely old man on his deathbed in a big apartment on Park Avenue—hanging on to life, begging for life, begging for somebody to care." He saw the scene vividly. "Kilraine calls out in the night, and who comes?" Ben smiled demurely. "*Rose*—the angel of mercy. She fluffs his pillow, rubs his back, tells him everything's going to be fine, and gives him his sleeping pills. She's the whole world to him."

Ben waggled his finger at the girl. "And you mean to tell me it didn't pop into Rose's little head that maybe he might leave her just a little something to remember him by?"

She dropped her gaze to the floor. "It might have crossed her mind," she murmured.

"Might?" said Ben triumphantly. "It *did*—and I don't mean once; I mean *hundreds* of times." He added up her bill. "I've never laid eyes on her," he said, "but, if

there's one thing I learned about in this business, it's how the human mind works."
He looked up. "Two ninety-five."

He was amazed to see tears on the rims of her eyes.

"Oh, hey—say, now," said Ben remorsefully. He touched her. "Gosh—hey, listen—don't mind me."

"I don't think it's very *nice* for you to talk that way about people you don't even know," she said tautly.

Ben nodded. "You're right, you're right. Don't mind me. You picked a lousy time to come in. I was looking around for something to hit. Why, hell—Rose is probably the salt of the earth."

"I didn't say that," she said. "I never claimed that."

"Well, whatever it was you *did* claim," said Ben. "Don't pay any attention to me." He shook his head, and he wondered at the two dead years in the grocery store. Anxiety and a million nagging details had held him prisoner all that time, numbed him, dried him out. There'd been no time for love or play—no time, even, for thoughts of them.

He worked his fingers, unsure that love and playfulness would ever come back into them.

"I shouldn't be ragging a nice girl like you," he said. "I should give you a smile and a gardenia."

"Gardenia?" she said.

"Sure," said Ben. "When I opened up two years ago, I gave every lady customer a smile and a gardenia. Since you're my last customer, seems like you ought to get a little something, too." He gave her the opening-day smile.

The smile and the offer of a gardenia pleased and confused the poor, pretty mouse of a girl, and made her blush.

Ben was fascinated. "Gee," he said, "now you make me *really* sorry the florist shop is closed."

Her pleasure went on and on, and so did Ben's. Ben could almost smell the gardenia, could almost see her pinning it on, her hands all thumbs.

"You're selling your store?" she said.

There was radiance between them now. There were overtones and undertones to everything they said. The talk itself was formal, lifeless.

"The business failed," said Ben. It didn't matter much anymore.

"What are you going to do now?" she said.

"Dig clams," said Ben, "unless you've got a better idea." He cocked his head, and, with the control of an actor, he showed in his face how keenly hungry for a girl he was.

Her fingers tightened on her purse, but she didn't look away. "Is that hard work?" she said.

"Cold work," said Ben. "Lonely work, out there with a fork."

"Is there a living in it?" she said.

"The way *I* live," said Ben. "No wife, no kids—no bad habits. Won't make as much as old man Kilraine spent on cigars."

"Toward the end, all he had was his cigars," she said.

"And his nurse," said Ben.

"He's dead, and you're young and alive," she said.

"Eeeeeeeeeeyup," said Ben. "Guess I'm the big winner after all."

He picked up her small bag of groceries, went outside, and saw the big car she'd come in.

"Rose let you take *this* big boat?" he said. "What does that leave her?"

"It's embarrassing," she said. "It's too big. It makes me want to hide under the dashboard when I go through towns."

Ben opened the front door for her, and she slid into the leather chauffeur's seat. She seemed no bigger than a ten-year-old, dwarfed by the great steering wheel and instrument panel.

Ben set the groceries on the floor beside her, and he sniffed. "If ghosts had smells," he said, "that's what the ghost of Joel Kilraine would smell like—*cigars*." He wasn't about to say goodbye to her. He sat down beside her, as though resting and gathering his thoughts. "You ever hear how he made his money? Clear back in 1922, he figured out that—" His words trailed off as he saw that the spell was broken, that she was about to cry again.

"Miss," said Ben helplessly, "you sure cry *easy*."

"I cry all the time," she said pipingly. "Everything makes me cry. I can't help it."

"About what?" said Ben. "What's there to cry about?"

"About *everything*," she said wretchedly. "I'm Rose," she said, "and everything makes me want to cry."

Ben's world yawed, shimmered, and righted itself. "You?" he said softly. "Rose? Twelve million dollars? Cloth coat? Cornflakes? Oleo margarine? Look at your purse! The patent leather's all chipping off."

"That's how I've always lived," she said.

"You haven't lived very long," said Ben.

"I feel like Alice in Wonderland," said Rose, "where she shrank and shrank and shrank until *everything* was too big for her."

Ben chuckled emptily. "You'll grow back," he said.

She rubbed her eyes. "I think Mr. Kilraine must have done it as some kind of joke on the world—making somebody like me so rich." She was trembling, white.

Ben took her arm firmly, to calm her.

She went limp gratefully. Her eyes glazed over. "Nobody to turn to, nobody to trust, nobody who understands," she said in a singsong. "I've never been so lonely and tired and scared in all my life. Everybody yammering, yammering, yammering." She closed her eyes and lay back like a rag doll.

"Would a drink help?" said Ben.

"I—I don't know," she said dully.

"*Do* you drink?" said Ben.

"Once," she said.

"Do you want to try again, Rose?" said Ben.

"Maybe—maybe that would help," she said. "Maybe. I dunno. I'm so sick of thinking, I'll just do anything anybody tells me to do."

Ben licked his lips. "I'll go get my truck and a bottle my creditors don't know about," he said. "Then you follow me."

Ben put away Rose's groceries in the vast kitchen of the Kilraine cottage. The tidbits were lost in canyons of porcelain and steel.

He mixed two drinks from his bottle, and carried them into the entrance hall. Rose, her coat still on, lay on the spiral staircase, looking at her wedding-cake ceiling far above.

"I got the oil burner going," said Ben. "It'll be a while before we feel it."

"I don't think I'll ever feel anything again," said Rose. "Nothing means anything anymore. There's too much of everything."

"Keep breathing," said Ben. "That's the big thing for now."

Rose inhaled and exhaled rattlingly.

Some of what she felt began to creep into Ben's bones, too. He had a spooky sense of a third person in the house—not the shade of Joel Kilraine, but the phantasm of twelve million dollars. Neither Rose nor Ben could speak without a polite, nervous nod to the Kilraine fortune. And the twelve million, a thousand dollars a day at three percent, took full advantage of their awe. It let nothing go by without comment—without giving the conversation a hard, rude wrench.

"Well, here we are," said Ben, giving Rose her drink.

"And here *I* am," said the twelve million dollars.

"Two sleepy people—" said Ben.

"I never sleep," said the Kilraine fortune.

"Fate's a funny thing," said Ben, "bring us together like this tonight."

"Heh heh heh," said the twelve million. The *heh*s were spaced far apart, and the sarcasm in them squawked like rusty hinges.

"What's this house and everything got to do with me?" said Rose. "I'm just a plain, ordinary person."

"With a plain, ordinary twelve million simoleons," said the Kilraine fortune.

"Sure you are," said Ben. "Just like the girls I used to go around with in high school."

"Only with twelve million iron men," said the Kilraine fortune.

"I was happy with what I had," said Rose. "I'd graduated from nursing school— was making my own way. I had nice friends, and a green '49 Chevy that was almost paid for."

The twelve million let out a long, wet raspberry.

"And I was *helping* people," said Rose.

"Like you *helped* Kilraine for twelve million spondulics," said the twelve million. Ben drank thirstily. So did Rose.

"I think it speaks very well for you that you feel the way you do," said Ben.

"And somebody's going to bamboozle her out of the whole works, if she doesn't brighten up," said the twelve million.

Ben rolled his eyes. "Gee—it's funny about troubles," he said. "You got troubles, I got troubles—everybody's got troubles, whether they've got a lot of money or a little money or no money. When you get right down to it, I guess love and friendship and doing good really *are* the big things."

"Still, it might be kind of interesting to shuffle the money around," said the twelve million, "just to see if somebody might not get happier."

Ben and Rose covered their ears at the same time.

"Let's get some music in this mausoleum," said Ben. He went into the living room, loaded the big phonograph with records, and turned the volume up loud. For a moment, he thought he'd driven the Kilraine fortune away. For a moment, he was free to appreciate Rose for what she was—pink, sweet, and affectionate.

And then the twelve million dollars started singing along with the music. "Bewa, scratch, and lucre," it sang. "Mopus, oof, and chink; Jack and bucks and rhino; Bawbees, specie, clink."

"Dance?" said Ben wildly. "Rose—you wanna dance?"

They didn't dance. They huddled together to music in a corner of the living room. Ben's arms ached, he was so grateful to have Rose in them. She was what he needed. With his store and his credit gone, only a woman's touch could make him whole.

And he knew he was what Rose needed, too. He pitted muscle against muscle, to make himself hard and bulging. Rose fawned against the rock he was.

Bundled up in each other, their heads down, they could almost ignore the hulla-baloo from the Kilraine fortune. But the twelve million dollars still seemed to prance around them, singing, cracking wise—hell-bent on being the life of the party.

Ben and Rose talked in whispers, hoping to keep a little something private.

"It's a funny thing about time," said Ben. "I think maybe that's the next big thing science is going to turn up."

"How you mean?" said Rose.

"Well, *you* know—" said Ben. "Sometimes two years seems like ten minutes. Sometimes ten minutes seems like two years."

"Like when?" said Rose.

"Like now, for instance," said Ben.

"How like now?" said Rose, letting him know with her tone that she was way ahead of him. "How you mean?"

"I mean," said Ben, "it seems like we've been dancing for hours. Seems like I've known you all my life."

"That's funny," said Rose.

"How you mean?" said Ben.

"I feel the same way," murmured Rose.

Ben caromed back through time to his high school senior prom—when childhood had ended, when the scrabbling curse of maturity had begun. The prom had been an orgy of unreality. Now that feeling was back. Ben was somebody. His girl was the prettiest thing on earth. Everything was going to be just fine.

"Rose," said Ben, "I—I feel kind of like I was coming home. You know what I mean?"

"Yes," said Rose.

She tilted her head back, her eyes closed.

Ben leaned down to kiss her.

"Make it good," said the Kilraine fortune. "That's a twelve-million-dollar kiss."

Ben and Rose froze.

"Four lips into twelve million dollars gives three million dollars a lip," said the Kilraine fortune.

"Rose, listen—I—" said Ben. No thoughts came.

"He's trying to say he'd love you," said the twelve million, "even if you *didn't* have a thousand dollars a day, without even touching the principal. He'd love you even if the principal *wasn't* going right through the roof in the bull market; even if he *had* two dimes of his own to rub together; even if he *wasn't* dead sick of working. He'd love you even if he *didn't* want money so bad he could taste it; even if he *hadn't* dreamed all his life of going bluefishing in his own Crosby Striper, with a Jacobson rod, a Strozier reel, a Matthews line, and a case of cold Schlitz."

The Kilraine fortune seemed to pause for breath.

Ben and Rose let each other go. Their hands fell away from each other lifelessly.

"He'd love you," said the twelve million dollars, "even if he *hadn't* said a hundred times that the only way to make big money, by God, was to marry it." The Kilraine fortune closed in for the final kill. There was no need of it. The perfect moment of love was already dead, stiff and bug-eyed.

"I guess I'd better say good night," said Rose to Ben. "Thanks a lot for starting the oil burner and everything."

"Glad to be of help," said Ben desolately.

The twelve million dollars administered the *coup de grâce*. "He loves you, Rose," it said, "even though you *aren't* what anybody'd call a raving beauty or a personality girl—even though nobody but a sick old man *ever* fell in love with you before."

"Good night," said Ben. "Sleep tight."

"Good night," said Rose. "Sweet dreams."

All night long, Ben, in his rumpled, narrow bed, took inventory of Rose's virtues—virtues any one of which was more tempting than twelve million dollars. In his agitation, he peeled wallpaper from the wall by his bed.

When dawn came, he knew that a kiss was all that could drown out the twelve million dollars. If he and Rose could kiss, ignoring all the nasty things the Kilraine fortune could say about it, they could prove to each other that they had love above all. And they'd live happily ever after.

Ben decided to take Rose by storm, to overwhelm her with his manliness. They were, after all, when all was said and done, a *man* and a *woman*.

At nine that morning, Ben lifted the massive knocker on the front door of the Kilraine cottage. He let it fall. The *boom* echoed and died in nineteen rooms.

Ben was in clamming clothes, as big as Paul Bunyan, in hip boots, two layers of trousers, four layers of sweaters, and a villainous black cap. He carried his clam rake like a battle-ax. Beside him was a bucket stuffed with a burlap bag.

The heiress to the Kilraine fortune, wearing an old bathrobe patterned with daisies a foot across, answered the door. "Yes?" said Rose. She took a step backward. "Oh—it's you," she said. "I'm not used to you in boots."

Ben, supported by his clothing, maintained an air of ponderous indifference. "I'd like to go clamming off your beach, if that's all right with you," he said.

Rose was shyly interested. "You mean there are clams right out there?"

"Yes, ma'am," said Ben. "Cherrystones."

"Well, I never," said Rose. "Like in a restaurant?"

"That's who'll buy 'em," said Ben.

"Now, isn't God good to Cape Codders," said Rose, "putting all that food out there for anybody who needs it?"

"Yes," said Ben. He touched his cap. "Well, thanks for everything." He timed his turn carefully, so she would be sure he was walking out of her life. And then he turned back to her suddenly, passionately, and grabbed her.

"Rose, Rose, Rose," said Ben.

"Ben, Ben, Ben," said Rose.

The Kilraine fortune seemed to yell at them from somewhere deep in the cottage. Before they could kiss, it was with them again. "This I've got to see—this twelve-million-dollar kiss," it said.

Rose ducked her head. "No, no, no, Ben, no," she said.

"Forget everything else," said Ben. "We're what matters."

"Forget twelve million dollars like you'd forget an old hat," said the Kilraine fortune lightly. "Forget all the lies most men would tell for twelve million dollars."

"I'll never know what matters again," said Rose. "I'll never be able to believe anything or anybody again." She wept quietly, and closed the door in Ben's face.

"Goodbye, Romeo," said the twelve million to Ben. "Don't look so blue. The world is full of girls just as good as Rose, and prettier. And they're all waiting to marry a man like you for love, love, love."

Ben walked away slowly, heartbroken.

"And love, as we all know," the Kilraine fortune called after him, "makes the world go 'round."

Ben laid the burlap bag on the beach before the Kilraine cottage, and waded into the sea with his bucket and rake. He buried the tines of the rake in the bay floor, and worried them through the sand.

A telltale click ran through the handle of the rake to Ben's gloved fingers. Ben tipped the handle back, and lifted the rake from the water. Resting on the tines were three fat clams.

Ben was glad to stop thinking about love and money. Swaddled in the good feel of thick wool, listening only to the voices of the sea, he lost himself in the hunt for treasure under the sand.

He lost himself for an hour, and in that time he gathered almost half a bushel of clams.

He waded back to the beach, emptied his bucket into the bag, and rested and smoked. His bones ached sweetly with manly satisfaction.

For the first time in two years, he saw what a fine day it was, saw what a beautiful part of the world he lived in.

And then his mind began to play with numbers: six dollars a bushel . . . three hours a bushel . . . six hours a day . . . six days a week . . . room rent, eight dollars a week . . . meals, a dollar and a half a day . . . cigarettes, forty cents a day . . . interest on bank loan, fifteen dollars a month . . .

Money began talking to Ben again—not big money this time, but little money. It niggled and nagged and carped and whined at him, as full of fears and bitterness as a spinster witch.

Ben's soul knotted and twisted like an old apple tree. He was hearing again the voice that had held him prisoner in the grocery store for two years, that had soured every smile since the milk and honey of high school.

Ben turned to look at the Kilraine cottage. Rose's haunted face peered out from an upstairs window.

Seeing the captive maiden, remembering his own captivity, Ben understood at last that money was one big dragon, with a billion dollars for a head, and a penny on the tip of its tail. It had as many voices as there were men and women, and it captured all who were fools enough to listen to it all the time.

Ben threw the bag of clams over his shoulder, and went to the door of the Kilraine cottage once more.

Again, Rose opened the door for him. "Please—please go away," she said weakly.

"Rose," said Ben, "I thought you might want some clams. They're very good, steamed, dipped in melted butter or oleo."

"No, thank you," said Rose.

"I want to give you *something*, Rose," said Ben. "Clams is all I've got. Nothing like twelve million clams, but clams, anyway."

Rose was startled.

"Of course," said Ben, strolling past her and into the living room, "if we fell in love and got married, then I'd be as rich as you are. That'd be a nutty break for me, just like the nutty break old man Kilraine gave you."

Rose was shocked. "Am I supposed to laugh?" she said. "Is this supposed to be funny, talking this way?"

"It's the truth," said Ben. "All depends on what you make of it. God's honest truth." He took an old cigar from a humidor. The outer leaves crumbled in his fingers and fell to the carpet.

"I asked you to leave nicely," said Rose angrily. "Now I'm going to tell you in no uncertain terms to please get out. I can see now how right I was—how little I knew about you." She quivered. "Rude, insulting—"

Ben put down his clams, and lit what was left of the cigar. He put one foot on a windowsill, and cocked his behind to one side, in a pose of superb male arrogance. "Rose," he said, "do you know where that damn fool bonanza of yours is?"

"It's invested all over the country," said Rose.

Ben pointed into a corner with his cigar. "It's sulking over there in the corner, where it belongs," he said, "because *I* said everything *it* was gonna say."

Rose looked into the corner, puzzled.

"The thing about money is," said Ben, "you can't be polite to it. Leave something suspicious to say, and it'll say it." He took his foot down from the windowsill. "Leave something greedy to say, and it'll say it." He put his cigar in an ashtray. "Leave something scary to say, and it'll say it.

"Give it an inch," said Ben, "and it'll take a mile." He took off his gloves, and laid them on the windowsill. "As near as I can tell, I love you, Rose," he said. "I'd do my best to make you happy. If you love me, kiss me, and make me rich beyond my wildest dreams. Then, after that, we'll steam these clams."

Rose thought a moment, still looking into the corner. And then she did what Ben had asked her to do.

The Kilraine fortune seemed to speak once more. "At your service," it said.

While Mortals Sleep

IF FRED HACKLEMAN and Christmas could have avoided each other, they would have. He was a bachelor, a city editor, and a newspaper genius, and I worked for him as a reporter for three insufferable years. As nearly as I could tell, he and the Spirit of Christmas had as little in common as a farm cat and the Audubon Society.

And he was like a farm cat in a lot of ways. He was solitary, deceptively complacent and lazy, and quick with the sharp claws of his authority and wit.

He was in his middle forties when I worked for him, and he had seemingly lost respect not just for Christmas but for government, matrimony, business, patriotism, and just about any other important institution you could name. The only ideals I ever heard him mention were terse leads, good spelling, accuracy, and speed in reporting the stupidity of mankind.

I can remember only one Christmas during which he radiated, faintly, anything like joy and goodwill. But that was a coincidence. A jailbreak happened to take place on December twenty-fifth.

I can remember another Christmas when he badgered a rewrite girl until she cried, because she'd said in a story that a man had passed on after having been hit by a freight train.

"Did he get up, dust himself off, giggle, and pass on to wherever he was headed before his little misunderstanding with the locomotive?" Hackleman wanted to know.

"No." She bit her lip. "He died, and—"

"Why didn't you say so in the first place? He died. After the locomotive, the tender, fifty-eight loaded freight cars and the caboose rolled over him, he died. That we can tell our readers without fear of contradiction. First-rate reporting—he died. Did he go to Heaven? Is that where he passed on to?"

"I—I don't know."

"Well, your story says we do know. Did the reporter say he had definite information that the dead man is now in Heaven—or en route? Did you check with the man's minister to see if he had a ghost of a chance of getting in?"

She burst into tears. "I hope he did!" she said furiously. "I tried to say I hoped he did, and I'm not sorry!" She walked away, blowing her nose, and paused by the door to glare at Hackleman. "Because it's Christmas!" she cried, and she left the newspaper world forever.

"Christmas?" said Hackleman. He seemed baffled, and looked around the room as though hoping someone would translate the strange word for him. "Christmas." He walked over to the calendar on the wall, and ran his finger along the dates until he came to the twenty-fifth. "Oh—that's the one with the red numbers. Huh."

But the Christmas season I remember best is the last one I spent with Hackleman—the season in which the great crime was committed, the robbery proclaimed by Hackleman, gleefully, as the most infamous crime in the history of the city.

It must have been on about the first of December that I heard him say, as he went over his morning mail, "Goddamn it, how much glory can come to a man in one short lifetime?"

He called me over to his desk. "It isn't right that all of the honors that pour into these offices every day should be shared only by management," he said. "It's to you, the working stiffs, that the honors really belong."

"That's very kind of you," I said uneasily.

"So, in lieu of the raise which you richly deserve, I am going to make you my assistant."

"Assistant city editor?"

"Bigger than that. My boy, you are now assistant publicity director of the Annual Christmas Outdoor Lighting Contest. Bet you thought I wasn't even aware of the brilliant, selfless job you've been doing for the paper, eh?" He shook my hand. "Well, here's your answer. Congratulations."

"Thanks. What do I do?"

"The reason executives die young is that they don't know how to delegate authority," said Hackleman. "This should add twenty years to my life, because I hereby delegate to you my full authority as publicity director, just tendered me by the Chamber of Commerce. The door of opportunity is wide open. If your publicity makes this year's Annual Christmas Outdoor Lighting Contest the biggest, brightest one yet, there'll be no ceiling on how high you can rise in the world of journalism. Who's to say you won't be the next publicity director of National Raisin Week?"

"I'm afraid I'm not very familiar with this particular art form," I said.

"Nothing to it," said Hackleman. "The contestants dangle colored electric lights all over the fronts of their houses, and the man whose meter goes around fastest wins. That's Christmas for you."

◎ ◎ ◎

As a dutiful assistant publicity director, I boned up on the history of the event, and learned that the contest had been held every year, except for the war years, since 1938. The first winner won with a two-story Santa Claus, outlined in lights on the front of his house. The next winner had a great pair of plywood bells, outlined in lights and hung from the eaves, which swung back and forth while a loudspeaker concealed in the shrubbery went ding-dong.

And so it went: each winner bettered the winner of the year before, until no entrant had a prayer of winning without the help of an electrical engineer, and the Power and Light Company had every bit of its equipment dangerously overloaded on the night of the judging, Christmas Eve.

As I said, Hackleman wanted nothing to do with it. But, unfortunately for Hackleman, the publisher of the paper had just been elected president of the Chamber of Commerce, and he was annoyed to learn that one of his employees was squirming out of a civic duty.

The publisher rarely appeared in the city room, but his visits were always memorable—particularly the visit he made two weeks before Christmas to educate Hackleman on his twofold role in the community.

"Hackleman," he said, "every man on this staff is not only a newspaper man, he's an active citizen."

"I vote," said Hackleman. "I pay my taxes."

"And there it stops," said the publisher reproachfully. "For ten years you've been city editor, and for ten years you've been ducking the civic duties that come to a man in such a position—foisting them off on the nearest reporter." He pointed at me. "It's a slap in the face of the community, sending out kids like this to do work that most citizens would consider a great honor."

"I haven't got time," said Hackleman sullenly.

"Make the time. Nobody asks you to spend eighteen hours a day in the office. That's your idea. It isn't necessary. Get out with your fellow men once in a while, Hackleman, especially now. It's the Christmas season, man. Get behind this contest and—"

"What's Christmas to me?" said Hackleman. "I'm not a religious man and I'm not a family man, and eggnog gives me gastritis, so the hell with Christmas."

The publisher was stunned. "The hell with Christmas?" he said, hollowly, hoarsely.

"Certainly," said Hackleman.

"Hackleman," said the publisher evenly, "I order you to take part in running the contest—to get into the swing of Christmas. It'll do you good."

"I quit," said Hackleman, "and I don't think that will do you much good."

And Hackleman was right. His quitting did the paper no good. It was a disaster, for in many ways he *was* the paper. However, there was no wailing or gnashing of teeth in the paper's executive offices—only a calm, patient wistfulness. Hackleman had quit before, but had never managed to stay away from the paper for more than twenty-four hours. His whole life was the paper, and his talking of quitting it was like a trout's talking of quitting a mountain stream to get a job clerking in a five-and-ten.

Setting a new record for an absence from the paper, Hackleman returned to his desk twenty-seven hours after quitting. He was slightly drunk and surly, and looked no one in the eye.

As I passed his desk, quietly and respectfully, he mumbled something to me.

"Beg your pardon?" I said.

"I said Merry Christmas," said Hackleman.

"And a Merry Christmas to you."

"Well, sir," he said, "it won't be long now, will it, until old soup-for-brains with the long white beard will come a-jingling over our housetops with goodies for us all."

"No—guess not."

"A man who whips little reindeer is capable of anything," said Hackleman.

"Yes—I suppose."

"Bring me up to date, will you, kid? What's this goddamn contest all about?"

The committee that was supposed to be running the contest was top-heavy with local celebrities who were too busy and important to do a lick of work on the contest—the mayor, the president of a big manufacturing company, and the chairman of the Real Estate Board. Hackleman kept me on as his assistant, and it was up to us and some small fry from the Chamber of Commerce to do the spadework.

Every night we went out to look at entries, and there were thousands of them. We were trying to make a list of the twenty best displays from which the committee would choose a winner on Christmas Eve. The Chamber of Commerce underlings scouted the south side of town, while Hackleman and I scouted the north.

It should have been pleasant. The weather was crisp, not bitter; the stars were out every night, bright, hard, and cold against a black velvet sky. Snow, while cleared from the streets, lay on yards and rooftops, making all the world seem soft and clean; and our car radio sang Christmas carols.

But it wasn't pleasant, because Hackleman talked most of the time, making a bitter indictment against Christmas.

One time, I was listening to a broadcast of a children's choir singing "Silent Night," and was as close to heaven as I could get without being pure and dead. Hackleman suddenly changed stations to fill the car with the clangor of a jazz band.

"Wha'd you do that for?" I said.

"They're running it into the ground," said Hackleman peevishly. "We've heard it eight times already tonight. They sell Christmas the way they sell cigarettes—just keep hammering away at the same old line over and over again. I've got Christmas coming out of my ears."

"They're not selling it," I said. "They're just happy about it."

"Just another form of department store advertising."

I twisted the dial back to the station carrying the children's choir. "If you don't mind, I'd enjoy hearing this to the end," I said. "Then you can change it again."

"Sleee-eeep in heav-en-ly peace," piped the small, sweet voices. And then the announcer broke in. "This fifteen-minute interlude of Christmas favorites," he said, "has been brought to you by Bullard Brothers Department Store, which is open until ten o'clock every evening except Sunday. Don't wait until the last minute to do your Christmas shopping. Avoid the rush."

"There!" said Hackleman triumphantly.

"That's a side issue," I said. "The main thing is that the Savior was born on Christmas."

"Wrong again," said Hackleman. "Nobody knows when he was born. There's nothing in the Bible to tell you. Not a word."

"You're the last man I'd come to for an expert opinion on the Bible," I said heatedly.

"I memorized it when I was a kid," said Hackleman. "Every night I had to learn a new verse. If I missed a word, by God, the old man knocked my block off."

"Oh?" This was an unexpected turn of events—unexpected because part of Hackleman's impressiveness lay in his keeping to himself, in his never talking about his past or about what he did or thought when he wasn't at work. Now he was talking about his childhood, and showing me for the first time an emotion more profound than impatience and cynicism.

"I didn't miss a single Sunday School session for ten years," said Hackleman. "Rain or shine, sick or well, I was there."

"Devout, eh?"

"Scared stiff of my old man's belt."

"Is he still alive—your father?"

"I don't know," said Hackleman without interest. "I ran away when I was fifteen, and never went back."

"And your mother?"

"Died when I was a year old."

"Sorry."

"Who the hell asked you to be sorry?"

We were pulling up before the last house we planned to look at that night. It was a salmon-pink mansion with a spike fence, iron flamingos, and five television aerials—combining in one monster the worst features of Spanish architecture, electronics, and sudden wealth. There was no Christmas lighting display that we could see—only ordinary lights inside the house.

We knocked on the door, to make sure we'd found the right place, and were told by a butler that there was indeed a lighting display, on the other side of the house, and that he would have to ask the master for permission to turn it on.

A moment later, the master appeared, fat and hairy, and with two prominent upper front teeth—looking like a groundhog in a crimson dressing gown.

"Mr. Fleetwood, sir," said the butler to his master, "these gentlemen here—"

The master waved his man to silence. "How have you been, Hackleman?" he said. "It's rather late to be calling, but my door is always open to old friends."

"Gribbon," said Hackleman incredulously, "Leu Gribbon. How long have you been living here?"

"The name is Fleetwood now, Hackleman—J. Sprague Fleetwood, and I'm strictly legitimate. There was a story the last time we met, but there isn't one tonight. I've been out for a year, living quietly and decently."

"Mad Dog Gribbon has been out for a year, and I didn't know it?" said Hackleman.

"Don't look at me," I said. "I cover the School Board and the Fire Department."

"I've paid my debt to society," said Gribbon.

Hackleman toyed with the visor of a suit of armor guarding the entrance into the baronial living room. "Looks to me like you paid your debt to society two cents on the dollar," he said.

"Investments," said Gribbon, "legitimate investments in the stock market."

"How'd your broker get the bloodstains out of your money to find out what the denominations were?" said Hackleman.

"If you're going to abuse my hospitality with rudeness, Hackleman, I'll have you thrown out," said Gribbon. "Now, what do you want?"

"They wish to see the lighting display, sir," said the butler.

Hackleman looked very sheepish when this mission was announced. "Yeah," he mumbled, "we're on a damn fool committee."

"I thought the judging was to take place Christmas Eve," said Gribbon. "I didn't plan to turn it on until then—as a pleasant surprise for the community."

"A mustard gas generator?" said Hackleman.

"All right, wise guy," said Gribbon haughtily, "tonight you're going to see what kind of a citizen J. Sprague Fleetwood is."

It was a world of vague forms and shades of blue in the snowy yard of J. Sprague Fleetwood, alias Mad Dog Gribbon. It was midnight and Hackleman and I stamped our feet and blew on our hands to keep warm, while Gribbon and three servants hurried about the yard, tightening electrical connections and working over what seemed to be statues with screwdrivers and oil cans.

Gribbon insisted that we stand far away from the display in order to get the impact of the whole, whenever it was ready to be turned on. We couldn't tell what it was we were about to see, and were particularly tantalized by what the butler was doing—filling an enormous weather balloon from a tank of gas. The balloon arose majestically, captive at the end of a cable, as the butler turned the crank of a winch.

"What's that for?" I whispered to Hackleman.

"Sending for final instructions from God," said Hackleman.

"What'd he get sent to prison for?"

"Ran the numbers in town for a while, and had about twenty people killed so he could keep his franchise. So they put him away for five years for not paying his income taxes."

"Lights ready?" bawled Gribbon, standing on a porch, his arms upraised, commanding a miracle.

"Lights ready," said a voice in the shrubbery.

"Sound ready?"

"Sound ready, sir."

"Balloon ready?"

"Balloon aloft, sir."

"Let 'er go!" cried Gribbon.

Demons shrieked from the treetops.

Suns exploded.

Hackleman and I cowered, instinctively threw our arms across our faces.

We uncovered our eyes slowly, fearfully, and saw stretching before us, in blinding, garish light, a life-sized nativity scene. Loudspeakers on every side blared earsplitting carols. Plaster cattle and sheep were everywhere, wagging their heads, while shepherds raised and lowered their right arms like railroad-crossing gates, jerkily pointing into the sky.

The Virgin Mary and Joseph looked down sweetly on the child in the manger, while mechanical angels flapped their wings and mechanical wise men bobbed up and down like pistons.

"Look!" cried Hackleman above the din, pointing where the shepherds pointed, where the balloon had disappeared into the sky.

There, over the salmon-pink palace of Mad Dog Gribbon, hung in the Christmas heavens from a bag of gas, shone an imitation of the star of Bethlehem.

Suddenly, all was black and still again. My mind was numb. Hackleman stared blankly at the place where the star had been, speechless.

Gribbon trotted toward us. "Anything else in town that can touch it?" he panted proudly.

"Nope," said Hackleman bleakly.

"Think it'll win?"

"Yup," murmured Hackleman. "Unless somebody's got an atomic explosion in the form of Rudolph the Red-nosed Reindeer."

"People will come from miles around to see it," said Gribbon. "Just tell 'em in the newspaper story to follow the star."

"Listen, Gribbon," said Hackleman, "you know there isn't any money that goes with the first prize, don't you? Nothing but a lousy little scroll worth maybe a buck."

Gribbon looked offended. "Of course," he said. "This is a public service, Hackleman."

Hackleman grunted. "Come on, kid, let's call it a night, eh?"

It was a real break, our finding the certain winner of the contest a week before the judging was to take place. It meant that the judges and assistants like myself could spend most of Christmas Eve with our families, instead of riding around town for hours, trying to decide which was the best of twenty or so equally good entries. All we had to do now was to drive to Gribbon's mansion, be blinded and deafened, shake his hand and give him his scroll, and return home in time to trim the tree, fill the stocking, and put away several rounds of eggnog.

As thoughts of Christmas made Hackleman's neurotic staff gentle and sentimental, and the preposterous rumor that he had a heart of gold gained wide circulation, Hackleman behaved in typical holiday fashion, declaring that heads were going to roll because Mad Dog Gribbon had been out of prison and back in town for a year without a single reporter's finding out about it.

"By God," he said, "I'm going to have to go out on the street again, or the paper'll fold up for want of news." And, during the next two days, the paper would have done just that, if it hadn't been for news from the wire services, because Hackleman sent out almost everybody to find out what Gribbon was up to.

Desperate as Hackleman made us, we couldn't find a hint of skulduggery in Gribbon's life since he'd left prison. The only conclusion to draw was that crime paid so well that Gribbon could retire in his early forties, and live luxuriously and lawfully for the rest of his days.

"His money really does come from stocks and bonds," I told Hackleman wearily at the end of the second day. "And he pays his taxes like a good boy, and never sees his old friends anymore."

"All right, all right, all right," said Hackleman irritably. "Forget it. Never mind." He was more nervous than I'd ever seen him be before. He drummed on his desk with his fingers, and jumped at unexpected sounds.

"You have something special against him?" I asked. It wasn't like Hackleman to go after anyone with such zeal. Ordinarily, he never seemed to care whether justice or crime won out. What interested him were the good news stories that came out of the conflict. "After all, the guy really is going straight."

"Forget it," said Hackleman. Suddenly, he broke his pencil in two, stood up, and strode out, hours before his usual departure time.

The next day was my day off. I would have slept till noon, but a paper boy was selling extras under my bedroom window. The headline was huge and black, and spelled one terrible word: KIDNAPPED! The story below said that plaster images of Jesus, Mary, and Joseph had been stolen from Mr. J. Sprague Fleetwood, and that he had offered a reward of one thousand dollars for information leading to their return before the judging of the Annual Christmas Outdoor Lighting Contest on Christmas Eve.

Hackleman called a few minutes later. I was to come to the office at once to help trace down the clues that were pouring in.

The police complained that, if there were any clues, hordes of amateur detectives had spoiled them. But there was no pressure at all on the police to solve the robbery. By evening the search had become a joyful craze that no one escaped—that no one wanted to escape. And the search was for the people to make, not for the police.

Throngs went from door to door, asking if anyone had seen the infant Jesus.

Movie theaters played to empty houses, and a local radio giveaway program said mournfully that nobody seemed to be home in the evenings to answer the telephone.

Thousands insisted on searching the only stable in the city, and the owner made a small fortune selling them hot chocolate and doughnuts. An enterprising hotel bought a full-page ad, declaring that if anyone found Jesus and Mary and Joseph, here was an inn that would make room for them.

The lead story in every edition of the paper dealt with the search and every edition was a sellout.

Hackleman remained as sarcastic and cynical and efficient as ever.

"It's a miracle," I told him. "By taking this little story and blowing it up big, you've made Christmas live."

Hackleman shrugged apathetically. "Just happened to come along when news was slow. If something better comes along, and I hope it will, I'll drop this one right out of sight. It's about time somebody was running berserk with an automatic shotgun in a kindergarten isn't it?"

"Sorry I opened my mouth."

"Have I remembered to wish you a merry Saturnalia?"

"Saturnalia?"

"Yeah—a nasty old pagan holiday near the end of December. The Romans used to close the schools, eat and drink themselves silly, say they loved everybody, and give each other gifts." He answered the phone. "No, ma'am, we haven't found Him yet. Yes, ma'am, there'll be an extra if He turns up. Yes, ma'am, the stable's already been checked pretty carefully. Thank you. Goodbye."

◎ ◎ ◎

The search was more a spontaneous, playful pageant than an earnest hunt for the missing figures. Realistically, the searchers didn't have much of a chance. They made a lot of noise, and went only where they thought it would be pleasant or interesting to go. The thief, who was apparently a nut, would have had little trouble keeping his peculiar loot out of sight.

But the searchers were so caught up in the allegory of what they were doing that a powerful expectation grew of its own accord, with no help from the paper. Everyone was convinced that the holy family would be found on Christmas Eve.

But on that eve, no new star shone over the city save the five-hundred-watt lamp hung from a balloon over the mansion of J. Sprague Fleetwood, alias Mad Dog Gribbon, the victim of the theft.

The mayor, the president of a big manufacturing company, and the chairman of the Real Estate Board rode in the back seat of the mayor's limousine, while Hackleman and I sat on the jump seats in front of them. We were on our way to award the first-prize scroll to Gribbon, who had replaced the missing figures with new ones.

"Turn down this street here?" said the chauffeur.

"Just follow the star," I said.

"It's a light, a goddamn electric light that anybody can hang over his house if he's got the money," said Hackleman.

"Follow the goddamn electric light," I said.

Gribbon was waiting for us, wearing a tuxedo, and he opened the car door himself. "Gentlemen—Merry Christmas." His eyes down, his hands folded piously across his round belly, he led us down a path, bounded by ropes, that led around the display and back to the street again. He passed by the corner of the mansion, just short of the point where we would be able to see the display. "I like to think of it as a shrine," he said, "with people coming from miles around, following the stars." He stepped aside, motioning us to go ahead.

And the dumbfounding panorama dazzled us again, looking like an outdoor class in calisthenics, with expressionless figures bobbing, waving their arms, flapping their wings.

"Gangster heaven," whispered Hackleman.

"Oh, my," said the mayor.

The chairman of the Real Estate Board looked appalled, but cleared his throat and recovered gamely. "Now, there's a display," he said, clinging doggedly to his integrity.

"Where'd you get the new figures?" said Hackleman.

"Wholesale from a department-store supply house," said Gribbon.

"What an engineering feat," said the manufacturer.

"Took four engineers to do it," said Gribbon proudly. "Whoever swiped the figures left the neon halos behind, thank God. They're rigged so I can make 'em blink, if you think that'd look better."

"No, no," said the mayor. "Mustn't gild the lily."

"Uh . . . do I win?" said Gribbon politely.

"Hmmm?" said the mayor. "Oh—do you win? Well, we have to deliberate, of course. We'll let you know this evening."

No one seemed able to think of anything more to say, and we shuffled back to the limousine.

"Thirty-two electric motors, two miles of wire, nine hundred and seventy-six lightbulbs, not counting neon," said Gribbon as we pulled away.

"I thought we were going to just hand him the scroll right then and there," said the real estate man. "That was the plan, wasn't it?"

"I just couldn't bring myself to do it then," sighed the mayor. "Suppose we could stop somewhere for a stirrup cup."

"He obviously won," said the manufacturer. "We wouldn't dare give the prize to anyone else. He won by brute force—brute dollars, brute kilowatts, no matter how terrible his taste is."

"There's one more stop," said Hackleman.

"I thought this was a one-stop expedition," said the manufacturer. "I thought we'd agreed on that."

Hackleman held up a card. "Well, it's a technicality. The official deadline for entries was noon today. This thing came in by special delivery about two seconds ahead of the deadline, and we haven't had a chance to check it."

"It certainly can't match this Fleetwood thing," said the mayor. "What could? What's the address?"

Hackleman told him.

"Shabby neighborhood out on the edge of town," said the real estate man. "No competition for our friend Fleetwood."

"Let's forget it," said the manufacturer. "I've got guests coming in, and . . ."

"Bad public relations," said Hackleman gravely. It was startling to hear the words coming from him, enunciated with respect. He'd once said that the three most repellent forms of life were rats, leeches, and public relations men . . . in descending order.

To the three important men in the back seat, though, the words were impressive and troubling. They mumbled and fidgeted, but didn't have the courage to fight.

"Let's make it quick," said the mayor, and Hackleman gave the driver the card.

Stopped by a traffic signal, we came abreast of a group of cheerful searchers, who called to us, asking if we knew where the holy family was hidden.

Impulsively, the mayor leaned out of the window. "You won't find them under that," he said, waggling his finger at the light over Gribbon's house.

Another group crossed the street before us, singing:

> For Christ is born of Mary,
> And gathered all above,
> While mortals sleep, the angels keep
> Their watch of wondering love.

The light changed, and we drove on, saying little as we left the fine homes behind, as the electric lamp over Gribbon's mansion was lost behind black factory chimneys.

"You sure the address is right?" said the chauffeur uncertainly.

"I guess the guy knows his own address," said Hackleman.

"This was a bad idea," said the manufacturer, looking at his watch. "Let's call up Gribbon or Fleetwood or whatever his name is, and tell him he's the big winner. The hell with this."

"I agree," said the mayor. "But, as long as we're this far along, let's see it through."

The limousine turned down a dark street, banged over a chuckhole, and stopped. "This is it gentlemen," said the chauffeur.

We were parked before an empty, leaning, roofless house, whose soundest part was its splintered siding, a sign declaring it to be unfit for human habitation.

"Are rats and termites eligible for the contest?" said the mayor.

"The address checks," said the chauffeur defensively.

"Turn around and go home," said the mayor.

"Hold it," said the real estate man. "There's a light in the barn in back. My God, I came all this way to judge and I'm going to judge."

"Go see who's in the barn," said the mayor to the chauffeur.

The chauffeur shrugged, got out, and walked through the snow-covered rubbish to the barn. He knocked. The door swung open under the impact of his fist. Silhouetted by a frail, wavering light from within, he sank to his knees.

"Drunk?" said Hackleman.

"I don't think so," murmured the mayor. He licked his lips. "I think he's praying—for the first time in his life." He got out of the car, and we followed him silently to the barn. When we reached the chauffeur, we went to our knees beside him.

Before us were the three missing figures. Joseph and Mary sheltered against a thousand drafts the sleeping infant Jesus in his bed of straw. The only illumination came from a single oil lantern, and its wavering light made them live, alive with awe and adoration.

On Christmas morning, the paper told the people where the holy family could be found.

All Christmas Day the people streamed to the cold, lonely barn to worship.

A small story inside announced that Mr. Sprague Fleetwood had won the Annual Christmas Outdoor Lighting Contest with thirty-two electric motors, two miles of wire, and nine hundred and seventy-six lightbulbs, not counting neon, and an Army surplus weather balloon.

Hackleman was on the job at his desk, critical and disillusioned as ever.

"It's a great, great story," I said.

"I'm good and sick of it," said Hackleman. He rubbed his hands. "What I'm looking forward to is January when the Christmas bills come in. A great month for homicides."

"Well, there's still got to be a follow-up on the Christmas story. We still don't know who did it."

"How you going to find out who did it? The name on the entry blank was a phony, and the guy who owns the barn hasn't been in town for ten years."

"Fingerprints," I said. "We could go over the figures for fingerprints."

"One more suggestion like that, and you're fired."

"Fired?" I said. "What for?"

"Sacrilege!" said Hackleman grandly, and the subject was closed. His mind, as he said, was on stories in the future. He never looked back.

Hackleman's last act with respect to the theft, the search, and Christmas was to send me out to the barn with a photographer on Christmas night. The mission was routine and trite, and it bored him.

"Get a crowd shot from the back, with the figures facing the camera," said Hackleman. "They must be pretty damn dusty by now, with all the sinners tramping through. Better go over 'em with a damp cloth before you make the shot."

Tango

EVERY JOB APPLICATION FORM I fill out asks for a tabulation, with dates, of what I've done with my adult life so far, and tells me sternly to leave no periods unaccounted for. I would give a great deal for permission to leave out the last three months, when I served as a tutor in a village called Pisquontuit. Anyone writing my former employer there for an appraisal of my character would get his ears burnt off.

On each application form there is a small blank section entitled *remarks*, where I might tell my side of the Pisquontuit story. But there seems little chance of anyone's understanding my side if he hasn't seen Pisquontuit. And the chances of an ordinary man's seeing Pisquontuit are about the same as his chances for being dealt two spade royal flushes in a row.

Pisquontuit is an Indian word said to mean "shining waters," and is pronounced *Ponit* by the few privileged to know that the village exists. It is a secret assemblage of mansions by the sea. The entrance is unmarked, an unpromising lane leading from the main road into a forest of scrub pine. A guard lives in the forest by a turnaround on the lane, and he makes all cars that do not belong in Pisquontuit turn around and go back where they came from. The cars that belong in Pisquontuit are either very big ones or very little ones.

I worked there as a tutor for Robert Brewer, an amiable, mildly fogbound young man who was preparing to take college entrance examinations and needed help.

I think I can say without fear of contradiction that Pisquontuit was the most exclusive community in America. While I was there, a gentleman sold his house on the grounds that his neighbors were "a pretty stuffy bunch." He went back to where he came from, Beacon Hill in Boston. My employer, Robert's father, Herbert Clewes Brewer, spent most of his time between sailboat races writing indignant letters to Washington. He was indignant because every mansion in the village was shown on United States Geodetic Survey maps, which could be bought by just anybody.

It was a quiet community. Its members had paid a handsome price for peace, and small ripples looked like tidal waves. At the heart of my troubles there was nothing more violent or barbaric than the tango.

The tango, of course, is a dance of Spanish-American origin, usually in four-four time, and is distinguished by low dips and twisting steps on the toes. One Saturday night, at the weekly dance of the Pisquontuit Yacht Club, young Robert Brewer, my student, who had never even seen the tango performed in his eighteen years of life, began to dip lowly and twist his toes. His movements were tentative at first, as involuntary as shudders. Robert's mind and face were blank when it happened. The heady Latin music wandered in through his ears, found nobody at home under his crew cut, and took command of his long, thin body.

Something clicked, locking Robert in the machinery of the music. His partner, a plain, wholesome girl with three million dollars and a low center of gravity, struggled in embarrassment, and then, seeing the fierce look in Robert's eyes, succumbed. The two became as one, a fast-moving one.

It simply was not done in Pisquontuit.

Dancing at Pisquontuit was an almost imperceptible shifting of weight from one foot to the other, with the feet remaining in place, from three to six inches apart. This seemly shifting of weight was all things to all music, samba, waltz, gavotte, fox-trot, bunny hug, or hokeypokey. No matter what new dance craze came along, Pisquontuit overpowered it easily. The ballroom could have been filled with clear gelatin to shoulder height without hampering the dancers. It could have been filled to a point just below the dancers' nostrils, for that matter, for agreement on every subject was so complete that discussion had been reduced to a verbal shorthand resembling asthma.

And there was Robert crossing and recrossing the ballroom floor like a Chris-Craft.

No one paid the slightest attention to Robert and his partner as they careered and careened. This indifference was equivalent to breaking a man on the wheel or throwing him down the oubliette in other times and places. Robert had put himself in the same class with the poor devil in Pisquontuit history who put lampblack on the bottom of his sailboat, another who found out too late that no one *ever* went swimming before eleven in the morning, and another who could not break the habit of saying okey dokey on the telephone.

When the music was over, Robert's partner, flushed and rattled, excused herself, and Robert's father joined him by the bandstand.

When Mr. Brewer was angry, he thrust his tongue between his teeth and talked around it, withdrawing it only to make s sounds. "Good Lord, Bubs!" he said to Robert. "What do you think you are, a gigolo?"

"I don't know what happened," said Robert, crimson. "I never did a dance right before, and I just kind of went crazy. Like flying."

"Consider yourself shot down in flames," said Mr. Brewer. "This isn't Coney Island, and it isn't going to become Coney Island. Now go apologize to your mother."

"Yessir," said Robert, shaken.

"Looked like a damn flamingo playing soccer," said Mr. Brewer. He nodded, pulled in his tongue, closed his teeth with a clack, and stalked away.

Robert apologized to his mother and went straight home.

Robert and I shared a suite, bathroom, sitting room, and two bedrooms, on the third floor of what was known as the Brewer cottage. Robert seemed to be asleep when I got home shortly after midnight.

But at three in the morning I was awakened by soft music from the sitting room, and by the sounds of someone striding around in agitation. I opened my door and surprised Robert in the act of tangoing by himself. In the instant before he saw me, his nostrils were flaring and his eyes were narrowed, the smoldering eyes of a sheik.

He gasped, turned off the phonograph, and collapsed on the couch.

"Keep it up," I said. "You were doing fine."

"I guess nobody's as civilized as he'd like to think," said Robert.

"Lots of nice people tango," I said.

He clenched and unclenched his hands. "Cheap, asinine, grotesque!"

"It isn't supposed to look good," I said. "It's supposed to feel good."

"It isn't done in Pisquontuit," he said.

I shrugged. "What's Pisquontuit?"

"I don't mean to be impolite," he said, "but you couldn't possibly understand."

"I've been around long enough to see the sort of thing they get exercised about around here," I said.

"It's very easy for you to make comments," said Robert. "It's easy to make fun of anything, if you don't have any responsibilities."

"Responsibilities?" I said. "You've got responsibilities? For what?"

Robert looked about himself moodily. "This—all this. Someday I'll be taking all this over, presumably. You, you're free as the air, to come and go as you please and laugh all you like."

"Robert!" I said. "It's just real estate. If it depresses you, why, when you take it over, sell it."

Robert was shocked. "Sell it? My grandfather built this place."

"Fine bricklayer," I said.

"It's a way of life that's rapidly disappearing all over the world," said Robert.

"Farewell," I said.

"If Pisquontuit goes under," said Robert gravely, "if we all abandon ship, who's going to preserve the old values?"

"What old values?" I said. "Being grim about tennis and sailing?"

"Civilization!" he said. "Leadership!"

"What civilization?" I said. "That book your mother keeps saying she's going to read someday, if it kills her? And who around here leads anything anywhere?"

"My great-grandfather," said Robert, "was lieutenant governor of Rhode Island."

For want of a reply to this thunderclap, I started the phonograph, filling the room with the tango once more.

There was a gentle knock on the door, and I opened it to find Marie, the young and beautiful upstairs maid, standing outside in her bathrobe.

"I heard voices," she said. "I thought maybe there were prowlers." Her shoulders were moving gently in time with the music.

I took her easily in my arms, and we tangoed together into the sitting room. "With every step," I said to her, "we betray our lower-middle-class origins and drive the stake deeper into the heart of civilization."

"Huh?" said Marie, her eyes closed.

I felt a hand on my shoulder. Robert, breathing shallowly and quickly, was cutting in.

"After us the deluge," I said, loading the record changer.

Thus began Robert's secret vice—and Marie's, and mine. Almost every night the ritual was repeated. We would start the phonograph, Marie would come to investigate, and Marie and I would dance, with Robert looking on sullenly. Then Robert would rise painfully from his couch, like an arthritic old man, and take her from me wordlessly. It was the Pisquontuit equivalent of the Black Mass.

In three weeks' time, Robert was an excellent dancer and hopelessly in love with Marie.

"How did it happen?" he said to me. "How could it?"

"You are a man and she is a woman," I said.

"We're utterly different," he said.

"Vive la utter difference," I said.

"What'll I do, what'll I do?" he said heartbrokenly.

"Proclaim your love," I said.

"For a maid?" he said incredulously.

"Royalty's all gone or spoken for, Robert," I said. "The descendants of the lieutenant governor of Rhode Island have no choice but to marry commoners. It's like musical chairs."

"You're not very funny," said Robert bitterly.

"Well, you can't marry anybody in Pisquontuit, can you?" I said. "There's been a guard in the woods for three generations, and now all the people inside are at least second cousins. The system carries the seeds of its own destruction, unless it's willing to start mixing in chauffeurs and upstairs maids."

"There's new blood coming in all the time," said Robert.

"He left," I said. "He went back to Beacon Hill."

"Oh? I didn't know that," said Robert. "I don't notice much of anything anymore but Marie." He laid his hand on his chest. "This force," he said, "it just does with you what it wants to do with you, makes you feel what it wants to make you feel."

"Steady, boy, steady," I said, and I went to question Marie rather sharply as to whether she loved Robert or not.

Over the noise of the vacuum cleaner, she gave me coy, equivocal answers. "I feel like I'd kind of created him," she said, "starting with nothing."

"He says you've showed him the savage in himself," I said.

"That's what I mean," she said. "I don't think there was any savage to begin with."

"What a pity," I said, "after they've gone to so much expense keeping the savages out. If you married him, you'd have a very rich savage, you know."

"It's just an incubator baby now," she said wickedly.

"Life is losing all meaning for Robert," I said. "You don't know what you're doing to him. He's stopped caring if he wins or loses at tennis and sailing."

As I spoke of another's love and looked into the wide, blue windows of her soul, a rich, insistent yearning flooded my senses. "He can't even manage a smile anymore when somebody pronounces Pisquontuit the way it's spelled," I murmured, my voice trailing off at the end.

"I'm very sorry, I'm sure," she said bewitchingly.

I lost my head. I seized her by the wrist. "Do you love me?" I whispered hoarsely.

"I might," she said.

"Do you or don't you?"

"It's hard," she said, "for a girl who's been brought up to be friendly and affectionate to tell. Now let an honest girl get about her work."

I told myself that I had never seen such an honest and pretty girl in all my life, and went back to Robert a jealous rival.

"I can't eat, I can't sleep," he said.

"Don't cry on my shoulder," I snapped. "Go talk to your father about it. Let *him* sympathize."

"God no!" he said. "What an idea!"

"Have you ever talked to him about *anything*?" I said.

"Well, for a while there, there was what he called *getting to know the boy*," said Robert. "He used to set aside Wednesday nights for that, when I was little."

"All right," I said, "you've got a precedent for talking to him. Recreate the spirit of those days." I wanted him to get off the couch so *I* could lie down and stare at the ceiling.

"Oh, we didn't talk exactly," said Robert. "The butler would come up to my room and set up a motion-picture projector, and then father would come up and run off Mickey Mouse for an hour. We just sat in the dark with the thing grinding away."

"As thick as thieves!" I said. "What brought an end to these emotional binges?"

"A combination of things," said Robert. "The war mostly. He was chief air-raid warden of Pisquontuit, in charge of the siren and all, and it took a lot out of him. And I got the hang of feeding the film through the spools and all myself."

"Kids mature early around here," I said, contemplating a nice dilemma. It was my duty as tutor to make Robert a mature individual. Yet, his immaturity gave me my biggest advantage over him in our rivalry for Marie. After much thought, I devised a plan that promised to make Robert a man and deliver Marie into my arms free and clear.

"Marie," I said, catching her in the hall, "is it Robert or is it me?"

"Shhhhh!" she said. "Keep your voice down. There's a cocktail party downstairs, and sound carries right down the stairway."

"Wouldn't you like to be taken away from all this?" I whispered.

"Why?" she said. "I like the smell of furniture polish, I make more money than my girlfriend at the airplane factory, and I meet a very high class of people."

"I'm asking you to marry me, Marie," I said. "*I'd* never be ashamed of you."

She took a step backward. "Now, what made you say a mean thing like that? Who's ashamed of me, I want to know?"

"Robert," I said. "He loves you, but his shame is bigger than his love."

"He's glad enough to dance with me," she said. "We have a lovely time."

"In private," I said. "Do you think, for all your charms, he'd dance one step with you at the Yacht Club? In a pig's eye."

"He would," she said slowly, "if I wanted him to, if I really wanted him to."

"He'd rather die," I said. "You've heard of closet drinkers? Well, you've got yourself a closet lover."

I left her with this annoying thought, and was gratified to see a challenging look in her eye when she came to dance late that night. She did nothing unusual, however, until Robert cut in. Ordinarily, she transferred from me to Robert without opening her eye or missing a step. This time she stopped, her eyes open wide.

"What is this?" said Robert, dipping lowly and twisting his toes, while she stood as rigid as an iron post. "Something wrong?"

"No," said Marie in a brittle tone. "Why would you think there was something wrong?"

Reassured, Robert started to dip and twist some more, but again failed to budge Marie.

"There *is* something wrong," he said.

"Do you think I'm at all attractive, Robert?" said Marie coolly.

"Attractive?" said Robert. "Attractive? Lord yes! I should say. I'll tell the world."

"As attractive as any girl my age in Pisquontuit?"

"More!" said Robert heartily, starting to dance again, and again getting nowhere. "Much more, much, much more," he said, his movements subsiding.

"And do I have good manners?"

"The best!" said Robert, puzzled. "Absolutely the best, Marie."

"Then why don't you take me to the next Yacht Club dance?" she said.

Robert became as rigid as Marie. "To the Yacht Club?" he said. "To the *Pisquontuit* Yacht Club?"

"That's the one," said Marie.

"What she's asking, Robert," I said helpfully, "is, are you a man or a mouse? Are you going to take her to the Yacht Club dance, or does she go out of your life forever and into the airplane factory?"

"They need a good girl at the airplane factory," said Marie.

"I never saw a better one," I said.

"They're not ashamed of their girls over at the airplane factory," said Marie. "They have picnics and Christmas parties and wedding showers and all kinds of things, and the foremen and the vice presidents and the works manager and the comptroller and all come to the parties and dance with the girls and have a fine time. My girlfriend gets taken out regularly everywhere by the comptroller."

"What's the comptroller?" said Robert, fighting for time.

"I don't know," said Marie, "except he works for a living, and he isn't any closet lover."

Robert was stung speechless.

"Man or mouse?" I said, bringing the issue back into focus.

Robert chewed his lip, and at last murmured something we couldn't understand.

"What was that?" said Marie.

"Mouse," said Robert with a sigh. "I said mouse."

"Mouse," said Marie softly.

"Don't say it *that* way," said Robert desolately.

"What other way is there to say mouse?" said Marie. "Good night."

I followed her out into the hall. "Well," I said, "it's been rough on him, but—"

"Marie—" said Robert, appearing in the doorway, wan. "You wouldn't like it. You'd hate it. You'd have a terrible time. Everybody has a terrible time. That's why I said mouse."

"As long as there's music," said Marie, "and the gentleman is proud of his lady, nothing else matters."

"Um," said Robert. He disappeared into the sitting room again, and we heard the couch springs creak.

"You were saying—?" said Marie.

"I was saying it was a rough thing to put him through," I said to Marie, "but it'll do him a world of good in the long run. This will eat into him for years, and there's a good chance he'll become the first rounded human being in Pisquontuit history. A long, slow, profound double take."

"Listen," said Marie. "He's talking to himself. What's he saying?"

"Mouse, mouse, mouse," said Robert. "Mouse, mouse—"

"We've lit the fuse," I whispered, "on a spiritual time bomb."

"Mouse, man, mouse, man—" said Robert.

"Couple of years from now," I said, "*kaboom!*"

"Man!" shouted Robert. "Man, man, man!" He was on his feet, charging out into the hall. "Man!" he said savagely, and he bent Marie over backwards, kissing her hotly. He straightened her up and pulled her after him down the stairs to the second floor.

I followed them down, appalled.

"Robert," gasped Marie. "Please, what's going on?"

Robert pounded on his parents' bedroom door. "You'll see," he said. "I'm going to tell all the world you're mine!"

"Robert—listen," I said, "maybe you ought to cool off first, and—"

"Aha! The great mouse exposer!" he said wildly. He knocked me down. "How was that for a mouse tap?" He pounded on the door again. "Out of the sack in there!"

"I don't want to be yours," said Marie.

"We'll go out West somewhere," said Robert, "and raise Herefords or soybeans."

"I just wanted to go to a Yacht Club dance," piped Marie fearfully.

"Don't you understand?" said Robert. "I'm yours!"

"But I'm his," said Marie, pointing to me. She twisted away from Robert and ran upstairs to her room, with Robert on her heels. She slammed her door and locked it.

I stood slowly, rubbing my bruised cheek.

Mr. and Mrs. Brewer's bedroom door opened suddenly. Mr. Brewer stood in the doorway, glaring at me, his tongue between his teeth. "Well?" he said.

"I uh—up wupp," I said. I smiled glassily. "Never mind, sir."

"Never mind!" he bellowed. "You beat on the door like the world's coming to an end, and now you say never mind. Are you drunk?"

"Nossir."

"Well, neither am I," he said. "My mind's clear as a bell, and you're fired." He slammed the door.

I went back to Robert's and my suite and began packing. Robert was lying on the couch again, staring at the ceiling.

"She's packing, too," he said.

"Oh?"

"I guess you'll be getting married, eh?"

"Looks that way. I'll have to find another job."

"Count your blessings," he said. "Here, but for the grace of God, lie you."

"Calmed down, have you?" I said.

"I'm still through with Pisquontuit," he said.

"I think you're wise," I said.

"I wonder," he said, "if you and Marie would do me a little favor before you leave?"

"Name it."

"I'd kind of like to dance her down the steps." Robert's eyes grew narrow and smoldered again, as they had when I'd surprised him tangoing by himself. "You know," he said, "like Fred Astaire."

"You bet," I said. "I wouldn't miss it for the world."

The volume of the phonograph was turned up high, and all twenty-six rooms of the Brewer cottage pulsed at dawn with the rhythm of the tango.

Robert and Marie, a handsome couple, dipped lowly and twisted their toes as they descended the spiral staircase. I followed with Marie's and my luggage.

Again Mr. Brewer burst from his bedroom, his tongue between his teeth. "Bubs! What does this mean?"

Robert's reply to his father's question, I realize with each job application form I fill out, was unnecessarily heroic. Had we left it unsaid, Mr. Brewer's attitude toward me might have softened in time. But now, when I write his name down as my last employer, I smear it with the ball of my thumb, hoping that prospective employers will take my honest smile as reference enough.

"It means, sir," said Robert, "that you should thank my two friends here for raising your son from the dead."

The Humbugs

LIFE HAD BEEN GOOD to Durling Stedman. He drove a new Cadillac the color of lobster bisque. And on the back bumper of the Cadillac was a big trailer-hitch that hauled Stedman's silver home on wheels to Cape Cod in the springtime and to Florida in the fall. Stedman was an artist—a picture painter. But he didn't look like one. Part of his stock-in-trade was looking like a four-square businessman, like a no-nonsense free-enterpriser who knew what it was to meet a payroll, like a man's man who thought most artists were dreamers, who thought most art was bunk. He was sixty years old, and he looked a good deal like George Washington.

The sign over his studio in the art colony of Seminole Highlands, Florida, said it all: "Durling Stedman—Art Without Bunk." He set up shop right in the middle of struggling abstract painters. That was slick of him, because a majority of the tourists were confused and angered by the abstractionists. And then, in the middle of all the gibberish, the disgruntled tourists came upon Stedman and his work. Stedman's paintings were as pretty as postcards. And Stedman himself looked like a friend from home.

"I am an oasis," he liked to say.

Every night he did a demonstration painting on an easel in front of his studio. He did a painting in an hour flat with a crowd watching. He signified that he was done by putting a golden frame around the painting. The crowd knew then that it was all right to talk and applaud. A sudden noise couldn't spoil the masterpiece now, because the masterpiece was done.

The price of the masterpiece was on a card tacked to the frame: "65.00, frame included. Ask about our lay-away plan." The "our" on the card referred to Stedman and his wife Cornelia. Cornelia didn't know much about art, but she thought her husband was another Leonardo da Vinci.

And Cornelia wasn't the only one who thought so.

"I swear," said a thunderstruck woman in the demonstration crowd one night, "when you was doing them birch trees, it looked like you was using some kind of birch-bark paint—like all a body had to do was gob it on and it'd come out birch bark. And the same with them clouds—like you was using cloud paint, and all a body had to do was scrootch it on up top without hardly thinking."

Stedman offered her his palette and brush playfully. "Help yourself, Madam," he said. He smiled serenely, but it was an empty smile—a case of the show's going on. All was not well. When he had come out to do his demonstration on schedule, he had left his wife in tears.

Cornelia, he supposed, was still weeping in the trailer behind the studio—was still weeping over the evening paper. In the paper, an art critic had called Stedman an iridescent humbug.

"Land-a-mercy, no!" said the woman to whom Stedman had offered his palette and brush. "I couldn't make nothing look like nothing." She drew back, put her hands behind her.

And then Cornelia appeared, white and trembling—came out of the studio and stood beside her husband. "I want to say something to all these people," she said.

All those people had never seen her before. But she made them understand instantly an awful lot about her. She was scared and humble and shy—had never spoken to a crowd before. Plainly, only a cataclysm of the first magnitude could have loosened her tongue. Cornelia Stedman was suddenly universal—representing all sweet, quiet, affectionate, bewildered housewives full of years.

Stedman was speechless. He had expected nothing like this.

"Ten days from now," said Cornelia unevenly, "my husband's gonna be sixty. And I just wonder how much longer we're gonna have to wait before the world finally wakes up and admits he's one of the greatest painters who ever lived." She bit her lip and fought back tears.

"Some high art muckety-muck from the paper says in the paper tonight that my husband's some kind of a humbug." Now the tears came. "There's a nice birthday present for a man who's given his whole life to art," she said.

The thought broke her up so much that she could hardly begin her next sentence. "My husband," she said at last, "entered ten beautiful pictures in the Annual Exhibition of the so-called Seminole Highlands Art Association, and every one of 'em got rejected." She pointed to a painting in the window of a studio across the street. Her lips moved. She was trying to say something about the painting, a huge, shocking abstract, but no coherent sounds came from her throat.

Cornelia's speech was over. Stedman led her tenderly into the studio, closed the door.

Stedman kissed his wife and made her a drink. He was in a peculiar position, since he knew perfectly well that he was a humbug. He knew his paintings were awful, knew what a good picture was, knew what a good painter was. But he had somehow never passed the information on to his wife. Cornelia's high opinion of his talent, while showing dreadful taste, was the most precious thing that Stedman had.

When Cornelia had finished her drink, she finished her speech, too. "All your beautiful pictures got rejected," she said. She pointed to the painting across the street with a hand that was now steady and deadly. "And that mess across the street won first prize," she said.

"Well, honey bunch," said Stedman, "like we've always said, we've got to take the bad with the good, and the good's been mighty good." The painting across the street was superbly imaginative, powerful, sincere—and Stedman knew it, felt it in his bones.

"There's all kinds of painting styles, honey bunch," he said, "and some kinds of people like one kind and some kinds of people like another kind, and that's the way the ball bounces."

Cornelia continued to stare across the street. "I wouldn't give that awful thing houseroom," she said darkly. "There's a big conspiracy going on against you," she said, "and it's high time somebody blew the whistle."

Cornelia stood up, slowly, dangerously, still staring across the street. "Now what's she think she's pasting in the window?" she said.

Across the street, Sylvia Lazarro was taping a newspaper article to the front window of her husband's studio. It was the article that called Stedman a humbug.

Sylvia was putting it up for all to see, not because of the humbug crack but because of what it said about her husband, John Lazarro. It said Lazarro was the most exciting young abstractionist in Florida. It said Lazarro was capable of expressing complex emotions with extraordinarily simple elements. It said Lazarro painted with the rarest of all pigments—Lazarro painted with soul.

It said also that Lazarro had begun his art career as a boy wonder, discovered in the Chicago slums. He was now only twenty-three. He had never been to art school. He was self-taught.

In the window with the clipping was the painting that had won all the praise and a two-hundred-dollar first prize besides.

In the painting, Lazarro had tried to trap on canvas the pregnant stillness, massive ache and cold sweat in the moment before the break of a thunderstorm. The clouds didn't look like real clouds. They looked like big gray boulders—as solid as granite, but somehow spongy and sopping, too. And the ground didn't look like real ground. It looked like hot, tarnished copper.

There was no shelter in sight. Anyone caught in that godforsaken moment in that godforsaken place would have to cower on that hot copper under those big wet boulders—would have to take whatever Nature was going to hurl down next.

It was an upsetting painting, a painting that only a museum or a dedicated collector would give houseroom to. Lazarro's sales were few.

Lazarro himself was upsetting—seemingly crude and angry. He liked to seem dangerous, to seem the hoodlum he'd almost been. He wasn't dangerous. He was afraid. He was afraid that he was the biggest humbug of all.

He lay fully dressed on his bed in the dark. The only light in his studio came from the overflow of Stedman's profligate lighting scheme across the way. He was thinking morosely about the presents he had hoped to buy with his two-hundred-dollar first prize. The presents would have gone to his wife, but creditors had snatched the prize money away.

Sylvia left the window, sat down on the edge of his bed. She had been a pert, uncomplicated waitress when Lazarro had wooed her. Three years with a complicated, brilliant husband had put circles under her eyes. And bill collectors had reduced her pertness to gamely gay despair. But Sylvia wasn't about to give up. She thought her husband was another Raphael.

"Why wouldn't you read what the man said about you in the paper?" she said.

"Art critics never make any sense to me," said Lazarro.

"You make a lot of sense to them," said Sylvia.

"Hooray," said Lazarro emptily. The more praise he got from critics, the more he secretly cowered on hot copper under a boulder sky. His hands and eyes were so poorly disciplined that he could not draw the simplest likeness. His paintings were brutal, not because he wished to express brutality, but because he could paint no other way. On the surface, Lazarro had only contempt for Stedman. Down deep, he was in awe of Stedman's hands and eyes—hands and eyes that could do anything Stedman asked them to do.

"Lord Stedman has a birthday in ten days," said Sylvia. She had nicknamed the Stedmans "Lord and Lady Stedman" because they were so rich—and because the Lazarros were so poor. "Lady Stedman just came out of the trailer and made a big speech about it."

"Speech?" said Lazarro. "I didn't know Lady Stedman had a voice."

"She had one tonight," said Sylvia. "She was clear off her rocker because the paper called her husband a humbug."

Lazarro took her hand tenderly. "Will you protect me, baby, if anybody ever says that about me?"

"I'd kill anybody who said that about you," said Sylvia.

"You haven't got a cigarette, have you?" said Lazarro.

"Out," said Sylvia. They had been out since noon.

"I thought maybe you'd found a pack hidden around," said Lazarro.

Sylvia was on her feet. "I'll borrow some next door," she said.

Lazarro clung to her hand. "No, no—no," he said. "Don't borrow anything more next door."

"If you want a cigarette so badly—" said Sylvia.

"Never mind. Forget it," said Lazarro, a little wildly. "I'm giving 'em up. The first few days are the hardest. Save a lot of money—feel a lot better."

Sylvia squeezed his hand, let go of it—went to the beaverboard wall and drummed with her fists. "It's so unfair," she said bitterly. "I hate them."

"Hate who?" said Lazarro, sitting up.

"Lord and Lady Stedman!" said Sylvia through clenched teeth. "Showing off all their money over there. Lord Stedman with his big, fat twenty-five-cent cigar stuck in his face—selling those silly pictures of his hand over fist—and here's you, trying to bring something new and wonderful and original into the world, and you can't even have a cigarette when you want one!"

There was a firm knock on the door. There were the sounds of a small crowd out there, too, as though Stedman's demonstration crowd had crossed the street.

And then Stedman himself spoke up outside the door, said plaintively, "Now, honey bunch—"

Sylvia went to the door, opened it.

Outside stood Lady Stedman, very proud, Lord Stedman, very wretched, and a crowd, very interested.

"Take that rotten thing out of your window this very instant," Cornelia Stedman said to Sylvia Lazarro.

"Take what out of my window?" said Sylvia.

"Take that clipping out of your window," said Cornelia.

"What about the clipping?" said Sylvia.

"You know what about the clipping," said Cornelia.

Lazarro heard the women's voices rising. The voices sounded harmless enough at first—merely business-like. But each sentence ended on a slightly higher note.

Lazarro reached the door of the studio just in time to witness the moment before the break of a fight between two nice women—between two nice women pushed too far. The clouds that seemed to hang over Cornelia and Sylvia weren't wet and massive. They were a luminous, poisonous green.

"You mean," said Sylvia crisply, "the part of the clipping that says your husband is a humbug or the part that says my husband is great?"

The storm broke.

The women didn't touch each other. They stood apart and whaled away with awful truths. And no matter what they yelled, they didn't hurt each other at all. The mad joy of a battle finally joined improved them both.

It was the husbands who were being dilapidated. Every time Cornelia hurled a taunt, it hit Lazarro hard. She knew him for the clumsy fraud he was.

Lazarro glanced at Stedman, saw that Stedman winced and sucked in air every time Sylvia let a good gibe fly.

When the fight entered its declining phase, the women's words were clearer, more deliberate.

"Do you honestly think my husband couldn't paint a silly old picture of an Indian in a birch-bark canoe or a cabin in a valley?" said Sylvia Lazarro. "He could do it without even thinking! He paints the way he paints because he's too honest to copy old calendars."

"You really think my husband couldn't paint big hunks of glunk just any which way, and think up some fancy name for it?" said Cornelia Stedman. "You think he couldn't ook and gook paint around so's one of your high muckety-muck critic friends would come around and look at the mess and say, 'Now there's what I call real soul'? You really think that?"

"You bet I think that," said Sylvia.

"You want to have a little contest?" said Cornelia.

"Anything you say," said Sylvia.

"All righty," said Cornelia. "Tonight your husband'll do a picture of something that really looks like something, and tonight my husband'll paint with what you call soul." She tossed her gray head. "And we'll just see who eats crow tomorrow."

"You're on," said Sylvia happily. "You're on."

◎ ◎ ◎

"Just squook the old paint on," said Cornelia Stedman. She felt marvelous, looked twenty years younger. She was looking over her husband's shoulder.

Stedman was seated bleakly before a blank canvas.

Cornelia picked up a tube of paint, squeezed it hard, laid a vermilion worm on the canvas. "All righty," she said, "now you take it from there." Stedman picked up a brush listlessly, did nothing with it. He knew he was going to fail.

He had been living cheerfully with artistic failure for years. He had managed to coat it with the sugar of ready cash. But now he was sure that his failure was going to be presented to him so nakedly, so dramatically, that he could only take it for the ghastly thing it was.

He did not doubt that Lazarro was now creating across the street a painting so well drawn, so vibrant, that even Cornelia and the demonstration crowds would be struck dumb. And Stedman would be so shamed that he would never touch a brush again.

He looked everywhere but at the canvas, studied the paintings and signs on the studio walls as though he had never seen them before. "A ten percent deposit holds anything Stedman does," said a sign. "At no extra charge," said a sign, "Stedman will work the colors of a customer's drapes, carpet, and upholstery into a sunset." "Stedman," said a sign, "will make a genuine oil painting from any photograph." Stedman found himself wondering who this bustling Stedman was.

Stedman now considered Stedman's work. One theme occurred in every painting—a cunning little cottage with smoke coming from its fieldstone chimney. It was a sturdy little cottage that no wolf could ever huff and puff down. And the cottage seemed to say, no matter where Stedman set it down, "Come in, weary stranger, whoever you are—come in and rest your bones."

Stedman wished he could drag himself inside the cottage, close the doors and shutters, and huddle before the fire. He comprehended vaguely that that was where he had been, in fact, for the last thirty-five years.

Now he was being dragged out.

"Sweetheart—" said Cornelia.

"Hm?" said Stedman.

"Aren't you glad?" she said.

"Glad?" said Stedman.

"About how we're having out about who's the real artist?" said Cornelia.

"Glad as can be," said Stedman. He managed a smile.

"Then why don't you go ahead and paint?" said Cornelia.

"Why not?" said Stedman. He raised his brush, made flicking thrusts at the vermilion worm. In seconds he had created a vermilion clump of birch. A dozen more thoughtless thrusts, and he had erected a small vermilion cottage next to the clump of trees.

"An Indian—do an Indian," said Sylvia Lazarro, and she laughed because Stedman was always doing Indians. Sylvia put a fresh canvas on Lazarro's easel, sketched on it with her fingertip. "Make him bright red," she said, "and give him a big eagle beak. And put a sunset over a mountain in the background, with a little cottage on the side of the mountain."

Lazarro's eyes were glazed. "All in one picture?" he said glumly.

"Sure," said Sylvia. She was a frisky bride again. "Put all kinds of stuff in, so people will shut up once and for all about how their kids can draw better than you can."

Lazarro hunched over, rubbed his eyes. It was absolutely true that he drew like a child. He drew like an astonishing, wildly imaginative child—but like a child all the same. Some of the things he did now, in fact, were almost indistinguishable from things he had done in childhood.

Lazarro found himself wondering if perhaps his greatest work hadn't been his very first. His first work of any importance had been in stolen colored chalk on a sidewalk in the shadows of a Chicago El. He had been twelve.

He had begun his first big work as a piece of slum-craftiness, part racket, part practical joke. Bigger and bigger the bright chalk picture had grown—and crazier and crazier. Green sheets of rain, laced with black lightning, fell on jumbled pyramids. It was daytime here and nighttime there, with a pale gray moon making daytime, with a hot red sun making night.

And the bigger and crazier the picture had become, the more a growing crowd had loved it. Change had showered on the sidewalk. Strangers had brought the artist more chalk. Police had come. Reporters had come. Photographers had come. The mayor himself had come.

When young Lazarro had arisen at last from his hands and knees, he had made himself, for one summer day at least, the most famous and beloved artist in the Middle West. Now he wasn't a boy anymore. He was a man who made his living painting like a boy, and his wife was asking him to paint an Indian that really looked like an Indian.

"It will be so easy for you," said Sylvia. "You won't have to put soul in it or anything." She scowled and shaded her eyes, pretended to scan the horizon like a Stedman Indian. "Just do um heap big Injun," she said.

By one in the morning, Durling Stedman had driven himself almost out of his wits. Pounds of paint had been laid on the canvas before him. Pounds had been scraped away. No matter how abstract Stedman made his beginnings, the hackneyed themes of a lifetime came through. He could not restrain a cube from turning into a cottage, a cone from turning into a snow-capped mountain, a sphere from becoming a harvest moon. And Indians popped up everywhere, numerous enough at times for a panorama of Custer's Last Stand.

"You just can't keep your talent from busting right through, can you?" his wife Cornelia said.

Stedman blew up, ordered her to bed.

"It would be a hell of a help if you wouldn't watch," John Lazarro said to his wife peevishly.

"I just want to keep you from working too hard at it," said Sylvia. She yawned. "If I leave you alone with it, I'm afraid you'll start putting soul in it and get it all complicated. Just paint an Indian."

"I *am* painting an Indian," said Lazarro, his nerves twanging.

"You—you mind if I ask a question?" said Sylvia.

Lazarro closed his eyes. "Not at all," he said.

"Where's the Indian?" she said.

Lazarro gritted his teeth, pointed to the middle of the canvas. "There's your lousy Indian," he said.

"A green Indian?" said Sylvia.

"That's the underpainting," said Lazarro.

Sylvia put her arms around him, babied him. "Honey," she said, "please don't underpaint. Just start right off with an Indian." She picked up a tube of paint. "Here—this is a good color for an Indian. Just draw the Indian, then color him with this—like in a Mickey Mouse coloring book."

Lazarro threw his brush across the room. "I couldn't even color a picture of Mickey Mouse with somebody looking over my shoulder!" he yelled.

Sylvia backed away. "Sorry. I'm just trying to tell you how easy it should be," she said.

"Go to bed!" said Lazarro. "You'll get your stinking Indian! Just go to bed."

Stedman heard Lazarro's yell, mistook it for a yell of joy. Stedman thought that the yell could mean one of two things—that Lazarro had finished his painting, or that the painting had jelled and would very soon be done.

He imagined Lazarro's painting—saw it now as a shimmering Tintoretto, now as a shadowy Caravaggio, now as a swirling Rubens.

Doggedly, not caring if he lived or died, Stedman began killing Indians with his palette knife again. His self-contempt was now at its peak.

He stopped working completely when he realized how profound his contempt for himself was. It was so profound that he could decide without shame to go across the street and buy a painting with soul from Lazarro. He would pay a great deal for a Lazarro painting, for the right to sign his own name to it, for Lazarro's keeping quiet about the whole shabby deal.

Having come to this decision, Stedman began to paint again. He painted now in an orgy of being his good old, vulgar, soulless self.

He created a mountain range with a dozen saber strokes. He dragged his brush above the mountains, and his brush trailed clouds behind. He shook his brush at the mountainsides, and Indians tumbled out.

The Indians formed at once for an attack on some poor thing in the valley. Stedman knew what the poor thing was. They were going to attack his precious cottage. He stood to paint the cottage angrily. He painted the front door ajar. He painted himself inside. "There's the essence of Stedman!" he sneered. He chuckled bitterly. "There the old fool is."

Stedman went back to the trailer, made sure Cornelia was sound asleep. He counted the money in his billfold, then stole back through his studio and across the street.

Lazarro was exhausted. He didn't feel that he had been painting for the past five hours. He felt that he had been trying to rescue a cigar-store Indian from quicksand. The quicksand was the paint on Lazarro's canvas.

Lazarro had given up on pulling the Indian to the surface. He had let the Indian slip away at last to the Happy Hunting Ground.

The surface of the painting closed over the Indian, closed over Lazarro's self-respect, too. Life had called Lazarro's bluff, as he'd always known it would.

He smiled like a racketeer, hoped to feel that he had gotten away with a very funny swindle for a good number of years. But he couldn't feel that way. He cared terribly about painting, wanted terribly to go on painting. If he was a racketeer, he was the racket's most pathetic victim, too.

As Lazarro dropped his clumsy hands into his lap, he thought of what the deft hands of Stedman must now be doing. If Stedman told those magical hands to be worldly, like Picasso's, they would be worldly. If he told those hands to be rigidly rectilinear, like Mondrian's, they would be rigidly rectilinear. If he told those hands to be wickedly childish, like Klee's, they would be wickedly childish. If he told those hands to be fumblingly angry, like Lazarro's, those magical hands of Stedman's could be that way, too.

Lazarro had sunk so low that it actually flashed into his mind to steal a painting of Stedman's, to sign his own name to it, to threaten the poor old man with violence if he dared to say a word.

Lazarro could sink no lower. He began to paint now about how low he felt—about how crooked, how crude, how dirty Lazarro was. The painting was mostly black. It was the last painting Lazarro was ever going to do, and its title was *No Damn Good.*

There was a sound at the studio's front door, as though a sick animal were outside. Lazarro went on painting feverishly.

The sound came again.

Lazarro went to the door, opened it.

Outside stood Lord Stedman. "If I look like a man who's just about to be hanged," said Stedman, "that's exactly how I feel."

"Come in," said Lazarro. "Come in."

Durling Stedman slept until eleven in the morning. He tried to make himself sleep longer, but he could not. He did not want to get up.

In analyzing his reasons for not wanting to get up, Stedman found that he wasn't afraid of the day. He had, after all, solved his problem of the night before neatly—by trading paintings with Lazarro. He no longer feared humiliation. He had signed his name to a painting with soul. Glory was probably awaiting him in the strange stillness outside.

What made Stedman not want to get up was a feeling that he had lost something priceless in the lunatic night.

As he shaved and examined himself in the mirror, he knew that the priceless thing he had lost wasn't integrity. He was still the same old genial humbug. Nor had he lost cash. He and Lazarro had traded even-Steven.

There was no one in his studio as he passed through it from his trailer to the front. It was too early for tourists to be coming through. They wouldn't appear until noon. Nor did Cornelia seem to be around.

The feeling that he had lost something important was now so strong that Stedman gave in to a compulsion to rummage through drawers and cabinets in the studio for only-God-knew-what. He wanted his wife to help him.

"Honey bunch—?" he called.

"There he is!" Cornelia cried outside. She came in, hustled him merrily out to the easel where he did his demonstrations. On the easel was Lazarro's black painting. It was signed by Stedman.

In daylight it had an altogether new quality. The blacks glistened, were alive. And the colors other than black no longer seemed merely muddy variations on black. They gave the painting the soft, holy, timeless translucence of a stained glass window. The painting, moreover, was not obviously a Lazarro. It was far better than a Lazarro, because it wasn't a picture of fear. It was a picture of beauty, pride, and vibrant affirmation.

Cornelia was radiant. "You won, honey—you *won*," she said.

In a grave semicircle before the painting stood a small audience altogether different from that to which Stedman was accustomed. The serious artists had come quietly to see what Stedman had done. They were confused, rueful, and respectful—for the shallow, foolish Stedman had proved that he was the master of them all. They saluted the new master with bittersweet smiles.

"And look at that mess over there!" crowed Cornelia. She pointed across the street. In the window of Lazarro's studio was the painting Stedman had done the night before. It was signed by Lazarro.

Stedman was amazed. The painting looked nothing like a Stedman. It looked something like a postcard, all right, but like a postcard mailed from a private hell.

The Indians and the cottage and the old man huddled in the cottage and the mountains and the clouds didn't conspire this time for bombastic romance and prettiness. With the storytelling quality of a Brueghel, with the sweep of a Turner, with the color of a Giorgione, the painting spoke of an old man's troubled soul.

The painting was the priceless thing that Stedman had lost in the night. It was the only fine thing he had ever done.

Lazarro was crossing the street now, coming toward Stedman, looking wild.

Sylvia Lazarro was with him, protesting as they came. "I've never seen you like this," she said. "What's the matter with you?"

"I want that picture," said Lazarro, loudly, indignantly. "How much you take for it?" he snarled at Stedman. "I haven't got any money now, but I'll pay you when I get some—anything you want. Name your price."

"Have you gone crazy?" said Sylvia. "That's a lousy painting. I wouldn't give it houseroom."

"Shut up!" said Lazarro.

Sylvia shut up.

"Would—would you by any chance consider an even trade?" said Stedman.

Cornelia Stedman laughed. "Trade this beautiful thing here for that slop pile over there?" she said.

"Silence!" said Stedman. For once he was really as grand as he seemed. He shook Lazarro's hand warmly. "Done," he said.

SECTION 6

Behavior

Human behavior has always been a prime topic for fiction writers, but in Kurt Vonnegut's case that behavior has an emphatically social cast. Especially in his short stories, community is often a factor in determing themes and their expression in character and plot. Interventions by representatives of specific communal functions are a favorite device. There's the bandmaster from Lincoln High School who solves problems with his students, the storm window and bathtub enclosure salesman who not only installs his work but serves as a reminder of communal sanity amid curious departures, and in some of the stories that follow an investments counsellor who handles matters that involve anything except money. In these and other stories the overriding truth is that as crazy as things might get, there is always a world of stable values that can support human endeavor.

Why should Vonnegut choose the salesman for an investments firm as his narrator, spokesperson, and catalyst for action in so many stories? The answer is that investment is a social act. An investor takes some of his or her own money and not only gives it to someone else, but puts it to work in a larger enterprise. If it succeeds, that enterprise will be beneficial to the community, such as the ferry service from Cape Cod to Nantucket in which Kurt himself invested at the same time he was writing these stories. The investment failed, by the way, a reminder that there is always a risk factor in such endeavors. And even the failures make good stories.

A very good one is "The Foster Portfolio," in which the financial adviser spends an evening with a client whose humble lifestyle belies the fact that he's worth a fortune. Why this investor neglects his portfolio with its treasures in favor of living in economically stressful conditions isn't the point. The point is that he does, no matter what. Money isn't everything, the counsellor learns, but happiness is. Appearing in *Collier's* on September 8, 1951, it sets the tone for others that follow. Vonnegut chose it to represent such efforts in both *Canary in a Cat House* and *Welcome to the Monkey House*. Much later he'd allow "Custom-Made Bride" from the March 27, 1954, *Saturday Evening Post* and "Unpaid Consultant" as first published in the March 1955 issue of *Cosmopolitan* to be collected in *Bagombo Snuff Box*. "Sucker's

669

Portfolio" was never accepted by a magazine, but is part of the posthumous collection with that title. "The Drone King" has rested until now among his papers in Indiana University's Lilly Library. In each case the client's behavior is different, on an ascending scale of behavior that pushes and finally exceeds rational limits.

Where is behavior normal? In the village, be it North Crawford, New Hampshire, or an unnamed small community on Cape Cod, very like where Kurt and his family lived throughout the 1950s and '60s. At the heart of these places is the local community theater, a natural place for Vonnegut to anchor his action. In his own life he was always community minded, serving in the volunteer fire department of Alplaus, New York (a suburb of Schenectady where he worked as a publicist for General Electric in the late 1940s), helping teach a Great Books course for neighbors on Cape Cod in the next decade, and participating in community theater into the 1960s. Even after moving to New York City in 1970, where he feasted on the fame of his novel *Slaughterhouse-Five*'s success, Kurt Vonnegut remained dependent for a time on the extended-family style of support a theater company provided as his play *Happy Birthday, Wanda June* was prepared for production. Village life of a more general sort stands at the center of two stories published posthumously in *Look at the Birdie*, "Hello, Red" and "The Honor of a Newsboy." Each has a protagonist, and each benefits from its own strong theme. But both depend upon community standards and social attitudes to work effectively, which they do.

What other social activities can generate stories? Like the opening line of so many old-fashioned jokes, "guy walks into a bar," the notion of a guy sitting on a park bench and being approached by a stranger can provide the starting point for any number of narratives. Two of them, one published in 1953, the other after Kurt's death, show what he could do with the situation. "Tom Edison's Shaggy Dog" was snapped up by *Collier's*, while "The Man Without No Kiddleys" waited until the posthumous volume *While Mortals Sleep*. The stories are companions in inception but differ in their endings. In other narratives, Vonnegut was tempering his barbed humor with redeeming sentiment at the end, perhaps softening his wit with hopes for a sale. It is instructive for his future success as a novelist that it was the "unredeemed" piece one of the higher-paying magazines of the time accepted, providing what must have been half of his short story income for that year. (That his family didn't go hungry was thanks to earnings from a Book Club edition of his novel *Player Piano* and a small advance for its paperback version coming out the next year, retitled as *Utopia 14*.)

Teenage behavior can have both lighter and more serious moments, and Kurt Vonnegut knew from his bandmaster stories that the family weeklies were eager to have such doings treated. "Runaways" provided the *Saturday Evening Post* with a text that fit popular radio's soundtrack of the era, young-love lyrics which Kurt wrote gleefully. As the father of teens at the time, he must have taken great pleasure in giving the parents this story's last laugh. The other great factor in teenagers' lives, at least among the boys, are cars, and an especially powerful one gives its name to *Cosmopolitan*'s "The Powder-Blue Dragon." Sadly, there are no laughs here.

Maturity and variations of how it can be displayed are factors in behavior as well. An unsold story appearing in *While Mortals Sleep* makes the case brilliantly. Here a young man just out of his teens meets with the uncle who has been his legal guardian. It is the situation of "Runaways" reversed, with telling consequences. Even at this very early stage of his career Vonnegut could counterpose the narrative progress of two characters on track to meet each other, a progress wrought with tension because the reader has learned how the intentions of these characters are at cross purposes. This style of developmental cross-cutting would serve the author well in his seventh novel, *Breakfast of Champions*, where writer Kilgore Trout travels halfway across the country to the hometown of Dwayne Hoover, a reader who has taken Trout's fiction far too seriously. In "Guardian of the Person," it is mutual misapprehension—mutual misreading, if you will—that seals the story's fate.

Finally, there is the behavior of the brothers Vonnegut, Kurt and Bernard, employed by General Electric in its public relations office and research laboratory respectively. In a book review Kurt wrote several years after the popularity of television had eroded his magazine market, "Money Talks to the New Man," the author was transitioning to a new style of personal journalism that would soon give special voice to his novels as well.) Here, in talking about Goffredo Parise's rather fantastic *The Boss*, Kurt compares its situation to his own. "Years ago, when I worked as a public-relations man for General Electric," he explains, "I was rated by three of my co-workers every six months—anonymously. Then I had to go over the comments with my boss, promising to improve." He even names his boss, Griffin, and gives him a personality. As ridiculous as Parise's fictive employer, "Griffin was something else again." When the employee in the novel is forced to marry a Mongolian idiot and submit to painful megavitamin injections, Kurt allows that "Griffin and I had our troubles, but nothing like that." The review goes on to locate the fantasy of Parise's novel in real water-cooler conversations that characterize any office, including Vonnegut's own.

The short story that Kurt Vonnegut did write about his office at GE, "Bomar," has its co-workers conspiring to fool a secretary about an oddly named stockholder who remains a character of fantasy—until the whole event blows up in their faces. Read today among other materials not published until after his death, it recalls his own monkey business with a fake letter on General Electric stationery he wrote to his uncle Alex late in 1947, when he'd only been on the job for a short time. Just as in "Bomar," the prank blew up in his face, as recounted in his epilogue to *Timequake*. Here the author discusses how his brother's recent death has brought back memories of all the fun they'd had together growing up, and how Bernard had saved this letter that had so infuriated their uncle. Nearly thirty years before, when writing the preface for *Welcome to the Monkey House*, Kurt had named Bernard and their sister Alice as inspirations for the two main themes of his work:"cleaning shit off of practically everything" and "no pain."

Bernard, whom Kurt testified as being funnier than himself, gets featured in a previously unpublished story found among his papers at Indiana University's Lilly Library. "And on Your Left" takes place in a similar corporation's quite similar research lab, with scientists who had to be based on the people Bernard worked with and on whom Kurt reported as the lab's publicist. Intended to function together, the two activities collide, as hilariously as anything Kurt later wrote about his brother and his own work at GE. Would his boss Griffin have approved? See if you can find Griffin in the story.

—JK

The Foster Portfolio

I'M A SALESMAN of good advice for rich people. I'm a contact man for an investment counseling firm. It's a living, but not a whale of a one—or at least not now, when I'm just starting out. To qualify for the job, I had to buy a Homburg, a navy-blue overcoat; a double-breasted banker's gray suit, black shoes, a regimental-stripe tie, half a dozen white shirts, half a dozen pairs of black socks and gray gloves.

When I call on a client, I come by cab, and I am sleek and clean and foursquare. I carry myself as though I've made a quiet killing on the stock market, and have come to call more as a public service than anything else. When I arrive in clean wool, with crackling certificates and confidential stock analyses in crisp Manila folders, the reaction—ideally and usually—is the same accorded a minister or physician. I am in charge, and everything is going to be just fine.

I deal mostly with old ladies—the meek, who by dint of cast-iron constitutions have inherited sizable portions of the earth. I thumb through the clients' lists of securities, and relay our experts' suggestions for ways of making their portfolios—or bonanzas or piles—thrive and increase. I can speak of tens of thousands of dollars without a catch in my throat, and look at a list of securities worth more than a hundred thousand with no more fuss than a judicious "Mmmmm, uh-huh."

Since *I* don't have a portfolio, my job is a little like being a hungry delivery boy for a candy store. But I never really felt that way about it until Herbert Foster asked me to have a look at his finances.

He called one evening to say a friend had recommended me, and could I come out to talk business. I washed, shaved, dusted my shoes, put on my uniform, and made my grave arrival by cab.

People in my business—and maybe people in general—have an unsavory habit of sizing up a man's house, car, and suit, and estimating his annual income. Herbert Foster was six thousand a year, or I'd never seen it. Understand, I have nothing against people in moderate circumstances, other than the crucial fact that I can't make any money off them. It made me a little sore that Foster would take my time, when the most he had to play around with, I guessed, was no more than a few hundred dollars. Say it was a thousand: my take would be a dollar or two at best.

673

Anyway, there I was in the Fosters' jerry-built postwar colonial with expansion attic. They had taken up a local furniture store on its offer of three rooms of furniture, including ashtrays, a humidor, and pictures for the wall, all for $199.99. Hell, I was there, and I figured I might as well go through with having a look at his pathetic problem.

"Nice place you have here, Mr. Foster," I said. "And this is your charming wife?"

A skinny, shrewish-looking woman smiled up at me vacuously. She wore a faded housecoat figured with a fox-hunting scene. The print was at war with the slipcover of the chair, and I had to squint to separate her features from the clash about her. "A pleasure, Mrs. Foster," I said. She was surrounded by underwear and socks to be mended, and Herbert said her name was Alma, which seemed entirely possible.

"And this is the young master," I said. "Bright little chap. Believe he favors his father." The two-year-old wiped his grubby hands on my trousers, snuffled, and padded off toward the piano. He stationed himself at the upper end of the keyboard, and hammered on the highest note for one minute, then two, then three.

"Musical—like his father," Alma said.

"You play, do you, Mr. Foster?"

"Classical," Herbert said. I took my first good look at him. He was lightly built, with the round, freckled face and big teeth I usually associate with a show-off or wise guy. It was hard to believe that he had settled for so plain a wife, or that he could be as fond of family life as he seemed. It may have been that I only imagined a look of quiet desperation in his eyes.

"Shouldn't you be getting on to your meeting, dear?" Herbert said.

"It was called off at the last minute."

"Now, about your portfolio—" I began.

Herbert looked rattled. "How's that?"

"Your portfolio—your securities."

"Yes, well, I think we'd better talk in the bedroom. It's quieter in there."

Alma put down her sewing. "What securities?"

"The bonds, dear. The government bonds."

"Now, Herbert, you're not going to cash them in."

"No, Alma, just want to talk them over."

"I see," I said tentatively. "Uh—approximately how much in government bonds?"

"Three hundred and fifty dollars," Alma said proudly.

"Well," I said, "I don't see any need for going into the bedroom to talk. My advice, and I give it free, is to hang on to your nest egg until it matures. And now, if you'll let me phone a cab—"

"Please," Herbert said, standing in the bedroom door, "there are a couple of other things I'd like to discuss."

"What?" Alma said.

"Oh, long-range investment planning," Herbert said vaguely.

"We could use a little short-range planning for next month's grocery bill."

"Please," Herbert said to me again.

I shrugged and followed him into the bedroom. He closed the door behind me. I sat on the edge of the bed and watched him open a little door in the wall, which bared the pipes servicing the bathroom. He slid his arm up into the wall, grunted, and pulled down an envelope.

"Oho," I said apathetically, "so that's where we've got the bonds, eh? Very clever. You needn't have gone to that trouble, Mr. Foster. I have an idea what government bonds look like."

"Alma," he called.

"Yes, Herbert."

"Will you start some coffee for us?"

"I don't drink coffee at night," I said.

"We have some from dinner," Alma said.

"I can't sleep if I touch it after supper," I said.

"Fresh—we want some fresh," Herbert said.

The chair springs creaked, and her reluctant footsteps faded into the kitchen.

"Here," said Herbert, putting the envelope in my lap. "I don't know anything about this business, and I guess I ought to have professional help."

All right, so I'd give the poor guy a professional talk about his three hundred and fifty dollars in government bonds. "They're the most conservative investment you can make. They haven't the growth characteristics of many securities, and the return isn't great, but they're very safe. By all means hang on to them." I stood up. "And now, if you'll let me call a cab—"

"You haven't looked at them."

I sighed, and untwisted the red string holding the envelope shut. Nothing would do but that I admire the things. The bonds and a list of securities slid into my lap. I riffled through the bonds quickly, and then read the list of securities slowly.

"Well?"

I put the list down on the faded bedspread. I composed myself. "Mmmmm, uh-huh," I said. "Do you mind telling me where the securities listed here came from?"

"Grandfather left them to me two years ago. The lawyers who handled the estate have them. They sent me that list."

"Do you know what these stocks are worth?"

"They were appraised when I inherited them." He told me the figure, and, to my bewilderment, he looked sheepish, even a little unhappy about it.

"They've gone up a little since then."

"How much?"

"On today's market—maybe they're worth seven hundred and fifty thousand dollars, Mr. Foster. Sir."

His expression didn't change. My news moved him about as much as if I'd told him it'd been a chilly winter. He raised his eyebrows as Alma's footsteps came back into the living room. "Shhhh!"

"She doesn't know?"

"Lord, no!" He seemed to have surprised himself with his vehemence. "I mean the time isn't ripe."

"If you'll let me have this list of securities, I'll have our New York office give you a complete analysis and recommendations," I whispered. "May I call you Herbert, sir?"

◎ ◎ ◎

My client, Herbert Foster, hadn't had a new suit in three years; he had never owned more than one pair of shoes at a time. He worried about payments on his second-hand car, and ate tuna and cheese instead of meat, because meat was too expensive. His wife made her own clothes, and those of Herbert, Jr., and the curtains and slipcovers—all cut from the same bargain bolt. The Fosters were going through hell, trying to choose between new tires or retreads for the car; and television was something they had to go two doors down the street to watch. Determinedly, they kept within the small salary Herbert made as a bookkeeper for a wholesale grocery house.

God knows it's no disgrace to live that way, which is better than the way I live, but it was pretty disturbing to watch, knowing Herbert had an income, after taxes, of perhaps twenty thousand a year.

I had our securities analysts look over Foster's holdings, and report on the stocks' growth possibilities, prospective earnings, the effects of war and peace, inflation and deflation, and so on. The report ran to twenty pages, a record for any of my clients. Usually, the reports are bound in cardboard covers. Herbert's was done up in red leatherette.

It arrived at my place on a Saturday afternoon, and I called up Herbert to ask if I could bring it out. I had exciting news for him. My by-eye estimate of the values had been off, and his portfolio, as of that day, was worth close to eight hundred and fifty thousand.

"I've got the analysis and recommendations," I said, "and things look good, Mr. Foster—*very* good. You need a little diversification here and there, and maybe more emphasis on growth, but—"

"Just go ahead and do whatever needs to be done," he said.

"When could we talk about this? It's something we ought to go over together, certainly. Tonight would be fine with me."

"I work tonight."

"Overtime at the wholesale house?"

"Another job—in a restaurant. Work Friday, Saturday, and Sunday nights."

I winced. The man had maybe seventy-five dollars a day coming in from his securities, and he worked three nights a week to make ends meet! "Monday?"

"Play organ for choir practice at the church."

"Tuesday?"

"Volunteer Fire Department drill."

"Wednesday?"

"Play piano for folk dancing at the church."

"Thursday?"

"Movie night for Alma and me."

"When, then?"

"You go ahead and do whatever needs to be done."

"Don't you want to be in on what I'm doing?"

"Do I have to be?"

"I'd feel better if you were."

"All right, Tuesday noon, lunch."

"Fine with me. Maybe you'd better have a good look at this report before then, so you can have questions ready."

He sounded annoyed. "Okay, okay, okay. I'll be here tonight until nine. Drop it off before then."

"One more thing, Herbert." I'd saved the kicker for last. "I was way off about what the stocks are worth. They're now up to about eight hundred and fifty thousand dollars."

"Um."

"I said, you're about a hundred thousand dollars richer than you thought!"

"Uh-huh. Well, you just go ahead and do whatever needs to be done."

"Yes, sir." The phone was dead.

◎ ◎ ◎

I was delayed by other business, and I didn't get out to the Fosters' until quarter of ten. Herbert was gone. Alma answered the door, and, to my surprise, she asked for the report, which I was hiding under my coat.

"Herbert said I wasn't supposed to look at it," she said, "so you don't need to worry about me peeking."

"Herbert told you about this?" I said carefully.

"Yes. He said it's confidential reports on stocks you want to sell him."

"Yes, uh-huh—well, if he said to leave it with you, here it is."

"He told me he had to promise you not to let *anybody* look at it."

"Mmm? Oh, yes, yes. Sorry, company rules."

She was a shade hostile. "I'll tell you one thing without looking at any reports, and that is he's not going to cash those bonds to buy any stocks with."

"I'd be the last one to recommend that, Mrs. Foster."

"Then why do you keep after him?"

"He may be a good customer at a later date." I looked at my hands, which I realized had become inkstained on the earlier call. "I wonder if I might wash up?"

Reluctantly, she let me in, keeping as far away from me as the modest floor plan would permit.

As I washed up, I thought of the list of securities Herbert had taken from between the plasterboard walls. Those securities meant winters in Florida, *filet mignon* and twelve-year-old bourbon, Jaguars, silk underwear and handmade shoes, a trip around the world . . . Name it; Herbert Foster could have it. I sighed heavily. The soap in the Foster soap dish was mottled and dingy—a dozen little chips moistened and pressed together to make a new bar.

I thanked Alma, and started to leave. On my way out, I paused by the mantel to look at a small tinted photograph. "Good picture of you," I said. A feeble effort at public relations. "I like that."

"Everybody says that. It isn't me; it's Herbert's mother."

"Amazing likeness." And it was. Herbert had married a girl just like the girl that married dear old dad. "And this picture is his father?"

"*My* father. We don't want a picture of *his* father."

This looked like a sore point that might prove informative. "Herbert is such a wonderful person, his father must have been wonderful, too, eh?"

"He deserted his wife and child. That's how wonderful he was. You'll be smart not to mention him to Herbert."

"Sorry. Everything good about Herbert comes from his mother?"

"She was a saint. She taught Herbert to be decent and respectable and God-fearing." Alma was grim about it.

"Was she musical, too?"

"He gets that from his father. But what he does with it is something quite different. His taste in music is his mother's—the classics."

"His father was a jazz man, I take it?" I hinted.

"He preferred playing piano in dives, and breathing smoke and drinking gin, to his wife and child and home and job. Herbert's mother finally said he had to choose one life or the other."

I nodded sympathetically. Maybe Herbert looked on his fortune as filthy, untouchable, since it came from his father's side of the family. "This grandfather of Herbert's, who died two years ago—?"

"He supported Herbert and his mother after his son deserted them. Herbert worshipped him." She shook her head sadly. "He was penniless when he died."

"What a shame."

"I'd so hoped he would leave us a little something, so Herbert wouldn't have to work weekends."

◙ ◙ ◙

We were trying to talk above the clatter, tinkle, and crash of the cafeteria where Herbert ate every day. Lunch was on me—or on my expense account—and I'd picked up his check for eighty-seven cents. I said, "Now, Herbert, before we go any further, we'd better decide what you want from your investments: growth or income." It was a cliché of the counseling business. God knows what *he* wanted from the securities. It didn't seem to be what everybody else wanted—money.

"Whatever you say," Herbert said absently. He was upset about something, and not paying much attention to me.

"Herbert—look, you've got to face this thing. You're a rich man. You've got to concentrate on making the most of your holdings."

"That's why I called you. I want *you* to concentrate. I want you to run things for me, so I won't have to bother with the deposits and proxies and taxes. Don't trouble me with it at all."

"Your lawyers have been banking the dividends, eh?"

"Most of them. Took out thirty-two dollars for Christmas, and gave a hundred to the church."

"So what's your balance?"

He handed me the deposit book.

"Not bad," I said. Despite his Christmas splurge and largess toward the church, he'd managed to salt away $50,227.33. "May I ask what a man with a balance like that can be blue about?"

"Got bawled out at work again."

"Buy the place and burn it down," I suggested.

"I could, couldn't I?" A wild look came into his eyes, then disappeared.

"Herbert, you can do anything your heart desires."

"Oh, I suppose so. It's all in the way you look at it."

I leaned forward. "How *do* you look at it, Herbert?"

"I think every man, for his own self-respect, should earn what he lives on."

"But, Herbert—"

"I have a wonderful wife and child, a nice house for them, and a car. And I've earned every penny of the way. I'm living up to the full measure of my responsibilities. I'm proud to say I'm everything my mother wanted me to be, and nothing my father was."

"Do you mind my asking what your father was?"

"I don't enjoy talking about him. Home and family meant nothing to him. His real love was for low-down music and honky-tonks, and for the trash in them."

"Was he a good musician, do you think?"

"Good?" For an instant, there was excitement in his voice, and he tensed, as though he were going to make an important point. But he relaxed again. "Good?" he repeated, flatly this time. "Yes, in a crude way, I suppose he was passable—technically, that is."

"And that much you inherited from him."

"His wrists and hands, maybe. God help me if there's any more of him in me."

"You've got his love of music, too."

"I love music, but I'd never let it get like dope to me!" he said, with more force than seemed necessary.

"Uh-huh. Well—"

"Never!"

"Beg your pardon?"

His eyes were wide. "I said I'll never let music get like dope to me. It's important to me, but I'm master of it, and not the other way around."

◎ ◎ ◎

Apparently it was a treacherous subject, so I switched back to the matter of his finances. "Yes, well, now about your portfolio again: just what use do you expect to make of it?"

"Use some of it for Alma's and my old age; leave most of it to the boy."

"The least you can do is take enough out of the kitty to let you out of working weekends."

He stood up suddenly. "Look. I want you to handle my securities, not my life. If you can't do one without the other, I'll find someone who can."

"Please, Herbert, Mr. Foster. I'm sorry, sir. I was only trying to get the whole picture for planning."

He sat down, red-faced. "All right then, respect my convictions. I want to make my own way. If I have to hold a second job to make ends meet, then that's my cross to bear."

"Sure, sure, certainly. And you're dead right, Herbert. I respect you for it." I thought he belonged in the bughouse for it. "You leave everything to me from now on. I'll invest those dividends and run the whole show." As I puzzled over Herbert, I glanced at a passing blonde. Herbert said something I missed. "What was that, Herbert?"

"I said, 'If thy right eye offend thee, pluck it out and cast it from thee.'"

I laughed appreciatively, then cut it short. Herbert was deadly serious. "Well, pretty soon you'll have the car paid for, and then you can take a well-earned rest on the weekends. And you'll really have something to be proud of, eh? Earned the whole car by the sweat of your brow, right down to the tip of the exhaust pipe."

"One more payment."

"*Then* by-by restaurant."

"There'll still be Alma's birthday present to pay for. I'm getting her television."

"Going to earn that, too, are you?"

"Think how much more meaningful it will be as a gift, if I do."

"Yes, sir, and it'll give her something to do on weekends, too."

"If I have to work weekends for twenty-eight more months, God knows it's little enough to do for her."

If the stock market kept doing what it had been doing for the past three years, Herbert would be a millionaire just about the time he made the last payment on Alma's birthday present. "Fine."

"I love my family," Herbert said earnestly.

"I'm sure you do."

"And I wouldn't trade the life I've got for anything."

"I can certainly see why," I said. I had the impression that he was arguing with me, that it was important to him that I be convinced.

"When I consider what my father was, and then see the life I've made for myself, it's the biggest thrill in all my experience."

A very small thrill could qualify for the biggest in Herbert's experience, I thought. "I envy you. It must be gratifying."

"Gratifying," he repeated determinedly. "It is, it is, it is."

◎ ◎ ◎

My firm began managing Herbert's portfolio, converting some of the slower-moving securities into more lucrative ones, investing the accumulated dividends, diversifying his holdings so he'd be in better shape to weather economic shifts—and in general making his fortune altogether shipshape. A sound portfolio is a thing of beauty in its way, aside from its cash value. Putting one together is a creative act, if done right, with solid major themes of industrials, rails, and utilities, and with the lighter, more exciting themes of electronics, frozen foods, magic drugs, oil and gas, aviation, and other more speculative items. Herbert's portfolio was our masterpiece. I was thrilled and proud of what the firm had done, and not being able to show it off, even to him, was depressing.

It was too much for me, and I decided to engineer a coincidence. I would find out in which restaurant Herbert worked, and then drop in, like any other citizen, for something to eat. I would happen to have a report on his overhauled portfolio with me.

I telephoned Alma, who told me the name of the place, one I'd never heard of. Herbert hadn't wanted to talk about the place, so I gathered that it was pretty grim—as he said, his cross to bear.

It was worse than I'd expected: tough, brassy, dark, and noisy. Herbert had picked one hell of a place, indeed, to do penance for a wayward father, or to demonstrate his gratitude to his wife, or to maintain his self-respect by earning his own way—or to do whatever it was he was doing there.

I elbowed my way between bored-looking women and racetrack types to the bar. I had to shout at the bartender to be heard. When I did get through to him, he yelled back that he'd never heard of no Herbert Foster. Herbert, then, was about as minor an employee as there was in the establishment. He was probably doing something greasy in the kitchen or basement. Typical.

In the kitchen, a crone was making questionable-looking hamburgers, and nipping at a quart of beer.

"I'm looking for Herbert Foster."

"Ain' no damn' Herbert Foster in here."

"In the basement?"

"Ain' no damn' basement."

"Ever hear of Herbert Foster?"

"Ain't never heard of no damn' Herbert Foster."

"Thanks."

I sat in a booth to think it over. Herbert had apparently picked the joint out of a telephone book, and told Alma it was where he spent his weekend evenings. In a way, it made me feel better, because it began to look as though Herbert maybe had better reasons than he'd given me for letting eight hundred and fifty thousand dollars get musty. I remembered that every time I'd mentioned his giving up the weekend job, he'd reacted like a man hearing a dentist tune up his drill. I saw it now: the minute he let Alma know he was rich, he'd lose his excuse for getting away from her on weekends.

But what was it that was worth more to Herbert than eight hundred and fifty thousand? Binges? Dope? Women? I sighed, and admitted I was kidding myself, that I was no closer to the answer than I'd ever been. Moral turpitude on Herbert's part was inconceivable. Whatever he was up to, it had to be for a good cause. His mother had done such a thorough job on him, and he was so awfully ashamed of his father's failings, that I was sure he couldn't operate any other way but righteously. I gave up on the puzzle, and ordered a nightcap.

And then Herbert Foster, looking drab and hunted, picked his way through the crowd. His expression was one of disapproval, of a holy man in Babylon. He was oddly stiff-necked and held his arms at his sides as he pointedly kept from brushing against anyone or from meeting any of the gazes that fell upon him. There was no question that being in the place was absolute, humiliating hell for him.

I called to him, but he paid no attention. There was no communicating with him. Herbert was in a near coma of see-no-evil, speak-no-evil, hear-no-evil.

The crowd in the rear parted for him, and I expected to see Herbert go into a dark corner for a broom or a mop. But a light flashed on at the far end of the aisle the crowd made for him, and a tiny white piano sparkled there like jewelry. The bartender set a drink on the piano, and went back to his post.

Herbert dusted off the piano bench with his handkerchief, and sat down gingerly. He took a cigarette from his breast pocket and lighted it. And then the cigarette started to droop slowly from his lips; and, as it drooped, Herbert hunched over the keyboard and his eyes narrowed as though he were focusing on something beautiful on a faraway horizon.

Startlingly, Herbert Foster disappeared. In his place sat an excited stranger, his hands poised like claws. Suddenly he struck, and a spasm of dirty, low-down, gorgeous jazz shook the air, a hot, clanging wraith of the twenties.

◙ ◙ ◙

Late that night I went over my masterpiece, the portfolio of Herbert Foster, alias "Firehouse" Harris. I hadn't bothered Firehouse with it or with myself.

In a week or so, there would be a juicy melon from one of his steel companies. Three of his oil stocks were paying extra dividends. The farm machinery company in which he owned five thousand shares was about to offer him rights worth three dollars apiece.

Thanks to me and my company and an economy in full bloom, Herbert was about to be several thousand dollars richer than he'd been a month before. I had a right to be proud, but my triumph—except for the commission—was gall and wormwood.

Nobody could do anything for Herbert. Herbert already had what he wanted. He had had it long before the inheritance or I intruded. He had the respectability his mother had hammered into him. But just as priceless as that was an income not quite big enough to go around. It left him no alternative but—in the holy names of wife, child, and home—to play piano in a dive, and breathe smoke, and drink gin, to be Firehouse Harris, his father's son, three nights out of seven.

Custom-Made Bride

I AM A CUSTOMER'S man for an investment counseling firm. I'm starting to build a clientele and to see my way clear to take, in a modest way, the good advice I sell. My uniform—gray suit, Homburg hat, and navy blue overcoat—is paid for, and after I get a half-dozen more white shirts, I'm going to buy some stock.

We in the investment counseling business have a standard question, which goes, "Mr. X, sir, before we can make our analyses and recommendations, we'd like to know just what it is you want from your portfolio: income or growth?" A portfolio is a nest egg in the form of stocks and bonds. What the question tries to get at is, does the client want to put his nest egg where it will grow, not paying much in dividends at first, or does he want the nest egg to stay about the same size but pay nice dividends?

The usual answer is that the client wants his nest egg to grow *and* pay a lot of dividends. He wants to get richer fast. But I've had plenty of unusual answers, particularly from clients who, because of some kind of mental block, can't take money in the abstract seriously. When asked what they want from their portfolio, they're likely to name something they're itching to blow money on—a car, a trip, a boat, a house.

When I put the question to a client named Otto Krummbein, he said he wanted to make two women happy: Kitty and Falloleen.

Otto Krummbein is a genius, designer of the Krummbein Chair, the Krummbein Di-Modular Bed, the body of the Marittima-Frascati Sports Racer, and the entire line of Mercury Kitchen Appliances.

He is so engrossed in beauty that his mental development in money matters is that of a chickadee. When I showed him the first stock certificate I bought for his portfolio, he wanted to sell it again because he didn't like the artwork.

"What difference do the looks of the certificate make, Otto?" I said, bewildered. "The point is that the company behind it is well managed, growing, and has a big cash reserve."

"Any company," said Otto, "that would choose as its symbol this monstrosity at the top of the certificate, this fat Medusa astride a length of sewer pipe and wrapped in cable, is certainly insensitive, vulgar, and stupid."

When I got Otto as a client, he was in no condition to start building a portfolio. I got him through his lawyer, Hal Murphy, a friend of mine.

"I laid eyes on him for the first time two days ago," said Hal. "He came wandering in here, and said in a casual, fogbound way that he thought he might need a little help." Hal chuckled. "They tell me this Krummbein is a genius, but I say he belongs on Skid Row or in a laughing academy. He's made over two hundred and thirty-five thousand dollars in the past seven years, and—"

"Then he is a genius," I said.

"He's blown every dime of it on parties, nightclubbing, his house, and clothes for his wife," said Hal.

"Hooray," I said. "That's the investment advice I always wanted to give, but nobody would pay for it."

"Well, Krummbein is perfectly happy with his investments," said Hal. "What made him think he might just possibly need a little help was a call from the Internal Revenue Service."

"Oh, oh," I said. "I'll bet he forgot to file a declaration of estimated income for the coming year."

"You lose," said Hal. "This genius has never paid a cent of income taxes—ever! He said he kept expecting them to send him a bill, and they never did." Hal groaned. "Well, brother, they finally got around to it. Some bill!"

"What can I do?" I asked.

"He's got bundles of money coming in all the time—and insists on being paid in cashier's checks," said Hal. "You take care of them while I try to keep him out of prison. I've told him all about you, and he says for you to come out to his house right away."

"What bank does he use?" I said.

"He doesn't use a bank, except to cash the checks, which he keeps in a wicker basket under his drafting table," said Hal. "Get that basket!"

Otto's home and place of business is thirty miles from town, in a wilderness by a waterfall. It looks, roughly, like a matchbox resting on a spool. The upper story, the matchbox, has glass walls all the way around, and the lower story, the spool, is a windowless brick cylinder.

There were four other cars in the guest parking area when I arrived. A small cocktail party was in progress. As I was skirting the house, wondering how to get into it, I heard somebody tapping on the inside of a glass wall above. I looked up to see the most startling and, in a bizarre way, one of the most beautiful women of my experience.

She was tall and slender, with a subtly muscled figure sheathed in a zebra-striped leotard. Her hair was bleached silver and touched with blue, and in the white and perfect oval of her face were eyes of glittering green, set off by painted eyebrows, jet black and arched. She wore one earring, a barbaric gold hoop. She was making spiral motions with her hand, and I understood at last that I was to climb the spiral ramp that wound around the brick cylinder.

The ramp brought me up to a catwalk outside the glass walls. A towering, vigorous man in his early thirties slid back a glass panel and invited me in. He wore lavender nylon coveralls and sandals. He was nervous, and there was tiredness in his deep-set eyes.

"Mr. Krummbein?" I said.

"Who else would I be?" said Otto. "And you must be the wizard of high finance. We can go into my studio, where we'll have more privacy, and then"—pointing to the woman—"you can join us in a drink."

His studio was inside the brick cylinder, and he led me through a door and down another spiral ramp into it. There were no windows. All light was artificial.

"Guess this is the most modern house I've ever been in," I said.

"Modern?" said Otto. "It's twenty years behind the times, but it's the best my imagination can do. Everything else is at least a hundred years behind the times, and that is why we have all the unrest, this running to psychiatrists, broken homes, wars. We haven't learned to design our living for our own times. Our lives clash with our times. Look at your clothes! Shades of 1910. You're not dressed for 1954."

"Maybe not," I said, "but I'm dressed for helping people handle money."

"You are being suffocated by tradition," said Otto. "Why don't you say, 'I am going to build a life for myself, for my time, and make it a work of art'? Your life isn't a work of art—it's a thirdhand Victorian whatnot shelf, complete with someone else's collection of seashells and hand-carved elephants."

"Yup," I said, sitting down on a twenty-foot couch. "That's my life, all right."

"Design your life like that Finnish carafe over there," said Otto, "clean, harmonious, alive with the cool, tart soul of truth in our time. Like Falloleen."

"I'll try," I said. "Mostly it's a question of getting my head above water first. What is Falloleen, a new miracle fiber?"

"My wife," said Otto. "She's hard to miss."

"In the leotard," I said.

"Did you ever see a woman who fitted so well into surroundings like this—who seems herself to be designed for contemporary living?" said Otto. "A rare thing, believe me. I've had many famous beauties out here, but Falloleen is the only one who doesn't look like a piece of 1920-vintage overstuffed furniture."

"How long have you been married?" I said.

"The party upstairs is in celebration of one month of blissful marriage," said Otto, "of a honeymoon that will never end."

"How nice," I said. "And now, about your financial picture—"

"Just promise me one thing," he said, "don't be depressing. I can't work if I'm depressed. The slightest thing can throw me off—that tie of yours, for instance.

It jars me. I can't think straight when I look at it. Would you mind taking it off? Lemon yellow is your color, not that gruesome maroon."

Half an hour later, tieless, I felt like a man prowling through a city dump surrounded by smoldering tire casings, rusting bedsprings, and heaps of tin cans, for that was the financial picture of Otto Krummbein. He kept no books, bought whatever caught his fancy, without considering the cost, owed ruinous bills all over town for clothes for Falloleen, and didn't have a cent in a savings account, insurance, or a portfolio.

"Look," said Otto, "I'm scared. I don't want to go to prison, I didn't mean to do anything wrong. I've learned my lesson. I promise to do anything you say. Anything! Just don't depress me.

"If you can be cheerful about this mess," I said, "the Lord knows I can. The thing to do, I think, is to save you from yourself by letting me manage your income, putting you on an allowance."

"Excellent," said Otto. "I admire a bold approach to problems. And that will leave me free to work out an idea I got on my honeymoon, an idea that is going to make millions. I'll wipe out all this indebtedness in one fell swoop!"

"Just remember," I said, "you're going to have to pay taxes on that, too. You're the first man I ever heard of who got a profitable idea on his honeymoon. Is it a secret?"

"Moonlight-engineered cosmetics," said Otto, "designed expressly, according to the laws of light and color, to make a woman look her best in the moonlight. Millions, zillions!"

"That's swell," I said, "but in the meantime, I'd like to go over your bills to see exactly how deep in you are, and also to figure out what allowance you could get by on at a bare minimum."

"You could go out to supper with us tonight," said Otto, "and then come back and work undisturbed here in the studio. I'm sorry we have to go out, but it's the cook's day off."

"That would suit me fine," I said. "That way I'll have you around to answer questions. There ought to be plenty of those. For instance, how much is in the basket?"

Otto paled. "Oh, you know about the basket?" he said. "I'm afraid we can't use that. That's special."

"In what way?" I said.

"I need it—not for me, for Falloleen," said Otto. "Can't I keep that much, and send you all the royalty checks that come in from now on? It isn't right to make Falloleen suffer because of my mistakes. Don't force me to do that, don't strip me of my self-respect as a husband."

I was fed up, and I stood irritably. "I won't strip you of anything, Mr. Krummbein," I said. "I've decided I don't want the job. I'm not a business manager, anyway. I offered to help as a favor to Hal Murphy, but I didn't know how bad working conditions were. You say I'm trying to strip you, when the truth is that your bones were bleached white on the desert of your own prodigality before I arrived. Is there a secret exit out of this silo," I said, "or do I go out the way I came in?"

"No, no, no," said Otto apologetically. "Please, sit down. You've got to help me. It's just that it's a shock for me to get used to how bad things really are. I thought you'd tell me to give up cigarettes or something like that." He shrugged. "Take the basket and give me my allowance." He covered his eyes. "Entertaining Falloleen on an allowance is like running a Mercedes on Pepsi-Cola."

In the basket was five thousand—odd dollars in royalty checks from manufacturers and about two hundred dollars in cash. As I was making out a receipt for Otto, the studio door opened above us, and Falloleen, forever identified in my mind with a Finnish carafe, came down the ramp gracefully, carrying a tray on which were three martinis.

"I thought your throats might be getting parched," said Falloleen.

"A voice like crystal chimes," said Otto.

"Must I go, or can I stay?" said Falloleen. "It's such a dull party without you, Otto, and I get self-conscious and run out of things to say."

"Beauty needs no tongue," said Otto.

I dusted my hands. "I think we've got things settled for the time being. I'll get down to work in earnest this evening."

"I'm awfully dumb about finances," said Falloleen. "I just leave all that to Otto—he's so brilliant. Isn't he!"

"Yup," I said.

"I was thinking what fun it would be to take our whole party to Chez Armando for dinner," said Falloleen.

Otto looked askance at me.

"We were just talking about love and money," I said to Falloleen, "and I was saying that if a woman loves a man, how much or how little money the man spends on her makes no difference to her. Do you agree?"

Otto leaned forward to hear her answer.

"Where were you brought up?" said Falloleen to me. "On a chicken farm in Saskatchewan?"

Otto groaned.

Falloleen looked at him in alarm. "There's more going on here than I know about," she said. "I was joking. Was that so awful, what I said? It seemed like such a silly question about love and money." Comprehension bloomed on her face. "Otto," she said, "are you broke?"

"Yes," said Otto.

Falloleen squared her lovely shoulders. "Then tell the others to go to Chez Armando without us, that you and I want to spend a quiet evening at home for a change."

"You belong where there are people and excitement," said Otto.

"I get tired of it," said Falloleen. "You've taken me out every night since God knows when. People must wonder if maybe we're afraid to be alone with each other."

Otto went up the ramp to send the guests on their way, leaving Falloleen and me alone on the long couch. Fuddled by her perfume and beauty, I said, "Were you in show business, Mrs. Krummbein?"

"Sometimes I feel like I am," said Falloleen. She looked down at her blue fingernails. "I certainly put on a show wherever I go, don't I?"

"A marvelous show," I said.

She sighed. "I guess it should be a good show," she said. "I've been designed by the greatest designer in the world, the father of the Krummbein Di-Modular Bed."

"Your husband designed you?"

"Didn't you know?" said Falloleen. "I'm a silk purse made out of a sow's ear. He'll design you, too, if he gets the chance. I see he's already made you take off your tie. I'll bet he's told you what your color is, too."

"Lemon yellow," I said.

"Each time he sees you," said Falloleen, "he'll make some suggestion about how to improve your appearance." She ran her hands dispassionately over her spectacular self. "Step by step, one goes a long way."

"You were never any sow's ear," I said.

"One year ago," she said, "I was a plain, brown-haired, dowdy thing, fresh out of secretarial school, starting to work as secretary to the Great Krummbein."

"Love at first sight?" I said.

"For me," murmured Falloleen. "For Otto it was a design problem at first sight. There were things about me that jarred him, that made it impossible for him to think straight when I was around. We changed those things one by one, and what became of Kitty Cahoun, nobody knows."

"Kitty Cahoun?" I said.

"The plain, brown-haired, dowdy thing, fresh out of secretarial school," said Falloleen.

"Then Falloleen isn't your real name?" I said.

"It's a Krummbein original," said Falloleen. "Kitty Cahoun didn't go with the decor." She hung her head. "Love—" she said, "don't ask me any more silly questions about love."

"They're off to Chez Armando," said Otto, returning to the studio. He handed me a yellow silk handkerchief. "That's for you," he said. "Put it in your breast pocket. That dark suit needs it like a forest needs daffodils."

I obeyed, and saw in a mirror that the handkerchief really did give me a little dash, without being offensive. "Thanks very much," I said. "Your wife and I've been having a pleasant time talking about the mysterious disappearance of Kitty Cahoun."

"What ever did become of her?" said Otto earnestly. A look of abject stupidity crossed his face as he realized what he'd said. He tried to laugh it off. "An amazing and amusing demonstration of how the human mind works, wasn't it?" he said. "I'm so used to thinking of you as Falloleen, darling." He changed the subject. "Well, now the maestro is going to cook supper." He laid his hand on my shoulder. "I absolutely insist that you stay. Chicken à la Krummbein, asparagus tips à la Krummbein, potatoes à la—"

"I think I ought to cook supper," said Falloleen. "It's high time the bride got her first meal."

"Won't hear of it," said Otto. "I won't have you suffering for my lack of financial acumen. It would make me feel terrible. Falloleen doesn't belong in a kitchen."

"I know what," said Falloleen, "we'll both get supper. Wouldn't that be cozy, just the two of us?"

"No, no, no, no," said Otto. "I want everything to be a surprise. You stay down here with J. P. Morgan, until I call you. No fair peeking."

"I refuse to worry about it," said Otto, as he, Falloleen, and I cleared away the supper dishes. "If I worry, I can't work, and if I can't work, I can't get any money to bail me out of this mess."

"The important thing is for somebody to worry," I said, "and I guess I'm it. I'll leave you two lovebirds alone up here in the greenhouse while I go to work."

"Man must spend half his time at one with Nature," said Otto, "and half at one with himself. Most houses provide only a muddy, murky in-between." He caught my sleeve. "Listen, don't rush off. All work and no play make Jack a dull boy. Why don't the three of us just have a pleasant social evening, so you can get to know us, and then tomorrow you can start getting down to brass tacks?"

"That's nice of you," I said. "But the quicker I get to work, the quicker you'll be out of the woods. Besides, newlyweds don't want to entertain on their first evening at home."

"Heavens!" said Otto. "We're not newlyweds anymore."

"Yes we are," said Falloleen meekly.

"Of course you are," I said, opening my briefcase. "And you must have an awful lot to say to each other."

"Um," said Otto.

There followed an awkward silence in which Otto and Falloleen stared out into the night through the glass walls, avoiding each other's eyes.

"Didn't Falloleen put on one too many earrings for supper?" said Otto.

"I felt lopsided with just one," said Falloleen.

"Let me be the judge of that," said Otto. "What you don't get is a sense of the whole composition—something a little off-balance here, but lo and behold, a perfect counterbalance down there."

"So you won't capsize," I said, opening the studio door. "Have fun."

"It didn't really jar you, did it, Otto?" said Falloleen guiltily.

I closed the door.

The studio was soundproofed, and I could hear nothing of the Krummbeins' first evening at home as I picked over the wreckage of their finances.

I intruded once, with a long list of questions, and found the upstairs perfectly quiet, save for soft music from the phonograph and the rustle of rich, heavy material. Falloleen was turning around in a lazy sort of ballet, wearing a magnificent evening gown. Otto, lying on the couch, watched her through narrowed lids and blew smoke rings.

"Fashion show?" I said.

"We thought it would be fun for me to try on all the things Otto's bought me that I haven't had a chance to wear," said Falloleen. Despite her heavy makeup, her face had taken on a haggard look. "Like it?" she said.

"Very much," I said, and I roused Otto from his torpor to answer my questions.

"Shouldn't I come down and work with you?" he asked.

"Thanks," I said, "but I'd rather you wouldn't. The perfect quiet is just what I need."

Otto was disappointed. "Well, please don't hesitate to call me for anything."

An hour later, Falloleen and Otto came down into the studio with cups and a pot of coffee. They smiled, but their eyes were glazed with boredom.

Falloleen had on a strapless gown of blue velveteen, with ermine around the hem and below her white shoulders. She slouched and shuffled. Otto hardly glanced at her.

"Ah-h-h!" I said. "Coffee! Just the thing! Style show all over?"

"Ran out of clothes," said Falloleen. She poured the coffee, kicked off her shoes, and lay down at one end of the couch. Otto lay down at the other end, grunting. The peace of the scene was deceptive. Neither Otto nor Falloleen was relaxed. Falloleen was clenching and unclenching her hands. Every few seconds Otto would click his teeth like castanets.

"You certainly look very lovely, Falloleen," I said. "Are those by any chance moonlight-engineered cosmetics you're wearing?"

"Yes," said Falloleen. "Otto had some samples made up, and I'm a walking laboratory. Fascinating work."

"You're not in moonlight," I said, "but I'd say the experiment was a smashing success."

Otto sat up, refreshed by praise of his work. "You really think so? We had moonlight for most of our honeymoon, and the idea practically forced itself on me."

Falloleen sat up as well, sentimentally interested in the subject of the honeymoon. "I loved going out to glamorous places every evening," she said, "but the evening I liked best was the one when we went canoeing, just the two of us, and the lake and the moon."

"I kept looking at her lips there in the moonlight," said Otto, "and—"

"I was looking at your eyes," said Falloleen.

Otto snapped his fingers. "And then it came to me! By heaven, something was all wrong with ordinary cosmetics in the moonlight. The wrong colors came out, blues and greens. Falloleen looked like she'd just swum the English Channel."

Falloleen slapped him with all her might.

"Whatja do that for?" bellowed Otto, his face crimson from the blow. "You think I've got no sense of pain?"

"You think I haven't?" seethed Falloleen. "You think I'm striated plywood and plastic?"

Otto gasped.

"I'm sick of being Falloleen and the style show that never ends!" Her voice dropped to a whisper. "She's dull and shallow, scared and lost, unhappy and unloved."

She twitched the yellow handkerchief from my breast pocket and wiped it across her face dramatically, leaving a smear of red, pink, white, blue, and black. "You designed her, you deserve her, and here she is!" She pressed the stained handkerchief into Otto's limp hand. Up the ramp she went. "Good-bye!"

"Falloleen!" cried Otto.

She paused in the doorway. "My name is Kitty Cahoun Krummbein," she said. "Falloleen is in your hand."

Otto waved the handkerchief at her. "She's as much yours as she is mine," he said. "You wanted to be Falloleen. You did everything you could to be Falloleen."

"Because I loved you," said Kitty. She was weeping. "She was all your design, all for you."

Otto turned his palms upward. "Krummbein is not infallible," he said. "There was widespread bloodshed when the American housewife took the Krummbein Vortex Can Opener to her bosom. I thought being Falloleen would make you happy, and it's made you unhappy instead. I'm sorry. No matter how it turned out, it was a work of love."

"You love Falloleen," said Kitty.

"I love the way she looked," said Otto. He hesitated. "Are you really Kitty again?"

"Would Falloleen show her face looking like this?"

"Never," said Otto. "Then I can tell you, Kitty, that Falloleen was a crashing bore when she wasn't striking a pose or making a dramatic entrance or exit. I lived in terror of being left alone with her."

"Falloleen didn't know who she was or what she was," Kitty sobbed. "You didn't give her any insides."

Otto went up to her and put his arms around her. "Sweetheart," he said, "Kitty Cahoun was supposed to be inside, but she disappeared completely."

"You didn't like anything about Kitty Cahoun," said Kitty.

"My dear, sweet wife," said Otto, "there are only four things on earth that don't scream for redesigning, and one of them is the soul of Kitty Cahoun. I thought it was lost forever."

She put her arms around him tentatively. "And the other three?" she said.

"The egg," said Otto, "the Model-T Ford, and the exterior of Falloleen."

"Why don't you freshen up," said Otto, "slip into your lavender negligee, and put a white rose behind your ear, while I straighten things out here with the Scourge of Wall Street?"

"Oh, dear," she said. "I'm starting to feel like Falloleen again."

"Don't be afraid of it," said Otto. "Just make sure this time that Kitty shines through in all her glory."

She left, supremely happy.

"I'll get right out," I said. "Now I know you want to be alone with her."

"Frankly, I do," said Otto.

"I'll open a checking account and hire a safe-deposit box in your name tomorrow," I said.

And Otto said, "Sounds like your kind of thing. Enjoy, enjoy."

Unpaid Consultant

MOST MARRIED WOMEN won't meet an old beau for cocktails, send him a Christmas card, or even look him straight in the eye. But if they happen to need something an old beau sells—anything from an appendectomy to Venetian blinds—they'll come bouncing back into his life, all pink and smiling, to get it for wholesale or less.

If a Don Juan were to go into the household appliance business, his former conquests would ruin him inside of a year.

What I sell is good advice on stocks and bonds. I'm a contact man for an investment counseling firm, and the girls I've lost, even by default, never hesitate to bring their investment problems to me.

I am a bachelor, and in return for my services, which after all cost me nothing, they sometimes offer me that jewel beyond price—the home-cooked meal.

The largest portfolio I ever examined, in return for nostalgia and chicken, country style, was the portfolio of Celeste Divine. I lost Celeste in high school, and we didn't exchange a word for seventeen years, until she called me at my office one day to say, "Long time no see."

Celeste Divine is a singer. Her hair is black and curly, her eyes large and brown, her lips full and glistening. Painted and spangled and sheathed in gold lamé, Celeste is before the television cameras for one hour each week, making love to all the world. For this public service she gets five thousand dollars a week.

"I've been meaning to have you out for a long time," said Celeste to me. "What would you say to home-cooked chicken, Idaho potatoes, and strawberry shortcake?"

"Mmmmmmmmmm," I said.

"And after supper," said Celeste, "you and Harry and I can sit before a roaring fire and talk about old times and old friends back home."

"Swell," I said. I could see the firelight playing over the columns of figures, *The Wall Street Journal*, the prospectuses and graphs. I could hear Celeste and her husband Harry murmuring about the smell of new-mown hay, American Brake Shoe preferred, moonlight on the Wabash, Consolidated Edison three-percent bonds, cornbread, and Chicago, Milwaukee, St. Paul, and Pacific common.

"We've only been away from here for two years," said Celeste, "but it seems like a lifetime, so much has happened. It'll be good to see somebody from back home."

"You really came up fast, didn't you, Celeste," I said.

"I feel like Cinderella," said Celeste. "One day, Harry and I were struggling along on his pay from Joe's Greasing Palace, and the next day, everything I touched seemed to turn to gold."

It wasn't until I'd hung up that I began wondering how Harry felt.

Harry was the man I'd lost Celeste to. I remembered him as a small, good-looking, sleepy boy, who asked nothing more of life than the prettiest wife in town and a decent job as an automobile mechanic. He got both one week after graduation.

When I went to the Divine home for supper, Celeste herself, with the body of a love goddess and the face of a Betsy Wetsy, let me in.

The nest she'd bought for herself and her mate was an old mansion on the river, as big and ugly as the Schenectady railroad station.

She gave me her hand to kiss, and befuddled by her beauty and perfume, I kissed it.

"Harry? Harry!" she called. "Guess who's here."

I expected to see either a cadaver or a slob, the remains of Harry, come shuffling in.

But there was no response from Harry.

"He's in his study," said Celeste. "How that man can concentrate! When he gets something on his mind, it's just like he was in another world." She opened the study door cautiously. "You see?"

Lying on his back on a tiger-skin rug was Harry. He was staring at the ceiling. Beside him was a frosty pitcher of martinis, and in his fingers he held a drained glass. He rolled the olive in it around and around and around.

"Darling," said Celeste to Harry, "I hate to interrupt, dear."

"What? What's that?" said Harry, startled. He sat up. "Oh! I beg your pardon. I didn't hear you come in." He stood and shook my hand forthrightly, and I saw that the years had left him untouched.

Harry seemed very excited about something, but underneath his excitement was the sleepy contentment I remembered from high school. "I haven't any right to relax," he said. "Everybody in the whole damn industry is relaxing. If I relax, down comes the roof. Ten thousand men out of jobs." He seized my arm. "Count their families, and you've got a city the size of Terre Haute hanging by a thread."

"I don't understand," I said. "Why are they hanging by a thread?"

"The industry!" said Harry.

"What industry?" I said.

"The catchup industry," said Celeste.

Harry looked at me. "What do *you* call it? Catchup? Ketchup? Catsup?"

"I guess I call it different things at different times," I said.

Harry slammed his hand down on the coffee table. "There's the story of the catchup-ketchup-catsup industry in a nutshell! They can't even get together on how to spell the name of the product. If we can't even hang together that much," he said, "we'll all hang separately. Does one automobile manufacturer call automobiles 'applemobiles,' and another one 'axlemobiles,' and another one 'urblemowheels'?"

"Nope," I said.

"You bet they don't," said Harry. He filled his glass, motioned us to chairs, and lay down again on the tiger skin.

"Harry's found himself," said Celeste. "Isn't it marvelous? He was at loose ends so long. We had some terrible scenes after we moved here, didn't we, Harry?"

"I was immature," said Harry. "I admit it."

"And then," said Celeste, "just when things looked blackest, Harry blossomed! I got a brand-new husband!"

Harry plucked tufts of hair from the rug, rolled them into little balls, and flipped them into the fireplace. "I had an inferiority complex," he said. "I thought all I could ever be was a mechanic." He waved away Celeste's and my objections. "Then I found out plain horse sense is the rarest commodity in the business world. Next to most of the guys in the catchup industry, I look like an Einstein."

"Speaking of people blossoming," I said, "your wife gets more gorgeous by the minute."

"Hmmmmm?" said Harry.

"I said, Celeste is really something—one of the most beautiful and famous women in the country. You're a lucky man," I said.

"Yeah, yeah—sure," said Harry, his mind elsewhere.

"You knew what you wanted, and you got it, didn't you?" I said to Celeste.

"I—" Celeste began.

"Tell me, Celeste," I said, "what's your life like now? Pretty wild, I'll bet, with the program and the nightclub appearances, publicity, and all that."

"It is," said Celeste. "It's the most—"

"It's a lot like the industry," said Harry. "Keep the show moving, keep the show moving—keep the catchup moving, keep the catchup moving. There are millions of people who take television for granted, and there are millions of people taking catchup for granted. They want it when they want it. It's got to be there—and it's got to be right. They don't stop to think about how it got there. They aren't interested." He dug his fingers into his thighs. "But they wouldn't get television, and they wouldn't get catchup if there weren't people tearing their hearts out to get it to 'em."

"I liked your record of 'Solitude' very much, Celeste," I said. "The last chorus, where you—"

Harry clapped his hands together. "Sure she's good. Hell, I said we'd sponsor her, if the industry'd ever get together on anything." He rolled over and looked up at Celeste. "What's the story on chow, Mother?" he said.

At supper, conversation strayed from one topic to another, but always settled, like a ball in a crooked roulette wheel, on the catchup industry.

Celeste tried to bring up the problem of her investments, but the subject, ordinarily a thriller, fizzled and sank in a sea of catchup again and again.

"I'm making five thousand a week now," said Celeste, "and there are a million people ready to tell me what to do with it. But I want to ask a friend—an old friend."

"It all depends on what you want from your investments," I said. "Do you want growth? Do you want stability? Do you want a quick return in dividends?"

"Don't put it in the catchup industry," said Harry. "If they wake up, if I can wake 'em up, OK. I'd say get in catchup and stay in catchup. But the way things are now, you might as well sink your money in Grant's Tomb, for all the action you'll get."

"Um," I said. "Well, Celeste, with your tax situation, I don't think you'd want dividends as much as you'd want growth."

"It's just crazy about taxes," said Celeste. "Harry figured out it was actually cheaper for him to work for nothing."

"For love," said Harry.

"What company are you with, Harry?" I said.

"I'm in a consulting capacity for the industry as a whole," said Harry.

The telephone rang, and a maid came in to tell Celeste that her agent was on the line.

I was left alone with Harry, and I found it hard to think of anything to say—anything that wouldn't be trivial in the face of the catchup industry's impending collapse.

I glanced around the room, humming nervously, and saw that the wall behind me was covered with impressive documents, blobbed with sealing wax, decked with ribbons, and signed with big black swirling signatures. The documents were from every conceivable combination of human beings, all gathered in solemn assembly to declare something nice about Celeste. She was a beacon to youth, a promoter of Fire Prevention Week, the sweetheart of a regiment, the television discovery of the year.

"Quite a girl," I said.

"See how they get those things up?" said Harry. "They really look like something, don't they?"

"Like nonaggression pacts," I said.

"When someone gets one of these, they think they've got something—even if what it says is just plain hogwash and not even good English. Makes 'em feel good," said Harry. "Makes 'em feel important."

"I suppose," I said. "But all these citations are certainly evidence of affection and respect."

"That's what a suggestion award should look like," said Harry. "It's one of the things I'm trying to put through. When a guy in the industry figures out a better way to do something, he ought to get some kind of certificate, a booby-dazzler he can frame and show off."

Celeste came back in, thrilled about something. "Honey," she said to Harry.

"I'm telling him about suggestion awards," said Harry. "Will it keep a minute?" He turned back to me. "Before you can understand a suggestion a guy made the other day," he said, "you've got to understand how catchup is made. You start with the tomatoes out on the farms, see?"

"Honey," said Celeste plaintively, "I hate to interrupt, but they want me to play Dolley Madison in a movie."

"Go ahead, if you want to," said Harry. "If you don't, don't. Now where was I?"

"Catchup," I said.

As I left the Divine home, I found myself attacked by a feeling of doom. Harry's anxieties about the catchup industry had become a part of me. An evening with Harry was like a year of solitary confinement in a catchup vat. No man could come away without a strong opinion about catchup.

"Let's have lunch sometime, Harry," I said as I left. "What's your number at the office?"

"It's unlisted," said Harry. He gave me the number very reluctantly. "I'd appreciate it if you'd keep it to yourself."

"People would always be calling him up to pick his brains, if the number got around," said Celeste.

"Good night, Celeste," I said. "I'm glad you're such a success. How could you miss with that face, that voice, and the name Celeste Divine? You didn't have to change a thing, did you?"

"It's just the opposite with catchup," said Harry. "The original catchup wasn't anything like what we call catchup or ketchup or catsup. The original stuff was made out of mushrooms, walnuts, and a lot of other things. It all started in Malaya. *Catchup* means 'taste' in Malaya. Not many people know that."

"I certainly didn't," I said. "Well, good night."

I didn't get around to calling Harry until several weeks later, when a prospective client, a Mr. Arthur J. Bunting, dropped into my office shortly before noon. Mr. Bunting was a splendid old gentleman, stout, over six feet tall, with the white mustache and fierce eyes of an old Indian fighter.

Mr. Bunting had sold his factory, which had been in his family for three generations, and he wanted my suggestions as to how to invest the proceeds. His factory had been a catchup factory.

"I've often wondered," I said, "how the original catchup would go over in this country—made the way they make it in Malaya."

A moment before, Mr. Bunting had been a sour old man, morbidly tidying his life. Now he was radiant. "You know catchup?" he said.

"As an amateur," I said.

"Was your family in catchup?" he said.

"A friend," I said.

Mr. Bunting's face clouded over with sadness. "I and my father," he said hoarsely, "and my father's father made the finest catchup this world has ever known. Never once did we cut corners on quality." He gave an anguished sigh. "I'm sorry I sold out!" he said. "There's a tragedy for someone to write: A man sells something priceless for a price he can't resist."

"There's a lot of that going on, I guess," I said.

"Being in the catchup business was ridiculous to a lot of people," said Mr. Bunting. "But by glory, if everybody did his job as well as my grandfather did, my father did, and I did, it would be a perfect world! Let me tell you that!"

I nodded, and dialed Harry's unlisted telephone number. "I've got a friend I'd like very much to have you meet, Mr. Bunting," I said. "I hope he can have lunch with us."

"Good, fine," said Mr. Bunting. "And now the work of three generations is in the hands of strangers," he said.

A man with a tough voice answered the telephone. "Yeah?"

"Mr. Harry Divine, please," I said.

"Out to lunch. Back at one," said the man.

"Gee, that's too bad. Mr. Bunting," I said, hanging up, "it would have been wonderful to get you two together."

"Who is this person?"

"Who is he?" I said. I laughed. "Why, my friend Harry is Mr. Catchup himself!"

Mr. Bunting looked as though he'd been shot in the belly. "Mr. Catchup?" he said hollowly. "That's what they used to call me. Who's he with?"

"He's a consultant for the whole industry," I said.

The corners of Mr. Bunting's mouth pulled down. "I never even heard of him," he said. "My word, things happen fast these days!"

As we sat down to lunch, Mr. Bunting was still very upset.

"Mr. Bunting, sir," I said, "I was using the term 'Mr. Catchup' loosely. I'm sure Harry doesn't claim the title. I just mean that catchup was a big thing in *his* life, too."

Mr. Bunting finished his drink grimly. "New names, new faces," he said. "These sharp youngsters, coming up fast, still wet behind the ears, knowing all the answers, taking over—do they know they've got a heritage to respect and protect?" His voice quivered. "Or are they going to tear everything down, without even bothering to ask why it was built that way?"

There was a stir in the restaurant. In the doorway stood Celeste, a bird of paradise, creating a sensation.

Beside her, talking animatedly, demanding her full attention, was Harry.

I waved to them, and they crossed the room to join us at our table. The headwaiter escorted them, flattering the life out of Celeste. And every face turned toward her, full of adoration.

Harry, seemingly blind to it all, was shouting at Celeste about the catchup industry.

"You know what I said to them?" said Harry, as they reached our table.

"No, dear," said Celeste.

"I told them there was only one thing to do," said Harry, "and that was burn the whole damn catchup industry down to the ground. And next time, when we build it, by heaven, let's *think!*"

Mr. Bunting stood, snow white, every nerve twanging.

Uneasily I made the introductions.

"How do you do?" said Mr. Bunting.

Celeste smiled warmly. Her smile faded as Mr. Bunting looked at Harry with naked hate.

Harry was too wound up to notice. "I am now making a historical study of the catchup industry," he announced, "to determine whether it never left the Dark Ages, or whether it left and then scampered back."

I chuckled idiotically. "Mr. Bunting, sir," I said, "you've no doubt seen Celeste on television. She's—"

"The communications industry," said Harry, "has reached the point where it can send the picture of my wife through the air to forty million homes. And the catchup industry is still bogged down, trying to lick thixotropy."

Mr. Bunting blew up. "Maybe the public doesn't *want* thixotropy licked!" he bellowed. "Maybe they'd rather have good catchup, and thixotropy be damned! It's flavor they want! It's quality they want! Lick thixotropy, and you'll have some new red bilge sold under a proud old name!" He was trembling all over.

Harry was staggered. "You know what thixotropy is?" he said.

"Of course I know!" said Bunting, furious. "And I know what good catchup is. And I know what you are—an arrogant, enterprising, self-serving little pipsqueak!" He turned to me. "And a man is judged by the company he keeps. Good day!" He strode out of the restaurant, grandly.

"There were tears in his eyes," said Celeste, bewildered.

"His life, his father's life, and his grandfather's life have been devoted to catchup," I said. "I thought Harry knew that. I thought everybody in the industry knew who Arthur J. Bunting was."

Harry was miserable. "I really hurt him, didn't I?" he said. "God knows, I didn't want to do that."

Celeste laid her hand on Harry's. "You're like Louis Pasteur, darling," she said. "Pasteur must have hurt the feelings of a lot of old men, too."

"Yeah," said Harry. "Like Louis Pasteur—that's me."

"The old collision between youth and age," I said.

"Big client, was he?" said Harry.

"Yes, I'm afraid so," I said.

"I'm sorry," said Harry. "I can't tell you how sorry. I'll call him up and make things right."

"I don't want you to say anything that will go against your integrity, Harry," I said. "Not on my account."

Mr. Bunting called the next day to say that he had accepted Harry's apology.

"He made a clean breast of how he got into catchup," said Mr. Bunting, "and he promised to get out. As far as I'm concerned, the matter is closed."

I called up Harry immediately. "Harry, boy, listen!" I said. "Mr. Bunting's business isn't *that* important to me. If you're right about catchup and the Buntings are wrong, stick with it and fight it out!"

"It's all right," said Harry, "I was getting sick of catchup. I was about to move on, anyway." He hung up. I called him back, and was told that he had gone to lunch.

"Do you know where he's eating?"

"Yeah, right across the street. I can see him going in."

I got the address of the restaurant and hailed a cab.

The restaurant was a cheap, greasy diner, across the street from a garage. I looked around for Harry for some time before realizing that he was on a stool at the counter, watching me in the cigarette machine mirror.

He was wearing coveralls. He turned on his stool, and held out a hand whose nails were edged in black. "Shake hands with the new birdseed king," he said. His grip was firm.

"Harry, you're working as a mechanic," I said.

"Not half an hour ago," said Harry, "a man with a broken fuel pump thanked God for me. Have a seat."

"What about the catchup business?" I said.

"It saved my marriage and it saved my life," said Harry. "I'm grateful to the pioneers, like the Buntings, who built it."

"And now you've quit, just like that?" I snapped my fingers.

"I was never in it," said Harry. "Bunting has promised to keep that to himself, and I'd appreciate it if you'd do the same."

"But you know so much about catchup!" I said.

"For eighteen months after Celeste struck it rich and we moved here," said Harry, "I walked the streets, looking for a job suitable for the husband of the famous and beautiful Celeste."

Remembering those dark days, he rubbed his eyes, reached for the catchup. "When I got tired, cold, or wet," he said, "I'd sit in the public library, and study all the different things men could do for a living. Making catchup was one of them."

He shook the bottle of catchup over his hamburger, violently. The bottle was almost full, but nothing came out. "There—you see?" he said. "When you shake catchup one way, it behaves like a solid. You shake it another way, and it behaves like a liquid." He shook the bottle gently, and catchup poured over his hamburger. "Know what that's called?"

"No," I said.

"Thixotropy," said Harry. He hit me playfully on the upper arm. "There—you learned something new today."

Sucker's Portfolio

EVERYBODY HAS THE ITCH to buy what I sell, because what I sell is advice on how to get richer, *probably*, and advice on what stocks and bonds to buy or sell—and when. It's expert advice, and I study hard to make it that way. But, good as my advice is, not everybody can be a customer, because not everybody has venture capital—money for the stock market and me.

More people have venture capital than are talking about it, and it's my job, if I care to go on eating, to discover these close-mouthed ones and convince them that they would be shrewd to accept my help. And they would be, too. But, America being what it is, it's a nightmare trying to guess who has venture capital and who doesn't.

It never occurred to me to talk about building a portfolio—accumulating a bonanza in securities—to the ragged, foul-mouthed old man who used to sell papers outside my apartment. But when he died, police found $58,000 in venture capital in his mattress. Worse—before I could rally from the shock, his heir had ventured the whole wad on a Florida motel.

Clothes furnish no clues. A Homburg hat, a banker's gray suit, a regimental tie, and highly polished black shoes are no more indications that a man has venture capital than the shape of his ears. I know. I wear a Homburg hat, a banker's gray suit, a regimental tie, and highly polished black shoes.

So—finding customers is pretty much a lottery, and they're likely to come from anywhere and look like anything.

I was inherited by one of my customers, and he is the most conservative-looking young man I've ever met. I didn't think I could interest him in any investments that were even remotely speculative—ones that might go up or down fast, but probably up. But, after I'd made his $20,000 portfolio as stable and conservative as possible, he threw away $10,000 of it, and I'm still looking for signs of regret.

His name is George Brightman. I was inherited by him from his adoptive parents, lovely people who were among my first customers. Shortly after I got their portfolio shipshape, they lost their lives in an automobile accident, and I went on taking care of the portfolio in the name of their adopted son and heir, George.

I take pride in my work, and I feel especially affectionate toward my early efforts.

The Brightman portfolio was a nice job—balanced and strong. In its own way, it was a work of love, because the Brightmans wanted George to have it someday, and they adored George. Well, the time for George to get it came sooner than anyone expected, and it made me sick when he began to dynamite the small but neat financial edifice we'd built for him.

George was a client of mine for six months before I met him. He was a divinity student at the University of Chicago, and the business we did was by correspondence and long-distance telephone calls.

His parents had told me what a clean, kind, splendid young chap he was, working his way through divinity school; and his letters and telephone conversations gave me no reason to think otherwise. I *did* think he was maybe a little too lighthearted and trusting about his financial affairs—but his financial affairs were in the hands of an honest man, fortunately, so he could afford to tell me to do what I pleased with his $20,000. Sometimes his responses to my questions and suggestions were so lackadaisical that I wondered if he cared at all about the portfolio, or had the vaguest idea of what it was or how it worked. Then he stopped being lackadaisical.

The first indication I had of the change was a letter from George, saying he was coming home for a week, and demanding $519.29. At first glance, the letter looked like a forgery, and I suspected that some confidence man had seen the wonderful possibility of going through George's pockets while his head was in the clouds. George's handwriting, as I knew it, was as regular and quietly powerful as slow rollers on the sea before a steady wind. The writing in demand of $519.29 was ragged and choppy.

It was only when I compared the letter with some of George's earlier ones that I saw they were all written by the same hand. The steady rollers had been hit by a squall.

◙ ◙ ◙

"I'm George Brightman," he said gently, stepping into my small office.

"I think I might have guessed," I said. "I saw a lot of snapshots of you when I worked with your parents. And I caught a glimpse of you at the funeral."

"I didn't feel much like meeting anyone then."

"Everybody understood."

He was remarkably small for a man, about five feet four inches tall, I'd say. His face wasn't the calm, bright, amiable moon remembered from the snapshots. And when I'd seen it at the funeral, of course, it had been distorted by grief. The face I saw now was restless and excited, a little wild—in contrast with his dark-gray flannel suit and black tie.

I'd looked forward to a pleasant, leisurely chat with him, but he was in a great hurry about something.

"Where's my money?" he said.

I handed him my personal check for the amount he'd asked for. I pressed my palms together, pursed my lips judiciously, and leaned back, the image of an expert. "Now then, that money is the proceeds from the sale of a hundred shares of Nevada Mining and Exploration," I said. "This leaves your portfolio somewhat unbalanced, weakened in natural resources. In my opinion—"

"Well, thanks for everything," said George. "You do whatever's best." He started to leave.

"Listen! Wait!" I said. "We got a thousand dollars for Nevada Mining, so you've got a cash surplus beyond that check of about $480. Now, there's a very fine, small but old and well-run zinc firm that we might be smart to put your $480 into. That would restore some of the balance we've lost, and—"

"Could I have it?"

"The stock in the zinc company?"

"The cash surplus," said George. "The $480."

"George," I said evenly, "may I ask what for?"

"Maybe I'll tell you later," said George, his eyes shining. "It *is* my money, isn't it?"

"It's your money, George. Don't let anybody tell you any different. But—"

"And if I want more, I just tell you to sell something. Isn't that the way it works?"

"Like a dollar watch, George," I said wretchedly. "But—"

"Good. Then you can write me a check for the . . . the cash surplus." The term pleased him.

I wrote the check slowly. "Maybe it isn't any of my business, George," I said, "but you haven't come across a clean-cut stranger who wants to double your money for you, have you?"

"When the right time comes, you'll hear all about it," said George.

"Then it'll be too late," I said, but he was gone.

◎ ◎ ◎

I'm no artist, but I honestly believe my business is a lot like painting. It drives me crazy to see a lopsided portfolio, just the way it hurts an artist to see a painting that isn't put together right. After George's raid on his portfolio, which was like cutting a hole in a painting, I couldn't think about anything else. And I couldn't get it out of my head that he—*we*—were being swindled. Before the afternoon was over, I'd convinced myself that I had a holy mandate to mind George's business. All of it.

I called the YMCA and found that he was staying there—of course. When he came to the phone, he sounded even more excited than he'd been in my office.

"We ought to get together for a business talk as soon as possible," I said. "What about supper?"

"Not tonight, not tonight," he said. "Not tonight of all nights. I don't feel like eating anyway."

"Lunch tomorrow?"

"Yes. All right, fine."

I named a restaurant where we would meet. "George," I said casually, "I've been thinking about your portfolio." What I'd been thinking about it was that, if someone was tempting him with prospects of huge profits in a hurry, it was up to me to tempt him into some highly speculative propositions where he had at least a small chance of winning. "If you can possibly hang on to the money you got this afternoon, just until our talk tomorrow, I think I could show you a way to invest it so that you might realize, in a very short time, an increase of—"

"Talk to me about it tomorrow," said George. "My mind is too full now to think about investments."

"Um," I said. "Well—you *will* hang on to the money until tomorrow, eh?"

"Can't," said George, and he hung up.

◎ ◎ ◎

I spent a fitful night, trying to imagine what it was that cost $519.29, would be delivered after nightfall, and would excite a divinity student.

I called the YMCA a dozen times in the morning, and was told each time, until noon, that George was resting and couldn't come to the phone.

At noon he agreed to come to the phone, and I could hear the sounds of his steps echoing down the hall as he approached. His footfalls sounded like the slaps of a wet washrag.

"Uh?" said George. His voice was the quack of a duck.

"George?"

"Uh."

"How was the night of nights?"

"Uh."

"Lunch, George—in an hour?"

"Uh."

"George, are you all right?"

"Only God," mumbled George, "could give a man a headache like this."

"We could call off lunch, I suppose. What is it—some virus thing?"

"Sin," said George thickly. "I'll come. I've got to talk to you."

◎ ◎ ◎

I knew without asking that the money was gone and that no satisfaction had been received for it—a thousand dollars out the window. I couldn't help feeling pleased, in a twisted way, as I waited in the restaurant for George. He'd bought something, anyway—a good, stiff lesson in economics that he wouldn't forget. It could have been much worse, I thought. He still had $19,000 to hang on to for dear life.

When George walked into the restaurant and peered around for me, his eyes looked like dying fires in the back of a cave. Whoever had taken him to the cleaners had gotten him drunk—a trick I would have considered impossible.

"Where'd you go last night, George?" I said lightheartedly.

"Never mind," he said desolately, and throughout the meal, which he couldn't eat, he hardly said a word.

"You said you had to talk to me?" I coaxed gently.

"I've got to think it out first," he said. "I've got to get it straight in my mind."

"Take your time, take your time," I said. And to make the time pass I spoke interestingly, I thought, about men who had lost their money to swindlers of one sort or another, and who had been doubly foolish in not going to the police about it. "That's how the con men stay in business," I said. "A guy feels so stupid after he's been taken that he doesn't want to let anybody know how stupid he was." I watched George carefully for some flicker of interest.

"Oh well," said George apathetically.

"Oh well?" I said indignantly. "Swindlers take honest people for millions of dollars a year. It's up to people with some guts to turn them in."

George shrugged. "'It is easier for a camel to go through the eye of a needle than for a rich man to enter into the kingdom of God.' Maybe swindlers are doing people a favor."

I was stunned. "George! Let's be practical."

"I thought I was being."

"Well there's certainly some middle ground between being stone broke and being filthy rich, George. I mean, after all, the time is going to come when you're going to be raising a family, and you'll certainly want to give your children certain advantages that cost money. A comfortable home, good schooling, plenty of healthful food. Those things are important to a child."

"That *is* true, isn't it?" said George with sudden intensity.

"If you hadn't been raised in a comfortable home, if your parents hadn't been able to help with your college education, you would have been an entirely different person, George. Those things matter."

"I know," said George gravely. "I'm learning. If I hadn't been adopted as a baby, if I'd been left in the orphanage—" His eyes widened. "There but for the grace of God, go I."

I was delighted. "So you see, George—you've got to take an interest in your portfolio and not do anything foolish with it, because it really belongs to your children. Now, as I told you yesterday, your portfolio is weak in natural resources, and I thought we might sell part of the chemicals, and—"

George stood. "Please," he said apologetically, "some other time. I'm feeling

KURT VONNEGUT

pretty woozy. I better go back to my room and lie down." He reached into his pocket for his billfold.

"No, no, George. This is on me."

"Thanks. Nice of you," said George. He'd taken something from his pocket and was looking at it with something close to nausea. It was a plastic swizzle stick. He broke it vengefully, dropped the pieces into an ashtray, smiled wanly, and fled.

Written on the swizzle stick was a name that must have struck George with horrible irony: Club Joy.

◎ ◎ ◎

All was right with the world, I thought, and I expected no more trouble from George. George had learned some important things, and I had helped to teach him. The thought made me happy, and I whistled at my work through most of the afternoon.

I was whistling as I locked up my office, when the telephone rang. "Oh!" I said cheerily, "It's *you*, George. You sound much better. A hundred percent recovered, I'd say."

"Yes, thank you," said George politely. "I wonder if you could tell me something."

"Glad to."

"How much was my portfolio worth before I sold some of it?"

"To the penny, George?"

"Please."

"Well—I'll have to do some figuring. Hold on." Five minutes later, I was able to give him the figures. "As of closing this afternoon, you were worth $19,021.50. With the cash you got yesterday, $20,021.50."

"And half of that would be—?"

"Well, let's see. Two into twenty goes ten . . . mmm. That'd be $10,010.75."

"Less $480.71 would be—?"

"Uh—$9,530.04, George. Why?"

"I want you to sell enough securities to get me that amount, please. Use your own discretion."

"George!"

"Can you do it tomorrow?"

"George—what are you up to?"

"If I cared to discuss it, I would," said George coolly.

"George," I said pleadingly, "you said you'd tell me what was going on when the right time came. There never was a righter time than now."

"Sorry," said George. "I'm afraid the right time will never come now. I'll come for the money tomorrow afternoon. Good-bye."

◎ ◎ ◎

The Club Joy was under the city streets. I found a smoke-filled bubble blown in the muck between the sewers and the subway.

"Have to check your coat and hat, sir," said the hatcheck girl, as I stood on the threshold of the Club Joy, in desperate search for George.

She was a pretty thing, tiny but fierce, blinking up at me with large brown eyes through the haze of hysterical jazz, blood, sweat, and tears coming from the main room. Her hair was bleached as white as a snowdrift, and rhinestone icicles hung from her ears. Her dress was cut so low that, from where I stood, she seemed to be wearing little more than the half door of her booth.

She caressed my Homburg and Chesterfield as she hung them up. "Just like Walter Pidgeon or an ambassador or something," she said. Her fingertips lingered in my palm for a moment as she handed me the brass check.

I started to ask her if she'd seen anyone fitting George's description, but I changed my mind. If someone at the Club Joy had gotten George into $10,000 worth of trouble, I reasoned, it might be unwise—suicide, that is—to show curiosity about George or the nature of his trouble.

The main room of the Club Joy confirmed this. It was joyless, populated with vicious drunks and sullen drunks, and a few men as sober as tombstones, cold and white faced and silent, watching everything in the blue mirror behind the bar. They watched me.

I ordered a drink and looked around casually for George. He wasn't there. I looked casually but many noticed and didn't seem to like it—especially the white-faced men.

I didn't plan to drink much, but in the nightmare of the Club Joy there was nothing to do but drink. Drinking was a physical necessity for those who weren't born numb. My whole system cried out for anesthesia if I were to stay any length of time, and I began to understand how George had come by his crashing hangover.

Two hours later, at midnight, George still hadn't appeared. But there was one important development: I'd come uncoupled from truth and was as tough as they came—a ruthless private eye, out to save George. With baleful eyes that had seen everything, I sized up people as they came in; a good many of them looked away uneasily.

I turned to the sodden fat man on the stool next to mine. "Can't imagine what happened to my buddy," I said craftily. "Supposed to meet me here. You seen him? Real little guy, with big brown eyes, dark-gray suit, black tie."

"Yeah, I know the one. Nah, hasn't been in t'night."

"You know him?"

"Saw him las' night. That's the only time." He nodded to himself. "Yeah—the kid looks like he don't know his elbow fr'm third base. I know, I know. The one that's so hot for li'l Jackie."

"Jackie?"

"Hatcheck girl. Your pal sat here all las' night, lookin' at 'er in the mirror. Sure couldn't drink."

"Oh?"

"Bartender kept rushin' him to drink more or let somebody else have his stool, and the kid got pretty boozed up."

"Alone?"

"Yeah—'til he took Jackie home. Sure can't tell by lookin' who's after what, can you? Kid looked like he ought to be a minister to me."

◎ ◎ ◎

It was no trick getting to take Jackie home. It seemed to be a custom of the house, and I was the best-dressed man in it—at a walkaway.

My recollections of the ride home and what followed are fuzzy. My intentions were perfectly honorable, I know that. I think my plan was to discover, without falling into it myself, what sort of trap she'd caught George in. The plan was crafty, whatever it was.

I dozed frequently in the taxi and caught only snatches of Jackie's conversation, which was bright and phony, brittle as glass. She pulled out all the stops for me: she was lonesome and helpless and poor, and had been raised in a tough orphanage, and had never been happy or understood.

My next recollection was of sitting on a couch in her apartment, trying to keep my eyes open, while she mixed a drink in the kitchen. But my eyes closed, and I didn't wake up until I heard a man yelling bloody murder.

"Hmm?" I said, my eyes still closed.

"So!" he shouted. "Here I've been a good husband for years, worked hard and tried to save, and this happens."

"What happens?" I mumbled, vaguely interested.

"This!"

"Oh," I said. "Huh."

"I thought you were in Los Angeles!" said Jackie.

"Ha!" he said. "I finished my work two days early. I hurry home, and what do I find?"

"What?" I said.

"You!"

"Oh."

"Caught!" said Jackie. "Forgive us, forgive us."

"You!" he said to her. "I'll take care of you, all right." He turned to me. "You've ruined my home, and now buster, I'm going to wreck yours. Your wife is going to hear about this outrage the first thing tomorrow morning. Let's see how you like that!"

"Haven't ruined anything," I said sleepily. "No wife, either. Wreck away."

"Then I'll wreck your career. See how you like that!"

"Make more money in a defense plant anyway," I said.

There was a lot more yelling that I can't remember, but it got feebler as time went on, and they finally threw me out into the hall and locked the door.

⊚ ⊚ ⊚

I slept until noon and didn't get to my office until after lunch, which I couldn't touch. When I got there, George was waiting for me.

"Have you got it?" he said.

"The money?" I chuckled, patted him like a father, and eased him into a chair. "No, George, I haven't. But I've got news for you. You're off the hook, my boy."

"What hook?" said George. He seemed annoyed.

"George, last night I met a cute little girl named Jackie. Took her home, in fact."

George turned bright red and stood. "I don't care to hear about it!"

"Take it easy, take it easy, George. It's the oldest racket in the world, the badger game is, and all you've got to do is to tell 'em to go to hell. They'll back right down. Tell 'em to take your reputation instead of your money, and that's the last you'll ever hear of 'em. Don't give 'em a dime!"

"I don't want to discuss it," said George. "Kindly get me the money this afternoon."

"George," I said, "if you don't stand up to those two, *I'll* go to the cops and press charges. They pulled the same stunt on me. And even if you gave them half of what you've got—that wouldn't be the end, George. You start paying them off, and they won't leave you alone until they get everything—and then some."

"If you have them arrested, we're through," said George.

"If I let you hand over all that money to them, I'll be through with myself," I said. "You've given them a thousand now, and that's a thousand too much."

"I didn't give them a thousand, or anything close to it," said George, "but I plan to. Please get me the money, and keep this matter to yourself. Or must I call a policeman?"

"For them? You bet!"

"For you," said George.

⊚ ⊚ ⊚

I was so mad that I walked out on him, and if he'd stood in my way, divinity school or not, I would have knocked him down.

With a clanging headache, I strode around town, piecing together what I knew of the stupid mess George had gotten himself into. Somebody had offered him something he wanted for $519.29, told him to come to the Club Joy to get it; and George, waiting for the seller to show up with the goods, had gotten drunk without meaning to, and had fallen for Jackie and the oldest swindle on earth. QED.

I went to the bank, cashed a check and picked up my statement, and then went into a bar next door for a hair of the dog that bit me—the dog I'd invited to bite me for George's sake.

I leafed through my cancelled checks in the twilight of the bar—nervously and without interest at first, just for something to do. And then I found the check for $519.29, made out by me to George. I turned it over and saw that it was endorsed by George—and by a Robert S. Noonan. I looked up Noonan in the phone directory. He was a private detective.

That's what George had bought, then—a piece of information. That's what had excited him so much, had made him leave his studies and hurry home. That's what he'd been waiting for at the Club Joy, waiting for all evening.

And then I guessed that Noonan hadn't stood up George. Noonan had delivered what he'd been paid for before George had set foot in the Club Joy.

◎ ◎ ◎

Late in the afternoon, I reached George by telephone at the YMCA. "George," I said, "I'm sorry I lost my temper."

"I waited around your office quite a while, hoping you'd come back," said George. "I don't blame you for getting angry. I was very rude."

"I think I understand what it's all about now, George."

"Please," said George, "let's not go through that again. It's a personal matter you couldn't possibly understand."

"George—I guess you've fired me because I didn't get you the money this afternoon. I couldn't, but I'm going to have my little say anyway."

"I don't think you could say anything about the situation that I don't know."

"I can say something that I didn't know until a little while ago. She's your sister, isn't she?"

George was silent for only a moment. "Yes," he said. His voice was dead when he said it.

"Don't get mad at Noonan. He wouldn't tell me a thing. I guessed it myself. Does she know who you are?"

"No. I went to that place just to look at her. I was going to tell her who I was, but apparently what happened to you happened to me."

"And you paid off?"

"Certainly. I was prepared to spend the money on celebrating our reunion anyway. Now, please—you've been very kind to me—won't you get me the money tomorrow? I'm in a hurry to get back to school."

"Sister or not, George—she's a real lady rat," I said.

"There's a child, and there's hope in that," said George. "I am what I am because good people gave me what no one owed me. The best I can do for her, now, too late, is the same. I intend to do the best. I'll see you tomorrow."

◎ ◎ ◎

George actually had to catch a late train back to Chicago. I'd sold off half his kingdom, and we'd mailed the proceeds to Jackie in the form of a bank check she'd never be able to trace.

George and I finished a splendid supper, and the question arose as to how we might most pleasantly kill the time remaining until his train.

There was only one place to go, we agreed—the Club Joy. Our visit was purely ceremonial. We ordered drinks, but neither of us could touch them. We just sat there, looking like killers.

Fifteen minutes before train time, we gathered up our coats and hats from Jackie. She looked at us again the way she'd looked at us when we came in: afraid we would turn her in, and hopeful that we were such idiots that we'd not only keep our mouths shut but come back for more.

"Good-night, Jackie," said George.

"Good-night," she said uneasily.

George dropped a dime into her little plate, into a nest of ones and fives.

"A lousy dime?" said Jackie derisively.

"That's all, sister," said George. "Sin no more."

The Drone King

ONE THING ABOUT the investment counseling business: the surroundings are almost always nice. Wherever my work takes me, prosperity has beat me there.

Prosperity beat me to the Millennium Club by about a hundred years. As I walked through the door for the first time, my cares dropped away. I felt as though I'd just finished two brandies and a good cigar. Here was peace.

It was a club downtown—six stories of snug hideaways and playthings and apartments for rich gentlemen. It overlooked a park.

The foyer was guarded by an elegant old man behind a rosewood desk.

I gave him my card. "Mr. Quick? Mr. Sheldon Quick?" I said. "He asked me to come over."

He examined the card for a long time. "Yes," he said at last. "Mr. Quick is expecting you. You'll find him in the small library—second door on the left, by the grandfather clock."

"Thank you," I said, and I started past him.

He caught my sleeve. "Sir—"

"Yes?" I said.

"You aren't wearing a boutonniere, are you?"

"No," I said guiltily. "Should I be?"

"If you were," he said, "I'd have to ask you to check it. No women or flowers allowed past the front desk."

I paused by the door of the small library. "Say," I said, "you know this clock has stopped?"

"Mr. Quick stopped it the night Calvin Coolidge died," he said.

I blushed. "Sorry," I said.

"We all are," he said. "But what can *anyone* do?"

◙ ◙ ◙

Sheldon Quick was alone in the small library. We were meeting for the first time.

He was about fifty—very tall, and handsome in a lazy ornamental way. His hair was golden, his eyes blue, and he stroked his mustache with his little finger as he shook my hand.

"You come highly recommended," he said.

"Thank you, sir," I said.

He brought his finger away from his mustache, and I saw that his upper lip was swollen on one side, as fat as a ping-pong ball. He touched the swelling. "A bee," he said.

"It must be very painful," I said.

"It is," he said. "I won't deceive you about that." He smiled sourly. "Don't let anybody tell you this isn't a woman's world."

"How's that, sir?" I said.

"Only a *female* bee can sting," he said.

"Oh," I said. "I didn't know that about bees."

"You knew that about *females*, didn't you?" he said. He closed one eye, and, with his face already lopsided with the bee sting, he looked crazy as a bedbug. "Law of life!" he said sharply. "If you get yellow fever, you'll have the female mosquito to thank. If a black widow spider does you in, my boy, again—*cherchez la femme.*"

"Huh," I said. "I'll be darned."

A sweet, doddering old waiter came in with coffee and cigars on a silver tray. "Is they anything else you wants, Mister Quick?" he said.

"Anything else I wants?" said quick. He rolled his eyes unhappily. "Wealth, George? Power? Instant success?"

The waiter shrugged and seemed close to tears. "Mister Quick, suh—we's goin' to miss you, sir," he said.

Quick threw back his head, and tried to laugh heartily. It was a horrible laugh, full of fear and peevishness. "Why must everybody act as though resigning from the Millennium Club was the same thing as death?" he said. "Don't depress me, man! Wish me luck!"

"Oh, I *do*, I *do*, sir!" said the waiter.

"I'll have plenty of expert help on the outside," said Quick. He nodded at me. "He'll he handling the financial end, while I take care of research and production."

The waiter looked at me miserably. "It ain't gonna he the same aroun' here without Mister Quick," he said. "I'll come to work in the mornin', an' I'll look in the barber shop, an' I'll look in the bar, an' I'll look in the shower room, an' I'll look up on the roof where the beehives is." His eyes widened, as though he were telling a ghost story. "An' Mister Quick, he won't be *none* of them places.

"An' when I gets ready to go home at night," said the waiter, "I'll look in the periodical room, an' Mister Quick, he won't *be* in there, sippin' his brandy—just a–underlinin' an' a–underlinin' an' a–underlinin'."

"Underlining?" I said.

"Important things in the magazines," said the waiter respectfully. "I reckon in the past twenty-five years Ah done throwed out tons of magazines Mister Quick done underlined."

Every word seemed to snap a vertebra in Sheldon Quick's back. When the waiter left, Quick lay down on the couch. He murmured something, and his voice was like wind in the treetops.

"Beg your pardon?" I said, leaning close to him.

"You are in the stock and bond business?" he said.

"I sell advice on them," I said.

"I want you to sell some stock for me," he said.

"I'll be glad to look at your portfolio, and give you my recommendations as to what to hold and what to sell," I said.

He waved his hand feebly. "You miss my meaning," he said. "I want you to sell stock in a new company of mine. That's the way new companies raise money, isn't it? Sell stock?"

"Yessir," I said. "But that's way out of my line. First of all, you'll need a lawyer."

Again he said something I missed.

"Are you sick, sir?" I said.

He sat up, blinking blindly. "I *wish* he hadn't said all those things," he said. "The agreement was that nobody was going to say goodbye. Some day soon, nobody knows when, I'm simply going to walk out, as though for a breath of fresh air. And I won't come back. The next thing they hear from me will be a letter, telling them where to send my things."

"Um," I said.

He looked around the room wistfully. "Well, I'm neither the first nor the last to go out into the world, to recoup my fortunes, to return."

"Something happened to your fortunes, sir?" I said uneasily.

"The money my father left to me is at an end," he said. "I've seen the end coming for some time." He curled his swollen lip, baring a long, white, wet fang. "I'm not unprepared. I've been planning this business for more than a year."

"Look—about this business of yours," I said, "I—"

"Business of *ours*," he said.

"*Ours?*" I said.

"I want you to be general manager," he said. "I want you to see the lawyer, and get us incorporated, and do whatever needs to be done to put us in business."

"I'm sorry, Mr. Quick," I said, "but I couldn't take an assignment like that."

Quick looked at me levelly. "Does two hundred thousand dollars a year sound like inadequate compensation for a man of your caliber?" he said.

The room seemed to go around slowly, like a stately merry-go-round. My own voice seemed to come back to me from a distance—sweet and flute-like. "Nossir," I said. "Are you offering me that?"

"Nature is offering us that," said Quick. He reached out and closed his hand on air. "We have only to reach out and take it."

"Uranium?" I whispered.

"Bees!" he said. His face twisted into a look of wild triumph.

"Bees?" I said. "What about bees?"

"Sometime in the next month I shall call you," he said, "and you shall see what you shall see."

"When, exactly?" I said.

"It's up to the bees," said Quick.

"Where are they?" I said.

"On the roof," said Quick. "Then you and I will call a press conference, to tell the world what it is we have to sell."

The clock on the mantelpiece struck noon.

Quick winced with each strike. "In exactly thirty days," he said, "my membership expires."

He shook my hand, and opened the door for me. "When I call, come at once," he said.

In the corridor outside, the old waiter was talking to a young one. "With Mister Quick gone," he said, "who's gonna be Santy Claus at the Christmas party for the help? You tell me that!"

◎ ◎ ◎

Ten days later, Quick called me up. He was awfully excited. "They're doing it!" he yelled into the phone. "It's going on right now!" He hung up.

The man behind the rosewood desk waved me into the Millennium Club. The old waiter was waiting for me. He handed me a beekeeper's mask and gloves, and hustled me to an elevator. The elevator operator took me straight to the roof.

On the roof was Sheldon Quick and ten beehives. He was gloved and masked, wearing plus-fours, a sports coat, and shoes with gum soles as thick as fruitcakes.

He was furious about what the bees were doing. He pointed to a hive. "Look! Just look, would you!"

Fat, clumsy, colorful bees were staggering out of the hive door, bumping into one another, floundering around in circles, buzzing in hurt surprise.

Then little bees came out, whining in high-pitched rage. They stung the big ones again and again, and tried to tear them to pieces.

Quick lashed out at the little bees with one gloved hand, and with the other hand he scooped up the big bees. He stepped back, and dropped the big bees into a Mason jar—tenderly.

"What is it?" I said. "A bee war?"

"War?" said Quick, his nostrils flaring. "I'll say it's a war! A war to the bitter finish! No quarter given!"

"Gee," I said, "you'd think the big ones would be knocking the stuffings out of the little ones, instead of the other way around."

"The big ones have no sting," said Quick.

"Whose hive was it in the first place?" I said.

Quick's laughter clanked with irony. "Your question is good enough to be chiseled in granite for all time to ponder," he said. "The little ones are the females. The big ones are the males."

◎ ◎ ◎

We went from the roof to the basement, with Quick carrying his jar of bees. We went to a big room opening off the stairwell. The only thing in the room was an office desk, which sat in the middle of the cement floor.

The old waiter had arrived ahead of us with cocktails and sandwiches. He bowed and left.

"Have you guessed it—the wonderful thing we're going to sell?" said Quick.

I shook my head.

"I will give you the key word, and it will hit you like a thunderlap," he said. "Are you ready?"

"Ready," I said.

"*Communications!*" he said. He raised his glass. "To the so-called drones! If Nature has no use for them, we do!" He nudged me. "Eh? Eh?"

He set his glass down hard on the desk, and a deep, lazy, fuzzy buzzing sound came from inside.

"This wholesale slaughter of the males takes place after the males have performed their most basic function," said Quick. "They have risen in an insane spiral, pursuing the queen—higher and higher and higher!"

He swung his arms around, portraying a swarm of drones chasing a queen. "Until—*presto!*" he said. "One lucky devil gets her, the jewel beyond price. He dies instantly." He bowed his head. "And when the rest go home, they are murdered—as you saw."

"Gosh," I said. "And you rescue the males?"

"Like the Scarlet Pimpernel in the French Revolution," said Quick. "I attend the executions, and spirit away the innocent victims. I feed them and shelter them, and teach them to lead useful lives."

Coyly, he offered me a riddle. "When is a drone *not* a drone?"

"I give up," I said.

"When is a file drawer *not* a file drawer?" said Quick. He opened the file drawer of the desk. In the drawer was a big wooden box with a hole in its top.

Two drones came out of the hole, buzzed stupidly, bumped into each other, waddled back to the hole, and fell in.

"Here," said Quick raptly, "we have the first all-male beehive in history—a sort of bee Millennium Club, if you like. The food, which I provide, is rich and plentiful. Fellowship is the order of the day. And there is time for reflection and a relishing of life, away from the senseless, thankless, harrowing, rush-rush-rush and moodiness of the female workers. Take a drone away from his Millennium Club, and he will be back like a shot!"

Quick opened the top drawer of the desk, and took from it a magnifying glass, a needle-sharp pencil, tissue paper, string, and soda straws chopped in half-inch lengths.

"A drone is not a drone," said Sheldon Quick, *"when he carries messages."*

He opened the lid of the bee Millennium Club. It was teeming with drones. He dumped in the drones from the Mason jar. "Welcome to civilization, little brothers," he said. "It's been a long time coming."

☉ ☉ ☉

"For the sake of drama," Quick called down to me as he climbed the basement stairs, "you will be the president of a motor car company, and I will be the president of a taxicab company. I am about to order a new fleet."

"Anything you say," I said, from my post by the desk.

Gaily, Quick waved a drone over his head, holding it firmly between his thumb and forefinger. The drone buzzed in alarm. Quick had kidnapped it from the file drawer.

He disappeared from sight, going to the top of the stairs. I heard him talking reassuringly to the drone.

A moment later, the drone plummeted down the stairwell, pulled up inches from the floor, and blundered across the room to the desktop. There was a piece of soda straw tied under his belly.

The drone rested, then started groggily for the open file drawer.

"Grab him!" yelled Quick. "Get the message!"

I chased the drone around the desktop with my cupped hands, but I didn't have the nerve to grab him.

Quick had to come down from the stairs to do the job. He handed me the straw with the message in it.

The drone, with a buzz of joy, dived into his club. There was a murmur of welcome inside.

The message was on a scrap of tissue paper. The writing was so tiny, I needed a magnifying glass to make it out. *"Quote price on 400 taxis,"* it said. *"Reply by begram. Quick Taxi Corp."*

"See?" said Quick. "You would have bees from my club, and I would have bees from *yours*. And a penny's worth of honey would keep one of our little messengers operating for a year."

"Don't they make their own honey?" I said bleakly. It was just something to say—something to cover up my feelings. I felt awful. Quick was so happy about the drone business, was staking so much on it—and it seemed to be up to me to tell him what a fat-headed enterprise it was.

"Only the female workers make honey," said Quick.

"Oh," I said. "Huh. I guess that's why the female workers knock off the males, eh? The males are nothing but a drain on the community."

The color left Quick's fine face. "What's so wonderful about making honey?" he said. "Can *you* make honey?"

"Nope," I said.

He was excited, upset. "Is that any reason to condemn you to death?" he said.

"Nope—heck no," I said.

Quick gathered up my lapel in his fist. "Consider the philosophical and moral implications of what you've just seen!" he said intensely. "Bees are just the beginning!"

"Yessir," I said, smiling and sweating.

His eyes narrowed. "The female praying mantis eats the male as you or I would eat a stalk of celery," he said. "The female tarantula pops her little lover into her mouth like a canapé!"

He backed me into the wall. "What are we going to do with the male praying mantis and the male tarantula?" he said. He stabbed my chest with his finger. "We're going to teach them to carry inter-office memos, to carry orders from foxhole to foxhole on the front lines!"

Quick let go of my lapel and looked at me disappointedly. "My God, man—" he said irritably, "you stand there with fishy eyes and a slack jaw, and I've just showed you the greatest thing in humanitarianism since the *New Testament*!"

"Yessir," I said, "but—"

"The greatest advance in communications since the invention of wireless telegraphy!" he said.

"Yup. Yessir," I said. I sighed and squared my shoulders. "If you'd discovered this *before* somebody else had discovered wireless telegraphy," I said, "maybe you'd have something. But, good gosh, what person in this day and age is going to want to write eensy-teensy messages on tissue paper and send them by bee?"

He leaned against the desk, closed his eyes, and nodded to himself. "I should have expected it," he said. "The chorus of 'No, no, no—it can't be done.' Every innovator has been faced by that."

"Yessir—I guess that's so," I said. "But sometimes the chorus is right. I mean, good gosh, what you've got here is competitive with carrier pigeons."

His eyes lit up. "Aha!" he said. "And look how wide open you have to leave a window for carrier pigeons!" He waggled his finger at me. "And tell me this: can you use carrier pigeons indoors as well as outdoors?"

I scratched my head. "Everything you say against carrier pigeons is true," I said. "But who uses carrier pigeons anymore?"

Quick looked at me blankly. His lips moved, but no sounds came. An automobile backfired in the outside world, and fear crossed Quick's face like a cloud.

"I'm no genius," he said softly, "I never claimed that, did I?"

"Nossir," I said.

"Living quietly and decently seemed to be the best I could expect of myself, with my small store of talents," said Quick. He was humble and reverent. "But once in this life, as I sat in the small library where we met, I was reading Maeterlinck's *Life of the Bee*—and I heard the thunderclap and saw the flash of inspiration."

"Um," I said.

"In that divine trance," he said, "I bought my bees, experimented—and here we are."

"Yup," I said, wretchedly.

He raised his chin bravely. "Very well," he said. "I have gone this far—I will go the rest of the way. I will put my findings before the greatest jury of all, the American public, and let them decide: have I got the seeds of something useful to humanity, or have I not?"

Quick laid his hand on my shoulder. "We will call a press conference at once. Will you help?"

There was a lump in my throat. "Yessir, I will," I said.

"Good boy!" he said. "You tear up tissue paper while I chop straws."

◙ ◙ ◙

For the press conference, Quick chose a sober blue suit and the air of an historian. His eyes were red, and his head ached. For three hours he had been writing tiny beegrams. The messages were a secret, known only to him and to God.

The conference took place in the auditorium of the Millennium Club. Quick had splurged a part of the little money he had left on a buffet and cocktails for the gentlemen of the press.

Five gentlemen of the press came—three reporters and two photographers. Quick had prepared for a hundred.

The five sat in the front row, eating and drinking. Quick stood on the stage. I stood behind him, with his entire fleet of drones in a wooden box. Each drone had a message tied under his belly. By a window stood the faithful old waiter, ready to open the window at a signal from Quick.

Quick had explained his experiments, his theories, and his inspiration. The time was coming when I was to open the box, and release the history-making cloud that would fly out the window, down three stories, into an open basement window, and into the first all-male beehive in the desk.

The bees themselves seemed to sense the excitement around them. They bumped their heads against the lid of the box, and kept up a steady, anxious, eager buzzing.

"The history of man's advance," said Quick impressively, "has been the history of encouraging that which is good in Nature, and discouraging that which is bad. For millions of years now, Nature has been throwing away, like so much garbage, one of her wisest, gentlest, most beautiful creations—the drone, whose only crime is that he does not make honey."

Quick raised his finger. "Now!" he said. "Man comes along, and declares in the face of this cruel waste: "'There is more to life than this crazy, sick-headed preoccupation with honey, honey, honey, everything for honey—and *death* to anybody who can't make honey!'"

Quick's voice became husky with emotion, as though he were praying for a multitude. "We welcome the drones today to the fruits of freedom and equality. Down with tyranny wherever we find it! Down with the tyranny of honey! Down with the tyranny of the self-centered and vain queen! Down with the tyranny of the narrow-minded, materialistic female workers!"

Quick turned to address the box. "Life and liberty are yours!"

I opened the lid and dumped the box.

The drones tumbled to the floor in a seething heap. And then, one by one, they took to the air, forming a ragged circle over our heads.

"Pursue happiness!" shouted Quick.

The old waiter threw open the window.

The drones bungled around the room for several minutes, until some found the open window. The swarm strung out in a line, and went out the window, over the park below.

The line started down, and we cheered. And then something went wrong. The line went up again, and drifted out over the park.

"Down! Down, boys!" cried Quick.

The drones seemed to be looking for something. And then they found it—not down, but up. They arose in an insane spiral, higher and higher above the park, until they were out of sight.

"A queen!" sobbed Quick. "A queen!"

◎ ◎ ◎

The press conference moved into the basement with its refreshments, to wait by the bee Millennium Club. The hive in the file drawer was empty. A basement window was propped open, but nothing came in but little gusts of soot.

Quick was strangely at peace. The appearance of the queen seemed to have blown every fuse in his nervous system.

After an hour of waiting, he said in a distant voice to me, "Go up on the roof, and keep a lookout for our faithful messengers from there."

I went to the roof, and found the drone fleet there. They were back from the mating, dragging their message cases, swaggering triumphantly into the homes of their birth—the hives from which Quick had rescued them.

The female workers came whining out to meet their brothers. In a matter of minutes, Quick's drones lay dead or dying, buzzing their last in mournful mystification.

◙ ◙ ◙

With a heart as heavy as a stone, I went back to the basement and told Quick the news.

He took the news calmly. He had banked the fires of his hopes during the long wait. And now, like the gentleman he was, he let the fires die quietly.

"You would think," he said, "that there would be one out of the many whose intellect would rise above his instincts." He stood and smiled gamely. "With him, we might have sired a new and nobler race of bees."

He shook hands all around. "A fiasco, gentlemen. I apologize." There were tears in his eyes. "Report me as a fool, if you must," he said. "But report me as a fool with one of the kinder, grander dreams of our time."

He bowed, and left, climbing the stairs alone.

◙ ◙ ◙

The newspaper men and the old waiter left soon after, and I was alone.

Footsteps passed the open window, and I saw Quick's feet go by. He had picked the moment in which to leave the Millennium Club, probably never to return.

I closed the window, and drank to the health of Sheldon Quick, to the memory of his drones.

There was a gentle bumping sound against the window.

I opened the window, and let in a single drone. He was horribly maimed, with wings torn, legs gone.

He flew to the file drawer, crawled to the hole in the bee Millennium Club, and fell in. There was a weak buzz inside—the buzz of a soul fulfilled.

He was dead.

I took his message, and read the words Quick had written over and over again for all his bees to carry.

"*What*," Quick had written, "*hath God wrought?*"

Hello, Red

THE SUN WAS SETTING behind the big black drawbridge. The bridge, with its colossal abutments and piers, weighed more than the whole river-mouth village in its shadows. On a revolving stool in a lunchroom at one end of the bridge sat Red Mayo, the new bridge tender. He had just come off duty.

The air of the lunchroom was cut by a cruel screech from a dry bearing in the revolving stool as Red turned away from his coffee and hamburger, and looked up at the bridge expectantly. He was a heavy young man, twenty-eight, with the flat, mean face of a butcher boy.

The frail counterman and the three other customers, all men, watched Red with amiable surmise, as though ready to bloom with broad smiles at the first sign of friendliness from him.

No friendliness was forthcoming. When Red's eyes met theirs briefly, Red sniffed, and returned his attention to his food. He toyed with his tableware, and the big muscles in his forearms fretted under his tattoos, under intertwined symbols of bloodlust and love—daggers and hearts.

The counterman, egged on by nods from the other three customers, spoke to Red with great politeness. "Excuse me, sir," he said, "but are you Red Mayo?"

"That's who I am," said Red, without looking up.

A universal sigh and happy murmur went up. "I knew it was . . . I thought it was . . . That's who it is," said the chorus of three.

"Don't you remember me, Red?" said the counterman. "Slim Corby?"

"Yeah—I remember you," said Red emptily.

"Remember *me*, Red?" said an elderly customer hopefully. "George Mott?"

"Hi," said Red.

"Sorry about your mother and father passing on, Red," said Mott. "That was years ago, but I never got to see you till now. Good people. *Real* good people." Finding Red's eyes filled with apathy, he hesitated. "You remember me, Red—George Mott?"

"I remember," said Red. He nodded to the other two customers. "And that's Harry Childs and that's Stan West."

"He remembers . . . Sure he remembers . . . How could Red forget?" said the nervous chorus. They continued to make tentative gestures of welcome.

724

"Gee," said Slim, the counterman, "I figured we'd never see *you* again. I figured you'd took off for good."

"Figured wrong," said Red. "Happens sometimes."

"How long since you been back, Red?" said Slim. "Eight, nine years?"

"Eight," said Red.

"You still in the merchant marines?" said Mott.

"Bridge tender," said Red.

"Whereabouts?" said Slim.

"This bridge right here," said Red.

"Heeeeeeey—you hear that?" said Slim. He started to touch Red familiarly, but thought better of it. "Red's the new bridge tender!"

"Home to stay . . . Got hisself a good job . . . Ain't that nice?" said the chorus.

"When you start?" said Mott.

"Started," said Red. "Been up there two days now."

All were amazed. "Never heard a word about it . . . Never thought to look up and see who's there . . . Two days, and we never noticed him," said the chorus.

"I cross the bridge four times a day," said Slim. "You should have said hello or something. You know—you get to kind of thinking of the bridge tender as just kind of part of the machinery. You must of seen me and Harry and Stan and Mr. Mott and Eddie Scudder and everybody else crossing the bridge, and you never said a word?"

"Wasn't ready to," said Red. "Somebody else I had to talk to first."

"Oh," said Slim. His face went blank. He looked to the other three for enlightenment, and got three shrugs. Rather than pry, Slim tried to fidget his curiosity into thin air with his fingers.

"Don't give me that," said Red irritably.

"Give you what, Red?" said Slim.

"Them innocent looks about who I been talking to," said Red.

"I honest to God don't know, Red," said Slim. "It's so long since you been home, it's kind of hard to figure out *who* you'd want to see *special*."

"So many people come and gone . . . So much water under the bridge . . . All your old friends growed up and settled down," said the chorus.

Red grinned unpleasantly, to let them know they weren't getting away with anything. "A girl," said Red. "I been talking to a girl."

"Ooooooooooooh," said Slim. He chuckled lecherously. "You old dog, you old sea dog. All of a sudden got a hankering for some of the old hometown stuff, eh?" His chuckle died as Red glared at him.

"Go on, enjoy yourself," said Red angrily. "Play dumb. You got about five minutes more, till Eddie Scudder gets here."

"Eddie, eh?" said Slim, helpless in the midst of the puzzle.

The chorus had fallen silent, their eyes straight ahead. Red had killed their welcome, and given them only fear and bewilderment in return.

Red pursed his lips prissily. "Can't imagine what Red Mayo'd be wanting to see Eddie Scudder about," he said in a falsetto. He was infuriated by the innocence all around him. "I really forgot what this village was like," he said. "By God—everybody agrees to tell the same big lie; pretty soon, everybody believes it like it was the gospel truth." He hit the counter with his fist. "My own folks, even!" he said. "My own flesh and blood—they never even said a word in their letters."

Slim, deserted by the chorus, was now terribly alone with the surly redhead. "What lie?" he said shakily.

"What lie, what lie?" said Red in a parrot's voice. "Polly wants a crack-*er*, Polly wants a crack-*er*! I guess I've seen just about everything in my travels, but I only seen one thing to come up to you guys."

"What's that, Red?" said Slim, who was now an automaton.

"There was this kind of South American snake, see?" said Red. "Liked to steal kids. It'd swipe a kid, and raise it just like it was a snake. Teach it to crawl and everything. And all the other snakes'd treat it just like it was a snake, too."

In the silence, the chorus felt obliged to murmur. "Never heard of such a thing . . . A snake do that? . . . If that don't take the cake."

"We'll ask Eddie about it when he gets here," said Red. "He always was real good at animals and nature." He hunched over, and stuffed his mouth with hamburger, indicating that the conversation was at an end. "Eddie's late," he said with a full mouth. "I hope he got my message."

He thought about his messenger, and how he'd sent her. With his jaws working, his eyes down, he was soon reliving his day. In his mind, it was noon again.

And it seemed to Red at noon that he was steering the village from his steel and glass booth, six feet above the roadway, on a girder at one end of the bridge. Only the clouds and massive counterweights of the bridge were higher than Red was.

There was a quarter of an inch of play in the lever that controlled the bridge, and it was with this quarter of an inch that Red pretended, God-like, to steer the village. It was natural for him to think of himself and his surroundings as moving, of the water below as standing still. He had been a merchant sailor for nine years—a bridge tender for less than two days.

Hearing the noon howl of the fire horn, Red stopped his steering, and looked through his spyglass at Eddie Scudder's oyster shack below. The shack was rickety and helpless-looking on pilings in the river mouth, connected to the salt marsh shore by two springy planks. The river bottom around it was a twinkling white circle of oyster shells.

Eddie's eight-year-old daughter, Nancy, came out of the shack, and bounced gently on the planks, her face lifted to the sunshine. And then she stopped bouncing, and became demure.

Red had taken the job for the opportunity it gave him to watch her. He knew what the demureness was. It was a prelude to a ceremony, the ceremony of Nancy's combing her bright red hair.

Red's fingers played along the spyglass as though it were a clarinet. "Hello, Red," he whispered.

Nancy combed and combed and combed that cascade of red hair. Her eyes were closed, and each tug of the comb seemed to fill her with bittersweet ecstasy.

The combing left her languid. She walked through the salt meadow gravely, and climbed the steep bank to the road that crossed the bridge. Every day at noon, Nancy crossed the bridge to the lunchroom at the other end, to fetch a hot lunch for herself and her father.

Red smiled down at Nancy as she came.

Seeing the smile, she touched her hair.

"It's still there," said Red.

"What is?" said Nancy.

"Your hair, Red."

"I told you yesterday," she said, "my name isn't Red. It's Nancy."

"How could anybody call you anything *but* Red?" said Red.

"That's *your* name," said Nancy.

"So I got a right to give it to you, if I want to," said Red. "I don't know anybody who's got a better right."

"I shouldn't even be talking to you," she said playfully, teasing him with propriety. There was no mistrust in her mind. Their meetings had a fairy-tale quality, with Red no ordinary stranger, but a genial sorcerer in charge of the wonderful bridge—a sorcerer who seemed to know more about the girl than she knew about herself.

"Didn't I tell you I grew up in this village, just like you're doing?" said Red. "Didn't I tell you I went to high school with your mother and father? Don't you believe that?"

"I believe it," said Nancy. "Only Mother used to say little girls should be introduced to strangers. They shouldn't just start talking to them."

Red kept the needles of sarcasm out of his voice. "Quite an upstanding lady, wasn't she?" he said. "Yup—*she* knew how good little boys and girls should act. Yessirreeee—good as gold, Violet was. Butter wouldn't melt in *her* mouth."

"Everybody says so," said Nancy proudly. "Not just Daddy and me."

"Daddy, eh?" said Red. He mimicked her. "'Daddy, Daddy, Daddy—Eddie Scudder is my great big Daddy.'" He cocked his head watchfully. "You didn't tell him I was up here, did you?"

Nancy blushed at the accusation. "I wouldn't break my word of honor."

Red grinned and wagged his head. "Gee, he'll really get a big boot out of it when I all of a sudden just kind of drop out of the sky, after all these years."

"One of the last things Mother said before she died," said Nancy, "was that I should never break my word of honor."

Red clucked piously. "Real serious girl, your mother," he said. "Back when we got out of high school, the other girls wanted to play around a little before they settled down. But not Violet. Nosir. I made my first voyage back then—and when I come back a year later, she was all married and settled down with Eddie, and she'd had you. Course, you didn't have any hair when I saw you that time."

"I've got to go now, and get my daddy's lunch," said Nancy.

"'Daddy, Daddy, Daddy,'" said Red. "'Got to do this for Daddy, got to do that for Daddy.' Must be nice to have a pretty, smart daughter like you. 'Daddy, Daddy.' You ask your daddy about red hair, like I told you?"

"He said he guessed it usually ran in families," said Nancy. "Only sometimes it pops up from nowhere, like it did with me." Her hand went up to her hair.

"It's still there," said Red.

"What is?" said Nancy.

"Your *hair*, Red!" He guffawed. "I swear, if anything was to happen to that hair, you'd just dry up and blow away. Comes from nowhere, does it? That's what Eddie said?" Red nodded judiciously. "*He'd* know. I expect Eddie's done a lot of thinking about red hair in his time. Now, you take *my* family: if *I* was ever to have a kid that *wasn't* redheaded, *that'd* start everybody to figuring and wondering. Been a red-headed family since the beginning of time."

"That's very interesting," said Nancy.

"Gets more interesting, the more you think about it," said Red. "You and me and my old man are about the only redheads this village ever had, that *I* know of. Now that the old man's gone, that just leaves two of us."

Nancy remained serene. "Huh," she said. "Bye, now."

"Bye, Red."

As she walked away, Red picked up his spyglass, and looked down at Eddie's oyster shack. Through the window, he could see Eddie, blue-gray in the twilight interior, shucking oysters. Eddie was a small man, with a large head majestic in sorrow. It was the head of a young Job.

"Hi," whispered Red. "Guess who's home."

When Nancy came back from the lunchroom with a warm, fat paper bag, Red stopped her again.

"Saaaaaay," he said, "maybe you'll grow up to be a nurse, after taking such good care of old Eddie. I wish there'd been nice nurses like you at the hospital I was at."

Nancy's face softened with pity. "You were in a hospital?"

"Three months, Red, in Liverpool, without a friend or a relative in this world to come see me, or even send me a get-well card." He grew wistful. "Funny, Red—I never realized how lonely I was, till I had to lie down and stay down, till I knew I couldn't ever go to sea again." He licked his lips. "Changed me, Red, like *that*." He snapped his fingers.

"All of a sudden, I needed a home," he said, "and somebody to care about me, and keep me company—maybe in that little cottage out there on the point. I didn't have nothing, Red, but mate's papers that wasn't worth the paper they were printed on for a man with one leg."

Nancy was shocked. "You've only got one leg?"

"One day I was the crazy, tough kid they all remember down there," said Red, including the village in a sweep of his hand. "The next day I was an old, old man."

Nancy bit her knuckle, sharing his pain. "Haven't you got a wife or a mother or a lady friend to look after you?" she said. By her stance, she offered her services as a daughter, as though it were a simple thing that any good girl would do.

Red hung his head. "Dead," he said. "My mother's dead, and the only girl I ever loved is dead. And the lady friends, Red—they're never what you'd call *real* friendly, not if you can't love *them*, not if you're in love with a ghost."

Nancy's sweet face twisted as Red forced her to look at the grisliness of life. "Why do you live up the river, if you're so lonesome?" she said. "Why don't you live down here, where you'd be with your old friends?"

Red raised an eyebrow. "Old friends? Funny kind of friends to have, who wouldn't even drop me a postcard to tell me Violet's kid had bright red hair. Not even my folks told me."

The wind freshened, and on the wind, from seemingly far away, came Nancy's voice. "Daddy's lunch is getting cold," she said. She started to walk away.

"Red!"

She stopped, and her hand went up to her hair. She kept her back to him.

Red wished to God he could see her face. "Tell Eddie I want to talk to him, would you? Tell him to meet me in the lunchroom after I get off work—about ten after five."

"I will," she said. Her voice was clear, calm.

"Word of honor?"

"Word of honor," she said. She started walking again.

"Red!"

Her hand went up to her hair, but she kept on walking.

Red followed her with his spyglass, but she knew she was being watched. She kept her head turned, so he couldn't see her face. And seconds after she went into the oyster shack, a shade was drawn across the window that faced the bridge.

For the rest of the afternoon, the shack might as well have been empty for all the life Red could see. Only once, toward sunset, did Eddie come out. He didn't so much as glance up at the bridge, and he kept *his* face hidden, too.

The screech from his own stool in the lunchroom brought Red back to the present. He blinked at the sunset, and saw the silhouette of Eddie Scudder crossing the bridge, big-headed and bandy-legged, carrying a small paper bag.

Red turned his back to the door, reached into a jacket pocket, and brought forth a packet of letters, which he set on the counter before him. He put his fingertips on them, like a cardplayer standing pat. "Here's the man of the hour," he said.

No one spoke.

Eddie came in without hesitation, with a formal greeting for everyone, Red last of all. His voice was surprisingly rich and deep. "Hello, Red," he said. "Nancy said you wanted to see me."

"That's right," said Red. "Nobody here can figure out what I'd have to say to you."

"Nancy had a little trouble figuring it out, too," said Eddie, without a trace of resentment.

"She finally got the drift?" said Red.

"She got it, about as well as an eight-year-old could," said Eddie. He sat down on the stool next to Red's, and set his bag on the counter, next to the letters. He showed mild surprise at the handwriting of the letters, and made no effort to hide his surprise from Red. "Coffee, please, Slim," he said.

"Maybe you'd rather have this private," said Red. He was a little disconcerted by Eddie's equanimity. He'd remembered Eddie as a homely clown.

"Makes no difference," said Eddie. "It's all before God, wherever we do it."

The straightforward inclusion of God in the meeting was also unexpected by Red. In his daydreams in his hospital bed, the resounding lines had all been his— irrefutable lines dealing with man's rights to the love of his own flesh and blood. Red felt the necessity of puffing himself up, of dramatizing his advantages in bulk and stature. "First of all," he said importantly, "I wanna say I don't care what the law has to say about this. This is bigger than that."

"Good," said Eddie. "Then we agree first of all. I'd hoped we would."

"So's we won't be talking about two different things," said Red, "lemme say right out that I'm the father of that kid—not you."

Eddie stirred his coffee with a steady hand. "We'll be talking about exactly the same thing," he said.

Slim and the three others looked out the windows desperately.

Around and around and around went Eddie's spoon in his coffee. "Go on," he said happily.

Red was rattled. Things were going faster than he had expected—and, at the same time, they were seemingly going nowhere. He'd passed the climax of what he'd come home to say, and nothing had changed—and nothing seemed about to change. "Everybody's gone right along with you, pretending she was your kid," he said indignantly.

"They've been good neighbors," said Eddie.

Red's mind was now a mare's nest of lines he hadn't used yet, lines that now didn't seem to fit anywhere. "I'm willing to take a blood test, to find out who's her father," he said. "Are you?"

"Do we all have to bleed, before we can believe each other?" said Eddie. "I told you I agreed with you. You are her father. Everybody knows that. How could they miss it?"

"Did she tell you I'd lost a leg?" said Red hectically.

"Yes," said Eddie. "That impressed her more than anything. That's what *would* impress an eight-year-old the most."

Red looked at his own reflection in the coffee urn and saw that his eyes were watery, his face bright pink. His reflection assured him that he'd spoken well—that he was being trifled with. "Eddie—that kid is mine, and I want her."

"I'm sorry for you, Red," said Eddie, "but you can't have her." For the first time, his hand trembled, making his spoon click against the side of his cup. "I think you'd better go away."

"You think this is a little thing?" said Red. "You think a man can back away from something like this like it was nothing—back away from his own kid, and just forget it?"

"Not being a father myself," said Eddie, "I can only guess at what you're going through."

"Is that a joke?" said Red.

"Not to me," said Eddie evenly.

"This is some smart way of saying you're more her old man that I am?" said Red.

"If I haven't said it, I will say it," said Eddie. His hand shook so uncontrollably that he was obliged to set his spoon down, to grip the counter's edge.

Red saw now how frightened Eddie was, saw how phony his poise and godliness were. Red felt his own strength growing, felt the flow of booming good health and righteousness he'd daydreamed of. He was suddenly in charge, with plenty to say, and plenty of time in which to say it.

It angered him that Eddie had tried to bluff and confuse him, had nearly succeeded. And on the crest of the anger rode all Red's hate for the cold and empty world. His whole will was now devoted to squashing the little man beside him.

"That's Violet's and my kid," said Red. "She never loved you."

"I hope she did," said Eddie humbly.

"She married you because she figured I wasn't ever coming back!" said Red. He picked up a letter from the top of the packet and waved it under Eddie's nose. "She told me so—just like that—in so many words."

Eddie refused to look at the letter. "That was a long time ago, Red. A lot can happen."

"I'll tell you one thing that didn't happen," said Red, "she never stopped writing, never stopped begging me to come back."

"I guess those things go on for a while," said Eddie softly.

"A *while*?" said Red. He riffled through the letters, and dropped one before Eddie. "Look at the date on that one, would you? Just look at the date on *that.*"

"I don't want to," said Eddie. He stood.

"You're afraid," said Red.

"That's right," said Eddie. He closed his eyes. "Go away, Red. Please go away."

"Sorry, Eddie," said Red, "but nothing's gonna make me go away. Red's home."

"God pity you," said Eddie. He walked to the door.

"You forgot your little paper bag," said Red. His feet danced.

"That's yours," said Eddie. "Nancy sent it. It was her idea, not mine. God knows I would have stopped her if I'd known." He was crying.

He left, and crossed the bridge in the gathering darkness.

Slim and the other three customers had turned to stone.

"My God!" Red cried at them. "My own flesh and blood! It's the deepest thing there is! What could ever make me leave?"

No one answered.

A terrible depression settled over Red, the aftermath of battle. He sucked the back of his hand, as though nursing a wound. "Slim," he said, "what's in that bag?"

Slim opened the bag and looked inside. "Hair, Red," he said. "Red hair."

The Honor of a Newsboy

CHARLEY HOWES WAS the police chief in a Cape Cod village. He was in command of four patrolmen in the summer and one in the winter. It was late winter now. The one patrolman was down with the flu, and Charley didn't feel too good himself. On top of that, there'd been a murder. Somebody had given Estelle Fulmer, the Jezebel waitress over at the Blue Dolphin, a beating that had killed her.

They found her in a cranberry bog on Saturday. The medical examiner said she'd been killed Wednesday night.

Charley Howes guessed he knew who'd done it. He guessed Earl Hedlund had done it. Earl was mean enough, and Earl had reason. Estelle had told Earl to go to hell one night at the Blue Dolphin, told him off the way he'd never been told off before. Nobody had ever told Earl off that way before because everybody knew Earl would kill anybody who did.

Charley's wife was bundling up Charley now so he could go up to Earl's house and question him. "If I'd known there was going to be a murder," said Charley, "I never would have taken the job of police chief."

"Now, you watch out for that big dog," said his wife, wrapping a muffler around his neck.

"He's all bark and no bite," said Charley.

"That's what they said about Earl Hedlund, too," said his wife.

The dog they were talking about was Satan. Satan was a crossbreed between a Great Dane and an Irish wolfhound. He was as big as a small horse. Satan didn't belong to Earl Hedlund, but he spent most of his time in Earl's woods, scaring people off the property. Earl fed him off and on, getting a cheap watchdog that way. And the dog and Earl liked each other fine besides. They both liked to make a lot of noise and act like man-eaters.

When Charley drove the patrol car up the long hill to Earl's house, way off in the woods, he expected to find Earl home. It was Saturday afternoon, but Charley would have expected to find Earl home any day of the week. Earl didn't work for a living. He'd inherited just enough money so he didn't have to work—if he was good and stingy, and kept a sharp eye on the stock market. The busiest Earl ever got was when the newspaper came. He'd turn to the financial page and make graphs of what all the stocks were doing.

When Charley got up to the house, he could hear Satan barking from a long way off. And Earl wasn't around, either. The house was locked up tight, and the newspapers had piled up on the front porch.

The newspapers were under a brick, so they couldn't blow away. Charley counted the papers. There were four. Friday's was the top one. Saturday's hadn't come yet. It began to look as though Earl hadn't killed Estelle after all, much as he would have liked to. It looked as though Earl hadn't been around to do the job.

Charley looked at the dates on the untouched papers, and he discovered something interesting. The Wednesday paper was missing.

The noise of the dog was coming closer now, coming closer fast. Charley figured the dog had got wind of him. Charley had to keep a grip on himself to keep from being scared. Charley had the same feeling about Satan everybody else in the village had. The dog was crazy. Satan hadn't bitten anybody yet—but if he ever did, he'd bite to kill.

Then Charley saw what Satan was barking at. Satan was cantering alongside of a boy on a bicycle, showing teeth like butcher knives. He was swinging his head from side to side, barking, and slashing air with those awful teeth.

The boy looked straight ahead, pretending the dog wasn't there. He was the bravest human being Charley had ever seen. The hero was Mark Crosby, the ten-year-old newsboy.

"Mark—" said Charley. The dog came after Charley now, did his best to turn Charley's thinning hair white with those butcher-knife teeth. If the boy hadn't set such high standards for bravery, Charley might have made a dive for the safety of the patrol car. "You seen anything of Mr. Hedlund, Mark?" said Charley.

"Nosir," said Mark, giving Charley's uniform the respect it deserved. He put the Saturday paper on top of the pile on the doorstep, put it under the brick. "He's been gone all week, sir."

Satan finally got bored with these two unscarable human beings. He lay down on the porch with a tremendous thump, and snarled lazily from time to time.

"Where'd he go? You know?" said Charley.

"Nosir," said Mark. "He didn't say he was going—didn't stop his paper."

"Did you deliver a paper Wednesday?" said Charley.

Mark was offended that his friend the policeman should ask. "Of course," he said. "It's the rule. If the papers pile up and nobody's said to stop, you keep on delivering for six days." He nodded. "It's the *rule*, Mr. Howes."

The serious way Mark talked about the rule reminded Charley what a marvelous age ten was. And Charley thought it was a pity that everybody couldn't stay ten for the rest of their lives. If everybody were ten, Charley thought, maybe rules and common decency and horse sense would have a Chinaman's chance.

"You—you sure you didn't maybe miss Wednesday, Mark?" said Charley. "Nobody'd blame you—sleet coming down, the papers piling up, the long hill to climb, the big dog to get past."

Mark held up his right hand. "My word of honor," he said, "a paper was delivered here Wednesday."

That was good enough for Charley. That certainly settled it once and for all.

Just about the time that was settled, up the road came Earl Hedlund's old coupe. Earl got out grinning, and Satan whimpered and got up and licked Earl's hand. Earl was the village bully of thirty-five years ago—gone to fat and baldness. His grin was still the bully-boy's grin, daring anybody not to love him. He'd never been able to bluff Charley, and he hated Charley for that.

His grin got wider when Charley, as a precaution, reached into his car and took out the ignition key. "You see a cop do that on television, Charley?" said Earl.

"Matter of fact, I did," said Charley. It was true.

"I'm not running off to nowheres," said Earl. "I read in the Providence papers about poor Estelle, and I figured you'd be wanting to see me, so I came back. Thought I could save you from wasting time—thinking it was me that killed her."

"Thanks," said Charley.

"I been at my brother's place in Providence all week," said Earl. "My brother'll swear to that. Every minute's accounted for." He winked. "O.K., Charley?"

Charley knew Earl's brother. Earl's brother had a mean streak, too—but he was too little to beat up on women, so he specialized in lying. All the same, his word might stand up in court.

Earl sat down on his doorstep, took the top paper off the pile, turned to the financial page. Then he remembered it was Saturday. There weren't any market quotations on Saturday. It was easy to see he hated Saturday for that.

"You have many visitors up here, Earl?" said Charley.

"Visitors?" said Earl scornfully. He was reading what little financial news there was. "What I want with visitors?"

"Repairmen? Strangers out for a walk? Kids?" said Charley. "Hunters maybe?"

Earl puffed himself up for his answer. He really enjoyed the idea that everybody was too scared to come near his place. "Anything needs repairing, I repair myself," he said. "And strangers and kids and hunters and anybody else finds out pretty quick from the dog that we don't want no visitors up this way."

"Then who picked up the paper Wednesday night?" said Charley.

Earl let his paper sag for just a second, then he straightened it out again, pretended to read something a lot more important than anything Charley was saying. "What's this bushwah about a Wednesday paper?" he grumbled.

Charley told him what the bushwah was—told him that it might prove that Earl had been back on Cape Cod the night Estelle was murdered. "If you did come back on Wednesday," said Charley, "I can't see you passing up the chance to look in the paper to see what the market was doing."

Earl put down the paper, and he looked straight at Mark. "There wasn't any Wednesday paper on account of the kid was too lazy to bring one," he said.

"He gave his word of honor he brought one," said Charley.

Earl started reading again. "The kid's not only lazy," he said, "he's a liar besides."

Charley was glad he hadn't brought his gun along. If he had, he might have shot Earl Hedlund. Charley forgot all about the murder. Here, for Charley's money, was a crime that was just as bad as murder—and there wasn't any name for it and there wasn't any law against it.

Poor Mark was ruined. The most priceless thing he'd built up for himself in this vale of tears was his word of honor. Earl had spit on it.

"He gave his word of honor!" Charley yelled at Earl.

Earl said a dirty word, didn't look up from his paper.

"Mr. Howes—" said Mark.

"Yes, Mark?" said Charley.

"I—I got something even better than my word of honor," said Mark.

Charley couldn't imagine what that would be. Earl was curious, too. Even Satan the dog seemed to want to know what could top a ten-year-old's word of honor.

Mark glowed, he was so sure he could prove, even to Earl's satisfaction, that the Wednesday paper had been delivered. "I was sick Wednesday," he said, "so my father delivered the papers." As far as Mark was concerned, he might as well have said God had done the route.

Charley Howes smiled feebly. Mark had just done him out of his one good clue. Mark's father was maybe brave in a lot of ways, but there were two things he wasn't brave about. All his life he'd been scared of Earl Hedlund and dogs.

Earl Hedlund guffawed.

Charley sighed. "Thanks—thanks for the information, Mark," he said. "You go on and carry the rest of your route now." He was going to let it go at that.

But Earl wouldn't let it go that easily. "Kid," he said to Mark, "I hate to tell you this, but that father of yours is the biggest yellow belly in the village." He put the paper aside and stood up, so Mark could see what a real man looked like.

"Shut up, Earl," said Charley.

"Shut up?" said Earl. "A minute ago, this kid was doing his best to get me in the electric chair."

Mark was flabbergasted. "Electric chair?" he said. "All I said was my father brought the paper."

Earl's piggy eyes glittered. The way those eyes glittered and the way Earl hunched over removed all doubt from Charley's mind that Earl was a murderer. Earl wanted to kill the boy. He couldn't do it with his hands with Charley there, so he was doing the next cruelest thing. He was doing it with words.

"Maybe your old man told you he brought the paper," said Earl, "but I promise you right now he wouldn't come near this dog for a million dollars, and he wouldn't come near me for ten million!" He held up his right hand. "Word of honor on that, kid!" He didn't stop there. He told Mark story after story about how Mark's father had run or hidden or cried or begged for mercy as a boy—how he'd slunk away from danger as a man. And in every story danger was one of two things—a dog or Earl Hedlund. "Scout's honor, word of honor, swear on a stack of Bibles—any kind of honor you want, kid," said Earl, "everything I've said is true."

There was nothing left for Mark to do but the thing he'd sworn never to do again. He cried. He climbed on his bicycle, and he rode away.

The dog didn't chase him this time. Satan understood that Mark wasn't fair game.

"Now you git, too," Earl said to Charley.

Charley was so heartsick about Mark, he leaned against Earl's house and closed his eyes for a minute. He opened his eyes and saw his reflection in a windowpane. He saw a tired old man, and he figured he'd grown old and tired trying to make the world be what ten-year-olds thought it was.

And then he saw the newspaper lying on the chair just inside the window, locked up nice and tight inside the house. Charley could read the date. It was Wednesday's paper, open to the financial page. It was proof enough that Earl had gone to Providence to build an alibi—that he'd sneaked back Wednesday to kill Estelle.

But Charley wasn't thinking about Earl or Estelle. He was thinking about Mark and his father.

Earl knew what Charley had seen through the window. He was on his feet, showing his teeth, ready to fight. And he held the dog by the scruff of his neck, getting the dog ready to fight, too.

But Charley didn't close in for a fight. He climbed into the patrol car instead. "Be here when I get back," he said, and he drove down the hill after Mark.

He caught up with Mark at the mouth of the road. "Mark!" he yelled. "Your father delivered the paper! It's up there! He delivered it through the sleet, past the dog and everything!"

"Good," said Mark. There wasn't any joy in the way he'd said it. He'd been through too much to be happy for a while. "Those things Mr. Hedlund said about Father," said Mark, "even if he gave his word of honor—they wouldn't necessarily be true, would they, Mr. Howes?"

There were two ways Charley could answer. He could lie, say no, the stories weren't true. Or he could tell the truth, and hope that Mark would catch on to the fact that all the stories made his father's delivery of the paper to Earl Hedlund's house one of the most glorious chapters in village history.

"Every one of those stories was true, Mark," said Charley. "Your father couldn't help being afraid, on account of he was born that way, just the way he was born with blue eyes and brown hair. You and me, we can't imagine what it's like to be loaded down with all that fear. It's a mighty brave man who can live with all that. So just think a minute how brave your father was to get that paper up to Earl Hedlund's rather than break a rule."

Mark thought, and then he nodded to show he understood. He was satisfied. His father was what a ten-year-old's father has to be—a hero.

"Did—did Mr. Hedlund do the murder?" said Mark.

"Gosh amighty!" said Charley. He banged the side of his head with the heel of his hand to make his brains work better. "Forgot all about the murder."

He turned the patrol car around and roared up to Earl's house again. Earl was gone, and so was the dog. They'd taken off through the woods.

Two hours later a search party found Earl. He'd been heading for the railroad tracks, and Satan the dog had killed him. At the coroner's inquest, all anybody could offer was theories about why the dog had done it.

The best theory was probably Charley's. Charley guessed that the dog had smelled Earl's fear and seen him running, so he'd chased him. "And Earl was the first person who'd ever let the dog see how scared he was," Charley said at the inquest, "so Satan killed him."

Tom Edison's Shaggy Dog

TWO OLD MEN sat on a park bench one morning in the sunshine of Tampa, Florida—one trying doggedly to read a book he was plainly enjoying while the other, Harold K. Bullard, told him the story of his life in the full, round, head tones of a public address system. At their feet lay Bullard's Labrador retriever, who further tormented the aged listener by probing his ankles with a large, wet nose.

Bullard, who had been, before he retired, successful in many fields, enjoyed reviewing his important past. But he faced the problem that complicates the lives of cannibals—namely: that a single victim cannot be used over and over. Anyone who had passed the time of day with him and his dog refused to share a bench with them again.

So Bullard and his dog set out through the park each day in quest of new faces. They had had good luck this morning, for they had found this stranger right away, clearly a new arrival in Florida, still buttoned up tight in heavy serge, stiff collar and necktie, and with nothing better to do than read.

"Yes," said Bullard, rounding out the first hour of his lecture, "made and lost five fortunes in my time."

"So you said," said the stranger, whose name Bullard had neglected to ask. "Easy, boy. No, no, no, boy," he said to the dog, who was growing more aggressive toward his ankles.

"Oh? Already told you that, did I?" said Bullard.

"Twice."

"Two in real estate, one in scrap iron, and one in oil and one in trucking."

"So you said."

"I did? Yes, guess I did. Two in real estate, one in scrap iron, one in oil, and one in trucking. Wouldn't take back a day of it."

"No, I suppose not," said the stranger. "Pardon me, but do you suppose you could move your dog somewhere else? He keeps—"

"Him?" said Bullard, heartily. "Friendliest dog in the world. Don't need to be afraid of him."

"I'm not afraid of him. It's just that he drives me crazy, sniffing at my ankles."

"Plastic," said Bullard, chuckling.

"What?"

"Plastic. Must be something plastic on your garters. By golly, I'll bet it's those little buttons. Sure as we're sitting here, those buttons must be plastic. That dog is nuts about plastic. Don't know why that is, but he'll sniff it out and find it if there's a speck around. Must be a deficiency in his diet, though, by gosh, he eats better than I do. Once he chewed up a whole plastic humidor. Can you beat it? *That's* the business I'd go into now, by glory, if the pill rollers hadn't told me to let up, to give the old ticker a rest."

"You could tie the dog to that tree over there," said the stranger.

"I get so darn' sore at all the youngsters these days!" said Bullard. "All of 'em mooning around about no frontiers any more. There never have been so many frontiers as there are today. You know what Horace Greeley would say today?"

"His nose is wet," said the stranger, and he pulled his ankles away, but the dog humped forward in patient pursuit. "Stop it, boy!"

"His wet nose shows he's healthy," said Bullard. "'Go plastic, young man!' That's what Greeley'd say. 'Go atom, young man!'"

The dog had definitely located the plastic buttons on the stranger's garters and was cocking his head one way and another, thinking out ways of bringing his teeth to bear on those delicacies.

"Scat!" said the stranger.

"'Go electronic, young man!'" said Bullard. "Don't talk to me about no opportunity any more. Opportunity's knocking down every door in the country, trying to get in. When I was young, a man had to go out and find opportunity and drag it home by the ears. Nowadays—"

"Sorry," said the stranger, evenly. He slammed his book shut, stood and jerked his ankle away from the dog. "I've got to be on my way. So good day, sir."

◎ ◎ ◎

He stalked across the park, found another bench, sat down with a sigh and began to read. His respiration had just returned to normal, when he felt the wet sponge of the dog's nose on his ankles again.

"Oh—it's you!" said Bullard, sitting down beside him. "He was tracking you. He was on the scent of something, and I just let him have his head. What'd I tell you about plastic?" He looked about contentedly. "Don't blame you for moving on. It was stuffy back there. No shade to speak of and not a sign of a breeze."

"Would the dog go away if I bought him a humidor?" said the stranger.

"Pretty good joke, pretty good joke," said Bullard, amiably. Suddenly he clapped the stranger on his knee. "Sa-ay, you aren't in plastics, are you? Here I've been blowing off about plastics, and for all I know that's your line."

"My line?" said the stranger crisply, laying down his book. "Sorry—I've never had a line. I've been a drifter since the age of nine, since Edison set up his laboratory next to my home, and showed me the intelligence analyzer."

"Edison?" said Bullard. "Thomas Edison, the inventor?"

"If you want to call him that, go ahead," said the stranger.

"If I *want* to call him that?"—Bullard guffawed— "I guess I just will! Father of the light bulb and I don't know what all."

"If you want to think he invented the light bulb, go ahead. No harm in it." The stranger resumed his reading.

"Say, what is this?" said Bullard, suspiciously. "You pulling my leg? What's this about an intelligence analyzer? I never heard of that."

"Of course you haven't," said the stranger. "Mr. Edison and I promised to keep it a secret. I've never told anyone. Mr. Edison broke his promise and told Henry Ford, but Ford made him promise not to tell anybody else—for the good of humanity."

Bullard was entranced. "Uh, this intelligence analyzer," he said, "it analyzed intelligence, did it?"

"It was an electric butter churn," said the stranger.

"Seriously now," Bullard coaxed.

"Maybe it *would* be better to talk it over with someone," said the stranger. "It's a terrible thing to keep bottled up inside me, year in and year out. But how can I be sure that it won't go any further?"

"My word as a gentleman," Bullard assured him.

"I don't suppose I could find a stronger guarantee than that, could I?" said the stranger, judiciously.

"There is no stronger guarantee," said Bullard, proudly. "Cross my heart and hope to die!"

"Very well." The stranger leaned back and closed his eyes, seeming to travel backward through time. He was silent for a full minute, during which Bullard watched with respect.

"It was back in the fall of eighteen seventy-nine," said the stranger at last, softly. "Back in the village of Menlo Park, New Jersey. I was a boy of nine. A young man we all thought was a wizard had set up a laboratory next door to my home, and there were flashes and crashes inside, and all sorts of scary goings on. The neighborhood children were warned to keep away, not to make any noise that would bother the wizard.

"I didn't get to know Edison right off, but his dog Sparky and I got to be steady pals. A dog a whole lot like yours, Sparky was, and we used to wrestle all over the neighborhood. Yes, sir, your dog is the image of Sparky."

"Is that so?" said Bullard, flattered.

"Gospel," replied the stranger. "Well, one day Sparky and I were wrestling around, and we wrestled right up to the door of Edison's laboratory. The next thing I knew, Sparky had pushed me in through the door, and bam! I was sitting on the laboratory floor, looking up at Mr. Edison himself."

"Bet he was sore," said Bullard, delighted.

"You can bet I was scared," said the stranger. "I thought I was face to face with Satan himself. Edison had wires hooked to his ears and running down to a little black box in his lap! I started to scoot, but he caught me by my collar and made me sit down.

"'Boy,' said Edison, 'it's always darkest before the dawn. I want you to remember that.'

"'Yes, sir,' I said.

"'For over a year, my boy,' Edison said to me, 'I've been trying to find a filament that will last in an incandescent lamp. Hair, string, splinters—nothing works. So while I was trying to think of something else to try, I started tinkering with another idea of mine, just letting off steam. I put this together,' he said, showing me the little black box. 'I thought maybe intelligence was just a certain kind of electricity, so I made this intelligence analyzer here. It works! You're the first one to know about it, my boy. But I don't know why you shouldn't be. It will be your generation that will grow up in the glorious new era when people will be as easily graded as oranges.'"

"I don't believe it!" said Bullard.

"May I be struck by lightning this very instant!" said the stranger. "And it did work, too. Edison had tried out the analyzer on the men in his shop, without telling them what he was up to. The smarter a man was, by gosh, the farther the needle on the indicator in the little black box swung to the right. I let him try it on me, and the needle just lay where it was and trembled. But dumb as I was, then is when I made my one and only contribution to the world. As I say, I haven't lifted a finger since."

"Whadja do?" said Bullard, eagerly.

"I said, 'Mr. Edison, sir, let's try it on the dog.' And I wish you could have seen the show that dog put on when I said it! Old Sparky barked and howled and scratched to get out. When he saw we meant business, that he wasn't going to get out, he made a beeline right for the intelligence analyzer and knocked it out of Edison's hands. But we cornered him, and Edison held him down while I touched the wires to his ears. And would you believe it, that needle sailed clear across the dial, way past a little red pencil mark on the dial face!"

"The dog busted it," said Bullard.

"'Mr. Edison, sir,' I said, 'what's that red mark mean?'

"'My boy,' said Edison, 'it means that the instrument is broken, because that red mark is me.'"

"I'll say it was broken," said Bullard.

The stranger said gravely, "But it wasn't broken. No, sir. Edison checked the whole thing, and it was in apple-pie order. When Edison told me that, it was then that Sparky, crazy to get out, gave himself away."

"How?" said Bullard, suspiciously.

"We really had him locked in, see? There were three locks on the door—a hook and eye, a bolt, and a regular knob and latch. That dog stood up, unhooked the hook, pushed the bolt back and had the knob in his teeth when Edison stopped him."

"No!" said Bullard.

"Yes!" said the stranger, his eyes shining. "And then is when Edison showed me what a great scientist he was. He was willing to face the truth, no matter how unpleasant it might be.

"'So!' said Edison to Sparky. 'Man's best friend, huh? Dumb animal, huh?'

"That Sparky was a caution. He pretended not to hear. He scratched himself and bit fleas and went around growling at ratholes—anything to get out of looking Edison in the eye.

"'Pretty soft, isn't it, Sparky?' said Edison. 'Let somebody else worry about getting food, building shelters and keeping warm, while you sleep in front of a fire or go chasing after the girls or raise hell with the boys. No mortgages, no politics, no war, no work, no worry. Just wag the old tail or lick a hand, and you're all taken care of.'

"'Mr. Edison,' I said, 'do you mean to tell me that dogs are smarter than people?'

"'Smarter?' said Edison. 'I'll tell the world! And what have I been doing for the past year? Slaving to work out a light bulb so dogs can play at night!'

"'Look, Mr. Edison,' said Sparky, 'why not—'"

"Hold on!" roared Bullard.

"Silence!" shouted the stranger, triumphantly. "'Look, Mr. Edison,' said Sparky, 'why not keep quiet about this? It's been working out to everybody's satisfaction for hundreds of thousands of years. Let sleeping dogs lie. You forget all about it, destroy the intelligence analyzer, and I'll tell you what to use for a lamp filament.'"

"Hogwash!" said Bullard, his face purple.

The stranger stood. "You have my solemn word as a gentleman. That dog rewarded *me* for my silence with a stock-market tip that made me independently wealthy for the rest of my days. And the last words that Sparky ever spoke were to Thomas Edison. 'Try a piece of carbonized cotton thread,' he said. Later, he was torn to bits by a pack of dogs that had gathered outside the door, listening."

The stranger removed his garters and handed them to Bullard's dog. "A small token of esteem, sir, for an ancestor of yours who talked himself to death. Good day." He tucked his book under his arm and walked away.

The Man Without No Kiddleys

"I DONE ATE TWELVE barium meals in my time," said Noel Sweeny. Sweeny had never felt really well, and now, on top of everything else, he was ninety-four years old. "Twelve times Sweeny's stomach's been x-rayed. Reckon that's some kind of a world's record."

Sweeny was on a bench by a shuffleboard court in Tampa, Florida. He was talking to another old man, a stranger who shared the bench with him.

The stranger had plainly just begun a new way of life in Florida. He wore black shoes, black silk socks, and the trousers of a blue serge business suit. His sports shirt and fighter-pilot cap were crackling, glossy new. A price tag was still stapled to the hem of his shirt.

"Um," said the stranger to Sweeny, without looking at him. The stranger was reading the *Sonnets* of William Shakespeare.

"*From fairest creatures we desire increase,/ That thereby beauty's rose might never die,*" Shakespeare said to the stranger.

"How many times *you* had *your* stomach x-rayed?" Sweeny said to the stranger.

"Um," said the stranger.

"*Music to hear, why hear'st thou music sadly?*" said Shakespeare. "*Sweets with sweets war not, joy delights in joy.*"

"I ain't got no spleen," said Sweeny. "You believe it?"

The stranger did not respond.

Considerately, Sweeny moved closer to the stranger and yelled in his ear. "Sweeny ain't had no spleen since nineteen hundred and forty-three," he yelled.

The stranger dropped his book and almost fell off the bench. He cowered and covered his ringing ears. "I'm not deaf," he said, full of pain.

Firmly, Sweeny pulled one of the stranger's hands away from his ear. "I didn't think you *heard* me," he said.

"I heard you," said the stranger, trembling. "I heard it all: barium meals, gall-stones, tired blood, and sleepy liver bile. I heard every word of what Dr. Sternweiss said about your gastric sphincter. Has Dr. Sternweiss thought of setting it to music?"

Sweeny picked up the book of sonnets and put it on the opposite end of the bench, out of the stranger's reach. "You want to make that little bet now?" he said.

"What bet?" said the stranger, very pale.

"See?" said Sweeny, beaming bleakly. "I was right—you *wasn't* listening! A while back I asked you did you want to bet how many kiddleys we got between us, and you said, 'Um.'"

"How many *kiddies*?" said the stranger. His expression softened—was cautiously interested! He liked children, and thought the bet was a charming one. "Do we count children and grandchildren—or how do we do it?" he said.

"Not *kiddies*," said Sweeny. "Kiddleys."

"Kiddleys?" said the stranger, puzzled.

Sweeny put his hands over the spots where his kidneys were—or had been. "Kiddleys," he said. His error was one of such long standing that it had the ring of authority.

The stranger was disappointed and annoyed. "If you don't mind, I don't want to think about kidneys," he said. "Please—could I have my book back?"

"After we bet," said Sweeny craftily.

The stranger sighed. "Would a dime be enough?" he said.

"Fine," said Sweeny. "The money's just to make it a little more interesting."

"Oh," said the stranger emptily.

Sweeny studied him for a long time. "I guess we got three kiddleys between us," he said at last. "How many you guess?"

"I guess none," said the stranger.

"None?" said Sweeny, amazed. "If there wasn't *no* kiddleys between us, we'd both be dead. A man can't live without *no* kiddleys. You got to guess two, three, or four."

"I have lived happily since eighteen hundred and eighty-four without a *trace* of a kiddley," said the stranger. "I gather that you *do* have a kiddley, which makes one kiddley between us. Therefore the bet ends in a tie, with no money changing hands. Now, please, sir—would you kindly hand me my book?"

Sweeny held up his hands, barring all access to the book. "How dumb you think I am?" he said challengingly.

"I've gone as deeply as I care to into that subject," said the stranger. "Please, sir—the book."

"If you ain't got no kiddleys," said Sweeny, "just tell me one thing."

The stranger rolled his eyes. "Can't we change the subject?" he said. "I used to have a garden up north. I'd like to start a little vegetable garden down here. Do people have little vegetable gardens down here? Do you have a garden?"

Sweeny would not be deflected. He stabbed the stranger in the chest with his finger. "How you eliminate waste?" he said.

The stranger hung his head. He stroked his face in helpless exasperation. He made soft raspberry sounds. He straightened up to smile benignly at a pretty girl jiggling by. "Look at those trim ankles, Mr. Sweeny—those rosy heels," he said. "Oh to be young—or to *pretend* to be young, dreaming here in the sunshine." He closed his eyes, dreamed.

"I guessed right, didn't I?" said Sweeny.

"Um," said the stranger.

"We only got three kiddleys between us, and now you're trying to change the subject and mix me up so's you can get out of paying off," said Sweeny. "Well—I don't mix up so easy."

The stranger dug a dime from his pocket without opening his eyes. He held it out to Sweeny.

Sweeny did not take it. "I ain't gonna take it till I know for sure I'm entitled to it," he said. "I gave you my word of honor I don't got but one kiddley. Now you got to give me your word of honor how many kiddleys you got."

The stranger bared his teeth dangerously in the sunshine. "I swear by all that's holy," he said tautly. "I have no kiddleys."

"What happened to 'em?" said Sweeny. "Bright's disease?"

"Sweeny's disease," said the stranger.

"Same name as me?" said Sweeny, surprised.

"Same name as you," said the stranger. "And a *horrible* disease it is."

"What's it like?" said Sweeny.

"Anybody who suffers from Sweeny's disease," snarled the stranger, "mocks beauty, Mr. *Sweeny*; invades privacy, Mr. *Sweeny*; disturbs the peace, Mr. *Sweeny*; shatters dreams, Mr. *Sweeny*; and drives all thoughts of love, Mr. *Sweeny*, away!"

The stranger stood. He put his face inches from Sweeny's. "Anyone suffering from Sweeny's disease, sir, makes life of the spirit impossible by reminding all around him that men are nothing but buckets of guts!"

The stranger made barking sounds of frantic indignation. He snatched up his book of sonnets, strode to another bench twenty feet away, and sat down with his back to Sweeny. He snuffled and snorted and turned the pages roughly.

"*The forward violet thus did I chide:*" Shakespeare said to him, "*Sweet thief, whence didst thou steal thy sweet that smells,/If not from my love's breath?*" The excitement of battle began to subside in the stranger.

"*The purple pride/Which on thy soft cheek for complexion dwells/In my love's veins thou hast too grossly dy'd,*" said Shakespeare, still chiding the violet.

The stranger tried to smile in pure, timeless, placeless pleasure. The smile, however, would not come. The almighty here-and-now was making itself too strongly felt.

The stranger had come to Tampa for only one reason—that his old bones had betrayed him. No matter how much his home in the North meant to him, no matter how little Florida meant to him—his old bones had cried out that they couldn't stand another winter in the snow and cold.

He had thought of himself, as he accompanied his old bones down South, as a silent, harmless cloud of contemplation.

He found himself instead, only hours after his arrival in Tampa, the author of a savage attack on another old man. The back that he'd turned to Sweeny saw far more than his eyes. His eyes had gone out of focus. His book was a blur.

His back sensed keenly that Sweeny, a kind and lonely man of simpleminded pleasures, was all but destroyed. Sweeny, who'd wanted to go on living, even if he had only half a stomach and one kidney, Sweeny, whose enthusiasm for life hadn't diminished an iota after he'd lost his spleen in nineteen hundred and forty-three—now Sweeny didn't want to live anymore. Sweeny didn't want to live anymore, because an old man he'd tried to befriend had been so savage and mean.

It was a hideous discovery for the stranger to make—that a man at the end of his days was as capable of inflicting pain as the rawest, loudest youth. With so little time left, the stranger had added one more item to his long, long list of regrets.

And he ransacked his mind for elaborate lies that would make Sweeny want to live again. He settled, finally, on an abject, manly, straightforward apology as the only thing to do.

He went to Sweeny, held out his hand. "Mr. Sweeny," he said, "I want to tell you how sorry I am that I lost my temper. There was no excuse for it. I'm a tired old fool, and my temper's short. But the last thing in my heart I want to do is hurt you."

He waited for some fire to return to Sweeny's eyes. But not even the faintest spark returned.

Sweeny sighed listlessly. "Never mind," he said. He didn't take the stranger's hand. Plainly, he wanted the stranger to go away again.

The stranger kept his hand extended, prayed to God for the right thing to say. He himself would lose the will to live if he abandoned Sweeny like this.

His prayer was answered. He became radiant even before he spoke, he was so sure his words were going to be the right ones. One regret, at least, was going to be wiped off the slate.

The stranger raised his proferred hand to a position of solemn oath. "Mr. Sweeny," he said, "I give you my solemn word of honor that I have two kiddleys. If you have one kiddley, that makes three kiddleys between us."

He handed Sweeny a dime. "So you win, Mr. Sweeny."

Sweeny was restored to health instantly. He jumped up, shook the stranger's hand. "I knowed you was a two-kiddley man by looking at you," he said. "You couldn't be nothing *but* a two-kiddley man."

"I just don't know what got into me to pretend I was ever anything else," said the stranger.

"Well," said Sweeny cheerfully, "nobody likes to lose." He looked at the dime one last time before pocketing it. "Anyways—you got a lesson cheap. Don't never bet nobody down here at his own game." He nudged the stranger, winked confidingly. "What's your game?"

"My game?" said the stranger. He thought awhile, amiably. "Shakespeare, I suppose."

"Now you see," said Sweeny, "if you was to come up to me and make me a little bet about Shakespeare—" Sweeny shook his head craftily. "I just wouldn't bet you. I wouldn't even listen."

Sweeny nodded and walked away.

The Powder-Blue Dragon

A THIN YOUNG MAN with big grimy hands crossed the sun-softened asphalt of the seaside village's main street, went from the automobile dealership where he worked to the post office. The village had once been a whaling port. Now its natives served the owners and renters of mansions on the beachfront.

The young man mailed some letters and bought stamps for his boss. Then he went to the drugstore next door on business of his own. Two summer people, a man and a woman his age, were coming out as he was going in. He gave them a sullen glance, as though their health and wealth and lazy aplomb were meant to mock him.

He asked the druggist, who knew him well, to cash his own personal check for five dollars. It was drawn on his account at a bank in the next town. There was no bank in the village. His name was Kiah.

Kiah had moved his money, which was quite a lot, from a savings account into checking. The check Kiah handed the druggist was the first he had ever written. It was in fact numbered 1. Kiah didn't need the five dollars. He worked off the books for the automobile dealer, and was paid in cash. He wanted to make sure a check written by him was really money, would really work.

"My name is written on top there," he said.

"I see that," said the druggist. "You're certainly coming up in the world."

"Don't worry," said Kiah, "it's good." Was it ever good! Kiah thought maybe the druggist would faint if he knew how good that check was.

"Why would I worry about a check from the most honest, hardworking boy in town?" The druggist corrected himself. "A checking account makes you a big man now, just like J. P. Morgan."

"What kind of a car does he drive?" asked Kiah.

"Who?"

"J. P. Morgan."

"He's dead. Is that how you judge people, by the cars they drive?" The druggist was seventy years old, very tired, and looking for somebody to buy his store. "You must have a very low opinion of me, driving a secondhand Chevy." He handed Kiah five one-dollar bills.

Kiah named the Chevy's model instantly: "Malibu."

"I think maybe working for Daggett has made you car-crazy." Daggett was the dealer across the street. He sold foreign sports cars there, and had another show-room in New York City. "How many jobs you got now, besides Daggett?"

"Wait tables at the Quarterdeck weekends, pump gas at Ed's nights." Kiah was an orphan who lived in a boardinghouse. His father had worked for a landscape con-tractor, his mother as a chambermaid at the Howard Johnson's out on the turnpike. They were killed in a head-on collision in front of the Howard Johnson's when Kiah was sixteen. The police had said the crash was their fault. His parents had no money, and their secondhand Plymouth Fury was totaled, so they didn't even have a car to leave him.

"I worry about you, Kiah," said the druggist. "All work and no play. Still haven't saved enough to buy a car?" It was generally known in the village that Kiah worked such long hours so he could buy a car. He had no girl.

"Ever hear of a Marittima-Frascati?"

"No. And I don't believe anybody else ever heard of one, either."

Kiah looked at the druggist pityingly. "Won the Avignon road race two years in a row—over Jaguars, Mercedes, and everything. Guaranteed to do a hundred and thirty on an open stretch. Most beautiful car in the world. Daggett's got one in his New York place." Kiah went up on his tiptoes. "Nobody's ever seen anything like it around here. Nobody."

"Why don't you ever talk about Fords or Chevrolets or something I've heard of? Marittima-Frascati!"

"No class. That's why I don't talk about them."

"Class! Listen who's talking about class all the time. He sweeps floors, polishes cars, waits tables, pumps gas, and he's got to have class or nothing."

"You dream your dreams, I'll dream mine," Kiah said.

"I dream of being young like you in a village that's as pretty and pleasant as this one is," said the druggist. "You can take class and—"

Daggett, a portly New Yorker who operated his branch showroom only in the summer, was selling a car to an urbane and tweedy gentleman as Kiah walked in.

"I'm back, Mr. Daggett," Kiah said.

Daggett paid no attention to him. Kiah sat down on a chair to wait and day-dream. His heart was beating hard.

"It's not for me, understand," the customer was saying. He looked down in amazement at the low, boxy MG. "It's for my boy. He's been talking about one of these things."

"A fine young-man's car," Daggett said. "And reasonably priced for a sports car."

"Now he's raving about some other car, a Mara-something."

"Marittima-Frascati," said Kiah.

Daggett and the customer seemed surprised to find him in the same room.

"Mmmm, yes, that's the name," the customer said.

"Have one in the city. I could get it out here early next week," said Daggett.

"How much?"

"Fifty-six hundred and fifty-one dollars," said Kiah.

Daggett gave a flat, unfriendly laugh. "You've got a good memory, Kiah."

"Fifty-six hundred!" the customer said. "I love my boy, but love's got to draw the line somewhere. I'll take this one." He took a checkbook from his pocket.

Kiah's long shadow fell across the receipt Daggett was making out.

"Kiah, please. You're in the light." Kiah didn't move. "Kiah, what is it you want? Why don't you sweep out the back room or something?"

"I just wanted to say," Kiah said, his breathing shallow, "that when this gentleman is through, I'd like to order the Marittima-Frascati."

"You what?" Daggett stood angrily.

Kiah took out his own checkbook.

"Beat it!" Daggett said.

The customer laughed.

"Do you want my business?" Kiah asked.

"I'll take care of your business, kid, but good. Now sit down and wait."

Kiah sat down until the customer left.

Daggett then walked toward Kiah slowly, his fists clenched. "Now, young man, your funny business almost lost me a sale."

"I'll give you two minutes, Mr. Daggett, to call up the bank and find out if I've got the money, or I'll get my car someplace else."

Daggett called the bank. "George, this is Bill Daggett." He interjected a supercilious laugh. "Look, George, Kiah Higgins wants to write me a check for fifty-six hundred dollars. . . . That's what I said. I swear he does. . . . Okay, I'll wait." He drummed on the desktop and avoided looking at Kiah.

"Fine, George. Thanks." He hung up.

"Well?" Kiah said.

"I made that call to satisfy my curiosity," said Daggett. "Congratulations. I'm very impressed. Back to work."

"It's my money. I earned it," Kiah said. "I worked and saved for four years—four lousy, long years. Now I want that car."

"You've got to be kidding."

"That car is all I can think about, and now it's going to be mine, the damnedest car anybody around here ever saw."

Daggett was exasperated. "The Marittima-Frascati is a plaything for maharajas and Texas oil barons. Fifty-six hundred dollars, boy! What would that leave of your savings?"

"Enough for insurance and a few tanks of gas." Kiah stood. "If you don't want my business . . ."

752

KURT VONNEGUT

"You must be sick," said Daggett.

"You'd understand if you'd been brought up here, Mr. Daggett, and your parents had been dead broke."

"Baloney! Don't tell me what it is to be broke till you've been broke in the city. Anyway, what's the car going to do for you?"

"It's going to give me one hell of a good time—and about time. I'm going to do some living, Mr. Daggett. The first of next week, Mr. Daggett?"

The midafternoon stillness of the village was broken by the whir of a starter and the well-bred grumble of a splendid engine.

Kiah sat deep in the lemon-yellow leather cushions of the powder-blue Marittima-Frascati, listening to the sweet thunder that followed each gentle pressure of his toe. He was scrubbed pink, and his hair was freshly cut.

"No fast stuff, now, for a thousand miles, you hear?" Daggett said. He was in a holiday mood, resigned to the bizarre wonder Kiah had wrought. "That's a piece of fine jewelry under the hood, and you'd better treat it right. Keep it under sixty for the first thousand miles, under eighty until three thousand." He laughed. "And don't try to find out what she can really do until you've put five thousand on her." He clapped Kiah on the shoulder. "Don't get impatient, boy. Don't worry—she'll do it!"

Kiah switched on the engine again, seeming indifferent to the crowd gathered around him.

"How many of these you suppose are in the country?" Kiah asked Daggett.

"Ten, twelve." Daggett winked. "Don't worry. All the others are in Dallas and Hollywood."

Kiah nodded judiciously. He hoped to look like a man who had made a sensible purchase and, satisfied with his money's worth, was going to take it home now. The moment for him was beautiful and funny, but he did not smile.

He put the car in gear for the first time. It was so easy. "Pardon me," he said to those in his way. He raced his engine rather than blow his brass choir of horns. "Thank you."

When Kiah got the car onto the six-lane turnpike, he ceased feeling like an intruder in the universe. He was as much a part of it as the clouds and the sea. With the mock modesty of a god traveling incognito, he permitted a Cadillac convertible to pass him. A pretty girl at its wheel smiled down on him.

Kiah touched the throttle lightly and streaked around her. He laughed at the speck she became in his rearview mirror. The temperature gauge climbed, and Kiah slowed the Marittima-Frascati, forgiving himself this one indulgence. Just this once—it had been worth it. This was the life!

The girl and the Cadillac passed him again. She smiled, and gestured disparagingly at the expanse of hood before her. She loved his car. She hated hers.

At the mouth of a hotel's circular driveway, she signaled with a flourish and turned in. As though coming home, the Marittima-Frascati followed, purred beneath the porte cochere and into the parking lot. A uniformed man waved, smiled, admired, and directed Kiah into the space next to the Cadillac. Kiah watched the girl disappear into the cocktail lounge, each step an invitation to follow.

As he crossed the deep white gravel, a cloud crossed the sun, and in the momentary chill, Kiah's stride shortened. The universe was treating him like an intruder again. He paused on the cocktail lounge steps and looked over his shoulder at the car. There it waited for its master, low, lean, greedy for miles—Kiah Higgins's car.

Refreshed, Kiah walked into the cool lounge. The girl sat alone in a corner booth, her eyes down. She amused herself by picking a wooden swizzle stick to bits. The only other person in the room was the bartender, who read a newspaper.

"Looking for somebody, sonny?"

Sonny? Kiah felt like driving the Marittima-Frascati into the bar. He hoped the girl hadn't heard. "Give me a gin and tonic," he said coldly, "and don't forget the lime."

She looked up. Kiah smiled with the camaraderie of privilege, horsepower, and the open road.

She nodded back, puzzled, and returned her attention to the swizzle stick.

"Here you are, sonny," said the bartender, setting the drink before him. He rattled his newspaper and resumed his reading.

Kiah drank, cleared his throat, and spoke to the girl. "Nice weather," he said.

She gave no sign that he'd said anything. Kiah turned to the bartender, as though it were to him he'd been speaking. "You like to drive?"

"Sometimes," the bartender said.

"Weather like this makes a man feel like really letting his car go full-bore." The bartender turned a page without comment. "But I'm just breaking her in, and I've got to keep her under fifty."

"I guess."

"Big temptation, knowing she's guaranteed to do a hundred and thirty."

The bartender put down his paper irritably. "What's guaranteed?"

"My new car, my Marittima-Frascati."

The girl looked up, interested.

"Your what?" the bartender said.

"My Marittima-Frascati. It's an Italian car."

"It sure don't sound like an American one. Who you driving it for?"

"Who'm I driving it for?"

"Yeah. Who owns it?"

"Who you think owns it? *I* own it."

The bartender picked up his paper again. "*He* owns it. He owns it, and it goes a hundred and thirty. Lucky boy."

Kiah replied by turning his back. "Hello," he said to the girl, with more assurance than he thought possible. "How's the Cad treating you?"

She laughed. "My car, my fiancé, or my father?"

"Your car," Kiah said, feeling stupid for not having a snappier retort.

"Cads always treat me nicely. I remember you now. You were in that darling little blue thing with yellow seats. I somehow didn't connect you with the car. You look different. What did you call it?"

"*A* Marittima-Frascati."

"Mmmmmm. I could never learn to say that."

"It's a very famous car in Europe," Kiah said. Everything was going swimmingly. "Won the Avignon road race two years running, you know."

She smiled a bewitching smile. "No! I *didn't* know that."

"Guaranteed to go a hundred and thirty."

"Goodness. I didn't think a car could go that fast."

"Only about twelve in the country, if *that.*"

"Certainly isn't many, is it? Do you mind my asking how much one of those wonderful cars costs?"

Kiah leaned back against the bar. "No, I don't mind. Seems to me it was somewhere between five and six."

"Oh, between *those*, is it? Quite something to be between."

"Oh, I think it's well worth it. I certainly don't feel I've thrown any money down a sewer."

"That's the important thing."

Kiah nodded happily, and stared into the wonderful eyes, whose admiration seemed bottomless. He opened his mouth to say more, to keep the delightful game going forever and ever, when he realized he had nothing more to say. "Nice weather."

A glaze of boredom formed on her eyes. "Have you got the time?" she asked the bartender.

"Yes, ma'am. Seven after four."

"What did you say?" asked Kiah.

"Four, sonny."

A ride, Kiah thought, maybe she'd like to go for a ride.

The door swung open. A handsome young man in tennis shorts blinked and grinned around the room, poised, vain, and buoyant. "Marion!" he cried. "Thank heaven you're still here. What an angel you are for waiting for me!"

Her face was stunning with adoration. "You're not very late, Paul, and I forgive you."

"Like a fool, I let myself get into a game of doubles, and it just went on and on. I finally threw the game. I was afraid I'd lose you forever. What've you been up to while you've been waiting?"

"Let me see. Well, I tore up a swizzle stick, and I, uh— Ohhhhhh! I met an extremely interesting gentleman who has a car that will go a hundred and thirty miles an hour."

"Well, you've been slickered, dear, because the man was lying about his car."

"Those are pretty strong words," Marion said.

Paul looked pleased. "They are?"

"Considering that the man you called a liar is right here in this room."

"Oh, my." Paul looked around the room with a playful expression of fear. His eyes passed over Kiah and the bartender. "There are only four of us here."

She pointed to Kiah. "That boy there. Would you mind telling Paul about your Vanilla Frappé?"

"Marittima-Frascati," Kiah said, his voice barely audible. He repeated it, louder. "Marittima-Frascati."

"Well," Paul said, "I must say it sounds like it'd go two hundred a second. Have you got it here?"

"Outside," Kiah said.

"That's what I meant," Paul said. "I must learn to express myself with more precision." He looked out over the parking lot. "Oho, I see. The little blue jobbie. Ver-ry nice, scary but gorgeous. And that's yours?"

"I said it was."

"Might be the second-fastest car in these parts. Probably is."

"Is that a fact?" Kiah said sarcastically. "I'd like to see the first."

"Would you? It's right outside, too. There, the green one."

The car was a British Hampton. Kiah knew the car well. It was the one he'd begun saving for before Daggett showed him pictures of the Marittima-Frascati.

"It'll do," Kiah said.

"Do, will it?" Paul laughed. "It'll do yours in, and I'll bet anything you like."

"Listen," said Kiah, "I'd bet the world on my car against yours, if mine was broken in."

"Pity," said Paul. "Another time, then." He explained to Marion, "Not broken in, Marion. Shall we go?"

"I'm ready, Paul," she said. "I'd better tell the attendant I'll be back for the Cadillac, or he'll think I've been kidnapped."

"Which is exactly what is about to happen," said Paul. "Be seeing you, Ralph," he said to the bartender. They knew each other.

"Always glad to see you, Paul," said Ralph.

So Kiah now knew the names of all three, but they didn't know what his name was. Nobody had asked. Nobody cared. What could matter less than what his name was?

Kiah watched through a window as Marion spoke to the parking attendant, and then eased herself down into the passenger seat of the low-slung Hampton.

Ralph asked the nameless one this: "You a mechanic? Somebody left that car with you, and you took it out for a road test? Better put the top up, because it's gonna rain."

The rear wheels of the powder-blue dragon with the lemon-yellow leather bucket seats sprayed gravel at the parking attendant's legs. A doorman beneath the porte cochere signaled for it to slow down, then jumped for his life.

Kiah was encouraging it softly, saying, "That's good, let's go, let's go. I love yah," and so on. He steered, and shifted the synchromesh gears so the car could go ever faster smoothly, but he felt doing all that was really unnecessary, that the car itself knew better than he did where to go and how to do what it had been born to do.

The only Marittima-Frascati for thousands of miles swept past cars and trucks as though they were standing still. The needle of the temperature gauge on the padded dashboard was soon trembling against the pin at the extreme end of the red zone.

"Good girl," said Kiah. He talked to the car sometimes as though it were a girl, sometimes as though it were a boy.

It overtook the Hampton, which was going only a hair over the speed limit. The Marittima-Frascati had to slow a lot, so it could run alongside the Hampton and Kiah could give Marion and Paul the finger.

Paul shook his head and waved Kiah on, then applied his brakes to drop far behind. There would be no race.

"He's got no guts, baby," said Kiah. "Let's show the world what guts are." He pressed the accelerator to the floor. As blurs loomed before him and vanished, he kept it there.

The engine was shrieking in agony now, and Kiah said in a matter-of-fact tone, "Explode, explode."

But the engine didn't explode or catch fire. Its precious jewels simply merged with one another, and the engine ceased to be an engine. Nor was the clutch a clutch anymore. That allowed the car to roll into the breakdown lane of the highway, powered by nothing but the last bit of momentum it would ever have on its own.

The Hampton, with Paul and Marion aboard, never passed. They must have gotten off at some exit far behind, Kiah thought.

Kiah left the car where it died. He thumbed a ride back to the village, without having to give his lift a story of any kind. He returned to Daggett's showroom and acted as though he was there to work. The MG was still on the floor. The man who said he would buy it for his son had changed his mind.

"I gave you the whole day off," said Daggett.

"I know," said Kiah.

"So where's the car?"

"I killed it."

"You what?"

"I got it up to one forty-four, when they said it could only do one thirty-five."

"You're joking."

"Wait'll you see," said Kiah. "That's one dead sports vehicle. You'll have to send the tow truck."

"My God, boy, why would you do such a thing?"

"Call me Kiah."

"Kiah," echoed Daggett, convinced he was dealing with a lunatic.

"Who knows why anybody does anything?" said Kiah. "I don't know why I killed it. All I know is I'm glad it's dead."

Runaways

THEY LEFT A NOTE saying teenagers were as capable of true love as anybody else—maybe more capable. And then they took off for parts unknown.

They took off in the boy's old blue Ford, with baby shoes dangling from the rearview mirror, with a pile of comic books on the burst backseat.

A police alarm went out for them right away, and their pictures were in the papers and on television. But they weren't caught for twenty-four hours. They got all the way to Chicago. A patrolman spotted them shopping together in a supermarket there, caught them buying what looked like a lifetime supply of candy, cosmetics, soft drinks, and frozen pizzas.

The girl's father gave the patrolman a two-hundred-dollar reward. The girl's father was Jesse K. Southard, governor of the state of Indiana.

That was why they got so much publicity. It was exciting when an ex–reform school kid, a kid who ran a lawn mower at the governor's country club, ran off with the governor's daughter.

When the Indiana State Police brought the girl back to the Governor's Mansion in Indianapolis, Governor Southard announced that he would take immediate steps to get an annulment. An irreverent reporter pointed out to him that there could hardly be an annulment, since there hadn't been a marriage.

The governor blew up. "That boy never laid a finger on her," he roared, "because she wouldn't let him! And I'll knock the block off any man who says otherwise."

The reporters wanted to talk to the girl, naturally, and the governor said she would have a statement for them in about an hour. It wouldn't be her first statement about the escapade. In Chicago she and the boy had lectured reporters and police on love, hypocrisy, persecution of teenagers, the insensitivity of parents, and even rockets, Russia, and the hydrogen bomb.

When the girl came downstairs with her new statement, however, she contradicted everything she'd said in Chicago. Reading from a three-page typewritten script, she said the adventure had been a nightmare, said she didn't love the boy and never had, said she must have been crazy, and said she never wanted to see the boy again.

She said the only people she loved were her parents, said she didn't see how she could make it up to them for all the heartaches she had caused, said she was going to concentrate on schoolwork and getting into college, and said she didn't want to pose for pictures because she looked so awful after the ordeal.

She didn't look especially awful, except that she'd dyed her hair red, and the boy had given her a terrible haircut in an effort to disguise her. And she'd been crying some. She didn't look tired. She looked young and wild and captured—that was all.

Her name was Annie—Annie Southard.

When the reporters left, when they went to show the boy the girl's latest statement, the governor turned to his daughter and said to her, "Well, I certainly want to thank you. I don't see how I can ever thank you enough."

"You thank me for telling all those lies?" she said.

"I thank you for making a very small beginning in repairing the damage you've done," he said.

"My own father, the governor of the state of Indiana," said Annie, "ordered me to lie. I'll never forget that."

"That isn't the last of the orders you'll get from me," he said.

Annie said nothing out loud, but in her mind she placed a curse on her parents. She no longer owed them anything. She was going to be cold and indifferent to them for the rest of her days. The curse went into effect immediately.

Annie's mother, Mary, came down the spiral staircase. She had been listening to the lies from the landing above. "I think you handled that very well," she said to her husband.

"As well as I could, under the circumstances," he said.

"I only wish we could come out and say what there really is to say," said Annie's mother. "If we could only just come out and say we're not against love, and we're not against people who don't have money." She started to touch her daughter comfortingly, but was warned against it by Annie's eyes. "We're not snobs, darling—and we're not insensitive to love. Love is the most wonderful thing there is."

The governor turned away and glared out a window.

"We *believe* in love," said Annie's mother. "You've seen how much I love your father and how much your father loves me—and how much your father and I love you."

"If you're going to come out and say something, say it," said the governor.

"I thought I was," said his wife.

"Talk money, talk breeding, talk education, talk friends, talk interests," said the governor, "and then you can get back to love if you want." He faced his women. "Talk happiness, for heaven's sake," he said. "See that boy again, keep this thing going, marry him when you can do it legally, when we can't stop you," he said to Annie, "and not only will you be the unhappiest woman alive, but he'll be the unhappiest man alive. It will be a mess you can truly be proud of, because you will have married without having met a single condition for a happy marriage—and by single condition I mean one single, solitary thing in common.

"What did you plan to do for friends?" he said. "His gang at the poolroom or your gang at the country club? Would you start out by buying him a nice house and nice furniture and a nice automobile—or would you wait for him to buy those things, which he'll be just about ready to pay for when hell freezes over? Do you like comic books as well as he does? Do you like the same kind of comic books?" cried the governor.

"Who do you think you are?" he asked Annie. "You think you're Eve, and God only made one Adam for you?"

"Yes," said Annie, and she went upstairs to her room and slammed the door. Moments later music came from her room. She was playing a record.

The governor and his wife stood outside the door and listened to the words of the song. These were the words:

> They say we don't know what love is,
> Boo-wah-wah, uh-huh, yeah.
> But we know what the message in the stars above is,
> Boo-wah-wah, uh-huh, yeah.
> So hold me, hold me, baby,
> And you'll make my poor heart sing,
> Because everything they tell us, baby,
> Why, it just don't mean a thing.

Eight miles away, eight miles due south, through the heart of town and out the other side, reporters were clumping onto the front porch of the boy's father's house.

It was old, cheap, a carpenter's special, a 1926 bungalow. Its front windows looked out into the perpetual damp twilight of a huge front porch. Its side windows looked into the neighbors' windows ten feet away. Light could reach the interior only through a window in the back. As luck would have it, the window let light into a tiny pantry.

The boy and his father and his mother did not hear the reporters knocking. The television set in the living room and the radio in the kitchen were both on, blatting away, and the family was having a row in the dining room, halfway between them.

The row was actually about everything in creation, but it had for its subject of the moment the boy's mustache. He had been growing it for a month and had just been caught by his father in the act of blacking it with shoe polish.

The boy's name was Rice Brentner. It was true, as the papers said, that Rice had spent time in reform school. That was three years behind him now. His crime had been, at the age of thirteen, the theft of sixteen automobiles within a period of a week. Except for the escapade with Annie, he hadn't been in any real trouble since.

"You march into the bathroom," said his mother, "and you shave that awful thing off."

Rice did not march. He stayed right where he was.

"You heard your mother," his father said. When Rice still didn't budge, his father tried to hurt him with scorn. "Makes him feel like a man, I guess—like a great big man," he said.

"Doesn't make him look like a man," said his mother. "It makes him look like an I-don't-know-what-it-is."

"You just named him," said his father. "That's exactly what he is: an I-don't-know-what-it-is." Finding a label like that seemed to ease the boy's father some. He was, as one newspaper and then all the newspapers had pointed out, an eighty-nine-dollar-and sixty-two-cent-a-week supply clerk in the main office of the public school system. He had reason to resent the thoroughness of the reporter who had dug that figure from the public records. The sixty-two cents galled him in particular. "An eighty-nine-dollar-and-sixty-two-cent-a-week supply clerk has an I-don't-know-what-it-is for a son," he said. "The Brentner family is certainly covered with glory today."

"Do you realize how lucky you are not to be in jail—rotting?" said Rice's mother. "If they had you in jail, they'd not only shave off your mustache, without even asking you about it—they'd shave off every hair on your head."

Rice wasn't listening much, only enough to keep himself smoldering comfortably. What he was thinking about was his car. He had paid for it with money he himself had earned. It hadn't cost his family a dime. Rice now swore to himself that if his parents tried to take his car away from him, he would leave home for good.

"He knows about jail. He's been there before," said his father.

"Let him keep his mustache if he wants to," said his mother. "I just wish he'd look in a mirror once to see how silly it makes him look."

"All right—let him keep it," said his father, "but I'll tell you one thing he isn't going to keep, and I give you my word of honor on that, and that's the automobile."

"Amen!" said his mother. "He's going to march down to a used-car lot, and he's going to sell the car, and then he's going to march over to the bank and put the money in his savings account, and then he's going to march home and give us the bankbook." As she uttered this complicated promise she became more and more martial until, at the end, she was marching in place like John Philip Sousa.

"You said a mouthful!" said her husband.

And now that the subject of the automobile had been introduced, it became the dominant theme and the loudest one of all. The old blue Ford was such a frightening symbol of disastrous freedom to Rice's parents that they could yammer about it endlessly.

And they just about did yammer about it endlessly this time.

"Well—the car is going," said Rice's mother, winded at last.

"That's the end of the car," said his father.

"And that's the end of me," said Rice. He walked out the back door, got into his car, turned on the radio, and drove away.

Music came from the radio. The song told of two teenagers who were going to get married, even though they were dead broke. The chorus of it went like this:

We'll have no fancy drapes—
No stove, no carpet, no refrigerator.
But our nest will look like a hunk of heaven,
Because love, baby, is our interior decorator.

Rice went to a phone booth a mile from the Governor's Mansion. He called the number that was the governor's family's private line.

He pitched his voice a half-octave higher, and he asked to speak to Annie.

It was the butler who answered. "I'm sorry, sir," he said, "but I don't think she's taking any calls just now. You want to leave your name?"

"Tell her it's Bob Counsel," said Rice. Counsel was the son of a man who had gotten very rich on coin-operated laundries. He spent most of his time at the country club. He was in love with Annie.

"I didn't recognize your voice for a minute there, Mr. Counsel," said the butler. "Please hold on, sir, if you'd be so kind."

Seconds later Annie's mother was on the phone. She wanted to believe so desperately that the caller was the polite and attractive and respectable Bob Counsel that she didn't even begin to suspect a fraud. And she did almost all the talking, so Rice had only to grunt from time to time.

"Oh Bob, oh Bob, oh Bob—you dear boy," she said. "How nice, how awfully nice of you to call. It was what I was *praying* for! She *has* to talk to somebody her own age. Oh, her father and I have talked to her, and I guess she heard us, but there's such a gap between the generations these days.

"This thing—this thing Annie's been through," said Annie's mother, "it's more like a nervous breakdown than anything else. It isn't really a nervous breakdown, but she isn't herself—isn't the Annie we know. Do you understand what I'm trying to say?"

"Yup," said Rice.

"Oh, she'll be so glad to hear from you, Bob—to know she's still got her old friends, her real friends to fall back on. Hearing your voice," said the governor's wife, "our Annie will know everything's going to get back to normal again."

She went to get Annie—and had a ding-dong wrangle with her that Rice could hear over the telephone. Annie said she hated Bob Counsel, thought he was a jerk, a stuffed shirt, and a mamma's boy. Somebody thought to cover the mouthpiece at that point, so Rice didn't hear anything more until Annie came on the line.

"Hullo," she said emptily.

"I thought you might enjoy a ride—to kind of take your mind off your troubles," said Rice.

"What?" said Annie.

"This is Rice," he said. "Tell your mother you're going to the club to play tennis with good old Bob Counsel. Meet me at the gas station at Forty-sixth and Illinois."

So half an hour later, they took off again in the boy's old blue Ford, with baby shoes dangling from the rearview mirror, with a pile of comic books on the burst backseat.

The car radio sang as Annie and Rice left the city limits behind:

> *Oh, baby, baby, baby,*
> *What a happy, rockin' day,*
> *'Cause your sweet love and kisses*
> *Chase those big, black blues away.*

And the exhilarating chase began again.

Annie and Rice crossed the Ohio border on a back road and listened to the radio talk about them above the sound of gravel rattling in the fenders.

They had listened impatiently to news of a riot in Bangalore, of an airplane collision in Ireland, of a man who blew up his wife with nitroglycerin in West Virginia. The newscaster had saved the biggest news for last—that Annie and Rice, Juliet and Romeo, were playing hare and hounds again.

The newscaster called Rice "Rick," something nobody had ever called him, and Rice and Annie liked that.

"I'm going to call you Rick from now on," said Annie.

"That's all right with me," said Rice.

"You look more like a Rick than a Rice," said Annie. "How come they named you Rice?"

"Didn't I ever tell you?" said Rice.

"If you did," she said, "I've forgot."

The fact was that Rice had told her about a dozen times why he was named Rice, but she never really listened to him. For that matter, Rice never really listened to her, either. Both would have been bored stiff if they had listened, but they spared themselves that.

So their conversations were marvels of irrelevance. There were only two subjects in common—self-pity and something called love.

"My mother had some ancestor back somewhere named Rice," said Rice. "He was a doctor, and I guess he was pretty famous."

"Dr. Siebolt is the only person who ever tried to understand me as a human being," said Annie. Dr. Siebolt was the governor's family physician.

"There's some other famous people back there somewhere, too—on my mother's side," said Rice. "I don't know what all they did, but there's good blood back there."

"Dr. Siebolt would hear what I was trying to say," said Annie. "My parents never had time to listen."

"That's why my old man always got burned up at me—because I've got so much of my mother's blood," said Rice. "You know—I want to do things and have things and live and take chances, and his side of the family isn't that way at all."

"I could talk to Dr. Siebolt about love—I could talk to him about anything," said Annie. "With my parents there were just all kinds of things I had to keep bottled up."

"Safety first—that's their motto," said Rice. "Well, that isn't my motto. They want me to end up the way they have, and I'm just not that kind of a person."

"It's a terrible thing to make somebody bottle things up," said Annie. "I used to cry all the time, and my parents never could figure out why."

"That's why I stole those cars," said Rice. "I just all of a sudden went crazy one day. They were trying to make me act like my father, and I'm just not that kind of man. They never understood me. They don't understand me yet."

"But the worst thing," said Annie, "was then my own father ordered me to lie. That was when I realized that my parents didn't care about truth. All they care about is what people think."

"This summer," said Rice, "I was actually making more money than my old man or any of his brothers. That really ate into him. He couldn't stand that."

"My mother started talking to me about love," said Annie, "and it was all I could do to keep from screaming, 'You don't know what love is! You never have known what it is!'"

"My parents kept telling me to act like a man," said Rice. "Then, when I really started acting like one, they went right through the roof. What's a guy supposed to do?" he said.

"Even if I screamed at her," said Annie, "she wouldn't hear it. She never listens. I think she's afraid to listen. Do you know what I mean?"

"My older brother was the favorite in our family," said Rice. "He could do no wrong, and I never could do anything right, as far as they were concerned. You never met my brother, did you?"

"My father killed something in me when he told me to lie," said Annie.

"We sure are lucky we found each other," said Rice.

"What?" said Annie.

"I said, 'We sure are lucky we found each other,'" said Rice.

Annie took his hand. "Oh yes, oh yes, oh yes," she said fervently. "When we first met out there on the golf course, I almost died because I knew how right we were for each other. Next to Dr. Siebolt, you're the first person I ever really felt close to."

"Dr. who?" said Rice.

In the study of the Governor's Mansion, Governor Southard had his radio on. Annie and Rice had just been picked up, twenty miles west of Cleveland, and Southard wanted to hear what the news services had to say about it.

So far he had heard only music, and was hearing it now:

Let's not go to school today,
Turtle dove, turtle dove.
Let's go out in the woods and play,
Play with love, play with love.

The governor turned the radio off. "How do they *dare* put things like that on the air?" he said. "The whole American entertainment industry does nothing but tell children how to kill their parents—and themselves in the bargain."

He put the question to his wife and to the Brentners, the parents of the boy, who were sitting in the study with him.

The Brentners shook their heads, meaning that they did not know the answer to the governor's question. They were appalled at having been called into the presence of the governor. They had said almost nothing—nothing beyond abject, rambling, ga-ga apologies at the very beginning. Since then they had been in numb agreement with anything the governor cared to say.

He had said plenty, wrestling with what he called the toughest decision of his life. He was trying to decide, with the concurrence of his wife and the Brentners, how to make the runaways grow up enough to realize what they were doing, how to fix them so they would never run away again.

"Any suggestions, Mr. Brentner?" he said to Rice's father.

Rice's father shrugged. "I haven't got any control over him, sir," he said. "If somebody'd tell me a way to get control of him, I'd be glad to try it, but . . ." He let the sentence trail off to nothing.

"But what?" said the governor.

"He's pretty close to being a man now, Governor," said Rice's father, "and he's just about as easy to control as any other man—and that isn't very easy." He murmured something else, which the governor didn't catch, and shrugged again.

"Beg your pardon?" said the governor.

Rice's father said it again, scarcely louder than the first time. "I said he doesn't respect me."

"By heaven, he would if you'd have the guts to lay down the law to him and make it stick!" said the governor with hot righteousness.

Rice's mother now did the most courageous thing in her life. She was boiling mad about having all the blame put on her son, and she now squared the governor of Indiana away. "Maybe if we'd raised our son the way you raised your daughter," she said, "maybe then we wouldn't have the trouble we have today."

The governor looked startled. He sat down at his desk. "Well said, madam," he said. He turned to his wife. "We should certainly give our child-rearing secret to the world."

"Annie isn't a bad girl," said his wife.

"Neither's our boy a bad boy," said Rice's mother, very pepped up, now that she'd given the governor the works.

"I—I'm sure he isn't," said the governor's wife.

"He isn't a bad boy anymore. That's the big thing," blurted Rice's father. And he took courage from his wife's example, and added something else. "And that little girl isn't what you'd call real little, either," he said.

"You recommend they get married?" said the governor, incredulous.

"I don't know what I recommend," said Rice's father. "I'm not a recommending man. But maybe they really do love each other. Maybe they really were made for each other. Maybe they really would be happy for the rest of their lives together, starting right now, if we'd let 'em." He threw his hands up. "I don't know!" he said. "Do you?"

Annie and Rice were talking to reporters in a state police barracks outside of Cleveland. They were waiting to be hauled back home. They claimed to be unhappy, but they appeared to be having a pretty fine time. They were telling the reporters about money now.

"People care too much about money," said Annie. "What is money, when you really stop to think about it?"

"We don't want money from her parents," said Rice. "I guess maybe her parents think I'm after their money. All I want is their daughter."

"It's all right with me, if they want to disinherit me," said Annie. "From what I've seen of the rich people I grew up with, money just makes people worried and unhappy. People with a lot of money get so worried about how maybe they'll lose it, they forget to live."

"I can always earn enough to keep a roof over our heads and keep from starving," said Rice. "I can earn more than my old man does. My car is completely paid for. It's all mine, free and clear."

"I can earn money, too," said Annie. "I would be a lot prouder of working than I would be of what my parents want me to do, which is hang around with a lot of other spoiled people and play games."

A state trooper now came in, told Annie her father was on the telephone. The governor of Indiana wanted to talk to her.

"What good will talk do?" said Annie. "Their generation doesn't understand our generation, and they never will. I don't want to talk to him."

The trooper left. He came back a few minutes later.

"He's still on the line?" said Annie.

"No, ma'am," said the trooper. "He gave me a message for you."

"Oh, boy," said Annie. "This should really be good."

"It's a message from your parents, too," the trooper said to Rice.

"I can hardly wait to hear it," said Rice.

"The message is this," said the trooper, keeping his face blankly official, "you are to come home in your own car whenever you feel like it. When you get home, they want you to get married and start being happy as soon as possible."

Annie and Rice crept home in the old blue Ford, with baby shoes dangling from the rearview mirror, with a pile of comic books on the burst backseat. They came home on the main highways. Nobody was looking for them anymore.

Their radio was on, and every news broadcast told the world the splendid news: Annie and Rice were to be married at once. True love had won another stunning victory.

By the time the lovers reached the Indiana border, they had heard the news of their indescribable happiness a dozen times. They were beginning to look like department store clerks on Christmas Eve, jangled and exhausted by relentless tidings of great joy.

Rice turned off the radio. Annie gave an involuntary sigh of relief. They hadn't talked much on the trip home. There didn't seem to be anything to talk about: everything was so settled—everything was so, as they say in business, finalized.

Annie and Rice got into a traffic jam in Indianapolis and were locked for stoplight after stoplight next to a car in which a baby was howling. The parents of the child were very young. The wife was scolding her husband, and the husband looked ready to uproot the steering wheel and brain her with it.

Rice turned on the radio again, and this is what the song on the radio said:

We certainly fooled them,
The ones who said our love wasn't true.
Now, forever and ever,
You've got me, and I've got you.

In almost a frenzy, with Annie's nerves winding ever tighter, Rice changed stations again and again. Every station bawled of either victories or the persecution of teenage love. And that's what the radio was bawling about when the old blue Ford stopped beneath the porte cochere of the Governor's Mansion.

Only one person came out to greet them, and that was the policeman who guarded the door. "Congratulations, sir . . . madam," he said blandly.

"Thank you," said Rice. He turned everything off with the ignition key. The last illusion of adventure died as the radio tubes lost their glow and the engine cooled.

The policeman opened the door on Annie's side. The door gave a rusty screech. Two loose jelly beans wobbled out the door and fell to the immaculate blacktop below.

Annie, still in the car, looked down at the jelly beans. One was green. The other was white. There were bits of lint stuck to them. "Rice?" she said.

"Hm?" he said.

"I'm sorry," she said, "I can't go through with it."

Rice made a sound like a faraway freight whistle. He was grateful for release.

"Could we talk alone, please?" Annie said to the policeman.

"Beg your pardon," said the policeman as he withdrew.

"Would it have worked?" said Annie.

Rice shrugged. "For a little while."

"You know what?" said Annie.

"What?" said Rice.

"We're too young," said Annie.

"Not too young to be in love," said Rice.

"No," said Annie, "not too young to be in love. Just too young for about every-thing else there is that goes with love." She kissed him. "Good-bye, Rice. I love you."

"I love you," he said.

She got out, and Rice drove away.

As he drove away, the radio came on. It was playing an old song now, and the words were these:

> Now's the time for sweet good-bye
> To what could never be,
> To promises we ne'er could keep,
> To a magic you and me.
> If we should try to prove our love,
> Our love would be in danger.
> Let's put our love beyond all harm.
> Good-bye—sweet, gentle stranger.

The Good Explainer

THE OFFICE OF DR. LEONARD ABEKIAN was in a bad part of Chicago. It was behind a false front of yellow brick and glass block built out from the first floor of a narrow Victorian mansion whose spine was spiked with lightning rods. Joe Cunningham, treasurer of a bank in a small town outside of Cincinnati, arrived at Dr. Abekian's office by taxicab. He had spent the night in a hotel. Joe had come all the way from Ohio, under the impression that Dr. Abekian had had phenomenal successes in curing sterility. Joe was thirty-five. He had been married ten years without fathering a child.

The waiting room was not impressive. Its walls were goose-fleshed pink Spackle. Its furnishings were cracked leatherette and chromium-plated tubes. Joe had to put down a feeling that the office gave him at once—a feeling that Dr. Abekian was a cheap quack. The air of the place was little more impressive than a barbershop's. Joe put down the feeling, told himself that Dr. Abekian was too absorbed in his work and too little interested in money to put up an impressive front.

There was no nurse or receptionist at the waiting room desk. The only other soul in the room was a boy about fourteen years old. He had his arm in a sling. The nature of this solitary patient disturbed Joe, too. He had expected to find the waiting room filled with people like himself—childless people who had traveled great distances to see the famous Dr. Abekian, to get the final word on what the trouble was.

"Is—is the doctor in?" Joe asked the boy.

"Ring the bell," said the boy.

"Bell?" said Joe.

"On the desk," said the boy.

Joe went to the desk, found a bell button on it, pressed it, heard a buzzer ring somewhere deep in the house. A moment later, a harried-looking young woman in a white uniform came in from the back part of the house, closed a door on the wailing of a child. "I'm sorry," she said, "the baby isn't well. I have to go back and forth between him and the office. Can I help you?"

"Are you Mrs. Abekian?" said Joe.

"Yes," she said.

"I talked to you on the phone last night," said Joe.

769

"Oh yes," she said. "You made appointments for yourself and your wife?"

"That's right," said Joe.

She referred to an appointment pad. "Mr. and Mrs. Joseph Cunningham?"

"Right," said Joe. "My wife had some shopping. She'll be along. I'll go in first."

"Fine," she said. She nodded at the boy with his arm in a sling. "You go in right after Peter here." She took a blank form from the desk drawer, tried to ignore the squalling of the baby in the back of the house. She wrote Joe's name at the top of the form, and she said, "You'll have to excuse the distractions."

Joe tried a shy smile. "To me," he said, "that's the most beautiful sound in the world."

She gave a tired laugh. "You've come to the right place to hear beautiful sounds like that," she said.

"How many children do you have?" said Joe.

"Four," she said. And then she added, "So far."

"You're very lucky," said Joe.

"I keep telling myself so," she said.

"You see," said Joe, "my wife and I don't have any."

"I'm *so* sorry," she said.

"That's why my wife and I have come to see your husband," said Joe.

"I see," she said.

"We came all the way from Ohio," said Joe.

"Ohio?" she said. She looked startled. "You mean you just moved to Chicago from Ohio?"

"Ohio's still our home," said Joe. "We're up here just to see your husband."

She looked so puzzled now that Joe had to ask, "Is there another Dr. Abekian?"

"No," she said. And then she said, too quickly, too watchfully, too brightly to make Joe think he really had come to the right place, "No, no—there's only one. My husband's the man you want."

"I heard he'd done some wonderful things with sterility cases," said Joe.

"Oh, yes, yes, yes—he has, he has," she said. "May—may I ask who recommended him?"

"My wife heard a lot of talk around about him," said Joe.

"I see," she said.

"We wanted the best," said Joe, "and my wife asked around, and she decided he *was* the best."

She nodded, frowned ever so slightly. "Uh-huh," she said.

Dr. Abekian himself now came out of his office, shepherding a mournful, old, old woman. He was a tall, flashily handsome man—flashy by reason of his even white teeth and dark skin. There was a lot of the sharpness and dazzle of a nightclub master of ceremonies about him. At the same time, Dr. Abekian revealed an underlying embarrassment about his looks, too. He gave Joe the impression that he would have preferred, on occasion anyway, a more conservative exterior.

"There must be something I could take that would make me feel better than I do," the old, old woman said to him.

"You take these new pills," he said to her gently. "They may be just what you've been looking for. If not, we'll try, try, try again." He waved the boy with the broken arm into his office.

"Len—" said his wife.

"Hm?" he said.

"This man," she said, indicating Joe, "this man and his wife came all the way from Ohio to see you."

In spite of herself, she made Joe's trip seem such a peculiar thing that Joe was now dead certain that a big, foolish mistake had been made.

"Ohio?" said Dr. Abekian. His incredulity was frank. He arched his thick, dark eyebrows. "All the way from Ohio?" he said.

"I heard people from all over the country came to see you," said Joe.

"Who told you that?" he said.

"My wife," said Joe.

"She knows me?" said Dr. Abekian.

"No," said Joe. "She just heard about you."

"From whom?" said the doctor.

"Woman talk," said Joe.

"I—I'm very flattered," said Dr. Abekian. "As you can see," he said, spreading his long-fingered hands, "I'm a neighborhood general practitioner. I won't pretend that I'm a specialist, and I won't pretend that anyone has ever traveled any great distance to see me before."

"Then I beg your pardon," said Joe. "I don't know how this happened."

"Ohio?" said Dr. Abekian.

"That's right," said Joe.

"Cincinnati?" said the doctor.

"No," said Joe. He named the town.

"Even if it were Cincinnati," said the doctor, "it wouldn't make much sense. Years ago, I was a medical student in Cincinnati, but I never practiced there."

"My wife was a nursing student in Cincinnati," said Joe.

"Oh, she was?" said the doctor, thinking for a moment that he'd found a clue. The clue faded. "But she doesn't know me."

"No," said Joe.

Dr. Abekian shrugged. "So the mystery remains a mystery," he said. "Since you've come all this distance—if there's anything I can do—"

"They want children," said the doctor's wife. "They haven't had any."

"You've no doubt been to many specialists before coming all this distance," said the doctor.

"No," said Joe.

"At least your own family doctor, anyway—" said Dr. Abekian.

Joe shook his head.

"You haven't taken this matter up with your own doctor?" said Dr. Abekian, unable to make sense of the fact.

"No," said Joe.

"May I ask why not?" said the doctor.

"You'd better ask my wife when she comes," said Joe. "I've been after her to go to a doctor for years. She not only wouldn't go—she made me promise I wouldn't go, either."

"This was a religious matter?" said the doctor. "Is she a Christian Scientist?"

"No, no," said Joe. "I told you—she was a nurse."

"Of course," said the doctor. "I forgot." He shook his head. "But she did agree to see me—under the impression that I was a famous specialist."

"Yes," said Joe.

"Amazing," said Dr. Abekian softly, rubbing the bridge of his nose. "Well—since you haven't even seen a general practitioner, there *is* a chance I can help."

"I'm game—God knows," said Joe.

"All right—fine," said the doctor. "After Peter, then, comes you."

When young Peter was gone, Dr. Abekian called Joe into his office. He had a directory open on his desk. He explained it. "I was trying to find," he said, "somebody with a name remotely like mine—somebody who might be really famous for handling cases like yours."

"What luck?" said Joe.

"There *is* Dr. Aarons—who's done a lot with a psychiatric approach," said Dr. Abekian. "His name is vaguely like mine."

"Look," said Joe, patiently, earnestly, "the name of the man we were coming to see, the name of the man who was going to do so much for us, the name wasn't Aarons, and it wasn't a name we could very well mix up with another name, because it was such an unusual name. My wife said we should come to Chicago and see Dr. Abekian—A-b-e-k-i-a-n. We came to Chicago, looked up Dr. Abekian—A-b-e-k-i-a-n—in the phone book. There he was—A-b-e-k-i-a-n—and here I am."

Dr. Abekian's sharp, gaudy features expressed tantalization and perplexity. "Tst," he said.

"You say this Aarons uses the psychiatric approach?" said Joe. He was undressing now for a physical examination, revealing himself as a chunky man, with muscles that looked powerful but slow.

"The psychiatric approach is meaningless, of course," said Dr. Abekian, "if there's anything physically wrong." He lit a cigarette. "I keep thinking," he said, "this whole mystery has to have something to do with Cincinnati."

"I'll tell you this," said Joe, "this isn't the only crazy thing that's happened lately.

The way things have been going, maybe Barbara and I ought to go over and see Dr. Aarons no matter what the physicals turn up."

"Barbara?" said Dr. Abekian, cocking his head.

"What?" said Joe.

"Barbara? You said your wife's name was Barbara?" said Dr. Abekian.

"Did I say that?" said Joe.

"I thought you did," said the doctor.

Joe shrugged. "There's one more crazy promise down the drain," he said. "I was supposed to keep her name a secret."

"I don't understand," said the doctor.

"Who the hell does?" said Joe, showing sudden fatigue and exasperation. "If you knew all the fights we've had this past couple of years, if you knew how much I had to go through before she'd agree to see a doctor, to find out if there was anything we could do . . ." Joe left the sentence unfinished, went on undressing. He was quite red now.

"If I knew that?" said Dr. Abekian, himself a little restless now.

"If you knew that," said Joe, "you'd understand why I promised her anything she wanted, whether it made sense or not. She said we had to come to Chicago, so we came to Chicago. She said she didn't want people to know what her real name was, so I promised I wouldn't tell. But I did tell, didn't I?"

Dr. Abekian nodded. Smoke from the cigarette in his mouth was making one eye water, but he did nothing to remedy the situation.

"Well—what the hell," said Joe. "If you can't tell a doctor the whole truth, what's the point of going to one? How's he going to help you?"

Dr. Abekian responded not at all.

"For years," said Joe, "Barbara and I were about as happily married as two people could be—I think. It's a pretty town where we live, full of nice people. We've got a nice big house I inherited from my father. I like my job. Money's never been a problem."

Dr. Abekian turned his back, stared at a rectangle of glass block that faced the street.

"And this no kid thing—" said Joe, "much as we both want kids, not having 'em wouldn't be enough to break us up. It's this doctor thing—or was. Do you know she hasn't gone to a doctor for *any* reason? For the whole ten years we've been married! 'Look, sweetheart,' I'd say to her, 'if you're the reason we can't have children, or if I'm the reason—it doesn't make any difference. I won't think any the less of you, if you're to blame, and I hope you won't think any the less of me, if I'm to blame, which I probably am. The big thing is to find out if there's anything we can do.'"

"It really wouldn't make any difference?" said Dr. Abekian, his back still to Joe.

"All I can speak for is myself," said Joe. "Speaking for myself—no. The love I've got for my wife is certainly big enough to rise above something accidental like that."

"Accidental?" said Dr. Abekian. He started to face Joe, but changed his mind.

"What the heck is it but an accident, who can have kids and who can't?" said Joe.

Joe came closer to Dr. Abekian and the glass block window, was surprised to see in every dimple of every glass block a tiny image of his wife, Barbara, getting out of a taxicab. "That's my wife," said Joe.

"I know," said Dr. Abekian.

"You know?" said Joe.

"You can get dressed, Mr. Cunningham," said the doctor.

"Dressed?" said Joe. "You haven't even looked at me."

"I don't have to," said Dr. Abekian. "I don't have to look at you to tell you that, as long as you're married to that woman, you can never have children." He turned on Joe with startling bitterness. "Are you a marvelous actor, Mr. Cunningham?" he said. "Or are you really as innocent as you seem?"

Joe backed away. "I don't know what's going on, if that's what you mean," he said.

"You came to the right doctor, Mr. Cunningham," said Dr. Abekian. He gave a rueful smile. "When I told you I wasn't a specialist, I was very much mistaken. In your particular case, I'm as specialized as it's possible for a man to be."

Joe heard the sharp heels of his wife as she crossed the waiting room outside. He heard her ask someone else out there whether the doctor was in. A moment later, the buzzer rang in the back of the house.

"The doctor is in," said Dr. Abekian. He raised his arms in mock admiration of all he was. "Ready for anything," he said.

Out in the waiting room, the door to the back of the house opened. The baby was still crying. Dr. Abekian's wife was still harassed.

Dr. Abekian strode to his office door, opened it on Barbara and his wife. "The doctor is in, Mrs. Cunningham," he said to Barbara. "He can see you right away."

Barbara, a little woman, a glistening trinket brunette, walked into the office, looking at everything with great curiosity. "You finished with Joe that fast?" she said.

"The faster the better, wouldn't you say?" said Dr. Abekian tautly. He closed the door. "I understand you haven't been quite honest with your husband," he said.

She nodded.

"We know each other, you see," Dr. Abekian said to Joe.

Joe licked his lips. "I see," he said.

"You now wish to be completely honest with your husband?" Dr. Abekian said to Barbara. "You want me to help you achieve that honesty?" he said.

Barbara shrugged weakly. "Whatever the doctor thinks best," she said.

Dr. Abekian closed his eyes. "The doctor thinks," he said, "that Mr. Cunningham should know that his wife, while a student nurse, was pregnant by me. An abortion was arranged for, the job was botched, and the patient was made sterile ever after."

Joe said nothing. It would be some time before anything coherent came to him.

"You went to a lot of trouble to bring this moment about," said Dr. Abekian to Barbara.

"Yes," she said emptily.

"Is the revenge sweet?" said Dr. Abekian.

"It isn't revenge," she said, and she went over to look at the thousands of identical images in the glass blocks.

"Then why would you go to so much trouble?" said the doctor.

"Because you were always so much better than I was at explaining why everything we did was all for the best," she said, "every step of the way."

Guardian of the Person

"I WISH THERE WASN'T all that money," said Nancy Holmes Ryan. "I really wish it wasn't there." Nancy had been married for an hour and a half now. She was driving with her husband from Boston to Cape Cod. The time was noon, late winter. The scenery was leaden sea, summer cottages boarded up, scrub oaks still holding their brown leaves tight, cranberry bogs with frosty beards—

"That much money is embarrassing," said Nancy. "I mean it." She didn't really mean it—not very much, anyway. She was enduring the peculiar Limbo between a wedding and a wedding night. Like many maidens in such a Limbo, Nancy found her own voice unreal, as though echoing in a great tin box, and she heard that voice speaking with unreasonable intensity, heard herself expressing extravagant opinions as though they were the bedrock of her soul.

They weren't the bedrock of her soul. Nancy was bluffing—pretending to love this and hate that—dealing as best she could with the confusing fact of Limbo, of being nothing and nobody and nowhere until her new life, until her married life could truly begin.

A moment before, Nancy had launched a startlingly bitter attack on stucco houses and the people who lived in them, had made her husband promise that they would never live in a stucco house. She hadn't really meant it.

Now, out of control, not really meaning it, Nancy was wishing that her husband were poor. He was a long way from being poor. He was worth about two hundred thousand dollars.

Nancy's husband was an engineering student at M.I.T. His name was Robert Ryan, Jr. Robert was tall, quiet—pleasant and polite, but often withdrawn. He had been orphaned at the age of nine. He had been raised from then on by his aunt and uncle on Cape Cod. Like most orphaned minors with a lot of money, Robert had two guardians—one for his finances and one for his person. The Merchants' Trust Company of Cape Cod was his financial guardian. His uncle Charley Brewer was the guardian of his person. And Robert was not only going to Cape Cod to honeymoon. He was going to take full control of his inheritance as well. His wedding day was also his twenty-first birthday, and the bank's financial guardianship was legally at an end.

Robert was in a Limbo of his own. He wasn't full of talk. He was almost completely mechanical, in harmony with the automobile and little else. His responses to his pink and garrulous new bride were as automatic as his responses to the road.

On and on Nancy talked.

"I would rather start out with nothing," she said. "I wish you'd kept the money a secret from me—just left it in the bank for emergencies."

"Forget about it then," said Robert. He pushed in the cigarette lighter. It clicked out a moment later, and Robert lit a cigarette without taking his eyes from the road.

"I'm going to keep my job," said Nancy. "We'll make our own way." She was a secretary in the admissions office at M.I.T. She and Robert had known each other for only two months before they were married. "We'll live within whatever we actually make ourselves," she said.

"Good," said Robert.

"I didn't know you had a dime when I said I'd marry you," said Nancy.

"I know," said Robert.

"I hope your uncle knows that," said Nancy.

"I'll tell him," said Robert. Robert hadn't even told his Uncle Charley that he was going to get married. That would be a surprise.

It was typical of Robert to deal in large surprises, to make his decisions in solitude. Even at the age of nine, he had found it somehow important to show very little emotional dependence on his uncle and aunt. In all the years Robert had lived with them, only one remark had been made about the way he kept his distance. His Aunt Mary had once called him her boarder.

Aunt Mary was dead now. Uncle Charley lived on, was going to meet Robert for lunch in the Atlantic House, a restaurant across the street from the bank. Charley roamed all over Cape Cod in a big, sad old Chrysler, knocking on strangers' doors. He was a straight-commission salesman of aluminum combination storm windows and screens.

"I hope your uncle likes me," said Nancy.

"He will," said Robert. "Don't worry about it."

"I worry about everything," said Nancy.

The Merchants' Trust Company of Cape Cod, as Robert's financial guardian, had certain duties to perform on Robert's twenty-first birthday. They had to get him to sign many documents, and they had to give him an accounting of their custodianship going back twelve years.

The bank was expecting him at one-thirty.

There wasn't anything in particular that Robert's other guardian, his Uncle Charley, the guardian of his person, had to do on the same day. Under law, Charley's responsibility for the boy's person simply evaporated on that day.

That was that—automatically.

But Charley couldn't let it go at that. After all, Charley had no other children, he loved Robert, and he thought that raising the boy was the best thing he and his wife had done with their lives. So Charley planned to make a sentimental little ceremony of surrendering Robert's person before the boy went into the bank.

Charley didn't know about Robert's marriage, so Charley's plan was for just two people.

Charley went into the Atlantic House a half an hour before Robert was supposed to arrive. Charley went into the bar side of the restaurant, and he picked a small table for two.

He sat down and waited.

Several people in the bar knew Charley, and they nodded to him. Those who knew Charley well were surprised to see him on the bar side, because Charley hadn't dared to take a drink for eight years. He hadn't dared to drink because he was an alcoholic. One small beer was enough to start Charley on a toot that could last for weeks.

A new waitress who didn't know Charley took his order, went over to the bar, announced the order loud and clear. "Bourbon on the rocks," she said. She said it emptily. She didn't know that she was announcing big news, announcing that Charley Brewer, after eight dry-as-dust years, was going to have a drink.

Charley got his drink.

Ned Crosby, the owner of the Atlantic House, came right along with it. When the waitress put the drink in front of Charley, Ned slipped into the chair facing him.

"Hello, Charley," said Ned, gently, watchfully.

Charley thanked the waitress for the drink, took his own sweet time in acknowledging Ned. "Hello, Ned," he said. "I'm afraid you're going to have to give up that chair pretty soon. My boy's going to walk in here any minute."

"The drink for him?" said Ned.

"For me," said Charley. He smiled serenely.

Both men were in their late forties, both were going bald, both were alcoholics. They had been boozing buddies years before. They had sworn off booze at the same time, had gone to their first meeting of Alcoholics Anonymous together.

"Today's the boy's twenty-first birthday, Ned," said Charley. "Today he is a man."

"Good for him," said Ned. He pointed to the drink. "That accounts for the celebration."

"That accounts for it," said Charley simply. He made no move to touch the drink. He wasn't going to drink it until Robert walked in.

Strangers looking at Charley and Ned would have guessed that Ned was broke and Charley was prosperous. They would have guessed exactly wrong. Ned, dumpy and humble, wearing rumpled sports clothes from plain pipe racks, took thirty thousand dollars a year out of the Atlantic House. Charley, tall and elegant, sporting a British mustache, made about a tenth that much selling storm windows and screens.

"That a new suit, Charley?" said Ned.

"It's one I've had a while," said Charley. The suit, dark, expensive, and gentle-manly, was in point of fact sixteen years old, dated back to the days when Charley had really been the rich man he seemed. Charley, like the person whose guardian he was, had inherited a lot of money, too. He had lost it all in one fantastic business enterprise after another. There had been a Venetian blind factory, a chain of frozen custard stands, a distributorship for Japanese vacuum cleaners, a ferry operating between Hyannis and Nantucket—even a scheme for harnessing steam that escaped from Italian volcanoes.

"Don't worry about the drink, Ned," said Charley.

"Did I say I was worried?" said Ned.

"Doesn't take much imagination to guess what you're thinking," said Charley. The most obvious trap that an alcoholic could fall into was a celebration, and Charley knew this perfectly well.

"That's the most flattering thing anybody's said to me all week," said Ned.

"This is no ordinary celebration," said Charley.

"They never are, Charley," said Ned.

"What I am celebrating today," said Charley, "is the one thing that really turned out well."

"Uh huh," said Ned. His face remained cheerfully quizzical. "Go on and cele-brate if you want to, Charley—but not in here."

Charley closed his hand around his glass. "Yes—" he said, "in here, and pretty darn soon, too." He had been planning the dramatic gesture of the drink too long to be talked out of it now. He was fully aware of the danger the drink represented. He was scared to death of it. It represented as terrifying a test as walking a tightrope across Niagara Falls.

But the danger was the whole point.

"Ned—" said Charley, "that boy is going to watch in horror while I swallow this drink. And would you like to know what is going to happen to me?" Charley leaned forward. "*Nothing*," he said. He sat back again. "You can watch in horror," he said, "and anybody else who wants to can watch in horror, too. Sell tickets. It ought to be worth a pretty good price of admission, because Charley Brewer is going to take his first drink in eight years—swallow it right down—and that drink isn't going to touch him!

"Why?" said Charley, and he put the question so loudly that it was heard across the room.

"Why isn't this stuff poison for me today?" he said, pointing down at his glass. He answered his own question softly, sibilantly. "Because today I have nothing but a complete success to think about, Ned. This is one day my failures won't come crowding in on me, gibbering and squawking."

Charley shook his head in incredulous gratitude. "That kid—that lovely kid of mine," he said. "I can take a drink today, Ned, because today I am not a disappointed man."

Robert Ryan, Jr., parked his car in the paved lot behind the Atlantic House. It was the first stop in his married life, and his new bride was keeping track of all firsts.

"This is our very first stop," said Nancy Holmes Ryan. She pretended to memorize the place, to find love poetry in the backs of a dime store, a shoe store, a radio store, and the Atlantic House. "I'll always remember this place as the very first place we stopped," she said.

Robert got out of the car promptly, went around to Nancy's side, opened her door.

"Wait," said Nancy. "Now that you're married, you'll have to learn how to wait a little." She turned the car mirror in order to see her own reflection in it. "You'll have to learn—" she said, "a woman can't just rush into things like a man. She's got to get ready a little."

"Sorry," said Robert.

"Especially if she's going to meet a new relative," said Nancy. She frowned at herself in the mirror—and then she tried, in quick succession, a whole series of expressions by which she might be judged. "I—I hardly know anything about him," she said.

"Uncle Charley?" said Robert.

"You haven't said much," said Nancy. "Tell me—tell me a few little things."

Robert shrugged. "Dreamer," he said.

Nancy tried to make something of this, could make very little. "Dreamer?" she echoed.

"Lost everything he had in different crazy businesses," said Robert.

Nancy nodded. "I see." She still saw very little. "Bob?"

"Hm?" said Robert.

"What does that have to do with dreams?" she said.

"Never sees things the way they really are," said Robert. His voice was just a little edgy.

"The way things really are—" he said, "that's never good enough for Uncle Charley."

The edginess increased. "Anything he's mixed up in—he'll fancy it up in his dreams till it's the most glorious thing he ever heard of."

"That sounds like a nice way to be." Her own tone, in involuntary response to Robert's, was mildly argumentative.

"It's a lousy way to be," said Robert harshly.

"I don't see why," said Nancy.

"The poor guy bets his life again and again and again on things that are just—" he shook his head wildly, "just nothing at all! Nothing!"

Robert's bitterness startled Nancy, dismayed her. "Don't you like him, Robert?" she said.

"Sure I like him!" said Robert loudly.

Robert's tone was now so harsh, so worldly, so alone and unromantic, so unsuitable for a wedding day, that it was like a slap to Nancy. After an instant of shock, she could not hold back her tears. The tears were few, and unaccompanied by sound—but there they were in plain view, twinkling on the rims of her eyes. She turned away from Robert.

Robert turned red. His hands worked the air cumbersomely. "Sorry," he said.

"You sound so mad," said Nancy.

"I'm not," said Robert.

"You sound that way," said Nancy. "What did I say wrong?"

"Nothing—nothing to do with you," said Robert. He sighed. "You about ready?"

"No," said Nancy, "not now—not after crying."

"Take your time," said Robert.

Ned Crosby, the innkeeper, looked old. He was still at the table for two with Charley in the bar. He had been unable to wheedle his old friend out of taking a drink. With each new line of argument, Charley had become more radiant with the glamour of his plan.

Ned stood, and Charley looked up at him with amused affection.

"Going?" said Charley.

"Going," said Ned.

"I hope I've put your mind at ease," said Charley lightly.

"Sure," said Ned. He managed to smile. "Prosit, skoal, and mud in your eye," he said.

"Join the boy and me in a drink, Ned?" said Charley playfully.

"I'm tempted," said Ned, "but I'm scared to death the world wouldn't cooperate."

"What could go wrong?" said Charley.

"I don't know, and neither do you," said Ned. "But it's an awfully busy world out there, full of fast-moving people with big, fancy ideas of their own. No sooner would we get that first drink down, counting on a perfect day, and somebody would come crashing in here and say or do exactly the wrong thing."

At the end of this speech, Ned intended to take Charley's drink away from him. But he wasn't quick enough. Before he could do it, Charley was on his feet, his glass on high, saluting Robert, who stood in the doorway.

In three brave, highly ceremonious gulps, Charley drank the drink down.

Nancy Holmes Ryan watched Charley do it through the small opening between her husband's shoulder and the doorjamb. The opening widened now, until Nancy was framed alone in the doorway. Robert had gone to his uncle's side.

There was a third man with them, frowsy, worried. The third man, of course, was the innkeeper, Ned. Of the three men, only Charley looked happy.

"Don't worry—" Charley said to Robert.

"I—I'm not," said Robert.

"I'm not starting on a binge," said Charley. "I haven't taken up drinking again since you've been gone. This is a special drink." He set the glass down with melodramatic finality. "One—just one. One drink, and that's the end." He turned to Ned. "Have I shamed the Atlantic House?" he said.

"No," said Ned quietly.

"Nor am I going to," said Charley. He motioned to the chair facing him. "Sit down, person," he said to Robert.

"Person?" said Robert.

"What I've been guarding for twelve solid years," said Charley. "What'll you have?"

"Uncle Charley—" said Robert, starting to introduce Nancy.

"Sit down, sit down!" said Charley heartily. "Whatever we've got to say to each other, let's say it in comfort."

"Uncle Charley—" said Robert, "I—I'd like you to meet my wife."

"Your what?" said Charley. So far, he hadn't noticed Nancy at all. Now, when Robert nodded in her direction, Charley remained sitting, looked at her blankly.

"My wife," Robert said again, lamely.

Now Charley stood, his eyes on Nancy. His eyes were strangely empty. "How do you do?" he said.

Nancy bowed slightly. "How do you do?" she said.

"I missed your name," said Charley.

"Nancy," said Nancy.

"Nancy," said Charley.

"We were married this morning," said Robert.

"I see," said Charley. He blinked hard several times, distorting his face, as though trying to make his eyes work better. And then, realizing that the expressions might be mistaken for drunkenness, he explained loudly, "Something in my eye." He turned to Ned. "I'm not drunk, Ned," he said.

"Nobody said you were, Charley," said Ned.

"I don't suppose this table will do any longer," said Charley.

Bomar

THERE WERE NO WINDOWS in the Stockholders' Records Section of the Treasurer's Department of the American Forge and Foundry Company. But the soft, sweet music from the loudspeaker on the green wall by the clock, music that increased the section's productivity by 3 percent, kept pace with the seasons, and provided windows of a sort for the staff—Bud Carmody and Lou Sterling, and Nancy Daily.

The loudspeaker was playing spring songs when Carmody and Sterling left the sixty-four-year-old Miss Daily in charge, and went out for morning coffee.

Both were lighthearted, unhaunted by ambition as they sauntered along the factory street to the main gate, outside of which was the Acme Grille. It had been made clear to both of them that they didn't have the priceless stuff of which executives were made. So, unlike so many wide-eyed and hustling men all around them, they were free to dress comfortably and inexpensively, and go out for coffee as often as they pleased.

They also had a field of humor that was closed to those with big futures in the organization. They could make jokes about the American Forge and Foundry Company, its products, its executives, and its stockholders.

Carmody, who was forty-five, was theoretically in charge of the section, of young Sterling, Miss Daily, and the files. But he was spiritually an anarchist, and never gave orders. He was a tall, thin dreamer, who prided himself on being creative rather than domineering, and his energies went into stuffing the suggestion box, decorating the office for holidays, and collecting limericks, which he kept in a locked file in his desk.

Carmody had been lonely and a little sour, as wave after wave of enterprising young men passed him on the ladder of success. But then the twenty-eight-year-old Sterling, also tall, thin, and dreamy, had joined the section after unappreciated performances in other departments, and life in the section had become vibrant. Carmody and Sterling stimulated each other to new peaks in creativity—and out of the incredibly fruitful union of their talents had come many things, the richest being the myth of Bomar Fessenden III.

There really was a Bomar Fessenden III, and he was a stockholder of the company, but neither Carmody nor Sterling knew anything about him save the number of shares he owned, one hundred, and his home address, 5889 Seaview Terrace, Great Neck, Long Island, New York. But Bomar's splendid name had caught Sterling's fancy. He started talking knowingly about the debauched life Fessenden led with the dividends the section mailed to him, claiming Fessenden as an old friend, a fraternity brother who wrote regularly from fleshpots around the world—Acapulco, Palm Beach, Nice, Capri . . . Carmody had been charmed by the myth, and had contributed heavily to it.

"Some day!" said Carmody, as they walked through the main gate. "Too bad Bomar Fessenden III isn't here to see it."

"That's one of the many reasons I would never trade places with Bomar," said Sterling. "Not for all his wealth and comfort and beautiful women. He never gets to see the seasons come and go."

"Cut off from life, that's what Bomar is," said Carmody. "He might as well be dead. When winter comes, what does he do?"

"Bomar runs away from it," said Sterling. "Pathetic. He runs away from everything. I just got a card from him saying he's pulling out of Buenos Aires because of the dampness."

"And all the time, what Bomar is really running away from is himself, the futility of his whole existence," said Carmody, sliding into a booth in the Acme Grille. "But his hollowness still pursues him as certainly as his dividend checks."

"Two crumb-buns and draw two, black," said Sterling to the waitress.

"By golly," said Carmody, "I wonder what old Bomar wouldn't give to be here with us right now, making plain, wholesome talk with plain, wholesome people over plain, wholesome food?"

"Plenty," said Sterling. "I can read that between the lines in his letters. There Bomar is, wherever he is, spending a fortune every day on liquor and beautiful women and expensive playthings, when he could find peace of mind right here with us, for a mere twenty cents."

"That'll be twenty-five apiece," said the waitress.

"Twenty-five!" said Carmody incredulously.

"Coffee's done went up a nickel," said the waitress.

Carmody smiled wanly. "So, for peace of mind, Bomar's got to pay a nickel more." He threw a quarter down on the table. "Damn the expense!"

"This is our day to howl," said Sterling. "Have another crumb-bun."

"Who's Bomar?" said the waitress. "All the time you talk about Bomar."

"Who is Bomar?" said Sterling. He looked at her pityingly. "Bomar? Bomar Fessenden III? Ask anybody!"

"Ask Miss Daily," said Carmody gleefully. "If you really want to get an earful about Bomar, ask Miss Daily. She can't think about anything else."

"Ask her what she thinks of Bomar's latest girlfriend," said Sterling.

Carmody pursed his lips in imitation of Miss Daily, and imitated her voice. "That hussy from the Copacabana!"

Poor Miss Daily, who had been with the company for thirty-nine years, had been assigned to the Stockholders' Records Section only a month before, and believed everything Sterling and Carmody told her about Bomar.

Carmody continued his expert imitation of Miss Daily. "There ought to be laws against somebody like Bomar having all that money, and throwing it around like it was water, with so many people going hungry everywhere," he said indignantly. "If I were a man, I'd go to wherever Bomar was, push his stuck-up old butler aside, and give him the thrashing of his life."

"What's the butler's name?" said Sterling.

"Dawson?" said Carmody. He shook his head. "Redfield? No, no, not Redfield."

"Come on, man—think," said Sterling. "You made him up."

"Perkins? Nope, no. Slipped my mind completely." He smiled and shrugged. "No matter. Miss Daily will remember. She hasn't forgotten a shred of the whole ugly story that is the life of Bomar Fessenden III."

"Oh," said Carmody vaguely, displaying his leadership, as he and Sterling returned to the basement office after coffee. "They're here. Guess we might as well fall to, huh?"

The office was filled with cardboard boxes containing the spring dividend checks, which the section would compare with the most up-to-date information on the whereabouts of and number of shares held by the company's thousands of owners. Miss Daily, tiny and shy, bright-eyed as a chicken, was sorting through the contents of one of the boxes.

"We don't have to go over them all, Miss Daily," said Carmody. "Just the ones with recent changes of address or changes in holdings."

"I know," said Miss Daily. "I've got the list on my desk."

"Good. Fine," said Carmody. "I see you're already in 'F.' Do you mean to say that in the short time Mr. Sterling and I have been gone, you've gotten that far?"

"I was looking up our fine Mr. Bomar Fessenden III," said Miss Daily grimly.

"Everything square with my old pal?" said Sterling.

Miss Daily was white with resentment. "Yes," she said crisply, "quite. Two hundred and fifty dollars."

"Spit in the ocean," said Sterling. "I doubt if Bomar even knows he owns a piece of this company, it's such a little piece. The big money comes in from Standard Oil, DuPont, General Motors, and all that."

"A hundred shares!" said Miss Daily. "You call that a little piece?"

"Well, that's only worth ten thousand dollars, after all," said Carmody patiently, "take or leave a hundred. The necklace he gave to Carmella down in Buenos Aires cost more than that."

"You mean Juanita," said Miss Daily.

"I beg your pardon," said Carmody. "I meant Juanita."

"Carmella was the bullfighter's daughter in Mexico City," said Miss Daily. "She got the Cadillac."

"Of course," said Sterling to Carmody, reproachfully, "how could you get Carmella and Juanita confused?"

"Stupid of me," said Carmody.

"They're not at all alike," said Miss Daily.

"Well, he's through with Juanita anyway," said Sterling. "He's left Buenos Aires. It got damp."

"Mercy me—damp!" said Miss Daily with bitter sarcasm. "It's more than a body can put up with!"

"What else has Bomar got to say for himself?" said Carmody.

"Oh—he's in Monte Carlo now. Flew up. Got a new girl now. Fifi. Met her while he was playing roulette. He says he dropped five thousand watching her instead of keeping his mind on the game," said Sterling.

Carmody chuckled appreciatively. "What a card, Bomar."

Miss Daily snorted.

"Now, now, Miss Daily, you mustn't get mad at Bomar," said Sterling. "He's just playful and high-spirited is all. We'd all live high, if we could."

"Speak for yourself," said Miss Daily hotly. "It's the wickedest thing I ever heard of. That nasty boy—and here we are, sending him more money, money he won't even notice, so he can throw it away. It isn't Christian. I wish I were already retired, so I wouldn't have to face doing this."

"Grit your teeth, the way Mr. Sterling and I do," said Carmody.

"Bite the bullet, Miss Daily," said Sterling.

Two weeks later, Carmody and his protégé, Sterling, were in the Acme Grille, with Carmody speaking to Sterling sternly for the first time in their relationship.

"Man, you've killed the goose that laid the golden eggs," said Carmody. "You're weak. You succumbed to temptation."

"You're right, you're right," said Sterling miserably. "I can see that now. I overdid. I wasn't myself. Twenty-four-hour flu."

"Overdid!" said Carmody. "You had Bomar charter the *Queen Elizabeth.*"

"Madcap Bomar," said Sterling ruefully. "When she doubted it, I tried to turn it into a joke."

"You turned the whole thing into a joke. When she started cross-examining you about everything we'd ever told her about Bomar, you went all to pieces."

"It was a lot of material to keep track of," said Sterling. "What can I say, after I've said I'm sorry? What gets me is how hard it hit her."

"Of course it hit her hard. She's humiliated, and it takes a big piece out of her life. The lonely old soul took to Bomar like a cannibal to a fat Baptist missionary. She loved Bomar, he made her feel so righteous. Now you've taken Bomar from her—and from us, boy."

"I didn't admit we'd made the whole thing up."

"It was plain enough. The only thing that would convince her now would be for Bomar to show up in the flesh."

Sterling stirred his coffee thoughtfully. "Well—is that *utterly* inconceivable?"

"Not utterly," Carmody admitted.

"There—you see?" said Sterling. "It's always darkest before the dawn. Think of what it would mean to Miss Daily to be able to square off Bomar Fessenden III, to his face! In three more months she retires after forty years of service. What a way to wind it up!"

Carmody nodded interestedly, and chewed. "Your crumb-bun taste a little funny?"

"Order a crumb-bun, you get a crumb-bun," said Sterling. "Now, about Bomar: he should be fat and dissipated, short and insolent—"

"With a sports coat down to his knees," said Carmody, "a tie like the flag of Liberia, and gum-soles as thick as fruitcakes."

Miss Daily was absent from the office when Carmody and Sterling returned after an extensive search for a replica of the Bomar Fessenden III of their imaginations. They'd found their man in a supply room of the Research and Development Laboratory, and bought his services for five dollars. His name was Stanley Broom, and, as Bomar, he was perfect.

"He doesn't have to *act* worthless," said Sterling happily, "he *is* worthless."

"Shh!" said Carmody, and Miss Daily walked in.

She looked terribly upset. "You're making fun of me again," she said.

"Why would we do that?" said Carmody.

"You two made it all up—about Bomar."

"Made it up?" said Sterling incredulously. "My dear Miss Daily, Bomar is going to be in this very office before twenty-four hours have passed. I just received a telegram. He's stopping off here on his way from Monte Carlo to Catalina."

"Please, please," said Miss Daily, "you've done too much already. You don't know what you've done."

"Miss Daily, it most certainly isn't a joke," said Sterling. "He'll be here tomorrow, and you can see him for yourself. Pinch him, even. He's real, all right." He watched her closely, puzzled by the importance she seemed to attach to Bomar. "If Bomar were a joke—what difference would that make?"

"He is real? You promise?" she said.

"You'll see him tomorrow," said Carmody.

"You swear he's done everything you say he's done?" said Miss Daily.

"I made that up about the *Queen Elizabeth*," said Sterling.

788

KURT VONNEGUT

"The rest is true?"

"Oh, Bomar's a wild one, Miss Daily," said Carmody.

Unaccountably, Miss Daily seemed vastly relieved. She sank down in her chair, and managed to smile. "It *is* true," she said faintly. "Thank the Lord. If it had all been made up, oh, I—" She shook her head, and left the sentence unfinished.

"If it had all been made up, you what?" said Carmody.

"Never mind, never mind," said Miss Daily absently. "If it's all true, I have no regrets."

"What sort of regrets might you have had?" said Carmody.

"Never you mind, never you mind," she crooned. "So, tomorrow I come face-to-face at last with Master Fessenden. Good!"

◎ ◎ ◎

At the Acme Grille, shortly after eight the next morning, Sterling and Carmody rehearsed Stanley Broom for the drama he was about to enact before Miss Daily in the Stockholders' Records Section.

Broom was dressed flamboyantly, and wore an insolent sneer that seemed to invite all the world to slap his fat face. "This can't take long," he said, "or I'll get canned."

"Fifteen minutes at the outside," said Sterling. "We walk in together, see—and I introduce you to Carmody and Miss Daily casually. You're stopping off to see me, your old college buddy, on your way from Monte Carlo to Catalina. Got it?"

"Check," said Broom. "Listen, she isn't going to take a swat at me or anything, is she?"

"Couldn't hurt a flea," said Sterling. "She isn't even five feet tall, and she weighs under a hundred."

"She could still be *wiry*," said Broom.

"Naaaah. Now listen, what's the name of your yacht?"

"*The Golden Eagle*, and it's anchored at Miami Beach," said Broom. "I may have the crew bring it around through the canal to the West Coast."

"Who you in love with now?" said Sterling.

"Fifi. I met her at Monte Carlo, and she's going to follow me to Catalina in a few days, at my expense. She's got to shake off a count she was engaged to."

"What have you given her so far?" said Sterling.

"Uh—emerald and a blue mink."

"*Silver*—blue mink," said Carmody. "OK, I'd say we're in pretty good shape. I'll go on back to the office, and make sure Miss Daily is there for Bomar's grand entrance."

◎ ◎ ◎

Miss Daily was pink with excitement as she sat in the office, waiting for Bomar, and her breathing was shallow. She shuffled papers nervously, accomplishing nothing. Her lips moved, but made no sounds.

"Eh?" said Carmody. "What was that, Miss Daily?"

"I wasn't speaking to you," said Miss Daily politely. "I was getting things straight in my mind."

"That's the stuff. Really going to give him a piece of your mind, eh?"

"Bomar, you old dog!" said Sterling in the hall, just outside the office door. "You're a sight for sore eyes!"

Miss Daily snapped the point on her pencil in a nervous spasm, and Sterling and Broom walked in.

Broom puffed on a preposterously big and foul cigar, and took in the office in a withering glance. "Steerage," he said. "How can you bear it? I've been in here ten seconds, and it's driving me mad."

Miss Daily was white and trembling, but as yet speechless, fascinated.

"Do you mean to say that people really live like this?" said Broom.

"They do," said Miss Daily in a small voice, "if they're not too lazy or spoiled to help do the world's work."

"I suppose that's an insult," said Broom, "but not a very good one, since most of the world's work isn't worth doing. Besides, someone has to give his full attention to the finer things in life, or there'd be no civilization."

"Fifi?" said Miss Daily. "Carmella? Juanita? Amber? Collette?"

"You *do* keep track of the stockholders down here, don't you?" said Broom.

"I've told her a little about you, Bomar," said Sterling.

"I just found out I owned stock in this thing the other day," said Broom, "but apparently Miss Pry here has known about me all along."

"My name is Miss Daily," said Miss Daily, "Miss Nancy Daily."

"Well, get off your high horse, Miss Daily," said Broom. "I haven't done anything to hurt the lower classes."

"You're what's wrong with the world," said Miss Daily bravely, her back straight, her lips trembling. "And now that I've met you, and seen that you're worse than I ever imagined you to be, I'm not sorry at all I did what I did. I'm glad."

"Huh?" said Broom, his stride broken. He looked questioningly at Carmody and Sterling, who in turn looked uneasily at Miss Daily.

"Your last dividend check, Mr. Fessenden," said Miss Daily. "I signed your name on the back, and sent it to the Red Cross."

Carmody and Sterling exchanged glances full of horror.

"I did it single-handed," said Miss Daily. "Mr. Carmody and Mr. Sterling know nothing about it. It was only two hundred and fifty dollars, so you won't miss it— and it's in better hands than if you'd given it to that shameless Fifi."

"Um," said Broom, completely at sea.

"Well, aren't you going to call the police?" said Miss Daily. "I'm quite ready to go, if it would satisfy you to prefer charges."

"Well, I—uh—" mumbled Broom. He got no help with his lines from Carmody and Sterling, who were thunderstruck. "Easy come, easy go," he said at last. "Isn't that right, Sterling?"

Sterling roused himself. "Root of all evil," he said desolately.

Broom tried to think of something more to say, but failed.

"Well, off to Monte Carlo," he said. "Ta ta."

"Catalina," said Miss Daily. "You just came from Monte Carlo."

"Catalina," said Broom.

"Don't you feel much better, Mr. Fessenden?" said Miss Daily. "Doesn't it make you happy to have done something unselfish for a change?"

"Yup," said Broom, nodding gravely, and he left.

"He took it like a little gentleman," said Miss Daily to Carmody and Sterling.

"Oh, it's easy enough for Bomar," said Carmody bleakly, looking with loathing at Sterling, the Frankenstein who'd invented the monster. A new check would have to be made out to the real Bomar, and Carmody could think of no graceful way of explaining to the powers upstairs what had happened to the old one. Carmody, Sterling, and Miss Daily were through at American Forge and Foundry. The monster had turned on them savagely, and destroyed all three.

"I think Mr. Fessenden learned something today," said Miss Daily.

Carmody laid his hand on Miss Daily's shoulder. "Miss Daily, there's something you'd better know," he said grimly. "We're in quite a mess, Miss Daily. That was not Bomar Fessenden III who was just in here, and nothing we've said about Bomar is true."

"A joke," said Sterling bitterly.

"Well, I must say it wasn't a very funny joke," said Miss Daily. "It was quite unkind, treating me like an idiot."

"No—it wasn't funny at all, the way it turned out," said Carmody.

"Not as funny as my joke about forging the check," said Miss Daily.

"That was a joke?" said Carmody.

"Certainly," said Miss Daily sweetly. "Aren't you going to smile, Mr. Carmody? Not even a little snicker, Mr. Sterling? Heavens—it really *is* time to retire. No one seems to be able to laugh at himself anymore."

Requiem for Zeitgeist

"DE MORTUIS NIL NISI BONUM!" said the man on the bar stool next to mine. It was nearly closing time, the bartender had excused himself momentarily, and we were alone. We had been sitting side by side for nearly two hours without speaking. I had studied his reflection in the blue mirror behind the bar now and then, but I hadn't looked into his eyes before he spoke—and what I saw there troubled me. He had the figure and features of an athletic youngster, not yet thirty, but his eyes—his eyes were those of a sick, baffled old man, a King Lear. "Say nothing but good about the dead!" he translated after a baleful silence.

"I know," I said, "and I do."

He seemed satisfied; so satisfied, in fact, as to lose interest in me altogether. He addressed himself to his own reflection, with gestures. "They don't make men like Omar Zeitgeist anymore," he said. "And where is he now? Where is the greatest mind of our time, of all time?" At this point, he burst into uncontrollable laughter, so full of irony as to almost clank.

I left a quarter tip beneath my half-filled glass, and moved toward the exit. He caught me roughly by the shoulder. "Omar Zeitgeist was a German, the only man on earth with the know-how of the cosmic bomb," be whispered. "I was his bodyguard."

"Cosmic bomb like the H-bomb?" I ventured.

"The cosmic bomb is to the H-bomb what an earthquake is to hiccups," he said acidly. "Works on the same principle as what holds the universe together, only backwards."

"Bully for it," I said.

"Zeitgeist had no laboratory, worked out everything in his head." My informant tapped his temple significantly and made clucking noises. "Our counterspies knew that he was very close to solving the riddle of the cosmic bomb when the war ended. No twig was left unbent in the search for him that followed Germany's surrender. Several full regiments of men from good families were assigned to the sole task of finding Zeitgeist. Not a few of these searchers were found floating facedown in the Rhine, the Rhône, the Elbe, the Ruhr, the Aller, the Altmühl, the Unstrut, and other waterways, with bullets in their heads. They were not alone in their quest."

"Communists, eh?"

"You already know about this?" he asked in surprise.

"Just a lucky guess."

"As I was saying," he continued irritably, "in the country between the Yapura and the Putumayo Rivers is a no-man's-land once claimed by both Colombia and Peru. Colombia won, if you can call getting the country between the Yapura and Putumayo Rivers winning anything. When I say no-man's-land, I mean to say that no Colombian or Peruvian ever wants to go there, and that the Witotos are not—in the civilized sense of the word—men. The Witotos live naked and in chronic fear of their neighbors, and are abominably omnivorous. How abominably omnivorous I shall presently relate." He tossed down the remainder of his drink. "They eat manios, maize, yams, peanuts, peppers, plantains, pineapples, deer, tapirs, peccaries, sloths, bears, monkeys, and—." His voice caught. He lapsed into a moody silence that lasted for perhaps ten minutes.

"Omar Zeitgeist—you were going to tell me what happened to him," I prodded.

"I'm coming to that," he said peevishly. "He was found in Wiesbaden, in an abandoned *Luftschutzraum*."

"Beg your pardon?"

He looked at me sympathetically. "Why, what did you do?"

"Nothing," I said in confusion. "I just didn't know what a *Luftschutzraum* was."

"No offense," he said, extending his hand. "It was decided that Zeitgeist should be spirited away to an area free of outside pressures and communists, where he might work out the final details of the cosmic bomb. As far as was known, there were no communist spies between the Yapura and Putumayo Rivers." He smiled sadly. "All that the Colombians said was, 'Watch out for them Peruvians,' and all the Peruvians said was, 'Watch out for them Colombians.' Nobody said boo about the Witotos, and nobody knew if it would stop raining when Omar Zeitgeist and I got there. If they had, we might now have the cosmic bomb."

"Perhaps we're too spoiled as it is," I suggested.

He closed his eyes and sighed. "Of all the words of mice and men, the saddest are 'It might have been.'" He hammered on the bar with his fists. "He was so brilliant, he didn't even notice he'd been spirited across the Atlantic and stuck away in a jungle hut. He thought he was still in an abandoned *Luftschutzraum*, that Germany was a democracy, and that von Hindenburg was president. Zeitgeist needed no laboratory, no assistants. He had only to think, while I guarded his body. There we were, just the two of us, hemmed in by tropical rain forest and Witotos. He had but one more problem to solve before the cosmic bomb would be ready for humanity. It was that close!"

"But no cigar, in a manner of speaking?" I said.

"No cigar—precisely." He wept unashamedly, then scowled. "The Witotos are ignorant and savage. How ignorant and savage I can perhaps make clear by telling you that they believe rain is caused by a little white elf-like creature. They call this creature 'Dilbo,' and believe that he lives hidden in the jungle. They believe that if they can catch and eat Dilbo and make a tom-tom out of his cranium, they can have rain anytime they want it just by beating on Dilbo's head. They know nothing of dry ice and silver iodide rain-making techniques." He bit his lip. "More's the pity.

"At any rate, there we were, just the two of us, and one more problem to be solved. Suddenly, one night, Zeitgeist jumped to his feet and rushed into the jungle before I could stop him, shouting, 'Eureka! Eureka! Eureka!,' which is Greek for 'I have found it! I have found it! I have found it!'" The man brushed away his tears and smiled bravely. "It was a triumphant moment. He was probably the first white man ever to shout Greek between the Putumayo and Yapura Rivers." He frowned. "If only it hadn't happened in a dry spell! If only the manios crop hadn't been withering and the peccaries moving south to new waterholes! The drought, worse luck, had made the Witotos skittish and testy.

"I was beside myself, at the end of my rope—you can imagine. For hours I combed the dark jungle, calling his name. Fruitless. Finally, as the rays of the rising sun struck the peaks of the Andes to the west, I resolved to enlist the aid of the Witotos." Here, my informant closed his eyes, as though he were concentrating every bit of his attention on his memory, on the terrible moments he was reliving.

"The Witotos have an effective telegraph system in the form of huge drums, which can be heard for miles," he continued, struggling to keep his voice even. "I was used to their infernal thumping, night and day, and so didn't take much notice of the din that grew louder as I approached the native village. It wasn't until I was almost through the gates that I realized there was a new quality in the sound of the village drum. It wasn't the same drum. It sounded unlike any drum I had ever heard before—like a man beating on an empty tank car with a ball-peen hammer." He grasped my arm and squeezed it until it hurt. "I suddenly knew that only one thing could make that unearthly clamor. The thirsty Witotos had found Dilbo!"

"Not—?" I began.

"Zeitgeist," gasped the man. "The father of the cosmic bomb was *kaput*, gone, *fini*—to say the least, the very least, dead. 'Clunk, clunk,' clunk' went the Witotos' brand-new tom-tom. As a bodyguard, I was through."

He whipped out a revolver, and fired six shots into the jukebox, which turned a blinding cherry red and died.

"Did it rain?" I asked, after a respectful silence.

"It did," said my informant gravely, "but not as much as the Witotos had hoped for."

And on Your Left

THE NEW RESEARCH LABORATORY of the Federal Apparatus Corporation was called a "temple of science" by three out of six chief speakers at the dedication ceremonies—by a cabinet member, a state governor, and a Nobel Prize winner. They said that no American should miss seeing it, that it was the finest laboratory on earth. Company spokesmen responded by saying that every day was open house to everybody, regardless of race, color, or creed, and that buses would provide free transportation from downtown every hour on the hour, and that guides would be on duty. When the state Chamber of Commerce issued its annual vacation guide, it gave more space to the laboratory as a tourist attraction than it did to the fifth highest waterfall in the East or to the picnic grounds where the family of Hendrik van Zyl had been massacred by drunk Natacoochie braves.

Inside the new temple of science, which was fieldstone and steel and glass, and whose windows looked out over woods and blue Lake Minango, Dr. Harold Meyers sat in his laboratory, coaxing a shaved rat from one cage to another, which the rat would share with a black vacuum tube the size and shape of a fat cigar.

Meyers, whose taste in haircuts and clothes was that of a college boy, though he was forty-five, made chirping sounds intended to be soothing and rat-like, and he prodded the behind of the naked and furious animal with the rounded end of his fountain pen.

"There now—eep, eep—easy, boy—tchk, tchk—attaboy." The rat was halfway into the new cage. "An inch more, baby, and—"

"And on your left," howled a guide, "is Dr. Harold Meyers, the man I'm sure you've all read about in the papers!"

Meyers dropped his pen, and the rat attacked it, tearing open the barrel and ink reservoir, spattering the tabletop and Meyers's white cuffs.

"Dr. Meyers," said the guide proudly, "is none other than the man who recently discovered the Z-rays you've all been reading about. At this very moment, you may be seeing history made, for Dr. Meyers is now at work on possible applications of Z-rays to everyday life."

Dr. Meyers smiled bleakly as the guide stepped into the laboratory, and forty Boy Scouts crowded into the room to peer under bell jars, open drawers, test faucets, and try to force jelly beans and peanuts through the wire mesh of the animal cages.

"Just take a minute of your time, Doctor," said the guide expansively. "This," he said, gesturing at the laboratory, "is where the miracles of the modern age come from—from modern research. Men like Dr. Meyers are the American pioneers of the present, working for a greater tomorrow."

Dr. Meyers looked down at his feet with what he hoped was "becoming modesty. Since moving from the old laboratory to the new, he had heard the same speech at least four times a day.

"Would you mind showing these fine young Americans a little something about Z-rays, Doctor?"

"No, not at all," sighed Meyers. "Glad to." He could do it in his sleep. He hadn't done much of anything else for six months. "Through the hoop, Rover," he said to himself, and he stood and closed the Venetian blinds.

"Z-rays," he said in a singsong voice, without reflection, "are interesting radiations which make human skin, and all bare animal skin, for that matter, fluoresce—that is, they make skin glow in the dark. This small tube here radiates Z-rays. I'll turn it on, and I want you to watch its effect on my face."

As Meyers talked and did his tricks, his thoughts were free to go wherever they liked, so automatic was his performance by now, and his thoughts did not care to remain in the laboratory with the guide and the Boy Scouts. They fled the world of tile and stainless steel and floor-to-ceiling windows, and returned to the antique warehouse downtown that had been partitioned and heated to house the first research scientists hired by the company in the late twenties—when the hiring of pure research scientists by industry had been something of an experiment in itself. Guides would have sooner conducted visitors on tours of the company's men's rooms than take them to the research laboratory in those days—the days before the temple.

The Boy Scouts laughed delightedly, and Meyers realized that he was approaching the finale of his act, and was playing Z-rays on the shaved laboratory animals in their cages along one wall. He chuckled through his apathy, as though having the time of his life, and suddenly played the rays over the Boy Scouts, who guffawed and nudged each other as they glowed in the dark.

Dr. Meyers turned off the tube, opened the Venetian blinds again, and sat down, smiling glassily at his guests, waiting for them to get out so he could get back to work.

"Thank you, Doctor," said the guide graciously.

"You're certainly welcome." He drummed on the desk as the guide made no move to leave.

"I suppose you boys are wondering what all these valves are for, eh?" said the guide, pointing to a battery of taps over a sink. "Well, a research scientist needs a lot more on tap than you and I do at home. He's got hot and cold water, sure, but, in addition, every scientist in this building has right at his fingertips nitrogen, hydrogen, oxygen, steam, vacuum, and . . ." The guide paused tantalizingly. "And who wants to guess what comes out of this one?"

Dr. Meyers clenched and unclenched his hands several times as the Boy Scouts fidgeted and offered no guesses, and the guide coyly refused to tell them. The guide at last gave up, and said, with an air of great wisdom, "Illuminating gas!"

Dr. Meyers exhaled with relief, and raised his eyebrows in an expression of cheery farewell.

The guide held fast. "Absolutely everything a research scientist could possibly need was put into this building," he said. "The company's first laboratory was in a makeshift building, and the scientists had to make it do as well as they could. But this building was built from the ground up for research." He turned to a Scout next to him. "Say you were Dr. Meyers, here, sitting at the desk, and all of a sudden a terrible fire broke out in the apparatus between you and the door. Remember, you're four stories up. What would you do?"

"Die?" said the Scout, looking at Meyers with awe.

"Here's what you'd do," said the guide happily, and he skirted Dr. Meyers and gave the wall behind him a savage kick. An escape panel in the wall snapped free from its latch, and swung open into the next laboratory. There was an outcry from the room next door, followed by the din of splintering glass.

"Goddammit, Meyers!" shouted Dr. Herpers, Meyers's neighbor, thrusting his head through the opening in the wall. "What are you doing—switching from Z-rays to battering rams?" He saw the guide. "Oh—it's you!"

"I was simply showing these boys the wonders of the laboratory," said the guide coolly.

"Knocking out partitions is your idea of simplicity?" said Herpers bitterly.

"Please," said the guide, "these young gentlemen are guests of the company." He started to shepherd them into the hall. "Thank you, Dr. Meyers. That was very interesting. Now, boys, on your right you're about to see something you can tell your grandchildren about. Could we have a minute of your time, Dr. Dawson?"

Meyers strode over to the door and slammed it.

Herpers had crawled through the escape hatch, and was looking gloomily out the window at Lake Minango. "There's one thing they forgot to pipe into every laboratory," he said at last.

"Helium?" said Meyers.

"Gin," said Herpers. "Nice view you have here. Must inspire you."

"Give me the Universal Clothing outlet and the Lehigh Valley switchyards any day," said Meyers. This was the view he'd had through a crusty window in the old laboratory. "You can get used to freight whistles, and the locomotives never came right into the laboratory. What are you working on now?"

"Working up a new act I think they'll like," said Herpers. "See—I come on with a buck and wing, balancing a ringstand on the end of my nose and playing the *1812 Overture* on a panpipe made out of test tubes. I was going to work in my vacuum pump, but the guide just broke it with the escape panel."

"It's just as well. Dr. Levi's got his whole act built around a vacuum pump, and the tours start there."

The door opened, and Dr. Elizabeth Dawson, a young woman physicist from across the hall, her hands clasped, her face grave and white, came in.

"Liz!" said Meyers, "what on earth happened?"

"For five days," she said hollowly, "I have been trying to get out a quarterly report that should have taken me four hours to write."

"In the bad old days," said Meyers.

"All I had to do today was add up a simple column of figures. You know—two plus two and things like that?" She hammered on the stainless steel, sinktop with her small fist. "Well, twenty times I've added the column, and twenty times I've been interrupted—to be oggled at and talked about and photographed like a Navaho rug weaver or something. And, just now, just after Troop 17 marched out, Dr. Berry called to ask me if I knew the report was overdue, and would I please try to be more business-like?" She burst into tears. "I wish to heaven I'd never started work on the infrared microscope!"

"It's good vaudeville, all right," said Herpers gloomily.

"This has got to stop!" said Meyers, patting Dr. Dawson's shoulder. "Nobody's getting anything done."

"And on your left," cried a guide, "is Dr. Harold Meyers, the man you've no doubt all read about in the papers."

"Places, everybody," said Herpers, "curtain going up." He crawled back into his own laboratory.

"We're doing our act just once more, Liz," whispered Dr. Meyers to Dr. Dawson, "and then we're going to Dr. Berry and tell him the hell with it. Buck up."

"Just take a minute of your time, Dr. Meyers," said the guide.

"No trouble," said Dr. Meyers hoarsely.

◙ ◙ ◙

Dr. Berry, head of the laboratory, stared glumly out at Lake Minango, his back to his white, kidney-shaped desk, and to the three tense scientists standing before it. Drs. Harold Meyers, Elizabeth Dawson, and Edward Herpers. "You've got to look at it from the viewpoint of the men in the line," he said, "because they're the ones who have their hands on the purse strings."

"The who?" said Meyers. Dr. Berry, whose position brought him into contact with company officers in production and sales and advertising and distribution, was full of jargon that meant nothing to the scientists under him.

"The men in the line," said Dr. Berry, "the people who make the money that built this place, the money that pays our salaries." He sighed. "Facts of life."

"We earn the money," said Dr. Meyers. "Or used to, and would again, if we had half a chance."

Dr. Berry turned around to face them. "They intend to see that we do," he said. "This place was supposed to cost seven million, and it's run over nine already. Did you see the manager of sales out here at the dedication?"

"Eugene Bullard?" said Herpers. "He was the one who went around saying, 'How much this cost, how much this cost?'"

"And rubbing the drapes between his thumb and forefinger," said Meyers.

"And asking which room was Marie Antoinette's bedroom," said Liz Dawson.

"That's Bullard," said Dr. Berry heavily. "And, as long as he keeps selling the way he's been selling, to all practical purposes this is his company."

"What's Bullard to us?" said Meyers. "We never had anything to do with him before."

"We never made a raid on the company treasury like this before," said Berry, "and Bullard has a profound interest in where the dollars go—and, God help us, he has the company president's ear. We wouldn't have this laboratory at all, if I hadn't been able to sell Bullard on its being a terrific investment in sales promotion. And you heard what he said at the dedication."

Dr. Meyers quoted from dismal memory: "'The basic job of every man and every dollar in this company is to sell, sell, sell!'"

"So," said Dr. Berry, "in exchange for our new facilities we have the new responsibility, according to Mr. Bullard, of being host to potential consumers of the company's products, and making sure that they leave with opened billfolds and stars in their eyes."

"But nobody's getting any research done!" said Dr. Meyers hotly. "Why don't you tell Bullard to keep his big nose out of what he doesn't know anything about?"

Dr. Berry turned white, and was about to say something bitter when the telephone rang. "Dr. Berry speaking. Oh—hello, sir. What's that? Oh, yes, I picked the color for the foyer walls—light blue. Seemed like a nice, cool, restful color. Uh-huh. I see. Well, perhaps we should strive for more of a feeling of excitement and adventure as the visitors come in." He chuckled without changing his grave expression. "Well, I'm not used to looking at things from the angle of sales psychology, but I'm learning. All right, sir—a warm yellow on the orange side." He glanced at his watch. "You and your party are coming out in an hour, you say? Well, sir, we can hardly have the foyer redecorated by then, but everything else will be ready. Thanks for calling, Mr. Bullard."

Dr. Berry hung up and tried to remember what he had been about to say to Dr. Meyers. "Oh—in reply to your question, Meyers: I don't tell Bullard to mind his own business for the same reason that you don't brush your teeth in hydrofluoric acid or mix ground glass with your breakfast cereal. My advice to you, to all three of you, is to count your blessings, keep your patience, and do the best you can. Bullard will be out here in an hour, incidentally, with some very important customers. White coats will be worn."

◎ ◎ ◎

Drs. Meyers, Herpers, and Dawson sat around Dr. Meyers's desk in stiff, brilliantly-white laboratory coats, talking and drinking coffee warmed on a Bunsen burner, while waiting for Eugene Bullard and his important customers to arrive.

"Well, if Berry won't stand up to Bullard, maybe we should. When he shows up, we can say we haven't got anything to show, because we've been doing nothing but greeting visitors since we've been out here," said Herpers, absently opening and shutting the valves that ran along the top of the sink like organ stops.

"Or put on such a dull, pointless show that Bullard would never want anybody to come out here again," said Dr. Liz Dawson.

"And have the research appropriation cut to nothing," said Meyers. He shook his head. "Poor Berry—I'll bet he wishes to God he were out of administration and back in research. Let that be an example to all of us. Budgets, power politics, policy. He's just got to play along."

"Or quit," said Harpers.

"Then somebody else would have to give up research and take his job, and it'd be the same damn thing all over again," said Meyers. "Berry can cooperate or get out, and that goes for all of us."

"No biz like showbiz," said Herpers.

Meyers looked at him thoughtfully. "But maybe we could be too cooperative."

"What do you mean?" said Liz Dawson.

Meyers rattled a pencil between his teeth. "Put on a real show, jam-packed with enthusiasm and sell, sell, sell, that'll make Bullard and the tours look so foolish that we'll have the place to ourselves forever after."

"Or get fired," said Liz Dawson.

"And on your left," bawled a guide, "is Dr. Harold Meyers, the man I'm sure you've all read about in the papers."

Dr. Meyers rolled his eyes. "So what's the matter with getting fired?"

◎ ◎ ◎

Eugene Bullard could drive a golf ball farther, hold his liquor better, and laugh louder than anyone else in the Federal Apparatus Corporation—feats that called for physical bulk carried proudly. His voice and heavy footfalls dominated the radiant-heated halls of the research laboratory, as a guide, subdued and polite in the presence of great rank, conducted him and a half-dozen important customers with millions to spend on a tour of the temple of science.

Dr. Meyers heard the party coming, tapped on the wall that separated his laboratory from that of Dr. Herpers, and telephoned Liz Dawson across the hall to whisper that the show was about to begin. He hung up.

"On your left," said the guide, "is Dr. Harold Meyers, the man you've no doubt all read about in the papers." He peered into the darkened laboratory with puzzlement, and cleared his throat. The only illumination in the room came from a spark gap in one corner. A blue-white spark formed at the bottom of a metal "V," climbed sizzling to its top, and broke with a loud snap and began at the bottom again. In this unearthly light, Dr. Meyers sat at his desk with his chin on his folded arms, staring moodily at a vast and intricate system of flasks, condensers, beakers, burettes, retorts, fractionating columns, and glass tubing, which burbled and gasped ominously, and was filled with brilliantly colored fluids.

Eugene Bullard's great voice was silenced by the scene, and the customers' eyes, as they entered the laboratory on tiptoe, were filled with awe and reverence.

"Working on some new project, are you, Dr. Meyers," said the guide uncertainly.

Dr. Meyers did not reply, did not seem to notice his visitors. Instead, he picked up a beaker that had been filling with a green solution dripping from one end of the glass jungle, and poured it down the sink, shaking his head ruefully. He opened a notebook and, with his callers looking on sympathetically, he crossed out something, and closed the book with a snap. "Five hundred and twenty-eight times I've tried," he said aloud, in soliloquoy, "and five hundred and twenty-eight times I've failed."

Dr. Herpers's head appeared in the opening of the escape panel. "Harold, my boy, vot iss de madder?" he said, in thick Milwaukee English.

Dr. Meyers groaned. "It's no use, Dr. Herpers. Solution 528 failed, just as all the others before it. It's no use. The theory is correct—it's got to be correct! But again I've failed. I give up."

"No, no, my poy," said Herpers, crawling into the laboratory and putting his arm around Meyers's shoulder. "Dot's not like you. Qvit? Not Meyers!"

"The hours, the years of failures, trying to make Federal Apparatus's paint even better than it is."

"As I told you von you came to us, a mere poy," said Herpers, "you picked a hard assignment, making de company's produgts even bedder zen dey are. Dey are already de greadest on eardt."

Dr. Meyers looked at the ceiling. "It can be done—it's got to be done. That's the job of research: better products for more people at less cost." He ran his hands through his hair. "But I have failed."

Liz Dawson came into the room, brushing heedlessly past the rapt audience. "Harold," she said softly, "what makes you so white?"

"Solution fife hundredt and tvenny-eight failed, Liebehen," said Herpers.

"Oh, you poor man," said Liz. "Your life's work."

Dr. Herpers took a step backward to let Liz get to Meyers, and knocked a bottle of amber fluid into the sink. "Ach! Vot a clumsy fool!"

"What difference does it make?" asked Meyers tragically, and he brushed a beaker filled with red fluid into the sink, where it splintered. He covered his eyes.

"Wait!" said Liz. "Look!" The mixture in the sink was fizzing, giving off bluish smoke.

"*Mein Gott*! Vot iss?" said Herpers.

Exaltedly, the three crowded one another for a glimpse of the miracle in the sink.

"That's it!" cried Meyers. "We've found it!"

"De qvest is over!" said Herpers.

"What will we call it?" said Liz.

"Five hundred and twenty-nine," said Dr. Meyers in a faraway voice. "Solution 529!"

The three embraced one another, and headed for the door arm in arm. "We must tell Dr. Berry!" said Meyers, and the audience parted for them, flushed and speechless.

"Anodder first for de gumpany!" said Herpers.

◎ ◎ ◎

In the hallway, Drs. Meyers, Herpers, and Dawson hurried toward a soundproofed conference room, where they could release the triumphant laughter quaking in their chests.

"Bullard was almost purple with embarrassment!" whispered Liz Dawson.

"And he can't say we didn't sell, sell, sell," said Herpers.

"And that's that for the tours!" said Meyers joyfully.

"Wait!" boomed Eugene Bullard, and he and his entourage came trotting after them. "By God," he said, catching Meyers's hand and crushing it affectionately. "Congratulations! I knew our research was pretty good, but it took you to show me it was great!"

The co-discoverers of solution 529 looked down at the floor and held their peace with modesty bordering on complete paralysis.

"I feel like a godfather to solution 529," said a customer breathlessly.

"We all do," said Bullard. "What we just saw was more thrilling, more inspiring than the Grand Canyon! Frankly, a lot of this outfit looks like it's piddling away the time. But you, by golly—you're doing work with some real guts to it. And if I have anything to say about it, nobody's going to come to this laboratory without seeing what we just saw—*eggs-ackly* the way we saw it!"

The Band Director

Lucky for me, barbershops as well as doctors' and dentists' offices keep magazines for weeks after the issues are published, so I was able to come across Kurt Vonnegut's story "Ambitious Sophomore" in *the Saturday Evening Post* of May 1, 1954, a few weeks after I'd come home from college for summer vacation. While waiting for my haircut from Bill Isbell, an ace barber in Broad Ripple, the Indianapolis neighborhood where I grew up, I was leafing through the barbershop's magazines, and found a story that especially delighted me. It was about a high school band, and "the head of the music department and director of the band" was "George M. Helmholtz"—who seemed remarkably like Robert W. Schultz, the director of the band at Shortridge, where I had gone to high school, ten years after Vonnegut had graduated.

Both of us had been editors of the *Shortridge Daily Echo*, the first high school daily paper in the US. The barbershop where I read the *Post* was across the street from Vonnegut's Hardware, our local branch of the city's well-known hardware store, whose headquarters were downtown. Even after I got to know Kurt Vonnegut, it was many years before I realized that the family of "the seller of nails," as an earlier relative of Kurt described the business, was also the family of the author; hardware and writing didn't go together in my limited imagination.

Helmholtz is described as "a good, fat man" (more kindly, in "A Song for Selma," he is "portly" rather than "fat") and although Mr. Schultz was not really fat—he was just "large, a big man," not in girth but in height and overall stature, as a classmate of mine reminds me—Mr. Schultz reminded me of Kurt's Mr. Helmholtz in more important ways—his devotion to the band and the students, his desire to get the best out of even the most untalented musicians, his pride in the "Lincoln High School Ten Square Band" (as Mr. Schultz took rightful pride in our excellent

Shortridge Marching Band), and his temper if the rules of decorum were broken, especially if a student was ever treated disrespectfully. These admirable qualities were upheld and elaborated in all the Helmholtz stories.

Our Mr. Schultz, as well as being director of the band, was in charge of proceedings in our school auditorium, Caleb Mills Hall, where plays, talks, musicals, and variety shows were staged. My classmate Dick Lugar (destined to serve with distinction as a senator of Indiana) once played the role of the Bishop in a drama called *The Bishop's Candlesticks*. Lugar was burdened with delivering the stilted dialogue, which he did with appropriately stilted intonations. Giggles broke out in the student audience and spread throughout the auditorium until the actors could not be heard above the hilarity. Mr. Schultz came charging onto the stage and stopped the proceedings, berating us with such ferocity that all laughter was muted; not a giggle was heard again as the play proceeded to its final curtain. Fortunately, Mr. Shultz never roved with a flashlight through the darkened auditorium during "Noon Movies," when stifled sounds of passion sometimes emanated from the back rows of the co-ed student audience.

No such evidence of outlawed teenage lust is found in the Helmholtz stories (or anywhere, as far as I know, in the pages of the *Saturday Evening Post*, whose fiction was mostly in keeping with its Norman Rockwell covers of an idealized America). All but one of the four Helmholtz stories seems to come from a time of such innocence it might be best summed up by the assessment of Madelyn Pugh Davis, who was in the fiction club at Shortridge with Vonnegut, and later became head writer of the *I Love Lucy* show. Mrs. Davis later recalled for Kurt's friend Majie Failey (*We Never Danced Cheek to Cheek*) that when she and Vonnegut were in high school (Indiana in the 1940s) "it was really an 'Andy Hardy' existence. I think back on it now with absolute wonder."

The only student who didn't fit the "Andy Hardy" image in the Helmholtz stories appears in "The Kid Nobody Could Handle," which was published in the *Post* in September 1955. The movie version of *The Blackboard Jungle*, the Evan Hunter best-selling novel, opened in March that year and *Rebel Without a Cause*, starring James Dean, came out in October. Teenage rebellion was suddenly a hot topic.

Jim Donnini comes from a broken home on the South Side of Chicago, and after a stint in foster homes, transfers to Lincoln High. He has come to town to live with a relative ("His mother's dead. His old man married my sister—walked out on her.") Now the angry relative is "stuck . . . with him," and plans to "ride his tail till he straightens up and flies right or winds up in the can for life." Donnini wears a black leather jacket and black boots with chains that jangle, more like the kids in *The Blackboard Jungle* than Lincoln High School.

It's not an "Andy Hardy" world for the band director either in "The Kid Nobody Could Handle," when he realizes as the story opens that he's "been had" by an arrogant, greedy businessman, and lost out in selling a small piece of real estate, his only inheritance. Helmholtz is married in this story (he seems to have no wife in the others). In "Ambitious Sophomore," Helmholtz is a far less worldly character, who tells himself, "If love was blinding, obsessing, demanding, beyond reason, and all the other wild things people said it was, then he had never known it . . . He sighed, and supposed he was missing something, not knowing romance."

In his valiant effort to save the "The Kid" in the black boots and black jacket from a bleak, unfeeling future, Helmholtz offers his prized trumpet and the lure of music, but nothing can penetrate Donnini's angry apathy. Helmholtz becomes so frustrated he hammers his prized trumpet out of shape and bends it around a coat tree. "Life is no damn good," he says. We have never heard a line like that come out of the mouth of George Helmholtz—and we never will again.

The anger Helmholtz displays when he bends the prized trumpet finally penetrates the "bad boy's" sullen hostility, and Donnini is last seen with the repaired trumpet in the last chair of the last row of the "C Band," but we know he's on the way to salvation.

Kurt wrote with pride in *Fates Worse Than Death* that when he was growing up in Indianapolis "there was a fine symphony orchestra, and I took lessons from Ernst Michaelis, its first-chair clarinet." That brings to mind the "Band Director" story "The Boy Who Hated Girls," when Bert Higgins suddenly has trouble marching, and Helmholtz wonders if the boy has "had any injury, any sickness recently?" The boy says he hasn't had any such problems and says, "Maybe it's stopping my lessons with you." When Bert qualified for the band, "Helmholtz had turned him over to the best trumpet teacher in town, Larry Fink, for the final touches of grace and color." But after that happened, there was a "collapse of the boy's spirits and coordination."

I doubt the ensuing plot and the boy's return to his old form were something Vonnegut experienced—as critics and readers often love to assume in trying to match life with fiction—but rather I believe that Kurt's band experience provided him as an author with seeds for story ideas built around a high school band director.

In his autobiographical *Fates Worse Than Death*, Kurt writes that "when I took up the clarinet, [my father] declared this instrument, black studded with silver, to be a masterpiece." In another "Band" story, "The No-Talent Kid," the boy in the C Band who has little talent but a lot of moxie keeps challenging and failing to unseat the best clarinetist in the A Band. When he asks Helmholtz to have another crack at it, and the band director tries to discourage him, the confident boy says, "'You don't understand . . . You haven't noticed I have a new clarinet' . . . Plummer stroked the satin-black barrel of the instrument as though it were King Arthur's sword, giving magical powers to whoever possessed it. 'It's as good as Flammer's . . . Better, even.'"

Every kid who starts out, as I did, with a metal, silver clarinet, knows that the black wood instrument with the silver keys is for real pros—as last chair in the School No. 80 band, I knew, unlike Plummer, that even such a fine instrument would not give me greater musical talent, and I dropped out after two dispiriting years as last chair. Unlike the Plummer of the story, whose ambitions for a band letter are fulfilled by giving up the clarinet and pulling the gigantic bass drum, Vonnegut stuck with the clarinet. According to the high school yearbook of his senior year, Vonnegut listed with his more impressive accomplishments ("Student Council, '38, '40. President, Social Committee. Co-editor, Tuesday Echo,'40 . . .") that he had also made B Band.

His high school clarinet experience later provided a more satisfying moment. He reported in *Fates Worse Than Death* that "a few years ago, I wound up with Benny Goodman in somebody else's car after a party. I was able to tell him truthfully 'Mr. Goodman, I used to play a little licorice stick myself.'"

That was even better than making A Band.

—DW

The Kid Nobody Could Handle

IT WAS SEVEN-THIRTY in the morning. Waddling, clanking, muddy machines were tearing a hill to pieces behind a restaurant, and trucks were hauling the pieces away. Inside the restaurant, dishes rattled on their shelves. Tables quaked, and a very kind fat man with a headful of music looked down at the jiggling yolks of his breakfast eggs. His wife was visiting relatives out of town. He was on his own.

The kind fat man was George M. Helmholtz, a man of forty, head of the music department of Lincoln High School, and director of the band. Life had treated him well. Each year he dreamed the same big dream. He dreamed of leading as fine a band as there was on the face of the earth. And each year the dream came true.

It came true because Helmholtz was sure that a man couldn't have a better dream than his. Faced by this unnerving sureness, Kiwanians, Rotarians, and Lions paid for band uniforms that cost twice as much as their best suits, school administrators let Helmholtz raid the budget for expensive props, and youngsters played their hearts out for him. When youngsters had no talent, Helmholtz made them play on guts alone.

Everything was good about Helmholtz's life save his finances. He was so dazzled by his big dream that he was a child in the marketplace. Ten years before, he had sold the hill behind the restaurant to Bert Quinn, the restaurant owner, for one thousand dollars. It was now apparent, even to Helmholtz, that Helmholtz had been had.

Quinn sat down in the booth with the bandmaster. He was a bachelor, a small, dark, humorless man. He wasn't a well man. He couldn't sleep, he couldn't stop working, he couldn't smile warmly. He had only two moods: one suspicious and self-pitying, the other arrogant and boastful. The first mood applied when he was losing money. The second mood applied when he was making it.

Quinn was in the arrogant and boastful mood when he sat down with Helmholtz. He sucked whistlingly on a toothpick, and talked of vision—his own.

"I wonder how many eyes saw the hill before I did?" said Quinn. "Thousands and thousands, I'll bet—and not one saw what I saw. How many eyes?"

"Mine, at least," said Helmholtz. All the hill had meant to him was a panting climb, free blackberries, taxes, and a place for band picnics.

"You inherit the hill from your old man, and it's nothing but a pain in the neck to you," said Quinn. "So you figure you'll stick me with it."

"I didn't figure to stick you," Helmholtz protested. "The good Lord knows the price was more than fair."

"You say that now," said Quinn gleefully. "Sure, Helmholtz, you say that now. Now you see the shopping district's got to grow. Now you see what I saw."

"Yes," said Helmholtz. "Too late, too late." He looked around for some diversion, and saw a fifteen-year-old boy coming toward him, mopping the aisle between booths.

The boy was small but with tough, stringy muscles standing out on his neck and fore-arms. Childhood lingered in his features, but when he paused to rest, his fingers went hopefully to the silky beginnings of sideburns and a mustache. He mopped like a robot, jerkily, brainlessly, but took pains not to splash suds over the toes of his black boots.

"So what do I do when I get the hill?" said Quinn. "I tear it down, and it's like some-body pulled down a dam. All of a sudden everybody wants to build a store where the hill was."

"Um," said Helmholtz. He smiled genially at the boy. The boy looked through him without a twitch of recognition.

"We all got something," said Quinn. "You got music; I got vision." And he smiled, for it was perfectly clear to both where the money lay. "Think big!" said Quinn. "Dream big! That's what vision is. Keep your eyes wider open than anybody else's."

"That boy," said Helmholtz, "I've seen him around school, but I never knew his name."

Quinn laughed cheerlessly. "Billy the Kid? The storm trooper? Rudolph Valentino? Flash Gordon?" He called the boy. . . . "Hey, Jim! Come here a minute."

Helmholtz was appalled to see that the boy's eyes were as expressionless as oysters.

"This is my brother-in-law's kid by another marriage—before he married my sister," said Quinn. "His name's Jim Donnini, and he's from the south side of Chi-cago, and he's very tough."

Jim Donnini's hands tightened on the mop handle.

"How do you do?" said Helmholtz.

"Hi," said Jim emptily.

"He's living with me now," said Quinn. "He's my baby now."

"You want a lift to school, Jim?"

"Yeah, he wants a lift to school," said Quinn. "See what you make of him. He won't talk to me." He turned to Jim. "Go on, kid, wash up and shave."

Robotlike, Jim marched away.

"Where are his parents?"

"His mother's dead. His old man married my sister, walked out on her, and stuck her with him. Then the court didn't like the way she was raising him, and put him in foster homes for a while. Then they decided to get him clear out of Chicago, so they stuck me with him." He shook his head. "Life's a funny thing, Helmholtz."

"Not very funny, sometimes," said Helmholtz. He pushed his eggs away.

"Like some whole new race of people coming up," said Quinn wonderingly. "Nothing like the kids we got around here. Those boots, the black jacket—and he won't talk. He won't run around with the other kids. Won't study. I don't think he can even read and write very good."

"Does he like music at all? Or drawing? Or animals?" said Helmholtz. "Does he collect anything?"

"You know what he likes?" said Quinn. "He likes to polish those boots—get off by himself and polish those boots. And when he's really in heaven is when he can get off by himself, spread comic books all around him on the floor, polish his boots, and watch television." He smiled ruefully. "Yeah, he had a collection too. And I took it away from him and threw it in the river."

"Threw it in the river?" said Helmholtz.

"Yeah," said Quinn. "Eight knives—some with blades as long as your hand."

Helmholtz paled. "Oh." A prickling sensation spread over the back of his neck. "This is a new problem at Lincoln High. I hardly know what to think about it." He swept spilled salt together in a neat little pile, just as he would have liked to sweep together his scattered thoughts. "It's a kind of sickness, isn't it? That's the way to look at it?"

"Sick?" said Quinn. He slapped the table. "You can say that again!" He tapped his chest. "And Doctor Quinn is just the man to give him what's good for what ails him."

"What's that?" said Helmholtz.

"No more talk about the poor little sick boy," said Quinn grimly. "That's all he's heard from the social workers and the juvenile court, and God knows who all. From now on, he's the no-good bum of a man. I'll ride his tail till he straightens up and flies right or winds up in the can for life. One way or the other."

"I see," said Helmholtz.

◙ ◙ ◙

"Like listening to music?" said Helmholtz to Jim brightly, as they rode to school in Helmholtz's car.

Jim said nothing. He was stroking his mustache and sideburns, which he had not shaved off.

"Ever drum with the fingers or keep time with your feet?" said Helmholtz. He had noticed that Jim's boots were decorated with chains that had no function but to jingle as he walked.

Jim sighed with ennui.

"Or whistle?" said Helmholtz. "If you do any of those things, it's just like picking up the keys to a whole new world—a world as beautiful as any world can be."

Jim gave a soft Bronx cheer.

"There!" said Helmholtz. "You've illustrated the basic principle of the family of brass wind instruments. The glorious voice of every one of them starts with a buzz on the lips."

The seat springs of Helmholtz's old car creaked under Jim, as Jim shifted his weight. Helmholtz took this as a sign of interest, and he turned to smile in comradely fashion. But Jim had shifted his weight in order to get a cigarette from inside his tight leather jacket.

Helmholtz was too upset to comment at once. It was only at the end of the ride, as he turned into the teachers' parking lot, that he thought of something to say.

"Sometimes," said Helmholtz, "I get so lonely and disgusted, I don't see how I can stand it. I feel like doing all kinds of crazy things, just for the heck of it—things that might even be bad for me."

Jim blew a smoke ring expertly.

"And then!" said Helmholtz. He snapped his fingers and honked his horn. "And then, Jim, I remember I've got at least one tiny corner of the universe I can make just the way I want it! I can go to it and gloat over it until I'm brand-new and happy again."

"Aren't you the lucky one?" said Jim. He yawned.

"I am, for a fact," said Helmholtz. "My corner of the universe happens to be the air around my band. I can fill it with music. Mr. Beeler, in zoology, has his butterflies. Mr. Trottman, in physics, has his pendulum and tuning forks. Making sure everybody has a corner like that is about the biggest job we teachers have. I—"

The car door opened and slammed, and Jim was gone. Helmholtz stamped out Jim's cigarette and buried it under the gravel of the parking lot.

◎ ◎ ◎

Helmholtz's first class of the morning was C Band, where beginners thumped and wheezed and tooted as best they could, and looked down the long, long, long road through B Band to A Band, the Lincoln High School Ten Square Band, the finest band in the world.

Helmholtz stepped onto the podium and raised his baton. "You are better than you think," he said. "A-one, a-two, a-three." Down came the baton.

C Band set out in its quest for beauty—set out like a rusty switch engine, with valves stuck, pipes clogged, unions leaking, bearings dry.

Helmholtz was still smiling at the end of the hour, because he'd heard in his mind the music as it was going to be someday. His throat was raw, for he had been singing with the band for the whole hour. He stepped into the hall for a drink from the fountain.

As he drank, he heard the jingling of chains. He looked up at Jim Donnini. Rivers of students flowed between classrooms, pausing in friendly eddies, flowing on again. Jim was alone. When he paused, it wasn't to greet anyone, but to polish the toes of his boots on his trousers legs. He had the air of a spy in a melodrama, missing nothing, liking nothing, looking forward to the great day when everything would be turned upside down.

"Hello, Jim," said Helmholtz. "Say, I was just thinking about you. We've got a lot of clubs and teams that meet after school. And that's a good way to get to know a lot of people."

Jim measured Helmholtz carefully with his eyes. "Maybe I don't want to know a lot of people," he said. "Ever think of that?" He set his feet down hard to make his chains jingle as he walked away.

When Helmholtz returned to the podium for a rehearsal of B Band, there was a note waiting for him, calling him to a special faculty meeting.

The meeting was about vandalism.

Someone had broken into the school and wrecked the office of Mr. Crane, head of the English Department. The poor man's treasures—books, diplomas, snapshots of England, the beginnings of eleven novels—had been ripped and crumpled, mixed, dumped and trampled, and drenched with ink.

Helmholtz was sickened. He couldn't believe it. He couldn't bring himself to think about it. It didn't become real to him until late that night, in a dream. In the dream Helmholtz saw a boy with barracuda teeth, with claws like baling hooks. The monster climbed into a window of the high school and dropped to the floor of the band rehearsal room. The monster clawed to shreds the heads of the biggest drum in the state. Helmholtz woke up howling. There was nothing to do but dress and go to the school.

◎ ◎ ◎

At two in the morning, Helmholtz caressed the drum heads in the band rehearsal room, with the night watchman looking on. He rolled the drum back and forth on its cart, and he turned the light inside on and off, on and off. The drum was unharmed. The night watchman left to make his rounds.

The band's treasure house was safe. With the contentment of a miser counting his money, Helmholtz fondled the rest of the instruments, one by one. And then he began to polish the sousaphones. As he polished, he could hear the great horns roaring, could see them flashing in the sunlight, with the Stars and Stripes and the banner of Lincoln High going before.

"Yump-yump, tiddle-tiddle, yump-yump, tiddle-tiddle!" sang Helmholtz happily. "Yump-yump-yump, ra-a-a-a-a, yump-yump, yump-yump—boom!"

As he paused to choose the next number for his imaginary band to play, he heard a furtive noise in the chemistry laboratory next door. Helmholtz sneaked into the hall, jerked open the laboratory door, and flashed on the lights. Jim Donnini had a bottle of acid in either hand. He was splashing acid over the periodic table of the elements, over the blackboards covered with formulas, over the bust of Lavoisier. The scene was the most repulsive thing Helmholtz could have looked upon.

Jim smiled with thin bravado.

"Get out," said Helmholtz.

"What're you gonna do?" said Jim.

"Clean up. Save what I can," said Helmholtz dazedly. He picked up a wad of cotton waste and began wiping up the acid.

"You gonna call the cops?" said Jim.

"I—I don't know," said Helmholtz. "No thoughts come. If I'd caught you hurting the bass drum, I think I would have killed you with a single blow. But I wouldn't have had any intelligent thoughts about what you were—what you thought you were doing."

"It's about time this place got set on its ear," said Jim.

"Is it?" said Helmholtz. "That must be so, if one of our students wants to murder it."

"What good is it?" said Jim.

"Not much good, I guess," said Helmholtz. "It's just the best thing human beings ever managed to do." He was helpless, talking to himself. He had a bag of tricks for making boys behave like men—tricks that played on boyish fears and dreams and loves. But here was a boy without fear, without dreams, without love.

"If you smashed up all the schools," said Helmholtz, "we wouldn't have any hope left."

"What hope?" said Jim.

"The hope that everybody will be glad he's alive," said Helmholtz. "Even you."

"That's a laugh," said Jim. "All I ever got out of this dump was a hard time. So what're you gonna do?"

"I have to do something, don't I?" said Helmholtz.

"I don't care what you do," said Jim.

"I know," said Helmholtz. "I know." He marched Jim into his tiny office off the band rehearsal room. He dialed the telephone number of the principal's home. Numbly, he waited for the bell to get the old man from his bed.

Jim dusted his boots with a rag.

Helmholtz suddenly dropped the telephone into its cradle before the principal could answer. "Isn't there anything you care about but ripping, hacking, bending, rending, smashing, bashing?" he cried. "Anything? Anything but those boots?"

"Go on! Call up whoever you're gonna call," said Jim.

Helmholtz opened a locker and took a trumpet from it. He thrust the trumpet into Jim's arms. "There!" he said, puffing with emotion. "There's my treasure. It's the dearest thing I own. I give it to you to smash. I won't move a muscle to stop you. You can have the added pleasure of watching my heart break while you do it."

Jim looked at him oddly. He laid down the trumpet.

"Go on!" said Helmholtz. "If the world has treated you so badly, it deserves to have the trumpet smashed!"

"I—" said Jim. Helmholtz grabbed his belt, put a foot behind him, and dumped him on the floor.

Helmholtz pulled Jim's boots off and threw them into a corner. "There!" said Helmholtz savagely. He jerked the boy to his feet again and thrust the trumpet into his arms once more.

Jim Donnini was barefoot now. He had lost his socks with his boots. The boy looked down. The feet that had once seemed big black clubs were narrow as chicken wings now—bony and blue, and not quite clean.

The boy shivered, then quaked. Each quake seemed to shake something loose inside, until, at last, there was no boy left. No boy at all. Jim's head lolled, as though he waited only for death.

Helmholtz was overwhelmed by remorse. He threw his arms around the boy. "Jim! Jim—listen to me, boy!"

Jim stopped quaking.

"You know what you've got there—the trumpet?" said Helmholtz. "You know what's special about it?"

Jim only sighed.

"It belonged to John Philip Sousa!" said Helmholtz. He rocked and shook Jim gently, trying to bring him back to life. "I'll trade it to you, Jim—for your boots. It's yours, Jim! John Philip Sousa's trumpet is yours! It's worth hundreds of dollars, Jim—thousands!"

Jim laid his head on Helmholtz's breast.

"It's better than boots, Jim," said Helmholtz. "You can learn to play it. You're somebody, Jim. You're the boy with John Philip Sousa's trumpet!"

Helmholtz released Jim slowly, sure the boy would topple. Jim didn't fall. He stood alone. The trumpet was still in his arms.

"I'll take you home, Jim," said Helmholtz. "Be a good boy and I won't say a word about tonight. Polish your trumpet, and learn to be a good boy."

"Can I have my boots?" said Jim dully.

"No," said Helmholtz. "I don't think they're good for you."

He drove Jim home. He opened the car windows and the air seemed to refresh the boy. He let him out at Quinn's restaurant. The soft pats of Jim's bare feet on the sidewalk echoed down the empty street. He climbed through a window, and into his bedroom behind the kitchen. And all was still.

◙ ◙ ◙

The next morning the waddling, clanking, muddy machines were making the vision of Bert Quinn come true. They were smoothing off the place where the hill had been behind the restaurant. They were making it as level as a billiard table.

Helmholtz sat in a booth again. Quinn joined him again. Jim mopped again. Jim kept his eyes down, refusing to notice Helmholtz. And he didn't seem to care when a surf of suds broke over the toes of his small and narrow brown Oxfords.

"Eating out two mornings in a row?" said Quinn. "Something wrong at home?"

"My wife's still out of town," said Helmholtz.

"While the cat's away—" said Quinn. He winked.

"When the cat's away," said Helmholtz, "this mouse gets lonesome."

Quinn leaned forward. "Is that what got you out of bed in the middle of the night, Helmholtz? Loneliness?" He jerked his head at Jim. "Kid! Go get Mr. Helmholtz his horn."

Jim raised his head, and Helmholtz saw that his eyes were oysterlike again. He marched away to get the trumpet.

Quinn now showed that he was excited and angry. "You take away his boots and give him a horn, and I'm not supposed to get curious?" he said. "I'm not supposed to start asking questions? I'm not supposed to find out you caught him taking the school apart? You'd make a lousy crook, Helmholtz. You'd leave your baton, sheet music, and your driver's license at the scene of the crime."

"I don't think about hiding clues," said Helmholtz. "I just do what I do. I was going to tell you."

Quinn's feet danced and his shoes squeaked like mice. "Yes?" he said. "Well, I've got some news for you too."

"What is that?" said Helmholtz uneasily.

"It's all over with Jim and me," said Quinn. "Last night was the payoff. I'm sending him back where he came from."

"To another string of foster homes?" said Helmholtz weakly.

"Whatever the experts figure out to do with a kid like that." Quinn sat back, exhaled noisily, and went limp with relief.

"You can't," said Helmholtz.

"I can," said Quinn.

"That will be the end of him," said Helmholtz. "He can't stand to be thrown away like that one more time."

"He can't feel anything," said Quinn. "I can't help him; I can't hurt him. Nobody can. There isn't a nerve in him."

"A bundle of scar tissue," said Helmholtz.

The bundle of scar tissue returned with the trumpet. Impassively, he laid it on the table in front of Helmholtz.

Helmholtz forced a smile. "It's yours, Jim," he said. "I gave it to you."

"Take it while you got the chance, Helmholtz," said Quinn. "He doesn't want it. All he'll do is swap it for a knife or a pack of cigarettes."

"He doesn't know what it is, yet," said Helmholtz. "It takes a while to find out."

"Is it any good?" said Quinn.

"Any good?" said Helmholtz, not believing his ears. "Any good?" He didn't see how anyone could look at the instrument and not be warmed and dazzled by it. "Any good?" he murmured. "It belonged to John Philip Sousa."

Quinn blinked stupidly. "Who?"

Helmholtz's hands fluttered on the table top like the wings of a dying bird. "Who was John Philip Sousa?" he piped. No more words came. The subject was too big for a tired man to cover. The dying bird expired and lay still.

After a long silence, Helmholtz picked up the trumpet. He kissed the cold mouthpiece and pumped the valves in a dream of a brilliant cadenza. Over the bell of the instrument, Helmholtz saw Jim Donnini's face, seemingly floating in space—all but deaf and blind. Now Helmholtz saw the futility of men and their treasures. He had thought that his greatest treasure, the trumpet, could buy a soul for Jim. The trumpet was worthless.

Deliberately, Helmholtz hammered the trumpet against the table edge. He bent it around a coat tree. He handed the wreck to Quinn.

"Ya busted it," said Quinn, amazed. "Why'dja do that? What's that prove?"

"I—I don't know," said Helmholtz. A terrible blasphemy rumbled deep in him, like the warning of a volcano. And then, irresistibly, out it came. "Life is no damn good," said Helmholtz. His face twisted as he fought back tears and shame.

Helmholtz, the mountain that walked like a man, was falling apart. Jim Donnini's eyes filled with pity and alarm. They came alive. They became human. Helmholtz had got a message through. Quinn looked at Jim, and something like hope flickered for the first time in his bitterly lonely old face.

◎ ◎ ◎

Two weeks later, a new semester began at Lincoln High.

In the band rehearsal room, the members of C Band were waiting for their leader—were waiting for their destinies as musicians to unfold.

Helmholtz stepped onto the podium, and rattled his baton against his music stand. "The Voices of Spring," he said. "Everybody hear that? The Voices of Spring?"

There were rustling sounds as the musicians put the music on their stands. In the pregnant silence that followed their readiness, Helmholtz glanced at Jim Donnini, who sat on the last seat of the worst trumpet section of the worst band in school.

His trumpet, John Philip Sousa's trumpet, George M. Helmholtz's trumpet, had been repaired.

"Think of it this way," said Helmholtz. "Our aim is to make the world more beautiful than it was when we came into it. It can be done. You can do it."

A small cry of despair came from Jim Donnini. It was meant to be private, but it pierced every ear with its poignancy.

"How?" said Jim.

"Love yourself," said Helmholtz, "and make your instrument sing about it. A-one, a-two, a-three." Down came his baton.

The No-Talent Kid

IT WAS AUTUMN, and the leaves outside Lincoln High School were turning the same rusty color as the bare brick walls in the band rehearsal room. George M. Helmholtz, head of the music department and director of the band, was ringed by folding chairs and instrument cases, and on each chair sat a very young man, nervously prepared to blow through something or, in the case of the percussion section, to hit something, the instant Mr. Helmholtz lowered his white baton.

Mr. Helmholtz, a man of forty, who believed that his great belly was a sign of health, strength, and dignity, smiled angelically, as though he were about to release the most exquisite sounds ever heard by human beings. Down came his baton.

Blooooomp! went the big sousaphones.

Blat! Blat! echoed the French horns, and the plodding, shrieking, querulous waltz was begun.

Mr. Helmholtz's expression did not change as the brasses lost their places, as the woodwinds' nerve failed and they became inaudible rather than have their mistakes heard, while the percussion section sounded like the Battle of Gettysburg.

"A-a-a-a-ta-ta, a-a-a-a-a-a, ta-ta-ta-ta!" In a loud tenor, Mr. Helmholtz sang the first-cornet part when the first cornetist, florid and perspiring, gave up and slouched in his chair, his instrument in his lap.

"Saxophones, let me hear you," called Mr. Helmholtz. "Good!"

This was the C Band, and for the C Band, the performance was good. It couldn't have been more polished for the fifth session of the school year. Most of the youngsters were just starting out as bandsmen, and in the years ahead of them they would acquire artistry enough to move into the B Band, which met the next hour. And finally the best of them would gain positions in the pride of the city, the Lincoln High School Ten Square Band.

The football team lost half its games and the basketball team lost two-thirds of theirs, but the band, in the ten years Mr. Helmholtz had been running it, had been second to none until the past June. It had been the first in the state to use flag twirlers, the first to use choral as well as instrumental numbers, the first to use triple-tonguing extensively, the first to march in breathtaking double time, the first to put a light in its bass drum. Lincoln High School awarded letter sweaters to the

816

members of the A Band, and the sweaters were deeply respected, and properly so. The band had won every statewide high school band competition for ten years—save the showdown in June.

While members of the C Band dropped out of the waltz, one by one, as though mustard gas were coming out of the ventilation, Mr. Helmholtz continued to smile and wave his baton for the survivors, and to brood inwardly over the defeat his band had sustained in June, when Johnstown High School had won with a secret weapon, a bass drum seven feet in diameter. The judges, who were not musicians but politicians, had had eyes and ears for nothing but this Eighth Wonder of the World, and since then Mr. Helmholtz had thought of little else. But the school budget was already lopsided with band expenses. When the school board had given him the last special appropriation he'd begged so desperately—money to wire the plumes of the bandsmen's hats with flashlight bulbs and batteries for night games—the board had made him swear like a habitual drunkard that, so help him God, this was the last time.

Only two members of the C Band were playing now, a clarinetist and a snare drummer, both playing loudly, proudly, confidently, and all wrong. Mr. Helmholtz, coming out of his wistful dream of a bass drum bigger than the one that had beaten him, administered the coup de grâce to the waltz by clattering his stick against his music stand. "All righty, all righty," he said cheerily, and he nodded his congratulations to the two who had persevered to the bitter end.

Walter Plummer, the clarinetist, responded gravely, like a concert soloist receiving an ovation led by the director of a symphony orchestra. He was small, but with a thick chest developed in summers spent at the bottom of swimming pools, and he could hold a note longer than anyone in the A Band, much longer, but that was all he could do. He drew back his tired, reddened lips, showing the two large front teeth that gave him the look of a squirrel, adjusted his reed, limbered his fingers, and awaited the next challenge to his virtuosity.

This would be Plummer's third year in the C Band, Mr. Helmholtz thought, with a mixture of pity and fear. Nothing could shake Plummer's determination to earn the right to wear one of the sacred letters of the A Band, so far, terribly far away.

Mr. Helmholtz had tried to tell Plummer how misplaced his ambitions were, to recommend other fields for his great lungs and enthusiasm, where pitch would be unimportant. But Plummer was in love, not with music, but with the letter sweaters. Being as tone-deaf as boiled cabbage, he could detect nothing in his own playing about which to be discouraged.

"Remember," said Mr. Helmholtz to the C Band, "Friday is challenge day, so be on your toes. The chairs you have now were assigned arbitrarily. On challenge day it'll be up to you to prove which chair you really deserve." He avoided the narrowed, confident eyes of Plummer, who had taken the first clarinetist's chair without consulting the seating plan posted on the bulletin board. Challenge day occurred every two weeks, and on that day any bandsman could challenge anyone ahead of him to a contest for his position, with Mr. Helmholtz as judge.

Plummer's hand was raised, its fingers snapping.

"Yes, Plummer?" said Mr. Helmholtz. He had come to dread challenge day because of Plummer. He had come to think of it as Plummer's day. Plummer never challenged anybody in the C Band or even the B Band, but stormed the organization at the very top, challenging, as was unfortunately the privilege of all, only members of the A Band. The waste of the A Band's time was troubling enough, but infinitely more painful for Mr. Helmholtz were Plummer's looks of stunned disbelief when he heard Mr. Helmholtz's decision that he hadn't out-played the men he'd challenged.

"Mr. Helmholtz," said Plummer, "I'd like to come to A Band session that day."

"All right—if you feel up to it." Plummer always felt up to it, and it would have been more of a surprise if Plummer had announced that he wouldn't be at the A Band session.

"I'd like to challenge Flammer."

The rustling of sheet music and clicking of instrument case latches stopped. Flammer was the first clarinetist in the A Band, a genius whom not even members of the A Band would have had the gall to challenge.

Mr. Helmholtz cleared his throat. "I admire your spirit, Plummer, but isn't that rather ambitious for the first of the year? Perhaps you should start out with, say, challenging Ed Delaney." Delaney held down the last chair in the B Band.

"You don't understand," said Plummer. "You haven't noticed I have a new clarinet."

"Hmm? Oh—well, so you do."

Plummer stroked the satin-black barrel of the instrument as though it were King Arthur's sword, giving magical powers to whoever possessed it. "It's as good as Flam-mer's," said Plummer. "Better, even."

There was a warning in his voice, telling Mr. Helmholtz that the days of discrimi-nation were over, that nobody in his right mind would dare to hold back a man with an instrument like this.

"Um," said Mr. Helmholtz. "Well, we'll see, we'll see."

After practice, he was forced into close quarters with Plummer again in the crowded hallway. Plummer was talking darkly to a wide-eyed freshman bandsman.

"Know why the band lost to Johnstown High last June?" asked Plummer, seem-ingly ignorant of the fact that he was back-to-back with Mr. Helmholtz. "Because they stopped running the band on the merit system. Keep your eyes open on Friday."

Mr. George M. Helmholtz lived in a world of music, and even the throbbing of his headache came to him musically, if painfully, as the deep-throated boom of a bass drum seven feet in diameter. It was late afternoon on the first challenge day of the new school year. He was sitting in his living room, his eyes covered, awaiting another sort of thump—the impact of the evening paper, hurled against the clapboards of the front of the house by Walter Plummer, the delivery boy.

As Mr. Helmholtz was telling himself that he would rather not have his newspaper on challenge day, since Plummer came with it, the paper was delivered with a crash.

"Plummer!" he cried.

"Yes, sir?" said Plummer from the sidewalk.

Mr. Helmholtz shuffled to the door in his carpet slippers. "Please, my boy," he said, "can't we be friends?"

"Sure—why not?" said Plummer. "Let bygones be bygones, is what I say." He gave a bitter imitation of an amiable chuckle. "Water over the dam. It's been two hours now since you stuck the knife in me."

Mr. Helmholtz sighed. "Have you got a moment? It's time we had a talk, my boy."

Plummer hid his papers under the shrubbery, and walked in. Mr. Helmholtz gestured at the most comfortable chair in the room, the one in which he'd been sitting. Plummer chose to sit on the edge of a hard one with a straight back instead.

"My boy," said the bandmaster, "God made all kinds of people: some who can run fast, some who can write wonderful stories, some who can paint pictures, some who can sell anything, some who can make beautiful music. But He didn't make anybody who could do everything well. Part of the growing-up process is finding out what we can do well and what we can't do well." He patted Plummer's shoulder. "The last part, finding out what we can't do, is what hurts most about growing up. But everybody has to face it, and then go in search of his true self."

Plummer's head was sinking lower and lower on his chest, and Mr. Helmholtz hastily pointed out a silver lining. "For instance, Flammer could never run a business like a paper route, keeping records, getting new customers. He hasn't that kind of a mind, and couldn't do that sort of thing if his life depended on it."

"You've got a point," said Plummer with unexpected brightness. "A guy's got to be awful one-sided to be as good at one thing as Flammer is. I think it's more worthwhile to try to be better rounded. No, Flammer beat me fair and square today, and I don't want you to think I'm a bad sport about that. It isn't that that gets me."

"That's mature of you," said Mr. Helmholtz. "But what I was trying to point out to you was that we've all got weak points, and—"

Plummer waved him to silence. "You don't have to explain to me, Mr. Helmholtz. With a job as big as you've got, it'd be a miracle if you did the whole thing right."

"Now, hold on, Plummer!" said Mr. Helmholtz.

"All I'm asking is that you look at it from my point of view," said Plummer. "No sooner'd I come back from challenging A Band material, no sooner'd I come back from playing my heart out, than you turned those C Band kids loose on me. You and I know we were just giving 'em the feel of challenge days, and that I was all played out. But did you tell them that? Heck, no, you didn't, Mr. Helmholtz, and those kids all think they can play better than me. That's all I'm sore about, Mr. Helmholtz. They think it means something, me in the last chair of the C Band."

"Plummer," said Mr. Helmholtz, "I have been trying to tell you something as kindly as possible, but the only way to get it across to you is to tell it to you straight."

"Go ahead and quash criticism," said Plummer, standing.

"Quash?"

"Quash," said Plummer with finality. He headed for the door. "I'm probably ruining my chances for getting into the A Band by speaking out like this, Mr. Helmholtz, but frankly, it's incidents like what happened to me today that lost you the band competition last June."

"It was a seven-foot bass drum!"

"Well, get one for Lincoln High and see how you make out then."

"I'd give my right arm for one!" said Mr. Helmholtz, forgetting the point at issue and remembering his all-consuming dream.

Plummer paused on the threshold. "One like the Knights of Kandahar use in their parades?"

"That's the ticket!" Mr. Helmholtz imagined the Knights of Kandahar's huge drum, the showpiece of every local parade. He tried to think of it with the Lincoln High School black panther painted on it. "Yes, sir!" When the bandmaster returned to earth, Plummer was astride his bicycle.

Mr. Helmholtz started to shout after Plummer, to bring him back and tell him bluntly that he didn't have the remotest chance of getting out of C Band ever, that he would never be able to understand that the mission of a band wasn't simply to make noises but to make special kinds of noises. But Plummer was off and away.

Temporarily relieved until next challenge day, Mr. Helmholtz sat down to enjoy his paper, to read that the treasurer of the Knights of Kandahar, a respected citizen, had disappeared with the organization's funds, leaving behind and unpaid the Knights' bills for the past year and a half. "We'll pay a hundred cents on the dollar, if we have to sell everything but the Sacred Mace," the Sublime Chamberlain of the Inner Shrine had said.

Mr. Helmholtz didn't know any of the people involved, and he yawned and turned to the funnies. He gasped, turned to the front page again. He looked up a number in the phone book and dialed.

"Zum-zum-zum-zum," went the busy signal in his ear. He dropped the telephone into its cradle. Hundreds of people, he thought, must be trying to get in touch with the Sublime Chamberlain of the Inner Shrine of the Knights of Kandahar at this moment. He looked up at his flaking ceiling in prayer. But none of them, he prayed, was after a bargain in a cart-borne bass drum.

He dialed again and again, and always got the busy signal. He walked out on his porch to relieve some of the tension building up in him. He would be the only one bidding on the drum, he told himself, and he could name his price. Good Lord! If he offered fifty dollars for it, he could probably have it! He'd put up his own money, and get the school to pay him back in three years, when the plumes with the electric lights in them were paid for in full.

He was laughing like a department store Santa Claus, when his gaze dropped from heaven to his lawn and he espied Plummer's undelivered newspapers lying beneath the shrubbery.

He went inside and called the Sublime Chamberlain again, with the same results. He then called Plummer's home to let him know where the papers were mislaid. But that line was busy, too.

He dialed alternately the Plummers' number and the Sublime Chamberlain's number for fifteen minutes before getting a ringing signal.

"Yes?" said Mrs. Plummer.

"This is Mr. Helmholtz, Mrs. Plummer. Is Walter there?"

"He was here a minute ago, telephoning, but he just went out of here like a shot."

"Looking for his papers? He left them under my spirea."

"He did? Heavens, I have no idea where he was going. He didn't say anything about his papers, but I thought I overheard something about selling his clarinet." She sighed, and then laughed. "Having money of their own makes them awfully independent. He never tells me anything."

"Well, you tell him I think maybe it's for the best, his selling his clarinet. And tell him where his papers are."

It was unexpected good news that Plummer had at last seen the light about his musical career. The bandmaster now called the Sublime Chamberlain's home again for more good news. He got through this time, but was disappointed to learn that the man had just left on some sort of lodge business.

For years, Mr. Helmholtz had managed to smile and keep his wits about him in C Band practice sessions. But on the day after his fruitless efforts to find out anything about the Knights of Kandahar's bass drum, his defenses were down, and the poisonous music penetrated to the roots of his soul.

"No, no, no!" he cried in pain. He threw his white baton against the brick wall. The springy stick bounded off the bricks and fell into an empty folding chair at the rear of the clarinet section—Plummer's empty chair.

As Mr. Helmholtz retrieved the baton, he found himself unexpectedly moved by the symbol of the empty chair. No one else, he realized, no matter how untalented, could fill the last chair in the organization as well as Plummer had. Mr. Helmholtz looked up to find many of the bandsmen contemplating the chair with him, as though they, too, sensed that something great, in a fantastic way, had disappeared, and that life would be a good bit duller on account of that.

During the ten minutes between the C Band and B Band sessions, Mr. Helmholtz hurried to his office and again tried to get in touch with the Sublime Chamberlain of the Knights of Kandahar. No luck! "Lord knows where he's off to now," Mr. Helmholtz was told. "He was in for just a second, but went right out again. I gave him your name, so I expect he'll call you when he gets a minute. You're the drum gentleman, aren't you?"

"That's right—the drum gentleman."

The buzzers in the hall were sounding, marking the beginning of another class period. Mr. Helmholtz wanted to stay by the phone until he'd caught the Sublime Chamberlain and closed the deal, but the B Band was waiting—and after that it would be the A Band.

An inspiration came to him. He called Western Union and sent a telegram to the man, offering fifty dollars for the drum and requesting a reply collect.

But no reply came during B Band practice. Nor had one come by the halfway point of the A Band session. The bandsmen, a sensitive, high-strung lot, knew immediately that their director was on edge about something, and the rehearsal went badly. Mr. Helmholtz stopped a march in the middle because somebody outside was shaking the large double doors at one end of the rehearsal room.

"All right, all right, let's wait until the racket dies down so we can hear ourselves," Mr. Helmholtz said.

At that moment, a student messenger handed him a telegram. Mr. Helmholtz tore open the envelope, and this is what he read:

> DRUM SOLD STOP COULD YOU USE A STUFFED
> CAMEL ON WHEELS STOP

The wooden doors opened with a shriek of rusty hinges. A snappy autumn gust showered the band with leaves. Plummer stood in the great opening, winded and perspiring, harnessed to a drum as big as a harvest moon!

"I know this isn't challenge day," said Plummer, "but I thought you might make an exception in my case."

He walked in with splendid dignity, the huge apparatus grumbling along behind him.

Mr. Helmholtz rushed to meet him. He crushed Plummer's right hand between both of his. "Plummer, boy! You got it for us. Good boy! I'll pay you whatever you paid for it," he cried, and in his joy he added rashly, "And a nice little profit besides. Good boy!"

"Sell it?" said Plummer. "I'll give it to you when I graduate. All I want to do is play it in the A Band as long as I'm here."

"But Plummer," said Mr. Helmholtz, "you don't know anything about drums."

"I'll practice hard," said Plummer. He backed his instrument into an aisle between the tubas and the trombones, toward the percussion section, where the amazed musicians were hastily making room.

"Now, just a minute," said Mr. Helmholtz, chuckling as though Plummer were joking, and knowing full well he wasn't. "There's more to drum playing than just lambasting the thing whenever you take a notion to, you know. It takes years to be a drummer."

"Well," said Plummer, "the quicker I get at it, the quicker I'll get good."

"What I meant was that I'm afraid you won't be quite ready for the A Band for a little while."

Plummer stopped his backing. "How long?" he asked.

"Oh, sometime in your senior year, perhaps. Meanwhile, you could let the band have your drum to use until you're ready."

Mr. Helmholtz's skin began to itch all over as Plummer stared at him coldly. "Until hell freezes over?" Plummer said at last.

Mr. Helmholtz sighed. "I'm afraid that's about right." He shook his head. "It's what I tried to tell you yesterday afternoon: Nobody can do everything well, and we've all got to face up to our limitations. You're a fine boy, Plummer, but you'll never be a musician—not in a million years. The only thing to do is what we all have to do now and then: smile, shrug, and say, 'Well, that's just one of those things that's not for me.'"

Tears formed on the rims of Plummer's eyes. He walked slowly toward the doorway, with the drum tagging after him. He paused on the doorsill for one more wistful look at the A Band that would never have a chair for him. He smiled feebly and shrugged. "Some people have eight-foot drums," he said, "and others don't, and that's just the way life is. You're a fine man, Mr. Helmholtz, but you'll never get this drum in a million years, because I'm going to give it to my mother for a coffee table."

"Plummer!" cried Mr. Helmholtz. His plaintive voice was drowned out by the rumble and rattle of the big drum as it followed its small master down the school's concrete driveway.

Mr. Helmholtz ran after him. Plummer and his drum had stopped at an intersection to wait for a light to change. Mr. Helmholtz caught him there and seized his arm. "We've got to have that drum," he panted. "How much do you want?"

"Smile," said Plummer. "Shrug! That's what I did." Plummer did it again. "See? So I can't get into the A Band, so you can't have the drum. Who cares? All part of the growing-up process."

"The situations aren't the same!" said Mr. Helmholtz. "Not at all the same!"

"You're right," said Plummer. "I'm growing up, and you're not."

The light changed, and Plummer left Mr. Helmholtz on the corner, stunned.

Mr. Helmholtz had to run after him again. "Plummer," he wheedled, "you'll never be able to play it well."

"Rub it in," said Plummer.

"But look at what a swell job you're doing of pulling it," said Mr. Helmholtz.

"Rub it in," Plummer repeated.

"No, no, no," said Mr. Helmholtz. "Not at all. If the school gets that drum, whoever's pulling it will be as crucial and valued a member of the A Band as the first-chair clarinet. What if it capsized?"

"He'd win a band letter if it didn't capsize?" said Plummer.

And Mr. Helmholtz said this: "I don't see why not."

Ambitious Sophomore

GEORGE M. HELMHOLTZ, head of the music department and director of the band of Lincoln High School, was a good, fat man who saw no evil, heard no evil, and spoke no evil, for wherever he went, the roar and boom and blast of a marching band, real or imagined, filled his soul. There was room for little else, and the Lincoln High School Ten Square Band he led was, as a consequence, as fine as any band on earth.

Sometimes, when he heard muted, wistful passages, real or imagined, Helmholtz would wonder if it wasn't indecent of him to be so happy in such terrible times. But then the brasses and percussion section would put sadness to flight, and Mr. Helmholtz would see that his happiness and its source could only be good and rich and full of hope for everyone.

Helmholtz often gave the impression of a man lost in dreams, but there was a side to him that was as tough as a rhinoceros. It was that side that raised money for the band, that hammered home to the school board, the Parent Teacher Association, Chamber of Commerce, Kiwanis, Rotary, and Lions that the goodness and richness and hope that his band inspired cost money. In his fund-raising harangues, he would recall for his audiences black days for the Lincoln High football team, days when the Lincoln stands had been silent, hurt, and ashamed.

"Half-time," he would murmur, and hang his head.

He would twitch a whistle from his pocket and blow a shrill blast. "Lincoln High School Ten Square Band!" he'd shout. "Forward—harch! Boom! Ta-ta-ta-taaaaaa!" Helmholtz, singing, marching in place, would become flag twirlers, drummers, brasses, woodwinds, glockenspiel and all. By the time he'd marched his one-man band up and down the imaginary football field once, his audience was elated and wringing wet, ready to buy the band anything it wanted.

But no matter how much money came in, the band was always without funds. Helmholtz was a spender when it came to band equipment, and was known among rival bandmasters as "The Plunger" and "Diamond Jim."

Among the many duties of Stewart Haley, Assistant Principal of Lincoln High, was keeping an eye on band finances. Whenever it was necessary for Haley to discuss band finances with Helmholtz, Haley tried to corner the bandmaster where he couldn't march and swing his arms.

Helmholtz knew this, and felt trapped when Haley appeared in the door of the bandmaster's small office, brandishing a bill for ninety-five dollars. Following Haley was a delivery boy from a tailor shop, who carried a suit box under his arm. As Haley closed the office door from inside, Helmholtz hunched over a drawing board, pretending deep concentration.

"Helmholtz," said Haley, "I have here an utterly unexpected, utterly unauthorized bill for—"

"Sh!" said Helmholtz. "I'll be with you in a moment." He drew a dotted line across a diagram that was already a black thicket of lines. "I'm just putting the finishing touches on the Mother's Day formation," he said. "I'm trying to make an arrow pierce a heart and then spell 'Mom.' It isn't easy."

"That's very sweet," said Haley, rattling the bill, "and I'm as fond of mothers as you are, but you've just put a ninety-five-dollar arrow through the public treasury."

Helmholtz did not look up. "I was going to tell you about it," he said, drawing another line, "but what with getting ready for the state band festival and Mother's Day, it seemed unimportant. First things first."

"Unimportant!" said Haley. "You hypnotize the community into buying you one hundred new uniforms for the Ten Square Band, and now—"

"Now?" said Helmholtz mildly.

"This boy brings me a bill for the hundred-and-first uniform!" said Haley. "Give you an inch and—"

Haley was interrupted by a knock. "Come in," said Helmholtz. The door opened, and there stood Leroy Duggan, a shy, droll, slope-shouldered sophomore. Leroy was so self-conscious that when anyone turned to look at him he did a sort of fan dance with his piccolo case and portfolio, hiding himself as well as he could behind them.

"Come right in, Leroy," said Helmholtz.

"Wait outside a moment, Leroy," said Haley. "This is rather urgent business."

Leroy backed out, mumbling an apology, and Haley closed the door again.

"My door is always open to my musicians," said Helmholtz.

"It will be," said Haley, "just as soon as we clear up the mystery of the hundred-and-first uniform."

"I'm frankly surprised and hurt at the administration's lack of faith in my judgment," said Helmholtz. "Running a precision organization of a hundred highly talented young men isn't the simple operation everyone seems to think."

"Simple!" said Haley. "Who thinks it's simple! It's plainly the most tangled, mysterious, expensive mess in the entire school system. You say a hundred young men, but this boy here just delivered the hundred-and-first uniform. Has the Ten Square Band added a tail gunner?"

"No," said Helmholtz. "It's still a hundred, much as I'd like to have more, much as I need them. For instance, I was just trying to figure out how to make *Whistler's Mother* with a hundred men, and it simply can't be done." He frowned. "If we could throw in the girls' glee club we might make it. You're intelligent and have good taste. Would you give me your ideas on the band festival and this Mother's Day thing?"

Haley lost his temper. "Don't try to fuddle me, Helmholtz! What's the extra uniform for?"

"For the greater glory of Lincoln High School!" barked Helmholtz. "For the third leg and permanent possession of the state band festival trophy!" His voice dropped to a whisper, and he glanced furtively at the door. "Specifically, it's for Leroy Duggan, probably the finest piccoloist in this hemisphere. Let's keep our voices down, because we can't discuss the uniform without discussing Leroy."

The conversation became tense whispers.

"And what's the matter with Leroy's wearing one of the uniforms you've already got?" said Haley.

"Leroy is bell-shaped," said Helmholtz. "We don't have a uniform that doesn't bag or bind on him."

"This is a public school, not a Broadway musical!" said Haley. "Not only have we got students shaped liked bells, we've got them shaped like telephone poles, pop bottles, chimpanzees, and Greek gods. There's going to have to be a certain amount of bagging and binding."

"My duty," said Helmholtz, standing, "is to bring the best music out of whoever chooses to come to me. If a boy's shape prevents him from making the music he's capable of making, then it's my duty to get him a shape that will make him play like an angel. This I did, and here we are." He sat down. "If I could be made to feel sorry for this, then I wouldn't be the man for my job."

"A special uniform is going to make Leroy play better?" said Haley.

"In rehearsals, with nobody but fellow musicians around," said Helmholtz, "Leroy has brilliance and feeling that would make you weep and faint. But when Leroy marches, with strangers watching, particularly girls, he gets out of step, stumbles, and can't even play 'Row, Row, Row Your Boat.'" Helmholtz brought his fist down on the desk. "And that's not going to happen at the state band festival!"

The bill in Haley's hand was rumpled and moist now. "The message I came to deliver today," he said, "remains unchanged: You can't get blood out of a turnip. The total cash assets of the band are seventy-five dollars, and there is absolutely no way for the school to provide the remaining twenty—absolutely none."

He turned to the delivery boy. "That is my somber message to you, as well," he said.

"Mr. Kornblum said he was losing money on it as it was," said the delivery boy. "He said Mr. Helmholtz came in and started talking, and before he knew it—"

"Don't worry about a thing," said Helmholtz. He brought out his checkbook and, with a smile and a flourish, wrote a check for twenty dollars.

Haley was ashen. "I'm sorry it has to turn out this way," he said.

Helmholtz ignored him. He took the parcel from the delivery boy and called to Leroy, "Would you come in, please?"

Leroy came in slowly, shuffling, doing his fan dance with the piccolo case and portfolio, apologizing as he came.

"Thought you might like to try on your new uniform for the band festival, Leroy," said Helmholtz.

"I don't think I'd better march," said Leroy. "I'd get all mixed up and ruin everything."

Helmholtz opened the box dramatically. "This uniform's special, Leroy."

"Every time I see one of those uniforms," said Haley, "all I can think of is a road company of *The Chocolate Soldier*. That's the uniform the stars wear, but you've got a hundred of the things—a hundred and one."

Helmholtz removed Leroy's jacket. Leroy stood humbly in his shirtsleeves, relieved of his piccolo case and portfolio, comical, seeing nothing at all comical in being bell-shaped.

Helmholtz slipped the new jacket over Leroy's narrow shoulders. He buttoned the great brass buttons and fluffed up the gold braid cascading from the epaulets. "There, Leroy."

"Zoot!" exclaimed the delivery boy. "Man, I mean zoot!"

Leroy looked dazedly from one massive, jutting shoulder to the other, and then down at the astonishing taper to his hips.

"Rocky Marciano!" said Haley.

"Walk up and down the halls, Leroy," said Helmholtz. "Get the feel of it."

Leroy blundered through the door, catching his epaulets on the frame.

"Sideways," said Helmholtz, "you'll have to learn to go through doors sideways."

"Only about ten percent of what's under the uniform is Leroy," said Haley, when Leroy was out of hearing.

"It's all Leroy," said Helmholtz. "Wait and see—wait until we swing past the reviewing stand at the band festival and Leroy does his stuff."

When Leroy returned to the office, he was marching, knees high. He halted and clicked his heels. His chin was up, his breathing shallow.

"You can take it off, Leroy," said Helmholtz. "If you don't feel up to marching in the band festival, just forget it." He reached across his desk and undid a brass button.

Leroy's hand came up quickly to protect the rest of the buttons. "Please," he said, "I think maybe I could march after all."

"That can be arranged," said Helmholtz. "I have a certain amount of influence in band matters."

Leroy buttoned the button. "Gee," he said, "I walked past the athletic office, and Coach Jorgenson came out like he was shot out of a cannon."

"What did the silent Swede have to say?" said Helmholtz.

"He said that only in this band-happy school would they make a piccolo player out of a man built like a locomotive," said Leroy. "His secretary came out, too."

"Did Miss Bearden like the uniform?" said Helmholtz.

"I don't know," said Leroy. "She didn't say anything. She just looked and looked."

Late that afternoon, George M. Helmholtz appeared in the office of Harold Crane, head of the English Department. Helmholtz was carrying a heavy, ornate gold picture frame and looking embarrassed.

"I hardly know how to begin," said Helmholtz. "I—I thought maybe I could sell you a picture frame." He turned the frame this way and that. "It's a nice frame, isn't it?"

"Yes, it is," said Crane. "I've admired it often in your office. That is the frame you had around John Philip Sousa, isn't it?"

Helmholtz nodded. "I thought maybe you'd like to frame some John Philip Sousa in your line—Shakespeare, Edgar Rice Burroughs."

"That might be nice," said Crane. "But frankly, the need hasn't made itself strongly felt."

"It's a thirty-nine-dollar frame," said Helmholtz. "I'll let it go for twenty."

"Look here," said Crane, "if you're in some sort of jam, I can let you have—"

"No, no, no," said Helmholtz, holding up his hand. Fear crossed his face. "If I started on credit, heaven only knows where it would end."

Crane shook his head. "That's a nice frame, all right, and a real bargain. Sad to say, though, I'm in no shape to lay out twenty dollars for something like that. I've got to buy a new tire for twenty-three dollars this afternoon and—"

"What size?" said Helmholtz.

"Size?" said Crane. "Six-seventy, fifteen. Why?"

"I'll sell you one for twenty dollars," said Helmholtz. "Never been touched."

"Where would you get a tire?" said Crane.

"By a stroke of luck," said Helmholtz, "I have an extra one."

"You don't mean your spare, do you?" said Crane.

"Yes," said Helmholtz, "but I'll never need it. I'll be careful where I drive. Please, you've got to buy it. The money isn't for me, it's for the band."

"What else would it be for?" said Crane helplessly. He took out his billfold.

When Helmholtz got back to his office, and was restoring John Philip Sousa to the frame, Leroy walked in, whistling. He wore the jacket with the boulder shoulders.

"You still here, Leroy?" said Helmholtz. "Thought you went home hours ago."

"Can't seem to take the thing off," said Leroy. "I was trying a kind of experiment with it."

"Oh?"

"I'd walk down the hall past a bunch of girls," said Leroy, "whistling the piccolo part of 'The Stars and Stripes Forever.'"

"And?" said Helmholtz.

"Kept step and didn't miss a note," said Leroy.

The city's main street was cleared of traffic for eight blocks, swept, and lined with bunting for the cream of the state's youth, its high school bands. At one end of the line of march was a great square with a reviewing stand. At the other end were the bands, hidden in alleys, waiting for orders to march.

The band that looked and sounded best to the judges in the reviewing stand would receive a great trophy, donated by the Chamber of Commerce. The trophy was two years old, and bore the name of Lincoln High School as winner twice.

In the alleys, twenty-five bandmasters were preparing secret weapons with which they hoped to prevent Lincoln's winning a third time—special effects with flash powder, flaming batons, pretty cowgirls, and at least one three-inch cannon. But everywhere hung the smog of defeat, save over the bright plumage of the ranks of Lincoln High.

Beside those complacent ranks stood Stewart Haley, Assistant Principal, and, wearing what Haley referred to privately as the uniform of a Bulgarian rear admiral, George M. Helmholtz, Director of the Band.

Lincoln High shared the alley with bands from three other schools, and the blank walls on either side echoed harshly with the shrieks and growls of bands tuning up.

Helmholtz was lighting pieces of punk with Haley's lighter, blowing on them, and passing them in to every fourth man, who had a straight, cylindrical firework under his sash.

"First will come the order 'Prepare to light!'" said Helmholtz. "Ten seconds later, 'Light!' When your left foot strikes the ground, touch your punk to the end of the fuse. The rest of you, when we hit the reviewing stand, I want you to stop playing as though you'd been shot in the heart. And Leroy—"

Helmholtz craned his neck to find Leroy. As he did so, he became aware of a rival drum major, seedy and drab by comparison with Lincoln's peacocks, who had been listening to everything he said.

"What can I do for you?" said Helmholtz.

"Is this the Doormen's Convention?" said the drum major.

Helmholtz did not smile. "You'd do well to stay with your own organization," he said crisply. "You're plainly in need of practice and sprucing up, and time is short."

The drum major walked away, sneering, insolently spinning his baton.

"Now, where's Leroy got to, this time?" said Helmholtz. "He's a disciplinary problem whenever he puts on that uniform. A new man."

"You mean Blabbermouth Duggan?" said Haley. He pointed to Leroy's broad back in the midst of another band. Leroy was talking animatedly to a fellow piccoloist, who happened to be a very pretty girl with golden curls tucked under her cap. "You mean Casanova Duggan?" said Haley.

"Everything's built around Leroy," said Helmholtz. "If anything went wrong with Leroy, we'd be lucky to place second. . . . Leroy!"

Leroy paid no attention.

Leroy was too engrossed to hear Helmholtz. He was too engrossed to notice that the insolent drum major, who had lately called Helmholtz's band a Doormen's Convention, was now examining his broad back with profound curiosity.

The drum major prodded one of Leroy's shoulder pads with the rubber tip of his baton. Leroy gave no sign that he felt it. The drum major laid his hand on Leroy's shoulder and dug his fingers several inches into it. Leroy went on talking.

With an audience gathering, the drum major began a series of probings with his baton, starting from the outside of Leroy's shoulder and moving in toward the middle, trying to locate the point where padding stopped and Leroy began.

The baton at last found flesh, and Leroy turned in surprise. "What's the idea?" he said.

"Making sure your stuffing's all in place, General," said the drum major. "Spring a leak, and we'll be up to our knees in sawdust."

Leroy reddened. "I don't know what you're talking about," he said.

"Ask your boyfriend to take off his jacket so we can all see his rippling muscles," the drum major said to Leroy's new girl. He challenged Leroy, "Go on, take it off."

"Make me," said Leroy.

"All righty, all righty," said Helmholtz, stepping between the two.

"You think I can't?" said the drum major.

Leroy swallowed and thought for a long time. "I know you can't," he said at last.

The drum major pushed Helmholtz aside and seized Leroy's jacket by its shoulders. Off came the epaulets, then the citation cord, then the sash. Buttons popped off, and Leroy's undershirt showed.

"Now," said the drum major, "we'll simply undo this, and—"

Leroy exploded. He hit the drum major's nose, stripped off his buttons, medals, and braid, hit him in the stomach, and went over to get his baton, with the apparent intention of beating him to death with it.

"Leroy! Stop!" cried Helmholtz in anguish. He wrenched the baton from Leroy. "Just look at you! Look at your new uniform—wrecked!" Trembling, he touched the rents, the threads of missing buttons, the misshapen padding. He raised his hands in a gesture of surrender. "It's all over. We concede—Lincoln High concedes."

Leroy was wild-eyed, unrepentant. "I don't care!" he yelled. "I'm glad!"

Helmholtz called over another bandsman and gave him the keys to his car. "There's a spare uniform in the back," he said numbly. "Go get it for Leroy."

The Lincoln High School Ten Square Band swung smartly along the street, moving toward the bright banners of the reviewing stand. George M. Helmholtz smiled as he marched along the curb beside it. Inside he was ill, angry, and full of dread. With

832

KURT VONNEGUT

one cruel stroke, Fate had transformed his plan for winning the trophy into the most preposterous anticlimax in band history.

He couldn't bear to look at the young man on whom he had staked everything. He could imagine Leroy with appalling clarity, slouching along, slovenly, lost in a misfit uniform, a jumble of neuroses and costly fabrics. Leroy was to play alone when the band passed in review. Leroy, Helmholtz reflected, would be incapable even of recalling his own name at that point.

Ahead was the first of a series of chalk marks Helmholtz had made on the curb earlier in the day, carefully measured distances from the reviewing stand.

Helmholtz blew his whistle as he passed the mark, and the band struck up "The Stars and Stripes Forever," full-blooded, throbbing, thrilling. It raised the crowd on its toes and put roses in its cheeks. The judges leaned out of the reviewing stand in happy anticipation of the coming splendor.

Helmholtz passed another mark. "Prepare to light!" he shouted. And a moment later, "Light!"

Helmholtz smiled glassily. In five seconds the band would be before the reviewing stand, the music would stop, the fireworks would send American flags into the sky. And then, playing alone, Leroy would tootle pathetically, ridiculously, if he played at all.

The music stopped. Fireworks banged, and up went the parachutes. The Lincoln High School Ten Square Band passed in review, lines straight, plumes high, brass flashing.

Helmholtz almost cried as American flags hung in air from parachutes. Among them, like a cloudburst of diamonds, was the Sousa piccolo masterpiece. Leroy! Leroy!

The bands were massed before the reviewing stand. George M. Helmholtz stood at parade rest before his band, between the great banner bearing the Lincoln High Black Panther on a scarlet field and Old Glory.

When he was called forward to receive the trophy, the bandmaster crossed the broad square to the accompaniment of a snare drum and a piccolo. As he returned with thirty pounds of bronze and walnut, the band played "Lincoln's Foes Shall Wail Tonight," words and music by George M. Helmholtz.

When the parade was dismissed, Assistant Principal Haley hurried from the crowd to shake Helmholtz's hand.

"Shake Leroy's hand," said Helmholtz. "He's the hero." He looked around for Leroy, beaming, and saw the boy was with the pretty blond piccolo player again, more animated than ever. She was responding warmly.

"She doesn't seem to miss the shoulders, does she?" said Helmholtz.

"That's because *he* doesn't miss them anymore," said Haley. "He's a man now, bell-shaped or not."

"He certainly gave his all for Lincoln High," said Helmholtz. "I admire school spirit in a boy."

Haley laughed. "That wasn't school spirit—that was the love song of a full-bodied American male. Don't you know anything about love?"

Helmholtz thought about love as he walked back to his car alone, his arms aching with the weight of the great trophy. If love was blinding, obsessing, demanding, beyond reason, and all the other wild things people said it was, then he had never known it, Helmholtz told himself. He sighed, and supposed he was missing something, not knowing romance.

When he got to his car, he found that the left front tire was flat. He remembered that he had no spare. But he felt nothing more than mild inconvenience. He boarded a streetcar, sat down with the trophy on his lap, and smiled. He was hearing music again.

The Boy Who
Hated Girls

GEORGE M. HELMHOLTZ, head of the music department and director of the band of Lincoln High School, could sound like any musical instrument. He could shriek like a clarinet, mumble like a trombone, bawl like a trumpet. He could swell his big belly and roar like a sousaphone, could purse his lips sweetly, close his eyes, and whistle like a piccolo.

At eight o'clock one Wednesday night, he was marching around the band rehearsal room at the school, shrieking, mumbling, bawling, roaring, and whistling "Semper Fidelis."

It was easy for Helmholtz to do. For almost half of his forty years, he'd been forming bands from the river of boys that flowed through the school. He'd sung along with them all. He'd sung so long and wished so hard for his bands that he dealt with life in terms of them alone.

Marching beside the lusty pink bandmaster, his face now white with awe and concentration, was a gangly sixteen-year-old named Bert Higgens. He had a big nose, and circles under his eyes. Bert marched flappingly, like a mother flamingo pretending to be injured, luring alligators from her nest.

"*Rump-yump, tiddle-tiddle, rump-yump, burdle-burdle,*" sang Helmholtz. "Left, right, *left*, Bert! El-bows *in*, Bert! Eyes off *feet*, Bert! Keep on *line*, Bert! Don't turn *head*, Bert! Left, right, *left*, Bert! Halt—one, *two*!"

Helmholtz smiled. "I think maybe there was some improvement there."

Bert nodded. "It's sure been a help to practice with you, Mr. Helmholtz."

"As long as you're willing to work at it, so am I," said Helmholtz. He was bewildered by the change that had come over Bert in the past week. The boy seemed to have lost two years, to become what he'd been in his freshman year: awkward, cowering, lonely, dull.

"Bert," said Helmholtz, "are you sure you haven't had any injury, any sickness recently?" He knew Bert well, had given him trumpet lessons for two years. He had watched Bert grow into a proud, straight figure. The collapse of the boy's spirits and coordination was beyond belief.

834

Bert puffed out his cheeks childishly as he thought hard. It was a mannerism Helmholtz had talked him out of long before. Now he was doing it again. Bert let out the air. "Nope," he said.

"I've taught a thousand boys to march," said Helmholtz, "and you're the first one who ever forgot how to do it." The thousand passed in review in Helmholtz's mind—ranks stretching to infinity, straight as sunbeams. "Maybe we ought to talk this over with the school nurse," said Helmholtz. A cheerful thought struck him. "Unless this is girl trouble."

Bert raised one foot, then the other. "Nope," he said. "No trouble like that."

"Pretty little thing," said Helmholtz.

"Who?" said Bert.

"That dewy pink tulip I see you walking home with," said Helmholtz.

Bert grimaced. "Ah-h-h-h—her," he said. "Charlotte."

"Charlotte isn't much good?" said Helmholtz.

"I dunno. I guess she's all right. I suppose she's OK. I haven't got anything against her. I dunno."

Helmholtz shook Bert gently, as though hoping to jiggle a loose part into place. "Do you remember it at all—the feeling you used to have when you marched so well, before this relapse?"

"I think it's kind of coming back," said Bert.

"Coming up through the C and B bands, you learned to march fine," said Helmholtz. These were the training bands through which the hundred men of the Lincoln High School Ten Square Band came.

"I dunno what the trouble is," said Bert, "unless it's the excitement of getting in the Ten Square Band." He puffed his cheeks. "Maybe it's stopping my lessons with you."

When Bert had qualified for the Ten Square Band three months before, Helmholtz had turned him over to the best trumpet teacher in town, Larry Fink, for the final touches of grace and color.

"Say, Fink isn't giving you a hard time, is he?" said Helmholtz.

"Nope," said Bert. "He's a nice gentleman." He rolled his eyes. "Mr. Helmholtz— if we could practice marching just a couple more times, I think I'll be fine."

"Gee, Bert," said Helmholtz, "I don't know when I can fit you in. When you went to Fink, I took on another boy. It just so happened he was sick tonight. But next week—"

"Who is he?" said Bert.

"Norton Shakely," said Helmholtz. "Little fellow—kind of green around the gills. He's just like you were when you started out. No faith in himself. Doesn't think he'll ever make the Ten Square Band, but he will, he will."

"He will," agreed Bert. "No doubt about it."

Helmholtz clapped Bert on the arm, to put some heart into him. "Chin up!" he sang. "Shoulders back! Go get your coat, and I'll take you home."

As Bert put on his coat, Helmholtz thought of the windows of Bert's home—windows as vacant as dead men's eyes. Bert's father had wandered away years before—and his mother was seldom there. Helmholtz wondered if that was where the trouble was.

Helmholtz was depressed. "Maybe we can stop somewhere and get a soda, and maybe play a little table tennis afterward in my basement," he said. When he'd given Bert trumpet lessons, they'd always stopped somewhere for a soda, and then played table tennis afterward.

"Unless you'd rather go see Charlotte or something," said Helmholtz.

"Are you kidding?" said Bert. "I hate the way she talks sometimes."

The next morning, Helmholtz talked with Miss Peach, the school nurse. It was a symposium between two hearty, plump people, blooming with hygiene and common sense. In the background, rickety and confused, stripped to the waist, was Bert.

"By 'blacked out,' you mean Bert fainted?" said Miss Peach.

"You didn't see him do it at the Whitestown game last Friday?" said Helmholtz.

"I missed that game," said Miss Peach.

"It was right after we'd formed the block L, when we were marching down the field to form the pinwheel that turned into the Lincoln High panther and the Whitestown eagle," said Helmholtz. The eagle had screamed, and the panther had eaten it.

"So what did Bert do?" said Miss Peach.

"He was marching along with the band, fine as you please," said Helmholtz. "And then he just drifted out of it. He wound up marching by himself."

"What did it feel like, Bert?" said Miss Peach.

"Like a dream at first," said Bert. "Real good, kind of. And then I woke up, and I was alone." He gave a sickly smile. "And everybody was laughing at me."

"How's your appetite, Bert?" said Miss Peach.

"He polished off a soda and a hamburger last night," said Helmholtz.

"What about your coordination when you play games, Bert?" said Miss Peach.

"I'm not in sports," said Bert. "The trumpet takes all the time I've got."

"Don't you and your father throw a ball sometimes?" said Miss Peach.

"I don't have a father," said Bert.

"He beat me at table tennis last night," said Helmholtz.

"All in all, it was quite a binge last night, wasn't it?" Miss Peach said.

"It's what we used to do every Wednesday night," said Bert.

"It's what I do with all the boys I give lessons to," said Helmholtz.

Miss Peach cocked her head. "You used to do it with Bert?"

"I take lessons from Mr. Fink now," said Bert.

"When a boy reaches the Ten Square Band," said Helmholtz, "he's beyond me, as far as individual lessons are concerned. I don't treat him like a boy anymore. I treat him like a man. And he's an artist. Only an artist like Fink can teach him anything from that point on."

"Ten Square Band," mused Miss Peach. "That's ten on a side—a hundred in all? All dressed alike, all marching like parts of a fine machine?"

"Like a block of postage stamps," said Helmholtz proudly.

"Uh-huh," said Miss Peach. "And all of them have had lessons from you?"

"Heavens, no," said Helmholtz. "I've only got time to give five boys individual lessons."

"A lucky, lucky five," said Miss Peach. "For a little while."

The door of the office opened, and Stewart Haley, the Assistant Principal, came in. He had begun his career as a bright young man. But now, after ten years of dealing with oversize spirits on undersize salaries, his brightness had mellowed to the dull gloss of pewter. A lot of his luster had been lost in verbal scuffles with Helmholtz over expenses of the band.

In Haley's hand was a bill. "Well, Helmholtz," he said, "if I'd known you were going to be here, I'd have brought another interesting bill with me. Five war-surplus Signal Corps wire-laying reels, complete with pack frames? Does that ring a bell?"

"It does," said Helmholtz, unabashed. "And may I say—"

"Later," said Haley. "Right now I have a matter to take up with Miss Peach—one that makes your peculation look like peanuts." He rattled the bill at Miss Peach. "Miss Peach—have you ordered a large quantity of bandages recently?"

Miss Peach paled. "I—I ordered thirty yards of sterile gauze," she said. "It came this morning. And it's thirty yards, and it's gauze."

Haley sat down on a white stool. "According to this bill," he said, "somebody in this grand institution has ordered and received two hundred yards of silver nylon ribbon, three inches wide—treated to glow in the dark."

He was looking blankly at Helmholtz when he said it. He went on looking at Helmholtz, and color crept into his cheeks. "Hello again, Helmholtz."

"Hi," said Helmholtz.

"Down for your daily shot of cocaine?" said Haley.

"Cocaine?" said Helmholtz.

"How else," said Haley, "could a man get dreams of cornering the world output of nylon ribbon treated to glow in the dark?"

"It costs much less to make things glow in the dark than most people realize," said Helmholtz.

Haley stood. "So it was you!"

Helmholtz laid his hand on Haley's shoulder and looked him in the eye. "Stewart," he said, "the question on everybody's lips is, How can the Ten Square Band possibly top its performance at the Westfield game last year?"

"The big question is," said Haley, "How can a high school with a modest budget like ours afford such a vainglorious, Cecil B. DeMille machine for making music? And the answer is," said Haley, "We can't!" He jerked his head from side to side. "Ninety-five-dollar uniforms! Biggest drum in the state! Batons and hats that light up! Everything treated to glow in the dark! Holy smokes!" he said wildly. "The biggest jukebox in the world!"

The inventory brought nothing but joy to Helmholtz. "You love it," he said. "Everybody loves it. And wait till you hear what we're going to do with those reels and that ribbon!"

"Waiting," said Haley. "Waiting."

"Now then," said Helmholtz, "any band can form block letters. That's about the oldest stuff there is. As of this moment our band is the only band, as far as I know, equipped to write longhand."

In the muddled silence that followed, Bert, all but forgotten, spoke up. He had put his shirt back on. "Are you all through with me?" he said.

"You can go, Bert," said Miss Peach. "I didn't find anything wrong with you."

"Bye," said Bert, his hand on the doorknob. "Bye, Mr. Helmholtz."

"So long," said Helmholtz. "Now what do you think of that?" he said to Haley. "Longhand!"

Just outside the door, Bert bumped into Charlotte, the dewy pink tulip of a girl who often walked home with him.

"Bert," said Charlotte, "they told me you were down here. I thought you were hurt. Are you all right?"

Bert brushed past her without a word, leaning, as though into a cold, wet gale.

"What do I think of the ribbon?" said Haley to Helmholtz. "I think this is where the spending of the Ten Square Band is finally stopped."

"That isn't the only kind of spree that's got to be stopped," said Miss Peach darkly.

"What do you mean by that?" said Helmholtz.

"I mean," said Miss Peach, "all this playing fast and loose with kids' emotions." She frowned. "George, I've been watching you for years—watching you use every emotional trick in the books to make your kids march and play."

"I try to be friends," said Helmholtz, untroubled.

"You try to be a lot more than that," said Miss Peach. "Whatever a kid needs, you're it. Father, mother, sister, brother, God, slave, or dog—you're it. No wonder we've got the best band in the world. The only wonder is that what's happened with Bert hasn't happened a thousand times."

"What's eating Bert?" said Helmholtz.

"You won him," said Miss Peach. "That's what. Lock, stock, and barrel—he's yours, all yours."

"Sure he likes me," said Helmholtz. "Hope he does, anyway."

"He likes you like a son likes a father," said Miss Peach. "There's a casual thing for you."

Helmholtz couldn't imagine what the argument was about. Everything Miss

Peach had said was obvious. "That's only natural, isn't it?" he said. "Bert doesn't have a father, so he's going to look around for one, naturally, until he finds some girl who'll take him over and—"

"Will you please open your eyes, and see what you've done to Bert's life?" said Miss Peach. "Look what he did to get your attention, after you stuck him in the Ten Square Band, then sent him off to Mr. Fink and forgot all about him. He was willing to have the whole world laugh at him, just to get you to look at him again."

"Growing up isn't supposed to be painless," said Helmholtz. "A baby's one thing, a child's another, and a man's another. Changing from one thing to the next is a famous mess." He opened his eyes wide. "If we don't know that, who does?"

"Growing up isn't supposed to be hell!" said Miss Peach.

Helmholtz was stunned by the word. "What do you want me to do?"

"It's none of my business," said Miss Peach. "It's a highly personal affair. That's the way you made it. That's the way you work. I'd think the least you could do would be to learn the difference between getting yourself tangled up in a boy and getting yourself tangled up in ribbon. You can cut the ribbon. You can't do that to a boy."

"About that ribbon—" said Haley.

"We'll pack it up and send it back," said Helmholtz. He didn't care about the ribbon anymore. He walked out of the office, his ears burning.

Helmholtz carried himself as though he'd done nothing wrong. But guilt rode on his back like a chimpanzee. In his tiny office off the band rehearsal room, Helmholtz removed stacks of sheet music from the washbasin in the corner and dashed cold water in his face, hoping to make the chimpanzee go away at least for the next hour. The next hour was the rehearsal period for the Ten Square Band.

Helmholtz telephoned his good friend Larry Fink, the trumpet teacher.

"What's the trouble this time, George?" said Fink.

"The school nurse just jumped all over me for being too nice to my boys. She says I get too involved, and that's a very dangerous thing."

"Oh?"

"Psychology's a wonderful science," said Helmholtz. "Without it, everybody'd still be making the same terrible mistake—being nice to each other."

"What brought this on?" said Fink.

"Bert," said Helmholtz.

"I finally let him go last week," said Fink. "He never practiced, came to the lessons unprepared. Frankly, George, I know you thought a lot of him, but he wasn't very talented. He wasn't even very fond of music, as near as I can tell."

Helmholtz protested with all his heart. "That boy went from the C Band to the Ten Square in two years! He took to music like a duck to water."

"Like a camel in quicksand, if you ask me," said Fink. "That boy busted his butt for you, George. And then you busted his heart when you handed him on to me. The school nurse is right: You've got to be more careful about who you're nice to."

"He's even forgotten how to march. He fell out of step and spoiled a formation, forgot where he was supposed to go, at half-time at the Findlay Tech game."

"He told me about it," said Fink.

"Did he have any explanation?"

"He was surprised you and the nurse didn't come up with it. Or maybe the nurse figured it out, but didn't want anybody else to know."

"I still can't imagine," said Helmholtz.

"He was drunk, George. He said it was his first time, and promised it would be his last. Unfortunately, I don't believe we can count on that."

"But he still can't march," said Helmholtz, shocked. "When just the two of us practice alone, with nobody watching, he finds it impossible to keep in step with me. Is he drunk all the time?"

"George," said Fink, "you and your innocence have turned a person who never should have been a musician into an actor instead."

From the rehearsal room outside Helmholtz's office came the cracks and slams of chairs being set up for the Ten Square Band. Bandsmen with a free period were doing that. The coming hour was ordinarily a perfect one for the bandmaster, in which he became weightless, as he sang the part of this instrument or that one, while his bandsmen played. But now he feared it.

He was going to have to face Bert again, having been made aware in the interim of how much he might have hurt the boy. And maybe others.

Would he be to blame, if Bert went on to become an alcoholic? He thought about the thousand or more boys with whom he had behaved like a father, whether they had a real father or not. To his knowledge, several had later become drunks. Two had been arrested for drugs, and one for burglary. He lost track of most. Few came back to see him after graduation. That was something else it was time to think about.

The rest of the band entered now, Bert among them. Helmholtz heard himself say to him, as privately as he could, "Could you see me in my office after school?" He hadn't a clue of what he would say then.

He went to his music stand in front, rapped his baton against it. The band fell silent. "Let's start off with 'Lincoln's Foes Shall Wail Tonight.'" The author of the words and music was Helmholtz himself. He had written them during his first year as bandmaster, when the school's bandsmen at athletic events and parades had numbered only fifty. Their uniforms fit them purely by chance, and in any case made them look, as Helmholtz himself had said at the time, like "deserters from Valley Forge." That was twenty years before.

"Everybody ready?" he said. "Good! Fortissimo! Con brio! A-one, a-two, a-three, a-four!" Helmholtz stayed earth-bound this time. He weighed a ton.

When Bert came to his office after school, Helmholtz had an agenda. He wanted the lonely boy to stop disliking Charlotte. She appeared to be a warm person, who

COMPLETE STORIES

could lead Bert into a social life apart from the band and Helmholtz. He thought it important, too, that the dangers of alcohol be discussed.

But the talk wouldn't go at all as planned, and Helmholtz sensed that it wouldn't as soon as Bert sat down. He had self-respect on a scale Helmholtz had never seen him exhibit before. Something big must have happened, thought Helmholtz. Bert was staring straight at him, challenging, as though they were equals, no longer man and boy.

"Bert," Helmholtz began, "I won't beat around the bush. I know you were drunk at the football game."

"Mr. Fink told you?"

"Yes, and it troubled me."

"Why didn't you realize it at the time?" said Bert. "Everybody else did. People were laughing at you because you thought I was sick."

"I had a lot on my mind," said Helmholtz.

"Music," said Bert, as though it were a dirty word.

"Certainly music," said Helmholtz, taken aback. "My goodness."

"*Nothin'* but music," said Bert, his gaze like laser beams.

"That's often the case, and why not?" Again Helmholtz added incredulously, "My goodness."

"Charlotte was right."

"I thought you hated her."

"I like her a lot, except for the things she said about you. Now I know how right she was, and I not only like her, I love her."

Helmholtz was scared now, and unused to that. This was a most unpleasant scene. "Whatever she said about me, I don't think I'd care to hear it."

"I won't tell you, because all you'd hear is music." Bert put his trumpet in its case on the bandmaster's desk. The trumpet was rented from the school. "Give this to somebody else, who'll love it more than I did," he said. "I only loved it because you were so good to me, and you told me to." He stood. "Good-bye."

Bert was at the door before Helmholtz asked him to stop, to turn around and look him in the eye again, and say what Charlotte had said about him.

Bert was glad to tell him. He was angry, as though Helmholtz had somehow swindled him. "She said you were completely disconnected from real life, and only pretended to be interested in people. She said all you paid attention to was music, and if people weren't playing it, you could still hear it in your head. She said you were nuts."

"Nuts?" echoed Helmholtz wonderingly.

"I told her to stop saying that," said Bert, "but then you showed me how really nutty you are."

"Please tell me how. I need to know," said Helmholtz. But a concert band in his head was striking up Tchaikovsky's *1812 Overture*, complete with the roar of cannons. It was all he could do not to sing along.

"When you gave me marching lessons," Bert was saying, "and I was acting drunk, you didn't even notice how crazy it was. You weren't even there!"

A brief silence followed a crescendo in the music in the bandmaster's head. Helmholtz asked this question: "How could that girl know anything about me?"

"She dates a lot of other bandsmen," said Bert. "She gets 'em to tell her the really funny stuff."

Before leaving for home at sunset that day, Helmholtz paid a visit to the school nurse. He said he needed to talk to her about something.

"Is it that Bert Higgens again?" she said.

"I'm afraid it's even closer to home than that," he said. "It's me this time. It's I. It's me."

A Song for Selma

AROUND LINCOLN HIGH SCHOOL, Al Schroeder's first name was hardly ever mentioned. He was simply Schroeder. Or not so simply Schroeder, either, because his last name was spoken with a strong accent, as though Schroeder were a famous dead European. He wasn't. He was as American as cornflakes, and, far from being dead, he was a vivid sixteen years old.

It was Helga Grosz, the German teacher at Lincoln, who first gave the name a rich accent. The other faculty members, hearing her do it, recognized instantly the rightness of the accent. It set Schroeder apart, reminded any faculty member who discussed him that Schroeder represented a thrilling responsibility.

For Schroeder's own good, it was kept from him and from the rest of the student body just why Schroeder was such a thrilling responsibility. He was the first authentic genius in the history of Lincoln High.

Schroeder's blinding I.Q., like the I.Q. of every student, was a carefully guarded secret in the confidential files in the office of the principal.

It was the opinion of George M. Helmholtz, portly head of the music department and director of the Lincoln Ten Square Marching Band, that Schroeder had the stuff to become as great as John Philip Sousa, composer of "Stars and Stripes Forever."

Schroeder, in his freshman year, learned to play a clarinet well enough in three months to take over the first chair in the band. By the end of his sophomore year, he was master of every instrument in the band. He was now a junior, and the composer of nearly a hundred marches.

As an exercise in sight reading, Helmholtz was now putting the beginners' band, the C Band, through an early Schroeder composition called "Hail to the Milky Way." It was an enthusiastic piece of music, and Helmholtz hoped that the straight-forward violence of it would tempt the beginners into really having a go at music. Schroeder's own comments on the composition pointed out that the star farthest from the earth in the Milky Way was approximately ten thousand light-years away. If the sound of the musical salute was to reach that farthest star, the music would have to be played good and loud.

The C Band bleated, shrieked, howled, and squawked at that farthest star gamely.

But the musicians dropped out one by one until, as was so often the case, the bass drummer played alone.

Blom, blom, bloom went the bass drum. It was being larruped by Big Floyd Hires, the biggest, the most pleasant, and the dumbest boy in school. Big Floyd was probably the wealthiest, as well. Someday he would own his father's dry-cleaning chain.

Bloom, bloom, bloom went Big Floyd's drum.

Helmholtz waved Big Floyd to silence. "Thank you for sticking with it, Floyd," he said. "Sticking with it to the end is an example the rest of you could well follow. Now, we're going to go through this again—and I want everybody to stick with it right to the end, no matter what."

Helmholtz raised his baton, and Schroeder, the school genius, came in from the hall. Helmholtz nodded a greeting. "All right, men," Helmholtz said to the C Band, "here's the composer himself. Don't let him down."

Again the band tried to hail the Milky Way, again it failed.

Bloom, bloom, bloom went Big Floyd's drum—alone, alone, terribly alone.

Helmholtz apologized to the composer, who was sitting on a folding chair by the wall. "Sorry," he said. "It's only the second time through. Today's the first they've seen of it."

"I understand," said Schroeder. He was a small person—nicely proportioned, but very light, and only five feet and three inches tall. He had a magnificent brow, high and already lined by scowling thought. Eldred Crane, head of the English department, called that brow "the white cliffs of Dover." The unrelenting brilliance of Schroeder's thoughts gave him an alarming aspect that had been best described by Hal Bourbeau, the chemistry teacher. "Schroeder," Bourbeau said one time, "looks as though he's sucking on a very sour lemon drop. And when the lemon drop is gone, he's going to kill everybody."

The part about Schroeder's killing everybody was, of course, pure poetic license. He had never been in the least temperamental.

"Perhaps you would like to speak to the boys about what you've tried to achieve with this composition," Helmholtz said to Schroeder.

"Nope," said Schroeder.

"Nope?" said Helmholtz, surprised. Negativism wasn't Schroeder's usual style. It would have been far more like Schroeder to speak to the bandsmen thrillingly, to make them optimistic and gay. "Nope?" said Helmholtz.

"I'd rather they didn't try it again," said Schroeder.

"I don't understand," said Helmholtz.

Schroeder stood, and he looked very tired. "I don't want anybody to play my music anymore," he said. "I'd like to have it all back, if you don't mind."

"What do you want it back for?" said Helmholtz.

"To burn it," said Schroeder. "It's trash—pure trash." He smiled wanly. "I'm through with music, Mr. Helmholtz."

"Through?" said Helmholtz, heartsick. "You can't mean it!"

Schroeder shrugged. "I simply haven't got what it takes," he said. "I know that now." He waved his small hand feebly. "All I ask is that you don't embarrass me any more by playing my foolish, crude, and no doubt comical compositions."

He saluted Helmholtz and left.

For the remainder of the period, Helmholtz could not keep his mind on the C Band. All he could think about was Schroeder's shocking and inexplicable decision to give up music entirely.

At the end of the period, Helmholtz set out for the teachers' cafeteria. It was lunchtime. He became gradually aware that he had company. Big Floyd Hires, the genially dumb drummer, was clumping along beside him.

There was nothing casual about Big Floyd's being there. His presence was massively intentional. Big Floyd had something of importance to say, and the novelty of that made him throw off heat like a steam locomotive.

And it made him wheeze.

"Mr. Helmholtz," wheezed Big Floyd.

"Yes?" said Helmholtz.

"I'm—I—I just wanted you to know I'm through loafing," wheezed Big Floyd.

"Excellent," said Helmholtz. He was all for people's trying their hardest, even in cases like Big Floyd's, where the results of trying and not trying were almost certain to be identical.

Big Floyd now flabbergasted Helmholtz by handing him a song he had composed. "I wish you'd look at this, Mr. Helmholtz," he said.

The music was written in great black gobs, and there wasn't much of it. But it must have been about as difficult for Big Floyd as the Fifth Symphony had been for Beethoven.

It had a title. It was called "A Song for Selma."

And there were words to go with the music:

> *I break the chains that bind me.*
> *I leave the clown I was behind me.*
> *It was wonderful of you to remind me*
> *That if I looked I would find me.*
> *Oh, Selma, Selma, thank you.*
> *I can never say good-bye.*

When Helmholtz looked up from the words and music, the poet-composer was gone.

There was a spry debate that noon in the teachers' cafeteria. The subject, as stated by Hal Bourbeau of the chemistry department: "Does the good news about Big Floyd

Hires deciding to be a musical genius offset the bad news about Schroeder deciding to withdraw from the field entirely?"

The obvious purpose of the debate was to twit Helmholtz. It was good fun for everybody but Helmholtz, since the problem was regarded as being purely a band matter, and since the band was regarded as being a not very serious enterprise anyway. It was not yet known that Schroeder despaired of amounting to anything in any field of learning.

"As I see it," said Bourbeau, "if a slow student decides to take band music seriously and a genius decides to give it up in favor of chemistry, say, it isn't a case of one person's going up and another person's going down. It's a case of two persons' going up."

"Yes," said Helmholtz mildly, "and the bright boy can give us a new poison gas, and the dumb one can give us a new tune to whistle."

Ernest Groper, the physics teacher, joined the group. He was a rude, realistic, bomb-shaped man, at war with sloppy thinking. As he transferred his lunch from his tray to the table, he gave the impression that he was obeying the laws of motion voluntarily, with gusto—not because he had to obey them but because he thought they were darn fine laws.

"You hear the news about Big Floyd Hires?" Bourbeau asked him.

"The great nucular fizzist?" said Groper.

"The what?" said Bourbeau.

"That's what Big Floyd told me he was going to be this morning," said Groper. "Said he was through loafing, said he was going to be a nucular fizzist. I think he means *nuclear physicist*, but he may mean *veterinarian*." He picked up the copy of Big Floyd's "A Song for Selma," which Helmholtz had passed around the table a few minutes before. "What's this?"

"Big Floyd wrote it," said Helmholtz.

Groper raised his eyebrows. "He *is* busy these days, isn't he!" he said. "Selma? Selma who? Selma Ritter?" He tucked his napkin under his collar.

"She's the only Selma we could think of," said Helmholtz.

"Must be Selma Ritter," said Groper. "She and Big Floyd sit at the same table in the physics lab." He closed his eyes, rubbed the bridge of his nose. "What a crazy, mixed-up table that is, too," he said tiredly. "Schroeder, Big Floyd, and Selma Ritter."

"They all three sit together?" said Helmholtz musingly, trying to find some pattern.

"I thought Schroeder might help to pull Big Floyd and Selma up," said Groper. He nodded wonderingly. "And he certainly has, hasn't he?" He looked quizzically at Helmholtz. "You don't happen to know what Big Floyd's I.Q. is, do you, George?"

"I wouldn't even know how to find out," said Helmholtz. "I don't believe in I.Q.s."

"There's a confidential file in the principal's office," said Groper. "If you want a real thrill, look up Schroeder, sometime."

"Which one is Selma Ritter?" said Hal Bourbeau, looking through the plate glass partition that separated the teachers' cafeteria from the students' cafeteria.

"She's a little thing," said Groper.

"A quiet little thing," said Eldred Crane, head of the English department. "Shy, and not very popular."

"She's certainly popular now—with Big Floyd," said Groper. "They've got a big love affair going, from all I can see." He shuddered. "I've got to get those two away from Schroeder. I don't know how they do it, but they certainly manage to depress him."

"I don't see her out there anywhere," said Helmholtz, still scanning the student cafeteria for Selma Ritter's face. He did see Schroeder, who was sitting by himself. The small, brilliant boy was looking very dejected, ruefully resigned. And Helmholtz saw Big Floyd. Big Floyd was sitting alone, too—massive, inarticulate, and inexpressibly hopeful about something. He was apparently thinking prodigiously. He squirmed and scowled, and bent imaginary iron bars.

"Selma isn't out there," said Helmholtz.

"I just remembered," said Eldred Crane, "Selma doesn't eat during the regular lunch hour. She eats during the next period."

"What does she do during the lunch hour?" said Helmholtz.

"She holds down the switchboard in the principal's office," said Crane, "while the staff is out to lunch."

Helmholtz excused himself, and he went to the principal's office to have a talk with Selma Ritter. The office was actually a suite, consisting of a foyer, a meeting room, two offices, and a file room.

When Helmholtz entered the suite, his first impression was that there was no one in it. The switchboard was deserted. The switches buzzed and blinked in dismal futility.

And then Helmholtz heard what was little more than a mouse noise in the file room. He went to the room quietly, peeked in.

Selma Ritter was kneeling by an open file drawer, writing something in her notebook.

Helmholtz was not shocked. He didn't jump to the conclusion that Selma was looking into something that wasn't any of her business—for the simple reason that he didn't believe in secrets. As far as Helmholtz was concerned, there weren't any secrets in Lincoln High School.

Selma took a rather different view of secrecy. What she had her hands in were the confidential files, the files that told, among other things, what everyone's I.Q. was. When Helmholtz caught her red-handed, Selma literally lost her balance, toppled to one side from her precarious kneel.

Helmholtz helped her up. And while he was doing it, he caught a glimpse of the file card Selma had been copying from. The card had unexplained numbers scattered over it, seemingly at random.

The numbers meant nothing to Helmholtz, since he had never used the files. They represented not only an individual's I.Q. but his sociability index, his dexterity, his weight, his leadership potential, his height, his work preferences, and his aptitudes in six different fields of human accomplishment. The Lincoln High School testing program was a thorough one.

It was a famous one, too—a favorite hunting ground for would-be Ph.D.s, since Lincoln's testing records went back more than twenty-five years.

In order to find out what each number meant, Helmholtz would have had to use a decoding card, a card with holes punched in it, which was kept locked up in the principal's safe. By placing the decoding card over the file card, Helmholtz might have found out what all the numbers meant.

But he didn't need the decoding card to find out whose file card Selma had been copying from. The name of the individual was typed big as life at the top of the card.

George M. Helmholtz was startled to read the name.

The name was HELMHOLTZ, GEO. M.

"What is this?" murmured Helmholtz, taking the card from the drawer. "What's this doing with my name on it? What's this got to do with me?"

Selma burst into tears. "Oh, Mr. Helmholtz," she wailed, "I didn't mean any harm. Please don't tell on me. I'll never do it again. Please don't tell."

"What is there to tell?" said Helmholtz, completely at sea.

"I was looking up your I.Q.," said Selma. "I admit it. You caught me. And I suppose I could get thrown out of school for it. But I had a reason, Mr. Helmholtz—a very important reason."

"I have no idea what my I.Q. is, Selma," said Helmholtz, "but you're certainly welcome to it, whatever it is."

Selma's crying abated some. "You won't report me?" she said.

"What's the crime?" said Helmholtz. "If my I.Q. is so interesting, I'll paint it on my office door for all to see."

Selma's eyes widened. "You don't know what your I.Q. is?" she said.

"No," said Helmholtz humbly. "Very submedium, I'd guess," he said.

Selma pointed to a number on the file card. "There," she said, "that's your I.Q., Mr. Helmholtz." She stepped back, as though she expected Helmholtz to collapse in astonishment. "That's it," she whispered.

Helmholtz studied the number. He pulled in his chin, creating a multitude of echoing chins beneath it. The number was 183. "I know nothing about I.Q.s," he said. "Is that high or low?" He tried to remember when his I.Q. had last been tested. As nearly as he could recall, it hadn't been tested since he himself had been a student in Lincoln High.

"It's very, very, very high, Mr. Helmholtz," said Selma earnestly. "Mr. Helmholtz," she said, "don't you even know you're a genius?"

"What *is* this card anyway?" said Helmholtz.

"It's from when you were a student," said Selma.

Helmholtz frowned at the card. He remembered fondly the sober, little, fat boy he'd been, and it offended him to see that boy reduced to numbers. "I give you my word of honor, Selma," he said, "I was no genius then, and I am not a genius now. Why on earth did you look me up?"

"You're a teacher of Big Floyd's," said Selma. At the mention of Big Floyd, she gained an inch in stature and became radiantly possessive. "I knew you'd gone to school here, so I looked you up," she said, "to see if you were smart enough to realize how really smart Big Floyd is."

Helmholtz cocked his head quizzically. "And just how smart do you think Big Floyd is?" said Helmholtz.

"Look him up, if you want to," said Selma. She was becoming self-righteous now. "I guess nobody ever bothered to look him up before I did."

"You looked him up, too?" said Helmholtz.

"I got so sick of everybody saying how dumb Big Floyd was, and how smart that stupid Alvin Schroeder was," said Selma. "I had to find out for myself."

"What did you find?" said Helmholtz.

"I found out Alvin Schroeder was a big bluffer," said Selma, "acting so smart all the time. He's actually dumb. And I found out Big Floyd wasn't dumb at all. Actually, he's a big loafer. Actually, he's a genius like you."

"Um," said Helmholtz. "And you told them so?"

Selma hesitated. And then, so steeped in crime she could hardly worsen her case, she nodded. "Yes—I told them," she said. "I told them for their own good."

From three until four that afternoon, Helmholtz was in charge of an extracurricular activity, the Railsplitters, the glee club of Lincoln High. On this particular occasion, the sixty voices of the Railsplitters were augmented by a grand piano, a brass choir of three trumpets, two trombones, and a tuba, and the bright, sweet chimes of a glockenspiel.

The musicians who backed the glee club so richly had been recruited by Helmholtz since the lunch hour. Helmholtz had been frantically busy in his tiny office since lunch, making plans and sending off messengers like the commander of a battalion under fire.

When the clock on the wall of the rehearsal room stood at one minute until four, Helmholtz pinched off with his thumb and forefinger the almost insufferably beautiful final chord of the song the augmented glee club had been rehearsing.

When Helmholtz had pinched it off, he and the group looked stunned.

They had found the lost chord.

Never had there been such beauty.

The undamped voice of the glockenspiel was the last to die. The high song of the last chime struck on the glockenspiel faded into infinity, and it seemed to promise that it would be forever audible to anyone willing to listen hard enough.

"That's it—that's certainly it," whispered Helmholtz raptly. "Ladies and gentlemen—I can't thank you enough."

The buzzer on the wall clock sounded. It was four o'clock.

Right on the dot of four, Schroeder, Selma, and Big Floyd came into the rehearsal room, just as Helmholtz had told them to do. Helmholtz stepped down from the podium, led the three into his office, and closed the door.

"I suppose you all know why I've asked you to come," said Helmholtz.

"I don't," said Schroeder.

"It's about I.Q.s, Schroeder," said Helmholtz. And he told Schroeder about catching Selma in the file room.

Schroeder shrugged listlessly.

"If any of you three talks about this to anybody," said Helmholtz, "it will get Selma into terrible trouble, and me, too. I haven't reported the very bad thing Selma's done, and that makes me an accessory."

Selma paled.

"Selma," said Helmholtz, "what made you think that one particular number on the file cards was an I.Q.?"

"I—I read up on I.Q.s in the library," said Selma, "and then I looked myself up in the files, and I found the number on my card that was probably my I.Q."

"Interesting," said Helmholtz, "and a tribute to your modesty. That number you thought was your I.Q., Selma—that was your weight. And when you looked up the rest of us here, all you found out was who was heavy and who was light. In my case, you discovered that I was once a very fat boy. Big Floyd and I are far from being geniuses, and small Schroeder here is far from being a moron."

"Oh," said Selma.

Big Floyd gave a sigh that sounded like a freight whistle. "I told you I was dumb," he said to Selma wretchedly. "I told you I wasn't any genius." He pointed helplessly at Schroeder. "He's the genius. He's the one who's got it. He's the one who's got the brains to carry him right up into the stars or somewhere! I told you that!"

Big Floyd pressed the heels of his hands against his temples, as though to jar his brains into working better. "Boy," he said tragically, "I sure proved how dumb I was, believing for even one minute I had something on the ball."

"There's only one test to pay any attention to," said Helmholtz, "and that's the test of life. That's where you'll make the score that counts. That's true for Schroeder, for Selma, for you, Big Floyd, for me—for everybody."

"You can tell who's going to amount to something," said Big Floyd.

"Can you?" said Helmholtz. "I can't. Life is nothing but surprises to me."

"Think of the surprises that are waiting for a guy like me," said Big Floyd. He nodded at Schroeder. "Then think of the surprises that are waiting for a guy like him."

"Think of the surprises that are waiting for everybody!" said Helmholtz. "My mind reels!" He opened his office door, indicating that the interview was at an end.

Selma, Big Floyd, and Schroeder shuffled from Helmholtz's office into the rehearsal room. Their chins were not held high. The talk from Helmholtz hadn't inspired them much. On the contrary, the talk, like so many pep talks on the high school level, had been fairly depressing.

And then, as Selma, Big Floyd, and Schroeder shuffled past the glee club, the glee club and the musicians in support of it stood up.

At a signal from Helmholtz, there was a brilliant fanfare of brass.

The fanfare brought Selma, Big Floyd, and Schroeder to a halt and to startled attention.

The fanfare went on and on—intricately. And the grand piano and the glockenspiel joined the fanfare—clanged, banged, and pealed triumphantly, like church bells celebrating a great victory.

The seeming church bells and the fanfare died reluctantly.

The sixty voices of the glee club began to murmur sweetly, to murmur low.

And then the sixty voices, crying out wordlessly, began to climb. They reached a plateau, and they seemed to want to stay there.

But the brasses and the grand piano and the glockenspiel taunted them into climbing again, taunted the voices into overcoming all obstacles above them, taunted the voices into aspiring to the stars.

Up and up the voices went, to unbelievable heights. And as the wordless voices climbed, they seemed to promise that, when they reached the uppermost limits of their aspirations, they would at last speak words. They seemed to promise too that, when they spoke those words, those words would be stunning truth.

The voices now could go no higher.

They strained melodramatically. Melodramatically, they could rise no more.

And then, musical miracle of miracles, a soprano sent her voice not a little above the rest, but far, far, far above the rest. And, soaring so far above the rest, she found words.

"*I break the chains that bind meeeeeeeeeeee,*" she sang. Her voice was a thread of pure sunlight.

The piano and the glockenspiel both made sounds like breaking chains.

The glee club groaned in harmonic wonder at the broken chains.

"*I leave the clown I was behind me,*" sang a rumbling bass.

The trumpets laughed ironically, and then the entire brass choir sang a haunting phrase from "Auld Lang Syne."

"*It was wonderful of you to remind me,*" sang a baritone, "*That if I looked I would find me.*"

In very swift order, the soprano sang a phrase from "Someday I'll Find You," the full glee club sang a phrase from "These Foolish Things," and the piano played a phrase from "Among My Souvenirs."

"*Oh, Selma, Selma, Selma, thank you,*" sang all the basses together.

"Selma?" echoed the real Selma in real life.

"You," said Helmholtz to Selma. "This is a song Big Floyd, the well-known genius, wrote for you."

"For me?" said Selma, astonished.

"Sh!" said Helmholtz.

"*I can never—*" sang the soprano.

"*Never, never, never, never, never, never, never, never—*" chanted the glee club.

"*Say—*" rumbled the basses.

"*Good—*" piped the soprano.

And now the entire ensemble, Helmholtz included, joined in a hair-raising final chord, "*Byeeeeeeeeeeeeeeeeeeeeeeeeeeeeeeeeeeeeeeeeeeeeeeeeeeeeeeeeeeeeeeeeeeeeeee!*"

Helmholtz pinched off the final chord with his thumb and forefinger.

Tears streamed down Big Floyd's cheeks. "Oh my, oh my, oh my," he murmured. "Who arranged it?" he said.

"A genius," said Helmholtz.

"Schroeder?" said Big Floyd.

"No," said Schroeder. "I—"

"How did you like it, Selma?" said Helmholtz.

There was no reply. Selma Ritter had fainted dead away.

SECTION 8

Futuristic

Kurt Vonnegut's generation not only won World War II, but came out of it amazed and perhaps a bit mystified by the brave new future that awaited them. The global conflict had put pressure on military development to be better, faster, and more mind-bendingly innovative than ever before. Within years such devices as radar and sonar transformed warfare in the air and sea. Contrails from jet aircraft crossed the skies of Germany in early 1945, and by August of that year mushroom clouds from two atomic bombs rose over Japan. Back home a new corporate structure awaited the returning vets, in a workplace now shared with the women who'd taken over their jobs while they were in service—a double-edged sword that prevented the would-be journalist from getting a permanent job with a major newspaper but also put him on the ladder at the General Electric Corporation's publicity department. Here, from autumn 1947 to spring 1951, he wrote media releases about the wonderful new future being concocted by his brother Bernard and other scientists in the GE Research Lab. In later years he was fond of recalling how Americans expected that someone, rather soon, would discover God Almighty, and sell a color photograph of Him to *Popular Mechanics*.

Not to *Scientific American*, readers should note. The editors of that journal knew very well that such a photo would never be published, at least not there. But alternately playful and ominous fantasies about the future were welcome in magazines that shared drugstore racks with the likes of *Collier's*, *Cosmopolitan*, and the *Saturday Evening Post*. These were the markets Kurt Vonnegut hoped to write for, and at which his agent Kenneth Littauer aimed. When stories fell short, there were always the lower-earning (but still paying) science fiction journals. And so, after two years of graduate study (anthropology) on the GI Bill while working parttime for Chicago's City News Bureau (pool reporting) and then after two and a half years doing publicity at GE, the young writer still in his twenties set out to describe a fictive future for his countrymen.

Some projections were intentionally frivolous. "Tomorrow and Tomorrow and Tomorrow" had a Shakespearian title meant to catch the eye of better editors, but they passed it up in favor of Kurt's stories featuring other subjects. Recast as "The Big Trip Up Yonder," it appeared in *Galaxy Science Fiction* for January 1954. Here readers could delight in a future of eternal life and then be surprised by its consequences. Although its premise was likely too incredible for those at *Collier's* and the *Post*, the story's characters behaved much like their counterparts in these more standard journals—there is no doubt that this is a classic Kurt Vonnegut short story.

Others were ominous. The true classic, for which Vonnegut became known as much as for his novel *Slaughterhouse-Five*, is "Welcome to the Monkey House," the title piece of his 1968 collection of short pieces that publisher Seymour Lawrence brought out with Delacorte Press. This volume, the initial work of a three-book contract that would bring the author his first widespread national attention, was reprinted as a special paperback edition in 2014, featuring scholar Gregory D. Sumner's analysis of the story's earlier versions, a full dozen in typescript that reflect the author's pursuit of a proper audience for his future of "ethical suicide parlors." The finished tale did not appear until January 1968, and then in a magazine that didn't even exist when Vonnegut began publishing in 1950: *Playboy*. Given page rates, it had to be his most remunerative short story ever. Seymour Lawrence knew that in the intervening years Kurt had not only come to know nearly every magazine editor in America thanks to his dependable short stories, but had since the mid-sixties (when the story market had disappeared) served these editors well by taking on book review assignments nobody else would touch. (The classic example is "New Dictionary," a *New York Times Book Review* piece saved in this same collection, in which Vonnegut jokes about an ongoing debate among dictionary makers: "Prescriptive [linguistics], as nearly as I could tell, was like an honest cop, and descriptive was like a boozed-up war buddy from Mobile, Ala.") Could there be any doubt about his sixth novel, scheduled to come out the next year, finally getting the media attention its author had so long deserved but never yet received?

How governments of the future might handle overpopulation worried Kurt Vonnegut. Besides "Welcome to the Monkey House," this theme occupied "Adam" and "2BR02B," two earlier stories that appeared respectively in *Cosmopolitan* and *Worlds of If*. The former was not always a "sex manual," as Kurt had to remind an interviewer when the book collecting the story, *Bagombo Snuff Box*, was released late in 1999. In the 1950s it was as respectable (and as conservatively mannered) as any of the family magazines, though with a slant toward women's interests (as opposed to today's women's issues). The latter was a hard-core science fiction journal, favoring exotic fantasy over speculative technology. Readers can note two things: that the readers of *Cosmo* appreciated certain plot devices while science fiction enthusiasts preferred others, and that both reaches of the short story market shared Kurt's futuristic fears that some lives would be sacrificed.

Then there's the ridiculous. Given Kurt Vonnegut's disdain for the science fiction market, which in the opening essay for *Wampeters, Foma & Granfalloons* he compares to a urinal, one has to ponder his motives in contributing a story (on request) to science fiction writer Harlan Ellison's anthology published in 1972, *Again, Dangerous Visions*. This was when Kurt had achieved his fame as a novelist that would carry him through the rest of his career, with no need to write short stories for small if steady income. But write one he did. In *Palm Sunday*, where he reprints "The Big Space Fuck" with other collected works, Kurt reveals that his was the first story to use the notorious F word in its title. What this could achieve, beyond disqualifying the anthology for high school library or curriculum adoption, is not clear. At this very same time *Slaughterhouse-Five* was being banned for lesser reasons. It is included in *Palm Sunday*'s otherwise nonfiction section on "Obscenity."

It is ironic that one of Kurt Vonnegut's most widely praised and frequently anthologized stories first appeared in a science fiction journal, *Galaxy Science Fiction*. A few years later William F. Buckley reprinted it in the *National Review* as an example of first-rate conservative thinking, even as a left-wing counterculture was embracing Vonnegut the paperback novelist as its guru for youth. "Harrison Bergeron" qualifies on both levels. The student revolutionaries of the 1960s disliked big government as much as did their Young Republican colleagues and their elders on the party's right wing. "Corporate liberalism" with its "phony liberals" as the young call them was the enemy. In this story may be found materials for study that will explain the author's almost universal appeal. The government that mandates equality as practiced in this story is neither liberal nor conservative, but rather self-styled government per se.

The previously unpublished "Unknown Soldier" is only slightly futuristic, looking forward to the new millenium's arrival when the world is already awash in late-twentieth-century devices, some of which are awarded to the new age's first-born as prizes. Are those devices honorable awards? Do they honor the baby, or disgrace themselves? In the story's ending may lie Vonnegut's answer. When he'd started writing so many decades before, they were almost unimaginable. Now they are disposable. So it goes.

—JK

Harrison Bergeron

THE YEAR WAS 2081, and everybody was finally equal. They weren't only equal before God and the law. They were equal every which way. Nobody was smarter than anybody else. Nobody was better looking than anybody else. Nobody was stronger or quicker than anybody else. All this equality was due to the 211th, 212th, and 213th Amendments to the Constitution, and to the unceasing vigilance of agents of the United States Handicapper General.

Some things about living still weren't quite right, though. April, for instance, still drove people crazy by not being springtime. And it was in that clammy month that the H-G men took George and Hazel Bergeron's fourteen-year-old son, Harrison, away.

It was tragic, all right, but George and Hazel couldn't think about it very hard. Hazel had a perfectly average intelligence, which meant she couldn't think about anything except in short bursts. And George, while his intelligence was way above normal, had a little mental handicap radio in his ear. He was required by law to wear it at all times. It was tuned to a government transmitter. Every twenty seconds or so, the transmitter would send out some sharp noise to keep people like George from taking unfair advantage of their brains.

George and Hazel were watching television. There were tears on Hazel's cheeks, but she'd forgotten for the moment what they were about.

On the television screen were ballerinas.

A buzzer sounded in George's head. His thoughts fled in panic, like bandits from a burglar alarm.

"That was a real pretty dance, that dance they just did," said Hazel.

"Huh?" said George.

"That dance—it was nice," said Hazel.

"Yup," said George. He tried to think a little about the ballerinas. They weren't really very good—no better than anybody else would have been, anyway. They were burdened with sash-weights and bags of birdshot, and their faces were masked, so that no one, seeing a free and graceful gesture or a pretty face, would feel like something the cat drug in. George was toying with the vague notion that maybe dancers shouldn't be handicapped. But he didn't get very far with it before another noise in his ear radio scattered his thoughts.

George winced. So did two out of the eight ballerinas.

Hazel saw him wince. Having no mental handicap herself, she had to ask George what the latest sound had been.

"Sounded like somebody hitting a milk bottle with a ball peen hammer," said George.

"I'd think it would be real interesting, hearing all the different sounds," said Hazel, a little envious. "All the things they think up."

"Um," said George.

"Only, if I was Handicapper General, you know what I would do?" said Hazel. Hazel, as a matter of fact, bore a strong resemblance to the Handicapper General, a woman named Diana Moon Glampers. "If I was Diana Moon Glampers," said Hazel, "I'd have chimes on Sunday—just chimes. Kind of in honor of religion."

"I could think, if it was just chimes," said George.

"Well—maybe make 'em real loud," said Hazel. "I think I'd make a good Handicapper General."

"Good as anybody else," said George.

"Who knows better'n I do what normal is?" said Hazel.

"Right," said George. He began to think glimmeringly about his abnormal son who was now in jail, about Harrison, but a twenty-one-gun salute in his head stopped that.

"Boy!" said Hazel, "that was a doozy, wasn't it?"

It was such a doozy that George was white and trembling, and tears stood on the rims of his red eyes. Two of the eight ballerinas had collapsed to the studio floor, were holding their temples.

"All of a sudden you look so tired," said Hazel. "Why don't you stretch out on the sofa, so's you can rest your handicap bag on the pillows, honeybunch." She was referring to the forty-seven pounds of birdshot in a canvas bag, which was padlocked around George's neck. "Go on and rest the bag for a little while," she said. "I don't care if you're not equal to me for a while."

George weighed the bag with his hands. "I don't mind it," he said. "I don't notice it any more. It's just a part of me."

"You been so tired lately—kind of wore out," said Hazel. "If there was just some way we could make a little hole in the bottom of the bag, and just take out a few of them lead balls. Just a few."

"Two years in prison and two thousand dollars fine for every ball I took out," said George. "I don't call that a bargain."

"If you could just take a few out when you came home from work," said Hazel. "I mean—you don't compete with anybody around here. You just set around."

"If I tried to get away with it," said George, "then other people'd get away with it—and pretty soon we'd be right back to the dark ages again, with everybody competing against everybody else. You wouldn't like that, would you?"

"I'd hate it," said Hazel.

"There you are," said George. "The minute people start cheating on laws, what do you think happens to society?"

If Hazel hadn't been able to come up with an answer to this question, George couldn't have supplied one. A siren was going off in his head.

"Reckon it'd fall all apart," said Hazel.

"What would?" said George blankly.

"Society," said Hazel uncertainly. "Wasn't that what you just said?"

"Who knows?" said George.

The television program was suddenly interrupted for a news bulletin. It wasn't clear at first as to what the bulletin was about, since the announcer, like all announcers, had a serious speech impediment. For about half a minute, and in a state of high excitement, the announcer tried to say, "Ladies and gentlemen—"

He finally gave up, handed the bulletin to a ballerina to read.

"That's all right—" Hazel said of the announcer, "he tried. That's the big thing. He tried to do the best he could with what God gave him. He should get a nice raise for trying so hard."

"Ladies and gentlemen—" said the ballerina, reading the bulletin. She must have been extraordinarily beautiful, because the mask she wore was hideous. And it was easy to see that she was the strongest and most graceful of all the dancers, for her handicap bags were as big as those worn by two-hundred-pound men.

And she had to apologize at once for her voice, which was a very unfair voice for a woman to use. Her voice was a warm, luminous, timeless melody. "Excuse me—" she said, and she began again, making her voice absolutely uncompetitive.

"Harrison Bergeron, age fourteen," she said in a grackle squawk, "has just escaped from jail, where he was held on suspicion of plotting to overthrow the government. He is a genius and an athlete, is under-handicapped, and should be regarded as extremely dangerous."

A police photograph of Harrison Bergeron was flashed on the screen—upside down, then sideways, upside down again, then right side up. The picture showed the full length of Harrison against a background calibrated in feet and inches. He was exactly seven feet tall.

The rest of Harrison's appearance was Halloween and hardware. Nobody had ever borne heavier handicaps. He had outgrown hindrances faster than the H-G men could think them up. Instead of a little ear radio for a mental handicap, he wore a tremendous pair of earphones, and spectacles with thick wavy lenses. The spectacles were intended to make him not only half blind, but to give him whanging headaches besides.

Scrap metal was hung all over him. Ordinarily, there was a certain symmetry, a military neatness to the handicaps issued to strong people, but Harrison looked like a walking junkyard in the race of life. Harrison carried three hundred pounds.

And to offset his good looks, the H-G men required that he wear at all times a red rubber ball for a nose, keep his eyebrows shaved off, and cover his even white teeth with black caps at snaggle-tooth random.

"If you see this boy," said the ballerina, "do not—I repeat, do not—try to reason with him."

There was the shriek of a door being torn from its hinges.

Screams and barking cries of consternation came from the television set. The photograph of Harrison Bergeron on the screen jumped again and again, as though dancing to the tune of an earthquake.

George Bergeron correctly identified the earthquake, and well he might have—for many was the time his own home had danced to the same crashing tune. "My God—" said George, "that must be Harrison!"

The realization was blasted from his mind instantly by the sound of an automobile collision in his head.

When George could open his eyes again, the photograph of Harrison was gone. A living, breathing Harrison filled the screen.

Clanking, clownish, and huge, Harrison stood in the center of the studio. The knob of the uprooted studio door was still in his hand. Ballerinas, technicians, musicians, and announcers cowered on their knees before him, expecting to die.

"I am the Emperor!" cried Harrison. "Do you hear? I am the Emperor! Everybody must do what I say at once!" He stamped his foot and the studio shook.

"Even as I stand here—" he bellowed, "crippled, hobbled, sickened—I am a greater ruler than any man who ever lived! Now watch me become what I can become!"

Harrison tore the straps of his handicap harness like wet tissue paper, tore straps guaranteed to support five thousand pounds.

Harrison's scrap-iron handicaps crashed to the floor.

Harrison thrust his thumbs under the bar of the padlock that secured his head harness. The bar snapped like celery. Harrison smashed his headphones and spectacles against the wall.

He flung away his rubber-ball nose, revealed a man that would have awed Thor, the god of thunder.

"I shall now select my Empress!" he said, looking down on the cowering people. "Let the first woman who dares rise to her feet claim her mate and her throne!"

A moment passed, and then a ballerina arose, swaying like a willow.

Harrison plucked the mental handicap from her ear, snapped off her physical handicaps with marvellous delicacy. Last of all, he removed her mask.

She was blindingly beautiful.

"Now—" said Harrison, taking her hand, "shall we show the people the meaning of the word dance? Music!" he commanded.

The musicians scrambled back into their chairs, and Harrison stripped them of their handicaps, too. "Play your best," he told them, "and I'll make you barons and dukes and earls."

The music began. It was normal at first—cheap, silly, false. But Harrison snatched two musicians from their chairs, waved them like batons as he sang the music as he wanted it played. He slammed them back into their chairs.

The music began again and was much improved.

Harrison and his Empress merely listened to the music for a while—listened gravely, as though synchronizing their heartbeats with it.

They shifted their weights to their toes.

Harrison placed his big hands on the girl's tiny waist, letting her sense the weightlessness that would soon be hers.

And then, in an explosion of joy and grace, into the air they sprang!

Not only were the laws of the land abandoned, but the law of gravity and the laws of motion as well.

They reeled, whirled, swiveled, flounced, capered, gamboled, and spun.

They leaped like deer on the moon.

The studio ceiling was thirty feet high, but each leap brought the dancers nearer to it.

It became their obvious intention to kiss the ceiling.

They kissed it.

And then, neutralizing gravity with love and pure will, they remained suspended in air inches below the ceiling, and they kissed each other for a long, long time.

It was then that Diana Moon Glampers, the Handicapper General, came into the studio with a double-barreled ten-gauge shotgun. She fired twice, and the Emperor and the Empress were dead before they hit the floor.

Diana Moon Glampers loaded the gun again. She aimed it at the musicians and told them they had ten seconds to get their handicaps back on.

It was then that the Bergerons' television tube burned out.

Hazel turned to comment about the blackout to George. But George had gone out into the kitchen for a can of beer.

George came back in with the beer, paused while a handicap signal shook him up. And then he sat down again. "You been crying?" he said to Hazel.

"Yup," she said.

"What about?" he said.

"I forget," she said. "Something real sad on television."

"What was it?" he said.

"It's all kind of mixed up in my mind," said Hazel.

"Forget sad things," said George.

"I always do," said Hazel.

"That's my girl," said George. He winced. There was the sound of a rivetting gun in his head.

"Gee—I could tell that one was a doozy," said Hazel.

"You can say that again," said George.

"Gee—" said Hazel, "I could tell that one was a doozy."

Welcome to the Monkey House

SO PETE CROCKER, the sheriff of Barnstable County, which was the whole of Cape Cod, came into the Federal Ethical Suicide Parlor in Hyannis one May afternoon—and he told the two six-foot Hostesses there that they weren't to be alarmed, but that a notorious nothinghead named Billy the Poet was believed headed for the Cape.

A nothinghead was a person who refused to take his ethical birth-control pills three times a day. The penalty for that was $10,000 and ten years in jail.

This was at a time when the population of Earth was 17 billion human beings. That was far too many mammals that big for a planet that small. The people were virtually packed together like drupelets.

Drupelets are the pulpy little knobs that compose the outside of a raspberry.

So the World Government was making a two-pronged attack on overpopulation. One pronging was the encouragement of ethical suicide, which consisted of going to the nearest Suicide Parlor and asking a Hostess to kill you painlessly while you lay on a Barcalounger. The other pronging was compulsory ethical birth control.

The sheriff told the Hostesses, who were pretty, tough-minded, highly intelligent girls, that roadblocks were being set up and house-to-house searches were being conducted to catch Billy the Poet. The main difficulty was that the police didn't know what he looked like. The few people who had seen him and known him for what he was were women—and they disagreed fantastically as to his height, his hair color, his voice, his weight, the color of his skin.

"I don't need to remind you girls," the sheriff went on, "that a nothinghead is very sensitive from the waist down. If Billy the Poet somehow slips in here and starts making trouble, one good kick in the right place will do wonders."

He was referring to the fact that ethical birth-control pills, the only legal form of birth control, made people numb from the waist down.

Most men said their bottom halves felt like cold iron or balsa-wood. Most women said their bottom halves felt like wet cotton or stale ginger ale. The pills were so effective that you could blindfold a man who had taken one, tell him to recite the Gettysburg Address, kick him in the balls while he was doing it, and he wouldn't miss a syllable.

The pills were ethical because they didn't interfere with a person's ability to reproduce, which would have been unnatural and immoral. All the pills did was take every bit of pleasure out of sex.

Thus did science and morals go hand in hand.

◎ ◎ ◎

The two Hostesses there in Hyannis were Nancy McLuhan and Mary Kraft. Nancy was a strawberry blonde. Mary was a glossy brunette. Their uniforms were white lipstick, heavy eye makeup, purple body stockings with nothing underneath, and black-leather boots. They ran a small operation—with only six suicide booths. In a really good week, say the one before Christmas, they might put sixty people to sleep. It was done with a hypodermic syringe.

"My main message to you girls," said Sheriff Crocker, "is that everything's well under control. You can just go about your business here."

"Didn't you leave out part of your main message?" Nancy asked him.

"I don't get you."

"I didn't hear you say he was probably headed straight for us."

He shrugged in clumsy innocence. "We don't know that for sure."

"I thought that was all anybody did know about Billy the Poet: that he specializes in deflowering Hostesses in Ethical Suicide Parlors." Nancy was a virgin. All Hostesses were virgins. They also had to hold advanced degrees in psychology and nursing. They also had to be plump and rosy, and at least six feet tall.

America had changed in many ways, but it had yet to adopt the metric system.

Nancy McLuhan was burned up that the sheriff would try to protect her and Mary from the full truth about Billy the Poet—as though they might panic if they heard it. She told the sheriff so.

"How long do you think a girl would last in the E. S. S.," she said, meaning the Ethical Suicide Service, "if she scared that easy?"

The sheriff took a step backward, pulled in his chin. "Not very long, I guess."

"That's very true," said Nancy, closing the distance between them and offering him a sniff of the edge of her hand, which was poised for a karate chop. All Hostesses were experts at judo and karate. "If you'd like to find out how helpless we are, just come toward me, pretending you're Billy the Poet."

The sheriff shook his head, gave her a glassy smile. "I'd rather not."

"That's the smartest thing you've said today," said Nancy, turning her back on him while Mary laughed. "We're not scared—we're *angry*. Or we're not even *that*. He isn't *worth* that. We're *bored*. How boring that he should come a great distance, should cause all this fuss, in order to—" She let the sentence die there. "It's just too absurd."

"I'm not as mad at *him* as I am at the women who let him do it to them without a struggle"—said Mary—"who let him do it and then couldn't tell the police what he looked like. Suicide Hostesses at that!"

"Somebody hasn't been keeping up with her karate," said Nancy.

◎ ◎ ◎

It wasn't just Billy the Poet who was attracted to Hostesses in Ethical Suicide Parlors. All nothingheads were. Bombed out of their skulls with the sex madness that came from taking nothing, they thought the white lips and big eyes and body stocking and boots of a Hostess spelled sex, sex, sex.

The truth was, of course, that sex was the last thing any Hostess ever had in mind.

"If Billy follows his usual M.O.," said the sheriff, "he'll study your habits and the neighborhood. And then he'll pick one or the other of you and he'll send her a dirty poem in the mail."

"Charming," said Nancy.

"He has also been known to use the telephone."

"How brave," said Nancy. Over the sheriff's shoulder, she could see the mailman coming.

A blue light went on over the door of a booth for which Nancy was responsible. The person in there wanted something. It was the only booth in use at the time.

The sheriff asked her if there was a possibility that the person in there was Billy the Poet, and Nancy said, "Well, if it is, I can break his neck with my thumb and forefinger."

"Foxy Grandpa," said Mary, who'd seen him, too. A Foxy Grandpa was any old man, cute and senile, who quibbled and joked and reminisced for hours before he let a Hostess put him to sleep.

Nancy groaned. "We've spent the past two hours trying to decide on a last meal."

And then the mailman came in with just one letter. It was addressed to Nancy in smeary pencil. She was splendid with anger and disgust as she opened it, knowing it would be a piece of filth from Billy.

She was right. Inside the envelope was a poem. It wasn't an original poem. It was a song from olden days that had taken on new meanings since the numbness of ethical birth control had become universal. It went like this, in smeary pencil again:

> *We were walking through the park,*
> *A-goosing statues in the dark.*
> *If Sherman's horse can take it,*
> *So can you.*

When Nancy came into the suicide booth to see what he wanted, the Foxy Grandpa was lying on the mint-green Barcalounger, where hundreds had died so peacefully over the years. He was studying the menu from the Howard Johnson's next door and beating time to the Muzak coming from the loudspeaker on the lemon-yellow wall. The room was painted cinder block. There was one barred window with a Venetian blind.

There was a Howard Johnson's next door to every Ethical Suicide Parlor, and vice versa. The Howard Johnson's had an orange roof and the Suicide Parlor had a purple roof, but they were both the Government. Practically everything was the Government.

Practically everything was automated, too. Nancy and Mary and the sheriff were lucky to have jobs. Most people didn't. The average citizen moped around home and,watched television, which was the Government. Every fifteen minutes his television would urge him to vote intelligently or consume intelligently, or worship in the church of his choice, or love his fellowmen, or obey the laws—or pay a call to the nearest Ethical Suicide Parlor and find out how friendly and understanding a Hostess could be.

The Foxy Grandpa was something of a rarity, since he was marked by old age, was bald, was shaky, had spots on his hands. Most people looked twenty-two, thanks to anti-aging shots they took twice a year. That the old man looked old was proof that the shots had been discovered after his sweet bird of youth had flown.

"Have we decided on a last supper yet?" Nancy asked him. She heard peevishness in her own voice, heard herself betray her exasperation with Billy the Poet, her boredom with the old man. She was ashamed, for this was unprofessional of her. "The breaded veal cutlet is very good."

The old man cocked his head. With the greedy cunning of second childhood, he had caught her being unprofessional, unkind, and he was going to punish her for it. "You don't sound very friendly. I thought you were all supposed to be friendly. I thought this was supposed to be a pleasant place to come."

"I beg your pardon," she said. "If I seem unfriendly, it has nothing to do with you."

"I thought maybe I bored you."

"No, no," she said gamely, "not at all. You certainly know some very interesting history." Among other things, the Foxy Grandpa claimed to have known J. Edgar Nation, the Grand Rapids druggist who was the father of ethical birth control.

"Then look like you're interested," he told her. He could get away with that sort of impudence. The thing was, he could leave any time he wanted to, right up to the moment he asked for the needle—and he had to ask for the needle. That was the law.

Nancy's art, and the art of every Hostess, was to see that volunteers didn't leave, to coax and wheedle and flatter them patiently, every step of the way.

So Nancy had to sit down there in the booth, to pretend to marvel at the freshness of the yarn the old man told, a story everybody knew, about how J. Edgar Nation happened to experiment with ethical birth control.

"He didn't have the slightest idea his pills would be taken by human beings someday," said the Foxy Grandpa. "His dream was to introduce morality into the monkey house at the Grand Rapids Zoo. Did you realize that?" he inquired severely.

"No. No, I didn't. That's very interesting."

"He and his eleven kids went to church one Easter. And the day was so nice and the Easter service had been so beautiful and pure that they decided to take a walk through the zoo, and they were just walking on clouds."

"Um." The scene described was lifted from a play that was performed on television every Easter.

The Foxy Grandpa shoehorned himself into the scene, had himself chat with the Nations just before they got to the monkey house. "'Good morning, Mr. Nation,' I said to him. 'It certainly is a nice morning.' 'And a good morning to you, Mr. Howard,' he said to me. 'There is nothing like an Easter morning to make a man feel clean and reborn and at one with God's intentions.'"

"Um." Nancy could hear the telephone ringing faintly, naggingly, through the nearly soundproof door.

"So we went on to the monkey house together, and what do you think we saw?"

"I can't imagine." Somebody had answered the phone.

"We saw a monkey playing with his private parts!"

"No!"

"Yes! and J. Edgar Nation was so upset he went straight home and he started developing a pill that would make monkeys in the springtime fit things for a Christian family to see."

There was a knock on the door.

"Yes—?" said Nancy.

"Nancy," said Mary, "telephone for you."

When Nancy came out of the booth, she found the sheriff choking on little squeals of law-enforcement delight. The telephone was tapped by agents hidden in the Howard Johnson's. Billy the Poet was believed to be on the line. His call had been traced. Police were already on their way to grab him.

"Keep him on, keep him on," the sheriff whispered to Nancy, and he gave her the telephone as though it were solid gold.

"Yes—?" said Nancy.

"Nancy McLuhan?" said a man. His voice was disguised. He might have been speaking through a kazoo. "I'm calling for a mutual friend."

"Oh?"

"He asked me to deliver a message."

"I see."

"It's a poem."

"All right."

"Ready?"

"Ready." Nancy could hear sirens screaming in the background of the call.

The caller must have heard the sirens, too, but he recited the poem without any emotion. It went like this:

> *Soak yourself in Jergen's Lotion.*
> *Here comes the one-man population*
> *explosion.*

They got him. Nancy heard it all—the thumping and clumping, the argle-bargle and cries.

The depression she felt as she hung up was glandular. Her brave body had prepared for a fight that was not to be.

The sheriff bounded out of the Suicide Parlor, in such a hurry to see the famous criminal he'd helped catch that a sheaf of papers fell from the pocket of his trench coat.

Mary picked them up, called after the sheriff. He halted for a moment, said the papers didn't matter any more, asked her if maybe she wouldn't like to come along. There was a flurry between the two girls, with Nancy persuading Mary to go, declaring that she had no curiosity about Billy. So Mary left, irrelevantly handing the sheaf to Nancy.

The sheaf proved to be photocopies of poems Billy had sent to Hostesses in other places. Nancy read the top one. It made much of a peculiar side effect of ethical birth-control pills: They not only made people numb—they also made people piss blue. The poem was called *What the Somethinghead Said to the Suicide Hostess*, and it went like this:

> *I did not sow, I did not spin,*
> *And thanks to pills I did not sin.*
> *I loved the crowds, the stink, the noise.*
> *And when I peed, I peed turquoise.*
>
> *I ate beneath a roof of orange;*
> *Swung with progress like a door hinge.*
> *'Neath purple roof I've come today*
> *To piss my azure life away.*
>
> *Virgin hostess, death's recruiter,*
> *Life is cute, but you are cuter.*
> *Mourn my pecker, purple daughter—*
> *All it passed was sky-blue water.*

"You never heard that story before—about how J. Edgar Nation came to invent ethical birth control?" the Foxy Grandpa wanted to know. His voice cracked.

"Never did," lied Nancy.

"I thought everybody knew that."

"It was news to me."

"When he got through with the monkey house, you couldn't tell it from the Michigan Supreme Court. Meanwhile, there was this crisis going on in the United Nations. The people who understood science said people had to quit reproducing so much, and the people who understood morals said society would collapse if people used sex for nothing but pleasure."

The Foxy Grandpa got off his Barcalounger, went over to the window, pried two slats of the blind apart. There wasn't much to see out there. The view was blocked by the backside of a mocked-up thermometer twenty feet high, which faced the street. It was calibrated in billions of people on Earth, from zero to twenty. The make-believe column of liquid was a strip of translucent red plastic. It showed how many people there were on Earth. Very close to the bottom was a black arrow that showed what the scientists thought the population ought to be.

The Foxy Grandpa was looking at the setting sun through that red plastic, and through the blind, too, so that his face was banded with shadows and red.

"Tell me—" he said, "when I die, how much will that thermometer go down? A foot?"

"No."

"An inch?"

"Not quite."

"You know what the answer is, don't you?" he said, and he faced her. The senility had vanished from his voice and eyes. "One inch on that thing equals 83,333 people. You knew that, didn't you?"

"That—that might be true," said Nancy, "but that isn't the right way to look at it, in my opinion."

He didn't ask her what the right way was, in her opinion. He completed a thought of his own, instead. "I'll tell you something else that's true: I'm Billy the Poet, and you're a very good-looking woman."

With one hand, he drew a snub-nosed revolver from his belt. With the other, he peeled off his bald dome and wrinkled forehead, which proved to be rubber. Now he looked twenty-two.

"The police will want to know exactly what I look like when this is all over," he told Nancy with a malicious grin. "In case you're not good at describing people, and it's surprising how many women aren't:

I'm five foot two,
With eyes of blue,
With Brown hair to my shoulders—
A manly elf
So full of self
The ladies say he smolders.

Billy was ten inches shorter than Nancy was. She had about forty pounds on him. She told him he didn't have a chance, but Nancy was much mistaken. He had unbolted the bars on the window the night before and he made her go out the window and then down a manhole that was hidden from the street by the big thermometer.

He took her down into the sewers of Hyannis. He knew where he was going. He had a flashlight and a map. Nancy had to go before him along the narrow catwalk, her own shadow dancing mockingly in the lead. She tried to guess where they were, relative to the real world above. She guessed correctly when they passed under the Howard Johnson's, guessed from noises she heard. The machinery that processed and served the food there was silent. But, so people wouldn't feel too lonesome when eating there, the designers had provided sound effects for the kitchen. It was these Nancy heard—a tape recording of the clashing of silverware and the laughter of Negroes and Puerto Ricans.

After that she was lost. Billy had very little to say to her other than "Right," or "Left," or "Don't try anything funny, Juno, or I'll blow your great big fucking head off."

Only once did they have anything resembling a conversation. Billy began it, and ended it, too. "What in hell is a girl with hips like yours doing selling death?" he asked her from behind.

She dared to stop. "I can answer that," she told him. She was confident that she could give him an answer that would shrivel him like napalm.

But he gave her a shove, offered to blow her fucking head off again.

"You don't even want to hear my answer," she taunted him. "You're afraid to hear it."

"I never listen to a woman till the pills wear off," sneered Billy. That was his plan, then—to keep her a prisoner for at least eight hours. That was how long it took for the pills to wear off.

"That's a silly rule."

"A woman's not a woman till the pills wear off."

"You certainly manage to make a woman feel like an object rather than a person."

"Thank the pills for that," said Billy.

◎ ◎ ◎

There were 80 miles of sewers under Greater Hyannis, which had a population of 400,000 drupelets, 400,000 souls. Nancy lost track of the time down there. When Billy announced that they had at last reached their destination, it was possible for Nancy to imagine that a year had passed.

She tested this spooky impression by pinching her own thigh, by feeling what the chemical clock of her body said. Her thigh was still numb.

Billy ordered her to climb iron rungs that were set in wet masonry. There was a circle of sickly light above. It proved to be moonlight filtered through the plastic polygons of an enormous geodesic dome. Nancy didn't have to ask the traditional victim's question, "Where am I?" There was only one dome like that on Cape Cod. It was in Hyannis Port and it sheltered the ancient Kennedy Compound.

It was a museum of how life had been lived in more expansive times. The museum was closed. It was open only in the summertime.

The manhole from which Nancy and then Billy emerged was set in an expanse of green cement, which showed where the Kennedy lawn had been. On the green cement, in front of the ancient frame houses, were statues representing the fourteen Kennedys who had been Presidents of the United States or the World. They were playing touch football.

The President of the World at the time of Nancy's abduction, incidentally, was an ex–Suicide Hostess named "Ma" Kennedy. Her statue would never join this particular touch-football game. Her name was Kennedy, all right, but she wasn't the real thing. People complained of her lack of style, found her vulgar. On the wall of her office was a sign that said, YOU DON'T HAVE TO BE CRAZY TO WORK HERE, BUT IT SURE HELPS, and another one that said THIMK!, and another one that said, SOMEDAY WE'RE GOING TO HAVE TO GET ORGANIZED AROUND HERE.

Her office was in the Taj Mahal.

◙ ◙ ◙

Until she arrived in the Kennedy Museum, Nancy McLuhan was confident that she would sooner or later get a chance to break every bone in Billy's little body, maybe even shoot him with his own gun. She wouldn't have minded doing those things. She thought he was more disgusting than a blood-filled tick.

It wasn't compassion that changed her mind. It was the discovery that Billy had a gang. There were at least eight people around the manhole, men and women in equal numbers, with stockings pulled over their heads. It was the women who laid firm hands on Nancy, told her to keep calm. They were all at least as tall as Nancy and they held her in places where they could hurt her like hell if they had to.

Nancy closed her eyes, but this didn't protect her from the obvious conclusion: These perverted women were sisters from the Ethical Suicide Service. This upset her so much that she asked loudly and bitterly, "How can you violate your oaths like this?"

She was promptly hurt so badly that she doubled up and burst into tears.

When she straightened up again, there was plenty more she wanted to say, but she kept her mouth shut. She speculated silently as to what on Earth could make Suicide Hostesses turn against every concept of human decency. Nothingheaded-ness alone couldn't begin to explain it. They had to be drugged besides.

Nancy went over in her mind all the terrible drugs she'd learned about in school, persuaded herself that the women had taken the worst one of all. That drug was so powerful, Nancy's teachers had told her, that even a person numb from the waist down would copulate repeatedly and enthusiastically after just one glass. That had to be the answer: The women, and probably the men, too, had been drinking gin.

◎ ◎ ◎

They hastened Nancy into the middle frame house, which was dark like all the rest, and Nancy heard the men giving Billy the news. It was in this news that Nancy perceived a glint of hope. Help might be on its way.

The gang member who had phoned Nancy obscenely had fooled the police into believing that they had captured Billy the Poet, which was bad for Nancy. The police didn't know yet that Nancy was missing, two men told Billy, and a telegram had been sent to Mary Kraft in Nancy's name, declaring that Nancy had been called to New York City on urgent family business.

That was where Nancy saw the glint of hope: Mary wouldn't believe that telegram. Mary knew Nancy had no family in New York. Not one of the 63,000,000 people living there was a relative of Nancy's.

The gang had deactivated the burglar-alarm system of the museum. They had also cut through a lot of the chains and ropes that were meant to keep visitors from touching anything of value. There was no mystery as to who and what had done the cutting. One of the men was armed with brutal lopping shears.

They marched Nancy into a servant's bedroom upstairs. The man with the shears cut the ropes that fenced off the narrow bed. They put Nancy into the bed and two men held Nancy while a woman gave her a knockout shot.

Billy the Poet had disappeared.

As Nancy was going under, the woman who had given her the shot asked her how old she was.

Nancy was determined not to answer, but discovered that the drug had made her powerless not to answer. "Sixty-three," she murmured.

"How does it feel to be a virgin at sixty-three?"

Nancy heard her own answer through a velvet fog. She was amazed by the answer, wanted to protest that it couldn't possibly be hers. "Pointless," she'd said.

Moments later, she asked the woman thickly, "What was in that needle?"

"What was in the needle, honey bunch? Why, honey bunch, they call that 'truth serum.'"

◎ ◎ ◎

The moon was down when Nancy woke up—but the night was still out there. The shades were drawn and there was candlelight. Nancy had never seen a lit candle before.

What awakened Nancy was a dream of mosquitoes and bees. Mosquitoes and bees were extinct. So were birds. But Nancy dreamed that millions of insects were swarming about her from the waist down. They didn't sting. They fanned her. Nancy was a nothinghead.

She went to sleep again. When she awoke next time, she was being led into a bathroom by three women, still with stockings over their heads. The bathroom was already filled with the steam from somebody else's bath. There were somebody else's wet footprints crisscrossing the floor and the air reeked of pine-needle perfume.

Her will and intelligence returned as she was bathed and perfumed and dressed in a white nightgown. When the women stepped back to admire her, she said to them quietly, "I may be a nothinghead now. But that doesn't mean I have to think like one or act like one."

Nobody argued with her.

◙ ◙ ◙

Nancy was taken downstairs and out of the house. She fully expected to be sent down a manhole again. It would be the perfect setting for her violation by Billy, she was thinking—down in a sewer.

But they took her across the green cement, where the grass used to be, and then across the yellow cement, where the beach used to be, and then out onto the blue cement, where the harbor used to be. There were twenty-six yachts that had belonged to various Kennedys, sunk up to their water lines in blue cement. It was to the most ancient of these yachts, the Marlin, once the property of Joseph P. Kennedy, that they delivered Nancy.

It was dawn. Because of the high-rise apartments all around the Kennedy Museum, it would be an hour before any direct sunlight would reach the microcosm under the geodesic dome.

Nancy was escorted as far as the companionway to the forward cabin of the Marlin. The women pantomimed that she was expected to go down the five steps alone.

Nancy froze for the moment and so did the women. And there were two actual statues in the tableau on the bridge. Standing at the wheel was a statue of Frank Wirtanen, once skipper of the Marlin. And next to him was his son and first mate, Carly. They weren't paying any attention to poor Nancy. They were staring out through the windshield at the blue cement.

Nancy, barefoot and wearing a thin white nightgown, descended bravely into the forward cabin, which was a pool of candlelight and pine-needle perfume. The companionway hatch was closed and locked behind her.

Nancy's emotions and the antique furnishings of the cabin were so complex that Nancy could not at first separate Billy the Poet from his surroundings, from all the mahogany and leaded glass. And then she saw him at the far end of the cabin, with his back against the door to the forward cockpit. He was wearing purple silk pajamas with a Russian collar. They were piped in red, and writhing across Billy's silken breast was a golden dragon. It was belching fire.

Anticlimactically, Billy was wearing glasses. He was holding a book.

Nancy poised herself on the next-to-the-bottom step, took a firm grip on the handholds in the companionway. She bared her teeth, calculated that it would take ten men Billy's size to dislodge her.

Between them was a great table. Nancy had expected the cabin to be dominated by a bed, possibly in the shape of a swan, but the Marlin was a day boat. The cabin was anything but a seraglio. It was about as voluptuous as a lower-middle-class dining room in Akron, Ohio, around 1910.

A candle was on the table. So were an ice bucket and two glasses and a quart of champagne. Champagne was as illegal as heroin.

Billy took off his glasses, gave her a shy, embarrassed smile, said, "Welcome."

"This is as far as I come."

He accepted that. "You're very beautiful there."

"And what am I supposed to say—that you're stunningly handsome? That I feel an overwhelming desire to throw myself into your manly arms?"

"If you wanted to make me happy, that would certainly be the way to do it." He said that humbly.

"And what about my happiness?"

The question seemed to puzzle him. "Nancy—that's what this is all about."

"What if my idea of happiness doesn't coincide with yours?"

"And what do you think my idea of happiness is?"

"I'm not going to throw myself into your arms, and I'm not going to drink that poison, and I'm not going to budge from here unless somebody makes me," said Nancy. "So I think your idea of happiness is going to turn out to be eight people holding me down on that table, while you bravely hold a cocked pistol to my head—and do what you want. That's the way it's going to have to be, so call your friends and get it over with!"

Which he did.

◎ ◎ ◎

He didn't hurt her. He deflowered her with a clinical skill she found ghastly. When it was all over, he didn't seem cocky or proud. On the contrary, he was terribly depressed, and he said to Nancy, "Believe me, if there'd been any other way—"

Her reply to this was a face like stone—and silent tears of humiliation.

His helpers let down a folding bunk from the wall. It was scarcely wider than a bookshelf and hung on chains. Nancy allowed herself to be put to bed in it, and she was left alone with Billy the Poet again. Big as she was, like a double bass wedged onto that narrow shelf, she felt like a pitiful little thing. A scratchy, war-surplus blanket had been tucked in around her. It was her own idea to pull up a corner of the blanket to hide her face.

Nancy sensed from sounds what Billy was doing, which wasn't much. He was sitting at the table, sighing occasionally, sniffing occasionally, turning the pages of a book. He lit a cigar and the stink of it seeped under her blanket. Billy inhaled the cigar, then coughed and coughed and coughed.

When the coughing died down, Nancy said loathingly through the blanket, "You're so strong, so masterful, so healthy. It must be wonderful to be so manly."

Billy only sighed at this.

"I'm not a very typical nothinghead," she said. "I hated it—hated everything about it."

Billy sniffed, turned a page.

"I suppose all the other women just loved it—couldn't get enough of it."

"Nope."

She uncovered her face. "What do you mean, 'Nope'?"

"They've all been like you."

This was enough to make Nancy sit up and stare at him. "The women who helped you tonight—"

"What about them?"

"You've done to them what you did to me?"

He didn't look up from his book. "That's right."

"Then why don't they kill you instead of helping you?"

"Because they understand." And then he added mildly, "They're grateful."

Nancy got out of bed, came to the table, gripped the edge of the table, leaned close to him. And she said to him tautly, "I am not grateful."

"You will be."

"And what could possibly bring about that miracle?"

"Time," said Billy.

Billy closed his book, stood up. Nancy was confused by his magnetism. Somehow he was very much in charge again.

"What you've been through, Nancy," he said, "is a typical wedding night for a strait-laced girl of a hundred years ago, when everybody was a nothinghead. The groom did without helpers, because the bride wasn't customarily ready to kill him. Otherwise, the spirit of the occasion was much the same. These are the pajamas my great-great-grandfather wore on his wedding night in Niagara Falls.

"According to his diary, his bride cried all that night, and threw up twice. But, with the passage of time, she became a sexual enthusiast."

It was Nancy's turn to reply by not replying. She understood the tale. It frightened her to understand so easily that, from gruesome beginnings, sexual enthusiasm could grow and grow.

"You're a very typical nothinghead," said Billy. "If you dare to think about it now, you'll realize that you're angry because I'm such a bad lover, and a funny-looking shrimp besides. And what you can't help dreaming about from now on is a really suitable mate for a Juno like yourself.

"You'll find him, too—tall and strong and gentle. The nothinghead movement is growing by leaps and bounds."

"But—" said Nancy, and she stopped there. She looked out a porthole at the rising sun.

"But what?"

"The world is in the mess it is today because of the nothingheadedness of olden times. Don't you see?" She was pleading weakly. "The world can't afford sex anymore."

"Of course it can afford sex," said Billy. "All it can't afford anymore is reproduction."

"Then why the laws?"

"They're bad laws," said Billy. "If you go back through history, you'll find that the people who have been most eager to rule, to make the laws, to enforce the laws and to tell everybody exactly how God Almighty wants things here on Earth—those people have forgiven themselves and their friends for anything and everything. But they have been absolutely disgusted and terrified by the natural sexuality of common men and women.

"Why this is, I do not know. That is one of the many questions I wish somebody would ask the machines. I do know this: The triumph of that sort of disgust and terror is now complete. Almost every man and woman looks and feels like something the cat dragged in. The only sexual beauty that an ordinary human being can see today is in the woman who will kill him. Sex is death. There's a short and nasty equation for you: 'Sex is death. Q. E. D.'

"So you see, Nancy," said Billy, "I have spent this night, and many others like it, attempting to restore a certain amount of innocent pleasure to the world, which is poorer in pleasure than it needs to be."

Nancy sat down quietly and bowed her head.

"I'll tell you what my grandfather did on the dawn of his wedding night," said Billy.

"I don't think I want to hear it."

"It isn't violent. It's—it's meant to be tender."

"Maybe that's why I don't want to hear it."

"He read his bride a poem." Billy took the book from the table, opened it. "His diary tells which poem it was. While we aren't bride and groom, and while we may not meet again for many years, I'd like to read this poem to you, to have you know I've loved you."

"Please—no. I couldn't stand it."

"All right, I'll leave the book here, with the place marked, in case you want to read it later. It's the poem beginning:

> *How do I love thee? Let me count the ways.*
> *I love thee to the depth and breadth and height*
> *My soul can reach, when feeling out of sight*
> *For the ends of Being and ideal Grace.*

Billy put a small bottle on top of the book. "I am also leaving you these pills. If you take one a month, you will never have children. And still you'll be a nothing-head."

And he left. And they all left but Nancy.

When Nancy raised her eyes at last to the book and bottle, she saw that there was a label on the bottle. What the label said was this: WELCOME TO THE MONKEY HOUSE.

Adam

IT WAS MIDNIGHT in a Chicago lying-in hospital.

"Mr. Sousa," said the nurse, "your wife had a girl. You can see the baby in about twenty minutes."

"I know, I know, I know," said Mr. Sousa, a sullen gorilla, plainly impatient with having a tiresome and familiar routine explained to him. He snapped his fingers. "Girl! Seven, now. Seven girls I got now. A houseful of women. I can beat the stuffings out of ten men my own size. But, what do I get? Girls."

"Mr. Knechtmann," said the nurse to the other man in the room. She pronounced the name, as almost all Americans did, a colorless Netman. "I'm sorry. Still no word on your wife. She is keeping us waiting, isn't she?" She grinned glassily and left.

Sousa turned on Knechtmann. "Some little son of a gun like you, Netman, you want a boy, bing! You got one. Want a football team, bing, bing, bing, eleven, you got it." He stomped out of the room.

The man he left behind, all alone now, was Heinz Knechtmann, a presser in a dry-cleaning plant, a small man with thin wrists and a bad spine that kept him slightly hunched, as though forever weary. His face was long and big-nosed and thin-lipped, but was so overcast with good-humored humility as to be beautiful. His eyes were large and brown, and deep-set and long-lashed. He was only twenty-two, but seemed and felt much older. He had died a little as each member of his family had been led away and killed by the Nazis, until only in him, at the age of ten, had life and the name of Knechtmann shared a soul. He and his wife, Avchen, had grown up behind barbed wire.

◙ ◙ ◙

He had been staring at the walls of the waiting room for twelve hours now, since noon, when his wife's labor pains had become regular, the surges of slow rollers coming in from the sea a mile apart, from far, far away. This would be his second child. The last time he had waited, he had waited on a straw tick in a displaced-persons camp in Germany. The child, Karl Knechtmann, named after Heinz's father, had died, and with it, once more, had died the name of one of the finest cellists ever to have lived.

When the numbness of weary wishing lifted momentarily during this second vigil, Heinz's mind was a medley of proud family names, gone, all gone, that could be brought to life again in this new being—if it lived. Peter Knechtmann, the surgeon; Kroll Knechtmann, the botanist; Friedrich Knechtmann, the playwright. Dimly recalled uncles. Or if it was a girl, and if it lived, it would be Helga Knechtmann, Heinz's mother, and she would learn to play the harp as Heinz's mother had, and for all Heinz's ugliness, she would be beautiful. The Knechtmann men were all ugly, the Knechtmann women were all lovely as angels, though not all angels. It had always been so—for hundreds and hundreds of years.

"Mr. Netman," said the nurse, "it's a boy, and your wife is fine. She's resting now. You can see her in the morning. You can see the baby in twenty minutes."

Heinz looked up dumbly.

"It weighs five pounds nine ounces." She was gone again, with the same prim smile and officious, squeaking footsteps.

"Knechtmann," murmured Heinz, standing and bowing slightly to the wall. "The name is Knechtmann." He bowed again and gave a smile that was courtly and triumphant. He spoke the name with an exaggerated Old World pronunciation, like a foppish footman announcing the arrival of nobility, a guttural drum roll, unsoftened for American ears. "*KhhhhhhhhhhhhhhhhNECHT! mannnnnnnnnnnn.*"

"Mr. Netman?" A very young doctor with a pink face and close-cropped red hair stood in the waiting-room door. There were circles under his eyes, and he spoke through a yawn.

"Dr. Powers!" cried Heinz, clasping the man's right hand between both of his. "Thank God, thank God, thank God, and thank you."

"Um," said Dr. Powers, and he managed to smile wanly.

"There isn't anything wrong, is there?"

"Wrong?" said Powers. "No, no. Everything's fine. If I look down in the mouth, it's because I've been up for thirty-six hours straight." He closed his eyes, and leaned against the doorframe. "No, no trouble with your wife," he said in a faraway voice. "She's made for having babies. Regular pop-up toaster. Like rolling off a log. Schnip-schnap."

"She is?" said Heinz incredulously.

Dr. Powers shook his head, bringing himself back to consciousness. "My mind—conked out completely. Sousa—I got your wife confused with Mrs. Sousa. They finished in a dead heat. Netman, you're Netman. Sorry. Your wife's the one with pelvis trouble."

"Malnutrition as a child," said Heinz.

"Yeah. Well, the baby came normally, but, if you're going to have another one, it'd better be a Caesarean. Just to be on the safe side."

"I can't thank you enough," said Heinz passionately.

Dr. Powers licked his lips, and fought to keep his eyes open. "Uh huh. 'S O.K.," he said thickly. "'Night. Luck." He shambled out into the corridor.

The nurse stuck her head into the waiting room. "You can see your baby, Mr. Netman."

"Doctor—" said Heinz, hurrying out into the corridor, wanting to shake Powers' hand again so that Powers would know what a magnificent thing he'd done. "It's the most wonderful thing that ever happened." The elevator doors slithered shut between them before Dr. Powers could show a glimmer of response.

◎ ◎ ◎

"This way," said the nurse. "Turn left at the end of the hall, and you'll find the nursery window there. Write your name on a piece of paper and hold it against the glass."

Heinz made the trip by himself, without seeing another human being until he reached the end. There, on the other side of a large glass panel, he saw a hundred of them cupped in shallow canvas buckets and arranged in a square block of straight ranks and files.

Heinz wrote his name on the back of a laundry slip and pressed it to the window. A fat and placid nurse looked at the paper, not at Heinz's face, and missed seeing his wide smile, missed an urgent invitation to share for a moment his ecstasy.

She grasped one of the buckets and wheeled it before the window. She turned away again, once more missing the smile.

"Hello, hello, hello, little Knechtmann," said Heinz to the red prune on the other side of the glass. His voice echoed down the hard, bare corridor, and came back to him with embarrassing loudness. He blushed and lowered his voice. "Little Peter, little Kroll," he said softly, "little Friederich—and there's Helga in you, too. Little spark of Knechtmann, you little treasure house. Everything is saved in you."

"I'm afraid you'll have to be more quiet," said a nurse, sticking her head out from one of the rooms.

"Sorry," said Heinz. "I'm very sorry." He fell silent, and contented himself with tapping lightly on the window with a fingernail, trying to get the child to look at him. Young Knechtmann would not look, wouldn't share the moment, and after a few minutes the nurse took him away again.

Heinz beamed as he rode on the elevator and as he crossed the hospital lobby, but no one gave him more than a cursory glance. He passed a row of telephone booths and there, in one of the booths with the door open, he saw a soldier with whom he'd shared the waiting room an hour before.

"Yeah, Ma—seven pounds six ounces. Got hair like Buffalo Bill. No, we haven't had time to make up a name for her yet . . . That you, Pa? Yup, mother and daughter doin' fine, just fine. Seven pounds six ounces. Nope, no name. . . . That you, Sis? Pretty late for you to be up, ain't it? Doesn't look like anybody yet. Let me talk to Ma again. . . . That you, Ma? Well, I guess that's all the news from Chicago. Now,

Mom, Mom, take it easy—don't worry. It's a swell-looking baby, Mom. Just the hair looks like Buffalo Bill, and I said it as a joke, Mom. That's right, seven pounds six ounces. . . ."

There were five other booths, all empty, all open for calls to anyplace on earth. Heinz longed to hurry into one of them breathlessly, and tell the marvelous news. But there was no one to call, no one waiting for the news.

◉ ◉ ◉

But Heinz still beamed, and he strode across the street and into a quiet tavern there. In the dank twilight there were only two men, tête-à-tête, the bartender and Mr. Sousa.

"Yes sir, what'll it be?"

"I'd like to buy you and Mr. Sousa a drink," said Heinz with a heartiness strange to him. "I'd like the best brandy you've got. My wife just had a baby!"

"That so?" said the bartender with polite interest.

"Five pounds nine ounces," said Heinz.

"Huh," said the bartender. "What do you know."

"Netman," said Sousa, "wha'dja get?"

"Boy," said Heinz proudly.

"Never knew it to fail," said Sousa bitterly. "It's the little guys, all the time the little guys."

"Boy, girl," said Heinz, "it's all the same, just as long as it lives. Over there in the hospital, they're too close to it to see the wonder of it. A miracle over and over again—the world made new."

"Wait'll you've racked up seven, Netman," said Sousa. "*Then* you come back and tell me about the miracle."

"You got seven?" said the bartender. "I'm one up on you. I got eight." He poured three drinks.

"Far as I'm concerned," said Sousa, "you can have the championship."

Heinz lifted his glass. "Here's long life and great skill and much happiness to—to Peter Karl Knechtmann." He breathed quickly, excited by the decision.

"*There's* a handle to take ahold of," said Sousa. "You'd think the kid weighed two hundred pounds."

"Peter is the name of a famous surgeon," said Heinz, "the boy's great-uncle, dead now. Karl was my father's name."

"Here's to Pete K. Netman," said Sousa, with a cursory salute.

"Pete," said the bartender, drinking.

"And here's to *your* little girl—the new one," said Heinz.

Sousa sighed and smiled wearily. "Here's to her. God bless her."

"And now, *I'll* propose a toast," said the bartender, hammering on the bar with his fist. "On your feet, gentlemen. Up, up, everybody up."

Heinz stood, and held his glass high, ready for the next step in camaraderie, a toast to the whole human race, of which the Knechtmanns were still a part.

"Here's to the White Sox!" roared the bartender.

"Minoso, Fox, Mele," said Sousa.

"Fain, Lollar, Rivera!" said the bartender. He turned to Heinz. "Drink up, boy! The White Sox! Don't tell me you're a Cub fan."

"No," said Heinz, disappointed. "No—I don't follow baseball, I'm afraid." The other two men seemed to be sinking away from him. "I haven't been able to think about much but the baby."

The bartender at once turned his full attention to Sousa. "Look," he said intensely, "they take Fain off of first, and put him at third, and give Pierce first. Then move Minoso in from left field to shortstop. See what I'm doing?"

"Yep, yep," said Sousa eagerly.

"And then we take that no-good Carrasquel and . . ."

Heinz was all alone again, with twenty feet of bar between him and the other two men. It might as well have been a continent.

He finished his drink without pleasure, and left quietly.

At the railroad station, where he waited for a local train to take him home to the South Side, Heinz's glow returned again as he saw a co-worker at the dry-cleaning plant walk in with a girl. They were laughing and had their arms around each other's waist.

"Harry," said Heinz, hurrying toward them. "Guess what, Harry. Guess what just happened." He grinned broadly.

Harry, a tall, dapper, snub-nosed young man, looked down at Heinz with mild surprise. "Oh—hello, Heinz. What's up, boy?"

The girl looked on in perplexity, as though asking why they should be accosted at such an odd hour by such an odd person. Heinz avoided her slightly derisive eyes.

"A baby, Harry. My wife just had a boy."

"Oh," said Harry. He extended his hand. "Well, congratulations." The hand was limp. "I think that's swell, Heinz, perfectly swell." He withdrew his hand and waited for Heinz to say something else.

"Yes, yes—just about an hour ago," said Heinz. "Five pounds nine ounces. I've never been happier in my life."

"Well, I think it's perfectly swell, Heinz. You should be happy."

"Yes, indeed," said the girl.

There was a long silence, with all three shifting from one foot to the other.

"Really good news," said Harry at last.

"Yes, well," said Heinz quickly, "well, that's all I had to tell you."

"Thanks," said Harry. "Glad to hear about it."

There was another uneasy silence.

"See you at work," said Heinz, and strode jauntily back to his bench, but with his reddened neck betraying how foolish he felt.

The girl giggled.

Back home in his small apartment, at two in the morning, Heinz talked to himself, to the empty bassinet, and to the bed. He talked in German, a language he had sworn never to use again.

"They don't care," said Heinz. "They're all too busy, busy, busy to notice life, to feel anything about it. A baby is born." He shrugged. "What could be duller? Who would be so stupid as to talk about it, to think there was anything important or interesting about it?"

He opened a window on the summer night, and looked out at the moonlit canyon of gray wooden porches and garbage cans. "There are too many of us, and we are all too far apart," said Heinz. "Another Knechtmann is born, another O'Leary, another Sousa. Who cares? Why should anyone care? What difference does it make? None."

He lay down in his clothes on the unmade bed, and, with a rattling sigh, went to sleep.

◎ ◎ ◎

He awoke at six, as always. He drank a cup of coffee, and with a wry sense of anonymity, he jostled and was jostled aboard the downtown train. His face showed no emotion. It was like all the other faces, seemingly incapable of surprise or wonder, joy or anger.

He walked across town to the hospital with the same detachment, a gray, uninteresting man, a part of the city.

In the hospital, he was as purposeful and calm as the doctors and nurses bustling about him. When he was led into the ward where Avchen slept behind white screens, he felt only what he had always felt in her presence—love and aching awe and gratitude for her.

"You go ahead and wake her gently, Mr. Netman," said the nurse.

"Avchen—" He touched her on her white-gowned shoulder. "Avchen. Are you all right, Avchen?"

"Mmmmmmmmmmm?" murmured Avchen. Her eyes opened to narrow slits. "Heinz. Hello, Heinz."

"Sweetheart, are you all right?"

"Yes, yes," she whispered. "I'm fine. How is the baby, Heinz?"

"Perfect. Perfect, Avchen."

"They couldn't kill us, could they, Heinz?"

"No."

"And here we are, alive as we can be."

"Yes."

"The baby, Heinz—" She opened her dark eyes wide. "It's the most wonderful thing that ever happened, isn't it?"

"Yes," said Heinz.

Tomorrow and Tomorrow and Tomorrow

THE YEAR WAS 2158 A.D., and Lou and Emerald Schwartz were whispering on the balcony outside Lou's family's apartment on the seventy-sixth floor of Building 257 in Alden Village, a New York housing development that covered what had once been known as Southern Connecticut. When Lou and Emerald had married, Em's parents had tearfully described the marriage as being between May and December; but now, with Lou one hundred and twelve and Em ninety-three, Em's parents had to admit that the match had worked out well.

But Em and Lou weren't without their troubles, and they were out in the nippy air of the balcony because of them.

"Sometimes I get so mad, I feel like just up and diluting his anti-gerasone," said Em.

"That'd be against Nature, Em," said Lou, "it'd be murder. Besides, if he caught us tinkering with his anti-gerasone, not only would he disinherit us, he'd bust my neck. Just because he's one hundred and seventy-two doesn't mean Gramps isn't strong as a bull."

"Against Nature," said Em. "Who knows what Nature's like anymore? Ohhhhh—I don't guess I could ever bring myself to dilute his anti-gerasone or anything like that, but, gosh, Lou, a body can't help thinking Gramps is never going to leave if somebody doesn't help him along a little. Golly—we're so crowded a person can hardly turn around, and Verna's dying for a baby, and Melissa's gone thirty years without one." She stamped her feet. "I get so sick of seeing his wrinkled old face, watching him take the only private room and the best chair and the best food, and getting to pick out what to watch on TV, and running everybody's life by changing his will all the time."

"Well, after all," said Lou bleakly, "Gramps *is* head of the family. And he can't help being wrinkled like he is. He was seventy before anti-gerasone was invented. He's going to leave, Em. Just give him time. It's his business. I know he's tough to live with, but be patient. It wouldn't do to do anything that'd rile him. After all, we've got it better'n anybody else, there on the daybed."

"How much longer do you think we'll get to sleep on the daybed before he picks another pet? The world's record's two months, isn't it?"

"Mom and Pop had it that long once, I guess."

"When *is* he going to leave, Lou?" said Emerald.

"Well, he's talking about giving up anti-gerasone right after the five-hundred-mile Speedway Race."

"Yes—and before that it was the Olympics, and before that the World's Series, and before that the Presidential Elections, and before that I-don't-know-what. It's been just one excuse after another for fifty years now. I don't think we're ever going to get a room to ourselves or an egg or anything."

"All right—call me a failure!" said Lou. "What can I do? I work hard and make good money, but the whole thing, practically, is taxed away for defense and old age pensions. And if it wasn't taxed away, where you think we'd find a vacant room to rent? Iowa, maybe? Well, who wants to live on the outskirts of Chicago?"

Em put her arms around his neck. "Lou, hon, I'm not calling you a failure. The Lord knows you're not. You just haven't had a chance to be anything or have anything because Gramps and the rest of his generation won't leave and let somebody else take over."

"Yeah, yeah," said Lou gloomily. "You can't exactly blame 'em, though, can you? I mean, I wonder how quick we'll knock off the anti-gerasone when we get Gramps' age."

"Sometimes I wish there wasn't any such thing as anti-gerasone!" said Emerald passionately. "Or I wish it was made out of something real expensive and hard-to-get instead of mud and dandelions. Sometimes I wish folks just up and died regular as clockwork, without anything to say about it, instead of deciding themselves how long they're going to stay around. There ought to be a law against selling the stuff to anybody over one hundred and fifty."

"Fat chance of that," said Lou, "with all the money and votes the old people've got." He looked at her closely. "You ready to up and die, Em?"

"Well, for heaven's sakes, what a thing to say to your wife. Hon! I'm not even one hundred yet." She ran her hands lightly over her firm, youthful figure, as though for confirmation. "The best years of my life are still ahead of me. But you can bet that when one hundred and fifty rolls around, old Em's going to pour her anti-gerasone down the sink, and quit taking up room, and she'll do it smiling."

"Sure, sure," said Lou, "you bet. That's what they all say. How many you heard of doing it?"

"There was that man in Delaware."

"Aren't you getting kind of tired of talking about him, Em? That was five months ago."

"All right, then—Gramma Winkler, right here in the same building."

"She got smeared by a subway."

"That's just the way she picked to go," said Em.

"Then what was she doing carrying a six-pack of anti-gerasone when she got it?"

Emerald shook her head wearily and covered her eyes. "I dunno, I dunno, I dunno. All I know is, something's just got to be done." She sighed. "Sometimes I wish they'd left a couple of diseases kicking around somewhere, so I could get one and go to bed for a little while. Too many people!" she cried, and her words cackled and gabbled and died in a thousand asphalt-paved, skyscraper-walled courtyards.

Lou laid his hand on her shoulder tenderly. "Aw, hon, I hate to see you down in the dumps like this."

"If we just had a car, like the folks used to in the old days," said Em, "we could go for a drive, and get away from people for a little while. Gee—if *those* weren't the days!"

"Yeah," said Lou, "before they'd used up all the metal."

"We'd hop in, and Pop'd drive up to a filling station and say, 'Fillerup!'"

"That *was* the nuts, wasn't it—before they'd used up all the gasoline."

"And we'd go for a carefree ride in the country."

"Yeah—all seems like a fairyland now, doesn't it, Em? Hard to believe there really used to be all that space between cities."

"And when we got hungry," said Em, "we'd find ourselves a restaurant, and walk in, bit as you please and say, 'I'll have a steak and French-fries, I believe,' or, 'How are the pork chops today?'" She licked her lips, and her eyes glistened.

"Yeah man!" growled Lou. "How'd you like a hamburger with the works, Em?"

"Mmmmmmmm."

"If anybody'd offered us processed seaweed in those days, we would have spit right in his eye, huh, Em?"

"Or processed sawdust," said Em.

Doggedly, Lou tried to find the cheery side of the situation. "Well, anyway, they've got the stuff so it tastes a lot less like seaweed and sawdust than it did at first; and they say it's actually better for us than what we used to eat."

"I felt fine!" said Em fiercely.

Lou shrugged. "Well, you've got to realize, the world wouldn't be able to support twelve billion people if it wasn't for processed seaweed and sawdust. I mean, it's a wonderful thing, really. I guess. That's what they say."

"They say the first thing that pops into their heads," said Em. She closed her eyes. "Golly—remember shopping, Lou? Remember how the stores used to fight to get our folks to buy something? You didn't have to wait for somebody to die to get a bed or chairs or a stove or anything like that. Just went in—bing!—and bought whatever you wanted. Gee whiz that was nice, before they used up all the raw materials. I was just a little kid then, but I can remember so plain."

Depressed, Lou walked listlessly to the balcony's edge, and looked up at the clean, cold, bright stars against the black velvet of infinity. "Remember when we used to be bugs on science fiction, Em? Flight seventeen, leaving for Mars, launching ramp twelve. 'Board! All non-technical personnel kindly remain in bunkers. Ten seconds . . . nine . . . eight . . . seven . . . six . . . five . . . four . . . three . . . two . . . one! Main Stage! Barrrrrroooom!"

"Why worry about what was going on on Earth?" said Em, looking up at the stars with him. "In another few years, we'd all be shooting through space to start life all over again on a new planet."

Lou sighed. "Only it turns out you need something about twice the size of the Empire State Building to get one lousy colonist to Mars. And for another couple of trillion bucks he could take his wife and dog. *That's* the way to lick overpopulation—*emigrate!*"

"Lou—?"

"Hmmm?"

"When's the Five-Hundred-Mile Speedway Race?"

"Uh—Memorial Day, May thirtieth."

She bit her lip. "Was that awful of me to ask?"

"Not very, I guess. Everybody in the apartment's looked it up to make sure."

"I don't want to be awful," said Em, "but you've just got to talk over these things now and then, and get them out of your system."

"Sure you do. Feel better?"

"Yes—and I'm not going to lose my temper anymore, and I'm going to be just as nice to him as I know how."

"That's my Em."

They squared their shoulders, smiled bravely, and went back inside.

○ ○ ○

Gramps Schwartz, his chin resting on his hands, his hands on the crook of his cane, was staring irascibly at the five-foot television screen that dominated the room. On the screen, a news commentator was summarizing the day's happenings. Every thirty seconds or so, Gramps would jab the floor with his cane-tip and shout, "Hell! We did that a hundred years ago!"

Emerald and Lou, coming in from the balcony, were obliged to take seats in the back row, behind Lou's father and mother, brother and sister-in-law, son and daughter-in-law, grandson and wife, granddaughter and husband, great-grandson and wife, nephew and wife, grandnephew and wife, great-grandniece and husband, great-grandnephew and wife, and, of course, Gramps, who was in front of everybody. All, save Gramps, who was somewhat withered and bent, seemed, by pre-anti-gerasone standards, to be about the same age—to be somewhere in their late twenties or early thirties.

"*Meanwhile,*" the commentator was saying, "*Council Bluffs, Iowa, was still threatened by stark tragedy. But two hundred weary rescue workers have refused to give up hope, and continue to dig in an effort to save Elbert Haggedorn, one hundred and eighty-three, who has been wedged for two days in a . . . "*

"I wish he'd get something more cheerful," Emerald whispered to Lou.

"Silence!" cried Gramps. "Next one shoots off his big bazoo while the TV's on is gonna find hisself cut off without a dollar—" and here his voice suddenly softened and sweetened—"when they wave that checkered flag at the Indianapolis Speedway, and old Gramps gets ready for the Big Trip Up Yonder." He sniffed sentimentally, while his heirs concentrated desperately on not making the slightest sound. For them the poignancy of the prospective Big Trip had been dulled somewhat by its having been mentioned by Gramps about once a day for fifty years.

"Dr. Brainard Keyes Bullard," said the commentator, *"President of Wyandotte College, said in an address tonight that most of the world's ills can be traced to the fact that Man's knowledge of himself has not kept pace with his knowledge of the physical world."*

"Hell!" said Gramps. "We said that a hundred years ago."

"In Chicago tonight," said the commentator, *"a special celebration is taking place in the Chicago Lying-in Hospital. The guest of honor is Lowell W. Hitz, age zero. Hitz, born this morning, is the twenty-five-millionth child to be born in the hospital."* The commentator faded, and was replaced on the screen by young Hitz, who squalled furiously.

"Hell," whispered Lou to Emerald, "we said that a hundred years ago."

"I heard that!" shouted Gramps. He snapped off the television set, and his petrified descendants stared silently at the screen. "You, there, boy—"

"I didn't mean anything by it, sir," said Lou.

"Get me my will. You know where it is. You kids *all* know where it is. Fetch, boy!"

Lou nodded dully, and found himself going down the hall, picking his way over bedding to Gramps' room, the only private room in the Schwartz apartment. The other rooms were the bathroom, the living room, and the wide, windowless hallway, which was originally intended to serve as a dining area, and which had a kitchenette in one end. Six mattresses and four sleeping bags were dispersed in the hallway and living room, and the daybed, in the living room, accommodated the eleventh couple, the favorites of the moment.

On Gramps' bureau was his will, smeared, dog-eared, perforated, and blotched with hundreds of additions, deletions, accusations, conditions, warnings, advice, and homely philosophy. The document was, Lou reflected, a fifty-year diary, all jammed onto two sheets—a garbled, illegible log of day after day of strife. This day, Lou would be disinherited for the eleventh time, and it would take him perhaps six months of impeccable behavior to regain the promise of a share in the estate.

"Boy!" called Gramps.

"Coming, sir." Lou hurried back into the living room, and handed Gramps the will.

"Pen!" said Gramps.

He was instantly offered eleven pens, one from each couple.

"Not *that* leaky thing," he said, brushing Lou's pen aside. "Ah, there's a nice one. Good boy, Willy." He accepted Willy's pen. That was the tip they'd all been waiting for. Willy, then, Lou's father, was the new favorite.

Willy, who looked almost as young as Lou, though one hundred and forty-two, did a poor job of concealing his pleasure. He glanced shyly at the daybed, which would become his, and from which Lou and Emerald would have to move back into the hall, back to the worst spot of all by the bathroom door.

Gramps missed none of the high drama he'd authored, and he gave his own familiar role everything he had. Frowning and running his finger along each line, as though he were seeing the will for the first time, he read aloud in a deep, portentous monotone, like a bass tone on a cathedral organ:

"I, Harold D. Schwartz, residing in Building 257 of Alden Village, New York City, do hereby make, publish, and declare this to be my last Will and Testament, hereby revoking any and all former wills and codicils by me at any time heretofore made." He blew his nose importantly, and went on, not missing a word, and repeating many for emphasis—repeating in particular his ever-more-elaborate specifications for a funeral.

At the end of these specifications, Gramps was so choked with emotion that Lou thought he might forget why he'd gotten out the will in the first place. But Gramps heroically brought his powerful emotions under control, and, after erasing for a full minute, he began to write and speak at the same time. Lou could have spoken his lines for him, he'd heard them so often.

"I have had many heartbreaks ere leaving this vale of tears for a better land," Gramps said and wrote. "But the deepest hurt of all has been dealt me by—" He looked around the group, trying to remember who the malefactor was.

Everyone looked helpfully at Lou, who held up his hand resignedly.

Gramps nodded, remembering, and completed the sentence: "my great-grandson, Louis J. Schwartz."

"Grandson, sir," said Lou.

"Don't quibble. You're in deep enough now, young man," said Gramps, but he changed the trifle. And from there he went without a misstep through the phrasing of the disinheritance, causes for which were disrespectfulness and quibbling.

In the paragraph following, the paragraph that had belonged to everyone in the room at one time or another, Lou's name was scratched out and Willy's substituted as heir to the apartment and, the biggest plum of all, the double bed in the private bedroom. "So!" said Gramps, beaming. He erased the date at the foot of the will, and substituted a new one, including the time of day. "Well—time to watch the McGarvey Family." The McGarvey Family was a television serial that Gramps had been following since he was sixty, or for one hundred and twelve years. "I can't wait to see what's going to happen next," he said.

Lou detached himself from the group and lay down on his bed of pain by the bathroom door. He wished Em would join him, and he wondered where she was.

He dozed for a few moments, until he was disturbed by someone's stepping over him to get into the bathroom. A moment later, he heard a faint gurgling sound, as though something were being poured down the washbasin drain. Suddenly, it entered his mind that Em had cracked up, and that she was in there doing something drastic about Gramps.

"Em—?" he whispered through the panel. There was no reply, and Lou pressed against the door. The worn lock, whose bolt barely engaged its socket, held for a second, then let the door swing inward.

"Morty!" gasped Lou.

Lou's great-grandnephew, Mortimer, who had just married and brought his wife home to the Schwartz menage, looked at Lou with consternation and surprise. Morty kicked the door shut, but not before Lou had glimpsed what was in his hand—Gramps' enormous economy-size bottle of anti-gerasone, which had been half-emptied, and which Morty was refilling to the top with tap water.

A moment later, Morty came out, glared defiantly at Lou, and brushed past him wordlessly to rejoin his pretty bride.

Shocked, Lou didn't know what on earth to do. He couldn't let Gramps take the mousetrapped anti-gerasone; but if he warned Gramps about it, Gramps would certainly make life in the apartment, which was merely insufferable now, harrowing.

Lou glanced into the living room, and saw that the Schwartzes, Emerald among them, were momentarily at rest, relishing the botches that McGarveys had made of *their* lives. Stealthily, he went into the bathroom, locked the door as well as he could, and began to pour the contents of Gramps' bottle down the drain. He was going to refill it with full-strength anti-gerasone from the twenty-two smaller bottles on the shelf. The bottle contained a half-gallon, and its neck was small, so it seemed to Lou that the emptying would take forever. And the almost imperceptible smell of anti-gerasone, like Worcestershire sauce, now seemed to Lou, in his nervousness, to be pouring out into the rest of the apartment through the keyhole and under the door.

"*Gloog-gloog-gloog-gloog-*," went the bottle monotonously. Suddenly, up came the sound of music from the living room, and there were murmurs and the scraping of chair legs on the floor. "*Thus ends,*" said the television announcer, "*the 29,121st chapter in the life of your neighbors and mine, the McGarveys.*" Footsteps were coming down the hall. There was a knock on the bathroom door.

"Just a sec," called Lou cheerily. Desperately, he shook the big bottle, trying to speed up the flow. His palms slipped on the wet glass, and the heavy bottle smashed to splinters on the tile floor.

The door sprung open, and Gramps, dumfounded, stared at the mess.

Lou grinned engagingly through his nausea, and, for want of anything remotely resembling a thought, he waited for Gramps to speak.

"Well, boy," said Gramps at last, "looks like you've got a little tidying up to do."

And that was all he said. He turned around, elbowed his way through the crowd, and locked himself in his bedroom.

The Schwartzes contemplated Lou in incredulous silence for a moment longer, and then hurried back to the living room, as though some of his horrible guilt would taint them, too, if they looked too long. Morty stayed behind long enough to give Lou a quizzical, annoyed glance. Then he, too, went into the living room, leaving only Emerald standing in the doorway.

Tears streamed over her cheeks. "Oh, you poor lamb—please don't look so awful. It was my fault. I put you up to this."

"No," said Lou, finding his voice, "really you didn't. Honest, Em, I was just—"

"You don't have to explain anything to me, hon. I'm on your side no matter what." She kissed him on his cheek, and whispered in his ear. "It wouldn't have been murder, hon. It wouldn't have killed him. It wasn't such a terrible thing to do. It just would have fixed him up so he'd be able to go any time God decided He wanted him."

"What's gonna happen next, Em?" said Lou hollowly. "What's he gonna do?"

◎ ◎ ◎

Lou and Emerald stayed fearfully awake almost all night, waiting to see what Gramps was going to do. But not a sound came from the sacred bedroom. At two hours before dawn, the pair dropped off to sleep.

At six o'clock they arose again, for it was time for their generation to eat breakfast in the kitchenette. No one spoke to them. They had twenty minutes in which to eat, but their reflexes were so dulled by the bad night that they had hardly swallowed two mouthfuls of egg-type processed seaweed before it was time to surrender their places to their son's generation.

Then, as was the custom for whomever had been most recently disinherited, they began preparing Gramps' breakfast, which would presently be served to him in bed, on a tray. They tried to be cheerful about it. The toughest part of the job was having to handle the honest-to-God eggs and bacon and oleomargarine on which Gramps spent almost all of the income from his fortune.

"Well," said Emerald, "I'm not going to get all panicky until I'm sure there's something to be panicky about."

"Maybe he doesn't know what it was I busted," said Lou hopefully.

"Probably thinks it was your watch crystal," said Eddie, their son, who was toying apathetically with his buckwheat-type processed sawdust cakes.

"Don't get sarcastic with your father," said Em, "and don't talk with your mouth full, either."

"I'd like to see anybody take a mouthful of this stuff and *not* say something," said

Eddie, who was seventy-three. He glanced at the clock. "It's time to take Gramps his breakfast, you know."

"Yeah, it is, isn't it," said Lou weakly. He shrugged. "Let's have the tray, Em."

"We'll both go."

Walking slowly, smiling bravely, they found a large semicircle of long-faced Schwartzes standing around the bedroom door.

Em knocked. "Gramps," she said brightly, "breakfast is ready."

There was no reply, and she knocked again, harder.

The door swung open before her fist. In the middle of the room, the soft, deep, wide, canopied bed, the symbol of the sweet by-and-by to every Schwartz, was empty.

A sense of death, as unfamiliar to the Schwartzes as Zoroastrianism or the causes of the Sepoy Mutiny, stilled every voice and slowed every heart. Awed, the heirs began to search gingerly under the furniture and behind the drapes for all that was mortal of Gramps, father of the race.

But Gramps had left not his earthly husk but a note, which Lou finally found on the dresser, under a paperweight which was a treasured souvenir from the 2000 World's Fair. Unsteadily, Lou read it aloud:

"'Somebody who I have sheltered and protected and taught the best I know how all these years last night turned on me like a mad dog and diluted my anti-gerasone, or tried to. I am no longer a young man. I can no longer bear the crushing burden of life as I once could. So, after last night's bitter experience, I say goodbye. The cares of this world will soon drop away like a cloak of thorns, and I shall know peace. By the time you find this, I will be gone.'"

"Gosh," said Willy brokenly, "he didn't even get to see how the Five-Hundred-Mile Speedway Race was going to come out."

"Or the World's Series," said Eddie.

"Or whether Mrs. McGarvey got her eyesight back," said Morty.

"There's more," said Lou, and he began reading aloud again: "'I, Harold D. Schwartz . . . do hereby make, publish and declare this to be my last Will and Testament, hereby revoking any and all former will and codicils by me at any time heretofore made.'"

"No!" cried Willy. "Not another one!"

"'I do stipulate,'" read Lou, "'that all of my property, of whatsoever kind and nature, not be divided, but do devise and bequeath it to be held in common by my issue, without regard for generation, equally, share and share alike.'"

"Issue?" said Emerald.

Lou included the multitude in a sweep of his hand. "It means we all own the whole damn shootin' match."

All eyes turned instantly to the bed.

"Share and share alike?" said Morty.

"Actually," said Willy, who was the oldest person present, "it's just like the old system, where the oldest people head up things with their headquarters in here, and—"

"I like *that!*" said Em. "Lou owns as much of it as you do, and I say it ought to be for the oldest one who's still working. You can snooze around here all day, waiting for your pension check, and poor Lou stumbles in here after work, all tuckered out, and—"

"How about letting somebody who's never had any privacy get a little crack at it?" said Eddie hotly. "Hell, you old people had plenty of privacy back when you were kids. I was born and raised in the middle of the goddam barracks in the hall! How about—"

"Yeah?" said Morty. "Sure, you've all had it pretty tough, and my heart bleeds for you. But try honeymooning in the hall for a real kick."

"Silence!" shouted Willy imperiously. "The next person who opens his mouth spends the next six months by the bathroom. Now clear out of my room. I want to think."

A vase shattered against the wall, inches above his head. In the next moment, a free-for-all was underway, with each couple battling to eject every other couple from the room. Fighting coalitions formed and dissolved with the lightning changes of the tactical situation. Em and Lou were thrown into the hall, where they organized others in the same situation, and stormed back into the room.

After two hours of struggle, with nothing like a decision in sight, the cops broke in.

For the next half-hour, patrol wagons and ambulances hauled away Schwartzes, and then the apartment was still and spacious.

◎ ◎ ◎

An hour later, films of the last stages of the riot were being televised to 500,000,000 delighted viewers on the Eastern Seaboard.

In the stillness of the three-room Schwartz apartment on the 76th floor of Building 257, the television set had been left on. Once more the air was filled with the cries and grunts and crashes of the fray, coming harmlessly now from the loud-speaker.

The battle also appeared on the screen of the television set in the police station, where the Schwartzes and their captors watched with professional interest.

Em and Lou were in adjacent four-by-eight cells, and were stretched out peace-fully on their cots.

"Em—" called Lou through the partition, "you got a washbasin all your own too?"

"Sure. Washbasin, bed, light—the works. Ha! And we thought Gramps' room was something. How long's this been going on?" She held out her hand. "For the first time in forty years, hon, I haven't got the shakes."

"Cross your fingers," said Lou, "the lawyer's going to try to get us a year."

"Gee," said Em dreamily, "I wonder what kind of wires you'd have to pull to get solitary?"

"All right, pipe down," said the turnkey, "or I'll toss the whole kit and caboodle of you right out. And first one who lets on to anybody outside how good jail is ain't never getting back in!"

The prisoners instantly fell silent.

The living room of the Schwartz apartment darkened for a moment, as the riot scenes faded, and then the face of the announcer appeared, like the sun coming from behind a cloud. "*And now, friends,*" he said, "*I have a special message from the makers of anti-gerasone, a message for all you folks over one hundred and fifty. Are you hampered socially by wrinkles, by stiffness of joints and discoloration or loss of hair, all because these things came upon you before anti-gerasone was developed? Well, if you are, you need no longer suffer, need no longer feel different and out of things.*

"*After years of research, medical science has now developed super-anti-gerosone! In weeks, yes weeks, you can look, feel, and act as young as your great-great-grandchildren! Wouldn't you pay $5,000 to be indistinguishable from everybody else? Well, you don't have to. Safe, tested super-anti-gerasone costs you only dollars a day. The average cost of regaining all the sparkle and attractiveness of youth is less than fifty dollars.*

"*Write now for your free trial carton. Just put your name and address on a dollar postcard, and mail it to 'Super,' Box 500,000, Schenectady, N.Y. Have you got that? I'll repeat it. 'Super.' Box . . .*" Underlining the announcer's words was the scratching of Gramps' fountain-pen, the one Willy had given him the night before. He had come in a few minutes previous from the Idle Hour Tavern, which commanded a view of Building 257 across the square of asphalt known as the Alden Village Green. He had called a cleaning woman to come straighten the place up, and had hired the best lawyer in town to get his descendants a conviction. Gramps had then moved the daybed before the television screen so that he could watch from a reclining position. It was something he'd dreamed of doing for years.

"Schen-*ec*-ta-dy," mouthed Gramps. "Got it." His face had changed remarkably. His facial muscles seemed to have relaxed, revealing kindness and equanimity under what had been taut, bad-tempered lines. It was almost as though his trial package of *Super*-anti-gerasone had already arrived. When something amused him on television, he smiled easily, rather than barely managing to lengthen the thin line of his mouth a millimeter. Life was good. He could hardly wait to see what was going to happen next.

The Big Space Fuck

IN 1987 IT BECAME possible in the United States of America for a young person to sue his parents for the way he had been raised. He could take them to court and make them pay money and even serve jail terms for serious mistakes they made when he was just a helpless little kid. This was not only an effort to achieve justice but to discourage reproduction, since there wasn't anything much to eat any more. Abortions were free. In fact, any woman who volunteered for one got her choice of a bathroom scale or a table lamp.

In 1989, America staged the Big Space Fuck, which was a serious effort to make sure that human life would continue to exist somewhere in the Universe, since it certainly couldn't continue much longer on Earth. Everything had turned to shit and beer cans and old automobiles and Clorox bottles. An interesting thing happened in the Hawaiian Islands, where they had been throwing trash down extinct volcanoes for years: a couple of the volcanoes all of a sudden spit it all back up. And so on.

This was a period of great permissiveness in matters of language, so even the President was saying shit and fuck and so on, without anybody's feeling threatened or taking offense. It was perfectly OK. He called the Space Fuck a Space Fuck and so did everybody else. It was a rocket ship with eight hundred pounds of freeze-dried jizzum in its nose. It was going to be fired at the Andromeda Galaxy, two million light years away. The ship was named the *Arthur C. Clarke*, in honor of a famous space pioneer.

It was to be fired at midnight on the Fourth of July. At ten o'clock that night, Dwayne Hoobler and his wife Grace were watching the countdown on television in the living room of their modest home in Elk Harbor, Ohio, on the shore of what used to be Lake Erie. Lake Erie was almost solid sewage now. There were man-eating lampreys in there thirty-eight feet long. Dwayne was a guard in the Ohio Adult Correctional Institution, which was two miles away. His hobby was making birdhouses out of Clorox bottles. He went on making them and hanging them around his yard, even though there weren't any birds any more.

Dwayne and Grace marveled at a film demonstration of how jizzum had been freeze-dried for the trip. A small beaker of the stuff, which had been contributed by the head of the Mathematics Department at the University of Chicago, was flash-frozen. Then it was placed under a bell jar, and the air was exhausted from the jar. The air evanesced, leaving a fine white powder. The powder certainly didn't look like much, and Dwayne Hoobler said so—but there were several hundred million sperm cells in there, in suspended animation. The original contribution, an average contribution, had been two cubic centimeters. There was enough powder, Dwayne estimated out loud, to clog the eye of a needle. And eight hundred pounds of the stuff would soon be on its way to Andromeda.

"Fuck you, Andromeda," said Dwayne, and he wasn't being coarse. He was echoing billboards and stickers all over town. Other signs said, "Andromeda, We Love You," and "Earth Has the Hots for Andromeda," and so on.

There was a knock on the door, and an old friend of the family, the County Sheriff, simultaneously let himself in. "How are you, you old motherfucker?" said Dwayne.

"Can't complain, shitface," said the sheriff, and they joshed back and forth like that for a while. Grace chuckled, enjoying their wit. She wouldn't have chuckled so richly, however, if she had been a little more observant. She might have noticed that the sheriff's jocularity was very much on the surface. Underneath, he had something troubling on his mind. She might have noticed, too, that he had legal papers in his hand.

"Sit down, you silly old fart," said Dwayne, "and watch Andromeda get the surprise of her life."

"The way I understand it," the sheriff replied, "I'd have to sit there for more than two million years. My old lady might wonder what's become of me." He was a lot smarter than Dwayne. He had jizzum on the *Arthur C. Clarke*, and Dwayne didn't. You had to have an I.Q. of over 115 to have your jizzum accepted. There were certain exceptions to this: if you were a good athlete or could play a musical instrument or paint pictures, but Dwayne didn't qualify in any of those departments, either. He had hoped that birdhouse-makers might be entitled to special consideration, but this turned out not to be the case. The Director of the New York Philharmonic, on the other hand, was entitled to contribute a whole quart, if he wanted to. He was sixty-eight years old. Dwayne was forty-two.

There was an old astronaut on the television now. He was saying that he sure wished he could go where his jizzum was going. But he would sit at home instead, with his memories and a glass of Tang. Tang used to be the official drink of the astronauts. It was a freeze-dried orangeade.

"Maybe you haven't got two million years," said Dwayne, "but you've got at least five minutes. Sit thee doon."

"What I'm here for—" said the sheriff, and he let his unhappiness show, "is something I customarily do standing up."

Dwayne and Grace were sincerely puzzled. They didn't have the least idea what was coming next. Here is what it was: the sheriff handed each one of them a subpoena, and he said, "It's my sad duty to inform you that your daughter, Wanda June, has accused you of ruining her when she was a child."

Dwayne and Grace were thunderstruck. They knew that Wanda June was twenty-one now, and entitled to sue, but they certainly hadn't expected her to do so. She was in New York City, and when they congratulated her about her birthday on the telephone, in fact, one of the things Grace said was, "Well, you can sue us now, honeybunch, if you want to." Grace was so sure she and Dwayne had been good parents that she could laugh when she went on, "If you want to, you can send your rotten old parents off to jail."

Wanda June was an only child, incidentally. She had come close to having some siblings, but Grace had aborted them. Grace had taken three table lamps and a bathroom scale instead.

"What does she say we did wrong?" Grace asked the sheriff.

"There's a separate list of charges inside each of your subpoenas," he said. And he couldn't look his wretched old friends in the eye, so he looked at the television instead. A scientist there was explaining why Andromeda had been selected as a target. There were at least eighty-seven chronosynclastic infundibulae, time warps, between Earth and the Andromeda Galaxy. If the *Arthur C. Clarke* passed through any one of them, the ship and its load would be multiplied a trillion times, and would appear everywhere throughout space and time.

"If there's any fecundity anywhere in the Universe," the scientist promised, "our seed will find it and bloom."

One of the most depressing things about the space program so far, of course, was that it had demonstrated that fecundity was one hell of a long way off, if anywhere. Dumb people like Dwayne and Grace, and even fairly smart people like the sheriff, had been encouraged to believe that there was hospitality out there, and that Earth was just a piece of shit to use as a launching platform.

Now Earth really was a piece of shit, and it was beginning to dawn on even dumb people that it might be the only inhabitable planet human beings would ever find.

Grace was in tears over being sued by her daughter, and the list of charges she was reading was broken into multiple images by the tears. "Oh God, oh God, oh God—" she said, "she's talking about things I forgot all about, but she never forgot a thing. She's talking about something that happened when she was only four years old."

Dwayne was reading charges against himself, so he didn't ask Grace what awful thing she was supposed to have done when Wanda June was only four, but here it was: Poor little Wanda June drew pretty pictures with a crayon all over the new living-room wallpaper to make her mother happy. Her mother blew up and spanked her instead. Since that day, Wanda June claimed, she had not been able to look at any sort of art materials without trembling like a leaf and breaking out into cold sweats. "Thus was I deprived," Wanda June's lawyer had her say, "of a brilliant and lucrative career in the arts."

Dwayne meanwhile was learning that he had ruined his daughter's opportunities for what her lawyer called an "advantageous marriage and the comfort and love therefrom." Dwayne had done this, supposedly, by being half in the bag whenever a suitor came to call. Also, he was often stripped to the waist when he answered the door, but still had on his cartridge belt and his revolver. She was even able to name a lover her father had lost for her: John L. Newcomb, who had finally married somebody else. He had a very good job now. He was in command of the security force at an arsenal out in South Dakota, where they stockpiled cholera and bubonic plague.

The sheriff had still more bad news to deliver, and he knew he would have an opportunity to deliver it soon enough. Poor Dwayne and Grace were bound to ask him, "What made her *do* this to us?" The answer to that question would be more bad news, which was that Wanda June was in jail, charged with being the head of a shoplifting ring. The only way she could avoid prison was to prove that everything she was and did was her parents' fault.

Meanwhile, Senator Flem Snopes of Mississippi, Chairman of the Senate Space Committee, had appeared on the television screen. He was very happy about the Big Space Fuck, and he said it had been what the American space program had been aiming toward all along. He was proud, he said, that the United States had seen fit to locate the biggest jizzum-freezing plant in his "l'il ol' home town," which was Mayhew.

The word "jizzum" had an interesting history, by the way. It was as old as "fuck" and "shit" and so on, but it continued to be excluded from dictionaries, long after the others were let in. This was because so many people wanted it to remain a truly magic word—the only one left.

And when the United States announced that it was going to do a truly magical thing, was going to fire sperm at the Andromeda Galaxy, the populace corrected its government. Their collective unconscious announced that it was time for the last magic word to come into the open. They insisted that *sperm* was nothing to fire at another galaxy. Only *jizzum* would do. So the Government began using that word, and it did something that had never been done before, either: it standardized the way the word was spelled.

The man who was interviewing Senator Snopes asked him to stand up so everybody could get a good look at his codpiece, which the Senator did. Codpieces were very much in fashion, and many men were wearing codpieces in the shape of rocket ships, in honor of the Big Space Fuck. These customarily had the letters "U.S.A."

embroidered on the shaft. Senator Snopes' shaft, however, bore the Stars and Bars of the Confederacy.

This led the conversation into the area of heraldry in general, and the interviewer reminded the Senator of his campaign to eliminate the bald eagle as the national bird. The Senator explained that he didn't like to have his country represented by a creature that obviously hadn't been able to cut the mustard in modern times.

Asked to name a creature that *had* been able to cut the mustard, the Senator did better than that: he named two—the lamprey and the bloodworm. And, unbeknownst to him or to anybody, lampreys were finding the Great Lakes too vile and noxious even for *them*. While all the human beings were in their houses, watching the Big Space Fuck, lampreys were squirming out of the ooze and onto land. Some of them were nearly as long and thick as the *Arthur C. Clarke*.

And Grace Hoobler tore her wet eyes from what she had been reading, and she asked the sheriff the question he had been dreading to hear: "What made her *do* this to us?"

The sheriff told her, and then he cried out against cruel Fate, too. "This is the most horrible duty I ever had to carry out—" he said brokenly, "to deliver news this heartbreaking to friends as close as you two are—on a night that's supposed to be the most joyful night in the history of mankind."

He left sobbing, and stumbled right into the mouth of a lamprey. The lamprey ate him immediately, but not before he screamed. Dwayne and Grace Hoobler rushed outside to see what the screaming was about, and the lamprey ate them, too.

It was ironical that their television set continued to report the countdown, even though they weren't around any more to see or hear or care.

"Nine!" said a voice. And then, "Eight!" And then, "Seven!" And so on.

2BR02B

EVERYTHING WAS PERFECTLY SWELL.

There were no prisons, no slums, no insane asylums, no cripples, no poverty, no wars.

All diseases were conquered. So was old age.

Death, barring accidents, was an adventure for volunteers.

The population of the United States was stabilized at forty million souls.

One bright morning in the Chicago Lying-In Hospital, a man named Edward K. Wehling, Jr., waited for his wife to give birth. He was the only man waiting. Not many people were born each day anymore.

Wehling was fifty-six, a mere stripling in a population whose average age was one hundred twenty-nine.

X rays had revealed that his wife was going to have triplets. The children would be his first.

Young Wehling was hunched in his chair, his head in his hands. He was so rumpled, so still and colorless as to be virtually invisible. His camouflage was perfect, since the waiting room had a disorderly and demoralized air, too. Chairs and ashtrays had been moved away from the walls. The floor was paved with spattered dropcloths.

The room was being redecorated. It was being redecorated as a memorial to a man who had volunteered to die.

A sardonic old man, about two hundred years old, sat on a stepladder, painting a mural he did not like. Back in the days when people aged visibly, his age would have been guessed at thirty-five or so. Aging had touched him that much before the cure for aging was found.

The mural he was working on depicted a very neat garden. Men and women in white, doctors and nurses, turned the soil, planted seedlings, sprayed bugs, spread fertilizer. Men and women in purple uniforms pulled up weeds, cut down plants that were old and sickly, raked leaves, carried refuse to trash burners.

Never, never, never—not even in medieval Holland or old Japan—had a garden been more formal, been better tended. Every plant had all the loam, light, water, air, and nourishment it could use.

A hospital orderly came down the corridor, singing under his breath a popular song:

> *If you don't like my kisses, honey,*
> *Here's what I will do:*
> *I'll go see a girl in purple,*
> *Kiss this sad world toodle-oo.*
> *If you don't want my lovin',*
> *Why should I take up all this space?*
> *I'll get off this old planet,*
> *Let some sweet baby have my place.*

The orderly looked in at the mural and the muralist. "Looks so real," he said, "I can practically imagine I'm standing in the middle of it."

"What makes you think you're not in it?" said the painter. He gave a satiric smile. "It's called *The Happy Garden of Life*, you know."

"That's good of Dr. Hitz," said the orderly.

He was referring to one of the male figures in white, whose head was a portrait of Dr. Benjamin Hitz, the hospital's chief obstetrician. Hitz was a blindingly handsome man.

"Lot of faces still to fill in," said the orderly. He meant that the faces of many of the figures in the mural were blank. All blanks were to be filled with portraits of important people either on the hospital staff or from the Chicago office of the Federal Bureau of Termination.

"Must be nice to be able to make pictures that look like something," said the orderly.

The painter's face curdled with scorn. "You think I'm proud of this drab? You think this is my idea of what life really looks like?"

"What's your idea of what life looks like?"

The painter gestured at a foul dropcloth. "There's a good picture of it," he said. "Frame that, and you'll have a picture a damn sight more honest than this one."

"You're a gloomy old duck, aren't you?" said the orderly.

"Is that a crime?" said the painter.

"If you don't like it here, Grandpa—" The orderly finished the thought with the trick telephone number that people who didn't want to live anymore were supposed to call. The zero in the telephone number he pronounced "naught."

The number was 2BR02B.

It was the telephone number of an institution whose fanciful sobriquets included "Automat," "Birdland," "Cannery," "Catbox," "Delouser," "Easy Go," "Good-bye, Mother," "Happy Hooligan," "Kiss Me Quick," "Lucky Pierre," "Sheepdip," "Waring Blender," "Weep No More," and "Why Worry?"

"To Be or Not to Be" was the telephone number of the municipal gas chambers of the Federal Bureau of Termination.

The painter thumbed his nose at the orderly. "When I decide it's time to go," he said, "it won't be at the Sheepdip."

"A do-it-yourselfer, eh?" said the orderly. "Messy business, Grandpa. Why don't you have a little consideration for the people who have to clean up after you?"

The painter expressed with an obscenity his lack of concern for the tribulations of his survivors. "The world could do with a good deal more mess, if you ask me," he said.

The orderly laughed and moved on.

Wehling, the waiting father, mumbled something without raising his head. And then he fell silent again.

A coarse, formidable woman strode into the waiting room on spike heels. Her shoes, stockings, trench coat, bag, and overseas cap were all purple, a purple the painter called "the color of grapes on Judgment Day."

The medallion on her purple musette bag was the seal of the Service Division of the Federal Bureau of Termination, an eagle perched on a turnstile.

The woman had a lot of facial hair—an unmistakable mustache, in fact. A curious thing about gas chamber hostesses was that no matter how lovely and feminine they were when recruited, they all sprouted mustaches within five years or so.

"Is this where I'm supposed to come?" she asked the painter.

"A lot would depend on what your business was," he said. "You aren't about to have a baby, are you?"

"They told me I was supposed to pose for some picture," she said. "My name's Leora Duncan." She waited.

"And you dunk people," he said.

"What?" she said.

"Skip it," he said.

"That sure is a beautiful picture," she said. "Looks just like heaven or something."

"Or something," said the painter. He took a list of names from his smock pocket. "Duncan, Duncan, Duncan," he said, scanning the list. "Yes—here you are. You're entitled to be immortalized. See any faceless body here you'd like me to stick your head on? We've got a few choice ones left."

She studied the mural. "Gee," she said, "they're all the same to me. I don't know anything about art."

"A body's a body, eh?" he said. "All righty. As a master of the fine art, I recommend this body here." He indicated the faceless figure of a woman who was carrying dried stalks to a trash burner.

"Well," said Leora Duncan, "that's more the disposal people, isn't it? I mean, I'm in service. I don't do any disposing."

The painter clapped his hands in mock delight. "You say you don't know any-

COMPLETE STORIES

thing about art, and then you prove in the next breath that you do know more about it than I do! Of course the sheaf carrier is wrong for a hostess! A snipper, a pruner—that's more your line." He pointed to a figure in purple who was sawing a dead branch from an apple tree. "How about her?" he said. "You like her at all?"

"Gosh—" she said, and she blushed and became humble. "That—that puts me right next to Dr. Hitz."

"That upsets you?" he said.

"Good gravy, no!" she said. "It's—it's just such an honor."

"Ah, you admire him, eh?" he said.

"Who doesn't admire him?" she said, worshipping the portrait of Hitz. It was the portrait of a tanned, white-haired, omnipotent Zeus, two hundred forty years old. "Who doesn't admire him?" she said again. "He was responsible for setting up the very first gas chamber in Chicago."

"Nothing would please me more," said the painter, "than to put you next to him for all time. Sawing off a limb—that strikes you as appropriate?"

"That is kind of like what I do," she said. She was demure about what she did. What she did was make people comfortable while she killed them.

And while Leora Duncan was posing for her portrait, into the waiting room bounded Dr. Hitz himself. He was seven feet tall, and he boomed with importance, accomplishments, and the joy of living.

"Well, Miss Duncan! Miss Duncan!" he said, and he made a joke. "What are you doing here? This isn't where the people leave. This is where they come in!"

"We're going to be in the same picture together," she said shyly.

"Good!" said Dr. Hitz. "And say, isn't that some picture?"

"I sure am honored to be in it with you," she said.

"Let me tell you, I'm honored to be in it with you. Without women like you, this wonderful world we've got wouldn't be possible."

He saluted her and moved toward the door that led to the delivery rooms. "Guess what was just born," he said.

"I can't," she said.

"Triplets!" he said.

"Triplets!" she said. She was exclaiming over the legal implications of triplets.

The law said that no newborn child could survive unless the parents of the child could find someone who would volunteer to die. Triplets, if they were all to live, called for three volunteers.

"Do the parents have three volunteers?" said Leora Duncan.

"Last I heard," said Dr. Hitz, "they had one, and were trying to scrape another two up."

"I don't think they made it," she said. "Nobody made three appointments with us. Nothing but singles going through today, unless somebody called in after I left. What's the name?"

"Wehling," said the waiting father, sitting up, red-eyed and frowzy. "Edward K. Wehling, Jr., is the name of the happy father-to-be."

He raised his right hand, looked at a spot on the wall, gave a hoarsely wretched chuckle. "Present," he said.

"Oh, Mr. Wehling," said Dr. Hitz, "I didn't see you."

"The invisible man," said Wehling.

"They just phoned me that your triplets have been born," said Dr. Hitz. "They're all fine, and so is the mother. I'm on my way in to see them now."

"Hooray," said Wehling emptily.

"You don't sound very happy," said Dr. Hitz.

"What man in my shoes wouldn't be happy?" said Wehling. He gestured with his hands to symbolize the carefree simplicity. "All I have to do is pick out which one of the triplets is going to live, then deliver my maternal grandfather to the Happy Hooligan, and come back here with a receipt."

Dr. Hitz became rather severe with Wehling, towered over him. "You don't believe in population control, Mr. Wehling?" he said.

"I think it's perfectly keen," said Wehling.

"Would you like to go back to the good old days, when the population of the earth was twenty billion—about to become forty billion, then eighty billion, then one hundred and sixty billion? Do you know what a drupelet is, Mr. Wehling?" said Hitz.

"Nope," said Wehling, sulking.

"A drupelet, Mr. Wehling, is one of the little knobs, one of the little pulpy grains, of a blackberry," said Dr. Hitz. "Without population control, human beings would now be packed on the surface of this old planet like drupelets on a blackberry! Think of it!"

Wehling continued to stare at the spot on the wall.

"In the year 2000," said Dr. Hitz, "before scientists stepped in and laid down the law, there wasn't even enough drinking water to go around, and nothing to eat but seaweed—and still people insisted on their right to reproduce like jackrabbits. And their right, if possible, to live forever."

"I want those kids," said Wehling. "I want all three of them."

"Of course you do," said Dr. Hitz. "That's only human."

"I don't want my grandfather to die, either," said Wehling.

"Nobody's really happy about taking a close relative to the Catbox," said Dr. Hitz sympathetically.

"I wish people wouldn't call it that," said Leora Duncan.

"What?" said Dr. Hitz.

"I wish people wouldn't call it the Catbox, and things like that," she said. "It gives people the wrong impression."

"You're absolutely right," said Dr. Hitz. "Forgive me." He corrected himself, gave the municipal gas chambers their official title, a title no one ever used in conversation. "I should have said 'Ethical Suicide Studios,'" he said.

"That sounds so much better," said Leora Duncan.

"This child of yours—whichever one you decide to keep, Mr. Wehling," said Dr. Hitz. "He or she is going to live on a happy, roomy, clean, rich planet, thanks to population control. In a garden like in that mural there." He shook his head. "Two centuries ago, when I was a young man, it was a hell that nobody thought could last another twenty years. Now centuries of peace and plenty stretch before us as far as the imagination cares to travel."

He smiled luminously.

The smile faded when he saw that Wehling had just drawn a revolver.

Wehling shot Dr. Hitz dead. "There's room for one—a great big one," he said.

And then he shot Leora Duncan. "It's only death," he said to her as she fell. "There! Room for two."

And then he shot himself, making room for all three of his children.

Nobody came running. Nobody, it seemed, had heard the shots.

The painter sat on the top of his stepladder, looking down reflectively on the sorry scene. He pondered the mournful puzzle of life demanding to be born and, once born, demanding to be fruitful . . . to multiply and to live as long as possible—to do all that on a very small planet that would have to last forever.

All the answers that the painter could think of were grim. Even grimmer, surely, than a Catbox, a Happy Hooligan, an Easy Go. He thought of war. He thought of plague. He thought of starvation.

He knew that he would never paint again. He let his paintbrush fall to the dropcloths below. And then he decided he had had about enough of the Happy Garden of Life, too, and he came slowly down from the ladder.

He took Wehling's pistol, really intending to shoot himself. But he didn't have the nerve.

And then he saw the telephone booth in a corner of the room. He went to it, dialed the well-remembered number: 2BR02B.

"Federal Bureau of Termination," said the warm voice of a hostess.

"How soon could I get an appointment?" he asked, speaking carefully.

"We could probably fit you in late this afternoon, sir," she said. "It might even be earlier, if we get a cancellation."

"All right," said the painter, "fit me in, if you please." And he gave her his name, spelling it out.

"Thank you, sir," said the hostess. "Your city thanks you, your country thanks you, your planet thanks you. But the deepest thanks of all is from future generations."

Unknown Soldier

IT WAS ALL NONSENSE, of course, when they said our baby was the first one to be born in New York City into the third millennium of the Christian era—at ten seconds past midnight on January 1, 2000. For starters, the third millennium, as countless people had pointed out, would not begin until January 1, 2001. Planetarily speaking, the new year was already six hours old when our child was born, since it had begun that much earlier at the Royal Observatory in Greenwich, England, where time begins. Never mind that the numbering of years since the birth of Christ could only be approximate. The datum was so obscure. And who can say in which minute a child was born? When its head appeared? When all of it was outside the mother? When the umbilical cord was cut? Since there were many valuable prizes to be given to the city's first baby of 2000, and its parents, and the chief physician in attendance, it was agreed well in advance of the contest that severing the cord should not count, since the moment could be delayed past the crucial midnight. There might be doctors all over the city with their eyes on the clock and their scissors poised, and of course with witnesses present, watching the scissors, watching the clock. The winning doctor would get an all-expense-paid vacation on one of the few islands where a tourist could still feel fairly secure, which was Bermuda. A battalion of British paratroops was stationed there. Understandably, doctors might be tempted to fudge the birthtime, given the opportunity.

No matter what the criteria, defining the moment of birth was a lot less controversial than declaring when a fertilized ovum was a human being in the mother's womb. For the purpose of the contest, the moment of birth was the moment when the baby's eyes or eyelids were first bathed in light from the outside world, when they could first be seen by the witnesses. So the baby, which was the case with ours, would still be partly inside the mother. If she had been a breech-birth, of course, the eyes would have been almost the last things to appear. And here comes the most nonsensical aspect of the contest we won: If she had been a breech-birth, or had Down's syndrome or spina bifida or been a crack baby or an AIDS baby or whatever, she surely would have been disqualified for the prizes on some supposed technicality having to do with timing rather than, or so the judges would have said, her variations from so-called norms. She was, after all, supposed to symbolize how healthy and delightful the next thousand years were supposed to be. One guarantee by the judges was that race and religion and national origin of the parents could not possibly skew their deliberations. And it is true that I am a native American black, and my wife, while classified as white, was born in Cuba. But it surely did not hurt that I was head of the Sociology Department at Columbia University, or that my wife was a physical therapist at New York Hospital. I am certain that our baby won over several other candidates, including a newborn boy found in a trashcan in Brooklyn, because we were middle class.

We got a Ford station wagon and three lifetime passes to Disney World and a home entertainment console, with a six-foot screen and a VCR and a sound system capable of playing every sort of record or tape, and equipment for a home gymnasium, and so on. And the baby got a government bond worth fifty thousand dollars at maturity, and a bassinet and a stroller and free diaper service and on and on. But then she died when she was only six weeks old. The doctor who helped her into the world was in Bermuda at the time, and he did not hear about her death there. Her death was no more big news there, or anywhere outside of New York City, than her birth had been. It wasn't big news here, either, since nobody but the promoters of the asinine contest and the business people who had donated the prizes took all the hoopla about her at all seriously, the blather about her representing so many wonderful things, the mingling of races in beauty and happiness, the rebirth of the spirit which had once made New York the greatest city in the world in the greatest nation in the world, and just plain peace, and I don't know what all. It seems to me now that she was like an unknown soldier in a war memorial, a little bit of flesh and bone and hair which was extolled to the point of lunacy. Hardly anybody came to her funeral, incidentally. The TV station whose idea the contest was sent a minor executive, not even a personality, and surely not a camera crew. Who wants to watch the burial of the next thousand years? If television refuses to look at something, it is as though it never happened. It can erase anything, even whole continents, such as Africa, one big desert now, where millions upon millions of babies, with a brand-new thousand years of history looming before them, starve to death. It was Crib Death Syndrome which killed our daughter, they say This is a genetic defect as yet, and perhaps forever, undetectable by amniocentesis. She was our first child. Ah me.

S O U R C E   A C K N O W L E D G M E N T S

"The Nice Little People," "The Petrified Ants," "Little Drops of Water," "Confi-do," "Hall of Mirrors," "Look at the Birdie," "FUBAR," "Shout About It from the Housetops," "Ed Luby's Key Club," "King and Queen of the Universe," "Hello, Red," "The Honor of a Newsboy," "The Good Explainer," and "A Song for Selma" from *Look at the Birdie: Unpublished Short Fiction* by Kurt Vonnegut, copyright © 2009 by the Kurt Vonnegut Jr. Trust. Used by permission of Delacorte Press, an imprint of Random House, a division of Penguin Random House LLC. All rights reserved.

"The Big Space Fuck" from *Palm Sunday: An Autobiographical Collage* by Kurt Vonnegut, copyright © 1981 by Kurt Vonnegut. Used by permission of Dell Publishing, an imprint of Random House, a division of Penguin Random House LLC. All rights reserved.

"Tom Edison's Shaggy Dog," copyright © 1953 by Kurt Vonnegut Jr. Copyright renewed © 1981 Kurt Vonnegut Jr.; "Who Am I This Time?," and "Harrison Bergeron," copyright © 1961 by Kurt Vonnegut. Copyright renewed © 1989 by Kurt Vonnegut; "The Lie," copyright © 1962 by Kurt Vonnegut. Copyright renewed © 1990 by Kurt Vonnegut; "Adam," copyright © 1954 by Kurt Vonnegut Jr. Copyright renewed © 1982 by Kurt Vonnegut Jr.; "The Euphio Question," copyright © 1951 by Kurt Vonnegut Jr. Copyright renewed © 1979 by Kurt Vonnegut Jr.; "Long Walk to Forever," copyright © 1960 by Kurt Vonnegut. Copyright renewed © 1988 by Kurt Vonnegut; "Go Back to Your Precious Wife and Son," copyright © 1962 by Kurt Vonnegut. Copyright renewed © 1990 by Kurt Vonnegut; "EPICAC," copyright © 1950 by Kurt Vonnegut Jr. Copyright renewed © 1978 by Kurt Vonnegut Jr.; "Tomorrow and Tomorrow and Tomor-row," copyright © 1954 by Kurt Vonnegut Jr.; "Deer in the Works," copyright © 1955 by Kurt Vonnegut. Copyright renewed © 1983 by Kurt Vonnegut; "Report on the Barnhouse Effect," copyright © 1950 by Kurt Vonnegut Jr.; "Welcome to the Monkey House," copyright © 1968 by Kurt Vonnegut Jr. Copyright © 1996

Born in 1922 in Indianapolis, Indiana, KURT VONNEGUT was one of the few grandmasters of modern American letters. Called by the *New York Times* "the counterculture's novelist," his works guided a generation through the miasma of war and greed that was life in the US in the second half of the twentieth century. Vonnegut rose to prominence with the publication of *Cat's Cradle* in 1963. Several modern classics, including *Slaughterhouse-Five*, soon followed. And he wrote and published dozens of short stories. "Given who and what I am," he once said, "it has been presumptuous of me to write so well." Kurt Vonnegut died in New York in 2007.

A longtime friend of Kurt Vonnegut's, DAN WAKEFIELD edited and introduced *Kurt Vonnegut: Letters*, and is the author of the memoirs *New York in the Fifties* and *Returning: A Spiritual Journey*, and the novel *Going All the Way*, which was made into a movie starring Ben Affleck. He lives in Indianapolis, Indiana.

JEROME KLINKOWITZ, a scholar of mid-century American literature in general and Kurt Vonnegut in particular, is a professor of English at the University of Northern Iowa. He is co-editor of *The Vonnegut Statement* and author of several books including *The American 1960s*. He lives in Cedar Falls, Iowa.

DAVE EGGERS is the founder of McSweeney's and is the author of many books, including *Heroes of the Frontier*, *The Circle*, *A Hologram for the King*, and *What Is the What*.